Exploring
the
Horizons

ALSO BY GARDNER DOZOIS

Anthologies

A DAY IN THE LIFE
ANOTHER WORLD
BEST SCIENCE FICTION STORIES OF
   THE YEAR #6–10
THE BEST OF ISAAC ASIMOV'S
   SCIENCE FICTION MAGAZINE
TIME-TRAVELLERS FROM ISAAC
   ASIMOV'S SCIENCE FICTION
   MAGAZINE
TRANSCENDENTAL TALES FROM ISAAC
   ASIMOV'S SCIENCE FICTION
   MAGAZINE
ISAAC ASIMOV'S ALIENS
ISAAC ASIMOV'S MARS
ISAAC ASIMOV'S SF LITE
ISAAC ASIMOV'S WAR
ISAAC ASIMOV'S PLANET EARTH
   (WITH SHEILA WILLIAMS)
ISAAC ASIMOV'S ROBOTS
   (WITH SHEILA WILLIAMS)
ISAAC ASIMOV'S CYBERDREAMS
   (WITH SHEILA WILLIAMS)
ISAAC ASIMOV'S VALENTINES
   (WITH SHEILA WILLIAMS)
ISAAC ASIMOV'S SKIN DEEP
   (WITH SHEILA WILLIAMS)
ISAAC ASIMOV'S GHOSTS
   (WITH SHEILA WILLIAMS)
ISAAC ASIMOV'S DETECTIVES
   (WITH SHEILA WILLIAMS)
ISAAC ASIMOV'S VAMPIRES
   (WITH SHEILA WILLIAMS)
ISAAC ASIMOV'S MOONS
   (WITH SHEILA WILLIAMS)
ISAAC ASIMOV'S CHRISTMAS
   (WITH SHEILA WILLIAMS)
ISAAC ASIMOV'S CAMELOT
   (WITH SHEILA WILLIAMS)
ISAAC ASIMOV'S WEREWOLVES
   (WITH SHEILA WILLIAMS)
ROADS NOT TAKEN
   (WITH STANLEY SCHMIDT)
THE YEAR'S BEST SCIENCE FICTION,
   #1–15
FUTURE EARTHS: UNDER AFRICAN
   SKIES (WITH MIKE RESNICK)
FUTURE EARTHS: UNDER SOUTH
   AMERICAN SKIES (WITH MIKE
   RESNICK)

SLOW DANCING THROUGH TIME
   (WITH JACK DANN, MICHAEL
   SWANWICK, SUSAN CASPER, AND
   JACK C. HALDEMAN II)
THE PEACEMAKER
GEODESIC DREAMS (COLLECTION)

Nonfiction

THE FICTION OF JAMES TIPTREE, JR.
FUTURE POWER
   (WITH JACK DANN)
ALIENS! (WITH JACK DANN)
UNICORNS! (WITH JACK DANN)
MAGICATS! (WITH JACK DANN)
MAGICATS 2 (WITH JACK DANN)
BESTIARY! (WITH JACK DANN)
MERMAIDS! (WITH JACK DANN)
SORCERERS! (WITH JACK DANN)
DEMONS! (WITH JACK DANN)
DOGTALES! (WITH JACK DANN)
RIPPER! (WITH SUSAN CASPER)
SEASERPENTS! (WITH JACK DANN)
DINOSAURS! (WITH JACK DANN)
LITTLE PEOPLE! (WITH JACK DANN)
DRAGONS! (WITH JACK DANN)
HORSES! (WITH JACK DANN)
UNICORNS 2 (WITH JACK DANN)
INVADERS! (WITH JACK DANN)
ANGELS! (WITH JACK DANN)
DINOSAURS II (WITH JACK DANN)
HACKERS (WITH JACK DANN)
TIMEGATES (WITH JACK DANN)
CLONES (WITH JACK DANN)
NANOTECH (WITH JACK DANN)
IMMORTALS (WITH JACK DANN)
ARMAGEDDONS (WITH JACK DANN)
MODERN CLASICS OF SCIENCE FICTION
MODERN CLASSIC SHORT NOVELS OF
   SCIENCE FICTION
MODERN CLASSICS OF FANTASY
KILLING ME SOFTLY
DYING FOR IT
THE GOOD OLD STUFF
THE GOOD NEW STUFF

Fiction

STRANGERS
THE VISIBLE MAN (COLLECTION)
NIGHTMARE BLUE
   (WITH GEORGE ALEC EFFINGER)

Exploring the Horizons

Explorers
The Furthest Horizon

Edited by
GARDNER DOZOIS

SCIENCE
FICTION

EXPLORERS Copyright © 2000 by Gardner Dozois
   Publishing History: St. Martin's/Griffin trade paperback, April 2000

THE FURTHEST HORIZON Copyright © 2000 by Gardner Dozois
   Publishing History: St. Martin's/Griffin trade paperback, May 2000

First SFBC Science Fiction Printing: May 2000

Because this page can not legibly contain all the relevant copyright notices, pages 913–916 constitutes an extension of this copyright page.

Published by arrangement with:
St. Martin's Press
175 Fifth Avenue
New York, NY 10010

Visit The SFBC online at *http://www.sfbc.com*

ISBN 0-7394-1009-1

PRINTED IN THE UNITED STATES OF AMERICA.

CONTENTS

Explorers

CONTENTS

PREFACE

At one time, all humans were explorers, nomads who wandered ceaselessly over the face of the Earth. And even now, thousands of years later, after the invention of agriculture and towns, when most of us stay at home most of the time, many of us still feel a twinge of restlessness every once in a while, a desire to see what's over the next hill or in the next valley—a desire that we can sublimate and satisfy by listening to the travel tales of those who *don't* stay home, the explorers . . . those brave and reckless and restless enough to venture into unknown, uncharted territory and return to tell us what they've found.

Certainly humans have been telling tales of exploration for millennia—it was a venerable tradition even when Homer was telling his tales of danger-filled voyaging around Bronze Age campfires, and who knows what prehistoric *Odysseys*, now lost and forgotten, were being told around campfires thousands of years before *that*? Not surprisingly, those tales have often contained elements of fantasy, elements that probably crept in on a slow night when the tale-teller noticed that his audience was becoming bored and threw in a dragon or a cockatrice or a hundred-headed monster to spice things up a bit . . . and thus we got stories about the men over the next hill who wore their heads upside down, or the people of a distant country who drank human blood, or the land where the ants were as big as horses and mined gold.

Possibly the more sophisticated members of Homer's fireside audiences recognized these fantasy elements *as* fantasy even then and suspected that there weren't really man-eating Cyclops or sorceresses who turned men into swine out there, but it made for a good story—and besides, who knew for sure that there *weren't* such things, eh? The world was wide. There were many corners of it that no one had ever seen. Who knew *what* could be out there?

This uncertainty as to what was Out There has served authors well ever since, from Herodotus to Sir John Mandeville and Baron Münchausen, and even as late as the nineteenth century was enabling authors to get away with peppering the still largely unexplored (from a European perspective) continents of Africa and Asia with fabulous Lost Cities and Lost Civilizations, chock-full of ugly subhuman

Beast-Men and beautiful Caucasian girls in skimpy slave-girl outfits and/or revealingly sheer diaphanous gowns. But by the twentieth century the We-Don't-Know-What's-Out-There alibi was beginning to wear a little thin. Edgar Rice Burroughs littered his Africa with Lost Civilizations, as had H. Rider Haggard before him, but even in the first few decades of the new century, the Dark Continent wasn't quite as dark as it used to be, and it was becoming hard for all except the most determinedly credulous reader to believe that those gleaming alabaster Lost Cities were really *out* there somewhere in the jungle, waiting for Scientific Expeditions consisting of an Absentminded Professor and his Beautiful Daughter to stumble across them in chapter 2. Perhaps this is what motivated Burroughs to set up a competing shop on Mars, where it was harder to check up on him.

In fact, as the twentieth century progressed, as even the remotest and most inaccessible places on Earth—the poles, the Gobi Desert, the Congo, the Matto Grosso—were visited by explorers, and the formerly blank areas on the map began to fill up with tidy countries, or at least with detailed information, it became increasingly obvious that to explore *really* unknown territory, places where *no*body had ever gone before, future explorers, both real and fictional ones, would have to move *off* Earth altogether—and into the depths of space.

Writers of Space Opera had been banging around the solar system since the late twenties or early thirties, of course, and had even launched paper armadas into interstellar space, but as World War II approached, perhaps influenced by visionaries such as Konstantin Tsiolkovsky, Herman Oberth, Robert Goddard (who had himself been influenced by H. G. Wells), Wernher von Braun, Willy Ley, and the founding fathers of the British Interplanetary Society, people who actually wanted to *go* into space, for *real*, and who were carrying out the first crude experiments that might someday make that a possibility (and influenced as well by the Campbellian Revolution in science fiction, circa 1939, when the new editor of *Astounding* magazine, John W. Campbell, began downplaying the melodramatic pulp stuff in favor of more thoughtful material that actually made a stab at rigor and scientific accuracy), we began to get stories that took the idea of space exploration *seriously*, as something that might *actually happen*, as something that could actually be done, in the real world . . . that treated space as a real frontier that one day could be— and *would* be!—explored, rather than just as a setting, a colorful backdrop for chase-and-fight pulp fantasies that wouldn't have been much different in their essentials if the setting had been the Spanish Main rather than the rings of Saturn.

By the fifties, as the science-fiction world began to get into full swing again after the partial interregnum of World War II, new writers such as Arthur C. Clarke, Robert A. Heinlein, Hal Clement, Poul Anderson, and a dozen others had perfected the realistic space exploration story—and, ironically, by so doing, had helped to invoke the very thing they dreamed about, to *call* it into being, as if by incantation, by impressing their dream upon hundreds of young men and women who, inspired, would then go on to become the very scientists and engineers and technicians and astronauts who would make manned space travel a physical reality in the sixties and seventies.

By the mid- and later seventies, though, perhaps because of the prominence of the "New Wave" revolution in science fiction, which concentrated both on introspective, stylistically "experimental" work and work with more immediate sociological and political "relevance" to the tempestuous social scene of the day, perhaps because the space probes of the late sixties and early seventies had "proved" that the solar system was nothing but an "uninteresting" collection of balls of rock and ice, dull as a supermarket parking lot, with no available abodes for life, perhaps because of the feeling that the Space Age was *behind* us, a social aberration fading away into nostalgic memory (a feeling that started in the seventies and grew throughout the eighties as years—and finally decades—went by without a return to the Moon or seemingly any further progress into space), science fiction as a genre would tend to turn away from the Space Exploration tale, with most of the stories published taking place on Earth, often in the near-future, and dealing centrally with the sociological and/ or dystopian problems of society.

But then, in one of those ironic reversals characteristic of the genre, in the late seventies and early eighties a new crew of writers such as John Varley, Gregory Benford, Michael Swanwick, Kim Stanley Robinson, Vernor Vinge, Jack McDevitt, and others began to become interested in exploring the solar system again, began to find the solar system romantic and fascinating *just as it was,* lifeless balls of rock and all, even before the later *Voyager* probes to the Jupiter and Saturn system had proved the solar system to be a lot more complex, contradictory, and surprising place than people thought that it was . . . and by now, by the end of the nineties, the realistic Space Exploration story, reinvented to better fit the aesthetic style and tastes of the day in the hands of writers such as Greg Egan, Stephen Baxter, Allen Steele, Paul J. McAuley, G. David Nordley, Charles Sheffield, Geoffrey A. Landis, Ian McDonald, Alexander Jablokov, and a dozen others, is once again at the artistic center of the field.

This anthology, then, brings you a sampling of some of the best stories about explorers and exploration from almost fifty years of science-fiction writing, from 1950 to 1998. This kind of story has gone out of fashion occasionally during that time and may go out of fashion again, but it always comes back, and I suspect that it will continue to fascinate us as long as we look up at the stars at night and wonder what, or *who*, is Out There, as long as something deep inside us feels that restless itch to know what's over the far horizon—in other words, as long as we remain *human*, as we currently recognize the term.

So sit back and relax—you're about to go on a series of marvelous voyages, to explore strange new worlds and uncharted territories, to face strange new dangers and even stranger wonders, dangers and wonders of a sort that could never be encountered on our familiar, present-day Earth, to learn for *yourself* what's around the bend and over the next hill . . . and all without leaving your chair!

Enjoy.

The Sentinel

ARTHUR C. CLARKE

Arthur C. Clarke is perhaps the most famous modern science-fiction writer in the world, seriously rivaled for that title only by the late Isaac Asimov and Robert A. Heinlein. Clarke is probably most widely known for his work on Stanley Kubrick's film *2001: A Space Odyssey* but is also renowned as a novelist, short-story writer, and a writer of nonfiction, usually on technological subjects such as spaceflight. He has won three Nebula Awards, three Hugo Awards, the British Science Fiction Award, the John W. Campbell Memorial Award, and a Grandmaster Nebula for Life Achievement. His best-known books include the novels *Childhood's End, The City and the Stars, The Deep Range, Rendezvous with Rama, A Fall of Moondust, 2001: A Space Odyssey, 2010: Odyssey Two, 2061: Odyssey Three, Songs of Distant Earth,* and *The Fountains of Paradise* and the collections *The Nine Billion Names of God, Tales of Ten Worlds,* and *The Sentinel.* He has also written many nonfiction books on scientific topics, the best-known of which are probably *Profiles of the Future* and *The Wind from the Sun,* and is generally considered to be the man who first came up with the idea of the communications satellite. His most recent books are the novel *3001: The Final Odyssey* and the nonfiction collection *Greetings, Carbon-Based Bipeds: Collected Works 1944–1998.* Born in Somerset, England, Clarke now lives in Sri Lanka and was recently knighted

Clarke may well have written more, and more memorably, about the theme of exploration, particularly space exploration, than any other science-fiction writer, dealing with it with one degree or another of centralness in novels and stories such as *Rendezvous with Rama,* "A Meeting with Medusa" (to be found elsewhere in this anthology), "Before Eden," *The Sands of Mars, The City and the Stars,* "Rescue Party," "Summertime on Icarus," "Out of the Sun," *Songs of Distant Earth,* "The Star," "Transit of Earth," and all of the *Odyssey* novels, as well as in scores of other stories and in dozens of nonfiction articles.

He's seldom handled the theme better, though, than in the classic story that follows, the inspiration for the later movie *2001: A Space Odyssey,* which I think actually works *better* than the film in some ways—a near-perfect miniature that captures the odd blend of minutely detailed scientific accuracy and sweeping

Stapeldonian mysticism that is the essence of Clark's work and a story still capable of delivering in its last few lines that shiver of mingled fear and wonder that is one of the hallmarks of science fiction at its best.

The next time you see the full Moon high in the south, look carefully at its right-hand edge and let your eye travel upward along the curve of the disk. Round about two o'clock you will notice a small, dark oval: anyone with normal eyesight can find it quite easily. It is the great walled plain, one of the finest on the Moon, known as the Mare Crisium—the Sea of Crises. Three hundred miles in diameter, and almost completely surrounded by a ring of magnificent mountains, it had never been explored until we entered it in the late summer of 1996.

Our expedition was a large one. We had two heavy freighters which had flown our supplies and equipment from the main lunar base in the Mare Serenitatis, five hundred miles away. There were also three small rockets which were intended for short-range transport over regions which our surface vehicles couldn't cross. Luckily, most of the Mare Crisium is very flat. There are none of the great crevasses so common and so dangerous elsewhere, and very few craters or mountains of any size. As far as we could tell, our powerful caterpillar tractors would have no difficulty in taking us wherever we wished to go.

I was geologist—or selenologist, if you want to be pedantic—in charge of the group exploring the southern region of the Mare. We had crossed a hundred miles of it in a week, skirting the foothills of the mountains along the shore of what was once the ancient sea, some thousand million years before. When life was beginning on Earth, it was already dying here. The waters were retreating down the flanks of those stupendous cliffs, retreating into the empty heart of the Moon. Over the land which we were crossing, the tideless ocean had once been half a mile deep, and now the only trace of moisture was the hoarfrost one could sometimes find in caves which the searing sunlight never penetrated.

We had begun our journey early in the slow lunar dawn, and still had almost a week of Earth time before nightfall. Half a dozen times a day we would leave our vehicle and go outside in the space suits to hunt for interesting minerals, or to place markers for the guidance of future travelers. It was an uneventful routine. There is nothing hazardous or even particularly exciting about lunar exploration. We could live comfortably for a month in our pressurized tractors, and if we ran into trouble we could always radio for help and sit tight until one of the spaceships came to our rescue.

I said just now that there was nothing exciting about lunar exploration, but of course that isn't true. One could never grow tired of those incredible mountains, so much more rugged than the gentle hills of Earth. We never knew, as we rounded the capes and promontories of that vanished sea, what new splendors would be revealed to us. The whole southern curve of the Mare Crisium is a vast delta where a score of rivers once found their way into the ocean, fed perhaps by the torrential rains that must have lashed the mountains in the brief volcanic age when the Moon was young. Each of these ancient valleys was an invitation, challenging us to climb into the unknown uplands beyond. But we had a hundred miles still to cover, and could only look longingly at the heights which others must scale.

We kept Earth time aboard the tractor, and precisely at 2200 hours the final radio message would be sent out to Base and we would close down for the day. Outside, the rocks would still be burning beneath the almost vertical sun, but to us it was night until we awoke again eight hours later. Then one of us would prepare breakfast, there would be a great buzzing of electric razors, and someone would switch on the shortwave radio from Earth. Indeed, when the smell of frying sausages began to fill the cabin, it was sometimes hard to believe that we were not back on our own world—everything was so normal and homely, apart from the feeling of decreased weight and the unnatural slowness with which objects fell.

It was my turn to prepare breakfast in the corner of the main cabin that served as a galley. I can remember that moment quite vividly after all these years, for the radio had just played one of my favorite melodies, the old Welsh air "David of the White Rock." Our driver was already outside in his space suit, inspecting our caterpillar treads. My assistant, Louis Garnett, was up forward in the control position, making some belated entries in yesterday's log.

As I stood by the frying pan waiting, like any terrestrial housewife, for the sausages to brown, I let my gaze wander idly over the mountain walls which covered the whole of the southern horizon, marching out of sight to east and west below the curve of the Moon. They seemed only a mile or two from the tractor, but I knew that the nearest was twenty miles away. On the Moon, of course, there is no loss of detail with distance—none of that almost imperceptible haziness which softens and sometimes transfigures all far-off things on Earth.

Those mountains were ten thousand feet high, and they climbed steeply out of the plain as if ages ago some subterranean eruption had smashed them skyward through the molten crust. The base of even the nearest was hidden from sight by the steeply curving surface of the plain, for the Moon is a very little world, and from where I was standing the horizon was only two miles away.

I lifted my eyes toward the peaks which no man had ever climbed, the peaks which, before the coming of terrestrial life, had watched the retreating oceans sink sullenly into their graves, taking with them the hope and the morning promise of a world. The sunlight was beating against those ramparts with a glare that hurt the eyes, yet only a little way above them the stars were shining steadily in a sky blacker than a winter midnight on Earth.

I was turning away when my eye caught a metallic glitter high on the ridge of a great promontory thrusting out into the sea thirty miles to the west. It was a dimensionless point of light, as if a star had been clawed from the sky by one of those cruel peaks, and I imagined that some smooth rock surface was catching the sunlight and heliographing it straight into my eyes. Such things were not uncommon. When the Moon is in her second quarter, observers on Earth can sometimes see the great ranges in the Oceanus Procellarum burning with a blue-white iridescence as the sunlight flashes from their slopes and leaps again from world to world. But I was curious to know what kind of rock could be shining so brightly up there, and I climbed into the observation turret and swung our four-inch telescope round to the west.

I could see just enough to tantalize me. Clear and sharp in the field of vision, the mountain peaks seemed only half a mile away, but whatever was catching the sunlight was still too small to be resolved. Yet it seemed to have an elusive symmetry, and the summit upon which it rested was curiously flat. I stared for a long time at that glittering enigma, straining my eyes into space, until presently a smell of burning from the galley told me that our breakfast sausages had made their quarter-million-mile journey in vain.

All that morning we argued our way across the Mare Crisium while the western mountains reared higher in the sky. Even when we were out prospecting in the space suits, the discussion would continue over the radio. It was absolutely certain, my companions argued, that there had never been any form of intelligent life on the Moon. The only living things that had ever existed there were a few primitive plants and their slightly less degenerate ancestors. I knew that as well as anyone, but there are times when a scientist must not be afraid to make a fool of himself.

"Listen," I said at last, "I'm going up there, if only for my own peace of mind. That mountain's less than twelve thousand feet high—that's only two thousand under Earth gravity—and I can make the trip in twenty hours at the outside. I've always wanted to go up into those hills, anyway, and this gives me an excellent excuse."

"If you don't break your neck," said Garnett, "you'll be the laughingstock of the expedition when we get back to Base. That mountain will probably be called Wilson's Folly from now on."

"I won't break my neck," I said firmly. "Who was the first man to climb Pico and Helicon?"

"But weren't you rather younger in those days?" asked Louis gently.

"That," I said with great dignity, "is as good a reason as any for going."

We went to bed early that night, after driving the tractor to within half a mile of the promontory. Garnett was coming with me in the morning; he was a good climber, and had often been with me on such exploits before. Our driver was only too glad to be left in charge of the machine.

At first sight, those cliffs seemed completely unscalable, but to anyone with a good head for heights, climbing is easy on a world where all weights are only a sixth of their normal value. The real danger in lunar mountaineering lies in over-confidence; a six-hundred-foot drop on the Moon can kill you just as thoroughly as a hundred-foot fall on Earth.

We made our first halt on a wide ledge about four thousand feet above the plain. Climbing had not been very difficult, but my limbs were stiff with the un-accustomed effort, and I was glad of the rest. We could still see the tractor as a tiny metal insect far down at the foot of the cliff, and we reported our progress to the driver before starting on the next ascent.

Inside our suits it was comfortably cool, for the refrigeration units were fighting the fierce sun and carrying away the body heat of our exertions. We seldom spoke to each other, except to pass climbing instructions and to discuss our best plan of ascent. I do not know what Garnett was thinking, probably that this was the craziest goose chase he had ever embarked upon. I more than half agreed with him, but the joy of climbing, the knowledge that no man had ever gone this way before and the exhilaration of the steadily widening landscape gave me all the reward I needed.

I don't think I was particularly excited when I saw in front of us the wall of rock I had first inspected through the telescope from thirty miles away. It would level off about fifty feet above our heads, and there on the plateau would be the thing that had lured me over these barren wastes. It was, almost certainly, nothing more than a boulder splintered ages ago by a falling meteor, and with its cleavage planes still fresh and bright in this incorruptible, unchanging silence.

There were no handholds on the rock face, and we had to use a grapnel. My tired arms seemed to gain new strength as I swung the three-pronged metal anchor round my head and sent it sailing up toward the stars. The first time it broke loose and came falling slowly back when we pulled the rope. On the third attempt, the prongs gripped firmly and our combined weights could not shift it.

Garnett looked at me anxiously. I could tell that he wanted to go first, but I smiled back at him through the glass of my helmet and shook my head. Slowly, taking my time, I began the final ascent.

Even with my space suit, I weighed only forty pounds here, so I pulled myself up hand over hand without bothering to use my feet. At the rim I paused and waved to my companion; then I scrambled over the edge and stood upright, staring ahead of me.

You must understand that until this very moment I had been almost completely convinced that there could be nothing strange or unusual for me to find here. Almost, but not quite; it was that haunting doubt that had driven me forward. Well, it was a doubt no longer, but the haunting had scarcely begun.

I was standing on a plateau perhaps a hundred feet across. It had once been smooth—too smooth to be natural—but falling meteors had pitted and scored its surface through immeasurable eons. It had been leveled to support a glittering, roughly pyramidal structure, twice as high as a man, that was set in the rock like a gigantic many-faceted jewel.

Probably no emotion at all filled my mind in those first few seconds. Then I felt a great lifting of my heart, and a strange, inexpressible joy. For I loved the Moon, and now I knew that the creeping moss of Aristarchus and Eratosthenes was not the only life she had brought forth in her youth. The old, discredited dream of the first explorers was true. There had, after all, been a lunar civilization—and I was the first to find it. That I had come perhaps a hundred million years too late did not distress me; it was enough to have come at all.

My mind was beginning to function normally, to analyze and to ask questions. Was this a building, a shrine—or something for which my language had no name? If a building, then why was it erected in so uniquely inaccessible a spot? I wondered if it might be a temple, and I could picture the adepts of some strange priesthood calling on their gods to preserve them as the life of the Moon ebbed with the dying oceans, and calling on their gods in vain.

I took a dozen steps forward to examine the thing more closely, but some sense of caution kept me from going too near. I knew a little of archaeology, and tried to guess the cultural level of the civilization that must have smoothed this mountain and raised the glittering mirror surfaces that still dazzled my eyes.

The Egyptians could have done it, I thought, if their workmen had possessed whatever strange materials these far more ancient architects had used. Because of the thing's smallness, it did not occur to me that I might be looking at the handiwork of a race more advanced than my own. The idea that the Moon had possessed intelligence at all was still almost too tremendous to grasp, and my pride would not let me take the final, humiliating plunge.

And then I noticed something that set the scalp crawling at the back of my neck—something so trivial and so innocent that many would never have noticed it at all. I have said that the plateau was scarred by meteors; it was also coated inches deep with the cosmic dust that is always filtering down upon the surface of any world where there are no winds to disturb it. Yet the dust and the meteor scratches ended quite abruptly in a wide circle enclosing the little pyramid, as though an invisible wall was protecting it from the ravages of time and the slow but ceaseless bombardment from space.

There was someone shouting in my earphones, and I realized that Garnett had been calling me for some time. I walked unsteadily to the edge of the cliff and signaled him to join me, not trusting myself to speak. Then I went back toward that circle in the dust. I picked up a fragment of splintered rock and tossed it gently toward the shining enigma. If the pebble had vanished at that invisible barrier I should not have been surprised, but it seemed to hit a smooth, hemispherical surface and slide gently to the ground.

I knew then that I was looking at nothing that could be matched in the antiquity of my own race. This was not a building, but a machine, protecting itself with forces that had challenged Eternity. Those forces, whatever they might be, were still operating, and perhaps I had already come too close. I thought of all the radiations man had trapped and tamed in the past century. For all I knew, I might be as irrevocably doomed as if I had stepped into the deadly, silent aura of an unshielded atomic pile.

I remember turning then toward Garnett, who had joined me and was now standing motionless at my side. He seemed quite oblivious to me, so I did not disturb him but walked to the edge of the cliff in an effort to marshal my thoughts. There below me lay the Mare Crisium—Sea of Crises, indeed—strange and weird to most men, but reassuringly familiar to me. I lifted my eyes toward the crescent Earth, lying in her cradle of stars, and I wondered what her clouds had covered when these unknown builders had finished their work. Was it the steaming jungle of the Carboniferous, the bleak shoreline over which the first amphibians must crawl to conquer the land—or, earlier still, the long loneliness before the coming of life?

Do not ask me why I did not guess the truth sooner—the truth that seems so obvious now. In the first excitement of my discovery, I had assumed without question that this crystalline apparition had been built by some race belonging to the Moon's remote past, but suddenly, and with overwhelming force, the belief came to me that it was as alien to the Moon as I myself.

In twenty years we had found no trace of life but a few degenerate plants. No lunar civilization, whatever its doom, could have left but a single token of its existence.

I looked at the shining pyramid again, and the more remote it seemed from anything that had to do with the Moon. And suddenly I felt myself shaking with a foolish, hysterical laughter, brought on by excitement and overexertion: for I had imagined that the little pyramid was speaking to me and was saying: "Sorry, I'm a stranger here myself."

It has taken us twenty years to crack that invisible shield and to reach the machine inside those crystal walls. What we could not understand, we broke at last with the savage might of atomic power and now I have seen the fragments of the lovely, glittering thing I found up there on the mountain.

They are meaningless. The mechanisms—if indeed they are mechanisms—of the pyramid belong to a technology that lies far beyond our horizon, perhaps to the technology of paraphysical forces.

The mystery haunts us all the more now that the other planets have been reached and we know that only Earth has ever been the home of intelligent life in our Universe. Nor could any lost civilization of our own world have built that machine, for the thickness of the meteoric dust on the plateau has enabled us to measure its age. It was set there upon its mountain before life had emerged from the seas of Earth.

When our world was half its present age, *something* from the stars swept through the Solar System, left this token of its passage, and went again upon its way. Until we destroyed it, that machine was still fulfilling the purpose of its builders; and as to that purpose, here is my guess.

Nearly a hundred thousand million stars are turning in the circle of the Milky Way, and long ago other races on the worlds of other suns must have scaled and passed the heights that we have reached. Think of such civilizations, far back in time against the fading afterglow of Creation, masters of a Universe so young that life as yet had come only to a handful of worlds. Theirs would have been a loneliness we cannot imagine, the loneliness of gods looking out across infinity and finding none to share their thoughts.

They must have searched the star clusters as we have searched the planets. Everywhere there would be worlds, but they would be empty or peopled with crawling, mindless things. Such was our own Earth, the smoke of the great volcanoes still staining the skies, when that first ship of the peoples of the dawn came sliding in from the abyss beyond Pluto. It passed the frozen outer worlds, knowing that life could play no part in their destinies. It came to rest among the inner planets, warming themselves around the fire of the Sun and waiting for their stories to begin.

Those wanderers must have looked on Earth, circling safely in the narrow zone between fire and ice, and must have guessed that it was the favorite of the Sun's children. Here, in the distant future, would be intelligence; but there were countless stars before them still, and they might never come this way again.

So they left a sentinel, one of millions they have scattered throughout the Universe, watching over all worlds with the promise of life. It was a beacon that down the ages has been patiently signaling the fact that no one had discovered it.

Perhaps you understand now why that crystal pyramid was set upon the Moon instead of on the Earth. Its builders were not concerned with races still struggling up from savagery. They would be interested in our civilization only if we proved our fitness to survive—by crossing space and so escaping from the Earth, our cradle. That is the challenge that all intelligent races must meet, sooner or later. It is a double challenge, for it depends in turn upon the conquest of atomic energy and the last choice between life and death.

Once we had passed that crisis, it was only a matter of time before we found the pyramid and forced it open. Now its signals have ceased, and those whose duty it is will be turning their minds upon Earth. Perhaps they wish to help our infant civilization. But they must be very, very old, and the old are often insanely jealous of the young.

I can never look now at the Milky Way without wondering from which of those banked clouds of stars the emissaries are coming. If you will pardon so commonplace a simile, we have set off the fire alarm and have nothing to do but to wait.

I do not think we will have to wait for long.

Moonwalk

H. B FYFE

Although H. B. Fyfe sold primarily to *Astounding* in the course of his twenty-seven-year career, it was the memorable story that follows, "Moonwalk," published in a second-string pulp magazine called *Space Science Fiction,* that would have the greatest impact on subsequent science fiction. A gritty, hard-edged, and realistic look at one man's struggle to survive in the face of almost overwhelming odds, stranded and alone on the surface of a hostile Moon, with his air running out, "Moonwalk" would inspire—consciously or unconsciously—dozens of similar stories in the years to come, an influence that persists right up to the present day. It remains one of the seminal classics of space exploration.

H. B. Fyfe sold his first story in 1940. By the time he retired in 1967, he had published more than sixty works of short fiction, most of them in his "Bureau of Slick Tricks" series for *Astounding,* and one novel, *D-99,* set in the same series. Fyfe died in 1996 and is survived by his widow, Sonia.

The radio operator stopped sending out his call and slumped back in the folding chair of canvas and aluminum. Concern showed through the impassivity of his broad, Mexican features.

The footsteps in the corridor outside the radio room pattered lightly because of the Lunar gravity, but with a haste that suggested urgency. Two men entered. Like the operator, they wore dungarees and heavy sweaters, but the gray-haired man had an air of authority.

"Dr. Burney wanted to check with you himself, Mike," said the youth with him.

The operator shrugged.

"Tractor One is okay, Doctor," he reported, "but as Joey must have told you, we've lost Two."

"When was the last time they called in?" asked Burney.

Mike gestured at the map on the side wall, and the elder man stepped over to study it. The area shown was that surrounding the fifty-mile-wide crater of Archi-medes.

"The blue line is One and the red is Two," said Mike. "I guess you know the planned routes. Well, the little *x*'s show the positions reported and the times."

Burney glanced briefly at the blue line. From the black square near the northern side of the crater that represented the first major base on Luna, it climbed slantingly over the ringwall. After zigzagging down the broken outer slope and skirting a ridge of vein mountains, the line swept in a wide curve north of Aristillus and Autolycus, the next largest craters of the region, and moved into that subregion of the Mare Imbrium, whimsically christened "Misty Swamp." Thereafter, the blue trail led toward possible passes through the Lunar Apennines to the Mare Sereni-tatis.

"I could expect to lose One," muttered the operator, "in spite of our tower here. But Two shouldn't be blocked by anything yet."

The red line was more direct. Parting from the blue north of the ringwall of Archimedes, it pushed out across the level plain, avoiding isolated mountain ridges and the seven-mile craters of Kirch and Piazza Smyth. After something like three hundred miles, it passed the towering lonely Mt. Pico and probed a dotted delta of possible routes up the ringwall of Plato. This route was *x*'ed almost to Pico.

"They were supposed to report before attempting the descent," mused Burney. "Maybe the depression of the Mare Imbrium isn't quite what we estimated. The normal curvature would put a lot of rock between us, in that case. An awful lot of rock."

"Maybe they went over the ringwall in a hurry," suggested Joey.

Burney considered that in a short silence. He ran a hand absently over his balding temple. His lean face became a mask of lines as he puckered up his eyes in thought.

"Number Two has Hansen driving, hasn't it? And Groswald, the mechanic . . . Van Ness, the astronomer . . . and who else?"

"Fernandez from Geology," said Joey.

The entire personnel of the base numbered scarcely fifty. They were just be-ginning their surface exploration projects after completing the low domes of their buildings. With such scanty resources, Burney was naturally worried about four men and one of the precious tractors.

"They were with us an hour ago," said Mike, fingering his microphone. "Their set must have gone sour."

When no one replied, he hitched around to face his own controls.

"Or else, they're in trouble—"

On the ledge atop the ringwall of Plato, Hansen teetered and tried to maintain his balance by pressing a gauntleted hand against an outcropping of gray Lunar rock. The thermal-eroded surface crumbled slightly beneath the metal-tipped mitten.

In his bulky space suit, he found it difficult to lean very far forward, but he could not bear not seeing. The landslip tumbled down the inner slope of the ring-wall with horrible deliberation.

"I told them 'Don't move her till I find a way down!' " Hansen muttered. "I told them, I *told* them!"

He was hardly conscious of speaking aloud. Somewhere in the churning mass was the vacuum tractor in which he had driven from Archimedes. Inside, unless it had already been split open, were Van Ness, Groswald, and Fernandez.

The collection of loose rock and dust passed out of sight for a moment over the edge of a terrace. It reappeared farther down. Once, Hansen thought he saw a glint of bright metal, but the slide almost immediately plunged down another sheer drop.

The phase of Luna being closer to "new" than to "first quarter," the sun was far too low on the horizon to light the floor of the crater, or even the three mountain peaks on the ringwall to Hansen's right front. The light from the gibbous Earth, however, was bright enough for him to see quite clearly the surface around him.

The slide finally reached the bottom, at this point nearly three thousand feet below the man's precarious position. He breathed deeply and tried to straighten the ache from his shoulders.

"Must have taken five minutes," he murmured, realizing that he had frozen in a cramped position as he stared.

It had seemed more like an hour. In the dim shadows of the crater floor, the dust settled rapidly because of the lack of air, but the debris remained heaped at an angle much steeper than would have been possible on Earth. Even the slight vibration Hansen had felt through his boots ceased.

He was alone in the dead silence of a world for eons dead.

He stood there, a spot of color in the chrome yellow of the protective chafing suit. The transparent faceplate of his unpainted helmet revealed a blond young man, perhaps twenty-six, with a lean, square-jawed face. Against the tanned skin, his eyebrows were ludicrously light, but the gray eyes under them were wide with horror.

He was of medium height, but the bulkiness of the suit hid his welterweight trimness; and the pack of oxygen tank and batteries for powering radio, heat pads, and air circulator increased the appearance of stubbiness.

The quiet hiss of the air being circulated through his suit finally aroused him. With painstaking care, he climbed from the ledge to the level terrace on which the tractor was to have remained while he scouted the route down. A hundred yards away, a great bite seemed to have been snapped out of the ridge.

"All the way from Archimedes, and we didn't even get a look at the floor," he whispered.

For a moment, following the raw scar of the slide with his eye, he considered climbing all the way down and venturing out onto the crater floor to examine the ground. For centuries, the floor of Plato had been reported by Earth observers to darken with the rising sun until at noon it was nearly black. Occasionally, there were stories of misty clouds obscuring the surface, and of shifts in the pattern of light streaks and spots.

One of the expedition's first assignments, therefore, had been the investigation of Plato, to check the unlikely possibility that there might be some primitive, airless form of life present. But the present sortie was clearly ended.

"Not one damn chance," Hansen told himself as he squinted downward. "None of them had a suit on when I got out."

On a terrace about a third of the way down lay an object with an oddly regular shape. It gleamed in the blue-green earthlight, and Hansen peered more intently. It looked like one of the spare oxygen cylinders that had been carried on top of the tractor.

Hansen abruptly became sensitive about the supply of his suit tank. Before he did anything, even sitting down to think the situation over, he wanted to get down there and find out if the cylinder was full.

Despite his eagerness, he held back until he thought he had spied a reasonable path. It involved going two or three hundred feet out of his way, but Hansen managed to work his way down to the lower level without serious difficulty. Once or twice, he slithered a few feet when loose rock shaled off under his grip, but even with his suit and equipment, he weighed little over forty pounds. As long as he did not drop very far, he could always stop himself one-handed.

He walked back along the level strip which was about fifty yards wide at this point, until he approached the path of the landslip. Near it, apparently having been scraped off as the tractor rolled, lay the cylinder.

He checked it hurriedly.

"Whew! Well, that's some help, anyway," he told himself, discovering that the tank had not been tapped.

He left the cylinder and walked over to the inner limit of the level band. Scanning the steep slope and the debris of the slide, he thought he could pick out two or three scraps of twisted metal. There was nothing to be done.

"I'd better get back up and think this out," he decided.

He took the broken chain that had held the tank to the tractor and hooked a broken link through it to make a sling. For the time being, he contented himself with using it as a handle to drag the lucky supply of oxygen after him.

After regaining his original position, the going was easier to the top of the ringwall. They had come over one of the several passes crossing the southern part of the cliffs, and Hansen walked through in a few minutes. The thickness of the ringwall here was only a mile or so, although at the base it probably approached ten miles.

He came out onto a little plateau, and the dim plain of the Mare Imbrium spread out before him. Hansen suddenly felt tiny, lost, and insignificant.

"What am I gonna do?" he asked himself.

For the first time, he had admitted his predicament to himself. His gauntlet crept up to his chest where the switch of his radio protruded through the chafing suit.

"Hello Base! Tractor Two to Base! Tractor Two to Base. Over."

He waited several minutes, and repeated the call five or six times. He screwed his eyes shut to throw every ounce of concentration into listening.

No human voice broke into the quiet hissing of the earphones. Hansen sighed.

"Never reach them, of course!" he grumbled. "This set is made to reach about your arm's length."

He remembered that Van Ness had complained about the reception the last time they had called in, and asked Hansen to maneuver to the top of a ridge of vein mountains near the hulking silhouette of Pico. Hansen was higher now, but also much farther from home.

"Mike Ramirez and Joey Friedman aren't the kind to miss a call," he muttered. "It seems to me, Paul E. Hansen, my boy . . . that you are . . . on your own!"

The radio had been but a faint hope, inspired by his height and tales of freak reception. He was not too disappointed. Looking down the rough outer slope of the ringwall, he saw that it was not by any means as steep as the inner, and that fact settled it.

"Guess I'd better see how far I can get," Hansen decided. "When they don't get the regular report over the tractor radio, they'll probably send out another crew to follow the trail. If I can meet them out a way, maybe even as far as Pico, it'll save that much time."

After considerable fumbling, he balanced the large cylinder on his back atop the other equipment with the chain sling across his chest. He started along the series of gentle slopes the tractor had climbed earlier. Deliberately, he pushed to the back of his mind the possibility he would have to face sometime: Base might decide the crew had been too eager to negotiate the ringwall to call back before being blanked out by the mass of rock.

He had to restrain a temptation to rush headlong down to the plain across miles of rough grades. Even with his tremendous load of equipment, he might still travel in twenty-foot bounds in Lunar gravity; but he had no desire to plunge all the way to the bottom with one misstep.

"It'll be easy enough going down," he murmured. "And after that, I can judge the direction well enough from Earth."

He looked up at the brightness of the planet. Earth was rather high in the Lunar sky, although not overhead because of his position far north. It would indicate roughly his southerly course toward Archimedes. As he looked, he noticed that much of the eastern coast of North America, which to his view was almost centered on the hemisphere, was blanketed in clouds.

"Wish I was there right now," he sighed. "Rain and all!"

He wondered about the next step as he worked his way around ridges radiating from the sizable minor craterlet in Plato's ringwall. He still had a good view of the gray plain at the foot of the heights. Although reasonably flat—probably leveled by the colossal flow of lava that had formed the Mare Imbrium, filling older craters and melting down or inundating existing mountains until merely their crests showed—it contained many hills and irregularities that would be even more apparent to a man on foot than from the tractor.

He worked past the craterlet, leaving it to his right. Whenever he struck a reasonably level stretch, he moved at a bounding trot. The first time he tried this, he tumbled head over heels and gave himself a fright lest he rupture the space suit on a projecting rock. Thereafter, he was more careful until he got used to being so top-heavy because of the huge oxygen tank.

Finally, scrambling down the last ridges of old debris, he found himself on the level floor of the Sea of Showers, in the region between Plato and the jutting, lonely Mt. Pico. Off to his right, an extension of the ringwall behind him thrust out to point at the group of other peaks known as the Teneriffe Mountains, which were somewhat like a flock of lesser Picos. The ground on which he stood had perhaps once been part of another crater, twin in size to Plato, but now only detectable by faint outlines and vein mountains. In the past, some astronomers had called it Newton, before deciding upon a more worthy landmark for Sir Isaac.

It had taken Hansen nearly half an hour, and he paused now to catch his breath.

"I feel pretty good," he exclaimed with relief. "I'm carrying quite a lot to go at that speed, but I don't seem to get tired." He thought a moment, and warned himself, "You'd better not, either!"

He turned partly to look at the ringwall towering behind him. It loomed grimly, scored with deep shadows of cracks into which the rays of Earth, seventy times brighter than moonlight it received from Luna, could not penetrate.

Hansen turned away hastily. The mountainous mass made him uneasy; he remembered how easily a landslip had started on the inner slope.

"I'd better get moving!"

He struck out at a brisk, bounding pace, a trot on Luna without the effort of a normal trot. The ground was fairly level, and he congratulated himself upon making good time. Once or twice, he staggered a little, having overbalanced; but he soon got into the rhythm of the pace and the load on his back ceased to bother him. He bore slightly to the right, toward the jutting point of the ringwall.

The footing was like powdery gray sand. Alternating extremes of temperature during the two-week Lunar day or night had cracked the rock surface until successive expansions and contractions had affected the crystalline structure of the top layers. When these had flaked off, the powder had formed an insulating layer, but the result as far as Hansen was concerned was that he trotted on a sandy footing. When he looked back, he could see the particles kicked up by his last few steps still above the surface. They fell rather neatly, there being no air to whirl them about.

Gradually, he realized that the unobtrusive noises of his space suit had risen a notch in tone. The clever little machines were laboring to dispel the effects of his faster breathing. He dropped down to an easy walk, which was still a goodly pace in the light gravity.

"Guess I'm sweating more, too," he told himself. "Now that I think of it, my mouth's a little dry."

He twisted his neck until he could get his lips on the thin rubber hose sticking up to the left of his chin. He closed his teeth on the clamp, and sucked up a few swallows of water from his tank. It was not particularly tasty, but at least it was cool. It would have been a lot colder if carried uninsulated, he reflected. The night temperature of Luna was something like minus one-fifty Centigrade, and it dropped like a shot as soon as the surface was shaded from the sun.

Refreshed, he started out again at a bounding run, rejoicing in his strength. He felt as if he were just jogging along, but the ground rolled back under his feet swiftly. Had he been on such a bleak desert on Earth, he knew he would be slogging ankle-deep in sand—if he could move at all. His own weight was between a hundred and fifty and a hundred and sixty pounds. With what he was wearing and carrying, he was probably close to three hundred. It did not bother him here.

"It isn't bad at all," he thought with satisfaction. "Feels like jogging around the track in school, warming up for a race. One . . . two . . . three . . . four—still got pretty good form! Not even breathing hard!"

It occurred to him that it resembled a footrace in one other particular. He was deliberately putting off consideration of the finish while he still felt good.

"Oh, I'll meet them somewhere along the way," he said aloud, despite a momentary doubt that he was talking too much to himself. "Pretty soon, I'll cross the tractor trail. I'll follow it out maybe as far as Pico and wait for them to pick me up. The relief crew can't miss a landmark like that. It's damn near nine thousand feet high, straight up out of the flat plain."

He slowed down somewhat to scrutinize a ridge ahead. It turned out to be an easy grade and he skimmed over it easily. Otherwise, however, he was beginning to lose his recent feeling of satisfaction. Now that he moved out into the flat, empty plain, the essential grimness of Lunar landscape was more apparent than when disguised by the majesty of the view from atop the ringwall. It was a study in gray and black, the powdery sand and the deep shadows groping toward him as he trotted into the earthshine. Above was the deep black of an airless sky, lit by the bright Earth and chilly stars.

Gray, black, green, white—and all of it cold and inhospitable.

"I feel like I'm not wanted here," Hansen thought. "Well, that makes it mutual, I guess!"

He looked back, and was amazed at the distance he had covered. Already, Plato looked more like a range of towering mountains than it did like a barrier of cliffs.

"This won't take so long," he reassured himself. "I must have covered five miles running like this. Maybe almost ten."

He circled a tiny craterlet, or "bead," a few hundred yards across. In the precise center, it had a tiny peak, corresponding to the central mountain masses found in nearly half the craters of Luna. For the first time, Hansen regretted the camera that had gone down with the tractor.

"Too busy driving to take any pix on the way," he growled, "and now that I come across a perfect miniature, I have no camera. A fine spare photographer for an expedition this size!"

He diverted himself for a few minutes by considering what a fool he was to come to Luna in the first place. He had not really wanted to, and he was sure there were plenty of others who would have been better qualified and better pleased at the opportunity. Still, it was strange sometimes how a man would do things he did not want to because someone else was doing them.

He glanced up at Earth, and kept moving southward with the shining globe on his left front.

Mike and Joey sat before their radio, on a folding chair and empty crate respectively, maintaining whenever not directly addressed an almost sullen silence. Their tiny cubicle was becoming entirely too crowded to suit them.

Dr. Burney paced up and down before the wall map of the Mare Imbrium. Opposite him, the lower section of the radiomen's double bunk—canvas and aluminum like their single chair—had collected an overload of three. Dr. Sherman, the chief astronomer, sat between Bucky O'Neil and Emil Wohl. Besides heading the geologists, Wohl was Burney's second in command; and O'Neil was present in case it was decided to send out a rocket to photograph the Plato region.

"Ya'd think they could use their own rooms," Joey whispered into Mike's ear. "All but Bucky got singles. How we gonna catch an incoming call with all this racket?"

The "racket" at the moment consisted mostly of sighs, finger drumming, and a tortured semiwhistle from where Sherman sat staring at the map with his chin cupped in one hand.

"There's little doubt of the general location," repeated Burney, once more reaching a familiar impasse. "But I hate to hold up the other work to send out a crew when we cannot with any certainty agree that something has gone wrong."

"Let's see," said Wohl. "There was some difficulty, was there not, the last time they communicated?"

When no one answered, Mike finally repeated his previous testimony.

"Van Ness said they drove up a sort of mountain to get us. Complained a little about reception. He might've been getting to the limit."

"Then," said Wohl, "there is really no reason for alarm, is there? They could just as well have decided that continuing the mission was more important than running around looking for a good radio position, couldn't they?"

Mike considered that glumly.

"It's funny they didn't back up far enough to make *one* call to let me know they were going out of reach," he grumbled. "The speed they make in that rig, it wouldn'ta taken them long."

"That would have been the proper action," admitted Burney, "but we must not demand perfect adherence to the rules when a group is in the field and may have perfectly good reasons for disregarding them. No, I think we had best—Who's that coming?"

Bucky O'Neil bounded up from the end of the bunk and stuck his head out the door. When he looked around, his freckled face was unhappy.

"Johnny Pierce from the map section," he announced. "He's got Louise with him. I guess you don't need me any more."

He edged out the door as two others of the base staff came in. The one who acted as if he had business there was a lean, bespectacled man who managed to achieve a vaguely scholarly air despite rough clothing.

Trailing him was a girl who looked as if the heating economy that necessitated the standard costume of the base also had the effect of cheating the male personnel of a brightening influence. The shapeless clothing, however, did not lessen the attractiveness of her lightly tanned features or lively black eyes. She wore her dark hair tucked into a knit cap that on Earth probably would have been donned only as a joke.

"We've looked at the photo maps," Pierce reported in a dry, husky voice. "They might very well be out of range. Lots of curvature in that distance, even with the depression caused by a mass of lava like that Mare Imbrium."

Burney accepted this with an expression of relief.

"I heard them talking about the Plato crew," the girl put in. "What's going on?"

Her voice was warm and, like a singer's, stronger than her petite outline would have suggested.

"Oh . . . just checking the radio reception," said Burney. "You can get the details from Mike, I suppose, if you have time off from the observatory. The rest of us are through here."

Mike scowled, and the girl looked puzzled; but Burney, Wohl, and Sherman crowded through the door as if intent upon some new project. Sherman muttered something about the problem of erecting a transparent dome for direct observations, and the voices receded down the corridor. Pierce slipped out after them.

"Did I say something?" inquired Louise. "I only thought there might be news."

"I guess they're just busy, Louise," Mike said. He turned to the radio, unplugged the speaker, and donned a set of earphones. "You know how it is. Why don't you catch Bucky? *He's* got nothing to do for a while."

Louise had started to show her even white teeth in a smile which now faded. Joey picked up his empty crate and busily moved it around to the other side of the radio setup.

"Sorry," said the girl, her dark eyes beginning to smolder. "I'll ask somebody else."

They listened to her footsteps as they faded away in the corridor. Mike looked at Joey and shrugged.

"What was I gonna tell her?" he asked. "That her husband either forgot to call in—or got himself quick-frozen when something in his tractor popped?"

Joey shook his head sympathetically. "Tough on her."

"Dunno why she had to come to Luna in the first place," Mike complained. "I can see a nurse like Jean doin' it, and a typewriter pusher like old Edna oughta be classed expendable. But a babe like Louise!"

"It's her science," said Joey. "She wants to see the stars better."

"We got enough astronomers now. She's a smart girl, all right—can't take that away from her. But if she was *my* woman, she wouldn'ta come up here!"

"If she was mine," countered Joey, "I wouldn'ta taken a second-rate job just to follow her up here either! But you're dreaming about the past, Boss."

"*Uh*-unh," grunted Mike, plugging in the speaker again. "I just believe in equal rights for men. How'd you like to be married to a dame like that and have to trail her to a place where there's three women to forty-eight men?"

"Ask me how I'd like to be married to a dame like that, period!" Joey invited him.

Mike adjusted the shade on the light so as to shadow half the room. He straightened the blanket where the three visitors had sat, appropriated the one from the upper bunk to cover himself, and lay down.

"Your watch," he announced coldly. "Wake me up if anything comes in!"

The rope lacing of the canvas creaked as he settled himself; then Joey was left with only the quiet hiss of the radio. He leaned back in the folding chair and relaxed.

Hansen paused and turned to survey the ground he had covered in the past half hour. The hiss of his air circulator and the whine of the tiny motors within his suit were a comfort in the face of his bleak surroundings.

He had found himself trotting along at such an easy pace that he had kept going past Mt. Pico. Now he wondered if he ought to stop.

"Might as well go on," he muttered. "Now that I've picked up the tractor trail from Archimedes, I can hardly be missed by the relief crew."

He eyed the twin tracks in the gray sand. Flanked by his own wide-spaced footprints, they stretched away into the dim distance. As a sign that man had passed, they did little but accentuate the coldness of the scene.

"Maybe I'll stop at the big triple peak," Hansen planned. "That's about thirty-five or forty miles . . . they ought to be along by then if they started right away."

Careful not to admit to himself that relief might be slow in starting from Archimedes, he took a last look at Pico. Rearing starkly upward, it projected a lonely, menacing grandeur, like a lurking iceberg or an ancient monument half buried in the creeping sands of a desert. In the light of the nearly full Earth, it was a pattern of gray angles and inky black patches—not a hospitable sight.

"Come on, come on!" Hansen reproved himself. "Let's get moving. You want to turn into a monument too?"

He had stopped just before reaching Pico to replenish his suit tank from the big cylinder, and still felt good at having managed the valves without the mishap he had feared. He did not feel like a man who had traveled seventy miles.

"Why, on Earth," he thought, "that would be a good three-day march! I feel it a little, but not to the point of being tired."

He looked up at Earth as he started out again. The cloudy eastern coast of North America had moved around out of sight in the narrow dark portion. Hansen guessed that he had been on the move for at least four or five hours.

"I'd like to see their faces when they meet me way out here," he chuckled.

It occurred to him that he might be more tired than he thought, and as he went on he tried to save himself by holding his pace to a brisk walk. He found that if he got up on his toes a bit, he could still bound along that way.

The gray sand flowed under his feet, relieved occasionally by a stretch of yellowish ground. Hansen kept his eyes on his path and avoided the empty waste. When he did glance into the distance, he felt a twinge of loneliness. It was like the wide plainsland of the western United States, but grimly bare of anything so living as a wheat field.

He tried to remember as he moved along where it was that they had driven the tractor up a mountain ridge. He decided that he would rather avoid the climb, and kept an eye open for the chain of vein mountain beyond Pico.

"It ought to be faster to go around the end of them," he thought. "I can always pick up the tracks again."

When he finally sighted the rise ahead, he bore to his right. He remembered from the maps he had studied that the mountains curved somewhat toward another isolated peak, and he watched for that. As far as he knew, it had no name, but although only half the height of Pico, it was an unmistakable landmark.

The mountains on his left gradually dwindled into ragged hills and sank beneath the layer of lava. Hansen turned toward the last outcroppings as the triple mountain he sought came into sight. He climbed onto a broad rock and started to sit down.

The end of the big cylinder slung across his back clanged on the back of his helmet. Hansen lost his balance and tumbled over the side of the rock. Under his groping hands, the heat-tortured surface of it flaked away, and he bounced once on the ground before sprawling full length.

"Damn!" he grunted. "When'll I learn to watch my balance with this load?"

He picked himself up and unslung the tank. Then, allowing for the normal bulk of his backpack of tank and batteries, he backed against the outcropping until he was resting at a comfortable angle.

"Maybe I ought to relax a few minutes," he told himself. "Give the air circulator time to filter out some of the sweat. Then, too, I don't want to get tired and miss them when they come along."

He idly scanned the arc between the peak toward which he was heading and Mt. Pico, still easily visible off to his right. The northern part of the Mare Imbrium drew his gaze coaxingly into the distance until he felt an insane desire to thrust his head forward. It almost seemed that if he could get beyond the double glass of his insulated faceplate, if he could escape from the restraint of his helmet, he might perceive his bleak surroundings with a better, more real sense of proportion.

There was nothing out there, of course, he forced himself to realize. Except for shadows of craterlets that looked like low mountains, there was nothing to see for fifty miles, and nothing even then more noteworthy than a couple of minor craters.

"Then what are you looking for?" Hansen snapped. "You want it to get on your nerves? And quit talking to yourself!"

He suppressed, however, the sudden urge to spring up and break into a run. Instead, he hitched around to stare along the ridge at whose end he sat.

He was far enough south to be able to see the side lit by earthlight. The ridge climbed higher the farther it went, like the back of some sea monster rising from placid waters. Several miles away, a spur seemed to project out to the south; and Hansen thought he could remember a mile-wide crater on the maps.

He was a bit more comfortable inside his suit by now. He shifted his position to expedite the drying of the coveralls he wore under the space suit. Then he raised his arms and tried to clasp his hands behind his neck, but found that his garb was not that flexible.

"Shouldn't kick, I guess," he thought. "Without plenty of springs in the joints, I wouldn't be able to bend anything, considering the pressure difference."

He spent a minute admiring the construction of the suit that alone stood between him and instant extinction. That led him to think of the marvelous mechanism of the vacuum tractor that had carried him so comfortably—though he had not appreciated it at the time—across the Lunar plain. That, logically, recalled the men who had come with him and now were buried beneath one of Plato's many landslips.

"Talk about borrowed time!" he thought. "I wonder how long I'll stay lucky? Any little thing might do it—"

He had already taken three or four tumbles, or was it more? On any one of them, had he rolled the wrong way perhaps, he might have cracked that faceplate on a projecting rock. It was made as tough as possible, true, but if he ever cracked the outer pane, the insulating sheet of air would spurt out to leave him with a slow leak. The inner plate would lose heat and cloud up from his breath, so that he would end up without even knowing where he was dying.

Or if he had slid over a surface jagged enough to tear through his yellow chafing suit, and then to rip the tough material of the inner suit—

A puncture here would be a real blowout!

He reminded himself to be careful about stepping into shadows, especially if they were more or less straight-edged. He did not remember encountering on the way out any of the canyonlike rills that ran like long cracks straight through all other surface features of Luna—except occasional small craters slammed into the rock after the rill had been formed—but there was always the chance that he might step into some other kind of a hole.

Fortunately, the earthlight shone into his face, so that he should be able to tell a shadow resulting from some elevation ahead of him.

"I'm getting the jitters squatting here," Hansen thought. "It won't do any harm to move on a little way. At least out past that mountain, where I'll have a good view toward Archimedes."

He arose and slung the big cylinder over his back again, jiggling on the toes of his boots to jockey it into place. With one last look over his shoulder at the trail of his footprints splotched in the ashy sand, he started off.

He was surprised to discover that the rest had stiffened him slightly, but that soon worked out. As soon as he was warmed up, he moved out in a brisk walk which on Luna sent him bounding along with fifteen-foot strides. Swinging his arms to keep his balance, he concentrated upon the footing ahead of him. Once more he was alone with the hissing and humming of his suit and the sound of his own breathing, undisturbed by either memory or anticipation.

Mike Ramirez stirred on his bunk with the change of the quiet hissing of the radio. Something more than the occasional crackle or creak of Joey's chair or footfall in the corridor brought him up with eyes still half closed. To his sleep-drugged mind, it seemed that nothing had existed until a second ago, when a faint, dreamlike voice had started to speak.

He started to push back his blanket—Joey's blanket—and said, "Joey! You got a call!"

". . . to Archimedes Base. Hello Base! Over."

"I hear him!" snarled Joey. "Go back to sleep!"

He pushed his switch and the rushing noise that had partly muffled the weak voice gave way before the surge of his own transmitter.

"Archimedes Base to Tractor One!" Joey answered, and Mike leaned back on one elbow and sighed.

He did not listen while Joey took the message, but swung his feet to the floor and sat up. Wiggling his toes uncomfortably, he wished he had taken off his shoes; but he had expected to lie down only half an hour or so. Until the call came in, he had been sound asleep.

Joey acknowledged the message and turned to Mike after dropping his pencil.

"The Serenitatis bunch," he said. "They left two of them at Linné to take photos and poke around while the other pair brought the tractor back through between the Apennines and Caucasus to call in."

"Everything okay?"

"Yeah, they're on the way back already, but they say Linné didn't look as if it was ever a volcano after all."

"Very true if interesting," said Mike. "Okay, take it to Burney. I'll bend an ear a while."

He tossed the blanket back onto the upper bunk and walked over to the chair. He stretched, and sat down as Joey's footsteps departed down the corridor.

He sat there, staring moodily at the softly lighted dials of the radio, wishing he had a cigarette. That was one habit he had had to cut off short when joining the expedition.

"I think I'm getting over it some," he congratulated himself. He looked up at the sound in the corridor, thinking that Joey had made good time to Burney's compartment and back. He raised an eyebrow as Louise entered.

"I just saw Joey go by," she announced hastily. "Did some news come in?"

"Tractor One reported—just routine. What are you doing, picketing this dive?"

"I—I just happened to be passing the Junction, and I saw the paper in Joey's hand."

"Uh-huh," grunted Mike.

What the members of the expedition had come to call the Junction was an intermediate dome equipped with the main airlock. The other buildings connected with it through safety doors so as to localize any danger of air loss in the event of a rupture in one of the domes. It was, in effect, the front hall of the whole base.

And if you stand there long enough, thought Mike, *everyone you know on Luna will pass by, and you'll find out everything that's going on.*

"Where is number Two now?" demanded Louise quietly.

Scared, thought Mike, noting the overcontrolled tenseness of her voice.

"I don't know for sure," he answered, not looking at her. "It's time they were inside Plato, and we can't expect to hear them from in there."

Louise walked jerkily to the bunk and sat on the foot of the lower section. She crossed her legs. Seeing the nervous manner in which she twitched her foot, Mike turned to his radio.

After a moment, she spoke again, and his shoulders quivered at the agonized harshness of her tone.

"Don't string me along, Mike! I want to know! You were worried about them hours ago, weren't you?"

Mike licked his lips.

"That don't mean anything," he muttered.

"The others backtracked to report, didn't they? To call in, I mean. Something happened to number Two, didn't it?"

"Now, take it easy, Louise!" Mike squirmed in his chair, then forced himself to sit still. It was not the sort of furniture that would stand much squirming. "Burney kinda considered that as a possibility, but in the end they decided things were probably okay."

"Then why did they have Bucky in here?" she demanded.

"Just in case they thought it worth the trouble of scouting the Plato region. Nothing special."

Louise bounced up from the bunk. She stood beside it, stiff, with her little fists clenched tightly at her sides.

"They wouldn't let this long a time go by without calling in and you know it!" she declared. "Even if they did, there ought to be a tractor on the way to check."

"You might have a point there," admitted Mike.

"It could always be called back."

"It's probably been thought of," said Mike. "Look, Louise, why don't you calm down and let the worryin' get done by the people supposed to do it?"

She did not look at him. The darkness of her eyes surprised him, and he realized how she had paled beneath her tan.

"I can't help it," she said. "It's my fault, in a way. He only came along because I got so excited about the expedition I couldn't stay down on Earth. He didn't want to come, and now he's out there—"

Mike rose and shoved his chair aside with his foot. He thought the girl was going to faint. Watching her narrowly, he reached out to put his hand on her arm.

He sighed with relief as he heard Joey whistling outside. Louise straightened and moved away from his hand as the younger operator entered.

"Why don't you go see Burney?" suggested Mike. "He'll explain how he figures the odds; or if you want to argue, it's more sense to do it with him than me. I got nothing to do with it."

The girl pulled herself together with a visible effort.

"I know, Mike. Thanks for listening, anyway."

"Joey, go along with her to Burney's quarters!"

"That's all right," said Louise. "I can find my way farther than that."

They watched her leave.

Once more, Joey took the chair before the set and the pair of them sat in glum silence. The ventilation system came to life in one of its efforts to homogenize the base atmosphere, and its sigh partly drowned out the hiss of the radio.

"You know something, Joey?" grunted Mike.

"What?"

"I got a feelin' we're not gonna see those guys again."

"Hope you're wrong," said Joey. "It's awful tough digging around here, after the first few inches."

Hansen trotted along steadily with the four-thousand-foot mountain rising in a sheer sweep out of the lava "sea" over to his right. There were three distinct peaks, he knew, but they ran in a line away from him so that the whole thing appeared one towering mass to him. Most of it, from his position, was black with the deepness of Lunar shadows, although he was gradually reaching a location where he could see the splashes of earthlight on the tortured rocks.

"Pretty soon I'll be out in the real flat, with nothing but a scattering of little craters to steer by," he reflected. "If I don't want to stop, how had I better head?"

Just in case the problem should arise, he began to estimate the direction he should take and the sort of ground he would find.

The first thing would be to bear slightly left until he picked up the trail of the tractor once more. Then he could expect a region of fairly frequent craterlets, leading up to Kirch, a modest but respectable seven miles in diameter. If he passed to the right of Kirch, he would be kept from wandering aimlessly out into the Mare Imbrium by a range of vein mountains. He might go farther astray by passing Kirch to the left, but there the going would probably be easier.

"Then what?" he murmured, trying to recall the map and the journey in the tractor.

There was another open area, he seemed to remember, and then the forty-mile string of peaks called the Kirch Mountains, bordered on the right by an even longer ridge of vein mountains which might once have been part of the range.

And then, another thirty miles or so would bring him to the ringwall of Archimedes!

Hansen shook his head.

"That would be going a little too far," he muttered.

His voice sounded husky to his own ears, and he paused to suck up a few swallows of water through the hose. He must have been half hypnotized by the steady streaming of the gray surface under his feet, for he suddenly realized that he had gone considerably beyond the triple peak.

Without his steady forward speed, he found it difficult for a moment to stand erect. He braced against the movement of the big tank on his back, and turned around to look back.

He stared at the dark, earthlit ground over which he had been trotting. With the looming mountain in the foreground, and the upthrust ringwalls of smaller craterlets here and there above the level, aseptic frigidity of the plain, it was a scene of complete desolation. It was more naked of life or any kind of softness than any desert on Earth; yet to Hansen, it did not really seem like a desert. There was some further overtone plucking at the fringe of his consciousness.

Then it came to him.

"It's like an *ocean!*" he exclaimed. "There's something about it that's like . . . like a cold, gray, winter sea smashing in on a rocky coast!"

There was the same monstrous, chilling power, the same effect upon the beholder that here was a massive, half-sentient entity against whose callous strength and cruelty nothing human could stand. It was a *thing* to observe from a safe distance, to cower from lest it somehow become aware of the puny structure of bone, blood, and flesh spying upon it. Then there would be no escape, no withstanding the crushing force of its malice. But he was on no safe cliff. He was down in the sea.

He looked around. Gray everywhere, mottled with inky shadows. Gray ash underfoot, gray-and-black lumps thrusting up from the surface like colossal vertebrae, gray distance in all directions.

"Been going for hours," he thought, "and there's no sign, really, that I'll ever get anywhere! I might as well be in the middle of the far side of Pluto!"

The huge mountain towered behind him, like a hulking beast from some alien world stalking the only object in all its frozen world that dared to move. Hansen suddenly could not bear to have his back turned to it. He faced it and edged clumsily away. The helmet that reduced his field of vision was his prison. If that black-shadowed mass of rock chose to topple over, it would easily reach him, and more. He would be ground under countless tons of weight, mangled and frozen in one instant—

Hansen whirled about and bolted.

On his first stride, he caught the toe of his right foot in the sand and sprawled forward with flailing arms. He plowed into the ground, throwing up spurts of sand like a speedboat tossing spray.

Somehow, he was up immediately, running in long, wobbling, forty-foot bounds. His eyes bulged and the breath rasped between his lips as he strove desperately to keep his balance.

It was like running in a dream, the nightmare come true. More than once, until he adapted to the pace, he found himself churning two or three steps at the zenith of his trajectory, too impatient to wait for the touch of boot on sand. There was sudden, dynamic power in his tiring muscles. All his joints felt loose.

His chest began to labor and he stumbled slightly. With a quick spasm, he blew his lungs and sucked in a deeper breath. After a few repetitions, he felt a trifle easier. In a minute he began to get his second wind. All this came like a half-perceived process of instinct, while he concentrated narrowly upon speeding ahead.

He flew up a slight grade and took off in a soaring leap to the next crest of an undulating stretch of pale yellow ash. The next thing he knew, he was rushing upon a long shadow that barred his path.

A hasty glance each way warned him there was no use trying to skirt it, for the shadow or hole or whatever it was ran for hundreds of yards right and left. Hansen stamped hard at the near edge and kicked off for at least sixty feet. Something seemed to snap in his right knee, but he came down all right and kept running, well clear of the shadow.

How long he ran, dodging this way and that to avoid hills and shadows obstructing his path, he did not know. In the end, the tiny motors of his suit fell behind the rate at which he consumed oxygen and gave off carbon dioxide and copious moisture.

When he began to feel like an underwater swimmer reaching his limit with writhing chest, Hansen gave up. He stopped.

That felt worse. He moved on at a gentle walk, accomplishing it mostly by motion from the ankles down. Amid the stifling warmth and stickiness inside his space suit, it was borne in upon him how badly he had lost his head.

He looked back, panting. Where was the mountain? Then, following the trail of isolated scars on the surface beyond where they faded into the gray distance, he saw a small knob of gray against the star-dotted black of the horizon.

"I guess . . . I've . . . really been traveling!" he panted. "Twenty minutes or half an hour—wonder how fast I went to put a mountain out of sight? Of course . . . I was well past when I started."

That reminded him of his bolt, and he closed his eyes in a paroxysm of shame.

The sweat beading his forehead began to trickle down his cheekbones or nose.

Now and then, a drop rolled into his eyes, despite efforts to shake his head inside the confines of the helmet. It stung, but he was too blown to get excited over that.

"Why did I have to go and do that?" he groaned inwardly.

He remembered how levelheaded he had been in the first minutes of the catastrophe. Calmly, he had judged the odds of there being any survivors; calmly, he had climbed down for the prime requisite, the tank of oxygen; calmly, he had started off by a well-chosen route that led him accurately to landmarks so plain that they could be spotted from Earth with a good pair of field glasses.

He had intended to go only as far as Pico, or perhaps the triple peak. Or had he?

Somewhere back there, he remembered, he had begun planning a further march. There could be no reason for that except—

Except that he was secretly aware that he could count upon no help to reach him in time!

"Why should they send anybody out yet?" he asked himself. "For all they know, we're still inside Plato, camping on the nice level lava floor. I *must* have been thinking that, underneath, when I was figuring which side to pass Kirch."

He had been skating on thin ice and should have expected a crack-up. For a moment, he considered the possibility that it would have been better had he broken down on the spot. But then he might have quit while still on the ringwall of the great crater.

"As it is," he said aloud, "I'll at least get the most possible mileage out of this suit. If I live long enough, I might even walk in on them at base, for a surprise."

He grinned a bit as he considered that pleasant fantasy:

"Hi, Paul; where you been?"

"Oh, just out for a little walk on the moon."

"And where did you go on your little moon walk?"

"Took a turn around Plato. Pretty boring but 'toujours gai, whatthehell whatthehell!' "

He managed a deeper breath as his equipment caught up somewhat to his physical needs. The half grin on his lean features faded, and he stepped up his plodding pace.

"Why kid myself?" he snorted. "I'm just about scared senseless! And I've got a right to be!"

Bucky O'Neil, as the pilot who was to take the scouting rocket, occupied the only extra chair in Dr. Burney's headquarters room. Burney sat across from him at the folding table and circled the proposed search area continuously with the butt of his pencil. Both men eyed the map reflectively. Burney looked as if he were trying to guess the precise location of his tractor crew. O'Neil, tracing his route with a blunt forefinger, was obviously attempting to estimate where he would have to punch his flare release in order to have his camera working by the time he whipped across Plato.

"Just to save us the wait," said Burney, leaning back in the silent, crowded room, "report by radio as soon as you loop back. Have you checked your set with Mike?"

The radio operator, standing to the rear of the little group, spoke up, "Joey's checking with the field now."

"Good!" approved Burney. "Does anyone have anything to add?"

He looked about. Sherman whistled quietly and tonelessly. Wohl shook his head. Johnny Pierce hovered, waiting to get his hands on his photomap again. Louise leaned against one wall near the door, worrying a pencil end between her white teeth.

"All right, then," said Burney, "you can get into your suit, Bucky. Good luck!"

The gathering broke up. Burney signaled for Wohl and Dr. Sherman to stay behind, and forestalled Johnny's move to reappropriate the map.

"We may want to consider further," he offered as an excuse, and Pierce left with Mike.

Outside, they watched Louise follow Bucky in the opposite direction.

"Wonder how it feels to have her man out there and maybe not coming back?" murmured Johnny.

His long face looked sad.

"What do you think their chances are?" he persisted after a brief pause as they turned a corner in the corridor.

Mike shrugged.

"Tractor One is starting back already," he said simply.

Hurrying along the other end of the corridor, Bucky was unable to shake off the following footsteps without putting on an obvious burst of speed. It sounded like Louise, and he wanted to think about his flight plan.

Finally, as he passed through the safety door—a double mounting that could be used in an emergency as an airlock—he had to pause long enough to acknowledge her presence.

"Do you mind if I ask you something, Bucky?" Louise inquired.

"Of course not, but I have to—"

"I know; I won't take more than a minute. The thing I don't like is that they just want you to photograph Plato."

Bucky released the door which swung shut automatically. He looked puzzled.

"Don't you think it's worth doing?" he asked.

"Oh, yes! Yes, I do. But how about all the other places?"

The pilot fidgeted.

"I can't take shots of the whole Mare Imbrium, Louise."

"You might take a few of the section this side of Plato, though. How do we know they ever reached the crater? If tracks show up on your pictures, we'll know how far they got."

"That's a good point," admitted Bucky, scratching his head. "But why didn't you bring it up in the meeting?"

Louise looked away. She shrugged slightly.

"Well, maybe Burney would have talked you out of it," Bucky conceded. "We all know you're worried."

"I know what everybody thinks," Louise replied. "I'm getting excited because one of the four happens to be my husband. I'm not thinking calmly about what's best for the base as a whole, whether it's worth taking people off other jobs to play hide-and-seek out on the surface. I probably shouldn't have come to Luna in the first place."

Bucky looked around, but there was no one passing through the Junction. Louise stepped closer and put a trembling hand on his arm.

"All right, Bucky, it's true enough. I'm frightened. I wish I'd never thought of coming here and making Paul feel he had to trail along! Are you married, Bucky, or engaged?"

"Well, there's a little blonde waiting down there for me—I hope. She'd better wait."

"How would you like it if *she* were out there?"

"Ummm," murmured the pilot. "I see what you mean."

He saw more than that. He saw how close she was to losing her grip, how she was keeping back the tears with an effort, trying to use every ounce of self-discipline so as to keep from being ignored as hysterical. Getting a few little things done, like influencing him to take extra photos, was all she could do at the moment to look out for her man. He remembered hearing from Pierce that Burney had refused her offer to take out a tractor herself.

"Well . . ." he yielded, "I'll see if I have a chance. I figure to cover the approaches to the ringwall anyway; maybe I can get a shot out around Pico, or thereabouts."

She did not thank him, but hid her face against his shoulder for a second. Bucky looked around again, touched her lightly on the head with one big, freckled hand, and disengaged himself gently.

When he glanced back over his shoulder, Louise was opening the safety door to go back.

"Heading for Mike and the radio, I bet," he thought. "Wonder when she slept last?"

He reminded himself that he had a job to do which involved delicate judgments at high speed, and he had no business going into it with hindering worries on his mind. If that girl did not watch herself, she would wind up under the care of Jean and "M.D." McLeod.

"I'm liable to, myself," he muttered, "if I don't snap out of it now! I wonder who'll pick me up if I zig out there when I ought to zag?"

He stopped at a phone connection and called the field control dome to learn if they were ready for him.

★ ★ ★

Dazzling glints of light flashed here and there from that part of the Pacific Ocean still in bright sunlight as Hansen came in sight of Kirch. The coast of California had faded into the darkness and Asia was partly in view. He estimated that he had been moving for nearly eight hours.

His pace was still a rhythmic lope, but the feeling of having vigorous reserves of strength had worn off. Hansen knew that he must rest soon. In traversing the flat, crater-speckled plain since his panic, he had paused only once when he took a few minutes to recharge the oxygen tank of his suit.

"But I'm due for a good half hour off my feet," he decided.

His legs, he noticed, had lost some of their snap, so that his bounding trot was less exuberant. On the other hand, this resulted in his getting slightly better control of his stride; he no longer broke his rhythm by bouncing too high. The thing that bothered him most was the growing ache across the small of his back.

He skirted the ringwall of the last of a series of small craters and saw the shadowed side of the seven-mile wall. He was approaching the left curve of it, for he had hours ago decided to abandon the tractor tracks when he had crossed them again.

"No use running up the right and getting into the Kirch Mountains," he had muttered. "I'd have to zig-zag through them and I doubt I'll feel like making any extra distance by then."

His guess now, from the angle of Earth in the starry sky, was that he was heading a shade left of his generally southerly route. He reminded himself that he must change after rounding Kirch.

"I'll keep going till I'm past," he promised himself. "Then I'll sit down and relax a while."

He could not see much point in making another few miles out into the empty wasteland beyond Kirch. The crater was a natural goal to mark a section of his journey. About halfway between Plato and Archimedes, it was farther than he had dreamed of going. Even now, after he had seen how fast he could travel in the light gravity, it struck him as almost unbelievable that he could have covered such a distance. It was nearly a hundred and fifty miles.

Yet here he was, not in bad shape at all. He glanced at the outer slope of the ringwall on his right, and mentally cataloged his various irritations. There was, of course, the general clamminess that resulted from spending hours in a space suit, plus the fact that his bladder was beginning to bother him and there was nothing he could do about it. The overheating due to his exertions had been partially adjusted when he had discovered during his last halt that he could regulate the heating unit by a small dial in his battery pack, which discovery left him slightly aggrieved at not having had the finer points of the care and handling of space suits more exhaustively explained to him.

"But then," he reflected, "I was probably expected to spend a lot of time in the darkroom as a spare photographer."

He could not say he was hungry, although he supposed that sooner or later he would discover feelings of weakness. His suit seemed to be functioning as well as could be expected, except for something that had given way in the right knee on that one leap. He wondered if a spring was working loose.

"That could end up giving me a beautiful limp," he thought. "With fourteen pounds inside, and no air at all outside, it'd be tough to bend a joint without some mechanical help."

By now he could see light-streaks along the ring-wall, and knew that he was rounding it. The lighting gradually increased as he continued, until when he began to move out into the open plain some time later, the walls were mostly gray with earthlight. Kirch had a "new" appearance, as craters went. Its floor was not lava-filled, nor its ringwall seemingly as long exposed to thermal erosion, so that the probability was that it had been formed after the "sea" around it.

Hansen began to keep an eye out for a suitable place to sit down. Presently, he located a rock the size of an auto.

"Time for a drink, and then I'll pick out a good spot," he sighed.

The second he stopped to grope with his lips for the little hose, he knew he was really tired.

The water, cool from being only partly surrounded by heating coils to protect it from the exterior cold, refreshed him but slightly. The running had left a thick taste in his mouth.

Hansen unslung the big cylinder he had carried on his back and set it down beside a comfortable indentation in the rock. He then unfastened his backpack of tank and batteries. The metal-covered connection protecting the hose and wires was long enough to permit the pack to be set at his side.

He lowered himself to the fine sand and leaned his back against the rock with a sigh of relief. He squirmed into a more comfortable position.

"Wish I hadn't drunk all that water," he growled.

He leaned the back of his neck against the neck-piece of his suit. It was not uncomfortable except that he found himself staring directly into the light of Earth.

"I'm getting used to it all right, if I think that's too bright," he thought. "Bet my pupils are big as a cat's now."

Ironically, his feet had not started to hurt until his weight was off them. It felt as if he were developing blisters. The coveralls he wore under the space suit, moreover, had begun to chafe in a few places—around the armpits as he swung his arms, behind his right knee, on the inside of his thighs.

He also was reminded of the sweat that had trickled around or into his eyes, for the lids felt sore.

"I want a different view," he grunted, picking himself up. "Facing the other way, maybe I can rest my eyes."

Carrying his backpack, he started around the rock, then prudently went back for his big oxygen cylinder. He could think of no good reason for dragging this with him, but he somehow felt more comfortable with it beside him.

The other face of the rock was blackly shadowed, and he was forced to find a convenient spot by groping about. With a sigh, he settled down, squirmed again into an easy position, and found himself contemplating the ringwall of Kirch a few miles away. The regular sough of air through his suit and the quiet hum of the mechanisms that were keeping him alive were so familiar by now that he hardly noticed them. It was the cessation of movement, not any diminishment of the normal sounds, that lent an impression of quiet to the scene.

He looked at the ringwall, squinting against the sting in his eyes that caused them to water occasionally. The left extremity was dim in the distance, but to the right, he could clearly see the slope of the wall as it curved to meet the plain. There was no feeling of a towering, insecurely balanced mass like that of the mountain.

"Although a crater at a distance does look like a mountain range," he thought. "Not so close as this; it goes up too steeply."

In a way, it was almost like looking at the skyscrapers of a big city, like looking at Manhattan from across the Hudson River. Except that there were no lights.

He closed his eyes for a moment and tried to visualize the sharp peak a little to his left atop the wall as it might look with a thousand lighted windows gleaming white and yellow.

It was hard to do. The stark fact was that there was only Lunar dimness, relieved by earthlight but tending to be uniform in intensity without the rays of the sun. If the silhouette of Kirch was like that of a city, the metropolis it resembled was a dead one.

A dead city in the midst of a cold, frozen sea of lava. A ghost city that had never lived, yet rose up from the gray sea over which no ship had sailed and whispered and whined ghostly warnings. "Stay with me, Man! I am dry and lonely. There are no people to warm me with light and sound. . . . There is none to see my massive strength and, by seeing, make it into reality. . . . Stay where you are, Man!"

"But it's dead," thought Hansen. "More than dead—sterile!"

"But you, Man, you too are dead. You are already turning cold. You will slowly congeal . . . become solid . . . a monument . . . a symbol of the tribute brought by folly and life to the sea of coldness and gray death—No, do not shake your head. . . . It is too late. . . . My shadows are about you. . . . You have no light. . . . All your prayers and wishes will not turn on a single light. The shadows reach you . . . touch you. . . . The pain in your leg is the cold of space. . . . You will sit there forever . . . drowned in the gray sea of frozen lava . . . imagining lights for me in the blackness . . . imagining life in me in the noon glare. . . . But now there is no light unless you have the force to see it . . . but you are cold . . . cold . . . cold . . . cold. . . ."

The sky flared with flickering light. It turned black while the image of light still remained in Hansen's eyes. Then a new light, tinier and higher streaked overhead. Hansen awoke with the hairs tingling on his neck and leaped to his feet with a hoarse shout.

"A rocket!"

★ ★ ★

In the stillness of the radio room, the incoming call from Bucky's rocket made Mike jump in his chair before the set. Hastily, he turned down the volume he had kept up in hope of picking up faint calls from Plato.

When he had answered and relayed the message by phone to the landing area, he turned to the others in the room.

Joey had been sleeping in the upper bunk. Louise had asked to stay and Mike had offered his bunk for her to sit on. She had not slept, as far as he knew; but he had turned to the radio and maintained a lengthy silence.

"Maybe I ought to talk to her," he thought, "but what is there to say? Four good guys; but they're awful late checking in."

But when he looked around, they were both watching him; and he had to tell them.

"Bucky's coming in," he said.

"Did he find anything?" demanded Louise.

"Don't know yet," Mike told her. "He said he took a snap of Plato coming and going and three more on the way back."

Louise moved toward the door.

"Thanks a lot, Mike," she said.

Joey slipped down from the bunk as she disappeared into the corridor.

"Never mind," advised Mike. "With Louise and Bucky in that hole they call a darkroom, dodging the photographer's elbow every time he breathes in, they won't have any place for you but up on a shelf."

"I just thought I'd—"

"We'll get told. Now, stay with me, kid, an' make sure *I* don't go wanderin' off to have a look too!"

Hansen stood stiffly by the rock and painfully tried his neck muscles. He searched the sky, but nothing moved among the stars.

"Now, *did* I see something?" he asked himself slowly. "Or was I still dreaming?"

He grimaced, and raised a hand to the back of his head before he remembered that he was still in his space suit. His neck was stiff and sore from lying across the rigid neckpiece of his suit, and he was chilled to the bone.

"Must have been asleep quite a while," he thought. "Maybe I ought to turn up the heating again—or should I just warm up as I walk?"

He paused a moment to stare in open-mouthed amazement at the ringwall of Kirch, rearing up three thousand feet toward the stars.

"When am I going to do something right?" he asked. "Why couldn't I stay where I was, facing Earth, and go to sleep dreaming I was home?"

He went on to wish that he had not gone to sleep at all. The aches that were irritations when he was warm from walking were now centers of agony.

He was sure he had blisters, and the chafed places under the suit jabbed little warnings of tenderness as he tried to move. Reaching for his battery pack, he nearly toppled over because his right leg was asleep. Even after he recovered and took a few steps to restore the circulation, the knee did not feel right.

"I wonder if I pulled a muscle?" he mused. "Or is it in the suit?"

He looked up at Earth. India was moving into the arc of shadow, but he could see Africa, the Mediterranean, and Europe.

When he realized he must have been out for three or perhaps four hours, he immediately checked his oxygen. It was none too soon. He refilled his suit tank and examined the pressure of the big cylinder. He guessed that he could do the trick once more.

"I wonder how long a man can live in a space suit?" he muttered. "Hansen, why aren't you dead?"

Groaning with stiffness, he adjusted his battery pack and tank and slung the cylinder atop the load. Although he seemed as wet as ever, he sucked up a drink of water while he listened to the hiss of his air circulator.

"Wish I wasn't so thirsty," he said. "I'll have to watch it. Beginning to feel lack of food, too."

He started off, moving mincingly to favor his sore muscles, and immediately felt the weakness brought on by hunger. It was hard to believe that a nightmare could last so long, but he remembered that it was almost a full day since he had eaten a sandwich in the tractor.

Gradually, as he moved along, marching away from Kirch into the open wasteland, he began to warm up. The stiffness left his muscles, although the chafing remained annoying. His feet felt sticky in the thick socks, suggesting that he would have trouble. He thought they might be bleeding.

What the hell was the matter with that knee? he wondered.

He thought of stopping to examine it, but the likelihood of his falling over on his face if he bent to feel the joint deterred him. He kept on. In half an hour, it became clear that a spring had snapped.

Not only was the knee harder to bend than it should have been, but something began to dig through his coveralls behind the knee.

"That's not so good," he told himself, but there was nothing he could think of to do.

He finally mustered the ambition to get up on his toes and bound along at a fairly brisk pace. The miles again floated under his feet, but he found that he could not maintain the trot the way he had earlier. Then, he had congratulated himself on his freshness, but he had come a long way since those few hours of immunity to fatigue.

The end of an hour found him moving at a moderate walk. One more, and he stopped noticing the pace particularly. There were few landmarks about him. He did not even strain ahead to catch a glimpse of the Kirch Mountains.

Finally, the nagging pain behind his knee became bad enough to make him stop.

"This is damn silly!" he growled. "I can't go along until that point of metal saws through a vein or something! Must be something I can do about it."

He thought it over, but it seemed that there simply was nothing he *could* do. The broken bit of metal was beyond his reach; he could not even feel it through the thickness of the space suit and the protective yellow chafing suit. Even if he should remove the latter by some weird contortion, the knee joint, as an obvious trouble spot, was reinforced by a bulge of metal. He would not be able to pinch or prod through that.

"Of course," he muttered, "I might take it off entirely. That would make things easy right away. A lot easier than just sitting down to wait for my air to run out."

He shook that out of mind with a jerk of his head, and struck out across the plain once more.

He had come to a stretch of gently rolling rises, and he tried to get most of his upward push from his left leg. Coming down the slopes, he hopped stiff-legged on his right. It was not too long before this became more tiring than it was worth.

"To hell with it!" he growled, and grimly drove onward with a more normal gait despite the sharp dig . . . dig . . . dig into his flesh at every stride.

Burney and Bucky again sat across the table in the former's room. Instead of the map they had consulted earlier, they gazed down at the new photographs. The room, as before, was crowded with others who had edged in to watch silently. Even "M.D." McLeod, so nicknamed to distinguish him from all the doctors of philosophy and doctors of science among the expedition, lingered with his stethoscope dangling after giving Bucky a routine, postflight check.

Johnny Pierce stood lankily behind Burney's shoulder, holding a spare magnifying glass and squinting down at the photos. Sherman, Wohl, and Joey stood around the table with the photographers who had developed and enlarged the pictures. Louise watched from behind Bucky, resting her hands on his shoulders.

Burney nodded slowly, examining the picture of the interior of Plato through his lens.

"I very much fear," he said, tapping a forefinger on the half-lit heap of material at the foot on the ringwall, "that there is only one conclusion. That is a new slide, is it not?"

"It is," said Dr. Sherman, gesturing slightly with an older photograph of the region.

"And it is quite clear that they reached the crater," Burney continued. "These are excellent pictures, and the trail of the tractor treads shows very definitely."

"How about this one, Dr. Burney?" asked Bucky, pushing across another photo.

It showed the region around Mt. Pico, and had been enlarged until tracks of the tractor could be clearly seen. Burney frowned when he looked at it.

"To be perfectly frank," he murmured, "I do not know what to make of it. Those marks accompanying the trail *could* be footprints, I suppose, as has been suggested. But why . . . or how?"

"A man running could make marks that far apart in this gravity," said Bucky. "I know Johnny estimates those little dots are twenty and thirty feet apart, but it's possible."

"It is also possible that they are nothing of the sort. You notice that they leave the trail after a time."

Louise spoke up.

"That at least rules out one interpretation," she said. "They certainly aren't footprints made by someone on the surface on the way *to* Plato. Anybody walking beside the tractor would have left a trail starting and ending at the tread tracks."

There was silence. Some of the men looked at her with pity, others stared very hard at the photographs on the table.

Burney prodded another picture with his finger.

"Bucky took this where the tracks passed Kirch," he reminded them. "There are none of these so-called footprints there. I regret to point out the obvious conclusion—"

"But can't you do something to make sure?" Louise burst out. "You aren't just going to leave them out there. You couldn't!"

"Of course not," said Burney, biting his lip uncomfortably. "As soon as the Serenitatis crew get a few hours' rest, I shall send them out to recover . . . ah . . . to check. But the time element has already become such—that—Well, my dear, there is simply no use in rushing things. Either there is no need, or it is already too late."

There was not much doubt as to which possibility seemed the more likely. The meeting began to break up in unhappy silence.

Hansen trudged along with his chin on the neckpiece of the suit. Every so often, when he lurched in the shifting sand, his forehead bumped against the face-plate of his helmet.

"And that's not so easy to do," he thought foolishly. "Takes a supple neck to accomplish it."

He concentrated for perhaps a hundred paces, and slowly arrived at the corollary.

"Takes a pretty soft and supple head to get out here in the first place. Shoulda stood at home in bed. Should've stayed on Plato and tried to build some kind of a marker. Base'll send out somebody . . . wonder if that was a rocket I saw? Maybe I'd be dead . . . but I'm gonna be dead anyway. Why don't I just sit down and wait? At least, it won't hurt anymore. And, I'll be easy."

No arguments to the contrary occurred to him, but some deep impulse refused to let him quit.

He had to pause again; his stops for rest were becoming frequent. He did not sit down.

Never get up again, he realized.

He planted his feet wide apart and stood there, panting and letting his hands hang limply at his sides. His face felt stiff as he bared his teeth against the throb of the cut behind his knee. By now, he was so used to the wetness of the leg that he could not be sure the blood trickled down any faster.

He saw that he was standing on ground lighter than usual, and tinted pale yellow. Remembering passing several such areas, he slowly realized that they must be rays from Aristillus, traces of vaporized minerals blown out across the surrounding territory when the crater had been formed. It meant, for what it might be worth, that he was getting near Archimedes. Some of the rays of Aristillus reached the larger crater.

He gritted his teeth and took the first step forward. A glance to his right assured him that the jagged peaks of the Kirch Mountains were where they should be. Once, as he walked along half awake, he had discovered himself turning away on a course that would have sent him circling back into the Mare Imbrium.

"Sea of Showers," he thought. "I wish there were some. I wish I even had a glass of water to pour over my head. Just a glass of water to rinse out these eyes. I wouldn't even care about a shave."

He began to notice his footsteps, besides the hiss of the air circulator and the laboring of the suit's motors. Through his boots, they had a distant, swishing sound that insidiously lowered his puffed eyelids little by little. His head bumped against the faceplate again.

Hansen jerked upright with a start. Clumsily, he turned to look back. His tracks were long, dragging gashes in the sandy surface.

"Hell! Going to sleep again," he croaked.

With the effort of speaking aloud—it was getting difficult to think clearly otherwise—the corner of his lower lip cracked. He opened his dry mouth, making a face at the morning-after taste, and gently touched the tip of his tongue to the spot. It stung.

No harm in taking a little water, he decided, though he knew it would offer only a fleeting relief. But he needed that.

He turned his head to the left and got the thin rubber tube between his teeth. The cracked lip stung as he sucked on the tube.

The water was cool. His tired eyes closed with the sheer pleasure of the sensation.

On the third swallow, it stopped flowing.

"Oh, *no!*" Hansen groaned.

He drew harder on the hose and eked out another mouthful. That was all. The tank was empty. It was supposed to be partly replenished by moisture removed from the air in the suit, but he had apparently reached the limit. The suit was not designed to be worn for twenty hours. It was a wonder that nothing had yet broken down.

He held the last mouthful without swallowing, letting it roll slowly about his mouth.

"Come on!" he thought. "That's all there is. What are you waiting for?"

He knew it was silly to feel angry at this latest pinprick. His growing rage was a sign of exhaustion, and some part of his mind recognized that fact; but he deliberately let his temper go . . . and drew extra strength from it.

The swallow of water gradually slipped down as he surged forward. With the stiff right knee, he staggered once and came so near falling flat that he skidded on all fours under him again.

"Dammit!" he raged. "What are they doing at base? Waiting for a weather report? Anybody with an ounce of brain would know by now things went sour!"

He lurched down a gentle slope and charged the next rise.

"I'll show them!" he grunted. "I don't need them, if they're too chicken to come out for me. I'll get there. . . . I don't know how I'll get up the goddamned wall . . . but I'll get *to* it! I'll get there!"

Mike sat before his radio and looked at the other three in the room.

Pierce looked thoughtful, Joey was frankly excited, and Louise Hansen paced nervously back and forth.

"The crew from Tractor One say they saw no tracks of any kind," he said, "but that doesn't prove a thing. They came nowheres near the line between Plato and Archimedes."

"Then you think we're justified in not waiting for the same crew?" asked Louise.

"Sure," said Mike. "I don't like to sound like I'm egging you on to something I wouldn't do myself, but—"

"Of course, Mike, of course," interrupted Johnny. "One of you has to stay on the radio, or we couldn't call back. We could get Bucky to take Joey's place, I guess, but why wake him up?"

"He did his share," Joey put in quickly.

Mike looked from face to face.

"Well, Joey can say I gave him permission," he said. "I don't know what you will say, but it'd be better if you got going and figured that out on the way back."

The shadowed ringwall loomed up before the yellow speck on the plain. Just enough earthlight reached this face to show where the seven-mile-wide outer slope was terraced by gentle inclines. Several of these led upward toward the pass used by the scouting expedition. Against the black sky, Hansen could not see the radio tower that had been erected, but he was no longer interested in that. He had jettisoned his radio batteries back on the plain to be rid of their weight as he tackled the long slope leading to Archimedes.

"There you are . . . there you are!" he mumbled. "Eureka, eureka! Damn near three hundred miles . . . maybe more the way I came. That's navigating, ain't it?"

The ringwall stood passively before him.

"Well, ain't it?" snarled Hansen thickly. "All right, here we go!"

He lurched forward. Despite having abandoned every bit of excess gear—the empty oxygen cylinder lay back beside the last craterlet he had passed—he could walk no faster than if he had been on Earth. It probably meant that on Earth he would have long since collapsed, but he was beyond thinking of that.

He found he could not climb the first seven-foot ledge he came to, and had to walk along it to a lower spot.

"No time, no time," he muttered against the delay. "You're on your last tankful now . . . in fact, well into it. You get up there . . . now . . . or not ever."

He found a long lateral slope and followed it up several hundred yards. He was cold and sluggish, and it seemed that his heating batteries were close to exhausted.

The ache across his back seemed normal. Even the dull misery of his legs, chafed, cut, rubbed raw, and the sogginess of his bleeding feet had come to be merely part of his general limpness.

He found himself finishing the last few yards of the slope on hands and knees.

"Funny," he croaked. "Don't remember fallin'."

He reached out for an outcropping of rock to pull himself up. The broken spring twisted in the mangled spot on the back of his thigh as he tried to rise. Getting both hands on the rock, he inched upward little by little.

It took him all of five minutes before he was on his feet again. At first, he thought he was dreaming again. The rock seemed to move under him.

Then he saw, peering blearily upward, that it was part of an old landslide. One slip on his part now might set it off again, and send him crashing down to the bottom of the ringwall again. Hansen groaned and stepped away as carefully as he could.

He was faced by a forty-five degree slope. If he could negotiate it for about thirty feet, he would reach another ramp. He looked down, and wondered if it would be easier to slide down to a lower terrace which would eventually lead higher than his present position.

"No time," he said dazedly.

He began to scrabble his way up the incline, not one too difficult to climb on Luna. The sun-powered rock flaked off beneath his hands, elbows, knees, and feet. He slid back about as fast as he climbed.

With a sob, he lunged for a projection the size of a man's head and got one mitten on it. The rock cracked off and he slid to the foot of the incline.

"Oh, God! It's too much!"

His face twisted up and he expected to feel tears running down his face. Apparently, however, he was too dried out for that.

★ ★ ★

He sat there dully, staring at the lower ramp and trying to tell himself he could always try that.

He knew better.

"This is the end of the line," he told himself. "Last stop. . . . You're done."

Even his conscience did not twitch at his surrender. He only wished he could see Earth and look at North America again where it was centered on the globe once more.

It was too much effort to turn around.

"Wonder if they'll find me," he mumbled. "Dunno if I want to get buried or not. . . ."

Something moved to his left. A light.

"I'm seeing things," he muttered. "Not long now."

But the light swung up and down, it lit the slope below him, and it kept moving. Nothing looked like that but a tractor.

But it would pass a hundred yards below him. The driver would have his eyes glued to the ground ahead, watching for holes or cracks.

Hansen started to laugh and managed to catch himself.

"The chance after the last chance!" he thought he said aloud, although his lips barely moved.

The effort of pulling himself to his knees brought out sweat he did not know he had left.

He waited for the tractor to reach a point below him. Waited . . . lifting the head-sized rock in both hands.

The tiny weight tired him, and he lowered the stone to his knees. The tractor lumbered along, heading down the slope into the plain.

Hansen swayed where he knelt, but concentrated everything upon estimating the distance.

With a grunt, he raised the rock and thrust it away from his chest, outward over the slope on which he sprawled with the motion.

He raised himself on his elbows and looked to see what happened. The tractor had slid to an abrupt halt.

Dimly, he could see the shattered pieces of his missile bouncing in and out of patches of earthlight below the vehicle. The driver could not have missed it crossing his path.

"Gotta get up . . . up!" Hansen thought desperately.

He did not realize that his air was turning foul, but the simple feat of getting his feet under him left his heart pounding wildly.

He planted his feet somehow until the light swept up the slope as those in the tractor searched for a possible slide.

Brightness filled his helmet. He was dazzled, and felt himself falling.

"Paul, try to help!"

"Paul, can't you get some grip when I shove you in? I can't keep you from sliding out the airlock. Paul!"

The voice was young and desperate.

When the other man backed away, parting the contact of their helmets, Hansen saw the features of Joey, the radio operator, through the other faceplate.

He stirred feebly.

"That's it, Paul," said the faraway voice as Joey bent to lift him again. "Just a little bit of help till I get you inside the airlock."

Something clanged, leaving him in blackness.

The next thing he knew, he was gulping in sobbing breaths of fresh, oxygen-rich air. His head ached, but he felt better.

Someone was mopping his sweaty face with a wet handkerchief. The handkerchief dripped, and the drops were salty.

He could not see Louise, because she held his head cradled against her breast, but Joey was looking at him wide-eyed over the back of another seat.

"How long ago did you start?" asked someone else, and Hansen saw that Johnny Pierce was driving.

"Right after we got to Plato," said Hansen. "Everything but me and a tank of oxygen went down in a slide."

"Musta been nearly twenty-four hours ago!" exclaimed Joey.

"Gol-darn!" said Pierce primly. "Three hundred miles, give or take a few!"

"You ain't human, Paul!" said Joey.

"Do you want your suit off now?" asked Louise. "We could only get your helmet loose in this space."

Without seeing her face, he could tell that she had been crying.

"Just leave it on," said Hansen. "Wait till we're in, and I can go right from the suit to a bath."

"We're coming over the crest," announced Johnny. "Louise, you better hold him in case I hit a few bumps."

Hansen relaxed with a sigh as he felt her hands tighten against him.

"Hold tight, honey!" he whispered as he closed his eyes against the lights in the tractor. "I . . . I'm a little tired."

Grandpa

JAMES H. SCHMITZ

James H. Schmitz made his first sale in 1943, to *Unknown*. He served in the U. S. Air Force during World War II and, after the war quickly established himself as one of the mainstays of the postwar *Astounding,* a role he would fill all through the fifties and sixties. Schmitz's action-packed space opera, especially stories such as his *Vega* series, later collected as *Agent of Vega,* holds up well for verve, imagination, and headlong pacing against the work of his contemporaries, although it's less intense, paranoid, ornate, and rabidly xenophobic than A. E. van Vogt's stuff, for instance. Unlike most of his peers, Schmitz even occasionally shows sympathy for the alien monsters his characters battle, who are sometimes seen in the end not to be monsters at all, but rather creatures with agendas and priorities and points of view of their own, from which perspectives their actions are justified and sometimes even admirable. Even more extreme, and unlike almost anyone else in the business at that time, Schmitz frequently used *women* as the heroes in swashbuckling tales of interplanetary adventure (sacrilege!) and portrayed them as the total equal of the male characters, every bit as competent and brave and smart (and ruthless, when need be) as the men.

Although he did write a few novels—*The Witches of Karres* is usually thought of as Schmitz's best novel and perhaps is his best work—Schmitz was also unlike his peers in that he did most of his best work at short lengths, most of it for *Astounding* (and later for *Analog,* after the magazine had changed its name) and for *Galaxy,* including such memorable stories as "Balanced Ecology," "Lion Loose . . . ," "Trouble Tide," "Greenface," "The Searcher," "The Winds of Time," "The Custodians," and dozens of others, plus a large number of stories about the adventures of a PSI-powered teenager, Telzey Amberdon. Schmitz's stories have been collected in *A Nice Day For Screaming and Other Tales of the Hub, A Pride of Monsters,* the aforementioned *Agent of Vega,* and, most recently, the posthumous collection *The Best of James H. Schmitz;* the "Telzey Amberdon" stories have been collected in *The Universe against Her* and *The Telzey Toy.* Schmitz's other books include *The Demon Breed, A Tale of Two Clocks,* and *The Eternal Frontiers.*

Schmitz was also known for his aliens, and especially for the construction of intricate and inventive alien ecosystems, with all the interlocking details of the bio-sphere carefully worked out. (He may have been one of the first authors, in fact, to use the word *ecology* in a story.) The alien ecosystem he describes here is partic-ularly ingenious and well thought out, as he takes us along for a hair-raising lesson in why explorers should never take *anything* for granted—even things they think they already know.

Most of Schmitz's work is out-of-print, although an occasional copy of *The Witches of Karres* still shows up in used-book stores. Your best choice of sampling his work would probably be his most recent book, published in 1991, *The Best of James H. Schmitz*, which does contain several of his best stories. You could try ordering it from the publisher, NESFA Press (NESFA Press, PO Box 809, Framingham, MA 97101-0203), although I have no idea whether they have any left in stock or not; the price was $18.95, but you'd better write first and ask for information.

A green-winged, downy thing as big as a hen fluttered along the hillside to a point directly above Cord's head and hovered there, twenty feet above him. Cord, a fifteen-year-old human being, leaned back against a skipboat parked on the equator of a world that had known human beings for only the past four Earth years, and eyed the thing speculatively. The thing was, in the free and easy terminology of the Sutang Colonial Team, a swamp bug. Concealed in the downy fur back of the bug's head was a second, smaller, semiparastical thing, classed as a bug rider.

The bug itself looked like a new species to Cord. Its parasite might or might not turn out to be another unknown. Cord was a natural research man; his first glimpse of the odd flying team had sent endless curiosities thrilling through him. How did that particular phenomenon tick, and why? What fascinating things, once you'd learned about it, could you get it to do?

Normally, he was hampered by circumstances in carrying out any such inves-tigation. The Colonial Team was a practical, hardworking outfit—two thousand people who'd been given twenty years to size up and tame down the brand-new world of Sutang to the point where a hundred thousand colonists could be settled on it, in reasonable safety and comfort. Even junior colonial students like Cord were expected to confine their curiosity to the pattern of research set up by the station to which they were attached. Cord's inclination toward independent exper-iments had got him into disfavor with his immediate superiors before this.

He sent a casual glance in the direction of the Yoger Bay Colonial Station behind him. No signs of human activity about that low, fortresslike bulk in the hill. Its central lock was still closed. In fifteen minutes, it was scheduled to be opened to let out the Planetary Regent, who was inspecting the Yoger Bay Station and its principal activities today.

Fifteen minutes was time enough to find out something about the new bug, Cord decided.

But he'd have to collect it first.

He slid out one of the two handguns holstered at his side. This one was his own property: a Vanadian projectile weapon. Cord thumbed it to position for an-esthetic small-game missiles and brought the hovering swamp bug down, drilled neatly and microscopically through the head.

As the bug hit the ground, the rider left its back. A tiny scarlet demon, round and bouncy as a rubber ball, it shot toward Cord in three long hops, mouth wide to sink home inch-long, venom-dripping fangs. Rather breathlessly, Cord triggered the gun again and knocked it out in midleap. A new species, all right! Most bug riders were harmless plant-eaters, mere suckers of vegetable juice—

"*Cord!*" A feminine voice.

Cord swore softly. He hadn't heard the central lock click open. She must have come around from the other side of the station.

"Hi, Grayan!" he shouted innocently without looking around. "Come see what I got! New species!"

Grayan Mahoney, a slender, black-haired girl two years older than himself, came trotting down the hillside toward him. She was Sutang's star colonial student, and the station manager, Nirmond, indicated from time to time that she was a fine example for Cord to pattern his own behavior on. In spite of that, she and Cord were good friends, but she bossed him around considerably.

"Cord, you dope!" she scowled as she came up. "Quit acting like a collector! If the Regent came out now, you'd be sunk. Nirmond's been telling her about you!"

"Telling her what?" Cord asked, startled.

"For one," Grayan reported, "that you don't keep up on your assigned work. Two, that you sneak off on one-man expeditions of your own at least once a month and have to be rescued—"

"Nobody," Cord interrupted hotly, "has had to rescue me yet!"

"How's Nirmond to know you're alive and healthy when you just drop out of sight for a week?" Grayan countered. "Three," she resumed checking the items off on slim fingertips, "he complained that you keep private zoological gardens of unidentified and possibly deadly vermin in the woods back of the station. And four ... well, Nirmond simply doesn't want the responsibility for you any more!" She held up the four fingers significantly.

"Golly!" gulped Cord, dismayed. Summed up tersely like that, his record *didn't* look too good.

"Golly is right! I keep warning you! Now Nirmond wants the Regent to send you back to Vanadia—and there's a starship coming in to New Venus forty-eight hours from now!" New Venus was the Colonial Team's main settlement on the opposite side of Sutang.

"What'll I do?"

"Start acting like you had good sense mainly." Grayan grinned suddenly. "I talked to the Regent, too—Nirmond isn't rid of you yet! But if you louse up on our tour of the Bay Farms today, you'll be off the Team for good!"

She turned to go. "You might as well put the skipboat back; we're not using it. Nirmond's driving us down to the edge of the Bay in a treadcar, and we'll take a raft from there. Don't let them know I warned you!"

Cord looked after her, slightly stunned. He hadn't realized his reputation had become as bad as all that! To Grayan, whose family had served on Colonial Teams for the past four generations, nothing worse was imaginable than to be dismissed and sent back ignominiously to one's own homeworld. Much to his surprise, Cord was discovering now that he felt exactly the same way about it!

Leaving his newly bagged specimens to revive by themselves and flutter off again, he hurriedly flew the skipboat around the station and rolled it back into its stall.

Three rafts lay moored just offshore in the marshy cove, at the edge of which Nirmond had stopped the treadcar. They looked somewhat like exceptionally broad-brimmed, well-worn sugarloaf hats floating out there, green and leathery. Or like lily pads twenty-five feet across, with the upper section of a big, gray-green pine-apple growing from the center of each. Plant animals of some sort. Sutang was too new to have had its phyla sorted out into anything remotely like an orderly clas-sification. The rafts were a local oddity which had been investigated and could be regarded as harmless and moderately useful. Their usefulness lay in the fact that they were employed as a rather slow means of transportation about the shallow, swampy waters of the Yoger Bay. That was as far as the Team's interest in them went at present.

The Regent had stood up from the back seat of the car, where she was sitting next to Cord. There were only four in the party; Grayan was up front with Nirmond.

"Are those our vehicles?" The Regent sounded amused.

Nirmond grinned, a little sourly. "Don't underestimate them, Dane! They could become an important economic factor in this region in time. But, as a matter of fact, these three are smaller than I like to use." He was peering about the reedy edges of the cove. "There's a regular monster parked here usually—"

Grayan turned to Cord. "Maybe Cord knows where Grandpa is hiding."

It was well-meant, but Cord had been hoping nobody would ask him about Grandpa. Now they all looked at him.

"Oh, you want Grandpa?" he said, somewhat flustered. "Well, I left him . . . I mean I saw him a couple of weeks ago about a mile south from here—"

Grayan sighed. Nirmond grunted and told the Regent, "The rafts tend to stay wherever they're left, providing it's shallow and muddy. They use a hair-root system to draw chemicals and microscopic nourishment directly from the bottom of the bay. Well—Grayan, would you like to drive us there?"

Cord settled back unhappily as the treadcar lurched into motion. Nirmond suspected he'd used Grandpa for one of his unauthorized tours of the area, and Nirmond was quite right.

"I understand you're an expert with these rafts, Cord," Dane said from beside him. "Grayan told me we couldn't find a better steersman, or pilot, or whatever you call it, for our trip today."

"I can handle them," Cord said, perspiring. "They don't give you any trouble!" He didn't feel he'd made a good impression on the Regent so far. Dane was a young, handsome-looking woman with an easy way of talking and laughing, but she wasn't the head of the Sutang Colonial Team for nothing. She looked quite capable of shipping out anybody whose record wasn't up to par.

"There's one big advantage our beasties have over a skipboat, too," Nirmond remarked from the front seat. "You don't have to worry about a snapper trying to climb on board with you!" He went on to describe the stinging ribbon-tentacles the rafts spread around them under water to discourage creatures that might make a meal off their tender underparts. The snappers and two or three other active and aggressive species of the Bay hadn't yet learned it was foolish to attack armed human beings in a boat, but they would skitter hurriedly out of the path of a leisurely perambulating raft.

Cord was happy to be ignored for the moment. The Regent, Nirmond and Grayan were all Earth people, which was true of most of the members of the Team; and Earth people made him uncomfortable, particularly in groups. Vanadia, his own homeworld, had barely graduated from the status of Earth colony itself, which might explain the difference. All the Earth people he'd met so far seemed dedicated to what Grayan Mahoney called the Big Picture, while Nirmond usually spoke of it as "Our Purpose Here." They acted strictly in accordance with their Team Regulations—sometimes, in Cord's opinion, quite insanely. Because now and then the Regulations didn't quite cover a new situation and then somebody was likely to get killed. In which case, the Regulations would be modified promptly, but Earth people didn't seem otherwise disturbed by such events.

Grayan had tried to explain it to Cord:

"We can't really ever *know* in advance what a new world is going to be like! And once we're there, there's too much to do, in the time we've got, to study it inch by inch. You get your job done, and you take a chance. But if you stick by the Regulations you've got the best chances of surviving anybody's been able to figure out for you—"

Cord felt he preferred to just use good sense and not let Regulations or the job get him into a situation he couldn't figure out for himself.

To which Grayan replied impatiently that he hadn't yet got the Big Picture—

The treadcar swung around and stopped, and Grayan stood up in the front seat, pointing. "That's Grandpa, over there!"

Dane also stood up and whistled softly, apparently impressed by Grandpa's fifty-foot spread. Cord looked around in surprise. He was pretty sure this was several hundred yards from the spot where he'd left the big raft two weeks ago; and as Nirmond said, they didn't usually move about by themselves.

Puzzled, he followed the others down a narrow path to the water, hemmed in by tree-sized reeds. Now and then he got a glimpse of Grandpa's swimming platform, the rim of which just touched the shore. Then the path opened out, and he saw the whole raft lying in sunlit, shallow water; and he stooped short, startled.

Nirmond was about to step up on the platform, ahead of Dane.

"Wait!" Cord shouted. His voice sounded squeaky with alarm. "Stop!"

He came running forward.

They had frozen where they stood, looked around swiftly. Then glanced back at Cord coming up. They were well trained.

"What's the matter, Cord?" Nirmond's voice was quiet and urgent.

"Don't get on that raft—it's changed!" Cord's voice sounded wobbly, even to himself. "Maybe it's not even Grandpa—"

He saw he was wrong on the last point before he'd finished the sentence. Scattered along the rim of the raft were discolored spots left by a variety of heatguns, one of which had been his own. It was the way you goaded the sluggish and mindless things into motion. Cord pointed at the cone-shaped central projection. "There—his head! He's sprouting!"

"Sprouting?" the station manager repeated uncomprehendingly. Grandpa's head, as befitted his girth, was almost twelve feet high and equally wide. It was armor-plated like the back of a saurian to keep off plant-suckers, but two weeks ago it had been an otherwise featureless knob, like those on all other rafts. Now scores of long, kinky, leafless vines had grown out from all surfaces of the cone, like green wires. Some were drawn up like tightly coiled springs, others trailed limply to the platform and over it. The top of the cone was dotted with angry red buds, rather like pimples, which hadn't been there before either. Grandpa looked unhealthy.

"Well," Nirmond said, "so it is. Sprouting!" Grayan made a choked sound. Nirmond glanced at Cord as if puzzled. "Is that all that was bothering you, Cord?"

"Well, sure!" Cord began excitedly. He hadn't caught the significance of the word "all"; his hackles were still up, and he was shaking. "None of them ever—"

Then he stopped. He could tell by their faces that they hadn't got it. Or rather, that they'd got it all right but simply weren't going to let it change their plans. The rafts were classified as harmless, according to the Regulations. Until proved otherwise, they would continue to be regarded as harmless. You didn't waste time quibbling with the Regulations—apparently even if you were the Planetary Regent. You didn't feel you had the time to waste.

He tried again. "Look—" he began. What he wanted to tell them was that Grandpa with one unknown factor added wasn't Grandpa any more. He was an unpredictable, oversized lifeform, to be investigated with cautious thoroughness till you knew what the unknown factor meant.

But it was no use. They knew all that. He stared at them helplessly. "I—"

Dane turned to Nirmond. "Perhaps you'd better check," she said. She didn't add, "—to reassure the boy!" but that was what she meant.

Cord felt himself flushing terribly. They thought he was scared—which he was—and they were feeling sorry for him, which they had no right to do. But there was nothing he could say or do now except watch Nirmond walk steadily across the platform. Grandpa shivered slightly a few times, but the rafts always did that when someone first stepped on them. The station manager stopped before one of the kinky sprouts, touched it and then gave it a tug. He reached up and poked at the lowest of the budlike growths. "Odd-looking things!" he called back. He gave Cord another glance. "Well, everything seems harmless enough, Cord. Coming aboard, everyone?"

It was like dreaming a dream in which you yelled and yelled at people and couldn't make them hear you! Cord stepped up stiff-legged on the platform behind Dane and Grayan. He knew exactly what would have happened if he'd hesitated even a moment. One of them would have said in a friendly voice, careful not to let it sound too contemptuous: "You don't have to come along if you don't want to, Cord!"

Grayan had unholstered her heat-gun and was ready to start Grandpa moving out into the channels of the Yoger Bay.

Cord hauled out his own heat-gun and said roughly, "I was to do that!"

"All right, Cord." She gave him a brief, impersonal smile, as if he were someone she'd met for the first time that day, and stood aside.

They were so infuriatingly polite! He was, Cord decided, as good as on his way back to Vanadia right now.

For a while, Cord almost hoped that something awesome and catastrophic would happen promptly to teach the Team people a lesson. But nothing did. As always, Grandpa shook himself vaguely and experimentally when he felt the heat on one edge of the platform and then decided to withdraw from it, all of which was standard procedure. Under the water, out of sight, were the raft's working sections: short, thick leaf-structures shaped like paddles and designed to work as such, along with the slimy nettle-streamers which kept the vegetarians of the Yoger Bay away, and a jungle of hair roots through which Grandpa sucked nourishments from the mud and the sluggish waters of the Bay, and with which he also anchored himself.

The paddles started churning, the platform quivered, the hair roots were hauled out of the mud; and Grandpa was on his ponderous way.

Cord switched off the heat, reholstered his gun, and stood up. Once in motion, the rafts tended to keep traveling unhurriedly for quite a while. To stop them, you gave them a touch of heat along their leading edge; and they could be turned in any direction by using the gun lightly on the opposite side of the platform.

It was simple enough. Cord didn't look at the others. He was still burning inside. He watched the reed beds move past and open out, giving him glimpses of the misty, yellow and green and blue expanse of the brackish Bay ahead. Behind the mist, to the west, were the Yoger Straits, tricky and ugly water when the tides were running; and beyond the Straits lay the open sea, the great Zlanti Deep, which was another world entirely and one of which he hadn't seen much as yet.

Suddenly he was sick with the full realization that he wasn't likely to see any more of it now! Vanadia was a pleasant enough planet; but the wildness and strangeness were long gone from it. It wasn't Sutang.

Grayan called from beside Dane, "What's the best route from here into the farms, Cord?"

"The big channel to the right," he answered. He added somewhat sullenly, "We're headed for it!"

Grayan came over to him. "The Regent doesn't want to see all of it," she said, lowering her voice. "The algae and plankton beds first. Then as much of the mutated grains as we can show her in about three hours. Steer for the ones that have been doing best, and you'll keep Nirmond happy!"

She gave him a conspiratorial wink. Cord looked after her uncertainly. You couldn't tell from her behavior that anything was wrong. Maybe—

He had a flare of hope. It was hard not to like the Team people, even when they were being rock-headed about their Regulations. Perhaps it was that purpose that gave them their vitality and drive, even though it made them remorseless about themselves and everyone else. Anyway, the day wasn't over yet. He might still redeem himself in the Regent's opinion. Something might happen—

Cord had a sudden cheerful, if improbable, vision of some Bay monster plunging up on the raft with snapping jaws, and of himself alertly blowing out what passed for the monster's brains before anyone else—Nirmond, in particular—was even aware of the threat. The Bay monsters shunned Grandpa, of course, but there might be ways of tempting one of them.

So far, Cord realized, he'd been letting his feelings control him. It was time to start thinking!

Grandpa first. So he'd sprouted—green vines and red buds, purpose unknown, but with no change observable in his behavior-patterns otherwise. He was the biggest raft in this end of the Bay, though all of them had been growing steadily in the two years since Cord had first seen one. Sutang's seasons changed slowly; its year was somewhat more than five Earth years long. The first Team members to land here hadn't yet seen a full year pass.

Grandpa then was showing a seasonal change. The other rafts, not quite so far developed, would be reacting similarly a little later. Plant animals—they might be blossoming, preparing to propagate.

"Grayan," he called, "how do the rafts get started? When they're small, I mean."

Grayan looked pleased; and Cord's hopes went up a little more. Grayan was on his side again anyway!

"Nobody knows yet," she said. "We were just talking about it. About half of the coastal marsh-fauna of the continent seems to go through a preliminary larval stage in the sea." She nodded at the red buds on the raft's cone. "It *looks* as if Grandpa is going to produce flowers and let the wind or ride take the seeds out through the Straits."

It made sense. It also knocked out Cord's still half-held hope that the change in Grandpa might turn out to be drastic enough, in some way, to justify his reluctance to get on board. Cord studied Grandpa's armored head carefully once more— unwilling to give up that hope entirely. There were a series of vertical gummy black slits between the armor plates, which hadn't been in evidence two weeks ago either. It looked as if Grandpa were beginning to come apart at the seams. Which might indicate that the rafts, big as they grew to be, didn't outlive a full seasonal cycle, but came to flower at about this time of Sutang's year and died. However, it was a safe bet that Grandpa wasn't going to collapse into senile decay before they completed their trip today.

Cord gave up on Grandpa. The other notion returned to him—perhaps he could coax an obliging Bay monster into action that would show the Regent he was no sissy!

Because the monsters were there, all right.

Kneeling at the edge of the platform and peering down into the wine-colored, clear water of the deep channel they were moving through, Cord could see a fair selection of them at almost any moment.

Some five or six snappers, for one thing. Like big, flattened crayfish, chocolate-brown mostly, with green and red spots on their carapaced backs. In some areas they were so thick you'd wonder what they found to live on, except that they ate almost anything, down to chewing up the mud in which they squatted. However, they preferred their food in large chunks and alive, which was one reason you didn't go swimming in the Bay. They would attack a boat on occasion; but the excited manner in which the ones he saw were scuttling off toward the edges of the channel showed they wanted to have nothing to do with a big moving raft.

Dotted across the bottom were two-foot round holes which looked vacant at the moment. Normally, Cord knew, there would be a head filling each of those holes. The heads consisted mainly of triple sets of jaws, held open patiently like so many traps to grab at anything that came within range of the long, wormlike bodies behind the heads. But Grandpa's passage, waving his stingers like transparent pennants through the water, had scared the worms out of sight, too.

Otherwise, mostly schools of small stuff—and then a flash of wicked scarlet, off to the left behind the raft, darting out from the reeds! Turning its needle-nose into their wake.

Cord watched it without moving. He knew that creature, though it was rare in the Bay and hadn't been classified. Swift, vicious—alert enough to snap swamp bugs out of the air as they fluttered across the surface. And he'd tantalized one with fishing tackle once into leaping up on a moored raft, where it had flung itself about furiously until he was able to shoot it.

No fishing tackle. A handkerchief might just do it, if he cared to risk an arm—

"What fantastic creatures!" Dane's voice just behind him.

"Yellowheads," said Nirmond. "They've got a high utility rating. Keep down the bugs."

Cord stood up casually. It was no time for tricks! The reed bed to their right was thick with yellowheads, a colony of them. Vaguely froggy things, man-sized and better. Of all the creatures he'd discovered in the Bay, Cord liked them least. The flabby, sacklike bodies clung with four thin limbs to the upper sections of the twenty-foot reeds that lined the channel. They hardly ever moved, but their huge, bulging eyes seemed to take in everything that went on about them. Every so often, a downy swamp bug came close enough; and a yellowhead would open its vertical, enormous, tooth-lined slash of a mouth, extend the whole front of its face like a bellows in a flashing strike; and the bug would be gone. They might be useful, but Cord hated them.

"Ten years from now we should know what the cycle of coastal life is like," Nirmond said. "When we set up the Yoger Bay Station there were no yellowheads here. They came the following year. Still with traces of the oceanic larval form; but the metamorphosis was almost complete. About twelve inches long—"

Dane remarked that the same pattern was duplicated endlessly elsewhere. The Regent was inspecting the yellowhead colony with field glasses; she put them down now, looked at Cord and smiled. "How far to the farms?"

"About twenty minutes."

"The key," Nirmond said, "seems to be the Zlanti Basin. It must be almost a soup of life in spring."

"It is," nodded Dane, who had been here in Sutang's spring, four Earth years ago. "It's beginning to look as if the Basin alone might justify colonization. The question is still—", she gestured towards the yellowheads—"how do creatures like that get there?"

They walked off toward the other side of the raft, arguing about ocean currents. Cord might have followed. But something splashed back of them, off to the left and not too far back. He stayed, watching.

After a moment, he saw the big yellowhead. It had slipped down from its reedy perch, which was what had caused the splash. Almost submerged at the water line, it stared after the raft with huge pale-green eyes. To Cord, it seemed to look directly at him. In that moment, he knew for the first time why he didn't like yellowheads. There was something very like intelligence in that look, an alien calculation. In creatures like that, intelligence seemed out of place. What use could they have for it?

A little shiver went over him when it sank completely under the water and he realized it intended to swim after the raft. But it was mostly excitement. He had never seen a yellowhead come down out of the reeds before. The obliging monster he'd been looking for might be presenting itself in an unexpected way.

Half a minute later, he watched it again, swimming awkwardly far down. It had no immediate intention of boarding at any rate. Cord saw it come into the area of the raft's trailing stingers. It maneuvered its way between them with curiously human swimming motions, and went out of sight under the platform.

He stood up, wondering what it meant. The yellowhead had appeared to know about the stingers; there had been an air of purpose in every move of its approach. He was tempted to tell the others about it, but there was the moment of triumph he could have if it suddenly came slobbering up over the edge of the platform and he nailed it before their eyes.

It was almost time anyway to turn the raft in toward the farms. If nothing happened before then—

He watched. Almost five minutes, but no sign of the yellowhead. Still wondering, a little uneasy, he gave Grandpa a calculated needling of heat.

After a moment, he repeated it. Then he drew a deep breath and forgot all about the yellowhead.

"Nirmond!" he called sharply.

The three of them were standing near the center of the platform, next to the big armored cone, looking ahead at the farms. They glanced around.

"What's the matter now, Cord?"

Cord couldn't say it for a moment. He was suddenly, terribly scared again. Something had gone wrong!

"The raft won't turn!" he told them.

"Give it a real burn this time!" Nirmond said.

Cord glanced up at him. Nirmond, standing a few steps in front of Dane and Grayan as if he wanted to protect them, had begun to look a little strained, and no wonder. Cord already had pressed the gun to three different points on the platform; but Grandpa appeared to have developed a sudden anesthesia for heat. They kept moving out steadily toward the center of the Bay.

Now Cord held his breath, switched the heat on full and let Grandpa have it. A six-inch patch on the platform blistered up instantly, turned brown, then black—

Grandpa stopped dead. Just like that.

"That's right! Keep burn—" Nirmond didn't finish his order.

A giant shudder. Cord staggered back toward the water. Then the whole edge of the raft came curling up behind him and went down again, smacking the Bay with a sound like a cannon shot. He flew forward off his feet, hit the platform face down and flattened himself against it. It swelled up beneath him. Two more enormous slaps and joltings. Then quiet. He looked round for the others.

He lay within twelve feet of the central cone. Some twenty or thirty of the mysterious new vines the cone had spouted were stretched out stiffly toward him now, like so many thin green fingers. They couldn't quite reach him. The nearest tip was still ten inches from his shoes.

But Grandpa had caught the others, all three of them. They were tumbled together at the foot of the cone, wrapped in a stiff network of green vegetable ropes, and they didn't move.

Cord drew his feet up cautiously, prepared for another earthquake reaction. But nothing happened. Then he discovered that Grandpa was back in motion on his previous course. The heatgun had vanished. Gently, he took out the Vanadian gun.

"Cord? It didn't get you?" It was the Regent.

"No," he said, keeping his voice low. He realized suddenly he'd simply assumed they were all dead. Now he felt sick and shaky.

"What are you doing?"

Cord looked at Grandpa's big armor-plated head with a certain hunger. The cones were hollowed out inside; the station's lab had decided their chief function was to keep enough air trapped under the rafts to float them. But in that central section was also the organ that controlled Grandpa's overall reactions.

He said softly, "I got a gun and twelve heavy-duty explosive bullets. Two of them will blow that cone apart."

"No good, Cord!" the pain-racked voice told him. "If the thing sinks, we'll die anyway. You have anesthetic charges for that gun of yours?"

He stared at her back. "Yes."

"Give Nirmond and the girl a shot each, before you do anything else. Directly into the spine, if you can. But don't come any closer—"

Somehow, Cord couldn't argue with that voice. He stood up carefully. The gun made two soft spitting sounds.

"All right," he said hoarsely. "What do I do now?"

Dane was silent a moment. "I'm sorry, Cord. I can't tell you that. I'll tell you what I can—"

She paused for some seconds again. "This thing didn't try to kill us, Cord. It could have easily. It's incredibly strong. I saw it break Nirmond's legs. But as soon as we stopped moving, it just held us. They were both unconscious then—"

"You've got that to go on. It was trying to pitch you within reach of its vines or tendrils, or whatever they are, wasn't it?"

"I think so," Cord said shakily. That was what had happened, of course; and at any moment Grandpa might try again.

"Now it's feeding us some sort of anesthetic of its own through those vines. Tiny thorns. A sort of numbness—" Dane's voice trailed off a moment. Then she said clearly, "Look, Cord—it seems we're food it's storing up! You get that?"

"Yes," he said.

"Seeding time for the rafts. There are analogues. Live food for its seed probably; not for the raft. One couldn't have counted on that. Cord?"

"Yes. I'm here."

"I want," said Dane, "to stay awake as long as I can. But there's really just one other thing—this raft's going somewhere. To some particularly favorable location. And that might be very near shore. You might make it in then; otherwise it's up to you. But keep your head and wait for a chance. No heroics, understand?"

"Sure, I understand," Cord told her. He realized then that he was talking reassuringly, as if it weren't the Planetary Regent but someone like Grayan.

"Nirmond's the worst," Dane said. "The girl was knocked unconscious at once. If it weren't for my arm—But, if we can get help in five hours or so, everything should be all right. Let me know if anything happens, Cord."

"I will," Cord said gently again. Then he sighted his gun carefully at a point between Dane's shoulder blades, and the anesthetic chamber made its soft, spitting sound once more. Dane's taut body relaxed slowly, and that was all.

There was no point Cord could see in letting her stay awake; because they weren't going anywhere near shore.

The reed beds and the channels were already behind them, and Grandpa hadn't changed direction by the fraction of a degree. He was moving out into the open Bay—and he was picking up company!

So far, Cord could count seven big rafts within two miles of them; and on the three that were closest he could make out a sprouting of new green vines. All of them were traveling in a straight direction; and the common point they were all headed for appeared to be the roaring center of the Yoger Straits, now some three miles away!

Behind the Straits, the cold Zlanti Deep—the rolling fogs, and the open sea! It might be seeding time for the rafts, but it looked as if they weren't going to distribute their seeds in the Bay—

For a human being, Cord was a fine swimmer. He had a gun and he had a knife, in spite of what Dane had said; he might have stood a chance among the killers of the Bay. But it would be a very small chance, at best. And it wasn't, he thought, as if there weren't still other possibilities. He was going to keep his head.

Except by accident, of course, nobody was going to come looking for them in time to do any good. If anyone did look, it would be around the Bay Farms. There were a number of rafts moored there; and it would be assumed they'd used one of them. Now and then something unexpected happened and somebody simply vanished—by the time it was figured out just what had happened on this occasion, it would be much too late.

Neither was anybody likely to notice within the next few hours that the rafts had started migrating out of the swamps through the Yoger Straits. There was a small weather station a little inland, on the north side of the Straits, which used a helicopter occasionally. It was about as improbable, Cord decided dismally, that they'd use it in the right spot just now as it would be for a jet transport to happen to come in low enough to spot them.

The fact that it was up to him, as the Regent had said, sank in a little more after that! Cord had never felt so lonely.

Simply because he was going to try it sooner or later, he carried out an experiment next that he knew couldn't work. He opened the gun's anesthetic chamber and counted out fifty pellets—rather hurriedly because he didn't particularly want to think of what he might be using them for eventually. There were around three hundred charges left in the chamber then; and in the next few minutes Cord carefully planted a third of them in Grandpa's head.

He stopped after that. A whale might have showed signs of somnolence under a lesser load. Grandpa paddled on undisturbed. Perhaps he had become a little numb in spots, but his cells weren't equipped to distribute the soporific effect of that type of drug.

There wasn't anything else Cord could think of doing before they reached the Straits. At the rate they were moving, he calculated that would happen in something less than an hour; and if they did pass through the Straits, he was going to risk a swim. He didn't think Dane would have disapproved, under the circumstances. If the raft simply carried them all out into the foggy vastness of the Zlanti Deep, there would be no practical chance of survival left at all.

Meanwhile, Grandpa was definitely picking up speed. And there were other changes going on—minor ones, but still a little awe-inspiring to Cord. The pimply-looking red buds that dotted the upper part of the cone were opening out gradually. From the center of most of them protruded now something like a thin, wet, scarlet worm: a worm that twisted weakly, extended itself by an inch or so, rested and twisted again, and stretched up a little farther, groping into the air. The vertical black slits between the armor plates looked somehow deeper and wider than they had been even some minutes ago; a dark, thick liquid dripped slowly from several of them.

Under other circumstances Cord knew he would have been fascinated by these developments in Grandpa. As it was, they drew his suspicious attention only because he didn't know what they meant.

Then something quite horrible happened suddenly. Grayan started moaning loudly and terribly and twisted almost completely around. Afterwards, Cord knew it hadn't been a second before he stopped her struggles and the sounds together with another anesthetic pellet; but the vines had tightened their grip on her first, not flexibly but like the digging, bony green talons of some monstrous bird of prey. If Dane hadn't warned him—

White and sweating, Cord put his gun down slowly while the vines relaxed again. Grayan didn't seem to have suffered any additional harm; and she would certainly have been the first to point out that his murderous rage might have been as intelligently directed against a machine. But for some moments Cord continued to luxuriate furiously in the thought that, at any instant he chose, he could still turn the raft very quickly into a ripped and exploded mess of sinking vegetation.

Instead, and more sensibly, he gave both Dane and Nirmond another shot, to prevent a similar occurrence with them. The contents of two such pellets, he knew, would keep any human being torpid for at least four hours. Five shots—

Cord withdrew his mind hastily from the direction it was turning into; but it wouldn't stay withdrawn. The thought kept coming up again; until at last he had to recognize it:

Five shots would leave the three of them completely unconscious, whatever else might happen to them, until they either died from other causes or were given a counteracting agent.

Shocked, he told himself he couldn't do it. It was exactly like killing them.

But then, quite steadily, he found himself raising the gun once more, to bring the total charge for each of the three Team people up to five. And if it was the first time in the last four years Cord had felt like crying, it also seemed to him that he had begun to understand what was meant by using your head—along with other things.

Barely thirty minutes later, he watched a raft as big as the one he rode go sliding into the foaming white waters of the Straits a few hundred yards ahead, and dart off abruptly at an angle, caught by one of the swirling currents. It pitched and spun, made some headway, and was swept aside again. And then it righted itself once more. Not like some blindly animated vegetable, Cord thought, but like a creature that struggled with intelligent purpose to maintain its chosen direction.

At least, they seemed practically unsinkable—

Knife in hand, he flattened himself against the platform as the Straits roared just ahead. When the platform jolted and tilted up beneath him, he rammed the knife all the way into it and hung on. Cold water rushed suddenly over him, and

Grandpa shuddered like a laboring engine. In the middle of it all, Cord had the horrified notion that the raft might release its unconscious human prisoners in its struggle with the Straits. But he underestimated Grandpa in that. Grandpa also hung on.

Abruptly, it was over. They were riding a long swell, and there were three other rafts not far away. The Straits had swept them together, but they seemed to have no interest in one another's company. As Cord stood up shakily and began to strip off his clothes, they were visibly drawing apart again. The platform of one of them was half-submerged; it must have lost too much of the air that held it afloat and, like a small ship, it was foundering.

From this point, it was only a two-mile swim to the shore north of the Straits, and another mile inland from there to the Straits Head Station. He didn't know about the current; but the distance didn't seem too much, and he couldn't bring himself to leave knife and gun behind. The Bay creatures loved warmth and mud, they didn't venture beyond the Straits. But Zlanti Deep bred its own killers, though they weren't often observed so close to shore.

Things were beginning to look rather hopeful.

Thin, crying voices drifted overhead, like the voices of curious cats, as Cord knotted his clothes into a tight bundle, shoes inside. He looked up. There were four of them circling there; magnified seagoing swamp bugs, each carrying an unseen rider. Probably harmless scavengers—but the ten-foot wingspread was impressive. Uneasily, Cord remembered the venomously carnivorous rider he'd left lying beside the station.

One of them dipped lazily and came sliding down toward him. It soared overhead and came back, to hover about the raft's cone.

The bug rider that directed the mindless flier hadn't been interested in him at all! Grandpa was baiting it!

Cord stared in fascination. The top of the cone was alive now with a softly wriggling mass of the scarlet, wormlike extrusions that had started sprouting before the raft left the Bay. Presumably, they looked enticingly edible to the bug rider.

The flier settled with an airy fluttering and touched the cone. Like a trap springing shut, the green vines flashed up and around it, crumpling the brittle wings, almost vanishing into the long soft body—

Barely a second later, Grandpa made another catch, this one from the sea itself. Cord had a fleeting glimpse of something like a small, rubbery seal that flung itself out of the water upon the edge of the raft, with a suggestion of desperate haste—and was flipped on instantly against the cone where the vines clamped it down beside the flier's body.

It wasn't the enormous ease with which the unexpected kill was accomplished that left Cord standing there, completely shocked. It was the shattering of his hopes to swim to shore from here. Fifty yards away, the creature from which the rubbery thing had been fleeing showed briefly on the surface, as it turned away from the raft; and the glance was all he needed. The ivory-white body and gaping jaws were similar enough to those of the sharks of Earth to indicate the pursuer's nature. The important difference was that, wherever the white hunters of the Zlanti Deep went, they went by the thousands.

Stunned by that incredible piece of bad luck, still clutching his bundled clothes, Cord stared toward shore. Knowing what to look for, he could spot the telltale roilings of the surface now—the long, ivory gleams that flashed through the swells and vanished again. Shoals of smaller things burst into the air in sprays of glittering desperation and fell back.

He would have been snapped up like a drowning fly before he'd covered a twentieth of that distance!

But almost another full minute passed before the realization of the finality of his defeat really sank in.

Grandpa was beginning to eat!

Each of the dark slits down the sides of the cone was a mouth. So far only one of them was in operating condition, and the raft wasn't able to open that one very wide as yet. The first morsel had been fed into, however: the bug rider the vines had plucked out of the flier's downy neck fur. It took Grandpa several minutes to work it out of sight, small as it was. But it was a start.

Cord didn't feel quite sane any more. He sat there, clutching his bundle of clothes and only vaguely aware of the fact that he was shivering steadily under the cold spray that touched him now and then, while he followed Grandpa's activities attentively. He decided it would be at least some hours before one of that black set of mouths grew flexible and vigorous enough to dispose of a human being. Under the circumstances, it couldn't make much difference to the other human beings here; but the moment Grandpa reached for the first of them would also be the moment he finally blew the raft to pieces. The white hunters were cleaner eaters, at any rate; and that was about the extent to which he could still control what was going to happen.

Meanwhile, there was the very faint chance that the weather station's helicopter might spot them—

Meanwhile also, in a weary and horrified fascination, he kept debating the mystery of what could have produced such a nightmarish change in the rafts. He could guess where they were going by now; there were scattered strings of them stretching back to the Straits or roughly parallel to their own course, and the direction was that of the plankton-swarming pool of the Zlanti Basin, a thousand miles to the north. Given time, even mobile lily pads like the rafts had been could make that trip for the benefit of their seedlings. But nothing in their structure explained the sudden change into alert and capable carnivores.

He watched the rubbery little seal-thing being hauled up to a mouth next. The vines broke its neck; and the mouth took it in up to the shoulders and then went on working patiently at what was still a trifle too large a bite. Meanwhile, there were more thin cat cries overhead; and a few minutes later, two more sea bugs were trapped almost simultaneously and added to the larder. Grandpa dropped the dead seal-thing and fed himself another bug rider. The second rider left its mount with a sudden hop, sank its teeth viciously into one of the vines that caught it again, and was promptly battered to death against the platform.

Cord felt a resurge of unreasoning hatred against Grandpa. Killing a bug was about equal to cutting a branch from a tree; they had almost no life-awareness. But the rider had aroused his partisanship because of its appearance of intelligent action—and it was in fact closer to the human scale in that feature than to the monstrous life-form that had, mechanically, but quite successfully, trapped both it and the human beings. Then his thoughts had drifted again; and he found himself. Speculating vaguely on the curious symbiosis in which the nerve systems of two creatures as dissimilar as the bugs and their riders could be linked so closely that they functioned as one organism.

Suddenly an expression of vast and stunned surprise appeared on his face. Why—now he knew!

Cord stood up hurriedly, shaking with excitement, the whole plan complete in his mind. And a dozen long vines snaked instantly in the direction of his sudden motion, and groped for him, taut and stretching. They couldn't reach him, but their savagely alert reaction froze Cord briefly where he was. The platform was shuddering under his feet, as if in irritation at his inaccessibility; but it couldn't be tilted up suddenly here to throw him within the grasp of the vines, as it could around the edges.

Still, it was a warning! Cord sidled gingerly around the cone till he had gained the position he wanted, which was on the forward half of the raft. And then he waited. Waited long minutes, quite motionless, until his heart stopped pounding and the irregular angry shivering of the surface of the raft-thing died away, and the last vine tendril had stopped its blind groping. It might help a lot if, for a second or two after he next started moving, Grandpa wasn't too aware of his exact whereabouts

He looked back once to check how far they had gone by now beyond the Straits Head Station. It couldn't, he decided, be even an hour behind them. Which was close enough, by the most pessimistic count—if everything else worked out all right! He didn't try to think out in detail what that "everything else" could include, because there were factors that simply couldn't be calculated in advance. And he had an uneasy feeling that speculating too vividly about them might make him almost incapable of carrying out his plan.

At last, moving carefully, Cord took the knife in his left hand but left the gun holstered. He raised the tightly knotted bundle of clothes slowly over his head, balanced in his right hand. With a long, smooth motion he tossed the bundle back across the cone, almost to the opposite edge of the platform.

It hit with a soggy thump. Almost immediately, the whole far edge of the raft buckled and flapped up to toss the strange object to the reaching vines.

Simultaneously, Cord was racing forward. For a moment, his attempt to divert Grandpa's attention seemed completely successful—then he was pitched to his knees as the platform came up.

He was within eight feet of the edge. As it slapped down again, he threw himself desperately forward.

An instant later, he was knifing down through cold, clear water, just ahead of the raft, then twisting and coming up again.

The raft was passing over him. Clouds of tiny sea creatures scattered through its dark jungle of feeding roots. Cord jerked back from a broad, wavering streak of glassy greenness, which was a stinger, and felt a burning jolt on his side, which meant he'd been touched lightly by another. He bumped on blindly through the slimy black tangles of hair roots that covered the bottom of the raft; then green half-light passed over him, and he burst up into the central bubble under the cone.

Half-light and foul, hot air. Water slapped around him, dragging him away again—nothing to hang on to here! Then above him, to his right, molded against the interior curve of the cone as if it had grown there from the start, the froglike, man-sized shape of the yellowhead.

The raft rider—

Cord reached up and caught Grandpa's symbiotic partner and guide by a flabby hind leg, pulled himself half out of the water and struck twice with the knife, fast while the pale-green eyes were still opening.

He'd thought the yellowhead might need a second or so to detach itself from its host, as the bug riders usually did, before it tried to defend itself. This one merely turned its head; the mouth slashed down and clamped on Cord's left arm above the elbow. His right hand sank the knife through one staring eye, and the yellowhead jerked away, pulling the knife from his grasp.

Sliding down, he wrapped both hands around the slimy leg and hauled with all his weight. For a moment more, the yellowhead hung on. Then the countless neural extensions that connected it now with the raft came free in a succession of sucking, tearing sounds; and Cord and the yellowhead splashed into the water together.

Black tangle of roots again—and two more electric burns suddenly across his back and legs! Strangling, Cord let go. Below him, for a moment, a body was turning over and over with oddly human motions; then a solid wall of water thrust him up and aside, as something big and white struck the turning body and went on.

Cord broke the surface twelve feet behind the raft. And that would have been that, if Grandpa hadn't already been slowing down.

After two tries, he floundered back up on the platform and lay there gasping and coughing awhile. There were no indications that his presence was resented now. A few vine tips twitched uneasily, as if trying to remember previous functions, when he came limping up presently to make sure his three companions were still breathing; but Cord never noticed that.

They were still breathing; and he knew better than to waste time trying to help them himself. He took Grayan's heat-gun from its holster. Grandpa had come to a full stop.

Cord hadn't had time to become completely sane again, or he might have worried now whether Grandpa, violently sundered from his controlling partner, was still capable of motion on his own. Instead, he determined the approximate direction of the Straits Head Station, selected a corresponding spot on the platform and gave Grandpa a light tap of heat.

Nothing happened immediately. Cord sighed patiently and stepped up the heat a little.

Grandpa shuddered gently. Cord stood up.

Slowly and hesitatingly at first, then with steadfast—though now again brainless—purpose, Grandpa began paddling back toward the Straits Head Station.

The Red Hills of Summer

EDGAR PANGBORN

The late Edgar Pangborn is almost forgotten these days and is rarely ever mentioned even in historical surveys of the fifties and sixties . . . which is a pity, since he had a depth and breadth of humanity that have rarely been matched inside the field or out. Although he was never a particularly prolific writer (five science-fiction novels, one or two mainstream novels, and a baker's dozen or so of short pieces) he was nevertheless one of that select crew of underappreciated authors (one thinks of Cordwainer Smith, Fritz Leiber, Jack Vance, Avram Davidson, and Richard McKenna) who have had an enormous underground effect on the field simply by impressing the hell out of other writers and numerous authors-in-the-egg. Pangborn wrote about "little people" for the most part, only rarely focusing on the famous and powerful. He was one of only a handful of science-fiction writers capable of writing about small-town or rural people with insight and sympathy (most science fiction is urban in orientation, written by city people *about* city people—or, when it *is* written by people from small towns, they are frequently kids who couldn't wait to get *out* of those small towns and off to the bright lights of the big city . . . which often amounts to the same thing, as far as sympathies are concerned), and he was also one of the few who could get inside the minds of both the very young and the very old with equal ease and compassion.

Pangborn's masterpiece was *Davy*, which, in spite of a somewhat weak ending (or, at least, a final third that doesn't quite live up to the two-thirds that came before it), may well be the finest postholocaust novel ever written—in my opinion, it is seriously rivaled only by Walter M. Miller's *A Canticle for Leibowitz* and John Wyndham's *Re-Birth*. In any fair world, *Davy* alone ought to be enough to guarantee Pangborn a distinguished place in the history of the genre, but there were also novels like *A Mirror for Observers*—his International Fantasy Award winner, somewhat dated now, but still powerful, in which alien observers from two opposing philosophical camps vie for the soul of a brilliant human boy—and *West of the Sun,* an underrated novel about the efforts of human castaways to survive on an alien world, as well as beautifully crafted short work such as "A Master of Babylon," "Longtooth," "The World Is a Sphere," and "Angel's Egg." Edgar Pangborn's other works include *The Judgment of Eve* and *The Company of Glory,* the mainstream novel *The Trial of Castilla Blake,* the collection *Good Neighbors and Other Strangers,* and the posthumously published collection *Still I Persist in Wondering.*

The story that follows, "The Red Hills of Summer," which was later expanded into *West of the Sun,* paints a vivid picture, both hardheadedly realistic and beautifully evocative, of humankind's first attempt to explore an alien world, and the landing party's discovery that no matter how far away you go, you can't outrun the monsters that dwell within your own heart. . . .

1

Miranda caught my hand, her own soft small hands gone hard with tension. Captain Madison on the speaker's platform had mentioned the pilot mission, and possible lethal elements on the shining dot below us—bacteria, viruses, qualities of the lower atmosphere not discoverable from orbit. It had not dawned on me till then that my troubled Miranda might be desiring the pilot mission for herself and me. For the last year she had been in the shadow of private unhappiness, often remote even when she was in my arms.

Below us. For the first time in fifteen years that word *below* was more than a reference to the place where your feet happened to be. It possessed a meaning in relation to the ship, to me as a unit of living matter, to black-haired Miranda.

Madison's square face recaptured my attention. I had first glimpsed it at the beginning of the voyage, when I came aboard with the unsparing eyes of a boy of twelve. That year he was thirty-five. Now at fifty he looked little changed—more tired, hair grayer, voice flatter. Who wouldn't be tired, after the job of bringing our enormous sphere into a safe orbit? My own healthy red-haired carcass felt exhausted too, from the excitement that had churned in all of us since the planet was sighted and we knew we must decide whether to risk a descent. We were in the meeting-room now, all three hundred, to make that decision.

I, David Leroy, am not a scientist nor a technician. Miranda and I were Randies—chosen like most of the kids for good health and what the Builders' Directives solemnly call Random Talents. There's a pride in it. You discover the virtues of comprehensive wide-ranging ignorance.

Captain Rupert Madison was saying: "If we go on, I don't suppose any of you, even children born in space, would live to see the end of the journey. The distances are too vast, Earth-type planets too far apart. The chance of finding another as promising as this one, within our lifetime, is small. The other choice is to go down—and stay."

It was that simple. A huge frail sphere like ours, built to transport a colony for generations if necessary, doesn't land anywhere. You don't take it into atmosphere. Compartmented and honeycombed, spheres within spheres down to the core where the computer hummed its mathematical daydreams, the ship *Galileo* was designed for one purpose only: to bear our splinter fragment of humanity away from a world that humanity had apparently ruined, away to some cleaner place where the sickness in our germ plasm might work itself out—perhaps, always perhaps, and only after many generations. That errand performed, the emptied shell of *Galileo* would shine on as a satellite, a golden moon circling a second-chance world.

When you live in close awareness of it for fifteen years, even the new curse of Cain can become a commonplace. But I had been obliged to learn it was not so for Miranda. Her trouble was there, a sense of futility forced on her by the radiation sickness of Earth: for what, her heart said, is the point of a million years of human evolution if it must end not even with a bang, only with the whimper of babies born armless, distorted, blind? She had grown terrified of the times when she couldn't *care* about anything. "Not even about you, Davy . . ."

Captain Madison was hammering home the truth of no return, speaking of what it requires—in terms of industry, labor, raw materials—to build just one launching center like the twelve that toiled eight years to send the bits and pieces of this vessel out of Earth's gravity. Earth had bled herself white for her children, after men once and for all faced the probability of racial extinction. They would build another *Galileo*, and another; would go on doggedly building, all else subordinated, so long as any courage and equipment remained. "The gravity of that planet down there is a bit greater than the gravity of Earth. Launching centers!" Madison said. "I remember. That was my life, you know, from teens into thirties, beginning as a grease monkey at Canaveral . . . Well, you know the arithmetic: three hundred colonists don't reproduce a technology that was based on a population of three billion.

"The know-how? We have it all, in the microfilm library. Raw materials, yes— down there we'll find the same minerals, same general chemical pattern. But the building of launching centers, new ships, the reconquest of space if you want that inflated language—let's say it just might be an enterprise of our great-great-grand- children, if we have any, if enough of them are healthy and active human beings, and if space travel happens to be what they want most, at any cost, in their own far-off time."

Nobody sighed or fidgeted, as many would have done if this had been another pep-talk by our Psychometric Coordinator Cecil Dorman, known to Miranda and me and others of the irreverent as Cecil Psycho.

"The planet is habitable," said Captain Madison, "so far as we know from orbit study." Miranda felt my look but would not return it; her hands grasping mine were cold. "So far as we know," he repeated, "in advance of the pilot mission— which will consist of two men and two women who will go down, maintain radio contact at least four weeks, and make the final tests we can't make up here. Your only vote in this meeting, I suppose, will be to decide whether the pilot mission starts at all—remembering that whatever they find, those four volunteers can't come back."

Behind me, I heard the suave voice of Andrea del Sentiero—fifty-eight, the only colonist older than Madison. His official title was Historian. "Does anything in the latest studies suggest a civilization?"

"Nothing, sir. Forest, savannah, large lakes, marshes, deserts, mountain ranges running generally north and south, a few of the summits snow-capped." He was talking for all of us, who had had only brief chances at the telescopes; the viewplate in the panel behind him gave a low magnification, the planet a blur of blue and reddish green. "Six continental land masses paired north and south, three main oceans, polar caps small and broken up. Bound to be dense tropics near the equator, the rest sub-tropical, with narrow temperate zones. No roads in the open areas, nothing like cities. No vessels on the seas, river mouths surrounded by the same vegetation that covers most of the land. The reddish green deepens on the seaward slopes of the hills, but that suggests—Dr. Bunuan agrees—a result of rainfall, not intelligent agriculture. Dr. Bunuan thinks we may find something like Earth in the time of dinosaurs. He calls that a half-educated guess."

"Quarter-educated," the biologist's mellow voice corrected him.

Captain Madison grinned. "If you insist, José. No, Andrea, if there's life at the social, technological level it would have to be hidden under forest cover—unlikely."

"Yes," said del Sentiero. "I have no other questions."

"Maybe something to add?"

"Only two things," said the Historian. "One, that my vote will be for going down and making the best of it. Two, that the pilot mission ought to be a privilege of the old."

Captain Madison winced. "You mean, why risk the young?"

Del Sentiero said nothing. I knew, without seeing, the stoical Latin shrug, the dark eyes contemplating eternity, the mild outward motion of eloquent hands.

"Anyone may volunteer for it," said Madison heavily, and he shut his eyes, his face freezing into difficult calm. "Responsibility for choosing the four is on me, Andrea, nowhere else." His eyes flew open, probing here and there. "Questions? Discussion?"

I had expected that Paul Cutter would seize this moment to sound off on the revision of the model constitution, which could not even begin to function until after a landing. The constitution was an attempt of the Builders to suggest the framework of such government as a colony of 300 might be expected to need. Mirthless and lonely Paul Cutter had grappled with it, conceiving amendment after amendment, identifying his unhappy self with each improvement to the point of monomania. He ate and drank the constitution, slept and got up with it. At any time his blaring monologue might nail you to the wall explaining how it *must* be amended or the whole expedition would Betray the Human Heritage.

Paul was younger than Miranda and myself, a boy of ten at the start of the voyage. Some hereditary slant made him grow from a normal-looking child into a small bandy-legged man, gnarled, not misshapen but seeming so, a bulging head connected by a weak neck to a tight barrel of torso. A bore, comical and ugly through no fault of his own. He had chosen psychology as his field of specialization, becoming a noisy satellite of Cecil Dorman. Unfortunately for Paul's ambitions, not Dorman but the learned, humorous and peaceful Dr. Carey was boss of the Psychology Department. (*Galileo* was certainly in its way a college; I still think of it so.) Paul Cutter never earned a title: a Randy still, the fact no source of pride to him but an ingrowing pain.

I saw Cutter in the front row, big head alertly cocked. Nothing happened. No fresh amendment, no bray of earnest argument. Maybe Cecil Dorman had persuaded him to let the constitution wait a minute or two . . .

We were voting, by a simple show of hands. No opposition. No one could bear the thought of another fifteen years, or another generation, or another century, in space. But I remember that when my own hand went up I was not thinking of that, but of red-green seaward hills, and of the sound of ocean that might resemble what I had heard when I was a boy at Martha's Vineyard watching the loud hurry and change of waves under the sudden winds of September.

I believe this was the only unanimous decision ever taken by the colonists of the planet Demeter.

Madison was speaking evenly: "The pilot mission. You know the Builders' Directives. You know the necessity. We can't take down the whole colony to be destroyed by something not discoverable from orbit. We haven't the means to break out of gravity and come back. Directives recommend the mission consist of two men and two women. Partly to avoid trusting the judgment of one volunteer. Partly because one sex might be immune to a lethal factor that would kill the other. Partly on the chance that the four might pull through with their survival equipment, and multiply, even if they had to tell the rest of us to stay away. So I want four guinea-pigs. Whoever they are, they'll be four individuals whom we love and can't spare. I am now calling for them."

This was the way it came, like all great questions, not with trumpets but plainly spoken and quiet as morning. I thought at first there was also a question in Miranda's brown-eyed gaze, one not weighted toward yes or no. Then I understood she was not asking me: *Are you going to stand up?* She was silently saying: *I must do this, I'm driven from within. Whether you stand up or not, Davy, I must and I will.*

I took her hand again and I was on my feet.

Five or six other couples were standing, and a surprising number, ten or a dozen, stood up alone. I heard a murmuring, voices here and there attempting the unsayable, as Rupert Madison looked us over through his captain's mask.

I supposed he would choose the volunteers from among the Randies. Breezy Arthur Clay for instance, standing alone two rows ahead of us, solemn as I had never seen him. Or Joe and Miriam Somers, solidly married with the formalities Miranda had never quite wanted for us, decent, unexciting Joe and Miriam who rather thought they'd like to be farmers if we ever landed. Or Laurette Vieuxtemps, a housewife temperament but not committed to any man, religious, reservedly sweet.

Madison told a few of them—all specialists—to sit down. Then he appeared to have reached a private impasse, brooding in his loneliness. Fussy and dapper Cecil Dorman, on the platform with him, leaned forward suggesting something, and shriveled in Madison's glare. Madison would not be saying again, in words, where responsibility lay, but the Psychometric Coordinator was just the one guy who wouldn't understand it unless he got his nose rubbed in it twice. Madison sighed and spoke names.

Just names. No request to sit down.

"Paul Cutter." I was unready to understand. I had not noticed till then that Paul Cutter had risen; his squat form had been hidden by Art Clay. "Laurette Vieuxtemps . . ." Miranda's fingers gripped tightly. I did understand. "Miranda Klein . . . David Leroy."

2

David Leroy, pilot. I had a title . . .

I don't recall much about the entry into atmosphere. I remember a tight-sealed pocket of heat skimming interminably above a world that gradually expanded in the viewplates above my controls. I remember fear, doubt of my own skill based on nothing but years of theoretical drill without experience. Most clearly, I recall Captain Madison's voice, linked to me by the tenuous nerve of radio, a true part of me, the one part that remained unshaken.

I had known there would be breaks in communication—static interference, other difficulties—and there was one when Madison was on the other side of the planet. No foreknowledge can prepare you for such a loneliness. Yet I'd always been lonely, like Miranda, like everyone else, a single human planet in the galaxy of the human race.

Then Madison, remote and *above*, in an orbit become incredibly *swift* relative to my *slow*, was speaking again. I was able to give him a much lower temperature reading, a respectably diminished altitude. He said: "You're past the worst. How do you feel?"

"Fine, dandy and lonesome." I glanced in the mirror that gave me the cabin. "Others in good shape. Colonizing with no pain."

"You'll be over that plateau in six minutes, then test your power. Better not use it much till you're down to say 90,000—but that's up to you, Davy. From here on you play it by the seat of your pants."

"I'll do that, Captain."

"We won't try calling from the blind side again. Reestablish contact 0940 hours *Galileo* time." Then with some dry noise that might have been static: "See you, boy."

Below me, ocean and red-green land, an infinity of brooding day. I found the 40-mile oval of my target, and tested the power in a long cautious turn—no trouble. Trust the Builders for that.

The Builders? There was no one, no one at all to trust except Miranda Klein, Laurette Vieuxtemps, Paul Cutter and myself. The Builders were finished with us, had done their magnificent best fifteen years ago, and by now many of them would be dead, and, groping somewhere through the unthinkable reaches, there might be a *Galileo II*, even a *Galileo III*. I would not think now about the Builders, who had known they could have no reward except consciousness of a piece of good work completed . . .

Our chosen landing spot was a roughly oval plateau, 40 miles at the greatest length, on one of the three continents of the southern hemisphere. It had been selected by the Council of *Galileo*—del Sentiero presiding, we four volunteers awkwardly attending. The choice had to be partly arbitrary, for the photographic map showed little to suggest that any one spot in the temperate belts would be better than another. I favored the notion of an island, but kept my Randy mouth shut. Del Sentiero suggested the same thing and was overruled: aircraft fuel would give out before our technology could replace it, the building of ships might be difficult, we might even find no suitable timber. And a plateau is, in a way, an island.

My turn carried us out over the sea, then inland, miles above the white summits of a mountain range that rose to the west of our plateau. I cut the power and we drifted soundless in the thickening air.

The plateau lay 30 miles in from the sea. Vegetation covered most of it, but reddish-white patches suggested open ground, possibly sand. We had noticed the same pinkish tinge on many of the ocean beaches. Easy for landing (I hoped) and an easy mark for *Galileo* to hold in observation. Westward for 500 miles spread the random masses of the mountains, our plateau a midget among their numberless foothills.

Prevailing winds in the southern hemisphere blew westward as on Earth; Dr. Bunuan was surely right in assuming plentiful rainfall on the seaward slopes. The region west of the range was no desert, however, but deep forest, 800 miles of it, divided by the silver furrow of a river flowing south. That forest ended at another, narrower range, following the continent's western shore. Our plateau stood at the 45th parallel south, where the continent dwindled in a triangular pattern rather like South America. No land bridge to the continent in the northern hemisphere, and no continental mass at the south polar region, but a myriad scattered islands, and drift ice, and occasional stretches of blue sea all the way to the pole.

"Handling right?" I had known Paul Cutter would be the first and only one to forget Madison's order about letting me alone on this job. I didn't mind the distraction; the little ship was gliding with almost no need of attention. I did mind the jitters in Paul's crashing voice.

I said: "Yes. You people happy back there?"

"Happy as three ticks on a dog—you're the dog." The voice I wanted, Miranda's. It went on, cool but not too sharp: "Let's keep a cork in it, Paul—the man's busy."

Wounded to the core, Paul boomed: "Sorry! Sorry!"

Two birds, or creatures in the shape of birds, were circling between me and the plateau, as a hawk soars, with unmoving wings. Frightened perhaps by our descending gleam, they sped away downwind—at least I thought, from the gust of speed without wing-motion, that they were heading downwind, and I tried to remember the games of seagulls over Martha's Vineyard. Only the color returned to me and the sense of an airy freedom, the taste of salt wind, the brown ghost of a Portuguese boy who used to play with me.

The smooth course of the ship told me nothing—maybe no wind at all was blowing. Maybe it was blowing some other way at a lower altitude. I saw no wind-motion of the forest, but I was still too high to be certain.

And too low to look down any longer on the mountain-tops. They were above me and would remain above me.

The spot of open ground I had selected for landing was the only one beginning at an edge of the plateau. If the wind was right—where *was* the wind?—I would circle out beyond the edge, come in slightly above it, and still have two miles clear for a landing. With this trim vessel, Madison said, I could manage with less than a thousand yards. But where was the wind?

The time to swing out beyond the plateau was now, right now. The plane made the turn in graceful ease—and dropped, hideously.

I think I yelled it was just an air pocket. But when I lurched out of it we were bound straight for the sullen wall of the plateau. In panic I somehow slammed the power on in time, and ran scared up a channel of hell like a dragonfly on fire. We cleared the cliff by a yard and shot a thousand feet up before I had the wits to level off and cut the jets. Paul was howling: "God Almighty, you almost—"

Miranda's voice came small and cold: "Have a tranquillizer, Paul, it's on the house. Have you noticed, by the way, we're all right?"

I began talking myself, though, when I realized I'd forgotten to lower the landing gear. The talk did me good. I got the gear down. I soared out further beyond the plateau, came in higher, ready for the air pocket, hitting it again and coming out happy, skittering over half a mile of reddish white and touching down in a landing soft as a baby's kiss. Miranda said: "Davy, when you get around to it, explain me some of those nouns and adjectives, huh? I thought I knew em all."

We equalized the pressure, a difference too small to bother the eardrums, and breathed the unknown atmosphere—nothing to gain by delaying. It was wild, warm, the freshness wholly sweet. I could have sat there half an hour doing nothing but breathe the air of Demeter—and wondering whether in a few weeks we would be voting on that name, a poetic whim of Andrea del Sentiero.

The stuff outside was mostly sand, sparse red grains mingled with the white. Miranda whispered: "Be first to set your foot on it." It seemed unimportant, a thing I might do to please her—until I had done it. Then absurd pride startled me, and I held up my arms for her.

Laurette and Paul emerged, Laurette moving away from us, looking toward the mountains in the west—praying I think, or merely wanting a small time of solitude. She had talked with the chaplain during most of our last hour on *Galileo*. Miranda and I had spent that time with the half dozen friends who had been closest to us through the voyage—not saying goodbye; they all wanted to take it for granted they would rejoin us in four weeks. Paul Cutter had employed the hour furiously writing in a corner of the common room—some intense document which he delivered into Madison's keeping. "Not to be opened," he blared for all of us to hear, "except in the event that *Galileo* must proceed without us." Captain Madison took it gravely, probably with no smothered impulse to laugh, and shook hands with the hero.

Impossible that I could ever have looked down on those mountain peaks. Yet I had done so. I would remember it.

Miranda kicked off her right shoe, pressed her bare foot in the reddish sand, drew it away, gazed curiously at the dainty human imprint. I asked: "Are you caring now?"

She held my shoulder, putting back the shoe; watched me a while with midnight eyes; said: "I think I am . . . Let's walk off a way."

We approached the somber edge of the woods. "You'd know it," I said, "wouldn't you, dear? You wouldn't just think."

"Maybe." She was frowning gravely at the sand, not wanting to touch me or be touched. "You've felt it yourself, Davy, that emptiness. Impulse to give up because nothing can make much difference."

"Sometimes. I found I could push it away by studying something new—holing up in the library—talking to del Sentiero."

"I couldn't. Not the last year anyway. It was partly the ship, the monotony. Suspended animation." She looked about rather blindly into the depth of morning. "We're—home, aren't we?"

"Yes."

"It wasn't only the ship. I kept thinking, even if we can have a baby, there'll be—ah, what do the damn Directives call it?—70 per cent chance of normal birth. I remember hearing my father say that even the 70 per cent was a sort of statistician's lie. The dice are loaded, Davy. . . . I loved Earth. You did too. I know. Inside me somewhere I've got every word you ever said about Martha's Vineyard. . . . Davy, it's just barely possible I'm pregnant. I can't be sure, hasn't been time, quite." She wanted nearness then, twisting her fingers in my shirt, clinging, suddenly crying. "Let it be true, Davy! Let it be right, not a—not a 30-per-center. I'd care—I'd care *then!*"

It meant nothing to Paul Cutter that she was crying in my arms. I felt his tap on my shoulder, his brazen voice exploding: "Who is leader?"

Miranda laughed; looked past me at the little man and laughed, with brimming eyes—which puzzled the hell out of him. Simply Paul's way. He was incapable of understanding other people's urgencies.

I straightened my face, suggesting that for the moment we hardly needed leadership: we all knew what work was to be done, maybe we'd already done the biggest part by breathing the air and continuing to live. I looked at my watch. "*Galileo* will be calling in fifteen minutes. Until then why don't we just look around? Only we'd better break out some armament, I suppose."

I should have thought of that sooner, too. The bland quiet here made the idea of guns downright obscene. Nothing was stirring. Two bird-like things soared high overhead, maybe curious at the alien brightness of our plane. The lack of vegetation at this landing spot puzzled me. In places the ground was clay instead of sand; small stones resembling the granites and composites of Earth lay here and there. Nothing suggested animal life. In a spot higher than the rest of the open land, I noticed a boulder thrusting from the ground and a wraith of vapor rising from it to dissolve in the still air. A geyser, perhaps, that periodically flooded the area, killing plant life. The trees, and the rim of very dark grass between them and the open ground, looked rich and healthy.

The trees were in the pattern of Earth, but I saw no such complex of a thousand species as in forests of the old world. One type was completely dominant, a broadleaf tree averaging fifty feet in height, thick-trunked, spreading only at the top, the young leaves and twigs red as maple buds, the mature leaves a hemlock green with wide red veining. The grass was like Earth's except for its darkness, shading almost to a cobalt blue; it grew hardly a foot high, dense as carpet-pile. We had seen that color solid in most of the open areas of the plateau, and it was the characteristic hue of the savannahs elsewhere on the planet.

We opened a storage compartment of the plane. Paul and I slung light carbines; Miranda strapped on a .32 automatic. The bullets for all three were designed to fragment on impact, releasing an anesthetic poison that would stop anything if the wound failed to—anything with an Earth-type bloodstream. Laurette Vieuxtemps when I called her, smiled and shook her head.

"Will you stand by the radio then, Laurette, till they call in?"

"Yes." She was good with instruments, deft and careful; delicate tests on soil and plants would be part of her work. She returned to the plane, after a last glance at the hills, their red-green mystery, cloud-trailing spires brilliant with snow.

I said: "I don't like carrying this thing either, Laurette. But just at first I don't want any of us wandering out here unarmed."

Laurette nodded amiably. And Paul Cutter said with some clang of bitterness: "Well, Dave, you've answered my question."

"I'm not leader unless you all three agree to it."

I think I spoke with friendliness. I meant to; we had need of it. His face, turned toward me in the mild heat of the sun of Demeter, had gone opaque. Miranda's arm slid around me; she studied the ground, perhaps waiting. Paul said politely, with none of his normal stridency: "Four weeks, they said. I agree you should be leader, for four weeks."

3

At the close of the second day we imagined we knew a little about that plateau. I had hedge-hopped over it twice, beginning to enjoy the plane, except for the always rugged instant of landing.

I flew alone both times—no sense risking two lives with an inexperienced pilot. In the first one I proved that the only part of the plateau safe for the larger landing ships of *Galileo* was the one I had first chosen. Then I indulged myself in a 30-mile flight to the sea above the course of a small river that skirted the northern base of the plateau and wound down through the piedmont past rolling land, meadow and forest, meeting the ocean at a harbor a mile wide. Madison wanted to know more about that harbor.

A small hilly island stood twenty miles out to sea from it, hazy and purple in the sun. It pulled me, called me. I was thinking, I know, of Martha's Vineyard. I thought also of fuel, danger, the need of my people for this plane and for me too; and I did not go.

On my flight to the harbor I noticed a few tawny deerlike animals bounding into the woods away from the shadow of the plane, and some flying creatures, none very close. On the way back something different showed itself, night-black, lizard-shaped, basking in a sunny meadow. I circled down for a better look. Hugely unconcerned, it did not retreat when I skimmed over it sixty feet up. Not dead, for I saw the great triangle of the head moving, and a twitch of a saurian tail. I shot up then; the sudden clamor of the jets did not disturb it. I guessed the length at twenty-five feet.

We slept in the plane on the first night. My second flight, next day, was for study of a smaller open area two miles from our landing site, that looked reasonable for a camp. It was a clearing of level dark grass half a mile square with a brook slipping across the northern side, widening to a pond near the edge of the woods. I landed and explored.

The pond-water shone deep ruby, reflecting red-leaved bushes. I found the banks pockmarked with prints of small divided hoofs, and noticed one set of tracks with pads and claw-marks, not frighteningly large. Mammals or something like them lived in this land, knew fear, ate each other, bred, died. I remembered my black lizard, his vastness curved rather like a question-mark.

The forms would be new to me. The forms themselves would change, must already have done so through millions of years in the manner of Earth. So far as I knew, so far as I know today, the meaning, if there was one, would be the same.

I was bothered by the absence of anything like humanly edible plants. Maybe the forest would take care of that. Here I found only the short grass and a few of the red-leaved bushes that grew by the pond. I brought a shovel from the plane and drove it into the sod. The loosened earth displayed brown worms, legless grubs, nothing like ants or beetles. In any such region on Earth I would have encountered a hundred forms of insect life. Grasshoppers would have shot up around my feet; bees and flies would have buzzed near me; beetles would have scampered away from the shovel. The grassblades should have been scarred by the nibbling of tiny mouths; butterflies ought to have been drifting and fluttering in innocent splendor.

No bugs. I supposed I could do without them . . .

The earth under the grass was dark, rich-looking, with a pleasing aromatic smell. We must learn what it could do. I collected a sample of pond water for testing and returned to the others. That was near noon of the second day.

By evening we had moved to that clearing and set up our camp around a light dome shelter—astonishingly large, strong against storms, capable of lasting indefinitely under any conditions the Builders could imagine for a planet that was bound to be much like their own.

We set out a wire-covered pen for a pair of rabbits, potential food. Those, and a few mice and rats for experiment, were the only animals that shared the pilot mission. From *Galileo* would come sheep, chickens, a few precious cattle of a recently developed breed hardly bigger than goats. Other animals would arrive (if anything arrived to join us) in the form of frozen ova and sperm that our skill might or might not be able to bring to maturity—still a rudimentary art when we left Earth.

These outside bunnies were pilot bunnies. Our three other pairs must get along on *Galileo* rations until we were sure the first pair was thriving. Laurette set up her miniature laboratory for soil and water tests. Paul Cutter dug magnificently until the light began to fail. I felt now a kind of permanency and sense of achievement, and Miranda felt it too, working like a little dynamo at whatever came to hand.

Toward sundown I roved the whole clearing again, with the carbine, not wanting it until I noticed the sun of Demeter slipping beyond the mountains, then pleased enough to be carrying that slim bit of functional wickedness. Once or twice I heard small life scuttering away in the grass, but if Demeter was blessed with field mice I didn't see them. We had set our camp not too near the pond; we wanted the wild things to continue using it if they would. As I approached it now, I thought I glimpsed some of those "deer" slipping into the shadows. Later we must shoot a few, for science if not for food. I felt no fear, only pleasure and curiosity, when a night flier, like a bat or bird, hurried over me and flickered into evening light above the trees. . . .

And before dawn on the third day, Miranda was ill.

She woke me before sunrise, during Paul's tour of guard duty. I could barely see her face. She was speaking soberly, carefully, as if describing someone else's trouble—pain in the right leg, in the right foot a numbness that had started as an itching, and now the beginning of fever, headache, nausea.

Under the light of my lantern, the sole of her right foot looked inflamed, but at that time I found no break in the skin; the leg was reddened up to the knee. She said she was afraid of blacking out, and her voice was blurring—but it was Miranda who had the wits to remember how she had made that barefoot imprint on the sand of our landing place.

By mid-morning, near the time of our next radio contact with *Galileo*, she was unconscious. No signs of pain or delirium. She was unreachable, breathing too rapidly in a fevered sleep.

We had given her MH-12, for lack of anything better, and because it's the most generally useful and safe of the antibiotics developed on Earth. Then Laurette had searched the medical information in our "library"—*Galileo's* great microfilm library cut to the essentials. We could expect no precise help there, since the diseases of Earth would not be paralleled closely enough for proper guidance, but what Laurette found concerning Earth's tropical fevers did give me the idea of searching Miranda's foot with a hand-lens. I discovered a puncture so small that without the lens I had missed it completely. It seemed to be a true eschar with a definite center. It could have been made by an infinitesimal wood or mineral sliver, admitting some poison latent in the ground, or it could have been the bite of an organism hidden under the sand or too tiny to see. For what it was worth, and so far as I could endure it, I might then consider the scrub typhus that was endemic in some regions of Earth's tropics, a rickettsial disease carried by a mite no bigger than a grain of pepper.

I remembered my black lizard in the meadow. I would take him on any time in preference to this. No man is born with any skill at fighting shadows. You have to learn it, and always the hard way.

I could not look at the implications. I could only stand by and wait for Miranda to come back to me; to bring back, if it might be so, the meaning and the purpose I knew I was losing. It was not a case of thinking how I loved her: that was deep-down, bloodstream knowledge requiring no thought, and to think of it then would have made me even more useless in trying to help her.

I was with her—needing to fight, and no antagonist; needing to talk with her, and she could not know it—when I heard the noise of Paul Cutter, subdued because it came from within the plane. Laurette had just rejoined me by Miranda's cot in the shelter; Paul would be talking to *Galileo*, and a black uneasiness vaguely tele-pathic nudged me to rise. "Stay with her, Laurette," I said, and hurried for the plane.

I saw him at the radio, the prominent, somehow pathetic cords at the back of his neck, his heavy head wobbling a little, his voice attempting a casualness denied by that tremor and by that sweating hands. He was saying: "Yes, the rabbits go for the grass and they're thriving. What? . . . Oh sure, everyone's fine. We—"

He jumped a foot when my fingers dug at his shoulder. I nodded at the transmitter, and he croaked: "Here's Leroy—wants to talk to you." He lurched away, but an animal warning of danger reached me—perhaps he made some half-completed motion. I drew the automatic I was carrying and held it aimed at his heart while I talked to the Captain.

Paul slumped to his haunches and dropped his face on his knees. I told Madison as quickly as I could about Miranda, and he said: "I'll switch you to Dr. Dana, he's right here—then I want to talk to you again, Dave."

Dr. Dana helped me—just the voice and the manner. I could imagine I was in touch with the three thousand years of his tradition; out of space, that was Hippocrates talking. He questioned me, approving what we had done, suggesting other supportive measures. He admitted no other important measures were possible, since we knew nothing of the disease, hence nothing of the prognosis. He agreed it might be similar in some ways to Earth's tropical fevers, though when I mentioned scrub typhus he roared at me to forget that. But then he mentioned methods of searching the dead sand area for a guilty organism if there was one, and warned against letting Demeter's earth come in contact with our skins; so he would be reviewing his knowledge of the rickettsial diseases, and the snarling statistics of mortality. Well, Paul and I in our digging had both shoved our hands in the dirt several times. It flickered through my mind that Paul himself might be ill. He was sick enough, avoiding the cold eye of the .32, but not with fever.

Madison was back. "Dave, why did Paul say everyone was fine?"

"Oh—didn't realize the seriousness. It's all new this morning, Captain. Laurette and I have been caring for her, while Paul was getting on with the work."

I suppose Madison knew I was lying, and knew Paul Cutter had to be my problem. Paul flashed me a sick and haunted thank-you-for-nothing glare. I gave Madison the rest of the report—water pure, test animals in good shape, no time yet for much aerial reconnaissance outside the plateau. At the close Madison said: "Dave, if you possibly can, be on hand yourself when we're due to call in."

"I'll do that, Captain."

"Soon as Miranda wakes up, give her my love. See you, Davy."

I closed the transmitter; studied the man suffering beyond the gunsights, and holstered the automatic. "Why, Paul?"

He was on his feet and swaying. "Why don't you shoot?"

"No cause, now. You were ready to jump me till I made the report. That was in your face . . . Why?"

"I'm ashamed," he said. "Is that enough?"

"Look: you knew I'd be reporting next time, if not now."

The tremor of his head ceased, his mouth steadied to tightness. A man of twenty-five, he looked forty. "Maybe I thought by that time you'd—understand."

"Or maybe you only saw them leaving, abandoning us, and didn't think."

"Have it your way."

"Paul, while there's any chance at all, they'll never abandon us."

"You're wrong there." He knotted his hands, white-knuckled. "They'll go. Dr. Carey will influence them. Dr. God-Almighty Carey will see to that if no one else does." I scolded myself for failing to recognize the paranoid pattern sooner; or maybe I was wrong now, and seeing spooks. I made a note that I must talk to Carey at the next contact. "Dave—I've said, I'm ashamed. I was afraid and foolish, and I admit it. Isn't that enough?"

"I suppose it is." It was true—he was sick with shame, and other inward disasters; but did shame fit the pattern? I thought, the hell with patterns—the poor devil was human; leave it at that. Of course he was also profoundly hating me. Because I had seen him in an act of dishonesty and betrayal, he would always hate me. I said: "Let's get on with the work."

He stumbled out of the cabin and resumed digging away sod for our test plot in open ground. Attacking it rather—driving the bright blade into the green face of an enemy.

Late in the morning of our fourth day on Demeter, Miranda recovered consciousness. Her fever had risen to a peak of 106° during an interminable night, when the green-white moon of Demeter was to me no longer enchanting, only sickly and baleful. Then, about dawn, the fever rapidly subsided. Miranda came back to me. I could forget about scrub typhus. I could sweep away all the horrors, because I saw memory and understanding and awareness of my kiss.

"How long, Davy? What's the time?"

"You've been out for one day of twenty-six hours. The computer upstairs has dreamed up a calendar for us—got it yesterday. This is Friday morning—sorry fresh out of fish."

"They know of course?"

"Yes, and since you're recovering it won't make any difference."

"So what's the man crying about?"

"Stardust up my nose—itches. How about your foot—does that itch now?"

"Little bit. No numbness. Feels about all right." Under the lens, the puncture spot looked healed, like any tiny injury.

"You got a bite. I'm going after the beast soon as you're up and around— earth samples, and so on. We'll run down the little devil." She couldn't smile much, but she was trying. "He won't stop anything."

"That's right, Bud—we'll rise above bugs and stuff." She was trying, but then her eyes dilated, she winced and turned her face away from me. "Ask Laurette to come, will you please?"

"Yes—what is it?"

"Oh, damn everything!"

"What is it, Miranda?"

"Don't you know?" I suppose I did. "My baby—it was going to be my—my— Demeter's killed my baby."

4

Saturday morning Miranda was able to sit up without help, and eat. She said she felt nothing wrong except exhaustion. She blamed that on the gravity of Demeter, but I think it was the after-effect of fever; we other three had adjusted to the gravity with almost no effort. Then after a decent meal, an hour of her old love Sibelius on the tapes, and another hour of just sitting with me in the temperate sunlight, Miranda let me talk to her, and suggest that she had not been pregnant at all. Rejecting the idea at first in despair, she presently came around to accepting it, and I felt she was at least half convinced that Demeter had nothing to do with our disappointment. Just before she fell asleep beside me in the sunshine, she murmured: "False-alarm Miranda. From here on out I'm going to try to behave like a rational mammal. But it's uphill work—you know? . . ."

Sunday morning Miranda climbed into the cabin of the plane, wanting to do it without the help of my arm, and talked to Captain Madison and Dr. Dana, rejoining me with a new quiet resembling cheerfulness.

Paul Cutter was speaking to me only when necessary, and with an intense politeness that affected me like a split fingernail. He made a point of asking, in private, for "official" permission to carry his carbine. There was no danger in him for the present. My leadership had become an immediate fact; I knew Paul felt terror at the thought of having to assume responsibility if anything happened to me. Actually he wouldn't have had to: Laurette would have stood aloof while Miranda assumed it, and Caliban-as-hero would have minded the chores.

When Miranda promised to loaf and rest, I took off that Sunday morning to blaze a trail alone through the woods to the dead-sand area. Miranda's recovery and her new calm had brought the kind of joy where recklessness bubbles near the surface. It had brought me too a burgeoning love for this one planet among all the stars. In such a mood the foot can slip—mine didn't. I went slowly, mindful of my blazes on the wood of these ancient trees.

The forest was all one hush, cool under the thickness of the canopy. I walked on a carpet formed from the rotted wood and leaves of centuries. Almost no undergrowth. At one place, a tree had fallen from old age; here a hundred saplings of the same species had already shot up high at the touch of the sun. Therefore they grew from seed; therefore the trees ought to bear *some* kind of fruit in their season, whenever that was.

Rarely and far apart, I noticed trees with holes high off the ground—natural holes left by the fall of dead branches and rotting of the sapwood. They were occupied. The corner of my eye caught a squirrely character popping into one of them, and I was aware of the scrutiny of harmless eyes.

After the first mile my ears told me of something larger following. I tried quick turns but learned nothing—once, maybe, a hint of motion retiring behind the reddish column of a tree-trunk. Anyhow not a twenty-five-foot lizard.

I was humming for a while—Schubert's *Die Forelle* I think it was, or some other memory of Earth equally light and happy.

Observing Dr. Dana's instructions, I was covered except for my face, and I took care not to let that be brushed by branches, though I was fairly sure the enemy I hunted lived under the sand. Close-fitting leggings, shirt tucked in, gloves. I carried a shovel, carbine, hand-ax, a sack with several small bags that could be tightly sealed, and a cage with four white mice.

Not much of a load. I supposed I could drop everything but the carbine, fast, but though I caught a few more dim sounds, nothing bothered me. If whatever followed me possessed anything like my kind of wits, it would know I was aware of its presence.

I came out on the dead sand near that vapor column idly rising from the fissured rock. The vapor gave off a slight sulfur smell. It drifted up with no pulsation, no force. Some age-old dirty business in the gut of Demeter, a planet that never asked for us. Yet I loved her.

Apologetically I set the wire-bottom cage of mice out on a patch of sand, with a cloth to shade them from the sun. Poor little rascals, as martyrs to science they even had their bellies shaved, to make it easier for our enemy to bite them—if it would, if there was such an enemy. I filled the small bags with samples of the sand, the clay patches, the good-seeming earth near the woods, the sod, the forest mold itself. One bag still empty, I searched for Miranda's barefoot print. It had been blurred by a breeze that must have stirred the sand at the edges without obliterating it. No rain had fallen since we landed. Nothing had made tracks out on this desolate ground. The ruts of our plane, our shoe-prints, patches where the jets had blasted sand hollows in take-off—all still plain to read.

For reasons of sentiment or superstition I took my final sample from a spot as near Miranda's footprint as I could set the shovel without destroying the mark— bad science, no excuse offered.

Nothing had followed me out here. If anything watched from the edge of the woods I caught no sense of it.

I had been away from the unfortunate mice for twenty minutes. As I removed the cloth they looked fair enough, but when I raised the cage a midget drop of blood splashed on the sand. I held the cage above the level of my eyes. Two of the mice flitted about in natural nervousness. The others were sluggish, and on the shaved belly of one of them I saw another blood-drop form and fall. No sign of normal coagulation.

I spread the cloth, drove in the shovel where the cage had rested, and spilled out the sand with care. That's where I found the thing, a worm two inches long gorged with blood. With a gloved fingertip I stirred the sand and found another, not distended, thin as a fine hair and barely visible, the same pinkish-white color as the sand. Exposed, the things moved feebly, obscene head ends lifting and blindly searching, mouth parts apparent as specks of black.

I drew the cloth into the form of a bag, tied it tightly for my collection and started home.

On the way back through the woods I tried to puzzle it out. If nothing ventured on that sand, where did the worms find their natural food supply? Subterranean maybe—burrowing animals, grubs, other worms. I could leave all that to Dr. Bunuan, but it teased my curiosity, reminding me how mystery is always with us. I could not live long enough to see our colony (if there was to be a colony) become more than a trifling spot of intrusion on a most ancient planet. If we had grandchildren to the seventh generation, this world would remain imperfectly explored— and yet some of them would certainly hunger for space flight.

We never really learned much about the beautiful planet Earth.

Twice I stopped to search the forest mold for more of the hair-worms. I found none, but did find more of the stocky brown worms than in the sod of our clearing. They were active, burrowing, wriggling, hunting. I saw one attack a grub. Grasping organs shot out from either side of the worm's head and squeezed the grub helpless while the mouth consumed it. Maybe these brown fellows ate the poison hair-worms.

I glanced up from the vanishing grub, and saw what was lying flat along a branch that overhung my trail.

That clawed track by the pond had deceived me about the size of its maker.

The paws were disproportionately large, the animal itself lean as an ocelot, not much bigger. The claws, hooked for efficient climbing and piercing, were relatively immense, partly retractile, though less so than a cat's. The creature was hairless, with a reddish-brown skin obscure against the color of the branch. I saw a narrow-nosed head, like a fox's except that the external ears were mere flaps of skin close to the skull. It had the wonderful deep eyes of a beast that must be mainly nocturnal.

I could bypass that part of the trail and circle around. I said aloud: "Would that sit all right with you, Jackson?"

Jackson winced at the sound of my voice—he shouldn't have, after hearing my no-account baritone murder *Die Forelle*—and flattened himself, or herself, close to the branch. I took up the carbine, seeing the narrow head begin a measuring motion from side to side. The hind-quarters quivered, the motion of the head ceased in a frozen readiness. Not happy about that, I said: "Look, I'm not a deer. I'm not even a darling."

After all, I suppose Jackson could hardly have forgiven that. He was fifteen feet above the ground, six yards from the muzzle of the carbine. He could jump it with no strain and evidently had it in mind. The mouth opened and closed on interesting daggers of orange teeth. My sights steadied on the thin neck. I said: "Sorry, Jackson!" and fired.

Beginner's luck. Jackson shuddered, dropped and lay twitching, orange-red blood gushing from the shattered neck. I turned the body over with my foot. Not ugly nor beautiful, just strange. The sex organs puzzled me—female I thought, but peculiar. I tied the body to my sack, finding it curiously light. We learned later that the bones are partly hollow, and most of the viscera lighter than the corresponding tissues of Earth animals.

Dissection and observation in the next few days also demonstrated that Jackson, the timid and stupid creatures resembling deer, and the mouse-like animals nesting in the grass, are mammals, in the sense that they bear their young alive and nurse them. And they are functional hermaphrodites. Demeter hasn't arranged for boy to meet girl. Well, we're here to fix that.

The brains, even to my uneducated eye, look primitively smooth.

Maybe we can fix that too . . .

We found poison hair-worms in all the samples of sand and clay from the open ground, none at all in the sod or forest mold. The two lively mice from my cage remained lively—not bitten, apparently. Of the other two, one went into stupor the following day, and died. The one that had been bleeding did not die. Its wound clotted normally soon after my return to camp, and after a period of sluggishness the mouse recovered with no observable after-effects.

We repeated the experiment with other mice—couldn't spare many—and hair-worms from my samples. The results were the same. Under Laurette's guidance Miranda gladly introduced a brown worm to a hair-worm, with delightful results. In sixty seconds, no hair-worm, the brown guy acting as contented as I do after a mince pie.

Conclusion, given me over the radio by Dr. Bunuan: "You've got a lovely little thing there, boy. Apparently the poison is, or is associated with, an anti-coagulant that probably helps the worm to feed. If the bite is interrupted, likely the poison stays in the wound, enters the bloodstream, generates some kind of systemic toxin. But if your trichinoid critter finishes the drink, I suggest he sucks back most of the poison with the blood and everybody's happy. And let me say, Davy, you people have put through a handsome little preliminary study." O my Miranda, burning that night with a fever of 106° and far away! But there was a sweet healthiness in the biologist's way of speaking; he had not forgotten the pain and terror any more than I had. I reserve judgment on physicists, but I'll drink beer with a biologist any day of the week—if we can make beer on Demeter. "Very handsome, Davy. I wish I was there."

I transmitted his remarks to Paul Cutter. Paul was alone in the clearing outside the shelter, with nothing much to do. We had dug as large a test plot as we needed, the seeds from Earth had been planted—in fact it was almost time for the radishes, rye-grass and other quick-sprouting plants to show themselves if they were going to. I passed on Dr. Bunuan's comment mostly for something pleasant to say. Paul had shown a polite interest in our study of the worms, saying that he had no talent himself for technician's work.

Paul faced me gravely, listened with bent head to my recital of Dr. Bunuan's words, nodded amiably, and replied: "The fundamental error is in the very first clause—as I tried so many times to make plain. If the colony is to be defined as a *republic*, in that opening clause, you bypass and throw away the entire experience of the 19th and 20th Centuries of Earth history, which is absurd. May I remind you that at the time of the founding of the United States of America, the word 'democracy' was a *bad* word, a term of *opprobrium*?" He smacked his fist into his palm; the tawny grazers could have heard his voice and quivered to the vibration half a mile away in the woods. "Now manifestly I am no Marxian. The Russian experiment, for all its important achievements, was ethically and politically a dead end. And why? Because dictatorship supervened. Because in Russia the essence of social democracy was never in effect, once more the cause of the common man was *lost*. Now in the very first amendment I proposed, or I should say *tried* to propose—"

I heard him out . . .

5

Rain fell heavily all through our sixteenth day on Demeter; warm rain without a wind; we huddled miserably in the shelter. Laurette put in the time mending some of our clothes. Paul read, glued to the scanner—politics I guess, or psychology. Miranda played chess with me, and listened to Sibelius.

Our seeds from Earth had rotted. The day before we had dug up a few—squash, corn, garden pea, bean seeds, all sodden pulp without life. But here and there a wheat kernel showed a feeble sprout. Even the busy grubs in Demeter's earth had not wanted them.

Of course, one can get along on a carnivorous diet. If our rabbits could flourish on Demeter's grass, probably the sheep and cattle from *Galileo* could do the same. I had shot two of the deer-like animals. We tried the meat on the white rats and then ate of it without harm—muttony and rank, but not impossible.

The rain stopped after sunrise of the seventeenth day. I took off for a wider reconnaissance. Captain Madison had suggested this after learning of the failure of our seeds. Somewhere in the meadows or hills there ought to be edible plants worth a try. Captain Madison had also made it plain that nothing so far reported had discouraged him; his intention was to bring the whole colony down at the end of our four weeks. "Keep in your calculations, Davy, that we'll bring machines and three hundred pairs of hands."

It didn't sound like talk for my morale. And I wondered, I think for the first time, what the mere fact of the pilot mission might be doing to those who remained on the ship. . . .

I left the plateau behind me and flew north, a broadening morning on my right hand. The world glittered from the rain, the forest a field of diamonds. At five thousand feet, I saw that island twenty miles out from the river mouth shining like dawn made tangible.

Del Sentiero's suggestion of an island for the colony had been overruled; but shouldn't I at least go and look? Wasn't I playing it by the seat of my pants, accepted leader of the pilot mission?

Accepted anyway by Miranda and partly by Laurette Vieuxtemps. Paul Cutter was still at his brittle play-acting, ludicrously deferring to me, contriving each time to drop a hint that my "glory" would end. He seemed unworried about a bloody nose—may have craved one.

With Laurette, the question of leadership hardly arose, for she was sensible, hard-working; given another year on *Galileo* she would have earned a title. There hadn't been more than two or three occasions when it was up to me to tell her what to do, and those unimportant. She was inevitably remote from us in her religious faith, which answered a need in her mind not present in my own. Unlike our kind, perpetually worried chaplain, Laurette paid Miranda and me the rare courtesy of not trying to change our agnosticism. She may have been privately sorry for us, but we were spared hearing about it. We were friends; we got along in the limited area of mental contact.

Again I did not go to look at my island. Perhaps I was afraid that its summoning beauty was an effect of haze, distance, memory and irrelevant dreams . . . Some of the time as I flew north I was reliving a moment of the day before, when Miranda grinned at me across the shambles of the chessboard and said: "The things that happen when your knights break loose are pitiful, that's all. I find myself caring deeply about that butchered pawn, Captain Leroy." Caring—she wasn't talking about chess. She proved that in the night, when the rain tapped on the roof of our shelter, and she was whispering we'd try again, maybe our child would be the first to be conceived on the planet Demeter. . . .

The seaward slopes of the foothills had changed color after the rain. From an even, reddish green they had become a riot of tomato-scarlet splashes. I supposed—and I was wrong—that the downpour must have brought some plant into sudden blossoming.

I skimmed past the hills searching for a level place to land. Not so easy; the terrain was nearly all sloping, vegetation thick. The radio was with me: I had thought it safer to leave it installed in the plane, on the chance we might have to take off from the plateau in a hurry. Now I could picture myself abandoning a wrecked plane and the only means of communicating with *Galileo*. I could observe a lost human fool groping back twenty-odd miles through unknown forest, no armament except the .32 at my hip, no assurance that I could scale the walls of the plateau if I reached it. Even snug in the perfectly functioning plane, wasn't I a very naked creature in a lonely place? But I think any planet is a lonely place.

At four hundred feet I learned it was no blooming of flowers down there. The brilliance was that of scarlet fruit, on great tangles of low-growing bushes unlike any we had found on the plateau.

Evidently, while it grows, the fruit of those bushes wears a dull powdery bloom. The samples I later secured carried traces of it. It must be that in the final ripening the bloom loosens, washed away by the rain, so that when the hills break out in a sudden gleaming it's time for harvest.

The lizards were at it.

On every hillside where the fruit was shining, a dozen or more of those monsters writhed and scampered on short saurian legs. They paid no heed to the plane, nor to the hundreds of small bird-like creatures that darted about sharing the meal. It was hot holiday for the lizards in the genial sun; their black enormous jaws munched and slobbered, dripping scarlet. Here and there about the slopes, gorged pairs were breeding. When I cut the jets for brief glides I could hear the bellowing and roaring, smashing of bushes and the monstrous slap of black primordial flesh against flesh.

Just hungry and lusty hermaphrodite vegetarians having themselves a Mesozoic ball. But not too good for a little thin-hided foreign mammal who hadn't been invited. I climbed back to a thousand feet and began to get mad. They were first comers by several million years, had a right to the red lush stuff and needed it. But so did I.

A few miles further on I located a small valley in a pocket of the hills, with enough level ground for landing. The eastern of the two slopes closing it in bore the red splashes; the lizards were present there too, but not so numerously. I noticed only five or six as I circled down. If I dared climb that slope on foot for a hundred yards, I would be at the edge of the area where the bushes grew.

It became a thing that had to be done. I don't believe I was trying to prove anything. I haven't much patience with heroes. I'm afraid many of them have been in the pattern of Paul Cutter, ridden by the devil of one idea, and legend has supplied the pleasing part of the picture after silence took them. I'm simply a Randy who loves the idea of staying alive. I just wanted some of that fruit for my people and me.

The clamor of the beasts surged up to me as soon as I shut off the jets. Only a few, they made uproar enough for a convention. I lit nicely, coming to rest in the shadow of a tall solitary tree, and knew I must start at once, or hesitation would demoralize me. I took a sack for the fruit, and my .32, which might at least make me look like a hero later if one of the boys happened to step on me.

I was counting on the dullness of a primitive brain in a saurian hulk, too dim even for curiosity about the plane. I forgot that while the lizards were enjoying rich food and love, something else might be planning to enjoy the lizards. And, yes, there was a slight error of a few million years, for which I had no excuse after shooting mammals on the plateau. If Demeter's evolution has paralleled Earth's as closely as I think, those "lizards" are a survival from long ago. I was mistaking pseudo-Cenozoic for quasi-Mesozoic—Dr. Bunuan wouldn't have liked that.

At the base of that eastern slope the grass admitted some vegetation different from any I had so far seen. Many individual plants—call them weeds—were bushy, some taller than my head. This tall growth thickened as I climbed. For several yards I glimpsed no more of the revels up yonder, only heard the sodden gurgling and the roaring.

In the thicket I won a good look at one of the small flying animals clinging to a tall weed. It let me blunder within ten feet and then sailed off swift and airy. Not a bird; furry, with small teeth; the size of a big robin. The triangular wings are anchored, not to the hind foot like a bat's, but to the animal's side just below a rather large rib-cage. The free hind legs pull up in flight and vanish in the belly-fur. It seemed to me that two of the modified phalanges were projecting beyond the upper angle of the wing, but I couldn't be sure. Maybe they hang themselves up to sleep, like bats.

At the upper limit of the thicket I halted to watch through the leaves. The nearest of the red-fruited bushes were still at some distance. I would have to step out in the open—not nice, but better than scuttling back from the riot empty-handed and licked. I told myself those jolly black nightmares were not aggressive. Their enormous grappling—just sex, Demeter style. I'd heard of sex.

The lizards' vision might be dim; maybe that was why they had ignored the plane. Really there was nothing terrible about them except their size. They wouldn't smell me—a light breeze blew toward me down the slope, bringing me their musky reek.

I crawfished into the sunlight holding open the mouth of my sack, and snatched at the red pear-shaped fruit, a little thieving mammal making off with whatever wasn't nailed down. The fruit, big and firm, separated readily from the stems, warm with sunshine, aromatic like muskmelon, smooth and delightful in the hand.

The lizards paid no attention, though the bushes where I was pilfering their steak and potatoes stood hardly twenty yards from the spot where the nearest one of them lurched about alone. And when the other beast crashed out of deep bushes up there on my left, the only lizard that acted aware of the attack was that nearest one—when he was knocked flat by the rushing impact, stricken in the belly by orange fangs.

Earth-born, I thought of it as a bear—shaggy block of body, massive head, thick long-clawed legs. The color was dull cinnamon. It was more than half the length of the lizard it assaulted, and taller—I suppose about the size of the brown Kodiak bear of Alaska. Now, being still alive, I peacefully remember, from boyhood reading, someone's statement that if a Kodiak bear stood upright inside an ordinary house his head would poke well into the second story—so it wouldn't do you much good to hightail into the bathroom and slam the door.

That killer was majestically casual, rearing over the lizard, driving down both forepaws as a bear might grab a log, twitching the black monster over on its back with impudent ease and tearing open the pale belly with a swipe of orange tusks. Then I think it sheared the muscles of the hind legs, the stabbing bites too swift for my eyes to follow. The lizard's legs quit threshing; they twitched without effect or purpose. I saw no teeth in the howling cavern of the lizard's mouth. And while the bear began to feed on the slow-dying thing, the other lizards up the slope continued gorging and mating.

I'm not sure a small mammal from Earth's 21st Century should have witnessed that kind of death. No more significant than other kinds, but at this moment of writing I tend to remember it too much: the gaudy mess of it, the other lizards' unconcern, the mindless cruelty that was not cruelty at all but only single-minded hunger. For a second or two there in the sun I myself was lizard and bear, killer and killed, knowing down in the gut how it was for both of them.

After all, in the home cave of one of my great-grandfathers, Homo Pekinensis, there was a rather messy assortment of human bones, well gnawed; difficult to hush up that kind of family history.

I backed slowly into the thicket, once more Homo Quasi-sapiens. I had my peewee .32 out; my left hand clung to the sack with its couple of dozen lumps of scarlet treasure. Some noise I made must have caused the bear's head to swing. It saw me and stood quiet, measuring me with little wicked orange-veined eyes. A chunk of the lizard's liver hung dripping from its under jaw.

No use trying to freeze; it knew I was alive and interesting. It turned unhurriedly to study me. The piece of liver, bigger than my head, dropped to the ground. Not losing sight of me, the bear snuffed it, swallowed it in a gulp, and walked toward me, head swaying from side to side. Under stress one still observes: for the record, the pair of upper teeth that would be called canine in an Earth animal are about ten inches long, and slant outward; I believe the ends thrusting down beyond the under jaw have a slicing edge on the inner side.

I fired twice, trying for the eyes. Then I was in the thicket, reeling to one side as the crazed roaring mass plunged for the spot where I had been, and shuddered past me down the hill. It fell, rose on its hind legs to an impossible height, fell again rolling, scrabbling pitiably at its head with both paws, as a human being might clutch at a mortal wound. It should have been dead or helpless from the anesthetic poison in those bullets. But it would not die.

I followed. My body was sick and shaking. When the beast fell the second time, I managed to control my right hand and place more shots. One of them pierced the spine, for the bear plainly could not rise. But since it could not even then die, I must suppose the poison of those bullets has no rapid effect in the bloodstream of the animals of Demeter. The deerlike things, and the ocelot-like thing, I had shot on the plateau received heart or head wounds severe enough to account for the way they toppled over without a struggle. That bear was still trying to crawl toward me, hauling with vast forelegs, when I stepped close and put him out with a bullet that shattered the skull.

My wits came back, too gradually. I knew I was hearing something besides the commotion of the lizards up the hill. I pawed at the sweat dribbling into my eyes. Well, of course—that shrill imperious buzz could only be our radio in the plane. *Galileo* calling, report overdue.

My left hand was locked in a grip on that sack or I might have lost it. I remembered it as I reached the plane and flung it in ahead of me. I croaked: "Leroy to *Galileo*, over."

"Where the *hell* were you?" Madison was shouting. "You all right?

"Yes. Recon, away from plane, sorry, ran into bit of delay."

"All right."

"Sure. I just—"

He cut in sharply: "Where are you? Where's the plane?"

"I'm about thirty miles north of the plateau. Went to look for edible plants, found 'em too I think. I—"

"Alone?"

"Yes."

"What's the fog, Davy? We can't even find the plateau."

"Fog?" I was panting, sick and stupid. "Fog, on the plateau?"

6

Madison said carefully: "There are several areas of thick fog over the region of the plateau and south of there. They were still developing when we got your territory in the sights ten minutes ago. Now they seem to have stopped spreading. I'm watching a white blur the same size and shape as the plateau. I can see five other fog areas along the foothills to the south, none up where you must be. Over."

"I'm taking off." I did, my hands thinking for me. The jets roared and I was climbing.

"I think I see you—sun on the wings. In a valley, weren't you?"

"Yes."

"You'll see the fog from six or seven thousand, then save your fuel. And don't get nerved up—it looks like ordinary fog, milky white. I don't see how it could be smoke, starting in so many different places at once . . . What about that geyser you reported? Are there others like it on the plateau?"

I had seen none; there could have been. A few of the open areas on the plateau were blank sand instead of grass. There could have been fissures with no vapor columns to reveal them. I remembered and mentioned the rain of the day before. "Could that have touched off something?"

Madison said: "Dr. Matsumoto thought of it when we saw the fog. He's sweating it out—I'm no geologist, Davy. He says it's reasonable—if a heavy seepage of water reached something hot underground, you might get a vapor cover like that. If it's just water vapor, it ought to dissipate fairly soon in this sunlight. Is there any wind?"

"Hardly any."

Now I could see it in the south, a horror of sluggishly heaving white where I had left my people at work and cheerful in a sparkling morning. And once again I glimpsed my island, far to the left, twenty miles out to sea. No fog there. A fringe of beach was peacefully gleaming; the low hills stood tranquil under the sun.

"You've reported there's never much wind."

"Only day before yesterday, wind and some overcast, the day before the rain. Inshore and offshore breezes night and morning, but at the camp we've hardly noticed them; the trees shut them away. . . . I'm at eight thousand and going down. I've got the landmarks beyond the plateau that show me where the camp is."

"You can't try to land till it clears—hell, what am I saying? You don't need to be told."

I didn't need to be told, but I wanted his voice, or failing that, my own. I reported on the morning's flight, the bushes on the hills, the shift to scarlet and the reason for it. I told him of the lizards' festival, the thing I had killed, the fruit, with me in the plane cabin.

"There'll be food," he said, "and ways of growing more. Ways of doing without most of the things we knew on Earth."

"Including war."

"Including war, I hope, though not the causes of it, which were bound to travel with us, Davy. Look, I must say again, I must make sure you understand—there's been nothing in the reports to change my mind. And this fog doesn't, no matter what the reason for it is. This is our planet and we must take it, never mind your damn dinosaurs and cave bears and hair-worms—that's all duck soup. Don't worry about it." He sounded tired, and hoarse. "Where are you now?"

"About five miles to go. It looks like—just fog."

"What matters," he said, "is our people. The ways of living we must find. New problems. What to do about the—30-per-centers. A lot of things not in the Builders' Directives, Davy."

"We make our own, don't we?"

"Of course. And the Builders knew that. All they could give us were sketches—history. You know, Davy, I'm rather ashamed, how ignorant of history I was until three or four years ago, when Andrea began to get through my engineer's crust. Well . . . With this world we must somehow do better." Then when I most needed to hear him, his voice was cut short by a cough. He spoke two or three more words, blurred as if he had turned his face away from the transmitter. I caught the meaningless hum of other voices near him.

Confusion and then silence from the control room of *Galileo*. Seething below me, a white nothing of fog.

★ ★ ★

Down in that sea of blindness, Miranda and the others—I couldn't think. I climbed high with full power and drifted down again. If they were alive they would hear the jets. Why shouldn't they be alive? It was only fog—only fog. If it meant some upheaval from underground, that would have happened before, at other rains—but animals and plants lived on the plateau. Why shouldn't my people be alive?

Meanwhile *Galileo* was slipping away to the blind side of the world. I called them a few times. Then at last: "*Galileo* to Leroy." I knew that voice.

"Receiving."

"Del Sentiero, David. The Captain was called away. One of the patches of fog south of you is clearing. Can you find anything yet?"

"Not yet. Thought I saw treetops, but can't be sure. I'm climbing again, to try it from six thousand."

"David, consider this an order, as if Captain Madison were transmitting it. When the fog clears, if you find the worst has happened and the others are lost—though there's no reason I can see to expect it—you will then do everything possible to keep your own self alive, and you will assist the rest of the colony in coming down. . . . Are you hearing me?"

"Yes. The rest of the—"

"We're coming down. Tomorrow or the day after."

"But—"

"Forget the four weeks. I can't give you details—no time, we'll soon be out of range. See anything yet?"

"Treetops—yes—it can't be anything else—yes!" I was babbling. The plane had gone dangerously low. I shot up away from the white confusion, but the spots of darkness I had seen could only be treetops.

Del Sentiero was saying: "You'll find them. Just fog. One place south of you looks almost normal. Did a minute ago, I mean. We're out of sight now." His voice was smooth but faint. I lost some other words in a crackle of static. They would be slipping to the other side, presently watching the depth of Demeter's night.

I rechecked the outer landmarks. The tallest trees near our clearing grew by the pond. I saw those tops rising from the swirl of fog and recognized them, dripping, steaming with a thinner vapor in the sun.

Then at the top of the tallest tree-motion, a flutter of white and blue. Why, on all the world of Demeter I don't suppose there's more than one such bit of color, and that one is a blouse Miranda wears. I was shouting like an idiot as I dipped the plane to let her know I had seen it. Then I swept around and rose—not high this time, no need.

Cottony white smothered the clearing still, but it was dwindling. Soon I made out the upper half of our dome shelter. I could find time now to fret about *Galileo*, and Captain Madison. He couldn't have been called away by trouble with the ship, could he? My ignorant mind pecked at the notion of an error in the orbit—then I was going down into a rolling ground-fog, knowing that the fog was no more than four or five feet thick on the landing strip. I touched down, and stepped into vapor barely waist-high, walked through it over the invisible grass.

Miranda was still waving her blouse like a flag as we ran to each other in the mist, speaking the same stumbling words and not by chance: "What am I without you?"

The damp air carried a faint reek of sulfur and something unidentifiable; not a sharp irritant, merely unpleasant. Some fog swirled to my nostrils; I breathed it with no apparent harm, as Miranda talked in a roughened, uncomfortable voice.

"The others must be all right. I breathed it, I'm alive. I think they're still in the shelter. I'd gone to the pond for drinking water when it began. I thought, just evaporation from wet ground, then it came thicker, I couldn't see my way back to the shelter. Couldn't see a foot ahead, eyes watered." I saw they were still slightly inflamed; her cute nose was reddened; but she was alive. "I called, I guess they didn't hear—it choked me some, couldn't make much noise. People can't live here, Davy, if this happens."

"No, but I've found a place where they can. Our island—wait till you see— no fog there." I couldn't talk well either.

She was rubbing her face in my shirt. "Couldn't think of anything but that tree."

"Good thinking."

"At the top, it was all around me still, but I knew you'd be coming back. I just hung on—"

I said: "How else would we ever win Demeter . . . ?"

Laurette was in the shelter, in her "room"—we used that word for the plastic-walled compartments that gave us a bit of privacy—and she was alone. I shouted for Paul and heard no answer. Laurette was red-eyed, red-nosed, from the vapor I think, and not from tears. As Miranda hurried in, Laurette looked up from the table where she sat, indifferently, almost as if puzzled by Miranda's urgency.

"Laurette, come out of this! It's clearing outside. Davy's got back." Laurette blinked; Miranda shook her. "What's the matter? Come out into the air, it's much cleaner outside."

Laurette stood up then drowsily and left the shelter with us. She gazed about the clearing, where now the fog was no more than a heaving, milky blur over the grass. She said: "We go on living a while?"

"Laurette, what's happened?"

"Why, nothing, Miranda." She was not speaking impatiently. "I understand it now, that's all. We weren't meant to come here."

"Not meant"—for once in my life I saw Miranda angry. She started once or twice to speak, then only said, with too much restraint: "Forgive me if I don't think you're that much wiser than the rest of us."

"Nothing to forgive." Laurette spoke gently, and with the note of forgiveness. "I'm not, dear, it's not *my* wisdom. You see, we've all been very stupid. The radiation sickness back on Earth—that was the judgment. We should have understood then."

Miranda's brown eyes went incandescent, then quiet. "Well," she said, "maybe you'd still better forgive me, for understanding my own little speck of life rather differently."

I noticed a table outside the shelter, part of Laurette's laboratory equipment, overturned, solutions spilled, glassware broken. No great damage except the loss of several hours of good work. I asked: "Did Paul do that? Where is he, Laurette?"

"No," she said remotely, "I did it. I'm sorry—I guess I got a bit emotional: silly of me. I know you don't look at these things the way I do. Paul—I don't know. He went off somewhere, into the fog." She shrugged, turning more matter-of-fact, more like the girl we had known. "I won't disgrace you again. I can see we're nothing but naughty children fighting against the will of God, but since we're still alive—well, that must be His will too—somehow. I won't say any more about it—you can't see it my way, you don't understand. . . . I couldn't see for sure, David, but I think Paul went—that way." She pointed toward the pond.

"You two stay together while I find him. That's an order . . ."

I found him soon, by the noise of his footsteps, a small man blundering toward me through misty tree-shadows, halting when he saw me, frowning with folded arms but letting me approach, too unhappy to be absurd. His mouth was tight, his inflamed eyes steady on me and aloof. "Leroy—did Captain Madison order you to go on that flight this morning?"

"Order me?" I was stupidly puzzled. "No. He suggested it. How do you feel?"

"As you can see, I am still alive." He tapped a foot on the ground, brooding, watching me. "He suggested it—I suppose after a conference with Dr. Matsu-moto?"

"What are you talking about?"

"I know—I'm not supposed to be able to figure things out . . . I dare say, as soon as you reported that vapor coming out of the rock, Matsumoto guessed what might happen after a rain. Then he, and Carey of course, and Madison—oh well, let it go. You're just a sort of—innocent tool, Leroy. You know that, don't you?"

In a way, I blame Paul's paranoid state at that time partly on the fog. I don't know its chemical qualities—I suppose our experts will study it when the colony comes down—but I do know one true name for the thing that rode that mist: Fear. Laurette had retreated, in her fashion. Paul had retreated, into this. Miranda—just hung on. And I was by force of circumstances a pilot. With a Randy's scattered knowledge of everything in general and nothing in particular, I groped after what I ought to do here and now. I said: "Paul, the colony is coming down tomorrow or the day after. Del Sentiero just told me so."

"Del Sentiero!" Something blazed up cleanly in him—courage or hope or common sense—and a great deal of the misery and sour suspicion drained away. I take no credit for it; I hadn't remembered that del Sentiero was one of the few he admired and, more important, trusted. "Well—that's different! Tomorrow? They're not waiting?"

"No. The ship went out of range before del Sentiero could explain it, but I got that much for sure. And I've found a place where there's no fog, an island. We're going there now, soon as we can pack up—let's get going."

"An island." He liked that too. He rubbed his face, and smiled, and delivered the greatest understatement so far made on the planet Demeter: "I suppose my judgment isn't always too good, Dave, and I've been under a—sort of strain."

"Sure," I said. "Let's move." I bumped his shoulder, and we walked peacefully back to the plane, damn near friends.

Today is the 21st of June, and the sound of ocean beyond our shelter is the music I remember from childhood.

It is not the month of June on the planet Earth. Andrea del Sentiero (whom I shall see tomorrow) suggested we might give that name to our first month here, because in the old world June was a month of beauty and beginnings, an end to the troubling dangerous time of spring.

The orbit of Demeter and the phases of the green moon give us a year of fourteen four-week months. We can name the others as we please, when June is over. Next year, if the bushes grow that quickly from the seed I took, the hills of this island will redden with the harvest of early summer. But this is the 21st of June in the Year One.

The island is quiet. I miss the morning and evening music of the birds I remember. I miss the butterflies and moths, the dragonflies. We shall gradually learn about other creatures of Demeter, and our children—if we can have them— will feel no such nostalgia.

A firm beach two miles long faces the mainland, and two promontories like the horns of a crescent create a bay there; it would be a good harbor for boats of shallow draft. I landed on the beach. The larger landing ships from *Galileo* can touch down on the water and ride in easily. East of the crescent, the island is an oval block of about thirty square miles, the only level land in small mountain valleys of the interior. I noticed lakes and streams, one large enough to be called a river. No red fruit grows on the slopes. I believe it will.

We flew low over every part of the island before landing. Miranda spotted a few "deer." No larger forms; no lizards. The bears could be living here—if they are they'll have to go the hard way. We have searched samples of the beach sand for hair-worms and found none. They may be here but didn't Captain Madison himself call that sort of thing duck soup?

We had the shelter up, under tree cover at the edge of the beach, when *Galileo* called in again. It was Andrea del Sentiero. Even that early, I could honestly give him a good report of the island, and he told me once more that the colony would come down without waiting for the four weeks. I asked for three or four days to explore and make sure and he agreed—I may have spent too much of that time in writing up this sketchy personal account. But we know the island is good. As for shortening the pilot mission—well, those people up there voted so.

In a sense, they voted against the Builders' Directives, or at least against the logic of the pilot mission, which so far as I can see is still perfectly unanswerable— as logic. Against it, our people mount the equally unanswerable logic of love. They said in effect that since we four had come down, they could do nothing but follow.

Del Sentiero said: "David, with regard to Captain Madison . . ."

The silence hurt. I said: "What?"

"I'm sorry, I was hunting for words, but there are none of the kind I need. I suggest you remember the legend of Moses. It happened very quickly, David. A coronary—he'd been getting warnings; no one else knew of it except Dr. Dana. After that coughing spell—I guess you heard it—he turned to us and said: 'Davy's going down, but the fog is clearing.' Then I think his eyes troubled him, because he stood up and tried to move nearer the viewplate. I reached him before he fell. He said: 'We'll do better—we must.'

"That was all, David—but I think he was satisfied that we would. . . . You agree?"

"Yes."

And I do. Laurette may see us as the naughty rebellious children of God. Paul may spin visions of a perfect state that can never exist except inside the sanctuary of a lonely mind. Miranda will just hang on. And I think we shall be able to deal with each other in charity, more or less, and mind our campfires.

The Longest Voyage

POUL ANDERSON

One of the best-known writers in science fiction, Poul Anderson made his first sale in 1947, while he was still in college, and in the course of his subsequent fifty-plus-year career has published almost a hundred books (in several different fields, as Anderson has written historical novels, fantasies, and mysteries, in addition to science fiction), sold hundreds of short pieces to every conceivable market, and won seven Hugo Awards, three Nebula Awards, the Grandmaster Nebula, and the Tolkien Memorial Award for life achievement.

Anderson had trained to be a scientist, taking a degree in physics from the University of Minnesota, but the writing life proved to be more seductive, and he never did get around to working in his original field of choice. Instead, the sales mounted steadily, until by the late fifties and early sixties he may have been one of the most prolific writers in the genre.

In spite of his high output of fiction, he somehow managed to maintain an amazingly high standard of literary quality as well, and by the early-to-mid sixties was also on his way to becoming one of the most honored and respected writers in the genre. At one point during this period (in addition to nonrelated work and lesser series such as the "Hoka" stories he was writing in collaboration with Gordon R. Dickson), Anderson was running three of the most popular and prestigious series in science fiction *all at the same time*: the *Technic History* series detailing the numerous exploits of the wily trader Nicholas Van Rijn (which includes novels such as *The Man Who Counts*, *The Trouble Twisters*, *Satan's World*, *Mirkheim*, and *The People of the Wind* and collections such as *Trader to the Stars* and *The Earth Book of Stormgate*); the extremely popular series relating the adventures of interstellar secret agent Dominic Flandry, probably the most successful attempt to cross science fiction with the spy thriller, next to Jack Vance's *Demon Princes* novels (the Flandry series includes novels such as *A Circus of Hells*, *The Rebel Worlds*, *The Day of Their Return*, *Flandry of Terra*, *A Knight of Ghosts and Shadows*, *A Stone in Heaven*, and *The Game of Empire* and collections such as *Agent of the Terran Empire*); and, my own personal favorite, a series that took us along on assignment with the agents of the Time Patrol (including the collections *The Guardians of Time, Time Patrolman, The Shield of Time,* and *The Time Patrol*).

When you add to this amazing collection of memorable titles the impact of the best of Anderson's nonseries novels, work such as *Brain Wave, Three Hearts and Three Lions, The Night Face, The Enemy Stars,* and *The High Crusade,* all of which were being published in *addition* to the series books, it becomes clear that Anderson dominated the late fifties and the pre–New Wave sixties in a way that only Robert A. Heinlein, Isaac Asimov, and Arthur C. Clarke could rival. And, like them, he remained an active and dominant figure right through the seventies and eighties. He is *still* producing strong new work and turning up on best-seller lists at the end of the decade of the nineties as well.

Explorers and exploration of all sorts have long fascinated Anderson, and several different stories by him would have fit into this anthology perfectly well, but "The Longest Voyage" details the meeting of two *different* explorers from two different worlds and is his purest examination of the restless, questing spirit of those who are driven to seek out the farthest horizon they can possibly reach—and then long for horizons farther still. It won him a Hugo Award in 1960, and for its lyricism, compassion, subtlety, thoughtfulness, and, above all, the relish it takes in the bristling strangeness and *wonder* of the world it still goes nearly unmatched in the field.

Anderson's other books (among *many* others) include: *The Broken Sword, Tau Zero, A Midsummer Tempest, Orion Shall Rise,* and *The Boat of a Million Years.* His short work has been collected in *The Queen of Air and Darkness and Other Stories, Fantasy, The Unicorn Trade* (with Karen Anderson), *Past Times, The Best of Poul Anderson,* and *Explorations.* His most recent books are the novels *Harvest of Stars, The Fleet of Stars, Starfarers,* and *Operation Luna* and the retrospective collection *All One Universe.* Upcoming is a new novel, *Genesis.* Anderson lives in Orinda, California, with his wife (and fellow writer) Karen.

When first we heard of the sky ship, we were on an island whose name, as nearly as Montalirian tongues can wrap themselves about so barbarous a noise, was Yarzik. That was almost a year after the *Golden Leaper* sailed from Lavre Town, and we judged we had come halfway round the world. So befouled was our poor caravel with weeds and shells that all sail could scarce drag her across the sea. What drinking water remained in the butts was turned green and evil, the biscuit was full of worms, and the first signs of scurvy had appeared on certain crewmen.

"Hazard or no," decreed Captain Rovic, "we must land somewhere." A gleam I remembered appeared in his eyes. He stroked his red beard and murmured, "Besides, it's long since we asked for the Aureate Cities. Perhaps this time they'll have intelligence of the place."

Steering by that ogre planet which climbed daily higher as we bore westward, we crossed such an emptiness that mutinous talk broke out afresh. In my heart I could not blame the crew. Imagine, my lords. Day upon day upon day when we saw naught but blue waters, white foam, high clouds in a tropic sky; heard only the wind, *whoosh* of waves, creak of timbers, sometimes at night the huge sucking and rushing as a sea monster breached. These were terrible enough to common sailors, unlettered men who still thought the world must be flat. But then to have Tambur hang forever above the bowsprit, and climb, so we could see we must eventually pass directly beneath the brooding thing . . . and what upbore it? the crew mumbled in the forecastle. Would an angered God not let it fall down on us?

At last a deputation waited on Captain Rovic. Very timid and respectful they were, those rough burly men, as they asked him to turn about. But their comrades massed below, muscled sun-blackened bodies taut in the ragged kilts, daggers and belaying pins ready to hand. We officers on the quarterdeck had swords and pistols, true. But we numbered a mere six, including that frightened boy who was myself, and aged Froad the astrologue, whose robe and white beard were reverend to see but of small use in a fight.

Rovic stood mute for a long while after the spokesman had voiced this demand. The stillness grew, until the empty shriek of wind in our shrouds, the empty glitter of ocean out to the world's rim, became all there was. Most splendid our master looked, for he had donned scarlet hose and bell-tipped shoon when he knew the deputation was coming, as well as helmet and corselet polished to mirror brightness. The plumes blew around that blinding steel head and the diamonds on his fingers flashed against the rubies in his sword hilt. Yet when he spoke, it was not as a knight of the Queen's court, but in the broad Anday of his fisher boyhood.

"So 'tis back ye'd wend, lads? Wi' a fair wind an' a warm sun, liefer ye'd come about an' beat half round the globe? How ye're changed from yere fathers! Ken ye nay the legend, that once everything did as man commanded, an' 'twas an Andayman's lazy fault that now we must work? For see ye, 'twas nay too much that he told his ax to cut down a tree for him, an' told the faggots to walk home, but when he told 'em to carry him, then God was wroth an' took the power away. Though to be sure, as recompense God gave Andaymen sea-luck, dice-luck, an' love-luck. What more d'ye ask for, lads?"

Bewildered at this response, the spokesman wrung his hands, flushed, looked at the deck, and stammered that we'd perish miserably . . . starve, or thirst, or drown, or be crushed under that horrible moon, or sail off the world's edge . . . the *Golden Leaper* had come farther than ship had sailed since the Fall of Man, and if we returned at once, our fame would live forever.

"But can ye eat fame, Etien?" asked Rovic, still mild and smiling. "We've had fights an' storms, aye, an' merry carouses too; but devil an Aureate City we've seen, though well ye ken they lie out here someplace, stuffed wi' treasure for the first bold gang who'll come plunder 'em. What ails yere gutworks, lad? Is't nay an easy cruise? What would the foreigners say? How will yon arrogant cavaliers o' Sathayn, yon grubby chapmen o' Wondland, laugh—nay alone at us, but at all Montalir—did we turn back!"

Thus he jollied them. Only once did he touch his sword, half drawing it, as if absentmindedly, when he recalled how we had weathered the hurricane off Xingu. But they remembered the mutiny that followed then, and how that same sword had pierced three armed sailors who attacked him together. His dialect told them he would let bygones lie forgotten, if they would. His bawdy promises of sport among lascivious heathen tribes yet to be discovered, his recital of treasure legends, his appeal to their pride as seamen and Montalirians, soothed fear. And then in the end, when he saw them malleable, he dropped the provincial speech. He stood forth on the quarterdeck in burning casque and tossing plumes, and the flag of Montalir blew its sea-faded colors above him, and he said as the knights of the Queen say:

"Now you know I do not propose to turn back until the great globe has been rounded and we bring to Her Majesty that gift which is most peculiarly ours to give. The which is not gold or slaves, nor even that lore of far places that she and her most excellent Company of Merchant Adventures desire. No, what we shall lift in our hands to give her, on that day when again we lie by the long docks of Lavre, shall be our achievement: that we did this thing which no men have dared in all the world ere now, and did it to her glory."

A while longer he stood, through a silence full of the sea's noise. Then he said quietly, "Dismissed," turned on his heel and went back into his cabin.

So we continued for some days more, the men subdued but not uncheerful, the officers taking care to hide their doubts. I found myself busied, less with the clerical duties for which I was paid or the study of captaincy for which I was apprenticed—both these amounting to little by now—than with assisting Froad the astrologue. In these balmy airs he could carry on his work even on shipboard. To him it scarce mattered whether we sank or swam; he had lived more than a common span of years already. But the knowledge of the heavens to be gained here, that was something else. At night, standing on the foredeck amidst quadrant, astrolabe, and telescope, drenched in the radiance from above, he resembled some frosty-bearded saint in the windows of Provien Minster.

"See there, Zhean." His thin hand pointed above waves that glowed and rippled with light, past the purple sky and the few stars still daring to show themselves, toward Tambur. Huge it was in full phase, sprawling over seven degrees of sky, a shield or barry of soft vert and azure, splotched with angry sable that could be seen to move across its face. The firefly moon we had named Siett twinkled near the hazy edge of the giant. Balant, espied rarely and low on the horizon in our part of the world, here stood high: a crescent, but the dark part of its disk tinged by luminous Tambur.

"Observe," declared Froad, "there's no doubt left; one can *see* how the globe rotates on an axis, and how storms boil up in its air. Tambur is no longer the dimmest of frightened legends, nor a dreadful apparition seen to rise as we entered unknown waters; Tambur is real. A world like our own. Immensely bigger, certes, but still a spheroid in space, around which our own world moves, always turning the same hemisphere to her monarch. The conjectures of the ancients are triumphantly confirmed. Not merely that our world is round—*pouf*, that's obvious to anyone—but that we move, about a greater center, which in turn has an annual path about the sun. But, then, how big is the sun?"

"Siett and Balant are inner satellites of Tambur," I rehearsed, struggling for comprehension. "Vieng, Darou, and the other moons commonly seen at home have paths outside our own world's. Aye. But what holds it all up?"

"That I don't know. Mayhap the crystal sphere containing the stars exerts an inward pressure. The same pressure, maybe, that hurled mankind down onto the earth, at the time of the Fall From Heaven."

The night was warm, but I shivered, as if those had been winter stars. "Then," I breathed, "there may also be men on . . . Siett, Balant, Vieng . . . even on Tambur?"

"Who knows? We'll need many lifetimes to find out. And what lifetimes they'll be! Thank the good God, Zhean, that you were born in this dawn of the coming age."

Froad returned to making measurements. A dull business, the other officers thought; but by now I had learned enough of the mathematic arts to understand that from these endless tabulations might come the true size of the earth, of Tambur, of sun and moons and stars, the paths they took through space and the direction of Paradise. So the common sailors, who muttered and made signs against evil as they passed our instruments, were closer to fact than Rovic's gentlemen, for indeed Froad practiced a most potent gramarye.

At length we saw weeds floating on the sea, birds, towering cloud masses, the signs of land. Three days later we raised an island. It was an intense green under those calm skies. Surf, still more violent than in our hemisphere, flung against high cliffs, burst in a smother of foam and roared back down again. We coasted carefully, the palomers aloft to seek an approach, the gunners standing by our cannon with lighted matches. For not only were there unknown currents and shoals—familiar hazards— but we had had brushes with canoe-sailing cannibals in the past. Especially did we fear the eclipses. My lords can visualize how in that hemisphere the sun each day must go behind Tambur. In our longitude the occurrence was about midafternoon and lasted nearly ten minutes. An awesome sight: the primary planet—for so Froad now called it, a planet akin to Diell or Coint, with our own world humbled to a mere satellite thereof!—became a black disk bordered red, up in a sky suddenly full of stars. A cold wind blew across the sea, and even the breakers seemed hushed. Yet so impudent is the soul of man that we continued about our duties, stopping only for the briefest prayer as the sun disappeared, thinking more about the chance of shipwreck in the gloom than of God's Majesty.

So bright is Tambur that we continued to work our way around the island at night. From sunup to sunup, twelve mortal hours, we kept the *Golden Leaper* slowly moving. Toward the second noon, Captain Rovic's persistence was re- warded. An opening in the cliffs revealed a long fjord. Swampy shores overgrown with saltwater trees told us that while the tides rose high in that bay, it was not one of those bores dreaded by mariners. The wind being against us, we furled sail and lowered the boats, towing in our caravel by the power of oars. This was a vulnerable moment, especially since we had perceived a village within the fjord. "Should we not stand out, master, and let them come first to us?" I ventured.

Rovic spat over the rail. "I've found it best never to show doubt," said he. "If a canoe fleet should assail us, we'll give 'em a whiff of grapeshot and trust to break their nerve. But I think, thus showing ourselves fearless of them from the very first, we're less likely to meet treacherous ambuscade later."

He proved right.

In the course of time, we learned we had come upon the eastern end of a large archipelago. The inhabitants were mighty seafarers, considering that they had only outrigger dugouts to travel in. These, though, were often a hundred feet long. With forty paddles, or with three bast-sailed masts, such a vessel could almost match our best speed, and was more maneuverable. However, the small cargo space limited their range of travel.

Albeit they lived in houses of wood and thatch, possessing only stone tools, the natives were cultivated folk. They farmed as well as fished; their priests had an alphabet. Tall and vigorous, somewhat darker and less hairy than we, they were impressive to behold, whether nude, as was common, or in full panoply of cloth and feathers and shell ornaments. They had formed a loose empire throughout the archipelago, raided islands lying farther north, and carried on a brisk trade within their own borders. Their whole nation they called the Hisagazi, and the island on which we had chanced was Yarzik.

This we learned slowly, as we mastered somewhat their tongue. For we were several weeks at that town. The duke of the island, Guzan, made us welcome, supplying us food, shelter, and helpers as we required. For our part, we pleased them with glassware, bolts of Wondish cloth, and suchlike trade goods. Nonetheless we encountered many difficulties. The shore above highwater mark being too swampy for beaching a vessel as heavy as ours, we must build a drydock before we could careen. Numerous of us took a flux from some disease, though all recovered in time, and this slowed us further.

"Yet I think our troubles will prove a blessing," Rovic told me one night. As had become his habit, once he learned I was a discreet amanuensis, he confided certain thoughts in me. The captain is ever a lonely man; and Rovic, fisher lad, freebooter, self-taught navigator, victor over the Grand Fleet of Sathayn and ennobled by the Queen herself, must have found the keeping of that necessary aloofness harder than would a gentleman born.

I waited silent, there in the grass hut they had given him. A soapstone lamp threw wavering light and enormous shadows over us; something rustled the thatch. Outside, the damp ground sloped past houses on stilts and murmurous fronded trees, to the fjord where it shimmered under Tambur. Faintly I heard drums throb, a chant and stamping of feet around a sacrificial fire. Indeed, the cool hills of Montalir seemed far.

Rovic leaned back his muscular form, clad in a mere seaman's kilt in this heat. He had had them fetch him a civilized chair from the ship. "For see you, young fellow," he continued, "at other times we'd have established just enough communication to ask about gold. Well, we might also try to get a few sailing directions. But all in all, we'd hear little except the old story—'aye, foreign lord, indeed there's a kingdom where the very streets are paved with gold . . . a hundred miles west'—anything to get rid of us, eh? But in this prolonged stay, I've asked out the duke and the idolater priests more subtly. I've been so coy about whence we came and what we already know, that they've let slip a gobbet of knowledge they'd not otherwise have disgorged on the rack itself."

"The Aureate Cities?" I cried.

"Hush! I'd not have the crew get excited and out of hand. Not yet."

His leathery, hook-nosed face turned strange with thought. "I've always believed those cities an old wives' tale," he said. My shock must have been mirrored to his gaze, for he grinned and went on, "A useful one. Like a lodestone on a stick, it's dragging us around the world." His mirth faded. Again he got that look, which was not unlike the look of Froad considering the heavens. "Aye, of course I want gold, too. But if we find none on this voyage, I'll not care. I'll capture a few ships of Eralia or Sathayn when we're back in home waters, and pay for the voyage thus. I spoke God's truth that day on the quarterdeck, Zhean, that this journey was its own goal, until I can give it to Queen Odela, who once gave me the kiss of ennoblement."

He shook himself out of his reverie and said in a brisk tone: "Having led him to believe I already knew the most of it, I teased from Duke Guzan the admission that on the main island of this Hisagazi empire is something I scarce dare think about. A ship of the gods, he says, and an actual live god who came from the stars therein. Any of the natives will tell you that much. The secret reserved to the noble folk is that this is no legend or mummery, but sober fact. Or so Guzan claims. I know not what to think. But . . . he took me to a holy cave and showed me an object from that ship. It was some kind of clockwork mechanism, I believe. What, I know not. But of a shining silvery metal such as I've never seen before. The priest challenged me to break it. The metal was not heavy, must have been thin. But it blunted my sword, splintered a rock I pounded with, and my diamond ring would not scratch it."

I made signs against evil. A chill went along me, spine and skin and scalp, until I prickled all over. For the drums were muttering in a jungle dark, and the waters lay like quicksilver beneath gibbous Tambur, and each afternoon that planet ate the sun. Oh, the bells of Provien, heard across windswept Anday downs!

When the *Golden Leaper* was seaworthy again, Rovic had no trouble gaining permission to visit the Hisagazian emperor on the main island. He would, indeed, have found difficulty in not doing so. By now the canoes had borne word of us from one end of the realm to another, and the great lords were agog to see these blue-eyed strangers. Sleek and content once more, we disentangled ourselves from the arms of tawny wenches and embarked. Up anchor, up sail, chanties whose echoes sent sea birds whirling above the steeps, and we stood out to sea. This time we were escorted. Guzan himself was our pilot, a big middle-aged man whose handsomeness was not much injured by the livid green tattoos his folk affected on face and body. Several of his sons spread their pallets on our decks, while a swarm of warriors paddled alongside.

Rovic summoned Etien the boatswain to him in his cabin. "You're a man of some wit," he said. "I give you charge of keeping our crew alert, weapons ready, however peaceful this may look."

"Why, master!" The scarred brown face sagged with near dismay. "Think you the natives plot a treachery?"

"Who can tell?" answered Rovic. "Now, say naught to the crew. They've no skill in dissembling. Did greed or fear rise among 'em, the natives would sense as much, and grow uneasy—which would worsen the attitude of our own men, until none but God's Daughter could tell what'd happen. Only see to it, as casually as you're able, that our arms are ever close by and that our folk stay together."

Etien collected himself, bowed, and left the cabin. I made bold to ask what Rovic had in mind.

"Nothing, yet," said he. "However, I did hold in these fists a piece of clockwork such as the Grand Ban of Giair never imagined; and yarns were spun me of a Ship which flew down from heaven, bearing a god or a prophet. Guzan thinks I know more than I do, and hopes we'll be a new, disturbing element in the balance of things, by which he may further his private ambitions. He did not take those many fighting men along by accident. As for me . . . I intend to learn more about this."

He sat awhile at his table, staring at a sunbeam which sickled up and down the wainscot as the ship rocked. Finally: "Scripture tells us man dwelt beyond the stars before the Fall. The astrologues of the past generation or two have told us the planets are corporeal bodies like this earth. A traveler from Paradise—"

I left with my head in a roar.

We made an easy passage among scores of islands. After several days we raised the main one, Ulas-Erkila. It is about a hundred miles long, forty miles across at the widest, rising steep and green toward central mountains dominated by a volcanic cone. The Hisagazi worship two sorts of gods, watery and fiery, and believe this Mount Ulas houses the latter. When I saw that snowpeak afloat in the sky above emerald ridges, staining the blue with smoke, I could feel what the pagans did. The holiest act a man can perform among them is to cast himself into the burning crater of Ulas, and often an aged warrior is carried up the mountain that he may do so. Women are not allowed on the slopes.

Nikum, the royal seat, is situated at the head of a fjord, like the village where we had been staying. But Nikum is rich and extensive, being about the size of Roann. Many houses are made from timber rather than thatch; there is also a massive basalt temple atop a cliff, overlooking the city, with orchards, jungle, and mountains at its back. So great are the tree trunks available to them for pilings, the Hisagazi have built here a regular set of docks like those at Lavre—instead of moorings and floats that can rise or fall with the tides, such as most harbors use throughout the world. We were offered a berth of honor at the central wharf, but Rovic made the excuse that our ship was awkward to handle and got us tied at the far end.

"In the middle, we'd have the watchtower straight above us," he muttered to me. "And they may not have discovered the bow here, but their javelin throwers are good. Furthermore, they'd have an easy approach to our ship, plus a clutter of moored canoes between us and the bay mouth. Here, though, a few of us could hold the pier whilst the others ready for quick departure."

"But have we anything to fear, master?" I asked.

He gnawed his mustache. "I know not. Much depends on what they really believe about this god-ship of theirs . . . as well as what the truth is. But come all death and hell against us, we'll not return without that truth for Queen Odela."

Drums rolled and feathered spearmen leaped as our officers disembarked. A royal catwalk stretched above highwater level. (Common townsfolk in this realm swim from house to house when the tide laps their thresholds, or take a coracle if they have burdens to carry.) Across the graceful span of vines and canes lay the palace, which was a long building made from logs, the roof pillars carved into fantastic god-shapes.

Iskilip, Priest-Emperor of the Hisagazi, was an old and corpulent man. A soaring headdress of plumes, a feather robe, a wooden scepter topped with a human skull, his facial tattoos, his motionlessness, all made him seem unhuman. He sat on a dais, under sweet-smelling torches. His sons sat crosslegged at his feet, his courtiers on either side. Down the long walls were ranged his guardsmen. They had not our custom of standing to attention; but they were big, supple young men, bearing shields and corselets of scaly sea-monster leather, flint axes and obsidian spears that could kill as easily as iron. Their heads were shaven, which made them look the fiercer.

Iskilip greeted us well, called for refreshment, bade us be seated on a bench little lower than his dais. He asked many perceptive questions. Wide ranging, the Hisagazi knew of islands far beyond their own chain. They could even point the direction and tell us roughly the distance of a many-castled country they named Yurakadak, though none of them had traveled that far himself. Judging by their third-hand description, what could this be but Giair, which the Wondish adventurer Hanas Tolasson had reached overland? It blazed in me that we were indeed rounding the world. Only after that glory had faded a little did I again heed the talk.

"As I told Guzan," Rovic was saying, "another thing which drew us hither was the tale that you were blessed with a Ship from Heaven. And he showed me this was true."

A hissing went down the hall. The princes grew stiff, the courtiers blanked their countenances, the guardsmen stirred and muttered. Remotely through the walls I heard the rumbling, nearing tide. When Iskilip spoke, through the mask of himself, his voice had gone whetted: "Have you forgotten that these things are not for the uninitiated to see, Guzan?"

"No, Holy One," said the duke. Sweat sprang forth among the devils on his face, though not the sweat of fear. "However, this captain knew. His people also . . . as nearly as I could learn . . . he still has trouble speaking so I can understand . . . his people are initiate too. The claim seems reasonable, Holy One. Look at the marvels they brought. The hard, shining stone-which-is-not-stone, as in this long knife I was given—is that not like the stuff of which the Ship is built? The tubes which make distant things look close at hand, such as he has given you, Holy One—is this not akin to the far-seer the Messenger possesses?"

Iskilip leaned forward, toward Rovic. His scepter hand trembled till the pegged jaws of the skull clattered together. "Did the Star People themselves teach you to make all this?" he cried. "I never imagined. . . . The Messenger never spoke of any others—"

Rovic held up both palms. "Not so fast, Holy One, I pray you," said he. "We are poorly versed in your tongue. I couldn't recognize a word just now."

This was his deceit. His officers had been ordered to feign a knowledge of Hisagazi less than they really possessed. (We had improved our command of it by secret practicing with each other.) Thus he had an unimpeachable device for equivocation.

"Best we talk in private, Holy One," suggested Guzan, with a glance at the courtiers. They returned him a jealous glare.

Iskilip slouched in his gorgeous regalia. His words fell blunt, but in the weak tone of an old, uncertain man. "I know not. If these strangers are already initiate, certes we can show them what we have. But otherwise—if profane ears heard the Messenger's own tale—"

Guzan raised a dominator's hand. Bold and ambitious, long thwarted in his petty province, he had taken fire today. "Holy One," he said, "why has the full story been withheld these many years? In part to keep the commoners obedient, aye. But also, did you and your councillors not fear the whole world might swarm hither, greedy for knowledge, if it knew, and we then be overwhelmed? Well, if we let the blue-eyed men go home with curiosity unsatisfied, I think they are sure to return in strength. Thus we have naught to lose by revealing the truth to them. If they have never had a Messenger of their own, if they can be of no real use to us, time enough to kill them. But if they have indeed been visited like us, what might we and they not do together!"

This was spoken fast and softly, lest we Montalirians understand. And, indeed, our gentlemen failed to. I, having young ears, got the gist; and Rovic preserved such a fatuous smile of incomprehension that I knew he was seizing every word.

In the end they decided to take our leader—and my insignificant self, for no Hisagazian magnate goes anywhere quite unattended—to the temple. Iskilip led the way in person, Guzan and two brawny princes behind. A dozen spearmen brought up the rear. I thought Rovic's blade would be scant use if trouble came, but set my lips firmly together and made myself walk beside him. He looked as eager as a child on Thanksday Morning, teeth agleam in the pointed beard, a plumed bonnet slanted rakish over his brow. None would have thought him aware of any peril.

We left about sundown; in Tambur's hemisphere, folk make less distinction between day and night than our people must. Having observed Siett and Balant in high tide position, I was not surprised that Nikum lay nearly drowned. And yet, as we climbed the cliff trail toward the temple, methought I had never seen a view more alien.

Below us lay a sheet of water, on which the long grass roofs of the city appeared to float; the crowded docks, where our own ship's masts and spars raked above heathen figureheads; the fjord, winding between precipices toward its mouth, where the surf broke white and terrible on the skerries. The heights above us seemed altogether black, against a fire-colored sunset that filled nigh half the sky and bloodied the waters. Wan through those clouds I glimpsed the thick crescent of Tambur, banded in a heraldry no man could read. A basalt column chipped into the shape of a head loomed in outline athwart the planet. Right and left of the path grew sawtoothed turf, summer dry. The sky was pale at the zenith, dark purple in the east, where the first few stars had appeared. Tonight I found no comfort in the stars. We walked silent. The bare native feet made no noise. My shoes went pad-pad and the bells on Rovic's toes raised a tiny jingle.

The temple was a bold piece of work. Within a quadrangle of basalt walls guarded by tall stone heads lay several buildings of the same material. Only the fresh-cut fronds that roofed them were alive. Iskilip leading us, we brushed past acolytes and priests to a wooden cabin behind the sanctum. Two guardsmen stood watch at its door. They knelt for him. The emperor rapped with his curious scepter.

My mouth was dry and my heart thunderous. I expected almost any being hideous or radiant to stand in the doorway as it was opened. Astonishing, then, to see just a man, and of no great stature. By lamplight within I discerned his room, clean, austere, but not uncomfortable; this could have been an ordinary Hisagazian dwelling. He himself wore a simple bast skirt. The legs beneath were bent and thin, old man's shanks. His body was likewise thin, but still erect, the white head proudly carried. In complexion he was darker than a Montalirian, lighter than a Hisagazian, with brown eyes and sparse beard. His visage differed subtly, in nose and lips and slope of jaw, from any other race I had ever encountered. But he was human.

Naught else.

We entered the cabin, shutting out the spearmen. Iskilip doddered through a half-religious ceremony of introduction. I saw Guzan and the princes shift their stance, restless and unawed. Their class had long been party to this. Rovic's face was unreadable. He bowed in courtly wise to Val Nira, Messenger of Heaven, and explained our presence in a few words. But as he spoke, their eyes met and I saw him take the star man's measure.

"Aye, this is my home," said Val Nira. Habit spoke for him; he had given the same account to so many young nobles that the edges were worn off it. As yet he had not observed our metallic instruments, or else had not grasped their significance to him. "For . . . forty-three years, is that right, Iskilip? I have been treated as well as might be. If at times I was near screaming from loneliness, that is what an oracle must expect."

The emperor stirred, uneasy in his robe. "His demon left him," he explained. "Now he is simple human flesh. That's the real secret we keep. It was not ever thus. I remember when he first came. He prophesied immense things, and the people wailed and went on their faces. But sithence his demon has gone back to the stars, and the once-potent weapon he bore has equally been emptied of its force. The people would not believe this, however, so we will still pretend otherwise, or there would be unrest among them."

"Affecting your own privileges," said Val Nira. His tone was tired and sardonic. "Iskilip was young then," he added to Rovic, "and the imperial succession was in doubt. I gave him my influence. He promised in return to do certain things for me."

"I tried, Messenger," said the monarch. "Ask all the sunken canoes and drowned men if I did not try. But the will of the gods was otherwise."

"Evidently." Val Nira shrugged. "These islands have few ores, Captain Rovic, and no person capable of recognizing those I required. It's too far to the mainland for Hisagazian canoes. But I don't deny you tried, Iskilip . . . then." He cocked an eyebrow back at us. "This is the first time foreigners have been taken deeply into the imperial confidence, my friends. Are you certain you can get back out again, alive?"

"Why, why, why, they're our guests!" blustered Iskilip and Guzan, almost in each other's mouths.

"Besides," smiled Rovic, "I had most of the secret already. My country has secrets of its own, to set against this. Yes, I think we might well do business, Holy One."

The emperor trembled. His voice cracked across. "Have you indeed a Messenger too?"

"What?" For a numbed moment Val Nira stared at us. Red and white pursued each other across his countenance. Then he sat down on the bench and began to weep.

"Well, not precisely." Rovic laid a hand on the shaking shoulder. "I confess no heavenly vessel has docked at Montalir. But we've certain other secrets, belike equally valuable." Only I, who knew his moods somewhat, could sense the tautness in him. He locked eyes with Guzan and stared the duke down as a wild animal tamer does. And meanwhile, motherly gentle, he spoke with Val Nira. "I take it, friend, your Ship was wrecked on these shores, but could be repaired if you had certain materials?"

"Yes . . . yes . . . listen—" Stammering and gulping at the thought he might see his home again ere he died, Val Nira tried to explain.

The doctrinal implications of what he said are so astounding, even dangerous, that I feel sure my lords would not wish me to repeat much. However, I do not believe they are false. If the stars are indeed suns like our own, each attended by planets like our own, this demolishes the crystal-sphere theory. But Froad, when he was told later, did not think that matters to the true religion. Scriptures have never said that Paradise lies directly above the birthplace of God's Daughter; this was merely assumed, during those centuries when the earth was believed to be flat. Why should Paradise not be those planets of distant suns, where men dwell in magnificence, who possess the ancient arts and flit from star to star as casually as we might go from Lavre to West Alayn?

Val Nira believed our ancestors had been cast away on this world, several thousand years ago. They must have been fleeing the consequences of some crime or heresy, to come so far from any human domain. Somehow their ship was wrecked, the survivors went back to savagery, and only by degrees have their descendants regained a little knowledge. I cannot see where this explanation contradicts the dogma of the Fall. Rather, it amplifies it. The Fall was not the portion of all mankind but only a few—our own tainted blood—while the others continued to dwell prosperous and content in the heavens.

Our world still lies far off the trade lanes of the Paradise folk. Very few of them nowadays have any interest in seeking new realms. Val Nira, though, was such a one. He traveled at hazard for months until he chanced upon our earth. Then the curse seized him, too. Something went wrong. He descended upon Ulas-Erkila, and the Ship would fly no more.

"I know what the damage is," he said ardently. "I've not forgotten. How could I? No day has passed throughout these years that I didn't recite to myself what must be done. A certain subtle engine in the Ship requires quicksilver." (He and Rovic must spend some time talking ere they deduced this must be what he meant by the word he used.) "When the engine failed, I landed so hard that its tanks burst. All the quicksilver, what I had in reserve as well as what I was employing, poured forth. That much, in a hot enclosed space, would have poisoned me. I fled outside, forgetting to close the doorway. The deck being canted, the quicksilver ran after me. By the time I had recovered from blind panic, a tropical rainstorm had carried off the fluid metal. A series of unlikely accidents, yes, that's what's condemned me to a life's exile. It really would have made more sense to perish outright!"

He clutched Rovic's hand, staring up from his seat at the captain who stood over him. "Can you actually get quicksilver?" he begged. "I need no more than the volume of a man's head. Only that, and a few repairs easily made with tools in the Ship. When this cult grew up around me, I must needs release certain things I possessed, that each provincial temple might have a relic. But I took care never to give away anything important. Whatever I need is waiting there. A gallon of quicksilver, and—oh, God, my wife may even be alive, on Terra!"

Guzan, at least, had begun to understand the situation. He gestured to the princes, who hefted their axes and stepped a little closer. The door was shut on the cabin. Rovic looked from Val Nira to Guzan, whose face was grown ugly with tension. My captain laid hand on hilt. In no other way did he seem to feel any nearness of trouble.

"I take it, milord," he said lightly, "you're willing that the Heaven Ship be made to fly again."

Guzan was jarred. He had never expected this. "Why, of course," he exclaimed. "Why not?"

"Your tame god would depart you. What then becomes of your power in Hisagazia?"

"I—I'd not thought of that," Iskilip stuttered.

Val Nira's eyes shuttled among us, as if watching a game of paddleball. His thin body shook. "No," he whispered. "You can't. You can't keep me!"

Guzan nodded. "In a few more years," he said, not unkindly, "you would depart in death's canoe anyhow. If meanwhile we held you against your will, you might not speak the right oracles for us. Nay, be at ease; we'll get your flowing stone." With a slitted glance at Rovic: "Who shall fetch it?"

"My folk," said the knight. "Our ship can readily reach Giair, where there are civilized nations who surely have the quicksilver. We could return within a year, I think."

"Accompanied by a fleet of adventurers, to help you seize the sacred vessel?" asked Guzan bluntly. "Or, once out of our islands, you might not proceed to Yu-rakadak at all. You might continue the whole way home, and tell your Queen, and return with the power she commands."

Rovic lounged against a roof post, like a big pounce-cat at its ease in ruffles and hose and scarlet cape. His right hand continued to rest on his sword pommel. "None save Val Nira could make that Ship go, I suppose," he drawled. "Does it matter who aids him in making repairs? Surely you don't think either of our nations could conquer Paradise!"

"The ship is very easy to operate," chattered Val Nira. "Anyone can fly it in air. I showed many nobles what levers to use. It's navigating among the stars which is more difficult. No nation on this world could even reach my people unaided—let alone fight them—but why should you think of fighting? I've told you a thousand times, Iskilip, the dwellers in the Milky Way are dangerous to nobody. They have so much wealth they're hard put to find a use for most of it. Gladly would they spend large amounts to help the peoples of this world become civilized again." With an anxious, half-hysterical look at Rovic: "Fully civilized, I mean. We'll teach you our arts. We'll give you engines, automata, homunculi, that do all the toilsome work; and boats that fly through the air; and regular passenger service on those ships that ply between the stars—"

"These things you have promised for forty years," said Iskilip. "We've naught but your word."

"And, finally, a chance to confirm his word," I blurted.

Guzan said with calculated grimness: "Matters are not that simple, Holy One. I've watched these men from across the ocean for weeks, while they lived on Yarzik. Even on their best behavior, they're a fierce and greedy lot. I trust them no further than my eyes reach. This very night I see how they've befooled us. They know our language better than they ever admitted. And they misled us to believe they might have some inkling of a Messenger. If the Ship were indeed made to fly again, them in possession, who knows what they might choose to do?"

Rovic's tone softened still further. "What do you propose, Guzan?"

"We can discuss that another time."

I saw knuckles tighten around stone axes. For a moment, only Val Nira's unsteady breathing was heard. Guzan stood heavy in the lamplight, rubbing his chin, the small black eyes turned downward in thoughtfulness. At last he shook himself. "Perhaps," he said crisply, "a crew mainly Hisagazian could sail your ship, Rovic, and fetch the flowing stone. A few of your men could go along to instruct ours. The rest could remain here as hostages."

My captain made no reply. Val Nira groaned, "You don't understand! You're squabbling over nothing! When my people come here, there'll be no more war, no more oppression. They'll cure you of every disease. They'll show friendship to all and favor to none. I beg you—"

"Enough," said Iskilip. His own words fell ragged. "We shall sleep on this. If anyone can sleep after so much strangeness."

Rovic looked past the emperor's plumes, into the face of Guzan. "Before we decide anything . . ." His fingers tightened on the sword hilt till the nails turned white. Some thought had sprung up within him. But he kept his tone even. "First I want to see that Ship. Can we go there tomorrow?"

Iskilip was the Holy One, but he stood huddled in his feather robe. Guzan nodded agreement.

★ ★ ★

We bade our good-nights and went forth under Tambur. The planet was waxing toward full, flooding the courtyard with cold luminance, but the hut was shadowed by the temple. It remained a black outline, a narrow lamplight rectangle of doorway in the middle. There was etched the frail body of Val Nira, who had come from the stars. He watched us till we had gone out of sight.

On the way down the path, Guzan and Rovic bargained in curt words. The Ship lay two days' march inland, on the slopes of Mount Ulas. We would go in a joint party to inspect it, but a mere dozen Montalirians were allowed. Afterward we would debate our course of action.

Lanthorns glowed yellow at our caravel's poop. Refusing Iskilip's hospitality, Rovic and I returned thither for the night. A pikeman on guard at the gangway inquired what I had learned. "Ask me tomorrow," I said feebly. "My head's in too much of a whirl."

"Come into my cabin, lad, for a stoup ere we retire," the captain invited me.

God knows I needed wine. We entered the low room, crowded with nautical instruments, books, and printed charts that looked quaint to me now I had seen a little of those spaces where the cartographer drew mermaids and windsprites. Rovic sat down behind his table, gestured me to a chair opposite, and poured from a carafe into two goblets of Quaynish crystal. Then I knew he had momentous thoughts in his head—far more than the problem of saving our lives.

We sipped a while, unspeaking. I heard the lap-lap of wavelets on our hull, the tramp of men on watch, the rustle of distant surf—otherwise nothing. At last Rovic leaned back, staring at the ruby wine on the table. I could not read his expression.

"Well, lad," said he, "what do you think?"

"I know not what to think, master."

"You and Froad are a trifle prepared for this idea that the stars are other suns. You're educated. As for me, I've seen sufficient eldritch in my day that this seems quite believable. The rest of our people, though . . ."

"An irony that barbarians like Guzan should long have been familiar with the concept, having had the old man from the sky to preach it privily to their class for more than forty years. Is he indeed a prophet, master?"

"He denies it. He plays prophet because he must, but it's evident that the dukes and earls of this realm know it's a trick. Iskilip is senile, more than half converted to his own artificial creed. He was mumbling about prophecies Val Nira made long ago, true prophecies. Bah! Tricks of memory and wishfulness. Val Nira is as human and fallible as I am. We Montalirians are the same flesh as these Hisagazi, even if we have learned the use of metal before they did. Val Nira's people know more in turn than us; they're still mortals, by Heaven. I must remember that they are."

"Guzan remembers."

"Bravo, lad!" Rovic's mouth bent upward, one-sidedly. "He's a clever one, and bold. When he came, he saw his chance to stop stagnating as the petty lord of an outlying island. He'll not let that chance slip without a fight. Like many a double-dealer before him, he accuses us of plotting the very things he hopes to do."

"But what does he hope for?"

"My guess would be, he wants the Ship for himself. Val Nira said it was easy to fly. Navigation between the stars would be too difficult for anyone save him; nor could any man in his right mind hope to play pirate along the Milky Way. However . . . if the Ship stayed right here, on this earth, rising no higher than a mile above ground . . . the warlord who used it might conquer more widely than Lame Darveth himself."

I was aghast. "Do you mean Guzan would not even try to seek out Paradise?"

Rovic scowled so blackly at his wine that I saw he wanted solitude. I stole off to my bunk in the poop.

The captain was awake before dawn, readying our folk. Plainly he he had reached some decision, and it was not pleasant. But once he set a course, he seldom veered. He was long in conference with Etien, who came out of the cabin looking frightened. As if to reassure himself, the boatswain ordered the men about harshly.

Our allowed dozen were to be Rovic, Froad, myself, Etien, and eight crewmen. We were issued helmets and corselets, muskets and edged weapons. Since Guzan had told us there was a beaten path to the Ship, we assembled a supply cart on the dock. Etien supervised its landing. I was astonished to see that nearly all it carried, till the axles groaned, was barrels of gunpowder. "But we're not taking cannon!" I protested.

"Skipper's orders," rapped Etien. He turned his back on me. After a glance at Rovic's face, nobody ventured to ask him the reason. I remembered we would be going up a mountainside. A wagonful of powder, with lit fuse, set rolling down toward a hostile army, might win a battle. But did Rovic anticipate open conflict?

Certes his orders to the men and officers remaining behind suggested as much. They were to stay aboard the *Golden Leaper*, holding her ready for instant fight or flight.

As the sun rose, we said our morning prayers to God's Daughter and marched down the docks. The wood banged hollow under our boots. A few thin mists drifted on the bay; Tambur's crescent hung wan above. Nikum town lay hushed as we passed through.

Guzan met us at the temple. A son of Iskilip was supposedly in charge, but the duke ignored that youth as much as we did. They had a hundred guardsmen along, scaly-coated, shaven-headed, tattooed with storms and dragons. The early sunlight gleamed off obsidian spearheads. Our approach was watched in silence. But when we halted' before those disorderly ranks, Guzan trod forth. He was also y-clad in leather, and carried the sword Rovic had given him on Yarzik. The dew shimmered on his feather cloak. "What have you in that wagon?" he demanded.

"Supplies," Rovic answered.

"For four days?"

"Send home all but ten of your men," said Rovic coolly, "and I'll send back this cart."

Their eyes clashed, until Guzan turned and gave his orders. We started off, a few Montalirians surrounded by pagan warriors. The jungle lay ahead of us, a deep and burning green, rising halfway up the slope of Ulas. Then the mountain became naked black, to the snow that edged its smoking crater.

Val Nira walked between Rovic and Guzan. Strange, I thought, that the instrument of God's will for us was so shriveled. He ought to have walked tall and haughty, a star on his brow.

During the day, at night when we made camp, and again the next day, Rovic and Froad questioned him eagerly about his home. Of course, their talk was in fragments. Nor did I hear everything, since I must take my turn at pulling our wagon along that narrow, steep, damnable trail. The Hisagazi have no draft animals, therefore they make slight use of the wheel and have no proper roads. But what I did hear kept me long awake.

Ah, greater marvels than the poets have imagined for Elf Land! Entire cities built in a single tower half a mile high. The sky made to glow so that there is no true darkness after sunset. Food not grown in the earth, but manufactured in alchemical elaboratories. The lowest peasant owning a score of machines which serve him more subtly and humbly than might a thousand slaves; owning an aerial carriage which can fly him around his world in less than a day; owning a crystal window on which theatrical images appear, to beguile his abundant leisure. Argosies between suns, stuffed with the wealth of a thousand planets; yet every ship unarmed and unescorted, for there are no pirates and this realm is on such good terms with the other starfaring nations that war has also ceased. (These foreign countries, it seems, are more akin to the supernatural than Val Nira's, in that the races composing them are not human, though able to speak and reason.) In this happy land is little crime. When it does occur, the criminal is soon captured by the arts of the provost corps; yet he is not hanged, nor even transported overseas. Instead, his mind is cured of the wish to violate any law. He returns home to live as an especially honored citizen, since folk know he is now completely trustworthy. As for the government—but here I lost the thread of discourse. I believe it is in form a republic, but in practice a devoted fellowship of men, chosen by examination, who see to the welfare of everyone else.

Surely, I thought, this was Paradise!

Our sailors listened agape. Rovic's mien was reserved, but he gnawed his mustaches incessantly. Guzan, to whom this was an old tale, grew rough of manner. Plain to see, he disliked our intimacy with Val Nira, and the ease wherewith we grasped ideas that were spoken.

But, then, we came of a nation which has long encouraged natural philosophy and improvement of the mechanic arts. I myself, in my short lifetime, had witnessed the replacement of the waterwheel in regions where there are few streams by the modern form of windmill. The pendulum clock was invented the year before I was born. I had read many romances about the flying machines which no few men have tried to devise. Living at such a dizzy pace of progress, we Montalirians were all prepared to entertain still vaster concepts.

At night, sitting with Froad and Etien around a campfire, I spoke somewhat of this to the savant. "Ah," he crooned, "today Truth stood unveiled before me. Did you hear what the starman said? The three laws of planetary motion about a sun, and the one great law of attraction which explains them? Dear saints, that law can be put in a single short sentence, and yet the development will keep mathematicians busy for three hundred years!"

He stared past the flames, and the other fires around which the heathen slept, and jungle gloom, and angry volcanic glow in heaven. I started to query him. "Leave be, lad," grunted Etien. "Can ye nay tell when a man's in love?"

I shifted a little closer to the boatswain's stolid, comforting bulk. "What do you think of this?" I asked, softly, for the jungle whispered and croaked on every side.

"Me, I stopped thinking a while back," he said. "After yon day on the quarterdeck, when the skipper jested us into sailing wi' him though we went off the world's edge an' tumbled down in foam amongst the nether stars . . . well, I'm but a poor sailor man, an' my one chance o' regaining home is to follow the skipper."

"Even beyond the sky?"

"Less hazard to that, maybe, than sailing on around the world. The little man swore his vessel was safe, an' no storms blow between the suns."

"Can you trust his word?"

"Oh, aye. Even a knocked-about old palomer like me has seen enough o' men to ken when a one's too timid an' eagersome to stand by a lie. I fear not the folk in Paradise, nor does the skipper. Except in some way . . ." Etien rubbed his bearded jaw, scowling. "In some way I can nay wholly grasp, they affright Rovic. He fears nay they'll come hither wi' torch an' sword; but there's somewhat else about 'em that frets him."

I felt the ground shudder the least bit. Ulas had cleared his throat. "It does seem we'd be daring God's anger—"

"That's nay what gnaws on the skipper's mind. He was never an over-pious man." Etien scratched himself, yawned, and climbed to his feet. "Glad I am to be nay the skipper. Let him think over what's best to do. Time ye an' me was asleep."

But I slept little that night.

Rovic, I think, rested well. Yet as the next day wore on, I could see haggardness on him. I wondered why. Did he think the Hisagazi would turn on us? If so, why had he come? As the slope steepened, the wagon grew so toilsome to push and drag that my fears died for lack of breath.

Yet when we came upon the Ship, toward evening, I forgot my weariness. And after an amazed volley of oaths, our mariners rested silent on their pikes. The Hisagazi, never talkative, crouched low in token of awe. Only Guzan remained erect among them. I glimpsed his expression as he stared at the marvel. It was a look of lust.

Wild was that place. We had gone above timberline. The land was a green sea below us, edged with silvery ocean. Here we stood among tumbled black boulders, cinders and spongy tufa underfoot. The mountain rose in steeps and scarps and ravines, on to snows and smoke, which rose another mile into a pale chilly sky. And here stood the Ship.

And the Ship was beauty.

I remember. In length—height, rather, since it stood on its tail—it was about equal to our caravel, in form not unlike a lance head, in color a shining white, untarnished after forty years. That was all. But words are paltry, my lords. What can they show of clean soaring curves, of iridescence on burnished metal, of a thing which was proud and lovely and in its very shape aquiver to be off? How can I conjure back the glamour which hazed that Ship whose keel had cloven starlight?

We stood there a long time. My vision blurred. I wiped my eyes, angry to be seen thus affected, until I noticed a tear glisten in Rovic's red beard. But the captain's visage was quite blank. When he spoke, he said merely, in a flat voice, "Come, let's make camp."

The Hisagazian guardsmen dared approach no closer than these several hundred yards to as potent an idol as the Ship had become. Our mariners were glad to maintain the same distance. But after dark, when everything else was in order, Val Nira led Rovic, Froad, Guzan, and myself to the vessel.

As we approached, a double door in the side swung noiselessly open and a metal gangplank descended therefrom. Glowing in Tambur's light, and in the dull clotted red reflected off the smoke clouds, the Ship was already as strange as I could endure. When it thus beckoned me, as if a ghost stood guard, I whimpered and fled. The cinders crunched beneath my boots; I caught a whiff of sulfurous air.

But at the edge of camp I rallied myself enough to look again. The dark ground blotted up light, so that the Ship appeared alone with its grandeur. Presently I went back.

The interior was lit by luminous panels, cool to the touch. Val Nira explained that the great engine which drove it—as if the troll of folklore were put on a treadmill—was intact, and would furnish power at the flick of a lever. As nearly as I could understand what he said, this was done by changing the metallic part of salt into light . . . thus I do not understand after all. The quicksilver was required for a part of the controls, which channeled power from the engine into another mechanism that hurtled the Ship skyward. We inspected the broken container. Enormous indeed had been the impact of landing, to twist and bend that thick alloy. And yet Val Nira had been shielded by invisible forces, and the rest of the Ship had not suffered important damage. He fetched some tools, which flamed and hummed and whirled, and demonstrated a few repair operations on the broken part. Obviously he would have no trouble completing the work—and then he need only pour in a gallon of quicksilver, to bring his vessel alive again.

Much else did he show us that night. I shall say naught of it, for I cannot even remember such strangeness very clearly, let alone find words. Suffice that Rovic, Froad, and Zhean spent a few hours in Elf Hill.

So, too, did Guzan. Though he had been taken here before, as part of his initiation, he had never been shown this much ere now. Watching him, however, I saw less marveling in him than greed.

No doubt Rovic observed the same. There was little which Rovic did not observe. When we departed the Ship, his silence was not stunned like Froad's or mine. At the time, I thought in a vague fashion that he fretted over the trouble Guzan was certain to make. Now, looking back, I believe his mood was sadness.

Sure it is that long after we others were in our bedrolls, he stood by himself, looking at the planet-lit Ship.

Early in a cold dawn, Etien shook me awake. "Up, lad, we've work to do. Load yere pistols an' belt on yere dirk."

"What? What's to happen?" I fumbled with a hoar-frosted blanket. Last night seemed a dream.

"The skipper's nay said, but plainly he awaits a fight. Report to the wagon an' help us move into yon flying tower." Etien's thick form heelsquatted a moment longer beside me. Then, slowly: "Methinks Guzan has some idea o' murdering us here on the mountain. One officer an' a few crewmen can be made to sail the *Golden Leaper* for him, to Giair an' back. The rest o' us would be less trouble to him wi' our weasands slit."

I crawled forth, teeth clattering in my head. After arming myself, I snatched some food from the common store. The Hisagazi on the march carry dried fish and a sort of bread made from a powdered weed. The saints alone knew when I'd next get a chance to eat. I was the last to join Rovic at the cart. The natives were drifting sullenly toward us, unsure what we intended.

"Let's go, lads," said Rovic. He gave his orders. Four men started manhandling the wagon across the rocky trail toward the Ship, where this gleamed among mists. We others stood by, weapons ready. Guzan hastened toward us, Val Nira toiled in his wake.

Anger darkened his countenance. "What are you doing?" he barked.

Rovic gave him a calm stare. "Why, milord, as we may be here for some time, inspecting the wonders aboard the Ship—"

"What?" exclaimed Guzan. "What do you mean? Have you not seen ample for a first visit? We must get home again, and prepare to sail after the flowing stone."

"Go if you wish," said Rovic. "I choose to linger. And since you don't trust me, I reciprocate the feeling. My folk will stay in the Ship, which can be defended if necessary."

Guzan stormed and raged, but Rovic ignored him. Our men continued hauling the cart over the uneven ground. Guzan signaled his spearmen, who approached in a disordered but alert mass. Etien spoke a command. We fell into line. Pikes slanted forward, muskets took aim.

Guzan stepped back. We had demonstrated firearms for him at his home island. Doubtless he could overwhelm us with sheer numbers, were he determined, but the cost would be heavy. "No reason to fight, is there?" purred Rovic. "I am only taking a sensible precaution. The Ship is a most valuable prize. It could bring Paradise for all . . . or dominion over this earth for a few. There are those who'd prefer the latter. I've not accused you of being among them. However, in prudence I'd liefer keep the Ship for my hostage and my fortress, as long as it pleases me to remain here."

I think then I was convinced of Guzan's real intentions, not as a surmise of ours but as plain fact. Had he truly wished to attain the stars, his single concern would have been to keep the Ship safe. He would not have reached out, snatched little Val Nira in his powerful hands, and dragged the starman backward like a shield against our fire. Not that his intent matters, save to my own conscience. Wrath distorted his patterned visage. He screamed at us, "Then I'll keep a hostage too! And much good may your shelter do you!"

The Hisagazi milled about, muttering, hefting their spears and axes, but not prepared to follow us. We grunted our way across the black mountainside. The sun strengthened. Froad twisted his beard. "Dear me, master captain," he said, "think you they'll lay siege to us?"

"I'd not advise anyone to venture forth alone," said Rovic dryly.

"But without Val Nira to explain things, what use for us to stay at the Ship? Best we go back. I've mathematic texts to consult. My head's aspin with the law that binds the turning planets. I must ask the man from Paradise what he knows of—"

Rovic interrupted with a gruff order to three men, that they help lift a wheel wedged between two stones. He was in a savage temper. I confess his action seemed mad to me. If Guzan intended treachery, we had gained little by immobilizing ourselves in the Ship, where he could starve us. Better to let him attack in the open, where we would have a chance of fighting our way through. And if Guzan did not plan to fall on us in the jungle—or any other time—then this was senseless provocation on our part. But I dared not question.

When we had brought our wagon to the Ship, its gangplank again descended for us. The sailors started and cursed. Rovic forced himself out of his bitterness, to speak soothing words. "Easy, lads. I've been aboard already, ye ken. Naught harmful within. Now we must tote our powder thither, an' stow it as I've planned."

Being slight of frame, I was not set to carrying the heavy casks, but put at the foot of the gangplank to watch the Hisagazi. Although we were too far away to distinguish words, I saw how Guzan stood on a boulder and harangued them. They shook their weapons at us and whooped. They did not venture to attack. I wondered wretchedly what this was all about. If Rovic had foreseen us besieged, that would explain why he brought the powder along. . . . No, it would not, for there was more than a dozen men could shoot off in weeks of musketry, even if we had enough bullets . . . and we had almost no food! I looked past the poisonous volcano clouds, to Tambur where storms raged that could engulf our whole earth, and wondered what demons lurked here to possess men.

I sprang to alertness at an indignant shout from within. Froad! Almost, I ran up the gangway, then remembered my duty. I heard Rovic roar him down and order the crewfolk to carry on. Froad and Rovic must have gone by themselves into the pilot's compartment and talked for an hour or more. When the old man emerged, he protested no longer. But as he walked down the gangway, he wept.

Rovic followed, grimmer of countenance than I had ever seen ere now. The sailors filed after, some looking appalled, some relieved, but chiefly watching the Hisagazian camp. They were simply mariners; the Ship was little to them save a weird and disquieting object. Last came Etien, walking backward down the metal plank as he uncoiled a long string.

"Form square!" barked Rovic. The men snapped into position. "Get at the middle, Zhean and Froad," said the captain. "You can better carry extra ammunition than fight." He placed himself in the van.

I tugged Froad's sleeve. "Please, I beg you, master, what's happening?" He sobbed too much to answer.

Etien crouched, flint and steel in his hands. He heard me—for otherwise we were deathly silent—and said in a hard voice: "We placed casks o' powder throughout this hull, lad, wi' powder trains to join 'em. Here's the fuse to the whole."

I could not speak, could not even think, so monstrous was this. As if from immensely far away, I heard the click of stone on metal in Etien's fingers, heard him blow on the spark and add: "A good idea, methinks. I said t'other eventide, I'd follow the skipper wi'out fear o' God's curse—but let's not tempt Him over-much."

"Forward march!" Rovic's sword blazed clear of the scabbard.

Our feet scrunched loud and horrible on the mountain as we quick-stepped away. I did not look back. I could not. I was still fumbling in a nightmare. Since Guzan would have moved to intercept us anyhow, we proceeded straight toward his band. He stepped forth as we halted at the camp's edge. Val Nira slunk shivering after him. I heard the words dimly.

"Well, Rovic, what now? Are you ready to go home?"

"Yes," said the captain. His voice was dull. "All the way home."

Guzan squinted in rising suspiciousness. "Why did you abandon your wagon? What did you leave behind?"

"Supplies. Come, let's march."

Val Nira stared at the cruel shapes of our pikes. He must wet his lips a few times ere he could quaver, "What are you talking about? There's no reason to leave food there. It would spoil in the time until . . . until—" He faltered as he looked into Rovic's eyes. The blood drained from him.

"What have you done?" he whispered.

Suddenly Rovic's free hand arose, to cover his face. "What I must," he said thickly. "Daughter of God, forgive me."

The starman regarded us an instant more. Then he turned and ran. Past the astonished warriors he burst, out onto the cindery slope, toward his Ship.

"Come back!" bellowed Rovic. "You fool, you'll never—"

He swallowed hard. As he looked after that small, stumbling, lonely shape, hurrying across a fire mountain toward the Beautiful One, the sword sank in his grasp. "Perhaps it's best," he said, like a benediction.

Guzan raised his own sword. In scaly coat and blowing feathers, he was a figure as impressive as steel-clad Rovic. "Tell me what you've done," he snarled, "or I'll kill you this moment!"

He paid our muskets no heed. He, too, had had dreams.

He, too, saw them end, when the Ship exploded.

Even that adamantine hull could not withstand a wagonload of carefully placed gunpowder, set off at the same time. A crash knocked me to my knees, and the hull cracked open. White-hot chunks of metal screamed across the slopes. I saw one of them strike a boulder and split it in twain. Val Nira vanished, destroyed too quickly to have seen what happened; thus, in the ultimate, God was merciful to him. Through the flames and smokes and doomsday noise which followed, I saw the Ship fall. It rolled down the slope, strewing its mangled guts behind. Then the mountainside grumbled and slid in pursuit, and buried it, and dust hid the sky.

More than this, I have no heart to remember.

The Hisagazi shrieked and fled. They must have thought hell was come to earth. Guzan stood his ground. As the dust enveloped us, hiding the grave of the Ship and the white volcano crater, turning the sun red, he sprang at Rovic. A musketeer raised his weapon. Etien slapped it down. We stood and watched those two men fight, up and over the shaken cinder land, and knew in our private darkness that this was their right. Sparks flew where the blades clamored together. At last Rovic's skill prevailed. He took his foe in the throat.

We gave Guzan decent burial and went down through the jungle.

That night the guardsmen rallied their courage to attack us. We were aided by our muskets, but must chiefly use sword and pike. We hewed our way through them because we had no place else to go than the sea.

They retreated, but carried word ahead of us. When we reached Nikum, all the forces Iskilip could raise were besieging the *Golden Leaper* and waiting to oppose Rovic's entry. We formed a square again, and no matter how many thousands they had, only a score or so could reach us at any time. Nonetheless, we left six good men in the crimsoned mud of those streets. When our people on the caravel realized Rovic was coming back, they bombarded the town. This ignited the thatch roofs and distracted the enemy enough that a sortie from the ship was able to effect a juncture with us. We chopped our way to the pier, got aboard, and manned the capstan.

Outraged and very brave, the Hisagazi paddled their canoes up to our hull, where our cannon could not be brought to bear. They stood on each other's shoulders to reach our rail. One band forced itself aboard, and the fight was fierce which cleared them from the decks. That was when I got the shattered collarbone which plagues me to this day.

But in the end, we came out of the fjord. A fresh east wind was blowing. Sail aloft, we outran the foe. We counted our dead, bound our wounds, and slept.

★ ★ ★

Next dawning, awakened by the pain of my wound and the worse pain within, I mounted the quarterdeck. The sky was overcast. The wind had stiffened; the sea ran cold and green, whitecaps out to a cloudy-gray horizon. Timbers groaned and rigging thrummed. I stood an hour facing aft, into the chill wind that numbs pain.

When I heard boots behind me, I did not turn around. I knew they were Rovic's. He stood beside me a long while, bareheaded. I noticed that he was starting to turn gray.

Finally, not yet regarding me, still squinting into the air that lashed tears from our eyes, he said: "I had a chance to talk Froad over, that day. He was grieved, but owned I was right. Has he spoken to you about it?"

"No," I said.

"None of us are ever likely to speak of it much," said Rovic.

After another time: "I was not afraid Guzan or anyone else would seize the Ship and try to turn conqueror. We men of Montalir should well be able to deal with any such rogues. Nor was I afraid of the Paradise dwellers. That poor little man could only have been telling truth. They would never have harmed us . . . willingly. They would have brought precious gifts, and taught us their esoteric arts, and let us visit their stars."

"Then why?" I got out.

"Someday Froad's successors will solve the riddles of the universe," he said. "Someday our descendants will build their own Ship, and go forth to whatever destiny they wish."

Spume blew around us until our hair was wet. I tasted the salt on my lips.

"Meanwhile," said Rovic, "we'll sail the seas of this earth, and walk its mountains, and chart and subdue and come to understand it. Do you see, Zhean? That is what the Ship would have taken from us."

Then I was also made able to weep. He laid his hand on my uninjured shoulder and stood with me while the *Golden Leaper*, all sail set, proceeded westward.

Hot Planet

HAL CLEMENT

Hal Clement—the writing name of longtime science teacher Harry Clement Stubbs—made his first sale in 1942, to *Astounding,* and became one of the mainstays of that magazine throughout the fifties and sixties, with much of his best short work appearing there. Clement's most famous novel is *Mission of Gravity,* which in retrospect still holds up as one of the best science-fiction books of the sixties, although I am also fond of the underrated *Cycle of Fire.* Clement's influence on later writers such as G. David Nordley, Stephen Baxter, Harry Turtledove, Janet Kagan, and others is clear and unmistakable. His other books include the novels *Star Light* (the sequel to *Mission of Gravity), Needle, Close to Critical, Iceworld, Ocean on Top,* and *The Nitrogen Fix* and the collections *Small Changes, Natives of Space,* and *The Best of Hal Clement.*

   Although known as one of the most scrupulously accurate of the "hard science" writers, someone careful to always get the scientific details right, Clement also has a rich and lively imagination, especially when it comes to alien lifeforms, and he has created some of the most memorable alien characters in science fiction. His major contribution to the theme of exploration happens also to be the book that features his most intriguing alien characters, *Mission of Gravity,* in which *two* different parties of explorers, one human and one native, find they must work together in order to succeed in a mission on the surface of the bizarre high-gravity world Mesklin, where the gravity varies from 3g at the equator to 700g at the poles, one of the strangest alien worlds ever explored in print.

   There are no aliens in the taut, suspenseful tale that follows, but it remains one of the classic stories of space exploration and a reminder of how humans exploring hostile environments must somehow be prepared even for the totally *unexpected*—or else! (Note: It's an irony in the face of Clement's reputation for rigorous hard science that almost everything he says here about the planet Mercury is wrong, but it's not *his* fault that later, fuller information led scientists to change their minds; at the time, in 1963, the story stuck scrupulously to the "facts" about Mercury as they were known—or thought to be known. This is one of the dangers of hard science writing—no matter how much research you do the facts *themselves* can always change tomorrow, undoing all your hard work. You still ought to get points for trying, though!)

Clement's most recent books are a new novel, *Half Life*, and an omnibus reprint of three of his previous novels (*Needle, Iceworld,* and *Close to Critical*), bound together as *The Essential Hal Clement, Volume 1: Trio for Slide Rule and Typewriter* (NESFA Press, PO Box 809, Framingham, MA 01701—$25 plus $2 postage). Keep an eye out for the next volume in this series, as it's bringing a lot of Clement's long-unavailable work back into print.

1

The wind which had nearly turned the *Albireo*'s landing into a disaster instead of a mathematical exercise was still playing tunes about the fins and landing legs as Schlossberg made his way down to Deck Five.

The noise didn't bother him particularly, though the endless seismic tremors made him dislike the ladders. But just now he was able to ignore both. He was curious—though not hopeful. "Is there anything at all obvious on the last set of tapes, Joe?"

Mardikian, the geophysicist, shrugged. "Just what you'd expect . . . on a planet which has at least one quake in each fifty-mile-square area every five minutes. You know yourself we had a nice seismic programme set up, but when we touched down we found we couldn't carry it out. We've done our best with the natural tremors—incidentally stealing most of the record tapes the other projects would have used. We have a lot of nice information for the computers back home; but it will take all of them to make any sense out of it."

Schlossberg nodded; the words had not been necessary. His astronomical programme had been one of those sabotaged by the transfer of tapes to the seismic survey.

"I just hoped," he said. "We each have an idea why Mercury developed an atmosphere during the last few decades, but I guess the high school kids on Earth will know whether it's right before we do. I'm resigned to living in a chess-type universe—few and simple rules, but infinite combinations of them. But it would be nice to know an answer sometime."

"So it would. As a matter of fact, I need to know a couple right now. From you. How close to finished are the other programmes—or what's left of them?"

"I'm all set," replied Schlossberg. "I have a couple of instruments still monitoring the sun just in case, but everything in the revised programme is on tape."

"Good. Tom, any use asking you?"

The biologist grimaced. "I've been shown two hundred and sixteen different samples of rock and dust. I have examined in detail twelve crystal growths which looked vaguely like vegetation. Nothing was alive or contained living things by any standards I could conscientiously set."

Mardikian's gesture might have meant sympathy.

"Camille?"

"I may as well stop now as any time. I'll never be through. Tape didn't make much difference to me, but I wish I knew what weight of specimens I could take home."

"Eileen?" Mardikian's glance at the stratigrapher took the place of the actual question.

"Cam speaks for me, except that I could have used any more tape you could have spared. What I have is gone."

"All right, that leaves me, the tape-thief. The last spools are in the seismographs now, and will start running out in seventeen hours. The tractors will start out on their last rounds in sixteen, and should be back in roughly a week. Will, does that give you enough to figure the weights we rockhounds can have on the return trip?"

The *Albireo*'s captain nodded. "Close enough. There really hasn't been much question since it became evident we'd find nothing for the mass tanks here. I'll have a really precise check in an hour, but I can tell right now that you have about one and a half metric tons to split up among the three of you.

"Ideal departure time is three hundred and ten hours away, as you all know. We can stay here until then, or go into a parking-and-survey orbit at almost any time before then. You have all the survey you need, I should think, from the other time. But suit yourselves."

"I'd just as soon be space-sick as seasick," remarked Camille Burkett. "I still hate to think that the entire planet is as shivery as the spot we picked."

Willard Rowson smiled. "You researchers told me where to land after ten days in orbit mapping this rockball. I set you just where you asked. If you'd found even five tons of juice we could use in the reaction tanks I could still take you to another one—if you could agree which one. I hate to say 'Don't blame me,' but I can't think of anything else that fits."

"So we sit until the last of the tractors is back with the precious seismo tapes, playing battleship while our back teeth are being shaken out by earthquakes—excuse the word. What a thrill! Glorious adventure!" Zaino, the communications specialist who had been out of a job almost constantly since the landing, spoke sourly. The captain was the only one who saw fit to answer.

"If you want adventure, you made a mistake exploring space. The only space adventures I've heard of are second-hand stories built on guesswork; the people who really had them weren't around to tell about it. Unless Dr. Marini discovers a set of Mercurian monsters at the last minute and they invade the ship or cut off one of the tractors, I'm afraid you'll have to do without adventures." Zaino grimaced.

"That sounds funny coming from a spaceman, Captain. I didn't really mean adventure, though; all I want is something to do besides betting whether the next quake will come in one minute or five. I haven't even had to fix a suit-radio since we touched down. How about my going out with one of the tractors on this last trip, at least?"

"It's all right with me," replied Rowson, "but Dr. Mardikian runs the professional part of this operation. I require that Spurr, Trackman, Hargedon and Aiello go as drivers, since without them even a minor mechanical problem would be more than an adventure. As I recall it, Dr. Harmon, Dr. Schlossberg, Dr. Marini and Dr. Mardikian are scheduled to go; but if any one of them is willing to let you take his or her place, I certainly don't mind."

The radioman looked around hopefully. The geologists and the biologist shook their heads negatively, firmly and unanimously; but the astronomer pondered for a moment. Zaino watched tensely.

"It may be all right," Schlossberg said at last. "What I want to get is a set of wind, gas pressure, gas temperature and gas composition measures around the route. I didn't expect to be more meteorologist than astronomer when we left Earth, and didn't have exactly the right equipment. Hargedon and Aiello helped me improve some, and this is the first chance to use it on the Darkside. If you can learn what has to be done with it before starting time, though, you are welcome to my place."

The communicator got to his feet fast enough to leave the deck in Mercury's feeble gravity.

"Lead me to it, Doc. I guess I can learn to read a home-made weathervane!"

"Is that merely bragging, or a challenge?" drawled a voice which had not previously joined the discussion. Zaino flushed a bit.

"Sorry, Luigi," he said hastily. "I didn't mean it just that way. But I still think can run the stuff."

"Likely enough," Aiello replied. "Remember though, it wasn't made just for talking into." Schlossberg, now on his feet, cut in quickly.

"Come on, Arnie. We'll have to suit up to see the equipment; it's outside."

He shepherded the radioman to the hatch at one side of the deck and shooed him down towards the engine and air lock levels. Both were silent for some moments; but, safely out of earshot of Deck Five, the younger man looked up and spoke.

"You needn't push, Doc. I wasn't going to make anything of it. Luigi was right, and I asked for it." The astronomer slowed a bit in his descent.

"I wasn't really worried," he replied, "but we have several months yet before we can get away from each other, and I don't like talk that could set up grudges. Matter of fact, I'm even a little uneasy about having the girls along, though I'm no misogynist."

"Girls? They're not—"

"There goes your foot again. Even Harmon is about ten years older than you, I suppose. But they're girls to me. What's more important, they no doubt think of themselves as girls."

"Even Dr. Burkett? That is—I mean—"

"Even Dr. Burkett. Here, get into your suit. And maybe you'd better take out the mike. It'll be enough if you can listen for the next hour or two." Zaino made no answer, suspecting with some justice that anything he said would be wrong.

Each made final check on the other's suit; then they descended one more level to the air lock. This occupied part of the same deck as the fusion plants, below the wings and reaction mass tanks but above the main engine. Its outer door was just barely big enough to admit a spacesuited person. Even with the low air pressure carried by spaceships, a large door area meant large total force on jamb, hinges and locks. It opened on to a small balcony from which a ladder led to the ground. The two men paused on the balcony to look over the landscape.

This hadn't changed noticeably since the last time either had been out, though there might have been some small difference in the volcanic cones a couple of miles away to the north-east. The furrows down the sides of these, which looked as though they had been cut by water but were actually bone-dry ash slides, were always undergoing alteration as gas from below kept blowing fresh scoria fragments out of the craters.

The spines—steep, jagged fragments of rock which thrust upward from the plain beyond and to both sides of the cones—seemed dead as ever.

The level surface between the *Albireo* and the cones was more interesting Mardikian and Schlossberg believed it to be a lava sheet dating from early in Mercury's history, when more volatile substances still existed in the surface rock to cut down their viscosity when molten. They supposed that much—perhaps most—of the surface around the "twilight" belt had been flooded by this very liquid lava, which had cooled to a smoother surface than most Earthly lava flows.

How long it had stayed cool they didn't guess. But both men felt sure that Mercury must have periodic upheavals as heat accumulated inside it—heat coming not from radioactivity but from tidal energy. Mercury's orbit is highly eccentric At perihelion, tidal force tries to pull it apart along the planet-to-sun line, while at aphelion the tidal force is less and the little world's own gravity tries to bring it back to a spherical shape. The real change in form is not great, but a large force working through even a small amount of distance can mean a good deal of energy

If the energy can't leak out—and Mercury's rocks conduct heat no better than those of Earth—the temperature must rise.

Sooner or later, the men argued, deeply buried rock must fuse to magma. Its liquefaction would let the bulk of the planet give farther under tidal stress, so heat would be generated even faster. Eventually a girdle of magma would have to form far below the crust all around the twilight strip, where the tidal strain would be greatest. Sooner or later this would melt its way to the surface, giving the zone a period of intense volcanic activity and, incidentally, giving the planet a temporary atmosphere.

The idea was reasonable. It had, the astronomer admitted, been suggested long before to account for supposed vulcanism on the moon. It justified the careful examination that Schlossberg and Zaino gave the plain before they descended the ladder; for it made reasonable the occasional changes which were observed to occur in the pattern of cracks weaving over its surface.

No one was certain just how permanent the local surface was—though no one could really justify feeling safer on board the *Albireo* than outside on the lava. If anything really drastic happened, the ship would be no protection.

The sun, hanging just above the horizon slightly to the watcher's right, cast long shadows which made the cracks stand out clearly; as far as either man could see, nothing had changed recently. They descended the ladder carefully—even the best designed spacesuits are somewhat vulnerable—and made their way to the spot where the tractors were parked.

A sheet-metal fence a dozen feet high and four times as long provided shade, which was more than a luxury this close to the sun. The tractors were parked in this shadow, and beside and between them were piles of equipment and specimens. The apparatus Schlossberg had devised was beside the tractor at the north end of the line, just inside the shaded area.

It was still just inside the shade when they finished, four hours later. Hargedon had joined them during the final hour and helped pack the equipment in the tractor he was to drive. Zaino had had no trouble in learning to make the observations Schlossberg wanted, and the youngster was almost unbearably cocky. Schlossberg hoped, as they returned to the *Albireo*, that no one would murder the communications expert in the next twelve hours. There would be nothing to worry about after the trip started; Hargedon was quite able to keep anyone in his place without being nasty about it. If Zaino had been going with Aiello or Harmon—but he wasn't, and it was pointless to dream up trouble.

And no trouble developed all by itself.

2

Zaino was not only still alive but still reasonably popular when the first of the tractors set out, carrying Eileen Harmon and Eric Trackman, the *Albireo*'s nuclear engineer.

It started more than an hour before the others, since the stratigrapher's drilling programme, "done" or not, took extra time. The tractor hummed off to the south, since both Darkside routes required a long detour to pass the chasm to the west. Routes had been worked out from the stereophotos taken during the orbital survey. Even Darkside had been covered fairly well with Uniquantum film under Venus light.

The Harmon-Trackman vehicle was well out of sight when Mardikian and Aiello started out on one of the Brightside routes, and a few minutes later Marini set out on the other with the spacesuit technician, Mary Spurr, driving.

Both vehicles disappeared quickly into a valley to the northeast, between the ash cones and a thousand-foot spine which rose just south of them. All the tractors were in good radio contact; Zaino made sure of that before he abandoned the radio watch to Rowson, suited up and joined Hargedon at the remaining one. They climbed in, and Hargedon set it in motion.

At about the same time, the first tractor came into view again, now travelling north on the farther side of the chasm. Hargedon took this as evidence that the route thus far was unchanged, and kicked in highest speed.

The cabin was pretty cramped, even though some of the equipment had been attached outside. The men could not expect much comfort for the next week.

Hargedon was used to the trips, however. He disapproved on principle of people who complained about minor inconveniences such as having to sleep in spacesuits; fortunately, Zaino's interest and excitement overrode any thought he might have had about discomfort.

This lasted through the time they spent doubling the vast crack in Mercury's crust, driving on a little to the north of the ship on the other side and then turning west towards the dark hemisphere. The route was identical to that of Harmon's machine for some time, though no trace of its passage showed on the hard surface. Then Hargedon angled off towards the southwest. He had driven this run often enough to know it well even without the markers which had been set out with the seismographs. The photographic maps were also aboard. With them, even Zaino had no trouble keeping track of their progress while they remained in sunlight.

However, the sun sank as they travelled west. In two hours its lower rim would have been on the horizon, had they been able to see the horizon; as it was, more of the "sea level" lava plain was in the shadow than not, even near the ship, and their route now lay in semi-darkness.

The light came from peaks projecting into the sunlight, from scattered sky-light which was growing rapidly fainter and from the brighter celestial objects such as Earth. Even with the tractor's lights it was getting harder to spot crevasses and seismometer markers. Zaino quickly found the fun wearing off . . . though his pride made him cover this fact as best he could.

If Hargedon saw this, he said nothing. He set Zaino to picking up every other instrument, as any partner would have, making no allowance for the work the youngster was doing for Schlossberg. This might, of course, have had the purpose of keeping the radioman too busy to think about discomfort. Or it might merely have been Hargedon's idea of normal procedure.

Whatever the cause, Zaino got little chance to use the radio once they had driven into the darkness. He managed only one or two brief talks with those left at the ship.

The talks might have helped his morale, since they certainly must have given the impression that nothing was going on in the ship while at least he had something to do in the tractor. However, this state of affairs did not last. Before the vehicle was four hours out of sight of the *Albireo*, a broadcast by Camille Burkett reached them.

The mineralogist's voice contained at least as much professional enthusiasm as alarm, but everyone listening must have thought promptly of the dubious stability of Mercury's crust. The call was intended for her fellow geologists Mardikian and Harmon. But it interested Zaino at least as much.

"Joe! Eileen! There's a column of what looks like black smoke rising over Northeast Spur. It can't be a real fire, of course; I can't see its point of origin, but if it's the convection current it seems to be the source must be pretty hot. It's the closest thing to a genuine volcano I've seen since we arrived; it's certainly not another of those ash mounds. I should think you'd still be close enough to make it out, Joe. Can you see anything?"

The reply from Mardikian's tractor was inaudible to Zaino and Hargedon, but Burkett's answer made its general tenor plain.

"I hadn't thought of that. Yes, I'd say it was pretty close to the Brightside route. It wouldn't be practical for you to stop your run now to come back to see. You couldn't do much about it anyway. I could go out to have a look and then report to you. If the way back is blocked there'll be plenty of time to work out another." Hargedon and Zaino passed questioning glances at each other during the shorter pause that followed.

"I know there aren't," the voice then went on, responding to the words they could not hear, "but it's only two or three miles, I'd say. Two to the spur and not much farther to where I could see the other side. Enough of the way is in shade so I could make it in a suit easily enough. I can't see calling back either of the Darkside tractors. Their work is just as important as the rest—anyway, Eileen is probably out of range. She hasn't answered yet." Another pause.

"That's true. Still, it would mean sacrificing that set of seismic records—no, wait. We could go out later for those. And Mel could take his own weather measures on the later trip. There's plenty of time!" Pause, longer this time.

"You're right, of course. I just wanted to get an early look at this volcano, if it is one. We'll let the others finish their runs, and when you get back you can check the thing from the other side yourself. If it is blocking your way there's time to find an alternate route. We could be doing that from the maps in the meantime, just in case."

Zaino looked again at his companion.

"Isn't that just my luck!" he exclaimed. "I jump at the first chance to get away from being bored to death. The minute I'm safely away, the only interesting thing of the whole operation happens—back at the ship!"

"Who asked to come on this trip?"

"Oh, I'm not blaming anyone but myself. If I'd stayed back there the volcano would have popped out here somewhere, or else waited until we were gone."

"If it is a volcano. Dr. Burkett didn't seem quite sure."

"No, and I'll bet a nickel she's suiting up right now to go out and see. I hope she comes back with something while we're still near enough to hear about it."

Hargedon shrugged. "I suppose it was also just your luck that sent you on a Darkside trip? You know the radio stuff. You knew we couldn't reach as far this way with the radios. Didn't you think of that in advance?"

"I didn't think of it, any more than you would have. It was bad luck, but I'm not grousing about it. Let's get on with this job." Hargedon nodded with approval, and possibly with some surprise, and the tractor hummed on its way.

The darkness deepened around the patches of lava shown by the driving lights; the sky darkened towards a midnight hue, with stars showing ever brighter through it; and radio reception from the *Albireo* began to get spotty. Gas density at the ion layer was high enough so that recombination of molecules with their radiation-freed electrons was rapid. Only occasional streamers of ionised gas reached far over Darkside. As these thinned out, so did radio reception. Camille Burkett's next broadcast came through very poorly.

There was enough in it, however, to seize the attention of the two men in the tractor.

She was saying: ". . . real all right, and dangerous. It's the . . . thing I ever saw . . . kinds of lava from what looks like . . . same vent. There's high viscosity stuff building a spatter cone to end all spatter cones, and some very thin fluid from somewhere at the bottom. The flow has already blocked the valley used by the Brightside routes and is coming along it. A new return route will have to be found for the tractors that . . . was spreading fast when I saw it. I can't tell how much will come. But unless it stops there's nothing at all to keep the flow away from the ship. It isn't coming fast, but it's coming. I'd advise all tractors to turn back. Captain Rowson reminds me that only one take-off is possible. If we leave this site, we're committed to leaving Mercury. Arnie and Ren, do you hear me?"

Zaino responded at once. "We got most of it, Doctor. Do you really think the ship is in danger?"

"I don't know. I can only say that *if* this flow continues the ship will have to leave, because this area will sooner or later be covered. I can't guess how likely . . . check further to get some sort of estimate. It's different from any Earthly lava source—maybe you heard—should try to get Eileen and Eric back, too. I can't raise them. I suppose they're well out from under the ion layer by now. Maybe you're close enough to them to catch them with diffracted waves. Try, anyway. Whether you can raise them or not you'd better start back yourself."

Hargedon cut in at this point. "What does Dr. Mardikian say about that? We still have most of the seismometers on this route to visit."

"I think Captain Rowson has the deciding word here, but if it helps your decision Dr. Mardikian has already started back. He hasn't finished his route, either.

So hop back here, Ren. And Arnie, put that technical skill you haven't had to use yet to work raising Eileen and Eric."

"What I can do, I will," replied Zaino, "but you'd better tape a recall message and keep it going out on. Let's see—band F."

"All right. I'll be ready to check the volcano as soon as you get back. How long?"

"Seven hours—maybe six and a half," replied Hargedon. "We have to be careful."

"Very well. Stay outside when you arrive; I'll want to go right out in the tractor to get a closer look." She cut off.

"And *that* came through clearly enough!" remarked Hargedon as he swung the tractor around. "I've been awake for fourteen hours, driving off and on for ten or them; I'm about to drive for another six; and then I'm to stand by for more."

"Would you like me to do some of the driving?" asked Zaino.

"I guess you'll have to, whether I like it or not," was the rather lukewarm reply. "I'll keep on for a while, though—until we're back in better light. You get at your radio job."

3

Zaino tried. Hour after hour he juggled from one band to another. Once he had Hargedon stop while he went out to attach a makeshift antenna which, he hoped, would change his output from broadcast to some sort of beam; after this he kept probing the sky with the "beam," first listening to the *Albireo*'s broadcast in an effort to find projecting wisps of ionosphere and then, whenever he thought he had one, switching on his transmitter and driving his own message at it.

Not once did he complain about lack of equipment or remark how much better he could do once he was back at the ship.

Hargedon's silence began to carry an undercurrent of approval not usual in people who spent much time with Zaino. The technician made no further reference to the suggestion of switching drivers. They came in sight of the *Albireo* and doubled the chasm with Hargedon still at the wheel, Zaino still at his radio and both of them still uncertain whether any of the calls had got through.

Both had to admit, even before they could see the ship, that Burkett had had a right to be impressed.

The smoke column showed starkly against the sky, blowing back over the tractor and blocking the sunlight which would otherwise have glared into the driver's eyes. Fine particles fell from it in a steady shower; looking back, the men could see tracks left by their vehicle in the deposit which had already fallen.

As they approached the ship the dark pillar grew denser and narrower, while the particles raining from it became coarser. In some places the ash was drifting into fairly deep piles, giving Hargedon some anxiety about possible concealed cracks. The last part of the trip, along the edge of the great chasm and around its end, was really dangerous; cracks running from its sides were definitely spreading. The two men reached the *Albireo* later than Hargedon had promised, and found Burkett waiting impatiently with a pile of apparatus beside her.

She didn't wait for them to get out before starting to organise.

"There isn't much here. We'll take off just enough of what you're carrying to make room for this. No—wait. I'll have to check some of your equipment; I'm going to need one of Milt Schlossberg's gadgets, I think, so leave that on. We'll take—"

"Excuse me, Doctor," cut in Hargedon. "Our suits need servicing, or at least mine will if you want me to drive you. Perhaps Arnie can help you load for a while, if you don't think it's too important for him to get at the radio—"

"Of course. Excuse me. I should have had someone out here to help me with this. You two go on in. Ren, please get back as soon as you can. I can do the work here; none of this stuff is very heavy."

Zaino hesitated as he swung out of the cab. True, there wasn't too much to be moved, and it wasn't very heavy in Mercury's gravity, and he really should be at the radio; but the thirty-nine-year-old mineralogist was a middle-aged lady by his standards, and shouldn't be allowed to carry heavy packages . . .

"Get along, Arnie!" the middle-aged lady interrupted this train of thought. "Eric and Eileen are getting farther away and harder to reach every second you dawdle!"

He got, though he couldn't help looking north-east as he went rather than where he was going.

The towering menace in that direction would have claimed anyone's attention. The pillar of sable ash was rising straighter, as though the wind were having less effect on it. An equally black cone had risen into sight beyond Northeast Spur— a cone that must have grown to some two thousand feet in roughly ten hours. It had far steeper sides than the cinder mounds near it; it couldn't be made of the same loose ash. Perhaps it consisted of half-melted particles which were fusing together as they fell—that might be what Burkett had meant by "spatter-cone." Still, if that were the case, the material fountaining from the cone's top should be lighting the plain with its incandescence rather than casting an inky shadow for its entire height.

Well, that was a problem for the geologists; Zaino climbed aboard and settled to his task.

The trouble was that he could do very little more here than he could in the tractor. He could have improvised longer-wave transmitting coils whose radiations would have diffracted a little more effectively beyond the horizon, but the receiver on the missing vehicle would not have detected them. He had more power at his disposal, but could only beam it into empty space with his better antennae. He had better equipment for locating any projecting wisps of charged gas which might reflect his waves, but he was already located under a solid roof of the stuff—the *Albireo* was technically on Brightside. Bouncing his beam from this layer still didn't give him the range he needed, as he had found both by calculation and trial.

What he really needed was a relay satellite. The target was simply too far around Mercury's sharp curve by now for anything less.

Zaino's final gesture was to set his transmission beam on the lowest frequency the tractor would pick up, aim it as close to the vehicle's direction as he could calculate from map and itinerary and set the recorded return message going. He told Rowson as much.

"Can't think of anything else?" the captain asked. "Well, neither can I, but of course it's not my field. I'd give a year's pay if I could. How long before they should be back in range?"

"About four days. A hundred hours, give or take a few. They'll be heading back anyway by that time."

"Of course. Well, keep trying."

"I am—or rather, the equipment is. I don't see what else I can do unless a really bright idea should suddenly sprout. Is there anywhere else I could be useful? I'm as likely to have ideas working as just sitting."

"We can keep you busy, all right. But how about taking a transmitter up one of those mountains? That would get your wave farther."

"Not as far as it's going already. I'm bouncing it off the ion layer, which is higher than any mountain we've seen on Mercury even if it's nowhere near as high as Earth's."

"Hmph. All right."

"I could help Ren and Dr. Burkett. I could hang on outside the tractor—"

"They've already gone. You'd better call them, though, and keep a log of what they do."

"All right." Zaino turned back to his board and with no trouble raised the tractor carrying Hargedon and the mineralogist. The latter had been trying to call the *Albireo* and had some acid comments about radio operators who slept on the job.

"There's only one of me, and I've been trying to get the Darkside team," he pointed out. "Have you found anything new about this lava flood?"

"Flow, not flood," corrected the professional automatically. "We're not in sight of it yet. We've just rounded the corner that takes us out of your sight. It's over a mile yet, and a couple of more corners, before we get to the spot where I left it. Of course, it will be closer than that by now. It was spreading at perhaps a hundred yards an hour then. That's one figure we must refine . . . Of course, I'll try to get samples, too. I wish there were some way to get samples of the central cone. The whole thing is the queerest volcano I've ever heard of. Have you got Eileen started back?"

"Not as far as I can tell. As with your cone samples, there are practical difficulties," replied Zaino. "I haven't quit yet, though."

"I should think not. If some of us were paid by the idea we'd be pretty poor, but the perspiration part of genius is open to all of us."

"You mean I should charge a bonus for getting this call through?" retorted the operator.

Whatever Burkett's reply to this might have been was never learned; her attention was diverted at that point.

"We've just come in sight of the flow. It's about five hundred yards ahead. We'll get as close as seems safe, and I'll try to make sure whether it's really lava or just mud."

"Mud? Is that possible? I thought there wasn't—couldn't be—any water on this planet!"

"It is, and there probably isn't. The liquid phase of mud doesn't have to be water, even though it usually is on Earth. Here, for example, it might conceivably be sulphur."

"But if it's just mud, it wouldn't hurt the ship, would it?"

"Probably not."

"Then why all this fuss about getting the tractors back in a hurry?"

The voice which answered reminded him of another lady in his past, who had ept him after school for drawing pictures in maths class.

"Because in my judgment the flow is far more likely to be lava than mud, and : I must be wrong I'd rather my error were one that left us alive. I have no time t the moment to explain the basis of my judgment. I will be reporting our activities uite steadily from now on, and would prefer that you not interrupt unless a serious mergency demands it, or you get a call from Eileen.

"We are about three hundred yards away now. The front is moving about as ast as before, which suggests that the flow is coming only along this valley. It's nly three or four feet high, so viscosity is very low or density very high. Probably ne former, considering where we are. It's as black as the smoke column."

"Not glowing?" cut in Zaino thoughtlessly.

"*Black*, I said. Temperature will be easier to measure when we get closer. The ront is nearly straight across the valley, with just a few lobes projecting ten or welve yards and one notch where a small spine is being surrounded. By the way, trust you're taping all this?" Again Zaino was reminded of the afternoon after chool.

"Yes, Ma'am," he replied. "On my one and only monitor tape."

"Very well. We're stopping near the middle of the valley one hundred yards rom the front. I am getting out, and will walk as close as I can with a sampler nd a radiometer. I assume that the radio equipment will continue to relay my suit roadcast back to you." Zaino cringed a little, certain as he was that the tractor's lectronic apparatus was in perfect order.

It struck him that Dr. Burkett was being more snappish than usual. It never rossed his mind that the woman might be afraid.

"Ren, don't get any closer with the tractor unless I call. I'll get a set of tem->erature readings as soon as I'm close enough. Then I'll try to get a sample. Then 'll come back with that to the tractor, leave it and the radiometer and get the narkers to set out."

"Couldn't I be putting out the markers while you get the sample, Doctor?"

"You could, but I'd rather you stayed at the wheel." Hargedon made no answer, nd Burkett resumed her description for the record.

"I'm walking towards the front, a good deal faster than it's flowing towards ne. I am now about twenty yards away, and am going to take a set of radiation-emperature measures." A brief pause. "Readings coming. Nine sixty. Nine eighty. Vine ninety—that's from the bottom edge near the spine that's being surrounded. Vine eighty-five—" The voice droned on until about two dozen readings had been aped. Then, "I'm going closer now. The sampler is just a ladle on a twelve-foot nandle we improvised, so I'll have to get that close. The stuff is moving slowly; here should be no trouble. I'm in reach now. The lava is very liquid; there's no rouble getting the sampler in—or out again—it's not very dense, either. I'm head-ng back towards the tractor now. No, Ren, don't come to meet me."

There was a minute of silence, while Zaino pictured the spacesuited figure, with its awkwardly long burden, walking away from the creeping menace to the relative safety of the tractor. "It's frozen solid already; we needn't worry about spilling. The temperature is about—five eighty. Give me the markers, please."

Another pause, shorter this time. Zaino wondered how much of that could be laid to a faster walk without the ladle and how much to the lessening distance

between flow and tractor. "I'm tossing the first marker close to the edge—it'
landed less than a foot from the lava. They're all on a light cord at ten-foot inter
vals; I'm paying out the cord as I go back to the tractor. Now we'll stand by and
time the arrival at each marker as well as we can."

"How close are you to the main cone?" asked Zaino.

"Not close enough to see its base, I'm afraid. Or to get a sample of it, which
is worse. We—goodness, what was that?"

Zaino had just time to ask, "What was what?" when he found out.

<h1 style="text-align:center">4</h1>

For a moment, he thought that the *Albireo* had been flung bodily into the air. Then
he decided that the great metal pillar had merely fallen over. Finally he realised
that the ship was still erect, but the ground under it had just tried to leave.

Everyone in the group had become so used to the almost perpetual ground
tremors that they had ceased to notice them; but this one demanded attention.
Rowson, using language which suggested that his career might not have been com
pletely free of adventure after all, flashed through the communication level on hi,
way down to the power section. Schlossberg and Babineau followed, the medic
pausing to ask Zaino if he were all right. The radioman merely nodded affirma
tively; his attention was already back at his job. Burkett was speaking a good dea
faster than before.

"Never mind if the sample isn't lashed tight yet—if it falls off there'll be
plenty more. There isn't time! Arnie, get in touch with Dr. Mardikian and Dr
Marini. Tell them that this volcano is explosive, that all estimates of what the flow
may do are off until we can make more measures, and in any case the whole
situation is unpredictable. Everyone should get back as soon as possible. Remem
ber, we decided that those big craters Eileen checked were not meteor pits. I don'
know whether this thing will let go in the next hour, the next year, or at all. Maybe
what's happening now will act as a safety valve—but let's get out. Ren, that flow
is speeding up and getting higher, and the ash rain is getting a lot worse. Can you
see to drive?"

She fell silent. Zaino, in spite of her orders, left his set long enough to leap to
the nearest port for a look at the volcano.

He never regretted it.

Across the riven plain, whose cracks were now nearly hidden under the new
ash, the black cone towered above the nearer elevations. It was visibly taller than
it had been only a few hours before. The fountain from its top was thicker, now
jetting straight up as though wind no longer meant a thing to the fiercely driven
column of gas and dust. The darkness was not so complete; patches of red and
yellow incandescence showed briefly in the pillar, and glowing sparks rather than
black cinders rained back on the steep slopes. Far above, a ring of smoke rolled
and spread about the column, forming an ever-broadening blanket of opaque cloud
above a landscape which had never before been shaded from the sun. Streamers
of lightning leaped between cloud and pillar, pillar and mountain, even cloud and
ground. Any thunder there might have been was drowned in the howl of the es
caping gas, a roar which seemed to combine every possible note from the shrillest

possible whistle to a bass felt by the chest rather than heard by the ears. Rowson's language had become inaudible almost before he had disappeared down the hatch.

For long moments the radioman watched the spreading cloud, and wondered whether the *Albireo* could escape being struck by the flickering, ceaseless lightning. Far above the widening ring of cloud the smoke fountain drove, spreading slowly in the thinning atmosphere and beyond it. Zaino had had enough space experience to tell at a glance whether a smoke or dust cloud was in air or not. This wasn't, at least at the upper extremity . . .

And then, quite calmly, he turned back to his desk, aimed the antenna straight up, and called Eileen Harmon. She answered promptly.

The stratigrapher listened without interruption to his report and the order to return. She conferred briefly with her companion, replied "We'll be back in twelve hours," and signed off. And that was that.

Zaino settled back with a sigh, and wondered whether it would be tactful to remind Rowson of his offer of a year's pay.

All four vehicles were now homeward bound; all one had to worry about was whether any of them would make it. Hargedon and Burkett were fighting their way through an ever-increasing ash rain a scant two miles away—ash which not only cut visibility but threatened to block the way with drifts too deep to negotiate. The wind, now blowing fiercely towards the volcano, blasted the gritty stuff against their front window as though it would erode through; and the lava flow, moving far faster than the gentle ooze they had never quite measured, surged—and glowed—grimly behind.

A hundred miles or more to the east, the tractors containing Mardikian, Marini and their drivers headed south-west along the alternate route their maps had suggested; but Mardikian, some three hours in the lead, reported that he could see four other smoke columns in that general direction.

Mercury seemed to be entering a new phase. The maps might well be out of date.

Harmon and Trackman were having no trouble at the moment, but they would have to pass the great chasm. This had been shooting out daughter cracks when Zaino and Hargedon passed it hours before. No one could say what it might be like now, and no one was going out to make sure.

"We can see you!" Burkett's voice came through suddenly. "Half a mile to go, and we're way ahead of the flow."

"But it's coming?" Rowson asked tensely. He had returned from the power level at Zaino's phoned report of success.

"It's coming."

"How fast? When will it get here? Do you know whether the ship can stand contact with it?"

"I don't know the speed exactly. There may be two hours, maybe five or six. The ship can't take it. Even the temperature measures I got were above the softening point of the alloys, and it's hotter and much deeper now. Anyway, if the others aren't back before the flow reaches the ship they won't get through. The tractor wheels would char away, and I doubt that the bodies would float. You certainly can't wade through the stuff in a spacesuit, either."

"And you think there can't be more than five or six hours before the flow arrives?"

"I'd say that was a very optimistic guess. I'll stop and get a better speed estimate if you want, but won't swear to it."

Rowson thought for a moment.

"No," he said finally, "don't bother. Get back here as soon as you can. We need the tractor and human muscles more than we need even expert guesses." He turned to the operator.

"Zaino, tell all the tractors there'll be no answer from the ship for a while, because no one will be aboard. Then suit up and come outside." He was gone.

★ ★ ★

Ten minutes later, six human beings and a tractor were assembled in the flame-lit near-darkness outside the ship. The cloud had spread to the horizon, and the sun was gone. Burkett and Hargedon had arrived, but Rowson wasted no time on congratulations.

"We have work to do. It will be easy enough to keep the lava from the ship, since there seems to be a foot or more of ash on the ground and a touch of main drive would push it into a ringwall around us, but that's not the main problem. We have to keep it from reaching the chasm anywhere south of us, since that's the way the others will be coming. If they're cut off, they're dead. It will be brute work. We'll use the tractor any way we can think of. Unfortunately it has no plough attachment, and I can't think of anything aboard which could be turned into one. You have shovels, such as they are. The ash is light, especially here, but there's a mile and a half of dam to be built. I don't see how it can possibly be done . . . but it's going to be."

"Come on, Arnie! You're young and strong," came the voice of the mineralogist. "You should be able to lift as much of this stuff as I can. I understand you were lucky enough to get hold of Eileen—have you asked for the bonus yet?—but your work isn't done."

"It wasn't luck," Zaino retorted. Burkett, in spite of her voice, seemed much less of a schoolmistress when encased in a spacesuit and carrying a shovel, so he was able to talk back to her. "I was simply alert enough to make use of existing conditions, which I had to observe for myself in spite of all the scientists around. I'm charging the achievement to my regular salary. I saw—"

He stopped suddenly, both with tongue and shovel. Then, "Captain!"

"What is it?"

"The only reason we're starting this wall here is to keep well ahead of the flow so we can work as long as possible, isn't it?"

"Yes, I suppose so. I never thought of trying anywhere else. The valley would mean a much shorter dam, but if the flow isn't through it by now it would be before we could get there—oh! Wait a minute!"

"Yes, sir. You can put the main switch anywhere in a D.C. circuit. Where are the seismology stores we never had to use?"

Four minutes later the tractor set out from the *Albireo*, carrying Rowson and Zaino. Six minutes after that it stopped at the base of the ash cone which formed the north side of the valley from which the lava was coming. They parked a quarter of the way around the cone's base from the emerging flood and started to climb on foot, both carrying burdens.

Forty-seven minutes later they returned empty-handed to the vehicle, to find that it had been engulfed by the spreading liquid.

With noticeable haste they floundered through the loose ash a few yards above the base until they had outdistanced the glowing menace, descended and started back across the plain to where they knew the ship to be, though she was invisible through the falling detritus. Once they had to detour around a crack. Once they encountered one which widened towards the chasm on their right, and they knew a detour would be impossible. Leaping it seemed impossible, too, but they did it. Thirty seconds after this, forty minutes after finding the tractor destroyed, the landscape was bathed in a magnesium-white glare as the two one-and-a-half kiloton charges planted just inside the crater rim let go.

"Should we go back and see if it worked?" asked Zaino.

"What's the use? The only other charges we had were in the tractor. Thank goodness they were nuclear instead of H.E. If it didn't work we'd have more trouble to get back than we're having now."

"If it didn't work, is there any point in going back?"

"Stop quibbling and keep walking. Dr. Burkett, are you listening?"

"Yes, Captain."

"We're fresh out of tractors, but if you want to try it on foot you might start a set of flow measures on the lava. Arnie wants to know whether our landslide slid properly."

However, the two were able to tell for themselves before getting back to the *Albireo.*

The flow didn't stop all at once, of course; but with the valley feeding it blocked off by a pile of volcanic ash four hundred feet high on one side, nearly fifty on the other and more than a quarter of a mile long, its enthusiasm quickly subsided. It was thin, fluid stuff, as Burkett had noted; but as it spread it cooled, and as it cooled it thickened.

Six hours after the blast it had stopped with its nearest lobe almost a mile from the ship, less than two feet thick at the edge.

When Markidian's tractor arrived, Burkett was happily trying to analyse samples of the flow, and less happily speculating on how long it would be before the entire area would be blown off the planet. When Marini's and Harmon's vehicles arrived, almost together, the specimens had been loaded and everything stowed for acceleration. Sixty seconds after the last person was aboard, the *Albireo* left Mercury's surface at two gravities.

The haste, it turned out, wasn't really necessary. She had been in parking orbit nearly forty-five hours before the first of the giant volcanoes reached its climax, and the one beside their former site was not the first. It was the fourth.

"And that seems to be that," said Camille Burkett rather tritely as they drifted a hundred miles above the little world's surface. "Just a belt of white-hot calderas all around the planet. Pretty, if you like symmetry."

"I like being able to see it from this distance," replied Zaino, floating weightless beside her. "By the way, how much bonus should I ask for getting that idea of putting the seismic charges to use after all?"

"I wouldn't mention it. Any one of us might have thought of that. We all knew about them."

"Anyone *might* have. Let's speculate on how long it would have been before anyone *did*."

"It's still not like the other idea, which involved your own specialty. I still don't see what made you suppose that the gas pillar from the volcano would be heavily charged enough to reflect your radio beam. How did that idea strike you?"

Zaino thought back, and smiled a little as the picture of lightning blazing around pillar, cloud and mountain rose before his eyes.

"You're not quite right," he said. "I was worried about it for a while, but it didn't actually strike me."

It fell rather flat; Camille Burkett, Ph.D., had to have it explained to her.

Drunkboat

CORDWAINER SMITH

The late Cordwainer Smith—in "real" life Dr. Paul M. A. Linebarger, scholar, states-man, and author of the definitive text (still taught from today) on the art of psycho-logical warfare—was a writer of enormous talents who, from 1948 until his untimely death in 1966, produced a double handful of some of the best short fiction this genre has ever seen: "Alpha Ralpha Boulevard," "A Planet Named Shayol," "On the Storm Planet," "The Ballad of Lost C'Mell," "The Dead Lady of Clown Town," "The Game of Rat and Dragon," "The Lady Who Sailed *The Soul*," "Under Old Earth," and "Scanners Live in Vain," as well as a large number of lesser, but still fascinating, stories, all twisted and blended and woven into an interrelated tapestry of incred-ible lushness and intricacy. Smith created a baroque cosmology unrivaled even today for its scope and complexity: a millennia-spanning Future History, logically outlandish and elegantly strange, set against a vivid, richly colored, mythically in-tense universe where animals assume the shape of men, vast planoform ships whis-per through multidimensional space, immense sick sheep are the most valuable objects in the universe, immortality can be bought, and the mysterious Lords of the Instrumentality rule a hunted Earth too old for history. . . .

It is a cosmology that looks as evocative and bizarre today in the 1990s as it did in the 1960s—certainly for sheer sweep and daring of conceptualization in its vision of how different and *strange* the future will be it rivals any contemporary vision conjured up by Young Turks such as Bruce Sterling and Greg Bear, and I suspect that it is timeless.

In the bizarre and dazzling story that follows, decades ahead of its time both stylistically and conceptually (I suspect that it would still be considered cutting-edge even here at the brink of a new century, in fact), Smith sends an explorer off on a voyage unlike anyone has ever made before, in a vessel unlike any explorer has ever used—his own naked flesh and blood and bone.

Cordwainer Smith's books include the novel *Norstrilia* and the collections *Space Lords*—one of the landmark collections of the genre—The Best of Cordwainer Smith, Quest of the Three Worlds, Stardreamer, You Will Never Be the Same, and

The Instrumentality of Mankind. As Felix C. Forrest, he wrote two mainstream novels, *Ria* and *Carola*, and as Carmichael Smith he wrote the thriller *Atomsk*.

His most recent book is the posthumous collection *The Rediscovery of Man: The Complete Short Science Fiction of Cordwainer Smith* (NESFA Press, P.O. Box 809, Framingham, MA 07101-0203), a huge book that collects almost all of his short fiction and will certainly stand as one of the very best collections of the decade—and a book that belongs in every good science-fiction collection.

Perhaps it is the saddest, maddest, wildest story in the whole long history of space. It is true that no one else had ever done anything like it before, to travel at such a distance, and at such speeds, and by such means. The hero looked like such an ordinary man—when people looked at him for the first time. The second time, ah! that was different.

And the heroine. Small she was, and ash-blonde, intelligent, perky, and hurt. Hurt—yes, that's the right word. She looked as though she needed comforting or helping, even when she was perfectly all right. Men felt more like men when she was near. Her name was Elizabeth.

Who would have thought that her name would ring loud and clear in the wild vomiting nothing which made up space³?

He took an old, old rocket, of an ancient design. With it he outflew, outfled, outjumped all the machines which had ever existed before. You might almost think that he went so fast that he shocked the great vaults of the sky, so that the ancient poem might have been written for him alone. "All the stars threw down their spears and watered heaven with their tears."

Go he did, so fast, so far that people simply did not believe it at first. They thought it was a joke told by men, a farce spun forth by rumor, a wild story to while away the summer afternoon.

We know his name now.

And our children and their children will know it for always.

Rambo. Artyr Rambo of Earth Four.

But he followed his Elizabeth where no space was. He went where men could not go, had not been, did not dare, would not think.

He did all this of his own free will.

Of course people thought it was a joke at first, and got to making up silly songs about the reported trip.

"Dig me a hole for that reeling feeling . . . !" sang one.

"Push me the call for the umber number . . . !" sang another.

"Where is the ship of the ochre joker . . . ?" sang a third.

Then people everywhere found it was true. Some stood stock still and got gooseflesh. Others turned quickly to everyday things. Space³ had been found, and it had been pierced. Their world would never be the same again. The solid rock had become an open door.

Space itself, so clean, so empty, so tidy, now looked like a million million light-years of tapioca pudding—gummy, mushy, sticky, not fit to breathe, not fit to swim in.

How did it happen?

Everybody took the credit, each in his own different way.

1

"He came for me," said Elizabeth. "I died and he came for me because the machines were making a mess of my life when they tried to heal my terrible, useless death."

2

"I went myself," said Rambo. "They tricked me and lied to me and fooled me, but I took the boat and I became the boat and I got there. Nobody made me do it. I was angry, but I went. And I came back, didn't I?"

He too was right, even when he twisted and whined on the green grass of earth, his ship lost in a space so terribly far and strange that it might have been beneath his living hand, or might have been half a galaxy away.

How can anybody tell, with space-three?

It was Rambo who got back, looking for his Elizabeth. He loved her. So the trip was his, and the credit his.

3

But the Lord Crudelta said, many years later, when he spoke in a soft voice and talked confidentially among friends, "The experiment was mine. I designed it. I picked Rambo. I drove the selectors mad, trying to find a man who would meet those specifications. And I had that rocket built to the old, old plans. It was the sort of thing which human beings first used when they jumped out of the air a little bit, leaping like flying fish from one wave to the next and already thinking that they were eagles. If I had used one of the regular planoform ships, it would have disappeared with a sort of reverse gurgle, leaving space milky for a little bit while it faded into nastiness and obliteration. But I did not risk that. I put the rocket on a launching pad. *And the launching pad itself was an interstellar ship!* Since we were using an ancient rocket, we did it up right, with the old, old writing, mysterious letters printed all over the machine. We even had the name of our Organization—I and O and M—for 'the Instrumentality of Mankind' written on it good and sharp.

"How would I know," went on the Lord Crudelta, "that we would succeed more than we wanted to succeed, that Rambo would tear space itself loose from its hinges and leave that ship behind, just because he loved Elizabeth so sharply much, so fiercely much?"

Crudelta sighed.

"I know it and I don't know it. I'm like that ancient man who tried to take a water boat the wrong way around the planet Earth and found a new world instead. Columbus, he was called. And the land, that was Australia or America or something like that. That's what I did. I sent Rambo out in that ancient rocket and he found a way through space³. Now none of us will ever know who might come bulking through the floor or take shape out of the air in front of us."

Crudelta added, almost wistfully: "What's the use of telling the story? Everybody knows it, anyhow. My part in it isn't very glorious. Now the end of it, that's pretty. The bungalow by the waterfall and all the wonderful children that other people gave to them, you could write a poem about that. But the next to the end, how he showed up at the hospital helpless and insane, looking for his own Elizabeth. That was sad and eerie, that was frightening. I'm glad it all came to the happy ending with the bungalow by the waterfall, but it took a crashing long time to get there. And there are parts of it that we will never quite understand, the naked skin against naked space, the eyeballs riding something much faster than light ever was. Do you know what an *aoudad* is? It's an ancient sheep that used to live on Old Earth, and here we are, thousands of years later, with a children's nonsense rhyme about it. The animals are gone but the rhyme remains. It'll be like that with Rambo someday. Everybody will know his name and all about his drunkboat, but they will forget the scientific milestone that he crossed, hunting for Elizabeth in an ancient rocket that couldn't fly from peetle to pootle. . . . Oh, the rhyme? Don't you know that? It's a silly thing. It goes,

> *Point your gun at a murky lurky.*
> *(Now you're talking ham or turkey!)*
> *Shoot a shot at a dying aoudad.*
> *(Don't ask the lady why or how, dad!)*

Don't ask me what 'ham' and 'turkey' are. Probably parts of ancient animals, like beefsteak or sirloin. But the children still say the words. They'll do that with Rambo and his drunken boat some day. They may even tell the story of Elizabeth. But they will never tell the part about how he got to the hospital. That part is too terrible, too real, too sad and wonderful at the end. They found him on the grass. Mind you, naked on the grass, and nobody knew where he had come from!"

4

They found him naked on the grass and nobody knew where he had come from. They did not even know about the ancient rocket which the Lord Crudelta had sent beyond the end of nowhere with the letters, I, O and M written on it. They did not know that this was Rambo, who had gone through space-three. The robots noticed him first and brought him in, photographing everything that they did. They had been programmed that way, to make sure that anything unusual was kept in the records.

Then the nurses found him in an outside room.

They assumed that he was alive, since he was not dead, but they could not prove that he was alive, either.

That heightened the puzzle.

The doctors were called in. Real doctors, not machines. They were very important men. Citizen Doctor Timofeyev, Citizen Doctor Grosbeck and the director himself, Sir and Doctor Vomact. They took the case.

(Over on the other side of the hospital Elizabeth waited, unconscious, and

obody knew it at all. Elizabeth, for whom he had jumped space, and pierced the stars, but nobody knew it yet!)

The young man could not speak. When they ran eyeprints and fingerprints through the Population Machine, they found that he had been bred on earth itself, but had been shipped out as a frozen and unborn baby to Earth Four. At tremendous cost, they queried Earth Four with an "instant message," only to discover that the young man who lay before them in the hospital had been lost from an experimental ship on an intergalactic trip.

Lost.

No ship and no sign of ship.

And here he was.

They stood at the edge of space, and did not know what they were looking at. They were doctors and it was their business to repair or rebuild people, not to ship them around. How should such men know about space^3 when they did not even know about space^2 except for the fact that people got on the planoform ships and made trips through it? They were looking for sickness when their eyes saw engineering. They treated him when he was well.

All he needed was time, to get over the shock of the most tremendous trip ever made by a human being, but the doctors did not know that and they tried to rush his recovery.

When they put clothes on him, he moved from coma to a kind of mechanical spasm and tore the clothing off. Once again stripped, he lay himself roughly on the floor and refused food or speech.

They fed him with needles while the whole energy of space, had they only known it, was radiating out of his body in new forms.

They put him all by himself in a locked room and watched him through the peephole.

He was a nice-looking young man, even though his mind was blank and his body was rigid and unconscious. His hair was very fair and his eyes were light blue but his face showed character—a square chin; a handsome, resolute, sullen mouth; old lines in the face which looked as though, when conscious, he must have lived many days or months on the edge of rage.

When they studied him the third day in the hospital, their patient had not changed at all.

He had torn off his pajamas again and lay naked, face down, on the floor.

His body was as immobile and tense as it had been on the day before.

(One year later, this room was going to be a museum with a bronze sign reading, "Here lay Rambo after he left the Old Rocket for Space Three," but the doctors still had no idea of what they were dealing with.)

His face was turned so sharply to the left that the neck muscles showed. His right arm stuck out straight from the body. The left arm formed an exact right angle from the body, with the left forearm and hand pointing rigidly upward at 90° from the upper arm. The legs were in the grotesque parody of a running position.

Doctor Grosbeck said, "It looks to me like he's swimming. Let's drop him in a tank of water and see if he moves." Grosbeck sometimes went in for drastic solutions to problems.

Timofeyev took his place at the peephole. "Spasm, still," he murmured. "I hope the poor fellow is not feeling pain when his cortical defenses are down. How can a man fight pain if he does not even know what he is experiencing?"

"And you, Sir and Doctor," and Grosbeck to Vomact, "what do you see?"

Vomact did not need to look. He had come early and had looked long and quietly at the patient through the peephole before the other doctors arrived. Vomact was a wise man, with good insight and rich intuitions. He could guess in an hour more than a machine could diagnose in a year; he was already beginning to understand that this was a sickness which no man had ever had before. Still, there were remedies waiting.

The three doctors tried them.

They tried hypnosis, electrotherapy, message, subsonics, atropine, surgital, a whole family of the digitalinids, and some quasi-narcotic viruses which had been grown in orbit where they mutated fast. They got the beginning of a response when they tried gas hypnosis combined with an electronically amplified telepath; this showed that something still went on inside the patient's mind. Otherwise the brain might have seemed to be mere fatty tissue, without a nerve in it. The other attempts had shown nothing. The gas showed a faint stirring away from fear and pain. The telepath reported glimpses of unknown skies. (The doctors turned the telepath over to the Space Police promptly, so they could try to code the star patterns which he had seen in the patient's mind, but the patterns did not fit. The telepath, though a keen-witted man, could not remember them in enough detail for them to be scanned against the samples of piloting sheets.)

The doctors went back to their drugs and tried ancient, simple remedies— morphine and caffeine to counteract each other, and a rough massage to make him dream again, so that the telepath could pick it up.

There was no further result that day, or the next.

Meanwhile the Earth authorities were getting restless. They thought, quite rightly, that the hospital had done a good job of proving that the patient had not been on Earth until a few moments before the robots found him on the grass. How had he gotten on the grass?

The airspace of earth reported no intrusion at all, no vehicle marking a blazing arc of air incandescing against metal, no whisper of the great forces which drove a planoform ship through space[2].

(Crudelta, using faster-than-light ships, was creeping slow as a snail back toward Earth, racing his best to see if Rambo had gotten there first.)

On the fifth day, there was the beginning of a breakthrough.

5

Elizabeth had passed.

This was found out only much later, by a careful check of the hospital records.

The doctors only knew this much:

Patients had been moved down the corridor, sheet-covered figures immobile on wheeled beds.

Suddenly the beds stopped rolling.

A nurse screamed.

The heavy steel-and-plastic wall was bending inward. Some slow, silent force was pushing the wall into the corridor itself.

The wall ripped.

A human hand emerged.

One of the quick-witted nurses screamed,

"*Push* those beds! *Push* them out of the way."

The nurses and robots obeyed.

The beds rocked like a group of boats crossing a wave when they came to the place where the floor, bonded to the wall, had bent upward to meet the wall as it tore inward. The peach-colored glow of the lights flicked. Robots appeared.

A second human hand came through the wall. Pushing in opposite directions, the hands tore the wall as though it had been wet paper.

The patient from the grass put his head through.

He looked blindly up and down the corridor, his eyes not quite focusing, his skin glowing a strange red-brown from the burns of open space.

"No," he said. Just that one word.

But that "No" was heard. Though the volume was not loud, it carried through the hospital. The internal telecommunications system relayed it. Every switch in the place went negative. Frantic nurses and robots, with even the doctors helping them, rushed to turn all the machines back on—the pumps, the ventilators, the artificial kidneys, the brain re-recorders, even the simple air engines which kept the atmosphere clean.

Far overhead an aircraft spun giddily. Its "off" switch, surrounded by triple safeguards, had suddenly been thrown into the negative position. Fortunately the robot-pilot got it going again before crashing into earth.

The patient did not seem to know that his word had this effect.

(*Later the world knew that this was part of the "drunkboat effect." The man himself had developed the capacity for using his neurophysical system as a machine control.*)

In the corridor, the machine robot who served as policeman arrived. He wore sterile, padded velvet gloves with a grip of sixty metric tons inside his hands. He approached the patient. The robot had been carefully trained to recognize all kinds of danger from delirious or psychotic humans; later he reported that he had an input of "danger, extreme" on every band of sensation. He had been expecting to seize the prisoner with irreversible firmness and to return him to his bed, but with this kind of danger sizzling in the air, the robot took no chances. His wrist itself contained a hypodermic pistol which operated on compressed argon.

He reached out toward the unknown, naked man who stood in the big torn gap of the wall. The wrist-weapon hissed and a sizeable injection of condamine, the most powerful narcotic in the known universe, spat its way through the skin of Rambo's neck. The patient collapsed.

The robot picked him up gently and tenderly, lifted him through the torn wall, pushed the door open with a kick which broke the lock and put the patient back on his bed. The robot could hear doctors coming, so he used his enormous hands to pat the steel wall back into its proper shape. Work-robots or underpeople could finish the job later, but meanwhile it looked better to have that part of the building set at right angles again.

Doctor Vomact arrived, followed closely by Grosbeck.

"What happened?" he yelled, shaken out of a lifelong calm. The robot pointed at the ripped wall.

"He tore it open. I put it back," said the robot.

The doctors turned to look at the patient. He had crawled off his bed again and was on the floor, but his breathing was light and natural.

"What did you give him?" cried Vomact to the robot.

"Condamine," said the robot, "according to rule 47-B. The drug is not to be mentioned outside the hospital."

"I know that," said Vomact absent-mindedly and a little crossly. "You can go along now. Thank you."

"It is not usual to thank robots," said the robot, "but you can read a commendation into my record if you want to."

"Get the blazes out of here!" shouted Vomact at the officious robot.

The robot blinked. "There are no blazes but I have the impression you mean me. I shall leave, with your permission." He jumped with odd gracefulness around the two doctors, fingered the broken doorlock absentmindedly, as though he might have wished to repair it, and then, seeing Vomact glare at him, left the room completely.

A moment later soft muted thuds began. Both doctors listened a moment and then gave up. The robot was out in the corridor, gently patting the steel floor back into shape. He was a tidy robot, probably animated by an amplified chicken-brain, and when he got tidy he became obstinate.

"Two questions, Grosbeck," said the Sir and Doctor Vomact.

"Your service, sir!"

"Where was the patient standing when he pushed the wall into the corridor, and how did he get the leverage to do it?"

Grosbeck narrowed his eyes in puzzlement. "Now that you mention it, I have no idea of how he did it. In fact, he could not have done it. But he has. And the other question?"

"What do you think of condamine?"

"Dangerous, of course, as always. Addiction can—"

"Can you have addiction with no cortical activity?" interrupted Vomact.

"Of course," said Grosbeck promptly. "Tissue addiction."

"Look for it, then," said Vomact.

Grosbeck knelt beside the patient and felt with his fingertips for the muscle endings. He felt where they knotted themselves into the base of the skull, the tips of the shoulders, the striped area of the back.

When he stood up there was a look of puzzlement on his face. "I never felt a human body like this one before. I am not even sure that it *is* human any longer."

Vomact said nothing. The two doctors confronted one another. Grosbeck fidgeted under the calm stare of the senior man. Finally he blurted out,

"Sir and Doctor, I know what we *could* do."

"And that," said Vomact levelly, without the faintest hint of encouragement or of warning, "is what?"

"It wouldn't be the first time that it's been done in a hospital."

"What?" said Vomact, his eyes—those dreaded eyes!—making Grosbeck say what he did not want to say.

Grosbeck flushed. He leaned toward Vomact so as to whisper, even though there was no one standing near them. His words, when they came, had the hasty indecency of a lover's improper suggestion,

"Kill the patient, Sir and Doctor. Kill him. We have plenty of records of him. We can get a cadaver out of the basement and make it into a good simulacrum. Who knows what we will turn loose among mankind if we let him get well?"

"Who knows?" said Vomact without tone or quality to his voice. "But citizen and doctor, what is the twelfth duty of a physician?"

" 'Not to take the law into his own hands, keeping healing for the healers and giving to the state or the Instrumentality whatever properly belongs to the state or the Instrumentality.' " Grosbeck sighed as he retracted his own suggestion. "Sir and Doctor, I take it back. It wasn't medicine which I was talking about. It was government and politics which were really in my mind."

"And now . . . ?" asked Vomact.

"Heal him, or let him be until he heals himself."

"And which would you do?"

"I'd try to heal him."

"How?" said Vomact.

"Sir and Doctor," cried Grosbeck, "do not ride my weaknesses in this case! I know that you like me because I am a bold, confident sort of man. Do not ask me to be myself when we do not even know where this body came from. If I were bold as usual, I would give him typhoid and condamine, stationing telepaths nearby. But this is something new in the history of man. We are people and perhaps he is not a person any more. Perhaps he represents the combination of people with some kind of a new force. How did he get here from the far side of nowhere? How many million times has he been enlarged or reduced? We do not know what he is or what has happened to him. How can we treat a man when we are treating the cold of space, the heat of suns, the frigidity of distance? We know what to do with flesh, but this is not quite flesh any more. Feel him yourself, Sir and Doctor! You will touch something which nobody has ever touched before."

"I have," Vomact declared, "already felt him. You are right. We will try typhoid and condamine for half a day. Twelve hours from now let us meet each other at this place. I will tell the nurses and the robots what to do in the interim."

They both gave the red-tanned spread-eagled figure on the floor a parting glance. Grosbeck looked at the the body with something like distaste mingled with fear; Vomact was expressionless, save for a wry wan smile of pity.

At the door the head nurse awaited them. Grosbeck was surprised at his chief's orders.

"Ma'am and nurse, do you have a weapon-proof vault in this hospital?"

"Yes, sir," she said. "We used to keep our records in it until we telemetered all our records into Computer Orbit. Now it is dirty and empty."

"Clean it out. Run a ventilator tube into it. Who is your military protector?"

"My what?" she cried, in surprise.

"Everyone on Earth has military protection. Where are the forces, the soldiers, who protect this hospital of yours?"

"My Sir and Doctor!" she called out, "my Sir and Doctor! I'm an old woman and I have been allowed to work here for three hundred years. But I never thought of that idea before. Why would I need soldiers?"

"Find who they are and ask them to stand by. They are specialists too, with a different kind of art from ours. Let them stand by. They may be needed before this day is out. Give my name as authority to their lieutenant or sergeant. Now here is the medication which I want you to apply to this patient."

Her eyes widened as he went on talking, but she was a disciplined woman and she nodded as she heard him out, point by point. Her eyes looked very sad and weary at the end but she was a trained expert herself and she had enormous respect for the skill and wisdom of the Sir and Doctor Vomact. She also had a warm, feminine pity for the motionless young male figure on the floor, swimming forever on the heavy floor, swimming between archipelagoes which no man living had ever dreamed before.

6

Crisis came that night.

The patient had worn handprints into the inner wall of the vault, but he had not escaped.

The soldiers, looking oddly alert with their weapons gleaming in the bright corridor of the hospital, were really very bored, as soldiers always become when they are on duty with no action.

Their lieutenant was keyed up. The wirepoint in his hand buzzed like a dangerous insect. Sir and Doctor Vomact, who knew more about weapons than the soldiers thought he knew, saw that the wirepoint was set to HIGH, with a capacity of paralyzing people five stories up, five stories down or a kilometer sideways. He said nothing. He merely thanked the lieutenant and entered the vault, closely followed by Grosbeck and Timofeyev.

The patient swam here too.

He had changed to an arm-over-arm motion, kicking his legs against the floor. It was as though he had swum on the other floor with the sole purpose of staying afloat, and had now discovered some direction in which to go, albeit very slowly. His motions were deliberate, tense, rigid, and so reduced in time that it seemed as though he hardly moved at all. The ripped pajamas lay on the floor beside him.

Vomact glanced around, wondering what forces the man could have used to make those handprints on the steel wall. He remembered Grosbeck's warning that the patient should die, rather than subject all mankind to new and unthought risks, but though he shared the feeling, he could not condone the recommendation.

Almost irritably, the great doctor thought to himself—where could the man be going?

(To Elizabeth, the truth was, to Elizabeth, now only sixty meters away. Not till much later did people understand what Rambo had been trying to do—crossing sixty mere meters to reach his Elizabeth when he had already jumped an un-count of light-years to return to her. To his own, his dear, his well-beloved who needed him!)

The condamine did not leave its characteristic mark of deep lassitude and glowing skin: perhaps the typhoid was successfully contradicting it. Rambo did seem more lively than before. The name had come through on the regular message system, but it still did not mean anything to the Sir and Doctor Vomact. It would. It would.

Meanwhile the other two doctors, briefed ahead of time, got busy with the apparatus which the robots and the nurses had installed.

Vomact murmured to the others. "I think he's better off. Looser all around. I'll try shouting."

So busy were they that they just nodded.

Vomact screamed at the patient, "Who are you? What are you? Where do you come from?"

The sad blue eyes of the man on the floor glanced at him with a surprisingly quick glance, but there was no other real sign of communication. The limbs kept up their swim against the rough concrete floor of the vault. Two of the bandages which the hospital staff had put on him had worn off again. The right knee, scraped and bruised, deposited a sixty-centimeter trail of blood—some old and black and coagulated, some fresh, new and liquid—on the floor as it moved back and forth.

Vomact stood up and spoke to Grosbeck and Timofeyev. "Now," he said, "let us see what happens when we apply the pain."

The two stepped back without being told to do so.

Timofeyev waved his hand at a small white-enamelled orderly-robot who stood in the doorway.

The pain net, a fragile cage of wires, dropped down from the ceiling.

It was Vomact's duty, as senior doctor, to take the greatest risk. The patient was wholly encased by the net of wires, but Vomact dropped to his hands and knees, lifted the net at one corner with his right hand, thrust his own head into it next to the head of the patient. Doctor Vomact's robe trailed on the clean concrete, touching the black old stains of blood left from the patient's "swim" throughout the night.

Now Vomact's mouth was centimeters from the patient's ear.

Said Vomact, "Oh."

The net hummed.

The patient stopped his slow motion, arched his back, looked steadfastly at the doctor.

Doctors Grosbeck and Timofeyev could see Vomact's face go white with the impact of the pain machine, but Vomact kept his voice under control and said evenly and loudly to the patient,

"Who-are-you?"

The patient said flatly, "Elizabeth."

The answer was foolish but the tone was rational.

Vomact pulled his head out from under the net, shouting again at the patient, *"Who—are—you?"*

The naked man replied speaking very clearly:

> *"Chwinkle, chwinkle, little chweeble,*
> *I am feeling very feeble!"*

Vomact frowned and murmured to the robot, "More pain. Turn it up to pain ultimate."

The body threshed under the net, trying to resume its swim on the concrete.

A loud wild braying cry came from the victim under the net. It sounded like a screamed distortion of the name Elizabeth, echoing out from endless remoteness.

It did not make sense.

Vomact screamed back, "Who—are-you?"

With unexpected clarity and resonance, the voice came back to the three doctors from the twisting body under the net of pain:

"I'm the shipped man, the ripped man, the gypped man, the dipped man, the hipped man, the tripped man, the tipped man, the slipped man, the flipped man, the nipped man, the ripped man, the clipped man—aah!" His voice choked off with a cry and he went back to swimming on the floor, despite the intensity of the pain net immediately above him.

The doctor lifted his hand. The pain net stopped buzzing and lifted high into the air.

He felt the patient's pulse. It was quick. He lifted an eyelid. The reactions were much closer to normal.

"Stand back," he said to the others.

"Pain on both of us," he said to the robot.

The net came down on the two of them.

"Who are you?" shrieked Vomact, right into the patient's ear, holding the man halfway off the floor and not quite knowing whether the body which tore steel walls might not, somehow, tear both of them apart as they stood.

The man babbled back at him: "I'm the most man, the post man, the host man, the ghost man, the coast man, the boast man, the dosed man, the grossed man, the toast man, the roast man, no! no! no!"

He struggled in Vomact's arms. Grosbeck and Timofeyev stepped forward to rescue their chief when the patient added, very calmly and clearly,

"Your procedure is all right, doctor, whoever you are. More fever, please. More pain, please. Some of that dope to fight the pain. You're pulling me back. I know I am on Earth. Elizabeth is near. For the love of God, get me Elizabeth! But don't rush me. I need days and days to get well."

The rationality was so startling that Grosbeck, without waiting for orders from Vomact, as chief doctor, ordered the pain net lifted.

The patient began babbling again: "I'm the three man, the he man, the tree man, the me man, the three man, the three man . . ." His voice faded and he slumped unconscious.

Vomact walked out of the vault. He was a little unsteady.

His colleagues took him by the elbows.

He smiled wanly at them: "I wish it were lawful. . . . I could use some of that condamine myself. No wonder the pain nets wake the patients up and even make dead people do twitches! Get me some liquor. My heart is old."

Grosbeck sat him down while Timofeyev ran down the corridor in search of medicinal liquor.

Vomact murmured, "How are we going to find his Elizabeth? There must be millions of them. And he's from Earth Four too."

"Sir and Doctor, you have worked wonders," said Grosbeck. "To go under the net. To take those chances. To bring him to speech. I will never see anything like it again. It's enough for any one lifetime, to have seen this day."

"But what do we do next?" asked Vomact wearily, almost in confusion. That particular question needed no answer.

7

The Lord Crudelta had reached Earth.

His pilot landed the craft and fainted at the controls with sheer exhaustion.

Of the escort cats, who had ridden alongside the space craft in the miniature space-ships, three were dead, one was comatose and the fifth was spitting and raving.

When the port authorities tried to slow the Lord Crudelta down to ascertain his authority, he invoked Top Emergency, took over the command of troops in the name of the Instrumentality, arrested everyone in sight but the troop commander, and requisitioned the troop commander to take him to the hospital. The computers at the port had told him that one Rambo, "sans origine," had arrived mysteriously on the grass of a designated hospital.

Outside the hospital, the Lord Crudelta invoked Top Emergency again, placed all armed men under his own command, ordered a recording monitor to cover all his actions if he should later be channeled into a court-martial, and arrested everyone in sight.

The tramp of heavily armed men, marching in combat order, overtook Timofeyev as he hurried back to Vomact with a drink. The men were jogging along on the double. All of them had live helmets and their wirepoints were buzzing.

Nurses ran forward to drive the intruders out, ran backward when the sting of the stun-rays brushed cruelly over them. The whole hospital was in an uproar.

The Lord Crudelta later admitted that he had made a serious mistake.

The Two Minutes' War broke out immediately.

You have to understand the pattern of the Instrumentality to see how it happened. The Instrumentality was a self-perpetuating body of men with enormous powers and a strict code. Each was a plenum of the low, the middle and the high justice. Each could do anything he found necessary or proper to maintain the Instrumentality and to keep the peace between the worlds. But if he made a mistake or committed a wrong—ah, then, it was suddenly different. Any Lord could put another Lord to death in an emergency, but he was assured of death and disgrace himself if he assumed this responsibility. The only difference between ratification and repudiation came in the fact that Lords who killed in an emergency and were proved wrong were marked down on a very shameful list, while those who killed other Lords rightly (as later examination might prove) were listed on a very honorable list, but still killed.

With three Lords, the situation was different. Three Lords made an emergency court; if they acted together, acted in good faith, and reported to the computers of the Instrumentality, they were exempt from punishment, though not from blame or even reduction to citizen status. Seven Lords, or all the Lords on a given planet at a given moment, were beyond any criticism except that of a dignified reversal of their actions should a later ruling prove them wrong.

This was all the business of the Instrumentality. The Instrumentality had the perpetual slogan: "Watch, but do not govern; stop war but do not wage it; protect, but do not control; and first, survive!"

The Lord Crudelta had seized the troops—not his troops, but the light regular troops of Manhome Government—because he feared that the greatest danger in the history of man might come from the person whom he himself had sent through space.

He never expected that the troops would be plucked out from his command— an overriding power reinforced by robotic telepathy and the incomparable communications net, both open and secret, reinforced by thousands of years in trickery, defeat, secrecy, victory, and sheer experience, which the Instrumentality had perfected since it emerged from the Ancient Wars.

Overriding, overridden!

These were the commands which the Instrumentality had used before recorded time began. Sometimes they suspended their antagonists on points of law, sometimes by the deft and deadly insertion of weapons, most often by cutting in on other peoples' mechanical and social controls and doing their will, only to drop the controls as suddenly as they had taken them.

But not Crudelta's hastily-called troops.

8

The war broke out with a change of pace.

Two squads of men were moving into that part of the hospital where Elizabeth lay, waiting the endless returns to the jelly-baths which would rebuild her poor ruined body.

The squads changed pace.

The survivors could not account for what happened.

They all admitted to great mental confusion—afterward.

At the time it seemed that they had received a clear, logical command to turn and to defend the women's section by counterattacking their own main battalion right in their rear.

The hospital was a very strong building. Otherwise it would have melted to the ground or shot up in flame.

The leading soldiers suddenly turned around, dropped for cover and blazed their wirepoints at the comrades who followed them. The wirepoints were cued to organic material, though fairly harmless to inorganic. They were powered by the power relays which every soldier wore on his back.

In the first ten seconds of the turnaround, twenty-seven soldiers, two nurses, three patients and one orderly were killed. One hundred and nine other people were wounded in that first exchange of fire.

The troop commander had never seen battle, but he had been well trained. He immediately deployed his reserves around the external exits of the building and sent his favorite squad, commanded by a Sergeant Lansdale whom he trusted well, down into the basement, so that it could rise vertically from the basement into the women's quarters and find out who the enemy was.

As yet, he had no idea that it was his own leading troops turning and fighting their comrades.

He testified later, at the trial, that he personally had no sensations of eerie interference with his own mind. He merely knew that his men had unexpectedly come upon armed resistance from antagonists—identity unknown!—who had weapons identical with theirs. Since the Lord Crudelta had brought them along in case there might be a fight with unspecified antagonists, he felt right in assuming that a Lord of the Instrumentality knew what he was doing. This was the enemy all right.

In less than a minute, the two sides had balanced out. The line of fire had moved right into his own force. The lead men, some of whom were wounded, simply turned around and began defending themselves against the men immediately behind them. It was as though an invisible line, moving rapidly, had parted the two sections of the military force.

The oily black smoke of dissolving bodies began to glut the ventilators.

Patients were screaming, doctors cursing, robots stamping around and nurses trying to call each other.

The war ended when the troop commander saw Sergeant Lansdale, whom he himself had sent upstairs, leading a charge out of the women's quarters—directly at his own commander!

The officer kept his head.

He dropped to the floor and rolled sidewise as the air chittered at him, the emanations of Lansdale's wirepoint killing all the tiny bacteria in the air. On his helmet phone he pushed the manual controls to TOP VOLUME and to NON-COMS ONLY and he commanded, with a sudden flash of brilliant mother-wit,

"Good job, Lansdale!"

Lansdale's voice came back as weak as if it had been off-planet, "We'll keep them out of this section yet, sir!"

The troop commander called back very loudly but calmly, not letting on that he thought his sergeant was psychotic.

"Easy now. Hold on. I'll be with you."

He changed to the other channel and said to his nearby men, "Cease fire. Take cover and wait."

A wild scream came to him from the phones.

It was Lansdale. "Sir! Sir! I'm fighting *you*, sir. I just caught on. It's getting me again. Watch out."

The buzz and burr of the weapons suddenly stopped.

The wild human uproar of the hospital continued.

A tall doctor, with the insignia of high seniority, came gently to the troop commander and said,

"You can stand up and take your soldiers out now, young fellow. The fight was a mistake."

"I'm not under your orders," snapped the young officer. "I'm under the Lord Crudelta. He requisitioned this force from the Manhome Government. Who are you?"

"You may salute me, captain," said the doctor, "I am Colonel General Vomact of the Earth Medical Reserve. But you had better not wait for the Lord Crudelta."

"But *where* is he?"

"In my bed," said Vomact.

"Your *bed*?" cried the young officer in complete amazement.

"In bed. Doped the to the teeth. I fixed him up. He was excited. Take your men out. We'll treat the wounded on the lawn. You can see the dead in the refrigerators downstairs in a few minutes, except for the ones that went smoky from direct hits."

"But the fight . . . ?"

"A mistake, young man, or else—"

"Or else what?" shouted the young officer, horrified at the utter mess of his own combat experience.

"Or else a weapon no man has ever seen before. Your troops fought each other. Your command was intercepted."

"I could see that," snapped the officer, "as soon as I saw Lansdale coming at me."

"But do you know what took him over?" said Vomact gently, while taking the officer by the arm and beginning to lead him out of the hospital. The captain went willingly, not noticing where he was going, so eagerly did he watch for the other man's words.

"I think I know," said Vomact. "Another man's dreams. Dreams which have learned how to turn themselves into electricity or plastic or stone. Or anything else. Dreams coming to us out of space three."

The young officer nodded dumbly. This was too much. "Space three?" he murmured. It was like being told that the really alien invaders, whom men had been expecting for fourteen thousand years and had never met, were waiting for him on the grass. Until now space three had been a mathematical idea, a romancer's day-dream, but not a fact.

★ ★ ★

The sir and doctor Vomact did not even ask the young officer. He brushed the young man gently at the nape of the neck and shot him through with tranquilizer. Vomact then led him out to the grass. The young captain stood alone and whistled happily at the stars in the sky. Behind him, his sergeants and corporals were sorting out the survivors and getting treatment for the wounded.

The Two Minutes' War was over.

Rambo had stopped dreaming that his Elizabeth was in danger. He had recognized, even in his deep sick sleep, that the tramping in the corridor was the movement of armed men. His mind had set up defenses to protect Elizabeth. He took over command of the forward troops and set them to stopping the main body. The powers which space^3 had worked into him made this easy for him to do, even though he did not know that he was doing it.

9

"How many dead?" said Vomact to Grosbeck and Timofeyev.

"About two hundred."

"And how many irrecoverable dead?"

"The ones that got turned into smoke. A dozen, maybe fourteen. The other dead can be fixed up, but most of them will have to get new personality prints."

"Do you know what happened?" asked Vomact.

"No, Sir and Doctor," they both chorused.

"I do. I think I do. No, *I know* I do. It's the wildest story in the history of man. Our patient did it—Rambo. He took over the troops and set them against each other. That Lord of the Instrumentality who came charging in—Crudelta. I've known him for a long long time. He's behind this case. He thought that troops would help, not sensing that troops would invite attack upon themselves. And there is something else."

"Yes?" they said, in unison.

"Rambo's woman—the one he's looking for. She must be here."

"Why?" said Timofeyev.

"Because *he's* here."

"You're assuming that he came here because of his own will, Sir and Doctor."

Vomact smiled the wise crafty smile of his family; it was almost a trademark of the Vomact house.

"I am assuming all the things which I cannot otherwise prove.

"First, I assume that he came here naked out of space itself, driven by some kind of force which we cannot even guess.

"Second, I assume he came *here* because he wanted something. A woman named Elizabeth, who must already be here. In a moment we can go inventory all our Elizabeths.

"Third, I assume that the Lord Crudelta knew something about it. He has led troops into the building. He began raving when he saw me. I know hysterical fatigue, as do you, my brothers, so I condamined him for a night's sleep.

"Fourth, let's leave our man alone. There'll be hearings and trials enough, Space knows, when all these events get scrambled out."

Vomact was right.

He usually was.

Trials did follow.

It was lucky that Old Earth no longer permitted newspapers or television news. The population would have been frothed up to riot and terror if they had ever found out what happened at the Old Main Hospital just to the west of Meeya Meefla.

10

Twenty-one days later, Vomact, Timofeyev and Grosbeck were summoned to the trial of the Lord Crudelta. A full panel of seven Lords of the Instrumentality was there to give Crudelta an ample hearing and, if required, a sudden death. The doctors were present both as doctors for Elizabeth and Rambo and as witnesses for the Investigating Lord.

Elizabeth, fresh up from being dead, was as beautiful as a newborn baby in exquisite, adult feminine form. Rambo could not take his eyes off her, but a look of bewilderment went over his face every time she gave him a friendly, calm, remote little smile. (She had been told that she was his girl, and she was prepared to believe it, but she had no memory of him or of anything else more than sixty hours back, when speech had been reinstalled in her mind; and he, for his part, was still thick of speech and subject to strains which the doctors could not quite figure out.)

The investigating Lord was a man named Starmount.

He asked the panel to rise.

They did so.

He faced the Lord Crudelta with great solemnity, "You are obliged, my Lord Crudelta, to speak quickly and clearly to this court."

"Yes, my Lord," he answered.

"We have the summary power."

"You have the summary power. I recognize it."

"You will tell the truth or else you will lie."

"I shall tell the truth or I will lie."

"You may lie, if you wish, about matters of fact and opinion, but you will in no case lie about human relationships. If you do lie, nevertheless, you will ask that your name be entered in the Roster of Dishonor."

"I understand the panel and the rights of this panel. I will lie if I wish—though I don't think I will need to do so—" and here Crudelta flashed a weary intelligent smile at all of them—"but I will not lie about matters of relationship. If I do, I will ask for dishonor."

"You have yourself been well trained as a Lord of the Instrumentality?"

"I have been so trained and I love the Instrumentality well. In fact, I am myself the Instrumentality, as are you, and as are the honorable Lords beside you. I shall behave well, for as long as I live this afternoon."

"Do you credit him, my Lords?" asked Starmount.

The members of the panel nodded their mitred heads. They had dressed ceremonially for the occasion.

"Do you have a relationship to the woman Elizabeth?"

The members of the trial panel caught their breath as they saw Crudelta turn white: "My Lords!" he cried, and answered no further.

"It is the custom," said Starmount firmly, "that you answer promptly or that you die."

The Lord Crudelta got control of himself. "I am answering. I did not know who she was, except for the fact that Rambo loved her. I sent her to Earth from Earth Four, where I then was. Then I told Rambo that she had been murdered and hung desperately at the edge of death, wanting only his help to return to the green fields of life."

Said Starmount: "Was that the truth?"

"My Lord and Lords, it was a lie."

"Why did you tell it?"

"To induce rage in Rambo and to give him an overriding reason for wanting to come to Earth faster than any man has ever come before."

"A-a-ah! A-a-ah!" Two wild cries came from Rambo, more like the call of an animal than like the sound of a man.

Vomact looked at his patient, felt himself beginning to growl with a deep internal rage. Rambo's powers, generated in the depths of space[3], had begun to operate again. Vomact made a sign. The robot behind Rambo had been coded to keep Rambo calm. Though the robot had been enamelled to look like a white gleaming hospital orderly, he was actually a police-robot of high powers, built up with an electronic cortex based on the frozen midbrain of an old wolf. (A wolf was a rare animal, something like a dog.) The robot touched Rambo, who dropped off to sleep. Doctor Vomact felt the anger in his own mind fade away. He lifted his hand gently; the robot caught the signal and stopped applying the narcoleptic radiation. Rambo slept normally; Elizabeth looked worriedly at the man whom she had been told was her own.

The Lords turned back from the glances at Rambo.

Said Starmount, icily: "And why did you do that?"

"Because I wanted him to travel through space-three."

"Why?"

"To show it could be done."

"And do you, my Lord Crudelta, affirm that this man has in fact travelled through space-three?"

"I do."

"Are you lying?"

"I have the right to lie, but I have no wish to do so. In the name of the Instrumentality itself, I tell you that this is the truth."

The panel members gasped. Now there was no way out. Either the Lord Crudelta was telling the truth, *which meant that all former times had come to an end and that a new age had begun for all the kinds of mankind*, or else he was lying in the face of the most powerful form of affirmation which any of them knew.

Even Starmount himself took a different tone. His teasing, restless, intelligent voice took on a new timbre of kindness.

"You do therefore assert that this man has come back from outside our galaxy with nothing more than his own natural skin to cover him? No instruments? No power?"

"I did not say that," said Crudelta. "Other people have begun to pretend I used such words. I tell you, my Lords, that I planoformed for twelve consecutive Earth Days and nights. Some of you may remember where Outpost Baiter Gator is. Well, I had a good Go-captain, and he took me four long jumps beyond there, out into intergalactic space. I left this man there. When I reached Earth, he had been here twelve days, more or less. I have assumed, therefore, that his trip was more or less instantaneous. I was on my way back to Baiter Gator, counting by Earth time, when the doctor here found this man on the grass outside the hospital."

Vomact raised his hand. The Lord Starmount gave him the right to speak, "My Sirs and Lords, we did not find this man on the grass. The robots did, and made a record. But even the robots did not see or photograph his arrival."

"We know that," said Starmount angrily, "and we know that we have been told that nothing came to Earth by any means whatever, in that particular quarter hour. Go on, my Lord Crudelta. What relation are you to Rambo?"

"He is my victim."

"Explain yourself!"

"I computed him out. I asked the machines where I would be most apt to

find a man with a tremendous lot of rage in him, and was informed that on Earth
Four the rage level had been left high because that particular planet had a considerable need for explorers and adventurers, in whom rage was a strong survival trait.
When I got to Earth Four, I commanded the authorities to find out which border
cases had exceeded the limits of allowable rage. They gave me four men. One was
much too large. Two were old. This man was the only candidate for my experiment.
I chose him."

"What did you tell him?"

"Tell him? I told him his sweetheart was dead or dying."

"No, no," said Starmount. "Not at the moment of crisis. What did you tell him
to make him cooperate in the first place?"

"I told him," said the Lord Crudelta evenly, "that I was myself a Lord of the
Instrumentality and that I would kill him myself if he did not obey, and obey
promptly."

"And under what custom or law did you act?"

"Reserved material," said the Lord Crudelta promptly. "There are telepaths
here who are not a part of the Instrumentality. I beg leave to defer until we have
a shielded place."

Several members of the panel nodded and Starmount agreed with them. He
changed the line of questioning.

"You forced this man, therefore, to do something which he did not wish to
do?"

"That is right," said the Lord Crudelta.

"Why didn't you go yourself, if it is that dangerous?"

"My Lords and honorables, it was the nature of the experiment that the ex-
perimenter himself should not be expended in the first try. Artyr Rambo has indeed
travelled through space-three. I shall follow him myself, in due course." (How the
Lord Crudelta did do so is another tale, told about another time.) "If I had gone
and if I had been lost, that would have been the end of the space-three trials. At
least for our time."

"Tell us the exact circumstances under which you last saw Artyr Rambo before
you met after the battle in the old Main Hospital."

"We had put him in a rocket of the most ancient style. We also wrote writing
on the outside of it, just the way the Ancients did when they first ventured into
space. Ah, that was a beautiful piece of engineering and archeology! We copied
everything right down to the correct models of fifteen thousand years ago, when
the Paroskii and Murkins were racing each other into space. The rocket was white,
with a red and white gantry beside it. The letters IOM were on the rocket, not that
the words mattered. The rocket has gone into nowhere, but the passenger sits here.
It rose on a stool of fire. The stool became a column. Then the landing field
disappeared."

"And the landing field," said Starmount quietly, "what was that?"

"A modified planoform ship. We have had ships go milky in space because
they faded molecule by molecule. We have had others disappear utterly. The engineers had changed this around. We took out all the machinery needed for circumnavigation, for survival or for comfort. The landing field was to last three or
four seconds, no more. Instead, we put in fourteen planoform devices, all operating
in tandem, so that the ship would do what other ships do when they planoform—

namely, drop one of our familiar dimensions and pick up a new dimension from some unknown category of space—but do it with such force as to get out of what people call space-two and move over into space-three."

"And space-three, what did you expect of that?"

"I thought that it was universal and instantaneous, in relation to our universe. That everything was equally distant from everything else. That Rambo, wanting to see his girl again, would move in a thousandth of a second from the empty space beyond Outpost Baiter Gator into the hospital where she was."

"And, my Lord Crudelta, what made you think so?"

"A hunch, my Lord, for which you are welcome to kill me."

Starmount turned to the panel. "I suspect, my Lord, that you are more likely to doom him to long life, great responsibility, immense rewards, and the fatigue of being his own difficult and complicated self."

The mitres moved gently and the members of the panel rose.

"You, my Lord Crudelta, will sleep till the trial is finished."

A robot stroked him and he fell asleep.

"Next witness," said the Lord Starmount, "in five minutes."

11

Vomact tried to keep Rambo from being heard as a witness. He argued fiercely with the Lord Starmount in the intermission. "You Lords have shot up my hospital, abducted two of my patients and now you are going to torment both Rambo and Elizabeth. Can't you leave them alone? Rambo is in no condition to give coherent answers and Elizabeth may be damaged if she sees him suffer."

The Lord Starmount said to him, "You have your rules, doctor, and we have ours. This trial is being recorded, inch by inch and moment by moment. Nothing is going to be done to Rambo unless we find that he has planet-killing powers. If that is true, of course, we will ask you to take him back to the hospital and to put him to death very pleasantly. But I don't think it will happen. We want his story so that we can judge my colleague Crudelta. Do you think that the Instrumentality would survive if it did not have fierce internal discipline?"

Vomact nodded sadly; he went back to Grosbeck and Timofeyev, murmuring sadly to them, "Rambo's in for it. There's nothing we could do."

The panel reassembled. They put on their judicial mitres. The lights of the room darkened and the weird blue light of justice was turned on.

The robot orderly helped Rambo to the witness chair.

"You are obliged," said Starmount, "to speak quickly and clearly to this court."

"You're not Elizabeth," said Rambo.

"I am the Lord Starmount," said the investigating Lord, quickly deciding to dispense with the formalities. "Do you know me?"

"No," said Rambo.

"Do you know where you are?"

"Earth," said Rambo.

"Do you wish to lie or to tell the truth?"

"A lie," said Rambo, "is the only truth which men can share with each other, so I will tell you lies, the way we always do."

"Can you report your trip?"

"No."

"Why not, citizen Rambo?"

"Words won't describe it."

"Do you remember your trip?"

"Do you remember your pulse of two minutes ago?" countered Rambo.

"I am not playing with you," said Starmount. "We think you have been space-three and we want you to testify about the Lord Crudelta?"

"Oh!" said Rambo. "I don't like him. I never did like him."

"Will you nevertheless try to tell us what happened also to you?"

"Should I, Elizabeth?" asked Rambo of the girl, who sat in the audience.

She did not stammer. "Yes," she said, in a clear voice which rang through big room. "Tell them, so that we can find our lives again."

"I will tell you," said Rambo.

"When did you last see the Lord Crudelta?"

"When I was stripped and fitted to the rocket, four jumps out beyond Outp Baiter Gator. He was on the ground. He waved good-by to me."

"And then what happened?"

"The rocket rose. It felt very strange, like no craft I had ever been in befo I weighed many, many gravities."

"And then?"

"The engines went on. I was thrown out of space itself."

"What did it seem like?"

"Behind me I left the working ships, the cloth and the food which goes throu space. I went down rivers which did not exist. I felt people around me thoug could not see them, red people shooting arrows at live bodies."

"*Where* were you?" asked a panel member.

"In the winter time where there is no summer. In an emptiness like a chil mind. In peninsulas which had torn loose from the land. And I *was* the ship."

"You were what?" asked the same panel member.

"The rocket nose. The cone. The boat. I was drunk. It was drunk. I was drunkboat myself," said Rambo.

"And where did you go?" resumed Starmount.

"Where crazy lanterns stared with idiot eyes. Where the waves washed ba and forth with the dead of all the ages. Where the stars became a pool and I sw in it. Where blue turns to liquor, stronger than alcohol, wilder than music, f mented with the *red red reds* of love. I saw all the things that men have e thought they saw, but it was me who really saw them. I've heard phosphorescer singing and tides that seemed like crazy cattle clawing their way out of the oce their hooves beating the reefs. You will not believe me, but I found Floridas wil than this, where the flowers had human skins and eyes like big cats."

"What are you talking about?" asked the Lord Starmount.

"What I found in space^3," snapped Artyr Rambo. "Believe it or not. This what I now remember. Maybe it's a dream, but it's all I have. It was years a years and it was the blink of an eye. I dreamed green nights. I felt places whe the whole horizon became one big waterfall. The boat that was me met childr and I showed them El Dorado, where the gold men live. The people drowned space washed gently past me. I was a boat where all the lost space ships lay ruin and still. Seahorses which were not real ran beside me. The summer month came and hammered down the sun. I went past archipelagoes of stars, where the delirious skies opened up for wanderers. I cried for me. I wept for man. I wanted to be the drunkboat sinking. I sank. I fell. It seemed to me that the grass was a lake, where a sad child, on hands and knees, sailed a toy boat as fragile as a butterfly in spring. I can't forget the pride of unremembered flags, the arrogance of prisons which I suspected, the swimming of the businessmen! Then I was on the grass."

"This may have scientific value," said the Lord Starmount, "but it is not of judicial importance. Do you have any comment on what you did during the battle in the hospital?"

Rambo was quick and looked sane: "What I did, I did not do. What I did not do, I cannot tell. Let me go, because I am tired of you and space, big men and big things. Let me sleep and let me get well."

Starmount lifted his hand for silence.

The panel members stared at him.

Only the few telepaths present knew that they had all said, "*Aye. Let the man go. Let the girl go. Let the doctors go.* But bring back the Lord Crudelta later on. He has many troubles ahead of him, and we wish to add to them."

12

Between the Instrumentality, the Manhome Government and the authorities at the Old Main Hospital, everyone wished to give Rambo and Elizabeth happiness.

As Rambo got well, much of his Earth Four memory returned. The trip faded from his mind.

When he came to know Elizabeth, he hated the girl.

This was not his girl—his bold, saucy, Elizabeth of the markets and the valleys, of the snowy hills and the long boat rides. This was somebody meek, sweet, sad and hopelessly loving.

Vomact cured that.

He sent Rambo to the Pleasure City of the Herperides, where bold and talkative women pursued him because he was rich and famous.

In a few weeks—a very few indeed—he wanted *his* Elizabeth, this strange shy girl who had been cooked back from the dead while he rode space with his own fragile bones.

"Tell the truth, darling." He spoke to her once gravely and seriously. "The Lord Crudelta did not arrange the accident which killed you?"

"They say he wasn't there," said Elizabeth. "They say it was an actual accident. I don't know. I will never know."

"It doesn't matter now," said Rambo. "Crudelta's off among the stars, looking for trouble and finding it. We have our bungalow, and our waterfall, and each other."

"Yes, my darling," she said, "each other. And no fantastic Floridas for us."

He blinked at this reference to the past, but he said nothing. A man who has been through space[3] needs very little in life, outside of *not* going back to space[3]. Sometimes he dreamed he was the rocket again, the old rocket taking off on an impossible trip. Let other men follow! he thought, let other men go! I have Elizabeth and I am here.

Becalmed in Hell

LARRY NIVEN

Larry Niven made his first sale to *Worlds of If* magazine in 1964 and soon established himself as one of the best new writers of "hard" science fiction since Robert Heinlein. By the end of the seventies, Niven had won several Hugo and Nebula Awards, published *Ringworld*, one of the most acclaimed technological novels of its decade, and written several best-selling novels in collaboration with Jerry Pournelle, including *The Mote in God's Eye*. Niven's influence can clearly be seen on many of the new writers of the seventies, eighties, and nineties, including authors such as John Varley, Gregory Benford, Stephen Baxter, Paul J. McAuley, G. David Nordley, Geoffrey A. Landis, and many others. Niven's other books include the novels *Protector, World of Ptavvs, A Gift from Earth-Ringworld Engineers, Smoke Ring,* and *Destiny's Road* and the collections *Tales of Known Space, Inconstant Moon, Neutron Star, N-Space,* and *Playground of the Mind.* His most recent book is an omnibus novel/collection, *Rainbow Mars.*

Niven has explored many exotic locales, including the aforementioned Ringworld, the core of the galaxy, and the heart of a neutron star. Here he visits a pair of explorers stranded in the sullen atmosphere of Venus, hot and poisonous enough to put Hell itself to shame, for a lesson in how believing can sometimes make it so—whether you *want* it to or not!

I could feel the heat hovering outside. In the cabin it was bright and dry and cool, almost too cool, like a modern office building in the dead of the summer. Beyond the two small windows it was as black as it ever gets in the solar system, and hot enough to melt lead, at a pressure equivalent to three hundred feet beneath the ocean.

"There goes a fish," I said, just to break the monotony.

"So how's it cooked?"

"Can't tell. It seems to be leaving a trail of breadcrumbs. Fried? Imagine that Eric! A fried jellyfish."

Eric sighed noisily. "Do I have to?"

"You have to. Only way you'll see anything worthwhile in this—this—" Soup? Fog? Boiling maple syrup?

"Searing black calm."

"Right."

"Someone dreamed up that phrase when I was a kid, just after the news of the Mariner II probe. An eternal searing black calm, hot as a kiln, under an atmosphere thick enough to keep any light or any breath of wind from ever reaching the surface."

I shivered. "What's the outside temperature now?"

"You'd rather not know. You've always had too much imagination, Howie."

"I can take it, Doc."

"Six hundred and twelve degrees."

"I can't take it, Doc!"

This was Venus, Planet of Love, favorite of the science-fiction writers of three decades ago. Our ship hung below the Earth-to-Venus hydrogen fuel tank, twenty miles up and all but motionless in the syrupy air. The tank, nearly empty now, made an excellent blimp. It would keep us aloft as long as the internal pressure matched the external. That was Eric's job, to regulate the tank's pressure by regulating the temperature of the hydrogen gas. We had collected air samples after each ten mile drop from three hundred miles on down, and temperature readings for shorter intervals, and we had dropped the small probe. The data we had gotten from the surface merely confirmed in detail our previous knowledge of the hottest world in the solar system.

"Temperature just went up to six-thirteen," said Eric. "Look, are you through bitching?"

"For the moment."

"Good. Strap down. We're taking off."

"Oh frabjous day!" I started untangling the crash webbing over my couch.

"We've done everything we came to do. Haven't we?"

"Am I arguing? Look, I'm strapped down."

"Yeah."

I knew why he was reluctant to leave. I felt a touch of it myself. We'd spent four months getting to Venus in order to spend a week circling her and less than two days in her upper atmosphere, and it seemed a terrible waste of time.

But he was taking too long. "What's the trouble, Eric?"

"You'd rather not know."

He meant it. His voice was a mechanical, inhuman monotone; he wasn't making the extra effort to get human expression out of his "prosthetic" vocal apparatus. Only a severe shock would affect him that way.

"I can take it," I said.

"Okay. I can't feel anything in the ramjet controls. Feels like I've just had a spinal anaesthetic."

The cold in the cabin drained into me, all of it. "See if you can send motor impulses the other way. You could run the rams by guess-and-hope even if you can't feel them."

"Okay." One split second later, "They don't. Nothing happens. Good thinking though."

I tried to think of something to say while I untied myself from the couch. What came out was, "It's been a pleasure knowing you, Eric. I've liked being half of this team, and I still do."

"Get maudlin later. Right now, start checking my attachments. Carefully."

I swallowed my comments and went to open the access door in the cabin's forward wall. The floor swayed ever so gently beneath my feet.

Beyond the four-foot-square access door was Eric. Eric's central nervous system, with the brain perched at the top and the spinal cord coiled in a loose spiral to fit more compactly into the transparent glass-and-sponge-plastic housing. Hundreds of wires from all over the ship led to the glass walls, where they were joined to selected nerves which spread like an electrical network from the central coil of nervous tissue and fatty protective membrane.

Space leaves no cripples; and don't call Eric a cripple, because he doesn't like it. In a way he's the ideal spaceman. His life support system weighs only half of what mine does, and takes up a twelfth as much room. But his other prosthetic aids take up most of the ship. The ramjets were hooked into the last pair of nerve trunks, the nerves which once moved his legs, and dozens of finer nerves in those trunks sensed and regulated fuel feed, ram temperature, differential acceleration, intake aperture dilation, and spark pulse.

These connections were intact. I checked them four different ways without finding the slightest reason why they shouldn't be working.

"Test the others," said Eric.

It took a good two hours to check every trunk nerve connection. They were all solid. The blood pump was chugging along, and the fluid was rich enough, which killed the idea that the ram nerves might have "gone to sleep" from lack of nutrients or oxygen. Since the lab is one of his prosthetic aids, I let Eric analyse his own blood sugar, hoping that the "liver" had goofed and was producing some other form of sugar. The conclusions were appalling. There was nothing wrong with Eric—inside the cabin.

"Eric, you're healthier than I am."

"I could tell. You looked worried, son, and I don't blame you. Now you'll have to go outside."

"I know. Let's dig out the suit."

It was in the emergency tools locker, the Venus suit that was never supposed to be used. NASA had designed it for use at Venusian ground level. Then they had refused to okay the ship below twenty miles until they knew more about the planet. The suit was a segmented armor job. I had watched it being tested in the heat-and-pressure box at Cal Tech, and I knew that the joints stopped moving after five hours, and wouldn't start again until they had been cooled. Now I opened the locker and pulled the suit out by the shoulders and held it in front of me. It seemed to be staring back.

"You still can't feel anything in the ramjets?"

"Not a twinge."

I started to put on the suit, piece by piece like medieval armor. Then I thought of something else. "We're twenty miles up. Are you going to ask me to do a balancing act on the hull?"

"No! Wouldn't think of it. We'll just have to go down."

The lift from the blimp tank was supposed to be constant until takeoff. When the time came Eric could get extra lift by heating the hydrogen to higher pressure then cracking a valve to let the excess out. Of course he'd have to be very careful that the pressure was higher in the tank, or we'd get Venusian air coming in, and the ship would fall instead of rising. Naturally that would be disastrous.

So Eric lowered the tank temperature and cracked the valve, and down we went.

"Of course there's a catch," said Eric.

"I know."

"The ship stood the pressure twenty miles up. At ground level it'll be six times that."

"I know."

We fell fast, with the cabin tilted forward by the drag on our tailfins. The temperature rose gradually. The pressure went up fast. I sat at the window and saw nothing, nothing but black, but I sat there anyway and waited for the window to crack. NASA had refused to okay the ship below twenty miles . . .

Eric said, "The blimp tank's okay, and so's the ship, I think. But will the cabin stand up to it?"

"I wouldn't know."

"Ten miles."

Five hundred miles above us, unreachable, was the atomic ion engine that was to take us home. We couldn't get to it on the chemical rocket alone. The rocket was for use after the air became too thin for the ramjets.

"Four miles. Have to crack the valve again."

The ship dropped.

"I can see ground," said Eric.

I couldn't. Eric caught me straining my eyes and said, "Forget it. I'm using deep infrared, and getting no detail."

"No vast, misty swamps with weird, terrifying monsters and man-eating plants?"

"All I see is hot, bare dirt."

But we were almost down, and there were no cracks in the cabin wall. My neck and shoulder muscles loosened. I turned away from the window. Hours had passed while we dropped through the poisoned, thickening air. I already had most of my suit on. Now I screwed on my helmet and three-finger gantlets.

"Strap down," said Eric. I did.

We bumped gently. The ship tilted a little, swayed back, bumped again. And again, with my teeth rattling and my armor-plated body rolling against the crash webbing. "Damn," Eric muttered. I heard the hiss from above. Eric said, "I don't know how we'll get back up."

Neither did I. The ship bumped hard and stayed down, and I got up and went to the airlock.

"Good luck," said Eric. "Don't stay out too long." I waved at his cabin camera. The outside temperature was seven hundred and thirty.

The outer door opened. My suit refrigerating unit set up a complaining whine. With an empty bucket in each hand, and with my headlamp blazing a way through the black murk, I stepped out onto the right wing.

My suit creaked and settled under the pressure, and I stood on the wing and waited for it to stop. It was almost like being under water. My headlamp beam went out thick enough to be solid, penetrating no more than a hundred feet. The air couldn't have been that opaque, no matter how dense. It must have been full of dust, or tiny droplets of some fluid.

The wing ran back like a knife-edged running board, widening toward the tail until it spread into a tailfin. The two tailfins met back of the fuselage. At the tailfin tip was the ram, a big sculptured cylinder with an atomic engine inside. It wouldn't be hot because it hadn't been used yet, but I had my counter anyway.

I fastened a line to the wing and slid to the ground. As long as we were *here* . . . The ground turned out to be a dry, reddish dirt, crumbly, and so porous that it was almost spongy. Lava etched by chemicals? Almost anything would be corrosive at this pressure and temperature. I scooped one pailful from the surface and another from underneath the first, then climbed up the line and left the buckets on the wing.

The wing was terribly slippery. I had to wear magnetic sandals to stay on. I walked up and back along the two hundred foot length of the ship, making a casual inspection. Neither wing nor fuselage showed damage. Why not? If a meteor or something had cut Eric's contact with his sensors in the rams, there should have been evidence of a break in the surface.

Then, almost suddenly, I realized that there was an alternative.

It was too vague a suspicion to put into words yet, and I still had to finish the inspection. Telling Eric would be very difficult if I was right.

Four inspection panels were set into the wing, well protected from the reentry heat. One was halfway back on the fuselage, below the lower edge of the blimp tank, which was molded to the fuselage in such a way that from the front the ship looked like a dolphin. Two more were in the trailing edge of the tailfin, and the fourth was in the ram itself. All opened, with powered screwdriver on recessed screws, on junctions of the ship's electrical system.

There was nothing out of place under any of the panels. By making and breaking contacts and getting Eric's reactions, I found that his sensation ended somewhere between the second and third inspection panels. It was the same story on the left wing. No external damage, nothing wrong at the junctions. I climbed back to ground and walked slowly beneath the length of each wing, my headlamp tilted up. No damage underneath.

I collected my buckets and went back inside.

"A bone to pick?" Eric was puzzled. "Isn't this a strange time to start an argument? Save it for space. We'll have four months with nothing else to do."

"This can't wait. First of all, did you notice anything I didn't?" He'd been watching everything I saw and did through the peeper in my helmet.

"No. I'd have yelled."

"Okay. Now get this.

"The break in your circuits isn't inside, because you get sensation up to the second wing inspection panels. It isn't outside because there's no evidence of damage, not even corrosion spots. That leaves only one place for the flaw."

"Go on."

"We also have the puzzle of why you're paralyzed in both rams. Why should hey both go wrong at the same time? There's only one place in the ship where he circuits join."

"What? Oh, yes, I see. They join through me."

"Now let's assume for the moment that you're the piece with the flaw in it. You're not a piece of machinery, Eric. If something's wrong with you it isn't medical. That was the first thing we covered. But it could be psychological."

"It's nice to know you think I'm human. So I've slipped a cam, have I?"

"Slightly. I think you've got a case of what used to be called trigger anaesthesia. A soldier who kills too often sometimes finds that his right index finger or even his whole hand has gone numb, as if it were no longer a part of him. Your comment about not being a machine is important, Eric. I think that's the whole problem. You've never really believed that any part of the ship is a part of *you*. That's intelligent, because it's true. Every time the ship is redesigned you get a new set of parts, and it's right to avoid thinking of a change of model as a series of amputations." I'd been rehearsing this speech, trying to put it so that Eric would have no choice but to believe me. Now I know that it must have sounded phony. "But now you've gone too far. Subconsciously you've stopped believing that the cams can *feel* like a part of you, which they were designed to do. So you've persuaded yourself that you don't feel anything."

With my prepared speech done, and nothing left to say, I stopped talking and waited for the explosion.

"You make good sense," said Eric.

I was staggered. "You agree?"

"I didn't say that. You spin an elegant theory, but I want time to think about t. What do we do if it's true?"

"Why . . . I don't know. You'll just have to cure yourself."

"Okay. Now here's *my* idea. I propose that you thought up this theory to relieve yourself of a responsibility for getting us home alive. It puts the whole problem in my lap, metaphorically speaking."

"Oh, for—"

"Shut up. I haven't said you're wrong. That would be an ad hominem argument. We need time to think about this."

It was lights-out, four hours later, before Eric would return to the subject.

"Howie, do me a favor. Assume for awhile that something mechanical is causing all our trouble. I'll assume it's psychosomatic."

"Seems reasonable."

"It is reasonable. What can you do if I've gone psychosomatic? What can I do if it's mechanical? I can't go around inspecting myself. We'd each better stick to what we know."

"It's a deal." I turned him off for the night and went to bed.

But not to sleep.

With the lights off it was just like outside. I turned them back on. It wouldn't wake Eric. Eric never sleeps normally, since his blood doesn't accumulate fatigue poisons, and he'd go mad from being awake all the time if he didn't have a Russian

sleep inducer plate near his cortex. The ship could implode without waking Eri
when his sleep inducer's on. But I felt foolish being afraid of the dark.

While the dark stayed outside it was all right.

But it wouldn't stay there. It had invaded my partner's mind. Because hi
chemical checks guard him against chemical insanities like schizophrenia, we'
assumed he was permanently sane. But how could any prosthetic device protec
him from his own imagination, his own misplaced common sense?

I couldn't keep my bargain. I knew I was right. But what could I do about it

Hindsight is wonderful. I could see exactly what our mistake had been, Eric'
and mine and the hundreds of men who had built his life support after the crash
There was nothing left of Eric then except the intact central nervous system, an
no glands except the pituitary. "We'll regulate his blood composition," they saic
"and he'll always be cool, calm, and collected. No panic reactions from Eric!"

I know a girl whose father had an accident when he was forty-five or so. H
was out with his brother, the girl's uncle, on a fishing trip. They were blind drun
when they started home and the guy was riding on the hood while the brothe
drove. Then the brother made a sudden stop. Our hero left two important gland
on the hood ornament.

The only change in his sex life was that his wife stopped worrying about lat
pregnancy. His *habits* were developed.

Eric doesn't need adrenal glands to be afraid of death. His emotional pattern
were fixed long before the day he tried to land a moonship without radar. He'
grab any excuse to believe that I'd fixed whatever was wrong with the ram con
nections.

But he was counting on me to do it.

The atmosphere leaned on the windows. Not wanting to, I reached out to touc
the quartz with my fingertips. I couldn't feel the pressure. But it was there, inex
orable as the tide smashing a rock into sand grains. How long would the cabi
hold it back?

If some broken part were holding us here, how could I have missed findin;
it? Perhaps it had left no break in the surface of either wing. But how?

That was the angle.

Two cigarettes later I got up to get the sample buckets. They were empty, th
alien dirt safely stored away. I filled them with water and put them in the cooler
set the cooler for 40° Absolute, then turned off the lights and went to bed.

The morning was blacker than the inside of a smoker's lungs. What Venus reall
needs, I decided, philosophizing on my back, is to lose ninety-nine percent of he
air. That would give her a bit more than half as much air as Earth, which woul
lower the greenhouse effect enough to make the temperature livable. Drop Venus
gravity to near zero for a few weeks and the work would do itself.

The whole damn universe is waiting for us to discover antigravity.

"Morning," said Eric. "Thought of anything?"

"Yes." I rolled out of bed. "Now don't bug me with questions, I'll explai
everything as I go."

"No breakfast?"

"Not yet."

Piece by piece I put my suit on, just like one of King Arthur's gentlemen, and went for the buckets only after the gauntlets were on. The ice, in the cold section, was in the chilly neighborhood of absolute zero. "This is two buckets of ordinary ice," I said, holding them up. "Now let me out."

"I should keep you here till you talk," Eric groused. But the doors opened and I went out onto the wing. I started talking while I unscrewed the number two right panel.

"Eric, think a moment about the tests they run on a manned ship before they'll let a man walk into the lifesystem. They test every part separately and in conjunction with other parts. Yet if something isn't working, either it's damaged or it wasn't tested right. Right?"

"Reasonable." He wasn't giving away anything.

"Well, nothing caused any damage. Not only is there no break in the ship's skin, but no coincidence could have made both rams go haywire at the same time. So something wasn't tested right."

I had the panel off. In the buckets the ice boiled gently where it touched the surfaces of the glass buckets. The blue ice cakes had cracked under their own internal pressure. I dumped one bucket into the maze of wiring and contacts and relays, and the ice shattered, giving me room to close the panel.

"So I thought of something last night, something that wasn't tested. Every part of the ship must have been in the heat-and-pressure box, exposed to artificial Venus conditions, but the ship as a whole, a unit, couldn't have been. It's too big." I'd circled around to the left wing and was opening the number three panel in the trailing edge. My remaining ice was half water and half small chips; I sloshed these in and fastened the panel. "What cut your circuits must have been the heat or the pressure or both. I can't help the pressure, but I'm cooling these relays with ice. Let me know which ram gets its sensation back first, and we'll know which inspection panel is the right one."

"Howie. Has it occurred to you what the cold water might do to those hot metals?"

"It could crack them. Then you'd lose all control over the ramjets, which is what's wrong right now."

"Uh. Your point, partner. But I still can't feel anything."

I went back to the airlock with my empty buckets swinging, wondering if they'd get hot enough to melt. They might have, but I wasn't out that long. I had my suit off and was refilling the buckets when Eric said, "I can feel the right ram."

"How extensive? Full control?"

"No. I can't feel the temperature. Oh, here it comes. We're all set, Howie."

My sigh of relief was sincere.

I put the buckets in the freezer again. We'd certainly want to take off with the relays cold. The water had been chilling for perhaps twenty minutes when Eric reported, "Sensation's going."

"What?"

"Sensation's going. No temperature, and I'm losing fuel feed control. It doesn't stay cold long enough."

"Ouch! Now what?"

"I hate to tell you. I'd almost rather let you figure it out for yourself."

I had. "We go as high as we can on the blimp tank, then I go out on the wing with a bucket of ice in each hand—"

We had to raise the blimp tank temperature to almost eight hundred degrees to get pressure, but from then on we went up in good shape. To sixteen miles. It took three hours.

"That's as high as we go," said Eric. "You ready?"

I went to get the ice. Eric could see me, he didn't need an answer. He opened the airlock for me.

Fear I might have felt, or panic, or determination or self-sacrifice—but there was nothing. I went out feeling like a used zombie.

My magnets were on full. It felt like I was walking through shallow tar. The air was thick, though not as heavy as it had been down there. I followed my headlamp to the number two panel, opened it, poured ice in, and threw the bucket high and far. The ice was in one cake. I couldn't close the panel. I left it open and hurried around to the other wing. The second bucket was filled with exploded chips; I sloshed them in and locked the number two left panel and came back with both hands free. It still looked like limbo in all directions, except where the headlamp cut a tunnel through the darkness, and—my feet were getting hot. I closed the right panel on boiling water and sidled back along the hull into the airlock.

"Come in and strap down," said Eric. "Hurry!"

"Gotta get my suit off." My hands had started to shake from reaction. I couldn't work the clamps.

"No you don't. If we start right now we may get home. Leave the suit on and come in."

I did. As I pulled my webbing shut, the rams roared. The ship shuddered a little, then pushed forward as we dropped from under the blimp tank. Pressure mounted as the rams reached operating speed. Eric was giving it all he had. I would have been uncomfortable even without the metal suit around me. With the suit on it was torture. My couch was afire from the suit, but I couldn't get breath to say so. We were going almost straight up.

We had gone twenty minutes when the ship jerked like a galvanized frog. "Ram's out," Eric said calmly. "I'll use the other." Another lurch as we dropped the dead one. The ship flew on like a wounded penguin, but still accelerating.

One minute . . . two . . .

The other ram quit. It was as if we'd run into molasses. Eric blew off the ram and the pressure eased. I could talk.

"Eric."

"What?"

"Got any marshmallows?"

"*What?* Oh, I see. Is your suit tight?"

"Sure."

"Live with it. We'll flush the smoke out later. I'm going to coast above some of this stuff, but when I use the rocket it'll be savage. No mercy."

"Will we make it?"

"I think so. It'll be close."

The relief came first, icy cold. Then the anger. "No more inexplicable numbnesses?" I asked.

"No. Why?"

"If any come up you'll be sure and tell me, won't you?"

"Are you getting at something?"

"Skip it." I wasn't angry any more.

"I'll be damned if I do. You know perfectly well it was mechanical trouble, you fool. You fixed it yourself!"

"No. I convinced you I must have fixed it. You needed to believe the rams *should* be working again. I gave you a miracle cure, Eric. I just hope I don't have to keep dreaming up new placebos for you all the way home."

"You thought that, but you went out on the wing sixteen miles up?" Eric's machinery snorted. "You've got guts where you need brains, Shorty."

I didn't answer.

"Five thousand says the trouble was mechanical. We let the mechanics decide after we land."

"You're on."

"Here comes the rocket. Two, one—"

It came, pushing me down into my metal suit. Sooty flames licked past my ears, writing black on the green metal ceiling, but the rosy mist before my eyes was not fire.

The man with the thick glasses spread a diagram of the Venus ship and jabbed a stubby finger at the trailing edge of the wing. "Right around here," he said. "The pressure from outside compressed the wiring channel a little, just enough so there was no room for the wire to bend. It had to act as if it were rigid, see? Then when the heat expanded the metal these contacts pushed past each other."

"I suppose it's the same design on both wings?"

He gave me a queer look. "Well, naturally."

I left my check for $5000 in a pile of Eric's mail and hopped a plane for Brasilia. How he found me I'll never know, but the telegram arrived this morning

HOWIE COME HOME ALL IS FORGIVEN
DONOVANS BRAIN

I guess I'll have to.

Nine Hundred Grandmothers

R. A. LAFFERTY

R. A. Lafferty started writing in 1960, at the relatively advanced age (for a new writer, anyway) of forty-six, and in the years before his retirement in 1987 published some of the freshest and funniest short stories ever written, almost all of them dancing on the borderlines between fantasy, science fiction, and the tall tale, that most boisterous and quintessentially American of forms.

Lafferty has published memorable novels that stand up quite well today—among the best of them are *Past Master, The Devil Is Dead, The Reefs of Earth,* the historical novel *Okla Hannali,* and the totally unclassifiable (a fantasy novel *disguised as* a nonfiction historical study, perhaps?) *The Fall of Rome*—but it was the prolific stream of short stories he began publishing in 1960 that would eventually establish his reputation. Stories like "Slow Tuesday Night," "Thus We Frustrate Charlemagne," "Hog-Belly Honey," "The Hole on the Corner," "All Pieces of a River Shore," "Among the Hairy Earthmen," "Seven Day Terror," "Continued on Next Rock," "All But the Words," and many others, all clearly demonstrating Lafferty's characteristic virtues: folksy exuberance, a singing lyricism of surprising depth and power, outlandish imagination, a store of offbeat erudition matched only by Avram Davidson, and a strong, shaggy sense of humor unrivaled by anyone.

Lafferty's short work has been gathered in the landmark collection *Nine Hundred Grandmothers,* as well as in *Strange Doings, Does Anyone Else Have Something Further to Add?, Golden Gate and Other Stories,* and *Ringing Changes.* Much of his later work is available only in small-press editions—like the very strange novel *Archipelago* and *My Heart Leaps Up,* which was serialized as a sequence of chapbooks—but his other novels available in trade editions (although many of them are long out-of-print) include *Fourth Mansions, Arrive at Easterwine, Space Chantey,* and *The Flame Is Green.* Lafferty won the Hugo Award in 1973 for his story "Eurema's Dam" and in 1990 received the prestigious World Fantasy Life Achievement Award. His most recent books are the collections *Lafferty In Orbit* and *Iron Tears.* He lives in Oklahoma.

It's hardly surprising that Lafferty would have his own unique and quirky take on the theme of space exploration, just as he did on just about every other conceivable concept. In the razor-sharp and very funny story that follows, he takes us along on a journey of discovery with an intrepid and persistent (if perhaps not terribly wise) explorer who is about to discover that, gee, maybe there *are* things that Man Was Not Meant to Know, after all!

Ceran Swicegood was a promising young Special Aspects Man. But, like all Special Aspects, he had one irritating habit. He was forever asking the question: How Did It All Begin?

They all had tough names except Ceran. Manbreaker Crag, Heave Huckle, Blast Berg, George Blood, Move Manion (when Move says "Move," you move), Trouble Trent. They were supposed to be tough, and they had taken tough names at the naming. Only Ceran kept his own—to the disgust of his commander, Manbreaker.

"Nobody can be a hero with a name like Ceran Swicegood!" Manbreaker would thunder. "Why don't you take Storm Shannon? That's good. Or Gutboy Barrelhouse or Slash Slagle or Nevel Knife? You barely glanced at the suggested list."

"I'll keep my own," Ceran always said, and that is where he made his mistake. A new name will sometimes bring out a new personality. It had done so for George Blood. Though the hair on George's chest was a graft job, yet that and his new name had turned him from a boy into a man. Had Ceran assumed the heroic name of Gutboy Barrelhouse he might have been capable of rousing endeavors and man-sized angers rather than his tittering indecisions and flouncy furies.

They were down on the big asteroid Proavitus—a sphere that almost tinkled with the potential profit that might be shaken out of it. And the tough men of the Expedition knew their business. They signed big contracts on the native velvet-like bark scrolls and on their own parallel tapes. They impressed, inveigled and somewhat cowed the slight people of Proavitus. Here was a solid two-way market, enough to make them slaver. And there was a whole world of oddities that could lend themselves to the luxury trade.

"Everybody's hit it big but you," Manbreaker crackled in kindly thunder to Ceran after three days there. "But even Special Aspects is supposed to pay its way. Our charter compels us to carry one of your sort to give a cultural twist to the thing, but it needn't be restricted to that. What we go out for every time, Ceran, is to cut a big fat hog in the rump—we make no secret of that. But if the hog's tail can be shown to have a cultural twist to it, that will solve a requirement. And if that twist in the tail can turn us a profit, then we become mighty happy about the whole thing. Have you been able to find out anything about the living dolls, for instance? They might have both a cultural aspect and a market value."

"The living dolls seem a part of something much deeper," Ceran said. "There's a whole complex of things to be unraveled. The key may be the statement of the Proavitoi that they do not die."

"I think they die pretty young, Ceran. All those out and about are young, and those I have met who do not leave their houses are only middling old."

"Then where are their cemeteries?"

"Likely they cremate the old folks when they die."

"Where are the crematories?"

"They might just toss the ashes out or vaporize the entire remains. Probably they have no reverence for ancestors."

"Other evidence shows their entire culture to be based on an exaggerated reverence for ancestors."

"You find out, Ceran. You're Special Aspects Man."

★ ★ ★

Ceran talked to Nokoma, his Proavitoi counterpart as translator. Both were expert, and they could meet each other halfway in talk. Nokoma was likely feminine. There was a certain softness about both the sexes of the Proavitoi, but the men of the Expedition believed that they had them straight now.

"Do you mind if I ask some straight questions?" Ceran greeted her today.

"Sure is not. How else I learn the talk well but by talking?"

"Some of the Proavitoi say that they do not die, Nokoma. Is this true?"

"How is not be true? If they die, they not be here to say they do not die. Oh, I joke, I joke. No, we do not die. It is a foolish alien custom which we see no reason to imitate. On Proavitus, only the low creatures die."

"None of you does?"

"Why, no. Why should one want to be an exception in this?"

"But what do you do when you get very old?"

"We do less and less then. We come to a deficiency of energy. Is it not the same with you?"

"Of course. But where do you go when you become exceedingly old?"

"Nowhere. We stay at home then. Travel is for the young and those of the active years."

"Let's try it from the other end," Ceran said. "Where are your father and mother, Nokoma?"

"Out and about. They aren't really old."

"And your grandfathers and grandmothers?"

"A few of them still get out. The older ones stay home."

"Let's try it this way. How many grandmothers do you have, Nokoma?"

"I think I have nine hundred grandmothers in my house. Oh, I know that isn't many, but we are the young branch of a family. Some of our clan have very great numbers of ancestors in their houses."

"And all these ancestors are alive?"

"What else? Who would keep things not alive? How would such be ancestors?"

Ceran began to hop around in his excitement.

"Could I see them?" he twittered.

"It might not be wise for you to see the older of them," Nokoma cautioned. "It could be an unsettling thing for strangers, and we guard it. A few tens of them you can see, of course."

Then it came to Ceran that he might be onto what he had looked for all his life. He went into a panic of expectation.

"Nokoma, it would be finding the key!" he fluted. "If none of you has ever died, then your entire race would still be alive!"

"Sure. Is like you count fruit. You take none away, you still have them all."

"But if the first of them are still alive, then they might know their origin! They would know how it began! Do they? Do you?"

"Oh, not I. I am too young for the Ritual."

"But who knows? Doesn't someone know?"

"Oh, yes, All the old ones know how it began."

"How old? How many generations back from you till they know?"

"Ten, no more. When I have ten generations of children, then I will also go to the Ritual."

"The Ritual, what is it?"

"Once a year, the old people go to the very old people. They wake them up and ask them how it all began. The very old people tell them the beginning. It is a high time. Oh, how they hottle and laugh! Then the very old people go back to sleep for another year. So it is passed down to the generations. That is the Ritual."

The Proavitoi were not humanoid. Still less were they "monkey-faces," though that name was now set in the explorers' lingo. They were upright and robed and swathed, and were assumed to be two-legged under their garments. Though, as Manbreaker said, "They might go on wheels, for all we know."

They had remarkable flowing hands that might be called everywhere-digited. They could handle tools, or employ their hands as if they were the most intricate tools.

George Blood was of the opinion that the Proavitoi were always masked, and that the men of the Expedition had never seen their faces. He said that those apparent faces were ritual masks, and that no part of the Proavitoi had ever been seen by the men except for those remarkable hands, which perhaps were their real faces.

The men reacted with cruel hilarity when Ceran tried to explain to them just what a great discovery he was verging on.

"Little Ceran is still on the how-did-it-begin-jag," Manbreaker jeered. "Ceran, will you never give off asking which came first, the chicken or the egg?"

"I will have that answer very soon," Ceran sang. "I have the unique opportunity. When I find how the Proavitoi began, I may have the clue to how everything began. All of the Proavitoi are still alive, the very first generation of them."

"It passes belief that you can be so simpleminded," Manbreaker moaned. "They say that one has finally mellowed when he can suffer fools gracefully. By God, I hope I never come to that."

But two days later, it was Manbreaker who sought out Ceran Swicegood on nearly the same subject. Manbreaker had been doing a little thinking and discovering of his own.

"You are Special Aspects Man, Ceran," he said, "and you have been running off after the wrong aspect."

"What is that?"

"It don't make a damn how it began. What is important is that it may not have to end."

"It is the beginning that I intend to discover," said Ceran.

"You fool, can't you understand anything? What do the Proavitoi possess so uniquely that we don't know whether they have it by science or by their nature or by fool luck?"

"Ah, their chemistry, I suppose."

"Sure. Organic chemistry has come of age here. The Proavitoi have every kind of nexus and inhibitor and stimulant. They can grow and shrink and telescope and prolong what they will. These creatures seem stupid to me; it is as if they had these things by instinct. But they have them, that is what is important. With these things, we can become the patent medicine kings of the universes, for the Proavitoi do not travel or make many outside contacts. These things can do anything or undo anything. I suspect that the Proavitoi can shrink cells, and I suspect that they can do something else."

"No, they couldn't shrink cells. It is you who talk nonsense now, Manbreaker."

"Never mind. Their things already make nonsense of conventional chemistry. With the pharmacopoeia that one could pick up here, a man need never die. That's the stick horse you've been riding, isn't it? But you've been riding it backward with your head to the tail. The Proavitoi say that they never die."

"They seem pretty sure that they don't. If they did, they would be the first to know it, as Nokoma says."

"What? Have these creatures humor?"

"Some."

"But, Ceran, you don't understand how big this is."

"I'm the only one who understands it so far. It means that if the Proavitoi have always been immortal, as they maintain, then the oldest of them are still alive. From them I may be able to learn how their species—and perhaps every species—began."

Manbreaker went into his dying buffalo act then. He tore his hair and nearly pulled out his ears by the roots. He stomped and pawed and went off bull-bellowing: "It don't make a damn how it began, you fool! It might not have to end!" so loud that the hills echoed back:

"It don't make a damn—you fool."

Ceran Swicegood went to the house of Nokoma, but not with her on her invitation. He went without her when he knew that she was away from home. It was a sneaky thing to do, but the men of the Expedition were trained in sneakery.

He would find out better without a mentor about the nine hundred grandmothers, about the rumored living dolls. He would find out what the old people did do if they didn't die, and find if they knew how they were first born. For his intrusion, he counted on the innate politeness of the Proavitoi.

The house of Nokoma, of all the people, was in the cluster on top of the large flat hill, the Acropolis of Proavitus. They were earthen houses, though finely done, and they had the appearance of growing out of and being a part of the hill itself.

Ceran went up the winding, ascending flagstone paths, and entered the house which Nokoma had once pointed out to him. He entered furtively, and encountered one of the nine hundred grandmothers—one with whom nobody need be furtive.

The grandmother was seated and small and smiling at him. They talked without real difficulty, though it was not as easy as with Nokoma, who could meet Ceran halfway in his own language. At her call, there came a grandfather who likewise smiled at Ceran. These two ancients were somewhat smaller than the Proavitoi of active years. They were kind and serene. There was an atmosphere about the scene hat barely missed being an odor—not unpleasant, sleepy, reminiscent of some-thing, almost sad.

"Are there those here older than you?" Ceran asked earnestly.

"So many, so many, who could know how many?" said the grandmother. She called in other grandmothers and grandfathers older and smaller than herself, these no more than half the size of the active Proavitoi—small, sleepy, smiling.

Ceran knew now that the Proavitoi were not masked. The older they were, the more character and interest there was in their faces. It was only of the immature active Proavitoi that there could have been a doubt. No masks could show such calm and smiling old age as this. The queer textured stuff was their real faces.

So old and friendly, so weak and sleepy, there must have been a dozen gen-erations of them there back to the oldest and smallest.

"How old are the oldest?" Ceran asked the first grandmother.

"We say that all are the same age since all are perpetual," the grandmother told him. "It is not true that all are the same age, but it is indelicate to ask how old."

"You do not know what a lobster is," Ceran said to them, trembling, "but it is a creature that will boil happily if the water on him is heated slowly. He takes no alarm, for he does not know at what point the heat is dangerous. It is that gradual here with me. I slide from one degree to another with you and my credulity is not alarmed. I am in danger of believing anything about you if it comes in small doses, and it will. I believe that you are here and as you are for no other reason than that I see and touch you. Well, I'll be boiled for a lobster, then, before I turn back from it. Are there those here even older than the ones present?"

The first grandmother motioned Ceran to follow her. They went down a ramp through the floor into the older part of the house, which must have been under ground.

Living dolls! They were here in rows on the shelves, and sitting in small chairs in their niches. Doll-sized indeed, and several hundred of them.

Many had wakened at the intrusion. Others came awake when spoken to or touched. They were incredibly ancient, but they were cognizant in their glances and recognition. They smiled and stretched sleepily, not as humans would, but as very old puppies might. Ceran spoke to them, and they understood each other surprisingly.

Lobster, lobster, said Ceran to himself, *the water has passed the danger point! And it hardly feels different. If you believe your senses in this, then you will be boiled alive in your credulity.*

He knew now that the living dolls were real and that they were the living ancestors of the Proavitoi.

Many of the little creatures began to fall asleep again. Their waking moments were short, but their sleeps seemed to be likewise. Several of the living mummies woke a second time while Ceran was still in the room, woke refreshed from very short sleeps and were anxious to talk again.

"You are incredible!" Ceran cried out, and all the small and smaller and still smaller creatures smiled and laughed their assent. Of course they were. All good creatures everywhere are incredible, and were there ever so many assembled in one place? But Ceran was greedy. A roomful of miracles wasn't enough.

"I have to take this back as far as it will go!" he cried avidly. "Where are the even older ones?"

"There are older ones and yet older and again older," said the first grandmother, "and thrice-over older ones, but perhaps it would be wise not to seek to be too wise. You have seen enough. The old people are sleepy. Let us go up again."

Go up again, out of this? Ceran would not. He saw passages and descending ramps, down into the heart of the great hill itself. There were whole worlds of rooms about him and under his feet. Ceran went on and down, and who was to stop him? Not dolls and creatures much smaller than dolls.

Manbreaker had once called himself an old pirate who reveled in the stream of his riches. But Ceran was the Young Alchemist who was about to find the Stone itself.

He walked down the ramps through centuries and millennia. The atmosphere he had noticed on the upper levels was a clear odor now—sleepy, half-remembered, smiling, sad and quite strong. That is the way Time smells.

"Are there those here even older than you?" Ceran asked a small grandmother whom he held in the palm of his hand.

"So old and so small that I could hold in my hand," said the grandmother in what Ceran knew from Nokoma to be the older uncompounded form of the Proavitus language.

Smaller and older the creatures had been getting as Ceran went through the rooms. He was boiled lobster now for sure. He had to believe it all: he saw and felt it. The wren-sized grandmother talked and laughed and nodded that there were those far older than herself, and in doing so she nodded herself back to sleep. Ceran returned her to her niche in the hive-like wall where there were thousands of others, miniaturized generations.

Of course he was not in the house of Nokoma now. He was in the heart of the hill that underlay all the houses of Proavitus, and these were the ancestors of everybody on the asteroid.

"Are there those here even older than you?" Ceran asked a small grandmother whom he held on the tip of his finger.

"Older and smaller," she said, "but you come near the end."

She was asleep, and he put her back in her place. The older they were, the more they slept.

He was down to solid rock under the roots of the hill. He was into the passages that were cut out of that solid rock, but they could not be many or deep. He had a sudden fear that the creatures would become so small that he could not see them or talk to them, and so he would miss the secret of the beginning.

But had not Nokoma said that all the old people knew the secret? Of course. But he wanted to hear it from the oldest of them. He would have it now, one way or the other.

"Who is the oldest? Is this the end of it? Is this the beginning? Wake up! Wake up!" he called when he was sure he was in the lowest and oldest room.

"Is it Ritual?" asked some who woke up. Smaller than mice they were, no bigger than bees, maybe older than both.

"It is a special Ritual," Ceran told them. "Relate to me how it was in the beginning."

What was that sound—too slight, too scattered to be a noise? It was like a billion microbes laughing. It was the hilarity of little things waking up to a high time.

"Who is the oldest of all?" Ceran demanded, for their laughter bothered him. "Who is the oldest and first?"

"I am the oldest, the ultimate grandmother," one said gaily. "All the others are my children. Are you also of my children?"

"Of course," said Ceran, and the small laughter of unbelief flittered out from the whole multitude of them.

"Then you must be the ultimate child, for you are like no other. If you be, then it is as funny at the end as it was in the beginning."

"How was it in the beginning?" Ceran bleated. "You are the first. Do you know how you came to be?"

"Oh, yes, yes," laughed the ultimate grandmother, and the hilarity of the small things became a real noise now.

"How did it begin?" demanded Ceran, and he was hopping and skipping about in his excitement.

"Oh, it was so funny a joke the way things began that you would not believe it," chittered the grandmother. "A joke, a joke!"

"Tell me the joke, then. If a joke generated your species, then tell me that cosmic joke."

"Tell yourself," tinkled the grandmother. "You are a part of the joke if you are of my children. Oh, it is too funny to believe. How good to wake up and laugh and go to sleep again."

Blazing green frustration! To be so close and to be balked by a giggling bee!

"Don't go to sleep again! Tell me at once how it began!" Ceran shrilled, and he had the ultimate grandmother between thumb and finger.

"This is not Ritual," the grandmother protested. "Ritual is that you guess what it was for three days, and we laugh and say 'No, no, no, it was something nine times as wild as that. Guess some more.'"

"I will *not* guess for three days! Tell me at once or I will crush you," Ceran threatened in a quivering voice.

"I look at you, you look at me, I wonder if you will do it," the ultimate grandmother said calmly.

Any of the tough men of the Expedition would have done it—would have crushed her, and then another and another and another of the creatures till the secret was told. If Ceran had taken on a tough personality and a tough name he'd have done it. If he'd been Gutboy Barrelhouse he'd have done it without a qualm. But Ceran Swicegood couldn't do it.

"Tell me," he pleaded in agony. "All my life I've tried to find out how it began, how anything began. And you know!"

"We know. Oh, it was so funny how it began. So joke! So fool, so clown, so grotesque thing! Nobody could guess, nobody could believe."

"Tell me! Tell me!" Ceran was ashen and hysterical.

"No, no, you are no child of mine," chortled the ultimate grandmother. "Is too joke a joke to tell a stranger. We could not insult a stranger to tell so funny, so unbelieve. Strangers can die. Shall I have it on conscience that a stranger died laughing?"

"Tell me! Insult me! Let me die laughing!" But Ceran nearly died crying from the frustration that ate him up as a million bee-sized things laughed and hooted and giggled:

"Oh, it was so funny the way it began!"

And they laughed. And laughed. And went on laughing . . . until Ceran Swicegood wept and laughed together, and crept away, and returned to the ship still laughing. On his next voyage he changed his name to Blaze Bolt and ruled for ninety-seven days as king of a sweet sea island in M-81, but that is another and much more unpleasant story.

The Keys to December

ROGER ZELAZNY

Like a number of other writers, the late Roger Zelazny began publishing in 1962 in the pages of Cele Goldsmith's *Amazing*. This was the so-called Class of '62, whose membership also included Thomas M. Disch, Keith Laumer, and Ursula K. Le Guin. Everyone in that "class" would eventually achieve prominence, but some of them would achieve it faster than others, and Zelazny's subsequent career was one of the most meteoric in the history of science fiction. The first Zelazny story to attract wide notice was "A Rose for Ecclesiastes," published in 1963. (It was later selected by vote of the SFWA membership as one of the best science-fiction stories of all time.) By the end of that decade, he had won two Nebula Awards and two Hugo Awards and was widely regarded as one of the two most important American science-fiction writers of the sixties. (The other was Samuel R. Delany). By the end of the seventies, although Zelazny's critical acceptance as an important science-fiction writer had dimmed, his long series of novels about the enchanted land of Amber—beginning with *Nine Princes in Amber*—had made him one of the most popular and best-selling fantasy writers of our time and inspired the founding of worldwide fan clubs and fanzines.

Zelazny's early novels were, on the whole, well received *(This Immortal* won a Hugo, as did his most famous novel, *Lord of Light),* but it was the strong and stylish short work he published in magazines like *F&SF* and *Amazing* and *Worlds of If* throughout the middle years of the decade that electrified the genre, and it was these early stories—stories like "This Moment of the Storm," "The Doors of His Face, the Lamps of His Mouth," "The Graveyard Heart," "He Who Shapes," "For a Breath I Tarry," and "This Mortal Mountain"—that established Zelazny as a giant of the field, and that many still consider to be his best work. These stories are still amazing for their invention and elegance and verve, for their good-natured effrontery and easy ostentation, for the risks Zelazny took in pursuit of eloquence without ruffling a hair, the grace and nerve he displayed as he switched from high-flown pseudo-Spenserian, to wisecracking Chandlerian slang, to vivid prose poetry, to Hemingwayesque starkness in the course of only a few lines—and for the way he made it all look easy and effortless, the same kind of illusion Fred Astaire used to generate when he danced.

Here's one of those eloquent and elegant stories, written by Zelazny at the top of his form, demonstrating that if you can't find the kind of world you're looking for out there in the galaxy somewhere, you may have to create it *yourself*—but that even then, *exploring* that world may turn up dangers and wonders that you never planned on, unexpected things that you now have to deal with, no matter what the consequences may be. . . .

Zelazny won another Nebula and Hugo Award in 1976 for his novella *Home Is the Hangman,* a Hugo in 1982 for "Unicorn Variation," another Hugo in 1986 for his novella *24 Views of Mt. Fuji,* by Hokusai, and a final Hugo in 1987 for his story "Permafrost." His other books include, in addition to the multivolume *Amber* series, the novels *This Immortal, The Dream Master, Isle of the Dead, Jack of Shadows, Eye of Cat, Doorways in the Sand, Today We Choose Faces, Bridge of Ashes, To Die in Italbar,* and *Roadmarks* and the collections *Four for Tomorrow, The Doors of His Face, the Lamps of His Mouth and Other Stories, The Last Defender of Camelot,* and *Frost and Fire.* Among his last books are two collaborative novels, *A Farce to Be Reckoned With,* with Robert Sheckley, and *Wilderness,* with Gerald Hausman, and, as editor, two anthologies, *Wheel of Fortune* and *Warriors of Blood and Dream.* Zelazny died in 1995. Since his death, several posthumous collaborative novels have been published, including *Psychoshop,* with the late Alfred Bester, and *Donnerjack* and *Lord Demon,* both with Jane Lindskold. A tribute anthology to Zelazny, featuring stories by authors who had been inspired by his work, *Lord of the Fantastic,* was published in 1998.

Born of man and woman, in accordance with Catform Y7 requirements, Coldworld Class (modified per Alyonal), 3.2E, G.M.I. option, Jarry Dark was not suited for existence anywhere in the universe which had guaranteed him a niche. This was either a blessing or a curse, depending on how you looked at it.

So look at it however you would, here is the story:

It is likely that his parents could have afforded the temperature control unit, but not much more than that. (Jarry required a temperature of at least −50°C. to be comfortable.)

It is unlikely that his parents could have provided for the air pressure control and gas mixture equipment required to maintain his life.

Nothing could be done in the way of 3.2-E grav-simulation, so daily medication and physiotherapy were required. It is unlikely that his parents could have provided for this.

The much-maligned option took care of him, however. It safeguarded his health. It provided for his education. It assured his economic welfare and physical well-being.

It might be argued that Jarry Dark would not have been a homeless Coldworld Catform (modified per Alyonal) had it not been for General Mining, Incorporated, which had held the option. But then it must be borne in mind that no one could have foreseen the nova which destroyed Alyonal.

When his parents had presented themselves at the Public Health Planned Parenthood Center and requested advice and medication pending offspring, they had been informed as to the available worlds and the bodyform requirements for them. They had selected Alyonal, which had recently been purchased by General Mining for purposes of mineral exploitation. Wisely, they had elected the option; that is to say, they had signed a contract on behalf of their anticipated offspring, who would be eminently qualified to inhabit that world, agreeing that he would work as an employee of General Mining until he achieved his majority, at which time he would be free to depart and seek employment wherever he might choose (though his choices would admittedly be limited). In return for this guarantee, General Mining agreed to assure his health, education and continuing welfare for so long as he remained in their employ.

When Alyonal caught fire and went away, those Coldworld Catforms covered by the option who were scattered about the crowded galaxy were, by virtue of the agreement, wards of General Mining.

This is why Jarry grew up in a hermetically sealed room containing temperature and atmosphere controls, and why he received a first-class closed circuit education, along with his physiotherapy and medicine. This is also why Jarry bore some resemblance to a large gray ocelot without a tail, had webbing between his fingers and could not go outside to watch the traffic unless he wore a pressurized refrigeration suit and took extra medication.

All over the swarming galaxy, people took the advice of Public Health Planned Parenthood Centers, and many others had chosen as had Jarry's parents. Twenty-eight thousand, five hundred sixty-six of them, to be exact. In any group of over twenty-eight thousand five hundred sixty, there are bound to be a few talented individuals. Jarry was one of them. He had a knack for making money. Most of his General Mining pension check was invested in well-chosen stocks of a speculative nature. (In fact, after a time he came to own considerable stock in General Mining.)

When the man from the Galactic Civil Liberties Union had come around, expressing concern over the pre-birth contracts involved in the option and explaining that the Alyonal Catforms would make a good test case (especially since Jarry's parents lived within jurisdiction of the 877th Circuit, where they would be assured a favorable courtroom atmosphere), Jarry's parents had demurred, for fear of jeopardizing the General Mining pension. Later on, Jarry himself dismissed the notion also. A favorable decision could not make him an E-world Normform, and what else mattered? He was not vindictive. Also, he owned considerable stock in G.M. by then.

He loafed in his methane tank and purred, which meant that he was thinking. He operated his cryo-computer as he purred and thought. He was computing the total net worth of all the Catforms in the recently organized December Club.

He stopped purring and considered a sub-total, stretched, shook his head slowly. Then he returned to his calculations.

When he had finished, he dictated a message into his speech-tube, to Sanza Barati, President of December and his betrothed:

"Dearest Sanza—The funds available, as I suspected, leave much to be desired.

All the more reason to begin immediately. Kindly submit the proposal to the business committee, outline my qualifications and seek immediate endorsement. I've finished drafting the general statement to the membership. (Copy attached.) From these figures, it will take me between five and ten years, if at least eighty percent of the membership backs me. So push hard, beloved. I'd like to meet you someday, in a place where the sky is purple. Yours, always, Jarry Dark, Treasurer. P.S. I'm pleased you were pleased with the ring."

Two years later, Jarry had doubled the net worth of December Incorporated.

A year and a half after that, he had doubled it again.

When he received the following letter from Sanza, he leapt onto his trampoline, bounded into the air, landed upon his feet at the opposite end of his quarters, returned to his viewer and replayed it:

Dear Jarry,

Attached are specifications and prices for five more worlds. The research staff likes the last one. So do I. What do you think? Alyonal II? If so, how about the price? When could we afford that much? The staff also says that an hundred Worldchange units could alter it to what we want in 5-6 centuries. Will forward costs of this machinery shortly.

Come live with me and be my love, in a place where there are no walls. . . .

Sanza

"One year," he replied, "and I'll buy you a world! Hurry up with the costs of machinery and transport . . ."

When the figures arrived Jarry wept icy tears. One hundred machines, capable of altering the environment of a world, plus twenty-eight thousand coldsleep bunkers, plus transportation costs for the machinery and his people, plus . . . Too high! He did a rapid calculation.

He spoke into the speech-tube:

". . . Fifteen additional years is too long to wait, Pussycat. Have them figure the time-span if we were to purchase only twenty Worldchange units. Love and kisses, Jarry."

During the days which followed, he stalked above his chamber, erect at first, then on all fours as his mood deepened.

"Approximately three thousand years," came the reply. "May your coat be ever shiny—Sanza."

"Let's put it to a vote, Greeneyes," he said.

Quick, a world in 300 words or less! Picture this. . . .

One land mass, really, containing three black and brackish looking seas; gray plains and yellow plains and skies the color of dry sand; shallow forests with trees like mushrooms which have been swabbed with iodine; no mountains, just hills brown, yellow, white, lavender; green birds with wings like parachutes, bills like sickles, feathers like oak leaves, an inside-out umbrella behind; six very distant moons, like spots before the eyes in daytime, snowflakes at night, drops of blood at dusk and dawn; grass like mustard in the moister valleys; mists like white fire on windless mornings, albino serpents when the air's astir; radiating chasms, like fractures in frosted windowpanes; hidden caverns, like chains of dark bubbles; seventeen known dangerous predators, ranging from one to six meters in length, excessively furred and fanged; sudden hailstorms, like hurled hammerheads from a clear sky; an icecap like a blue beret at either flattened pole; nervous bipeds a meter and a half in height, short on cerebrum, which wander the shallow forests and prey upon the giant caterpillar's larva, as well as the giant caterpillar, the green bird, the blind burrower, and the offal-eating murk-beast; seventeen mighty rivers; clouds like pregnant purple cows, which quickly cross the land to lie-in beyond the visible east; stands of windblasted stones like frozen music; nights like soot, to obscure the lesser stars; valleys which flow like the torsos of women or instruments of music; perpetual frost in places of shadow; sounds in the morning like the cracking of ice, the trembling of tin, the snapping of steel strands. . . .

They knew they would turn it to heaven.

The vanguard arrived, decked out in refrigeration suits, installed ten Worldchange units in either hemisphere, began setting up cold-sleep bunkers in several of the larger caverns.

Then came the members of December down from the sand-colored sky.

They came and they saw, decided it was almost heaven, then entered their caverns and slept. Over twenty-eight thousand Coldworld Catforms (modified per Alyonal) came into their own world to sleep for a season in silence the sleep of ice and of stone, to inherit the new Alyonal. There is no dreaming in that sleep. But had there been, their dreams might have been as the thoughts of those yet awake.

"It is bitter, Sanza."

"Yes, but only for a time—"

". . . To have each other and our own world, and still to go forth like divers at the bottom of the sea. To have to crawl when you want to leap . . ."

"It is only for a short time, Jarry, as the senses will reckon it."

"But it is really three thousand years! An ice age will come to pass as we doze. Our former worlds will change so that we would not know them were we to go back for a visit—and none will remember us."

"Visit what? Our former cells? Let the rest of the worlds go by! Let us be forgotten in the lands of our birth! We are a people apart and we have found our home. What else matters?"

"True. . . . It will be but a few years, and we shall stand our tours of wakefulness and watching together."

"When is the first?"

"Two and a half centuries from now—three months of wakefulness."

"What will it be like then?"

"I don't know. Less warm . . ."

"Then let us return and sleep. Tomorrow will be a better day."

"Yes."

"Oh! See the green bird! It drifts like a dream . . ." When they awakened that first time, they stayed within the World-change installation at the place called Deadland. The world was already colder and the edges of the sky were tinted with pink. The metal walls of the great installation were black and rimed with frost. The atmosphere was still lethal and the temperature far too high. They remained within their special chambers for most of the time, venturing outside mainly to make necessary tests and to inspect the structure of their home.

Deadland. . . . Rocks and sand. No trees, no marks of life at all.

The time of terrible winds was still upon the land, as the world fought back against the fields of the machines. At night great clouds of real estate smoothed and sculpted the stands of stone, and when the winds departed the desert would shimmer as if fresh-painted and the stones would stand like flames within the morning and its singing. After the sun came up into the sky and hung there for a time, the winds would begin again and a dun-colored fog would curtain the day. When the morning winds departed, Jarry and Sanza would stare out across Deadland through the east window of the installation, for that was their favorite—the one on the third floor—where the stone that looked like a gnarly Normform waved to them, and they would lie upon the green couch they had moved up from the first floor, and would sometimes make love as they listened for the winds to rise again, or Sanza would sing and Jarry would write in the log or read back through it, the scribblings of friends and unknowns through the centuries, and they would purr often but never laugh, because they did not know how.

One morning, as they watched, they saw one of the biped creatures of the iodine forests moving across the land. It fell several times, picked itself up, continued, fell once more, lay still.

"What is it doing this far from its home?" asked Sanza.

"Dying," said Jarry. "Let's go outside."

They crossed a catwalk, descended to the first floor, donned their protective suits and departed the installation.

The creature had risen to its feet and was staggering once again. It was covered with a reddish down, had dark eyes and a long wide nose, lacked a true forehead. It had four brief digits, clawed, upon each hand and foot.

When it saw them emerge from the Worldchange unit, it stopped and stared at them. Then it fell.

They moved to its side and studied it where it lay.

It continued to stare at them, its dark eyes wide, as it lay there shivering.

"It will die if we leave it here," said Sanza.

". . . And it will die if we take it inside," said Jarry.

It raised a forelimb toward them, let it fall again. Its eyes narrowed, then closed.

Jarry reached out and touched it with the toe of his boot. There was no response.

"It's dead," he said.

"What will we do?"

"Leave it here. The sands will cover it."

They returned to the installation, and Jarry entered the event in the log.

During their last month of duty, Sanza asked him, "Will everything die here but us? The green birds and the big eaters of flesh? The funny little trees and the hairy caterpillars?"

"I hope not," said Jarry. "I've been reading back through the biologists' notes. I think life might adapt. Once it gets a start anywhere, it'll do anything it can to keep going. It's probably better for the creatures of this planet that we could afford only twenty Worldchangers. That way they have three millennia to grow more hair and learn to breathe our air and drink our water. With a hundred units we might have wiped them out and had to import coldworld creatures or breed them. This way, the ones who live here might be able to make it."

"It's funny," she said, "but the thought just occurred to me that we're doing here what was done to us. They made us for Alyonal, and a nova took it away . . . These creatures came to life in this place, and we're taking it away. We're turning all of life on this planet into what we were on our former worlds—misfits."

"The difference, however, is that we are taking our time," said Jarry, "and giving them a chance to get used to the new conditions."

"Still, I feel that all that—outside there"—she gestured toward the window—"is what this world is becoming: one big Deadland."

"Deadland was here before we came. We haven't created new deserts."

"All the animals are moving south. The trees are dying. When they get as far south as they can go and still the temperature drops, and the air continues to burn in their lungs—then it will be all over for them."

"By then they might have adapted. The trees are spreading, are developing thicker barks. Life will make it."

"I wonder . . ."

"Would you prefer to sleep until it's all over?"

"No; I want to be by your side, always."

"Then you must reconcile yourself to the fact that something is always hurt by any change. If you do this, you will not be hurt yourself."

Then they listened for the winds to rise.

Three days later, in the still of sundown, between the winds of day and the winds of night, she called him to the window. He climbed to the third floor and moved to her side. Her breasts were rose in the sundown light and the places beneath them silver and dark. The fur of her shoulders and haunches was like an aura of smoke. Her face was expressionless and her wide, green eyes were not turned toward him.

He looked out.

The first big flakes were falling, blue, through the pink light. They drifted past the stone and gnarly Normform; some stuck to the thick quartz windowpane; they fell upon the desert and lay there like blossoms of cyanide; they swirled as more of them came down and were caught by the first puffs of the terrible winds. Dark clouds had mustered overhead and from them, now, great cables and nets of blue descended. Now the flakes flashed past the window like butterflies, and the outline of Deadland flickered on and off. The pink vanished and there was only blue, blue and darkening blue, as the first great sigh of evening came into their ears and the billows suddenly moved sidewise rather than downwards, becoming indigo as they raced by.

★ ★ ★

"The machine is never silent," Jarry wrote. "Sometimes I fancy I can hear voices in its constant humming, its occasional growling, its crackles of power. I am alone here at the Deadland station. Five centuries have passed since our arrival. I thought it better to let Sanza sleep out this tour of duty, lest the prospect be too bleak. (It is.) She will doubtless be angry. As I lay half-awake this morning, I thought I heard my parents' voices in the next room. No words. Just the sounds of their voices as I used to hear them over my old intercom. They must be dead by now, despite all geriatrics. I wonder if they thought of me much after I left? I couldn't even shake my father's hand without my gauntlet, or kiss my mother goodbye. It is strange, the feeling, to be this alone, with only the throb of the machinery about me as it rearranges the molecules of the atmosphere, refrigerates the world, here in the middle of the blue place. Deadland. This, despite the fact that I grew up in a steel cave. I call the other nineteen stations every afternoon. I am afraid I am becoming something of a nuisance. I won't call them tomorrow, or perhaps the next day.

"I went outside without my refrig-pack this morning, for a few moments. It is still deadly hot. I gulped a mouthful of air and choked. Our day is still far off. But I can notice the difference from the last time I tried it, two and a half hundred years ago. I wonder what it will be like when we have finished?—And I, an economist! What will my function be in our new Alyonal? Whatever, so long as Sanza is happy. . . .

"The Worldchanger stutters and groans. All the land is blue for so far as I can see. The stones still, but their shapes are changed from what they were. The sky is entirely pink now, and it becomes almost maroon in the morning and the evening. I guess it's really a wine-color, but I've never seen wine, so I can't say for certain. The trees have not died. They've grown hardier. Their barks are thicker, their leaves are darker and larger. They grow much taller now, I've been told. There are no trees in Deadland.

"The caterpillars still live. They seem much larger, I understand, but it is actually because they have become woolier than they used to be. It seems that most of the animals have heavier pelts these days. Some apparently have taken to hibernating. A strange thing: Station Seven reported that they had thought the bipeds were growing heavier coats. There seem to be quite a few of them in that area, and they often see them off in the distance. They looked to be shaggier. Closer observation, however, revealed that some of them were either carrying or were wrapped in the skins of dead animals! Could it be that they are more intelligent than we have given them credit for? This hardly seems possible, since they were tested quite thoroughly by the Bio Team before we set the machines in operation. Yet, it is very strange.

"The winds are still severe. Occasionally, they darken the sky with ash. There has been considerable vulcanism southwest of here. Station Four was relocated because of this. I hear Sanza singing now, within the sounds of the machine. I will let her be awakened the next time. Things should be more settled by then. No, that is not true. It is selfishness. I want her here beside me. I feel as if I were the only living thing in the whole world. The voices on the radio are ghosts. The clock ticks loudly and the silences between the ticks are filled with the humming of the machine, which is a kind of silence, too, because it is constant. Sometimes I think it is not there; I listen for it, I strain my ears, and I do not know whether there is a humming or not. I check the indicators then, and they assure me that the machine is functioning. Or perhaps there is something wrong with the indicators. But they seem to be all right. No. It is me. And the blue of Deadland is a kind of visual silence. In the morning even the rocks are covered with blue frost. It is beautiful or ugly? There is no response within me. It is a part of the great silence, that's all. Perhaps I shall become a mystic. Perhaps I shall develop occult powers to achieve something bright and liberating as I sit here at the center of the great silence. Perhaps I shall see visions. Already I hear voices. Are there ghosts in Deadland? No, there was never anything here to be ghosted. Except perhaps for the little biped. Why did it cross Deadland, I wonder? Why did it head for the center of destruction rather than away, as its fellows did? I shall never know. Unless perhaps I have a vision. I think it is time to suit up and take a walk. The polar icecaps are heavier. The glaciation has begun. Soon, soon things will be better. Soon the silence will end, I hope. I wonder, though, whether silence is not the true state of affairs in the universe, our little noises serving only to accentuate it, like a speck of black on a field of blue. Everything was once silence and will be so again—is now, perhaps. Will I ever hear real sounds, or only sounds out of the silence? Sanza is singing again. I wish I could wake her up now, to walk with me, out there. It is beginning to snow."

Jarry awakened again on the eve of the millennium.

Sanza smiled and took his hand in hers and stroked it, as he explained why he had let her sleep, as he apologized.

"Of course I'm not angry," she said, "considering I did the same thing to you last cycle."

Jarry stared up at her and felt the understanding begin.

"I'll not do it again," she said, "and I know you couldn't. The aloneness is almost unbearable."

"Yes," he replied.

"They warmed us both alive last time. I came around first and told them to put you back to sleep. I was angry then, when I found out what you had done. But I got over it quickly, so often did I wish you were there."

"We will stay together," said Jarry.

"Yes, always."

They took a flier from the cavern of sleep to the World-change installation at Deadland, where they relieved the other attendants and moved the new couch up to the third floor.

The air of Deadland, while sultry, could now be breathed for short periods of time, though a headache invariably followed such experiments. The heat was still oppressive. The rock, once like an old Normform waving, had lost its distinctive outline. The winds were no longer so severe.

On the fourth day, they found some animal tracks which seemed to belong to one of the larger predators. This cheered Sanza, but another, later occurrence produced only puzzlement.

One morning they went forth to walk in Deadland.

Less than a hundred paces from the installation, they came upon three of the giant caterpillars, dead. They were stiff, as though dried out rather than frozen, and they were surrounded by rows of markings within the snow. The footprints which led to the scene and away from it were rough of outline, obscure.

"What does it mean?" she asked.

"I don't know, but I think we had better photograph this," said Jarry.

They did. When Jarry spoke to Station Eleven that afternoon, he learned that similar occurrences had occasionally been noted by attendants of other installations. These were not too frequent, however.

"I don't understand," said Sanza.

"I don't want to," said Jarry.

It did not happen again during their tour of duty. Jarry entered it into the log and wrote a report. Then they abandoned themselves to lovemaking, monitoring, and occasional nights of drunkenness. Two hundred years previously, a biochemist had devoted his tour of duty to experimenting with compounds which would produce the same reactions in Catforms as the legendary whiskey did in Normforms. He had been successful, had spent four weeks on a colossal binge, neglected his duty and been relieved of it, was then retired to his coldbunk for the balance of the Wait. His basically simple formula had circulated, however, and Jarry and Sanza found a well-stocked bar in the storeroom and a hand-written manual explaining its use and a variety of drinks which might be compounded. The author of the document had expressed the hope that each tour of attendance might result in the discovery of a new mixture, so that when he returned for his next cycle the manual would have grown to a size proportionate to his desire. Jarry and Sanza worked at it conscientiously, and satisfied the request with a Snowflower Punch which warmed their bellies and made their purring turn into giggles, so that they discovered laughter also. They celebrated the millennium with an entire bowl of it, and Sanza insisted on calling all the other installations and giving them the formula, right then, on the graveyard watch, so that everyone could share in their joy. It is quite possible that everyone did, for the recipe was well-received. And always, even after that bowl was but a memory, they kept the laughter. Thus are the first simple lines of tradition sometimes sketched.

★ ★ ★

"The green birds are dying," said Sanza, putting aside a report she had been reading.

"Oh?" said Jarry.

"Apparently they've done all the adapting they're able to," she told him.

"Pity," said Jarry.

"It seems less than a year since we came here. Actually, it's a thousand."

"Time flies," said Jarry.

"I'm afraid," she said.

"Of what?"

"I don't know. Just afraid."

"Why?"

"Living the way we've been living, I guess. Leaving little pieces of ourselves in different centuries. Just a few months ago, as my memory works, this place was a desert. Now it's an ice field. Chasms open and close. Canyons appear and disappear. Rivers dry up and new ones spring forth. Everything seems so very transitory. Things look solid, but I'm getting afraid to touch things now. They might go away. They might turn into smoke, and my hand will keep on reaching through the smoke and touch—something . . . God, maybe. Or worse yet, maybe not. No one really knows what it will be like here when we've finished. We're traveling toward an unknown land and it's too late to go back. We're moving through a dream, heading toward an idea. . . . Sometimes I miss my cell . . . and all the little machines that took care of me there. Maybe *I* can't adapt. Maybe I'm like the green bird . . ."

"No, Sanza. You're not. We're real. No matter what happens out there, *we* will last. Everything is changing because we want it to change. We're stronger than the world, and we'll squeeze it and paint it and poke holes in it until we've made it exactly the way we want it. Then we'll take it and cover it with cities and children. You want to see God? Go look in the mirror. God has pointed ears and green eyes. He is covered with soft gray fur. When He raises His hand there is webbing between His fingers."

"It is good that you are strong, Jarry."

"Let's get out the power sled and go for a ride."

"All right."

Up and down, that day, they drove through Deadland, where the dark stones stood like clouds in another sky.

It was twelve and a half hundred years.

Now they could breathe without respirators, for a short time.

Now they could bear the temperature, for a short time.

Now all the green birds were dead.

Now a strange and troubling thing began.

The bipeds came by night, made markings upon the snow, left dead animals in the midst of them. This happened now with much more frequency than it had in the past. They came long distances to do it, many of them with fur which was not their own upon their shoulders.

Jarry searched through the history files for all the reports on the creatures.

"This one speaks of lights in the forest," he said. "Station Seven."

"What . . . ?"

"Fire," he said. "What if they've discovered fire?"

"Then they're not really beasts!"

"But they were!"

"They wear clothing now. They make some sort of sacrifice to our machines. They're not beasts any longer."

"How could it have happened?"

"How do you think? *We* did it. Perhaps they would have remained stupid—animals—if we had not come along and forced them to get smart in order to go on living. We've accelerated their evolution. They had to adapt or die, and they adapted."

"D'you think it would have happened if we hadn't come along?" he asked.

"Maybe—some day. Maybe not, too."

Jarry moved to the window, stared out across Deadland.

"I have to find out," he said. "If they are intelligent, if they are—human, like us," he said, then laughed, "then we must consider their ways."

"What do you propose?"

"Locate some of the creatures. See whether we can communicate with them."

"Hasn't it been tried?"

"Yes."

"What were the results?"

"Mixed. Some claim they have considerable understanding. Others place them far below the threshold where humanity begins."

"We may be doing a terrible thing," she said. "Creating men, then destroying them. Once, when I was feeling low, you told me that we were the gods of this world, that ours was the power to shape and to break. Ours is the power to shape and break, but I don't feel especially divine. What can we do? They have come this far, but do you think they can bear the change that will take us the rest of the way? What if they are like the green birds? What if they've adapted as fast and as far as they can and it is not sufficient? What would a god do?"

"Whatever he wished," said Jarry.

That day, they cruised over Deadland in the flier, but the only signs of life they saw were each other. They continued to search in the days that followed, but they did not meet with success.

Under the purple morning, however, two weeks later, it happened.

"They've been here," said Sanza.

Jarry moved to the front of the installation and stared out.

The snow was broken in several places, inscribed with the lines he had seen before, about the form of a small, dead beast.

"They can't have gone very far," he said.

"No."

"We'll search in the sled."

Now over the snow and out, across the land called Dead they went, Sanza driving and Jarry peering at the lines of footmarks in the blue.

They cruised through the occurring morning, hinting of fire and violet, and the wind went past them like a river, and all about them there came sounds like the cracking of ice, the trembling of tin, the snapping of steel strands. The bluefrosted stones stood like frozen music, and the long shadow of their sled, black as ink, raced on ahead of them. A shower of hailstones drumming upon the roof of their vehicle like a sudden visitation of demon dancers, as suddenly was gone. Deadland sloped downward, slanted up again.

Jarry placed his hand upon Sanza's shoulder.

"Ahead!"

She nodded, began to brake the sled.

They had it at bay. They were using clubs and long poles which looked to have fire-hardened points. They threw stones. They threw pieces of ice.

Then they backed away and it killed them as they went.

The Catforms had called it a bear because it was big and shaggy and could rise up onto its hind legs. . . .

This one was about three and a half meters in length, was covered with bluish fur and had a thin, hairless snout like the business end of a pair of pliers.

Five of the little creatures lay still in the snow. Each time that it swung a paw and connected, another one fell.

Jarry removed the pistol from its compartment and checked the charge.

"Cruise by slowly," he told her. "I'm going to try to burn it about the head."

His first shot missed, scoring the boulder at its back. His second singed the fur of its neck. He leapt down from the sled then, as they came abreast of the beast, thumbed the power control up to maximum, and fired the entire charge into its breast, point-blank.

The bear stiffened, swayed, fell, a gaping wound upon it, front to back.

Jarry turned and regarded the little creatures. They stared up at him.

"Hello," he said. "My name is Jarry. I dub thee Redforms—"

He was knocked from his feet by a blow from behind.

He rolled across the snow, lights dancing before his eyes, his left arm and shoulder afire with pain.

A second bear had emerged from the forest of stone.

He drew his long hunting knife with his right hand and climbed back to his feet.

As the creature lunged, he moved with the catspeed of his kind, thrusting upward, burying his knife to the hilt in its throat.

A shudder ran through it, but it cuffed him and he fell once again, the blade torn from his grasp.

The Redforms threw more stones, rushed toward it with their pointed sticks.

Then there was a thud and a crunching sound, and it rose up into the air and came down on top of him.

He awakened.

He lay on his back, hurting, and everything he looked at seemed to be pulsing, as if about to explode.

How much time had passed, he did not know.

Either he or the bear had been moved.

The little creatures crouched, watching.

Some watched the bear. Some watched him.

Some watched the broken sled. . . .

The broken sled. . . .

He struggled to his feet.

The Redforms drew back.

He crossed to the sled and looked inside.

He knew she was dead when he saw the angle of her neck. But he did all the things a person does to be sure, anyway, before he would let himself believe it.

She had delivered the deathblow, crashing the sled into the creature, breaking its back. It had broken the sled. Herself, also.

He leaned against the wreckage, composed his first prayer, then removed her body.

The Redforms watched.

He lifted her in his arms and began walking, back toward the installation, across Deadland.

The Redforms continued to watch as he went, except for the one with the strangely high brow-ridge, who studied instead the knife that protruded from the shaggy and steaming throat of the beast.

Jarry asked the awakened executives of December: "What should we do?"

"She is the first of our race to die on this world," said Yan Turl, Vice President.

"There is no tradition," said Selda Kein, Secretary. "Shall we establish one?"

"I don't know," said Jarry. "I don't know what is right to do."

"Burial or cremation seem to be the main choices. Which would you prefer?"

"I don't—No, not the ground. Give her back to me. Give me a large flier . . . I'll burn her."

"Then let us construct a chapel."

"No. It is a thing I must do in my own way. I'd rather do it alone."

"As you wish. Draw what equipment you need, and be about it."

"Please send someone else to keep the Deadland installation. I wish to sleep again when I have finished this thing—until the next cycle."

"Very well, Jarry. We are sorry."

"Yes—we are."

Jarry nodded, gestured, turned, departed.

Thus are the heavier lines of life sometimes drawn.

At the southeastern edge of Deadland there was a blue mountain. It stood to slightly over three thousand meters in height. When approached from the northwest, it gave the appearance of being a frozen wave in a sea too vast to imagine. Purple clouds rent themselves upon its peak. No living thing was to be found on its slopes. It had no name, save that which Jarry Dark gave it.

He anchored the flier.

He carried her body to the highest point to which a body might be carried.

He placed her there, dressed in her finest garments, a wide scarf concealing the angle of her neck, a dark veil covering her emptied features.

He was about to try a prayer when the hail began to fall. Like thrown rocks, the chunks of blue ice came down upon him, upon her.

"God damn you!" he cried and he raced back to the flier.

He climbed into the air, circled.

Her garments were flapping in the wind. The hail was a blue, beaded curtain that separated them from all but these final caresses: fire aflow from ice to ice, from clay aflow immortally through guns.

He squeezed the trigger and a doorway into the sun opened in the side of the mountain that had been nameless. She vanished within it, and he widened the doorway until he had lowered the mountain.

Then he climbed upward into the cloud, attacking the storm until his guns were empty.

He circled then above the molten mesa, there at the southeastern edge of Deadland.

He circled above the first pyre this world had seen.

Then he departed, to sleep for a season in silence the sleep of ice and of stone, to inherit the new Alyonal. There is no dreaming in that sleep.

★ ★ ★

Fifteen centuries. Almost half the Wait. Two hundred words or less. . . . Picture—

. . . Nineteen mighty rivers flowing, but the black seas rippling violet now.

. . . No shallow iodine-colored forests. Mighty shag-barked barrel trees instead, orange and lime and black and tall across the land.

. . . Great ranges of mountains in the place of hills brown, yellow, white, lavender. Black corkscrews of smoke unwinding from smoldering cones.

. . . Flowers, whose roots explore the soil twenty meters beneath their mustard petals, unfolded amidst the blue frost and the stones.

. . . Blind burrowers burrowing deeper; offal-eating murk-beasts now showing formidable incisors and great rows of ridged molars; giant caterpillars growing smaller but looking larger because of increasing coats.

. . . The contours of valleys still like the torsos of women, flowing and rolling, or perhaps like instruments of music.

. . . Gone much windblasted stone, but ever the frost.

. . . Sounds in the morning as always, harsh, brittle, metallic.

They were sure they were halfway to heaven.

Picture that.

The Deadland log told him as much as he really needed to know. But he read back through the old reports, also.

Then he mixed himself a drink and stared out the third floor window.

". . . Will die," he said, then finished his drink, outfitted himself, and abandoned his post.

It was three days before he found a camp.

He landed the flier at a distance and approached on foot. He was far to the south of Deadland, where the air was warmer and caused him to feel constantly short of breath.

They were wearing animal skins—skins which had been cut for a better fit and greater protection, skins which were tied about them. He counted sixteen lean-to arrangements and three campfires. He flinched as he regarded the fires, but he continued to advance.

When they saw him, all their little noises stopped, a brief cry went up, and then there was silence.

He entered the camp.

The creatures stood unmoving about him. He heard some bustling within the large lean-to at the end of the clearing.

He walked about the camp.

A slab of dried meat hung from the center of a tripod of poles. Several long spears stood before each dwelling place. He advanced and studied one. A stone which had been flaked into a leaf-shaped spearhead was affixed to its end.

There was the outline of a cat carved upon a block of wood. . . .

He heard a footfall and turned.

One of the Redforms moved slowly toward him. It appeared older than the others. Its shoulders sloped; as it opened its mouth to make a series of popping noises, he saw that some of its teeth were missing; its hair was grizzled and thin. It bore something in its hands, but Jarry's attention was drawn to the hands themselves.

Each hand bore an opposing digit.

He looked about him quickly, studying the hands of the others. All of them seemed to have thumbs. He studied their appearance more closely.

They now had foreheads.

He returned his attention to the old Redform.

It placed something at his feet, and then it backed away from him.

He looked down.

A chunk of dried meat and a piece of fruit lay upon a broad leaf.

He picked up the meat, closed his eyes, bit off a piece, chewed and swallowed. He wrapped the rest in the leaf and placed it in the side pocket of his pack.

He extended his hand and the Redform drew back.

He lowered his hand, unrolled the blanket he had carried with him and spread it upon the ground. He seated himself, pointed to the Redform, then indicated a position across from him at the other end of the blanket.

The creature hesitated, then advanced and seated itself.

"We are going to learn to talk with one another," he said slowly. Then he placed his hand upon his breast and said, "Jarry."

★ ★ ★

Jarry stood before the reawakened executives of December.

"They are intelligent," he told them. "It's all in my report."

"So?" asked Yan Turl.

"I don't think they will be able to adapt. They have come very far, very rapidly. But I don't think they can go much further. I don't think they can make it all the way."

"Are you a biologist, an ecologist, a chemist?"

"No."

"Then on what do you base your opinion?"

"I observed them at close range for six weeks."

"Then it's only a feeling you have . . . ?"

"You know there are no experts on a thing like this. It's never happened before."

"Granting their intelligence—granting even that what you have said concerning their adaptability is correct—what do you suggest we do about it?"

"Slow down the change. Give them a better chance. If they can't make it the rest of the way, then stop short of our goal. It's already livable here. *We* can adapt the rest of the way."

"Slow it down? How much?"

"Supposing we took another seven or eight thousand years?"

"Impossible!"

"Entirely!"

"Too much!"

"Why?"

"Because everyone stands a three-month watch every two hundred fifty years. That's one year of personal time for every thousand. You're asking too much of everyone's time."

"But the life of an entire race may be at stake!"

"You do not know for certain."

"No, I don't. But do you feel it is something to take a chance with?"

"Do you want to put it to an executive vote?"

"No—I can see that I'll lose. I want to put it before the entire membership."

"Impossible. They're all asleep."

"Then wake them up."

"That would be quite a project."

"Don't you think that the fate of a race is worth the effort? Especially since we're the ones who forced intelligence upon them? We're the ones who made them evolve, cursed them with intellect."

"Enough! They were right at the threshhold. They might have become intelligent had we *not* come along—"

"But you can't say for certain! You don't really know! And it doesn't really matter how it happened. They're here and we're here, and they think we're gods— maybe because we do nothing for them but make them miserable. We have some responsibility to an intelligent race though. At least to the extent of not murdering it."

"Perhaps we could do a long-range study . . ."

"They could be dead by then. I formally move, in my capacity as Treasurer, that we awaken the full membership and put the matter to a vote."

"I don't hear any second to your motion."

"Selda?" he said.

She looked away.

"Tarebell? Clond? Bondici?"

There was silence in the cavern that was high and wide about him.

"All right. I can see when I'm beaten. We will be our own serpents when we come into our Eden. I'm going now, back to Deadland, to finish my tour of duty."

"You don't have to. In fact, it might be better if you sleep the whole thing out . . ."

"No. If it's going to be this way, the guilt will be mine also. I want to watch, share it fully."

"So be it," said Turl.

Two weeks later, when Installation Nineteen tried to raise the Deadland Station on the radio, there was no response.

After a time, a flier was dispatched.

The Deadland Station was a shapeless lump of melted metal.

Jarry Dark was nowhere to be found.

Later that afternoon, Installation Eight went dead.

A flier was immediately dispatched.

Installation Eight no longer existed. Its attendants were found several miles away, walking. They told how Jarry Dark had forced them from the station at gunpoint. Then he burnt it to the ground, with the fire-cannons mounted upon his flier.

At about the time they were telling this story, Installation Six became silent.

The order went out: MAINTAIN CONTINUOUS RADIO CONTACT WITH TWO OTHER STATIONS AT ALL TIMES.

The other order went out: GO ARMED AT ALL TIMES. TAKE ANY VISITOR PRISONER.

Jarry waited. At the bottom of a chasm, parked beneath a shelf of rock, Jarry waited. An opened bottle stood upon the control board of his flier. Next to it was a small case of white metal.

Jarry took a long, last drink from the bottle as he waited for the broadcast he knew would come.

When it did, he stretched out on the seat and took a nap.

When he awakened, the light of day was waning.

The broadcast was still going on. . . .

". . . Jarry. They will be awakened and a referendum will be held. Come back to the main cavern. This is Yan Turl. Please do not destroy any more installations. This action is not necessary. We agree with your proposal that a vote be held. Please contact us immediately. We are waiting for your reply, Jarry . . ."

He tossed the empty bottle through the window and raised the flier out of the purple shadow into the air and up.

When he descended upon the landing stage within the main cavern, of course they were waiting for him. A dozen rifles were trained upon him as he stepped from the flier.

"Remove your weapons, Jarry," came the voice of Yan Turl.

"I'm not wearing any weapons," said Jarry. "Neither is my flier," he added; and this was true, for the fire-cannons no longer rested within their mountings.

Yan Turl approached, looked up at him.

"Then you may step down."

"Thank you, but I like it right where I am."

"You are a prisoner."

"What do you intend to do with me?"

"Put you back to sleep until the end of the Wait. Come down here!"

"No. And don't try shooting—or using a stun charge or gas, either. If you do, we're all of us dead the second it hits."

"What do you mean?" asked Turl, gesturing gently to the riflemen.

"My flier," said Jarry, "is a bomb, and I'm holding the fuse in my right hand." He raised the white metal box. "So long as I keep the lever on the side of this box depressed, we live. If my grip relaxes, even for an instant, the explosion which ensues will doubless destroy this entire cavern."

"I think you're bluffing."

"You know how you can find out for certain."

"You'll die too, Jarry."

"At the moment, I don't really care. Don't try burning my hand off either, to destroy the fuse," he cautioned, "because it doesn't really matter. Even if you should succeed, it will cost you at least two installations."

"Why is that?"

"What do you think I did with the fire-cannons? I taught the Redforms how to use them. At the moment, these weapons are manned by Redforms and aimed at two installations. If I do not personally visit my gunners by dawn, they will open fire. After destroying their objectives, they will move on and try for two more."

"You trusted those beasts with laser projectors?"

"That is correct. Now, will you begin awakening the others for the voting?"

Turl crouched as if to spring at him, appeared to think better of it, relaxed.

"Why did you do it, Jarry?" he asked. "What are they to you that you would make your own people suffer for them?"

"Since you do not feel as I feel," said Jarry, "my reasons would mean nothing to you. After all, they are only based upon my feelings, which are different than your own—for mine are based upon sorrow and loneliness. Try this one, though: I am their god. My form is to be found in their every camp. I am the Slayer of Bears from the Desert of the Dead. They have told my story for two and a half centuries, and I have been changed by it. I am powerful and wise and good, so far as they are concerned. In this capacity, I owe them some consideration. If I do not give them their lives, who will there be to honor me in snow and chant my story around the fires and cut for me the best portions of the woolly caterpillar? None, Turl. And these things are all that my life is worth now. Awaken the others. You have no choice."

"Very well," said Turl. "And if their decision should go against you?"

"Then I'll retire, and you can be god," said Jarry.

Now every day when the sun goes down out of the purple sky, Jarry Dark watches it in its passing, for he shall sleep no more the sleep of ice and of stone, wherein there is no dreaming. He has elected to live out the span of his days in a tiny instant of the Wait, never to look upon the New Alyonal of his people. Every morning, at the new Deadland installation, he is awakened by sounds like the cracking of ice, the trembling of tin, the snapping of steel strands, before they come to him with their offerings, singing and making marks upon the snow. They praise him and he smiles upon them. Sometimes he coughs.

Born of man and woman, in accordance with Catform Y7 requirements, Cold-world Class, Jarry Dark was not suited for existence anywhere in the universe which had guaranteed him a niche. This was either a blessing or a curse, depending on how you looked at it. So look at it however you would, that was the story. Thus does life repay those who would serve her fully.

Vaster than Empires and
More Slow

URSULA K. LE GUIN

Like Roger Zelazny, Ursula K. Le Guin started publishing in 1962 in the pages of Cele
Goldsmith's *Amazing,* but her career would rise in a less meteoric way, even if, in
the end, its arc would take her even higher. Her first novel, *Rocannon's World,*
published in 1966 at the bottom of the novel market as half of a garishly covered
Ace Double, was resolutely ignored by almost every critic in the field. Her next few
novels, the excellent and still-underrated *Planet of Exile* and the complex, van Vog-
tian *City of Illusions,* were also mostly overlooked and would only be discovered
retrospectively by most readers (in the same fashion as was Samuel R. Delany's early
work), after her plunge into wide public notice was accomplished by the publication of her most famous and acclaimed novel, *The Left Hand of Darkness,* in 1969,
as part of Terry Carr's new Ace Specials line. Rarely has a novel had as sharp and
sudden an impact or been accepted as widely as a modem masterpiece.

   Here at the end of the nineties, thirty years further on, it's probably fair to say
that Le Guin is one of the best-known and most universally respected science-
fiction writers in the world today, and one of the few living science-fiction writers
widely known and accepted outside the boundaries of genre. *The Left Hand of
Darkness* may have been the most influential science-fiction novel of its decade
and shows every sign of becoming one of the enduring classics of the genre—even
ignoring the rest of Le Guin's work, the impact of this one novel alone on future
science-fiction and future science-fiction writers would be incalculably strong. (Her
1968 fantasy novel, *A Wizard of Earthsea,* would be almost as influential on future
generations of High Fantasy writers.) *The Left Hand of Darkness* won both the Hugo
and Nebula Awards, as did Le Guin's monumental novel *The Dispossessed* a few
years later. Her novel *Tehanu* won her another Nebula in 1990, and she has also
won three other Hugo Awards and a Nebula Award for her short fiction, as well as
the National Book Award for Children's Literature for her novel *The Farthest Shore,*
part of her acclaimed *Earthsea* trilogy. Her other novels include *The Lathe of Heaven,*
The Beginning Place, A Wizard of Earthsea, The Tombs of Atuan, Tehanu, Searoad,

nd the controversial multimedia novel *Always Coming Home.* She has had six :ollections: *The Wind's Twelve Quarters, Orsinian Tales, The Compass Rose, Buffalo 3als and Other Animal Presences, A Fisherman of the Inland Sea,* and her most ecent book, *Four Ways to Forgiveness.* Upcoming is a new novel, *The Telling,* and ı collection of fantasy stories set in the Earthsea universe.

Most of Le Guin's science-fiction novels and stories share a common back-3round, the star-spanning, interstellar community known as the Ekumen. Since the nany races of the Ekumen (including Terran humans) were seeded by a race of :xplorers, the Hainish, thousands of years ago, exploration themes are fundamental ɔ the background of all the Ekumen stories, but occasionally Le Guin focuses more directly on explorers in the foreground action as well, as she does in *The Left Hand ɔf Darkness* and *City of Illusion* and in the recent sequence of stories, such as Another World," "The Shobbies's Story," and "Dancing to Ganam," that document he development of a method of instantaneous travel called *churten.* Rarely, though, ıas she concentrated on the lives and journeys of explorers more closely or with 3reater effect than in the story that follows, which shows us that explorers are often ı special breed of people—in fact, that may be the *problem!*

t was only during the earliest decades of the League that the Earth sent ships out ɔn the enormously long voyages, beyond the pale, over the stars and far away. They were seeking for worlds which had not been seeded or settled by the Founders ɔn Hain, truly alien worlds. All the Known Worlds went back to the Hainish Origin, ınd the Terrans, having been not only founded but salvaged by the Hainish, re-;ented this. They wanted to get away from the family. They wanted to find some-ɔody new. The Hainish, like tiresomely understanding parents, supported their ɛxplorations, and contributed ships and volunteers, as did several other worlds of he League.

All these volunteers to the Extreme Survey crews shared one peculiarity: they were of unsound mind.

What sane person, after all, would go out to collect information that would not ɔe received for five or ten centuries? Cosmic mass interference had not yet been ɛliminated from the operation of the ansible, and so instantaneous communication was reliable only within a range of 120 lightyears. The explorers would be quite isolated. And of course they had no idea what they might come back to, if they came back. No normal human being who had experienced time-slippage of even a few decades between League worlds would volunteer for a round trip of centuries. The Surveyors were escapists, misfits. They were nuts.

Ten of them climbed aboard the ferry at Smeming Port, and made varyingly inept attempts to get to know one another during the three days the ferry took getting to their ship, *Gum.* Gum is a Cetian nickname, on the order of Baby or Pet. There were two Cetians on the team, two Hainishmen, one Beldene, and five Terrans; the Cetian-built ship was chartered by the Government of Earth. Her motley crew came aboard wriggling through the coupling tube one by one like apprehensive spermatozoa trying to fertilize the universe. The ferry left, and the navigator put *Gum* underway. She flittered for some hours on the edge of space a few hundred million miles from Smeming Port, and then abruptly vanished.

When, after 10 hours 29 minutes, or 256 years, *Gum* reappeared in normal space, she was supposed to be in the vicinity of Star KG-E-96651. Sure enough there was the gold pinhead of the star. Somewhere within a four-hundred-million kilometer sphere there was also a greenish planet, World 4470, as charted by a Cetian mapmaker. The ship now had to find the planet. This was not quite so easy as it might sound, given a four-hundred-million-kilometer haystack. And *Gum* couldn't bat about in planetary space at near lightspeed; if she did, she and Star KG-F-96651 and World 4470 might all end up going bang. She had to creep, using rocket propulsion, at a few hundred thousand miles an hour. The Mathematician. Navigator, Asnanifoil, knew pretty well where the planet ought to be, and though they might raise it within ten E-days. Meanwhile the members of the Survey team got to know one another still better.

"I can't stand him," said Porlock, the Hard Scientist (chemistry, plus physics astronomy, geology, etc.), and little blobs of spittle appeared on his mustache. "The man is insane. I can't imagine why he was passed as fit to join a Survey team unless this is a deliberate experiment in noncompatibility, planned by the Authority with us as guinea pigs."

"We generally use hamsters and Hainish gholes," said Mannon, the Soft Scientist (psychology, plus psychiatry, anthropology, ecology, etc.), politely; he was one of the Hainishmen. "Instead of guinea pigs. Well, you know, Mr. Osden is really a very rare case. In fact, he's the first fully cured case of Render's Syndrome—a variety of infantile autism which was thought to be incurable. The great Terran analyst Hammergeld reasoned that the cause of the autistic condition in this case is a supernormal empathic capacity, and developed an appropriate treatment Mr. Osden is the first patient to undergo that treatment, in fact he lived with Dr. Hammergeld until he was eighteen. The therapy was completely successful."

"Successful?"

"Why, yes. He certainly is not autistic."

"No, he's intolerable!"

"Well, you see," said Mannon, gazing mildly at the saliva-flecks on Porlock's mustache, "the normal defensive-aggressive reaction between strangers meeting—let's say you and Mr. Osden just for example—is something you're scarcely aware of; habit, manners, inattention get you past it; you've learned to ignore it, to the point where you might even deny it exists. However, Mr. Osden, being an empath, feels it. Feels his feelings, and yours, and is hard put to say which is which. Let's say that there's a normal element of hostility towards any stranger in your emotional reaction to him when you meet him, plus a spontaneous dislike of his looks, or clothes, or handshake—it doesn't matter what. He feels that dislike. As his autistic defense has been unlearned, he resorts to an aggressive-defense mechanism, a response in kind to the aggression which you have unwittingly projected onto him." Mannon went on for quite a long time.

"Nothing gives a man the right to be such a bastard," Porlock said.

"He can't tune us out?" asked Harfex, the Biologist, another Hainishman.

"It's like hearing," said Olleroo, Assistant Hard Scientist, stooping over to paint her toenails with fluorescent lacquer. "No eyelids on your ears. No Off switch on empathy. He hears our feelings whether he wants to or not."

"Does he know what we're *thinking?*" asked Eskwana, the Engineer, looking round at the others in real dread.

"No," Porlock snapped. "Empathy's not telepathy! Nobody's got telepathy."

"Yet," said Mannon, with his little smile. "Just before I left Hain there was a most interesting report in from one of the recently rediscovered worlds, a hilfer named Rocannon reporting what appears to be a teachable telepathic technique existent among a mutated hominid race; I only saw a synopsis in the HILF Bulletin, but—" He went on. The others had learned that they could talk while Mannon went on talking; he did not seem to mind, nor even to miss much of what they said.

"Then why does he hate us?" Eskwana said.

"Nobody hates you, Ander honey," said Olleroo, daubing Eskwana's left thumbnail with fluorescent pink. The engineer flushed and smiled vaguely.

"He acts as if he hated us," said Haito, the Coordinator. She was a delicate-looking woman of pure Asian descent, with a surprising voice, husky, deep, and soft, like a young bullfrog. "Why, if he suffers from our hostility, does he increase it by constant attacks and insults? I can't say I think much of Dr. Hammergeld's cure, really, Mannon; autism might be preferable. . . ."

She stopped. Osden had come into the main cabin.

He looked flayed. His skin was unnaturally white and thin, showing the channels of his blood like a faded road map in red and blue. His Adam's apple, the muscles that circled his mouth, the bones and ligaments of his wrists and hands, all stood out distinctly as if displayed for an anatomy lesson. His hair was pale rust, like long-dried blood. He had eyebrows and lashes, but they were visible only in certain lights; what one saw was the bones of the eye sockets, the veining of the lids, and the colorless eyes. They were not red eyes, for he was not really an albino, but they were not blue or grey; colors had cancelled out in Osden's eyes, leaving a cold water-like clarity, infinitely penetrable. He never looked directly at one. His face lacked expression, like an anatomical drawing, or a skinned face.

"I agree," he said in a high, harsh tenor, "that even autistic withdrawal might be preferable to the smog of cheap secondhand emotions with which you people surround me. What are you sweating hate for now, Porlock? Can't stand the sight of me? Go practice some auto-eroticism the way you were doing last night, it improves your vibes. Who the devil moved my tapes, here? Don't touch my things, any of you. I won't have it."

"Osden," said Asnanifoil in his large slow voice, "why *are* you such a bastard?"

Ander Eskwana cowered and put his hands in front of his face. Contention frightened him. Olleroo looked up with a vacant yet eager expression, the eternal spectator.

"Why shouldn't I be?" said Osden. He was not looking at Asnanifoil, and was keeping physically as far away from all of them as he could in the crowded cabin. "None of you constitute, in yourselves, any reason for my changing my behavior."

Harfex, a reserved and patient man, said, "The reason is that we shall be spending several years together. Life will be better for all of us if—"

"Can't you understand that I don't give a damn for all of you?" Osden said, took up his microtapes, and went out. Eskwana had suddenly gone to sleep. Asnanifoil was drawing slipstreams in the air with his finger and muttering the Ritual Primes. "You cannot explain his presence on the team except as a plot on the part of the Terran Authority. I saw this almost at once. This mission is meant to fail," Harfex whispered to the Coordinator, glancing over his shoulder. Porlock was fumbling with his fly-button; there were tears in his eyes. I did tell you they were all crazy, but you thought I was exaggerating.

All the same, they were not unjustified. Extreme Surveyors expected to find their fellow team members intelligent, well-trained, unstable, and personally sympathetic. They had to work together in close quarters and nasty places, and could expect one another's paranoias, depressions, manias, phobias and compulsions to be mild enough to admit of good personal relationships, at least most of the time. Osden might be intelligent, but his training was sketchy and his personality was disastrous. He had been sent only on account of his singular gift, the power of empathy: properly speaking, of wide-range bioempathic receptivity. His talent wasn't species-specific; he could pick up emotion or sentience from anything that felt. He could share lust with a white rat, pain with a squashed cockroach, and phototropy with a moth. On an alien world, the Authority had decided, it would be useful to know if anything nearby is sentient, and if so, what its feelings towards you are. Osden's title was a new one: he was the team's Sensor.

"What is emotion, Osden?" Haito Tomiko asked him one day in the main cabin, trying to make some rapport with him for once. "What is it, exactly, that you pick up with your empathic sensitivity?"

"Muck," the man answered in his high, exasperated voice. "The psychic excreta of the animal kingdom. I wade through your faeces."

"I was trying," she said, "to learn some facts." She thought her tone was admirably calm.

"You weren't after facts. You were trying to get at me. With some fear, some curiosity, and a great deal of distaste. The way you might poke a dead dog, to see the maggots crawl. Will you understand once and for all that I don't want to be got at, that I want to be left alone?" His skin was mottled with red and violet, his voice had risen. "Go roll in your own dung, you yellow bitch!" he shouted at her silence.

"Calm down," she said, still quietly, but she left him at once and went to her cabin. Of course he had been right about her motives; her question had been largely a pretext, a mere effort to interest him. But what harm in that? Did not that effort imply respect for the other? At the moment of asking the question she had felt at most a slight distrust of him; she had mostly felt sorry for him, the poor arrogant venomous bastard, Mr. No-Skin as Olleroo called him. What did he expect, the way he acted? Love?

"I guess he can't stand anybody feeling sorry for him," said Olleroo, lying on the lower bunk, gilding her nipples.

"Then he can't form any human relationship. All his Dr. Hammergeld did was turn an autism inside out. . . ."

"Poor frot," said Olleroo. "Tomiko, you don't mind if Harfex comes in for a while tonight, do you?"

"Can't you go to his cabin? I'm sick of always having to sit in Main with that damned peeled turnip."

"You do hate him, don't you? I guess he feels that. But I slept with Harfex last night too, and Asnanifoil might get jealous, since they share the cabin. It would be nicer here."

"Service them both," Tomiko said with the coarseness of offended modesty.

Her Terran subculture, the East Asian, was a puritanical one; she had been brought up chaste.

"I only like one a night," Olleroo replied with innocent serenity. Beldene, the Garden Planet, had never discovered chastity, or the wheel.

"Try Osden, then," Tomiko said. Her personal instability was seldom so plain as now: a profound self-distrust manifesting itself as destructivism. She had volunteered for this job because there was, in all probability, no use in doing it.

The little Beldene looked up, paintbrush in hand, eyes wide. "Tomiko, that was a dirty thing to say."

"Why?"

"It would be vile! I'm not attracted to Osden!"

"I didn't know it mattered to you," Tomiko said indifferently, though she did know. She got some papers together and left the cabin, remarking, "I hope you and Harfex or whoever it is finish by last bell; I'm tired."

Olleroo was crying, tears dripping on her little gilded nipples. She wept easily. Tomiko had not wept since she was ten years old.

It was not a happy ship; but it took a turn for the better when Asnanifoil and his computers raised World 4470. There it lay, a dark-green jewel, like truth at the bottom of a gravity well. As they watched the jade disc grow, a sense of mutuality grew among them. Osden's selfishness, his accurate cruelty, served now to draw the others together. "Perhaps," Mannon said, "he was sent as a beating gron. What Terrans call a scapegoat. Perhaps his influence will be good after all." And no one, so careful were they to be kind to one another, disagreed.

They came into orbit. There were no lights on nightside, on the continents none of the lines and clots made by animals who build.

"No men," Harfex murmured.

"Of course not," snapped Osden, who had a viewscreen to himself, and his head inside a polythene bag. He claimed that the plastic cut down on the empathic noise he received from the others. "We're two lightcenturies past the limit of the Hainish Expansion, and outside that there are no men. Anywhere. You don't think Creation would have made the same hideous mistake twice?"

No one was paying him much heed; they were looking with affection at that jade immensity below them, where there was life, but not human life. They were misfits among men, and what they saw there was not desolation, but peace. Even Osden did not look quite so expressionless as usual; he was frowning.

Descent in fire on the sea; air reconnaissance; landing. A plain of something like grass, thick, green, bowing stalks, surrounded the ship, brushed against extended viewcameras, smeared the lenses with a fine pollen.

"It looks like a pure phytosphere," Harfex said. "Osden, do you pick up anything sentient?"

They all turned to the Sensor. He had left the screen and was pouring himself a cup of tea. He did not answer. He seldom answered spoken questions.

The chitinous rigidity of military discipline was quite inapplicable to these teams of mad scientists; their chain of command lay somewhere between parliamentary procedure and peck-order, and would have driven a regular service officer out of his mind. By the inscrutable decision of the Authority, however, Dr. Haito Tomiko had been given the title of Coordinator, and she now exercised her prerogative for the first time. "Mr. Sensor Osden," she said, "please answer Mr. Harfex."

"How could I 'pick up' anything from outside," Osden said without turning, "with the emotions of nine neurotic hominids pullulating around me like worms in a can? When I have anything to tell you, I'll tell you. I'm aware of my responsibility as Sensor. If you presume to give me an order again, however, Coordinator Haito, I'll consider my responsibility void."

"Very well, Mr. Sensor. I trust no orders will be needed henceforth." Tomiko's bullfrog voice was calm, but Osden seemed to flinch slightly as he stood with his back to her, as if the surge of her suppressed rancor had struck him with physical force.

The biologist's hunch proved correct. When they began field analyses they found no animals even among the microbiota. Nobody here ate anybody else. All life-forms were photosynthesizing or saprophagous, living off light or death, not off life. Plants: infinite plants, not one species known to the visitors from the house of Man. Infinite shades and intensities of green, violet, purple, brown, red. Infinite silences. Only the wind moved, swaying leaves and fronds, a warm soughing wind laden with spores and pollens, blowing the sweet pale-green dust over prairies of great grasses, heaths that bore no heather, flowerless forests where no foot had ever walked, no eye had ever looked. A warm, sad world, sad and serene. The Surveyors, wandering like picnickers over sunny plains of violet filicaliformes, spoke softly to each other. They knew their voices broke a silence of a thousand million years, the silence of wind and leaves, leaves and wind, blowing and ceasing and blowing again. They talked softly; but being human, they talked.

"Poor old Osden," said Jenny Chong, Bio and Tech, as she piloted a helijet on the North Polar Quadrating run. "All that fancy hi-fi stuff in his brain and nothing to receive. What a bust."

"He told me he hates plants," Olleroo said with a giggle.

"You'd think he'd like them, since they don't bother him like we do."

"Can't say I much like these plants myself," said Porlock, looking down at the purple undulations of the North Circumpolar Forest. "All the same. No mind. No change. A man alone in it would go right off his head."

"But it's all alive," Jenny Chong said. "And if it lives, Osden hates it."

"He's not really so bad," Olleroo said, magnanimous. Porlock looked at her sidelong and asked, "You ever slept with him, Olleroo?"

Olleroo burst into tears and cried, "You Terrans are obscene!"

"No she hasn't," Jenny Chong said, prompt to defend. "Have you, Porlock?"

The chemist laughed uneasily: ha, ha, ha. Flecks of spittle appeared on his mustache.

"Osden can't bear to be touched," Olleroo said shakily. "I just brushed against him once by accident and he knocked me off like I was some sort of dirty . . . thing. We're all just things, to him."

"He's evil," Porlock said in a strained voice, startling the two women. "He'll end up shattering this team, sabotaging it, one way or another. Mark my words. He's not fit to live with other people!"

They landed on the North Pole. A midnight sun smouldered over low hills. Short, dry, greenish-pink bryoform grasses stretched away in every direction, which was all one direction, south. Subdued by the incredible silence, the three Surveyors set up their instruments and set to work, three viruses twitching minutely on the hide of an unmoving giant.

Nobody asked Osden along on runs as pilot or photographer or recorder, and he never volunteered, so he seldom left base camp. He ran Harfex's botanical taxonomic data through the onship computers, and served as assistant to Eskwana, whose job here was mainly repair and maintenance. Eskwana had begun to sleep a great deal, twenty-five hours or more out of the thirty-two-hour day, dropping off in the middle of repairing a radio or checking the guidance circuits of a helijet. The Coordinator stayed at base one day to observe. No one else was home except Poswet To, who was subject to epileptic fits; Mannon had plugged her into a therapy-circuit today in a state of preventive catatonia. Tomiko spoke reports into the storage banks, and kept an eye on Osden and Eskwana. Two hours passed.

"You might want to use the 860 microwaldoes in sealing that connection," Eskwana said in his soft, hesitant voice.

"Obviously!"

"Sorry. I just saw you had the 840's there—"

"And will replace them when I take the 860's out. When I don't know how to proceed, Engineer, I'll ask your advice."

After a minute Tomiko looked round. Sure enough, there was Eskwana sound asleep, head on the table, thumb in his mouth.

"Osden."

The white face did not turn, he did not speak, but conveyed impatiently that he was listening.

"You can't be unaware of Eskwana's vulnerability."

"I am not responsible for his psychopathic reactions."

"But you are responsible for your own. Eskwana is essential to our work here, and you're not. If you can't control your hostility, you must avoid him altogether."

Osden put down his tools and stood up. "With pleasure!" he said in his vindictive, scraping voice. "You could not possibly imagine what it's like to experience Eskwana's irrational terrors. To have to share his horrible cowardice, to have to cringe with him at everything!"

"Are you trying to justify your cruelty towards him? I thought you had more self-respect." Tomiko found herself shaking with spite. "If your empathic power really makes you share Ander's misery, why does it never induce the least compassion in you?"

"Compassion," Osden said. "Compassion. What do you know about compassion?"

She stared at him, but he would not look at her.

"Would you like me to verbalize your present emotional affect regarding myself?" he said. "I can do so more precisely than you can. I'm trained to analyze such responses as I receive them. And I do receive them."

"But how can you expect me to feel kindly towards you when you behave as you do?"

"What does it matter how I *behave*, you stupid sow, do you think it makes any difference? Do you think the average human is a well of loving-kindness? My choice is to be hated or to be despised. Not being a woman or a coward, I prefer to be hated."

"That's rot. Self-pity. Every man has—"

"But I am not a man," Osden said. "There are all of you. And there is myself. I am *one*."

Awed by that glimpse of abysmal solipsism, she kept silent a while; finally she said with neither spite nor pity, clinically, "You could kill yourself, Osden."

"That's your way, Haito," he jeered. "I'm not depressive, and *seppuku* isn't my bit. What do you want me to do here?"

"Leave. Spare yourself and us. Take the aircar and a data-feeder and go do a species count. In the forest; Harfex hasn't even started the forests yet. Take a hundred-square-meter forested area, anywhere inside radio range. But outside empathy range. Report in at 8 and 24 o'clock daily."

Osden went, and nothing was heard from him for five days but laconic all-well signals twice daily. The mood at base camp changed like a stage-set. Eskwana stayed awake up to eighteen hours a day. Poswet To got out her stellar lute and chanted the celestial harmonies (music had driven Osden into a frenzy). Mannon, Harfex, Jenny Chong, and Tomiko all went off tranquillizers. Porlock distilled something in his laboratory and drank it all by himself. He had a hangover. Asnanifoil and Poswet To held an all-night Numerical Epiphany, that mystical orgy of higher mathematics which is the chief pleasure of the religious Cetian soul. Olleroo slept with everybody. Work went well.

The Hard Scientist came towards base at a run, laboring through the high, fleshy stalks of the graminiformes. "Something—in the forest—" His eyes bulged, he panted, his mustache and fingers trembled. "Something big. Moving, behind me. I was putting in a benchmark, bending down. It came at me. As if it was swinging down out of the trees. Behind me." He stared at the others with the opaque eyes of terror or exhaustion.

"Sit down, Porlock. Take it easy. Now wait, go through this again. You *saw* something—"

"Not clearly. Just the movement. Purposive. A—an—I don't know what it could have been. Something self-moving. In the trees, the arboriformes, whatever you call 'em. At the edge of the woods."

Harfex looked grim. "There is nothing here that could attack you, Porlock. There are not even microzoa. There *could not* be a large animal."

"Could you possibly have seen an epiphyte drop suddenly, a vine come loose behind you?"

"No," Porlock said. "It was coming down at me, through the branches, fast. When I turned it took off again, away and upward. It made a noise, a sort of crashing. If it wasn't an animal, God knows what it could have been! It was big—as big as a man, at least. Maybe a reddish color. I couldn't see, I'm not sure."

"It was Osden," said Jenny Chong, "doing a Tarzan act." She giggled nervously, and Tomiko repressed a wild feckless laugh. But Harfex was not smiling.

"One gets uneasy under the arboriformes," he said in his polite, repressed voice. "I've noticed that. Indeed that may be why I've put off working in the forests. There's a hypnotic quality in the colors and spacing of the stems and branches, especially the helically-arranged ones; and the spore-throwers grow so regularly spaced that it seems unnatural. I find it quite disagreeable, subjectively speaking. I wonder if a stronger effect of that sort mightn't have produced a hallucination . . . ?"

Porlock shook his head. He wet his lips. "It was there," he said. "Something. Moving with purpose. Trying to attack me from behind."

When Osden called in, punctual as always, at 24 o'clock that night, Harfex told him Porlock's report. "Have you come on anything at all, Mr. Osden, that could substantiate Mr. Porlock's impression of a motile, sentient life-form, in the forest?"

Ssss, the radio said sardonically. "No. Bullshit," said Osden's unpleasant voice.

"You've been actually inside the forest longer than any of us," Harfex said with unmitigable politeness. "Do you agree with my impression that the forest ambiance has a rather troubling and possibly hallucinogenic effect on the perceptions?"

Ssss. "I'll agree that Porlock's perceptions are easily troubled. Keep him in his lab, he'll do less harm. Anything else?"

"Not at present," Harfex said, and Osden cut off.

Nobody could credit Porlock's story, and nobody could discredit it. He was positive that something, something big, had tried to attack him by surprise. It was hard to deny this, for they were on an alien world, and everyone who had entered the forest had felt a certain chill and foreboding under the "trees." ("Call them trees, certainly," Harfex had said. "They really are the same thing, only, of course, altogether different.") They agreed that they had felt uneasy, or had had the sense that something was watching them from behind.

"We've got to clear this up," Porlock said, and he asked to be sent as a temporary Biologist's Aide, like Osden, into the forest to explore and observe. Olleroo and Jenny Chong volunteered if they could go as a pair. Harfex sent them all off into the forest near which they were encamped, a vast tract covering four-fifths of Continent D. He forbade side-arms. They were not to go outside a fifty-mile half-circle, which included Osden's current site. They all reported in twice daily, for three days. Porlock reported a glimpse of what seemed to be a large semi-erect shape moving through the trees across the river; Olleroo was sure she had heard something moving near the tent, the second night.

"There are no animals on this planet," Harfex said, dogged.

Then Osden missed his morning call.

Tomiko waited less than an hour, then flew with Harfex to the area where Osden had reported himself the night before. But as the helijet hovered over the sea of purplish leaves, illimitable, impenetrable, she felt a panic despair. "How can we find him in this?"

"He reported landing on the riverbank. Find the aircar; he'll be camped near it, and he can't have gone far from his camp. Species-counting is slow work. There's the river."

"There's his car," Tomiko said, catching the bright foreign glint among the vegetable colors and shadows. "Here goes, then."

She put the ship in hover and pitched out the ladder. She and Harfex descended. The sea of life closed over their heads.

As her feet touched the forest floor, she unsnapped the flap of her holster; then glancing at Harfex, who was unarmed, she left the gun untouched. But her hand kept coming back up to it. There was no sound at all, as soon as they were a few meters away from the slow, brown river, and the light was dim. Great boles stood well apart, almost regularly, almost alike; they were soft-skinned, some appearing smooth and others spongy, grey or greenish-brown or brown, twined with cable-like creepers and festooned with epiphytes, extending rigid, entangled armfuls of big, saucer-shaped, dark leaves that formed a roof-layer twenty to thirty meters thick. The ground underfoot was springy as a mattress, every inch of it knotted with roots and peppered with small, fleshy-leaved growths.

"Here's his tent," Tomiko said, cowed at the sound of her voice in that huge community of the voiceless. In the tent was Osden's sleeping bag, a couple of books, a box of rations. We should be calling, shouting for him, she thought, but did not even suggest it; nor did Harfex. They circled out from the tent, careful to keep each other in sight through the thick-standing presences, the crowding gloom. She stumbled over Osden's body, not thirty meters from the tent, led to it by the whitish gleam of a dropped notebook. He lay face down between two huge-rooted trees. His head and hands were covered with blood, some dried, some still oozing red.

Harfex appeared beside her, his pale Hainish complexion quite green in the dusk. "Dead?"

"No. He's been struck. Beaten. From behind." Tomiko's fingers felt over the bloody skull and temples and nape. "A weapon or a tool . . . I don't find a fracture."

As she turned Osden's body over so they could lift him, his eyes opened. She was holding him, bending close to his face. His pale lips writhed. A deathly fear came into her. She screamed aloud two or three times and tried to run away, shambling and stumbling into the terrible dusk. Harfex caught her, and at his touch and the sound of his voice, her panic decreased. "What is it? What is it?" he was saying.

"I don't know," she sobbed. Her heartbeat still shook her, and she could not see clearly. "The fear—the . . . I panicked. When I saw his eyes."

"We're both nervous. I don't understand this—"

"I'm all right now, come on, we've got to get him under care."

Both working with senseless haste, they lugged Osden to the riverside and hauled him up on a rope under his armpits; he dangled like a sack, twisting a little, over the glutinous dark sea of leaves. They pulled him into the helijet and took off. Within a minute they were over open prairie. Tomiko locked onto the homing beam. She drew a deep breath, and her eyes met Harfex's.

"I was so terrified I almost fainted. I have never done that."

"I was . . . unreasonably frightened also," said the Hainishman, and indeed he looked aged and shaken. "Not so badly as you. But as unreasonably."

"It was when I was in contact with him, holding him. He seemed to be conscious for a moment."

"Empathy? . . . I hope he can tell us what attacked him."

Osden, like a broken dummy covered with blood and mud, half lay as they had bundled him into the rear seats in their frantic urgency to get out of the forest.

More panic met their arrival at base. The ineffective brutality of the assault was sinister and bewildering. Since Harfex stubbornly denied any possibility of animal life they began speculating about sentient plants, vegetable monsters, psychic projections. Jenny Chong's latent phobia reasserted itself and she could talk about nothing except the Dark Egos which followed people around behind their backs. She and Olleroo and Porlock had been summoned back to base; and nobody was much inclined to go outside.

Osden had lost a good deal of blood during the three or four hours he had lain alone, and concussion and severe contusions had put him in shock and semi-coma. As he came out of this and began running a low fever he called several times for "Doctor," in a plaintive voice: "Doctor Hammergeld . . ." When he regained full consciousness, two of those long days later, Tomiko called Harfex into his cubicle.

"Osden: can you tell us what attacked you?"

The pale eyes flickered past Harfex's face.

"You were attacked," Tomiko said gently. The shifty gaze was hatefully familiar, but she was a physician, protective of the hurt. "You may not remember it yet. Something attacked you. You were in the forest—"

"Ah!" he cried out, his eyes growing bright and his features contorting. "The forest—in the forest—"

"What's in the forest?"

He gasped for breath. A look of clearer consciousness came into his face. After a while he said, "I don't know."

"Did you see what attacked you?" Harfex asked.

"I don't know."

"You remember it now."

"I don't know."

"All our lives may depend on this. You must tell us what you saw!"

"I don't know," Osden said, sobbing with weakness. He was too weak to hide the fact that he was hiding the answer, yet he would not say it. Porlock, nearby, was chewing his pepper-colored mustache as he tried to hear what was going on in the cubicle. Harfex leaned over Osden and said, "You *will* tell us—" Tomiko had to interfere bodily.

Harfex controlled himself with an effort that was painful to see. He went off silently to his cubicle, where no doubt he took a double or triple dose of tranquilizers. The other men and women, scattered about the big frail building, a long main hall and ten sleeping-cubicles, said nothing, but looked depressed and edgy. Osden, as always, even now, had them all at his mercy. Tomiko looked down at him with a rush of hatred that burned in her throat like bile. This monstrous egotism that fed itself on others' emotions, this absolute selfishness, was worse than any hideous deformity of the flesh. Like a congenital monster, he should not have lived. Should not be alive. Should have died. Why had his head not been split open?

As he lay flat and white, his hands helpless at his sides, his colorless eyes were wide open, and there were tears running from the corners. He tried to flinch away. "Don't," he said in a weak hoarse voice, and tried to raise his hands to protect his head. "Don't!"

She sat down on the folding-stool beside the cot, and after a while put her hand on his. He tried to pull away, but lacked the strength.

A long silence fell between them.

"Osden," she murmured, "I'm sorry. I'm very sorry. I will you well. Let me will you well, Osden. I don't want to hurt you. Listen, I do see now. It was one of us. That's right, isn't it. No, don't answer, only tell me if I'm wrong; but I'm not . . . Of course there are animals on this planet. Ten of them. I don't care who it was. It doesn't matter, does it. It could have been me, just now. I realize that. I didn't understand how it is, Osden. You can't see how difficult it is for us to understand. . . . But listen. If it were love, instead of hate and fear . . . Is it never love?"

"No."

"Why not? Why should it never be? Are human beings all so weak? That is terrible. Never mind, never mind, don't worry. Keep still. At least right now it isn't hate, is it? Sympathy at least, concern, well-wishing. You do feel that, Osden? Is it what you feel?"

"Among . . . other things," he said, almost inaudibly.

"Noise from my subconscious, I suppose. And everybody else in the room . . . Listen, when we found you there in the forest, when I tried to turn you over, you partly wakened, and I felt a horror of you. I was insane with fear for a minute. Was that your fear of me I felt?"

"No."

Her hand was still on his, and he was quite relaxed, sinking towards sleep, like a man in pain who has been given relief from pain. "The forest," he muttered; she could barely understand him. "Afraid."

She pressed him no further, but kept her hand on his and watched him go to sleep. She knew what she felt, and what therefore he must feel. She was confident of it: there is only one emotion, or state of being, that can thus wholly reverse itself, polarize, within one moment. In Great Hainish indeed there is one word, *ontá*, for love and for hate. She was not in love with Osden, of course, that was another kettle of fish. What she felt for him was *ontá*, polarized hate. She held his hand and the current flowed between them, the tremendous electricity of touch, which he had always dreaded. As he slept the ring of anatomy-chart muscles around his mouth relaxed, and Tomiko saw on his face what none of them had ever seen, very faint, a smile. It faded. He slept on.

He was tough; next day he was sitting up, and hungry. Harfex wished to interrogate him, but Tomiko put him off. She hung a sheet of polythene over the cubicle door, as Osden himself had often done. "Does it actually cut down your empathic reception?" she asked, and he replied, in the dry, cautious tone they were now using to each other, "No."

"Just a warning, then."

"Partly. More faith-healing. Dr. Hammergeld thought it worked. . . . Maybe it does, a little."

There had been love, once. A terrified child, suffocating in the tidal rush and battering of the huge emotions of adults, a drowning child, saved by one man. Taught to breathe, to live, by one man. Given everything, all protection and love, by one man. Father/Mother/God: no other. "Is he still alive?" Tomiko asked, thinking of Osden's incredible loneliness, and the strange cruelty of the great doctors. She was shocked when she heard his forced, tinny laugh. "He died at least two and a half centuries ago," Osden said. "Do you forget where we are, Coordinator? We've all left our little families behind. . . ."

Outside the polythene curtain the eight other human beings on World 4470 moved vaguely. Their voices were low and strained. Eskwana slept; Poswet To was in therapy; Jenny Chong was trying to rig lights in her cubicle so that she wouldn't cast a shadow.

"They're all scared," Tomiko said, scared. "They've all got these ideas about what attacked you. A sort of ape-potato, a giant fanged spinach, I don't know. . . .

Even Harfex. You may be right not to force them to see. That would be worse, to lose confidence in one another. But why are we all so shaky, unable to face the fact, going to pieces so easily? Are we really all insane?"

"We'll soon be more so."

"Why?"

"There *is* something." He closed his mouth, the muscles of his lips stood out rigid.

"Something sentient?"

"A sentience."

"In the forest?"

He nodded.

"What is it, then—?"

"The fear." He began to look strained again, and moved restlessly. "When I fell, there, you know, I didn't lose consciousness at once. Or I kept regaining it. I don't know. It was more like being paralyzed."

"You were."

"I was on the ground. I couldn't get up. My face was in the dirt, in that soft leaf mold. It was in my nostrils and eyes. I couldn't move. Couldn't see. As if I was in the ground. Sunk into it, part of it. I knew I was between two trees even though I never saw them. I suppose I could feel the roots. Below me in the ground, down under the ground. My hands were bloody, I could feel that, and the blood made the dirt around my face sticky. I felt the fear. It kept growing. As if they'd finally known I was there, lying on them there, under them, among them, the thing they feared, and yet part of their fear itself. I couldn't stop sending the fear back, and it kept growing, and I couldn't get away. I would pass out, I think, and then the fear would bring me to again, and I still couldn't move. Any more than they can."

Tomiko felt the cold stirring of her hair, the readying of the apparatus of terror. "They: who are they, Osden?"

"They, it—I don't know. The fear."

"What is he talking about?" Harfex demanded when Tomiko reported this conversation. She would not let Harfex question Osden yet, feeling that she must protect Osden from the onslaught of the Hainishman's powerful, over-repressed emotions. Unfortunately this fueled the slow fire of paranoid anxiety that burned in poor Harfex, and he thought she and Osden were in league, hiding some fact of great importance or peril from the rest of the team.

"It's like the blind man trying to describe the elephant. Osden hasn't seen or heard the . . . the sentience, any more than we have."

"But he's felt it, my dear Haito," Harfex said with just-suppressed rage. "Not empathically. On his skull. It came and knocked him down and beat him with a blunt instrument. Did he not catch *one* glimpse of it?"

"What would he have seen, Harfex?" Tomiko asked, but he would not hear her meaningful tone; even he had blocked out that comprehension. What one fears is alien. The murderer is an outsider, a foreigner, not one of us. The evil is not in me!

"The first blow knocked him pretty well out," Tomiko said a little wearily, "he didn't see anything. But when he came to again, alone in the forest, he felt a great fear. Not his own fear, an empathic effect. He is certain of that. And certain it was nothing picked up from any of us. So that evidently the native life-forms are not all insentient."

Harfex looked at her a moment, grim. "You're trying to frighten me, Haito. I do not understand your motives." He got up and went off to his laboratory table, walking slowly and stiffly, like a man of eighty not of forty.

She looked round at the others. She felt some desperation. Her new, fragile, and profound interdependence with Osden gave her, she was well aware, some added strength. But if even Harfex could not keep his head, who of the others would? Porlock and Eskwana were shut in their cubicles, the others were all working or busy with something. There was something queer about their positions. For a while the Coordinator could not tell what it was, then she saw that they were all sitting facing the nearby forest. Playing chess with Asnanifoil, Olleroo had edged her chair around until it was almost beside his.

She went to Mannon, who was dissecting a tangle of spidery brown roots, and told him to look for the pattern-puzzle. He saw it at once, and said with unusual brevity, "Keeping an eye on the enemy."

"What enemy? What do *you* feel, Mannon?" She had a sudden hope in him as a psychologist, on this obscure ground of hints and empathies where biologists went astray.

"I feel a strong anxiety with a specific spatial orientation. But I am not an empath. Therefore the anxiety is explicable in terms of the particular stress-situation, that is, the attack on a team member in the forest, and also in terms of the total stress-situation, that is, my presence in a totally alien environment, for which the archetypical connotations of the word 'forest' provide an inevitable metaphor."

Hours later Tomiko woke to hear Osden screaming in nightmare; Mannon was calming him, and she sank back into her own dark-branching pathless dreams. In the morning Eskwana did not wake. He could not be roused with stimulant drugs. He clung to his sleep, slipping farther and farther back, mumbling softly now and then until, wholly regressed, he lay curled on his side, thumb at his lips, gone.

"Two days; two down. Ten little Indians, nine little Indians . . ." That was Porlock.

"And you're the next little Indian," Jenny Chong snapped. "Go analyze your urine, Porlock!"

"He is driving us all insane," Porlock said, getting up and waving his left arm. "Can't you feel it? For God's sake, are you all deaf and blind? Can't you feel what he's doing, the emanations? It all comes from him—from his room there—from his mind. He is driving us all insane with fear!"

"Who is?" said Asnanifoil, looming precipitous and hairy over the little Terran.

"Do I have to say his name? Osden, then. Osden! Osden! Why do you think I tried to kill him? In self-defense! To save all of us! Because you won't see what he's doing to us. He's sabotaged the mission by making us quarrel, and now he's going to drive us all insane by projecting fear at us so that we can't sleep or think, like a huge radio that doesn't make any sound, but it broadcasts all the time, and you can't sleep, and you can't think. Haito and Harfex are already under his control but the rest of you can be saved. I had to do it!"

"You didn't do it very well," Osden said, standing half-naked, all rib and bandage, at the door of his cubicle. "I could have hit myself harder. Hell, it isn't me that's scaring you blind, Porlock, it's out there—there, in the woods!"

Porlock made an ineffectual attempt to assault Osden; Asnanifoil held him back, and continued to hold him effortlessly while Mannon gave him a sedative shot. He was put away shouting about giant radios. In a minute the sedative took effect, and he joined a peaceful silence to Eskwana's.

"All right," said Harfex. "Now, Osden, you'll tell us what you know and all you know."

Osden said, "I don't know anything."

He looked battered and faint. Tomiko made him sit down before he talked.

"After I'd been three days in the forest, I thought I was occasionally receiving some kind of affect."

"Why didn't you report it?"

"Thought I was going spla, like the rest of you."

"That, equally, should have been reported."

"You'd have called me back to base. I couldn't take it. You realize that my inclusion in the mission was a bad mistake. I'm not able to coexist with nine other neurotic personalities at close quarters. I was wrong to volunteer for Extreme Survey, and the Authority was wrong to accept me."

No one spoke; but Tomiko saw, with certainty this time, the flinch in Osden's shoulders and the tightening of his facial muscles, as he registered their bitter agreement.

"Anyhow, I didn't want to come back to base because I was curious. Even going psycho, how could I pick up empathic affects when there was no creature to emit them? They weren't bad, then. Very vague. Queer. Like a draft in a closed room, a flicker in the corner of your eye. Nothing really."

For a moment he had been borne up on their listening: they heard, so he spoke. He was wholly at their mercy. If they disliked him he had to be hateful; if they mocked him he became grotesque; if they listened to him he was the storyteller. He was helplessly obedient to the demands of their emotions, reactions, moods. And there were seven of them, too many to cope with, so that he must be constantly knocked about from one to another's whim. He could not find coherence. Even as he spoke and held them, somebody's attention would wander: Olleroo perhaps was thinking that he wasn't unattractive, Harfex was seeking the ulterior motive of his words, Asnanifoil's mind, which could not be long held by the concrete, was roaming off towards the eternal peace of number, and Tomiko was distracted by pity, by fear. Osden's voice faltered. He lost the thread. "I . . . I thought it must be the trees," he said, and stopped.

"It's not the trees," Harfex said. "They have no more nervous system than do plants of the Hainish Descent on Earth. None."

"You're not seeing the forest for the trees, as they say on Earth," Mannon put in, smiling elfinly; Harfex stared at him. "What about those root-nodes we've been puzzling about for twenty days—eh?"

"What about them?"

"They are, indubitably, connections. Connections among the trees. Right? Now let's just suppose, most improbably, that you knew nothing of animal brain-structure. And you were given one axon, or one detached glial cell, to examine.

Would you be likely to discover what it was? Would you see that the cell was capable of sentience?"

"No. Because it isn't. A single cell is capable of mechanical response to stimulus. No more. Are you hypothesizing that individual arboriformes are 'cells' in a kind of brain, Mannon?"

"Not exactly. I'm merely pointing out that they are all interconnected, both by the root-node linkage and by your green epiphytes in the branches. A linkage of incredible complexity and physical extent. Why, even the prairie grass-forms have those root-connectors, don't they? I know that sentience or intelligence isn't a thing, you can't find it in, or analyze it out from, the cells of a brain. It's a function of the connected cells. It is, in a sense, the connection: the connectedness. It doesn't exist. I'm not trying to say it exists. I'm only guessing that Osden might be able to describe it."

And Osden took him up, speaking as if in trance. "Sentience without senses. Blind, deaf, nerveless, moveless. Some irritability, response to touch. Response to sun, to light, to water, and chemicals in the earth around the roots. Nothing comprehensible to an animal mind. Presence without mind. Awareness of being, without object or subject. Nirvana."

"Then why do you receive fear?" Tomiko asked in a low voice.

"I don't know. I can't see how awareness of objects, of others, could arise: an unperceiving response . . . But there was an uneasiness, for days. And then when I lay between the two trees and my blood was on their roots—" Osden's face glittered with sweat. "It became fear," he said shrilly, "only fear."

"If such a function existed," Harfex said, "it would not be capable of conceiving of a self-moving, material entity, or responding to one. It could no more become aware of us than we can 'become aware' of Infinity."

" 'The silence of those infinite expanses terrifies me,' " muttered Tomiko. "Pascal was aware of Infinity. By way of fear."

"To a forest," Mannon said, "we might appear as forest fires. Hurricanes. Dangers. What moves quickly is dangerous, to a plant. The rootless would be alien, terrible. And if it is mind, it seems only too probable that it might become aware of Osden, whose own mind is open to connection with all others so long as he's conscious, and who was lying in pain and afraid within it, actually inside it. No wonder it was afraid—"

"Not 'it,' " Harfex said. "There is no being, no huge creature, no person! There could at most be only a function—"

"There is only a fear," Osden said.

They were all still a while, and heard the stillness outside.

"Is that what I feel all the time coming up behind me?" Jenny Chong asked, subdued.

Osden nodded. "You all feel it, deaf as you are. Eskwana's the worst off, because he actually has some empathic capacity. He could send if he learned how, but he's too weak, never will be anything but a medium."

"Listen, Osden," Tomiko said, "you can send. Then send to it—the forest, the fear out there—tell it that we won't hurt it. Since it has, or is, some sort of affect that translates into what we feel as emotion, can't you translate back? Send out a message, We are harmless, we are friendly."

"You must know that nobody can emit a false empathic message, Haito. You an't send something that doesn't exist."

"But we don't intend harm, we are friendly."

"Are we? In the forest, when you picked me up, did you feel friendly?"

"No. Terrified. But that's—it, the forest, the plants, not my own fear, isn't it?"

"What's the difference? It's all you felt. Can't you see," and Osden's voice ose in exasperation, "why I dislike you and you dislike me, all of you? Can't you ee that I retransmit every negative or aggressive affect you've felt towards me ince we first met? I return your hostility, with thanks. I do it in self-defense. Like ²orlock. It is self-defense, though; it's the only technique I developed to replace ny original defense of total withdrawal from others. Unfortunately it creates a :losed circuit, self-sustaining and self-reinforcing. Your initial reaction to me was he instinctive antipathy to a cripple; by now of course it's hatred. Can you fail to ee my point? The forest-mind out there transmits only terror, now, and the only nessage I can send it is terror, because when exposed to it I can feel nothing :xcept terror!"

"What must we do, then?" said Tomiko, and Mannon replied promptly, "Move :amp. To another continent. If there are plant-minds there, they'll be slow to notice is, as this one was; maybe they won't notice us at all."

"It would be a considerable relief," Osden observed stiffly. The others had been watching him with a new curiosity. He had revealed himself, they had seen him as he was, a helpless man in a trap. Perhaps, like Tomiko, they had seen that the trap itself, his crass and cruel egotism, was their own construction, not his. They had built the cage and locked him in it, and like a caged ape he threw filth out through the bars. If, meeting him, they had offered trust, if they had been strong enough to offer him love, how might he have appeared to them?

None of them could have done so, and it was too late now. Given time, given solitude, Tomiko might have built up with him a slow resonance of feeling, a consonance of trust, a harmony; but there was no time, their job must be done. There was not room enough for the cultivation of so great a thing, and they must make do with sympathy, with pity, the small change of love. Even that much had given her strength, but it was nowhere near enough for him. She could see in his flayed face now his savage resentment of their curiosity, even of her pity.

"Go lie down, that gash is bleeding again," she said, and he obeyed her.

Next morning they packed up, melted down the sprayform hangar and living quarters, lifted *Gum* on mechanical drive and took her halfway round World 4470, over the red and green lands, the many warm green seas. They had picked out a likely spot on Continent G: a prairie, twenty thousand square kilos of windswept graminiformes. No forest was within a hundred kilos of the site, and there were no lone trees or groves on the plain. The plant-forms occurred only in large species-colonies, never intermingled, except for certain tiny ubiquitous saprophytes and spore-bearers. The team sprayed holomeld over structure forms, and by evening of the thirty-two-hour day were settled in to the new camp. Eskwana was still asleep and Porlock still sedated, but everyone else was cheerful. "You can breathe here!" they kept saying.

Osden got on his feet and went shakily to the doorway; leaning there he looked through twilight over the dim reaches of the swaying grass that was not grass. There was a faint, sweet odor of pollen on the wind; no sound but the soft, vast sibilance of wind. His bandaged head cocked a little, the empath stood motionless for a long time. Darkness came, and the stars, lights in the windows of the distant house of Man. The wind had ceased, there was no sound. He listened.

In the long night Haito Tomiko listened. She lay still and heard the blood in her arteries, the breathing of sleepers, the wind blowing, the dark veins running, the dreams advancing, the vast static of stars increasing as the universe died slowly, the sound of death walking. She struggled out of her bed, fled the tiny solitude of her cubicle. Eskwana alone slept. Porlock lay straitjacketed, raving softly in his obscure native tongue. Olleroo and Jenny Chong were playing cards, grim-faced. Poswet To was in the therapy niche, plugged in. Asnanifoil was drawing a mandala, the Third Pattern of the Primes. Mannon and Harfex were sitting up with Osden.

She changed the bandages on Osden's head. His lank, reddish hair, where she had not had to shave it, looked strange. It was salted with white, now. Her hands shook as she worked. Nobody had yet said anything.

"How can the fear be here too?" she said, and her voice rang flat and false in the terrific silence.

"It's not just the trees; the grasses too . . ."

"But we're twelve thousand kilos from where we were this morning, we left it on the other side of the planet."

"It's all one," Osden said. "One big green thought. How long does it take a thought to get from one side of your brain to the other?"

"It doesn't think. It isn't thinking," Harfex said, lifelessly. "It's merely a network of processes. The branches, the epiphytic growths, the roots with those nodal junctures between individuals: they must all be capable of transmitting electrochemical impulses. There are no individual plants, then, properly speaking. Even the pollen is part of the linkage, no doubt, a sort of windborne sentience, connecting overseas. But it is not conceivable. That all the biosphere of a planet should be one network of communications, sensitive, irrational, immortal, isolated. . . ."

"Isolated," said Osden. "That's it! That's the fear. It isn't that we're motile, or destructive. It's just that we are. We are other. There has never been any other."

"You're right," Mannon said, almost whispering. "It has no peers. No enemies. No relationship with anything but itself. One alone forever."

"Then what's the function of its intelligence in species-survival?"

"None, maybe," Osden said. "Why are you getting teleological, Harfex? Aren't you a Hainishman? Isn't the measure of complexity the measure of the eternal joy?"

Harfex did not take the bait. He looked ill. "We should leave this world," he said.

"Now you know why I always want to get out, get away from you," Osden said with a kind of morbid geniality. "It isn't pleasant, is it—the other's fear . . . ? If only it were an animal intelligence. I can get through to animals. I get along with cobras and tigers; superior intelligence gives one the advantage. I should have been used in a zoo, not on a human team. . . . If I could get through to the damned stupid potato! If it wasn't so overwhelming . . . I still pick up more than the fear, you know. And before it panicked it had a—there was a serenity. I couldn't take it in, then, I didn't realize how big it was. To know the whole daylight, after all, the whole night. All the winds and lulls together. The winter stars and the summer stars at the same time. To have roots, and no enemies. To be entire. Do you see? No invasion. No others. To be whole . . ."

He had never spoken before, Tomiko thought.

"You are defenseless against it, Osden," she said. "Your personality has changed already. You're vulnerable to it. We may not all go mad, but you will, if we don't leave."

He hesitated, then he looked up at Tomiko, the first time he had ever met her eyes, a long, still look, clear as water.

"What's sanity ever done for me?" he said, mocking. "But you have a point, Haito. You have something there."

"We should get away," Harfex muttered.

"If I gave in to it," Osden mused, "could I communicate?"

"By 'give in,' " Mannon said in a rapid, nervous voice, "I assume that you mean, stop sending back the empathic information which you receive from the plant-entity: stop rejecting the fear, and absorb it. That will either kill you at once, or drive you back into total psychological withdrawal, autism."

"Why?" said Osden. "Its message is *rejection*. But my salvation is rejection. It's not intelligent. But I am."

"The scale is wrong. What can a single human brain achieve against something so vast?"

"A single human brain can perceive pattern on the scale of stars and galaxies," Tomiko said, "and interpret it as Love."

Mannon looked from one to the other of them; Harfex was silent.

"It'd be easier in the forest," Osden said. "Which of you will fly me over?"

"When?"

"Now. Before you all crack up or go violent."

"I will," Tomiko said.

"None of us will," Harfex said.

"I can't," Mannon said. "I . . . I am too frightened. I'd crash the jet."

"Bring Eskwana along. If I can pull this off, he might serve as a medium."

"Are you accepting the Sensor's plan, Coordinator?" Harfex asked formally.

"Yes."

"I disapprove. I will come with you, however."

"I think we're compelled, Harfex," Tomiko said, looking at Osden's face, the ugly white mask transfigured, eager as a lover's face.

Olleroo and Jenny Chong, playing cards to keep their thoughts from their haunted beds, their mounting dread, chattered like scared children. "This thing, it's in the forest, it'll get you—"

"Scared of the dark?" Osden jeered.

"But look at Eskwana, and Porlock, and even Asnanifoil—"

"It can't hurt you. It's an impulse passing through synapses, a wind passing through branches. It is only a nightmare."

They took off in a helijet, Eskwana curled up still sound asleep in the rear compartment, Tomiko piloting, Harfex and Osden silent, watching ahead for the dark line of forest across the vague grey miles of starlit plain.

They neared the black line, crossed it; now under them was darkness.

She sought a landing place, flying low, though she had to fight her frantic wish to fly high, to get out, get away. The huge vitality of the plant-world was far stronger here in the forest, and its panic beat in immense dark waves. There was a pale patch ahead, a bare knoll-top a little higher than the tallest of the black shapes around it; the not-trees; the rooted; the parts of the whole. She set the helijet down in the glade, a bad landing. Her hands on the stick were slippery, as if she had rubbed them with cold soap.

About them now stood the forest, black in darkness.

Tomiko cowered and shut her eyes. Eskwana moaned in his sleep. Harfex's breath came short and loud, and he sat rigid, even when Osden reached across him and slid the door open.

Osden stood up; his back and bandaged head were just visible in the dim glow of the control panel as he paused stooping in the doorway.

Tomiko was shaking. She could not raise her head. "No, no, no, no, no, no, no," she said in a whisper. "No. No. No."

Osden moved suddenly and quietly, swinging out of the doorway, down into the dark. He was gone.

I am coming! said a great voice that made no sound.

Tomiko screamed. Harfex coughed; he seemed to be trying to stand up, but did not do so.

Tomiko drew in upon herself, all centered in the blind eye in her belly, in the center of her being; and outside that there was nothing but the fear.

It ceased.

She raised her head; slowly unclenched her hands. She sat up straight. The night was dark, and stars shone over the forest. There was nothing else.

"Osden," she said, but her voice would not come. She spoke again, louder, a lone bullfrog croak. There was no reply.

She began to realize that something had gone wrong with Harfex. She was trying to find his head in the darkness, for he had slipped down from the seat, when all at once, in the dead quiet, in the dark rear compartment of the craft, a voice spoke. "Good," it said.

It was Eskwana's voice. She snapped on the interior lights and saw the engineer lying curled up asleep, his hand half over his mouth.

The mouth opened and spoke. "All well," it said.

"Osden—"

"All well," said the soft voice from Eskwana's mouth.

"Where are you?"

Silence.

"Come back."

A wind was rising. "I'll stay here," the soft voice said.

"You can't stay—"

Silence.

"You'd be alone, Osden!"

"Listen." The voice was fainter, slurred, as if lost in the sound of wind. "Listen. I will you well."

She called his name after that, but there was no answer. Eskwana lay still. Harfex lay stiller.

"Osden!" she cried, leaning out the doorway into the dark, windshaken silence of the forest of being. "I will come back. I must get Harfex to the base. I will come back, Osden!"

Silence and wind in leaves.

★ ★ ★

Ihey finished the prescribed survey of World 4470, the eight of them; it took them forty-one days more. Asnanifoil and one or another of the women went into the forest daily at first, searching for Osden in the region around the bare knoll, though Tomiko was not in her heart sure which bare knoll they had landed on that night in the very heart and vortex of terror. They left piles of supplies for Osden, food enough for fifty years, clothing, tents, tools. They did not go on searching; there was no way to find a man alone, hiding, if he wanted to hide, in those unending labyrinths and dim corridors vine-entangled, root-floored. They might have passed within arm's reach of him and never seen him.

But he was there; for there was no fear any more.

Rational, and valuing reason more highly after an intolerable experience of the immortal mindless, Tomiko tried to understand rationally what Osden had done. But the words escaped her control. He had taken the fear into himself, and, accepting, had transcended it. He had given up his self to the alien, an unreserved surrender, that left no place for evil. He had learned the love of the Other, and thereby had been given his whole self.—But this is not the vocabulary of reason.

The people of the Survey team walked under the trees, through the vast colonies of life, surrounded by a dreaming silence, a brooding calm that was half aware of them and wholly indifferent to them. There were no hours. Distance was no matter. Had we but world enough and time . . . The planet turned between the sunlight and the great dark; winds of winter and summer blew fine, pale pollen across the quiet seas.

Gum returned after many surveys, years, and lightyears, to what had several centuries ago been Smeming Port. There were still men there, to receive (incredulously) the team's reports, and to record its losses: Biologist Harfex, dead of fear, and Sensor Osden, left as a colonist.

A Meeting with Medusa

ARTHUR C. CLARKE

Here's another seminal story by Arthur C. Clarke, whose "The Sentinel" appeared earlier in this anthology. In this one, he takes us on a terrifying plunge *into* the hellish interior of the immense, banded gas-giant, Jupiter, where storms rage large enough to swallow the entire Earth and a lone explorer in a frail little craft will need every bit of skill and courage and determination he possesses to steer his way *out* again— *if* he can keep himself from being distracted by some very big surprises he runs into along the way. . . .

1. A DAY TO REMEMBER

The *Queen Elizabeth* was over three miles above the Grand Canyon, dawdling along at a comfortable hundred and eighty, when Howard Falcon spotted the camera platform closing in from the right. He had been expecting it—nothing else was cleared to fly at this altitude—but he was not too happy to have company. Although he welcomed any signs of public interest, he also wanted as much empty sky as he could get. After all, he was the first man in history to navigate a ship three-tenths of a mile long. . . .

So far, this first test flight had gone perfectly; ironically enough, the only problem had been the century-old aircraft carrier *Chairman Mao*, borrowed from the San Diego Naval Museum for support operations. Only one of *Mao*'s four nuclear reactors was still operating, and the old battlewagon's top speed was barely thirty knots. Luckily, wind speed at sea level had been less than half this, so it had not been too difficult to maintain still air on the flight deck. Though there had been a few anxious moments during gusts, when the mooring lines had been dropped, the great dirigible had risen smoothly, straight up into the sky, as if on an invisible elevator. If all went well, *Queen Elizabeth IV* would not meet *Chairman Mao* again for another week.

Everything was under control; all test instruments gave normal readings. Commander Falcon decided to go upstairs and watch the rendezvous. He handed over

o his second officer, and walked out into the transparent tubeway that led through
he heart of the ship. There, as always, he was overwhelmed by the spectacle of
he largest single space ever enclosed by man.

The ten spherical gas cells, each more than a hundred feet across, were ranged
ne behind the other like a line of gigantic soap bubbles. The tough plastic was
o clear that he could see through the whole length of the array, and make out
letails of the elevator mechanism, more than a third of a mile from his vantage
oint. All around him, like a three-dimensional maze, was the structural framework
f the ship—the great longitudinal girders running from nose to tail, the fifteen
oops that were the circular ribs of this skyborne colossus, and whose varying sizes
lefined its graceful, streamlined profile.

At this low speed, there was little sound—merely the soft rush of wind over
he envelope and an occasional creak of metal as the pattern of stresses changed.
The shadowless light from the rows of lamps far overhead gave the whole scene
a curiously submarine quality, and to Falcon this was enhanced by the spectacle
f the translucent gasbags. He had once encountered a squadron of large but harm-
ess jellyfish, pulsing their mindless way above a shallow tropical reef, and the
lastic bubbles that gave *Queen Elizabeth* her lift often reminded him of these—
especially when changing pressures made them crinkle and scatter new patterns of
eflected light.

He walked down the axis of the ship until he came to the forward elevator,
between gas cells one and two. Riding up to the Observation Deck, he noticed that
t was uncomfortably hot, and dictated a brief memo to himself on his pocket
ecorder. The *Queen* obtained almost a quarter of her buoyancy from the unlimited
mounts of waste heat produced by her fusion power plant. On this lightly loaded
light, indeed, only six of the ten gas cells contained helium; the remaining four
vere full of air. Yet she still carried two hundred tons of water as ballast. However,
unning the cells at high temperatures did produce problems in refrigerating the
ccess ways; it was obvious that a little more work would have to be done there.

A refreshing blast of cooler air hit him in the face when he stepped out onto
he Observation Deck and into the dazzling sunlight streaming through the Plexi-
glas roof. Half a dozen workmen, with an equal number of superchimp assistants,
vere busily laying the partly completed dance floor, while others were installing
electric wiring and fixing furniture. It was a scene of controlled chaos, and Falcon
found it hard to believe that everything would be ready for the maiden voyage,
only four weeks ahead. Well, that was not *his* problem, thank goodness. He was
merely the Captain, not the Cruise Director.

The human workers waved to him, and the "simps" flashed toothy smiles, as
he walked through the confusion, into the already completed Skylounge. This was
his favorite place in the whole ship, and he knew that once she was operating he
vould never again have it all to himself. He would allow himself just five minutes
of private enjoyment.

He called the bridge, checked that everything was still in order, and relaxed
into one of the comfortable swivel chairs. Below, in a curve that delighted the eye,
vas the unbroken silver sweep of the ship's envelope. He was perched at the
highest point, surveying the whole immensity of the largest vehicle ever built. And
when he had tired of that—all the way out to the horizon was the fantastic wil-
lerness carved by the Colorado River in half a billion years of time.

Apart from the camera platform (it had now fallen back and was filming from amidships), he had the sky to himself. It was blue and empty, clear down to the horizon. In his grandfather's day, Falcon knew, it would have been streaked with vapor trails and stained with smoke. Both had gone: the aerial garbage had vanished with the primitive technologies that spawned it, and the long-distance transportation of this age arced too far beyond the stratosphere for any sight or sound of it to reach Earth. Once again, the lower atmosphere belonged to the birds and the clouds—and now to *Queen Elizabeth IV*.

It was true, as the old pioneers had said at the beginning of the twentieth century: this was the only way to travel—in silence and luxury, breathing the air around you and not cut off from it, near enough to the surface to watch the ever-changing beauty of land and sea. The subsonic jets of the 1980s, packed with hundreds of passengers seated ten abreast, could not even begin to match such comfort and spaciousness.

Of course, the *Queen* would never be an economic proposition, and even if her projected sister ships were built, only a few of the world's quarter of a billion inhabitants would ever enjoy this silent gliding through the sky. But a secure and prosperous global society could afford such follies and indeed needed them for their novelty and entertainment. There were at least a million men on Earth whose discretionary income exceeded a thousand new dollars a year, so the *Queen* would not lack for passengers.

Falcon's pocket communicator beeped. The copilot was calling from the bridge.

"O.K. for rendezvous, Captain? We've got all the data we need from this run, and the TV people are getting impatient."

Falcon glanced at the camera platform, now matching his speed a tenth of a mile away.

"O.K.," he replied. "Proceed as arranged. I'll watch from here."

He walked back through the busy chaos of the Observation Deck so that he could have a better view amidships. As he did so, he could feel the change of vibration underfoot; by the time he had reached the rear of the lounge, the ship had come to rest. Using his master key, he let himself out onto the small external platform flaring from the end of the deck; half a dozen people could stand here, with only low guardrails separating them from the vast sweep of the envelope—and from the ground, thousands of feet below. It was an exciting place to be, and perfectly safe even when the ship was traveling at speed, for it was in the dead air behind the huge dorsal blister of the Observation Deck. Nevertheless, it was not intended that the passengers would have access to it; the view was a little too vertiginous.

The covers of the forward cargo hatch had already opened like giant trap doors, and the camera platform was hovering above them, preparing to descend. Along this route, in the years to come, would travel thousands of passengers and tons of supplies. Only on rare occasions would the *Queen* drop down to sea level and dock with her floating base.

A sudden gust of cross wind slapped Falcon's cheek, and he tightened his grip on the guardrail. The Grand Canyon was a bad place for turbulence, though he did not expect much at this altitude. Without any real anxiety, he focused his attention on the descending platform, now about 150 feet above the ship. He knew that the highly skilled operator who was flying the remotely controlled vehicle had performed this simple maneuver a dozen times already; it was inconceivable that he would have any difficulties.

Yet he seemed to be reacting rather sluggishly. That last gust had drifted the platform almost to the edge of the open hatchway. Surely the pilot could have corrected before this. . . . Did he have a control problem? It was very unlikely; these remotes had multiple redundancy, fail-safe takeovers, and any number of backup systems. Accidents were almost unheard of.

But there he went again, off to the left. Could the pilot be *drunk*? Improbable though that seemed, Falcon considered it seriously for a moment. Then he reached for his microphone switch.

Once again, without warning, he was slapped violently in the face. He hardly felt it, for he was staring in horror at the camera platform. The distant operator was fighting for control, trying to balance the craft on its jets—but he was only making matters worse. The oscillations increased—twenty degrees, forty, sixty, ninety. . . .

"Switch to automatic, you fool!" Falcon shouted uselessly into his microphone. "Your manual control's not working!"

The platform flipped over on its back. The jets no longer supported it, but drove it swiftly downward. They had suddenly become allies of the gravity they had fought until this moment.

Falcon never heard the crash, though he felt it; he was already inside the Observation Deck, racing for the elevator that would take him down to the bridge. Workmen shouted at him anxiously, asking what had happened. It would be many months before he knew the answer to that question.

Just as he was stepping into the elevator cage, he changed his mind. What if there was a power failure? Better be on the safe side, even if it took longer and time was the essence. He began to run down the spiral stairway enclosing the shaft.

Halfway down he paused for a second to inspect the damage. That damned platform had gone clear through the ship, rupturing two of the gas cells as it did so. They were still collapsing slowly, in great falling veils of plastic. He was not worried about the loss of lift—the ballast could easily take care of that, as long as eight cells remained intact. Far more serious was the possibility of structural damage. Already he could hear the great latticework around him groaning and protesting under its abnormal loads. It was not enough to have sufficient lift; unless it was properly distributed, the ship would break her back.

He was just resuming his descent when a superchimp, shrieking with fright, came racing down the elevator shaft, moving with incredible speed, hand over hand, along the *outside* of the latticework. In its terror, the poor beast had torn off its company uniform, perhaps in an unconscious attempt to regain the freedom of its ancestors.

Falcon, still descending as swiftly as he could, watched its approach with some alarm. A distraught simp was a powerful and potentially dangerous animal, especially if fear overcame its conditioning. As it overtook him, it started to call out a string of words, but they were all jumbled together, and the only one he could recognize was a plaintive, frequently repeated "boss." Even now, Falcon realized, it looked toward humans for guidance. He felt sorry for the creature, involved in a man-made disaster beyond its comprehension, and for which it bore no responsibility.

It stopped opposite him, on the other side of the lattice; there was nothing to prevent it from coming through the open framework if it wished. Now its face was only inches from his, and he was looking straight into the terrified eyes. Never before had he been so close to a simp, and able to study its features in such detail. He felt that strange mingling of kinship and discomfort that all men experience when they gaze thus into the mirror of time.

His presence seemed to have calmed the creature. Falcon pointed up the shaft, back toward the Observation Deck, and said very clearly and precisely: "Boss—boss—go." To his relief, the simp understood; it gave him a grimace that might have been a smile, and at once started to race back the way it had come. Falcon had given it the best advice he could. If any safety remained aboard the *Queen*, it was in that direction. But his duty lay in the other.

He had almost completed his descent when, with a sound of rending metal, the vessel pitched nose down, and the lights went out. But he could still see quite well, for a shaft of sunlight streamed through the open hatch and the huge tear in the envelope. Many years ago he had stood in a great cathedral nave watching the light pouring through the stained-glass windows, forming pools of multicolored radiance on the ancient flagstones. The dazzling shaft of sunlight through the ruined fabric high above reminded him of that moment. He was in a cathedral of metal, falling down the sky.

When he reached the bridge, and was able for the first time to look outside, he was horrified to see how close the ship was to the ground. Only three thousand feet below were the beautiful and deadly pinnacles of rock and the red rivers of mud that were still carving their way down into the past. There was no level area anywhere in sight where a ship as large as the *Queen* could come to rest on an even keel.

A glance at the display board told him that all the ballast had gone. However, rate of descent had been reduced to a few yards a second; they still had a fighting chance.

Without a word, Falcon eased himself into the pilot's seat and took over such control as still remained. The instrument board showed him everything he wished to know; speech was superfluous. In the background, he could hear the Communications Officer giving a running report over the radio. By this time, all the news channels of Earth would have been preempted, and he could imagine the utter frustration of the program controllers. One of the most spectacular wrecks in history was occurring—without a single camera to record it. The last moments of the *Queen* would never fill millions with awe and terror, as had those of the *Hindenburg*, a century and a half before.

Now the ground was only about 1,700 feet away, still coming up slowly. Though he had full thrust, he had not dared to use it, lest the weakened structure collapse; but now he realized that he had no choice. The wind was taking them toward a fork in the canyon, where the river was split by a wedge of rock like the prow of some gigantic, fossilized ship of stone. If she continued on her present course, the *Queen* would straddle that triangular plateau and come to rest with a least a third of her length jutting out over nothingness; she would snap like a rotten stick.

Far away, above the sound of straining metal and escaping gas, came the familiar whistle of the jets as Falcon opened up the lateral thrusters. The ship staggered, and began to slew to port. The shriek of tearing metal was now almost continuous—and the rate of descent had started to increase ominously. A glance at the damage-control board showed that cell number five had just gone.

The ground was only yards away. Even now, he could not tell whether his maneuver would succeed or fail. He switched the thrust vectors over to vertical, giving maximum lift to reduce the force of impact.

The crash seemed to last forever. It was not violent—merely prolonged, and irresistible. It seemed that the whole universe was falling about them.

The sound of crunching metal came nearer, as if some great beast were eating its way through the dying ship.

Then floor and ceiling closed upon him like a vise.

2. "BECAUSE IT'S THERE"

"Why do you want to go to Jupiter?"

"As Springer said when he lifted for Pluto—'because it's there.' "

"Thanks. Now we've got that out of the way—the real reason."

Howard Falcon smiled, though only those who knew him well could have interpreted the slight, leathery grimace. Webster was one of them; for more than twenty years they had been involved in each other's projects. They had shared triumphs and disasters—including the greatest disaster of all.

"Well, Springer's cliché is still valid. We've landed on all the terrestrial planets, but none of the gas giants. They are the only real challenge left in the solar system."

"An expensive one. Have you worked out the cost?"

"As well as I can; here are the estimates. Remember, though—this isn't a one-shot mission, but a transportation system. Once it's proved out, it can be used over and over again. And it will open up not merely Jupiter, but all the giants."

Webster looked at the figures, and whistled.

"Why not start with an easier planet—Uranus, for example? Half the gravity, and less than half the escape velocity. Quieter weather, too—if that's the right word for it."

Webster had certainly done his homework. But that, of course, was why he was head of Long-Range Planning.

"There's very little saving—when you allow for the extra distance and the logistics problems. For Jupiter, we can use the facilities of Ganymede. Beyond Saturn, we'd have to establish a new supply base."

Logical, thought Webster; but he was sure that it was not the important reason. Jupiter was lord of the solar system; Falcon would be interested in no lesser challenge.

"Besides," Falcon continued, "Jupiter is a major scientific scandal. It's more than a hundred years since its radio storms were discovered, but we still don't know what causes them—and the Great Red Spot is as big a mystery as ever. That's why I can get matching funds from the Bureau of Astronautics. Do you know how many probes they have dropped into that atmosphere?"

"A couple of hundred, I believe."

"*Three* hundred and twenty-six, over the last fifty years—about a quarter of them total failures. Of course, they've learned a hell of a lot, but they've barely scratched the planet. Do you realize how *big* it is?"

"More than ten times the size of Earth."

"Yes, yes—but do you know what that really means?"

Falcon pointed to the large globe in the corner of Webster's office.

"Look at India—how small it seems. Well, if you skinned Earth and spread it out on the surface of Jupiter, it would look about as big as India does here."

There was a long silence while Webster contemplated the equation: Jupiter is to Earth as Earth is to India. Falcon had—deliberately, of course—chosen the best possible example. . . .

Was it already ten years ago? Yes, it must have been. The crash lay seven years in the past (that date was engraved on his heart), and those initial tests had taken place three years before the first and last flight of the *Queen Elizabeth.*

Ten years ago, then, Commander (no, Lieutenant) Falcon had invited him to a preview—a three-day drift across the northern plains of India, within sight of the Himalayas. "Perfectly safe," he had promised. "It will get you away from the office—and will teach you what this whole thing is about."

Webster had not been disappointed. Next to his first journey to the Moon, it had been the most memorable experience of his life. And yet, as Falcon had assured him, it had been perfectly safe, and quite uneventful.

They had taken off from Srinagar just before dawn, with the huge silver bubble of the balloon already catching the first light of the Sun. The ascent had been made in total silence; there were none of the roaring propane burners that had lifted the hot-air balloons of an earlier age. All the heat they needed came from the little pulsed-fusion reactor, weighing only about 220 pounds, hanging in the open mouth of the envelope. While they were climbing, its laser was zapping ten times a second, igniting the merest whiff of deuterium fuel. Once they had reached altitude, it would fire only a few times a minute, making up for the heat lost through the great gasbag overhead.

And so, even while they were almost a mile above the ground, they could hear dogs barking, people shouting, bells ringing. Slowly the vast, Sun-smitten landscape expanded around them. Two hours later, they had leveled out at three miles and were taking frequent draughts of oxygen. They could relax and admire the scenery; the on-board instrumentation was doing all the work—gathering the information that would be required by the designers of the still-unnamed liner of the skies.

It was a perfect day. The southwest monsoon would not break for another month, and there was hardly a cloud in the sky. Time seemed to have come to a stop; they resented the hourly radio reports, which interrupted their reverie. And all around, to the horizon and far beyond, was that infinite, ancient landscape, drenched with history—a patchwork of villages, fields, temples, lakes, irrigation canals. . . .

With a real effort, Webster broke the hypnotic spell of that ten-year-old memory. It had converted him to lighter-than-air flight—and it had made him realize the enormous size of India, even in a world that could be circled within ninety minutes. And yet, he repeated to himself, Jupiter is to Earth as Earth is to India. . . .

"Granted your argument," he said, "and supposing the funds are available, there's another question you have to answer. Why should you do better than the—what is it—326 robot probes that have already made the trip?"

"I am better qualified than they were—as an observer, and as a pilot. *Especially* as a pilot. Don't forget—I've more experience of lighter-than-air flight than anyone in the world."

"You could still serve as controller, and sit safely on Ganymede."

"*But that's just the point!* They've already done that. Don't you remember what killed the *Queen*?"

Webster knew perfectly well; but he merely answered: "Go on."

"*Time lag—time lag!* That idiot of a platform controller thought he was using a local radio circuit. But he'd been accidentally switched through a satellite—oh, maybe it wasn't his fault, but he should have noticed. That's a half-second time lag for the round trip. Even then it wouldn't have mattered flying in calm air. It was the turbulence over the Grand Canyon that did it. When the platform tipped, and he corrected for that—it had already tipped the other way. Ever tried to drive a car over a bumpy road with a half-second delay in the steering?"

"No, and I don't intend to try. But I can imagine it."

"Well, Ganymede is a million kilometers from Jupiter. That means a round-trip delay of six seconds. No, you need a controller on the spot—to handle emergencies in real time. Let me show you something. Mind if I use this?"

"Go ahead."

Falcon picked up a postcard that was lying on Webster's desk; they were almost obsolete on Earth, but this one showed a 3-D view of a Martian landscape, and was decorated with exotic and expensive stamps. He held it so that it dangled vertically.

"This is an old trick, but helps to make my point. Place your thumb and finger on either side, not quite touching. That's right."

Webster put out his hand, almost but not quite gripping the card.

"Now catch it."

Falcon waited for a few seconds; then, without warning, he let go of the card. Webster's thumb and finger closed on empty air.

"I'll do it again, just to show there's no deception. You see?"

Once again, the falling card had slipped through Webster's fingers.

"Now you try it on me."

This time, Webster grasped the card and dropped it without warning. It had scarcely moved before Falcon had caught it. Webster almost imagined he could hear a click, so swift was the other's reaction.

"When they put me together again," Falcon remarked in an expressionless voice, "the surgeons made some improvements. This is one of them—and there are others. I want to make the most of them. Jupiter is the place where I can do it."

Webster stared for long seconds at the fallen card, absorbing the improbable colors of the Trivium Charontis Escarpment. Then he said quietly: "I understand. How long do you think it will take?"

"With your help, plus the Bureau, plus all the science foundations we can drag in—oh, three years. Then a year for trials—we'll have to send in at least two test models. So, with luck—five years."

"That's about what I thought. I hope you get your luck; you've earned it. But there's one thing I won't do."

"What's that?"

"Next time you go ballooning, don't expect *me* as passenger."

3. THE WORLD OF THE GODS

The fall from Jupiter V to Jupiter itself takes only three and a half hours. Few men could have slept on so awesome a journey. Sleep was a weakness that Howard Falcon hated, and the little he still required brought dreams that time had not yet been able to exorcise. But he could expect no rest in the three days that lay ahead, and must seize what he could during the long fall down into that ocean of clouds, some sixty thousand miles below.

As soon as *Kon-Tiki* had entered her transfer orbit and all the computer checks were satisfactory, he prepared for the last sleep he might ever know. It seemed appropriate that at almost the same moment Jupiter eclipsed the bright and tiny Sun as he swept into the monstrous shadow of the planet. For a few minutes a strange golden twilight enveloped the ship; then a quarter of the sky became an utterly black hole in space, while the rest was a blaze of stars. No matter how far one traveled across the solar system, *they* never changed; these same constellations now shone on Earth, millions of miles away. The only novelties here were the small, pale crescents of Callisto and Ganymede; doubtless there were a dozen other moons up there in the sky, but they were all much too tiny, and too distant, for the unaided eye to pick them out.

"Closing down for two hours," he reported to the mother ship, hanging almost a thousand miles above the desolate rocks of Jupiter V, in the radiation shadow of the tiny satellite. If it never served any other useful purpose, Jupiter V was a cosmic bulldozer perpetually sweeping up the charged particles that made it unhealthy to linger close to Jupiter. Its wake was almost free of radiation, and there a ship could park in perfect safety, while death sleeted invisibly all around.

Falcon switched on the sleep inducer, and consciousness faded swiftly out as the electric pulses surged gently through his brain. While *Kon-Tiki* fell toward Jupiter, gaining speed second by second in that enormous gravitational field, he slept without dreams. They always came when he awoke; and he had brought his nightmares with him from Earth.

Yet he never dreamed of the crash itself, though he often found himself again face to face with that terrified superchimp, as he descended the spiral stairway between the collapsing gasbags. None of the simps had survived; those that were not killed outright were so badly injured that they had been painlessly "euthed." He sometimes wondered why he dreamed only of this doomed creature—which he had never met before the last minutes of its life—and not of the friends and colleagues he had lost aboard the dying *Queen*.

The dreams he feared most always began with his first return to consciousness. There had been little physical pain; in fact, there had been no sensation of any kind. He was in darkness and silence, and did not even seem to be breathing. And—strangest of all—he could not locate his limbs. He could move neither his hands nor his feet, because he did not know where they were.

The silence had been the first to yield. After hours, or days, he had become aware of a faint throbbing, and eventually, after long thought, he deduced that this was the beating of his own heart. That was the first of his many mistakes.

Then there had been faint pinpricks, sparkles of light, ghosts of pressures upon still-unresponsive limbs. One by one his senses had returned, and pain had come with them. He had had to learn everything anew, recapitulating infancy and babyhood. Though his memory was unaffected, and he could understand words that were spoken to him, it was months before he was able to answer except by the flicker of an eyelid. He could remember the moments of triumph when he had spoken the first word, turned the page of a book—and, finally, learned to move under his own power. *That* was a victory indeed, and it had taken him almost two years to prepare for it. A hundred times he had envied that dead superchimp, but *he* had been given no choice. The doctors had made their decision—and now, twelve years later, he was where no human being had ever traveled before, and moving faster than any man in history.

Kon-Tiki was just emerging from shadow, and the Jovian dawn bridged the sky ahead in a titanic bow of light, when the persistent buzz of the alarm dragged Falcon up from sleep. The inevitable nightmares (he had been trying to summon a nurse, but did not even have the strength to push the button) swiftly faded from consciousness. The greatest—and perhaps last—adventure of his life was before him.

He called Mission Control, now almost sixty thousand miles away and falling swiftly below the curve of Jupiter, to report that everything was in order. His velocity had just passed thirty-one miles a second (that was one for the books) and in half an hour *Kon-Tiki* would hit the outer fringes of the atmosphere, as he started on the most difficult reentry in the entire solar system. Although scores of probes had survived this flaming ordeal, they had been tough, solidly packed masses of instrumentation, able to withstand several hundred gravities of drag. *Kon-Tiki* would hit peaks of thirty g's, and would average more than ten, before she came to rest in the upper reaches of the Jovian atmosphere. Very carefully and thoroughly, Falcon began to attach the elaborate system of restraints that would anchor him to the walls of the cabin. When he had finished, he was virtually a part of the ship's structure.

The clock was counting backward; one hundred seconds to reentry. For better or worse, he was committed. In a minute and a half, he would graze the Jovian atmosphere, and would be caught irrevocably in the grip of the giant.

The countdown was three seconds late—not at all bad, considering the unknowns involved. From beyond the walls of the capsule came a ghostly sighing, which rose steadily to a high-pitched, screaming roar. The noise was quite different from that of a reentry on Earth or Mars; in this thin atmosphere of hydrogen and helium, all sounds were transformed a couple of octaves upward. On Jupiter, even thunder would have falsetto overtones.

With the rising scream came mounting weight; within seconds, he was completely immobilized. His field of vision contracted until it embraced only the clock and the accelerometer; fifteen g, and 480 seconds to go. . . .

He never lost consciousness; but then, he had not expected to. *Kon-Tiki's* trail through the Jovian atmosphere must be really spectacular—by this time, thousands of miles long. Five hundred seconds after entry, the drag began to taper off: ten g, five g, two. . . . Then weight vanished almost completely. He was falling free, all his enormous orbital velocity destroyed.

There was a sudden jolt as the incandescent remnants of the heat shield were jettisoned. It had done its work and would not be needed again; Jupiter could have it now. He released all but two of the restraining buckles, and waited for the automatic sequencer to start the next, and most critical, series of events.

He did not see the first drogue parachute pop out, but he could feel the slight jerk, and the rate of fall diminished immediately. *Kon-Tiki* had lost all her horizontal speed and was going straight down at almost a thousand miles an hour. Everything depended on what happened in the next sixty seconds.

There went the second drogue. He looked up through the overhead window and saw, to his immense relief, that clouds of glittering foil were billowing out behind the falling ship. Like a great flower unfurling, the thousands of cubic yards of the balloon spread out across the sky, scooping up the thin gas until it was fully inflated. *Kon-Tiki's* rate of fall dropped to a few miles an hour and remained constant. Now there was plenty of time; it would take him days to fall all the way down to the surface of Jupiter.

But he would get there eventually, even if he did nothing about it. The balloon overhead was merely acting as an efficient parachute. It was providing no lift; nor could it do so, while the gas inside and out was the same.

With its characteristic and rather disconcerting crack the fusion reactor started up, pouring torrents of heat into the envelope overhead. Within five minutes, the rate of fall had become zero; within six, the ship had started to rise. According to the radar altimeter, it had leveled out at about 267 miles above the surface—or whatever passed for a surface on Jupiter.

Only one kind of balloon will work in an atmosphere of hydrogen, which is the lightest of all gases—and that is a hot-hydrogen balloon. As long as the fuser kept ticking over, Falcon could remain aloft, drifting across a world that could hold a hundred Pacifics. After traveling over 300,000,000 miles, *Kon-Tiki* had at last begun to justify her name. She was an aerial raft, adrift upon the currents of the Jovian atmosphere.

★ ★ ★

Though a whole new world was lying around him, it was more than an hour before Falcon could examine the view. First he had to check all the capsule's systems and test its response to the controls. He had to learn how much extra heat was necessary to produce a desired rate of ascent, and how much gas he must vent in order to descend. Above all, there was the question of stability. He must adjust the length of the cables attaching his capsule to the huge, pear-shaped balloon, to damp out vibrations and get the smoothest possible ride. Thus far, he was lucky; at this level, the wind was steady, and the Doppler reading on the invisible surface gave him a ground speed of 217.5 miles an hour. For Jupiter, that was modest; winds of up to a thousand had been observed. But mere speed was, of course, unimportant; the real danger was turbulence. If he ran into that, only skill and experience and swift reaction could save him—and these were not matters that could yet be programmed into a computer.

Not until he was satisfied that he had got the feel of his strange craft did Falcon pay any attention to Mission Control's pleadings. Then he deployed the booms carrying the instrumentation and the atmospheric samplers. The capsule now resembled a rather untidy Christmas tree, but still rode smoothly down the Jovian winds while it radioed its torrents of information to the recorders on the ship miles above. And now, at last, he could look around. . . .

His first impression was unexpected, and even a little disappointing. As far as the scale of things was concerned, he might have been ballooning over an ordinary cloudscape on Earth. The horizon seemed at a normal distance; there was no feeling at all that he was on a world eleven times the diameter of his own. Then he looked at the infrared radar, sounding the layers of atmosphere beneath him—and knew how badly his eyes had been deceived.

That layer of clouds apparently about three miles away was really more than thirty-seven miles below. And the horizon, whose distance he would have guessed at about 125, was actually 1,800 miles from the ship.

The crystalline clarity of the hydrohelium atmosphere and the enormous curvature of the planet had fooled him completely. It was even harder to judge distances here than on the Moon; everything he saw must be multiplied by at least ten.

It was a simple matter, and he should have been prepared for it. Yet somehow, it disturbed him profoundly. He did not feel that Jupiter was huge, but that *he* had shrunk—to a tenth of his normal size. Perhaps, with time, he would grow accustomed to the inhuman scale of this world; yet as he stared toward that unbelievably distant horizon, he felt as if a wind colder than the atmosphere around him was blowing through his soul. Despite all his arguments, this might never be a place for man. He could well be both the first and the last to descend through the clouds of Jupiter.

The sky above was almost black, except for a few wisps of ammonia cirrus perhaps twelve miles overhead. It was cold up there, on the fringes of space, but both pressure and temperature increased rapidly with depth. At the level where *Kon-Tiki* was drifting now, it was fifty below zero, and the pressure was five atmospheres. Sixty-five miles farther down, it would be as warm as equatorial Earth, and the pressure about the same as at the bottom of one of the shallower seas. Ideal conditions for life . . .

A quarter of the brief Jovian day had already gone; the sun was halfway up the sky, but the light on the unbroken cloudscape below had a curious mellow quality. That extra three hundred million miles had robbed the Sun of all its power. Though the sky was clear, Falcon found himself continually thinking that it was a heavily overcast day. When night fell, the onset of darkness would be swift indeed; though it was still morning, there was a sense of autumnal twilight in the air. But autumn, of course, was something that never came to Jupiter. There were no seasons here.

Kon-Tiki had come down in the exact center of the equatorial zone—the least colorful part of the planet. The sea of clouds that stretched out to the horizon was tinted a pale salmon; there were none of the yellows and pinks and even reds that banded Jupiter at higher altitudes. The Great Red Spot itself—most spectacular of all of the planet's features—lay thousands of miles to the south. It had been a temptation to descend there, but the south tropical disturbance was unusually active, with currents reaching over nine hundred miles an hour. It would have been asking for trouble to head into that maelstrom of unknown forces. The Great Red Spot and its mysteries would have to wait for future expeditions.

The Sun, moving across the sky twice as swiftly as it did on Earth, was now nearing the zenith and had become eclipsed by the great silver canopy of the balloon. *Kon-Tiki* was still drifting swiftly and smoothly westward at a steady 217.5, but only the radar gave any indication of this. Was it always as calm here? Falcon asked himself. The scientists who had talked learnedly of the Jovian doldrums, and had predicted that the equator would be the quietest place, seemed to know what they were talking about, after all. He had been profoundly skeptical of all such forecasts, and had agreed with one unusually modest researcher who had told him bluntly: "There are *no* experts on Jupiter." Well, there would be at least one by the end of this day.

If he managed to survive until then.

4. THE VOICES OF THE DEEP

That first day, the Father of the Gods smiled upon him. It was as calm and peaceful here on Jupiter as it had been, years ago, when he was drifting with Webster across the plains of northern India. Falcon had time to master his new skills, until *Kon-Tiki* seemed an extension of his own body. Such luck was more than he had dared to hope for, and he began to wonder what price he might have to pay for it.

The five hours of daylight were almost over; the clouds below were full of shadows, which gave them a massive solidity they had not possessed when the Sun was higher. Color was swiftly draining from the sky, except in the west itself, where a band of deepening purple lay along the horizon. Above this band was the thin crescent of a closer moon, pale and bleached against the utter blackness beyond.

With a speed perceptible to the eye, the Sun went straight down over the edge of Jupiter, over 1,800 miles away. The stars came out in their legions—and there was the beautiful evening star of Earth, on the very frontier of twilight, reminding him how far he was from home. It followed the Sun down into the west. Man's first night on Jupiter had begun.

With the onset of darkness, *Kon-Tiki* started to sink. The balloon was no longer heated by the feeble sunlight and was losing a small part of its buoyancy. Falcon did nothing to increase lift; he had expected this and was planning to descend.

The invisible cloud deck was still over thirty miles below, and he would reach it about midnight. It showed up clearly on the infrared radar, which also reported that it contained a vast array of complex carbon compounds, as well as the usual hydrogen, helium, and ammonia. The chemists were dying for samples of that fluffy, pinkish stuff; though some atmospheric probes had already gathered a few grams, that had only whetted their appetites. Half the basic molecules of life were here, floating high above the surface of Jupiter. And where there was food, could life be far away? That was the question that, after more than a hundred years, no one had been able to answer.

The infrared was blocked by the clouds, but the microwave radar sliced right through and showed layer after layer, all the way down to the hidden surface almost 250 miles below. That was barred to him by enormous pressures and temperatures;

not even robot probes had ever reached it intact. It lay in tantalizing inaccessibility at the bottom of the radar screen, slightly fuzzy, and showing a curious granular structure that his equipment could not resolve.

An hour after sunset, he dropped his first probe. It fell swiftly for about sixty miles, then began to float in the denser atmosphere, sending back torrents of radio signals, which he relayed to Mission Control. Then there was nothing else to do until sunrise, except to keep an eye on the rate of descent, monitor the instruments, and answer occasional queries. While she was drifting in this steady current, *Kon-Tiki* could look after herself.

Just before midnight, a woman controller came on watch and introduced herself with the usual pleasantries. Ten minutes later she called again, her voice at once serious and excited.

"Howard! Listen in on channel forty-six—high gain."

Channel forty-six? There were so many telemetering circuits that he knew the numbers of only those that were critical; but as soon as he threw the switch, he recognized this one. He was plugged in to the microphone on the probe, floating more than eighty miles below him in an atmosphere now almost as dense as water.

At first, there was only a soft hiss of whatever strange winds stirred down in the darkness of that unimaginable world. And then, out of the background noise, there slowly emerged a booming vibration that grew louder and louder, like the beating of a gigantic drum. It was so low that it was felt as much as heard, and the beats steadily increased their tempo, though the pitch never changed. Now it was a swift, almost infrasonic throbbing. Then, suddenly, in mid-vibration, it stopped—so abruptly that the mind could not accept the silence, but memory continued to manufacture a ghostly echo in the deepest caverns of the brain.

It was the most extraordinary sound that Falcon had ever heard, even among the multitudinous noises of Earth. He could think of no natural phenomenon that could have caused it; nor was it like the cry of any animal, not even one of the great whales. . . .

It came again, following exactly the same pattern. Now that he was prepared for it, he estimated the length of the sequence; from first faint throb to final crescendo, it lasted just over ten seconds.

And this time there was a real echo, very faint and far away. Perhaps it came from one of the many reflecting layers, deeper in this stratified atmosphere; perhaps it was another, more distant source. Falcon waited for a second echo, but it never came.

Mission Control reacted quickly and asked him to drop another probe at once. With two microphones operating, it would be possible to find the approximate location of the sources. Oddly enough, none of *Kon-Tiki's* own external mikes could detect anything except wind noises. The boomings, whatever they were, must have been trapped and channeled beneath an atmospheric reflecting layer far below.

They were coming, it was soon discovered, from a cluster of sources about 1,200 miles away. The distance gave no indication of their power; in Earth's oceans, quite feeble sounds could travel equally far. And as for the obvious assumption that living creatures were responsible, the Chief Exobiologist quickly ruled that out.

"I'll be very disappointed," said Dr. Brenner, "if there are no microorganisms or plants there. But nothing like animals, because there's no free oxygen. All biochemical reactions on Jupiter must be low-energy ones—there's just no way an active creature could generate enough power to function."

Falcon wondered if this was true; he had heard the argument before, and reserved judgment.

"In any case," continued Brenner, "some of those sound waves are a hundred yards long! Even an animal as big as a whale couldn't produce them. They *must* have a natural origin."

Yes, that seemed plausible, and probably the physicists would be able to come up with an explanation. What would a blind alien make, Falcon wondered, of the sounds he might hear when standing beside a stormy sea, or a geyser, or a volcano, or a waterfall? He might well attribute them to some huge beast.

About an hour before sunrise the voices of the deep died away, and Falcon began to busy himself with preparation for the dawn of his second day. *Kon-Tiki* was now only three miles above the nearest cloud layer; the external pressure had risen to ten atmospheres, and the temperature was a tropical thirty degrees. A man could be comfortable here with no more equipment than a breathing mask and the right grade of heliox mixture.

"We've some good news for you," Mission Control reported, soon after dawn. "The cloud layer's breaking up. You'll have partial clearing in an hour—but watch out for turbulence."

"I've already noticed some," Falcon answered. "How far down will I be able to see?"

"At least twelve miles, down to the second thermocline. *That* cloud deck is solid—it never breaks."

And it's out of my reach, Falcon told himself; the temperature down there must be over a hundred degrees. This was the first time that any balloonist had ever had to worry, not about his ceiling, but about his basement!

Ten minutes later he could see what Mission Control had already observed from its superior vantage point. There was a change in color near the horizon, and the cloud layer had become ragged and humpy, as if something had torn it open. He turned up his little nuclear furnace and gave *Kon-Tiki* another three miles of altitude, so that he could get a better view.

The sky below was clearing rapidly, completely, as if something was dissolving the solid overcast. An abyss was opening before his eyes. A moment later he sailed out over the edge of a cloud canyon about twelve miles deep and six hundred miles wide.

A new world lay spread beneath him; Jupiter had stripped away one of its many veils. The second layer of clouds, unattainably far below, was much darker in color than the first. It was almost salmon pink, and curiously mottled with little islands of brick red. They were all oval-shaped, with their long axes pointing east-west, in the direction of the prevailing wind. There were hundreds of them, all about the same size, and they reminded Falcon of puffy little cumulus clouds in the terrestrial sky.

He reduced buoyancy, and *Kon-Tiki* began to drop down the face of the dissolving cliff. It was then that he noticed the snow.

White flakes were forming in the air and drifting slowly downward. Yet it was much too warm for snow—and, in any event, there was scarcely a trace of water at this altitude. Moreover, there was no glitter or sparkle about these flakes as they went cascading down into the depths. When, presently, a few landed on an instrument boom outside the main viewing port, he saw that they were a dull, opaque white—not crystalline at all—and quite large—several inches across. They looked like wax, and Falcon guessed that this was precisely what they were. Some chemical reaction was taking place in the atmosphere around him, condensing out the hydrocarbons floating in the Jovian air.

About sixty miles ahead, a disturbance was taking place in the cloud layer. The little red ovals were being jostled around, and were beginning to form a spiral—the familiar cyclonic pattern so common in the meteorology of Earth. The vortex was emerging with astonishing speed; if that was a storm ahead, Falcon told himself, he was in big trouble.

And then his concern changed to wonder—and to fear. What was developing in his line of flight was not a storm at all. Something enormous—something scores of miles across—was rising through the clouds.

The reassuring thought that it, too, might be a cloud—a thunderhead boiling up from the lower levels of the atmosphere—lasted only a few seconds. No; this was *solid.* It shouldered its way through the pink-and-salmon overcast like an iceberg rising from the deeps.

An *iceberg* floating on hydrogen? That was impossible, of course; but perhaps it was not too remote an analogy. As soon as he focused the telescope upon the enigma, Falcon saw that it was a whitish, crystalline mass, threaded with streaks of red and brown. It must be, he decided, the same stuff as the "snowflakes" falling around him—a mountain range of wax. And it was not, he soon realized, as solid as he had thought; around the edges it was continually crumbling and re-forming. . . .

"I know what it is," he radioed Mission Control, which for the last few minutes had been asking anxious questions. "It's a mass of bubbles—some kind of foam. Hydrocarbon froth. Get the chemists working on . . . *Just a minute!*"

"What is it?" called Mission Control. "What is it?"

He ignored the frantic pleas from space and concentrated all his mind upon the image in the telescope field. He had to be sure; if he made a mistake, he would be the laughing stock of the solar system.

Then he relaxed, glanced at the clock, and switched off the nagging voice from Jupiter V.

"Hello, Mission Control," he said, very formally. "This is Howard Falcon aboard *Kon-Tiki.* Ephemeris Time nineteen hours twenty-one minutes fifteen seconds. Latitude zero degrees five minutes North. Longitude 105 degrees forty-two minutes, System One.

"Tell Dr. Brenner that there is life on Jupiter. And it's *big.* . . ."

5. THE WHEELS OF POSEIDON

"I'm very happy to be proved wrong," Dr. Brenner radioed back cheerfully. "Nature always has something up her sleeve. Keep the long-focus camera on target and give us the steadiest pictures you can."

The things moving up and down those waxen slopes were still too far away for Falcon to make out many details, and they must have been very large to be visible at all at such a distance. Almost black, and shaped like arrowheads, they maneuvered by slow undulations of their entire bodies, so that they looked rather like giant manta rays, swimming above some tropical reef.

Perhaps they were skyborne cattle, browsing on the cloud pastures of Jupiter, for they seemed to be feeding along the dark, red-brown streaks that ran like dried-up river beds down the flanks of the floating cliffs. Occasionally, one of them would dive headlong into the mountain of foam and disappear completely from sight.

Kon-Tiki was moving only slowly with respect to the cloud layer below; it would be at least three hours before she was above those ephemeral hills. She was in a race with the Sun. Falcon hoped that darkness would not fall before he could get a good view of the mantas, as he had christened them, as well as the fragile landscape over which they flapped their way.

It was a long three hours. During the whole time, he kept the external microphones on full gain, wondering if here was the source of that booming in the night. The mantas were certainly large enough to have produced it; when he could get an accurate measurement, he discovered that they were almost a hundred yards across the wings. That was three times the length of the largest whale—though he doubted if they could weigh more than a few tons.

Half an hour before sunset, *Kon-Tiki* was almost above the "mountains."

"No," said Falcon, answering Mission Control's repeated questions about the mantas, "they're still showing no reaction to me. I don't think they're intelligent—they look like harmless vegetarians. And even if they try to chase me, I'm sure they can't reach my altitude."

Yet he was a little disappointed when the mantas showed not the slightest interest in him as he sailed high above their feeding ground. Perhaps they had no way of detecting his presence. When he examined and photographed them through the telescope, he could see no signs of any sense organs. The creatures were simply huge black deltas, rippling over hills and valleys that, in reality, were little more substantial than the clouds of Earth. Though they looked solid, Falcon knew that anyone who stepped on those white mountains would go crashing through them as if they were made of tissue paper.

At close quarters he could see the myriads of cellules or bubbles from which they were formed. Some of these were quite large—a yard or so in diameter—and Falcon wondered in what witches' cauldron of hydrocarbons they had been brewed. There must be enough petrochemicals deep down in the atmosphere of Jupiter to supply all Earth's needs for a million years.

The short day had almost gone when he passed over the crest of the waxen hills, and the light was fading rapidly along their lower slopes. There were no mantas on this western side, and for some reason the topography was very different. The foam was sculptured into long, level terraces, like the interior of a lunar crater. He could almost imagine that they were gigantic steps leading down to the hidden surface of the planet.

And on the lowest of those steps, just clear of the swirling clouds that the mountain had displaced when it came surging skyward, was a roughly oval mass, one or two miles across. It was difficult to see, since it was only a little darker than the gray-white foam on which it rested. Falcon's first thought was that he was looking at a forest of pallid trees, like giant mushrooms that had never seen the Sun.

Yes, it must be a forest—he could see hundreds of thin trunks, springing from the white waxy froth in which they were rooted. But the trees were packed astonishingly close together; there was scarcely any space between them. Perhaps it was not a forest, after all, but a single enormous tree—like one of the giant multitrunked banyans of the East. Once he had seen a banyan tree in Java that was over 650 yards across; this monster was at least ten times that size.

The light had almost gone. The cloudscape had turned purple with refracted sunlight, and in a few seconds that, too, would have vanished. In the last light of his second day on Jupiter, Howard Falcon saw—or thought he saw—something that cast the gravest doubts on his interpretation of the white oval.

Unless the dim light had totally deceived him, those hundreds of thin trunks were beating back and forth, in perfect synchronism, like fronds of kelp rocking in the surge.

And the tree was no longer in the place where he had first seen it.

"Sorry about this," said Mission Control, soon after sunset, "but we think Source Beta is going to blow within the next hour. Probability 70 percent."

Falcon glanced quickly at the chart. Beta—Jupiter latitude 140 degrees—was over 18,600 miles away and well below his horizon. Even though major eruptions ran as high as ten megatons, he was much too far away for the shock wave to be a serious danger. The radio storm that it would trigger was, however, quite a different matter.

The decameter outbursts that sometimes made Jupiter the most powerful radio source in the whole sky had been discovered back in the 1950s, to the utter astonishment of the astronomers. Now, more than a century later, their real cause was still a mystery. Only the symptoms were understood; the explanation was completely unknown.

The "volcano" theory had best stood the test of time, although no one imagined that this word had the same meaning on Jupiter as on Earth. At frequent intervals—often several times a day—titanic eruptions occurred in the lower depths of the atmosphere, probably on the hidden surface of the planet itself. A great column of gas, more than six hundred miles high, would start boiling upward as if determined to escape into space.

Against the most powerful gravitational field of all the planets, it had no chance. Yet some traces—a mere few million tons—usually managed to reach the Jovian ionosphere; and when they did, all hell broke loose.

The radiation belts surrounding Jupiter completely dwarf the feeble Van Allen belts of Earth. When they are short-circuited by an ascending column of gas, the result is an electrical discharge millions of times more powerful than any terrestrial flash of lightning; it sends a colossal thunderclap of radio noise flooding across the entire solar system and on out to the stars.

It had been discovered that these radio outbursts came from four main areas of the planet. Perhaps there were weaknesses there that allowed the fires of the interior to break out from time to time. The scientists on Ganymede, largest of

Jupiter's many moons, now thought that they could predict the onset of a decameter storm; their accuracy was about as good as a weather forecaster's of the early 1900s.

Falcon did not know whether to welcome or to fear a radio storm; it would certainly add to the value of the mission—if he survived it. His course had been planned to keep as far as possible from the main centers of disturbance, especially the most active one, Source Alpha. As luck would have it, the threatening Beta was the closest to him. He hoped that the distance, almost three-fourths the circumference of Earth, was safe enough.

"Probability 90 percent," said Mission Control with a distinct note of urgency. "And forget that hour. Ganymede says it may be any moment."

The radio had scarcely fallen silent when the reading on the magnetic field-strength meter started to shoot upward. Before it could go off scale, it reversed and began to drop as rapidly as it had risen. Far away and thousands of miles below, something had given the planet's molten core a titanic jolt.

"There she blows!" called Mission Control.

"Thanks, I already know. When will the storm hit me?"

"You can expect onset in five minutes. Peak in ten."

Far around the curve of Jupiter, a funnel of gas as wide as the Pacific Ocean was climbing spaceward at thousands of miles an hour. Already, the thunderstorms of the lower atmosphere would be raging around it—but they were nothing compared with the fury that would explode when the radiation belt was reached and began dumping its surplus electrons onto the planet. Falcon began to retract all the instrument booms that were extended out from the capsule. There were no other precautions he could take. It would be four hours before the atmospheric shock wave reached him—but the radio blast, traveling at the speed of light, would be here in a tenth of a second, once the discharge had been triggered.

The radio monitor, scanning back and forth across the spectrum, still showed nothing unusual, just the normal mush of background static. Then Falcon noticed that the noise level was slowly creeping upward. The explosion was gathering its strength.

At such a distance he had never expected to *see* anything. But suddenly a flicker as of far-off heat lightning danced along the eastern horizon. Simultaneously, half the circuit breakers jumped out of the main switchboard, the lights failed, and all communications channels went dead.

He tried to move, but was completely unable to do so. The paralysis that gripped him was not merely psychological; he seemed to have lost all control of his limbs and could feel a painful tingling sensation over his entire body. It was impossible that the electric field could have penetrated this shielded cabin. Yet there was a flickering glow over the instrument board, and he could hear the unmistakable crackle of a brush discharge.

With a series of sharp bangs, the emergency systems went into operation, and the overloads reset themselves. The lights flickered on again. And Falcon's paralysis disappeared as swiftly as it had come.

After glancing at the board to make sure that all circuits were back to normal, he moved quickly to the viewing ports.

There was no need to switch on the inspection lamps—the cables supporting the capsule seemed to be on fire. Lines of light glowing an electric blue against the darkness stretched upward from the main lift ring to the equator of the giant balloon; and rolling slowly along several of them were dazzling balls of fire.

The sight was so strange and so beautiful that it was hard to read any menace in it. Few people, Falcon knew, had ever seen ball lightning from such close quarters—and certainly none had survived if they were riding a hydrogen-filled balloon back in the atmosphere of Earth. He remembered the flaming death of the *Hindenburg*, destroyed by a stray spark when she docked at Lakehurst in 1937; as it had done so often in the past, the horrifying old newsreel film flashed through his mind. But at least that could not happen here, though there was more hydrogen above his head than had ever filled the last of the Zeppelins. It would be a few billion years yet, before anyone could light a fire in the atmosphere of Jupiter.

With a sound like briskly frying bacon, the speech circuit came back to life.

"Hello, *Kon-Tiki*—are you receiving? Are you receiving?"

The words were chopped and badly distorted, but intelligible. Falcon's spirits lifted; he had resumed contact with the world of men.

"I receive you," he said. "Quite an electrical display, but no damage—so far."

"Thanks—thought we'd lost you. Please check telemetry channels three, seven, twenty-six. Also gain on camera two. And we don't quite believe the readings on the external ionization probes. . . ."

Reluctantly Falcon tore his gaze away from the fascinating pyrotechnic display around *Kon-Tiki*, though from time to time he kept glancing out of the windows. The ball lightning disappeared first, the fiery globes slowly expanding until they reached a critical size, at which they vanished in a gentle explosion. But even an hour later, there were still faint glows around all the exposed metal on the outside of the capsule; and the radio circuits remained noisy until well after midnight.

The remaining hours of darkness were completely uneventful—until just before dawn. Because it came from the east, Falcon assumed that he was seeing the first faint hint of sunrise. Then he realized that it was twenty minutes too early for this—and the glow that had appeared along the horizon was moving toward him even as he watched. It swiftly detached itself from the arch of stars that marked the invisible edge of the planet, and he saw that it was a relatively narrow band, quite sharply defined. The beam of an enormous searchlight appeared to be swinging beneath the clouds.

Perhaps sixty miles behind the first racing bar of light came another, parallel to it and moving at the same speed. And beyond that another, and another—until all the sky flickered with alternating sheets of sheets of light and darkness.

By this time, Falcon thought, he had been inured to wonders, and it seemed impossible that this display of pure, soundless luminosity could present the slightest danger. But it was so astonishing, and so inexplicable, that he felt cold, naked fear gnawing at his self-control. No man could look upon such a sight without feeling like a helpless pygmy in the presence of forces beyond his comprehension. Was it possible that, after all, Jupiter carried not only life but also intelligence? And, perhaps, an intelligence that only now was beginning to react to his alien presence?

"Yes, we see it," said Mission Control, in a voice that echoed his own awe. "We've no idea what it is. Stand by, we're calling Ganymede."

The display was slowly fading; the bands racing in from the far horizon were much fainter, as if the energies that powered them were becoming exhausted. In five minutes it was all over; the last faint pulse of light flickered along the western sky and then was gone. Its passing left Falcon with an overwhelming sense of relief. The sight was so hypnotic, and so disturbing, that it was not good for any man's peace of mind to contemplate it too long.

He was more shaken than he cared to admit. The electrical storm was something that he could understand; but *this* was totally incomprehensible.

Mission Control was still silent. He knew that the information banks up on Ganymede were now being searched as men and computers turned their minds to the problem. If no answer could be found there, it would be necessary to call Earth; that would mean a delay of almost an hour. The possibility that even Earth might be unable to help was one that Falcon did not care to contemplate.

He had never before been so glad to hear the voice of Mission Control as when Dr. Brenner finally came on the circuit. The biologist sounded relieved, yet subdued—like a man who has just come through some great intellectual crisis.

"Hello, *Kon-Tiki*. We've solved your problem, but we can still hardly believe it.

"What you've been seeing is bioluminescence, very similar to that produced by microorganisms in the tropical seas of Earth. Here they're in the atmosphere, not the ocean, but the principle is the same."

"But the pattern," protested Falcon, "was so regular—so *artificial*. And it was hundreds of miles across!"

"It was even larger than you imagine; you observed only a small part of it. The whole pattern was over three thousand miles wide and looked like a revolving wheel. You merely saw the spokes, sweeping past at you at about six-tenths of a mile a second. . . ."

"A *second*!" Falcon could not help interjecting. "No animals could move that fast!"

"Of course not. Let me explain. What you saw was triggered by the shock wave from Source Beta, moving at the speed of sound."

"But what about the pattern?" Falcon insisted.

"That's the surprising part. It's a very rare phenomenon, but identical wheels of light—except that they're a thousand times smaller—have been observed in the Persian Gulf and the Indian Ocean. Listen to this: British India Company's *Patna*, Persian Gulf, May 1880, 11:30 P.M.—'an enormous luminous wheel, whirling round, the spokes of which appeared to brush the ship along. The spokes were two hundred or three hundred yards long . . . each wheel contained about sixteen spokes. . . .' And here's one from the Gulf of Omar, dated May 23, 1906: 'The intensely bright luminescence approached us rapidly, shooting sharply defined light rays to the west in rapid succession, like the beam from the searchlight of a warship. . . . To the left of us, a gigantic fiery wheel formed itself, with spokes that reached as far as one could see. The whole wheel whirled around for two or three minutes. . . .' The archive computer on Ganymede dug up about five hundred cases. It would have printed out the lot if we hadn't stopped it in time."

"I'm convinced—but still baffled."

"I don't blame you. The full explanation wasn't worked out until late in the twentieth century. It seems that these luminous wheels are the results of submarine earthquakes, and always occur in shallow waters where the shock waves can be reflected and cause standing wave patterns. Sometimes bars, sometimes rotating wheels—the 'Wheels of Poseidon,' they've been called. The theory was finally proved by making underwater explosions and photographing the results from a satellite. No wonder sailors used to be superstitious. Who would have believed a thing like *this*?"

So that was it, Falcon told himself. When Source Beta blew its top, it must have sent shock waves in all directions—through the compressed gas of the lower atmosphere, through the solid body of Jupiter itself. Meeting and crisscrossing, those waves must have canceled here, reinforced there; the whole planet must have rung like a bell.

Yet the explanation did not destroy the sense of wonder and awe; he would never be able to forget those flickering bands of light, racing through the unattainable depths of the Jovian atmosphere. He felt that he was not merely on a strange planet, but in some magical realm between myth and reality.

This was a world where absolutely *anything* could happen, and no man could possibly guess what the future would bring.

And he still had a whole day to go.

6. MEDUSA

When the true dawn finally arrived, it brought a sudden change of weather. *Kon-Tiki* was moving through a blizzard; waxen snowflakes were falling so thickly that visibility was reduced to zero. Falcon began to worry about the weight that might be accumulating on the envelope. Then he noticed that any flakes settling outside the windows quickly disappeared; *Kon-Tiki's* continual outpouring of heat was evaporating them as swiftly as they arrived.

If he had been ballooning on Earth, he would also have worried about the possibility of collision. At least that was no danger here; any Jovian mountains were several hundred miles below him. And as for the floating islands of foam, hitting them would probably be like plowing into slightly hardened soap bubbles.

Nevertheless, he switched on the horizontal radar, which until now had been completely useless; only the vertical beam, giving his distance from the invisible surface, had thus far been of any value. Then he had another surprise.

Scattered across a huge sector of the sky ahead were dozens of large and brilliant echoes. They were completely isolated from one another and apparently hung unsupported in space. Falcon remembered a phrase the earliest aviators had used to describe one of the hazards of their profession: "clouds stuffed with rocks." That was a perfect description of what seemed to lie in the track of *Kon-Tiki*.

It was a disconcerting sight; then Falcon again reminded himself that nothing *really* solid could possibly hover in this atmosphere. Perhaps it was some strange meteorological phenomenon. In any case, the nearest echo was about 125 miles.

He reported to Mission Control, which could provide no explanation. But it gave the welcome news that he would be clear of the blizzard in another thirty minutes.

It did not warn him, however, of the violent cross wind that abruptly grabbed *Kon-Tiki* and swept it almost at right angles to its previous track. Falcon needed all his skill and the maximum use of what little control he had over his ungainly vehicle to prevent it from being capsized. Within minutes he was racing northward at over three hundred miles an hour. Then, as suddenly as it had started, the tur-

bulence ceased; he was still moving at high speed, but in smooth air. He wondered
if he had been caught in the Jovian equivalent of a jet stream.

The snow storm dissolved; and he saw what Jupiter had been preparing for
him.

Kon-Tiki had entered the funnel of a gigantic whirlpool, some six hundred
miles across. The balloon was being swept along a curving wall of cloud. Overhead,
the sun was shining in a clear sky; but far beneath, this great hole in the atmosphere
drilled down to unknown depths until it reached a misty floor where lightning
flickered almost continuously.

Though the vessel was being dragged downward so slowly that it was in no
immediate danger, Falcon increased the flow of heat into the envelope until *Kon-Tiki* hovered at a constant altitude. Not until then did he abandon the fantastic
spectacle outside and consider again the problem of the radar.

The nearest echo was now only about twenty-five miles away. All of them, he
quickly realized, were distributed along the wall of the vortex, and were moving
with it, apparently caught in the whirlpool like *Kon-Tiki* itself. He aimed the telescope along the radar bearing and found himself looking at a curious mottled cloud
that almost filled the field of view.

It was not easy to see, being only a little darker than the whirling wall of mist
that formed its background. Not until he had been staring for several minutes did
Falcon realize that he had met it once before.

The first time it had been crawling across the drifting mountains of foam, and
he had mistaken it for a giant, many-trunked tree. Now at last he could appreciate
its real size and complexity and could give it a better name to fix its image in his
mind. It did not resemble a tree at all, but a jellyfish—a medusa, such as might be
met trailing its tentacles as it drifted along the warm eddies of the Gulf Stream.

This medusa was more than a mile across and its scores of dangling tentacles
were hundreds of feet long. They swayed slowly back and forth in perfect unison,
taking more than a minute for each complete undulation—almost as if the creature
was clumsily rowing itself through the sky.

The other echoes were more distant medusae. Falcon focused the telescope on
half a dozen and could see no variations in shape or size. They all seemed to be
of the same species, and he wondered just why they were drifting lazily around in
this six-hundred-mile orbit. Perhaps they were feeding upon the aerial plankton
sucked in by the whirlpool, as *Kon-Tiki* itself had been.

"Do you realize, Howard," said Dr. Brenner, when he had recovered from his
initial astonishment, "that this thing is about a hundred thousand times as large as
the biggest whale? And even if it's only a gasbag, it must still weigh a million
tons! I can't even guess at its metabolism. It must generate megawatts of heat to
maintain its buoyancy."

"But if it's just a gasbag, why is it such a damn good radar reflector?"

"I haven't the faintest idea. Can you get any closer?"

Brenner's question was not an idle one. If he changed altitude to take advantage
of the differing wind velocities, Falcon could approach the medusa as closely as
he wished. At the moment, however, he preferred his present twenty-five miles and
said so, firmly.

"I see what you mean," Brenner answered, a little reluctantly. "Let's stay where we are for the present." That "we" gave Falcon a certain wry amusement; an extra sixty thousand miles made a considerable difference in one's point of view.

For the next two hours *Kon-Tiki* drifted uneventfully in the gyre of the great whirlpool, while Falcon experimented with filters and camera contrast, trying to get a clear view of the medusa. He began to wonder if its elusive coloration was some kind of camouflage; perhaps, like many animals of Earth, it was trying to lose itself against its background. That was a trick used by both hunters and hunted.

In which category was the medusa? That was a question he could hardly expect to have answered in the short time that was left to him. Yet just before noon, without the slightest warning, the answer came. . . .

Like a squadron of antique jet fighters, five mantas came sweeping through the wall of mist that formed the funnel of the vortex. They were flying in a V formation directly toward the pallid gray cloud of the medusa; and there was no doubt, in Falcon's mind, that they were on the attack. He had been quite wrong to assume that they were harmless vegetarians.

Yet everything happened at such a leisurely pace that it was like watching a slow-motion film. The mantas undulated along at perhaps thirty miles an hour; it seemed ages before they reached the medusa, which continued to paddle imperturbably along at an even slower speed. Huge though they were, the mantas looked tiny beside the monster they were approaching. When they flapped down on its back, they appeared about as large as birds landing on a whale.

Could the medusa defend itself, Falcon wondered. He did not see how the attacking mantas could be in danger as long as they avoided those huge clumsy tentacles. And perhaps their host was not even aware of them; they could be insignificant parasites, tolerated as are fleas upon a dog.

But now it was obvious that the medusa was in distress. With agonizing slowness, it began to tip over like a capsizing ship. After ten minutes it had tilted forty-five degrees; it was also rapidly losing altitude. It was impossible not to feel a sense of pity for the beleaguered monster, and to Falcon the sight brought bitter memories. In a grotesque way, the fall of the medusa was almost a parody of the dying *Queen's* last moments.

Yet he knew that his sympathies were on the wrong side. High intelligence could develop only among predators—not among the drifting browsers of either sea or air. The mantas were far closer to him than was this monstrous bag of gas. And anyway, who could *really* sympathize with a creature a hundred thousand times larger than a whale?

Then he noticed that the medusa's tactics seemed to be having some effect. The mantas had been disturbed by its slow roll and were flapping heavily away from its back—like gorged vultures interrupted at mealtime. But they did not move very far, continuing to hover a few yards from the still-capsizing monster.

There was a sudden, blinding flash of light synchronized with a crash of static over the radio. One of the mantas, slowly twisting end over end, was plummeting straight downward. As it fell, a plume of black smoke trailed behind it. The resemblance to an aircraft going down in flames was quite uncanny.

In unison, the remaining mantas dived steeply away from the medusa, gaining speed by losing altitude. They had, within minutes, vanished back into the wall of cloud from which they had emerged. And the medusa, no longer falling, began to roll back toward the horizontal. Soon it was sailing along once more on an even keel, as if nothing had happened.

"Beautiful!" said Dr. Brenner, after a moment of stunned silence. "It's developed electric defenses, like some of our eels and rays. But that must have been about a million volts! Can you see any organs that might produce the discharge? Anything looking like electrodes?"

"No," Falcon answered, after switching to the highest power of the telescope. "But here's something odd. Do you see this pattern? Check back on the earlier images. I'm sure it wasn't there before."

A broad, mottled band had appeared along the side of the medusa. It formed a startlingly regular checkerboard, each square of which was itself speckled in a complex subpattern of short horizontal lines. They were spaced at equal distances in a geometrically perfect array of rows and columns.

"You're right," said Dr. Brenner, with something very much like awe in his voice. "That's just appeared. And I'm afraid to tell you what I think it is."

"Well, I have no reputation to lose—at least as a biologist. Shall I give my guess?"

"Go ahead."

"That's a large meter-band radio array. The sort of thing they used back at the beginning of the twentieth century."

"I was afraid you'd say that. Now we know why it gave such a massive echo."

"But why has it just appeared?"

"Probably an aftereffect of the discharge."

"I've just had another thought," said Falcon, rather slowly. "Do you suppose it's *listening* to us?"

"On this frequency? I doubt it. Those are meter—no, *decameter* antennas—judging by their size. Hmm . . . that's an idea!"

Dr. Brenner fell silent, obviously contemplating some new line of thought. Presently he continued: "I bet they're tuned to the radio outbursts! That's something nature never got around to doing on Earth. . . . We have animals with sonar and even electric senses, but nothing ever developed a radio sense. Why bother where there was so much light?"

"But it's different here. Jupiter is *drenched* with radio energy. It's worthwhile using it—maybe even tapping it. That thing could be a floating power plant!"

A new voice cut into the conversation.

"Mission Commander here. This is all very interesting, but there's a much more important matter to settle. *Is it intelligent?* If so, we've got to consider the First Contact directives."

"Until I came here," said Dr. Brenner, somewhat ruefully, "I would have sworn that anything that could make a short-wave antenna system *must* be intelligent. Now, I'm not sure. This could have evolved naturally. I suppose it's no more fantastic than the human eye."

"Then we have to play safe and assume intelligence. For the present, therefore, this expedition comes under all the clauses of the Prime directive."

There was a long silence while everyone on the radio circuit absorbed the implications of this. For the first time in the history of space flight, the rules that had been established through more than a century of argument might have to be applied. Man had—it was hoped—profited from his mistakes on Earth. Not only moral considerations, but also his own self-interest demanded that he should not repeat them among the planets. It could be disastrous to treat a superior intelligence as the American settlers had treated the Indians, or as almost everyone had treated the Africans. . . .

The first rule was: keep your distance. Make no attempt to approach, or even to communicate, until "they" have had plenty of time to study you. Exactly what was meant by "plenty of time," no one had ever been able to decide. It was left to the discretion of the man on the spot.

A responsibility of which he had never dreamed had descended upon Howard Falcon. In the few hours that remained to him on Jupiter, he might become the first ambassador of the human race.

And *that* was an irony so delicious that he almost wished the surgeons had restored to him the power of laughter.

7. PRIME DIRECTIVE

It was growing darker, but Falcon scarcely noticed as he strained his eyes toward that living cloud in the field of the telescope. The wind that was steadily sweeping *Kon-Tiki* around the funnel of the great whirlpool had now brought him within twelve miles of the creature. If he got much closer than six, he would take evasive action. Though he felt certain that the medusa's electric weapons were short-ranged, he did not wish to put the matter to the test. That would be a problem for future explorers, and he wished them luck.

Now it was quite dark in the capsule. That was strange, because sunset was still hours away. Automatically, he glanced at the horizontally scanning radar, as he had done every few minutes. Apart from the medusa he was studying, there was no other object within about sixty miles of him.

Suddenly, with startling power, he heard the sound that had come booming out of the Jovian night—the throbbing beat that grew more and more rapid, then stopped in mid-crescendo. The whole capsule vibrated with it like a pea in a kettledrum.

Falcon realized two things almost simultaneously during the sudden, aching silence. *This* time the sound was not coming from thousands of miles away, over a radio circuit. It was in the very atmosphere around him.

The second thought was even more disturbing. He had quite forgotten—it was inexcusable, but there had been other apparently more important things on his mind—that most of the sky above him was completely blanked out by *Kon-Tiki's* gasbag. Being lightly silvered to conserve its heat, the great balloon was an effective shield both to radar and to vision.

He had known this, of course; it had been a minor defect of the design, tolerated because it did not appear important. It seemed very important to Howard Falcon now—as he saw that fence of gigantic tentacles, thicker than the trunks of any tree, descending all around the capsule.

He heard Brenner yelling: "Remember the Prime directive! Don't alarm it!" Before he could make an appropriate answer that overwhelming drumbeat started again and drowned all other sounds.

The sign of a really skilled test pilot is how he reacts not to foreseeable emergencies, but to ones that nobody could have anticipated. Falcon did not hesitate for more than a second to analyze the situation. In a lightning-swift movement, he pulled the rip cord.

That word was an archaic survival from the days of the first hydrogen balloons; on *Kon-Tiki*, the rip cord did not tear open the gasbag, but merely operated a set of louvers around the upper curve of the envelope. At once the hot gas started to rush out; *Kon-Tiki*, deprived of her lift, began to fall swiftly in this gravity field two and a half times as strong as Earth's.

Falcon had a momentary glimpse of great tentacles whipping upward and away. He had just time to note that they were studded with large bladders or sacs, presumably to give them buoyancy, and that they ended in multitudes of thin feelers like the roots of a plant. He half expected a bolt of lightning—but nothing happened.

His precipitous rate of descent was slackening as the atmosphere thickened and the deflated envelope acted as a parachute. When *Kon-Tiki* had dropped about two miles, he felt that it was safe to close the louvers again. By the time he had restored buoyancy and was in equilibrium once more, he had lost another mile of altitude and was getting dangerously near his safety limit.

He peered anxiously through the overhead windows, though he did not expect to see anything except the obscuring bulk of the balloon. But he had sideslipped during his descent, and part of the medusa was just visible a couple of miles above him. It was much closer than he expected—and it was still coming down, faster than he would have believed possible.

Mission Control was calling anxiously. He shouted: "I'm O.K.—but it's still coming after me. I can't go any deeper."

That was not quite true. He could go a lot deeper—about 180 miles. But it would be a one-way trip, and most of the journey would be of little interest to him.

Then, to his great relief, he saw that the medusa was leveling off, not quite a mile above him. Perhaps it had decided to approach this strange intruder with caution; or perhaps it, too, found this deeper layer uncomfortably hot. The temperature was over fifty degrees centigrade, and Falcon wondered how much longer his life-support system could handle matters.

Dr. Brenner was back on the circuit, still worrying about the Prime directive.

"Remember—it may only be inquisitive!" he cried, without much conviction. "Try not to frighten it!"

Falcon was getting rather tired of this advice and recalled a TV discussion he had once seen between a space lawyer and an astronaut. After the full implications of the Prime directive had been carefully spelled out, the incredulous spacer had exclaimed: "Then if there was no alternative, I must sit still and let myself be eaten?" The lawyer had not even cracked a smile when he answered: "That's an *excellent* summing up."

It had seemed funny at the time; it was not at all amusing now.

And then Falcon saw something that made him even more unhappy. The medusa was still hovering about a mile above him—but one of its tentacles was becoming incredibly elongated, and was stretching down toward *Kon-Tiki*, thinning out at the same time. As a boy he had once seen the funnel of a tornado descending from a storm cloud over the Kansas plains. The thing coming toward him now evoked vivid memories of that black, twisting snake in the sky.

"I'm rapidly running out of options," he reported to Mission Control. "I now have only a choice between frightening it—and giving it a bad stomach ache. I don't think it will find *Kon-Tiki* very digestible, if that's what it has in mind."

He waited for comments from Brenner, but the biologist remained silent.

"Very well. It's twenty-seven minutes ahead of time, but I'm starting the ignition sequencer. I hope I'll have enough reserve to correct my orbit later."

He could no longer see the medusa; once more it was directly overhead. But he knew that the descending tentacle must now be very close to the balloon. It would take almost five minutes to bring the reactor up to full thrust. . . .

The fusor was primed. The orbit computer had not rejected the situation as wholly impossible. The air scoops were open, ready to gulp in tons of the surrounding hydrohelium on demand. Even under optimum conditions, this would have been the moment of truth—for there had been no way of testing how a nuclear ramjet would really work in the strange atmosphere of Jupiter.

Very gently something rocked *Kon-Tiki*. Falcon tried to ignore it.

Ignition had been planned at six miles higher, in an atmosphere of less than a quarter of the density and thirty degrees cooler. Too bad.

What was the shallowest dive he could get away with, for the air scoops to work? When the ram ignited, he'd be heading toward Jupiter with two and a half g's to help him get there. Could he possibly pull out in time?

A large, heavy hand patted the balloon. The whole vessel bobbed up and down, like one of the Yo-yo's that had just become the craze on Earth.

Of course, Brenner *might* be perfectly right. Perhaps it was just trying to be friendly. Maybe he should try to talk to it over the radio. Which should it be: "Pretty pussy"? "Down, Fido"? Or "Take me to your leader"?

The tritium-deuterium ratio was correct. He was ready to light the candle, with a hundred-million-degree match.

The thin tip of the tentacle came slithering around the edge of the balloon some sixty yards away. It was about the size of an elephant's trunk, and by the delicate way it was moving appeared to be almost as sensitive. There were little palps at its end, like questing mouths. He was sure that Dr. Brenner would be fascinated.

This seemed about as good a time as any. He gave a swift scan of the entire control board, started the final four-second ignition count, broke the safety seal, and pressed the Jettison switch.

There was a sharp explosion and an instant loss of weight. *Kon-Tiki* was falling freely, nose down. Overhead, the discarded balloon was racing upward, dragging the inquisitive tentacle with it. Falcon had no time to see if the gasbag actually hit the medusa, because at that moment the ramjet fired and he had other matters to think about.

A roaring column of hot hydrohelium was pouring out of the reactor nozzles, swiftly building up thrust—but *toward* Jupiter, not away from it. He could not pull out yet, for vector control was too sluggish. Unless he could gain complete control and achieve horizontal flight within the next five seconds, the vehicle would dive too deeply into the atmosphere and would be destroyed.

With agonizing slowness—those five seconds seemed like fifty—he managed to flatten out, then pull the nose upward. He glanced back only once and caught a final glimpse of the medusa, many miles away. *Kon-Tiki's* discarded gasbag had apparently escaped from its grasp, for he could see no sign of it.

Now he was master once more—no longer drifting helplessly on the winds of Jupiter, but riding his own column of atomic fire back to the stars. He was confident that the ramjet would steadily give him velocity and altitude until he had reached near-orbital speed at the fringes of the atmosphere. Then, with a brief burst of pure rocket power, he would regain the freedom of space.

Halfway to orbit, he looked south and saw the tremendous enigma of the Great Red Spot—that floating island twice the size of Earth—coming up over the horizon. He stared into its mysterious beauty until the computer warned him that conversion to rocket thrust was only sixty seconds ahead. He tore his gaze reluctantly away.

"Some other time," he murmured.

"What's that?" said Mission Control. "What did you say?"

"It doesn't matter," he replied.

8. BETWEEN TWO WORLDS

"You're a hero now, Howard," said Webster, "not just a celebrity. You've given them something to think about—injected some excitement into their lives. Not one in a million will actually travel to the Outer Giants, but the whole human race will go in imagination. And that's what counts."

"I'm glad to have made your job a little easier."

Webster was too old a friend to take offense at the note of irony. Yet it surprised him. And this was not the first change in Howard that he had noticed since the return from Jupiter.

The Administrator pointed to the famous sign on his desk, borrowed from an impresario of an earlier age: ASTONISH ME!

"I'm not ashamed of my job. New knowledge, new resources—they're all very well. But men also need novelty and excitement. Space travel has become routine; you've made it a great adventure once more. It will be a long, long time before we get Jupiter pigeonholed. And maybe longer still before we understand those medusae. I still think that one *knew* where your blind spot was. Anyway, have you decided on your next move? Saturn, Uranus, Neptune—you name it."

"I don't know. I've thought about Saturn, but I'm not really needed there. It's only one gravity, not two and a half like Jupiter. So men can handle it."

Men, thought Webster. He said "men." He's never done that before. And when did I last hear him use the word "we"? He's changing, slipping away from us. . . .

"Well," he said aloud, rising from his chair to conceal his slight uneasiness, "let's get the conference started. The cameras are all set up and everyone's waiting. You'll meet a lot of old friends."

He stressed the last word, but Howard showed no response. The leathery mask of his face was becoming more and more difficult to read. Instead, he rolled back from the Administrator's desk, unlocked his undercarriage so that it no longer formed a chair, and rose on his hydraulics to his full seven feet of height. It had been good psychology on the part of the surgeons to give him that extra twelve inches, to compensate somewhat for all that he had lost when the *Queen* had crashed.

Falcon waited until Webster had opened the door, then pivoted neatly on his balloon tires and headed for it at a smooth and silent twenty miles an hour. The display of speed and precision was not flaunted arrogantly; rather, it had become quite unconscious.

Howard Falcon, who had once been a man and could still pass for one over a voice circuit, felt a calm sense of achievement—and, for the first time in years, something like peace of mind. Since his return from Jupiter, the nightmares had ceased. He had found his role at last.

He now knew why he had dreamed about that superchimp aboard the doomed *Queen Elizabeth*. Neither man nor beast, it was between two worlds; and so was he.

He alone could travel unprotected on the lunar surface. The life-support system inside the metal cylinder that had replaced his fragile body functioned equally well in space or under water. Gravity fields ten times that of Earth were an inconvenience, but nothing more. And no gravity was best of all. . . .

The human race was becoming more remote, the ties of kinship more tenuous. Perhaps these air-breathing, radiation-sensitive bundles of unstable carbon compounds had no right beyond the atmosphere; they should stick to their natural homes—Earth, Moon, Mars.

Some day the real masters of space would be machines, not men—and he was neither. Already conscious of his destiny, he took a somber pride in his unique loneliness—the first immortal midway between two orders of creation.

He would, after all, be an ambassador; between the old and the new—between the creatures of carbon and the creatures of metal who must one day supersede them.

Both would have need of him in the troubled centuries that lay ahead.

The Man Who Walked Home

JAMES TIPTREE, JR.

As most of you probably know by now, multiple Hugo and Nebula–winning author James Tiptree, Jr.—at one time a figure reclusive and mysterious enough to be regarded as the B. Traven of science fiction—was actually the pseudonym of the late Dr. Alice Sheldon, a semiretired experimental psychologist who also wrote occasionally under the name of Raccoona Sheldon. Dr. Sheldon's tragic death in 1987 put an end to "both" authors' careers, but, before that, she had won two Nebula and two Hugo Awards as Tiptree, won another Nebula Award as Raccoona Sheldon, and established herself, under whatever name, as one of the best writers in science fiction.

Although "Tiptree" published two reasonably well received novels—*Up the Walls of the World* and *Brightness Falls from the Air*—she was, like Damon Knight and Theodore Sturgeon (two writers she aesthetically resembled and by whom she was strongly influenced) more comfortable with the short story and more effective with it. She wrote some of the very best short stories of the seventies: "The Screwfly Solution," "The Girl Who Was Plugged In," "The Women Men Don't See," "Beam Us Home," "And I Awoke and Found Me Here on the Cold Hill's Side," "I'm Too Big but I Love to Play," "Slow Music," and "His Smoke Rose Up Forever." Already it's clear that these are stories that will last. They—and a dozen others almost as good—show that Alice Sheldon was simply one of the best short-story writers to work in the genre in our times.

Exploration played an important part in Sheldon's work, although, ironically, often what her explorers were obsessively searching for was a way to get *home* again—a theme she never expressed more clearly than in the vivid and compelling story that follows, which takes us home by the longest way imaginable and shows us although home may only be a step away, sometimes that step can be very hard to *take*. . . .

As James Tiptree, Jr., Alice Sheldon also published nine short-story collections: *Ten Thousand Light Years from Home*, *Warm Worlds and Otherwise*, *Starsongs of an Old Primate*, *Out of the Everywhere*, *Tales of the Quintana Roo*, *Byte Beautiful*, *he Starry Rift,* the posthumously published *Crown of Stars,* and the retrospective ollection *Her Smoke Rose Up Forever.*

ransgression! Terror! And he thrust and lost there—punched into impossibility, bandoned, never to be known how, the wrong man in the most wrong of all wrong laces in that unimaginable collapse of never-to-be-reimagined mechanism—he tranded, undone, his lifeline severed, he in that nanosecond knowing his only ther parting, going away, the longest line to life withdrawing, winking out, disppearing forever beyond his grasp—telescoping away from him into the closing ortex beyond which lay his home, his life, his only possibility of being; seeing it ucked back into the deepest maw, melting, leaving him orphaned on what never-to-e-known shore of total wrongness—of beauty beyond joy, perhaps? Of horror?)f nothingness? Of profound otherness only, certainly whatever it was, that place ito which he transgressed, certainly it could not support his life there, his violent nd violating aberrance; and he, fierce, brave, crazy—clenched into one total rotest, one body-fist of utter repudiation of himself there in that place, forsaken here—what did he do? Rejected, exiled, hungering homeward more desperate than ny lost beast driving for its unreachable home, his home, his—HOME—and no vay, no transport, no vehicle, means, machinery, no force but his intolerable re-olve aimed homeward along that vanishing vector, that last and only lifeline—he lid, what?

He walked.

Home.

Precisely what hashed up in the work of the major industrial lessee of the 3onneville Particle Acceleration Facility in Idaho was never known. Or rather, all hose who might have been able to diagnose the original malfunction were them-elves obliterated almost at once in the greater catastrophe which followed.

The nature of this second cataclysm was not at first understood either. All that vas ever certain was that at 1153.6 of May 2, 1989 Old Style, the Bonneville aboratories and all their personnel were transformed into an intimately disrupted orm of matter resembling a high-energy plasma, which became rapidly airborne o the accompaniment of radiating seismic and atmospheric events.

The disturbed area unfortunately included an operational MIRV Watchdog)omb.

In the confusions of the next hours the Earth's population was substantially educed, the biosphere was altered, and the Earth itself was marked with numbers)f more conventional craters. For some years thereafter the survivors were exis-entially preoccupied and the peculiar dust bowl at Bonneville was left to weather)y itself in the changing climatic cycles.

It was not a large crater; just over a kilometer in width and lacking the usual lisplacement lip. Its surface was covered with a finely divided substance which lried into dust. Before the rains began it was almost perfectly flat. Only in certain lights, had anyone been there to inspect it, a small surface marking or abraded)lace could be detected almost exactly at the center.

Two decades after the disaster a party of short brown people appeared from he south, together with a flock of somewhat atypical sheep. The crater at this time appeared as a wide shallow basin in which the grass did not grow well, doubtless

from the almost complete lack of soil micro-organisms. Neither this nor the sur
rounding vigorous grass were found to harm the sheep. A few crude hogans went
up at the southern edge and a faint path began to be traced across the crater itself
passing by the central by the bare spot.

One spring morning two children who had been driving sheep across the crater
came screaming back to camp. A monster had burst out of the ground before them
a huge flat animal making a dreadful roar. It vanished in a flash and a shaking of
the earth, leaving an evil smell. The sheep had run away.

Since this last was visibly true, some elders investigated. Finding no sign of
the monster and no place in which it could hide, they settled for beating the chil
dren, who settled for making a detour around the monster-spot, and nothing more
occurred for a while.

The following spring the episode was repeated. This time an older girl was
present but she could add only that the monster seemed to be rushing flat out along
the ground without moving at all. And there was a scraped place in the dirt. Again
nothing was found; an evil-ward in a cleft stick was placed at the spot.

When the same thing happened for the third time a year later, the detour was
extended and other charm-wands were added. But since no harm seemed to come
of it and the brown people had seen far worse, sheep-tending resumed as before
A few more instantaneous apparitions of the monster were noted, each time in the
spring.

At the end of the third decade of the new era a tall old man limped down the
hills from the south, pushing his pack upon a bicycle wheel. He camped on the
far side of the crater, and soon found the monster-site. He attempted to question
people about it, but no one understood him, so he traded a knife for some meat.
Although he was obviously feeble, something about him dissuaded them from
killing him, and this proved wise because he later assisted the women to treat
several sick children.

He spent much time around the place of the apparition and was nearby when
it made its next appearance. This excited him very much, and he did several inexplicable but apparently harmless things, including moving his camp into the
crater by the trail. He stayed on for a full year watching the site and was close by
for its next manifestation. After this he spent a few days making a charmstone for
the spot and then left, northward, hobbling, as he had come.

More decades passed. The crater eroded and a rain-gully became an intermittent steamlet across one edge of the basin. The brown people and their sheep were
attacked by a band of grizzled men, after which the survivors went away eastward.
The winters of what had been Idaho were now frost-free; aspen and eucalyptus
sprouted in the moist plain. Still the crater remained treeless, visible as a flat bowl
of grass, and the bare place at the center remained. The skies cleared somewhat.

After another three decades a larger band of black people with ox-drawn carts
appeared and stayed for a time, but left again when they too saw the thunderclap-
monster. A few other vagrants straggled by.

Five decades later a small permanent settlement had grown up on the nearest
range of hills, from which men riding on small ponies with dark stripes down their
spines herded humped cattle near the crater. A herdsman hut was built by the
streamlet, which in time became the habitation of an oliveskinned, red-haired family. In due course one of this clan again observed the monster-flash, but these

people did not depart. The stone the tall man had placed was noted and left undisturbed.

The homestead at the crater's edge grew into a group of three and was joined by others, and the trail across it became a cartroad with a log bridge over the stream. At the center of the still-faintly-discernible crater the cartroad made a bend, leaving a grassy place which bore on its center about a square meter of curiously impacted bare earth and a deeply-etched sandstone rock.

The apparition of the monster was now known to occur regularly each spring on a certain morning in this place, and the children of the community dared each other to approach the spot. It was referred to in a phrase that could be translated as "the Old Dragon." The Old Dragon's appearance was always the same: a brief, violent thunderburst which began and cut off abruptly, in the midst of which a dragon-like creature was seen apparently in furious motion on the earth although it never actually moved. Afterward there was a bad smell and the earth smoked. People who saw it from close by spoke of a shivering sensation.

Early in the second century two young men rode into town from the north. Their ponies were shaggier than the local breed and the equipment they carried included two boxlike objects which the young men set up at the monster-site. They stayed in the area a full year, observing two materializations of the Old Dragon, and they provided much news and maps of roads and trading-towns in the cooler regions to the north. They built a windmill which was accepted by the community and offered to build a lighting machine, which was refused. Then they departed with their boxes after unsuccessfully attempting to persuade a local boy to learn to operate one.

In the course of the next decades other travelers stopped by and marveled at the monster, and there was sporadic fighting over the mountains to the south. One of the armed bands made a cattle-raid into the crater hamlet. It was repulsed, but the raiders left a spotted sickness which killed many. For all this time the bare place at the crater's center remained, and the monster made his regular appearances, observed or not.

The hill-town grew and changed and the crater hamlet grew to be a town. Roads widened and linked into networks. There were gray-green conifers in the hills now, spreading down into the plain, and chirruping lizards lived in their branches.

At century's end a shabby band of skin-clad squatters with stunted milk-beasts erupted out of the west and were eventually killed or driven away, but not before the local herds had contracted a vicious parasite. Veterinaries were fetched from the market-city up north, but little could be done. The families near the crater left, and for some decades the area was empty. Finally cattle of a new strain reappeared in the plain and the crater hamlet was reoccupied. Still the bare center continued annually to manifest the monster and he became an accepted phenomenon of the area. On several occasions parties came from the distant Northwest Authority to observe it.

The crater hamlet flourished and grew into the fields where cattle had grazed and part of the old crater became the town park. A small seasonal tourist industry based on the monstersite developed. The townspeople rented rooms for the appearances and many more-or-less authentic monster-relics were on display in the local taverns.

Several cults now grew up around the monster. Some held that it was a devil or damned soul forced to appear on Earth in torment to expiate the catastrophe of two centuries back. Others believed that it, or he, was some kind of messenger whose roar portended either doom or hope according to the believer. One very vocal sect taught that the apparition registered the moral conduct of the townspeople over the past year, and scrutinized the annual apparition for changes which could be interpreted for good or ill. It was considered lucky, or dangerous, to be touched by some of the dust raised by the monster. In every generation at least one small boy would try to hit the monster with a stick, usually acquiring a broken arm and a lifelong tavern tale. Pelting the monster with stones or other objects was a popular sport, and for some years people systematically flung prayers and flowers at it. Once a party tried to net it and were left with strings and vapor. The area itself had long since been fenced off at the center of the park.

Through all this the monster made his violently enigmatic annual appearance, sprawled furiously motionless, unreachably roaring.

Only as the fourth century of the new era went by was it apparent that the monster had been changing slightly. He was now no longer on the earth but had an arm and a leg thrust upward in a kicking or flailing gesture. As the years passed he began to change more quickly until at the end of the century he had risen to a contorted crouching pose, arms outflung as if frozen in gyration. His roar, too, seemed somewhat differently pitched and the earth after him smoked more and more.

It was then widely felt that the man-monster was about to do something, to make some definitive manifestation, and a series of natural disasters and marvels gave support to a vigorous cult teaching this doctrine. Several religious leaders journeyed to the town to observe the apparitions.

However, the decades passed and the man-monster did nothing more than turn slowly in place, so that he now appeared to be in the act of sliding or staggering while pushing himself backward like a creature blown before a gale. No wind, of course, could be felt, and presently the general climate quieted and nothing came of it all.

Early in the fifth century New Calendar three survey parties from the North Central Authority came through the area and stopped to observe the monster. A permanent recording device was set up at the site, after assurances to the townfolk that no hardscience was involved. A local boy was trained to operate it; he quit when his girl left him but another volunteered. At this time nearly everyone believed that the apparition was a man, or the ghost of one. The record-machine boy and a few others, including the school mechanics teacher, referred to him as The Man John. In the next decades the roads were greatly improved; all forms of travel increased and there was talk of building a canal to what had been the Snake River.

One May morning at the end of Century Five a young couple in a smart green mule-trap came jogging up the highroad from the Sandreas Rift Range to the southwest. The girl was golden-skinned and chatted with her young husband in a language unlike that ever heard by the Man John either at the end or the beginning of his life. What she said to him has, however, been heard in every age and tongue.

"Oh Serli, I'm so glad we're taking this trip now! Next summer I'll be so busy with baby."

To which Serli replied as young husbands often have, and so they trotted up to the town's inn. Here they left trap and bags and went in search of her uncle who was expecting them there. The morrow was the day of the Man John's annual appearance, and her Uncle Laban had come from the MacKenzie History Museum to observe it and to make certain arrangements.

They found him with the town school instructor of mechanics, who was also the recorder at the monster-site. Presently Uncle Laban took them all with him to the town mayor's office to meet with various religious personages. The mayor was not unaware of tourist values, but he took Uncle Laban's part in securing the cultists' grudging assent to the MacKenzie authorities' secular interpretation of the "monster," which was made easier by the fact that they disagreed among themselves. Then, seeing how pretty the niece was, the mayor took them all home to dinner.

When they returned to the inn for the night it was abrawl with holiday makers.

"Whew," said Uncle Laban. "I've talked myself dry, sister's daughter. What a weight of holy nonsense is that Morsha female! Serli, my lad, I know you have questions. Let me hand you this to read; it's the guide book we're giving 'em to sell. Tomorrow I'll answer for it all." And he disappeared into the crowded tavern.

So Serli and his bride took the pamphlet upstairs to bed with them, but it was not until the next morning at breakfast that they found time to read it.

"'All that is known of John Delgano,'" read Serli with his mouth full, "'comes from two documents left by his brother Carl Delgano in the archives of the MacKenzie Group in the early years after the holocaust.' Put some honey on this cake, Mira my dove. 'Verbatim transcript follows; this is Carl Delgano speaking.

"'I'm not an engineer or an astronaut like John. I ran an electronics repair shop in Salt Lake City. John was only trained as a spaceman, he never got to space, the slump wiped all that out. So he tied up with this commercial group who were leasing part of Bonneville. They wanted a man for some kind of hard vacuum tests; that's all I knew about it. John and his wife moved to Bonneville, but we all got together several times a year, our wives were like sisters. John had two kids, Clara and Paul.

"'The tests were all supposed to be secret, but John told me confidentially they were trying for an anti-gravity chamber. I don't know if it ever worked. That was the year before.

"'Then that winter they came down for Christmas and John said they had something new. He was really excited. A temporal displacement, he called it; some kind of time effect. He said the chief honcho was like a real mad scientist. Big ideas. He kept adding more angles every time some other project would quit and leave equipment he could lease. No, I don't know who the top company was— maybe an insurance conglomerate, they had all the cash, didn't they? I guess they'd pay to catch a look at the future; that figures. Anyway, John was go, go, go. Katharine was scared; that's natural. She pictured him like, you know, H. G. Wells—walking around in some future world. John told her it wasn't like that at all. All they'd get would be this kind of flicker, like a second or two. All kinds of complications'—Yes, yes, my greedy piglet, some brew for me too. This is thirsty work!

"So . . . 'I remember I asked him, what about the Earth moving? I mean, you could come back in a different place, right? He said they had that all figured. A spatial trajectory. Katherine was so scared we dropped it. John told her, don't worry, I'll come home. But he didn't. Not that it makes any difference, of course; everything was wiped out. Salt Lake too. The only reason I'm here is that I went up by Calgary to see Mom, April twenty-ninth. May second it all blew. I didn't find you folks at MacKenzie until July. I guess I may as well stay. That's all I know about John, except that he was an all-right guy. If that accident started all this it wasn't his fault.

"'The second document'—In the name of love, little mother, do I have to read all this! Oh very well; but you will kiss me first, madam. Must you look so ineffable? . . . 'The second document. Dated in the year eighteen, New Style, writter by Carl'—see the old handwriting, my plump pigeon. Oh, very well, very well.

"'Written at Bonneville Crater. I have seen my brother John Delgano. When I knew I had the rad sickness I came down here to look around. Salt Lake's still hot. So I hiked up here by Bonneville. You can see the crater where the labs were; it's grassed over. It's different, it's not radioactive, my film's OK. There's a bare place in the middle. Some Indios here told me a monster shows up here every year in the spring. I saw it myself a couple of days after I got here but I was too far away to see much, except I was sure it's a man. In a vacuum suit. There was a lot of noise and dust, took me by surprise. It was all over in a second. I figure it's pretty close to the day, I mean, May second, old.

"'So I hung around a year and he showed up again yesterday. I was on the face side and I could see his face through the faceplate. It's John all right. He's hurt. I saw blood on his mouth and his suit is frayed some. He's lying on the ground. He didn't move while I could see him but the dust boiled up, like a man sliding onto base without moving. His eyes are open like he was looking. I don't understand it anyway, but I know it's John, not a ghost. He was in exactly the same position each time and there's a loud crack like thunder and another sound like a siren, very fast. And an ozone smell, and smoke. I felt a kind of shudder.

"'I know it's John there and I think he's alive. I have to leave here now to take this back while I can still walk. I think somebody should come here and see. Maybe you can help John. Signed, Carl Delgano.

"'These records were kept by the MacKenzie Group but it was not for several years—' Etcetera, first light-print, etcetera, archives, analysts, etcetera—very good! Now it is time to meet your uncle, my edible one, after we go upstairs for just a moment."

"No, Serli, I will wait for you downstairs," said Mira prudently.

When they came into the town park Uncle Laban was directing the installation of a large durite slab in front of the enclosure around the Man John's appearance-spot. The slab was wrapped in a curtain to await the official unveiling. Townspeople and tourists and children thronged the walks and a Ride-For-Good choir was singing in the bandshell. The morning was warming up fast. Vendors hawked ices and straw toys of the monster and flowers and good-luck confetti to throw at him. Another religious group stood by in dark robes; they belonged to the Repentance church beyond the park. Their pastor was directing somber glares at the crowd in general and Mira's uncle in particular.

Three official-looking strangers who had been at the inn came up and introduced themselves to Uncle Laban as observers from Alberta Central. They went on into the tent which had been erected over the enclosure, carrying with them several pieces of equipment which the town-folk eyed suspiciously.

The mechanics teacher finished organizing a squad of students to protect the slab's curtain, and Mira and Serli and Laban went on into the tent. It was much hotter inside. Benches were set in rings around a railed enclosure about twenty feet in diameter. Inside the railing the earth was bare and scuffed. Several bunches of flowers and blooming poinciana branches leaned against the rail. The only thing inside the rail was a rough sandstone rock with markings etched on it.

Just as they came in a small girl raced across the open center and was yelled at by everybody. The officials from Alberta were busy at one side of the rail, where the light-print box was mounted.

"Oh, no," muttered Mira's uncle, as one of the officials leaned over to set up a tripod stand inside the rails. He adjusted it and a huge horsetail of fine feathery filaments blossomed out and eddied through the center of the space.

"Oh, *no*," Laban said again. "Why can't they let it be?"

"They're trying to pick up dust from his suit, is that right?" Serli asked.

"Yes, insane. Did you get time to read?"

"Oh yes," said Serli.

"Sort of," added Mira.

"Then you know. He's falling. Trying to check his—well, call it velocity. Trying to slow down. He must have slipped or stumbled. We're getting pretty close to when he lost his footing and started to fall. What did it? Did somebody trip him?" Laban looked from Mira to Serli, dead serious now. "How would you like to be the one who made John Delgano fall?"

"Ooh," said Mira in quick sympathy. Then she said, "Oh."

"You mean," asked Serli, "whoever made him fall caused all the, caused—"

"Possible," said Laban.

"Wait a minute," Serli frowned. "He did fall. So somebody had to do it—I mean, he has to trip or whatever. If he doesn't fall the past would all be changed, wouldn't it? No war, no—"

"Possible," Laban repeated. "God knows. All *I* know is that John Delgano and the space around him is the most unstable, improbable, highly charged area ever known on Earth and I'm damned if I think anybody should go poking sticks in it."

"Oh come now, Laban!" One of the Alberta men joined them, smiling. "Our dust-mop couldn't trip a gnat. It's just vitreous monofilaments."

"Dust from the future," grumbled Laban. "What's it going to tell you? That the future has dust in it?"

"If we could only get a trace from that thing in his hand."

"In his hand?" asked Mira. Serli started leafing hurriedly through the pamphlet.

"We've had a recording analyzer aimed at it," the Albertan lowered his voice, glancing around. "A spectroscope. We know there's something there, or was. Can't get a decent reading. It's severely deteriorated."

"People poking at him, grabbing at him," Laban muttered. "You—"

"*Ten minutes!*" shouted a man with a megaphone. "Take your places, friends and strangers."

The Repentance people were filing in at one side, intoning an ancient incantation, "mi-seri-cordia, ora pro nobis!"

The atmosphere suddenly took on tension. It was now very close and hot in the big tent. A boy from the mayor's office wiggled through the crowd, beckoning Laban's party to come and sit in the guest chairs on the second level on the "face" side. In front of them at the rail one of the Repentance ministers was arguing with an Albertan official over his right to occupy the space taken by a recorder, it being his special duty to look into the Man John's eyes.

"Can he really see us?" Mira asked her uncle.

"Blink your eyes," Laban told her. "A new scene every blink, that's what he sees. Phantasmagoria. Blink-blink-blink—for god knows how long."

"Mi-sere-re, pec-cavi," chanted the penitentials. A soprano neighed "May the red of sin pa-aa-ass from us!"

"They believe his oxygen tab went red because of the state of their souls." Laban chuckled. "Their souls are going to have to stay damned a while; John Delgano has been on oxygen reserve for five centuries—or rather, he *will be* low for five centuries more. At a half-second per year his time, that's fifteen minutes. We know from the audio trace he's still breathing more or less normally and the reserve was good for twenty minutes. So they should have their salvation about the year seven hundred, if they last that long."

"*Five minutes!* Take your seats, folks. Please sit down so everyone can see. Sit down, folks."

"It says we'll hear his voice through his suit speaker," Serli whispered. "Do you know what he's saying?"

"You get mostly a twenty-cycle howl," Laban whispered back. "The recorders have spliced up something like *ayt*, part of an old word. Take centuries to get enough to translate."

"Is it a message?"

"Who knows? Could be his word for 'date' or 'hate.' 'Too late,' maybe. Anything."

The tent was quieting. A fat child by the railing started to cry and was pulled back onto a lap. There was a subdued mumble of praying. The Holy Joy faction on the far side rustled their flowers.

"Why don't we set our clocks by him?"

"It's changing. He's on sidereal time."

"One minute."

In the hush the praying voices rose slightly. From outside a chicken cackled. The bare center space looked absolutely ordinary. Over it the recorder's silvery filaments eddied gently in the breath from a hundred lungs. Another recorder could be heard ticking faintly.

For long seconds nothing happened.

The air developed a tiny hum. At the same moment Mira caught a movement at the railing on her left.

The hum developed a beat and vanished into a peculiar silence and suddenly everything happened at once.

Sound burst on them, raced shockingly up the audible scale. The air cracked as something rolled and tumbled in the space. There was a grinding, wailing roar and—

He was there.

Solid, huge—a huge man in a monster suit, his head was a dull bronze transparent globe holding a human face, dark smear of open mouth. His position was impossible, legs strained forward thrusting himself back, his arms frozen in a whirlwind swing. Although he seemed to be in a frantic forward motion nothing moved, only one of his legs buckled or sagged slightly—

—And then he was gone, utterly and completely gone in a thunderclap, leaving only the incredible afterimage in a hundred pairs of staring eyes. Air boomed, shuddering, dust roiled out mixed with smoke.

"Oh, oh my God," gasped Mira, unheard, clinging to Serli. Voices were crying out, choking. "He saw me, he saw me!" a woman shrieked. A few people dazedly threw their confetti into the empty dust-cloud; most had failed to throw at all. Children began to howl. "He *saw* me!" the woman screamed hysterically. "Red, Oh Lord have mercy!" a deep male voice intoned.

Mira heard Laban swearing furiously and looked again into the space. As the dust settled she could see that the recorder's tripod had tipped over into the center. There was a dusty mound lying against it—flowers. Most of the end of the stand seemed to have disappeared or been melted. Of the filaments nothing could be seen.

"Some damn fool pitched flowers into it. Come on, let's get out."

"Was it under, did it trip him?" asked Mira, squeezed in the crowd.

"It was still red, his oxygen thing," Serli said over her head. "No mercy this trip, eh, Laban?"

"Shsh!" Mira caught the Repentance pastor's dark glance. They jostled through the enclosure gate and were out in the sunlit park, voices exclaiming, chattering loudly in excitement and relief.

"It was terrible," Mira cried softly. "Oh, I never thought it was a real live man. There he is, he's *there*. Why can't we help him? Did we trip him?"

"I don't know; I don't think so," her uncle grunted. They sat down near the new monument, fanning themselves. The curtain was still in place.

"Did we change the past?" Serli laughed, looked lovingly at his little wife. He wondered for a moment why she was wearing such odd earrings. Then he remembered he had given them to her at that Indian pueblo they'd passed.

"But it wasn't just those Alberta people," said Mira. She seemed obsessed with the idea. "It was the flowers really." She wiped at her forehead.

"Mechanics or superstition," chuckled Serli. "Which is the culprit, love or science?"

"Shsh." Mira looked about nervously. "The flowers were love, I guess . . . I feel so strange. It's hot. Oh, thank you." Uncle Laban had succeeded in attracting the attention of the iced-drink vendor.

People were chatting normally now and the choir struck into a cheerful song. At one side of the park a line of people were waiting to sign their names in the visitors' book. The mayor appeared at the park gate, leading a party up the bougainvillea alley for the unveiling of the monument.

"What did it say on that stone by his foot?" Mira asked. Serli showed her the guidebook picture of Carl's rock with the inscription translated below: WELCOME HOME JOHN.

"I wonder if he can see it."

The mayor was about to begin his speech.

Much later when the crowd had gone away the monument stood alone in the dark, displaying to the moon the inscription in the language of that time and place:

On this spot there appears annually the form of Major John Delgano, the first and only man to travel in time.

Major Delgano was sent into the future some hours before the holocaust of Day Zero. All knowledge of the means by which he was sent is lost, perhaps forever. It is believed that an accident occurred which sent him much farther than was intended. Some analysts speculate that he may have gone as far as fifty thousand years ahead. Having reached this unknown point Major Delgano apparently was recalled, or attempted to return, along the course in space and time through which he was sent. His trajectory is thought to start at the point which our solar system will occupy at a future time and is tangent to the complex helix which our Earth describes around the sun.

He appears on this spot in the annual instants in which his course intersects our planet's orbit and he is apparently able to touch the ground in those instants. Since no trace of his passage into the future has been manifested, it is believed that he is returning by a different means than he went forward. He is alive in our present. Our past is his future and our future is his past. The time of his appearances is shifting gradually in solar time to converge on the moment of 1153.6 on may 2nd 1989 old style, or Day Zero.

The explosion which accompanied his return to his own time and place may have occurred when some elements of the past instants of his course were carried with him into their own prior existence. It is certain that this explosion precipitated the worldwide holocaust which ended forever the Age of Hardscience.

—He was falling, losing control, failing in his fight against the terrible momentum he had gained, fighting with his human legs shaking in the inhuman stiffness of his armor, his soles charred, not gripping well now, not enough traction to brake, battling, thrusting as the flashes came, the punishing alternation of light, dark, light, dark, which he had borne so long, the claps of air thickening and thinning against his armor as he skidded through space which was time, desperately braking as the flickers of earth hammered against his feet—only his feet mattered now, only to slow and stay on course—and the pull, the beacon was getting slacker; as he came near home it was fanning out, hard to stay centered: he was becoming, he supposed, more probable; the wound he had punched in time was healing itself. In the beginning it had been so tight—a single ray in a closing tunnel—he had hurled himself after it like an electron flying to the anode, aimed surely along that exquisitely complex single vector of possibility of life, shot and been shot like a squeezed pip into the last chink in that rejecting and rejected nowhere through which he, John Delgano, could conceivably continue to exist, the hole leading to home—had pounded down it across time, across space, pumping with his human legs as the real Earth of that unreal time came under him, his course as certain

as the twisting dash of an animal down its burrow, he a cosmic mouse on an interstellar, intertemporal race for his nest with the wrongness of everything closing round the rightness of that one course, the atoms of his heart, his blood, his every well crying Home—HOME!—as he drove himself after that fading breathhole, each step faster, surer, stronger, until he raced with invincible momentum upon the rolling flickers of Earth as a man might race a rolling log in a torrent! Only the stars stayed constant around him from flash to flash, he looked down past his feet at a million strobes of Crux, of Triangulum; once at the height of his stride he had risked a century's glance upward and seen the Bears weirdly strung out from Polaris—But a Polaris not the Pole Star now, he realized, jerking his eyes back to his racing feet, thinking, I am walking home to Polaris, home to the strobing beat. He had ceased to remember where he had been, the beings, people or aliens or things he had glimpsed in the impossible moment of being where he could not be; had ceased to see the flashes of worlds around him, each flash different, the jumble of bodies, walls, landscapes, shapes, and colors beyond deciphering— some lasting a breath, some changing pell-mell—the faces, limbs, things poking at him; the nights he had pounded through, dark or lit by strange lamps; roofed or unroofed; the days flashing sunlight, gales, dust, snow, interiors innumerable, strobe after strobe into night again; he was in daylight now, a hall of some kind; I am getting closer at last, he thought, the feel is changing—but he had to slow down, to check; and that stone near his feet, it had stayed there some time now, he wanted to risk a look but he did not dare, he was so tired, and he was sliding, was going out of control, fighting to kill the merciless velocity that would not let him slow down; he was hurt, too, something had hit him back there, they had done something, he didn't know what back somewhere in the kaleidoscope of faces, arms, hooks, beams, centuries of creatures grabbing at him—and his oxygen was going, never mind, it would last—it had to last, he was going home, home! And he had forgotten now the message he had tried to shout, hoping it could be picked up somehow, the important thing he had repeated; and the thing he had carried, it was gone now, his camera was gone too, something had torn it away—but he was coming home! Home! If only he could kill this momentum, could stay on the failing course, could slip, scramble, slide, somehow ride this avalanche down to home, to home—and his throat said Home!—said Kate, Kate! And his heart shouted, his lungs almost gone now, as his legs fought, fought and failed, as his feet gripped and skidded and held and slid, as he pitched, flailed, pushed, strove in the gale of timerush across space, across time, at the end of the longest path ever: the path of John Delgano, coming home.

Long Shot

VERNOR VINGE

Born in Waukesha, Wisconsin, Vernor Vinge now lives in San Diego, California, where he is an associate professor of math sciences at San Diego State University. He sold his first story, "Apartness," to *New Worlds* in 1965; it immediately attracted a good deal of attention, was picked up for Donald A. Wollheim and Terry Carr's collaborative *World's Best Science Fiction* anthology the following year, and still strikes me as one of the strongest stories of that entire period, holding up well even in comparison with more-famous stories also reprinted in that same anthology, such as Clarke's "Sunjammer" or Ellison's " 'Repent, Harlequin!' Said the Ticktockman." Since this impressive debut, Vinge has become a frequent contributor to *Analog;* he has also sold to *Orbit, Far Frontiers, If, Stellar,* and other markets. His novella *"True Names"* was a finalist for both the Nebula and Hugo Awards in 1981 and is famous in Internet circles and among computer enthusiasts well outside the usual limits of the genre, cited by some as having been the *real* progenitor of cyberpunk rather than William Gibson's "Burning Chrome" or *Neuromancer*. Vinge's novel *A Fire upon the Deep,* one of the most epic and sweeping of modern Space Operas, won him a Hugo Award in 1993, and these days he is regarded as one of the best of the new breed of American hard science writers, along with people such as Charles Sheffield and Greg Bear.

In the poignant story that follows, Vinge takes us to the outer reaches of the galaxy in company with a *most* unusual sort of explorer. . . .

Vinge's other books include *Tatja Grimm's World* and *The Witling,* two Hugo finalists, *The Peace War* and *Marooned in Realtime,* which have been released in an omnibus volume as *Across Realtime,* and two short-story collections, *True Names and Other Dangers* and *Threats and Other Promises*. His most recent book is a major new novel, *A Deepness in the Sky,* a sequel to *A Fire upon the Deep.* Coming up is *True Names and the Opening of the Cyberspace Frontier,* an anthology of essays edited by James Frenkel related to Vinge's story "True Names."

They named her Ilse, and of all Earth's creatures, she was to be the longest lived— and perhaps the last. A prudent tortoise might survive three hundred years and a bristle-cone pine six thousand, but Ilse's designed span exceeded one hundred centuries. And though her brain was iron and germanium doped with arsenic, and her heart was a tiny cloud of hydrogen plasma, Ilse *was*—in the beginning—one of Earth's creatures: she could feel, she could question, and—as she discovered during the dark centuries before her fiery end—she could also forget.

Ilse's earliest memory was a fragment, amounting to less than fifteen seconds. Someone, perhaps inadvertently, brought her to consciousness as she sat atop her S-5N booster. It was night, but their launch was imminent and the booster stood white and silver in the light of a dozen spotlights. Ilse's sharp eye scanned rapidly around the horizon, untroubled by the glare from below. Stretching away from her to the north was a line of thirty launch pads. Several had their own boosters, though none were lit up as Ilse's was. Three thousand meters to the west were more lights, and the occasional sparkle of an automatic rifle. To the east, surf marched in phosphorescent ranks against the Merrit Island shore.

There the fragment ended: she was not conscious during the launch. But that scene remained forever her most vivid and incomprehensible memory.

When next she woke, Ilse was in low Earth orbit. Her single eye had been fitted to a one hundred and fifty centimeter reflecting telescope so that now she could distinguish stars set less than a tenth of an arcsecond apart, or, if she looked straight down, count the birds in a flock of geese two hundred kilometers below. For more than a year Ilse remained in this same orbit. She was not idle. Her makers had allotted this period for testing. A small manned station orbited with her, and from it came an endless sequence of radioed instructions and exercises.

Most of the problems were ballistic: hyperbolic encounters, transfer ellipses, and the like. But it was often required that Ilse use her own telescope and spectrometer to discover the parameters of the problems. A typical exercise: determine the orbits of Venus and Mercury; compute a minimum energy flyby of both planets. Another: determine the orbit of Mars; analyze its atmospheric; plan a hyperbolic entry subject to constraints. Many observational problems dealt with Earth: determine atmospheric pressure and composition; perform multispectrum analysis of vegetation. Usually she was required to solve organic analysis problems in less than thirty seconds. And in these last problems, the rules were often changed even while the game was played. Her orientation jets would be caused to malfunction. Critical portions of her mind and senses would be degraded.

One of the first things Ilse learned was that in addition to her private memories, she had a programmed memory, a "library" of procedures and facts. As with most libraries, the programmed memory was not as accessible as Ilse's own recollections, but the information contained there was much more complete and precise. The solution program for almost any ballistic, or chemical, problem could be lifted from this "library," used for seconds, or hours, as an integral part of Ilse's mind, and then returned to the "library." The real trick was to select the proper program on the basis of incomplete information, and then to modify that program to meet various combinations of power and equipment failure. Though she did poorly at first, Ilse eventually surpassed her design specifications. At this point her training stopped and for the first—but not the last—time, Ilse was left to her own devices.

Though she had yet to wonder on her ultimate purpose, still she wanted to see as much of her world as possible. She spent most of each daylight pass looking straight down, trying to see some order in the jumble of blue and green and white.

She could easily follow the supply rockets as they climbed up from Merritt Island and Baikonur to rendezvous with her. In the end, more than a hundred of the rockets were floating about her. As the weeks passed, the squat white cylinders were fitted together on a spidery frame.

Now her ten-meter-long body was lost in the webwork of cylinders and girders that stretched out two hundred meters behind her. Her programmed memory told her that the entire assembly massed 22,563.901 tons—more than most ocean-going ships—and a little experimenting with her attitude control jets convinced her that this figure was correct.

Soon her makers connected Ilse's senses to the mammoth's control mechanisms. It was as if she had been given a new body, for she could feel, and see, and use each of the hundred propellant tanks and each of the fifteen fusion reactors that made up the assembly. She realized that now she had the power to perform some of the maneuvers she had planned during her training.

Finally the great moment arrived. Course directions came over the maser link with the manned satellite. Ilse quickly computed the trajectory that would result from these directions. The answer she obtained was correct, but it revealed only the smallest part of what was in store for her.

In her orbit two hundred kilometers up, Ilse coasted smoothly toward high noon over the Pacific. Her eye was pointed forward, so that on the fuzzy blue horizon she could see the edge of the North American continent. Nearer, the granulated cloud cover obscured the ocean itself. The command to begin the burn came from the manned satellite, but Ilse was following the clock herself, and she had determined to take over the launch if any mistakes were made. Two hundred meters behind her, deep in the maze of tanks and beryllium girders, Ilse felt magnetic fields establish themselves, felt hydrogen plasma form, felt fusion commence. Another signal from the station, and propellant flowed around each of ten reactors.

Ilse and her twenty-thousand-ton booster were on their way.

Acceleration rose smoothly to one gravity. Behind her, vidicons on the booster's superstructure showed the Earth shrinking. For half an hour the burn continued, monitored by Ilse, and the manned station now fallen far behind. Then Ilse was alone with her booster, coasting away from Earth and her creators at better than twenty kilometers a second.

So Ilse began her fall toward the sun. For eleven weeks she fell. During this time, there was little to do: monitor the propellants, keep the booster's sunshade properly oriented, relay data to Earth. Compared to much of her later life, however, it was a time of hectic activity.

A fall of eleven weeks toward a body as massive as the sun can result in only one thing: speed. In those last hours, Ilse hurtled downward at better than two hundred and fifty kilometers per second—an Earth to Moon distance every half hour. Forty-five minutes before her closest approach to the sun—perihelion—Ilse jettisoned the empty first stage and its sunshade. Now she was left with the two-thousand-ton second stage, whose insulation consisted of a bright coat of white paint. She felt the pressure in the propellant tanks begin to rise.

Though her telescope was pointed directly away from the sun, the vidicons on the second stage gave her an awesome view of the solar fireball. She was moving so fast now that the sun's incandescent prominences changed perspective even as she watched.

Seventeen minutes to perihelion. From somewhere beyond the flames, Ilse got the expected maser communication. She pitched herself and her booster over so that she looked along the line of her trajectory. Now her own body was exposed to the direct glare of the sun. Through her telescope she could see luminous tracery within the solar corona. The booster's fuel tanks were perilously close to bursting, and Ilse was having trouble keeping her own body at its proper temperature.

Fifteen minutes to perihelion. The command came from Earth to begin the burn. Ilse considered her own trajectory data, and concluded that the command was thirteen seconds premature. Consultation with Earth would cost at least sixteen minutes, and her decision must be made in the next four seconds. Any of Man's earlier, less sophisticated creations would have accepted the error and taken the mission on to catastrophe, but independence was the essence of Ilse's nature: she overrode the maser command, and delayed ignition till the instant she thought correct.

The sun's northern hemisphere passed below her, less than three solar diameters away.

Ignition, and Ilse was accelerated at nearly two gravities. As she swung toward what was to have been perihelion, her booster lifted her out of elliptic orbit and into a hyperbolic one. Half an hour later she shot out from the sun into the spaces south of the ecliptic at three hundred and twenty kilometers per second—about one solar diameter every hour. The booster's now empty propellant tanks were between her and the sun, and her body slowly cooled.

Shortly after burnout, Earth offhandedly acknowledged the navigation error. This is not to say that Ilse's makers were without contrition for their mistake, or without praise for Ilse. In fact, several men lost what little there remained to confiscate for jeopardizing this mission, and Man's last hope. It was simply that Ilse's makers did not believe that she could appreciate apologies or praise.

Now Ilse fled up out of the solar gravity well. It had taken her eleven weeks to fall from Earth to Sol, but in less than two weeks she had regained this altitude, and still she plunged outward at more than one hundred kilometers per second. That velocity remained her inheritance from the sun. Without the gravity well maneuver, her booster would have had to be five hundred times as large, or her voyage three times as long. It had been the very best that men could do for her, considering the time remaining to them.

So began the voyage of one hundred centuries. Ilse parted with the empty booster and floated on alone: a squat cylinder, twelve meters wide, five meters long, with a large telescope sticking from one end. Four light-years below her in the well of the night she saw Alpha Centauri, her destination. To the naked human eye, it appears a single bright star, but with her telescope Ilse could clearly see two stars, one slightly fainter and redder than the other. She carefully measured their position and her own, and concluded that her aim had been so perfect that a midcourse correction would not be necessary for a thousand years.

For many months, Earth maintained maser contact—to pose problems and ask after her health. It was almost pathetic, for if anything went wrong now, or in the centuries to follow, there was very little Earth could do to help. The problems were interesting, though. Ilse was asked to chart the nonluminous bodies in the Solar System. She became quite skilled at this and eventually discovered all nine planets, most of their moons, and several asteroids and comets.

In less than two years, Ilse was farther from the sun than any known planet, than any previous terrestrial probe. The sun itself was no more than a very bright star behind her, and Ilse had no trouble keeping her frigid innards at their proper temperature. But now it took sixteen hours to ask a question of Earth and obtain an answer.

A strange thing happened. Over a period of three weeks, the sun became steadily brighter until it gleamed ten times as luminously as before. The change was not really a great one. It was far short of what Earth's astronomers would have called a nova. Nevertheless, Ilse puzzled over the event, in her own way, for many months, since it was at this time that she lost maser contact with Earth. That contact was never regained.

Now Ilse changed herself to meet the empty centuries. As her designers had planned, she split her mind into three co-equal entities. Theoretically each of these minds could handle the entire mission alone, but for any important decision, Ilse required the agreement of at least two of the minds. In this fractionated state, Ilse was neither as bright nor as quick-thinking as she had been at launch. But scarcely anything happened in interstellar space, the chief danger being senile decay. Her three minds spent as much time checking each other as they did overseeing the various subsystems.

The one thing they did not regularly check was the programmed memory, since Ilse's designers had—mistakenly—judged that such checks were a greater danger to the memories than the passage of time.

Even with her mentality diminished, and in spite of the caretaker tasks assigned her, Ilse spent much of her time contemplating the universe that spread out forever around her. She discovered binary star systems, then watched the tiny lights swing back and forth around each other as the decades and centuries passed. To her the universe became a moving, almost a living, thing. Several of the nearer stars drifted almost a degree every century, while the great galaxy in Andromeda shifted less than a second of arc in a thousand years.

Occasionally, she turned about to look at Sol. Even ten centuries out she could still distinguish Jupiter and Saturn. These were auspicious observations.

Finally it was time for the midcourse correction. She had spent the preceding century refining her alignment and her navigational observations. The burn was to be only one hundred meters per second, so accurate had been her perihelion impulse. Nevertheless, without that correction she would miss the Centauran system entirely. When the second arrived and her alignment was perfect, Ilse lit her tiny rocket—and discovered that she could obtain at most only three-quarters of the rated thrust. She had to make two burns before she was satisfied with the new course.

For the next fifty years, Ilse studied the problem. She tested the rocket's electrical system hundreds of times, and even fired the rocket in microsecond bursts. She never discovered how the centuries had robbed her, but extrapolating from her observations, Ilse realized that by the time she entered the Centauran system, she would have only a thousand meters per second left in her rocket—less than half its designed capability. Even so it was possible that, without further complications, she would be able to survey the planets of both stars in the system.

But before she finished her study of the propulsion problem, Ilse discovered another breakdown—the most serious she was to face:

She had forgotten her mission. Over the centuries the pattern of magnetic fields on her programmed memory had slowly disappeared—the least used programs going first. When Ilse recalled those programs to discover how her reduced maneuverability affected the mission, she discovered that she no longer had any record of her ultimate purpose. The memories ended with badly faded programs for biochemical reconnaissance and planetary entry, and Ilse guessed that there was something crucial left to do after a successful landing on a suitable planet.

Ilse was a patient sort—especially in her cruise configuration—and she didn't worry about her ultimate purpose, so far away in the future. But she did do her best to preserve what programs were left. She played each program into her own memory and then back to the programmed memory. If the process were repeated every seventy years, she found that she could keep the programmed memories from fading. On the other hand, she had no way of knowing how many errors this endless repetition was introducing. For this reason she had each of her subminds perform the process separately, and she frequently checked the ballistic and astronomical programs by doing problems with them.

Ilse went further: she studied her own body for clues as to its purpose. Much of her body was filled with a substance she must keep within a few degrees of absolute zero. Several leads disappeared into this mass. Except for her thermometers, however, she had no feeling in this part of her body. Now she raised the temperature in this section a few thousandths of a degree, a change well within design specifications, but large enough for her to sense. Comparing her observations and the section's mass with her chemical analysis programs, Ilse concluded that the mysterious area was a relatively homogeneous body of frozen water, doped with various impurities. It was interesting information, but no matter how she compared it with her memories she could not see any significance to it.

Ilse floated on—and on. The period of time between the midcourse maneuver and the next important event on her schedule was longer than Man's experience with agriculture had been on Earth.

As the centuries passed, the two closely set stars that were her destination became brighter until, a thousand years from Alpha Centauri, she decided to begin her search for planets in the system. Ilse turned her telescope on the brighter of the two stars . . . call it Able. She was still thirty-five thousand times as far from Able—and the smaller star . . . call it Baker—as Earth is from Sol. Even to her sharp eye, Able didn't show as a disk but rather as a diffraction pattern: a round blob of light—many times larger than the star's true disk—surrounded by a ring of light. The faint gleam of any planets would be lost in the diffraction pattern. For five years Ilse watched the pattern, analyzed it with one of her most subtle programs. Occasionally she slid occulting plates into the telescope and studied the resulting, distorted, pattern. After five years she had found suggestive anomalies in the diffraction pattern, but no definite signs of planets.

No matter. Patient Ilse turned her telescope a tiny fraction of a degree, and during the next five years she watched Baker. Then she switched back to Able. Fifteen times Ilse repeated this cycle. While she watched, Baker completed two revolutions about Able, and the stars' maximum mutual separation increased to nearly a tenth of a degree. Finally Ilse was certain: she had discovered a planet orbiting Baker, and perhaps another orbiting Able. Most likely they were both gas giants. No matter: she knew that any small, inner planets would still be lost in the glare of Able and Baker.

There remained less than nine hundred years before she coasted through the Centauran system.

Ilse persisted in her observations. Eventually she could see the gas giants as tiny spots of light—not merely as statistical correlations in her carefully collected diffraction data. Four hundred years out, she decided that the remaining anomalies in Able's diffraction pattern must be another planet, this one at about the same distance from Able as Earth is from Sol. Fifteen years later she made a similar discovery for Baker.

If she were to investigate both of these planets she would have to plan very carefully. According to her design specifications, she had scarcely the maneuvering capability left to investigate one system. But Ilse's navigation system had survived the centuries better than expected, and she estimated that a survey of both planets might still be possible.

Three hundred and fifty years out, Ilse made a relatively large course correction, better than two hundred meters per second. This change was essentially a matter of pacing: it would delay her arrival by four months. Thus she would pass near the planet she wished to investigate and, if no landing were attempted, her path would be precisely bent by Able's gravitational field and she would be cast into Baker's planetary system.

Now Ilse had less than eight hundred meters per second left in her rocket— less than one percent of her velocity relative to Able and Baker. If she could be at the right place at the right time, that would be enough, but otherwise . . .

Ilse plotted the orbits of the bodies she had detected more and more accurately. Eventually she discovered several more planets: a total of three for Able, and four for Baker. But only her two prime candidates—call them Able II and Baker II— were at the proper distance from their suns.

Eighteen months out, Ilse sighted moons around Able II. This was good news. Now she could accurately determine the planet's mass, and so refine her course even more. Ilse was now less than fifty astronomical units from Able, and eighty from Baker. She had no trouble making spectroscopic observations of the planets. Her prime candidates had plenty of oxygen in their atmosphere—though the farther one, Baker II, seemed deficient in water vapor. On the other hand, Able II had complex carbon compounds in its atmosphere, and its net color was blue-green. According to Ilse's damaged memory, these last were desirable features.

The centuries had shrunk to decades, then to years, and finally to days. Ilse was within the orbit of Able's gas giant. Ten million kilometers ahead her target swept along a nearly circular path about its sun, Able. Twenty-seven astronomical units beyond Able gleamed Baker.

But Ilse kept her attention on that target, Able II. Now she could make out its gross continental outlines. She selected a landing site, and performed a two hundred meter per second burn. If she chose to land, she would come down in a greenish, beclouded area.

Twelve hours to contact. Ilse checked each of her subminds one last time. She deleted all malfunctioning circuits, and reassembled herself as a single mind out of what remained. Over the centuries, one third of all her electrical components had failed, so that besides her lost memories, she was not nearly as bright as she had been when launched. Nevertheless, with her subminds combined she was much cleverer than she had been during the cruise. She needed this greater alertness, because in the hours and minutes preceding her encounter with Able II, she would do more analysis and make more decisions than ever before.

One hour to contact. Ilse was within the orbit of her target's outer moon. Ahead loomed the tentative destination, a blue and white crescent two degrees across. Her landing area was around the planet's horizon. No matter. The important task for these last moments was a biochemical survey—at least that's what her surviving programs told her. She scanned the crescent, looking for traces of green through the clouds. She found a large island in a Pacific sized ocean, and began the exquisitely complex analysis necessary to determine the orientation of amino acids. Every fifth second, she took one second to reestimate the atmospheric densities. The problems seemed even more complicated than her training exercises back in Earth orbit.

Five minutes to contact. She was less than forty thousand kilometers out, and the planet's hazy limb filled her sky. In the next ten seconds she must decide whether or not to land on Able II. Her ten-thousand-year mission was at stake here. For once Ilse landed, she knew that she would never fly again. Without the immense booster that had pushed her out along this journey, she was nothing but a brain and an entry shield and a chunk of frozen water. If she decided to bypass Able II, she must now use a large portion of her remaining propellants to accelerate at right angles to her trajectory. This would cause her to miss the upper edge of the planet's atmosphere, and she would go hurtling out of Able's planetary system. Thirteen months later she would arrive in the vicinity of Baker, perhaps with enough left in her rocket to guide herself into Baker II's atmosphere. But, if that planet should be inhospitable, there would be no turning back: she would have to land there, or else coast on into interstellar darkness.

Ilse weighed the matter for three seconds and concluded that Able II satisfied every criterion she could recall, while Baker II seemed a bit too yellow, a bit too dry.

Ilse turned ninety degrees and jettisoned the small rocket that had given her so much trouble. At the same time she ejected the telescope which had served her so well. She floated indivisible, a white biconvex disk, twelve meters in diameter, fifteen tons in mass.

She turned ninety degrees more to look directly back along her trajectory. There was not much to see now that she had lost her scope, but she recognized the point of light that was Earth's sun and wondered again what had been on all those programs that she had forgotten.

Five seconds. Ilse closed her eye and waited.

Contact began as a barely perceptible acceleration. In less than two seconds that acceleration built to two hundred and five gravities. This was beyond Ilse's experience, but she was built to take it: her body contained no moving parts and—

except for her fusion reactor—no empty spaces. The really difficult thing was to keep her body from turning edgewise and burning up. Though she didn't know it, Ilse was repeating—on a grand scale—the landing technique that men had used so long ago. But Ilse had to dissipate more than eight hundred times the kinetic energy of any returning Apollo capsule. Her maneuver was correspondingly more dangerous, but since her designers could not equip her with a rocket powerful enough to decelerate her, it was the only option.

Now Ilse used her wits and every dyne in her tiny electric thrusters to arc herself about Able II at the proper attitude and altitude. The acceleration rose steadily toward five hundred gravities, or almost five kilometers per second in velocity lost every second. Beyond that Ilse knew that she would lose consciousness. Just centimeters away from her body the air glowed at fifty thousand degrees. The fireball that surrounded her lit the ocean seventy kilometers below as with daylight.

Four hundred and fifty gravities. She felt a cryostat shatter, and one branch of her brain short through. Still Ilse worked patiently and blindly to keep her body properly oriented. If she had calculated correctly, there were less than five seconds to go now.

She came within sixty kilometers of the surface, then rose steadily back into space. But now her velocity was only seven kilometers per second. The acceleration fell to a mere fifteen gravities, then to zero. She coasted back through a long ellipse to plunge, almost gently, into the depths of Able II's atmosphere.

At twenty thousand meters altitude, Ilse opened her eye and scanned the world below. Her lens had been cracked, and several of her gestalt programs damaged, but she saw green and knew her navigation hadn't been too bad.

It would have been a triumphant moment if only she could have remembered what she was supposed to do *after* she landed.

At ten thousand meters, Ilse popped her paraglider from the hull behind her eye. The tough plastic blossomed out above her, and her fall became a shallow glide. Ilse saw that she was flying over a prairie spotted here and there by forest. It was near sunset and the long shadows cast by trees and hills made it easy for her to gauge the topography.

Two thousand meters. With a glide ratio of one to four, she couldn't expect to fly more than another eight kilometers. Ilse looked ahead, saw a tiny forest, and a stream glinting through the trees. Then she saw a glade just inside the forest, and some vagrant memory told her this was an appropriate spot. She pulled in the paraglider's forward lines and slid more steeply downward. As she passed three or four meters over the trees surrounding the glade, Ilse pulled in the rear lines, stalled her glider, and fell into the deep, moist grass. Her dun and green paraglider collapsed over her charred body so that she might be mistaken for a large black boulder covered with vegetation.

The voyage that had crossed one hundred centuries and four light-years was ended.

Ilse sat in the gathering twilight and listened. Sound was an undreamed-of dimension to her: tiny things burrowing in their holes, the stream gurgling nearby, a faint chirping in the distance. Twilight ended and a shallow fog rose in the dark glade. Ilse knew her voyaging was over. She would never move again. No matter. That had been planned, she was sure. She knew that much of her computing machinery—her mind—had been destroyed in the landing. She would not survive as a conscious being for more than another century or two. No matter.

What did matter was that she knew that her mission was not completed, and that the most important part remained, else the immense gamble her makers had undertaken would finally come to nothing. That possibility was the only thing which could frighten Ilse. It was part of her design.

She reviewed all the programmed memories that had survived the centuries and the planetary entry, but discovered nothing new. She investigated the rest of her body, testing her parts in a thorough, almost destructive, way she never would have dared while still centuries from her destination. She discovered nothing new. Finally she came to that load of ice she had carried so far. With one of her cryostats broken, she couldn't keep it at its proper temperature for more than a few years. She recalled the apparently useless leads that disappeared into that mass. There was only one thing left to try.

Ilse turned down her cryostats, and waited as the temperature within her climbed. The ice near her small fusion reactor warmed first. Somewhere in the frozen mass a tiny piece of metal expanded just far enough to complete a circuit, and Ilse discovered that her makers had taken one last precaution to insure her reliability. At the base of the icy hulk, next to the reactor, they had placed an auxiliary memory unit, and now Ilse had access to it. Her designers had realized that no matter what dangers they imagined, there would be others, and so they had decided to leave this backup cold and inactive till the very end. And the new memory unit was quite different from her old ones, Ilse vaguely realized. It used optical rather than magnetic storage.

Now Ilse knew what she must do. She warmed a cylindrical tank filled with frozen amniotic fluid to thirty-seven degrees centigrade. From the store next to the cylinder, she injected a single microorganism into the tank. In a few minutes she would begin to suffuse blood through the tank.

It was early morning now and the darkness was moist and cool. Ilse tried to probe her new memory further, but was balked. Apparently the instructions were delivered according to some schedule to avoid unnecessary use of the memory. Ilse reviewed what she had learned, and decided that she would know more in another nine months.

In the Hall of the Martian Kings

JOHN VARLEY

John Varley appeared on the science-fiction scene in 1974, and by the end of 1976—in what was a meteoric rise to prominence even for a field known for meteoric rises—he was already being recognized as one of the hottest new writers of the seventies. His first story, "Picnic on Nearside," appeared in 1974 in the *Magazine of Fantasy & Science Fiction* and was followed by as concentrated an outpouring of first-rate stories as the genre has ever seen, stories such as "The Phantom of Kansas," "Retrograde Summer," "In the Bowl," "Gotta Sing, Gotta Dance," "Equinoctial," "The Black Hole Passes," "Overdrawn at the Memory Bank," and many others, smart, bright, fresh, brash, audacious, effortlessly imaginative stories that seemed to suddenly shake the field out of its uneasy slumber like a wake-up call from a brand-new trumpet. It's hard to think of a group of short stories that has had a greater, more concentrated impact on the field, with the exception of Robert Heinlein's early work for John W. Campbell's *Astounding* or perhaps Roger Zelazny's early stories in the mid-sixties.

Varley was one of the first new writers to become interested in the solar system again, after several years in which it had been largely abandoned as a setting for stories because the space probes of the late sixties and early seventies had "proved" that it was nothing but an "uninteresting" collection of balls of rock and ice, with no available abodes for life. Instead, Varley seemed to find the solar system lushly romantic *just as it was*, lifeless balls of rock and all (and this was even before the later *Mariner* probes to the Jupiter and Saturn system had proved the solar system to be a lot more surprising than people thought that it was), an aesthetic shift in perception that will go ringing on down through the eighties and nineties in the work of writers such as G. David Nordley, Stephen Baxter, and a dozen others. Varley makes this obvious in the complex and inventive story that follows which takes us along with a team of explorers to Mars—not Burroughs's Mars, laced with canals, chockablock with giant green warriors, sword-wielding heroes, and beautiful egg-laying princesses, but rather the bleak, oxidized, apparently lifeless Mars of the *Mariner* probes—for a strange tale about the different kinds of rebirth . . . a tale that may well have served as the rebirth of the Martian story as well, after long years of neglect.

Varley somehow never had as great an impact with his novels as he did with his short fiction, with the possible exception of his first novel, *Ophiuchi Hotline.* His other novels include the somewhat disappointing *Gaean* trilogy, consisting of *Titan, Wizard,* and *Demon;* a novelization of one of his own short stories that was also made into a movie, *Millennium;* and the collections *The Persistence of Vision, The Barbie Murders, Picnic on Nearside,* and *Blue Champagne.*

In the eighties Varley moved away from the print world to produce a number of screenplays for Hollywood producers, most of which were never produced. He produced one last significant story, 1984's "Press Enter ☐," which won him both the Hugo and the Nebula Award. (He also won a Hugo in 1982 for his story "The Pusher," and a Hugo and a Nebula in 1979 for his novella *The Persistence of Vision.*) After "Press Enter ☐," little was heard from Varley in the genre until the publication of a major new novel, *Steel Beach,* in 1992, which was successful commercially but received a lukewarm reception from many critics. He was largely silent throughout most of the rest of the decade of the nineties but seems to be making something of a comeback here at the end of the century, publishing a major new novel, *The Golden Globe,* in 1998, with another new novel, *Irontown Blues,* coming up soon. He has won two Nebulas and two Hugos for his short fiction.

It took perseverance, alertness and a willingness to break the rules to watch the sunrise in Tharsis Canyon. Matthew Crawford shivered in the dark, his suit heater turned to emergency setting, his eyes trained toward the east. He knew he had to be watchful. Yesterday he had missed it entirely, snatched away from him in the middle of a long, unavoidable yawn. His jaw muscles stretched, but he controlled it and kept his eyes firmly open.

And there it was. Like the lights in a theater after the show is over: just a quick brightening, a splash of localized bluish purple over the canyon rim, and he was surrounded by footlights. Day had come, the truncated Martian day that would never touch the blackness over his head.

This day, like the nine before it, illuminated a Tharsis radically changed from what it had been over the last sleepy ten thousand years. Wind erosion of rocks can create an infinity of shapes, but it never gets around to carving out a straight line or a perfect arc. The human encampment below him broke up the jagged lines of the rocks with regular angles and curves.

The camp was anything but orderly. No one would get the impression that any care had been taken in the haphazard arrangement of dome, lander, crawlers, crawler tracks, and scattered equipment. It had grown, as all human base camps seem to grow, without pattern. He was reminded of the footprints around Tranquility Base, though on a much larger scale.

Tharsis Base sat on a wide ledge about halfway up from the uneven bottom of the Tharsis arm of the Great Rift Valley. The site had been chosen because it was a smooth area, allowing easy access up a gentle slope to the flat plains of the Tharsis Plateau, while at the same time only a kilometer from the valley floor. No one could agree which area was more worthy of study: plains or canyon. So this site had been chosen as a compromise. What it meant was that the exploring parties had to either climb up or go down; because there wasn't a damn thing worth seeing near the camp. Even the exposed layering and its areological records could not be seen without a half-kilometer crawler ride up to the point where Crawford had climbed to watch the sunrise.

He examined the dome as he walked back to camp. There was a figure hazily visible through the plastic. At this distance he would have been unable to tell who it was if it weren't for the black face. He saw her step up to the dome wall and wipe a clear circle to look through. She spotted his bright red suit and pointed at him. She was suited except for her helmet, which contained her radio. He knew he was in trouble. He saw her turn away and bend to the ground to pick up her helmet, so she could tell him what she thought of people who disobeyed her orders, when the dome shuddered like a jellyfish.

An alarm started in his helmet, flat and strangely soothing coming from the tiny speaker. He stood there for a moment as a perfect smoke ring of dust billowed up around the rim of the dome. Then he was running.

He watched the disaster unfold before his eyes, silent except for the rhythmic beat of the alarm bell in his ears. The dome was dancing and straining, trying to fly. The floor heaved up in the center, throwing the black woman to her knees. In another second the interior was a whirling snowstorm. He skidded on the sand and fell forward, got up in time to see the fiberglass ropes on the side nearest him snap free from the steel spikes anchoring the dome to the rock.

The dome now looked like some fantastic Christmas ornament, filled with snowflakes and the flashing red and blue lights of the emergency alarms. The top of the dome heaved over away from him, and the floor raised itself high in the air, held down by the unbroken anchors on the side farthest from him. There was a gush of snow and dust; then the floor settled slowly back to the ground. There was no motion now but the leisurely folding of the depressurized dome roof as it settled over the structures inside.

The crawler skidded to a stop, nearly rolling over, beside the deflated dome. Two pressure-suited figures got out. They started for the dome hesitantly, in fits and starts. One grabbed the other's arm and pointed to the ladder. The two of them changed course and scrambled up the rope ladder hanging over the side.

Crawford was the only one to look up when the lock started cycling. The two people almost tumbled over each other coming out of the lock. They wanted to *do* something, and quickly, but didn't know what. In the end, they just stood there silently twisting their hands and looking at the floor. One of them took off her helmet. She was a large woman in her thirties, with red hair shorn off close to the scalp.

"Matt, we got here as . . ." She stopped, realizing how obvious it was. "How's Lou?"

"Lou's not going to make it." He gestured to the bunk where a heavyset man lay breathing raggedly into a clear plastic mask. He was on pure oxygen. There was blood seeping from his ears and nose.

"Brain damage?"

Crawford nodded. He looked around at the other occupants of the room. There was the Surface Mission Commander, Mary Lang, the black woman he had seen inside the dome just before the blowout. She was sitting on the edge of Lou Prager's cot, her head cradled in her hands. In a way, she was a more shocking sight than Lou. No one who knew her would have thought she could be brought to this limp state of apathy. She had not moved for the last hour.

Sitting on the floor huddled in a blanket was Martin Ralston, the chemist. His shirt was bloody, and there was dried blood all over his face and hands from the nosebleed he'd only recently gotten under control, but his eyes were alert. He shivered, looking from Lang, his titular leader, to Crawford, the only one who seemed calm enough to deal with anything. He was a follower, reliable but unimaginative.

Crawford looked back to the newest arrivals. They were Lucy Stone McKillian, the redheaded ecologist, and Song Sue Lee, the exobiologist. They still stood numbly by the airlock, unable as yet to come to grips with the fact of fifteen dead men and women beneath the dome outside.

"What do they say on the *Burroughs*?" McKillian asked, tossing her helmet on the floor and squatting tiredly against the wall. The lander was not the most comfortable place to hold a meeting; all the couches were mounted horizontally since their purpose was cushioning the acceleration of landing and takeoff. With the ship sitting on its tail, this made ninety percent of the space in the lander useless. They were all gathered on the circular bulkhead at the rear of the life system, just forward of the fuel tank.

"We're waiting for a reply," Crawford said. "But I can sum up what they're going to say: not good. Unless one of you two has some experience in Mars-lander handling that you've been concealing from us."

Neither of them bothered to answer that. The radio in the nose sputtered, then clanged for their attention. Crawford looked over at Lang, who made no move to go answer it. He stood up and swarmed up the ladder to sit in the copilot's chair. He switched on the receiver.

"Commander Lang?"

"No, this is Crawford again. Commander Lang is . . . indisposed. She's busy with Lou, trying to do something."

"That's no use. The doctor says it's a miracle he's still breathing. If he wakes up at all, he won't be anything like you knew him. The telemetry shows nothing like the normal brain wave. Now I've got to talk to Mission Commander Lang. Have her come up." The voice of Mission Commander Weinstein was accustomed to command, and about as emotional as a weather report.

"Sir, I'll ask her, but I don't think she'll come. This is still her operation, you know." He didn't give Weinstein time to reply to that. Weinstein had been trapped by his own seniority into commanding the *Edgar Rice Burroughs*, the orbital ship that got them to Mars and had been intended to get them back. Command of the *Podkayne*, the disposable lander that would make the lion's share of the headlines, had gone to Lang. There was little friendship between the two especially when Weinstein fell to brooding about the very real financial benefits Lang stood to reap by being the first woman on Mars, rather than the lowly mission commander. He saw himself as another Michael Collins.

Crawford called down to Lang, who raised her head enough to mumble something.

"What'd she say?"

"She said take a message." McKillian had been crawling up the ladder as she said this. Now she reached him and said in a lower voice, "Matt, she's pretty broken up. You'd better take over for now."

"Right, I know." He turned back to the radio, and McKillian listened over his shoulder as Weinstein briefed them on the situation as he saw it. It pretty much jibed with Crawford's estimation, except at one crucial point. He signed off and they joined the other survivors.

He looked around at the faces of the others and decided it wasn't the time to speak of rescue possibilities. He didn't relish being a leader. He was hoping Lang would recover soon and take the burden from him. In the meantime he had to get them started on something. He touched McKillian gently on the shoulder and motioned her to the lock.

"Let's go get them buried," he said. She squeezed her eyes shut tight, forcing out tears, then nodded.

It wasn't a pretty job. Halfway through it, Song came down the ladder with the body of Lou Prager.

"Let's go over what we've learned. First, now that Lou's dead there's very little chance of ever lifting off. That is, unless Mary thinks she can absorb everything she needs to know about piloting the *Podkayne* from those printouts Weinstein sent down. How about it, Mary?"

Mary Lang was lying sideways across the improvised cot that had recently held the *Podkayne* pilot, Lou Prager. Her head was nodding listlessly against the aluminum hull plate behind her, her chin was on her chest. Her eyes were half open.

Song had given her a sedative from the dead doctor's supplies on the advice of the medic aboard the *E.R.B.* It had enabled her to stop fighting so hard against the screaming panic she wanted to unleash. It hadn't improved her disposition. She had quit, she wasn't going to do anything for anybody.

When the blowout started, Lang had snapped on her helmet quickly. Then she had struggled against the blizzard and the undulating dome bottom, heading for the roofless framework where the other members of the expedition were sleeping. The blowout was over in ten seconds, and she then had the problem of coping with the collapsing roof, which promptly buried her in folds of clear plastic. It was far too much like one of those nightmares of running knee-deep in quicksand. She had to fight for every meter, but she made it.

She made it in time to see her shipmates of the last six months gasping soundlessly and spouting blood from all over their faces as they fought to get into their pressure suits. It was a hopeless task to choose which two or three to save in the time she had. She might have done better but for the freakish nature of her struggle to reach them; she was in shock and half believed it was only a nightmare. So she grabbed the nearest, who happened to be Doctor Ralston. He had nearly finished donning his suit; so she slapped his helmet on him and moved to the next one. It was Luther Nakamura, and he was not moving. Worse, he was only half suited. Pragmatically, she should have left him and moved onto save the ones who still had a chance. She knew it now but didn't like it any better than she had liked it then.

While she was stuffing Nakamura into his suit, Crawford arrived. He had walked over the folds of plastic until he reached the dormitory, then sliced through it with his laser normally used to vaporize rock samples.

And he had had time to think about the problem of whom to save. He went straight to Lou Prager and finished suiting him up. But it was already too late. He didn't know if it would have made any difference if Mary Lang had tried to save him first.

Now she lay on the bunk, her feet sprawled carelessly in front of her. She slowly shook her head back and forth.

"You sure?" Crawford prodded her, hoping to get a rise, a show of temper, *anything*.

"I'm sure," she mumbled. "You people know how long they trained Lou to fly this thing? And he almost cracked it up as it was. I . . . ah, nuts. It isn't possible."

"I refuse to accept that as a final answer," he said. "But in the meantime we should explore the possibilities if what Mary says is true."

Ralston laughed. It wasn't a bitter laugh; he sounded genuinely amused. Crawford plowed on.

"Here's what we know for sure. The *E.R.B.* is useless to us. Oh, they'll help us out with plenty of advice, maybe more than we want, but any rescue is out of the question."

"We know that," McKillian said. She was tired and sick from the sight of the faces of her dead friends. "What's the use of all this talk?"

"Wait a moment," Song broke in. "Why can't they . . . I mean they have plenty of time, don't they? They have to leave in six months, as I understand it, because of the orbital elements, but in that time . . ."

"Don't you know anything about spaceships?" McKillian shouted. Song went on, unperturbed.

"I do know enough to know the *Edgar* is not equipped for an atmosphere entry. My idea was, not to bring down the whole ship but only what's aboard the ship that we need. Which is a pilot. Might that be possible?"

Crawford ran his hands through his hair, wondering what to say. That possibility had been discussed, and was being studied. But it had to be classed as extremely remote.

"You're right," he said. "What we need is a pilot, and that pilot is Commander Weinstein. Which presents problems legally, if nothing else. He's the captain of a ship and should not leave it. That's what kept him on the *Edgar* in the first place. But he did have a lot of training on the lander simulator, back when he was so sure he'd be picked for the ground team. You know Winey, always the instinct to be the one-man show. So if he thought he could do it, he'd be down here in a minute to bail us out and grab the publicity. I understand they're trying to work out a heat-shield parachute system, from one of the drop capsules that were supposed to ferry down supplies to us during the stay here. But it's very risky. You don't modify an aerodynamic design lightly, not one that's supposed to hit the atmosphere at ten thousand-plus kilometers. So I think we can rule that out. They'll keep working on it, but when it's done, Winey won't step into the damn thing. He wants to be a hero, but he wants to live to enjoy it, too."

There had been a brief lifting of spirits among Song, Ralston, and McKillian at the thought of a possible rescue. The more they thought about it, the less happy they looked. They all seemed to agree with Crawford's assessment.

"So we'll put that one in the Fairy Godmother file and forget about it. If it happens, fine. But we'd better plan on the assumption that it won't. As you may know, the *E.R.B.* and the *Podkayne* are the only ships in existence that can reach Mars and land on it. One other pair is in the congressional funding stage. Winey talked to Earth and thinks there'll be a speedup in the preliminary paperwork and the thing'll start building in a year. The launch was scheduled for five years from now, but it might get as much as a year's boost. It's a rescue mission now, easier to sell. But the design will need modification, if only to include five more seats to bring us all back. You can bet on there being more modifications when we send in our report on the blowout. So we'd better add another six months to the schedule."

McKillian had had enough. "Matt, what the hell are you talking about? Rescue mission? Damn it, you know as well as I that if they find us here, we'll be long dead. We'll probably be dead in another year."

"That's where you're wrong. We'll survive."

"How?"

"I don't have the faintest idea." He looked her straight in the eye as he said this. She almost didn't bother to answer, but curiosity got the best of her.

"Is this just a morale session? Thanks, but I don't need it. I'd rather face the situation as it is. Or do you really have something?"

"Both. I don't have anything concrete except to say that we'll survive the same way humans have always survived: by staying warm, by eating, by drinking. To that list we have to add 'by breathing.' That's a hard one, but other than that, we're no different than any other group of survivors in a tough spot. I don't know what we'll have to do, specially, but I know we'll find the answers."

"Or die trying," Song said.

"Or die trying." He grinned at her. She at least had grasped the essence of the situation. Whether survival was possible or not, it was necessary to maintain the illusion that it was. Otherwise, you might as well cut your throat. You might as well not even be born, because life is an inevitably fatal struggle to survive.

"What about air?" McKillian asked, still unconvinced.

"I don't know," he told her cheerfully. "It's a tough problem, isn't it?"

"What about water?"

"Well, down in that valley there's a layer of permafrost about twenty meters down."

She laughed. "Wonderful. So that's what you want us to do? Dig down there and warm the ice with our pink little hands? It won't work, I tell you."

Crawford waited until she had run through a long list of reasons why they were doomed. Most of them made a great deal of sense. When she was through, he spoke softly.

"Lucy, listen to yourself."

"I'm just—"

"You're arguing on the side of death. Do you want to die? Are you so determined that you won't listen to someone who says you can live?"

She was quiet for a long time, then shuffled her feet awkwardly. She glanced at him, then at Song and Ralston. They were waiting, and she had to blush and smile slowly at them.

"You're right. What do we do first?"

"Just what we were doing. Taking stock of our situation. We need to make a list of what's available to us. We'll write it down on paper, but I can give you a general rundown." He counted off the points on his fingers.

"One, we have food for twenty people for three months. That comes to about a year for the five of us. With rationing, maybe a year and a half. That's assuming all the supply capsules reach us all right. In addition, the *Edgar* is going to clean the pantry to the bone and give us everything they can possibly spare and send it to us in the three spare capsules. That might come to two years or even three.

"Two, we have enough water to last us forever if the recyclers keep going. That'll be a problem, because our reactor will run out of power in two years. We'll need another power source, and maybe another water source.

"The oxygen problem is about the same. Two years at the outside. We'll have to find a way to conserve it a lot more than we're doing. Offhand, I don't know how. Song, do you have any ideas?"

She looked thoughtful, which produced two vertical punctuation marks between her slanted eyes.

"Possibly a culture of plants from the *Edgar*. If we could rig some way to grow plants in Martian sunlight and not have them killed by the ultraviolet..."

McKillian looked horrified, as any good ecologist would.

"What about contamination?" she asked. "What do you think that sterilization was for before we landed? Do you want to louse up the entire ecological balance of Mars? No one would ever be sure if samples in the future were real Martian plants or mutated Earth stock."

"What ecological balance?" Song shot back. "You know as well as I do that this trip has been nearly a zero. A few anaerobic bacteria, a patch of lichen, both barely distinguishable from Earth forms—"

"That's just what I mean. You import Earth forms now, and we'll never tell the difference."

"But it could be done, right? With the proper shielding so the plants won't be wiped out before they ever sprout, we could have a hydroponics plant functioning—"

"Oh, yes, it could be done. I can see three or four dodges right now. But you're not addressing the main question, which is—"

"Hold it," Crawford said. "I just wanted to know if you had any ideas." He was secretly pleased at the argument; it got them both thinking along the right lines, moved them from the deadly apathy they must guard against.

"I think this discussion has served its purpose, which was to convince everyone here that survival is possible." He glanced uneasily at Lang, still nodding, her eyes glassy as she saw her teammates die before her eyes.

"I just want to point out that instead of an expedition, we are now a colony. Not in the usual sense of planning to stay here forever, but all our planning will have to be geared to that fiction. What we're faced with is not a simple matter of stretching supplies until rescue comes. Stopgap measures are not likely to do us much good. The answers that will save us are the long-term ones, the sort of answers a colony would be looking for. About two years from now we're going to have to be in a position to survive with some sort of life-style that could support us forever. We'll have to fit into this environment where we can and adapt it to us where we can. For that, we're better off than most of the colonists of the past, at least for the short term. We have a large supply of everything a colony needs: food, water, tools, raw materials, energy, brains, and women. Without these things, no colony has much of a chance. All we lack is a regular resupply from the home country, but a really good group of colonists can get along without that. What do you say? Are you all with me?"

Something had caused Mary Lang's eyes to look up. It was a reflex by now, a survival reflex conditioned by a lifetime of fighting her way to the top. It took root in her again and pulled her erect on the bed, then to her feet. She fought off the effects of the drug and stood there, eyes bleary but aware.

"What makes you think that women are a natural resource, Crawford?" she said, slowly and deliberately.

"Why, what I meant was that without the morale uplift provided by members of the opposite sex, a colony will lack the push needed to make it."

"That's what you meant, all right. And you meant women, available to the *real* colonists as a reason to live. I've heard it before. That's a male-oriented way to look at it, Crawford." She was regaining her stature as they watched, seeming to grow until she dominated the group with the intangible power that marks a leader. She took a deep breath and came fully awake for the first time that day.

"We'll stop that sort of thinking right now. I'm the mission commander. I appreciate your taking over while I was ... how did you say it? Indisposed. But you should pay more attention to the social aspects of our situation. If anyone is a commodity here, it's you and Ralston, by virtue of your scarcity. There will be some thorny questions to resolve there, but for the meantime we will function as a unit, under my command. We'll do all we can to minimize social competition among the women for the men. That's the way it must be. Clear?"

She was answered by quiet assent and nods of the head. She did not acknowledge it but plowed right on.

"I wondered from the start why you were along, Crawford." She was pacing slowly back and forth in the crowded space. The others got out of her way almost without thinking, except for Ralston, who still huddled under his blanket. "A historian? Sure, it's a fine idea, but pretty impractical. I have to admit that I've been thinking of you as a luxury, and about as useful as the nipples on a man's chest. But I was wrong. All the NASA people were wrong. The Astronaut Corps fought like crazy to keep you off this trip. Time enough for that on later flights. We were blinded by our loyalty to the test-pilot philosophy of space flight. We wanted as few scientists as possible and as many astronauts as we could manage. We don't like to think of ourselves as ferryboat pilots. I think we demonstrated during Apollo that we could handle science jobs as well as anyone. We saw you as a kind of insult, a slap in the face by the scientists in Houston to show us how low our stock has fallen."

"If I might be able to—"

"Shut up. But we were wrong. I read in your résumé that you were quite a student of survival. What's your honest assessment of our chances?"

Crawford shrugged, uneasy at the question. He didn't know if it was the right time to even postulate that they might fail.

"Tell me the truth."

"Pretty slim. Mostly the air problem. The people I've read about never sank so low that they had to worry about where their next breath was coming from."

"Have you ever heard of Apollo 13?"

He smiled at her. "Special circumstances. Short-term problems."

"You're right, of course. And in the only two other real space emergencies since that time, all hands were lost." She turned and scowled at each of them in turn.

"But we're *not* going to lose." She dared any of them to disagree, and no one was about to. She relaxed and resumed her stroll around the room. She turned to Crawford again.

"I can see I'll be drawing on your knowledge a lot in the years to come. What do you see as the next order of business?"

Crawford relaxed. The awful burden of responsibility, which he had never wanted, was gone. He was content to follow her lead.

"To tell you the truth, I was wondering what to say next. We have to make a thorough inventory. I guess we should start on that."

"That's fine, but there is an even more important order of business. We have to go out to the dome and find out what the hell caused the blowout. The damn thing should *not* have blown; it's the first of its type to do so. And from the *bottom*. But it did blow, and we should know why, or we're ignoring a fact about Mars that might still kill us. Let's do that first. Ralston, can you walk?"

When he nodded, she sealed her helmet and started into the lock. She turned and looked speculatively at Crawford.

"I swear, man, if you had touched me with a cattle prod you couldn't have got a bigger rise out of me than you did with what you said a few minutes ago. Do I dare ask?"

Crawford was not about to answer. He said, with a perfectly straight face, "Me? Maybe you should just assume I'm a chauvinist."

"We'll see, won't we?"

"What is that stuff?"

Song Sue Lee was on her knees, examining one of the hundreds of short, stiff spikes extruding from the ground. She tried to scratch her head but was frustrated by her helmet.

"It looks like plastic. But I have a strong feeling it's the higher life-form Lucy and I were looking for yesterday."

"And you're telling me those little spikes are what poked holes in the dome bottom? I'm not buying that."

Song straightened up, moving stiffly. They had all worked hard to empty out the collapsed dome and peel back the whole, bulky mess to reveal the ground it had covered. She was tired and stepped out of character for a moment to snap at Mary Lang.

"I didn't tell you that. We pulled the dome back and found spikes. It was your inference that they poked holes in the bottom."

"I'm sorry," Lang said quietly. "Go on with what you were saying."

"Well," Song admitted, "it wasn't a bad inference, at that. But the holes I saw were not punched through. They were eaten away." She waited for Lang to protest that the dome bottom was about as chemically inert as any plastic yet devised. But Lang had learned her lesson. And she had a talent for facing facts.

"So. We have a thing here that eats plastic. And seems to be made of plastic, into the bargain. Any ideas why it picked this particular spot to grow, and no other?"

"I have an idea on that," McKillian said. "I've had it in mind to do some studies around the dome to see if the altered moisture content we've been creating here had any effect on the spores in the soil. See, we've been here nine days, spouting out water vapor, carbon dioxide, and quite a bit of oxygen into the atmosphere. Not much, but maybe more than it seems, considering the low concentrations that are naturally available. We've altered the biome. Does anyone know where the exhaust air from the dome was expelled?"

Lang raised her eyebrows. "Yes, it was under the dome. The air we exhausted was warm, you see, and it was thought it could be put to use one last time before we let it go, to warm the floor of the dome and decrease heat loss."

"And the water vapor collected on the underside of the dome when it hit the cold air. Right. Do you get the picture?"

"I think so," Lang said. "It was so little water, though. You know we didn't want to waste it; we condensed it out until the air we exhausted was dry as a bone."

"For Earth, maybe. Here it was a torrential rainfall. It reached seeds or spores in the ground and triggered them to start growing. We're going to have to watch it when we use anything containing plastic. What does that include?"

Lang groaned. "All the airlock seals, for one thing." There were grimaces from all of them at the thought of that. "For another, a good part of our suits. Song, watch it, don't step on that thing. We don't know how powerful it is or if it'll eat the plastic in your boots, but we'd better play it safe. How about it, Ralston? Think you can find out how bad it is?"

"You mean identify the solvent these things use? Probably, if we can get some sort of workspace and I can get to my equipment."

"Mary," McKillian said, "it occurs to me that I'd better start looking for airborne spores. If there are some, it could mean that the airlock on the *Podkayne* is vulnerable. Even thirty meters off the ground."

"Right. Get on that. Since we're sleeping in it until we can find out what we can do on the ground, we'd best be sure it's safe. Meantime, we'll all sleep in our suits." There were helpless groans at this, but no protests. McKillian and Ralston headed for the pile of salvaged equipment, hoping to rescue enough to get started on their analyses. Song knelt again and started digging around one of the ten-centimeter spikes.

Crawford followed Lang back toward the *Podkayne*.

"Mary, I wanted . . . is it all right if I call you Mary?"

"I guess so. I don't think 'Commander Lang' would wear well over five years. But you'd better still think commander."

He considered it. "All right, Commander Mary." She punched him playfully. She had barely known him before the disaster. He had been a name on a roster and a sore spot in the estimation of the Astronaut Corps. But she had borne him no personal malice and now found herself beginning to like him.

"What's on your mind?"

"Ah, several things. But maybe it isn't my place to bring them up now. First, I want to say that if you're . . . ah, concerned, or doubtful of my support or loyalty because I took over command for a while . . . earlier today, well . . ."

"Well?"

"I just wanted to tell you that I have no ambitions in that direction," he finished lamely.

She patted him on the back. "Sure, I know. You forget, I read your dossier. It mentioned several interesting episodes that I'd like you to tell me about someday, from your 'soldier-of-fortune' days—"

"Hell, those were grossly overblown. I just happened to get into some scrapes and managed to get out of them."

"Still, it got you picked for this mission out of hundreds of applicants. The thinking was that you'd be a wild card, a man of action with proven survivability. Maybe it worked out. But the other thing I remember on your card was that you're not a leader. No, that you're a loner who'll cooperate with a group and be no discipline problem, but you work better alone. Want to strike out on your own?"

He smiled at her. "No, thanks. But what you said is right. I have no hankering to take charge of anything. But I do have some knowledge that might prove useful."

"And we'll use it. You just speak up, I'll be listening." She started to say something, then thought of something else. "Say, what are your ideas on a woman bossing this project? I've had to fight that all the way from my Air Force days. So if you have any objections you might as well tell me up front."

He was genuinely surprised. "You didn't take that crack seriously, did you? I might as well admit it. It was intentional, like that cattle prod you mentioned. You looked like you needed a kick in the ass."

"And thank you. But you didn't answer my question."

"Those who lead, lead," he said, simply. "I'll follow you as long as you keep leading."

"As long as it's in the direction you want?" She laughed and poked him in the ribs. "I see you as my Grand Vizier, the man who holds the arcane knowledge and advises the regent. I think I'll have to watch out for you. I know a little history, myself."

Crawford couldn't tell how serious she was. He shrugged it off.

"What I really wanted to talk to you about is this: You said you couldn't fly this ship. But you were not yourself, you were depressed and feeling hopeless. Does that still stand?"

"It stands. Come on up and I'll show you why."

In the pilot's cabin, Crawford was ready to believe her. Like all flying machines since the days of the windsock and open cockpit, this one was a mad confusion of dials, switches, and lights designed to awe anyone who knew nothing about it. He sat in the copilot's chair and listened to her.

"We had a backup pilot, of course. You may be surprised to learn that it wasn't me. It was Dorothy Cantrell, and she's dead. Now I know what everything does on this board, and I can cope with most of it easily. What I don't know, I could learn. Some of the systems are computer driven; give it the right program and it'll fly itself in space." She looked longingly at the controls, and Crawford realized that, like Weinstein, she didn't relish giving up the fun of flying to boss a gang of explorers. She was a former test pilot, and above all things she loved flying. She patted an array of hand controls on her right side. There were more like them on the left.

"This is what would kill us, Crawford. What's your first name? Matt. Matt, this baby is a flyer for the first forty thousand meters. It doesn't have the juice to orbit on the jets alone. The wings are folded up now. You probably didn't see them on the way in, but you saw the models. They're very light, supercritical, and designed for this atmosphere. Lou said it was like flying a bathtub, but it flew. And it's a *skill*, almost an art. Lou practiced for three years on the best simulators we could build and still had to rely on things you can't learn in a simulator. And he barely got us down in one piece. We didn't noise it around, but it was a *damn* close thing. Lou was young; so was Cantrell. They were both fresh from flying. They flew every day, they had the *feel* for it. They were tops." She slumped back into her chair. "I haven't flown anything but trainers for eight years."

Crawford didn't know if he should let it drop.

"But you were one of the best, everyone knows that. You still don't think you could do it?"

She threw up her hands. "How can I make you understand? This is nothing like anything I've ever flown. You might as well . . ." She groped for a comparison, trying to coax it out with gestures in the air. "Listen. Does the fact that someone can fly a biplane, maybe even be the best goddamn biplane pilot that ever was, does that mean they're qualified to fly a helicopter?"

"I don't know."

"It doesn't. Believe me."

"All right. But the fact remains that you're the closest thing on Mars to a pilot for the *Podkayne*. I think you should consider that when you're deciding what we should do." He shut up, afraid to sound like he was pushing her.

She narrowed her eyes and gazed at nothing.

"I have thought about it." She waited for a long time. "I think the chances are about a thousand to one against us if I try to fly it. But I'll do it, if we come to that. And that's *your* job. Showing me some better odds. If you can't, let me know."

Three weeks later, the Tharsis Canyon had been transformed into a child's garden of toys. Crawford had thought of no better way to describe it. Each of the plastic spikes had blossomed into a fanciful windmill, no two of them just alike. There were tiny ones, with the vanes parallel to the ground and no more than ten centimeters tall. There were derricks of spidery plastic struts that would not have looked too out of place on a Kansas farm. Some of them were five meters high. They came in all colors and many configurations, but all had vanes covered with a transparent film like cellophane, and all were spinning into colorful blurs in the stiff Martian breeze. Crawford thought of an industrial park built by gnomes. He could almost see them trudging through the spinning wheels.

Song had taken one apart as well as she could. She was still shaking her head in disbelief. She had not been able to excavate the long insulated taproot, but she could infer how deep it went. It extended all the way to the layer of permafrost, twenty meters down.

The ground between the windmills was coated in shimmering plastic. This was the second part of the plants' ingenious solution to survival on Mars. The windmills utilized the energy in the wind, and the plastic coating on the ground was in reality two thin sheets of plastic with a space between for water to circulate. The water was heated by the sun then pumped down to the permafrost, melting a little more of it each time.

"There's still something missing from our picture," Song had told them the night before, when she delivered her summary of what she had learned. "Marty hasn't been able to find a mechanism that would permit these things to grow by ingesting sand and rock and turning it into plasticlike materials. So we assume there is a reservoir of something like crude oil down there, maybe frozen in with the water."

"Where would that have come from?" Lang had asked.

"You've heard of the long-period Martian seasonal theories? Well, part of it is more than a theory. The combination of the Martian polar inclination, the precessional cycle, and the eccentricity of the orbit produces seasons that are about twelve thousand years long. We're in the middle of winter, though we landed in the nominal 'summer.' It's been theorized that if there were any Martian life it would have adapted to these longer cycles. It hibernates in spores during the cold cycle, when the water and carbon dioxide freeze out at the poles, then comes out when enough ice melts to permit biological processes. We seem to have fooled these plants; they thought summer was here when the water vapor content went up around the camp."

"So what about the crude?" Ralston asked. He didn't completely believe that part of the model they had evolved. He was a laboratory chemist, specializing in inorganic compounds. The way these plants produced plastics without high heat, through purely catalytic interactions, had him confused and defensive. He wished the crazy windmills would go away.

"I think I can answer that," McKillian said. "These organisms barely scrape by in the best of times. The ones that have made it waste nothing. It stands to reason that any really ancient deposits of crude oil would have been exhausted in only a few of these cycles. So it must be that what we're thinking of as crude oil must be something a little different. It has to be the remains of the last generation."

"But how did the remains get so far below ground?" Ralston asked. "You'd expect them to be high up. The winds couldn't bury them that deep in only twelve thousand years."

"You're right," said McKillian. "I don't really know. But I have a theory. Since these plants waste nothing, why not conserve their bodies when they die? They sprouted from the ground; isn't it possible they could withdraw when things start to get tough again? They'd leave spores behind them as they retreated, distributing them all through the soil. That way, if the upper ones blew away or were sterilized by the ultraviolet, the ones just below them would still thrive when the right conditions returned. When they reached the permafrost, they'd decompose into this organic slush we've postulated, and . . . well, it does get a little involved, doesn't it?"

"Sounds all right to me," Lang assured her. "It'll do for a working theory. Now what about airborne spores?"

It turned out that they were safe from that imagined danger. There were spores in the air now, but they were not dangerous to the colonists. The plants attacked only certain kinds of plastics, and then only in certain stages of their lives. Since they were still changing, it bore watching, but the airlocks and suits were secure. The crew was enjoying the luxury of sleeping without their suits.

And there was much work to do. Most of the physical sort devolved on Crawford and, to some extent, on Lang. It threw them together a lot. The other three had to be free to pursue their researches, as it had been decided that only in knowing their environment would they stand a chance.

The two of them had managed to salvage most of the dome. Working with patching kits and lasers to cut the tough material, they had constructed a much smaller dome. They erected it on an outcropping of bare rock, rearranged the exhaust to prevent more condensation on the underside, and added more safety features. They now slept in a pressurized building inside the dome, and one of them stayed awake on watch at all times. In drills, they had come from a deep sleep to full pressure-integrity in thirty seconds. They were not going to get caught again.

Crawford looked away from the madly whirling rotors of the windmill farm. He was with the rest of the crew, sitting in the dome with his helmet off. That was as far as Lang would permit anyone to go except in the cramped sleeping quarters. Song Sue Lee was at the radio giving her report to the *Edgar Rice Burroughs*. In her hand was one of the pump modules she had dissected out of one of the plants. It consisted of a half-meter set of eight blades that turned freely on Teflon bearings. Below it were various tiny gears and the pump itself. She twirled it idly as she spoke.

"I don't really get it," Crawford admitted, talking quietly to Lucy McKillian. "What's so revolutionary about little windmills?"

"It's just a whole new area," McKillian whispered back. "Think about it. Back on Earth, nature never got around to inventing the wheel. I've sometimes wondered why not. There are limitations, of course, but it's such a good idea. Just look what *we've* done with it. But all motion in nature is confined to up and down, back and forth, in and out, or squeeze and relax. Nothing on Earth goes round and round, unless we built it. Think about it."

Crawford did, and began to see the novelty of it. He tried in vain to think of some mechanism in an animal or plant of earthly origin that turned and kept on turning forever. He could not.

Song finished her report and handed the mike to Lang. Before she could start, Weinstein came on the line.

"We've had a change in plan up here," he said, with no preface. "I hope this doesn't come as a shock. If you think about it, you'll see the logic in it. We're going back to Earth in seven days."

It didn't surprise them too much. The *Burroughs* had given them just about everything it could in the form of data and supplies. There was one more capsule load due; after that, its presence would only be a frustration to both groups. There was a great deal of irony in having two such powerful ships so close to each other and being so helpless to do anything concrete. It was telling on the crew of the *Burroughs*.

"We've recalculated everything based on the lower mass without the twenty of you and the six tons of samples we were allowing for. By using the fuel we would have ferried down to you for takeoff, we can make a faster orbit down toward Venus. The departure date for that orbit is seven days away. We'll rendezvous with a drone capsule full of supplies we hadn't counted on." And besides, Lang thought to herself, it's much more dramatic. *Plunging sunward on the chancy cometary orbit, their pantries stripped bare, heading for the fateful rendezvous. . . .*

"I'd like your comments," he went on. "This isn't absolutely final as yet."

They all looked at Lang. They were reassured to find her calm and unshaken.

"I think it's the best idea. One thing: you've given up on any thoughts of me flying the *Podkayne*?"

"No insult intended, Mary," Weinstein said, gently. "But, yes, we have. It's the opinion of the people Earthside that you couldn't do it. They've tried some experiments, coaching some very good pilots and putting them into the simulators. They can't do it, and we don't think you could, either."

"No need to sugarcoat it. I know it as well as anyone. But even a billion to one shot is better than nothing. I take it they think Crawford is right, that survival is at least theoretically possible?"

There was a long hesitation. "I guess that's correct. Mary, I'll be frank. I don't think it's possible. I hope I'm wrong, but I don't expect . . ."

"Thank you, Winey, for the encouraging words. You always did know what it takes to buck a person up. By the way, that other mission, the one where you were going to ride a meteorite down here to save our asses, that's scrubbed, too?"

The assembled crew smiled, and Song gave a high-pitched cheer. Weinstein was not the most popular man on Mars.

"Mary, I told you about that already," he complained. It was a gentle complaint, and, even more significant, he had not objected to the use of his nickname. He was being gentle with the condemned. "We worked on it around the clock. I even managed to get permission to turn over command temporarily. But the mock-ups they made Earthside didn't survive the re-entry. It was the best we could do. I couldn't risk the entire mission on a configuration the people back on Earth wouldn't certify."

"I know. I'll call you back tomorrow." She switched the set off and sat back on her heels. "I swear, if the Earthside tests on a roll of toilet paper didn't . . . he wouldn't . . ." She cut the air with her hands. "What am I saying? That's petty. I don't like him, but he's right." She stood up, puffing out her cheeks as she exhaled a pent-up breath.

"Come on, crew, we've got a lot of work."

They named their colony New Amsterdam, because of the windmills. The name of whirligig was the one that stuck on the Martian plants, though Crawford held out for a long time in favor of spinnakers.

They worked all day and tried their best to ignore the *Burroughs* overhead. The messages back and forth were short and to the point. Helpless as the mother ship was to render them more air, they knew they would miss it when it was gone. So the day of departure was a stiff, determinedly nonchalant affair. They all made a big show of going to bed hours before the scheduled breakaway.

When he was sure the others were asleep, Crawford opened his eyes and looked around the darkened barracks. It wasn't much in the way of a home; they were crowded against each other on rough pads made of insulating material. The toilet facilities were behind a flimsy barrier against one wall, and smelled. But none of them would have wanted to sleep outside in the dome, even if Lang had allowed it.

The only light came from the illuminated dials that the guard was supposed to watch all night. There was no one sitting in front of them. Crawford assumed the guard had gone to sleep. He would have been upset, but there was no time. He had to suit up, and he welcomed the chance to sneak out. He began to furtively don his pressure suit.

As a historian, he felt he could not let such a moment slip by unobserved. Silly, but there it was. He had to be out there, watch it with his own eyes. It didn't matter if he never lived to tell about it, he must record it.

Someone sat up beside him. He froze, but it was too late. She rubbed her eyes and peered into the darkness.

"Matt?" she yawned. "What's . . . what is it? Is something—"

"Shh. I'm going out. Go back to sleep, Song."

"Um hmmm." She stretched, dug her knuckles fiercely into her eyes and smoothed her hair back from her face. She was dressed in a loose-fitting bottom of a ship suit, a gray piece of dirty cloth that badly needed washing, as did all their clothes. For a moment, as he watched her shadow stretch and stand up, he wasn't interested in the *Burroughs*. He forced his mind away from her.

"I'm going with you," she whispered.

"All right. Don't wake the others."

Standing just outside the airlock was Mary Lang. She turned as they came out, and did not seem surprised.

"Were you the one on duty?" Crawford asked her.

"Yeah. I broke my own rule. But so did you two. Consider yourselves on report." She laughed and beckoned them over to her. They linked arms and stood staring up at the sky.

"How much longer?" Song asked, after some time had passed.

"Just a few minutes. Hold tight." Crawford looked over to Lang and thought he saw tears, but he couldn't be sure in the dark.

There was a tiny new star, brighter than all the rest, brighter than Phobos. It hurt to look at it but none of them looked away. It was the fusion drive of the *Edgar Rice Burroughs*, heading sunward, away from the long winter on Mars. It stayed on for long minutes, then sputtered and was lost. Though it was warm in the dome, Crawford was shivering. It was ten minutes before any of them felt like facing the barracks.

They crowded into the airlock, carefully not looking at each other's faces as they waited for the automatic machinery. The inner door opened and Lang pushed forward—and right back into the airlock. Crawford had a glimpse of Ralston and Lucy McKillian; then Mary shut the door.

"Some people have no poetry in their souls," Mary said.

"Or too much," Song giggled.

"You people want to take a walk around the dome with me? Maybe we could discuss ways of giving people a little privacy."

The inner lock door was pulled open, and there was McKillian, squinting into the bare bulb that lighted the lock while she held her shirt in front of her with one hand.

"Come on in," she said, stepping back. "We might as well talk about this." They entered, and McKillian turned on the light and sat down on her mattress. Ralston was blinking, nervously tucked into his pile of blankets. Since the day of the blowout he never seemed to be warm enough.

Having called for a discussion, McKillian proceeded to clam up. Song and Crawford sat on their bunks, and eventually as the silence stretched tighter, they all found themselves looking to Lang.

She started stripping out of her suit. "Well, I guess that takes care of that. So glad to hear all your comments. Lucy, if you were expecting some sort of reprimand, forget it. We'll take steps first thing in the morning to provide some sort of privacy for that, but, no matter what, we'll all be pretty close in the years to come. I think we should all relax. Any objections?" She was half out of her suit when she paused to scan them for comments. There were none. She stripped to her skin and reached for the light.

"In a way it's about time," she said, tossing her clothes in a corner. "The only thing to do with these clothes is burn them. We'll all smell better for it. Song, you take the watch." She flicked out the lights and reclined heavily on her mattress.

There was much rustling and squirming for the next few minutes as they got out of their clothes. Song brushed against Crawford in the dark and they murmured apologies. Then they all bedded down in their own bunks. It was several tense, miserable hours before anyone got to sleep.

The week following the departure of the *Burroughs* was one of hysterical over-reaction by the New Amsterdamites. The atmosphere was forced and false; an eat-drink-and-be-merry feeling pervaded everything they did.

They built a separate shelter inside the dome, not really talking aloud about what it was for. But it did not lack for use. Productive work suffered as the five of them frantically ran through all the possible permutations of three women and two men. Animosities developed, flourished for a few hours, and dissolved in tearful reconciliations. Three ganged up on two, two on one, one declared war on all the other four. Ralston and Song announced an engagement, which lasted ten hours. Crawford nearly came to blows with Lang, aided by McKillian. McKillian renounced men forever and had a brief, tempestuous affair with Song. Then Song discovered McKillian with Ralston, and Crawford caught her on the rebound, only to be thrown over for Ralston.

Mary Lang let it work itself out, only interfering when it got violent. She herself was not immune to the frenzy but managed to stay aloof from most of it. She went to the shelter with whoever asked her, trying not to play favorites, and gently tried to prod them back to work. As she told McKillian toward the first of the week, "At least we're getting to know one another."

Things did settle down, as Lang had known they would. They entered their second week alone in virtually the same position they had started: no romantic entanglements firmly established. But they knew each other a lot better, were re-laxed in the close company of each other, and were supported by a new framework of interlocking friendships. They were much closer to being a team. Rivalries never died out completely, but they no longer dominated the colony. Lang worked them harder than ever, making up for the lost time.

Crawford missed most of the interesting work, being more suited for the semi-skilled manual labor that never seemed to be finished. So he and Lang had to learn about the new discoveries at the nightly briefings in the shelter. He remembered nothing about any animal life being discovered, and so when he saw something crawling through the whirligig garden, he dropped everything and started over to it.

At the edge of the garden he stopped, remembering the order from Lang to stay out unless collecting samples. He watched the thing—bug? turtle?—for a moment, satisfied himself that it wouldn't get too far away at its creeping pace, and hurried off to find Song.

"You've got to name it after me," he said as they hurried back to the garden. "That's my right, isn't it, as the discoverer?"

"Sure," Song said, peering along his pointed finger. "Just show me the damn thing and I'll immortalize you."

The thing was twenty centimeters long, almost round, and dome-shaped. It had a hard shell on top.

"I don't know quite what to do with it," Song admitted. "If it's the only one, I don't dare dissect it, and maybe I shouldn't even touch it."

"Don't worry, there's another over behind you." Now that they were looking for them, they quickly spied four of the creatures. Song took a sample bag from her pouch and held it open in front of the beast. It crawled halfway into the bag, then seemed to think something was wrong. It stopped, but Song nudged it in and picked it up. She peered at the underside and laughed in wonder.

"Wheels," she said. "The thing runs on wheels."

★ ★ ★

"I don't know where it came from," Song told the group that night. "I don't even quite believe in it. It'd make a nice educational toy for a child, though. I took it apart into twenty or thirty pieces, put it back together, and it still runs. It has a high-impact polystyrene carapace, nontoxic paint on the outside—"

"Not really polystyrene," Ralston interjected.

"—and I guess if you kept changing the batteries it would run forever. And it's *nearly* polystyrene, that's what you said."

"Were you serious about the batteries?" Lang asked.

"I'm not sure. Marty thinks there's a chemical metabolism in the upper part of the shell, which I haven't explored yet. But I can't really say if it's alive in the sense we use. I mean, it runs on *wheels*! It has three wheels, suited for sand, and something that's a cross between a rubber-band drive and a mainspring. Energy is stored in a coiled muscle and released slowly. I don't think it could travel more than a hundred meters. Unless it can re-coil the muscle, and I can't tell how that might be done."

"It sounds very specialized," McKillian said thoughtfully. "Maybe we should be looking for the niche it occupies. The way you describe it, it couldn't function without help from a symbiote. Maybe it fertilizes the plants, like bees, and the plants either donate or are robbed of the power to wind the spring. Did you look for some mechanism the bug could use to steal energy from the rotating gears in the whirligigs?"

"That's what I want to do in the morning," Song said. "Unless Mary will let us take a look tonight?" She said it hopefully, but without real expectation. Mary Lang shook her head decisively.

"It'll keep. It's *cold* out there, baby."

A new exploration of the whirligig garden the next day revealed several new species, including one more thing that might be an animal. It was a flying creature, the size of a fruit fly, that managed to glide from plant to plant when the wind was down by means of a freely rotating set of blades, like an autogiro.

Crawford and Lang hung around as the scientists looked things over. They were not anxious to get back to the task that had occupied them for the last two weeks: that of bringing the *Podkayne* to a horizontal position without wrecking her. The ship had been rigged with stabilizing cables soon after landing, and provision had been made in the plans to lay the ship on its side in the event of a really big windstorm. But the plans had envisioned a work force of twenty, working all day with a maze of pulleys and gears. It was slow work and could not be rushed. If the ship were to tumble and lose pressure, they didn't have a prayer.

So they welcomed an opportunity to tour fairyland. The place was even more bountiful than the last time Crawford had taken a look. There were thick vines that Song assured him were running with water, both hot and cold, and various other fluids. There were more of the tall variety of derrick, making the place look like a pastel oilfield.

They had little trouble finding where the "matthews" came from. They found dozens of twenty-centimeter lumps on the sides of the large derricks. They evidently grew from them like tumors and were released when they were ripe. What they were for was another matter. As well as they could discover, the matthews simply crawled in a straight line until their power ran out. If they were wound up again, they would crawl farther. There were dozens of them lying motionless in the sand within a hundred-meter radius of the garden.

Two weeks of research left them knowing no more. They had to abandon the matthews for the time, as another enigma had cropped up which demanded their attention.

This time Crawford was the last to know. He was called on the radio and found the group all squatted in a circle around a growth in the graveyard.

The graveyard, where they had buried their fifteen dead crewmates on the first day of the disaster, had sprouted with life during the week after the departure of the *Burroughs*. It was separated from the original site of the dome by three hundred meters of blowing sand. So McKillian assumed this second bloom was caused by the water in the bodies of the dead. What they couldn't figure out was why this patch should differ so radically from the first one.

There were whirligigs in the second patch, but they lacked the variety and disorder of the originals. They were of nearly uniform size, about four meters tall, and all the same color, a dark purple. They had pumped water for two weeks, then stopped. When Song examined them, she reported the bearings were frozen, dried out. They seemed to have lost the plasticizer that kept the structures fluid and living. The water in the pipes was frozen. Though she would not commit herself in the matter, she felt they were dead. In their place was a second network of pipes which wound around the derricks and spread transparent sheets of film to the sunlight, heating the water which circulated through them. The water was being pumped, but not by the now-familiar system of windmills. Spaced along each of the pipes were expansion-contraction pumps with valves very like those in a human heart.

The new marvel was a simple affair in the middle of that living petrochemical complex. It was a short plant that sprouted up half a meter, then extruded two stalks parallel to the ground. At the end of each stalk was a perfect globe, one gray, one blue. The blue one was much larger than the gray one.

Crawford looked at it briefly, then squatted down beside the rest, wondering what all the fuss was about. Everyone looked very solemn, almost scared.

"You called me over to see this?"

Lang looked over at him, and something in her face made him nervous.

"Look at it, Matt. Really look at it." So he did, feeling foolish, wondering what the joke was. He noticed a white patch near the top of the larger globe. It was streaked, like a glass marble with swirls of opaque material in it. It looked very familiar, he realized, with the hair on the back of his neck starting to stand up.

"It turns," Lang said quietly. "That's why Song noticed it. She came by here one day and it was in a different position than it had been."

"Let me guess," he said, much more calmly than he felt. "The little one goes around the big one, right?"

"Right. And the little one keeps one face turned to the big one. The big one rotates once in twenty-four hours. It has an axial tilt of twenty-three degrees."

"It's a . . . what's the word? Orrery. It's an orrery." Crawford had to stand up and shake his head to clear it.

"It's funny," Lang said, quietly. "I always thought it would be something flashy, or at least obvious. An alien artifact mixed in with caveman bones, or a spaceship entering the system. I guess I was thinking in terms of pottery shards and atom bombs."

"Well, that all sounds pretty ho-hum to me up against *this*," Song said. "Do you . . . do you *realize* . . . what are we talking about here? Evolution, or . . . or engineering? Is it the plants themselves that did this, or were they made to do it by whatever built them? Do you see what I'm talking about? I felt funny about those wheels for a long time. I just won't believe they'd evolve naturally."

"What do you mean?"

"I mean I think these plants we've been seeing were designed to be the way they are. They're *too* perfectly adapted, *too* ingenious to have just sprung up in response to the environment." Her eyes seemed to wander, and she stood up and gazed into the valley below them. It was as barren as anything that could be imagined: red and yellow and brown rock outcroppings and tumbled boulders. And in the foreground, the twirling colors of the whirligigs.

"But why this thing?" Crawford asked, pointing to the impossible artifact-plant. "Why a model of the Earth and Moon? And why right here, in the graveyard?"

"Because we were expected," Song said, still looking away from them. "They must have watched the Earth, during the last summer season. I don't know; maybe they even went there. If they did, they would have found men and women like us, hunting and living in caves. Building fires, using clubs, chipping arrowheads. You know more about it than I do, Matt."

"Who are *they*?" Ralston asked. "You think we're going to be meeting some Martians? People? I don't see how. I don't believe it."

"I'm afraid I'm skeptical, too," Lang said. "Surely there must be some other way to explain it."

"No! There's no other way. Oh, not people like us, maybe. Maybe we're seeing them right now, spinning like crazy." They all looked uneasily at the whirligigs. "But I think they're not here yet. I think we're going to see, over the next few years, increasing complexity in these plants and animals as they build up a biome here and get ready for the builders. Think about it. When summer comes, the conditions will be very different. The atmosphere will be almost as dense as ours, with about the same partial pressure of oxygen. By then, thousands of years from now, these early forms will have vanished. These things are adapted for low pressure, no oxygen, scarce water. The later ones will be adapted to an environment much like ours. And *that's* when we'll see the makers, when the stage is properly set." She sounded almost religious when she said it.

Lang stood up and shook Song's shoulder. Song came slowly back to them and sat down, still blinded by a private vision. Crawford had a glimpse of it himself, and it scared him. And a glimpse of something else, something that could be important but kept eluding him.

"Don't you see?" she went on, calmer now. "It's too pat, too much of a coincidence. This thing is like a . . . a headstone, a monument. It's growing right here in the graveyard, from the bodies of our friends. Can you believe in that as just a coincidence?"

Evidently no one could. But likewise, Crawford could see no reason why it should have happened the way it did.

It was painful to leave the mystery for later, but there was nothing to be done about it. They could not bring themselves to uproot the thing, even when five more like it sprouted in the graveyard. There was a new consensus among them to leave the Martian plants and animals alone. Like nervous atheists, most of them didn't believe Song's theories but had an uneasy feeling of trespassing when they went through the gardens. They felt subconsciously that it might be better to leave them alone in case they turned out to be private property.

And for six months, nothing really new cropped up among the whirligigs. Song was not surprised. She said it supported her theory that these plants were there only as caretakers to prepare the way for the less hardy, air-breathing varieties to come. They would warm the soil and bring the water closer to the surface, then disappear when their function was over.

The three scientists allowed their studies to slide as it became more important to provide for the needs of the moment. The dome material was weakening as the temporary patches lost strength, and so a new home was badly needed. They were dealing daily with slow leaks, any of which could become a major blowout.

The *Podkayne* was lowered to the ground, and sadly decommissioned. It was a bad day for Mary Lang, the worst since the day of the blowout. She saw it as a necessary but infamous thing to do to a proud flying machine. She brooded about it for a week, becoming short-tempered and almost unapproachable. Then she asked Crawford to join her in the private shelter. It was the first time she had asked any of the other four. They lay in each other's arms for an hour, and Lang quietly sobbed on his chest. Crawford was proud that she had chosen him for her companion when she could no longer maintain her tough, competent show of strength. In a way, it was a strong thing to do, to expose weakness to the one person among the four who might possibly be her rival for leadership. He did not betray the trust. In the end, she was comforting him.

After that day Lang was ruthless in gutting the old *Podkayne*. She supervised the ripping out of the motors to provide more living space, and only Crawford saw what it was costing her. They drained the fuel tanks and stored the fuel in every available container they could scrounge. It would be useful later for heating, and for recharging batteries. They managed to convert plastic packing crates into fuel containers by lining them with sheets of the double-walled material the whirligigs used to heat water. They were nervous at this vandalism, but had no other choice. They kept looking nervously at the graveyard as they ripped up meter-square sheets of it.

They ended up with a long cylindrical home, divided into two small sleeping rooms, a community room, and a laboratory-storehouse-workshop in the old fuel tank. Crawford and Lang spent the first night together in the "penthouse," the former cockpit, the only room with windows.

Lying there wide awake on the rough mattress, side by side in the warm air with Mary Lang, whose black leg was a crooked line of shadow lying across his body, looking up through the port at the sharp, unwinking stars—with nothing done yet about the problems of oxygen, food, and water for the years ahead and no assurance he would live out the night on a planet determined to kill him— Crawford realized he had never been happier in his life.

★ ★ ★

On a day exactly eight months after the disaster, two discoveries were made. One was in the whirligig garden and concerned a new plant that was bearing what might be fruit. They were clusters of grape-sized white balls, very hard and fairly heavy. The second discovery was made by Lucy McKillian and concerned the absence of an event that up to that time had been as regular as the full moon.

"I'm pregnant," she announced to them that night, causing Song to delay her examination of the white fruit.

It was not unexpected; Lang had been waiting for it to happen since the night the *Burroughs* left. But she had not worried about it. Now she must decide what to do.

"I was afraid that might happen," Crawford said. "What do we do, Mary?"

"Why don't you tell me what you think? You're the survival expert. Are babies a plus or a minus in our situation?"

"I'm afraid I have to say they're a liability. Lucy will be needing extra food during her pregnancy, and afterward, and it will be an extra mouth to feed. We can't afford the strain on our resources." Lang said nothing, waiting to hear from McKillian.

"Now wait a minute. What about all this line about 'colonists' you've been feeding us ever since we got stranded here? Who ever heard of a colony without babies? If we don't grow, we stagnate, right? We *have* to have children." She looked back and forth from Lang to Crawford, her face expressing formless doubts.

"We're in special circumstances, Lucy," Crawford explained. "Sure, I'd be all for it if we were better off. But we can't be sure we can even provide for ourselves, much less a child. I say we can't afford children until we're established."

"Do you want the child, Lucy?" Lang asked quietly.

McKillian didn't seem to know what she wanted. "No. I . . . but, yes. Yes, I guess I do." She looked at them, pleading for them to understand.

"Look, I've never had one, and never planned to. I'm thirty-four years old and never, never felt the lack. I've always wanted to go places, and you can't with a baby. But I never planned to become a colonist on Mars, either. I . . . things have changed, don't you see? I've been depressed." She looked around, and Song and Ralston were nodding sympathetically. Relieved to see that she was not the only one feeling the oppression, she went on, more strongly. "I think if I go another day like yesterday and the day before—and today—I'll end up screaming. It seems so pointless, collecting all that information, for what?"

"I agree with Lucy," Ralston said, surprisingly. Crawford had thought he would be the only one immune to the inevitable despair of the castaway. Ralston in his laboratory was the picture of carefree detachment, existing only to observe.

"So do I," Lang said, ending the discussion. But she explained her reasons to them.

"Look at it this way, Matt. No matter how we stretch our supplies, they won't take us through the next four years. We either find a way of getting what we need from what's around us, or we all die. And if we find a way to do it, then what does it matter how many of us there are? At the most, this will push our deadline a few weeks or a month closer, the day we have to be self-supporting."

"I hadn't thought of it that way," Crawford admitted.

"But that's not important. The important thing is what you said from the first, and I'm surprised you didn't see it. If we're a colony, we expand. By definition. Historian, what happened to colonies that failed to expand?"

"Don't rub it in."

"They died out. I know that much. People, we're not intrepid space explorers anymore. We're not the career men and women we set out to be. Like it or not, and I suggest we start liking it, we're pioneers trying to live in a hostile environment. The odds are very much against us, and we're not going to be here forever, but like Matt said, we'd betteer plan as if we were. Comment?"

There was none, until Song spoke up, thoughtfully.

"I think a baby around here would be fun. Two should be twice as much fun. I think I'll start. Come on, Marty."

"Hold on, honey," Lang said, dryly. "If you conceive now, I'll be forced to order you to abort. We have the chemicals for it, you know."

"That's discrimination."

"Maybe so. But just because we're colonists doesn't mean we have to behave like rabbits. A pregnant woman will have to be removed from the work force at the end of her term, and we can only afford one at a time. After Lucy has hers, then come ask me again. But watch Lucy carefully, dear. Have you really thought what it's going to take? Have you tried to visualize her getting into her pressure suit in six or seven months?"

From their expressions, it was plain that neither Song nor McKillian had thought of it.

"Right," Lang went on. "It'll be literal confinement for her, right here in the *Poddy*. Unless we can rig something for her, which I seriously doubt. Still want to go through with it, Lucy?"

"Can I have a while to think it over?"

"Sure. You have about two months. After that, the chemicals aren't safe."

"I'd advise you to do it," Crawford said. "I know my opinion means nothing after shooting my mouth off. I know I'm a fine one to talk; I won't be cooped up in here. But the colony needs it. We've all felt it: the lack of a direction or a drive to keep going. I think we'd get it back if you went through with this."

McKillian tapped her teeth thoughtfully with the tip of a finger.

"You're right," she said. "Your opinion *doesn't* mean anything." She slapped his knee delightedly when she saw him blush. "I think it's yours, by the way. And I think I'll go ahead and have it."

The penthouse seemed to have gone to Lang and Crawford as an unasked-for prerogative. It just became a habit, since they seemed to have developed a bond between them and none of the other three complained. Neither of the other women seemed to be suffering in any way. So Lang left it at that. What went on between the three of them was of no concern to her as long as it stayed happy.

Lang was leaning back in Crawford's arms, trying to decide if she wanted to make love again, when a gunshot rang out in the *Podkayne*.

She had given a lot of thought to the last emergency, which she still saw as partly a result of her lag in responding. This time she was through the door almost before the reverberations had died down, leaving Crawford to nurse the leg she had stepped on in her haste.

She was in time to see McKillian and Ralston hurrying into the lab at the back of the ship. There was a red light flashing, but she quickly saw it was not the worst it could be; the pressure light still glowed green. It was the smoke detector. The smoke was coming from the lab.

She took a deep breath and plunged in, only to collide with Ralston as he came out, dragging Song. Except for a dazed expression and a few cuts, Song seemed to be all right. Crawford and McKillian joined them as they laid her on the bunk.

"It was one of the fruit," she said, gasping for breath and coughing. "I was heating it in a beaker, turned away, and it blew. I guess it sort of stunned me. The next thing I knew, Marty was carrying me out here. Hey, I have to get back in there! There's another one . . . it could be dangerous, and the damage, I have to check on that—" She struggled to get up but Lang held her down.

"You take it easy. What's this about another one?"

"I had it clamped down, and the drill—did I turn it on, or not? I can't remember. I was after a core sample. You'd better take a look. If the drill hits whatever made the other one explode, it might go off."

"I'll get it," McKillian said, turning toward the lab.

"You'll stay right here," Lang barked. "We know there's not enough power in them to hurt the ship, but it could kill you if it hit you right. We stay right here until it goes off. The hell with the damage. And shut that door, quick!"

Before they could shut it they heard a whistling, like a teakettle coming to boil, then a rapid series of clangs. A tiny white ball came through the doorway and bounced off three walls. It moved almost faster than they could follow. It hit Crawford on the arm, then fell to the floor where it gradually skittered to a stop. The hissing died away, and Crawford picked it up. It was lighter than it had been. There was pinhole drilled in one side. The pinhole was cold when he touched it with his fingers. Startled, thinking he was burned, he stuck his finger in his mouth, then sucked on it absently long after he knew the truth.

"These 'fruit' are full of compressed gas," he told them. "We have to open up another, carefully this time. I'm afraid to say what gas I think it is, but I have a hunch that our problems are solved."

By the time the rescue expedition arrived, no one was calling it that. There had been the little matter of a long, brutal war with the Palestinian Empire, and a growing conviction that the survivors of the first expedition had not had any chance in the first place. There had been no time for luxuries like space travel beyond the Moon and no billions of dollars to invest while the world's energy policies were being debated in the Arabian Desert with tactical nuclear weapons.

When the ship finally did show up, it was no longer a NASA ship. It was sponsored by the fledgling International Space Agency. Its crew came from all over Earth. Its drive was new, too, and a lot better than the old one. As usual, war had given research a kick in the pants. Its mission was to take up the Martian exploration where the first expedition had left off and, incidentally, to recover the remains of the twenty Americans for return to Earth.

The ship came down with an impressive show of flame and billowing sand, three kilometers from Tharsis Base.

The captain, an Indian named Singh, got his crew started on erecting the permanent buildings, then climbed into a crawler with three officers for the trip to Tharsis. It was almost exactly twelve Earth-years since the departure of the *Edgar Rice Burroughs.*

The *Podkayne* was barely visible behind a network of multicolored vines. The vines were tough enough to frustrate their efforts to push through and enter the old ship. But both lock doors were open, and sand had drifted in rippled waves through the opening. The stern of the ship was nearly buried.

Singh told his people to stop, and he stood back admiring the complexity of the life in such a barren place. There were whirligigs twenty meters tall scattered around him, with vanes broad as the wings of a cargo aircraft.

"We'll have to get cutting tools from the ship," he told his crew. "They're probably in there. What a place this is! I can see we're going to be busy." He walked along the edge of the dense growth, which now covered several acres. He came to a section where the predominant color was purple. It was strangely different from the rest of the garden. There were tall whirligig derricks but they were frozen, unmoving. And covering all the derricks was a translucent network of ten-centimeter-wide strips of plastic, which was thick enough to make an impenetrable barrier. It was like a cobweb made of flat, thin material instead of fibrous spider-silk. It bulged outward between all the crossbraces of the whirligigs.

"Hello, can you hear me now?"

Singh jumped, then turned around, looked at the three officers. They were looking as surprised as he was.

"Hello, hello, hello? No good on this one, Mary. Want me to try another channel?"

"Wait a moment. I can hear you. Where are you?"

"Hey, he hears me! Uh, that is, this is Song Sue Lee, and I'm right in front of you. If you look real hard into the webbing, you can just make me out. I'll wave my arms. See?"

Singh thought he saw some movement when he pressed his face to the trans-lucent web. The web resisted his hands, pushing back like an inflated balloon.

"I think I see you." The enormity of it was just striking him. He kept his voice under tight control, as his officers rushed up around him, and managed not to stammer. "Are you well? Is there anything we can do?"

There was a pause. "Well, now that you mention it, you might have come on time. But that's water through the pipes, I guess. If you have some toys or some-thing, it might be nice. The stories I've told little Billy of all the nice things you people were going to bring! There's going to be no living with him, let me tell you."

This was getting out of hand for Captain Singh.

"Ms. Song, how can we get in there with you?"

"Sorry. Go to your right about ten meters, where you see the steam coming from the web. There, see it?" They did, and as they looked, a section of the webbing was pulled open and a rush of warm air almost blew them over. Water condensed out of it in their faceplates, and suddenly they couldn't see very well.

"Hurry, hurry, step in! We can't keep it open too long." They groped their way in, scraping frost away with their hands. The web closed behind them, and they were standing in the center of a very complicated network made of single strands of the webbing material. Singh's pressure gauge read 30 millibars.

Another section opened up and they stepped through it. After three more gates were passed, the temperature and pressure were nearly Earth-normal. And they were standing beside a small oriental woman with skin tanned almost black. She had no clothes on, but seemed adequately dressed in a brilliant smile that dimpled her mouth and eyes. Her hair was streaked with gray. She would be—Singh stopped to consider—forty-one years old.

"This way," she said, beckoning them into a tunnel formed from more strips of plastic. They twisted around through a random maze, going through more gates that opened when they neared them, sometimes getting on their knees when the clearance lowered. They heard the sound of children's voices.

They reached what must have been the center of the maze and found the people everyone had given up on. Eighteen of them. The children became very quiet and stared solemnly at the new arrivals, while the other four adults . . .

The adults were standing separately around the space while tiny helicopters flew around them, wrapping them from head to toe in strips of webbing like human maypoles.

"Of course we don't know if we would have made it without the assist from the Martians," Mary Lang was saying, from her perch on an orange thing that might have been a toadstool. "Once we figured out what was happening here in the graveyard, there was no need to explore alternative ways of getting food, water, and oxygen. The need just never arose. We were provided for."

She raised her feet so a group of three gawking women from the ship could get by. They were letting them come through in groups of five every hour. They didn't dare open the outer egress more often than that, and Lang was wondering if it was too often. The place was crowded, and the kids were nervous. But better to have the crew satisfy their curiosity in here where we can watch them, she reasoned, than have them messing things up outside.

The inner nest was free-form. The New Amsterdamites had allowed it to stay pretty much the way the whirlibirds had built it, only taking down an obstruction here and there to allow humans to move around. It was a maze of gauzy walls and plastic struts, with clear plastic pipes running all over and carrying fluids of pale blue, pink, gold, and wine. Metal spigots from the *Podkayne* had been inserted in some of the pipes. McKillian was kept busy refilling glasses for the visitors who wanted to sample the antifreeze solution that was fifty percent ethanol. It was good stuff, Captain Singh reflected as he drained his third glass, and that was what he still couldn't understand.

He was having trouble framing the questions he wanted to ask, and he realized he'd had too much to drink. The spirit of celebration, the rejoicing at finding these people here past any hope; one could hardly stay aloof from it. But he refused a fourth drink regretfully.

"I can understand the drink," he said, carefully. "Ethanol is a simple compound and could fit into many different chemistries. But it's hard to believe that you've survived eating the food these plants produced for you."

"Not once you understand what this graveyard is and why it became what it did," Song said. She was sitting cross-legged on the floor nursing her youngest, Ethan.

"First you have to understand that all this you see," she waved around at the meters of hanging soft-sculpture, causing Ethan to nearly lose the nipple, "was designed to contain beings who are no more adapted to *this* Mars than we are. They need warmth, oxygen at fairly high pressures, and free water. It isn't here now, but it can be created by properly designed plants. They engineered these plants to be triggered by the first signs of free water and to start building places for them to live while they waited for full summer to come. When it does, this whole planet will bloom. Then we can step outside without wearing suits or carrying airberries."

"Yes, I see," Singh said. "And it's all very wonderful, almost too much to believe." He was distracted for a moment, looking up to the ceiling where the airberries—white spheres about the size of bowling balls—hung in clusters from the pipes that supplied them with high-pressure oxygen.

"I'd like to see that process from the start," he said. "Where you suit up for the outside, I mean."

"We were suiting up when you got here. It takes about half an hour; so we couldn't get out in time to meet you."

"How long are those . . . suits good for?"

"About a day," Crawford said. "You have to destroy them to get out of them. The plastic strips don't cut well, but there's another specialized animal that eats that type of plastic. It's recycled into the system. If you want to suit up, you just grab a whirlibird and hold onto its tail and throw it. It starts spinning as it flies, and wraps the end product around you. It takes some practice, but it works. The stuff sticks to itself, but not to us. So you spin several layers, letting each one dry, then hook up an airberry, and you're inflated and insulated."

"Marvelous," Singh said, truly impressed. He had seen the tiny whirlibirds weaving the suits, and the other ones, like small slugs, eating them away when the colonists saw they wouldn't need them. "But without some sort of exhaust, you wouldn't last long. How is that accomplished?"

"We use the breather valves from our old suits," McKillian said. "Either the plants that grow valves haven't come up yet or we haven't been smart enough to recognize them. And the insulation isn't perfect. We only go out in the hottest part of the day, and our hands and feet tend to get cold. But we manage."

Singh realized he had strayed from his original question.

"But what about the food? Surely it's too much to expect for these Martians to eat the same things we do. Wouldn't you think so?"

"We sure did, and we were lucky to have Marty Ralston along. He kept telling us the fruits in the graveyard were edible by humans. Fats, starches, proteins; all identical to the ones we brought along. The clue was in the orrery, of course."

Lang pointed to the twin globes in the middle of the room, still keeping perfect Earth-time.

"It was a beacon. We figured that out when we saw they grew only in the graveyard. But what was it telling us? We felt it meant that we were expected. Song felt that from the start, and we all came to agree with her. But we didn't realize just how much they had prepared for us until Marty started analyzing the fruits and nutrients here.

"Listen, these Martians-and I can see from your look that you still don't really believe in them, but you will if you stay here long enough—they know genetics. They really know it. We have a thousand theories about what they may be like, and I won't bore you with them yet, but this is one thing we do know. They can build anything they need, make a blueprint in DNA, encapsulate it in a spore and bury it, knowing exactly what will come up in forty thousand years. When it starts to get cold here and they know the cycle's drawing to an end, they seed the planet with the spores and . . . do something. Maybe they die, or maybe they have some other way of passing the time. But they know they'll return.

"We can't say how long they've been prepared for a visit from us. Maybe only this cycle; maybe twenty cycles ago. Anyway, at the last cycle they buried the kind of spores that would produce these little gismos." She tapped the blue ball representing the Earth with one foot.

"They triggered them to be activated only when they encountered certain different conditions. Maybe they knew exactly what it would be; maybe they only provided for a likely range of possibilities. Song thinks they've visited us, back in the Stone Age. In some ways it's easier to believe than the alternative. That way they'd know our genetic structure and what kinds of food we'd eat, and could prepare.

" 'Cause if they didn't visit us, they must have prepared other spores. Spores that would analyze new proteins and be able to duplicate them. Further than that, some of the plants might have been able to copy certain genetic material if they encountered any. Take a look at that pipe behind you." Singh turned and saw a pipe about as thick as his arm. It was flexible, and had a swelling in it that continuously pulsed in expansion and contraction.

"Take that bulge apart and you'd be amazed at the resemblance to a human heart. So there's another significant fact; this place started out with whirligigs, but later modified itself to use human heart pumps from the genetic information *taken from the bodies of the men and women we buried*." She paused to let that sink in, then went on with a slightly bemused smile.

"The same thing for what we eat and drink. That liquor you drank, for instance. It's half alcohol, and that's probably what it would have been without the corpses. But the rest of it is very similar to hemoglobin. It's sort of like fermented blood. Human blood."

Singh was glad he had refused the fourth drink. One of his crew members quietly put his glass down.

"I've never eaten human flesh," Lang went on, "but I think I know what it must taste like. Those vines to your right; we strip off the outer part and eat the meat underneath. It tastes good. I wish we could cook it, but we have nothing to burn and couldn't risk it with the high oxygen count, anyway."

Singh and everyone else was silent for a while. He found he really was beginning to believe in the Martians. The theory seemed to cover a lot of otherwise inexplicable facts.

Mary Lang sighed, slapped her thighs, and stood up. Like all the others, she was nude and seemed totally at home with it. None of them had worn anything but a Martian pressure suit for eight years. She ran her hand lovingly over the gossamer wall, the wall that had provided her and her fellow colonists and their children protection from the cold and the thin air for so long. He was struck by her easy familiarity with what seemed to him outlandish surroundings. She looked at home. He couldn't imagine her anywhere else.

He looked at the children. One wide-eyed little girl of eight years was kneeling at his feet. As his eyes fell on her, she smiled tentatively and took his hand.

"Did you bring any bubblegum?" the girl asked.

He smiled at her. "No, honey, but maybe there's some in the ship." She seemed satisfied. She would wait to experience the wonders of earthly science.

"We were provided for," Mary Lang said, quietly. "They knew we were coming and they altered their plants to fit us in." She looked back to Singh. "It would have happened even without the blowout and the burials. The same sort of thing was happening around the *Podkayne*, too, triggered by our waste; urine and feces and such. I don't know if it would have tasted quite as good in the food department, but it would have sustained life."

Singh stood up. He was moved, but did not trust himself to show it adequately. So he sounded rather abrupt, though polite.

"I suppose you'll be anxious to go to the ship," he said. "You're going to be a tremendous help. You know so much of what we were sent here to find out. And you'll be quite famous when you get back to Earth. Your back pay should add up to quite a sum."

There was a silence, then it was ripped apart by Lang's huge laugh. She was joined by the others, and the children, who didn't know what they were laughing about but enjoyed the break in the tension.

"Sorry, Captain. That was rude. But we're not going back."

Singh looked at each of the adults and saw no trace of doubt. And he was mildly surprised to find that the statement did not startle him.

"I won't take that as your final decision," he said. "As you know, we'll be here six months. If at the end of that time any of you want to go, you're still citizens of Earth."

"We are? You'll have to brief us on the political situation back there. We were United States citizens when we left. But it doesn't matter. You won't get any takers, though we appreciate the fact that you came. It's nice to know we weren't forgotten." She said it with total assurance, and the others were nodding. Singh was uncomfortably aware that the idea of a rescue mission had died out only a few years after the initial tragedy. He and his ship were here now only to explore.

Lang sat back down and patted the ground around her, ground that was covered in a multiple layer of the Martian pressure-tight web, the kind of web that would have been made only by warm-blooded, oxygen-breathing, water-economy beings who needed protection for their bodies until the full bloom of summer.

"We *like* it here. It's a good place to raise a family, not like Earth the last time I was there. And it couldn't be much better now, right after another war. And we can't leave, even if we wanted to." She flashed him a dazzling smile and patted the ground again.

"The Martians should be showing up any time now. And we aim to thank them."

Ginungagap

MICHAEL SWANWICK

One of the most popular and respected of all the new writers who entered the field in the eighties, Michael Swanwick made his debut in 1980 with two strong and compelling stories, "The Feast of St. Janis" and "Ginungagap," both of which were Nebula Award finalists that year and both selected either for a Best of the Year anthology or for that year's annual Nebula Awards volume—as auspicious a debut as anyone has ever made.

He stayed in the public eye and on major award ballots throughout the rest of the eighties with intense and powerful stories such as "Mummer Kiss," "The Man Who Met Picasso," "Trojan Horse," "Dogfight" (written with William Gibson), "Covenant of Souls," "The Dragon Line," "Snow Angles," "A Midwinter's Tale," and many others, all of which earned him a reputation as one of the most powerful and consistently inventive short-story writers of his generation. Nor has his output of short fiction slackened noticeably in the nineties, in spite of a burgeoning career as a novelist, and recent years have seen the appearance of major Swanwick stories such as "The Edge of the World," "The Changeling's Tale," "Griffin's Egg," "Cold Iron," and "The Dead," which was on the final Hugo ballot in 1997 and on the Nebula final ballot in 1998; he remains one of science fiction's most prolific writers at short lengths. By the end of the nineties, his short work would have won him several *Asimov's* Reader's Awards (including, most recently, one in 1999 for his story "Radiant Doors"), a Sturgeon Award, the World Fantasy Award, and a Hugo Award.

At first, Swanwick's reputation as a novelist lagged behind his reputation as a short-story writer, with his first novel, *In the Drift*—published in 1985 as part of Terry Carr's resurrected Ace Specials line, along with first novels by William Gibson, Kim Stanley Robinson, and Lucius Shepard—largely ignored by the critics and panned by some of them. His second novel, though, the critically-acclaimed *Vacuum Flowers*, caused a stir, and with his third and perhaps best-known novel, *Stations of the Tide*, he established himself firmly as among the vanguard of the hot new novelists of the nineties; *Stations of the Tide* won him a Nebula Award in 1991. His next novel, *The Iron Dragon's Daughter*, a finalist for both the World Fantasy Award *and* the Arthur C. Clarke Award (a unique distinction!), explored new literary territory on the ambiguous borderland of science fiction and fantasy and has been hailed by some critics as the first example of an as-yet-still-nascent subgenre called hard fantasy (sort of a mix between the Dickensian sensibilities of "steampunk," high-tech science fiction, and traditional Tolkienesque fantasy). His most recent novel, *Jack Faust,* a sly reworking of the Faust legend that explores the unexpected impact of technology on society, blurs genre boundaries even more and has garnered rave reviews from nearly every source, from the Washington Post to *Interzone.* He's currently at work on another novel, featuring time travelers and hungry dinosaurs.

During the late eighties, Swanwick was sometimes, unfairly, judged to be derivative of William Gibson, although "Ginungagap" was published in 1980 and Gibson's "Burning Chrome" and *Neuromancer* weren't published until 1982 and 1985, respectively—in fact, science fiction rarely evolves in such a straightforward way, and the resemblances between Swanwick and Gibson are better explained as convergent evolution, by *both* writers being influenced by people such as Samuel R. Delany, Alfred Bester, James Tiptree, Jr., and John Varley than by their influence on each other. (When it's steam engine time, somebody invents the steam engine.) For instance, the vivid and inventive adventure that follows clearly prefigures many of what would later come to be considered cyberpunk tropes, as well as a few *post*cyberpunk tropes, all wrapped up in the same package years before either "Movement" was identified by critics and all wrapped *around* the story of a young explorer who finds that the cost of achievement may ultimately turn out to be more than you wanted to *spend.*

Swanwick's other books include the novella-length *Griffin's Egg,* one of the most brilliant and compelling of modern-day Moon-colony stories. His short fiction has been assembled in *Gravity's Angels* and in a collection of his collaborative short work with other writers, *Slow Dancing through Time.* His most recent books are a collection of critical articles, *The Postmodern Archipelago,* and a new collection, A Geography of Unknown Lands. Swanwick lives in Philadelphia with his wife, Marianne Porter, and their son, Sean.

Abigail checked out of Mother of Mercy and rode the translator web to Toledo Cylinder in Juno Industrial Park. Stars bloomed, dwindled, disappeared five times. It was a long trek, halfway around the sun.

Toledo was one of the older commercial cylinders, now given over almost entirely to bureaucrats, paper pushers, and free-lance professionals. It was not Abigail's favorite place to visit, but she needed work and 3M had already bought out of her contract.

The job broker had dyed his chest hairs blond and his leg hairs red. They clashed wildly with his green *cache-sexe* and turquoise jewelry. His fingers played on a key-out, bringing up an endless flow of career trivia. "Cute trick you played," he said.

Abigail flexed her new arm negligently. It was a good job, but pinker than the rest of her. And weak, of course, but exercise would correct that. "Thanks," she said. She laid the arm underneath one breast and compared the colors. It matched the nipple perfectly. Definitely too pink. "Work outlook any good?"

"Naw," the broker said. A hummingbird flew past his ear, a nearly undetectable parting of the air. "I see here that you applied for the Proxima colony."

"They were full up," Abigail said. "No openings for a gravity bum, hey?"

"I didn't say that," the broker grumbled. "I'll find—Hello! What's this?" Abigail craned her neck, couldn't get a clear look at the screen. "There's a tag on your employment record."

"What's that mean?"

"Let me read." A honeysuckle flower fell on Abigail's hair and she brushed it off impatiently. The broker had an open-air office, framed by hedges and roofed over with a trellis. Sometimes Abigail found the older Belt cylinders a little too lavish for her taste.

"Mmp." The broker looked up. "Bell-Sandia wants to hire you. Indefinite term one-shot contract." He swung the keyout around so she could see. "*Very* nice terms, but that's normal for a high risk contract."

"High risk? From B-S, the Friendly Communications People? What kind of risk?"

The broker scrolled up new material. "There." He tapped the screen with a finger. "The language is involved, but what it boils down to is they're looking for a test passenger for a device they've got that uses black holes for interstellar travel."

"Couldn't work," Abigail said. "The tidal forces—"

"Spare me. Presumably they've found a way around that problem. The question is, are you interested or not?"

Abigail stared up through the trellis at a stream meandering across the curved land overhead. Children were wading in it. She counted to a hundred very slowly, trying to look as if she needed to think it over.

★ ★ ★

Abigail strapped herself into the translation harness and nodded to the technician outside the chamber. The tech touched her console and a light stasis field immobilized Abigail and the air about her while the chamber wall irised open. In a fluid bit of technological sleight of hand, the translator rechanneled her inertia and gifted her with a velocity almost, but not quite, that of the speed of light.

Stars bloomed about her and the sun dwindled. She breathed in deeply and—was in the receiver device. Relativity had cheated her of all but a fraction of the transit time. She shrugged out of harness and frog-kicked her way to the lip station's tug dock.

The tug pilot grinned at her as she entered, then turned his attention to his controls. He was young and wore streaks of brown makeup across his chest and thighs—only slightly darker than his skin. His mesh vest was almost in bad taste, but he wore it well and looked roguish rather than overdressed. Abigail found herself wishing she had more than a *cache-sexe* and nail polish on—some jewelry or makeup, perhaps. She felt drab in comparison.

The star-field wraparound held two inserts routed in by synchronous cameras. Alphanumerics flickered beneath them. One showed her immediate destination, the Bell-Sandia base *Arthur C. Clarke*. It consisted of five wheels, each set inside the other and rotating at slightly differing speeds. The base was done up in red-and-orange supergraphics. Considering its distance from the Belt factories, it was respectably sized.

Abigail latched herself into the passenger seat as the engines cut in. The second insert—

Ginungagap, the only known black hole in the sun's gravity field, was discovered in 2023, a small voice murmured. *Its presence explained the long-puzzling variations in the orbits of the outer planets. The* Arthur C. Clarke *was . . .*

"Is this necessary?" Abigail asked.

"Absolutely," the pilot said. "We abandoned the tourist program a year or so ago, but somehow the rules never caught up. They're very strict about the regs here." He winked at Abigail's dismayed expression. "Hold tight a minute while—" His voice faded as he tinkered with the controls.

. . . established forty years later and communications with the Proxima colony began shortly thereafter. Ginungagap . . .

The voice cut off. She grinned thanks. "Abigail Vanderhoek."

"Cheyney," the pilot said. "You're the gravity bum, right?"

"Yeah."

"I used to be a vacuum bum myself. But I got tired of it, and grabbed the first semipermanent contract that came along."

"I kind of went the other way."

"Probably what I should have done," Cheyney said amiably. "Still, it's a rough road. I picked up three scars along the way." He pointed them out: a thick slash across his abdomen, a red splotch beside one nipple, and a white crescent half obscured by his scalp. "I could've had them cleaned up, but the way I figure, life is just a process of picking up scars and experience. So I kept 'em."

If she had thought he was trying to impress her, Abigail would have slapped him down. But it was clearly just part of an ongoing self-dramatization, possibly justified, probably not. Abigail suspected that, tour trips to Earth excepted, the *Clarke* was as far down a gravity well as Cheyney had ever been. Still he did have an irresponsible, boyish appeal. "Take me past the net?" she asked.

Cheyney looped the tug around the communications net trailing the *Clarke.* Kilometers of steel lace passed beneath them. He pointed out a small dish antenna on the edge and a cluster of antennae on the back. "The loner on the edge transmits into Ginungagap," he said. "The others relay information to and from Mother."

"Mother?"

"That's the traditional name for the *Arthur C. Clarke.*" He swung the tug about with a careless sweep of one arm, and launched into a long and scurrilous story about the origin of the nickname. Abigail laughed, and Cheyney pointed a finger. "There's Ginungagap."

Abigail peered intently. "Where? I don't see a thing." She glanced at the second wraparound insert, which displayed a magnified view of the black hole. It wasn't at all impressive: a red smear against black nothingness. In the star-field it was all but invisible.

"Disappointing, hey? But still dangerous. Even this far out, there's a lot of ionization from the accretion disk."

"Is that why there's a lip station?"

"Yeah. Particle concentration varies, but if the translator was right at the *Clarke,* we'd probably lose about a third of the passengers."

Cheyney dropped Abigail off at Mother's crew lock and looped the tug off and away. Abigail wondered where to go, what to do now.

"You're the gravity bum we're dumping down Ginungagap." The short, solid man was upon her before she saw him. His eyes were intense. His *cache-sexe* was a conservative orange. "I liked the stunt with the arm. It takes a lot of guts to do something like that." He pumped her arm. "I'm Paul Girard. Head of external security. In charge of your training. You play verbal Ping Pong?"

"Why do you ask?" she countered automatically.

"Don't you know?"

"Should I?"

"Do you mean now or later?"

"Will the answer be different later?"

A smile creased Paul's solid face. "You'll do." He took her arm, led her along a sloping corridor. "There isn't much prep time. The dry run is scheduled in two weeks. Things will move pretty quickly after that. You want to start your training now?"

"Do I have a choice?" Abigail asked, amused.

Paul came to a dead stop. "Listen," he said. "Rule number one: don't play games with *me*. You understand? Because I always win. Not sometimes, not usually—always."

Abigail yanked her arm free. "You maneuvered me into that," she said angrily.

"Consider it part of your training." He stared directly into her eyes. "No matter how many gravity wells you've climbed down, you're still the product of a near-space culture—protected, trusting, willing to take things at face value. This is a dangerous attitude, and I want you to realize it. I want you to learn to look behind the mask of events. I want you to grow up. And you will."

Don't be so sure. A small smile quirked Paul's face as if he could read her thoughts. Aloud, Abigail said, "That sounds a little excessive for a trip to Proxima."

"Lesson number two," Paul said: "don't make easy assumptions. You're not going to Proxima." He led her outward-down the ramp to the next wheel, pausing briefly at the juncture to acclimatize to the slower rate of revolution. "You're going to visit spiders." He gestured. "The crew room is this way."

★ ★ ★

The crew room was vast and cavernous, twilight gloomy, Keyouts were set up along winding paths that wandered aimlessly through the work space. Puddles of light fell on each board and operator. Dark-loving foliage was set between the keyouts.

"This is the heart of the beast," Paul said. "The green keyouts handle all Proxima communications—pretty routine by now. But the blue . . ." His eyes glinting oddly, he pointed. Over the keyouts hung silvery screens with harsh, grainy images floating on their surfaces, black-and-white blobs that Abigail could not resolve into recognizable forms.

"Those," Paul said, "are the spiders. We're talking to them in real-time. Response delay is almost all due to machine translation."

In a sudden shift of perception, the blobs became arachnid forms. That mass of black fluttering across the screen was a spider leg and *that* was its thorax. Abigail felt an immediate, primal aversion, and then it was swept away by an all-encompassing wonder.

"Aliens?" she breathed.

"Aliens."

They actually looked no more like spiders than humans looked like apes. The eight legs had an extra joint each, and the mandible configuration was all wrong. But to an untrained eye they would do.

"But this is—How long have you—? Why in God's name are you keeping this a secret?" An indefinable joy arose in Abigail. This opened a universe of possibilities, as if after a lifetime of being confined in a box someone had removed the lid.

"Industrial security," Paul said. "The gadget that'll send you through Ginungagap to their black hole is a spider invention. We're trading optical data for it, but the law won't protect our rights until we've demonstrated its use. We don't want the other corporations cutting in." He nodded toward the nearest black-and-white screen. "As you can see, they're weak on optics."

"I'd love to talk . . ." Abigail's voice trailed off as she realized how little-girl hopeful she sounded.

"I'll arrange an introduction."

There was a rustling to Abigail's side. She turned and saw a large black tomcat with white boots and belly emerge from the bushes. "This is the esteemed head of Alien Communications," Paul said sourly.

Abigail started to laugh, then choked in embarrassment as she realized that he was not speaking of the cat. "Julio Dominguez, section chief for translation," Paul said. "Abigail Vanderhoek, gravity specialist."

The wizened old man smiled professorially. "I assume our resident gadfly has explained how the communications net works, has he not?"

"Well—" Abigail began.

Dominguez clucked his tongue. He wore a yellow *cache-sexe* and matching bow tie, just a little too garish for a man his age. "Quite simple, actually. Escape velocity from a black hole is greater than the speed of light. Therefore, within Ginungagap the speed of light is no longer the limit to the speed of communications."

He paused just long enough for Abigail to look baffled. "Which is just a stuffy way of saying that when we aim a stream of electrons into the boundary of the stationary limit, they emerge elsewhere—out of another black hole. And if we aim them just so"—his voice rose whimsically—"they'll emerge from the black hole of our choosing. The physics is simple. The finesse is in aiming the electrons."

The cat stalked up to Abigail, pushed its forehead against her leg, and mewed insistently. She bent over and picked it up. "But nothing can emerge from a black hole," she objected.

Dominguez chuckled. "Ah, but anything can fall in, hey? A positron falling into Ginungagap in positive time is only an electron falling out in negative time. Which means that a positron falling into a black hole in negative time is actually an electron falling out in positive time—exactly the effect we want. Think of Ginungagap as being the physical manifestation of an equivalence sign in mathematics."

"Oh," Abigail said, feeling very firmly put in her place. White moths flittered along the path. The cat watched, fascinated, while she stroked its head.

"At any rate, the electrons do emerge, and once the data are in, the theory has to follow along meekly."

"Tell me about the spiders," Abigail said before he could continue. The moths were darting up, sideward, down, a chance ballet in three dimensions.

"The *aliens*," Dominguez said, frowning at Paul, "are still a mystery to us. We exchange facts, descriptions, recipes for tools, but the important questions do not lend themselves to our clumsy mathematical codes. Do they know of love? Do they appreciate beauty? Do they believe in God, hey?"

"Do they want to eat us?" Paul threw in.

"Don't be ridiculous," Dominguez snapped. "Of course they don't."

The moths parted when they came to Abigail. Two went to either side; one flew over her shoulder. The cat batted at it with one paw. "The cat's name is Garble," Paul said. "The kids in Bio cloned him up."

Dominguez opened his mouth, closed it again.

Abigail scratched Garble under the chin. He arched his neck and purred all but noiselessly. "With your permission," Paul said. He stepped over to a keyout and waved its operator aside.

"Technically you're supposed to speak a convenience language, but if you keep it simple and non-idiomatic, there shouldn't be any difficulty." He touched the keyout. "Ritual greetings, spider." There was a blank pause. Then the spider moved, a hairy leg flickering across the screen.

"Hello, human."

"Introductions: Abigail Vanderhoek. She is our representative. She will ride the spinner." Another pause. More leg waving.

"Hello, Abigail Vanderhoek. Transition of vacuum garble resting garble commercial benefits garble still point in space."

"Tricky translation," Paul said. He signed to Abigail to take over.

Abigail hesitated, then said, "Will you come to visit us? The way we will visit you?"

"No, you see—" Dominguez began, but Paul waved him to silence.

"No, Abigail Vanderhoek. We are sulfur-based life."

"I do not understand."

"You can garble black hole through garble spinner because you are carbon-based life. Carbon forms chains easily but sulfur combines in lattices or rosettes. Our garble simple form garble. Sometimes sulfur forms short chains."

"We'll explain later," Paul said. "Go on, you're doing fine."

Abigail hesitated again. What do you say to a spider, anyway? Finally, she asked, "Do you want to eat us?"

"Oh, Christ, get her off that thing," Dominguez said, reaching for the keyout. Paul blocked his arm. "No," he said. "I want to hear this."

Several of the spider legs wove intricate patterns. "The question is false. Sulfur-based life derives no benefit from eating carbon-based life."

"You see," Dominguez said.

"But if it were possible," Abigail persisted. "If you could eat us and derive benefit. Would you?"

"Yes, Abigail Vanderhoek. With great pleasure."

Dominguez pushed her aside. "We're terribly sorry," he said to the alien. "This is a horrible, horrible misunderstanding. You!" he shouted to the operator. "Get back on and clear this mess up."

Paul was grinning wickedly. "Come," he said to Abigail. "We've accomplished enough here for one day."

As they started to walk away, Garble twisted in Abigail's arms and leaped free. He hit the floor on all fours and disappeared into the greenery. "Would they really eat us?" Abigail asked. Then amended it to, "Does that mean they're hostile?"

Paul shrugged. "Maybe they thought we'd be insulted if they *didn't* offer to eat us." He led her to her quarters. "Tomorrow we start training for real. In the meantime, you might make up a list of all the ways the spiders could hurt us if we set up transportation and they are hostile. Then another list of all the reasons we shouldn't trust them." He paused. "I've done it myself. You'll find that the lists get rather extensive."

Abigail's quarters weren't flashy, but they fit her well. A full star field was routed to the walls, floor, and ceiling, only partially obscured by a trellis inner frame that supported fox-grape vines. Somebody had done research into her tastes.

"Hi." The cheery greeting startled her. She whirled, saw that her hammock was occupied.

Cheyney sat up, swung his legs over the edge of the hammock, causing it to rock lightly. "Come on in." He touched an invisible control and the star field blue-shifted down to a deep, erotic purple.

"Just what do you think you're doing here?" Abigail asked.

"I had a few hours free," Cheyney said, "so I thought I'd drop by and seduce you."

"Well, Cheyney, I appreciate your honesty," Abigail said. "So I won't say no."

"Thank you."

"I'll say maybe some other time. Now get lost. I'm tired."

"Okay." Cheyney hopped down, walked jauntily to the door. He paused. "You said 'Later,' right?"

"I said *maybe* later."

"Later. Gotcha." He winked and was gone.

Abigail threw herself into the hammock, red-shifted the star field until the universe was a sparse smattering of dying embers. Annoying creature! There was no hope for anything more than the most superficial of relationships with him. She closed her eyes, smiled. Fortunately, she wasn't currently in the market for a serious relationship.

She slept.

She was falling . . .

Abigail had landed the ship an easy walk from 3M's robot laboratory. The lab's geodesic dome echoed white clouds to the north, where Nix Olympus peeked over the horizon. Otherwise all—land, sky, rocks—was standard issue Martian orange. She had clambered to the ground and shrugged on the supply backpack.

Resupplying 3M-RL stations was a gut contract, easy but dull. So perhaps she was less cautious than usual going down the steep, rock-strewn hillside, or perhaps the rock would have turned under her no matter how carefully she placed her feet. Her ankle twisted and she lurched sideways, but the backpack had shifted her center of gravity too much for her to be able to recover.

Arms windmilling, she fell.

The rock slide carried her downhill in a panicky flurry of dust and motion, tearing her flesh and splintering her bones. But before she could feel pain, her suit shot her full of a nerve synesthetic, translating sensation into colors—reds, russets, and browns, with staccato yellow spikes when a rock smashed into her ribs. So that she fell in a whirling rainbow of glorious light.

She came to rest in a burst of orange. The rocks were settling about her. A spume of dust drifted away, out toward the distant red horizon. A large, jagged slab of stone slid by, gently shearing off her backpack. Tools, supplies, airpacks flew up and softly rained down.

A spanner as long as her arm slammed down inches from Abigail's helmet. She flinched, and suddenly events became real. She kicked her legs and sand and dust fountained up. Drawing her feet under her body—the one ankle bright gold—she started to stand.

And was jerked to the ground by a sudden tug on one arm. Even as she turned her head, she became aware of a deep purple sensation in her left hand. It was pinioned to a rock not quite large enough to stake a claim to. There was no color in the fingers.

"Cute," she muttered. She tugged at the arm, pushed at the rock. Nothing budged.

Abigail nudged the radio switch with her chin. "Grounder to Lip Station," she said. She hesitated, feeling foolish, then said, "Mayday. Repeat, Mayday. Could you guys send a rescue party down for me?"

There was no reply. With a sick green feeling in the pit of her stomach, Abigail reached a gloved hand around the back of her helmet. She touched something jagged, a sensation of mottled rust, the broken remains of her radio.

"I think I'm in trouble." She said it aloud and listened to the sound of it. Flat, unemotional—probably true. But nothing to get panicky about.

She took quick stock of what she had to work with. One intact suit and helmet. One spanner. A worldful of rocks, many close at hand. Enough air for—she checked the helmet readout—almost an hour. Assuming the lip station ran its checks on schedule and was fast on the uptake, she had almost half the air she needed.

Most of the backpack's contents were scattered too far away to reach. One rectangular gaspack, however, had landed nearby. She reached for it but could not touch it, squinted but could not read the label on its nozzle. It was almost certainly liquid gas—either nitrogen or oxygen—for the robot lab. There was a slim chance it was the spare airpack. If it was, she might live to be rescued.

Abigail studied the landscape carefully, but there was nothing more. "Okay, then, it's an airpack." She reached as far as her tethered arm would allow. The gaspack remained a tantalizing centimeter out of reach.

For an instant she was stymied. Then, feeling like an idiot, she grabbed the spanner. She hooked it over the gaspack. Felt the gaspack move grudgingly. Slowly nudged it toward herself.

By the time Abigail could drop the spanner and draw in the gaspack, her good arm was blue with fatigue. Sweat running down her face, she juggled the gaspack to read its nozzle markings.

It was liquid oxygen—useless. She could hook it to her suit and feed in the contents, but the first breath would freeze her lungs. She released the gaspack and lay back, staring vacantly at the sky.

Up there was civilization: tens of thousands of human stations strung together by webs of communication and transportation. Messages flowed endlessly on laser cables. Translators borrowed and lent momentum, moving streams of travelers and cargo at almost (but not quite) the speed of light. A starship was being readied to carry a third load of colonists to Proxima. Up there, free from gravity's relentless clutch, people lived in luxury and ease. Here, however . . .

"I'm going to die." She said it softly and was filled with wondering awe. Because it was true. She was going to die.

Death was a black wall. It lay before her, extending to infinity in all directions, smooth and featureless and mysterious. She could almost reach out an arm and touch it. Soon she would come up against it and, if anything lay beyond, pass through. Soon, very soon, she would *know*.

She touched the seal to her helmet. It felt gray—smooth and inviting. Her fingers moved absently, tracing the seal about her neck. With sudden horror, Abigail realized that she was thinking about undoing it, releasing her air, throwing away the little time she had left. . . .

She shuddered. With sudden resolve, she reached out and unsealed the shoulder seam of her captive arm.

The seal clamped down, automatically cutting off air loss. The flesh of her damaged arm was exposed to the raw Martian atmosphere. Abigail took up the gaspack and cradled it in the pit of her good arm. Awkwardly, she opened the nozzle with the spanner.

She sprayed the exposed arm with liquid oxygen for over a minute before she was certain it had frozen solid. Then she dropped the gaspack, picked up the spanner, and swung.

Her arm shattered into a thousand fragments.

She stood up.

Abigail awoke, tense and sweaty. She blue-shifted the walls up to normal light, and sat up. After a few minutes of clearing her head, she set the walls to cycle from red to blue in a rhythm matching her normal pulse. Eventually the womb-cycle lulled her back to sleep.

"Not even close," Paul said. He ran the tape backward, froze it on a still shot of the spider twisting two legs about each other. "That's the morpheme for 'extreme disgust,' remember. It's easy to pick out, and the language kids say that any statement with this gesture should be reversed in meaning. Irony, see? So when the spider says that the strong should protect the weak, it means—"

"How long have we been doing this?"

"Practically forever," Paul said cheerfully. "You want to call it a day?"

"Only if it won't hurt my standing."

"Hah! Very good." He switched off the keyout. "Nicely thought out. You're absolutely right; it would have. However, as reward for realizing this, you can take off early *without* it being noted on your record."

"Thank you," Abigail said sourly.

Like most large installations, the *Clarke* had a dozen or so smaller structures tagging along after it in minimum maintenance orbits. When Abigail discovered that these included a small wheel gymnasium, she had taken to putting in an hour's exercise after each training shift. Today she put in two.

The first hour she spent shadowboxing and practicing *savate* in heavy-gee to work up a sweat. The second hour she spent in the axis room, performing free-fall gymnastics. After the first workout, it made her feel light and nimble and good about her body.

She returned from the wheel gym sweaty and cheerful to find Cheyney in her hammock again: "Cheyney," she said, "this is not the first time I've had to kick you out of there. Or even the third, for that matter."

Cheyney held his palms up in mock protest. "Hey, no," he said. "Nothing like that today. I just came by to watch the raft debate with you."

Abigail felt pleasantly weary, decidedly uncerebral. "Paul said something about it, but . . ."

"Turn it on, then. You don't want to miss it." Cheyney touched her wall, and a cluster of images sprang to life at the far end of the room.

"Just what is a raft debate anyway?" Abigail asked, giving in gracefully. She hoisted herself onto the hammock, sat beside him. They rocked gently for a moment.

"There's this raft, see? It's adrift and powerless and there's only enough oxygen on board to keep one person alive until rescue. Only there are three on board—two humans and a spider."

"Do spiders breathe oxygen?"

"It doesn't matter. This is a hypothetical situation." Two thirds of the image area was taken up by Dominguez and Paul, quietly waiting for the debate to begin. The remainder showed a flat spider image.

"Okay, what then?"

"They argue over who gets to survive. Dominguez argues that he should, since he's human and human culture is superior to spider culture. The spider argues for itself and its culture." He put an arm around her waist. "You smell nice."

"Thank you." She ignored the arm. "What does Paul argue?"

"He's the devil's advocate. He argues that no one deserves to live and they should dump the oxygen."

"Paul would enjoy that role," Abigail said. Then, "What's the point to this debate?"

"It's an entertainment. There isn't supposed to be a point."

Abigail doubted it was that simple. The debate could reveal a good deal about the spiders and how they thought, once the language types were done with it. Conversely, the spiders would doubtless be studying the human responses. *This could be interesting*, she thought. Cheyney was stroking her side now, lightly but with great authority. She postponed reaction, not sure whether she liked it or not.

Louise Chang, a vaguely high-placed administrator, blossomed in the center of the image cluster. "Welcome," she said, and explained the rules of the debate. "The winner will be decided by acclaim," she said, "with half the vote being human and half alien. Please remember not to base your vote on racial chauvinism, but on the strengths of the arguments and how well they are presented." Cheyney's hand brushed casually across her nipples; they stiffened. The hand lingered. "The debate will begin with the gentleman representing the aliens presenting his thesis."

The image flickered as the spider waved several legs. "Thank you, Ms. Chairman. I argue that I should survive. My culture is superior because of our technological advancement. Three examples. Humans have used translation travel only briefly, yet we have used it for sixteens of garble. Our black hole technology is superior. And our garble has garble for the duration of our society."

"Thank you. The gentleman representing humanity?"

"Thank you, Ms. Chairman." Dominguez adjusted an armlet. Cheyney leaned back and let Abigail rest against him. Her head fit comfortably against his shoulder. "My argument is that technology is neither the sole nor the most important measure of a culture. By these standards dolphins would be considered brute animals. The aesthetic considerations—the arts, theology, and the tradition of philosophy—are of greater import. As I shall endeavor to prove."

"He's chosen the wrong tactic," Cheyney whispered in Abigail's ear. "That must have come across as pure garble to the spiders."

"Thank you. Mr. Girard?"

Paul's image expanded. He theatrically swigged from a small flask and hoisted it high in the air. "Alcohol! There's the greatest achievement of the human race!" Abigail snorted. Cheyney laughed out loud. "But I hold that neither Mr. Dominguez nor the distinguished spider deserves to live, because of the disregard both cultures have for sentient life." Abigail looked at Cheyney, who shrugged. "As I shall endeavor to prove." His image dwindled.

Chang said, "The arguments will now proceed, beginning with the distinguished alien."

The spider and then Dominguez ran through their arguments, and to Abigail they seemed markedly lackluster. She didn't give them her full attention, because Cheyney's hands were moving most interestingly across unexpected parts of her body. He might not be too bright, but he was certainly good at some things. She nuzzled her face into his neck, gave him a small peck, returned her attention to the debate.

Paul blossomed again. He juggled something in his palm, held his hand open to reveal three ball bearings. "When I was a kid I used to short out the school module and sneak up to the axis room to play marbles." Abigail smiled, remembering similar stunts she had played. "For the sake of those of us who are spiders, I'll explain that marbles is a game played in free-fall for the purpose of developing coordination and spatial perception. You make a six-armed star of marbles in the center . . ."

One of the bearings fell from his hand, bounced noisily, and disappeared as it rolled out of camera range. "Well, obviously it can't be played here. But the point is that when you shoot the marble just right, it hits the end of one arm and its kinetic energy is transferred from marble to marble along that arm. So that the shooter stops and the marble at the far end of the arm flies away." Cheyney was stroking her absently now, engrossed in the argument.

"Now, we plan to send a courier into Ginungagap and out the spiders' black hole. At least, that's what we say we're going to do.

"But what exits from a black hole is not necessarily the same as what went into its partner hole. We throw an electron into Ginungagap and another one pops out elsewhere. It's identical. It's a direct causal relationship. But it's like the marbles—they're identical to each other and have the same kinetic force. It's simply not the same electron."

Cheyney's hand was still, motionless. Abigail prodded him gently, touching his inner thigh. "Anyone who's interested can see the equations. Now, when we send messages, this doesn't matter. The message is important, not the medium. However, when we send a human being in . . . what emerges from the other hole will be cell for cell, gene for gene, atom for atom identical. *But it will not be the same person*." He paused a beat, smiled.

"I submit, then, that this is murder. And further, that by conspiring to commit murder, both the spider and human races display absolute disregard for intelligent life. In short, no one on the raft deserves to live. And I rest my case."

"Mr. Girard!" Dominguez objected, even before his image was restored to full size. "The simplest mathematical proof is an identity: that A equals A. Are you trying to deny this?"

Paul held up the two ball bearings he had left. "These marbles are identical too. But they are not the same marble."

"We know the phenomenon you speak of," the spider said. "It is as if garble the black hole bulges out simultaneously. There is no violation of continuity. The two entities are the same. There is no death."

Abigail pulled Cheyney down, so that they were both lying on their sides, still able to watch the images. "So long as you happen to be the second marble and not the first," Paul said. Abigail tentatively licked Cheyney's ear.

"He's right," Cheyney murmured.

"No he's not," Abigail retorted. She bit his earlobe.

"You mean that?"

"Of course I mean that. He's confusing semantics with reality." She engrossed herself in a study of the back of his neck.

"Okay."

Abigail suddenly sensed that she was missing something. "Why do you ask?" She struggled into a sitting position. Cheyney followed.

"No particular reason." Cheyney's hands began touching her again. But Abigail was sure something had been slipped past her.

They caressed each other lightly while the debate dragged to an end. Not paying much attention, Abigail voted for Dominguez, and Cheyney voted for Paul. As a result of a nearly undivided spider vote, the spider won. "I told you Dominguez was taking the wrong approach," Cheyney said. He hopped off the hammock. "Look, I've got to see somebody about something. I'll be right back."

"You're not leaving *now*?" Abigail protested, dumbfounded. The door irised shut.

Angry and hurt, she leaped down, determined to follow him. She couldn't remember ever feeling so insulted.

Cheyney didn't try to be evasive; it apparently did not occur to him that she might follow. Abigail stalked him down a corridor, up an in-ramp, and to a door that irised open for him. She recognized that door.

Thoughtfully she squatted on her heels behind an untrimmed boxwood and waited. A minute later, Garble wandered by, saw her, and demanded attention. "Scat!" she hissed. He butted his head against her knee. "Then be quiet, at least." She scooped him up. His expression was smug.

The door irised open and Cheyney exited, whistling. Abigail waited until he was gone, stood, went to the door, and entered. Fish darted between long fronds under a transparent floor. It was an austere room, almost featureless. Abigail looked, but did not see a hammock.

"So Cheyney's working for you now," she said coldly. Paul looked up from a corner keyout.

"As a matter of fact, I've just signed him to permanent contract in the crew room. He's bright enough. A bit green. Ought to do well."

"Then you admit that you put him up to grilling me about your puerile argument in the debate?" Garble struggled in her arms. She juggled him into a more comfortable position. "And that you staged the argument for my benefit in the first place?"

"Ah," Paul said. "I knew the training was going somewhere. You've become very wary in an extremely short time."

"Don't evade the question."

"I needed your honest reaction," Paul said. "Not the answer you would have given me, knowing your chances of crossing Ginungagap rode on it."

Garble made an angry noise. "You tell him, Garble!" she said. "That goes double for me." She stepped out the door. "You lost the debate," she snapped.

Long after the door had irised shut, she could feel Paul's amused smile burning into her back.

Two days after she returned to kick Cheyney out of her hammock for the final time, Abigail was called to the crew room. "Dry run," Paul said. "Attendance is mandatory." And cut off.

The crew room was crowded with technicians, triple the number of keyouts. Small knots of them clustered before the screens, watching. Paul waved her to him.

"There," he motioned to one screen. "That's Clotho—the platform we built for the transmission device. It's a hundred kilometers off. I wanted more, but Dominguez overruled me. The device that'll unravel you and dump you down Ginungagap is that doohickey in the center." He tapped a keyout and the platform zoomed up to fill the screen. It was covered by a clear, transparent bubble. Inside, a spacesuited figure was placing something into a machine that looked like nothing so much as a giant armor-clad clamshell. Abigail looked, blinked, looked again.

"That's Garble," she said indignantly.

"Complain to Dominguez. I wanted a baboon."

The clamshell device closed. The space-suited tech left in his tug, and alpha-numerics flickered, indicating the device was in operation. As they watched, the spider-designed machinery immobilized Garble, transformed his molecules into one long continuous polymer chain, and spun it out an invisible opening at near light speed. The water in his body was separated out, piped away, and preserved. The electrolyte balances were recorded and simultaneously transmitted in a parallel stream of electrons. It would reach the spider receiver along with the lead end of the cat-polymer, to be used in the reconstruction.

Thirty seconds passed. Now Garble was only partially in Clotho. The polymer chain, invisible and incredibly long, was passing into Ginungagap. On the far side the spiders were beginning to knit it up.

If all was going well . . .

Ninety-two seconds after they flashed on, the alphanumerics stopped twinkling on the screen. Garble was gone from Clotho. The clamshell opened and the remote cameras showed it to be empty. A cheer arose.

Somebody boosted Dominguez atop a keyout. Intercom cameras swiveled to follow. He wavered fractionally, said "My friends," and launched into a speech. Abigail didn't listen.

Paul's hand fell on her shoulder. It was the first time he had touched her since their initial meeting. "He's only a scientist," he said. "He had no idea how close you are to that cat."

"Look, I *asked* to go. I knew the risks. But Garble's just an animal; he wasn't given the choice."

Paul groped for words. "In a way, this is what your training has been about— the reason you're going across instead of someone like Dominguez. He projects his own reactions onto other people. If—"

Then, seeing that she wasn't listening, he said, "Anyway, you'll have a cat to play with in a few hours. They're only keeping him long enough to test out the life systems."

There was a festive air to the second gathering. The spiders reported that Garble had translated flawlessly. A brief visual display showed him stalking about Clotho's sister platform, irritable but apparently unharmed.

"There," somebody said. The screen indicated that the receiver net had taken in the running end of the cat's polymer chain. They waited a minute and a half and the operation was over.

It was like a conjuring trick: the clamshell closed on emptiness. Water was piped in. Then it opened and Garble floated over its center, quietly licking one paw.

Abigail smiled at the homeliness of it. "Welcome back, Garble," she said quietly. "I'll get the guys in Bio to brew up some cream for you."

Paul's eyes flicked in her direction. They lingered for no time at all, long enough to file away another datum for future use, and then his attention was elsewhere. She waited until his back was turned and stuck out her tongue at him.

The tub docked with Clotho and a technician floated in. She removed her helmet self-consciously, aware of her audience. One hand extended, she bobbed toward the cat, calling softly.

"Get that jerk on the line," Paul snapped. "I want her helmet back on. That's sloppy. That's real—"

And in that instant Garble sprang.

Garble was a black-and-white streak that flashed past the astonished tech, through the air lock, and into the open tug. The cat pounced on the pilot panel. Its forelegs hit the controls. The hatch slammed shut, and the tug's motors burst into life.

Crew room techs grabbed wildly at their keyouts. The tech on Clotho frantically tried to fit her helmet back on. And the tug took off, blasting away half the protective dome and all the platform's air.

The screens showed a dozen different scenes, lenses shifting from close to distant and back. "Cheyney," Paul said quietly. Dominguez was frozen, looking bewildered. "Take it out."

"It's coming right at us!" somebody shouted.

Cheyney's fingers flicked: rap-tap-rap.

A bright nuclear flower blossomed.

There was silence, dead and complete, in the crew room. *I'm missing something*, Abigail thought. *We just blew up 5 percent of our tug fleet to kill a cat.*

"*Pull* that transmitter!" Paul strode through the crew room, scattering orders. "Nothing goes out! You, you, and you"—he yanked techs away from their keyouts—"*off* those things. I want the whole goddamned net shut *down*."

"Paul, . . ." an operator said.

"Keep on receiving." He didn't bother to look. "Whatever they want to send. Dump it all in storage and don't merge any of it with our data until we've gone over it."

Alone and useless in the center of the room, Dominguez stuttered, "What—what happened?"

"You blind idiot!" Paul turned on him viciously. "Your precious aliens have just made their first hostile move. The cat that came back was nothing like the one we sent. They made changes. They retransmitted it with instructions wet-wired into its brain."

"But why would they want to steal a tug?"

"*We don't know!*" Paul roared. "Get that through your head. We don't know their motives and we don't know how they think. But we would have known a lot more about their intentions than we wanted if I hadn't rigged that tug with an abort device."

"You didn't—" Dominguez began. He thought better of the statement.

"—have the authority to rig that device," Paul finished for him. "That's right. I didn't." His voice was heavy with sarcasm.

Dominguez seemed to shrivel. He stared bleakly, blankly, about him, then turned and left, slightly hunched over. Thoroughly discredited in front of the people who worked for him.

That was cold, Abigail thought. She marveled at Paul's cruelty. Not for an instant did she believe that the anger in his voice was real, that he was capable of losing control.

Which meant that in the midst of confusion and stress, Paul had found time to make a swift play for more power. To Abigail's newly suspicious eye, it looked like a successful one, too.

For five days Paul held the net shut by sheer willpower and force of personality. Information came in but did not go out. Bell-Sandia administration was not behind him; too much time and money had been sunk into Clotho to abandon the project. But Paul had the support of the tech crew, and he knew how to use it.

"Nothing as big as Bell-Sandia runs on popularity," Paul explained. "But I've got enough sympathy from above, and enough hesitation and official cowardice to keep this place shut down long enough to get a message across."

The incoming information flow fluctuated wildly, shifting from subject to subject. Data sequences were dropped halfway through and incomplete. Nonsense came in. The spiders were shifting through strategies in search of the key that would reopen the net.

"When they start repeating themselves," Paul said, "we can assume they understand the threat."

"But we *wouldn't* shut the net down permanently," Abigail pointed out.

Paul shrugged. "So it's a bluff."

They were sharing an after-shift drink in a fifth-level bar. Small red lizards scuttled about the rock wall behind the bartender. "And if your bluff doesn't work?" Abigail asked. "If it's all for nothing—what then?"

Paul's shoulders sagged, a minute shifting of tensions. "Then we trust in the goodwill of the spiders," he said. "We let them call the shots. And they will treat us benevolently or not, depending. In either case," his voice became dark, "I'll have played a lot of games and manipulated a lot of people for no reason at all." He took her hand. "If that happens, I'd like to apologize." His grip was tight, his knuckles pale.

That night Abigail dreamed she was falling.

Light rainbowed all about her, in a violent splintering of bone and tearing of flesh. She flung out an arm and it bounced on something warm and yielding.

"Abigail."

She twisted and tumbled and something smashed into her ribs. Bright spikes of yellow darted up.

"Abigail!" Someone was shaking her, speaking loudly into her face. The rocks and sky went gray, were overlaid by unresolved images. Her eyelids struggled apart, fell together, opened.

"Oh," she said.

Paul rocked back on his heels. Fish darted about in the water beneath him. "There now," he said. Blue-green lights shifted gently underwater, moving in long, slow arcs. "Dream over?"

Abigail shivered, clutched his arm, let go of it almost immediately. She nodded.

"Good. Tell me about it."

"I—" Abigail began. "Are you asking me as a human being or in your official capacity?"

"I don't make that distinction."

She stretched out a leg and scratched her big toe, to gain time to think. She really didn't have any appropriate thoughts. "Okay," she said, and told him the entire dream.

Paul listened intently, rubbed a thumb across his chin thoughtfully when she was done. "We hired you on the basis of that incident, you know," he said. "Coolness under stress. Weak body image. There were a lot of gravity bums to choose from. But I figured you were just a hair tougher, a little bit grittier."

"What are you trying to tell me? That I'm replaceable?"

Paul shrugged. "Everybody's replaceable. I just wanted to be sure you knew that you could back out if you want. It wouldn't wreck our project."

"I don't want to back out." Abigail chose her words carefully, spoke them slowly, to avoid giving vent to the anger she felt building up inside. "Look, I've been on the gravity circuit for ten years. I've been everywhere in the system there is to go. Did you know that there are less than two thousand people alive who've set foot on Mercury *and* Pluto? We've got a little club; we get together once a year." Seaweed shifted about her; reflections of the floor lights formed nebulous swimming shapes on the walls. "I've spent my entire life going around and around and around the sun, and never really getting anywhere. I want to travel, and there's nowhere left for me to go. So you offer me a way out and then ask if I want to back down. Like hell I do!"

"Why don't you believe that going through Ginungagap is death?" Paul asked quietly. She looked into his eyes, saw cool calculations going on behind them. It frightened her, almost. He was measuring her, passing judgment warping events into long logical chains that did not take human factors into account. He was an alien presence.

"It's—common sense, is all. I'll be the same when I exit as when I go in. There'll be no difference, not an atom's worth, not a scintilla."

"The *substance* will be different. Every atom will be different. Not a single electron in your body will be the same one you have now."

"Well, how does that differ so much from normal life?" Abigail demanded. "All our bodies are in constant flux. Molecules come and go. Bit by bit, we're replaced. Does that make us different people from moment to moment? 'All that is body is as coursing vapors,' right?"

Paul's eyes narrowed. "Marcus Aurelius. Your quotation isn't complete, though. It goes on: 'All that is of the soul is dreams and vapors.' "

"What's that supposed to mean?"

"It means that the quotation doesn't say what you claimed it did. If you care to read it literally, it argues the opposite of what you're saying."

"Still, you can't have it both ways. Either the me that comes out of the spider black hole is the same as the one who went in, or I'm not the same person as I was an instant ago."

"I'd argue differently," Paul said. "But no matter. Let's go back to sleep."

He held out a hand, but Abigail felt no inclination to accept it. "Does this mean I've passed your test?"

Paul closed his eyes, stretched a little. "You're still reasonably afraid of dying, and you don't believe that you will," he said. "Yeah. You pass."

"Thanks a heap," Abigail said. They slept, not touching, for the rest of the night.

Three days later Abigail woke up, and Paul was gone. She touched the wall and spoke his name. A recording appeared. "Dominguez has been called up to Administration," it said. Paul appeared slightly distracted; he had not looked directly into the recorder and his image avoided Abigail's eyes. "I'm going to reopen the net before he returns. It's best we beat him to the punch." The recording clicked off.

Abigail routed an intercom call through to the crew room. A small chime notified him of her call, and he waved a hand in combined greeting and direction to remain silent. He was hunched over a keyout. The screen above it came to life.

"Ritual greetings, spider," he said.

"Hello, human. We wish to pursue our previous inquiry: the meaning of the term 'art' which was used by the human Dominguez six-sixteenths of the way through his major presentation."

"This is a difficult question. To understand a definition of art, you must first know the philosophy of aesthetics. This is a comprehensive field of knowledge comparable to the study of perception. In many ways it is related."

"What is the trade value of this field of knowledge?"

Dominguez appeared, looking upset. He opened his mouth, and Paul touched a finger to his own lips, nodding his head toward the screen.

"Significant. Our society considers art and science as being of roughly equal value."

"We will consider what to offer in exchange."

"Good. We also have a question for you. Please wait while we select the phrasing." He cut the translation lines, turned to Dominguez. "Looks like your raft gambit paid off. Though I'm surprised they bit at that particular piece of bait."

Dominguez looked weary. "Did they mention the incident with the cat?"

"No, nor the communications blackout."

The old man sighed. "I always felt close to the aliens," he said. "Now they seem—cold, inhuman." He attempted a chuckle. "That was almost a pun, wasn't it?"

"In a human, we'd call it a professional attitude. Don't let it spoil your accomplishment," Paul said. "This could be as big as optics." He opened the communications line again. "Our question is now phrased." Abigail noted he had not told Dominguez of her presence.

"Please go ahead."

"Why did you alter our test animal?"

Much leg waving. "We improved the ratios garble centers of perception garble wetware garble making the animal twelve-sixteenths as intelligent as a human. We thought you would be pleased."

"We were not. Why did the test animal behave in a hostile manner toward us?"

The spider's legs jerked quickly and it disappeared from the screen. Like an echo, the machine said, "Please wait."

Abigail watched Dominguez throw Paul a puzzled look. In the background, a man with a leather sack looped over one shoulder was walking slowly along the twisty access path. His hand dipped into the sack, came out, sprinkled fireflies among the greenery. Dipped in, came out again. Even in the midst of crisis the trivia of day-to-day existence went on.

The spider reappeared, accompanied by two of its own kind. Their legs interlaced and retreated rapidly, a visual pantomime of an excited conversation. Finally one of their number addressed the screen.

"We have discussed the matter."

"So I see."

"It is our conclusion that the experience of translation through Ginungagap had a negative effect on the test animal. This was not anticipated. It is new knowledge. We know little of the psychology of carbon-based life."

"You're saying the test animal was driven mad?"

"Key word did not translate. We assume understanding. Steps must be taken to prevent a recurrence of this damage. Can you do this?"

Paul said nothing.

"Is this the reason why communications were interrupted?"

No reply.

"There is a cultural gap. Can you clarify?"

"Thank you for your cooperation," Paul said, and switched the screen off. "You can set your people to work," he told Dominguez. "No reason why they should answer the last few questions, though."

"Were they telling the truth?" Dominguez asked wonderingly.

"Probably not. But at least now they'll think twice before trying to jerk us around again." He winked at Abigail, and she switched off the intercom.

They re-ran the test using a baboon shipped out from the Belt Zoological Gardens. Abigail watched it arrive from the lip station, crated and snarling.

"They're a lot stronger than we are," Paul said. "Very agile. If the spiders want to try any more tricks, we couldn't offer them better bait."

The test went smooth as silk. The baboon was shot through Ginungagap, held by the spiders for several hours, and returned. Exhaustive testing showed no tampering with the animal.

Abigail asked how accurate the tests were. Paul hooked his hands behind his back. "We're returning the baboon to the Belt. We wouldn't do that if we had any doubts. But—" He raised an eyebrow, asking Abigail to finish the thought.

"But if they're really hostile, they won't underestimate us twice. They'll wait for a human to tamper with."

Paul nodded.

★ ★ ★

The night before Abigail's send-off they made love. It was a frenzied and desperate act, performed wordlessly and without tenderness. Afterward they lay together, Abigail idly playing with Paul's curls.

"Gail . . ." His head was hidden in her shoulder; she couldn't see his face. His voice was muffled.

"Mmmm?"

"Don't go."

She wanted to cry. Because as soon as he said it, she knew it was another test, the final one. And she also knew that Paul wanted her to fail it. That he honestly believed transversing Ginungagap would kill her, and that the woman who emerged from the spiders' black hole would not be herself.

His eyes were shut; she could tell by the creases in his forehead. He knew what her answer was. There was no way he could avoid knowing.

Abigail sensed that this was as close to a declaration of emotion as Paul was capable of. She felt how he despised himself for using his real emotions as yet another test, and how he could not even pretend to himself that there were circumstances under which he would *not* so test her. *This must be how it feels to think as he does,* she thought. *To constantly scrabble after every last implication, like eternally picking at a scab.*

"Oh, Paul," she said.

He wrenched about, turning his back to her. "Sometimes I wish"—his hands rose in front of his face like claws; they moved toward his eyes, closed into fists— "that for just ten goddamned minutes I could turn my mind off." His voice was bitter.

Abigail huddled against him, looped a hand over his side and onto his chest. "Hush," she said.

The tug backed away from Clotho, dwindling until it was one of a ring of bright sparks pacing the platform. Mother was a point source lost in the star field. Abigail shivered, pulled off her arm bands and shoved them into a storage sack. She reached for her *cache-sexe*, hesitated.

The hell with it, she thought. *It's nothing they haven't seen before.* She shucked it off, stood naked. Gooseflesh rose on the backs of her legs. She swam to the transmittal device, feeling awkward under the distant watching eyes.

Abigail groped into the clamshell. "Go," she said.

The metal closed about her seamlessly, encasing her in darkness. She floated in a lotus position, bobbing slightly.

A light, gripping field touched her, stilling her motion. On cue, hypnotic commands took hold in her brain. Her breathing became shallow; her heart slowed. She felt her body ease into stasis. The final command took hold.

Abigail weighed 50 keys. Even though the water in her body would not be transmitted, the polymer chain she was to be transformed into would be 275 kilometers long. It would take 15 minutes and 17 seconds to unravel at light speed, negligibly longer at translation speed. She would still be sitting in Clotho when the spiders began knitting her up.

It was possible that Garble had gone mad from a relatively swift transit. Paul doubted it, but he wasn't taking any chances. To protect Abigail's sanity, the meds had wet-wired a travel fantasy into her brain. It would blind her to external reality while she traveled.

She was an eagle. Great feathered wings extended out from her shoulders. Clotho was gone, leaving her alone in space. Her skin was red and leathery, her breasts hard and unyielding. Feathers covered her thighs, giving way at the knees to talons.

She moved her wings, bouncing lightly against the thin solar wind swirling down into Ginungagap. The vacuum felt like absolute freedom. She screamed a predator's exultant shrill. Nothing enclosed her; she was free of restrictions forever.

Below her lay Ginungagap, the primal chasm, and invisible challenge marked by a red smudge of glowing gases. It was inchoate madness, a gibbering, impersonal force that wanted to draw her in, to crush her in its embrace. Its hunger was fierce and insatiable.

Abigail held her place briefly, effortlessly. Then she folded her wings and dove.

A rain of X rays stung through her, the scattering of Ginungagap's accretion disk. They were molten iron passing through a ghost. Shrieking defiance, she attacked, scattering sparks in her wake.

Ginungagap grew, swelled until it swallowed up her vision. It was purest black, unseeable, unknowable, a thing of madness. It was Enemy.

A distant objective part of her knew that she was still in Clotho, the polymer chain being unraveled from her body, accelerated by a translator, passing through two black holes, and simultaneously being knit up by the spiders. It didn't matter.

She plunged into Ginungagap as effortlessly as if it were the film of a soap bubble.

In—

—And out.

It was like being reversed in a mirror, or watching an entertainment run backward. She was instantly flying out the way she came. The sky was a mottled mass of violet light.

The stars before her brightened from violet to blue. She craned her neck, looked back at Ginungagap, saw its disk-shaped nothingness recede, and screamed in frustration because it had escaped her. She spread her wings to slow her flight and—

—was sitting in a dark place. Her hand reached out, touched metal, recognized the inside of a clamshell device.

A hairline crack of light looped over her, widened. The clamshell opened.

Oceans of color bathed her face. Abigail straightened, and the act of doing so lifted her up gently. She stared through the transparent bubble at a phosphorescent foreverness of light.

My God, she thought. *The stars.*

The stars were thicker, more numerous than she was used to seeing them— large and bright and glittery rich. She was probably someplace significant, in a star cluster or the center of the galaxy; she couldn't guess. She felt irrationally happy to simply be; she took a deep breath, then laughed.

"Abigail Vanderhoek."

She turned to face the voice, and found that it came from a machine. Spiders crouched beside it, legs moving silently. Outside, in the hard vacuum, were more spiders.

"We regret any pain this may cause," the machine said.

Then the spiders rushed forward. She had no time to react. Sharp mandibles loomed before her, then dipped to her neck. Impossibly swift, they sliced through her throat, severed her spine. A sudden jerk and her head was separated from her body.

It happened in an instant. She felt brief pain, and the dissociation of actually *seeing* her decapitated body just beginning to react. And then she died.

A spark. A light. *I'm alive*, she thought. Consciousness returned like an ancient cathode tube warming up. Abigail stretched slowly, bobbing gently in the air, collecting her thoughts. She was in the sister-Clotho again—not in pain, her head and neck firmly on her shoulders. There were spiders in the platform, and a few floating outside.

"Abigail Vanderhoek," the machine said. "We are ready to begin negotiations."

Abigail said nothing.

After a moment, the machine said, "Are you damaged? Are your thoughts impaired?" A pause, then, "Was your mind not protected during transit?"

"Is that you waving the legs there? Outside the platform?"

"Yes. It is important that you talk with the other humans. You must convey our questions. They will not communicate with us."

"I have a few questions of my own," Abigail said. "I won't cooperate until you answer them."

"We will answer any questions provided you neither garble nor garble."

"What do you take me for?" Abigail asked. "Of course I won't."

Long hours later she spoke to Paul and Dominguez. At her request the spiders had withdrawn, leaving her alone. Dominguez looked drawn and haggard. "I swear we had no idea the spiders would attack you," Dominguez said. "We saw it on the screens. I was certain you'd been killed. . . ." His voice trailed off.

"Well, I'm alive, no thanks to you guys. Just what is this crap about an explosive substance in my bones, anyway?"

"An explosive—I swear we know nothing of anything of the kind."

"A close relative to plastique," Paul said. "I had a small editing device attached to Clotho's translator. It altered roughly half the bone marrow in your sternum, pelvis, and femurs in transmission. I'd hoped the spiders wouldn't pick up on it so quickly."

"You actually did," Abigail marveled. "The spiders weren't lying; they decapitated me in self-defense. What the holy hell did you think you were *doing?*"

"Just a precaution," Paul said. "We wet-wired you to trigger the stuff on command. That way, we could have taken out the spider installation if they'd tried something funny."

"Um," Dominguez said, "this *is* being recorded. What I'd like to know, Ms. Vanderhoek, is how you escaped being destroyed."

"I didn't," Abigail said. "The spiders killed me. Fortunately, they anticipated the situation, and recorded the transmission. It was easy for them to recreate me—after they edited out the plastique."

Dominguez gave her a odd look. "You don't—feel anything particular about this?"

"Like what?"

"Well—" He turned to Paul helplessly.

"Like the real Abigail Vanderhoek died and you're simply a very realistic copy," Paul said.

"Look, we've been through this garbage before," Abigail began angrily.

Paul smiled formally at Dominguez. It was hard to adjust to seeing the two in flat black-and-white. "She doesn't believe a word of it."

"If you guys can pull yourselves up out of your navels for a minute," Abigail said, "I've got a line on something the spiders have that you want. They claim they've sent probes through their black hole."

"Probes?" Paul stiffened. Abigail could sense the thoughts coursing through his skull, of defenses and military applications.

"Carbon-hydrogen chain probes. Organic probes. Self-constructing transmitters. They've got a carbon-based secondary technology."

"Nonsense," Dominguez said. "How could they convert back to coherent matter with a receiver?"

Abigail shrugged. "They claim to have found a loophole."

"How does it work?" Paul snapped.

"They wouldn't say. They seemed to think you'd pay well for it."

"That's very true," Paul said slowly. "Oh, yes."

The conference took almost as long as her session with the spiders had. Abigail was bone weary when Dominguez finally said, "That ties up the official minutes. We now stop recording." A line tracked across the screen, was gone. "If you want to speak to anyone off the record, now's your chance. Perhaps there is someone close to you . . ."

"Close? No." Abigail almost laughed. "I'll speak to Paul alone, though."

A spider floated by outside Clotho II. It was a golden, crablike being, its body slightly opalescent. It skittered along unseen threads strung between the open platforms of the spider star-city. "I'm listening," Paul said.

"You turned me into a *bomb*, you freak."

"So?"

"I could have been killed."

"Am I supposed to care?"

"You damn well ought to, considering the liberties you've taken with my fair white body."

"Let's get one thing understood," Paul said. "The woman I slept with, the woman I cared for, is dead. I have no feelings toward or obligations to you whatsoever."

"Paul," Abigail said. "*I'm not dead*. Believe me, I'd know if I were."

"How could I possibly trust what you think or feel? It could all be attitudes the spiders wet-wired into you. We know they have the technology."

"How do you know that *your* attitudes aren't wet-wired in? For that matter, how do you know anything is real? I mean, these are the most sophomoric philosophic ideas there are. But I'm the same woman I was a few hours ago. My memories, opinions, feelings—they're all the same as they were. There's absolutely no difference between me and the woman you slept with on the *Clarke*."

"I know." Paul's eyes were cold. "That's the horror of it." He snapped off the screen.

Abigail found herself staring at the lifeless machinery. *God, that hurt*, she thought. *It shouldn't, but it hurt.* She went to her quarters.

The spiders had done a respectable job of preparing for her. There were no green plants, but otherwise the room was the same as the one she'd had on the *Clarke*. They'd even been able to spin the platform, giving her an adequate down-orientation. She sat in her hammock, determined to think pleasanter thoughts. About the offer the spiders had made, for example. The one she hadn't told Paul and Dominguez about.

Banned by their chemistry from using black holes to travel, the spiders needed a representative to see to their interests among the stars. They had offered her the job.

Or perhaps the plural would be more appropriate—they had offered her the jobs. Because there were too many places to go for one woman to handle them all. They needed a dozen—in time, perhaps, a hundred—Abigail Vanderhoeks.

In exchange for licensing rights to her personality, the right to make as many duplicates of her as were needed, they were willing to give her the rights to the self-reconstructing black hole platforms.

It would make her a rich woman—a hundred rich woman—back in human space. And it would open the universe. She hadn't committed herself yet, but there was no way she was going to turn down the offer. The chance to see a thousand stars? No, she would not pass it by.

When she got old, too, they could create another Abigail from their recording, burn her new memories into it, and destroy her old body.

I'm going to see the stars, she thought. I'm going to *live forever*. She couldn't understand why she didn't feel elated, wondered at the sudden rush of melancholy that ran through her like the precursor of tears.

Garble jumped into her lap, offered his belly to be scratched. The spiders had recorded him, too. They had been glad to restore him to his unaltered state when she made the request. She stroked his stomach and buried her face in his fur.

"Pretty little cat," she told him. "I thought you were dead."

Exploring Fossil Canyon

KIM STANLEY ROBINSON

Kim Stanley Robinson sold his first story in 1976 and quickly established himself as one of the most respected and critically acclaimed writers of his generation. His story "Black Air" won the World Fantasy Award in 1984, and his novella "The Blind Geometer," won the Nebula Award in 1987. His novel *The Wild Shore* was published in 1984 as the first title in the resurrected Ace Special line, along with first novels by other new writers such as William Gibson, Michael Swanwick, and Lucius Shepard, and was quickly followed up by other novels such as *Icehenge, The Memory of Whiteness, A Short, Sharp Shock, The Gold Coast,* and *The Pacific Shore* and by collections such as *The Planet on the Table, Escape from Kathmandu,* and *Remaking History.*

Robinson's already-distinguished literary reputation took a quantum jump in the decade of the nineties, however, with the publication of his acclaimed *Mars* trilogy, *Red Mars, Green Mars,* and *Blue Mars. Red Mars* won a Nebula Award, both *Green Mars* and *Blue Mars* won Hugo Awards, and the trilogy has come to be widely recognized as the genre's most accomplished, detailed, sustained, and substantial look at the colonization and terraforming of another world, rivaled only by Arthur C. Clarke's *The Sands of Mars.*

The *Mars* trilogy will probably associate Robinson's name forever with the Red Planet, but it was not the *first* time he would explore a fictional Mars; Robinson visited Mars in several stories of the eighties, including the memorable novella "Green Mars," and the evocative story of exploration that follows, during which occurs one of those perceptual shifts that come along every once in a while, one of the first appearances of the idea that, rather than terraforming Mars and reshaping it into a mirror image of the Earth, we should leave it *alone,* leave it just as it is, rocks, rust, red dirt, and all.

Robinson's latest books are the novel *Antarctica* and a collection of stories and poems set on his fictional Mars, *The Martians.* He lives with his family in California.

Two hours before sunset their guide, Roger Clayborne, declared it was time to set camp, and the eight members of the tour trooped down from the ridges or up out of the side canyons they had been exploring that day as the group slowly progressed west, toward Olympus Mons. Eileen Monday, who had had her intercom switched off all day (the guide could override her deafness) turned to the common band and heard the voices of her companions, chattering. Dr. Mitsumu and Cheryl Martinez had pulled the equipment wagon all day, down a particularly narrow canyon bottom, and their vociferous complaints were making Mrs. Mitsumu laugh. John Nobleton was suggesting, as usual, that they camp farther down the ancient water-formed arroyo they were following; Eileen could not be sure which of the dusty-suited figures was him, but she guessed it was the one enthusiastically bounding up the wash, kicking up sand with every jump, and floating like an impala. Their guide, on the other hand, was unmistakable: tall even when sitting against a tall boulder, high on the spine flanking one side of the deep canyon. When the others spotted him, they groaned. The equipments wagon weighed less than seven hundred kilograms in Mars's gravity, but still it would take several of them to pull it up the slope to the spot Clayborne had in mind.

"Roger, why don't we just pull it down the road we've got here and camp around the corner?" John insisted.

"Well, we certainly could," Roger said—he spoke so quietly that the intercoms barely transmitted his dry voice—"but I haven't yet learned to sleep comfortably at a forty-five-degree angle."

Mrs. Mitsumu giggled. Eileen snicked in irritation, hoping Roger could identify the maker of the sound. His remark typified all she disliked about the guide; he was both taciturn and sarcastic, a combination Eileen did not like any more for considering it unusual. And his wide derisive grin was no help either.

"I found a good flat down there," John protested.

"I saw it. But I suspect out tent needs a little more room."

Eileen joined the crew hauling the wagon up the slope. "I suspect," she mimicked as she began to pant and sweat inside her suit.

"See?" came Roger's voice in her ear. "Ms. Monday agrees with me."

She snicked again, more annoyed than she cared to show. So far, in her opinion, this expedition was a flop. And their guide was a very significant factor in its failure, even if he was so quiet that she had barely noticed him for the first three or four days. But eventually his sharp tongue had caught her attention.

She slipped in some soft dirt and went to her knees; bounced back up and heaved again, but the contact reminded her that Mars itself shared the blame for her disappointment. She wasn't as willing to admit that as she was her dislike for Clayborne, but it was true, and it disturbed her. All through her many years at the University of Mars Burroughs, she had studied the planet—first in literature (she had read every Martian tale every written, she once boasted), then in areology, particularly seismology. But she had spent most of her twenty four years in Burroughs itself, and the big city was not like the canyons. Her previous exposure to the Martian landscape consisted visits to the magnificent domed section of Hephaestus Chasma called Lazuli Canyon, where icy water ran in rills and springs, in waterfalls and pools, and tundra grass grew on every wet red beach. Of course she knew that the virgin Martian landscape was not like Lazuli, but somewhere in her mind, when she had seen the advertisement for the hike—"Guaranteed to be terrain *never before trodden* by human feet"—she must have had an image of something similar to that green world. The thought made her curse herself a fool. The slope they were struggling up at that very moment was a perfect representative sample of the untrodden terrain they had been hiking over for the week: It was composed of dirt of every consistency and hue, so that it resembled an immense layered cake slowly melting, made of ingredients that looked like baking soda, sulfur, brick dust, curry powder, coal slag, and alum. And it was only one cake out of thousands of them, all stacked crazily for as far as the eye could see. Dirt piles.

Just short of Roger's flat campsite, they stopped to rest. Sweat was stinging in Eileen's left eye. "Let's get the wagon up here," Roger said, coming down to help. His clients stared at him mutinously, unmoving. The doctor leaned over to adjust his boot, and as he had been holding the wagon's handle, the others were caught off guard; a pebble gave way under the wagon's rear wheel, and suddenly it was out of their grasp and rolling down the slope—

In an explosion of dust Roger dived headfirst down the hill, chocking the rear wheel with a stone the size of a breadloaf. The wagon plowed the chock downhill a couple of meters and came to a halt. The group stood motionlessly, staring at the prone guide, Eileen as surprised as the rest of them; she had never seen him move so fast. He stood up at his usual lazy pace and started wiping dust from his face-plate. "Best to put the chock down before it starts rolling," he murmured, smiling to himself. They gathered to pull the wagon up the flat, chattering again. But Eileen considered it; if the wagon had careened all the way down to the canyon bottom, there would have been at least the possibility that it would have been damaged. And if it had been damaged badly enough, it could have killed them all. She pursed her lips and climbed up to the flat.

Roger and Ivan Corallton were pulling the base of the tent from the wagon. They stretched it out over the posts that kept it level and off the frozen soil; Ivan and Kevin Ottalini assembled the curved poles of the tension dome. The three of them and John carefully got the poles in place, and pulled the transparent tent material out of the base to stretch it under the framework. When they were done the others stood, a bit stiffly—they had traveled some twenty kilometers that day—and walked in through the flaccid airlock, hauling the wagon in behind them. Roger twisted valves on the side of the wagon, and compressed air pushed violently into their protective bag. Before it was full, Dr. Mitsumu and his wife were disengaging the bath and the latrine assemblies from the wagon. Roger switched on the heaters, and after a few minutes of gazing at the gauges, he nodded. "Home again home again," he said as always. Condensation was beading on the inside of their dome's clear skin. Eileen unclipped her helmet from her suit and pulled it off. "It's too hot." No one heard her. She walked to the wagon and turned down the heater, catching Roger's sardonic grin out of the corner of her eye; she always thought the tent's air was too hot. Dr. Mitsumu, regular as clockwork, ducked into the latrine as soon as his suit was off. The air was filled with the smells of sweat and urine, as everyone stripped their suits off and poured the contents of the runoffs into the water purifier on the wagon. Doran Stark got to the bath first as always— Eileen was amused by how quickly a group established its habits and customs— and stood in the ankle-deep water, sponging himself down and singing "I Met Her in a Phobos Restaurant." As she emptied her suit into the purifier Eileen found herself smiling at all their domestic routines, performed in a transparent bubble in the midst of an endless rust desolation.

She took her sponge bath last except for Roger. There was a shower curtain that could be pulled around the tiny tub at shoulder level, but nobody else used it, so Eileen didn't either, although she was made a bit uncomfortable by the surreptitious glances of John and the doctor. Nevertheless, she sponged down thoroughly, and in the constantly moving air her clean wet skin felt good. Besides it was rather a splendid sight, all the ruddy naked bodies standing about on the ledge of a spine extending thousands of meters above and below them, the convolutions of canyon after canyon scoring the titled landscape, Olympus Mons bulging to the west, rising out of the atmosphere so that it appeared to puncture the dome of the sky, and the blood-red sun about to set behind it. Roger did know how to pick a campsite, Eileen admitted to herself (he somehow sponged down with his back always to her, shower curtain partly pulled out, and dressed while still wet, signaling the gradual rehabiliment of the others). It was truly a sublime sight, as all of their campsite prospects had been. Sublime: to have your senses telling you you are in danger, when you know you are not; that was Burke's definition of the sublime, more or less, and it fit practically every moment of these days, from dawn to dusk. But that in itself could get wearing. The sublime is not the beautiful, after all, and one cannot live comfortably in a perpetual sense of danger. But at sunset, in the tent, it was an apprehension that could be enjoyed: the monstrous bare landscape, her bare skin; the utter serenity of the slow movement of Beethoven's last string quartet, which Ivan played every day during the sun's dying moments. . . . "Listen to this," Cheryl said, and read from her constant companion, the volume *If Wang Wei Lived on Mars:*

> *Sitting out all night thinking.*
> *Sun half-born five miles to the east.*
> *Blood pulses through all this still air:*
> *The edge of a mountain, great distance away.*
> *Nothing moves but the sun,*
> *Blood to fire as it rises.*
> *How many, these dawns?*
> *How far, our home?*
> *Stars fade. Big rocks splinter*
> *The mind's great fear:*
> *Peace here. Peace, here.*

It was a fine moment, Eileen thought, made so by what was specifically human in the landscape. She dressed with the rest of them, deliberately turning away from John Nobleton as she rooted around in her drawer of the wagon, and they fell to making dinner. For more than an hour after Olympus Mons blotted out the sun the sky stayed light; pink in the west, shading to brick-black in the east. They cooked and ate by this illumination. Their meal, planned by Roger, was a thick vegetable stew, seemingly fresh French bread, and coffee. Most of them kept off the common band during long stretches of the day, and now they discussed what they had seen, for they explored different side canyons as they went. The main canyon they were following was a dry outflow wash, formed by flash floods working down a small fault line in a large tilted plateau. It was relatively young, Roger said—meaning two billion years old, but younger than most of the water-carved canyons on Mars. Wind erosion and the marvelous erratics created by volcanic bombardment from Olympus Mons gave the expedition members a lot of features to discuss: beach terracing from long-lost lakes, meandering streambeds, lava bombs shaped like giant teardrops, or colored in a way that implied certain gases in copious quantities in the Hesperian atmosphere. . . . This last, plus the fact that these canyons had been carved by water, naturally provoked a lot of speculation about the possibilities of ancient Martian life. And the passing water, and the resiliencies of the rock, had created forms fantastical enough to seem the sculpture of some alien art. So they talked, with the enthusiasm and free speculation that only amateurs seem to bring to a subject: Sunday paper areologists, Eileen thought. There wasn't a proper scientist among them; she was the closest thing to it, and the only thing she knew was the rudiments of areology. Yet she listened to the talk with interest.

Roger, on the other hand, never contributed to these free-ranging discussions, and didn't even listen. At the moment he was engaged in setting up his cot and "bedroom" wall. There were panels provided so that each sleeper, or couple, could block off an area around their cot; no one took advantage of them but Roger, the rest preferring to lie out under the stars together. Roger set two panels against the sloping side of the dome, leaving just enough room for his cot under the clear low roof. It was yet another way that he set himself apart, and watching him, Eileen shook her head. Expedition guides were usually so amiable—how did he keep his job? Did he ever get repeat customers? She set out her cot, observing his particular preparations: He was one of the tall Martians, well over two meters (Lamarckianism was back in vogue, as it appeared that the more generations of ancestors you had on Mars, the taller you grew; it was true for Eileen herself, who was fourth-generation, or *yonsei*)—long-faced, long-nosed, homely as English royalty . . . long feet that were clumsy once out of their boots. . . . He rejoined them, however, this evening, which was not always his custom, and they lit a lantern as the wine-dark sky turned black and filled with stars. Bedding arranged, they sat down on cots and the floor around the lantern's dim light and talked some more. Kevin and Doran began a chess game.

For the first time, they asked Eileen questions about her area of expertise. Was it true that the southern highlands now held the crust of both primeval hemispheres? Did the straight line of the three great Tharsis volcanoes indicate a hot spot in the mantle? Sunday paper areology again, but Eileen answered as best she could. Roger appeared to be listening.

"Do you think there'll ever be a marsquake we can actually feel?" he asked with a grin.

The others laughed, and Eileen felt herself blush. It was a common jest; sure enough, he followed it up: "You sure you seismologists aren't just inventing these marsquakes to keep yourself in employment?"

"You're out here enough," she replied. "One of these days a fault will open up and swallow you."

"She hopes," Ivan said. The sniping between them had of course not gone unnoticed.

"So you think I might actually feel a quake someday," Roger said.

"Sure. There's thousands every day, you know."

"But that's because your seismographs register every footstep on the planet. I mean, a big one?"

"Of course. I can't think of anyone who deserves a shaking more."

"Might even have to use the Richter scale, eh?"

Now that was unfair, because the Harrow scale was necessary to make finer distinctions between low-intensity quakes. But later in the same conversation, she got hers back. Cheryl and Mrs. Mitsumu were asking Roger about where he had traveled before in his work, how many expeditions he had guided and the like. "I'm a canyon guide," he replied at one point.

"So when will you graduate to Marineris?" Eileen asked.

"Graduate?"

"Sure, isn't Marineris the ultimate goal of every canyon man?"

"Well, to a certain extent—"

"You'd better get assigned there in a hurry, hadn't you—I hear it takes a whole lifetime to learn those canyons." Roger looked to be about forty.

"Oh not for our Roger," Mrs. Mitsumu said, joining in the ribbing.

"No one ever learns Marineris," Roger protested. "It's eight thousand kilometers long, with hundreds of side canyons—"

"What about Gustafsen?" Eileen said. "I thought he and a couple others knew every inch of it."

"Well . . ."

"Better start working on that transfer."

"Well, I'm a Tharsis fan myself," he explained, in a tone so apologetic that the whole group burst out laughing. Eileen smiled at him and went to get some tea started.

After the tea was distributed, John and Ivan turned the conversation to another favorite topic, the terraforming of the canyons. "This system would be as beautiful as Lazuli," John said. "Can you imagine water running down the drops we took today? Tundra grass everywhere, finches in the air, little horned toads down in the cracks . . . alpine flowers to give it some color."

"Yes, it will be exquisite," Ivan agreed. With the same material that made their tent, several canyons and craters had been domed, and thin cold air pumped beneath, allowing arctic and alpine life to exist. Lazuli was the greatest of these terraria, but many more were springing up.

"Unnh," Roger muttered.

"You don't agree?" Ivan asked.

Roger shook his head. "The best you can do is make an imitation Earth. That's not what Mars is for. Since we're on Mars, we should adjust to what it is, and enjoy it for that."

"Oh but there will always be natural canyons and mountains," John said. "There's as much land surface on Mars as on Earth, right?"

"Just barely."

"So with all that land, it will take centuries for it all to be terraformed. In this gravity, maybe never. But centuries, at least."

"Yes, but that's the direction it's headed," Roger said. "If they start orbiting mirrors and blowing open volcanoes to provide gases, they'll change the whole surface."

"But wouldn't that be marvelous!" Ivan said.

"You don't seriously object to making life on the open surface possible, do you?" Mrs. Mitsumu asked.

Roger shrugged. "I like it the way it is."

John and the rest continued to discuss the considerable problems of terraforming, and after a bit Roger got up and went to bed. An hour later Eileen got up to do the same, and the others followed her, brushing teeth, visiting the latrine, talking more. . . . Long after the others had settled down, Eileen stood under one edge of the tent dome, looking up at the stars. There near Scorpio, as a high evening star, was the Earth, a distinctly bluish point, accompanied by its fainter companion the moon. A double planet of resonant beauty in the host of constellations. Tonight it gave her an inexplicable yearning to see it, to stand on it.

Suddenly John appeared at her side, standing too close to her, shoulder to shoulder, his arm rising, as if with a life of its own, to circle her waist. "Hike'll be over soon," he said. She didn't respond. He was a very handsome man; aquiline features, jet-black hair. He didn't know how tired Eileen was of handsome men. She had been as impetuous in her affairs as a pigeon in a park, and it had brought her a lot of grief. Her last three lovers had all been quite good-looking, and the last of them, Eric, had been rich as well. His house in Burroughs was made of rare stones, as all the rich new houses were: a veritable castle of dark purple chert, inlaid with chalcedony and jade, rose quartz and jasper, its floors intricately flagged patterns of polished yellow slate, coral, and bright turquoise. And the parties! Croquet picnics in the maze garden, dances in the ballroom, masques all about the extensive grounds. . . . But Eric himself, brilliant talker though he was, had turned out to be rather superficial, and promiscuous as well, a discovery that Eileen had been slow to make. It had hurt her feelings. And since that had been the third intimate relationship to go awry in four years, she felt tired and unsure of herself, unhappy, and particularly sick of that easy mutual attraction of the attractive which had gotten her into such painful trouble, and which was what John was relying on at that very moment.

Of course he knew nothing of all this, as his arm hugged her waist (he certainly didn't have Eric's way with words), but she wasn't inclined to excuse his ignorance. She mulled over methods of diplomatically slipping out of his grasp and back to a comfortable distance. This was certainly the most he had made so far in the way of a move. She decided on one of her feints—leaning into him to peck his cheek, then pulling away when his guard was down—and had started the maneuver, when with a bump one of Roger's panels knocked aside and Roger stumbled out, in his shorts, bleary-eyed. "Oh?" he said sleepily, as he noticed them; then saw who they were, and their position—"Ah," he said, and stumped away toward the latrine.

Eileen took advantage of the disturbance to slip away from John and go to bed, which was no-trespass territory, as John well knew. She lay down in some agitation. That smile, that "Ah"—the whole incident irritated her so much that she had trouble falling asleep. And the double star, one blue, one white, returned her stare all the while.

★ ★ ★

The next day it was Eileen and Roger's turn to pull the wagon. This was the first time they had pulled together, and while the rest ranged ahead or to the sides, they solved the many small problems presented by the task of getting the wagon down the canyon. An occasional drop-off was high enough to require winch, block, and tackle—sometimes even one or two of the other travelers—but mostly it was a matter of guiding the flexible little cart down the center of the wash. They agreed on band 33 for their private communication, but aside from the business at hand, they conversed very little. "Look out for that rock." "How nice, that triangle of shards." To Eileen it seemed clear that Roger had very little interest in her or her observations. Or else, it occurred to her, he thought the same of her.

At one point she asked, "What if we let the wagon slip right now?" It was poised over the edge of a six-or seven-meter drop, and they were winching it down.

"It would fall," his voice replied solemnly in her ear, and through his faceplate she could see him smiling.

She kicked pebbles at him. "Come on, would it break? Are we in danger of our lives most every minute?"

"No way. These things are practically indestructible. Otherwise, it would be too dangerous to use them. They've dropped them off four-hundred-meter cliffs— not sheer you understand, but steep—and it doesn't even dent them."

"I see. So when you saved the wagon from slipping down that slope yesterday, you weren't actually saving our lives."

"Oh no. Did you think that? I just didn't want to climb down that hill and recover it."

"Ah." She let the wagon thump down, and they descended to it. After that there were no exchanges between them for a long time. Eileen contemplated the fact that she would be back in Burroughs in three or four days, with nothing in her life resolved, nothing different about it.

Still, it would be good to get back to the open air, the illusion of open air. Running water. Plants.

Roger clicked his tongue in distress.

"What?" Eileen asked.

"Sandstorm coming." He switched to the common band, which Eileen could now hear. "Everyone get back to the main canyon, please, there's a sandstorm on the way."

There were groans over the common band. No one was actually in sight. Roger bounced down the canyon with impeccable balance, bounced back up. "No good campsites around," he complained. Eileen watched him; he noticed and pointed at the western horizon. "See that feathering in the sky?"

All Eileen could see was a patch where the sky's pink was perhaps a bit yellow, but she said "Yes?"

"Dust storm. Coming our way, too. I think I feel the wind already." He put a hand up. Eileen thought that feeling the wind through a suit when the atmospheric pressure was thirty millibars was strictly a myth, a guide's boast, but she stuck her hand up as well, and thought that there might be a faint fluctuating pressure on it.

Ivan, Kevin, and the Mitsumus appeared far down the canyon. "Any campsites down there?" Roger asked.

"No, the canyon gets even narrower."

Then the sandstorm was upon them, sudden as a flash flood. Eileen could see fifty meters at the most; they were in a shifting dome of flying sand, it seemed, and it was as dark as their long twilights, or darker.

Over band 33, in her left ear, Eileen heard a long sigh. Then in her right ear, over the common band, Roger's voice: "You all down the canyon there, stick together and come on up to us. Doran, Cheryl, John, let's hear from you—where are you?"

"Roger?" It was Cheryl on the common band, sounding frightened.

"Yes, Cheryl, where are you?"

A sharp thunder roll of static: "We're in a sandstorm, Roger! I can just barely hear you."

"Are you with Doran and John?"

"I'm with Doran, and he's just over this ridge, I can hear him, but he says he can't hear you."

"Get together with him and start back for the main canyon. What about John?"

"I don't know, I haven't seen him in over an hour."

"All right. Stay with Doran—"

"Roger?"

"Yes?"

"Doran's here now."

"I can hear you again," Doran's voice said. He sounded more scared than Cheryl. "Over that ridge there was too much interference."

"Yeah, that's what's happening with John I expect," Roger said.

Eileen watched the dim form of their guide move up the canyon's side slope in the wavering amber dusk of the storm. The "sand" in the thin air was mostly dust, or fines even smaller than dust particles, like smoke; but occasional larger grains made a light *tik tik tik* against her faceplate.

"Roger, we can't seem to find the main canyon," Doran declared, scratchy in the interference.

"What do you mean?"

"Well, we've gone up the canyon we descended, but we must have taken a different fork, because we've run into a box canyon."

Eileen shivered in her warm suit. Each canyon system lay like a lightning bolt on the tilted land, a pattern of ever-branching forks and tributaries; in the storm's gloom it would be very easy to get lost; and they still hadn't heard from John.

"Well, drop back to the last fork and try the next one to the south. As I recall, you're over in the next canyon north of us."

"Right," Doran said. "We'll try that."

The four who had been farther down the main canyon appeared like ghosts in mist. "Here we are," Ivan said with satisfaction.

"Nobleton! John! Do you read me?"

No answer.

"He must be off a ways," Roger said. He approached the wagon. "Help me pull this up the slope."

"Why?" Dr. Mitsumu asked.

"We're setting the tent up there. Sleep on an angle tonight, you bet."

"But why up there?" Dr. Mitsumu persisted. "Couldn't we set up the tent here in the wash?"

"It's the old arroyo problem," Roger replied absently. "If the storm keeps up the canyon could start spilling sand as if it were water. We don't want to be buried."

They pulled it up the slope with little difficulty, and secured it with chock rocks under the wheels. Roger set up the tent mostly by himself, working too quickly for the others to help.

"Okay, you four get inside and get everything going. Eileen—"

"Roger?" It was Doran.

"Yes."

"We're still having trouble finding the main canyon."

"We thought we were in it," Cheryl said, "but when we descended we came to a big drop-off!"

"Okay. Hold on a minute where you are. Eileen, I want you to come up the main canyon with me and serve as a radio relay. You'll stay in the wash, so you'll be able to walk right back down to the tent if we get separated."

"Sure," Eileen said. The others were carefully rolling the wagon into the lock. Roger paused to oversee that operation, and then he gestured at Eileen through the tawny murk and took off upcanyon. Eileen followed.

They made rapid time. On band 33 Eileen heard the guide say, in an unworried conversational tone, "I hate it when this happens." It was as if he were referring to a shoelace breaking.

"I bet you do!" Eileen replied. "How are we going to find John?"

"Go high. Always go high when lost. I believe I told John that with the rest of you."

"Yes." Eileen had forgotten, however, and she wondered if John had too.

"Even if he's forgotten," Roger said, "when we get high enough, the radios will be less obstructed and we'll be able to talk to him. Or at the worst, we can bounce our signals off a satellite and back down. But I doubt we'll have to do that. Hey, Doran!" he said over the common band.

"Yeah?" Doran sounded very worried.

"What can you see now?"

"Um—we're on a spine—it's all we can see. The canyon to the right—"

"South?"

"Yeah, the south, is the one we were in. We thought the one here to the north would be the main one, but it's too little, and there's a drop-off in it."

"Okay, well, my APS has you still north of us, so cross back to the opposite spine and we'll talk from there. Can you do that?"

"Sure," Doran said, affronted. "It'll take a while, maybe."

"That's all right, take your time." The lack of concern in Roger's voice was almost catching, but Eileen felt that John was in danger; the suits would keep one alive for forty-eight hours at least, but these sandstorms often lasted a week, or more.

"Let's keep moving up," Roger said on band 33. "I don't think we have to worry about those two."

They climbed up the canyon floor, which rose at an average angle of about thirty degrees. Eileen noticed all the dust sliding loosely downhill, sand grains rolling, dust wafting down; sometimes she couldn't see her feet, or make out the ground, so that she had to step by feeling.

"How are you doing back in camp?" Roger asked on the common band.

"Just fine," Dr. Mitsumu answered. "It's on too much of a tilt to stand, so we're just sitting around and listening to the developments up there."

"Still in your suits?"

"Yes."

"Good. One of you stay suited for sure."

"Whatever you say."

Roger stopped where the main canyon was joined by two large tributary canyons, brancing in each direction. "Watch out, I'm going to turn up the gain on the radio," he warned Eileen and the others. She adjusted the controls on her wrist.

"JOHN! Hey, John! Oh, Jo-uhnnn! Come in, John! Respond on common band. Please."

The radio's static sounded like the hiss of flying sand grains. Nothing within it but crackling.

"Hmm," Roger said in Eileen's left ear.

"Hey Roger!"

"Cheryl! How are you doing?"

"Well, we're in what we think is the main canyon, but . . ."

Doran continued, embarrassed: "We really can't be sure, now. Everything looks the same."

"You're telling me," Roger replied. Eileen watched him bend over and, apparently, inspect his feet. He moved around some in this jacknifed position. "Try going to the wash at the lowest point in the canyon you're in."

"We're there."

"Okay, lean down and see if you find any boot prints. Make sure they aren't yours. They'll be faint by now, but Eileen and I just went upcanyon, so there should still be—"

"Hey! Here's some," Cheryl said.

"Where?" said Doran.

"Over here, look."

Radio hiss.

"Yeah, Roger, we've found some going upcanyon and down."

"Good. Now start downcanyon. Dr. M, are you still in your suit?"

"Just as you said, Roger."

"Good. Why don't you get out of the tent and go down to the wash. Keep your bearing, count your steps and all. Wait for Cheryl and Doran. That way they'll be able to find the tent as they come down."

"Sounds good."

After some chatter: "You all down there switch to band 5 to talk on, and just listen to common. We need to hear up here." Then on band 33: "Let's go up some more. I believe I remember a gendarme on the ridge up here with a good vantage."

"Fine. Where do you think he could be?"

"You got me."

When Roger located the outcropping he had in mind, they called again, and again got no response. Eileen then installed herself on top of the rocky knob on the ridge: an eerie place with nothing to see but the fine sand whipped about her, in a ghost wind barely felt on her back like the lightest puff of an air conditioner, despite the visual resemblance to some awful typhoon. She called for John from time to time. Roger ranged to north and south over difficult terrain, always staying within radio distance of Eileen, although once he had a hard time relocating her.

Three hours passed that way, and Roger's easygoing tone changed—not to worry, Eileen judged, but rather to boredom, and annoyance with John. Eileen herself was extremely concerned. If John had mistaken north for south, or fallen . . .

"I suppose we should go higher." Roger sighed. "Although I thought I saw him back when we brought the wagon down here, and I doubt he'd go back up."

Suddenly Eileen's earphones crackled. *"Pss flunk bdzz,"* and it was clear again. *"Ckk ssss ger, lo! ckk."*

"Sounds like he may have indeed gone high," Roger said with satisfaction, and, Eileen noticed, just a touch of relief. "Hey, John Nobleton! Do you read us?"

"Ckk sssssssss yeah, hey! *sssss kuh sssss."*

"We read you badly, John! Keep moving, keep talking! Are you all—"

"Roger! *ckk.* Hey, Roger!"

"John! We read you, are you all right?"

". . . *sssss* not exactly sure where I am."

"Are you all right?"

"Yes! Just lost."

"Well not anymore, we hope. Tell us what you see."

"Nothing!"

So began the long process of locating him and bringing him back. Eileen ranged left and right on her own, helping to get a fix on John, who had been instructed to stay still and keep talking.

"You won't believe it." John's voice was entirely free of fear; in fact, he sounded elated. "You won't believe it, Eileen, Roger. *crk!* Just before the storm hit I was way off down a tributary to the south, and I found . . ."

"Found what?"

"Well . . . I've found some things I'm sure must be fossils. I swear! A whole rock formation of them!"

"Oh yeah?"

"No seriously, I've got some with me. Very small shells, like little sea snails, or crustacea. Miniature nautiloids, like. They just couldn't be anything else. I have a couple in my pocket, but there's a whole wall of them back there! I figure if I just left I wouldn't be able to find the same canyon ever again, what with this storm, so I built a duck trail on the way back over to the main canyon, if that's where I am. So it took me a while to get back in radio clear."

"What color are they?" Ivan asked from below.

"You down there, be quiet," Roger ordered. "We're still trying to find him."

"We'll be able to get back to the site. Eileen, can you believe it? We'll all be—*Hey!"*

"It's just me," Roger said.

"Ah! You gave me a start, there."

Eileen smiled as she imagined John startled by the ghostlike appearance of the lanky, suited Roger. Soon enough Roger had led John downcanyon to Eileen, and after John hugged her, they proceeded down the canyon to Dr. Mitsumu, who again led them up the slope to the tent, which rested at a sharper angle than Eileen had recalled.

Once inside, the reunited group chattered for an hour concerning their adventure, while Roger showered and got the wagon on an even keel, and John revealed the objects he had brought back with him:

Small shell-shaped rocks, some held in crusts of sandstone. Each shell had a spiral swirl on its inside surface, and they were mottled red and black. By and large they were black.

They were unlike any rocks Eileen had ever seen; they looked exactly like the few Terran shells she had seen in school. Seeing them there in John's hand, she caught her breath. Life on Mars; even if only fossil traces of it, *life on Mars*. She took one of the shells from John and stared and stared at it. It very well could be. . . .

They had to arrange their cots across the slope of the tent floor and prop them level with clothes and other domestic objects from the wagon. Long after they were settled they discussed John's discovery, and Eileen found herself more and more excited by the idea of it. The sand pelting the tent soundlessly only made its presence known by the complete absence of stars. She stared at the faint curved reflection of them all on the dome's surface, and thought of it. The Clayborne Expedition, in the history books. And Martian life . . . The others talked and talked.

"So we'll go there tomorrow, right?" John asked Roger. The tilt of the tent made it impossible for Roger to set up his bedroom.

"Or as soon as the storm ends, sure." Roger had only glanced at the shells, shaking his head and muttering, "I don't know, don't get your hopes up too high." Eileen wondered about that. "We'll follow that duck trail of yours, if we can." Perhaps he was jealous of John now?

On and on they talked. Yet the hunt had taken it out of Eileen; to the sound of their voices she suddenly fell asleep.

★ ★ ★

She woke up when her cot gave way and spilled her down the floor; before she could stop herself, she had rolled over Mrs. Mitsumu and John. She got off John quickly and saw Roger over at the wagon, smiling down at the gauges. Her cot had been by the wagon; had he yanked out some crucial item of clothing? There was something of the prankster in the man. . . .

The commotion woke the rest of the sleepers. Immediately the conversation returned to the matter of John's discovery, and Roger agreed that their supplies were sufficient to allow a trip back up-canyon. And the storm had stopped; dust coated their dome, and was piled half a centimeter high on its uphill side, but they could see that the sky was clear. So after breakfast they suited up, more awkward than ever on the tilted floor, and emerged from their shelter.

The distance back up to where they had met John was much shorter than it had seemed to Eileen in the storm. All of their tracks had been covered, even the sometimes deep treadmarks of the wagon. John led the way, leaping upward in giant bounds that were almost out of his control.

"There's the gendarme where we found you," Roger said from below, pointing to the spine on their right for John's benefit. John waited for them, talking nervously all the while. "There's the first duck," he told them. "I see it way over there, but with all the sand, it looks almost like any other mound. This could be hard."

"We'll find them," Roger assured him.

When they had all joined John, they began to traverse the canyons to the south, each one a deep multifingered trench in the slope of Mars facing Olympus Mons. John had very little sense of where he had been, except that he had not gone much above or below the level they were on. Some of the ducks were hard to spot, but Roger had quite a facility for it, and the others spotted some as well. More than once none of them saw it, and they had to trek off in nine slightly different directions, casting about in hopes of running into it. Each time someone would cry, "Here it is," as if they were children hunting Easter eggs, and they would convene and search again. Only once were they unable to locate the next duck, and then Roger pumped John's memory of his hike; after all, as Ivan pointed out, it had been the full light of day when he walked to the site. A crestfallen John admitted that, each little red canyon looking so much like the next one, he couldn't really recall where he had gone from there.

"Well, but there's the next duck," Roger said with surprise, pointing at a little niche indicating a side ravine. And after they had reached the niche John cried, "This is it! Right down this ravine, in the wall itself. And some of them have fallen."

The common band was a babble of voices as they dropped into the steep-sided ravine one by one. Eileen stepped down through the narrow entrance and confronted the nearly vertical south wall. There, embedded in hard sandstone, were thousands of tiny black stone snail shells. The bottom of the ravine was covered with them; all of them were close to the same size, with holes that opened into the hollow interior of the shells. Many of them were broken, and inspecting some fragments, Eileen saw the spiral ribbing that so often characterized life. Her earphones rang with the excited voices of her companions. Roger had climbed the canyon wall and was inspecting a particular section, his faceplate only centimeters from stone. "See what I mean?" John was asking. "Martian snails! It's like those fossil bacterial mats they talk about, only further advanced. Back when Mars had surface water and an atmosphere, life *did* begin. It just didn't have time to get very far."

"Nobleton snails," Cheryl said, and they laughed. Eileen picked up fragment after fragment, her excitement growing. They were all very similar. She was taxing her suit's cooling system, starting to sweat. She examined a well-preserved specimen carefully, pulling it out of the rock to do so. The common band was distractingly noisy, and she was about to turn it off when Roger's voice said slowly, "Uh-ohh. . . . Hey, people. Hey."

When it was silent he said hesitantly, "I hate to spoil the party, but . . . these little things aren't fossils."

"What?"

"What do you mean?" John and Ivan challenged. "How do you know?"

"Well, there are a couple reasons," Roger said. Everyone was still now, and watching him. "First, I believe that fossils are created by a process that requires millions of years of water seepage, and Mars never had that."

"So we think now," Ivan objected. "But it may not be so, because it's certain that there was water on Mars all along. And after all, here are these things."

"Well . . ." Eileen could tell he was deciding to let that argument pass. "Maybe you're right, but a better reason is, I think I know what these are. They're lava pellets—bubble pellets, I've heard them called—although I've never seen ones this small. Little lava bombs from one of the Olympus Mons eruptions. A sort of spray."

Everyone stared at the objects in their hands.

"See, when lava pellets land hot in a certain sort of sand, they sink right through it and melt the sand fast, releasing gas that forms the bubble, and these glassy interiors. When the pellet is spinning, you get these spiral chambers. So I've heard, anyway. It must have happened on a flat plain long ago, and when the whole plain tilted and started falling down this slope, these layers broke up and were buried by later deposits."

"I don't believe that's necessarily so," John declared, while the others looked at the wall. But even he sounded pretty convinced to Eileen.

"Of course we'll have to take some back to be sure," Roger agreed in a soothing tone.

"Why didn't you tell us this last night?" Eileen asked.

"Well, I couldn't tell till I had seen the rock they were in. But this is lava-sprayed sandstone, they call it. That's why it's so hard in its upper layers. But you're an areologist, right?" He wasn't mocking.

"Don't they look like they're made of lava?"

Eileen nodded, reluctantly. "Looks like it."

"Well, lava doesn't make fossils."

Half an hour later a dispirited group was stretched out over the duck trail, straggling along in silence. John and Ivan trailed far behind, weighted down by several kilos of lava pellets. Pseudofossils, as both areologists and geologists called them. Roger was ahead, talking with the Mitsumus, attempting to cheer them all up, Eileen guessed. She felt bad about not identifying the rock the previous night. She felt more depressed than she could easily account for, and it made her angry. Everything was so empty out here, so meaningless, so without form. . . .

"Once I thought I had found traces of aliens," Roger was saying. "I was off by myself around the other side of Olympus, hiking canyons as usual, except I was by myself. I was crossing really broken fretted terrain, when suddenly I came across a trail duck. Stones never stack up by themselves. Now the Explorer's Society keeps a record of every single hike and expedition, you know, and I had checked before and I knew I was in fresh territory, just like we are now. No humans had ever been in that part of the badlands, as far as the Society knew. Yet here was this duck. And I started finding other ones right away. Set not in a straight line, but zigzagging, tacking like. And little. Tiny piles of flat rock, four or five high. Like they were set up by little aliens who saw best out of the sides of their eyes."

"You must have been astounded," Mrs. Mitsumu said.

"Exactly. But, you know—there were three possibilities. It was a natural rock formation—extremely unlikely, but it could be that breadloaf formations had slid onto their sides and then been eroded into separate pieces, still stacked on each other. Or they were set up by aliens. Also unlikely, in my opinion. Or someone had hiked through there without reporting it, and had played a game, maybe, for someone later to find. To me, that was the most likely explanation. But for a while there . . ."

"You must have been disappointed," said Mrs. Mitsumu.

"Oh no," Roger replied easily. "More entertained than anything, I think."

Eileen stared at the form of their guide, far ahead with the others. He truly didn't care that John's discovery had not been the remnants of life, she judged. In that way he was different, unlike John or Ivan, unlike herself; for she felt his obviously correct explanation of the little shells as a loss larger than she ever would have guessed. She wanted life out there as badly as John or Ivan or any of the rest of them did, she realized. All those books she had read, when studying literature. . . . That was why she had not let herself remember that igneous rock would never be involved with fossilization. If only life had once existed here— snails, lichen, bacteria, anything—it would somehow take away some of this land-scape's awful barrenness.

And if Mars itself could not provide, it became necessary to supply it—to do whatever was necessary to make life possible on its desolate surface, to transform it as soon as possible, to *give it life*. Now she understood the connection between the two main topics of evening conversation in their isolated camps: terraforming, and the discovery of extinct Martian life-forms; and the conversations took place all over the planet, less intently than out here in the canyons, perhaps, but still, all her life Eileen had been hoping for this discovery, had *believed* in it.

She pulled the half dozen lava pellets she had saved from one of her suit pockets and stared at them. Abruptly, bitterly, she tossed them aside, and they floated out into the rust waste. They would never find remnants of Martian life; no one ever would. She knew that was true in every cell of her. All the so-called discoveries, all the Martians in her books—they were all part of a simple case of projection, nothing more. Humans wanted Martians, that was all there was to it. But there were not, and never had been, any canal-builders; no lamppost creatures with heat-beam eyes, no brilliant lizards or grasshoppers, no manta ray intelli-gences, no angels and no devils; there were no four-armed races battling in blue jungles, no big-headed skinny thirsty folk, no sloe-eyed dusky beauties dying for Terran sperm, no wise little Bleekmen wandering stunned in the desert, no golden-eyed golden-skinned telepaths, no doppelgänger race—not a fun-house mirror im-age of any kind; there weren't any ruined adobe palaces, no dried-oasis castles, no mysterious cliff dwellings packed like a museum, no hologrammatic towers waiting to drive humans mad, no intricate canal systems with their locks all filled with sand, no not a single canal; there were not even any mosses creeping down from the polar caps every summer, nor any rabbitlike animals living far underground; no plastic windmill-creatures, no lichen capable of casting dangerous electrical fields, no lichen of any kind; no algae in the hot springs, no microbes in the soil, no microbacteria in the regolith, no stromatolites, no nanobacteria in the deep bedrock . . . no primeval soup.

All so many dreams. Mars was a dead planet. Eileen scuffed the freeze-dried dirt and watched through damp eyes as the pinkish sand lofted away from her boot. All dead. That was her home: dead Mars. Not even dead, which implied a life and a dying. Just . . . nothing. A red void.

They turned down the main canyon. Far below was their tent, looking like it would slide down its slope any instant. Now there was a sign of life. Eileen grinned bleakly behind her faceplate. Outside her suit it was forty degrees below zero, and the air was not air.

Roger was hurrying down the canyon ahead of them, no doubt to turn on the air and heat in the tent, or pull the wagon out to move it all downcanyon. In the alien gravity she had lived in all her life, he dropped down the great trench as in a dream, not bounding gazelle-like in the manner of John or Doran, but just on the straightest line, the most efficient path, in a sort of boulder ballet all the more graceful for being so simple. Eileen liked that. Now there, she thought, is a man reconciled to the absolute deadness of Mars. It seemed his home, his landscape. An old line occurred to her: "We have met the enemy, and he is us." And then something from Bradbury: "The Martians were there . . . Timothy and Robert and Michael and Mom and Dad."

She pondered the idea as she followed Clayborne down their canyon trying to imitate that stride.

"But there *was* life on Mars." That evening she watched him. Ivan and Doran talked to Cheryl; John sulked on his coat. Roger chatted with the Mitsumus, who liked him. At sunset when they showered (they had moved the tent to another fine flat site) he walked over to his paneled cubicle naked, and the flat onyx bracelet he wore around his left wrist suddenly seemed to Eileen the most beautiful ornamentation. She realized she was glancing at him in the same way John and the doctor looked at her—only differently—and she blushed.

After dinner the others were quiet, returning to their cots. Roger continued telling the Mitsumus and Eileen stories. She had never heard him talk so much. He was still sarcastic with her, but that wasn't what his smile was saying. She watched him move . . . and sighed, exasperated with herself; wasn't this just what she had come out here to get away from? Did she really need or want this feeling again, this quickening interest?

"They still can't decide if there's some ultrasmall nanobacteria down in the bedrock. The arguments go back and forth in the scientific journals all the time. Could be down there, so small we can't even see it. There's been reports of drilling contamination. . . . But I don't think so."

Yet he certainly was different from the men she had known in recent years. After everyone had gone to bed, she concentrated on that difference, that quality; he was . . . Martian. He was that alien life, and she wanted him in a way she had never wanted her other lovers. Mrs. Mitsumu had been smiling at them, as if she saw something going on, something she had seen developing long before, when the two of them were always at odds . . . Earth girl lusts for virile Martian; she laughed at herself, but there it was. Still constructing stories to populate this planet, still falling in love, despite herself. And she wanted to do something about it. She had always lived by Eulert's saying: If you don't act on it, it wasn't a true feeling. It had gotten her in trouble, too, but she was forgetting that. And tomorrow they would be at the little outpost that was their destination, and the chance would be gone. For an hour she thought about it, evaluating the looks he had given her that evening. How did you evaluate an alien's glances? Ah, but he was human—just adapted to Mars in a way she wished she could be—and there had been something in his eyes very human, very understandable. Around her the black hills loomed against the black sky, the double star hung overhead, that home she had never set foot on. It was a lonely place.

Well, she had never been particularly shy in these matters, but she had always favored a more inpulling approach, encouraging advances rather than making them (usually) so that when she quietly got off her cot and slipped into shorts and a shirt, her heart was knocking like a tympani roll. She tiptoed to the panels, thinking *Fortune favors the bold*, and slipped between them, went to his side.

He sat up; she put her hand to his mouth. She didn't know what to do next. Her heart was knocking harder than ever. That gave her an idea, and she leaned over and pulled his head around and placed it against her ribs, so he could hear her pulse. He looked up at her, pulled her down to the cot. They kissed. Some whispers. The cot was too narrow and creaky, and they moved to the floor, lay next to each other kissing. She could feel him, hard against her thigh; some sort of Martian stone, she reckoned, like that flesh jade. . . . They whispered to each other, lips to each other's ears like headpiece intercoms. She found it difficult to stay so quiet making love, exploring that Martian rock, being explored by it. . . . She lost her mind for a while then, and when she came to she was quivering now and again; an occasional aftershock, she thought to herself. A seismology of sex. He appeared to read her mind, for he whispered happily in her ear, "Your seismographs are probably picking us up right now."

She laughed softly, then made the joke current among literature majors at the university: "Yes, very nice . . . the Earth moved."

After a second he got it and stifled a laugh. "Several thousand kilometers."

Laughter is harder to suppress than the sounds of love.

Of course it is impossible to conceal such activity in a group—not to mention a tent—of such small size, and the next morning Eileen got some pointed looks from John, some smiles from Mrs. M. It was a clear morning, and after they got the tent packed into the wagon and were on their way, Eileen hiked off whistling to herself. As they descended toward the broad plain at the bottom of the canyon mouth, she and Roger tuned in to their band 33 and talked.

"You really don't think this wash would look better with some cactus and sage in it, say? Or grasses?"

"Nope. I like it the way it is. See that pentagon of shards there?" He pointed. "How nice."

With the intercom they could wander far apart from each other and still converse, and no one could know they were talking, while each voice hung in the other's ear. So they talked and talked. Everyone has had conversations that have been crucial in their lives: clarity of expression, quickness of feeling, attentiveness to the other's words, a belief in the reality of the other's world—of these and other elements are such conversations made, and at the same time the words themselves can be concerned with the simplest, most ordinary things:

"Look at that rock."

"How nice that ridge is against the sky—it must be a hundred kilometers away, and it looks like you could touch it."

"Everything's so red."

"Yeah. Red Mars, I love it. I'm for red Mars."

She considered it. They hiked down the widening canyon ahead of the others, on opposite slopes. Soon they would be back in the world of cities, the big wide world. There were lots and lots of people out there, and anyone you met you might never see again. On the other hand . . . she looked across at the tall awkwardly proportioned man, striding with feline Martian grace over the dunes, in the dream gravity. Like a dancer.

"How old are you?" she asked.

"Twenty-six."

"My God!" He was already quite wrinkled. More sun than most.

"What?"

"I thought you were older."

"No."

"How long have you been doing this?"

"Hiking canyons?"

"Yes."

"Since I was six."

"Oh." That explained how he knew all this world so well.

She crossed the canyon to walk by his side; seeing her doing it, he descended his slope and they walked down the center of the wash.

"Can I come on another trip with you?"

He looked at her: behind the faceplate, a grin. "Oh yes. There are a lot of canyons to see."

The canyon opened up, then flattened out, and its walls melted into the broad boulder-studded plain on which the little outpost was set, some kilometers away. Eileen could just see it in the distance, like a castle made of glass: a tent like theirs, really, only much bigger. Behind it Olympus Mons rose straight up out of the sky.

Promises to Keep

JACK McDEVITT

Born in Philadelphia, Jack McDevitt now lives in Brunswick, Georgia, with his family. He is a frequent contributor to *Asimov's Science Fiction* and has also sold stories to *Analog, The Magazine of Fantasy & Science Fiction, Full Spectrum, Universe, The Twilight Zone Magazine, Chess Life* and elsewhere. An ex–naval officer, ex–English teacher, and ex–customs inspector, he retired in 1995 and now works full-time as a writer. His first novel, *The Hercules Text,* won a special citation for the Philip K. Dick award. His novels *Ancient Shores* and *Moonfall* have been Nebula finalists, and *The Engines of God* was a finalist for the Arthur C. Clarke Award. His other books include the story collection *Standard Candles* and most recently, *Infinity Beach.*

Here he takes us across the solar system to the moons of Jupiter, to the desolate frozen snowscapes of Callisto, for a very human drama of risk and exploration played out against the cold, inhuman immensity of space. . . .

I received a Christmas card last week from Ed Iseminger. The illustration was a rendering of the celebrated Christmas Eve telecast from Callisto: a lander stands serenely on a rubble-strewn plain, spilling warm yellow light through its windows. Needle-point peaks rise behind it, and the rim of a crater curves across the fore-ground. An enormous belted crescent dominates the sky.

In one window, someone has hung a wreath.

It is a moment preserved, a tableau literally created by Cathie Perth, extracted from her prop bag. Somewhere here, locked away among insurance papers and the deed to the house, is the tape of the original telecast, but I've never played it. In fact, I've seen it only once, on the night of the transmission. But I know the words, Cathie's words, read by Victor Landolfi in his rich baritone, blending the timeless values of the season with the spectral snows of another world. They appear in schoolbooks now, and on marble.

Inside the card, in large, block, defiant letters, Iseminger had printed "SEP-TEMBER!" It is a word with which he hopes to conquer a world. Sometimes, at night, when the snow sparkles under the hard cold stars (the way it did on Callisto), I think about him, and his quest. And I am very afraid.

I can almost see Cathie's footprints on the frozen surface. It was a good time, and I wish there were a way to step into the picture, to toast the holidays once more with Victor Landolfi, to hold onto Cathie Perth (and not let go!), and somehow to save us all. It was the end of innocence, a final meeting place for old friends.

We made the Christmas tape over a period of about five days. Cathie took literally hours of visuals, but Callisto is a place of rock and ice and deadening sameness: there is little to soften the effect of cosmic indifference. Which is why all those shots of towering peaks and tumbled boulders were taken at long range, and in half-light. Things not quite seen, she said, are always charming.

Her biggest problem had been persuading Landolfi to do the voice-over. Victor was tall, lean, ascetic. He was equipped with laser eyes and a huge black mustache. His world was built solely of subatomic particles, and driven by electromagnetics. Those who did not share his passions excited his contempt; which meant that he understood the utility of Cathie's public relations function at the same time that he deplored its necessity. To participate was to compromise one's integrity. His sense of delicacy, however, prevented his expressing that view to Cathie: he begged off rather on the press of time, winked apologetically, and straightened his mustache. "Sawyer will read it for you," he said, waving me impatiently into the conversation.

Cathie sneered, and stared irritably out a window (it was the one with the wreath) at Jupiter, heavy in the fragile sky. We knew, by then, that it had a definable surface, that the big planet was a world sea of liquid hydrogen, wrapped around a rocky core. "It must be frustrating," she said, "to know you'll never see it." Her tone was casual, almost frivolous, but Landolfi was not easily baited.

"Do you really think," he asked, with the patience of the superior being (Landolfi had no illusions about his capabilities), "that these little pieces of theater will make any difference? Yes, Catherine, of course it's frustrating. Especially when one realizes that we have the technology to put vehicles down there. . . ."

"And scoop out some hydrogen," Cathie added.

He shrugged. "It may happen someday."

"Victor, it never will if we don't sell the Program. This is the last shot. These ships are old, and nobody's going to build any new ones. Unless things change radically at home."

Landolfi closed his eyes. I knew what he was thinking: Cathie Perth was an outsider, an ex-television journalist who had probably slept her way on board. She played bridge, knew the film library by heart, read John Donne (for style, she said), and showed no interest whatever in the scientific accomplishments of the mission. We'd made far-reaching discoveries in the fields of plate tectonics, planetary climatology, and a dozen other disciplines. We'd narrowed the creation date down inside a range of a few million years. And we finally understood how it had happened! But Cathie's televised reports had de-emphasized the implications, and virtually ignored the mechanics of such things. Instead, while a global audience watched, Marjorie Aubuchon peered inspirationally out of a cargo lock at Ganymede (much in the fashion that Cortez must have looked at the Pacific on that first bright morning), her shoulder flag patch resplendent in the sunlight. And while the camera moved in for a close-up (her features were illuminated by a lamp Cathie had placed for the occasion in her helmet), Herman Selma solemnly intoned Cathie's comments on breaking the umbilical.

That was her style: brooding alien vistas reduced to human terms. In one of her best-known sequences, there had been no narration whatever: two spacesuited figures, obviously male and female, stood together in the shadow of the monumental Cadmus Ice Fracture on Europa, beneath three moons.

"Cathie," Landolfi said, with his eyes still shut, "I don't wish to be offensive: but do you really care? For the Program, that is? When we get home, you will write a book, you will be famous, you will be at the top of your profession. Are you really concerned with where the Program will be in twenty years?"

It was a fair question: Cathie'd made no secret of her hopes for a Pulitzer. And she stood to get it, no matter what happened after this mission. Moreover, although she'd tried to conceal her opinions, we'd been together a long time by then, almost three years, and we could hardly misunderstand the dark view she took of people who voluntarily imprisoned themselves for substantial portions of their lives to go 'rock-collecting.'

"No," she said. "I'm not, because there won't be a Program in twenty years." She looked around at each of us, weighing the effect of her words. Iseminger, a blond giant with a reddish beard, allowed a smile of lazy tolerance to soften his granite features. "We're in the same class as the pyramids," she continued, in a tone that was unemotional and irritatingly condescending. "We're a hell of an expensive operation, and for what? Do you think the taxpayers give a good goddam about the weather on Jupiter? There's nothing out here but gas and boulders. Playthings for eggheads!"

I sat and thought about it while she smiled sweetly, and Victor smoldered. I had not heard the solar system ever before described in quite those terms; I'd heard people call it *vast, awesome, magnificent, serene,* stuff like that. But never *boring.*

In the end, Landolfi read his lines. He did it, he said, to end the distraction.

Cathie was clearly pleased with the result. She spent three days editing the tapes, commenting frequently (and with good-natured malice) on the *resonance* and tonal qualities of the voice-over. She finished on the morning of the 24th (ship time, of course), and transmitted the report to *Greenswallow* for relay to Houston. "It'll make the evening newscasts," she said with satisfaction.

It was our third Christmas out. Except for a couple of experiments-in-progress, we were finished on Callisto and, in fact, in the Jovian system. Everybody was feeling good about that, and we passed an uneventful afternoon, playing bridge and talking about what we'd do when we got back. (Cathie had described a deserted beach near Tillamook, Oregon, where she'd grown up. "It would be nice to walk on it again, under a *blue* sky," she said. Landolfi had startled everyone at that point: he looked up from the computer console at which he'd been working, and his eyes grew very distant. "I think," he said, "when the time comes, I would like very much to walk with you. . . .")

For the most part, Victor kept busy that afternoon with his hobby: he was designing a fusion engine that would be capable, he thought, of carrying ships to Jupiter within a few weeks, and, possibly, would eventually open the stars to direct exploration. But I watched him: he turned away periodically from the display screen, to glance at Cathie. Yes (I thought), she would indeed be lovely against the rocks and the spume, her black hair free in the wind.

Just before dinner, we watched the transmission of Cathie's tape. It was very strong, and when it was finished we sat silently looking at one another. By then, Herman Selma and Esther Crowley had joined us. (Although two landers were down, Cathie had been careful to give the impression in her report that there had only been one. When I asked why, she said, "In a place like this, one lander is the Spirit of Man. Two landers is just two landers.") We toasted Victor, and we toasted Cathie. Almost everyone, it turned out, had brought down a bottle for the occasion. We sang and laughed, and somebody turned up the music. We'd long since discovered the effect of low-gravity dancing in cramped quarters, and I guess we made the most of it.

Marj Aubuchon, overhead in the linkup, called to wish us season's greetings, and called again later to tell us that the telecast, according to Houston, had been "well-received." That was government talk, of course, and it meant only that no one in authority could find anything to object to. Actually, somebody high up had considerable confidence in her: in order to promote the illusion of spontaneity, the tapes were being broadcast directly to the commercial networks.

Cathie, who by then had had a little too much to drink, gloated openly. "It's the best we've done," she said. "Nobody'll ever do it better."

We shared that sentiment. Landolfi raised his glass, winked at Cathie, and drained it.

We had to cut the evening short, because a lander's life-support system isn't designed to handle six people. (For that matter, neither was an Athena's.) But before we broke it up, Cathie surprised us all by proposing a final toast: "To Frank Steinitz," she said quietly. "And his crew."

Steinitz: there was a name, as they say, to conjure with. He had led the first deep-space mission, five Athenas to Saturn, fifteen years before. It had been the first attempt to capture the public imagination for a dying program: an investigation of a peculiar object filmed by a Voyager on Iapetus. But nothing much had come of it, and the mission had taken almost seven years. Steinitz and his people had begun as heroes, but in the end they'd become symbols of futility. The press had portrayed them mercilessly as personifications of outworn virtues. Someone had compared them to the Japanese soldiers found as late as the 1970s on Pacific islands, still defending a world long since vanished.

The Steinitz group bore permanent reminders of their folly: prolonged weightlessness had loosened ligaments and tendons, and weakened muscles. Several had developed heart problems, and all suffered from assorted neuroses. As one syndicated columnist had observed, they walked like a bunch of retired big-league catchers.

"That's a good way to end the evening," said Selma, beaming benevolently.

Landolfi looked puzzled. "Cathie," he rumbled, "you've questioned Steinitz's good sense any number of times. And ours, by the way. Isn't it a little hypocritical to drink to him?"

"I'm not impressed by his intelligence," she said, ignoring the obvious parallel. "But he and his people went all the way out to Saturn in those damned things—"

she waved in the general direction of the three Athenas orbiting overhead in linkup "—hanging onto baling wire and wing struts. I have to admire that."

"Hell," I said, feeling the effects a little myself, "we've got the same ships he had."

"Yes, you do," said Cathie pointedly.

I had trouble sleeping that night. For a long time, I lay listening to Landolfi's soft snore, and the electronic fidgeting of the operations computer. Cathie was bundled inside a gray blanket, barely visible in her padded chair.

She was right, of course. I knew that rubber boots would never again cross that white landscape, which had waited a billion years for us. The peaks glowed in the reflection of the giant planet: fragile crystalline beauty, on a world of terrifying stillness. Except for an occasional incoming rock, nothing more would ever happen here. Callisto's entire history was encapsuled within twelve days.

Pity there hadn't been something to those early notions about Venusian rain forests and canals on Mars. The Program might have had easier going had Burroughs or Bradbury been right. My God: how many grim surprises had disrupted fictional voyages to Mars? But the truth had been far worse than anything Wells or the others had ever committed to paper: the red planet was so dull that we hadn't even gone there.

Instead, we'd lumbered out to the giants. In ships that drained our lives and our health.

We could have done better; our ships could have been better. The computer beside which Landolfi slept contained his design for the fusion engine. And at JPL, an Army team had demonstrated that artificial gravity was possible: a real gravity field, not the pathetic fraction created on the Athenas by spinning the inner hull. There were other possibilities as well: infrared ranging could be adapted to replace our elderly scanning system; new alloys were under development. But it would cost billions to build a second-generation vehicle. And unless there were an incentive, unless Cathie Perth carried off a miracle, it would not happen.

Immediately overhead, a bright new star glittered, moving visibly (though slowly) from west to east. That was the linkup, three ships connected nose to nose by umbilicals and a magnetic docking system. Like the Saturn mission, we were a multiple vehicle operation. We were more flexible that way, and we had a safety factor: two ships would be adequate to get the nine-man mission home. Conditions might become a little stuffy, but we'd make it.

I watched it drift through the icy starfield.

Cathie had pulled the plug on the Christmas lights. But it struck me that Callisto would only have one Christmas, so I put them back on.

Victor was on board *Tolstoi* when we lost it. No one ever really knew precisely what happened. We'd begun our long fall toward Jupiter, gaining the acceleration which we'd need on the flight home. Cathie, Herman Selma (the mission commander), and I were riding *Greenswallow*. The ships had separated, and would not rejoin until we'd rounded Jupiter, and settled into our course for home. (The Athenas are really individually-powered modular units which travel, except when maneuvering, as a single vessel. They're connected bow-to-bow by electromagnets. Coils of segmented tubing, called "umbilicals" even though the term does not accurately describe their function, provide ready access among the forward areas of the ships. As many as six Athenas can be linked in this fashion, although only five have ever been built. The resulting structure would resemble a wheel.)

Between Callisto and Ganymede, we hit something: a drifting cloud of fine particles, a belt of granular material stretched so thin it never appeared on the LGD, before or after. Cathie later called it a cosmic sandbar; Iseminger thought it an unformed moon. It didn't matter: whatever it was, the mission plowed into it at almost 50,000 kilometers per hour. Alarms clattered, and red lamps blinked on.

In those first moments, I thought the ship was going to come apart. Herman was thrown across a bank of consoles and through an open hatch. I couldn't see Cathie, but a quick burst of profanity came from her direction. Things were being ripped off the hull. Deep within her walls, *Greenswallow* sighed. The lights dipped, came back, and went out. Emergency lamps cut in, and something big glanced off the side of the ship. More alarms howled, and I waited for the clamor of the throaty klaxon which would warn of a holing, and which consequently would be the last sound I could expect to hear in this life.

The sudden deceleration snapped my head back on the pads. (The collision had occurred at the worst possible time: *Greenswallow* was caught in the middle of an attitude alignment. We were flying backwards.)

The exterior monitors were blank: that meant the cameras were gone.

Cathie's voice: "Rob, you okay?"

"Yes."

"Can you see Herman?"

My angle was bad, and I was pinned in my chair. "No. He's back in cargo."

"Is there any way you can close the hatch?"

"Herman's in there," I protested, thinking she'd misunderstood.

"If something tears a hole out back there, we're all going to go. Keeping the door open won't help him."

I hesitated. Sealing up seemed to be the wrong thing to do. (Of course, the fact that the hatch had been open in the first place constituted a safety violation.) "It's on your console," I told her. "Hit the numerics on your upper right."

"Which one?"

"Hit them all." She was seated at the status board, and I could see a row of red lights: several other hatches were open. They should have closed automatically when the first alarms sounded.

We got hit again, this time in front. *Greenswallow* trembled, and loose pieces of metal rattled around inside the walls like broken teeth.

"Rob," she said. "I don't think it's working."

The baleful lights still glowed across the top of her board.

It lasted about three minutes.

When it was over, we hurried back to look at Herman. We were no longer rotating, and gravity had consequently dropped to zero. Selma, gasping, pale, his skin damp, was floating grotesquely over a pallet of ore-sample canisters. We got him to a couch and applied compresses. His eyes rolled shut, opened, closed again. "Inside," he said, gently fingering an area just off his sternum. "I think I've been chewed up a little." He raised his head slightly. "What kind of shape are we in?"

I left Cathie with him. Then I restored power, put on a suit and went outside.

The hull was a disaster: antennas were down, housings scored, lenses shattered. The lander was gone, ripped from its web. The port cargo area had buckled, and an auxiliary hatch was sprung. On the bow, the magnetic dock was hammered into slag. Travel between the ships was going to be a little tougher.

Greenswallow looked as if she had been sandblasted. I scraped particles out of her thruster nozzles, replaced cable, and bolted down mounts. I caught a glimpse of Amity's lights, sliding diagonally across the sky. As were the constellations.

"Cathie," I said. "I see Mac. But I think we're tumbling."

"Okay."

Iseminger was also on board Amity. And, fortunately, Marj Aubuchon, our surgeon. Herman's voice broke in, thick with effort. "Rob, we got no radio contact with anyone. Any sign of Victor?"

Ganymede was close enough that its craters lay exposed in harsh solar light. Halfway round the sky, the Pleiades glittered. *Tolstoi*'s green and red running lights should have been visible among, or near, the six silver stars. But the sky was empty. I stood a long time and looked, wondering how many other navigators on other oceans had sought lost friends in that constellation. What had they called it in antiquity? The rainy Pleiades. . . . "Only Amity," I said.

I tore out some cable and lobbed it in the general direction of Ganymede. Jupiter's enormous arc was pushing above the maintenance pods, spraying October light across the wreckage. I improvised a couple of antennas, replaced some black boxes, and then decided to correct the tumble, if I could.

"Try it now," I said.

Cathie acknowledged.

Two of the thrusters were useless. I went inside for spares, and replaced the faulty units. While I was finishing up, Cathie came back on. "Rob," she said, "radio's working, more or less. We have no long-range transmit, though."

"Okay. I'm not going to try to do anything about that right now."

"Are you almost finished?"

"Why?"

"Something occurred to me. Maybe the cloud, whatever that damned thing was that we passed through: maybe it's U-shaped."

"Thanks," I said. "I needed something to worry about."

"Maybe you should come back inside."

"Soon as I can. How's the patient doing?"

"Out," she said. "He was a little delirious when he was talking to you. Anyhow, I'm worried: I think something's broken internally. He never got his color back, and he's beginning to bring up blood. Rob, we need Marj."

"You hear anything from *Amity* yet?"

"Just a carrier wave." She did not mention *Tolstoi*. "How bad is it out there?"

From where I was tethered, about halfway back on the buckled beam, I could see a crack in the main plates that appeared to run the length of the port tube. I climbed out onto the exhaust assembly, and pointed my flashlight into the combustion chamber. Something glittered where the reflection should have been subdued. I got in and looked: silicon. Sand, and steel, had fused in the white heat of passage. The exhaust was blocked.

Cathie came back on. "What about it, Rob?" she asked. "Any serious problems?"

"Cathie," I said, "*Greenswallow*'s going to Pluto."

Herman thought I was Landolfi: he kept assuring me that everything was going to be okay. His pulse was weak and rapid, and he alternated between sweating and shivering. Cathie had got a blanket under him and buckled him down so he wouldn't hurt himself. She bunched some pillows under his feet, and held a damp compress to his head.

"That's not going to help much. Raising his legs, I mean."

She looked at me, momentarily puzzled. "Oh," she said. "Not enough gravity."

I nodded.

"Oh, Rob." Her eyes swept the cases and cannisters, all neatly tagged, silicates from Pasiphae, sulfur from Himalia, assorted carbon compounds from Callisto. We had evidence now that Io had formed elsewhere in the solar system, and been well along in middle age when it was captured. We'd all but eliminated the possibility that life existed in Jupiter's atmosphere. We understood why rings formed around gas giants, and we had a new clue to the cause of terrestrial ice ages. And I could see that Cathie was thinking about trading lives to satisfy the curiosity of a few academics. "We don't belong out here," she said, softly. "Not in these primitive shells."

I said nothing.

"I got a question for you," she continued. "We're not going to find *Tolstoi*, right?"

"Is that your question?"

"No. I wish it were. But the LGD can't see them. That means they're just not there." Her eyes filled with tears, but she shook her head impatiently. "And we can't steer this thing. Can *Amity* carry six people?"

"It might have to."

"That wasn't what I asked."

"Food and water would be tight. Especially since we're running out of time, and wouldn't be able to transfer much over. If any. So we'd all be a little thinner when we got back. But yes, I think we could survive."

We stared at one another, and then she turned away. I became conscious of the ship: the throb of power deep in her bulkheads (power now permanently bridled by conditions in the combustion chambers), the soft amber glow of the navigation lamps in the cockpit.

McGuire's nasal voice, from *Amity*, broke the uneasy silence. "Herman, you okay?"

Cathie looked at me, and I nodded. "Mac," she said, "this is Perth. Herman's hurt. We need Marj."

"Okay," he said. "How bad?"

"We don't know. Internal injuries, looks like. He appears to be in shock."

We heard him talking to someone else. Then he came back. "We're on our way. I'll put Marj on in a minute; maybe she can help from here. How's the ship?"

"Not good: the dock's gone, and the engine might as well be."

He asked me to be specific. "If we try a burn, the rear end'll fall off."

McGuire delivered a soft, venomous epithet. And then: "Do what you can for Herman. Marj'll be right here."

Cathie was looking at me strangely. "He's worried," she said.

"Yes. He's in charge now. . . ."

"Rob, you say you *think* we'll be okay. What's the problem?"

"We might," I said, "run a little short of air."

Greenswallow continued her plunge toward Jupiter at a steadily increasing rate and a sharp angle of approach: we would pass within about 60,000 kilometers, and then drop completely out of the plane of the solar system. We appeared to be heading in the general direction of the Southern Cross.

Cathie worked on Herman. His breathing steadied, and he slipped in and out of his delirium. We sat beside him, not talking much. After awhile, Cathie asked, "What happens now?"

"In a few hours," I said, "we'll reach our insertion point. By then, we have to be ready to change course." She frowned, and I shrugged. "That's it," I said. "It's all the time we have to get over to *Amity*. If we don't make the insertion on time, *Amity* won't have the fuel to throw a U-turn later."

"Rob, how are we going to get Herman over there?"

That was an uncomfortable question. The prospect of jamming him down into a suit was less than appealing, but there was no other way. "We'll just have to float him over," I said. "Marj won't like it much."

"Neither will Herman."

"You wanted a little high drama," I said, unnecessarily. "The next show should be a barnburner."

Her mouth tightened, and she turned away from me.

One of the TV cameras had picked up the approach of *Amity*. Some of her lights were out, and she too looked a bit bent. The Athena is a homely vessel in the best of times, whale-shaped and snub-nosed, with a midship flare that suggests middle-age spread. But I was glad to see her.

Cathie snuffled at the monitor, and blew her nose. "Your Program's dead, Rob." Her eyes blazed momentarily, like a dying fire into which one has flung a few drops of water. "We're leaving three of our people out here; and if you're right about the air, we'll get home with a shipload of detectives, or worse. Won't that look good on the six o'clock news?" She gazed vacantly at *Amity*'s image. "I'd hoped," she said, "that if things went well, Victor would have lived to see a ship carry his fusion engine. And maybe his name, as well. Ain't gonna happen, though. Not ever."

I had not allowed myself to think about the oxygen problem we were going to face. The Athenas recycle their air supply: the converters in a single ship can maintain a crew of three, or even four, indefinitely. But six?

I was not looking forward to the ride home.

A few minutes later, a tiny figure detached itself from the shadow of the Athena and started across: Marj Aubuchon on a maintenance sled. McGuire's voice erupted from the ship's speakers. "Rob, we've taken a long look at your engines, and we agree with your assessment. The damage complicates things." Mac had a talent for understatement. It derived, not from a sophisticated sense of humor, but from a genuine conviction of his own inferiority. He preferred to solve problems by denying their existence. He was the only one of the nine astronauts who could have been accurately described as passive: other people's opinions carried great weight with him. His prime value to the mission was his grasp of Athena systems. But he'd been a reluctant crewman, a man who periodically reminded us that he wanted only to retire to his farm in Indiana. He wouldn't have been along at all except that one guy died and somebody else came down with an unexpected (but thoroughly earned) disease. Now, with Selma incapacitated and Landolfi gone, McGuire was in command. It must have been disconcerting for him. "We've got about five hours," he continued. "Don't let Marj get involved in major surgery. She's already been complaining to me that it doesn't sound as if it'll be possible to move him. *We have no alternative.* She knows that, but you know how she is. Okay?"

One of the monitors had picked him up. He looked rumpled, and nervous. Not an attitude to elicit confidence. "Mac," said Cathie, "we may kill him trying to get him over there."

"You'll kill him if you don't," he snapped. "Get your personal stuff together, and bring it with you. You won't be going back."

"What about trying to transfer some food?" I asked.

"We can't dock," he said. "And there isn't time to float it across."

"Mac," said Cathie, "is *Amity* going to be able to support six people?"

I listened to McGuire breathing. He turned away to issue some trivial instructions to Iseminger. When he came back he said, simply and tonelessly, "Probably not." And then, coldbloodedly (I thought), "How's Herman doing?"

Maybe it was my imagination. Certainly there was nothing malicious in his tone, but Cathie caught it too, and turned sharply round. "McGuire is a son-of-a-bitch," she hissed. I don't know whether Mac heard it.

Marjorie Aubuchon was short, blond, and irritable. When I relayed McGuire's concerns about time, she said, "God knows, that's all I've heard for the last half-hour." She observed that McGuire was a jerk, and bent over Herman. The blood was pink and frothy on his lips. After a few minutes she said, to no one in particular, "Probably a punctured lung." She waved Cathie over, and began filling a hypo; I went for a walk.

At sea, there's a long tradition of sentiment between mariners and their ships. Enlisted men identify with them, engineers baby them, and captains go down with them. No similar attitude has developed in space flight. We've never had an *Endeavor*, or a *Golden Hind*. Always, off Earth, it has been the mission, rather than the ship. Friendship VII and Apollo XI were far more than vehicles. I'm not sure why that is; maybe it reflects Cathie's view that travel between the worlds is still in its Kon-Tiki phase: the voyage itself is of such epic proportions that everything else is overwhelmed.

But I'd lived almost three years on *Greenswallow*. It was a long time to be confined to her narrow spaces. Nevertheless, she was shield and provider against that enormous abyss, and I discovered (while standing in the doorway of my cabin) a previously unfelt affection for her.

A few clothes were scattered round the room, a shirt was hung over my terminal, and two pictures were mounted on the plastic wall. One was a Casnavan print of a covered bridge in New Hampshire; the other was a telecopy of an editorial cartoon that had appeared in the *Washington Post*. The biggest human problem we had, of course, was sheer boredom. And Cathie had tried to capture the dimensions of the difficulty by showing crewmembers filling the long days on the outbound journey with bridge. ("It would be nice," Cathie's narrator had said at one point, "if we could take everybody out to an Italian restaurant now and then.") The *Post* cartoon had appeared several days later: it depicted four astronauts holding cards. (We could recognize Selma, Landolfi, and Marj. The fourth, whose back was turned, was exceedingly feminine, and appeared to be Esther Crowley.) An enormous bloodshot eye is looking in through one window; a tentacle and a UFO are visible through another. The "Selma" character, his glasses characteristically down on his nose, is examining his hand, and delivering the caption. *Dummy looks out the window and checks the alien.*

I packed the New Hampshire bridge, and left the cartoon. If someone comes by, in 20 million years or so, he might need a laugh. I went up to the cockpit with my bag.

McGuire checked with me to see how we were progressing. "Fine," I told him. I was still sitting there four hours later when Cathie appeared behind me.

"Rob," she said, "we're ready to move him." She smiled wearily. "Marj says he should be okay if we can get him over there without breaking anything else."

We cut the spin on the inner module to about point-oh-five. Then we lifted Herman onto a stretcher, and carried him carefully down to the airlock.

Cathie stared straight ahead, saying nothing. Her fine-boned cheeks were pale, and her eyes seemed focused far away. These, I thought, were her first moments to herself, unhampered by other duties. The impact of events was taking hold.

Marj called McGuire and told him we were starting over, and that she would need a sizable pair of shears when we got there to cut Herman's suit open. "Please have them ready," she said. "We may be in a hurry."

I had laid out his suit earlier: we pulled it up over his legs. That was easy, but the rest of it was slow, frustrating work. "We need a special kind of unit for this," Marj said. "Probably a large bag, without arms or legs. If we're ever dumb enough to do anything like this again, I'll recommend it."

McGuire urged us to hurry.

Once or twice, Cathie's eyes met mine. Something passed between us, but I was too distracted to define it. Then we were securing his helmet, and adjusting the oxygen mixture.

"I think we're okay," Marj observed, her hand pressed against Selma's chest. "Let's get him over there . . ."

I opened the inner airlock, and pulled my own helmet into place. Then we guided Herman in, and secured him to *Greenswallow*'s maintenance sled. (The sled was little more than a toolshed with jet nozzles.) I recovered my bag and stowed it on board.

"I'd better get my stuff," Cathie said. "You can get Herman over all right?"

"Of course," said Marj. "*Amity*'s sled is secured outside the lock. Use that."

She hesitated in the open hatchway, raised her left hand, and spread the fingers wide. Her eyes grew very round, and she formed two syllables that I was desperately slow to understand: in fact, I don't think I translated the gesture, the word, until we were halfway across to *Amity*, and the lock was irrevocably closed behind us.

"Good-bye."

Cathie's green eyes sparkled with barely controlled emotion across a dozen or so monitors. Her black hair, which had been tied back earlier, now framed her angular features and fell to her shoulders. It was precisely in that partial state of disarray that tends to be most appealing. She looked as if she'd been crying, but her jaw was set, and she stood erect. Beneath the gray tunic, her breast rose and fell.

"What the hell are you doing, Perth?" demanded McGuire. He looked tired, almost ill. He'd gained weight since we'd left the Cape, his hair had whitened and retreated, his flesh had grown blotchy, and he'd developed jowls. The contrast with his dapper image in the mission photo was sobering. "Get moving!" he said, striving to keep his voice from rising. "We're not going to make our burn!"

"I'm staying where I am," she said. "I couldn't make it over there now anyway. I wouldn't even have time to put on the suit."

McGuire's puffy eyelids slid slowly closed. "Why?" he asked.

She looked out of the cluster of screens, a segmented Cathie, a group Cathie. "Your ship won't support six people, Mac."

"Dammit!" His voice was a harsh rasp. "It would have just meant we'd cut down activity. Sleep a lot." He waved a hand in front of his eyes, as though his vision were blurred. "Cathie, we've lost you. There's no way we can get you back!"

"I know."

No one said anything. Iseminger stared at her.

"Is Herman okay?" she asked.

"Marj is still working on him," I said. "She thinks we got him across okay."

"Good."

A series of yellow lamps blinked on across the pilot's console. We had two minutes. "Damn," I said, suddenly aware of another danger: *Amity* was rotating, turning toward its new course. Would *Greenswallow* even survive the ignition? I looked at McGuire, who understood. His fingers flicked over press pads, and rows of numbers flashed across the navigation monitor. I could see muscles working in Cathie's jaws; she looked down at Mac's station as though she could read the result.

"It's all right," he said. "She'll be clear."

"Cathie . . ." Iseminger's voice was almost strangled. "If I'd known you intended anything like this . . ."

"I know, Ed." Her tone was gentle, a lover's voice, perhaps. Her eyes were wet: she smiled anyway, full face, up close.

Deep in the systems, pumps began to whine. "I wish," said Iseminger, absolutely without expression, "that we could do something."

She turned her back, strode with unbearable grace across the command center, away from us, and passed into the shadowy interior of the cockpit. Another camera picked her up there, and we got a profile: she was achingly lovely in the soft glow of the navigation lamps.

"There is something . . . you can do," she said. "Build Landolfi's engine. And come back for me."

For a brief moment, I thought Mac was going to abort the burn. But he sat frozen, fists clenched, and did the right thing, which is to say, nothing. It struck me that McGuire was incapable of intervening.

And I knew also that the woman in the cockpit was terrified of what she had done. It had been a good performance, but she'd utterly failed to conceal the fear that looked out of her eyes. And I realized with shock that she'd acted, not to prolong her life, but to save the Program. I watched her face as *Amity*'s engines ignited, and we began to draw away. Like McGuire, she seemed paralyzed, as though the nature of the calamity which she'd embraced was just becoming clear to her. Then it—she—was gone.

"What happened to the picture?" snapped Iseminger.

"She turned it off," I said. "I don't think she wants us to see her just now."

He glared at me, and spoke to Mac. "Why the hell," he demanded, "couldn't he have brought her back with him?" His fists were knotted.

"I didn't know," I said. "How could I know?" And I wondered, how could I not?

When the burn ended, the distance between the two ships had opened to only a few kilometers. But it was a gulf, I thought, wider than any across which men had before looked at each other.

Iseminger called her name relentlessly. (We knew she could hear us.) But we got only the carrier wave.

Then her voice crackled across the command center. "Good," she said. "Excellent. Check the recorders: make sure you got everything on tape." Her image was back. She was in full light again, tying up her hair. Her eyes were hooded, and her lips pursed thoughtfully. "Rob," she continued, "fade it out during Ed's response, when he's calling my name. Probably, you'll want to reduce the background noise at that point. Cut all the business about who's responsible. We want a sacrifice, not an oversight."

"My God, Cathie," I said. I stared at her, trying to understand. "What have you done?"

She took a deep breath. "I meant what I said. I have enough food to get by here for eight years or so. More if I stretch it. *And plenty of fresh air.* Well, relatively fresh. I'm better off than any of us would be if six people were trying to survive on *Amity*."

"Cathie!" howled McGuire. He sounded in physical agony. "Cathie, we didn't know for sure about life support. The converters might have kept up. There might have been enough air! It was just an estimate!"

"This is a hell of a time to tell me," she said. "Well, it doesn't matter now. Listen, I'll be fine. I've got books to read, and maybe one to write. My long-range communications are *kaput*, Rob knows that, so you'll have to come back for the book, too." She smiled. "You'll like it, Mac." The command center got very still. "And on nights when things really get boring, I can play bridge with the computer."

McGuire shook his head. "You're sure you'll be all right? You seemed pretty upset a few minutes ago."

She looked at me and winked.

"The first Cathie was staged, Mac," I said.

"I give up," McGuire sighed. "Why?" He swiveled round to face the image on his screen. "Why would you do that?"

"That young woman," she replied, "was committing an act of uncommon valor, as they say in the Marines. And she had to be vulnerable." And compellingly lovely, I thought. In those last moments, I was realizing what it might mean to love Cathie Perth. "This Cathie," she grinned, "is doing the only sensible thing. And taking a sabbatical as well. Do what you can to get the ship built. I'll be waiting." She paused. "Somebody should suggest they name it after Victor."

This is the fifth Christmas since that one on Callisto. It's a long time by any human measure. We drifted out of radio contact during the first week. There was some talk of broadcasting instructions to her for repairing her long-range transmission equipment. But she'd have to go outside to do it, so the idea was prudently tabled.

She was right about that tape. In my lifetime, I've never seen people so singlemindedly aroused. It created a global surge of sympathy and demands for action that seem to grow in intensity with each passing year. Funded partially by contributions and technical assistance from abroad, NASA has been pushing the construction of the fusion vessel that Victor Landolfi dreamed of.

Iseminger was assigned to help with the computer systems, and he's kept me informed of progress. The most recent public estimates had anticipated a spring launch. But that single word *September* in Iseminger's card suggests that one more obstacle has been encountered; and it means still another year before we can hope to reach her.

We broadcast to her on a regular basis. I volunteered to help, and I sit sometimes and talk to her for hours. She gets a regular schedule of news, entertainment, sports, whatever. And, if she's listening, she knows that we're coming.

And she also knows that her wish that the fusion ship be named for Victor Landolfi has been disregarded. The rescue vehicle will be the *Catherine Perth*.

If she's listening: we have no way of knowing. And I worry a lot. Can a human being survive six years of absolute solitude? Iseminger was here for a few days last summer, and he tells me he is confident. "She's a tough lady," he said, any number of times. "Nothing bothers her. She even gave us a little theater at the end."

And that's what scares me: Cathie's theatrical technique. I've thought about it, on the long ride home, and here. I kept a copy of the complete tape of that final conversation, despite McGuire's instructions to the contrary, and I've watched it a few times. It's locked downstairs in a file cabinet now, and I don't look at it anymore. I'm afraid to. There are two Cathie Perths on the recording: the frightened, courageous one who galvanized a global public; and our Cathie, preoccupied with her job, flexible, almost indifferent to her situation. A survivor.

And, God help me, I can't tell which one was staged.

Lieserl

STEPHEN BAXTER

Like many of his colleagues here at the end of the nineties—Greg Egan comes to mind, as do people like Paul J. McAuley, Michael Swanwick, Iain M. Banks, Bruce Sterling, Pat Cadigan, Brian Stableford, Gregory Benford, Ian McDonald, Gwyneth Jones, Vernor Vinge, Greg Bear, David Marusek, Geoff Ryman, and a half-dozen others—British writer Stephen Baxter has been engaged for the last ten years or so with the task of revitalizing and reinventing the hard-science story for a new generation of readers, producing work on the cutting edge of science that bristles with weird new ideas and often takes place against vistas of almost outrageously cosmic scope.

Arthur C. Clarke's work has clearly been a strong influence on Baxter's own (he's even written a story in collaboration with Clarke), and, like Clarke, Baxter seems to have a special fascination with the theme of exploration, delighting in taking us to places never visited by anyone before, including ice caverns deep inside Mercury, the core of the Moon, the surface of a sentient Venus, an artificial planet made of dark matter, and many other outré locations. Like Clarke, however, and like his colleagues named earlier, Baxter rarely loses track of the *human* side of the equation— as amply demonstrated by "Lieserl," which introduces us to one of the strangest and most haunting characters you're ever likely to meet and shows us that sometimes explorers aren't born; they're *made*.

Baxter made his first sale to *Interzone* in 1987 and since then has become one of that magazine's most frequent contributors, as well as making sales to *Asimov's Science Fiction, Science Fiction Age, Zenith,* and *New Worlds* and elsewhere. He's one of the most prolific of the new writers of the nineties and is rapidly becoming one of the most popular and acclaimed of them as well. Baxter's first novel, *Raft,* was released in 1991 to wide and enthusiastic response and was rapidly followed by other well-received novels such as *Timelike Infinity, Anti-Ice, Flux,* and the H. G. Wells homage—a sequel to *The Time Machine*—*The Time Ships,* which won both the Arthur C. Clarke Award and the Philip K. Dick Award. Baxter's other books include the novels *Voyage, Titan,* and *Moonseed* and the collections *Vacuum Diagrams: Stories of the Xeelee Sequence* and *Traces.* His most recent book is the novel *Mammoth,* Book One: *Silverhair.* Upcoming is a new novel, *Manifold: Time* and a collaboration with Sir Arthur C. Clarke, *The Light of Other Days.*

Lieserl was suspended inside the body of the Sun.

She spread her arms wide and lifted up her face. She was deep within the Sun's convective zone, the broad mantle of turbulent material beneath the glowing photosphere; convective cells larger than the Earth, tangled with ropes of magnetic flux, filled the world around her. She could hear the roar of the great convective founts, smell the stale photons diffusing out towards space from the remote fusing core.

She felt as if she were inside some huge cavern. Looking up she could see how the photosphere formed a glowing roof over her world perhaps fifty thousand miles above her, and the boundary of the inner radiative zone was a shining, impenetrable floor another fifty thousand miles beneath.

Lieserl? Can you hear me? Are you all right?

Kevan Scholes. It sounded like her mother's voice, she thought.

She thrust her arms down by her sides and swooped up, letting the floor and roof of the cavern-world wheel around her. She opened up her senses, so that she could feel the turbulence as a whisper against her skin, the glow of hard photons from the core as a gentle warmth against her face.

Lieserl? Lieserl?

She remembered how her mother had enfolded her in her arms. 'The Sun, Lieserl. *The Sun* . . .'

Even at the moment she was born she knew something was wrong.

A face loomed over her: wide, smooth, smiling. The cheeks were damp, the glistening eyes huge. 'Lieserl. Oh, Lieserl . . .'

Lieserl. My name, then.

She explored the face before her, studying the lines around the eyes, the humorous upturn of the mouth, the strong nose. It was an intelligent, lived-in face. *This is a good human being,* she thought. *Good stock* . . .

Good stock? What am I thinking of?

This was impossible. She felt terrified of her own explosive consciousness. She shouldn't even be able to focus her eyes yet . . .

She tried to touch her mother's face. Her own hand was still moist with amniotic fluid—*but it was growing visibly,* the bones extending and broadening, filling out the loose skin like a glove.

She opened her mouth. It was dry, her gums already sore with budding teeth. She tried to speak.

Her mother's eyes brimmed with tears. 'Oh, Lieserl. My impossible baby.'

Strong arms reached beneath her. She felt weak, helpless, consumed by growth. Her mother lifted her up, high in the air. Bony adult fingers dug into the aching flesh of her back; her head lolled backwards, the expanding muscles still too weak to support the burgeoning weight of her head. She could sense other adults surrounding her, the bed in which she'd been born, the outlines of a room.

She was held before a window, with her body tipped forward. Her head lolled; spittle laced across her chin.

An immense light flooded her eyes.

She cried out.

Her mother enfolded her in her arms. 'The Sun, Lieserl. *The Sun . . .*'

The first few days were the worst. Her parents—impossibly tall, looming figures—took her through brightly lit rooms, a garden always flooded with sunlight. She learned to sit up. The muscles in her back fanned out, pulsing as they grew. To distract her from the unending pain, clowns tumbled over the grass before her, chortling through their huge red lips, then popping out of existence in clouds of pixels.

She grew explosively, feeding all the time, a million impressions crowding into her soft sensorium.

There seemed to be no limit to the number of rooms in this place, this House. Slowly she began to understand that some of the rooms were Virtual chambers—blank screens against which any number of images could be projected. But even so, the House must comprise hundreds of rooms. And she—with her parents—wasn't alone here, she slowly realized. There were other people, but at first they kept away, out of sight, apparent only by their actions: the meals they prepared, the toys they left her.

On the third day her parents took her on a trip by flitter. It was the first time she'd been away from the House, its grounds. She stared through the bulbous windows, pressing her nose to heated glass. The journey was an arc over a toylike landscape; a breast of blue ocean curved away from the land, all around her. This was the island of Skiros, her mother told her, and the sea was called Aegean. The House was the largest construct on the island; it was a jumble of white, cube-shaped buildings, linked by corridors and surrounded by garden-grass, trees. Further out there were bridges and roads looping through the air above the ground, houses like a child's bricks sprinkled across glowing hillsides.

Everything was drenched in heavy, liquid sunlight.

The flitter snuggled at last against a grassy sward close to the shore of an ocean. Lieserl's mother lifted her out and placed her—on her stretching, unsteady legs—on the rough, sandy grass.

Hand in hand, the little family walked down a short slope to the beach.

The Sun burned through thinned air from an unbearably blue sky. Her vision seemed telescopic. She looked at distant groups of children and adults playing—far away, half-way to the horizon—and it was as if she was among them herself. Her feet, still uncertain, pressed into gritty, moist sand. She could taste the brine salt on the air; it seemed to permeate her very skin.

She found mussels clinging to a ruined pier. She prised them away with a toy spade, and gazed, fascinated, at their slime-dripping feet.

She sat on the sand with her parents, feeling her light costume stretch over her still-stretching limbs. They played a simple game, of counters moving over a floating Virtual board, pictures of ladders and hissing snakes. There was laughter, mock complaints by her father, elaborate pantomimes of cheating.

Her senses were electric. It was a wonderful day, full of light and joy, extraordinarily vivid sensations. Her parents loved her—she could see that in the way they moved with each other, came to her, played with her.

They must know she was different; but they didn't seem to care.

She didn't want to be different—to be *wrong*. She closed her mind against the thoughts, and concentrated on the snakes, the ladders, the sparkling counters.

Every morning she woke up in a bed that felt too small.

Lieserl liked the garden. She liked to watch the flowers straining their tiny, pretty faces towards the Sun, as the great light climbed patiently across the sky. The sunlight made the flowers grow, her father told her. Maybe she was like a flower, she thought, growing too quickly in all this sunlight.

On the fifth day she was taken to a wide, irregularly shaped, colourful classroom. This room was full of children—*other children!*—and toys, drawings, books. Sunlight flooded the room; perhaps there was some clear dome stretched over the open walls.

The children sat on the floor and played with paints and dolls, or talked earnestly to brilliantly-coloured Virtual figures—smiling birds, tiny clowns. The children turned to watch as she came in with her mother, their faces round and bright, like dapples of sunlight through leaves. She'd never been so close to other children before. Were these children *different* too?

One small girl scowled at her, and Lieserl quailed against her mother's legs. But her mother's familiar warm hands pressed into her back. 'Go ahead. It's all right.'

As she stared at the unknown girl's scowling face, Lieserl's questions, her too-adult, too-sophisticated doubts, seemed to evaporate. Suddenly, all that mattered to her—all that mattered in the world—was that she should be accepted by these children—that they wouldn't know she was *different*.

An adult approached her: a man, young, thin, his features bland with youth. He wore a jumpsuit coloured a ludicrous orange; in the sunlight, the glow of it shone up over his chin. He smiled at her. 'Lieserl, isn't it? My name's Michael. We're glad you're here.' In a louder, exaggerated voice, he said, 'Aren't we, people?'

He was answered by a rehearsed, chorused 'Yes'.

'Now come and we'll find something for you to do,' Michael said. He led her across the child-littered floor to a space beside a small boy. The boy—red-haired, with startling blue eyes—was staring at a Virtual puppet which endlessly formed and reformed: the figure two, collapsing into two snowflakes, two swans, two dancing children; the figure three, followed by three bears, three fish swimming in the air, three cakes. The boy mouthed the numbers, following the tinny voice of the Virtual. 'Two. One. Two and one is three.'

Michael introduced her to the boy—Tommy—and she sat down with him. Tommy, she was relieved to find, was so fascinated by his virtual that he scarcely seemed aware that Lieserl was present—let alone *different*.

The number Virtual ran through its cycle and winked out of existence. 'Bye-bye, Tommy! Goodbye, Lieserl!'

Tommy was resting on his stomach, his chin cupped in his palms. Lieserl, awkwardly, copied his posture. Now Tommy turned to her—without appraisal, merely looking at her, with unconscious acceptance.

Lieserl said, 'Can we see it again?'

He yawned and poked a finger into one nostril. 'No. Let's see another. There's a great one about the pre-Cambrian explosion—'

'The what?'

He waved a hand dismissively. 'You know, the Burgess Shale and all that. Wait till you see *Hallucigenia* crawling over your neck . . .'

The children played, and learned, and napped. Later, the girl who'd scowled at Lieserl—Ginnie—started some trouble. She poked fun at the way Lieserl's bony wrists stuck out of her sleeves (Lieserl's growth rate was slowing, but she was still growing out of her clothes during a day). Then—unexpectedly, astonishingly—Ginnie started to bawl, claiming that Lieserl had walked through her Virtual. When Michael came over Lieserl started to explain, calmly and rationally, that Ginnie must be mistaken; but Michael told her not to cause such distress, and for punishment she was forced to sit away from the other children for ten minutes, without stimulation.

It was all desperately, savagely unfair. It was the longest ten minutes of Lieserl's life. She glowered at Ginnie, filled with resentment.

The next day she found herself looking forward to going to the room with the children again. She set off with her mother through sunlit corridors. They reached the room Lieserl remembered—there was Michael, smiling a little wistfully to her, and Tommy, and the girl Ginnie—but Ginnie seemed different: childlike, unformed . . .

At least a head shorter than Lieserl.

Lieserl tried to recapture that delicious enmity of the day before, but it vanished even as she conjured it. Ginnie was just a kid.

She felt as if something had been stolen from her.

Her mother squeezed her hand. 'Come on. Let's find a new room for you to play in.'

★ ★ ★

Every day was unique. Every day Lieserl spent in a new place, with new people.

The world glowed with sunlight. Shining points trailed endlessly across the sky: low-orbit habitats and comet nuclei, tethered for power and fuel. People walked through a sea of information, with access to the Virtual libraries available anywhere in the world, at a subvocalized command. Lieserl learned quickly. She read about her parents. They were scientists, studying the Sun. They weren't alone; there were many people, huge resources, devoted to the Sun.

In the libraries there was a lot of material about the Sun, little of which she could follow. But she sensed some common threads.

Once, people had taken the Sun for granted. No longer. Now—for some reason—they *feared* it.

On the ninth day Lieserl studied herself in a Virtual holo-mirror. She had the image turn around, so she could see the shape of her skull, the lie of her hair. There was still some childish softness in her face, she thought, but the woman inside her was emerging already, as if her childhood was a receding tide. She would look like her mother—Phillida—in the strong-nosed set of her face, her large, vulnerable eyes; but she would have the sandy colouring of her father, George.

Lieserl looked about nine years old. But she was just nine *days* old.

She bade the Virtual break up; it shattered into a million tiny images of her face which drifted away like flies in the sunlit air.

Phillida and George were fine parents, she thought. They spent their time away from her working through technical papers—which scrolled through the air like falling leaves—and exploring elaborate, onion-ring Virtual models of stars. Although they were both clearly busy they gave themselves to her without hesitation. She moved in a happy world of smiles, sympathy and support.

Her parents loved her unreservedly. But that wasn't always enough.

She started to come up with more complicated, detailed questions. Like, what was the mechanism by which she was growing so rapidly? She didn't seem to eat more than the other children she encountered; what could be fuelling her absurd growth rates?

How did she *know* so much? She'd been born self-aware, with even the rudiments of language in her head. The Virtuals she interacted with in the classrooms were fun, and she always seemed to learn something new; but she absorbed no more than scraps of knowledge through them compared to the feast of insight with which she awoke each morning.

What had taught her, in the womb? What was teaching her now?

She had no answers. But perhaps—somehow—it was all connected with this strange, global obsession with the Sun. She remembered her childish fantasy—that she might be like a flower, straining up too quickly to the Sun. Maybe, she wondered now, there was some grain of truth in that insight.

The strange little family had worked up some simple, homely rituals together. Lieserl's favourite was the game, each evening, of snakes and ladders. George brought home an old set—a *real* board made of card, and wooden counters. Already Lieserl was too old for the game; but she loved the company of her parents, her father's elaborate jokes, the simple challenge of the game, the feel of the worn, antique counters.

Phillida showed her how to use Virtuals to produce her own game boards. Her first efforts, on her eleventh day, were plain, neat forms, little more than copies of the commercial boards she'd seen. But soon she began to experiment. She drew a huge board of a million squares, which covered a whole room—she could walk through the board, a planar sheet of light at about waist-height. She crammed the board with intricate, curling snakes, vast ladders, vibrantly glowing squares—detail piled on detail.

The next morning she walked with eagerness to the room where she'd built her board—and was immediately disappointed. Her efforts seemed pale, static, derivative—obviously the work of a child, despite the assistance of the Virtual software.

She wiped the board clean, leaving a grid of pale squares floating in the air. Then she started to populate it again—but this time with animated half-human snakes, slithering 'ladders' of a hundred forms. She'd learned to access the Virtual libraries, and she plundered the art and history of a hundred centuries to populate her board.

Of course it was no longer possible to play games on the board, but that didn't matter. The board was the thing, a little world in itself. She withdrew a little from her parents, spending long hours in deep searches through the libraries. She gave up her classes. Her parents didn't seem to mind; they came to speak to her regularly, and showed an interest in her projects, and respected her privacy.

The board kept her interest the next day. But now she evolved elaborate games, dividing the board into countries and empires with arbitrary bands of glowing light. Armies of ladder-folk joined with legions of snakes in crude reproductions of the great events of human history.

She watched the symbols flicker across the Virtual board, shimmering, coalescing; she dictated lengthy chronicles of the histories of her imaginary countries.

By the end of the day, though, she was starting to grow more interested in the history texts she was plundering than in her own elaborations on them. She went to bed, eager for the next morning to come.

She awoke in darkness, doubled in agony.

She called for light, which flooded the room, sourceless. She sat up in bed.

Blood spotted the sheets. She screamed.

Phillida sat with her, cradling her head. Lieserl pressed herself against her mother's warmth, trying to still her trembling.

'I think it's time you asked me your questions.'

Lieserl sniffed. 'What questions?'

'The ones you've carried around with you since the moment you were born.' Phillida smiled. 'I could see it in your eyes, even at that moment. You poor thing . . . to be burdened with so much *awareness*. I'm sorry, Lieserl.'

Lieserl pulled away. Suddenly she felt cold, vulnerable.

'Tell me why you're sorry,' she said at last.

'You're my daughter.' Phillida placed her hands on Lieserl's shoulders and pushed her face close; Lieserl could feel the warmth of her breath, and the soft room light caught the grey in her mother's blonde hair, making it seem to shine. 'Never forget that. You're as human as I am. But—' She hesitated.

'But what?'

'But you're being—*engineered.*'

Nanobots swarmed through Lieserl's body, Phillida said. They plated calcium over her bones, stimulated the generation of new cells, force-growing her body like some absurd human sunflower—they even implanted memories, artificial learning, directly into her cortex.

Lieserl felt like scraping at her skin, gouging out this artificial infection. '*Why?* Why did you let this be done to me?'

Phillida pulled her close, but Lieserl stayed stiff, resisting mutely. Phillida buried her face in Lieserl's hair; Lieserl felt the soft weight of her mother's cheek on the crown of her head. 'Not yet,' Phillida said. 'Not yet. A few more days, my love. That's all . . .'

Phillida's cheeks grew warmer, as if she was crying, silently, into her daughter's hair.

Lieserl returned to her snakes-and-ladders board. She found herself looking on her creation with affection, but also nostalgic sadness; she felt distant from this elaborate, slightly obsessive concoction.

Already she'd outgrown it.

She walked into the middle of the sparkling board and bade a Sun, a foot wide, rise out from the center of her body. Light swamped the board, shattering it.

She wasn't the only adolescent who had constructed fantasy worlds like this. She read about the Brontes, in their lonely parsonage in the north of England, and their elaborate shared world of kings and princes and empires. And she read about the history of the humble game of snakes and ladders. The game had come from India, where it was a morality teaching aid called *Moksha-Patamu*. There were twelve vices and four virtues, and the objective was to get to Nirvana. It was easier to fail than to succeed . . . The British in the nineteenth century had adopted it as an instructional guide for children called *Kismet*; Lieserl stared at images of claustrophobic boards, forbidding snakes. Thirteen snakes and eight ladders showed children that if they were good and obedient their life would be rewarded.

But by a few decades later the game had lost its moral subtexts. Lieserl found images from the early twentieth century of a sad-looking little clown; he slithered haplessly down snakes and heroically clambered up ladders. Lieserl stared at him, trying to understand the appeal of his baggy trousers, walking cane and little moustache.

The game, with its charm and simplicity, had survived through the twenty centuries which had worn away since the death of that forgotten clown.

She grew interested in the *numbers* embedded in the various versions of the game. The twelve-to-four ratio of *Moksha-Patamu* clearly made it a harder game to win than *Kismet's* thirteen-to-eight—but how much harder?

She began to draw new boards in the air. But these boards were abstractions—clean, colourless, little more than sketches. She ran through high-speed simulated games, studying their outcomes. She experimented with ratios of snakes to ladders, with their placement. Phillida sat with her and introduced her to combinatorial mathematics, the theory of games—to different forms of wonder.

On her fifteenth day she tired of her own company and started to attend classes again. She found the perceptions of others a refreshing counterpoint to her own, high-speed learning.

The world seemed to open up around her like a flower; it was a world full of sunlight, of endless avenues of information, of stimulating people.

She read up on nanobots.

Body cells were programmed to commit suicide. A cell itself manufactured enzymes which cut its DNA into neat pieces, and quietly closed down. The suicide of cells was a guard against uncontrolled growth—tumours—and a tool to sculpt the developing body: in the womb, the withering of unwanted cells carved fingers and toes from blunt tissue buds. Death was the default state of a cell. Chemical signals were sent by the body, to instruct cells to remain alive.

The nanotechnological manipulation of this process made immortality simple. It also made the manufacture of a Lieserl simple.

Lieserl studied this, scratching absently at her inhabited, engineered arms. She still didn't know *why*.

With a boy called Matthew, from her class, she took a trip away from the House—without her parents for the first time. They rode a flitter to the shore where she'd played as a child, twelve days earlier. She found the broken pier where she'd discovered mussels. The place seemed less vivid—less magical—and she felt a sad nostalgia for the loss of the freshness of her childish senses.

But there were other compensations. Her body was strong, lithe, and the sunlight was like warm oil on her skin. She ran and swam, relishing the sparkle of the ozone-laden air in her lungs. She and Matthew mock-wrestled and chased in the surf, clambering over each other like young apes—like children, she thought, but not quite with complete innocence . . .

As sunset approached they allowed the flitter to return them to the House. They agreed to meet the next day, perhaps take another trip somewhere. Matthew kissed her lightly, on the lips, as they parted.

That night she could barely sleep. She lay in the dark of her room, the scent of salt still strong in her nostrils, the image of Matthew alive in her mind. Her body seemed to pulse with hot blood, with its endless, continuing growth.

The next day—her sixteenth—Lieserl rose quickly. She'd never felt so alive; her skin still glowed from the salt and sunlight of the shore, and there was a hot tension inside her, an ache deep in her belly, a tightness.

When she reached the flitter bay at the front of the House, Matthew was waiting for her. His back was turned, the low sunlight causing the fine hairs at the base of his neck to glow.

He turned to face her.

He reached out to her, uncertainly, then allowed his hands to drop to his sides. He didn't seem to know what to say; his posture changed, subtly, his shoulders slumping slightly; before her eyes he was becoming shy of her.

She was taller than him. Visibly *older*. She became abruptly aware of the still-childlike roundness of his face, the awkwardness of his manner. The thought of *touching* him—the memory of her feverish dreams during the night—seemed absurd, impossibly adolescent.

She felt the muscles in her neck tighten; she felt as if she must scream. Matthew seemed to recede from her, as if she was viewing him through a tunnel.

Once again the labouring nanobots—the damned, unceasing nanotechnological infection of her body—had taken away part of her life.

This time, though, it was too much to bear.

'Why? *Why?*' She wanted to scream abuse at her mother—to *hurt* her.

Phillida had never looked so old. Her skin seemed drawn tight across the bones of her face, the lines etched deep. 'I'm sorry,' she said. 'Believe me. When we—George and I—volunteered for this programme, we knew it would be painful. But we never dreamed how much. Neither of us had had children before. Perhaps if we had, we'd have been able to anticipate how this would feel.'

'I'm a freak—an absurd experiment,' Lieserl shouted. 'A *construct*. Why did you make me human? Why not some insentient animal? Why not a Virtual?'

'Oh, you had to be human. As human as possible . . .' Phillida seemed to come to a decision. 'I'd hoped to give you a few more days of—life, normality—before it had to end. You seemed to be finding some happiness—'

'In fragments,' Lieserl said bitterly. 'This is no life, Phillida. It's *grotesque*.'

'I know. I'm sorry, my love. Come with me.'

'Where?'

'Outside. To the garden. I want to show you something.'

Suspicious, hostile, Lieserl allowed her mother to take her hand; but she made her fingers lie lifeless, cold in Phillida's warm grasp.

It was mid-morning now. The Sun's light flooded the garden; flowers—white and yellow—strained up towards the sky.

Lieserl looked around; the garden was empty. 'What am I supposed to be seeing?'

Phillida, solemnly, pointed upwards.

Lieserl tilted back her head, shading her eyes to block out the light. The sky was a searing blue dome, marked only by a high vapour trail and the lights of habitats.

'No.' Gently, Phillida pulled Lieserl's hand down from her face, and, cupping her chin, tipped her face flower-like towards the Sun.

The star's light seemed to fill her head. Dazzled, she dropped her eyes, stared at Phillida through a haze of blurred, streaked retinal images.

The Sun. Of course . . .

★ ★ ★

Kevan Scholes said, *Damn it, Lieserl, you're going to have to respond properly. Things are difficult enough without—*

'I know. I'm sorry. How are you feeling, anyway?'

Me? I'm fine. But that's hardly the point, is it? Now come on, Lieserl, the team here are getting on my back; let's run through the tests.

'You mean I'm not down here to enjoy myself?'

Scholes, speaking from his safe habitat far beyond the photosphere, didn't respond.

'Yeah. The tests. Okay, electromagnetic first.' She adjusted her sensorium. 'I'm plunged into darkness,' she said drily. 'There's very little free radiation at any frequency—perhaps an X-ray glow from the photosphere; it looks a little like a late evening sky. And—'

We know the systems are functioning. I need to know what you see, what you feel.

'What I feel?'

She spread her arms and sailed backwards through the 'air' of the cavern. The huge convective cells buffeted and merged like living things, whales in this insubstantial sea of gas.

'I see convection fountains,' she said. 'A cave full of them.'

She rolled over onto her belly, so that she was gliding face down, surveying the plasma sea below her. She *opened* her eyes, changing her mode of perception. The convective honeycomb faded into the background of her senses, and the magnetic flux tubes came into prominence, solidifying out of the air; beyond them the convective pattern was a sketchy framework, overlaid. The tubes were each a hundred yards broad, channels cutting through the air; they were thousands of miles long, and they filled the air around her, all the way down to the plasma sea.

Lieserl dipped into a tube; she felt the tingle of enhanced magnetic strength. Its walls rushed past her, curving gracefully. 'It's wonderful,' she said. 'I'm inside a flux tube. It's an immense tunnel; it's like a fairground ride. I could follow this path all the way round the Sun.'

Maybe. I don't know if we need the poetry, Lieserl. Kevan Scholes hesitated, and when he spoke again he sounded severely encouraging, as if he'd been instructed to be nice to her. *We're glad you're feeling—ah—happy in yourself, Lieserl.*

'My new self. Maybe. Well, it was an improvement on the old; you have to admit that.'

Yes. I want you to think back to the downloading. Can you do that?

'The downloading? Why?'

Come on, Lieserl. It's another test, obviously.

'A test of what?'

Your trace functions. We want to know if—

'My trace functions. You mean my memory.'

. . . Yes. He had the grace to sound embarrassed. *Think back, Lieserl. Can you remember?*

Downloading . . .

It was her ninetieth day, her ninetieth physical-year. She was impossibly frail—unable even to walk, or feed herself, or clean herself.

They'd taken her to a habitat close to the Sun. They'd almost left the download too late; they'd had one scare when an infection had somehow got through to her and settled into her lungs, nearly killing her.

She wanted to die.

Physically she was the oldest human in the System. She felt as if she were underwater: she could barely feel, or taste, or see anything, as if she was encased in some deadening, vicious fluid. And she knew her mind was failing.

It was so fast she could *feel* it. It was like a ghastly reverse run of her accelerated childhood. She woke every day to a new diminution of her self. She had come to dread sleep, yet could not avoid it.

She couldn't bear the indignity of it. Everybody else was immortal, and young; and the AS technology which had made them so was being used to kill Lieserl. She hated those who had put her in this position.

Her mother visited her for the last time, a few days before the download.

Lieserl, through her ruined, rheumy old eyes, was barely able to recognize Phillida—this young, weeping woman, only a few months older than when she had held up her baby girl to the Sun.

Lieserl cursed her, sent her away.

At last she was taken, in her bed, to a downloading chamber at the heart of the habitat.

Do you remember, Lieserl? Was it—continuous?

' . . . No.'

It was a sensory explosion.

In an instant she was young again, with every sense alive and vivid. Her vision was sharp, her hearing impossibly precise. And slowly, slowly, she had become aware of new senses—senses beyond the human. She could see the dull infra-red glow of the bellies and heads of the people working around the shell of her own abandoned body, the sparkle of X-ray photons from the Solar photosphere as they leaked through the habitat's shielding.

She'd retained her human memories, but they were qualitatively different from the experiences she was accumulating now. Limited, partial, subjective, imperfectly recorded: like fading paintings, she thought.

. . . Except, perhaps, for that single, golden, day at the beach.

She studied the husk of her body. It was almost visibly imploding now, empty . . .

'I remember,' she told Kevan Scholes. 'Yes, I remember.'

Now the flux tube curved away to the right; and, in following it, she became aware that she was tracing out a spiral path. She let herself relax into the motion, and watched the cave-world beyond the tube wheel around her. The flux tubes neighbouring her own had become twisted into spirals too, she realized; she was following one strand in a rope of twisted-together flux tubes.

Lieserl, what's happening? We can see your trajectory's altering, fast.

'I'm fine. I've got myself into a flux rope, that's all . . .'

Lieserl, you should get out of there . . .

She let the tube sweep her around. 'Why? This is fun.'

Maybe. But it isn't a good idea for you to break the surface; we're concerned about the stability of the wormhole—

Lieserl sighed and let herself slow. 'Oh, damn it, you're just no fun. I would have enjoyed bursting out through the middle of a sunspot. What a great way to go.'

We're not done with the tests yet, Lieserl.

'What do you want me to do?'

One more . . .

'Just tell me.'

Run a full self-check, Lieserl. Just for a few minutes . . . Drop the Virtual constructs.

She hesitated. 'Why? The systems are obviously functioning to specification.'

Lieserl, you don't need to make this difficult for me. Scholes sounded defensive. *This is a standard suite of tests for any AI which—*

'All right, damn it.'

She closed her eyes, and with a sudden, impulsive stab of will, let her Virtual image of herself-the illusion of a human body around her-crumble.

It was like waking from a dream: a soft, comfortable dream of childhood, waking to find herself entombed in a machine, a crude construct of bolts and cords and gears.

She considered herself.

The tetrahedral Interface of the wormhole was suspended in the body of the Sun. The thin, searing-hot gas of the convective zone poured into its four triangular faces, so that the Interface was surrounded by a sculpture of inflowing gas, a flower carved dynamically from the Sun's flesh, almost obscuring the Interface itself. The solar material was, she knew, being pumped through the wormhole to the second Interface in orbit around the Sun; convection zone gases emerged, blazing, from the drifting tetrahedron, making it into a second, miniature Sun around which human habitats could cluster.

By pumping away the gas, and the heat it carried, the Interface refrigerated itself, enabling it to survive—with its precious, fragile cargo of datastores . . .

The stores which sustained the awareness of herself, Lieserl.

She inspected herself, at many levels, simultaneously.

At the physical level she studied crisp matrices of data, shifting, coalescing. And overlaid on that was the logical structure of data storage and access paths which represented the components of her mind.

Good . . . Good, Lieserl. You're sending us good data. How are you feeling?

'You keep asking me that, damn it. I feel—'

Enhanced . . .

No longer trapped in a single point, in a box of bone behind eyes made of jelly.

What made her conscious? It was the ability to be aware of what was happening in her mind, and in the world around her, and what had happened in the past.

By any test, she was more conscious than any other human—because she had more of the *machinery* of consciousness.

She was supremely conscious—the most conscious human who had ever lived.

If, she thought uneasily, she was still human.

Good. Good. All right, Lieserl. We have work to do.

She let her awareness implode, once more, into a Virtual-human form. Her perception was immediately simplified. To be seeing through apparently-human eyes was comforting . . . and yet, she thought, restrictive.

Perhaps it wouldn't be much longer before she felt ready to abandon even this last vestige of humanity. And then what?

Lieserl?

'I hear you.'

She turned her face towards the core.

★ ★ ★

'There is a *purpose*, Lieserl,' her mother said. 'A justification. You aren't simply an experiment. You have a mission.' She waved her hand at the sprawling, friendly buildings that comprised the House. 'Most of the people here, particularly the children, don't know anything about you. They have jobs, goals—lives of their own to follow. But they're here for *you*.

'Lieserl, your experiences have been designed—George and I were selected, even—to ensure that the first few days of your existence would *imprint* you with humanity.'

'The first few days?' Suddenly the unknowable future was like a black wall, looming towards her; she felt as out of control of her life as if she was a counter on some immense, invisible snakes-and-ladders board.

'I don't want this. I want to be me. I want my freedom, Phillida.'

'No, Lieserl. You're not free, I'm afraid; you never can be. You have a goal.'

'What goal?'

'Listen to me. The Sun gave us life. Without it—without the other stars—we couldn't survive.

'We're a strong species. We believe we can live as long as the stars—for tens of billions of years. And perhaps even beyond that. But we've had—glimpses—of the future, the far distant future . . . Disturbing glimpses. People are starting to plan for that future—to work on projects which will take millions of years to come to fruition . . .

'Lieserl, you're one of those projects.'

'I don't understand.'

Phillida took her hand, squeezed it gently; the simple human contact seemed incongruous, the garden around them transient, a chimera, before this talk of megayears and the future of the species.

'Lieserl, something is wrong with the Sun. *You* have to find out what. The Sun is dying; something—or someone—is *killing* it.'

Phillida's eyes were huge before her, staring, probing for understanding. 'Don't be afraid. My dear, you will live forever. If you want to. You are a new form of human. And you will see wonders of which I—and everyone else who has ever lived—can only dream.'

Lieserl listened to her tone, coldly, analysing it. 'But you don't *envy* me. Do you, Phillida?'

Phillida's smile crumbled. 'No,' she said quietly.

Lieserl tipped back her head. An immense light flooded her eyes.

She cried out.

Her mother enfolded her in her arms. 'The Sun, Lieserl. *The Sun . . .*'

Crossing Chao Meng Fu

G. DAVID NORDLEY

Like John Varley, Michael Swanwick, Stephen Baxter, Kim Stanley Robinson, and others, G. David Nordley is a writer who finds the solar system an exotic-enough setting for adventures just as it *is*, as he's demonstrated with stories of exploration and conflict on a grand scale, such as "Into the Miranda Rift," "Out of the Quiet Years," "Dawn Venus," "Comet Gypsies," "Alice's Asteroid," "The Day of Their Coming," "Messengers of Chaos," and others. Many of these stories make effective use of the latest data from the *Voyager* space probes, data that show just how bizarre, complex, surprising, and mysterious a place our solar system really is, a far cry from the conception of the solar system as a dull collection of rock, ice, and cinders that was common in the seventies.

In the suspenseful tale that follows, Nordley shows us that while the determination to stick to a task until you complete it, to push through no matter what the odds or how overwhelming the problems you face, can be a positive quality, particularly in an explorer, on the airless, sun-blasted surface of Mercury, with death only inches away at any moment, sometimes it may not be such a *good idea . . .*

G. David Nordley is a retired air force officer and physicist who has become a frequent contributor to *Analog* in the last couple of years, winning that magazine's Analytical Laboratory readers poll in 1992 for his story "Poles Apart"; he also won the same award for his story "Into the Miranda Rift," to which the story that follows "Crossing Chao Meng Fu" is a "prequel." He has also sold stories to *Asimov's Science Fiction, Tomorrow, and Mindsparks* and elsewhere. Although fairly prolific at short lengths, Nordley has yet to publish a novel—even though he has several series in progress that could be worked up into novels without too much difficulty. Until then, you'll just have to look for him in the science fiction magazines, where he appears with pleasing frequency. Nordley lives in Sunnyvale, California.

Begin a ghostly plain
Dim white in pale starlight.
Flat as far as you can see
To where a distant black ridge

Divides reality.
Above the stars shine
Below the ground crunches;
Hillary, Byrd, Peary and Amundsen,
Are your guides. It is beautiful.
But you cannot stop long;
The plain is life itself;
Move on now, trod onward,
Or stand and freeze, they say.

—W.B.

I am in the middle of a line of people walking determinedly across the most everything-forsaken boring waste in the Solar System. I am so sore and tired I could scream—if there were a warm bed around somewhere, I'd crawl in it to shudder. My attitude has hit rock bottom, but it is time to file my report and if I want anything good out of this pain, I'd best sound positive:

"I am Wojciech Bubka, college teacher, occasional poet and now your . . ." I take a breath of sterile suit air, ". . . guide to the natural universe, courtesy of the Solar System Astrographic Society and its many sponsors and members. Welcome to my personal journey through exotic, dangerous, and unusual places of the Solar System." I take another deep breath—got to keep up with everyone else. "Come with me while there are still such places to explore—for as we approach the twenty-third century, this frontier, too, is receding."

I try to gain a little ground to stop briefly and pan my helmet cam over the dirty ice field. Despite the exertion, the change of pace lifts my spirits a bit. But not even a ten-to-one vertical exaggeration will make this landscape interesting. Come on, Bubka. You're a poet? Find meaning.

"These are not robot explorations to be experienced in a video display, but personal ones. I seek authentic, not virtual, reality. I seek the *go there, see there*, and *be there* experience of the human explorer, not sterile pixels." Breathe deep. "There is nothing between me and the crunch of crampon spikes on this frozen mud, the strike of an axe into virgin scarps, the strain of muscles, the hiss of sliding ropes, and the sight of wonders. Such is the dream and the experience I seek to share with you here, today, on the frozen wastes of Chao Meng Fu crater on Mercury."

Said strain of muscles gets my attention as I start walking again, and I groan involuntarily. I am tired from the almost week of walking under a pack that brought my weight close to Earth normal—when what is normal for me is Mars. I wiggle my toes as hard as I can—despite vacuum insulation, thermistor environmental control and loose, fluffy socks, I think my feet are beginning to get cold.

"Come on, mate. Another hour will get us there." That is Ed Blake, a gentleman adventurer from New Zealand with Antarctic experience. Ed is my tent-mate, lanky, mostly bald and prematurely gray, confident, competent, and reserved—unless he gets that kind of twinkle in his eye. Then beware a terrible pun. He's cheerful enough to me, but I sense a certain condescension.

Understandable, I think. What the frozen hell am I doing here?

★ ★ ★

I had been getting bored at Jovis Tholis University. Poetry, these days, includes video as well as text—something which would have delighted Will Shakespeare, I assure you—and has blended with drama so much that we distinguish the two by picking nits over length and symbolic content. But even in its media-inflated majesty, a dozen years of going over the same basic stuff while fighting battles with New Reformation censors and left-wing nihilists—neither of whom take kindly to the display of material contrary to their philosophies—has me well on my way to burnout.

JTU is in a dome over an ostensibly extinct volcano on Tharsis, roughly half-way to Olympus Mons from the tether tube terminal on Ascraeus. The location worked, and it became the biggest university on Mars—of which I was an increasingly small and out-of-step part.

As the politics of being an important academic became increasingly burdensome, my dreams of "out there" grew. I might teach at Saturn High Station with its magnificent view of the rings. Or I could compose random meter verse at Hyperion institute, the lonely retreat of mathematical philosophers set on a detached mountain peak that careens about Saturn as metaphor of an uncertain future. Or I could volunteer to ride a comet and watch robots turn it into Martian air while writing my epics in the freedom of isolation as the comet fell for a decade into the inner Solar System. Or, and this was my most favorite, I might become a journalist in the old sense on the first expedition to Pluto and Charon.

Thus did I dream. But so, of course, dream millions of others. Only a chosen few can go anywhere the first time or do anything the first time. I dabbled at trail writing; journals of hikes and visits to parts of the vanishing "Red" Mars, but got little notice beyond a reasonably nice "been there, done that" rejection from the Solar System Astrographic Society. I needed an entree, a contact, an idea, something to lift me out of the background.

Then, last year (Martian year, everyone; almost two standard years ago), Miranda Lotati, the daughter of the man in charge of Solar System Astrographic Society's expeditions division, walked into my literature class at Jovis Tholis University, a junior transfer from Stanford on Earth. She looked to be a hard, vigorous, and exciting person but could barely choke two words out in succession—about as contrary to stereotype as one could be and still have breasts.

She was not really beautiful—too muscular, too thin in the face, too boyish a figure, but I saw the possibilities in that. Less competition, and perhaps a complement to my esthetic, well, softness, I told myself. I saw the romance of an attraction of opposites who themselves were opposites of conventionality, and I was looking for some romance somewhere—the women of my normal circles were hopeless and helpless in anything but words, and even seemed to take pride in that. I saw in her an invitation to beyond and away from here. If I played it right—and I resolved to do so.

It wasn't easy. Miranda was a rough-edged, prickly student, and her essays were condensed dullness, never more than the required length. A spoken sentence of more than a half dozen words was a rarity from her, and she sometimes seemed to speak a language so far evolved from today's English in its lack of articles and verbs that, had it been deliberate, would have been considered art in some circles. Nonetheless I was intent. I persisted in bringing her along. I bided my time.

I had to expend some moral capital, but convinced myself that she covered the ground on her final well enough to let me pass her. She liked me, I think. But I said nothing unethical to her, nor hinted at anything romantic while she was my student—I have my standards.

I saw her on the last day of classes of the winter semester, after the final grades were in.

"You're off to Mercury, I hear, to be along on your father's attempt to walk across Chao Meng Fu Crater?" Shielded from the Sun, that huge crater was an ice field—Mercury's Antarctica.

She nodded.

"Have you set the expedition membership?"

She shook her head, confirming what was known publicly.

"Will you have any journalists along? It would make a very exciting nature piece."

She smiled a bit. "Like your Aseraeus Mons hike piece? Dad liked that and sent me here."

He'd seen that? I tried to remember the rejection letter. I was flattered but a bit worried that it was a little light for a Lotati expedition. Then the alarm bells rang in my head. My competition for the position of expedition bard was standing in front of me.

I reached for a tone of professional authority. "Randi, uh. You've come a long way in your composition . . ."

She shrugged. "Yeah. Thanks to you. Someone's got to do the article. Someone who fits on the team. Wish I wrote better."

"Randi, I suppose I shouldn't be obscure. Is there any chance I might come myself?"

Her eyes lit up for a moment, then she frowned. "Rough business, exploring."

"Then my accounts of it should draw interest, maybe enough to push Solar System Astrographic's allocation priorities a little further up." Not to mention that a single Astrographic article could bring in the equivalent in allocations of my entire Jovis Tholus University stipend for a year. A *Martian* year.

"Uh, huh." A doubtful assent on her part.

"Might even help you get to your namesake, out by Uranus. Now there would be an angle that people would notice!"

That got her attention. "Dad's idea too. My name. Not that easy, though. No place for amateurs, out there."

I smiled at her. "I bet I'll make a good explorer. I'm observant, handy, and in reasonably good shape."

She gave me a somewhat skeptical look and a sigh. "Mercury first. Chao Meng Fu. Hundred fifty kilometer-wide. Never sees the Sun. Covered with granite-hard permafrost. Probably take us two, three weeks to walk it."

"Walk?"

She nodded. "Unassisted. Carry everything. Vacuum suits, tents, supplies, samples."

"Walk it? Uh, why?"

She looked at me as if I was born in some other cosmos. "Because we can."

There is this recklessness about me that allows me to throw words around without fully considering the consequences. "Well, I think I can too. I've done enough hiking around Tharsis—I even have a cinder cone named after me."

She looked skeptically at me. "Oh? How high?"

She had me there. I grinned sheepishly. "Well, 'Bubka Mons' is only a hundred meters above local mean. But it's kind of impressive because there's nothing else around it." And I knew someone in the Martian Geology Institute that was laying out the local real estate.

She giggled.

"It *is* registered, Randi. Anyway, my Ascraeus trip was solo, and by a new route."

She looked judiciously at me and sighed. "Lose ten kilos. Do fifty kilometers a day." We stood silent for a couple of seconds as I tried to digest that.

She turned away. "Physics final—see you." And she was gone, gliding easily down the hall.

Dreams are free; but realizing them has a price. And I resolved to pay it.

By the end of last semester. I had walked up a few Martian mountains and lost the ten kilos. I talked to her again and we arranged a checkout hike down to the base of Jovis Tholis and back up to the town again with full packs, breather gear, and by the most difficult route she could pick. She watched every move I made, and seemed satisfied enough to make another "date."

As this went on, I grew utterly fascinated with her. She was a busy woman. Reporters called her, outfitters called her. She was always meeting young women explorers who knew her reputation as a companion of her father, and old men explorers who had been somewhere with her father. My metaphor for Randi was a black hole; people and things seem to swirl around and accrete to her without any significant verbal effort on her part, as if her presence distorts space so that all roads simply lead to her and none away.

The week she was to leave Mars for Mercury she called me.

"You're in, Professor Bubka. Can you make the Shannon inbound? Friday?"

By moving heaven and Mars, I could, and did. I had, it seemed, been within her event horizon for some time now.

So, Mercury. Mercury gravity is the same as Mars gravity, which some say is more than a coincidence, but a coincidence as yet unexplained. The gravity here is exactly the same as on Mars, but I'm carrying three times my mass in supplies and vacuum survival equipment. I might as well be hiking in Antarctica with a light pack. Indeed, I could use the conditioning to visit Earth! Despite the extra mass, we try to keep up the fifty kilometers a day—a pace I must maintain.

There are eight of us strung out along the Chao Meng Fu crater floor, Dr. Lotati in the lead. Dr. Juanita Tierzo, a Harvard-trained geologist, follows him. Juanita is actually on the JTU faculty—in the Martian Geology Institute—but I had to come to Mercury to meet her. Randi follows her. Then come Ed, myself, and one of Dr. Tierzo's graduate students, Eloni Wakhweya, a slight Kenyan woman with a big grin. Solar System Astrographic expedition staffers Mike and Karen Svenson come last, pulling an equipment pallet on two large wire wheels.

They meant it; no robots, no powered vehicles, and in my now humbled opinion, no sense. If Mercury had a breathable atmosphere, they'd have done without the spacesuits and all their built-in communications and amenities, too. I'm exhausted, uncomfortable, and increasingly uneasy with this exercise in cosmic hubris.

The view is simple, unrelieved flatness, the kind of view that should reach one's soul in the way of all great expanses. The crater's stark lines go its namesake's art one spareness better; the vertical dimension is almost absent. It too is painted in an ink of five colors, all gray. It is Aldrin's magnificent desolation, without relief. I appreciate it more in intellectual abstract than in person.

There is light to see: the tips of the peaks behind us blaze like distant arc lamps, and fill the bowl of Chao Meng Fu with a ghostly kind of moonlight. Small, rounded crater rims dot this frozen plane—very few higher than a man, for ice flows in time. The brighter stars shine down on us hard and free. Brilliant Earth hangs just over the horizon, a tiny dazzling blue-white star. Luna lies well away from it, a faint gray dot lost in Sagittarius.

Invisible to us in the Earth's glare is the beginning of Earth's Sunshield. This mammoth project will partly shade the heat-polluted atmosphere from the fires of Apollo's chariot someday. It is taking form at the Earth-Sun L-1 point, balanced there with the help of reflected light—they plan to reduce insolation by 1 percent. But more relevant to our endeavor is that it is the home of Solar System Astrographic's solar radio antenna, which we use to apprise the rest of the Solar System of the status of this madcap adventure. I look that way wondering why I ever left.

"Another five kilometers to the crevasse," Dr. Lotati tells us on the comnet.

This desolate flat sameness is an illusion; we have real work ahead. The crevasse is a major obstacle, or a major objective if you are a geologist. Halfway between the rim of Chao Meng Fu crater and its central peaks lies a huge crack in the permafrost caused, they think, by an almost infinitely slow lifting of the crater floor, still rebounding from the billion-year-old impact that formed the crater. To this poet, overhead views make the crevasse look like the mouth of the planet—and I worry about being devoured.

By noon, universal time, the mouth of Mercury yawns directly in front of us, an ugly black crack that makes the dark gray plain around us look silvery by comparison. We halt to plan our crossing. Juanita proposes that we simply go down into this thing, down into a darkness that has never known the Sun, and out again on the other side. That idea creates enough interest to scare me. But not now. A descent will take planning, and, in the meantime, I luxuriate in not having to move my body.

Yet, standing still, I forget my pain and become curious. The crevasse seems to run to the horizon to my right and left. The other side is the length of a football field away. I shudder—it is impossible to repress the thought that such darkness is not meant for human beings, that the laws of physics will become conscious and punish us for trying it. Perversely, the challenge of that danger attracts me.

Yet, there are reasons to go down beyond the simple thrill of it. Solar Astrographic's expedition is half stunt, half science—and here is where the other half gets its due. There is a mystery here and the root of it lies in a contrary mysticism of celestial dynamics. Here, a mere sixty million kilometers from its fiery photosphere, are surfaces that have not seen the Sun since the Caloris impact defined Mercury's final orientation.

This same counterintuitive magic then decrees that the ices of comets that orbit impossibly far—beyond even Pluto, Charon, and Persephone—are actually closer to the Sun, and Mercury, in the *energy* of their motion than anything in the inner Solar System. Something on Venus would have to be kicked at almost 11 km/s to reach Mercury, best case—but merely nudge a pair of Oort belt comets together and parts of them may fall into Mercury, decades hence. Sometimes these collisions *give* the planet a very temporary, tenuous atmosphere, which condenses in the deep freeze of Chao Meng Fu. Blame this on Kepler and Newton, not Ptolemy.

So near is far, and far is near, and the crevasse yawns from 'ere to 'ere. Does it have teeth? Do its open jaws reveal molecules from the beginning of time, such as measured in the Solar System? Lotati confers with his daughter, and Ed. Randi and Ed have a thing, I've found, and spend a fair amount of time touching helmets.

What great ideas I have! I despair of ever being able to itch again, let alone going to Miranda with its namesake. My rented vacuum gear fits like the skin of a hundred-year-old man; stretched taut digging into my flesh here, loose and bulging there. Randi says there's an art to it and I should take more time getting in. Next time I will.

I edge closer to the brink, attracted to the danger perhaps, or perhaps wanting to demonstrate courage to Randi. I gaze down. Here and there the dust has fallen from the sheer ice walls, and the layered structure is clear. There are Mercury's sediments. Each comet or meteor creates a temporary atmosphere for Mercury, and that which is not boiled away by the Sun condenses in the polar craters, mixed with ejecta dust. The bedrock lies perhaps a kilometer below us. After three days of the most physical labor I've done in decades, I now contemplate a rappel down to the bottom of a bottomless crevasse and the climb back up again.

I look away as though by not observing it, I can create the possibility that it does not exist.

But I have my journalist's duty. At my command, my helmet camera plays back the view, and it floats, reflected off my face plate, against the stars. It doesn't fit in the standard field of view, I realize, so I look over the edge again and slowly turn my head from horizon to horizon. An object of professional interest now, it begins to lose some of its scariness for me.

Bubka's prescription for fear of something—study the hell out of it.

How long and wide! Then I turn off all my lights, let my eyes relax, and turn back to see the solar corona, a peacock's tail of icy fire spreading from the Sun that sits just under those utterly black mountains that ring our horizon. If Chao Meng Fu did not flatten Mercury's globe here, we would not be able to see those mountains this far into the trek, so close is Mercury's horizon—but we have been heading ever so slightly inward, downhill, as well as south.

The furthest streamers of the corona glow far above that rim behind, looking almost like the aurora borealis back on Earth. Awed, I step back, and back again to catch my balance.

I happen to glance down—my boot is barely centimeters from the edge of the chasm.

"Bubka, freeze." Randi's voice echoes in my helmet.

I am already frozen.

"Now. Raise right hand," she continues.

I am carrying a strobe lamp in my right hand so I automatically start to raise my left—

"Your other right!" she snaps, instantly.

This time I get it right, raising both my arms and the strobe lamp.

"Now lean *that* way. Walk slowly. Away from edge."

I understand now: if I teeter, she wants me to teeter in the direction of safety. I walk away from the edge with as much dignity as I can muster, as if there were nothing at all wrong, knowing that anyone monitoring my heartbeat will know that I am anything but calm.

She detaches herself from the management group and strides toward me, ghostly dust glittering in my helmet light behind her footsteps. She halts in a cloud of fairy sparkles, grabs my hand, and leads me well away from the edge of the crevasse.

"Professor Bubka, near crevasses, tether. Always, always, tether."

"Professor" hangs in my mind dripping with irony. On Mars, I taught her literature. Here, I am her student—and I had just come close to failing a test where failure is judged somewhat more harshly than at Jovis Tholis University.

Nodding ruefully, I pull a piton gun from my pack and harpoon the planet. A test pull shows that it's secure, and I clip the line to my belt. Randi fires a piton in too, clips on, then clips another line between her belt and mine. "Ed, some baby-sitter you'd make! Going to take a look."

"Sorry, mate. Watching, Randi."

Baby-sitter?

"Now, Professor Bubka. Let's go look." Dark eyes, on a tanned face with a snub nose, twinkle at me behind the clear, non-reflecting visor.

We retrace my footprints together. We walk to the edge together. This time. I think to clip my strobe light to my belt as well.

One of the things I see is half a footprint at the edge of the crevasse. The toe half. Mine.

What I had done was, I realize, foolish, but I think I am forgiven. She pulls on her line, then actually leans out over the cut, to inspect its near side.

"Light." The word is a request and a command. Crystals from far down glitter in response.

Nervously, wrapping my line around my left hand and playing it out through a "smart slot" belay device, centimeter by centimeter, I lean out with her and shine my strobe on the wall under us. On a clean vertical, the layering resembles a diffraction grating—fine thin grooves, perfectly horizontal, broken occasionally by what must be the sections of ancient buried craters.

The strobe light looks continuous, but contains off-pulses for range—it times a journey of the absence of light. So. The crack goes down, a hundred meters, two hundred, three hundred. At five hundred, I can no longer see the light returning, but it can. I swing it slowly from side to side, as my helmet display paints a graph of angle and range. The walls seem to almost converge about twelve hundred meters below us here, with some flatness between them. I move the beam a bit to the left.

There is something across the chasm at eight hundred meters, just to our left. "Randi?"

"I see it. Bridge. Dad, channel seven."

"I have it, Randi! I'll think that is a billion years down if it's a day! What do you say, Juanita, my Randi's found a bridge!"

There seemed no point in immediately explaining that I'd found it.

"Eight hundred meters down and all the way across! Can we do it?" Juanita answers, thrill in her voice. "Do we have enough line?"

"Yes and yes," Randi's father answers after a moment of thought. Then he points to a slight dip almost above the bridge. "Probably half of an old crater, broken by the crack. That will get us a few meters closer. We could rappel down from there. Perhaps two billion years down, if the crevasse goes to the bottom of Chao Meng Fu. Do you want the bottom, Juanita?"

"God, yes, Emilio, if it isn't too dangerous."

Dr. Lotati shrugs. "It has been this way for millions of years of impacts; the walls should tolerate a few ants crawling on them. We'll go ourselves, instead of waiting for some robots to do it."

I look across the chasm for the other half of the ancient crater, but, like the other half of my footprint, there is no sign of it. Where did it go? I feel a curiosity as powerful as any hunger. What formed the bridge? What lies at the bottom? We shall find out, if the Laws of the Universe let us.

We all have some climbing experience, but only the Lotatis and Ed have very much. It is, however, a very easy climb down in 38 percent gravity. The ropes are well secured to the plain above, the slope is usually less than vertical. Mike and Karen Svenson will remain on the rim with the bulk of the equipment until we are all safely down. They call themselves the "human robots" and have been in excellent humor. When Randi and Dr. Lotati scale the other wall, they will fire a rope across. The Lotatis will then pull over a larger rope on which a tram will carry the equipment. Meanwhile, at the bottom, Dr. Tierzo will supervise sample gathering by the rest of us. That is the plan.

It becomes dark quickly as we descend. The sky contracts to a starry band overhead, one edge of which glows a faint, frozen, shadowy pearl, a reflection lit by a reflection of sunlight on distant peaks. We turn on our helmet lights, and their glare banishes any other source of illumination. They spread sparkly pools of light on the wall—tiny crystals everywhere. I am conscious of a fine mist or fog, just on the edge of the perceivable. Our suits allow the skin's waste gases to diffuse slowly outward, our footsteps create microscopic dust clouds on which it may condense, our helmet lights evaporate hydrogen gas that has condensed on the wall. Our progress appears tinged with the ethereal.

We are three hundred meters down: a football field on end. The descent is easy, simple, routine. You ease rope out under friction, take a pair of steps down, and ease out some more. This descent is demanding and terrifying. You dare not lose concentration. Pitons can pull out, crampons can slip, and you will be just as dead from a fall of a kilometer in Mercury's gravity as Earth's. Yes, it will take a few seconds longer and an academic might note that you hit with less velocity—only about five times instead of fifteen times what is needed to smash your helmet and the skull within it.

You dare not cause problems for everyone else. One foot after another.

A person in fear of his or her life needs no more excitement—but if you want it, you glance at the wall in front of you, at layers of ice laid down when dinosaurs were young. This is not on a screen, not a simulation, but never-seen-before reality that puts ice hard in front of your own eyes.

"Ed," I ask, "do you wonder if anyone might have been here a billion years ago?"

"Eh? Interesting thought, that. The feature would attract someone with enough curiosity to build spaceships, I should think. But the crack itself wouldn't be that old, now, would it?"

"No, I guess not." When the layers were laid down, of course, this had been a part of the plain.

Still, my eyes scan every layer, hoping.

"Has everyone got positive pressure in their suits?" Dr. Lotati asks, and receives chuckles. "There is," he continues, "a significant build-up of nitrogen gas, and a bare trace of nitrogen tri-flouride, which I would not recommend breathing."

I call up a temp display and find that it is cold in the crack—about eighty kelvins, versus a hundred twenty at the surface. As I think about it, I notice traces of frost on the outside of my gloves: our insulation is that good. I have no idea what the biological implications of nitrogen tri-fluoride are, but I would rather someone else perform the experiments. A drop rolls down my face plate.

"Watch your footing, Juanita," Dr. Lotati says. "It's slippery here."

So far, my crampons dig into the dirty clathrate walls with ease, but I can tell it is wet. The wall is mostly ice, but ice that is heavily mixed with crater ejecta, pocked with more volatile ices, and stiffened far harder than anything on Earth by cryogenic temperatures. Dr. Lotati says it's something like sandstone, but if it weren't for the gas in the ice, it would be like concrete. There are few cracks, but the piton gun works well, as does the ax.

"Nitrogen trifluoride data," I ask. Floating in the wall, by virtue of my helmet display hardware, are glowing numbers telling me that nitrogen tri-fluoride is liquid over a range of about 80 kelvins—from about 77 up to 145—which is over 120 Celsius degrees below the freezing point of water. Somehow, stating such temperatures in kelvins above absolute zero is less scary than using negative Celsius degrees below freezing. The vapor pressure of this big, heavy molecule is almost nil at the low end of this temperature range—a wet vacuum.

A hundred meters to go, and I can see the bridge clearly in the shifting pools of our helmet lights.

"A sliver of wall appears to have detached itself and slid down until it jammed," Dr. Tierzo tells us. "The top is a jumble with, here and there, flat spaces that may have been part of the original surface, including part of a crater. I wonder if that's what knocked it down?"

"Hello down there," Karen Svenson calls. "Yes, that crater would explain what looks like a ray network around where you went down. Now that I know what I'm looking at, this spiderweb network of cracks is a real giveaway."

I hadn't remembered any cracks. I ask my suit to play back my recording of our approach to the side. The surface in the depression was smooth. My pulse races. "Playback two hours ago," I command. In a ghostly video window, my suit shows me almost falling in to the crevasse, but . . .

"Hey, everyone!" I shout. "Those cracks weren't there before. Dr. Lotati, I've got it on channel six."

There is a moment of silence.

"Quickly now," Dr. Lotati speaks briefly and very businesslike. "Those of you still on the wall come down as quickly as possible without panic and without yanking on anything. Mike and Karen, set another belay well back of the cracked area."

I have my full attention on climbing down, gingerly as possible. Dr. Tierzo is off belay just below me. I remember to lock my crampon spikes *out*—the bridge is slippery.

Meanwhile, Dr. Lotati has set an ice bolt in at the far end of our bridge. Dr. Tierzo sets another one in the biggest hunk of bridge she can find at our end and pulls the line tight.

Then I am off the wall. I quickly clip my line to the bridge line and release myself from the wall ropes. "Off belay."

Miranda Lotati and the grad student, Eloni, are still on the wall.

I hear, I think, at very low frequency, a kind of groan.

"We have the protection in," Karen says. "The cracks are larger!"

"Wojciech can get your line, Ed," Dr. Lotati says, "release from the wall immediately!"

"No worry. Here." He tosses me the end of his spare line and I hit it with the loop of a smart 'biner, which opens, takes the line, and shuts faster than I can see—like that old magic trick with hoops. I take up the slack.

Ed releases and scrambles off the wall, holding the taut line for balance until he reaches me. We move further down the bridge.

"Come on, Eloni," Ed says encouragingly. The young Kenyan woman is the least experienced of our group—she descends slowly, but flawlessly, a few meters right of where Ed came down. "Toss me the end of your spare line."

She stops to find it. Miranda Lotati's feet are but a few meters above her. I hear another groan.

"Come on . . ." Ed says again.

Finally, Eloni tosses a coiled line toward Ed. It jerks short and dangles below her, a hopeless tangle.

"Sorry, I try to do this too fast."

"That's OK, mate," Ed says. "Just come on down now. We'll improvise."

We feel a slight tremor. She freezes.

"Down, Eloni. Fast," Randi says.

Eloni starts moving again. I can see her tremble.

"Ice!" Karen shouts. Our radios level amplitude, magnifying whispers and buffering shouts—that shout was well buffered.

Eloni freezes.

"Go," Randi snaps, and clips Eloni's helmet with the side of her boot. "Get going!"

Galvanized, Eloni half scrambles and half falls the remaining fifty meters, landing on her seat where the bridge butts against the wall. She starts fumbling with the 'biner holding her line to the wall belay line. Ed, clipped to a line, moves to help her—I think he has a knife in his hand. Needless, I follow him using crampons and ax. Ed reaches Eloni.

I look up and see the sky falling.

Randi releases and leaps from almost twenty meters up on the wall, unbelayed, right at me. "Catch," she shouts.

I have time to set my crampon spikes and open my arms. She hits hard, and various pieces of her gear dig into my chest. I grab her as the boots tear free and we skitter together down the side of the bridge. My line stops us after a three-meter slide.

Ten meters from us, with a roar clearly conducted through the ice we lie against, an avalanche of clathrate pours down. There is no sign of Ed and Eloni.

Randi clips a line to my belt, rolls off, and starts to scramble back to the top of the bridge, ice dust streaming around her.

"Ed!" she shouts. "Eloni!"

The fall increases, becoming a white wall. Randi scrambles into it. I follow and am enveloped in a stream of pulverized clathrate, and I can see nothing. It flows over me, not like sand or water, but something in between—not dense, but still exerting pressure.

I wait. My helmet is filled with the sound of my breathing.

"Ed!" Randi shouts again.

"We're alive." Ed's voice is hoarse and strained. "Trapped next to the wall. The fall created a bit of a pocket. No injuries, but it's getting somewhat cold."

In spacesuits with rebreathers and plenty of energy, we are in no danger of suffocating. But under our coveralls we wear skintight vacuum suits that depend on a surrounding vacuum for much of their thermal control and the fabric of the vacuum suits, while smart and extremely tough, is necessarily thin. Conduction of heat could quickly freeze Ed and Eloni. But, clinging to the side of the bridge with the landslide still in progress, there is nothing I can do to reach them.

"Got you on locator. Can move." That is Randi Lotati, for me. Move? How?

I roll over prone to the face of the bridge, reach forward into the flow with my hands, and find purchase. With both arms and legs, I find I can edge forward, too.

"Solid piece—here," Randi says. "Ice boulder. Think you're on other side."

"S—sounds that w—way," Ed replies.

"Line charge. My side. Push like hell when I say."

"No, Randi," Ed pleads, "too dangerous—"

"Push, damn it! Now!"

I hear the crack of the detonation.

"Randi?" I call, and claw my way toward the signals, white sand and occasional rocks still streaming by me. Somehow, though, it seems a bit easier. "Randi, Ed?"

"Wojciech, Ed. We—we're free. At—at least the rock's split. Need help with Eloni."

"I'm trying." I pant. "Where's Randi?" I am exhausted struggling against the continuing stream of material from above. I reach forward with my hand and hit flesh. Someone there. The world is gray in my helmet lamp; I can see nothing. "Ed, is that you?"

"Not me, mate. It's slackening a little. I've got some space."

The someone moans. The groan is female.

"Eloni?" I push the person in front of me again, harder.

"She's with me, Wojciech," Ed says.

"Randi?"

She grunts. "Wojciech. I'm OK, I'm just . . . stuck. Legs won't move." I feel a hand brush mine, then lock with mine. "Drag me back."

"I'll try." Trusting the precarious hand link, I sit up into the flow of clathrate mud. It tries to take me away with tremendous force, but my line holds me. Slowly I get my legs around in front of me and pull as hard as I dare. She doesn't move.

"It's no good. I'll hurt you if I pull any harder."

"Freezing's worse. Hurt me. Pull."

God knows how much force I put on her arm, but something seems to unstick, and she comes toward me, slowly at first; then something breaks free and we scoot back about four meters. I can see through whirls of snow here. I can see my clip still on the bridge line, see Randi strung out at the end of my arm.

"Dr. Lotati, she's out. Over here."

"What? Wojciech? Where? . . . There, I have you! I'll be right over."

He is there in a moment. "Had you on the other side of the bridge for a moment—propagation freak, I think. Randi, will you be all right for a few minutes?"

"Hurts like hell, Dad, but yes. Thanks, Wojciech."

Dr. Lotati gives her a pat and plunges into the remains of the ice fall. Minutes later, he and Ed emerge, carrying Eloni between them. "Mike, Karen, this is Emilio," he says. "We're all out of the avalanche. I don't know in what shape yet, but we're all out."

"Roger. We suggest all of you rest a bit until this plays itself out."

"Mike . . ." He pauses, catching his breath. "We'll consider that."

There are several rueful chuckles, and we spend the next five minutes or so watching the river of white dust slowly come to a halt.

Finally the ice fall abates entirely and we take stock. Randi reports a severe sprain in her right shoulder. Ed is recovering from hypothermia and is severely bruised as well. Eloni is better, physically, but appears to be in some kind of psychological shock. The rest of us have minor bruises.

The side of the crevasse looks like a giant took a huge, semicircular bite out of it. Karen and Mark wave at us from an edge that is now at least fifty meters back from where it was. We lost two long lines, buried in the debris. The avalanche has buried half the bridge and I worry that it could start again at any time and bury us along with the other half. I try to do some mental calculations on how long it would take a suborbital hopper to get here and pull us out.

"I think we are here for a while," Dr. Lotati says, "at least until we're all up to climbing out again. We might overnight on the bridge." If he's worried about the avalanche restarting, he isn't saying so.

"We'll need to revise the schedule a bit," Ed adds. "Another five kilometers per day would do it, I should think. Now, how do we get the gear down here?"

"Toboggan the big tent down to us," Randi says. "Meantime, collect data." I stare at Randi, stupefied.

"Are you OK, Eloni?" I ask, mainly out of concern but perhaps with a secondary agenda of reminding people of something.

Eloni raises her head and looks around in wonder. If she expects a chewing out, it seems she is in the wrong group. I lay a hand very on her shoulder, and, as if I touched some kind of hidden button, she leans into me and lets out a very long sigh, which I hear clearly where my helmet touches her. Randi is looking right at us, but in the glare of our headlights, her face is unreadable. Warning bells ring in my head.

"My mistake, Eloni," Ed says, "pressuring you like that for something that's not automatic. You needed to think it through, and with me talking at you like that, you couldn't. My mistake."

"Eloni," Dr. Lotati asks, "can you help Juanita get her samples tomorrow?"

Eloni takes a breath and slips away from me. "I—I can do that." A smile of relief creases the young woman's features.

"That a way!"

"Randi?" I ask, dumbfounded. "Your arm?"

"I'll live. Still go for the bottom, Juanita?"

"There may be a pond of liquid nitrogen trifluoride down there—it's unprecedented."

"Ed?"

He looks down, then at the crevasse sides. "Why don't I help Randi with the camp and prepare for climbing out of here?"

Apparently, we *will* sleep here—under the sword of Damocles.

"Wojciech?" Dr. Lotati asks.

I am at a loss for words. I am more tired and sore than I have ever been. How much more tired and sore can I be before I am a danger, I wonder? Everyone has been pummeled and challenged. But these people, these comrades of mine, will not admit disaster. They will press on. It is a collective decision—a spontaneous informal vote of voices that is already a majority. Voicing misgivings on my part would do no good at all, and my fate is tied to theirs. But I wonder that such things can still be in this age of robots. May the ghosts of Byrd, Amundsen, Lewis and Clark, and Bering fill my mind with whatever it is that gets one through. I came here to prove myself worthy and now the question is upon me. I look at the crevasse sides and down into its deep.

"Three climbers would be best," Dr. Lotati says.

"I'm . . . I can go with a little rest."

Dr. Lotati nods. "We can all use some. It's only 1100. We'll set up on the bridge. Mike and Karen, we'll take the big tent—you can probably slide it down on ropes."

This only takes a few minutes. We anchor the large vacuum tent to the bridge. It fits with about a meter to spare in width—with the door toward the intact wall. Room in the tent is limited. It was meant to sleep four and it is crowded with six of us. Our body odors again mingle in a forgettable stew of smells, and the drop curtain for its tiny commode is woefully inadequate for privacy. But we are relieved and happy—we have been through a memorable adventure and nobody has gotten killed.

Ed is quiet, eats quickly, and is asleep in his sack, fully clothed, in minutes. He says nothing. We will take a very real risk shortly far, far, from help—for the sake of samples that could easily be gathered by robots a month from now.

As a certified—and some might say certifiable—poet, suicidal undertakings are perhaps in my nature. But the milieu of the Gentleman Adventurer requires that one return from the adventure to recount it. While Ed was gallant in the crisis, the closeness of his brush with death might only now be sinking into him. I, with far less experience, accepted a challenge he did not—does he resent this? No, I tell myself, he is just exhausted.

I have to make myself eat—I'm hungry, but more tired. A warm sleep-sack never felt so good, I realize. It seems I have barely closed my eyes when Dr. Lotati is gently rocking me awake.

"It's 1400," he says. "Time to go."

The trip to the bottom of the crevasse is a straightforward rappel. With Randi resting her arm, Eloni and I head for the bottom with Juanita in the lead.

"This could be Calorian clathrate—proof that Chao Meng Fu is older."

"But doesn't its flatness mean it's young?" I ask. Old surfaces are heavily cratered.

"Watch for a hollow to your left. No, the surface is young due to deposition—the crater itself is ancient. I'd guess we're about 3.8 billion years down, below the original crater floor. The walls are shock-fractured rock, not exposed sediment layers. No strata—" a swing of her ax tears a rough section of about a square meter from the wall "—underneath."

"Look, more signs of erosion," she adds later.

"Erosion?" The wall is a rough breccia, a compressed clathrate and gravel mixture. The larger stones are sharp, not rounded.

"There is evidence of atmosphere all around us—you can see icicles in the hollows, and a cold glistening wetness on the walls."

I turn off my radio. "Can you hear me?" I shout.

There is no answer—the vapor is still too thin, even at the bottom, to conduct sound.

We hang from the wall and gaze into the utterly still pool of nitrogen trifluoride in the circles of our helmet lamps below us. Unable to resist the temptation. I reach into one of Mercury's nostrils and break off an icicle and toss it into the pool. It ripples like oily water.

"Wojciech," Eloni says in a mildly scolding voice, "have some respect! That pool has been built up, molecule by molecule, probably over billions of years."

"How?" Juanita asks, gently. "Even if the crater is that old, the crevasse isn't."

Eloni is silent, then says, "Oh, of course. But where does it come from then?"

"The pool is a mystery, for now," Juanita says. "Perhaps some comet with an unusual concentration of fluorine ices struck not too long ago. Or something else." She laughs. "Fortunately, not all mysteries can be solved now. We would run out of things to do!"

I envision tentacles reaching out of that deep to pluck us from the crevasse wall. "Could something have evolved to base its blood on that, the way we use seawater?"

"Not my field," Juanita answers. "But let's take a sample."

She is closest, and deftly dips a sample capsule into the liquid. Nothing emerges to bite her hand off—so much for that fantasy. I might not have had the nerve. Then I have a moment of insight, to do this requires the right balance of imagination and nerve.

"I do not think," Eloni offers, "that there would be enough energy for life. If there were, the liquid would boil away. Hydrocarbons at these temperatures would be frozen solid, so what could one use to build life molecules? How could anything that would work at these temperatures get here without being destroyed by the Sun first? Still, it is an interesting thought, Wojciech."

"If the crack could go down a hundred kilometers or so," Juanita remarks, "it would be warm enough to evaporate everything, possibly warm enough to walk around with the right atmosphere. But Mercury would close a crack that deep; its crust is surprisingly thin, even now. This is not Mars."

She sounds like my fifth-year teacher back in Krakow. I suddenly feel far, far over my head. These people understand where they are and what they are doing: it holds no terror for them, no fear of sticking a hand where it might not come back. But for me, my overripe literary imagination haunts my mind like the tale of the bogeyman that kept me out of grandfather's basement until I was seven. I am not comfortable here—but, I tell myself, I will enjoy having been here more when, and if—always if—we get back.

"It's time to go back," Juanita says, her vials filled. "Climbing."

"Climbing," we all say.

"Belay on," Dr. Lotati says, from far above us.

The climb back up to the bridge is slow. Once we hit the layered material, we stop to take half-meter cores, drilled slantwise, at those layers which Juanita estimates to have been laid down during the great events of the inner Solar System: layers that may contain glass beads from the Imbrium impact on Luna, Caloris here, Hellas on Mars, and, just possibly, a few grains with the right isotope ratios to be from the K-T impact on Earth. If we find these, we can bring the geological history of the planets together. If, the paradigm goes, we understand better why the Solar System is the way it is, we will understand better why we are the way we are—the forces that have shaped our evolution and those of other sentient races. But we won't know if the samples contain what we suspect for many months, by which time we will have scattered to the nether ends of the Solar System.

We are tired and bruises remind us of yesterday's avalanche with each bump, but there is a sense of elation about us. We are the first people to see a pool of liquid on an alien planet in its natural state. And no machine saw it first.

When we arrive back at the ice bridge, Juanita sees me staring nervously at the slide.

"I've calculated the slope and the coefficient of friction, Wojciech—I think it's fully relaxed. It may stay that way for a billion years."

"Now you tell me!" But would the trip have been as thrilling if she had? "What caused it to go in the first place?"

"Our weight, I think, plus an accumulation of stresses. I'm beginning to think the crevasse is fairly young—otherwise a meteor impact would have caused the slump before we did."

"There could be more than physical tension," Eloni says. "Near the surface, over many years, radiation will cause chemical changes and produce unstable molecules in crystalline ice. A physical shock, such as an ax, might release these energies."

"Possibly," Juanita says.

I look down at the ice bridge under me. If the crevasse is fairly recent, this would be even more recent—and not, I hope, have had time to accumulate radiation "energies."

We are physically tired but the midday nap and the feeling of accomplishment leave us too hyper to sleep immediately. After rations, I suggest the idea that had led me to join their expedition in the first place.

"Randi?" I ask. "Dr. Lotati?"

They turn their heads to me.

"Are you aware of the theories of a Dr. Nikhil Ray?"

Dr. Lotati purses his lips as if he had something to say, then thought better of it.

Juanita answers. "He tries to explain the low density of Miranda and some other outer satellites, by making them a sponge of caverns. It is an innovative idea, but, I'm afraid, not well accepted."

Dr. Lotati grunts. "I've met the man. His theories are unorthodox and he has this infuriatingly superior manner about him. . . . Well, we'll know soon enough anyway. The IPA is finally getting around to dropping sonography stations on the major Uranian satellites."

As "free" robot-produced resources grew exponentially, so did the Interplanetary Association's influence on who goes where and does what. The IPA, whose main members are the United Nations of Earth, the Mars Council, and the Cislunar Republic, responds, in large measure, to politicians. They in turn respond to the media and the public—I am counting on this.

"I was," I venture, "thinking that it might be time to visit Miranda—and that, with the coincidence in their names, Randi might be the one to do it. It would certainly be an interesting angle. Especially if Dr. Ray could be persuaded to come."

Dr. Lotati frowns. "That would be rather commercial, wouldn't it?" Ed contributes with a wink in my direction. He is not taking this too seriously.

"Finish school," Randi says, "do some low g work in the asteroids, Saturn, then maybe." She grins at me. "My world. Caves?"

"There are certainly caves there," Juanita says with a grin, "but if they are big ones, you might be sorry about taking Nikhil. He's already insufferable with the issue in doubt. God help us if he's right!"

Dr. Lotati and Ed laugh heartily. Randi shrugs, and a flicker of pain crosses her face at the gesture. The shoulder hurts more than she wants us to know, I suspect.

"You can make too much of that," Ed says. "He's not a monster, Juanita. He can be very much the gentleman, and his conversation is always interesting. I sometimes wonder if the personality conflicts don't have more to do with his peer review problems than the merits of his work."

Dr. Lotati turns and tugs on his beard. "Uranus is the frontier," he finally says. "There's only one small inhabited scientific station in the Uranus system, in its outer satellite, Mustardseed. Within the Uranian magnetosphere, radiation is a concern." He stares briefly at me, then Randi. "Also, I don't want to associate the Society with Ray's claims just yet. Let's see what happens with the seismic study. And let's see how well Wojciech's presentation of this expedition is received."

I glance at Randi. She stares back at me, intently, and the ghost of a smile crosses her face as she wrinkles her nose.

"I could use a shower," I say—humorously. There will be no showers for several days yet.

But Randi hands me a silver foil wrapper. Her nose has decided that it's bath time—understandable in view of our exertions. The foil contains a light towelette soaked in a cleaning solution that does not have to be rinsed. She offers them to the others, removes her coveralls, and then releases the seam of her vacuum suit. Her father turns his back to us and, facing the wall of the tent, does the same. Eloni also turns to the wall of the tent. Ed watches Randi, and they exchange a brief smile.

We are a cross section of the Solar System, and a cross section of attitudes about our bodies. I still feel a slight twinge, as if in nostalgia for an old cultural taboo, but the observer of people in me rejoices in the passing of taboos. Ed, surprisingly, seems the one uncomfortable with communal bathing.

Juanita, whose family left Earth a century ago, is already sponging, oblivious to anything else. She is a well-endowed woman in excellent condition, as is everyone on this kind of endeavor. Her hair, unbound, hangs to her shoulders. It is almost all white and makes her skin look darker than it is in contrast. Her only other concessions to her fifty standard years are a slight gut and a bit of looseness on her neck and under her arms.

Randi is still watching Ed watch her, as if she enjoys it. She is a rangy young woman of jet-black hair and well defined, though not exaggerated muscles. Her female features seem like the afterthoughts of a god who in making an athlete decided at the last minute to make a woman, too. There is an intriguing hardness about the rest of her, including an untouched scar on her side. But her face, her smile, and her manner are womanly.

Embarrassed at myself for staring, I turn around like Dr. Lotati and finish undressing—applying the cleaning cloth to my body. But I love women too much to resist another look. When I do, both Eloni and Juanita are looking at me. Our eyes meet, we smile and I relax. My feelings as they watch me bathe are hard to describe—would it make sense to say that I felt first forgiven? I feel something of a sense of camaraderie.

Then Eloni reaches with both hands and turns me to the side of the tent. Its drum-tight bulge instantly reminds me of the vacuum, just beyond that millimeter of tough, impervious fabric.

I feel a damp cloth on my back, up and down, hitting every needful spot. When she is done, I return the favor. She sighs just on the edge of audibility. Almost like a purr.

I feel suddenly very good, and useful—should poetry and nature writing fail me completely, I could do this for a living. Well, maybe.

Dr. Lotati turns to crawl into his sleeping bag, and I accidentally get a brief glimpse of injuries he has chosen not to show the rest of us. Gunshot wounds? Before he can seal the side, Juanita touches his shoulder and crawls in with him.

Eloni turns from the wall then and sees Randi and me, not yet in our sleeping bags. She looks down, then looks up again, then crawls into her sleeping bag. I can't read the expression on her face.

I get into my bag, pull my suit and helmet in with me, and seal the hood behind me. Its flaps will close and hold pressure if there is an accident while I sleep.

"Lights off," Randi says, and the tent complies. It is utterly, totally dark. There is movement. As my eyes adapt, I glance in her direction, but her sleeping bag is empty. She is probably not sleeping with Eloni, which leaves Ed. I feel a twinge of jealousy, though I know Ed has known the Lotatis for many years, and gone on several expeditions with them.

The exhaustion of this day does not permit sexual regrets, however. It seems like only a moment, and then I awake to light, discussions about the ascent, and the smell of freshly opened breakfast bars. The discussion is between Ed and Emilio, and it concerns who is to go up the wall with Randi, to set the ropes for the rest of us.

"We need to make time," Dr. Lotati says.

"All the more reason for you to go with Randi. You're a team."

"Thank you, friend, but I am sixty-two years old and you are thirty-eight. You and Randi climb well together." There is a slight hint of humor in Emilio's voice to suggest to my perhaps oversensitive mind that he knows they do more than climb well together.

"It's only a kilometer, mate. You're as good as ever."

"I'll second that," Juanita says.

Dr. Lotati smiles and shakes his head. "The group comes first."

Randi embraces her father, wordlessly, but I can see her eyes glisten. Then Dr. Lotati reaches over to Ed and they grasp hands.

Something has passed, I realize, and who am I to witness such a passing? More than ever, I feel an ambitious interloper. I look over at Eloni. She is looking at me. Wistfully? I smile back.

We pack quickly and efficiently, filling the soft pressure packs first with the things that can stand vacuum, then the hard ones. When the tent is bare, the last pack is sealed and we take it down to a tenth of an atmosphere. We check each other's seals and fit. Randi frowns at mine, and has me depressurize to readjust my fit. If the pressure were much lower, I think, my blood would boil. We normally breathe a fifty-fifty oxygen-nitrogen mix at four-tenths atmosphere, so I still have a quarter of Earth normal oxygen partial pressure. I try not to get excited.

Randi treats this like an everyday event. She tugs, pulls, and smooths all my joint areas. She is utterly clinical about this, but happens to glance up with a wink when she adjusts my leg seams. "It's all in the family," her look seems to say.

I find myself slipping as if to an event horizon. Do I want to befriend this woman to pursue fame and fortune on her distant namesake moon, or has my idea for an expedition to the moon become an excuse to be near the woman? I suddenly realize that I am very, very taken by her.

She reseals my suit and I tell it to bring its pressure up again. She has indeed worked wonders, and I am much more comfortable than I was the day before. She apparently likes what she sees, grins, and squeezes my arm, then turns to the business at hand.

The tent finishes taking itself down to near vacuum. When the sides are noticeably softer, we open the main seal, and the tent ripples as the remaining millibar or so of air escapes. We turn our helmet lights on and emerge into the crevasse again.

The wall is suddenly lit with flood-lights—Mike and Karen have seen us emerge. It is one kilometer of gray-banded dirty clathrate, vertical, except for the parts that are more than vertical.

Randi leads; if she falls, she is less weight on the bolts and pitons that hold our ropes.

"This stuff is like soft sandstone," Ed says. "I can almost push a piton in by hand, here and there."

"Use more," Randi says. "Angle down."

"OK." He is silent for a while. "There. I suggest we do this before I lose my nerve. Belay on."

"Climbing," Randi answers. They proceed upward carefully but steadily, taking turns.

I happen to be looking up when it happens. Randi is climbing when her foothold crumbles. She grabs for a line, says, "Damn!" then, "Falling." Her effort to grab has pushed her out from the wall, and when the rope goes taut, one of the pitons pops out of the wall with a shower of dust and ice. After a brief hesitation, the other two follow, and Ed yells, "Slack!"

Desperately, Randi tries to slow her fall by digging her hands and crampons into the wall beside her, throwing up a wake of dust. The smoothness of the wall helps; it is not completely vertical, and there are no bumps to throw her out.

The next set of pitons catches her rope, and for half a second it looks like it might hold. But before she comes to a complete halt, they pull out too and she starts to slide down again. Now, only Ed's own precarious hold on the wall stands between them and a five-hundred-meter fall. He is furiously trying to hammer in more pitons, but there is little rope left between him and Randi.

They need another secure line. Why, with six other more experienced explorers present, I am the one to think of something is a mystery. Perhaps it has something to do with creativity, or with not having a mind full of the knowledge of things that wouldn't work.

"Mike, Wojciech. Can you fire a rocket line right into the wall above them? It ought to penetrate that stuff and anchor itself."

He doesn't take time to answer me. There is a flash from overhead and an impact ten meters above Ed. The line it carries is much thinner than climbing rope, but drapes down beside them quickly in the vacuum. It continues to play out, draping all the way down to our little camp.

The line between Randi and Ed snaps tight, and his foot and arm come free in a shower of ice. He should hit the release, I think. Better one death than two, but he tries to hold on to the wall. He doesn't dare let go and reach for the new, untested line, hanging less than a meter away.

It almost works. Randi, caught short, manages to reach her ax and digs into the wall like a desperate fly. Working with her right hand, she sets one piton and then another, hammering them in with her fist.

Above her, the rest of the ice holding Ed begins to give way as he tries to regain his handhold. "Can't hold, falling!" He flails for the new line as he starts to slip, but it is out of reach.

They would, I think, be dead on Earth—but Mercury gravity is more forgiving. Working as Ed slides, Randi reaches the new line and yanks hard on it. She yanks hard again—it must not have been firmly set. Another hard pull and she seems satisfied. Ed slides down beside her in a plume of dust and ice, barely in contact with the wall.

Quickly Randi connects the new line to the line that still connects them, slack now, and loops it around the piton she has just set. "Protection in!"

Thirty meters below her, Ed bounces as the line pulls taut and pops the piton out of the wall in another shower of debris. Ed's weight pulls Randi free of her holds as well.

They both slide another ten meters, but now the slack in the line from the rocket has been taken up. They slide some more as it stretches, then, finally, stop. All told, Randi has fallen about a hundred meters and Ed perhaps fifty.

"Jupiter!" Karen, on the crevasse rim, exclaims. "Randi, Ed, set yourselves if you can. I can see the rocket: it's wedged itself vertically in the hole it made when it hit the wall, only about ten centimeters from the face. Try to hold tight while we think of something."

"OK," Ed says. "But don't take too long. I think I'm about at the end of my rope about this."

The laughter, fueled by relief, is perhaps a little too loud for the quality of the pun. Ed quickly starts hammering in additional protection. Randi, however, is simply hanging passively in her harness.

"Randi?" Mike calls.

"Injured. Both arms." Her voice attempts calm, but I can hear the pain in it.

"Can you climb?" Mike asks.

Randi tries to lift an arm up to her rope and gasps. "Not now."

"Descending," Ed says. "I'd like another belay if you can think of something."

What we think of is setting our remaining line rocket for maximum range and steering it about six meters under the far edge of the crevasse. It slams in hard, burying itself too far in for Karen to see. "Ice," Mike says, instantly, as a patch of icy regolith loosened by the rocket impact snows down left of the climbers. The upper layers, as we know, are softer. They pull the line from the far edge until it sets hard—ten kilonewtons tension, Mike estimates. Then they let the line drape down to us, and we walk it over to where Ed can reach it.

He connects the lines, and continues down.

Randi tries to descend. We hear the slightest hint of a cry of pain over the radio, then a loud "Damn! Dad, I can't lift my hands over my shoulders. Both shoulders shot."

"That's all right, Randi, I'm coming." Dr. Lotati turns and looks at me. "Come on, Wojciech. I want your head on that wall."

Juanita gives me a pat on the rear, and surprisingly, Eloni gives me a silent hug. Inside her visor, her dark eyes are glistening. I think of how frightened the

Kenyan student must be, but she has just contributed in the only way she could think of.

"Thanks, team," I say, and squeeze her hand.

I clip my ascent ratchet on and start climbing. There are no problems and we reach Randi and Ed in half an hour.

Randi is calm. "Right arm. Won't go above shoulder. Maybe dislocated. Left arm works, sort of. But hurts too much. Might faint. OK as long as I keep my hands down."

"I'll take you down, papoose-style," Ed offers. "Then we'll ride the elevator up."

Dr. Lotati touches Randi. "OK?"

"I'll make it, Dad."

"Good, Wojciech and I will go up then, and set the anchor," Dr. Lotati decides. His voice crackles with leadership and confidence. I smile. Everyone, including him, has forgotten about his age. It won't be obvious on this climb; if anything, I will slow *him* down.

We replace Ed's backpack with Randi, tying her to his shoulder harness, and help guide them down. When they are safe below, Dr. Lotati nods to me, and says, "We have to consider everything we put into this surface to be hazardous, no?"

I nod. We are leaning out from a wall almost half a kilometer above a bridge about half a kilometer above a pool of cryogenic nitrogen trifluoride, talking about how the various things that hold our ropes to said wall may give way at any time.

"OK. We use four pitons, or bolts, or a combination, on each belay, and arrange the ropes like so." He demonstrates, creating what looks at first glance to be a cat's cradle of ropes between carabiners and pitons. "This equalizes forces among the pitons and minimizes the shock if one lets go." It takes me a couple of tries to get it right. He finally pats me on the shoulder, and without further ado says, "Climbing."

"On belay," I answer, wondering about people who seem to come alive only when staring death in the face. He ascends deliberately, and deceptively fast.

Actually, I keep up, but exhaust myself in the process. Dr. Lotati is only a centimeter or two taller than his daughter, and hardly much heavier. He is wiry strong; occasional rest stops are the only concession he makes to age—and I need them more than he does. We stop where the second line-bearing rocket buried itself in the fragile clathrate, six meters below the crater floor. The ledge is overhung by about a meter, more where the rocket impact dislodged a large hunk of wall.

"Can you stand a short fall?" he asks me. "I think we'll need several tries to get around that edge." I've never fallen on a belay line before. I want to impress Emilio; my Mirandas, moon and woman, are at stake. But the idea of trying to scramble almost upside down and free-falling six to ten meters, with only a questionable anchor to stop me if I slip, scares the crap out me. If there were any other way . . .

"Wojciech?"

"Yes." Then, perhaps because my mind works best in an emergency, or under a deadline, the idea comes to me. "Dr. Lotati—this is fairly soft stuff. You don't suppose we could just tunnel through it, up to the surface?"

He looks down at me. "Perhaps! I wouldn't consider desecrating an Earth climb like that, but I think we will be forgiven here. I knew your head would be good for something!" Then he takes an ax from his belt and swings it into the ice overhead. A good sized hunk falls and shatters into tiny chips on my helmet.

"Ice!" He looks at his handiwork, says, "Si," and swings again, and again, cutting a notch more than a tunnel as it turns out. We are through and up to the crater floor in less than an hour.

There is a round of cheers when we say, "On top!" Mike and Karen wave from the other side of the crevasse—only a hundred meters away. It has taken us two days to go that hundred meters.

I help set the next set of anchors a hundred meters back from the edge, in firm regolith. The rest is ropes, ascenders and pulleys. Mike and Karen send the remaining gear, and themselves, across in an ersatz tram, and help us hoist the rest of the party. Juanita is the last one to emerge from the crevasse and we all cheer, intoxicated with our close call and our final victory. By the time everything is up or over, we have been awake for thirty hours. Dr. Lotati decides to set up camp immediately.

We have four two-person tents in addition to the large one. They can be independent or their entrances can be sealed to connecting ports in the large tent, forming a mini-base looking something like an inflated starfish minus an arm. That way, early risers can let others sleep.

Randi's left shoulder is bad—a possible separation—and we have at least three days' march ahead of us to our pickup point. We discuss an evacuation, but she won't hear of it. Mike and Ed both have field medical training but Mike has more practice, so he is the closest thing to a doctor we have, and he consults with Earth. It turns out that our optical scattering imager is good enough to build up a picture of the injury; Randi's humerus is not quite in its socket.

Earth recommends evacuation. Randi says no. Dr. Lotati supports her—we are in an age where injuries can be healed if they can be endured, but the opportunities to do something more significant than entertain oneself and collect one's automation stipend are few and far between.

Randi, Ed told me several nights ago, is Dr. Lotati's only son. I laughed and asked Ed what that made him. "The gayest man on Mercury," he answered—and threw such a convincing leer at me that it took me an unsettling second to get the joke. But the humor disguises a poignant situation—a young woman trying to be, for her father, the son he could never have. How much was from her nature, how much was from her love? Or was there a difference? And what of her mother? Randi's mother was never mentioned by anyone, and the only public biographical info was that Emilio had divorced her when Randi was six and never married again.

Following instructions from the doctors on Earth, Mike resets the shoulder. It takes him two tries. Randi shuts her eyes and gasps—that is all. Then it is in. Painkillers, anti-inflammatory drugs, and reconstructive stimulants we have—she will be sore, but as good as new in a few months. Climbing is out, but she can walk the rest of the way.

Ed and Randi retire together, her arm immobilized to her body with tape.

Juanita decides to sleep with Emilio. Mike and Karen are a given.

Eloni is looking at me with dark pools of eyes and what could be a hopeful smile on her face. I look at the shy graduate student who had given me a hug to send me up a treacherous wall that had just come within the width of an idea of killing two people. I shrug and reach a hand out to her and she comes and sits by me with the widest grin on her face I have ever seen.

"You wish I were Randi, don't you?" Eloni asks me.

"That's not your fault."

Her smile fades. "I almost got us all killed by being too slow. That was my fault."

There are times when sympathy can do things lust cannot. I have my arms around her in a second. "No one blames you. You're part of us, now. Time to enjoy it."

She kind of melts into me and gently pushes me down onto my back on my sleepsack. She has a low, incredibly sexy voice. "That is about as much as I can enjoy. I hope I do not disappoint you."

Tired as I am, I'm relieved; and confused. "Eloni, I write about the male and female thing, more from reading than experience, I'm afraid. I may sigh, but disappointment would be putting things a bit strong. But I'm curious. Do you believe in abstinence, and if so, can you tell me why?"

No contraception, I speculate? In this day, I find that hard to believe—but she is studying at Jovis Tholis on Mars, I remind myself, in the middle of the New Reformation.

A certain hardness comes over her face. "You want to know? I spoke literal truth. Abstinence has nothing to do with it. I was mutilated so I cannot enjoy what most women can enjoy. So I hike across glaciers and climb mountains instead," she smiles wryly. "That is how I get high. Try to understand. I am not Kenyan by birth. Kenya is a civilized nation."

I have it then. Female circumcision. Back on Earth, the villages all have nice premanufactured houses, with bathrooms, electricity, diagnostic comm ports, and regular food deliveries. But here and there, otherwise gentle people protect primitive cultures from "western interference," and so we still permit this to be done to children.

"How old were you?"

"Ten. They were very thorough. But in a few years, doctors will be able to fix it, I think. Regenerate the tissue that was taken from me. That's a spin-off from the interstellar project. They needed to solve tissue regeneration to do cold sleep reliably. For now, I must enjoy giving and being enjoyed while I fantasize what it might really be like."

What can one say? I take her hand and she squeezes it.

"Oh, yes." Her voice is low and throaty. "They mutilated me, they tried to keep me barefoot and stupid to carry on their primitive culture. They even tried to keep me from school. But they could not shut off my mind. And here I am, yes, here I am where they thought I could never go doing what they thought to keep from me forever. So I am a space person now, part of another tribe."

Eloni and I are both, I realize, refugees from cultures that do not want who we are. Hers a primitive one, mine too sophisticated to see itself. I only want to hold her, smother her hurt, and bring a smile to her face. I try to kiss her.

She holds me off. "Someday I have to go back there and try to change what the people do to each other there. I cannot be a space person forever. Do you understand?" She buries her face in my shoulder. "For now. Just for now."

I understand. This is for now—and whatever our feelings for each other now, our destinies lie in different directions. I nod and she is in my arms. Our lips touch again and the future vanishes. "What do you do want me to do?" I ask.

In answer, she releases the seal of my tight suit.

We remove each other's remaining clothes and slip into my sleep sack. She wriggles against me and we do kiss, and our hands do stroke and caress, and begin to defy the cold dead gray cruelty outside our bubble with yet another act of life.

But there really isn't very much room and we are both very tired. So, in each other's arms, we fall asleep, content with a mostly symbolic defiance.

The remaining walk toward the center of Chao Meng Fu is two by two, the time filled mostly with conversations that share what we are and what we know, but sometimes with those comfortable silences in which your mind digests what you have learned, playing this way and that with it. There are more crevasses to cross, but we do so expeditiously.

During one of these crossings, I say, "On belay, Dr. Lotati."

"Climbing. Wojciech, call me Emilio, it's quicker."

A small thing, but it suggests to me a future more interesting than correcting undergraduate papers.

Juanita suggests we share a piece of music for our final approach to the central depot. It is by a twentieth-century composer named Alan Hovhaness, a symphony called "City of Light." She says it is his symphony number twenty-two.

"Twenty-two?" I ask. "Did I hear you right? I know Haydn wrote over a hundred, but that was when they were short and highly formatted. Beethoven wrote only nine. Tchaikovsky, six. I thought they'd pretty much stopped doing symphonies by the twenty-first century."

Juanita laughed. "We geologists call Hovhaness our patron composer because he actually wrote a symphony about a volcano—and that was number *fifty*. By the mid-twenty-first century, they were calling him 'the American Haydn.' Now let's just listen."

As we approach the brilliant peaks of the Chao Meng Fu central crown—great massive round Sun-gilded domes that speak of power and eternity—I am incapable of understanding why I once thought of this expedition as a stunt. I feel like a piece of steel, bent, hammered, bent and hammered again in the fire with greater strength and balance than I have ever known before.

It is a feeling I want to have again, if I must pursue it to the ends of the Solar System. Perhaps I am not in a class with Ed Blake and perhaps any fantasies I had of a match with Randi must remain fantasies, but I have found in my own backyard a delicate and precious union with Eloni and a friend and colleague in Juanita. And I think I have succeeded in my main objective—I have, I think, the friendship and respect of the people who could bring me out to the frontier which calls my spirit.

As I walk I feel the voices of a more broad-shouldered century calling me; Stanley, Peary, Scott, Teddy Roosevelt, and among poets, of course, Kipling. As I trudge, I amuse myself with a doggerel:

> *Perhaps those prudent people*
> *Who never risk the pit,*

> *Also never know the joy*
> *Of coming out of it.*

Not prize material, perhaps, but sums my experience, and in my present state of deranged ecstasy, I am no critic!

And if my words fail you—as they fail many others of highly educated tastes— then listen to the finale of Hovhaness' symphony. For if you cannot understand after hearing that, you have left the human race. What I learned, in the crossing of Chao Meng Fu, was that such things still can be, in any age, for anyone who will do them.

Wang's Carpets

GREG EGAN

As the new century approaches, it's obvious that Australian writer Greg Egan is one of the Big New Names to emerge in science fiction in the nineties, probably the best new hard-science writer to enter the field since Greg Bear, and already one of the most widely known of all Australian genre writers. In the last few years, Egan has become a frequent contributor to *Interzone* and *Asimov's Science Fiction* and has made sales as well as to *Pulphouse, Analog, Aurealis, Eidolon* and elsewhere; many of his stories have also appeared in various "Best of the Year" series, and he was on the final Hugo ballot in 1995 for his story "Cocoon," which won the Ditmar Award and the *Asimov's* Readers' Award. His novella "Oceanic" won another *Asimov's* Readers' Award and is on this year's final Hugo ballot as I type these words. His first novel, *Quarantine,* appeared in 1992, to wide critical acclaim, and was followed by a second novel in 1994, *Permutation City,* which won the John W. Campbell Memorial Award. His most recent books are two new novels, *Distress* and *Diaspora,* and three collections of his short fiction, *Axiomatic, Luminous,* and *Our Lady of Chernobyl.* Upcoming is a new novel, *Teranesia.* He has a Web site at http://www.netspace.netau/^gregegan/.

Although he often writes incisive studies of near-future sociological problems and the way they are complicated (for both better *and* worse) by technological change, such as "Cocoon," "Tap," "Yeyuka," "Silver Fire," and many others, Egan has also written his share of stories about explorers of one kind or another, including "Luminous," in which scientists explore congruent mathematical realms with a computer made of light, "Dust," in which a hacker investigates firsthand what "life" as a program running inside a virtual construct would be like, and one of 1997's *two* stories about explorers who plunge into a black hole, "The Planck Dive" (the other is Geoffrey A. Landis's "Approaching Perimelasma," reprinted later in this book). In the brilliant story that follows, though—one of those seminal stories that come along only every once in a long while, where the conceptualization is so original that it persuades other writers to change their *own* thinking about what the future is going to be like—Egan succeeded in reinventing the space travel/space exploration tale for a new generation, and I suspect that you'll be seeing the mark of "Wang's Carpet" on many such stories for long years to come.

Waiting to be cloned one thousand times and scattered across ten million cubic light-years, Paolo Venetti relaxed in his favorite ceremonial bathtub: a tiered hexagonal pool set in a courtyard of black marble flecked with gold. Paolo wore full traditional anatomy, uncomfortable garb at first, but the warm currents flowing across his back and shoulders slowly eased him into a pleasant torpor. He could have reached the same state in an instant, by decree—but the occasion seemed to demand the complete ritual of verisimilitude, the ornate curlicued longhand of imitation physical cause and effect.

As the moment of diaspora approached, a small gray lizard darted across the courtyard, claws scrabbling. It halted by the far edge of the pool, and Paolo marveled at the delicate pulse of its breathing, and watched the lizard watching him, until it moved again, disappearing into the surrounding vineyards. The environment was full of birds and insects, rodents and small reptiles—decorative in appearance, but also satisfying a more abstract aesthetic: softening the harsh radial symmetry of the lone observer; anchoring the simulation by perceiving it from a multitude of viewpoints. Ontological guy lines. No one had asked the lizards if they wanted to be cloned, though. They were coming along for the ride, like it or not.

The sky above the courtyard was warm and blue, cloudless and sunless, isotropic. Paolo waited calmly, prepared for every one of half a dozen possible fates.

An invisible bell chimed softly, three times. Paolo laughed, delighted.

One chime would have meant that he was still on Earth: an anti-climax, certainly—but there would have been advantages to compensate for that. Everyone who really mattered to him lived in the Carter-Zimmerman polis, but not all of them had chosen to take part in the diaspora to the same degree; his Earth-self would have lost no one. Helping to ensure that the thousand ships were safely dispatched would have been satisfying, too. And remaining a member of the wider Earth-based community, plugged into the entire global culture in real-time, would have been an attraction in itself.

Two chimes would have meant that this clone of Carter-Zimmerman had reached a planetary system devoid of life. Paolo had run a sophisticated—but nonsapient—self-predictive model before deciding to wake under those conditions. Exploring a handful of alien worlds, however barren, had seemed likely to be an enriching experience for him—with the distinct advantage that the whole endeavor would be untrammeled by the kind of elaborate precautions necessary in the presence of alien life. C-Z's population would have fallen by more than half—and many of his closest friends would have been absent—but he would have forged new friendships, he was sure.

Four chimes would have signaled the discovery of intelligent aliens. Five, a technological civilization. Six, spacefarers.

Three chimes, though, meant that the scout probes had detected unambiguous signs of life—and that was reason enough for jubilation. Up until the moment of the pre-launch cloning—a subjective instant before the chimes had sounded—no reports of alien life had ever reached Earth. There'd been no guarantee that any part of the diaspora would find it.

Paolo willed the polis library to brief him; it promptly rewired the declarative memory of his simulated traditional brain with all the information he was likely to need to satisfy his immediate curiosity. This clone of C-Z had arrived at Vega, the second closest of the thousand target stars, twenty-seven light-years from Earth. Paolo closed his eyes and visualized a star map with a thousand lines-radiating out from the sun, then zoomed in on the trajectory which described his own journey. It had taken three centuries to reach Vega—but the vast majority of the polis's twenty thousand inhabitants had programmed their exoselves to suspend them prior to the cloning, and to wake them only if and when they arrived at a suitable destination. Ninety-two citizens had chosen the alternative: experiencing every voyage of the diaspora from start to finish, risking disappointment, and even death. Paolo now knew that the ship aimed at Fomalhaut, the target nearest Earth, had been struck by debris and annihilated *en route*. He mourned the ninety-two, briefly. He hadn't been close to any of them, prior to the cloning, and the particular versions who'd willfully perished two centuries ago in interstellar space seemed as remote as the victims of some ancient calamity from the era of flesh.

Paolo examined his new home star through the cameras of one of the scout probes—and the strange filters of the ancestral visual system. In traditional colors, Vega was a fierce blue-white disk, laced with prominences. Three times the mass of the sun, twice the size and twice as hot, sixty times as luminous. Burning hydrogen fast—and already halfway through its allotted five hundred million years on the main sequence.

Vega's sole planet, Orpheus, had been a featureless blip to the best lunar interferometers; now Paolo gazed down on its blue-green crescent, ten thousand kilometers below Carter-Zimmerman itself. Orpheus was terrestrial, a nickel-iron-silicate world; slightly larger than Earth, slightly warmer—a billion kilometers took the edge off Vega's heat—and almost drowning in liquid water. Impatient to see the whole surface firsthand, Paolo slowed his clock rate a thousandfold, allowing C-Z to circumnavigate the planet in twenty subjective seconds, daylight unshrouding a broad new swath with each pass. Two slender ocher-colored continents with mountainous spines bracketed hemispheric oceans, and dazzling expanses of pack ice covered both poles—far more so in the north, where jagged white peninsulas radiated out from the midwinter arctic darkness.

The Orphean atmosphere was mostly nitrogen—six times as much as on Earth; probably split by UV from primordial ammonia—with traces of water vapor and carbon dioxide, but not enough of either for a runaway greenhouse effect. The high atmospheric pressure meant reduced evaporation—Paolo saw not a wisp of cloud— and the large, warm oceans in turn helped feed carbon dioxide back into the crust, locking it up in limestone sediments destined for subduction.

The whole system was young, by Earth standards, but Vega's greater mass, and a denser protostellar cloud, would have meant swifter passage through most of the traumas of birth: nuclear ignition and early luminosity fluctuations; planetary coalescence and the age of bombardments. The library estimated that Orpheus had enjoyed a relatively stable climate, and freedom from major impacts, for at least the past hundred million years.

Long enough for primitive life to appear—

A hand seized Paolo firmly by the ankle and tugged him beneath the water. He offered no resistance, and let the vision of the planet slip away. Only two other people in C-Z had free access to this environment—and his father didn't play games with his now-twelve-hundred-year-old son.

Elena dragged him all the way to the bottom of the pool, before releasing his foot and hovering above him, a triumphant silhouette against the bright surface. She was ancestor-shaped, but obviously cheating; she spoke with perfect clarity, and no air bubbles at all.

"Late sleeper! I've been waiting seven weeks for this!"

Paolo feigned indifference, but he was fast running out of breath. He had his exoself convert him into an amphibious human variant—biologically and historically authentic, if no longer the definitive ancestral phenotype. Water flooded into his modified lungs, and his modified brain welcomed it.

He said, "Why would I want to waste consciousness, sitting around waiting for the scout probes to refine their observations? I woke as soon as the data was unambiguous."

She pummeled his chest; he reached up and pulled her down, instinctively reducing his buoyancy to compensate, and they rolled across the bottom of the pool, kissing.

Elena said, "You know we're the first C-Z to arrive, anywhere? The Fomalhaut ship was destroyed. So there's only one other pair of us. Back on Earth."

"So?" Then he remembered. Elena had chosen not to wake if any other version of her had already encountered life. Whatever fate befell each of the remaining ships, every other version of him would have to live without her.

He nodded soberly, and kissed her again. "What am I meant to say? You're a thousand times more precious to me, now?"

"Yes."

"Ah, but what about the you-and-I on Earth? Five hundred times would be closer to the truth."

"There's no poetry in five hundred."

"Don't be so defeatist. Rewire your language centers."

She ran her hands along the sides of his ribcage, down to his hips. They made love with their almost-traditional bodies—and brains; Paolo was amused to the point of distraction when his limbic system went into overdrive, but he remembered enough from the last occasion to bury his self-consciousness and surrender to the strange hijacker. It wasn't like making love in any civilized fashion—the rate of information exchange between them was minuscule, for a start—but it had the raw insistent quality of most ancestral pleasures.

Then they drifted up to the surface of the pool and lay beneath the radiant sunless sky.

Paolo thought: *I've crossed twenty-seven light-years in an instant. I'm orbiting the first planet ever found to hold alien life. And I've sacrificed nothing—left nothing I truly value behind. This is too good, too good.* He felt a pang of regret for his other selves—it was hard to imagine them faring as well, without Elena, without Orpheus—but there was nothing he could do about that, now. Although there'd be time to confer with Earth before any more ships reached their destinations, he'd decided—prior to the cloning—not to allow the unfolding of his manifold future to be swayed by any change of heart. Whether or not his Earth-self agreed, the two of them were powerless to alter the criteria for waking. The self with the right to choose for the thousand had passed away.

No matter, Paolo decided. The others would find—or construct—their own reasons for happiness. And there was still the chance that one of them would wake to the sound of *four chimes*.

Elena said, "If you'd slept much longer, you would have missed the vote."

The vote? The scouts in low orbit had gathered what data they could about Orphean biology. To proceed any further, it would be necessary to send micro-probes into the ocean itself—an escalation of contact which required the approval of two-thirds of the polis. There was no compelling reason to believe that the presence of a few million tiny robots could do any harm; all they'd leave behind in the water was a few kilojoules of waste heat. Nevertheless, a faction had arisen which advocated caution. The citizens of Carter-Zimmerman, they argued, could continue to observe from a distance for another decade, or another millennium, refining their observations and hypotheses before intruding . . . and those who dis-agreed could always sleep away the time, or find other interests to pursue.

Paolo delved into his library-fresh knowledge of the "carpets"—the single Or-phean lifeform detected so far. They were free-floating creatures living in the equa-torial ocean depths—apparently destroyed by UV if they drifted too close to the surface. They grew to a size of hundreds of meters, then fissioned into dozens of fragments, each of which continued to grow. It was tempting to assume that they were colonies of single-celled organisms, something like giant kelp—but there was no real evidence yet to back that up. It was difficult enough for the scout probes to discern the carpets' gross appearance and behavior through a kilometer of water, even with Vega's copious neutrinos lighting the way; remote observations on a microscopic scale, let alone biochemical analyses, were out of the question. Spec-troscopy revealed that the surface water was full of intriguing molecular debris—but guessing the relationship of any of it to the living carpets was like trying to reconstruct human biochemistry by studying human ashes.

Paolo turned to Elena. "What do you think?"

She moaned theatrically; the topic must have been argued to death while he slept. "The microprobes are harmless. They could tell us exactly what the carpets are made of, without removing a single molecule. What's the risk? *Culture shock?*"

Paolo flicked water onto her face, affectionately; the impulse seemed to come with the amphibian body. "You can't be sure that they're not intelligent."

"Do you know what was living on Earth, two hundred million years after it was formed?"

"Maybe cyanobacteria. Maybe nothing. This isn't Earth, though."

"True. But even in the unlikely event that the carpets are intelligent, do you think they'd notice the presence of robots a millionth their size? If they're unified organisms, they don't appear to react to anything in their environment—they have no predators, they don't pursue food, they just drift with the currents—so there's no reason for them to possess elaborate sense organs at all, let alone anything working on a sub-millimeter scale. And if they're colonies of single-celled crea-tures, one of which happens to collide with a microprobe and register its presence with surface receptors . . . what conceivable harm could that do?"

"I have no idea. But my ignorance is no guarantee of safety."

Elena splashed him back. "The only way to deal with your *ignorance* is to vote to send down the microprobes. We have to be cautious, I agree—but there's no point *being here* if we don't find out what's happening in the oceans, right now.

I don't want to wait for this planet to evolve something smart enough to broadcast biochemistry lessons into space. If we're not willing to take a few infinitesimal risks, Vega will turn red giant before we learn anything."

It was a throwaway line—but Paolo tried to imagine witnessing the event. In a quarter of a billion years, would the citizens of Carter-Zimmerman be debating the ethics of intervening to rescue the Orpheans—or would they all have lost interest, and departed for other stars, or modified themselves into beings entirely devoid of nostalgic compassion for organic life?

Grandiose visions for a twelve-hundred-year-old. The Fomalhaut clone had been obliterated by one tiny piece of rock. There was far more junk in the Vegan system than in interstellar space; even ringed by defenses, its data backed up to all the far-flung scout probes, this C-Z was not invulnerable just because it had arrived intact. Elena was right; they had to seize the moment—or they might as well retreat into their own hermetic worlds and forget that they'd ever made the journey.

Paolo recalled the honest puzzlement of a friend from Ashton-Laval: *Why go looking for aliens? Our polis has a thousand ecologies, a trillion species of evolved life. What do you hope to find, out there, that you couldn't have grown at home?*

What had he hoped to find? Just the answers to a few simple questions. Did human consciousness bootstrap all of space-time into existence, in order to explain itself? Or had a neutral, pre-existing universe given birth to a billion varieties of conscious life, all capable of harboring the same delusions of grandeur—until they collided with each other? Anthrocosmology was used to justify the inward-looking stance of most polises: if the physical universe was created by human thought, it had no special status which placed it above virtual reality. It might have come first—and every virtual reality might need to run on a physical computing device, subject to physical laws—but it occupied no privileged position in terms of "truth" versus "illusion." If the ACs were right, then it was no more *honest* to value the physical universe over more recent artificial realities than it was honest to remain flesh instead of software, or ape instead of human, or bacterium instead of ape.

Elena said, "We can't lie here forever; the gang's all waiting to see you."

"Where?" Paolo felt his first pang of homesickness; on Earth, his circle of friends had always met in a real-time image of the Mount Pinatubo crater, plucked straight from the observation satellites. A recording wouldn't be the same.

"I'll show you."

Paolo reached over and took her hand. The pool, the sky, the courtyard vanished—and he found himself gazing down on Orpheus again . . . nightside, but far from dark, with his full mental palette now encoding everything from the pale wash of ground-current long-wave radio, to the multi-colored shimmer of isotopic gamma rays and back-scattered cosmic-ray bremsstrahlung. Half the abstract knowledge the library had fed him about the planet was obvious at a glance, now. The ocean's smoothly tapered thermal glow spelt *three-hundred Kelvin* instantly— as well as backlighting the atmosphere's telltale infrared silhouette.

He was standing on a long, metallic-looking girder, one edge of a vast geodesic sphere, open to the blazing cathedral of space. He glanced up and saw the star-rich dust-clogged band of the Milky Way, encircling him from zenith to nadir; aware of the glow of every gas cloud, discerning each absorption and emission line, Paolo could almost feel the plane of the galactic disk transect him. Some constellations were distorted, but the view was more familiar than strange—and he recognized most of the old signposts by color. He had his bearings, now. Twenty degrees away from Sirius—south, by parochial Earth reckoning—faint but unmistakable: the sun.

Elena was beside him—superficially unchanged, although they'd both shrugged off the constraints of biology. The conventions of this environment mimicked the physics of real macroscopic objects in free-fall and vacuum, but it wasn't set up to model any kind of chemistry, let alone that of flesh and blood. Their new bodies were human-shaped, but devoid of elaborate microstructure—and their minds weren't embedded in the physics at all, but were running directly on the processor web.

Paolo was relieved to be back to normal; ceremonial regression to the ancestral form was a venerable C-Z tradition—and being human was largely self-affirming, while it lasted—but every time he emerged from the experience, he felt as if he'd broken free of billion-year-old shackles. There were polises on Earth where the citizens would have found his present structure almost as archaic: a consciousness dominated by sensory perception, an illusion of possessing solid form, a single time coordinate. The last flesh human had died long before Paolo was constructed, and apart from the communities of Gleisner robots, Carter-Zimmerman was about as conservative as a transhuman society could be. The balance seemed right to Paolo, though—acknowledging the flexibility of software, without abandoning interest in the physical world—and although the stubbornly corporeal Gleisners had been first to the stars, the C-Z diaspora would soon overtake them.

Their friends gathered round, showing off their effortless free-fall acrobatics, greeting Paolo and chiding him for not arranging to wake sooner; he was the last of the gang to emerge from hibernation.

"Do you like our humble new meeting place?" Hermann floated by Paolo's shoulder, a chimeric cluster of limbs and sense-organs, speaking through the vacuum in modulated infrared. "We call it Satellite Pinatubo. It's desolate up here, I know—but we were afraid it might violate the spirit of caution if we dared pretend to walk the Orphean surface."

Paolo glanced mentally at a scout probe's close-up of a typical stretch of dry land, an expanse of fissured red rock. "More desolate down there, I think." He was tempted to touch the ground—to let the private vision become tactile—but he resisted. Being elsewhere in the middle of a conversation was bad etiquette.

"Ignore Hermann," Liesl advised. "He wants to flood Orpheus with our alien machinery before we have any idea what the effects might be." Liesl was a green-and-turquoise butterfly, with a stylized human face stippled in gold on each wing.

Paolo was surprised; from the way Elena had spoken, he'd assumed that his friends must have come to a consensus in favor of the microprobes—and only a late sleeper, new to the issues, would bother to argue the point. "What effects? The carpets—"

"Forget the carpets! Even if the carpets are as simple as they look, we don't know what else is down there." As Liesl's wings fluttered, her mirror-image faces seemed to glance at each other for support. "With neutrino imaging, we barely achieve spatial resolution in meters, time resolution in seconds. We don't know anything about smaller lifeforms."

"And we never will, if you have your way." Karpal—an ex-Gleisner, human-shaped as ever—had been Liesl's lover, last time Paolo was awake.

"We've only been here for a fraction of an Orphean year! There's still a wealth of data we could gather non-intrusively, with a little patience. There might be rare beachings of ocean life—"

Elena said dryly, "Rare indeed. Orpheus has negligible tides, shallow waves, very few storms. And anything beached would be fried by UV before we glimpsed anything more instructive than we're already seeing in the surface water."

"Not necessarily. The carpets seem to be vulnerable—but other species might be better protected, if they live nearer to the surface. And Orpheus is seismically active; we should at least wait for a tsunami to dump a few cubic kilometers of ocean onto a shoreline, and see what it reveals."

Paolo smiled; he hadn't thought of that. A tsunami might be worth waiting for.

Liesl continued, "What is there to lose, by waiting a few hundred Orphean years? At the very least, we could gather baseline data on seasonal climate patterns—and we could watch for anomalies, storms and quakes, hoping for some revelatory glimpses."

A few hundred Orphean years? *A few terrestrial millennia?* Paolo's ambivalence waned. If he'd wanted to inhabit geological time, he would have migrated to the Lokhande polis, where the Order of Contemplative Observers watched Earth's mountains erode in subjective seconds. Orpheus hung in the sky beneath them, a beautiful puzzle waiting to be decoded, demanding to be understood.

He said, "But what if there *are* no 'revelatory glimpses'? How long do we wait? We don't know how rare life is—in time, or in space. If this planet is precious, *so is the epoch it's passing through.* We don't know how rapidly Orphean biology is evolving; species might appear and vanish while we agonize over the risks of gathering better data. The carpets—and whatever else—could die out before we'd learnt the first thing about them. What a waste that would be!"

Liesl stood her ground.

"And if we damage the Orphean ecology—or culture—by rushing in? That wouldn't be a waste. It would be a tragedy."

Paolo assimilated all the stored transmissions from his Earth-self—almost three hundred years' worth—before composing a reply. The early communications included detailed mind grafts—and it was good to share the excitement of the diaspora's launch; to watch—very nearly firsthand—the thousand ships, nanomachine-carved from asteroids, depart in a blaze of fusion fire from beyond the orbit of Mars. Then things settled down to the usual prosaic matters: Elena, the gang, shameless gossip, Carter-Zimmerman's ongoing research projects, the buzz of interpolis cultural tensions, the not-quite-cyclic convulsions of the arts (the perceptual aesthetic overthrows the emotional, again . . . although Valladas in Konishi polis claims to have constructed a new synthesis of the two).

After the first fifty years, his Earth-self had begun to hold things back; by the time news reached Earth of the Fomalhaut clone's demise, the messages had become pure audiovisual linear monologues. Paolo understood. It was only right; they'd diverged, and you didn't send mind grafts to strangers.

Most of the transmissions had been broadcast to all of the ships, indiscriminately. Forty-three years ago, though, his Earth-self had sent a special message to the Vega-bound clone.

"The new lunar spectroscope we finished last year has just picked up clear signs of water on Orpheus. There should be large temperate oceans waiting for you, if the models are right. So . . . good luck." Vision showed the instrument's domes growing out of the rock of the lunar farside; plots of the Orphean spectral data; an ensemble of planetary models. "Maybe it seems strange to you—all the trouble we're taking to catch a glimpse of what you're going to see in close-up, so soon. It's hard to explain: I don't think it's jealousy, or even impatience. Just a need for independence.

"There's been a revival of the old debate: should we consider redesigning our minds to encompass interstellar distances? One self spanning thousands of stars, not via cloning, but through acceptance of the natural time scale of the light-speed lag. Millennia passing between mental events. Local contingencies dealt with by non-conscious systems." Essays, pro and con, were appended; Paolo ingested summaries. "I don't think the idea will gain much support, though—and the new astronomical projects are something of an antidote. We have to make peace with the fact that we've stayed behind . . . so we cling to the Earth—looking outwards, but remaining firmly anchored.

"I keep asking myself, though: where do we go from here? History can't guide us. Evolution can't guide us. The C-Z charter says *understand and respect the universe* . . . but in what form? On what scale? With what kind of senses, what kind of minds? We can become anything at all—and that space of possible futures dwarfs the galaxy. Can we explore it without losing our way? Flesh humans used to spin fantasies about aliens arriving to 'conquer' Earth, to steal their 'precious' physical resources, to wipe them out for fear of 'competition' . . . as if a species capable of making the journey wouldn't have had the power, or the wit, or the imagination, to rid itself of obsolete biological imperatives. *Conquering the galaxy* is what bacteria with spaceships would do—knowing no better, having no choice.

"Our condition is the opposite of that: we have no end of choices. That's why we need to find alien life—not just to break the spell of the anthrocosmologists. We need to find aliens who've faced the same decisions—and discovered how to live, what to become. We need to understand what it means to inhabit the universe."

Paolo watched the crude neutrino images of the carpets moving in staccato jerks around his dodecahedral room. Twenty-four ragged oblongs drifted above him, daughters of a larger ragged oblong which had just fissioned. Models suggested that shear forces from ocean currents could explain the whole process, triggered by nothing more than the parent reaching a critical size. The purely mechanical break-up of a colony—if that was what it was—might have little to do with the life cycle of the constituent organisms. It was frustrating. Paolo was accustomed to a torrent of data on anything which caught his interest; for the diaspora's great discovery to remain nothing more than a sequence of coarse monochrome snapshots was intolerable.

He glanced at a schematic of the scout probes' neutrino detectors, but there was no obvious scope for improvement. Nuclei in the detectors were excited into unstable high-energy states, then kept there by fine-tuned gamma-ray lasers picking off lower-energy eigenstates faster than they could creep into existence and attract a transition. Changes in neutrino flux of one part in ten-to-the-fifteenth could shift the energy levels far enough to disrupt the balancing act. The carpets cast a shadow so faint, though, that even this near-perfect vision could barely resolve it.

Orlando Venetti said, "You're awake."

Paolo turned. His father stood an arm's length away, presenting as an ornately clad human of indeterminate age. Definitely older than Paolo, though; Orlando never ceased to play up his seniority—even if the age difference was only twenty-five percent now, and falling.

Paolo banished the carpets from the room to the space behind one pentagonal window, and took his father's hand. The portions of Orlando's mind which meshed with his own expressed pleasure at Paolo's emergence from hibernation, fondly dwelt on past shared experiences, and entertained hopes of continued harmony between father and son. Paolo's greeting was similar, a carefully contrived "revelation" of his own emotional state. It was more of a ritual than an act of communication—but then, even with Elena, he set up barriers. No one was totally honest with another person—unless the two of them intended to permanently fuse.

Orlando nodded at the carpets. "I hope you appreciate how important they are."

"You know I do." He hadn't included that in his greeting, though. "First alien life." *C-Z humiliates the Gleisner robots, at last*—that was probably how his father saw it. The robots had been first to Alpha Centauri, and first to an extrasolar planet—but first life was Apollo to their Sputniks, for anyone who chose to think in those terms.

Orlando said, "This is the hook we need, to catch the citizens of the marginal polises. The ones who haven't quite imploded into solipsism. This will shake them up—don't you think?"

Paolo shrugged. Earth's transhumans were free to implode into anything they liked; it didn't stop Carter-Zimmerman from exploring the physical universe. But thrashing the Gleisners wouldn't be enough for Orlando; he lived for the day when C-Z would become the cultural mainstream. Any polis could multiply its population a billionfold in a microsecond, if it wanted the vacuous honor of outnumbering the rest. Luring other citizens to migrate was harder—and persuading them to rewrite their own local charters was harder still. Orlando had a missionary streak: he wanted every other polis to see the error of its ways, and follow C-Z to the stars.

Paolo said, "Ashton-Laval has intelligent aliens. I wouldn't be so sure that news of giant seaweed is going to take Earth by storm."

Orlando was venomous. "Ashton-Laval intervened in its so-called 'evolutionary' simulations so many times that they might as well have built the end products in an act of creation lasting six days. They wanted talking reptiles, and—*mirabile dictu!*—they got talking reptiles. There are self-modified transhumans in *this polis* more alien than the aliens in Ashton-Laval."

Paolo smiled. "All right. Forget Ashton-Laval. But forget the marginal polises, too. We choose to value the physical world. That's what defines us—but it's as arbitrary as any other choice of values. Why can't you accept that? It's not the One True Path which the infidels have to be bludgeoned into following." He knew he was arguing half for the sake of it—he desperately wanted to refute the anthro-cosmologists, himself—but Orlando always drove him into taking the opposite position. Out of fear of being nothing but his father's clone? Despite the total absence of inherited episodic memories, the stochastic input into his ontogenesis, the chaotically divergent nature of the iterative mind-building algorithms.

Orlando made a beckoning gesture, dragging the image of the carpets halfway back into the room. "You'll vote for the microprobes?"

"Of course."

"Everything depends on that, now. It's good to start with a tantalizing glimpse—but if we don't follow up with details soon, they'll lose interest back on Earth very rapidly."

"Lose interest? It'll be fifty-four years before we know if anyone paid the slightest attention in the first place."

Orlando eyed him with disappointment, and resignation. "If you don't care about the other polises, think about C-Z. This helps us, it strengthens us. We have to make the most of that."

Paolo was bemused. "The charter is the charter. What needs to be strengthened? You make it sound like there's something at risk."

"What do you think a thousand lifeless worlds would have done to us? Do you think the charter would have remained intact?"

Paolo had never considered the scenario. "Maybe not. But in every C-Z where the charter was rewritten, there would have been citizens who'd have gone off and founded new polises on the old lines. You and I, for a start. We could have called it Venetti-Venetti."

"While half your friends turned their backs on the physical world? While Carter Zimmerman, after two thousand years, went solipsist? You'd be happy with that?"

Paolo laughed. "No—but it's not going to happen, is it? *We've found life.* All right, I agree with you: this strengthens C-Z. The diaspora might have 'failed' . . . but it didn't. We've been lucky. I'm glad, I'm grateful. Is that what you wanted to hear?"

Orlando said sourly, "You take too much for granted."

"And you care too much what I think! I'm not your . . . heir." Orlando was first-generation, scanned from flesh—and there were times when he seemed unable to accept that the whole concept of generation had lost its archaic significance. "You don't need me to safeguard the future of Carter-Zimmerman on your behalf. Or the future of transhumanity. You can do it in person."

Orlando looked wounded—a conscious choice, but it still encoded something. Paolo felt a pang of regret—but he'd said nothing he could honestly retract.

His father gathered up the sleeves of his gold and crimson robes—the only citizen of C-Z who could make Paolo uncomfortable to be naked—and repeated as he vanished from the room: "You take too much for granted."

The gang watched the launch of the microprobes together—even Liesl, though she came in mourning, as a giant dark bird. Karpal stroked her feathers nervously.

Hermann appeared as a creature out of Escher, a segmented worm with six human-shaped feet—on legs with elbows—given to curling up into a disk and rolling along the girders of Satellite Pinatubo. Paolo and Elena kept saying the same thing simultaneously; they'd just made love.

Hermann had moved the satellite to a notional orbit just below one of the scout probes—and changed the environment's scale, so that the probe's lower surface, an intricate landscape of detector modules and attitude-control jets, blotted out half the sky. The atmospheric-entry capsules—ceramic teardrops three centimeters wide—burst from their launch tube and hurtled past like boulders, vanishing from sight before they'd fallen so much as ten meters closer to Orpheus. It was all scrupulously accurate, although it was part real-time imagery, part extrapolation, part *faux*. Paolo thought: *We might as well have run a pure simulation . . . and pretended to follow the capsules down.* Elena gave him a guilty/admonishing look. *Yeah—and then why bother actually launching them at all? Why not just simulate a plausible Orphean ocean full of plausible Orphean lifeforms? Why not simulate the whole diaspora?* There was no crime of heresy in C-Z; no one had ever been exiled for breaking the charter. At times it still felt like a tightrope walk, though, trying to classify every act of simulation into those which contributed to an understanding of the physical universe (good), those which were merely convenient, recreational, aesthetic (acceptable) . . . and those which constituted a denial of the primacy of real phenomena (time to think about emigration).

The vote on the microprobes had been close: seventy-two percent in favor, just over the required two-thirds majority, with five percent abstaining. (Citizens created since the arrival at Vega were excluded . . . not that anyone in Carter-Zimmerman would have dreamt of stacking the ballot, perish the thought.) Paolo had been surprised at the narrow margin; he'd yet to hear a single plausible scenario for the microprobes doing harm. He wondered if there was another, unspoken reason which had nothing to do with fears for the Orphean ecology, or hypothetical culture. A *wish to prolong the pleasure of unraveling the planet's mysteries?* Paolo had some sympathy with that impulse—but the launch of the microprobes would do nothing to undermine the greater long-term pleasure of watching, and understanding, as Orphean life evolved.

Liesl said forlornly, "Coastline erosion models show that the northwestern shore of Lambda is inundated by tsunami every ninety Orphean years, on average." She offered the data to them; Paolo glanced at it, and it looked convincing—but the point was academic now. "We could have waited."

Hermann waved his eye-stalks at her. "Beaches covered in fossils, are they?"

"No, but the conditions hardly—"

"No excuses!" He wound his body around a girder, kicking his legs gleefully. Hermann was first-generation, even older than Orlando; he'd been scanned in the twenty-first century, before Carter-Zimmerman existed. Over the centuries, though, he'd wiped most of his episodic memories, and rewritten his personality a dozen times. He'd once told Paolo, "I think of myself as my own great-great-grandson. Death's not so bad, if you do it incrementally. Ditto for immortality."

Elena said, "I keep trying to imagine how it will feel if another C-Z clone stumbles on something infinitely better—like aliens with wormhole drives—while we're back here studying rafts of algae." The body she wore was more stylized than usual—still humanoid, but sexless, hairless and smooth, the face inexpressive and androgynous.

"If they have wormhole drives, they might visit us. Or share the technology, so we can link up the whole diaspora."

"If they have wormhole drives, where have they been for the last two thousand years?"

Paolo laughed. "Exactly. But I know what you mean: *first alien life* . . . and it's likely to be about as sophisticated as seaweed. It breaks the jinx, though. Seaweed every twenty-seven light-years. Nervous systems every fifty? Intelligence every hundred?" He fell silent, abruptly realizing what she was feeling: electing not to wake again after first life was beginning to seem like the wrong choice, a waste of the opportunities the diaspora had created. Paolo offered her a mind graft expressing empathy and support, but she declined.

She said, "I want sharp borders, right now. I want to deal with this myself."

"I understand." He let the partial model of her which he'd acquired as they'd made love fade from his mind. It was non-sapient, and no longer linked to her—but to retain it any longer when she felt this way would have seemed like a transgression. Paolo took the responsibilities of intimacy seriously. His lover before Elena had asked him to erase all his knowledge of her, and he'd more or less complied—the only thing he still knew about her was the fact that she'd made the request.

Hermann announced, "Planetfall!" Paolo glanced at a replay of a scout probe view which showed the first few entry capsules breaking up above the ocean and releasing their microprobes. Nanomachines transformed the ceramic shields (and then themselves) into carbon dioxide and a few simple minerals—nothing the micrometeorites constantly raining down onto Orpheus didn't contain—before the fragments could strike the water. The microprobes would broadcast nothing; when they'd finished gathering data, they'd float to the surface and modulate their UV reflectivity. It would be up to the scout probes to locate these specks, and read their messages, before they self-destructed as thoroughly as the entry capsules.

Hermann said, "This calls for a celebration. I'm heading for the Heart. Who'll join me?"

Paolo glanced at Elena. She shook her head. "You go."

"Are you sure?"

"Yes! Go on." Her skin had taken on a mirrored sheen; her expressionless face reflected the planet below. "I'm all right. I just want some time to think things through, on my own."

Hermann coiled around the satellite's frame, stretching his pale body as he went, gaining segments, gaining legs. "Come on, come on! Karpal? Liesl? Come and celebrate!"

Elena was gone. Liesl made a derisive sound and flapped off into the distance, mocking the environment's airlessness. Paolo and Karpal watched as Hermann grew longer and faster—and then in a blur of speed and change stretched out to wrap the entire geodesic frame. Paolo demagnetized his feet and moved away, laughing; Karpal did the same.

Then Hermann constricted like a boa, and snapped the whole satellite apart.

They floated for a while, two human-shaped machines and a giant worm in a cloud of spinning metal fragments, an absurd collection of imaginary debris, glinting by the light of the true stars.

The Heart was always crowded, but it was larger than Paolo had seen it—even though Hermann had shrunk back to his original size, so as not to make a scene. The huge muscular chamber arched above them, pulsating wetly in time to the music, as they searched for the perfect location to soak up the atmosphere. Paolo had visited public environments in other polises, back on Earth; many were designed to be nothing more than a perceptual framework for group emotion-sharing. He'd never understood the attraction of becoming intimate with large numbers of strangers. Ancestral social hierarchies might have had their faults—and it was absurd to try to make a virtue of the limitations imposed by minds confined to wetware—but the whole idea of mass telepathy as an end in itself seemed bizarre to Paolo . . . and even old-fashioned, in a way. Humans, clearly, would have benefited from a good strong dose of each other's inner life, to keep them from slaughtering each other—but any civilized transhuman could respect and value other citizens without the need to have *been them*, firsthand.

They found a good spot and made some furniture, a table and two chairs—Hermann preferred to stand—and the floor expanded to make room. Paolo looked around, shouting greetings at the people he recognized by sight, but not bothering to check for identity broadcasts from the rest. Chances were he'd met everyone here, but he didn't want to spend the next hour exchanging pleasantries with casual acquaintances.

Hermann said, "I've been monitoring our modest stellar observatory's data stream—my antidote to Vegan parochialism. Odd things are going on around Sirius. We're seeing electron-positron annihilation gamma rays, gravity waves . . . and some unexplained hot spots on Sirius B." He turned to Karpal and asked innocently, "What do you think those robots are up to? There's a rumor that they're planning to drag the white dwarf out of orbit, and use it as part of a giant spaceship."

"I never listen to rumors." Karpal always presented as a faithful reproduction of his old human-shaped Gleisner body—and his mind, Paolo gathered, always took the form of a physiological model, even though he was five generations removed from flesh. Leaving his people and coming into C-Z must have taken considerable courage; they'd never welcome him back.

Paolo said, "Does it matter what they do? Where they go, how they get there? There's more than enough room for both of us. Even if they shadowed the diaspora—even if they came to Vega—we could study the Orpheans together, couldn't we?"

Hermann's cartoon insect face showed mock alarm, eyes growing wider, and wider apart. "Not if they dragged along a white dwarf! Next thing they'd want to start building a Dyson sphere." He turned back to Karpal. "You don't still suffer the urge, do you, for . . . *astrophysical* engineering?"

"Nothing C-Z's exploitation of a few megatons of Vegan asteroid material hasn't satisfied."

Paolo tried to change the subject. "Has anyone heard from Earth, lately? I'm beginning to feel unplugged." His own most recent message was a decade older than the time lag.

Karpal said, "You're not missing much; all they're talking about is Orpheus . . . ever since the new lunar observations, the signs of water. They seem more excited by the mere possibility of life than we are by the certainty. And they have very high hopes."

Paolo laughed. "They do. My Earth-self seems to be counting on the diaspora to find an advanced civilization with the answers to all of transhumanity's existential problems. I don't think he'll get much cosmic guidance from kelp."

"You know there was a big rise in emigration from C-Z after the launch? Emigration, and suicides." Hermann had stopped wriggling and gyrating, becoming almost still, a sign of rare seriousness. "I suspect that's what triggered the astronomy program in the first place. And it seems to have stanched the flow, at least in the short term. Earth C-Z detected water before any clone in the diaspora—and when they hear that we've found life, they'll feel more like collaborators in the discovery because of it."

Paolo felt a stirring of unease. *Emigration and suicides? Was that why Orlando had been so gloomy?* After three hundred years of waiting, how high had expectations become?

A buzz of excitement crossed the floor, a sudden shift in the tone of the conversation. Hermann whispered reverently, "First microprobe has surfaced. And the data is coming in now."

The non-sapient Heart was intelligent enough to guess its patrons' wishes. Although everyone could tap the library for results, privately, the music cut out and a giant public image of the summary data appeared, high in the chamber. Pado had to crane his neck to view it, a novel experience.

The microprobe had mapped one of the carpets in high resolution. The image showed the expected rough oblong, some hundred meters wide—but the two- or three-meter-thick slab of the neutrino tomographs was revealed now as a delicate convoluted surface—fine as a single layer of skin, but folded into an elaborate space-filling curve. Paolo checked the full data: the topology was strictly planar, despite the pathological appearance. No holes, no joins—just a surface which meandered wildly enough to look ten thousand times thicker from a distance than it really was.

An inset showed the microstructure, at a point which started at the rim of the carpet and then—slowly—moved toward the center. Paolo stared at the flowing molecular diagram for several seconds before he grasped what it meant.

The carpet was not a colony of single-celled creatures. Nor was it a multicellular organism. It was a *single molecule*, a two-dimensional polymer weighing twenty-five million kilograms. A giant sheet of folded polysaccharide, a complex mesh of interlinked pentose and hexose sugars hung with alkyl and amide side chains. A bit like a plant cell wall—except that this polymer was far stronger than cellulose, and the surface area was twenty orders of magnitude greater.

Karpal said, "I hope those entry capsules were perfectly sterile. Earth bacteria would gorge themselves on this. One big floating carbohydrate dinner, with no defenses."

Hermann thought it over. "Maybe. If they had enzymes capable of breaking off a piece—which I doubt. No chance we'll find out, though: even if there'd been bacterial spores lingering in the asteroid belt from early human expeditions, every ship in the diaspora was double-checked for contamination *en route*. We haven't brought smallpox to the Americas."

Paolo was still dazed. "But how does it assemble? How does it . . . grow?" Hermann consulted the library and replied, before Paolo could do the same.

"The edge of the carpet catalyzes its own growth. The polymer is irregular, aperiodic—there's no single component which simply repeats. But there seem to be about twenty thousand basic structural units—twenty thousand different polysaccharide building blocks." Paolo saw them: long bundles of cross-linked chains running the whole two-hundred-micron thickness of the carpet, each with a roughly square cross-section, bonded at several thousand points to the four neighboring units. "Even at this depth, the ocean's full of UV-generated radicals which filter down from the surface. Any structural unit exposed to the water converts those radicals into more polysaccharide—and builds another structural unit."

Paolo glanced at the library again, for a simulation of the process. Catalytic sites strewn along the sides of each unit trapped the radicals in place, long enough for new bonds to form between them. Some simple sugars were incorporated straight into the polymer as they were created; others were set free to drift in solution for a microsecond or two, until they were needed. At that level, there were only a few basic chemical tricks being used . . . but molecular evolution must have worked its way up from a few small autocatalytic fragments, first formed by chance, to this elaborate system of twenty thousand mutually self-replicating structures. If the "structural units" had floated free in the ocean as independent molecules, the "lifeform" they comprised would have been virtually invisible. By bonding together, though, they became twenty thousand colors in a giant mosaic.

It was astonishing. Paolo hoped Elena was tapping the library, wherever she was. A colony of algae would have been more "advanced"—but this incredible primordial creature revealed infinitely more about the possibilities for the genesis of life. Carbohydrate, here, played every biochemical role: information carrier, enzyme, energy source, structural material. Nothing like it could have survived on Earth, once there were organisms capable of feeding on it—and if there were ever intelligent Orpheans, they'd be unlikely to find any trace of this bizarre ancestor.

Karpal wore a secretive smile.

Paolo said, "What?"

"Wang tiles. The carpets are made out of Wang tiles."

Hermann beat him to the library, again.

"*Wang* as in twentieth-century flesh mathematician, Hao Wang. *Tiles* as in any set of shapes which can cover the plane. Wang tiles are squares with various shaped edges, which have to fit complementary shapes on adjacent squares. You can cover the plane with a set of Wang tiles, as long as you choose the right one every step of the way. Or in the case of the carpets, grow the right one."

Karpal said, "We should call them Wang's Carpets, in honor of Hao Wang. After twenty-three hundred years, his mathematics has come to life."

Paolo liked the idea, but he was doubtful. "We may have trouble getting a two-thirds majority on that. It's a bit obscure . . ."

Hermann laughed. "Who needs a two-thirds majority? If we want to call them Wang's Carpets, we can call them Wang's Carpets. There are ninety-seven lan guages in current use in C-Z—half of them invented since the polis was founded. I don't think we'll be exiled for coining one private name."

Paolo concurred, slightly embarrassed. The truth was, he'd completely forgotten that Hermann and Karpal weren't actually speaking Modern Roman.

The three of them instructed their exoselves to consider the name adopted: henceforth, they'd hear "carpet" as "Wang's Carpet"—but if they used the term with anyone else, the reverse translation would apply.

Paolo sat and drank in the image of the giant alien: the first lifeform encountered by human or transhuman which was not a biological cousin. The death, at last, of the possibility that Earth might be unique.

They hadn't refuted the anthrocosmologists yet, though. Not quite. If, as the ACs claimed, human consciousness was the seed around which all of space-time had crystallized—if the universe was nothing but the simplest orderly explanation for human thought—then there was, strictly speaking, no need for a single alien to exist, anywhere. But the physics which justified human existence couldn't help generating a billion other worlds where life could arise. The ACs would be unmoved by Wang's Carpets; they'd insist that these creatures were physical, if not biological cousins—merely an unavoidable by-product of anthropogenic, life-enabling physical laws.

The real test wouldn't come until the diaspora—or the Gleisner robots—finally encountered conscious aliens: minds entirely unrelated to humanity, observing and explaining the universe which human thought had supposedly built. Most ACs had come right out and declared such a find impossible; it was the sole falsifiable prediction of their hypothesis. Alien consciousness, as opposed to mere alien life would always build itself a separate universe—because the chance of two unrelated forms of self-awareness concocting exactly the same physics and the same cosmology was infinitesimal—and any alien biosphere which seemed capable of evolving consciousness would simply never do so.

Paolo glanced at the map of the diaspora, and took heart. *Alien life already*— and the search had barely started; there were nine hundred and ninety-eight target systems yet to be explored. And even if every one of them proved no more conclusive than Orpheus . . . he was prepared to send clones out farther—and prepared to wait. Consciousness had taken far longer to appear on Earth than the quarter-of-a-billion years remaining before Vega left the main sequence—but the whole point of being here, after all, was that Orpheus wasn't Earth.

Orlando's celebration of the microprobe discoveries was a very first-generation affair. The environment was an endless sunlit garden strewn with tables covered in *food*, and the invitation had politely suggested attendance in fully human form. Paolo politely faked it—simulating most of the physiology, but running the body as a puppet, leaving his mind unshackled.

Orlando introduced his new lover, Catherine, who presented as a tall, dark-skinned woman. Paolo didn't recognize her on sight, but checked the identity code she broadcast. It was a small polis, he'd met her once before—as a man called Samuel, one of the physicists who'd worked on the main interstellar fusion drive employed by all the ships of the diaspora. Paolo was amused to think that many of the people here would be seeing his father as a woman. The majority of the citizens of C-Z still practiced the conventions of relative gender which had come into fashion in the twenty-third century—and Orlando had wired them into his own son too deeply for Paolo to wish to abandon them—but whenever the paradoxes were revealed so starkly, he wondered how much longer the conventions would endure. Paolo was same-sex to Orlando, and hence saw his father's lover as a woman, the two close relationships taking precedence over his casual knowledge of Catherine as Samuel. Orlando perceived himself as being male and heterosexual, as his flesh original had been . . . while Samuel saw himself the same way . . . and each perceived the other to be a heterosexual woman. If certain third parties ended up with mixed signals, so be it. It was a typical C-Z compromise: nobody could bear to overturn the old order and do away with gender entirely (as most other polises had done) . . . but nobody could resist the flexibility which being software, not flesh, provided.

Paolo drifted from table to table, sampling the food to keep up appearances, wishing Elena had come. There was little conversation about the biology of Wang's Carpets; most of the people here were simply celebrating their win against the opponents of the microprobes—and the humiliation that faction would suffer, now that it was clearer than ever that the "invasive" observations could have done no harm. Liesl's fears had proved unfounded; there was no other life in the ocean, just Wang's Carpets of various sizes. Paolo, feeling perversely even-handed after the fact, kept wanting to remind these smug movers and shakers: *There might have been anything down there. Strange creatures, delicate and vulnerable in ways we could never have anticipated. We were lucky, that's all.*

He ended up alone with Orlando almost by chance; they were both fleeing different groups of appalling guests when their paths crossed on the lawn.

Paolo asked, "How do you think they'll take this, back home?"

"It's first life, isn't it? Primitive or not. It should at least maintain interest in the diaspora, until the next alien biosphere is discovered." Orlando seemed subdued; perhaps he was finally coming to terms with the gulf between their modest discovery, and Earth's longing for world-shaking results. "And at least the chemistry is novel. If it had turned out to be based on DNA and protein, I think half of Earth C-Z would have died of boredom on the spot. Let's face it, the possibilities of DNA have been simulated to death."

Paolo smiled at the heresy. "You think if nature hadn't managed a little originality, it would have dented people's faith in the charter? If the solipsist polises had begun to look more inventive than the universe itself . . ."

"Exactly."

They walked on in silence, then Orlando halted, and turned to face him.

He said, "There's something I've been wanting to tell you. My Earth-self is dead."

"*What?*"

"Please, don't make a fuss."

"But . . . why? Why would he—?" *Dead* meant suicide; there was no other cause—unless the sun had turned red giant and swallowed everything out to the orbit of Mars.

"I don't know why. Whether it was a vote of confidence in the diaspora"—Orlando had chosen to wake only in the presence of alien life—"or whether he despaired of us sending back good news, and couldn't face the waiting, and the risk of disappointment. He didn't give a reason. He just had his exoself send a message, stating what he'd done."

Paolo was shaken. If a clone of *Orlando* had succumbed to pessimism, he couldn't begin to imagine the state of mind of the rest of Earth C-Z.

"When did this happen?"

"About fifty years after the launch."

"My Earth-self said nothing."

"It was up to me to tell you, not him."

"I wouldn't have seen it that way."

"Apparently, you would have."

Paolo fell silent, confused. How was he supposed to mourn a distant version of Orlando, in the presence of the one he thought of as real? Death of one clone was a strange half-death, a hard thing to come to terms with. His Earth-self had lost a father; his father had lost an Earth-self. What exactly did that mean to *him*?

What Orlando cared most about was Earth C-Z. Paolo said carefully, "Hermann told me there'd been a rise in emigration and suicide—until the spectroscope picked up the Orphean water. Morale has improved a lot since then—and when they hear that it's more than just water . . ."

Orlando cut him off sharply. "You don't have to talk things up for me. I'm in no danger of repeating the act."

They stood on the lawn, facing each other. Paolo composed a dozen different combinations of mood to communicate, but none of them felt right. He could have granted his father perfect knowledge of everything he was feeling—but what exactly would that knowledge have conveyed? In the end, there was fusion, or separateness. There was nothing in between.

Orlando said, "Kill myself—and leave the fate of transhumanity in your hands? You must be out of your fucking mind."

They walked on together, laughing.

Karpal seemed barely able to gather his thoughts enough to speak. Paolo would have offered him a mind graft promoting tranquillity and concentration—distilled from his own most focused moments—but he was sure that Karpal would never have accepted it. He said, "Why don't you just start wherever you want to? I'll stop you if you're not making sense."

Karpal looked around the white dodecahedron with an expression of disbelief. "You live here?"

"Some of the time."

"But this is your base environment? No trees? No sky? No *furniture*?"

Paolo refrained from repeating any of Hermann's naive-robot jokes. "I add them when I want them. You know, like . . . music. Look, don't let my taste in decor distract you."

Karpal made a chair and sat down heavily.

He said, "Hao Wang proved a powerful theorem, twenty-three hundred years ago. Think of a row of Wang Tiles as being like the data tape of a Turing Machine." Paolo had the library grant him knowledge of the term; it was the original conceptual form of a generalized computing device, an imaginary machine which moved back and forth along a limitless one-dimensional data tape, reading and writing symbols according to a given set of rules.

"With the right set of tiles, to force the right pattern, the next row of the tiling will look like the data tape after the Turing Machine has performed one step of its computation. And the row after that will be the data tape after two steps, and so on. For any given Turing Machine, there's a set of Wang Tiles which can imitate it."

Paolo nodded amiably. He hadn't heard of this particular quaint result, but it was hardly surprising. "The carpets must be carrying out billions of acts of computation every second . . . but then, so are the water molecules around them. There are no physical processes which don't perform arithmetic of some kind."

"True. But with the carpets, it's not quite the same as random molecular motion."

"Maybe not."

Karpal smiled, but said nothing.

"What? You've found a pattern? Don't tell me: our set of twenty thousand polysaccharide Wang Tiles just happens to form the Turing Machine for calculating pi."

"No. What they form is a universal Turing Machine. They can calculate anything at all—depending on the data they start with. Every daughter fragment is like a program being fed to a chemical computer. Growth executes the program."

"Ah." Paolo's curiosity was roused—but he was having some trouble picturing where the hypothetical Turing Machine put its read/write head. "Are you telling me only one tile changes between any two rows, where the 'machine' leaves its mark on the 'data tape' . . . ?" The mosaics he'd seen were a riot of complexity, with no two rows remotely the same.

Karpal said, "No, no. Wang's original example worked exactly like a standard Turing Machine, to simplify the argument . . . but the carpets are more like an arbitrary number of different computers with overlapping data, all working in parallel. This is biology, not a designed machine—it's as messy and wild as, say . . . a mammalian genome. In fact, there are mathematical similarities with gene regulation: I've identified Kauffman networks at every level, from the tiling rules up; the whole system's poised on the hyperadaptive edge between frozen and chaotic behavior."

Paolo absorbed that, with the library's help. Like Earth life, the carpets seemed to have evolved a combination of robustness and flexibility which would have maximized their power to take advantage of natural selection. Thousands of different autocatalytic chemical networks must have arisen soon after the formation of Orpheus—but as the ocean chemistry and the climate changed in the Vegan system's early traumatic millennia, the ability to respond to selection pressure had itself been selected for, and the carpets were the result. Their complexity seemed redundant, now, after a hundred million years of relative stability—and no predators or competition in sight—but the legacy remained.

"So if the carpets have ended up as universal computers . . . with no real need anymore to respond to their surroundings . . . what are they *doing* with all that computing power?"

Karpal said solemnly, "I'll show you."

Paolo followed him into an environment where they drifted above a schematic of a carpet, an abstract landscape stretching far into the distance, elaborately wrinkled like the real thing, but otherwise heavily stylized, with each of the polysaccharide building blocks portrayed as a square tile with four different colored edges. The adjoining edges of neighboring tiles bore complementary colors—to represent the complementary, interlocking shapes of the borders of the building blocks.

"One group of microprobes finally managed to sequence an entire daughter fragment," Karpal explained, "although the exact edges it started life with are largely guesswork, since the thing was growing while they were trying to map it." He gestured impatiently, and all the wrinkles and folds were smoothed away, an irrelevant distraction. They moved to one border of the ragged-edged carpet, and Karpal started the simulation running.

Paolo watched the mosaic extending itself, following the tiling rules perfectly—an orderly mathematical process, here: no chance collisions of radicals with catalytic sites, no mismatched borders between two new-grown neighboring "tiles" triggering the disintegration of both. Just the distillation of the higher-level consequences of all that random motion.

Karpal led Paolo up to a height where he could see subtle patterns being woven, overlapping multiplexed periodicities drifting across the growing edge, meeting and sometimes interacting, sometimes passing right through each other. Mobile pseudo-attractors, quasi-stable waveforms in a one-dimensional universe. The carpet's second dimension was more like time than space, a permanent record of the history of the edge.

Karpal seemed to read his mind. "One dimensional. Worse than flatland. No connectivity, no complexity. What can possibly happen in a system like that? Nothing of interest, right?"

He clapped his hands and the environment exploded around Paolo. Trails of color streaked across his sensorium, entwining, then disintegrating into luminous smoke.

"Wrong. Everything goes on in a multidimensional frequency space. I've Fourier-transformed the edge into over a thousand components, and there's independent information in all of them. We're only in a narrow cross-section here, a sixteen-dimensional slice—but it's oriented to show the principal components, the maximum detail."

Paolo spun in a blur of meaningless color, utterly lost, his surroundings beyond comprehension. "You're a *Gleisner robot*, Karpal! *Only* sixteen dimensions! How can you have done this?"

Karpal sounded hurt, wherever he was. "Why do you think I came to C-Z? I thought you people were flexible!"

"What you're doing is . . ." *What*? Heresy? There was no such thing. Officially. "Have you shown this to anyone else?"

"Of course not. Who did you have in mind? Liesl? *Hermann*?"

"Good. I know how to keep my mouth shut." Paolo invoked his exoself and moved back into the dodecahedron. He addressed the empty room. "How can I put this? The physical universe has three spatial dimensions, plus time. Citizens of Carter-Zimmerman inhabit the physical universe. Higher dimensional mind games are for the solipsists." Even as he said it, he realized how pompous he sounded. It was an arbitrary doctrine, not some great moral principle.

But it was the doctrine he'd lived with for twelve hundred years.

Karpal replied, more bemused than offended, "It's the only way to see what's going on. The only sensible way to apprehend it. Don't you want to know what the carpets are *actually like*?"

Paolo felt himself being tempted. Inhabit a *sixteen-dimensional slice of a thousand-dimensional frequency space*? But it was in the service of understanding a real physical system—not a novel experience for its own sake.

And nobody had to find out.

He ran a quick—non-sapient—self-predictive model. There was a ninety-three percent chance that he'd give in, after fifteen subjective minutes of agonizing over the decision. It hardly seemed fair to keep Karpal waiting that long.

He said, "You'll have to loan me your mind-shaping algorithm. My exoself wouldn't know where to begin."

When it was done, he steeled himself, and moved back into Karpal's environment. For a moment, there was nothing but the same meaningless blur as before.

Then everything suddenly crystallized.

Creatures swam around them, elaborately branched tubes like mobile coral, vividly colored in all the hues of Paolo's mental palette—Karpal's attempt to cram in some of the information that a mere sixteen dimensions couldn't show? Paolo glanced down at his own body—nothing was missing, but he could see *around* it in all the thirteen dimensions in which it was nothing but a pin-prick; he quickly looked away. The "coral" seemed far more natural to his altered sensory map, occupying sixteen-space in all directions, and shaded with hints that it occupied much more. And Paolo had no doubt that it was "alive"—it looked more organic than the carpets themselves, by far.

Karpal said, "Every point in this space encodes some kind of quasi-periodic pattern in the tiles. Each dimension represents a different characteristic size—like a wavelength, although the analogy's not precise. The position in each dimension represents other attributes of the pattern, relating to the particular tiles it employs. So the localized systems you see around you are clusters of a few billion patterns, all with broadly similar attributes at similar wavelengths."

They moved away from the swimming coral, into a swarm of something like jellyfish: floppy hyperspheres waving wispy tendrils (each one of them more substantial than Paolo). Tiny jewel-like creatures darted among them. Paolo was just beginning to notice that nothing moved here like a solid object drifting through normal space; motion seemed to entail a shimmering deformation at the leading hypersurface, a visible process of disassembly and reconstruction.

Karpal led him on through the secret ocean. There were helical worms, coiled together in groups of indeterminate number—each single creature breaking up into a dozen or more wriggling slivers, and then recombining . . . although not always from the same parts. There were dazzling multicolored stemless flowers, intricate hypercones of "gossamer-thin" fifteen-dimensional petals—each one a hypnotic fractal labyrinth of crevices and capillaries. There were clawed monstrosities, writhing knots of sharp insectile parts like an orgy of decapitated scorpions.

Paolo said, uncertainly, "You could give people a glimpse of this in just three dimensions. Enough to make it clear that there's . . . *life* in here. This is going to shake them up badly, though." Life—embedded in the accidental computations of Wang's Carpets, with no possibility of ever relating to the world outside. This was an affront to Carter-Zimmerman's whole philosophy: if nature had evolved "organisms" as divorced from reality as the inhabitants of the most inward-looking polis, where was the privileged status of the physical universe, the clear distinction between truth and illusion?

And after three hundred years of waiting for good news from the diaspora, how would they respond to this back on Earth?

Karpal said, "There's one more thing I have to show you."

He'd named the creatures squids, for obvious reasons. *Distant cousins of the jellyfish, perhaps?* They were prodding each other with their tentacles in a way which looked thoroughly carnal—but Karpal explained, "There's no analog of light here. We're viewing all this according to ad hoc rules which have nothing to do with the native physics. All the creatures here gather information about each other by contact alone—which is actually quite a rich means of exchanging data, with so many dimensions. What you're seeing is communication by touch."

"Communication about what?"

"Just gossip, I expect. Social relationships."

Paolo stared at the writhing mass of tentacles.

"You think they're *conscious*?"

Karpal, point-like, grinned broadly. "They have a central control structure with more connectivity than the human brain—and which correlates data gathered from the skin. I've mapped that organ, and I've started to analyze its function."

He led Paolo into another environment, a representation of the data structures in the "brain" of one of the squids. It was—mercifully—three-dimensional, and highly stylized, built of translucent colored blocks marked with icons, representing mental symbols, linked by broad lines indicating the major connections between them. Paolo had seen similar diagrams of transhuman minds; this was far less elaborate, but eerily familiar nonetheless.

Karpal said, "Here's the sensory map of its surroundings. Full of other squids' bodies, and vague data on the last known positions of a few smaller creatures. But you'll see that the symbols activated by the physical presence of the other squids are linked to these"—he traced the connection with one finger—"representations. Which are crude miniatures of *this whole structure* here."

"This whole structure" was an assembly labeled with icons for memory retrieval, simple tropisms, short-term goals. The general business of being and doing.

"The squid has maps, not just of other squids' bodies, but their minds as well. Right or wrong, it certainly tries to know what the others are thinking about. And"—he pointed out another set of links, leading to another, less crude, miniature squid mind—"it thinks about its own thoughts as well. I'd call that *consciousness*, wouldn't you?"

Paolo said weakly, "You've kept all this to yourself? You came this far, without saying a word—?"

Karpal was chastened. "I know it was selfish—but once I'd decoded the interactions of the tile patterns, I couldn't tear myself away long enough to start explaining it to anyone else. And I came to you first because I wanted your advice on the best way to break the news."

Paolo laughed bitterly. "The best way to break the news that *first alien consciousness* is hidden deep inside a biological computer? That everything the diaspora was trying to prove has been turned on its head? The best way to explain to the citizens of Carter-Zimmerman that after a three-hundred-year journey, they might as well have stayed on Earth running simulations with as little resemblance to the physical universe as possible?"

Karpal took the outburst in good humor. "I was thinking more along the lines of the *best way to point out* that if we hadn't traveled to Orpheus and studied Wang's Carpets, we'd never have had the chance to tell the solipsists of Ashton-Laval that all their elaborate invented lifeforms and exotic imaginary universes pale into insignificance compared to what's really out here—and which only the Carter-Zimmerman diaspora could have found."

Paolo and Elena stood together on the edge of Satellite Pinatubo, watching one of the scout probes aim its maser at a distant point in space. Paolo thought he saw a faint scatter of microwaves from the beam as it collided with iron-rich meteor dust. *Elena's mind being diffracted all over the cosmos?* Best not think about that.

He said, "When you meet the other versions of me who haven't experienced Orpheus, I hope you'll offer them mind grafts so they won't be jealous."

She frowned. "Ah. Will I or won't I? I can't be bothered modeling it. I expect I will. You should have asked me before I cloned myself. No need for jealousy, though. There'll be worlds far stranger than Orpheus."

"I doubt it. You really think so?"

"I wouldn't be doing this if I didn't believe that." Elena had no power to change the fate of the frozen clones of her previous self—but everyone had the right to emigrate.

Paolo took her hand. The beam had been aimed almost at Regulus, UV—hot and bright, but as he looked away, the cool yellow light of the sun caught his eye.

Vega C-Z was taking the news of the squids surprisingly well, so far. Karpal's way of putting it had cushioned the blow: it was only by traveling all this distance across the real, physical universe that they could have made such a discovery—and it was amazing how pragmatic even the most doctrinaire citizens had turned out to be. Before the launch, "alien solipsists" would have been the most unpalatable idea imaginable, the most abhorrent thing the diaspora could have stumbled upon—but now that they were here, and stuck with the fact of it, people were finding ways to view it in a better light. Orlando had even proclaimed, "This will be the perfect hook for the marginal polises. 'Travel through real space to witness a truly alien virtual reality.' We can sell it as a synthesis of the two world views."

Paolo still feared for Earth, though—where his Earth-self and others were waiting in hope of alien guidance. Would they take the message of Wang's Carpets to heart, and retreat into their own hermetic worlds, oblivious to physical reality?

And he wondered if the anthrocosmologists had finally been refuted . . . or not Karpal had discovered alien consciousness—but it was sealed inside a cosmos of its own, its perceptions of itself and its surroundings neither reinforcing nor conflicting with human and transhuman explanations of reality. It would be millennia before C-Z could untangle the ethical problems of daring to try to make contact . . . assuming that both Wang's Carpets, and the inherited data patterns of the squids, survived that long.

Paolo looked around at the wild splendor of the star-choked galaxy, felt the disk reach in and cut right through him. *Could all this strange haphazard beauty be nothing but an excuse for those who beheld it to exist? Nothing but the sum of all the answers to all the questions humans and transhumans had ever asked the universe—answers created in the asking?*

He couldn't believe that—but the question remained unanswered.

So far.

A Dance to Strange Musics

GREGORY BENFORD

Gregory Benford is one of the modern giants of the field. His 1980 novel *Timescape* won the Nebula Award, the John W. Campbell Memorial Award, the British Science Fiction Association Award, and the Australian Ditmar Award and is widely considered to be one of the classic novels of the last two decades. His other novels include *The Stars in Shroud, In the Ocean of Night, Against Infinity, Artifact, Across the Sea of Suns, Great Sky River, Tides of Light, Furious Gulf,* and *Sailing Bright Eternity.* His short work has been collected in *Matter's End.* His most recent books are a new addition to Isaac Asimov's *Foundation* series, *Foundation's Fear;* a new solo novel, *Cosm;* and a nonfiction collection, *Deep Time.* Coming up is a new novel, about the exploration of Mars, *The Martian Race.* Benford is a professor of physics at the University of California, Irvine, and is one of the regular science columnists for *The Magazine of Fantasy & Science Fiction.*

Benford has written almost as much about explorers and exploration as Arthur C. Clarke, certainly as much or more than any other writer of his generation. His most popular series, the *Galactic Center* series of novels and stories (the latest of which is *Sailing Bright Eternity),* takes us tens of thousand of years into the future and into the core of the galaxy itself, where imical machine civilizations relentlessly hunt down the few remaining survivors of the organic societies they've destroyed, including that of Earth; he's also given us vivid glimpses of the tribulations of the first astronauts to explore Mars, in stories such as "All the Beer on Mars" and (with Elisabeth Malartre) "A Cold, Dry Cradle."

Here he takes us along with the first Earth expedition to leave the solar system and attempt to explore the planets of another star . . . explorers who soon learn that you shouldn't look into the abyss if you don't want the abyss to look *back.*

1

The first crewed starship, the *Adventurer*, hung like a gleaming metallic moon among the gyre of strange worlds. Alpha Centauri was a triple-star system. A tiny flare star dogged the two big suns. At this moment in its eternal dance, the brilliant mote swung slightly toward Sol. Even though it was far from the two bright stars it was the nearest star to Earth: Proxima.

The two rich, yellow stars defined the Centauri system. Still prosaically termed A and B, they swam about each other, ignoring far Proxima.

The *Adventurer*'s astronomer, John, dopplered in on both stars, refreshing memories that were lodged deep. The climax of his career loomed before him. He felt apprehension, excitement, and a thin note of something like fear.

Sun B had an orbital eccentricity of 0.52 about its near-twin, with the extended axis of its ellipse 23.2 astronomical units long. This meant that the closest approach between A and B was a bit farther than the distance of Saturn from Sol.

A was a hard yellow-white glare, a G star with 1.08 the Sun's mass. Its companion, B, was a K-class star that glowed a reddish yellow, since it had 0.88 times the Sun's mass. B orbited with a period of 80 years around A. These two were about 4.8 billion years of age, slightly older than Sol. Promising.

Sun A's planetary children had stirred *Adventurer*'s expedition forth from Earth. From Luna, the system's single Earth-class planet was a mere mote, first detected by an oxygen absorption line in its spectrum. Only a wobbly image could be resolved by Earth's kilometer-sized interferometric telescope, a long bar with mirror-eyes peering in the spaces between A and B. Just enough of an image to entice.

A new Earth? John peered at its shrouded majesty, feeling the slight hum and surge of their ship beneath him. They were steadily moving inward, exploring the Newtonian gavotte of worlds in this two-sunned ballroom of the skies. Proxima was so far away, it was not even a wall-flower.

The Captain had named the fresh planet Shiva. It hung close to A, wreathed in water cirrus, a cloudball dazzling beneath A's simmering yellow-white glare. Shimmering with promise, it had beckoned to John for years during their approach.

Like Venus, but the gases don't match, he thought. The complex tides of the star system massaged Shiva's depths, releasing gases and rippling the crust. John's many-frequency probings had told him a lot, but how to stitch data into a weave of a world? He was the first astronomer to try out centuries of speculative thinking on a real planet.

Shiva was drier than Earth, oceans taking only 40 percent of the surface. Its air was heavy in nitrogen, with giveaway tags of 18 percent oxygen and traces of carbon dioxide; remarkably Earth-like Shiva was too warm for comfort, in human terms, but not fatally so; no Venusian runaway greenhouse had developed here. How had Shiva escaped that fate?

Long before, the lunar telescopes had made one great fact clear: The atmosphere here was far, far out of chemical equilibrium. Biological theory held that this was inevitably the signature of life. And indeed, the expedition's first mapping had shown that green, abundant life clung to two well-separated habitable belts, each beginning about 30 degrees from the equator.

Apparently the weird tidal effects of the Centauri system had stolen Shiva's initial polar tilt. Such steady workings had now made its spin align to within a single degree with its orbital angular momentum, so that conditions were steady and calm. The equatorial belt was a pale, arid waste of perpetual tornadoes and blistering gales.

John close-upped in all available bands, peering at the planet's crescent. Large blue-green seas, but no great oceans. Particularly, no water links between the two milder zones, so no marine life could migrate between them. Land migrations, calculations showed, were effectively blocked by the great equatorial desert. Birds might make the long flight, John considered, but what evolutionary factor would condition them for such hardship? And what would be the reward? Why fight the jagged mountain chains? Better to lounge about in the many placid lakes.

A strange world, well worth the decades of grinding, slow, starship flight, John thought. He asked for the full display and the observing bowl opened like a flower around him. He swam above the entire disk of the Centauri system now, the images sharp and rich.

To be here at last! *Adventurer* was only a mote among many—yet *here*, in the lap of strangeness. Far Centauri.

It did not occur to him that humanity had anything truly vital to lose here. The doctrine of expansion and greater knowledge had begun seven centuries before, making European cultures the inheritors of Earth. Although science had found unsettling truths, even those revelations had not blunted the agenda of ever-greater knowledge. After all, what harm could come from merely looking?

The truth about Shiva's elevated ocean only slowly emerged. Its very existence was plainly impossible, and therefore was not at first believed.

Odis was the first to notice the clues. Long days of sensory immersion in the data-streams repaid her. She was rather proud of having plucked such exotica from the bath of measurements their expedition got from their probes—the tiny speeding, smart spindle-eyes that now cruised all over the double-stars realm.

The Centauri system was odd, but even its strong tides could not explain this anomaly. Planets should be spherical, or nearly so; Earth bulged but a fraction of a percent at its equator, due to its spin. Not Shiva, though.

Odis found aberrations in this world's shape. The anomalies were far away from the equator, principally at the 1,694-kilometer-wide deep blue sea, immediately dubbed the Circular Ocean. It sat in the southern hemisphere, its nearly perfect ring hinting at an origin as a vast crater. Odis could not take her gaze from it, a blue eye peeking coyly at them through the clouds: a planet looking back.

Odis made her ranging measurements, gathering in her data like number-clouds, inhaling their cottony wealth. Beneath her, *Adventurer* prepared to go into orbit about Shiva.

She breathed in the banks of data-vapor, translated by her kinesthetic programming into intricate scent-inventories. Tangy complex.

At first she did not believe the radar reflections. Contours leap into view, artfully sketched by the mapping radars. Calibratio checked, though, so she tried other methods: slow, analytic tedious hard to do in her excitement. They gave the same result.

The Circular Ocean stood a full 10 kilometers higher than the continent upon which it rested.

No mountains surrounded it. It sat like some cosmic magic trick, insolently demanding an explanation.

Odis presented her discovery at the daily Oversight Group meeting. There was outright skepticism, even curled lips of derision, snorts of disbelief. "The range of methods is considerable," she said adamantly. "These results cannot be wrong."

"Only thing to resolve this," a lanky geologist said, "is get an edge-on view."

"I hoped someone would say that." Odis smiled. "Do I have the authorized observing time?"

They gave it reluctantly. *Adventurer* was orbiting in a severe ellipse about Shiva's cloud-wrack. Her long swing brought her into a side view of the target area two days later. Odis used the full panoply optical, IR, UV, and microwave instruments to peer at the Circular Ocean's perimeter, probing for the basin that supported the round slab of azure water.

There was none. No land supported the hanging sea.

This result was utterly clear. The Circular Ocean was 1.36 kilometers thick and a brilliant blue. Spectral evidence suggested water rich in salt, veined by thick currents. It looked exactly like an enormous, troubled mountain lake, with the mountain subtracted.

Beneath that layer there was nothing but the thick atmosphere. No rocky mountain range to support the ocean-in-air. Just a many-Kilometer gap.

All other observations halted. The incontrovertible pictures showed an immense layer of unimaginable weight, blissfully poised above mere thin gases, contradicting all known mechanics. Until this moment Odis had been a lesser figure in the expedition. Now her work captivated everyone and she was the center of every conversation. The concrete impossibility yawned like an inviting abyss.

Lissa found the answer to Shiva's mystery, but no one was happy with it.

An atmospheric chemist, Lissa's job was mostly done well before they achieved orbit around Shiva. She had already probed and labeled the gasses, shown clearly that they implied a thriving biology below. After that, she had thought, the excitement would shift elsewhere, to the surface observers.

Not so. Lissa took a deep breath and began speaking to the Oversight Group. She had to show that she was not wasting their time. With all eyes on the Circular Ocean, few cared for mere air.

Yet it was the key, Lissa told them. The Circular Ocean had intrigued her, too: so she looked at the mixture of oxygen, nitrogen, and carbon dioxide that apparently supported the floating sea. These proved perfectly ordinary, almost Earth-standard, except for one oddity. Their spectral lines were slightly split, so that she found two small spikes to the right and left of where each line should be.

Lissa turned from the images she projected before the Oversight Group. "The only possible interpretation," she said crisply, "is that an immensely strong electric field is inducing the tiny electric dipoles of these molecules to move. That splits the lines."

"An *electric* shift?" a grizzled skeptic called. "In a charge-neutral atmosphere? Sure, maybe when lightning flashes you could get momentary effect, but—"

"It is steady."

"You looked for lightning?" a shrewd woman demanded.

"It's there, sure. We see if forking between the clouds below the Circular Ocean. But that's not what causes the electric fields."

"What does?" This from the grave captain, who never spoke in scientific disputes. All heads turned to him, then to Lissa.

She shrugged. "Nothing reasonable." It pained her to admit it, but ignorance was getting to be a common currency.

A voice called, "So there must be an impossibly strong electric field *everywhere* in that 10 kilometers of air below the ocean?" Murmurs of agreement. Worried frowns.

"Everywhere, yes." The bald truth of it stirred the audience. "Everywhere."

Tagore was in a hurry. Too much so.

He caromed off a stanchion but did not let that stop him from rebounding from the opposite wall, absorbing his momentum with his knees, and springing off with a full push. Rasters streaked his augmented vision, then flickered and faded.

He coasted by a full-view showing Shiva and the world below, a blazing crescent transcendent in its cloud-wrapped beauty. Tagore ignored the spectacle; marvels of the mind preoccupied him.

He was carrying the answer to it all, he was sure of that. In his haste he did not even glance at how blue-tinged sunlight glinted from the Circular Ocean. The thick disk of open air below it made a clear line under the blue wedge. At this angle the floating water refracted sunlight around the still-darkened limb of the planet. The glittering azure jewel heralded dawn, serene in its impudent impossibility.

The youngest of the entire expedition, Tagore was a mere theorist. He had specialized in planetary formation at university, but managed to snag a berth on this expedition by developing a ready, quick facility at explaining vexing problems the observers turned up. That, and a willingness to do scutwork.

"Cap'n, I've got it," he blurted as he came through the hatch. The captain greeted him, sitting at small oak desk, the only wood on the whole ship—then got to business. Tagore had asked for this audience because he knew the effect his theory could have on the others; so the captain should see first.

"The Circular Ocean is held up by electric field pressure," he announced. The captain's reaction was less than he had hoped: unblinking calm, waiting for more information.

"See, electromagnetic fields exert forces on the electrons in atoms," Tagore persisted, going through the numbers, talking fast. "The fields down there are so strong—I got that measurement out of Lissa's data—they can act like a steady support."

He went on to make comparisons: the energy density of a hand grenade, contained in every suitcase-sized volume of air. Even though the fields could simply stand there, as trapped waves, they had to suffer some losses. The power demands were *huge*. Plus, how the hell did such a gargantuan construction *work*?

By now Tagore was thoroughly pumped, oblivious to his audience.

Finally the captain blinked and said, "Anything like this ever seen on Earth?"

"Nossir, not that I've ever heard."

"No natural process can do the stunt?"

"Nossir, not that I can imagine."

"Well, we came looking for something different."

Tagore did not know whether to laugh or not; the captain was unreadable. Was this what exploration was like—the slow anxiety of not knowing? On Earth such work had an abstract distance, but here . . .

He would rather have some other role. Bringing uncomfortable truths to those in power put him more in the spotlight than he wished.

Captain Badquor let the Tagore kid go on a bit longer before he said anything more. It was best to let these technical types sing their songs first. So few of them ever thought about anything beyond their own warblings.

He gave Tagore a captainly smile. Why did they all look so young? "So this whole big thing on Shiva is artificial."

"Well, yeah, I suppose so . . ."

Plainly Tagore hadn't actually thought about that part very much; the wonder of such strong fields had stunned him. Well, it was stunning. "And all that energy, just used to hold up a lake?"

"I'm sure of it, sir. The numbers work out, see? I equated the pressure exerted by those electric fields, assuming they're trapped in the volume under the Circular Ocean, the way waves can get caught if they're inside a conducting box—"

"You think that ocean's conductor?" Might as well show the kid that even the captain knew a little physics. In fact, though he never mentioned it, he had a doctorate from MIT Not that he had learned much about command there.

"Uh, well, no. I mean, it is a fairly good conductor, but for my model, it's only a way of speaking—"

"It has salt currents, true? They could carry electrical currents." The captain rubbed his chin, the machinery of his mind trying to grasp how such a thing could be. "Still, that doesn't explain why the thing doesn't evaporate away, at those altitudes."

"Uh, I really hadn't thought . . ."

The captain waved a hand. "Go on." *Sing for me.*

"Then the waves exert an upward force on the water every time they reflect from the underside of the ocean—"

"And transfer that weight down, on invisible waves, to the rock that's 10 kilometers below."

"Uh, yessir."

Tagore looked a bit constipated, bursting with enthusiasm, with the experience of the puzzle, but not knowing how to express it. The captain decided to have mercy on the kid. "Sounds good. Not anything impossible about it."

"Except the *size* of it, sir."

"That's one way to put it."

"Sir?"

A curious, powerful feeling washed over the captain. Long decades of antici-pation had steeled him, made him steady in the presence of the crew. But now he felt his sense of the room tilt, as though he were losing control of his status-space.

The mind could go whirling off, out here in the inky immensities between twin alien suns. He frowned. "This thing is bigger than anything humanity ever built. And there's not a clue what it's for. The majesty of it, son, that's what strikes me. Grandeur."

John slipped into his helmet and Shiva enclosed him. *To be wrapped in a world—* His pov shifted, strummed, arced with busy fretworks—then snapped into solidity, stabilized.

Astronomy had become intensely interactive in the past century, the spectral sensoria blanketing the viewer. Through *Adventurer*'s long voyage he had tuned the system to his every whim. Now it gave him a nuanced experience like a true, full-bodied immersion.

He was eager to immerse himself in the *feel* of Shiva, in full 3-D wraparound. Its crescent swelled below like a ripe, mottled fruit. He plunged toward it. A planet, fat in bandwidth.

For effect—decades before he had been a sky-diver—John had arranged the data-fields so that he accelerated into it. From their arcing orbit he shot directly toward Shiva's disk. Each mapping rushed toward him, exploding upward in finer detail. *There—*

The effect showed up first in the grasslands of the southern habitable belt. He slewed toward the plains, where patterns emerged in quilted confusions. After Tagore's astonishing theory about the Circular Ocean—odd, so audacious, and coming from a nonscientist—John had to be ready for anything. Somewhere in the data-fields must lurk the clue to who or what had made the ocean.

Below, the great grassy shelves swelled. But in places the grass was thin. Soon he saw why. The natural grass was only peeking out across plains covered with curious orderly patterns—hexagonals folding into triangles where necessary to cover hills and valleys, right up to the muddy banks of the slow-moving brown rivers.

Reflection in the UV showed that the tiles making this pattern were often small, but with some the size of houses, meters thick . . . and moving. They all jostled and worked with restless energy to no obvious purpose.

Alive? The UV spectrum broke down into a description of a complex polymer. Cross-linked chains bonded at many oblique angles to each other, flexing like sleek micro-muscles.

John brought in chemists, biologists in an ensemble suite: Odis and Lissa chimed in the scientific choir. In the wraparound display he felt them by the shadings they gave the data.

The tiles, Lissa found, fed on their own sky. Simple sugars rained from the clotted air, the fruit of an atmosphere that resembled an airy chicken soup. *Atmospheric electro-chemistry seems responsible, somehow*, Lissa sent. Floating microbial nuggets moderated the process.

The tiles were prime eaters. Oxidizing radicals the size of golf balls patroled their sharp linear perimeters. These pack-like rollers attacked invader chemicals, ejecting most, harvesting those they could use.

Lissa brought in two more biologists, who of course had many questions. *Are these tiles like great turtles?* one ventured, then chuckled uneasily. They yearned to flip one over.

Diurnal or nocturnal? *Some are, most aren't.*

Are there any small one? *A few.*

Do they divide by fission? *No, but.* . . . Nobody understood the complicated process the biologists witnessed. Reproduction seems a tricky matter.

There is some periodicity to their movements, some slow rhythms, and particularly a fast Fourier-spectrum spike at 1.27 seconds—but again, no clear reason for it.

Could they be all one life form?—could that be?

A whole planet taken over by a tiling-thing that co-opts all resources?

The senior biologists scoffed. How could a species evolve to have only one member? And an ecosystem—a whole world!—with so few parts?

Evolution ruled that out. Bio-evolution, that is. But not social evolution.

John plunged further into the intricate matrices of analysis. The endless tile-seas cloaking mountains and valleys shifted and nuilled, fidgety, only occasionally leaving bare ground visible as a square fissioned into triangles. Oblongs met and butted with fevered energy.

Each hemisphere of the world was similar, though the tiles in the north had different shapes—pentagonals, mostly. Nowhere did the tiles cross rivers but they could ford streams. A Centauri variant of chlorophyll was everywhere, in the oceans and rivers, but not in the Circular Ocean.

The ground was covered with a thin grass, the sprigs living off the momentary sunlight that slipped between the edges in the jostling, jiggling, bumping, and shaking. Tiles that moved over the grass sometimes cropped it, sometimes not, leaving stubs that seemed to have been burned off.

The tiles' fevered dance ran incessantly, without sleep. Could these things be performing some agitated discourse, a lust-fest without end?

John slowed his descent. The tiles were a shock. Could these be the builders of the Circular Ocean? Time for the biologists to get to work.

★ ★ ★

The computer folk thought one way, the biologists—after an initial rout, when they rejected the very possibility of a single entity filling an entire biosphere—quite another.

After some friction, their views converged somewhat. A biologist remarked that the larger tiles came together like dwarf houses making love . . . gingerly, always presenting the same angles and edges.

Adventurer had scattered micro-landers all over the world. These showed only weak electromagnetic fringing fields among the tiles. Their deft collisions seemed almost like neurons in a two-dimensional plan.

The analogy stirred the theorists. Over the usual after-shift menu of beer, soy nuts, and friendly insults, one maven of the digital realm ventured an absurd idea: Could the planet have become a computer?

Everybody laughed. They kidded the advocate of this notion . . . and then lapsed into frowning silence. Specialists find quite unsettling those ideas that cross disciplines.

Could a species turn itself into a biological computer? The tiles did rub and caress each other in systematic ways. Rather than carrying information in digital fashion, maybe they used a more complex language of position and angle, exploiting their planar geometry. If so, the information density flowing among them was immense. Every collision carried a sort of Euclidean talk, possibly rich in nuance.

The computer analogy brought up a next question—not that some big ones weren't left behind, perhaps lying in wait to bite them on their conceptual tail. Could the tiles know anything more than themselves? Or were they strange, geometroid solipsists? Should they call the tiles a single. It?

Sealed inside a cosmos of Its own making, was It even in principle interested in the outside world? Alpha Centauri fed It gratuitous energy, the very soupy air fueled It: the last standing power on the globe. What reason did it have to converse with the great Outside?

Curiosity, perhaps? The biologists frowned at the prospect. Curiosity in early prehumans was rewarded in the environment. The evolving ape learned new tricks, found fresh water, killed a new kind of game, invented a better way to locate those delicious roots—and the world duly paid it back.

Apparently—*but don't ask us why just yet!* the biologists cried—the game was different here. What reward came from the tiles' endless smacking together?

So even if the visiting humans rang the conceptual doorbell on the tile-things, maybe nobody would answer. Maybe nobody was home.

Should they try?

John and Odis and Lissa, Tagore and the captain, over a hundred other crew—they all pondered.

2

While they wrestled with the issue, exploration continued.

A flitter craft flew near the elevated ocean and inspected its supporting volume with distant sensors and probing telescopes. Even Shiva's weather patterns seemed wary of the Circular Ocean. Thunderclouds veered away from the gap between the ocean and the rugged land below. In the yawning height clouds formed but quickly dispersed, as if dissolved by unseen forces.

Birds flew through the space, birds like feathery kites.

Somehow they had missed noticing this class of life. Even the micro-landers had not had the speed to capture their darting lives. And while the kite-birds did seem to live mostly on tiny floating balloon-creatures that hovered in the murky air of the valleys, they were unusually common beneath the Circular Ocean.

John proposed that he send in a robo-craft of bird size, to measure physical parameters in the heart of the gap. Captain Badquor approved. The shops fabricated a convincing fake. Jet-powered and featuring fake feathers, it was reasonably convincing.

John flew escort in a rocket-plane. The bird-probe got 17 kilometers inside and then disappeared in a dazzling blue-white electrical discharge. Telemetry showed why: The Circular Ocean's support was a complex weave of electrical fields, supplying an upward pressure. These fields never exceeded the breakdown level of a megavolt per meter, above which Shiva's atmosphere would ionize. Field strength was about a million volts per meter.

The robo-craft had hit a critical peak in the field geometry. A conductor, it caused a flashover that dumped millions of watts into the bird within a millisecond.

As the cinder fell, John banked away from his monitoring position five kilometers beyond the gap perimeter. There was no particular reason to believe a discharge that deep within the gap would somehow spread, engulfing the region in a spontaneous discharge of the enormous stored energies. Surely whoever—no, whatever—had designed the Circular Ocean's supports would not allow the electromagnetic struts to collapse from the frying of a mere bird.

But something like that happened. The system responded.

The burned brown husk of the pseudo-bird turned lazily as it fell and sparks jumped from it. These formed a thin orange discharge that fed on the energy coursing through the now-atomized bird. The discharging line snaked away, following unerringly the bird's prior path. It raced at close to the speed of light back along the arc.

The system had *memory*, John realized. He saw a tendril of light at the corner of his vision as he turned his flitter craft. He had time only to think that it was like a huge, fast finger jabbing at him. An apt analogy, though he had no time to consider ironies. The orange discharge touched the flitter. John's hair stood on end as charge flooded into the interior.

Ideally, electrons move to the outer skin of a conductor. But when antennae connect deep into the interior, circuits can close.

Something had intended to dump an immense charge on the flitter, the origin of the pseudo-bird. Onboard instruments momentarily reported a charge exceeding 17 coulombs. By then John had, for all intents and purposes, ceased to exist as an organized bundle of electrical information.

John's death did yield a harvest of data. Soon enough Lissa saw the true function of the Circular Ocean. It was but an ornament, perhaps an artwork.

Ozone fizzed all around it. Completely natural-seeming, the lake crowned a huge cavity that functioned like a steady, standing laser.

The electrical fields both supported ohe Ocean and primed the atoms of the entire atmosphere they permeated. Upon stimulus—from the same system that had fried John—the entire gap could release the stored energy into an outgoing electromagnetic wave. It was an optical bolt, powerful and complex in structure—triggered by John.

Twice more the ocean's gap discharged naturally as the humans orbited Shiva. The flash lasted but a second, not enough to rob the entire ocean structure of its stability. The emission sizzled out through the atmosphere and off into space.

Laser beams are tight, and this one gave away few of its secrets. The humans, viewing it from a wide angle, caught little of the complex structure and understood less.

Puzzled, mourning John, they returned to a careful study of the Shiva surface. Morale was low. The captain felt that a dramatic gesture could lift their spirits. He would have to do it himself.

To Captain Badquor fell the honor of the first landing. A show of bravery would overcome the crew's confusions, surely. He would direct the complex exploring machines in real-time, up close.

He left the landing craft fully suited up, impervious to the complex biochem mix of the atmosphere.

The tiles jostled downhill from him. Only in the steep flanks of this equatorial mountain range did the tiles not endlessly surge. Badquor's boots crunched on a dry, crusty soil. He took samples, sent them back by runner-robo.

A warning signal from orbit: The tiles in his area seemed more agitated than usual. A reaction to his landing?

The tile polygons were leathery, with no obvious way to sense him. No eyes or ears. They seemed to caress the ground lovingly, though Badquor knew that they tread upon big crabbed feet.

He went forward cautiously. Below, the valley seemed alive with rippling turf, long waves sweeping to the horizon in the twinkling of an instant. He got an impression of incessant pace, of enthusiasm unspoken but plainly endless.

His boots were well insulated thermally, but not electrically; thus, when his headphones crackled he thought he was receiving noise in his transmission lines. The dry sizzle began to make his skin tingle.

Only when the frying noise rose and buried all other signals did he blink, alarmed. By then it was too late.

Piezoelectric energy arises when mechanical stress massages rock. Pressure on an electrically neutral stone polarizes it at the lattice level by slightly separating the center of positive charge from the negative. The lattice moves, the shielding electron cloud does not. This happens whenever the rock crystal structure does not have a center of structural symmetry, and so occurs in nearly all bedrock.

The effect was well known on Earth, though weak. Stressed strata sometimes discharged, sending glow discharges into the air. Such plays of light were now a standard precursor warning of earthquakes. But Earth was a mild case.

Tides stressed the stony mantle of Shiva, driven by the eternal gravitational gavotte of both stars, A and B. Periodic alignments of the two stars stored enormous energy in the full body of the planet. Evolution favored life that could harness these electrical currents that rippled through the planetary crust. This, far more than the kilowatt per square meter of sunlight, drove the tile-forms.

All this explanation came after the fact, and seemed obvious in retrospect. The piezoelectric energy source was naturally dispersed and easily harvested. A sizzle of electric micro-fields fed the tiles' large, crusted footpads. After all, on Earth fish and eels routinely use electrical fields as both sensors and weapons.

This highly organized ecology sensed Badquor's intrusion immediately. To them, he probably had many of the signatures of a power-parasite. These were small creatures like stick insects that Badquor himself had noticed after landing; they lived by stealing electrical charge from the tile polygons.

Only later analysis made it clear what had happened. The inter-linked commonality of piezo-driven life moved to expel the intruder by overpowering it—literally.

Badquor probably had no inkling of how strange a fate he had met, for the several hundreds of amperes caused his muscles to seize up, his heart to freeze in a clamped frenzy, and his synapses to discharge in a last vision that burned into his eyes a vision of an incandescent rainbow.

Lissa blinked. The spindly trees looked artificial, but weren't.

Groves of them spiraled around hills, zigzagged up razor-backed ridges and shot down the flanks of denuded rock piles. Hostile terrain for any sort of tree that earthly biologists understood. The trees, she noted, had growing patterns that bore no discernible relation to water flow, sunlight exposure, or wind patterns.

That was why Lissa went in to see. Her team of four had already sent the smart-eyes, rugged robots, and quasi-intelligent processors. Lightweight, patient, durable, these ambassadors had discovered little. Time for something a bit more interactive on the ground.

That is, a person. Captain Badquor's sacrifice had to mean something, and his death had strengthened his crew's resolve.

Lissa landed with electrically insulated boots. They now understood the piezoelectric ecology in broad outline, or thought they did. Courageous caution prevailed.

The odd beanpole trees made no sense. Their gnarled branches followed a fractal pattern and had no leaves. Still, there was ample fossil evidence—gathered by automatic prospectors sent down earlier—that the bristly trees had evolved from more traditional trees within the past few million years. But they had come so quickly into the geological record that Lissa suspected they were "driven" evolution—biological technology.

She carefully pressed her instruments against the sleek black sides of the trees. Their surfaces seethed with electric currents, but none strong enough to be a danger.

On Earth, the natural potential difference between the surface and the upper atmosphere provides a voltage drop of a hundred volts for each meter in height. A woman two meters tall could be at a significantly higher potential than her feet, especially if her feet had picked up extra electrons by walking across a thick carpet.

On Shiva this effect was much larger. The trees, Lissa realized, were harvesting the large potentials available between Shiva's rocky surface and the charged layers skating across the upper reaches of the atmosphere.

The "trees" were part of yet another way to reap the planetary energies—whose origin was ultimately the blunt forces of gravity, mass and torque—all for the use of life.

The potential-trees felt Lissa's presence quickly enough. They had evolved defenses against poachers who would garner stray voltages and currents from the unwary.

In concert—for the true living entity was the grove, comprising perhaps a million trees—they reacted.

Staggering back to her lander, pursued by vagrant electrical surges through both ground and the thick air, she shouted into her suit mike her conclusions. These proved useful in later analysis.

She survived, barely.

3

When the sum of these incidents sank in, the full import become clear. The entire Shiva ecology was electrically driven. From the planet's rotation and strong magnetosphere, from the tidal stretching of the Centauri system, from geological rumblings and compressions, came far more energy than mere sunlight could ever provide.

Seen this way, all biology was an afterthought. The geologists, who had been feeling rather neglected lately, liked this turn of events quite a bit. They gave lectures on Shiva seismology which, for once, everybody attended.

To be sure, vestigial chemical processes still ran alongside the vastly larger stores of charges and potentials; these were important for understanding the ancient biosphere that had once governed here.

Much could be learned from classic, old-style biology: from samples of the bushes and wiry trees and leafy plants, from the small insect-like creatures of 10 legs each, from the kite-birds, from the spiny, knife-like fish that prowled the lakes.

All these forms were ancient, unchanging. Something had fixed them in evolutionary amber. Their forms had not changed for many hundreds of millions of years.

There had once been higher forms, the fossil record showed. Something like mammals, even large tubular things that might have resembled reptiles.

But millions of years ago they had abruptly ceased. Not due to some trauma, either—they all ended together, but without the slightest sign of a shift in the biosphere, of disease or accident.

The suspicion arose that something had simply erased them, having no further need.

The highest form of life—defined as that with the highest brain/body volume ratio—had vanished slightly later than the others. It had begun as a predator wider than it was tall, and shaped like a turtle, though without a shell.

It had the leathery look of the tile-polygons, though.

Apparently it had not followed the classic mode of pursuit, but rather had outwitted its prey, boxing it in by pack-animal tactics. Later, it had arranged deadfalls and traps. Or so the sociobiologists suspected, from narrow evidence.

These later creatures had characteristic bony structures around the large, calculating brain. Subsequent forms were plainly intelligent, and had been engaged in a strange manipulation of their surroundings. Apparently without their inventing cities or agriculture, they had domesticated many other species.

Then, the other high life forms vanished from the fossil record. The scheme of the biosphere shifted. Electrical plant forms, like the spindly trees and those species that fed upon piezoelectric energy, came to the fore.

Next, the dominant, turtle-like predators vanished as well. Had they been dispatched?

On Shiva, all the forms humans thought of as life, plant and animal alike, were now in fact mere . . . well, maintenance workers. They served docilely in a far more complex ecology. They were as vital and as unnoticeable and as ignorable as the mitochondria in the stomach linings of *Adventurer*'s crew.

Of the immensely more complex electrical ecology, they were only beginning to learn even the rudiments. If Shiva was in a sense a single interdependent, colonial organism, what were its deep rules?

By focusing on the traditional elements of the organic biosphere they had quite missed the point.

Then the Circular Ocean's laser discharged again. The starship was nearer the lancing packet of emission, and picked up a side lobe. They learned more in a millisecond than they had in a month.

★ ★ ★

A human brain has about 10 billion neurons, each connected with about 100,000 of its neighbors. A firing neuron carries one bit of information. But the signal depends upon the path it follows, and in the labyrinth of the brain there are 1,015 pathways. This torrent of information flows through the brain in machine-gun packets of electrical impulses, coursing through myriad synapses. Since a single book has about a million bits in it, a single human carries the equivalent of a billion books of information—all riding around in a two-kilogram lump of electrically wired jelly.

Only one to 10 percent of a human brain's connections are firing at any one time. A neuron can charge and discharge at best a hundred times in a second. Human brains, then, can carry roughly 1,010 bits of information in a second.

Thus, to read out a brain containing 1,015 bits would take 100,000 seconds, or about a day.

The turtle-predators had approximately the same capacity. Indeed, there were theoretical arguments that a mobile, intelligent species would carry roughly the same load of stored information as a human could. For all its limitations, the human brain has an impressive datastore capability, even if, in many, it frequently went unused.

The Circular Ocean had sent discrete packets of information of about this size, 1015 bits compressed into its powerful millisecond pulse. The packets within it were distinct, well bordered by banks of marker code. The representation was digital, an outcome mandated by the fact that any number enjoys a unique representation only in base 2.

Within the laser's millisecond burst were fully a thousand brain-equivalent transmissions. A trove. What the packets actually said was quite undecipherable.

The target was equally clear: a star 347 light years away. Targeting was precise; there could be no mistake. Far cheaper, if one knows the recipient, to send a focused message, rather than to broadcast wastefully in the low-grade, narrow bandwidth radio frequencies.

Earth had never heard such powerful signals, of course, not because humans were not straining to hear, but because Shiva was ignoring them.

After Badquor's death and Lissa's narrow escape, *Adventurer* studied the surface with elaborately planned robot expeditions. The machines skirted the edge of a vast tile-plain, observing the incessant jiggling, fed on the piezoelectric feast welling from the crusted rocks.

After some days, they came upon a small tile lying still. The others had forced it out of the eternal jostling jam. It lay stiff and discolored, baking in the double suns' glare. Scarcely a meter across and thin, it looked like construction material for a patio in Arizona.

The robots carried it off. Nothing pursued them. The tile-thing was dead, apparently left for mere chemical processes to harvest its body.

This bonanza kept the ship's biologists sleepless for weeks as they dissected it. Gray-green, hard of carapace, and extraordinarily complex in its nervous system—these they had expected. But the dead alien devoted fully a quarter of its body volume to a brain that was broken into compact, separate segments.

The tile-creatures were indeed part of an ecology driven by electrical harvesting of the planetary energies. The tiles alone used a far higher percentage of the total energetic wealth than did Earth's entire sluggish, chemically driven biosphere.

And deep within the tile-thing was the same bone structure as they had seen in the turtle-like predator. The dominant, apparently intelligent species had not gone to the stars. Instead, they had formed the basis of an intricate ecology of the mind.

Then the engineers had a chance to study the tile-thing, and found even more.

As a manifestation of their world, the tiles were impressive. Their neurological system fashioned a skein of interpretations, of lived scenarios, of expressive renderings—all apparently for communication outward in well-sculpted bunches of electrical information, intricately coded. They had large computing capacity and ceaselessly exchanged great gouts of information with each other. This explained their rough skins, which maximized piezo connections when they rubbed against each other. And they "spoke" to each other through the ground, as well, where their big, crabbed feet carried currents, too.

Slowly it dawned that Shiva was an unimaginably huge computational complex, operating in a state of information flux many orders of magnitude greater than the entire sum of human culture. Shiva was to Earth as humans are to beetles.

The first transmissions about Shiva's biosphere reached Earth four years later. Already, in a culture more than a century into the dual evolution of society and computers, there were disturbing parallels.

Some communities in the advanced regions of Earth felt that real-time itself was a pallid, ephemeral experience. After all, one could not archive it for replay, savor it, return until it became a true part of oneself. Real-time was for one time only, then lost.

So increasingly, some people lived instead in worlds made totally volitional—truncated, chopped, governed by technologies they could barely sense as ghostlike constraints on an otherwise wide compass.

"Disposable realities," some sneered—but the fascination of such lives was clear.

Shiva's implication was extreme: An entire world could give itself over to life-as-computation.

Could the intelligent species of Shiva have executed a huge fraction of their fellow inhabitants? And then themselves gone extinct? For what? Could they have fled—perhaps from the enormity of their own deeds?

Or had those original predators become the tile-polygons?

The *Adventurer* crew decided to return to Shiva's surface in force, to crack the puzzles. They notified Earth and descended.

Shortly after, the Shiva teams ceased reporting back to Earth. Through the hiss of interstellar static there came no signal.

After years of anxious waiting, Earth launched the second expedition. They too survived the passage. Cautiously they approached Shiva.

Adventurer still orbited the planet, but was vacant.

This time they were wary. Further years of hard thinking and careful study passed before the truth began to come.

4

—John/Odis/Lissa/Tagore/Cap'n—

   —all assembled/congealed/thickened—

   —into a composite veneer persona—

   —on the central deck of their old starship,

   —to greet the second expedition.

Or so they seemed to intend.

They came up from the Shiva surface in a craft not of human construction. The sleek, webbed thing seemed to ride upon electromagnetic winds.

They entered through the main lock, after using proper hailing protocols.

But what came through the lock was an ordered array of people no one could recognize as being from the *Adventurer* crew.

They seemed younger, unworn. Smooth, bland features looked out at the bewildered second expedition. The party moved together, maintaining a hexagonal array with a constant spacing of four centimeters. Fifty-six pairs of eyes surveyed the new Earth ship, each momentarily gazing at a different portion of the field of view, as if to memorize only a portion, for later integration.

To convey a sentence, each person spoke a separate word. The effect was jarring, with no clue to how an individual knew what to say, or when, for the lines were not rehearsed. The group reacted to questions in a blur of scattershot talk, words like volleys.

Sentences ricocheted and bounced around the assembly deck where the survivors of the first expedition all stood, erect and clothed in a shapeless gray garment. Their phrases made sense when isolated, but the experience of hearing them was unsettling. Long minutes stretched out before the second expedition realized that these hexagonally spaced humans were trying to greet them, to induct them into something they termed the Being Suite.

This offer made, the faces within the hexagonal array began to show separate expressions. Tapes of this encounter show regular facial alterations with a fixed periodicity of 1.27 seconds. Each separate face racheted, jerking among a menu of finely graduated countenances—anger, sympathy, laughter, rage, curiosity, shock, puzzlement, ecstasy—flickering, flickering, endlessly flickering.

A witness later said that it were as if the hexagonals (as they came to be called) knew that human expressiveness centered on the face, and so had slipped into a kind of language of facial aspects. This seemed natural to them, and yet the 1.27 second pace quickly gave the witnesses a sense of creeping horror.

High-speed tapes of the event showed more. Beneath the 1.27 frequency there was a higher harmonic, barely perceptible to the human eye, in which other expressions shot across the hexagonals' faces. These were like waves, muscular twitches that washed over the skin like tidal pulls.

This periodicity was the same as the tile-polygons had displayed. The subliminal aspects were faster than the conscious human optical processor can manage, yet research showed that they were decipherable in the target audience.

Researchers later concluded that this rapid display was the origin of the growing unease felt by the second expedition. The hexagonals said nothing throughout all this.

The second expedition crew described the experience as uncanny, racking, unbearable. Their distinct impression was that the first expedition now manifested as like the *tile-things*. Such testimony was often followed by an involuntary twitch.

Tapes do not yield such an impression upon similar audiences: they have become the classic example of having to be in a place and time to sense the meaning of an event. Still, the tapes are disturbing, and access is controlled. Some Earth audiences experienced breakdowns after viewing them.

But the second expedition agreed even more strongly upon a second conclusion. Plainly, the *Adventurer* expedition had joined the computational labyrinth that was Shiva. How they were seduced was never clear, the second expedition feared finding out.

Indeed, their sole, momentary brush with {—John/Odis/Lissa/Tagore/ Cap'n . . . —} convinced the second expedition that there was no point in pursuing the maze of Shiva.

The hostility radiating from the second expedition soon drove the hexagonals back into their ship and away. The fresh humans from Earth felt something gut-level and instinctive, a reaction beyond words. The hexagonals retreated without showing a coherent reaction. They simply turned and walked away, holding to the four centimeter spacing. The 1.27 second flicker stopped and they returned to a bland expression, alert but giving nothing away.

The vision these hexagonals conveyed was austere, jarring . . . and yet, plainly intended to be inviting.

The magnitude of their failure was a measure of the abyss that separated the two parties. The hexagonals were now both more and less than human.

The hexagonals left recurrent patterns that told much, though only in retrospect. Behind the second expedition's revulsion lay a revelation: of a galaxy spanned by intelligences formal and remote, far developed beyond the organic stage. Such intelligences had been born variously, of early organic forms, or of later machine civilizations which had arisen upon the ashes of extinct organic societies. The gleam of the stars was in fact a metallic glitter.

This vision was daunting enough: of minds so distant and strange, hosted in bodies free of sinew and skin. But there was something more, an inexpressible repulsion in the manifestation of {—John/Odis/Lissa/Tagore/Cap'n . . . —}.

A 19th century philosopher, Goethe, had once remarked that if one stared into the abyss long enough, it stared back. This proved true. A mere moment's lingering look, quiet and almost casual, was enough. The second expedition panicked. It is not good to stare into a pit that has no bottom.

They had sensed the final implication of Shiva's evolution. To alight upon such interior worlds of deep, terrible exotica exacted a high cost: the body itself. Yet all those diverse people had joined the *syntony* of Shiva—an electrical harmony that danced to unheard musics. Whether they had been seduced, or even raped, would forever be unclear.

Out of the raw data-stream the second expedition could sample transmissions from the tile-things, as well. The second expedition caught a link-locked sense of repulsive grandeur. Still organic in their basic organization, still tied to the eternal wheel of birth and death, the tiles had once been lords of their own world, holding dominion over all they knew.

Now they were patient, willing drones in a hive they could not comprehend. But—and here human terms undoubtedly fail they loved their immersion.

Where was their consciousness housed? Partially in each, or in some displaced, additive sense? There was no clear way to test either idea.

The tile-things were like durable, patient machines that could best carry forward the first stages of a grand computation. Some biologists compared them with insects, but no evolutionary mechanism seemed capable of yielding a reason why a species would give itself over to computation. The insect analogy died, unable to predict the response of the polygons to stimulus, or even why they existed.

Or was their unending jostling only in the service of calculation? The tile-polygons would not say. They never responded to overtures.

The Circular Ocean's enormous atmospheric laser pulsed regularly, as the planet's orbit and rotation carried the laser's field of targeting onto a fresh partner-star system. Only then did the system send its rich messages out into the galaxy. The pulses carried mind-packets of unimaginable data, bound on expeditions of the intellect.

The second expedition reported, studied. Slowly at first, and then accelerating, the terror overcame them.

They could not fathom Shiva, and steadily they lost crew members to its clasp. Confronting the truly, irreducibly exotic, there is no end of ways to perish.

In the end they studied Shiva from a distance, no more. Try as they could, they always met a barrier in their understanding. Theories came and went, fruitlessly. Finally, they fled.

It is one thing to speak of embracing the new, the fresh, the strange. It is another to feel that one is an insect, crawling across a page of the *Encyclopedia Britannica*, knowing only that something vast is passing by beneath, all without your sensing more than a yawning vacancy. Worse, the lack was clearly in oneself, and was irredeemable.

This was the first contact humanity had with the true nature of the galaxy. It would not be the last. But the sense of utter and complete diminishment never left the species, in all the strange millennia that rolled on thereafter.

Approaching Perimelasma

GEOFFREY A. LANDIS

A physicist who works for NASA and who has recently been working on the Martian Lander program, Geoffrey A. Landis is a frequent contributor to *Analog* and to *Asimov's Science Fiction* and has also sold stories to markets such as *Interzone, Amazing,* and *Pulphouse*. Landis is not a prolific writer by the high-production standards of the genre, but he is popular. His story "A Walk in the Sun" won him a Hugo Award in 1992, his story "Ripples in the Dirac Sea" won him a Nebula Award in 1990, and his story "Elemental" was on the final Hugo ballot a few years back. His first book was the collection *Myths, Legends, and True History,* and he has just sold his first novel, *Mars Crossing*. He lives in Berea, Ohio.

Here he takes us along on a suspenseful and hair-raising cosmic ride unlike any you've ever taken before, in company with an intrepid future adventurer bound for someplace *no*body has ever gone before: a headlong plunge into a black hole and out of it again—if he *can* figure a way to get out of it, that is, with all the forces of the universe against him. . . .

There is a sudden frisson of adrenaline, a surge of something approaching terror (if I could still feel terror), and I realize that this is it, this time I am the one who is doing it.

I'm the one who is going to drop into a black hole.

Oh, my god. This time I'm not you.

This is real.

Of course, I have experienced this exact feeling before. We both know exactly what it feels like.

My body seems weird, too big and at once too small. The feel of my muscles, my vision, my kinesthetic sense, everything is wrong. Everything is strange. My vision is fuzzy, and colors are oddly distorted. When I move, my body moves unexpectedly fast. But there seems to be nothing wrong with it. Already I am getting used to it. "It will do," I say.

There is too much to know, too much to be all at once. I slowly coalesce the fragments of your personality. None of them are you. All of them are you.

A pilot, of course, you must have, you must be, a pilot. I integrate your pilot persona, and he is me. I will fly to the heart of a darkness far darker than any mere unexplored continent. A scientist, somebody to understand your experience, yes. I synthesize a persona. You are him, too, and I understand.

And someone to simply *experience* it, to tell the tale (if any of me will survive to tell the tale) of how you dropped into a black hole, and how you survived. If you survive. Me. I will call myself Wolf, naming myself after a nearby star, for no reason whatsoever, except maybe to claim, if only to myself, that I am not you.

All of we are me are you. But in a real sense, you're not here at all. None of me are you. You are far away. Safe.

Some black holes, my scientist persona whispers, are decorated with an accretion disk, shining like a gaudy signal in the sky. Dust and gas from the interstellar medium fall toward the hungry singularity, accelerating to nearly the speed of light in their descent, swirling madly as they fall. It collides; compresses; ionizes. Friction heats the plasma millions of degrees, to emit a brilliant glow of hard X-rays. Such black holes are anything but black; the incandescence of the infalling gas may be the most brilliantly glowing thing in a galaxy. Nobody and nothing would be able to get near it; nothing would be able to survive the radiation.

The Virgo hole is not one of these. It is ancient, dating from the very first burst of star-formation when the universe was new, and has long ago swallowed or ejected all the interstellar gas in its region, carving an emptiness far into the interstellar medium around it.

The black hole is fifty-seven light years from Earth. Ten billion years ago, it had been a supermassive star, and exploded in a supernova that for a brief moment had shone brighter than the galaxy, in the process tossing away half its mass. Now there is nothing left of the star. The burned-out remnant, some thirty times the mass of the sun, has pulled in space itself around it, leaving nothing behind but gravity.

Before the download, the psychologist investigated my—your—mental soundness. We must have passed the test, obviously, since I'm here. What type of man would allow himself to fall into a black hole? That is my question maybe if I can answer that, I would understand ourself.

But this did not seem to interest the psychologist. She did not, in fact, even look directly at me. Her face had the focusless abstract gaze characteristic of somebody hotlinked by the optic nerve to a computer system. Her talk was perfunctory. To be fair, the object of her study was not the flesh me, but my computed reflection, the digital maps of my soul. I remember the last thing she said.

"We are fascinated with black holes because of their depth of metaphor," she said, looking nowhere. "A black hole is, literally, the place of no return. We see it as a metaphor for how we, ourselves, are hurled blindly into a place from which no information ever reaches us, the place from which no one ever returns. We live our lives falling into the future, and we will all inevitably meet the singularity." She paused, expecting, no doubt, some comment. But I remained silent.

"Just remember this," she said, and for the first time her eyes returned to the outside world and focused on me. "This is a real black hole, not a metaphor. Don't treat it like a metaphor. Expect reality." She paused, and finally added, "Trust the math. It's all we really know, and all that we have to trust."

Little help.

Wolf versus the black hole! One might think that such a contest is an unequal one, that the black hole has an overwhelming advantage.

Not quite so unequal.

On my side, I have technology. To start with, the wormhole, the technological sleight-of-space which got you fifty-seven light years from Earth in the first place.

The wormhole is a monster of relativity no less than the black hole, a trick of curved space allowed by the theory of general relativity. After the Virgo black hole was discovered, a wormhole mouth was laboriously dragged to it, slower than light, a project that took over a century. Once the wormhole was here, though, the trip became only a short one, barely a meter of travel. Anybody could come here and drop into it.

A wormhole—a far too cute name, but one we seem to be stuck with—is a shortcut from one place to another. Physically, it is nothing more than a loop of exotic matter. If you move through the hoop on this side of the wormhole, you emerge out the hoop on that side. Topologically, the two sides of the wormhole are pasted together, a piece cut out of space glued together elsewhere.

Exhibiting an excessive sense of caution, the proctors of Earthspace refused to allow the other end of the Virgo wormhole to exit at the usual transportation nexus, the wormhole swarm at Neptune-Trojan 4. The far end of the wormhole opens instead to an orbit around Wolf-562, an undistinguished red dwarf sun circled by two airless planets that are little more than frozen rocks, twenty-one light-years from Earthspace. To get here we had to take a double wormhole hop: Wolf, Virgo.

The black hole is a hundred kilometers across. The wormhole is only a few meters across. I would think that they were overly cautious.

The first lesson of relativity is that time and space are one. For a long time after the theoretical prediction that such a thing as a traversable wormhole ought to be possible, it was believed that a wormhole could also be made to traverse time as well. It was only much later, when wormhole travel was tested, that it was found that the Cauchy instability makes it impossible to form a wormhole that leads backward in time. The theory was correct—space and time are indeed just aspects of the same reality, spacetime—but any attempt to move a wormhole in such a way that it becomes a timehole produces a vacuum polarization to cancel out the time effect.

After we—the spaceship I am to pilot, and myself/yourself—come through the wormhole, the wormhole engineers go to work. I have never seen this process close up, so I stay nearby to watch. This is going to be interesting.

A wormhole looks like nothing more than a circular loop of string. It is, in fact, a loop of exotic material, negative-mass cosmic string. The engineers, working telerobotically via vacuum manipulator pods, spray charge onto the string. They charge it until it literally glows with Paschen discharge, like a neon light in the dirty vacuum, and then use the electric charge to manipulate the shape. With the application of invisible electromagnetic fields, the string starts to twist. This is a slow process. Only a few meters across, the wormhole loop has a mass roughly equal to that of Jupiter. Negative to that of Jupiter, to be precise, my scientist persona reminds me, but either way, it is a slow thing to move.

Ponderously, then, it twists further and further, until at last it becomes a lemniscate, a figure of eight. The instant the string touches itself, it shimmers for a moment, and then suddenly there are two glowing circles before us, twisting and oscillating in shape like jellyfish.

The engineers spray more charge onto the two wormholes, and the two wormholes, arcing lightning into space, slowly repel each other. The vibrations of the cosmic string are spraying out gravitational radiation like a dog shaking off water—even where I am, floating ten kilometers distant, I can feel it, like the swaying of invisible tides—and as they radiate energy, the loops enlarge. The radiation represents a serious danger. If the engineers lose control of the string for even a brief instant, it might enter the instability known as "squiggle mode," and catastrophically enlarge. The engineers damp out the radiation before it gets critical, though—they are, after all, well practiced at this—and the loops stabilize into two perfect circles. On the other side, at Wolf, precisely the same scene has played out, and two loops of exotic string now circle Wolf-562 as well. The wormhole has been cloned.

All wormholes are daughters of the original wormhole, found floating in the depths of interstellar space eleven hundred years ago, a natural loop of negative cosmic string as ancient as the Big Bang, invisible to the eyes save for the distortion of spacetime. That first one led from nowhere interesting to nowhere exciting, but from that one we bred hundreds, and now we casually move wormhole mouths from star to star, breeding new wormholes as it suits us, to form an ever-expanding network of connections.

I should not have been so close. Angry red lights have been flashing in my peripheral vision, warning blinkers that I have been ignoring. The energy radiated in the form of gravitational waves had been prodigious, and would have, to a lesser person, been dangerous. But in my new body, I am nearly invulnerable, and if I can't stand a mere wormhole cloning, there is no way I will be able to stand a black hole. So I ignore the warnings, wave briefly to the engineers—though I doubt that they can even see me, floating kilometers away—and use my reaction jets to scoot over to my ship.

The ship I will pilot is docked to the research station, where the scientists have their instruments and the biological humans have their living quarters. The wormhole station is huge compared to my ship, which is a tiny ovoid occupying a berth almost invisible against the hull. There is no hurry for me to get to it.

I'm surprised that any of the technicians can even see me, tiny as I am in the void, but a few of them apparently do, because in my radio I hear casual greetings called out: how's it, *ohayo gozaimasu*, hey glad you made it, how's the bod? It's hard to tell from the radio voices which ones are people I know, and which are only casual acquaintances. I answer back: how's it, *ohayo*, yo, surpassing spec. None of them seem inclined to chat, but then, they're busy with their own work.

They are dropping things into the black hole.

Throwing things in, more to say. The wormhole station orbits a tenth of an astronomical unit from the Virgo black hole, closer to the black hole than Mercury is to the sun. This is an orbit with a period of a little over two days, but, even so close to the black hole, there is nothing to see. A rock, released to fall straight downward, takes almost a day to reach the horizon.

One of the scientists supervising, a biological human named Sue, takes the time to talk with me a bit, explaining what they are measuring. What interests me most is that they are measuring whether the fall deviates from a straight line. This will let them know whether the black hole is rotating. Even a slight rotation would mess up the intricate dance of the trajectory required for my ship. However, the best current theories predict that an old black hole will have shed its angular momentum long ago, and, as far as the technicians can determine, their results show that the conjecture holds.

The black hole, or the absence in space where it is located, is utterly invisible from here. I follow the pointing finger of the scientist, but there is nothing to see. Even if I had a telescope, it is unlikely that I would be able to pick out the tiny region of utter blackness against the irregular darkness of an unfamiliar sky.

My ship is not so different from the drop probes. The main difference is that I will be on it.

Before boarding the station, I jet over in close to inspect my ship, a miniature egg of perfectly reflective material. The hull is made of a single crystal of a synthetic material so strong that no earthly force could even dent it.

A black hole, though, is no earthly force.

Wolf versus the black hole! The second technological trick I have in my duel against the black hole is my body.

I am no longer a fragile, fluid-filled biological human. The tidal forces at the horizon of a black hole would rip a true human apart in mere instants; the accelerations required to hover would squash one into liquid. To make this journey, I have downloaded your fragile biological mind into a body of more robust material. As important as the strength of my new body is the fact that it is tiny. The force produced by the curvature of gravity is proportional to the size of the object. My new body, a millimeter tall, is millions of times more resistant to being stretched to spaghetti.

The new body has another advantage as well. With my mind operating as software on a computer the size of a pinpoint, my thinking and my reflexes are thousands of times faster than biological. In fact, I have already chosen to slow my thinking down, so that I can still interact with the biologicals. At full speed, my microsecondreactions are lightning compared to the molasses of neuron speeds in biological humans. I see far in the ultraviolet now, a necessary compensation for the fact that my vision would consist of nothing but a blur if I tried to see by visible light.

You could have made my body any shape, of course, a tiny cube or even a featureless sphere. But you followed the dictates of social convention. A right human should be recognizably a human, even if I am to be smaller than an ant, and so my body mimics a human body, although no part of it is organic, and my brain faithfully executes your own human brain software. From what I see and feel, externally and internally, I am completely, perfectly human.

As is right and proper. What is the value of experience to a machine?

Later, after I return—*if* I return—I can upload back. I can become you.

But return is, as they say, still somewhat problematical.

You, my original, what do you feel? Why did I think I would do it? I imagine you laughing hysterically about the trick you've played, sending me to drop into the black hole while you sit back in perfect comfort, in no danger. Imagining your laughter comforts me, for all that I know that it is false. I've been in the other place before, and never laughed.

I remember the first time I fell into a star.

We were hotlinked together, that time, united in online-realtime, our separate brains reacting as one brain. I remember what I thought, the incredible electric feel: ohmigod, am I really going to do this? Is it too late to back out?

The idea had been nothing more than a whim, a crazy idea, at first. We had been dropping probes into a star, Groombridge 1830B, studying the dynamics of a flare star. We were done, just about, and the last-day-of-project party was just getting in swing. We were all fuzzed with neurotransmitter randomizers, creativity spinning wild and critical thinking nearly zeroed. Somebody, I think it was Jenna, said, we could ride one down, you know. Wait for a flare, and then plunge through the middle of it. Helluva ride!

Helluva *splash* at the end, too, somebody said, and laughed.

Sure, somebody said. It might have been me. What do you figure? Download yourself to temp storage and then uplink frames from yourself as you drop?

That works, Jenna said. Better: we copy our bodies first, then link the two brains. One body drops; the other copy hotlinks to it.

Somehow, I don't remember when, the word "we" had grown to include me.

"Sure," I said. "And the copy on top is in null-input suspension; experiences the whole thing realtime!"

In the morning, when we were focused again, I might have dismissed the idea as a whim of the fuzz, but for Jenna the decision was already immovable as a droplet of neutronium. *Sure* we're dropping, let's start now.

We made a few changes. It takes a long time to fall into a star, even a small one like Bee, so the copy was reengineered to a slower thought-rate, and the original body in null-input was frame-synched to the drop copy with impulse-echoers. Since the two brains were molecule by molecule identical, the uplink bandwidth required was minimal.

The probes were reworked to take a biological, which meant mostly that a cooling system had to be added to hold the interior temperature within the liquidus range of water. We did that by the simplest method possible: we surrounded the probes with a huge block of cometary ice. As it sublimated, the ionized gas would carry away heat. A secondary advantage of the ice was that our friends, watching from orbit, would have a blazing cometary trail to cheer on. When the ice was used up, of course, the body would slowly vaporize. None of us would actually survive to hit the star.

But that was no particular concern. If the experience turned out to be too undesirable, we could always edit the pain part of it out of the memory later.

It would have made more sense, perhaps, to have simply recorded the brain-uplink from the copy onto a local high-temp buffer, squirted it back, and linked to it as a memory upload. But Jenna would have none of that. She wanted to experience it in realtime, or at least in as close to realtime as speed-of-light delays allow.

Three of us—Jenna, Martha, and me—dropped. Something seems to be missing from my memory here; I can't remember the reason I decided to do it. It must have been something about a biological body, some a-rational consideration that seemed normal to my then-body, that I could never back down from a crazy whim of Jenna's.

And I had the same experience, the same feeling then, as I, you, did, always do, the feeling that my god *I* am the copy and I am going to die. But that time, of course, thinking every thought in synchrony, there was no way at all to tell the copy from the original, to split the me from you.

It is, in its way, a glorious feeling.

I dropped.

You felt it, you remember it. Boring at first, the long drop with nothing but freefall and the chatter of friends over the radio-link. Then the ice shell slowly flaking away, ionizing and beginning to glow, a diaphanous cocoon of pale violet, and below the red star getting larger and larger, the surface mottled and wrinkled, and then suddenly we fell into and through the flare, a huge luminous vault above us, dwarfing our bodies in the immensity of creation.

An unguessable distance beneath me, the curvature of the star vanished, and, still falling at three hundred kilometers per second, I was hanging motionless over an infinite plane stretching from horizon to horizon.

And then the last of the ice vaporized, and I was suddenly suspended in nothing, hanging nailed to the burning sky over endless crimson horizons of infinity, and pain came like the inevitability of mountains—I didn't edit it—pain like infinite oceans, like continents, like a vast, airless world.

Jenna, now I remember. The odd thing is, I never did really connect in any significant way with Jenna. She was already in a quadrad of her own, a quadrad she was fiercely loyal to, one that was solid and accepting to her chameleon character, neither needing nor wanting a fifth for completion.

Long after, maybe a century or two later, I found out that Jenna had disassem bled herself. After her quadrad split apart, she'd downloaded her character to a mainframe, and then painstakingly cataloged everything that made her Jenna: all her various skills and insights, everything she had experienced, no matter how minor, each facet of her character, every memory and dream and longing: the myriad subroutines of personality. She indexed her soul, and she put the ten thousand pieces of it into the public domain for download. A thousand people, maybe a million people, maybe even more, have pieces of Jenna, her cleverness, her insight, her skill at playing antique instruments.

But nobody has her sense of self. After she copied her subroutines, she deleted herself.

And who am I?

Two of the technicians who fit me into my spaceship and who assist in the ten thousand elements of the preflight check are the same friends from that drop, long ago; one of them even still in the same biological body as he had then, although eight hundred years older, his vigor undiminished by biological reconstruction. My survival, if I am to survive, will be dependent on microsecond timing, and I'm embarrassed not to be able to remember his name.

He was, I recall, rather stodgy and conservative even back then.

We joke and trade small talk as the checkout proceeds. I'm still distracted by my self-questioning, the implications of my growing realization that I have no understanding of why I'm doing this.

Exploring a black hole would be no adventure if only we had faster-than-light travel, but of the thousand technological miracles of the third and fourth millennia, this one miracle was never realized. If I had the mythical FTL motor, I could simply drive out of the black hole. At the event horizon, space falls into the black hole at the speed of light; the mythical motor would make that no barrier.

But such a motor we do not have. One of the reasons I'm taking the plunge—not the only one, not the main one, but one—is in the hope that scientific measurements of the warped space inside the black hole will elucidate the nature of space and time, and so I myself will make one of the innumerable small steps to bring us closer to an FTL drive.

The spaceship I am to pilot has a drive nearly—but not quite—as good. It contains a microscopic twist of spacetime inside an impervious housing, a twist that will parity-reverse ordinary matter into mirror-matter. This total conversion engine gives my ship truly ferocious levels of thrust. The gentlest nudge of my steering rockets will give me thousands of gravities of acceleration. Unthinkable acceleration for a biological body, no matter how well cushioned. The engine will allow the rocket to dare the unthinkable, to hover at the very edge of the event horizon, to maneuver where space itself is accelerating at nearly light-speed. This vehicle, no larger than a peanut, contains the engines of an interstellar probe.

Even with such an engine, most of the ship is reaction mass.

The preflight checks are all green. I am ready to go. I power up my instruments, check everything out for myself, verify what has already been checked three times, and then check once again. My pilot persona is very thorough. Green.

"You still haven't named your ship," comes a voice to me. It is the technician, the one whose name I have forgotten. "What is your call sign?"

One way journey, I think. Maybe something from Dante? No, Sartre said it better: no exit. *"Huis Clos,"* I say, and drop free.

Let them look it up.

Alone.

The laws of orbital mechanics have not been suspended, and I do not drop into the black hole. Not yet. With the slightest touch of my steering engines—I do not dare use the main engine this close to the station—I drop into an elliptical orbit, one with a perimelasma closer to, but still well outside, the dangerous zone of the black hole. The black hole is still invisible, but inside my tiny kingdom I have enhanced senses of exquisite sensitivity, spreading across the entire spectrum from radio to gamma radiation. I look with my new eyes to see if I can detect an X-ray glow of interstellar hydrogen being ripped apart, but if there is any such, it is too faint to be visible with even my sensitive instruments. The interstellar medium is so thin here as to be essentially nonexistent. The black hole is invisible.

I smile. This makes it better, somehow. The black hole is pure, unsullied by any outside matter. It consists of gravity and nothing else, as close to pure mathematical abstraction as anything in the universe can ever be.

It is not too late to back away. If I were to choose to accelerate at a million gravities, I would reach relativistic velocities in about thirty seconds. No wormholes would be needed for me to run away; I would barely even need to slow down my brain to cruise at nearly the speed of light to anywhere in the colonized galaxy.

But I know I won't. The psychologist knew it, too, damn her, or she would never have approved me for the mission. Why? What is it about me?

As I worry about this with part of my attention, while the pilot persona flies the ship, I flash onto a realization, and at this realization another memory hits. It is the psychologist, and in the memory I'm attracted to her sexually, so much so that you are distracted from what she is saying.

I feel no sexual attraction now, of course. I can barely remember what it is. That part of the memory is odd, alien.

"We can't copy the whole brain to the simulation, but we can copy enough that, to yourself, you will still feel like yourself," she said. She is talking to the air, not to you. "You won't notice any gaps."

I'm brain-damaged. This is the explanation.

You frowned. "How could I not notice that some of my memories are missing?"

"The brain makes adjustments. Remember, at any given time, you never even use 1 percent of 1 percent of your memories. What we'll be leaving out will be stuff that you will never have any reason to think about. The memory of the taste of strawberries, for example; the floor-plan of the house you lived in as a teenager. Your first kiss."

This bothered you somewhat—you want to remain yourself. I concentrate hard. What do strawberries taste like? I can't remember. I'm not even certain what color they are. Round fruits, like apples, I think, only smaller. And the same color as apples, or something similar, I'm sure, except I don't remember what color that is.

You decided that you can live with the editing, as long as it doesn't change the essential you. You smiled. "Leave in the first kiss."

So I can never possibly solve the riddle: what kind of a man is it that would deliberately allow himself to drop into a black hole. I cannot, because I don't have the memories of you. In a real sense, I am not you at all.

But I do remember the kiss. The walk in the darkness, the grass wet with dew, the moon a silver sliver on the horizon, turning to her, and her face already turned up to meet my lips. The taste indescribable, more feeling than taste (not like strawberries at all), the small hardness of her teeth behind the lips—all there. Except the one critical detail: I don't have any idea at all who she *was*.

What else am I missing? Do I even know what I don't know?

I was a child, maybe nine, and there was no tree in the neighborhood that you could not climb. I was a careful, meticulous, methodical climber. On the tallest of the trees, when you reached toward the top, you were above the forest canopy (did I live in a forest?) and, out of the dimness of the forest floor, emerged into brilliant sunshine. Nobody else could climb like you; nobody ever suspected how high I climbed. It was your private hiding place, so high that the world was nothing but a sea of green waves in the valley between the mountains.

It was my own stupidity, really. At the very limit of the altitude needed to emerge into sunlight, the branches were skinny, narrow as your little finger. They bent alarmingly with your weight, but I knew exactly how much they would take. The bending was a thrill, but I was cautious, and knew exactly what I was doing.

It was further down, where the branches were thick and safe, that I got careless. Three points of support, that was the rule of safety; but I was reaching for one branch, not paying attention, when one in my other hand broke, and I was off balance. I slipped. For a prolonged instant I was suspended in space, branches all about me, I reached out and grasped only leaves, and I fell and fell, and all I could think as leaves and branches fell upward past me was, oh my, I made a miscalculation; I was really stupid.

The flash memory ends with no conclusion. I must have hit the ground but I cannot remember it. Somebody must have found me, or else I wandered or crawled back, perhaps in a daze, and found somebody, but I cannot remember it.

Half a million kilometers from the hole. If my elliptical orbit were around the sun instead of a black hole, I would already have penetrated the surface. I now hold the record for the closest human approach. There is still nothing to see with unmagnified senses. It seems surreal that I'm in the grip of something so powerful that is utterly invisible. With my augmented eyes used as a telescope, I can detect the black hole by what isn't there, a tiny place of blackness nearly indistinguishable from any other patch of darkness except for an odd motion of the stars near it.

My ship is sending a continuous stream of telemetry back to the station. I have an urge to add a verbal commentary—there is plenty of bandwidth—but I have nothing to say. There is only one person I have any interest in talking to, and you are cocooned at absolute zero, waiting for me to upload myself and become you.

My ellipse takes me inward, moving faster and faster. I am still in Newton's grip, far from the sphere where Einstein takes hold.

A tenth of a solar radius. The blackness I orbit is now large enough to see without a telescope, as large as the sun seen from Earth, and swells as I watch with time-distorted senses. Due to its gravity, the blackness in front of the star pattern is a bit larger than the disk of the black hole itself. Square root of twenty-seven over two—about two and a half times larger, the physicist persona notes. I watch in fascination.

What I see is a bubble of purest blackness. The bubble pushes the distant stars away from it as it swells. My orbital motion makes the background stars appear to sweep across the sky, and I watch them approach the black hole and then, smoothly pushed by the gravity, move off to the side, a river of stars flowing past an invisible obstacle. It is a gravitational lensing effect, I know, but the view of flowing stars is so spectacular that I cannot help but watch it. The gravity pushes each star to one side or the other. If a star were to pass directly behind the hole, it would appear to split and for an instant become a perfect circle of light, an Einstein ring. But this precise alignment is too rare to see by accident.

Closer, I notice an even odder effect. The sweeping stars detour smoothly around the bubble of blackness, but very close to the bubble, there are other stars, stars that actually move in the opposite direction, a counterflowing river of stars. It takes me a long time (microseconds perhaps) before my physicist persona tells me that I am seeing the image of the stars in the Einstein mirror. The entire external universe is mirrored in a narrow ring outside the black hole, and the mirror image flows along with a mirror of my own motion.

In the center of the ring there is nothing at all.

Five thousand kilometers, and I am moving fast. The gravitational acceleration here is over ten million gees, and I am still fifty times the Schwarzschild radius from the black hole. Einstein's correction is still tiny, though, and if I were to do nothing, my orbit would whip around the black hole and still escape into the outside world.

One thousand kilometers. Perimelasma, the closest point of my elliptical orbit. Ten times the Schwarzschild radius, close enough that Einstein's correction to Newton now makes a small difference to the geometry of space. I fire my engines. My speed is so tremendous that it takes over a second of my engine firing at a million gravities to circularize my orbit.

My time sense has long since speeded up back to normal, and then faster than normal. I orbit the black hole about ten times per second.

My god, this is why I exist, this is why I'm here!

All my doubts are gone in the rush of naked power. No biological could have survived this far; no biological could have even survived the million-gee circularization burn, and I am only at the very beginning! I grin like a maniac, throb with a most unscientific excitement that must be the electronic equivalent of an adrenaline high.

Oh, this ship is good. This ship is sweet. A million-gee burn, smooth as magnetic levitation, and I barely cracked the throttle. I should have taken it for a spin before dropping in, should have hot-rodded *Huis Clos* around the stellar neighborhood. But it had been absolutely out of the question to fire the main engine close to the wormhole station. Even with the incredible efficiency of the engine, that million-gee perimelasma burn must have lit up the research station like an unexpected sun.

I can't wait to take *Huis Clos* in and see what it will *really* do.

My orbital velocity is a quarter of the speed of light.

The orbit at nine hundred kilometers is only a parking orbit, a chance for me to configure my equipment, make final measurements, and, in principle, a last chance for me to change my mind. There is nothing to reconnoiter that the probes have not already measured, though, and there is no chance that I will change my mind, however sensible that may seem.

The river of stars swirls in a dance of counterflow around the blackness below me. The horizon awaits.

The horizon below is invisible, but real. There is no barrier at the horizon, nothing to see, nothing to feel. I will even be unable to detect it, except for my calculations.

An event horizon is a one-way membrane, a place you can pass into but neither you nor your radio signals can pass out of. According to the mathematics, as I pass through the event horizon, the directions of space and time change identity. Space rotates into time; time rotates into space. What this means is that the direction to the center of the black hole, after I pass the event horizon, will be the future. The direction out of the black hole will be the past. This is the reason that no one and nothing can ever leave a black hole; the way inward is the one direction we always must go, whether we will it or not: into the future.

Or so the mathematics says.

The future, inside a black hole, is a very short one.

So far the mathematics has been right on. Nevertheless, I go on. With infinitesimal blasts from my engine, I inch my orbit lower.

The bubble of blackness gets larger, and the counterflow of stars around it becomes more complex. As I approach three times the Schwarzschild radius, 180 kilometers, I check all my systems. This is the point of no rescue: inside three Schwarzschild radii, no orbits are stable, and my automatic systems will be constantly thrusting to adjust my orbital parameters to keep me from falling into the black hole or being flung away to infinity. My systems are all functional, in perfect form for the dangerous drop. My orbital velocity is already half the speed of light. Below this point, centrifugal force will decrease toward zero as I lower my orbit, and I must use my thrusters to increase my velocity as I descend, or else plunge into the hole.

When I grew up, in the last years of the second millennium, nobody thought that they would live forever. Nobody would have believed me if I told them that by my thousandth birthday, I would have no concept of truly dying.

Even if all our clever tricks fail, even if I plunge through the event horizon and am stretched into spaghetti and crushed by the singularity, I will not die. You, my original, will live on, and if *you* were to die, we have made dozens of backups and spin-off copies of myselves in the past, some versions of which must surely still be living on. My individual life has little importance. I can, if I chose, uplink my brain-state to the orbiting station right at this instant, and reawake, whole, continuing this exact thought, unaware (except on an abstract intellectual level) that I and you are not the same.

But we are not the same, you and I. I am an edited-down version of you, and the memories that have been edited out, even if I never happen to think them, make me different, a new individual. Not *you*.

On a metaphorical level, a black hole stands for death, the blackness that is sucking us all in. But what meaning does death have in a world of matrix backups and modular personality? Is my plunge a death wish? Is it thumbing my nose at death? Because I intend to survive. Not you. *Me*.

I orbit the black hole over a hundred times a second now, but I have revved my brain processing speed accordingly, so that my orbit seems to me leisurely enough. The view here is odd. The black hole has swollen to the size of a small world below me, a world of perfect velvet darkness, surrounded by a belt of madly rotating stars.

No engine, no matter how energetic, can put a ship into an orbit at 1.5 times the Schwarzschild radius; at this distance, the orbital velocity is the speed of light, and not even my total-conversion engine can accelerate me to that speed. Below that, there are no orbits at all. I stop my descent at an orbit just sixty kilometers from the event horizon, when my orbital velocity reaches 85 percent of the speed of light. Here I can coast, ignoring the constant small adjustments of the thrusters that keep my orbit from sliding off the knife-edge. The velvet blackness of the black hole is almost half of the universe now, and if I were to trust the outside view, I am diving at a slant downward into the black hole. I ignore my pilot's urge to override the automated navigation and manually even out the trajectory. The downward slant is only relativistic aberration, nothing more, an illusion of my velocity.

And 85 percent of the speed of light is as fast as I dare orbit; I must conserve my fuel for the difficult part of the plunge to come.

In my unsteady orbit sixty kilometers above the black hole, I let my ship's computer chat with the computer of the wormhole station, updating and downloading my sensors' observations.

At this point, according to the mission plan, I am supposed to uplink my brain state, so that should anything go wrong further down the well, you, my original, will be able to download my state and experiences to this point. To hell with that, I think, a tiny bit of rebellion. I am not you. If you awaken with my memories, I will be no less dead.

Nobody at the wormhole station questions my decision not to upload.

I remember one other thing now. "You're a type N personality," the psychologist had said, twitching her thumb to leaf through invisible pages of test results. The gesture marked her era; only a person who had grown up before computer hotlinks would move a physical muscle in commanding a virtual. She was twenty-first century, possibly even twentieth. "But I suppose you already know that."

"Type N?" you asked.

"Novelty-seeking," she said. "Most particularly, one not prone to panic at new situations."

"Oh," you said. You did already know that. "Speaking of novelty seeking, how do you feel about going to bed with a type N personality?"

"That would be unprofessional." She frowned. "I think."

"Not even one who is about to jump down a black hole?"

She terminated the computer link with a flick of her wrist, and turned to look at you. "Well—"

From this point onward, microsecond timing is necessary for the dance we have planned to succeed. My computer and the station computer meticulously compare clocks, measuring Doppler shifts to exquisite precision. My clocks are running slow, as expected, but half of the slowness is relativistic time dilation due to my velocity. The gravitational redshift is still modest. After some milliseconds—a long wait for me, in my hyped-up state—they declare that they agree. The station has already done their part, and I begin the next phase of my descent.

The first thing I do is fire my engine to stop my orbit. I crack the throttle to fifty million gees of acceleration, and the burn takes nearly a second, a veritable eternity, to slow my flight.

For a moment I hover, and start to drop. I dare not drop too fast, and I ramp my throttle up, to a hundred megagee, five hundred, a billion gravities. At forty billion gravities of acceleration, my engine thrust equals the gravity of the black hole, and I hover.

The blackness has now swallowed half of the universe. Everything beneath me is black. Between the black below and the starry sky above, a spectacularly bright line exactly bisects the sky. I have reached the altitude at which orbital velocity is just equal to the speed of light, and the light from my rocket exhaust is in orbit around the black hole. The line I see around the sky is my view of my own rocket, seen by light that has traveled all the way around the black hole. All I can see is the exhaust, far brighter than anything else in the sky.

The second brightest thing is the laser beacon from the wormhole station above me, shifted from the original red laser color to a greenish blue. The laser marks the exact line between the station and the black hole, and I maneuver carefully until I am directly beneath the orbiting station.

At forty billion gravities, even my ultrastrong body is at its limits. I cannot move, and even my smallest finger is pressed against the form-fitting acceleration couch. But the controls, hardware-interfaced to my brain, do not require me to lift a finger to command the spacecraft. The command I give *Huis Clos* is: down.

My engine throttles down slightly, and I drop inward from the photon sphere, the bright line of my exhaust vanishes. Every stray photon from my drive is now sucked downward.

Now my view of the universe has changed. The black hole has become the universe around me, and the universe itself, all the galaxies and stars and the wormhole station, is a shrinking sphere of sparkling dust above me.

Sixty billion gravities. Seventy. Eighty.

Eighty billion gravities is full throttle. I am burning fuel at an incredible rate, and only barely hold steady. I am still twenty kilometers above the horizon.

There is an unbreakable law of physics: incredible accelerations require incredible fuel consumption. Even though my spaceship is, by mass, comprised mostly of fuel, I can maintain less than a millisecond worth of thrust at this acceleration. I cut my engine and drop.

It will not be long now. This is my last chance to uplink a copy of my mind back to the wormhole station to wake in your body, with my last memory the decision to upload my mind.

I do not.

The stars are blueshifted by a factor of two, which does not make them noticeably bluer. Now that I have stopped accelerating, the starlight is falling into the hole along with me, and the stars do not blueshift any further. My instruments probe the vacuum around me. The theorists say that the vacuum close to the horizon of a black hole is an exotic vacuum, abristle with secret energy. Only a ship plunging through the event horizon would be able to measure this. I do, recording the results carefully on my ship's on-board recorders, since it is now far too late to send anything back by radio.

There is no sign to mark the event horizon, and there is no indication at all when I cross it. If it were not for my computer, there would be no way for me to tell that I have passed the point of no return.

Nothing is different. I look around the tiny cabin, and can see no change. The blackness below me continues to grow, but is otherwise not changed. The outside universe continues to shrink above me; the brightness beginning to concentrate into a belt around the edge of the glowing sphere of stars, but this is only an effect of my motion. The only difference is that I have only a few hundred microseconds left.

From the viewpoint of the outside world, the light from my spacecraft has slowed down and stopped at the horizon. But I have far outstripped my lagging image, and am falling toward the center at incredible speed. At the exact center is the singularity, far smaller than an atom, a mathematical point of infinite gravity and infinite mystery.

Whoever I am, whether or not I survive, I am now the first person to penetrate the event horizon of a black hole. That's worth a cheer, even with nobody to hear. Now I have to count on the hope that the microsecond timing of the technicians above me had been perfect for the second part of my intricate dance, the part that might, if all goes well, allow me to survive.

Above me, according to theory, the stars have already burned out, and even the most miserly red dwarf has sputtered the last of its hydrogen fuel and grown cold. The universe has already ended, and the stars have gone out. I still see a steady glow of starlight from the universe above me, but this is fossil light, light that has been falling down into the black hole with me for eons, trapped in the infinitely stretched time of the black hole.

For me, time has rotated into space, and space into time. Nothing feels different to me, but I cannot avoid the singularity at the center of the black hole any more than I can avoid the future. Unless, that is, I have a trick.

Of course, I have a trick.

At the center of the spherical universe above me is a dot of bright blue-violet; the fossil light of the laser beacon from the orbiting station. My reaction jets have kept on adjusting my trajectory to keep me centered in the guidance beam, so I am directly below the station. Anything dropped from the station will, if everything works right, drop directly on the path I follow.

I am approaching close to the center now, and the tidal forces stretching my body are creeping swiftly toward a billion gees per millimeter. Much higher, and even my tremendously strong body will be ripped to spaghetti. There are only microseconds left for me. It is time.

I hammer my engine, full throttle. Far away, and long ago, my friends at the wormhole station above dropped a wormhole into the event horizon. If their timing was perfect—

From a universe that has already died, the wormhole cometh.

Even with my enhanced time sense, things happen fast. The laser beacon blinks out, and the wormhole sweeps down around me like the vengeance of God, far faster than I can react. The sparkle-filled sphere of the universe blinks out like a light, and the black hole—and the tidal forces stretching my body—abruptly disappears. For a single instant I see a black disk below me, and then the wormhole rotates, twists, stretches, and then silently vanishes.

Ripped apart by the black hole.

My ship is vibrating like a bell from the abrupt release of tidal stretching. "I did it," I shout. "It worked! God damn it, it really worked!"

This was what was predicted by the theorists, that I would be able to pass through the wormhole before it was shredded by the singularity at the center. The other possibility, that the singularity itself, infinitesimally small and infinitely powerful, might follow me through the wormhole, was laughed at by everyone who had any claim to understand wormhole physics. This time, the theorists were right.

But where am I?

There should be congratulations pouring into my radio by now, teams of friends and technicians swarming over to greet me, cheering and shouting.

"*Huis Clos,*" I say, over the radio. "I made it! *Huis Clos* here. Is anybody there?"

In theory, I should have reemerged at Wolf-562. But I do not see it. In fact, what I see is not recognizably the universe at all.

There are no stars.

Instead of stars, the sky is filled with lines, parallel lines of white light by the uncountable thousands. Dominating the sky, where the star Wolf-562 should have been, is a glowing red cylinder, perfectly straight, stretching to infinity in both directions.

Have I been transported into some other universe? Could the black hole's gravity sever the wormhole, cutting it loose from our universe entirely, and connect it into this strange new one?

If so, it has doomed me. The wormhole behind me, my only exit from this strange universe, is already destroyed. Not that escaping through it could have done me any good—it would only have brought me back to the place I escaped, to be crushed by the singularity of the black hole.

I could just turn my brain off, and I will have lost nothing, in a sense. They will bring you out of your suspended state, tell you that the edition of you that dropped into the black hole failed to upload, and they lost contact after it passed the event horizon. The experiment failed, but you had never been in danger.

But, however much you think we are the same, *I am not you.* I am a unique individual. When they revive you, without your expected new memories, I will still be gone.

I want to survive, I want to return.

A universe of tubes of light! Brilliant bars of an infinite cage. The bright lines in the sky have slight variations in color, from pale red to plasma-arc blue. They must be similar to the red cylinder near me, I figure, but light-years away. How could a universe have lines of light instead of stars?

I am amazingly well equipped to investigate that question, with senses that range from radio through X-ray, and I have nothing else to do for the next thousand years or so. So I take a spectrum of the light from the glowing red cylinder.

I have no expectation that the spectrum will reveal anything I can interpret, but oddly, it looks normal. Impossibly, it looks like the spectrum of a star.

The computer can even identify, from its data of millions of spectra, precisely which star. The light from the cylinder has the spectral signature of Wolf-562.

Coincidence? It cannot possibly be coincidence, out of billions of possible spectra, that this glowing sword in the sky has exactly the spectrum of the star that should have been there. There can be no other conclusion but that the cylinder *is* Wolf-562.

I take a few more spectra, this time picking at random three of the lines of light in the sky, and the computer analyzes them for me. A bright one: the spectrum of 61 Virginis. A dimmer one: a match to Wolf-1061. A blue-white streak: Vega.

The lines in the sky are stars.

What does this mean?

I'm not in another universe. I am in *our* universe, but the universe has been transformed. Could the collision of a wormhole with a black hole destroy our entire universe, stretching suns like taffy into infinite straight lines? Impossible. Even if it had, I would still see far-away stars as dots, since the light from them has been traveling for hundreds of years.

The universe cannot have changed. Therefore, by logic, it must be *me* who has been transformed.

Having figured out this much, the only possible answer is obvious.

When the mathematicians describe the passage across the event horizon of a black hole, they say that the space and time directions switch identity. I had always thought this only a mathematical oddity, but if it were true, if I had rotated when I passed the event horizon, and was now perceiving time as a direction in space, and one of the space axes as time—this would explain everything. Stars extend from billions of years into the past to long into the future; perceiving time as space, I see lines of light. If I were to come closer and find one of the rocky planets of Wolf-562, it would look like a braid around the star, a helix of solid rock. Could I land on it? How would I interact with a world where what I perceive as time is a direction in space?

My physicist persona doesn't like this explanation, but is at a loss to find a better one. In this strange sideways existence, I must be violating the conservation laws of physics like mad, but the persona could find no other hypothesis and must reluctantly agree: time is rotated into space.

To anybody outside, I must look like a string, a knobby long rope with one end at the wormhole and the other at my death, wherever that might be. But nobody could see me fast enough, since with no extension in time I must only be a transient event that bursts everywhere into existence and vanishes at the same instant. There is no way I can signal, no way I can communicate—

Or? Time, to me, is now a direction I can travel in as simply as using my rocket. I could find a planet, travel parallel to the direction of the surface—

But, no, all I could do would be to appear to the inhabitants briefly as a disk, a cross-section of myself, infinitely thin. There is no way I could communicate.

But I can travel in time, if I want. Is there any way I can use this?

Wait. If I have rotated from space into time, then there is one direction in space that I cannot travel. Which direction is that? The direction that used to be away from the black hole.

Interesting thoughts, but not ones which help me much. To return, I need to once again flip space and time. I could dive into a black hole. This would again rotate space and time, but it wouldn't do me any good: once I left the black hole—if I could leave the black hole—nothing would change.

Unless there were a wormhole inside the black hole, falling inward to destruction just at the same instant I was there? But the only wormhole that has fallen into a black hole was already destroyed. Unless, could I travel forward in time? Surely some day the research team would drop a new wormhole into the black hole—

Idiot. Of course there's a solution. Time is a spacelike dimension to me, so I can travel either direction in time now, forward or back. I need only to move back to an instant just after the wormhole passed through the event horizon, and, applying full thrust, shoot through. The very moment that my original self shoots through the wormhole to escape the singularity, I can pass through the opposite direction, and rotate myself back into the real universe.

The station at Virgo black hole is forty light years away, and I don't dare use the original wormhole to reach it. My spacetime-rotated body must be an elongated snake in this version of space-time, and I do not wish to find out what a wormhole passage will do to it until I have no other choice. Still, that is no problem for me. Even with barely enough fuel to thrust for a few microseconds, I can reach an appreciable fraction of light-speed, and I can slow down my brain to make the trip appear only an instant.

To an outside observer, it takes literally no time at all.

"No," says the psych tech, when I ask her. "There's no law that compels you to uplink back into your original. You're a free human being. Your original can't force you."

"Great," I say. Soon I'm going to have to arrange to get a biological body built for myself. This one is superb, but it's a disadvantage in social intercourse being only a millimeter tall.

The transition back to real space worked perfectly. Once I figured out how to navigate in time-rotated space, it had been easy enough to find the wormhole and the exact instant it had penetrated the event horizon.

"Are you going to link your experiences to public domain?" the tech asks. "I think he would like to see what you experienced. Musta been pretty incredible."

"Maybe," I said.

"For that matter," the psych tech added, "I'd like to link it, too."

"I'll think about it."

So I am a real human being now, independent of you, my original.

There had been cheers and celebrations when I had emerged from the wormhole, but nobody had an inkling quite how strange my trip had been until I told them. Even then, I doubt that I was quite believed until the sensor readings and computer logs of *Huis Clos* confirmed my story with hard data.

The physicists had been ecstatic. A new tool to probe time and space. The ability to rotate space into time will open up incredible capabilities. They were already planning new expeditions, not the least of which was a trip to probe right to the singularity itself.

They had been duly impressed with my solution to the problem, although, after an hour of thinking it over, they all agreed it had been quite obvious. "It was lucky," one of them remarked, "that you decided to go through the wormhole from the opposite side, that second time."

"Why?" I asked.

"If you'd gone through the same direction, you'd have rotated an additional ninety degrees, instead of going back."

"So?"

"Reversed the time vector. Turns you into antimatter. First touch of the interstellar medium—Poof."

"Oh," I said. I hadn't thought of that. It made me feel a little less clever.

Now that the mission is over, I have no purpose, no direction for my existence. The future is empty, the black hole that we all must travel into. I will get a biological body, yes, and embark on the process of finding out who I am. Maybe, I think, this is a task that everybody has to do.

And then I will meet you. With luck, perhaps I'll even like you.

And maybe, if I should like you enough, and I feel confident, I'll decide to upload you into myself, and once more, we will again be one.

The Furthest Horizon

ACKNOWLEDGMENTS

Acknowledgment is made for permission to print the following material:

"Guyal of Sfere," by Jack Vance. Copyright © 1950 by Hillman Publications, Inc.; copyright renewed © 1978 by Jack Vance. First published in *The Dying Earth* (Hillman), 1950. Reprinted by permission of the author and the author's agent, Ralph M. Vicinanza, Ltd.

"Old Hundredth," by Brian W. Aldiss. Copyright © 1960 by Brian W. Aldiss. First published in *New Worlds,* November 1960. Reprinted by permission of the author.

"Alpha Ralpha Boulevard," by Cordwainer Smith. Copyright © 1961 by Mercury Press, Inc; copyright © 1963 by Cordwainer Smith. First published in *The Magazine of Fantasy & Science Fiction,* June 1961. Reprinted by permission of the author's estate and the agents for the estate, Scott Meredith Literary Associates, Inc., 845 Third Avenue, New York, NY 10022.

"Day Million," by Frederik Pohl. Copyright © 1966 by Rogue Magazine. First published in *Rogue Magazine,* February 1966. Reprinted by permission of the author.

"Bumberboom," by Avram Davidson. Copyright © 1966 by Mercury Press, Inc. First published in *The Magazine of Fantasy & Science Fiction,* December 1966. Reprinted by permission of the author's estate and the executor of the estate, Grania Davis.

"Coranda," by Keith Roberts. Copyright © 1967 by New Worlds. First published in *New Worlds,* January 1967. Reprinted by permission of the author and the author's agents, The Owlswick Literary Agency.

CONTENTS

PREFACE

Most science fiction takes place in the future, but even within the genre, few writers have ever had the imagination, poetic skills, and visionary scope to write convincingly about the *really* far future, and stories of that sort, which usually take place at least thousands and often millions of years from now, are among the rarest in science fiction.

Of course, the very *idea* of the far future, of a time thousands or millions of years removed from our own present day, is itself comparatively recent. To postulate a future millions of years from now, you first have to have a sense of a *past* that stretches millions of years behind us, an intuition into what has been called "deep time," the kind of time, measured out in geological eras, in which mountains rise and fall, rock is laid down in patiently accumulating strata at the bottom of the sea before being thrust up into the air as naked new peaks, continents drift lazily around the globe, whole species of animals die, and new species evolve to replace them. When the officially sanctioned concept of the age of the Earth is that the Earth is no more than 6,000 years old (Creation having happened at 9:00 A.M. on October 26, 4004 B.C., according to the calculations of Bishop Ussher in the seventeenth century), and when it's intensely controversial, if not downright dangerous, to declare otherwise, little thinking about either the really distant past or the really far future gets done (or if it does, it doesn't get *talked* about much in public).

The idea of deep time, of a past that stretches back for millions and millions of years, rather than a few thousand, is a concept that really doesn't begin to crop up in public discourse and scientific debate until the late eighteenth and early nineteenth centuries, when people such as James Hutton, Charles Lyell, Jean Louis Agassiz (with his then-radical concept of an Ice Age, with the face of Europe covered by and reshaped by immense mile-thick glaciers instead of by Noah's Flood), and Charles Darwin (whose *On the Origin of Species* proposed not only that species could become extinct—itself a fiercely controversial, much-debated concept—but also that all species *evolved,* the incremental result of many small changes over a period of time that certainly must have been immensely longer than any span imagined by Bishop Ussher) launched the first serious challenges to the concept of the Earth as a place only six thousand years old, gradually beginning to replace it with a vision of an Earth that was countless millions of years old—a span of time so staggeringly huge, so dismayingly vast, that it is difficult for the human mind, used to measuring things on the mayfly scale of our own eye-blink lives, to even grasp it.

It's probable that you have to have an understanding of this concept of deep time, though, of time stretching endlessly back into the past, before it's even possible to conceive of the idea of the *far future*, to wrap your mind around the concept that time will continue on *past* the current day and keep on going for millions of years more . . . a concept that, through extrapolation, leads inevitably to the realization that changes as sweeping and dramatic as those that took place in remote geological ages past will *continue* to happen in the future—that the Earth of the future will be as radically different from the Earth of today as today's Earth is from the Earth of the Cretaceous or the Mesozoic.

That being so, it's not surprising that it isn't until 1895, after the concept of deep time had become part of the intellectual/scientific discourse of the day, that we get the first clear vision of the far future in fiction, from H. G. Wells's *The Time Machine*, as the Time Traveller presses ever onward through time:

> . . . *the dim outlines of a desolate beach grew visible.*
>
> *I stopped very gently and sat upon the Time Machine, looking round. The sky was no longer blue. Northeastward it was inky black, and out of the blackness shone brightly and steadily the pale white stars. Overhead it was a deep Indian red and starless, and southeastward it grew brighter to a glowing scarlet where, cut by the horizon, lay the huge hull of the sun, red and motionless.*
>
> *. . . I cannot convey the sense of abominable desolation that hung over the world. The red eastern sky, the northward blackness, the salt Dead Sea, the stony beach crawling with these foul, slow-stirring monsters [giant crab-like creatures], the uniform poisonous-looking green of the lichenous plants, the thin air that hurts one's lungs: all contributed to an appalling effect. I moved on a hundred years, and there was the same red sun—a little larger, a little duller—the same dying sea, the same chill air, and the same crowd of earthy crustacea creeping in and out among the green weed and the red rocks. . . .*
>
> *So I traveled, stopping ever and again, in great strides of a thousand years or more, drawn on by the mystery of the earth's fate, watching with a strange fascination the sun grow larger and duller in the westward sky, and the life of the old earth ebb away . . .*

He ends up at last in bitter cold and near-total "great darkness" on the same desolate beach, now empty even of crawling crab-things. He is nauseated and sick, and he can hardly breathe. He can't go on. He can penetrate no further into the future, having reached Earth's furthest horizon, the End of Time. Appalled by the "remote and awful twilight" of the distant future, he flees back toward the warmer and more hospitable past.

Although Wells himself was certainly influenced by thinkers such as Lyell,

Agassiz, and Darwin, it is this vision of the far future, concentrated and intensified through the lens of fiction, Wells's vision of a bleak and desolate landscape brooded over by the dull red ball of the dying sun, that would for the next hundred years be the dominant vision of what the far future would be like—and which, for the most part, is still the dominant vision even today. It's possible to trace that vision through early works such as William Hope Hodgson's *The Night Land* and *The House on the Borderland* to J. B. S. Haldane's "The Last Judgement" and Olaf Stapledon's monumental (and extravagantly imaginative) *Last and First Men*, and on to the point where it enters the hothouse of the genre SF market in the early thirties via stories such as John W. Campbell's classic "Twilight" (written under the pseudonym of Don A. Stuart) and, perhaps even more significant, the *Zothique* stories of Clark Ashton Smith (which would go on to influence directly the work of Jack Vance in the fifties, whose work would then go on to influence directly Gene Wolfe in the eighties, whose work . . . and so on). With startling rapidity after that, we quickly come to the first great "modern" far-future SF novel (and still one of the very best), Arthur C. Clarke's *Against the Fall of Night,* in 1948.

Which brings us down to the territory of this anthology, which covers the years 1950 to 1998, an arbitrary period, chosen mostly for symmetry, but one that is not wholly indefensible: By 1950, the SF world was beginning to get back into full swing again after the partial interregnum of World War II, and the Campbellian Revolution in science fiction—circa 1939, when the new editor of *Astounding* magazine, John W. Campbell, began downplaying the melodramatic pulp stuff in favor of more thoughtful material that actually made a stab at rigor and scientific accuracy—had already taken place, with its lessons in the process of being absorbed and applied. Although "literary" writers such as Wells had been able to play in the far future only a few decades before, from this point on the development of the far-future story would take place almost entirely within the boundaries of the SF genre; indeed, the really far future is literary territory almost totally ignored by "mainstream" writers to this very day, even here, nearly to the beginning of a new millennium.

Perhaps this is not surprising, since, as I said in opening, even within science fiction itself, even within a genre whose writers are trained to think about the future and the majority of stories are set at least some distance into it, stories dealing with the really far future are, if not quite as rare as hens' teeth, then at least *comparatively* rare. Perhaps this is because the special scope and sweep of vision called for to conjure up an evocative and poetically intense portrait of the far future calls for a degree—and a *kind*—of imagination rare even among SF writers. (Why so *many* Brits write far-future stories, and why so *few* women do, way out of proportion demographically in both cases, I'll leave for wiser critics than me to try to puzzle out.)

This anthology, then, gives you an overview of the evolution of the far-future story—and of the evolution of ideas about what the far future will be like—from the middle of the twentieth century almost to the beginning of the twenty-first. Not at all incidentally, it also brings you some of the most vivid, evocative, entertaining, and mind-stretchingly imaginative science fiction ever written, stories that will take you so far into the future that our familiar everyday world, everything that we see around us, all our history and culture, everything we *are*, is at best a fading distant memory, blurred almost to nothing by time—if, indeed, it is remembered at all . . .

if, indeed, our remote descendants in that future are even *human* at all, as we today would understand the term. . . .

And, far from having to pant and shiver on that desolate terminal beach, you won't even have to get up from your chair!

Enjoy.

Guyal of Sfere

JACK VANCE

Here's one of the classic visions of the far future, from Jack Vance's *The Dying Earth*, taking us millions of years into the future, to the Earth at the end of time, when the sun is growing cold and the world is on the brink of being plunged into eternal Night, grues and deodands creep through the haunted forests, and technology has (as per Arthur C. Clarke's famous dictum) become indistinguishable from magic . . .

Born in San Francisco in 1920, Jack Vance served throughout World War II in the U.S. Merchant Navy. Most of the individual stories that would later be melded into his first novel, *The Dying Earth*, were written while Vance was at sea—he was unable to sell them, a problem he would also have with the book itself, the market for fantasy being almost nonexistent at the time. *The Dying Earth* was eventually published in an obscure edition in 1950 by a small semi-professional press, went out of print almost immediately, and remained out of print for more than a decade thereafter. Nevertheless, this slender little volume of stories became an underground cult classic, and was of immense evolutionary importance to the development of both modern fantasy *and* modern science fiction, as well as being one of the keystone works in the development of the hybrid form sometimes referred to as science-fantasy. Although it itself was clearly influenced by earlier work such as Clark Ashton Smith's *Zothique* and William Hope Hodgson's *The Night Land*, the effect of *The Dying Earth* on future generations of writers is incalculable: for one example, out of many, *The Dying Earth* is one of the most recognizable influences on Gene Wolfe's *The Book of the New Sun*. (Wolfe has said, for instance, that *The Book of Gold*, which is mentioned by Severian, is supposed to be *The Dying Earth*.) Vance returned to this milieu in 1965, with a series of stories that would be melded into *The Eyes of the Overworld*, and, in the early eighties, returned yet again with *Cugel's Saga* and *Rhialto the Marvellous*—taken together, *The Dying Earth* and the three volumes of *Cugel* stories represent one of the most impressive achievements in science-fantasy.

Vance is also a towering ancestral figure in science fiction proper, where he has produced some of the very best work of the last forty years. His most famous SF novels—*The Dragon Masters, The Last Castle, Big Planet, Emphyrio*, the five-

468 EXPLORING THE HORIZONS
468 EXPLORING THE HORIZONS468   EXPLORING THE HORIZONS
468 EXPLORING THE HORIZONS

468 EXPLORING THE HORIZONSvolume *Demon Princes* series (the best known of which are *The Star King* and *The Killing Machine*), *Blue World, The Anome, The Languages of Pao,* among many others—as well as dazzling short works such as "The New Prime," "The Miracle Workers," "The Last Castle," and "The Moon Moth" have had such a widespread impact that writers describing distant worlds and alien societies with strange alien customs write inevitably in the shadow of Vance: no one in the history of the field has brought more intelligence, imagination, or inexhaustible fertility of invention to that theme than he has, a fertility that shows no sign of slackening even here at the end of the nineties, with recent books such as *Night Lamp* as richly and lushly imaginative as the stuff he was writing in the fifties; even ostensible potboilers such as his *Planet of Adventure* series are full of vivid and richly portrayed alien societies and bizarre and often profoundly disturbing insights into the ways in which human psychology might be altered by immersion in alien values and cultural systems.

Vance has won two Hugo Awards, a Nebula Award, two World Fantasy Awards (one the prestigious Life Achievement Award), a Grandmaster Nebula Award for Life Achievement, and the Edgar Award for best mystery novel. His other books include *The Palace of Love, City of the Chasch, To Live Forever, The Dirdir, The Pnume, The Gray Prince, The Brave Free Men, Space Opera, Showboat World, Marune: Alastor 933, Wyst: Alastor 1716, Lyonesse, The Green Pearl, Madouc, Araminta Station, Ecce and Olde Earth,* and *Throy,* among many others. His short fiction has been collected in *Eight Fantasms and Magics, The Best of Jack Vance, Green Magic, Lost Moons, The Complete Magnus Ridolph, The World Between and Other Stories, The Dark Side of the Moon,* and *The Narrow Land.* His most recent books are an omnibus volume, *Alastor,* collecting three of his *Alastor* novels, and the new novels *Night Lamp* and *Ports of Call.*

Guyal of Sfere had been born one apart from his fellows and early proved vexation for his sire. Normal in outward configuration, there existed within his mind a void which ached for nourishment. It was as if a spell had been cast upon his birth, a harassment visited on the child in a spirit of sardonic mockery, so that every occurrence, *no* matter how trifling, became a source of wonder. Even as young as four seasons he was expounding such inquiries as:

"Why do squares have more sides than triangles?"

"How will we see when the sun goes dark?"

"Do flowers grow under the ocean?"

"Do stars hiss and sizzle when rain comes by night?"

To which his impatient sire gave answers:

"So it was ordained by the Pragmatica; squares and triangles must obey the rote."

"We will be forced to grope and feel our way."

"I have not verified this matter; only the Curator would know."

"Never. The stars are above the rain, higher even than the highest clouds, and swim in a rarified air where rain can never breed."

As Guyal grew to youth, this void in his mind, instead of dwindling becoming sedimented with wax, throbbed with a more violent ache. And so he asked:

"Why do people die when they are killed?"

"Where does beauty vanish when it goes?"

"How long have men lived on Earth?"

"What is beyond the sky?"

To which his sire, biting acerbity back from his lips, would respond:

"Death is the heritage of life; a man's vitality is like air in a bladder. Poinct his bubble and away, away, away, flees life, like the color of fading dream."

"Beauty is a luster which love bestows to guile the eye. Therefore it may be said that only when the brain is without love will the eye look and see no beauty."

"Some say men germinated in the soil like grubs in a corpse; others aver that the first men desired residence and so created Earth by sorcery. The question is shrouded in technicality; only the Curator may answer with exactness."

"An endless waste."

Guyal pondered and postulated, proposed and expounded, until he found himself the subject of surreptitious humor. The demesne was visited by a rumor that a gleft, coming upon Guyal's mother in labor, had stolen part of Guyal's brain, which deficiency he now industriously sought to restore.

Guyal therefore drew himself apart and roamed the grassy hills of Sfere in solitude. But ever was his mind acquisitive, ever did he seek to exhaust the lore of all around him, until at last his father in vexation refused to hear further inquiries, declaring that all knowledge had been known, that the trivial and useless had been discarded, leaving only that residue necessary to a sound man.

At this time Guyal was in his first manhood, a slight but erect youth with wide clear eyes, a penchant for severely elegant dress, a firm somewhat compressed mouth.

Hearing his father's angry statement, Guyal said, "One more question, then I ask no more."

"Speak," declared his father. "One more question I grant you."

"You have often referred me to the Curator; who is he, and where may I find him?"

A moment the father scrutinized the son whom he now considered past the verge of madness. Then he responded in a quiet voice, "The Curator guards the Museum of Man, which antique legend places in the Land of the Falling Wall— beyond the mountains of Fer Aquila and north of Ascolais. It is not certain that either Curator or Museum still exist; still it would seem that if the Curator knows all things, as is the legend, then surely he would know the wizardly foil to death."

Guyal said, "I would seek the Curator and the Museum of Man, that I likewise may know all things."

The father said with patience, "I will bestow on you my fine white horse, my Expansible Egg for your shelter, my Scintillant Dagger to illuminate the night. In addition, I lay a blessing along the trail, and danger will slide you by so long as you never wander aside."

Guyal quelled the hundred new questions at his tongue, including an inquisition as to where his father had learned these manifestations of sorcery, and accepted the gifts: the horse, the magic shelter, the dagger with the luminous pommel, and the blessing to guard him from the disadvantageous circumstances which plagued those who travelled the dim trails of Ascolais.

He caparisoned the horse, honed the dagger, cast a last glance around the old manse at Sfere, and set forth to the north.

He ferried the River Scaum on an old barge. Aboard the barge, and so off the

trail, the blessing lost its cogency and in fact seemed to stimulate a counterinflu-
ence, so that the barge-tender, who coveted Guyal's rich accoutrements, struck out
suddenly with his cudgel. Guyal fended off the blow and tripped the man into the
murky deep.

Mounting the north bank of the Scaum he saw ahead the Porphiron Scar, the
dark poplars and white columns of Kaiin, the dull gleam of Sanreale Bay.

Wandering the crumbled streets, he put the languid inhabitants such a spate of
questions that one in wry jocularity commended him to a professional augur.

This, a lank hermetic with red-rimmed eyes and a stained white beard, dwelled
in a booth painted with the Signs of the Aumoklopelastianic Cabal.

"What are your fees?" inquired Guyal cautiously.

"I respond to three questions," stated the augur. "For twenty terces I phrase
the answer in clear and decisive language; for ten I use a professional cant, which
occasionally admits of ambiguity; for five I speak a parable which you must interpret as you will; and for one terce I babble in an unknown tongue."

"First I must inquire, how profound is your knowledge?"

"I know all," responded the augur. "The secrets of red and the secrets of black,
the lost spells of Grand Motholam, the way of the fish and the voice of the bird."

"And where have you learned all these things?"

"By pure induction," explained the augur. "I retire into my booth, I closet
myself with never a glint of light and, so sequestered, I resolve the mysteries of
the world."

"Controlling such efficacy," ventured Guyal, "why do you live so meagerly,
with not an ounce of fat to your frame and miserable rags to your back?"

The augur stood back in fury. "Go along with you! Already I have wasted fifty
terces of wisdom on you who have never a copper to your pouch. If you desire
free enlightenment," and he cackled in mirth, "seek out the Curator." He sheltered
himself in his booth.

Guyal took lodging for the night, and in the morning went on his way. The
trail made a wide detour around the haunted ruins of Old Town, then took to the
fabulous forest.

For many a day Guyal rode toward the north. By night he surrounded himself
and his horse in the Expansible Egg, a membrane impermeable to thew, claw,
pressure, sound, and chill, and rested at ease despite the avid creatures of the dark.

The dull sun fell behind; the days grew wan and the nights bitter, and at last
the crags of Fer Aquila showed as a tracing on the north horizon. In this region
the forest was a scattering of phalurge and daobado; these last, massive construc-
tions of heavy bronze branches clumped with dark balls of foliage. Beside a giant
of the species Guyal came upon a village of turf huts. A group of surly louts
appeared and surrounded him with expressions of curiosity. Guyal, no less than
the villagers, had questions to ask, but none would speak till the hetman strode
up—a burly man in a shaggy fur hat, a cloak of brown fur, and a bristling beard,
so that it was hard to see where one ended and the other began. He exuded a rancid
odor which displeased Guyal, although from motives of courtesy, he took pains to
keep his distaste concealed.

"Where go you?" asked the hetman.

"I wish to cross the mountains to the Museum of Man," said Guyal. "Which
way does the trail lead?"

The hetman pointed out a notch on the silhouette of the mountains. "There is Omona Gap, which is the shortest and best route, though there is no trail. None comes and none goes, since when you pass the Gap, you walk an unknown land. And with no traffic there manifestly need be no trail."

The news did not cheer Guyal.

"How then is it known that Omona Gap is on the way to the Museum?"

The hetman shrugged. "Such is our tradition."

Guyal turned his head at a hoarse snuffling and saw a pen of woven wattles. In a litter of filth and matted straw stood a number of hulking men eight or nine feet tall. They were naked, with wax-colored faces, shocks of dirty yellow hair and watery blue eyes. As Guyal watched, one of them ambled to a trough and noisily began to gulp gray mash.

Guyal said, "What manner of things are these?"

The hetman guffawed at Guyal's ignorance. "They are oasts, naturally." He indicated Guyal's white horse. "Never have I seen a stranger oast than the one you bestride. Ours carry us more easily and appear to be less vicious; in addition, no flesh is more delicious than oast properly braised and kettled."

Standing close he fondled the metal of Guyal's saddle and the red and yellow embroidered quilt. "Your deckings however are rich and of superb quality. I will therefore bestow you my large and weighty oast in return for this creature with its accoutrements."

Guyal politely declared himself satisfied with his present mount, and the hetman shrugged his shoulders.

A horn sounded. The hetman looked about, then turned back to Guyal. "Food is prepared; will you eat?"

Guyal glanced toward the oast-pen. "I am not presently hungry, and I must hasten forward. However, I am grateful for your kindness."

He departed; as he passed under the arch of the great daobado he turned a glance back toward the village. There seemed an unwonted activity among the huts. Remembering the hetman's covetous touch at his saddle, and aware that no longer did he ride the trail, Guyal urged his horse forward and pounded fast under the trees.

As he neared the foothills the forest dwindled to a savanna, floored with a dull, jointed grass that creaked under the horse's hooves. Guyal glanced up and down the plain. The sun wallowed in the southwest; the light across the plain was dim and watery. Another hour, then the dark night of the latter-day Earth. Guyal twisted in the saddle, looked behind him. Four oasts, carrying men on their shoulders, came trotting from the forest. Sighting Guyal they broke into a lumbering run. With a crawling skin Guyal wheeled his horse and eased the reins; the white horse loped across the plain toward Omona Gap. Behind ran the oasts, bestraddled by the fur-cloaked villagers.

The sun touched the horizon. Guyal looked back to his pursuers, bounding now a mile behind, then turned his gaze to the forest ahead. An ill place to ride by night, but where was his choice?

The foliage loomed above him; he passed under the first gnarled daobados. He changed directions, turned once, twice, a third time, then stood his horse to listen. Far away a crashing in the brake reached his ears. Guyal dismounted, led the horse into a deep hollow where a bank of foliage made a screen. Presently the four men on their hulking oasts passed across the afterglow, black double-shapes in attitudes suggestive of ill-temper and disappointment.

The thud and pad of feet dwindled and died.

The horse moved restlessly; the foliage rustled.

A damp air passed down the hollow and chilled the back of Guyal's neck. Darkness stood in the hollow like ink in a basin.

Guyal urged his horse up to the height and sat listening. Far down the wind he heard a hoarse call. Turning in the opposite direction he let the horse choose its own path.

Branches and boughs knit patterns on the fading sky; the air smelt of moss and mold. The horse stopped short. Guyal, tensing in every muscle, leaned a little forward. The air was still, uncanny; his eyes could plumb not ten feet into the black. Somewhere near was death—grinding death, to come as a sudden shock.

Sweating cold, afraid to stir a muscle, he forced himself to dismount. Stiffly he slid from the saddle, brought forth the Expansible Egg and flung it around his horse and himself. Safety. Guyal released the pressure of his breath.

Guyal of Sfere had lost his way in a land of wind and naked crags. As night came he slouched numbly in the saddle while his horse took him where it would. Somewhere the ancient way through Omona Gap led to the northern tundra, but now, under a chilly overcast, north, east, south, and west were alike.

The horse halted and Guyal found himself at the brink of a quiet valley. Guyal leaned forward, staring. Below spread a dark city. Mist blew along the streets; the afterglow fell dull on slate roofs.

The horse snorted and scraped the stony ground.

"A strange town," said Guyal, "with no lights, no sound, no smell of smoke. . . . Doubtless an abandoned ruin from ancient times. . . ."

He debated descending to the streets. At times the old ruins were haunted by peculiar distillations. On the other hand such a ruin might be joined to the tundra by a trail. With this thought in mind he started his horse down the slope.

He entered the town and the hooves rang loud and sharp on the cobbles. The buildings were stone and dark mortar and seemed in uncommonly good preservation. A few lintels had cracked and sagged, a few walls gaped open, but for the most part the stone houses had successfully met the gnaw of time. . . . Guyal scented smoke. Did people live here still? He would proceed with caution.

Before a building which seemed to be a hostelry flowers bloomed in an urn. Guyal reined his horse and reflected that flowers were rarely cherished by persons of hostile disposition.

"Hello!" he called—once, twice.

No heads peered from the doors, no orange flicker brightened the windows. Guyal slowly turned and rode on.

The street widened and twisted toward a large hall, where Guyal saw a light. The building had a high façade, broken by four large windows, each shielded by two blinds of corroded bronze filigree. A marble balustrade fronting the terrace shimmered bone-white behind, a portal of massive wood stood slightly ajar; from here came the beam of light and also a strain of music.

Guyal of Sfere, halting, gazed not at the house nor at the light through the door. He dismounted and bowed to the young woman who sat pensively along the course of the balustrade. Though it was very cold, she wore but a simple gown, yellow-orange, a daffodil's color. Topaz hair fell loose to her shoulders and gave her face a cast of gravity and thoughtfulness.

As Guyal straightened from his greeting, the woman nodded, smiled slightly, and absently fingered the hair by her cheek.

"A bitter night for travelers."

"A bitter night for musing on the stars," responded Guyal.

She smiled again. "I am not cold. I sit and dream. . . . I listen to the music."

"What place is this?" inquired Guyal, looking up the street, down the street, and once more to the girl. "Are there any here but yourself?"

"This is Carchasel," said the girl, "abandoned by all ten thousand years ago. Only I and my aged uncle live here, finding this place a refuge from the Saponids of the tundra." She rose to her feet. "But you are cold and weary," said the girl, "and I keep you standing in the street. Our hospitality is yours."

"Which I gladly accept," said Guyal, "First I must stable my horse."

"He will be content in the house yonder. We have no stable." She indicated a long stone building with a door opening into blackness.

Guyal took the white horse thither and removed the bridle and saddle; then, standing in the doorway, he listened to the music he had noted before, the piping of an ancient air.

"Strange," he muttered, stroking the horse's muzzle. "The uncle plays music, the girl stares alone at the stars of the night. . . ." He considered a moment. "I may be over-suspicious. If witch she be, there is naught to be gained from me. If they be simple refugees as she says, and lovers of music, they may enjoy the airs from Ascolais; it will repay, in some measure, their hospitality." He reached into his saddlebag, brought forth his flute, and tucked it into his boot.

He returned to where the girl awaited him.

"You have not told me your name," she reminded him, "that I may introduce you to my uncle."

"I am Guyal of Sfere, by the River Scaum in Ascolais. And you?"

She smiled, pushing the portal wider. Warm yellow light fell into the cobbled street.

"I have no name. I need none. There has never been any but my uncle; and when he speaks there is no one to answer but I."

Guyal stared in astonishment; then, deeming his wonder too apparent for courtesy he controlled his expression. Perhaps she suspected him of wizardry and feared to pronounce her name lest he make magic with it.

They entered a flagged hall and the sound of piping grew louder.

"I will call you Ameth, if I may," said Guyal. "That is a flower of the south, as golden and kind as you seem to be."

She nodded. "You may call me Ameth."

They entered a tapestry-hung chamber. A great fire glowed at one wall, and here stood a table bearing food. On a bench sat the musician—an old man, untidy, unkempt. White hair hung tangled down his back; his beard, in no better case, was dirty and yellow. He wore a ragged kirtle, by no means clean, and the leather of his sandals had broken into dry cracks. Strangely, he did not take the flute from his mouth but kept up his piping; and the girl in yellow, so Guyal noted, seemed to move in rhythm to the tones.

"Uncle Ludowik," she cried in a gay voice, "I bring you a guest, Sir Guyal of Sfere."

Guyal looked into the man's face and wondered. The eyes, though somewhat rheumy with age, were gray and intelligent and, so Guyal thought, bright with a strange joy, which further puzzled Guyal, for the lines of the face indicated nothing other than years of misery.

"Perhaps you play?" inquired Ameth. "My uncle is a great musician, and this is his time for music. He has kept the routine for many years. . . ." She turned and smiled at Ludowik the musician, who jerked his head and contrived an acquiescent grin, never taking the flute from his mouth.

Ameth motioned to the bounteous table. "Eat, Guyal, and I will pour you wine. Afterwards perhaps you will play the flute for us."

"Gladly," said Guyal, and he noticed how the joy on Ludowik's face grew more apparent, quivering around the corners of his mouth.

He ate and Ameth poured him golden wine until his head went to reeling. And never did Ludowik cease his piping—a tender melody of running water, then a grave tune that told of the lost ocean to the west, then a simple melody such as a child might sing at his games. Guyal noted with wonder how Ameth fitted her mood to the music—grave and gay as the music led her. Strange! thought Guyal. But then—people thus isolated were apt to develop peculiar mannerisms, and they seemed kindly withal.

He finished his meal and stood erect, steadying himself against the table. Ludowik was lilting a melody of glass birds swinging round and round in the sunlight. Ameth came dancing over to him and stood close, so that he smelled the perfume of her loose golden hair. Her face was happy and wild. . . . Peculiar how Ludowik watched so grimly, and yet without a word. Perhaps he misdoubted a stranger's intent. Still . . .

"Now," breathed Ameth, "perhaps you will play the flute; you are strong and young." Then she said, as she saw Guyal's eyes widen. "I mean you will play on the flute for old Uncle Ludowik, and he will be happy and go off to bed—and then we will sit and talk far into the night."

"Gladly will I play the flute," said Guyal. "I am accounted quite skillful at my home in Sfere." Glancing at Ludowik, he surprised an expression of crazy gladness. Marvelous that a man should be so fond of music!

"Then—play!" breathed Ameth, urging him a little toward Ludowik and the flute.

"Perhaps," suggested Guyal, "I had better wait till your uncle pauses. I would seem discourteous—"

"No, as soon as you indicate that you wish to play, he will let off. Merely take the flute. You see," she confided, "he is rather deaf."

"Very well," said Guyal, "except that I have my own flute." And he brought it out from his boot. "Why—what is the matter?" For a change had come over the girl and the old man. A quick light had risen in her eyes, and Ludowik's strange gladness had gone, and there was but dull hopelessness in his eyes, stupid resignation.

Guyal slowly stood back, bewildered. "Do you not wish me to play?"

There was a pause. "Of course," said Ameth, young and charming once more. "But I'm sure that Uncle Ludowik would enjoy hearing you play his flute. He is accustomed to the pitch; another scale might be unfamiliar. . . ."

Ludowik nodded, and hope again shone in the rheumy old eyes. It was indeed a fine flute, Guyal saw, a rich piece of white metal, chased and set with gold, and Ludowik clutched this flute as if he would never let go.

"Take the flute," suggested Ameth. "He will not mind in the least." Ludowik shook his head, to signify the absence of objection. But Guyal, noting with distaste the long, stained beard, also shook his head. "I can play any scale, any tone on my flute. There is no need for me to use that of your uncle and possibly distress him. Listen," and he raised his instrument. "Here is a song of Kaiin, called 'The Opal, the Pearl, and the Peacock.' "

He put the pipe to his lips and began to play, very skillfully indeed, and Ludowik followed him, filling in gaps, making chords. Ameth, forgetting her vexation, listened with eyes half closed, and moved her arm to the rhythm.

"Did you enjoy that?" asked Guyal when he had finished.

"Very much. Perhaps you would try it on Uncle Ludowik's flute? It is a fine flute to play, very soft and easy to the breath."

"No," said Guyal, with sudden obstinacy. "I am able to play only my own instrument." He blew again, and it was a dance of the festival, a quirking carnival air. Ludowik, playing with supernal skill, ran merry phrases as might fit, and Ameth, carried away by the rhythm, danced a dance of her own, a merry step in time to the music.

Guyal played a tarantella of the peasant folk, and Ameth danced wilder and faster, flung her arms, wheeled, jerked her head in a fine display. And Ludowik's flute played a brilliant obbligato, hurtling over, now under, chording, veering, warping little silver strings of sound around Guyal's melody, adding urgent little grace-phrases.

Ludowik's eyes now clung to the whirling figure of the dancing girl. And suddenly he struck up a theme of his own, a tune of wildest abandon, of a frenzied beating rhythm; and Guyal, carried away by the force of the music, blew as he never had blown before, invented trills and runs, gyrating arpeggios, blew high and shrill, loud and fast and clear.

It was as nothing to Ludowik's music. His eyes were starting; sweat streamed from his seamed old forehead; his flute tore the air into shreds.

Ameth danced frenzy; she was no longer beautiful, she appeared grotesque and unfamiliar. The music became something more than the senses could bear. Guyal's vision turned pink and gray; he saw Ameth fall in a faint, in a foaming fit; and Ludowik, fiery-eyed, staggered erect, hobbled to her body and began a terrible intense concord, slow measures of most solemn and frightening meaning.

Ludowik played death.

Guyal of Sfere turned and ran wide-eyed from the hall. Ludowik, never noticing, continued his terrible piping, played as if every note were a skewer through the twitching girl's shoulder blades.

Guyal ran through the night and cold air bit at him like sleet. He burst into the shed, and the white horse nickered. On with the saddle, on with the bridle, away down the streets of old Carchasel, along the starlit cobbles, past the gaping black windows, away from the music of death!

Guyal of Sfere galloped up the mountain with the stars in his face, and not until he came to the shoulder did he turn in the saddle to look back.

The verging of dawn trembled into the stony valley. Where was Carchasel? There was no city, only a crumble of ruins. . . .

Hark! A far sound?

No. All was silence.

And yet . . .

Only dark stones on the floor of the valley.

Guyal, fixed of eye, turned and went his way along the trail which stretched north before him.

The walls of the defile were gray granite, stained dull scarlet and black by lichen. The horse's hooves made a clop-clop-clop on the stone. After the sleepless night Guyal began to sag in the saddle. He resolved to round one more bend in the trail and then take rest.

The rock looming above hid the sky. The trail twisted around a shoulder of rock; ahead shone a patch of indigo. One more turning, Guyal told himself. The defile fell open, the mountains were at his back. He looked out across a hundred miles of steppe: a land shaded with subtle colors, fading and melting into the haze at the horizon. To the east he saw a lone eminence cloaked by a a dark company of trees, the glisten of a lake at its foot. To the west a ranked mass of gray-white ruins was barely discernible. The Museum of Man? . . . Guyal dismounted and sought sleep within the Expansible Egg.

The sun rolled in sad majesty behind the mountains; murk fell across the tundra. Guyal awoke and refreshed himself. He gave meal to his horse, ate dry fruit and bread; then he mounted and rode down the trail. Gloom deepened; the plain sank from sight like a drowned land. Guyal reined his horse. Better, he thought, to ride in the morning. If he lost the trail in the dark, who could tell what he might encounter?

A mournful sound. Guyal turned his face to the sky. A sigh? A moan? . . . Another sound, closer: the rustle of cloth. Guyal cringed into his saddle. Floating slowly across the darkness came a shape robed in white. Under the cowl and glowing with witch-light was a drawn face with eyes like the holes in a skull.

It breathed a sad sound and drifted away.

Guyal drew a shuddering breath and slumped against the pommel. Then he slipped to the ground and established the Egg about himself and his horse; presently, as he lay staring into the dark, sleep came on him and so the night passed.

He awoke before dawn and set forth. The trail was a ribbon of white sand between banks of gray furze; the miles passed swiftly.

As he neared the tree-shrouded hillock he saw roofs through the foliage and smoke rising into the sharp air. And presently to right and left spread fields of spikenard, callow, and mead-apple. Guyal continued with eyes watchful for men.

The trail passed beside a fence of stone and black timber enclosing a region of churned and scorched earth, which Guyal paused to examine. The horse started nervously; Guyal, turning, saw three men who had come quietly upon him: individuals tall and well-formed, somewhat solemn, with golden-ivory skin and jet black hair. Their garments implied an ancient convention: tight suits of maroon leather trimmed with black lace and silver chain, maroon cloth hats crumpled in precise creases, with black leather flaps extended horizontally over each ear. Their attitudes expressed neither threat nor welcome. "Greetings, stranger," said one. "Whither bound?"

"I go as fate directs," replied Guyal cautiously. "You are Saponids?"

"That is our race, though now we are few. Before you is our final city, Issane." He inspected Guyal with frank curiosity. "And what of yourself?"

"I am Guyal of Sfere, which is in Ascolais, far to the south."

The Saponids regarded Guyal with respect. "You have come a long and perilous way."

Guyal looked back at the mountains. "Through the north forests and the wastes of Fer Aquila. At nightfall yesterday I passed through the mountains. In the dark a ghost hovered above till I thought the grave had marked me for its own."

He paused in surprise; his words seemed to have released a powerful emotion in the Saponids. Their features lengthened, their mouths grew white. The spokesman, his polite detachment a trifle diminished, searched the sky. "A ghost. . . . In a white garment, floating on high?"

"Yes; is it a known familiar of the region?"

There was a pause.

"In a certain sense," said the Saponid. "It is a signal of woe. . . . But I interrupt your tale."

"There is little to tell. I took shelter for the night, and this morning I fared down to the plain."

"Were you not molested further? By the Walking Serpent, who ranges the slopes like fate?"

"I saw neither walking serpent nor so much as a lizard; still, a blessing protects my trail and I come to no harm so long as I keep my course."

"Interesting, interesting."

"Now," said Guyal, "permit me to inquire of you, since there is much I would learn; what is this ghost, what event does he commemorate, and what are the portents?"

"You ask beyond my certain knowledge," replied the Saponid cautiously. "Of this ghost it is well not to speak lest our attention reinforce its malignity."

"As you will," replied Guyal. "Perhaps—" He caught his tongue. Before inquiring for the Museum of Man it would be wise to learn in what regard the Saponids held it, lest learning his interest they should seek to deny him knowledge.

"Yes?" inquired the Saponids. "What is your lack?"

Guyal indicated the seared area behind the fence of stone and timber. "What is the cause of this devastation?"

The Saponid looked across the area with a blank expression.

"It is one of the ancient places; so much is known, no more. You will desire to rest and refresh yourself at Issane. Come; we will guide you."

He turned down the trail; Guyal finding neither words nor reasons to reject the idea, urged his horse forward.

The Saponids walked in silence; Guyal, though he seethed with a thousand questions, likewise held his tongue. They skirted a placid lake. The surface mirrored the sky, shoals of reeds, boats in the shape of sickles, with bow and stern curving high from the water.

So they entered Issane: a town of no great pretense. The houses were hewn timber, golden brown, russet, weathered black. The construction was intricate and ornate, the walls rising three stories to steep gables. Pillars and piers were carved with complex designs: meshing ribbons, tendrils, leaves, lizards. The screens that guarded the windows were likewise carved, with foliage patterns, animal faces, radiant stars; rich textures in the mellow wood. Much effort, much expressiveness, had been expended on the carving.

They proceeded up a steep lane under the gloom cast by the trees, and the Saponids came forth to stare. They moved quietly and spoke in low voices, and their garments were of an elegance Guyal had not expected to see on the northern steppe.

One of the men turned to Guyal. "Will you oblige us by waiting until the First Elder is informed, so that he may prepare a suitable reception?"

The request was framed in candid words and with guileless eyes. Guyal thought to perceive ambiguity in the phrasing, but since the hooves of his horse were planted in the center of the road, and since he did not propose leaving the road, Guyal assented with an open face. The Saponids disappeared and Guyal sat musing on the pleasant town perched so high above the plain.

A group of girls came to look at Guyal with curious eyes. Guyal returned the inspection, and sensed a lack about their persons, a discrepancy which he could not instantly identify. They wore graceful garments of woven wool, striped and dyed various colors; they were supple and slender, and seemed not lacking in coquetry. And yet . . .

The Saponid returned. "Now, Sir Guyal, may we proceed?"

Guyal, endeavoring to remove any flavor of suspicion from his words, said, "You will understand that by the very nature of my father's blessing I dare not leave the delineated trail; for then, instantly, I would become liable to any curse placed on me along the way."

The Saponid made an understanding gesture. "Naturally; you follow a sound principle."

Guyal bowed in gratification, and they continued up the road.

A hundred paces and the road leveled, crossing a common planted with small, fluttering, heart-shaped leaves, colored in all shades of purple, red, and black.

The Saponid turned to Guyal. "As a stranger I must caution you never to set foot on the common. It is one of our sacred places, and tradition requires that a severe penalty be exacted for transgressions and sacrilege."

"I note your warning," said Guyal. "I will respectfully obey your law."

They passed a dense thicket; with hideous clamor a bestial shape sprang from concealment, a creature with tremendous fanged jaws. Guyal's horse shied, bolted, sprang out upon the sacred common and trampled the fluttering leaves.

A number of Saponid men rushed forth, grasped the horse, seized Guyal and dragged him from the saddle.

"Wait!" cried Guyal. "What means this? Release me!"

The Saponid who had been his guide advanced, shaking his head in reproach. "Indeed, and only had I just impressed upon you the gravity of such an offense!"

"But the monster frightened my horse!" said Guyal. "I am nowise responsible for this trespass; release me, let us proceed to the reception."

The Saponid said, "I fear that the penalties prescribed by tradition must first come into effect. Your protests, though of superficial plausibility, will not sustain examination. For instance, the creature you term a monster is in reality a harmless domesticated beast. Secondly, I observe the animal you bestride; he will not make a turn or twist without the twitch of the reins. Thirdly, even if your postulates were conceded, you thereby admit to guilt by virtue of negligence and omission. You should have secured a mount less apt to unpredictable action, or upon learning of the sanctitude of the common, you should have considered such a contingency as even now occurred, and therefore dismounted, leading your beast. Therefore, Sir Guyal, though loath, I am forced to believe you guilty of impertinence, impiety, disregard and impudicity. Therefore, as Castellan and Sergeant-Reader of the Litany, so responsible for the detention of law-breakers, I must order you secured, contained, pent, incarcerated and confined until such time as the penalties will be exacted."

"The entire episode is mockery!" raged Guyal. "Are you savages, then, thus to mistreat a lone wayfarer?"

"By no means," replied the Castellan. "We are a civilized people, with customs bequeathed us by the past. Since the past was more glorious than the present, we would show presumption by questioning these laws!"

Guyal fell quiet. "And what are the usual penalties for my act?"

The Castellan made a reassuring motion. "The rote prescribes three acts of penance, which in your case, I am sure will be nominal. But—the forms must be observed, and it is necessary that you be constrained in the Felon's Caseboard." He motioned to the men who held Guyal's arm. "Away with him, cross neither track nor trail, for then your grasp will be nerveless and he will be delivered from justice."

Guyal was pent in a well aired but poorly lighted cellar of stone. The floor he found dry, the ceiling free of crawling insects. He had not been searched, nor had his Scintillant Dagger been removed from his sash. With suspicions crowding his brain he lay on the rush bed and, after a period, slept.

Now ensued the passing of a day. He was given food and drink; and at last the Castellan came to visit him.

"You are indeed fortunate," said the Saponid, "in that, as a witness, I was able to suggest your delinquencies to be more the result of negligence than malice. The last penalties exacted for the crime were stringent; the felon was ordered to perform the following three acts: First, to cut off his toes and sew the severed members into the skin at his neck; second, to revile his forbears for three hours, commencing with a Common Bill of Anathema, including feigned madness and hereditary disease, and at last defiling the hearth of his clan; and third, walking a mile under the lake with leaded shoes in search of the Lost Book of Caraz." And the Castellan regarded Guyal with complacency.

"What deeds must I perform?" inquired Guyal drily.

The Castellan joined the tips of his fingers together. "As I say, the penances are nominal, by decree of the Elder. First, you must swear never again to repeat your crime."

"That I gladly do," said Guyal, and so bound himself.

"Second," said the Castellan with a slight smile, "you must adjudicate at a Grand Pageant of Pulchritude among the maids of the village and select her whom you consider the most beautiful."

"Scarcely an arduous task," commented Guyal. "Why does it fall to my lot?"

The Castellan looked vaguely to the ceiling. "There are a number of concomitants to victory in this contest. . . . Every person in the town would find relations among the participants—a daughter, a sister, a niece—and so would hardly be considered unprejudiced. The charge of favoritism could never be leveled against you; therefore you make an ideal selection for this important post."

Guyal seemed to hear the ring of sincerity in the Saponid's voice; still he wondered why the selection of the town's loveliest was a matter of such import.

"And third?" he inquired.

"That will be revealed after the contest, which occurs this afternoon."

The Saponid departed the cell.

Guyal, who was not without vanity, spent several hours restoring himself and his costume from the ravages of travel. He bathed, trimmed his hair, shaved his face, and, when the Castellan came to unlock the door, he felt that he made no discreditable picture.

He was led out upon the road and directed up the hill toward the summit of the terraced town of Saponce. Turning to the Castellan he said, "How is it that you permit me to walk the trail once more? You must know that now I am safe from molestation. . . ."

The Castellan shrugged. "True. But you would gain little by insisting upon your temporary immunity. Ahead the trail crosses a bridge which we could demolish; behind we need but breach the dam to Green Torrent; then, should you walk the trail you would be swept to the side and so rendered vulnerable. No, Sir Guyal of Sfere, once the secret of your immunity is abroad then you are liable to a variety of stratagems. For instance, a large wall might be placed athwart the way, before and behind you. No doubt the spell would preserve you from thirst and hunger but what then? So would you sit till the sun went out."

Guyal said no word. Across the lake he noticed a trio of the crescent boats approaching the docks, prows and sterns rocking and dipping into the shaded water with a graceful motion. The void in his mind made itself known. "Why are your boats constructed in such fashion?"

The Castellan looked blankly at him. "It is the only practicable method. Do not the oe-pods grow thusly to the south?"

"Never have I seen oe-pods."

"They are the fruit of a great vine, and grow in scimitar-shape. When sufficiently large we cut and clean them, slit the inner edge, grapple end to end with strong line, and constrict till the pod opens as is desirable. When cured, dried, varnished, carved, burnished and lacquered, fitted with deck, thwarts and gussets—then have we our boats."

They entered the plaza, a flat area at the summit surrounded on three sides by tall houses. To Guyal's surprise there seemed to be no preliminary ceremonies or formalities to the contest, and small spirit of festivity was manifest among the townspeople. Indeed they seemed beset by subdued despondency and eyed him without enthusiasm.

A hundred girls stood in a disconsolate group. It seemed to Guyal that they had gone to few pains to embellish themselves. To the contrary, they wore shape-less rags, their hair seemed deliberately misarranged, their faces were dirty and scowling.

Guyal turned to his guide. "The girls seem not to covet the garland of pul-chritude."

The Castellan nodded wryly. "As you see, they are by no means jealous for distinction; modesty has always been a Saponid trait."

Guyal hesitated. "What is the form of procedure? I do not desire in my igno-rance to violate another of your arcane regulations."

The Castellan said with a blank face, "There are no formalities. We conduct these pageants with expedition and the least possible ceremony. You need but pass among these maidens and point out her whom you deem the most attractive."

Guyal advanced to his task, feeling more than half foolish. Then he reflected: this is a penalty for contravening an absurd tradition; I will conduct myself with efficiency and so the quicker rid myself of the obligation.

He stood before the hundred girls who eyed him with hostility and anxiety, and Guyal saw that his task would not be simple, since, on the whole, they were of a comeliness which even the dirt, grimacing, and rags could not disguise.

"Range yourselves, if you please, into a line," said Guyal. "In this way, none will be at disadvantage."

Sullenly the girls formed a line.

Guyal surveyed the group. He saw at once that a number could be eliminated: the squat, the obese, the lean, the pocked and coarse-featured—perhaps a quarter of the group. He said suavely, "Never have I seen such unanimous loveliness; each of you might legitimately claim the cordon. My task is arduous; I must weigh fine imponderables; in the end my choice will undoubtedly be based on subjectivity and those of real charm will no doubt be the first discharged from the competition." He stepped forward. "Those whom I indicate may retire."

He walked down the line, pointing, and the ugliest, with expressions of un-mistakable relief, hastened to the sidelines.

A second time Guyal made his inspection, and now, somewhat more familiar with those he judged, he was able to discharge those who, while suffering no whit from ugliness, were merely plain.

Roughly a third of the original group remained. These stared at Guyal with varying degrees of apprehension and truculence as he passed before them, studying each in turn.

. . . All at once his mind was determined, and his choice definite.

Guyal made one last survey down the line. No, he had been accurate in his choice. There were girls here as comely as the senses could desire, girls with opal-glowing eyes and hyacinth features, girls as lissome as reeds, with hair silky and fine despite the dust which they seemed to have rubbed upon themselves.

The girl whom Guyal had selected was slighter than the others and possessed of a beauty not at once obvious. She had a small triangular face, great wistful eyes, and thick black hair cut short at the ears. Her skin was of a transparent paleness, like the finest ivory; her form slender, graceful, and of a compelling magnetism. She seemed to have sensed his decision and her eyes widened.

Guyal took her hand, led her forward, and turned to the Elder—an old man sitting stolidly in a heavy chair.

"This is she whom I find the loveliest among your maidens."

There was silence through the square. Then there came a hoarse sound, a cry of sadness from the Castellan and Sergeant-Reader. He came forward, sagging of face, limp of body. "Guyal of Sfere, you have wrought a great revenge for my tricking you. This is my beloved daughter, Shierl, whom you have designated."

Guyal stammered, "I meant but complete impersonality. Your daughter Shierl I find the loveliest creature of my experience; I cannot understand where I have offended."

"No, Guyal," said the Castellan, "you have chosen fairly, for such indeed is my own thought."

"Well, then," said Guyal, "reveal to me now my third task that I may finish, and then continue my pilgrimage."

The Castellan said, "Three leagues to the north lies the ruin which tradition tells us to be the olden Museum of Man."

"Ah," said Guyal, "go on, I attend."

"You must, as your third charge, conduct my daughter Shierl to the Museum of Man. At the portal you will strike on a copper gong and announce to whoever responds: 'We are those summoned from Issane.' "

Guyal frowned. "How is this? 'We'?"

"Such is your charge," said the Castellan in a voice like thunder.

Guyal looked to left, right, forward, and behind. But he stood in the center of the plaza surrounded by the hardy men of Issane.

"When must this charge be executed?" he inquired in a controlled voice.

The Castellan said in a voice bitter as gall: "Even now Shierl goes to clothe herself in yellow. In one hour shall she appear; in one hour shall you set forth for the Museum of Man."

"And then?"

"And then—for good or for evil, it is not known. You fare as thirteen thousand have fared before you."

Down from the plaza, down the leafy lanes of Issane came Guyal, indignant and clamped of mouth, though the pit of his stomach felt heavy with trepidation. The ritual carried distasteful overtones. Guyal's step faltered.

The Castellan seized his elbow with a hard hand. "Forward."

The faces along the lane swam with morbid curiosity, inner excitement.

The eminence, with the tall trees and carved dark houses was at his back; he walked out into the claret sunlight of the tundra. Eighty women in white gowns with ceremonial buckets of woven straw over their heads surrounded a tall tent of yellow silk. Here the Castellan halted Guyal and beckoned to the Ritual Matron. She flung back the hangings at the door of the tent; Shierl came slowly forth, eyes dark with fright. She wore a stiff gown of yellow brocade, and the wand of her body seemed pent and constrained within. She stared at Guyal, at her father, as if she had never seen them before. The Ritual Matron put a hand on her waist, propelled her forward. Shierl stepped once, twice, irresolutely halted. The Castellan brought Guyal forward and placed him at the girl's side; now two children, a boy and a girl, came hastening up with cups which they proffered to Guyal and Shierl. Dully she accepted the cup. Guyal glanced suspiciously at the murky brew. He asked the Castellan: "What is the nature of this potion?"

"Drink," said the Castellan. "So will your way seem the shorter; you will march to the Museum with a steadier step."

"I will not drink," said Guyal. "My senses must be my own when I meet the Curator. I have come far for the privilege; I would not stultify the occasion stumbling and staggering."

Shierl stared dully at the cup she held. Said Guyal: "I advise you likewise to avoid the drug; so will we come to the Museum of Man with our dignity."

She returned the cup. The Castellan's brow clouded, but he made no protest.

An old man in a black costume brought forward a satin pillow on which rested a whip with a handle of carved steel. The Castellan now lifted this whip, and advancing, laid three light strokes across the shoulders of both Shierl and Guyal.

"Now," said the Castellan, "go from Issane outlawed forever. Seek succor at the Museum of Man. Never look back, leave all thoughts of past and future here. Go, I command; go, go, go!"

Shierl sunk her teeth into her lower lip; tears coursed her cheek though she made no sound. With hanging head she started across the tundra. Guyal, with a swift stride, joined her.

For a space the murmurs, the nervous sounds followed their ears; then they were alone. The north lay across the horizon; the tundra filled the foreground and background, an expanse dreary and dun. The Museum of Man rose before them; along the faint trail they walked.

Guyal said in a tentative tone, "There is much I would understand."

"Speak," said Shierl.

"Why are we forced to this mission?"

"It is thus because it has always been thus. Is this not reason enough?"

"Sufficient possibly for you," said Guyal, "but not for me. In fact, my thirst for knowledge drew me here, to find the Museum of Man."

She looked at him in wonder. "Are all to the south as scholarly as you?"

"In no degree," said Guyal. "The habitants perform the acts which fed them yesterday, last week, a year ago. 'Why strive for a pedant's accumulation?' I have been asked. 'Why seek and search? Earth grows cold; man gasps his last; why forgo merriment, music, and revelry for the abstract?' "

"Indeed," said Shierl. "Such is the consensus at Issane. But ask what you will; I will try to answer."

He studied the charming triangle of her face, the heavy black hair, the lustrous eyes, dark as sapphires. "In happier circumstances, there would be other yearnings for you to ease."

"Ask," said Shierl of Issane. "The Museum of Man is close; there is occasion for naught but words."

"Why are we thus sent to the Museum?"

"The immediate cause is the ghost you saw on the hill. When the ghost appears, then we of Issane know that the most beautiful maiden and the most handsome youth must be dispatched to the Museum. The basis of the custom I do not know. So it is; so it has been; so it will be till the sun gutters out like a coal in the rain."

"But what is our mission? Who greets us, what is our fate?"

"Such details are unknown."

Guyal mused, "The likelihood of pleasure seems small. . . . You are beyond doubt the loveliest creature of the Saponids, the loveliest creature of Earth—but I, a casual stranger, am hardly the most well-favored youth of the town."

She smiled. "You are not uncomely."

Guyal said somberly, "More cogent is the fact that I am a stranger and so bring little loss to Issane."

"That aspect has no doubt been considered."

Guyal searched the horizon. "Let us then avoid the Museum of Man, let us circumvent this unknown fate and take to the mountains."

She shook her head. "Do you suppose that we would gain by the ruse? The eyes of a hundred warriors will follow until we pass through the portals of the Museum. Should we attempt to avoid our duty we should be bound to stakes, stripped of our skins by the inch, and at last placed in bags with a thousand scorpions. Such is the traditional penalty; twelve times in history has it been invoked."

Guyal threw back his shoulders. He spoke in a nervous voice, "Ah, well—the Museum of Man has been my goal for many years. On this motive I set forth from Sfere, so now I would seek the Curator and satisfy my obsession for brain-filling."

"You are blessed with great fortune," said Shierl, "for you are being granted your heart's desire."

Guyal could find nothing to say, so for a space they walked in silence.

Presently she touched his arm. "Guyal, I am greatly frightened."

Guyal gazed at the ground beneath his feet, and a blossom of hope sprang alive in his brain. "See the marking through the lichen?"

"Yes; what then?"

"Is it a trail?"

Dubiously she responded, "It is a way worn by the passage of many feet. So then—it is a trail."

"Here then is safety," declared Guyal. "But I must guard you; you must never leave my side, you must swim in the charm which protects me; perhaps then we will survive."

Shierl said sadly, "Let us not delude our reason, Guyal of Sfere."

But as they walked, the trail grew plainer, and Guyal became correspondingly sanguine. And ever larger bulked the crumble that marked the Museum of Man.

If a storehouse of knowledge had existed here, little sign remained. There was a great flat floor, flagged in white stone, now chalky, broken and grown over with weeds. The surrounding monoliths, pocked and worn, were toppled off at various heights. The rains had washed the marble, the dust from the mountains had been laid on and swept off, laid on and swept off, and those who had built the Museum were less than a mote of this dust, so far and forgotten were they.

"Think," said Guyal, "think of the vastness of knowledge which once was gathered here and which is now one with the soil—unless, of course, the Curator has salvaged and preserved."

Shierl looked about apprehensively. "I think rather of the portal, and that which awaits us. . . . Guyal," she whispered, "I fear, I fear greatly. . . . Suppose they tear us apart? Suppose there is torture and death? I fear a tremendous impingement."

Guyal's own throat was hot and full. He looked about with challenge. "While I still breathe and hold power in my arms to fight, there will be none to harm us."

Shierl groaned softly. "Guyal, Guyal, Guyal of Sfere—why did you choose me?"

"Because," said Guyal, "you were the loveliest and I thought nothing but good in store for you."

Shierl said, "I must be courageous; after all, if it were not I it would be some other maid equally fearful. . . . And there is the portal."

Guyal inhaled deeply, inclined his head, and strode forward. "Let us be to it, and know."

The portal opened into a wall supporting the first floor; a door of flat black metal. Guyal followed the trail to the door and rapped staunchly with his fist on the small copper gong to the side.

The door groaned wide on its hinges, and cool air, smelling of the under-earth, billowed forth.

"Hello within!" cried Guyal.

A soft voice, full of catches and quavers, as if just after weeping, said, "Come you, come you forward. You are desired and awaited."

Guyal leaned his head forward, straining to see. "Give us light, that we may not wander from the trail and bottom ourselves."

The breathless quaver of a voice said, "Light is not needed; anywhere you step, that will be your trail, by an arrangement so agreed with the Way-Maker."

"No," said Guyal, "we would see the visage of our host. We come at his invitation; the minimum of his courtesy is light; light there must be before we set foot inside the dungeon. Know we come as seekers after knowledge; we are visitors to be honored."

"Ah, knowledge, knowledge," came the sad breathlessness. "That shall be yours, in fullness; oh, you shall swim in a tide of knowledge——"

Guyal interrupted the sad, sighing voice. "Are you the Curator? Hundreds of leagues have I come to know the Curator and put him my inquiries. Are you he?"

"By no means. I revile the name of the Curator as a nonessential."

"Who then may you be?"

"I am no one, nothing. I am an abstraction, an emotion, the shake in the air when a scream has departed."

"You speak with the voice of man."

"Why not? Such things as I speak lie in the dearest center of the human brain."

Guyal said in a subdued voice, "You do not make your invitation as enticing as might be hoped."

"No matter, no matter; enter you must, into the dark and on the instant."

"If light there be, we enter."

"No light, no insolent scorch, is ever found in the Museum."

"In this case," said Guyal, drawing forth his Scintillant Dagger, "I innovate a welcome reform. For see, now there is light!"

From the under-pommel issued a searching glare; the ghost tall before them screeched and fell into twinkling ribbons like pulverized tinsel. There were a few vagrant motes in the air; he was gone.

Shierl, who had stood stark and stiff as one mesmerized, gasped a soft warm gasp and fell against Guyal. "How can you be so defiant?"

Guyal said in a voice, half-laugh, half-quaver, "In truth I do not know. . . . Perhaps I find it incredible that I should come from Sfere, through forest and across crag, into the northern waste, merely to play the role of victim. I disbelieve; I am bold."

He moved the dagger to right and left, and they saw themselves to be at the portal of a keep, cut from concreted rock. At the back opened a black depth. Crossing the floor swiftly, Guyal kneeled and listened.

He heard no sound. Shierl, at his back, stared with eyes as black and deep as the pit itself.

Leaning with his glowing dagger, Guyal saw a crazy rack of stairs voyaging down into the dark, and his light showed them and their shadows in so confusing a guise that he blinked and drew back.

Shierl said, "What do you fear?"

Guyal rose. "We are momentarily untended here in the Museum of Man. If we stay here we shall be once more arranged in harmony with the hostile pattern. If we go forward boldly we may come to a position of advantage. I propose that we descend these stairs and seek the Curator."

"But does he exist?"

"The ghost spoke fervently against him."

"Let us go, then," said Shierl. "I am resigned."

"We go."

They started down the stairs.

Back, forth, back, forth, down flights at varying angles, stages of varying heights, treads at varying widths, so that each step was a matter for concentration. Back, forth, down, down, down, and the black barred shadows moved and jerked in bizarre modes on the wall.

The flight ended; they stood in a room similar to the entry above, facing another black door, polished at one spot by use. On the walls to either side brass plaques carried messages in unfamiliar characters.

Guyal opened the door against a pressure of cold air, which, blowing through the aperture, made a slight rush, ceasing when Guyal opened the door farther.

"Listen."

It was a far sound, an intermittent clacking, and it raised the hairs at Guyal's neck. He felt Shierl's hand gripping his with clammy pressure.

Dimming the dagger's glow to a glimmer, Guyal passed through the door, with Shierl coming after. From afar came the evil sound, and by the echoes they knew they stood in a great hall.

Guyal directed the light to the floor: it was of a black resilient material. Next the wall: polished stone. He permitted the light to glow in the direction opposite to the sound, and a few paces distant they saw a bulky black case, studded with copper bosses.

With the purpose of the black case not apparent, they followed the wall, and as they walked similar cases appeared, looming heavy and dull, at regular intervals. The clacking receded as they walked; then they came to a right angle, and turning the corner, they seemed to approach the sound. Black case after black case passed; slowly, tense as foxes, they walked, eyes groping for sight through the darkness.

The wall made another angle, and here there was a door. Guyal hesitated. To follow the new direction of the wall would mean approaching the source of the sound. Would it be better to discover the worst quickly or to reconnoiter as they went?

He propounded the dilemma to Shierl, who shrugged. "It is all one; sooner or later the ghosts will flit down to pluck at us; then we are lost."

"Not while I possess light to stare them away to wisps and shreds," said Guyal. "Now I would find the Curator. Possibly he is behind this door. We will so discover."

He laid his shoulder to the door; it eased ajar with a crack of golden light. Guyal peered through. He sighed, a muffled sound of wonder.

Now he opened the door farther; Shierl clutched at his arm.

"This is the Museum," said Guyal in rapt tone. "Here there is no danger." He flung wide the door.

The light came from an unknown source, from the air itself, as if leaking from the discrete atoms; every breath was luminous, the room floated full of invigorating glow. Beautiful works of human fashioning ranked the walls: panels of rich woods; scenes of olden times; formulas of color, designed to convey emotion rather than reality. Here were representations of three hundred marvelous flowers no longer extant on waning Earth; as many star-burst patterns; a multitude of other creations.

The door thudded softly behind them; the two from Earth's final time moved forward through the hall.

"Somewhere near must be the Curator," whispered Guyal. "There has been careful tending and great effort here."

"Look."

Opposite was a door which Guyal was unable to open, for it bore no latch, key, handle knob, or bar. He rapped with his knuckles and waited; no sound returned.

Shierl tugged at his arm. "These are private regions. It is best not to venture too rudely."

Guyal turned away and they continued down the gallery, past the real expression of man's brightest dreamings, until the concentration of so much fire and spirit put them into awe. "Great minds lie on the dust," said Guyal. "Gorgeous souls have vanished. Nevermore will there be the like."

The room turned a corner, widened. And now the clacking sound they had noticed in the dark outer hall returned, louder, more suggestive of unpleasantness. It seemed to enter the gallery through an arched doorway opposite.

Guyal moved quietly to this door, with Shierl at his heels, and so they peered into the next chamber.

A great face looked from the wall, a face taller than Guyal, as tall as Guyal might reach with hands on high. The chin rested on the floor, the scalp slanted back into the panel.

Guyal stared, taken aback. In this pageant of beautiful objects, the grotesque visage was the disparity and dissonance a lunatic might have created. Ugly and vile was the face. The skin shone a gun-metal sheen, the eyes gazed from slanting folds. The nose was a lump, the mouth a pulp.

Guyal turned to Shierl. "Does this not seem an odd work to be honored here in the Museum of Man?"

With hands jerking, she grabbed his arm, staggered back into the gallery.

"Guyal," she cried, "Guyal, come away!"

He faced her in surprise. "What are you saying?"

"That horrible thing in there——"

"The diseased effort of an elder artist."

"It lives."

"How is this?"

"It lives!" she babbled. "It looked at me, then looked at you."

Guyal shrugged off her hand; in disbelief he looked through the doorway.

The face had changed. The torpor had evaporated; the glaze had departed the eye. The mouth squirmed; a hiss of escaping gas sounded. The mouth opened; a gray tongue protruded, and from this tongue darted a tendril. It terminated in a grasping hand, which groped for Guyal's neck. He jumped aside; the hand missed its clutch, the tendril coiled.

Guyal sprang back into the gallery. The hand seized Shierl, grasped her ankle. The eyes glistened; and now the flabby tongue sprouted a new member. . . . Shierl stumbled, fell limp, her eyes staring, foam at her lips. Guyal shouting in a voice he could not hear, ran forward with his dagger. He cut at the gray wrist, but his knife sprang away as if the steel itself were horrified. He seized the tendril; with a mighty effort he broke it against his knee.

The face winced, the tendril jerked back. Guyal dragged Shierl into the gallery, back out of reach.

Through the doorway now, Guyal glared in hate and fear. The mouth had closed; it sneered disappointment. From the dank nostril oozed a wisp of white which swirled, writhed, formed a tall thing in a white robe—a thing with a drawn face and eyes like holes in a skull. Whimpering and mewing in distaste for the light, it wavered forward into the gallery, moving with curious little pauses and hesitancies.

Guyal stood still. Fear had exceeded its power; fear no longer persuaded. A brain could react only to the maximum of its intensity; how could this thing harm him now? He would smash it with his hands, beat it into sighing fog.

"Hold, hold, hold!" came a new voice. "Hold, hold, hold. My charms and tokens, an ill day for Thorsingol. . . . Be off with you, ghost, back to the orifice, back, I say! Go, else I loose the actinics; trespass is not allowed, by supreme command from the Lycurgat; aye, the Lycurgat of Thorsingol." This was the voice of the old man who had hobbled into the gallery.

Back to the snoring face wandered the ghost, and let itself be sucked up into the nostril.

The face rumbled and belched a white fiery lick, flapping at the old man who moved not an inch. From a rod high on the door frame came a whirling disk of golden sparks, which cut and dismembered the white sheet, destroyed it back to the mouth of the face, whence now issued a black bar. This bar edged into the whirling disk and absorbed the sparks. There was an instant of dead silence.

Then the old man crowed, "Ah, you evil episode; you seek to interrupt my tenure. My clever baton holds you in abeyance; you are as naught. Disengage! Retreat into Jeldred!"

The mouth opened to display a gray viscous cavern; the eyes glittered in titanic emotion. The mouth yelled, a wave of sound to buffet the head and drive shock like a nail into the mind.

The baton sprayed a mist; the sound was captured and consumed; it was never heard.

The old man said, "You are captious today! You would disturb poor old Kerlin in his duties? So ho. Baton!" He turned and peered at the rod. "You have tasted that sound? Spew out a penalty."

The fog balled, struck at the nose, buried itself in the pulp. An explosion; the face seethed; the nose was a clutter of shredded gray plasms. They waved like starfish arms and grew together once more, and now the nose was pointed like a cone.

Kerlin the Curator laughed, a shrill yammer on a single tone. He stopped short and the laugh vanished as if it had never begun. He turned to Guyal and Shierl, who stood pressed together in the door frame.

"How now? You are after the gong; the study hours are ended. Why do you linger?" He shook a stern finger. "The Museum is not the site for roguery; this I admonish. So now be off, home to Thorsingol; be more prompt the next time; you disturb the order. . . ." He paused and threw a fretful glance over his shoulder. "The day has gone ill; the Nocturnal Key-keeper is inexcusably late. . . . I have waited an hour on the sluggard; the Lycurgat shall be so informed. I would be home to couch and hearth; here is ill use for old Kerlin. And, further, the encroachment of you two laggards; away now, and be off; out into the twilight!" And he advanced, making directive motions with his hands.

Guyal said, "My lord Curator, I must speak with you."

The old man halted, peered. "Eh? What now? At the end of a long day's effort? No, no, you are out of order; regulation must be observed. Attend my audiarium at the fourth circuit tomorrow morning; then we shall hear you. So go now, go."

Guyal stood back, nonplussed. Shierl fell on her knees. "Sir Curator, we beg you for help; we have no place to go."

Kerlin the Curator looked at her blankly. "No place to go! What folly you utter! Go to your domicile, or to the Pubescentarium, or to the Temple, or to the Outward Inn. The Museum is no casual tavern."

"My lord," cried Guyal desperately, "will you hear me? We speak from emergency."

"Say on then."

"Some malignancy has bewitched your brain. Will you credit this?"

"Ah, indeed?" ruminated the Curator.

"There is no Thorsingol. There is naught but dark waste. Your city is an aeon gone."

The Curator smiled benevolently. "A sad case. So it is with these younger minds." He shook his head. "My duty is clear. Tired bones, you must wait your rest. Fatigue—begone; duty to humanity makes demands; here is madness to be countered and cleared. And in any event the Nocturnal Key-keeper is not here to relieve me of my tedium." He beckoned. "Come."

Hesitantly, Guyal and Shierl followed him. He opened one of his doors, passed through muttering and expostulating. Guyal and Shierl came after.

The room was cubical, floored with dull black stuff. A hooded chair occupied the center of the room and beside it was a chest-high lectern whose face displayed a number of toggles and knurled wheels.

"This is the Curator's own Chair of Clarity," explained Kerlin. "As such it will, upon proper adjustment, impose the Pattern of Hynomeneural Clarity." He manipulated the manuals. "Now, if you will compose yourself I will repair your hallucination. It is beyond my call of duty, but I would not be spoken of as mean or unwilling."

Guyal inquired anxiously, "Lord Curator, this Chair of Clarity, how will it affect me?"

Kerlin the Curator said grandly, "The fibers of your brain are snarled and frayed, and so make contact with unintentional areas. By the marvelous craft of our modern cerebrologists this hood will compose your synapses with the correct readings from the library—those of normality, you must understand—and so repair the skein, and make you once more a whole man."

"Once I sit in the chair," Guyal inquired, "What will you do?"

"Merely close this contact, engage this arm, throw in this toggle—then you daze. In thirty seconds, this bulb glows, signaling the success and completion of the treatment. Then I reverse the manipulation and you arise a creature of renewed sanity."

Guyal looked at Shierl. "Did you hear and comprehend?"

"Yes, Guyal."

"Remember." Then to the Curator: "Marvelous. But how must I sit?"

"Merely relax in the seat. Then I pull the hood slightly forward, to shield the eyes from distraction."

Guyal leaned forward, peered gingerly into the hood. "I fear I do not understand."

The Curator hopped forward impatiently. "It is an act of the utmost facility. Like this." He sat in the chair.

"And how will the hood be applied?"

"In this wise." Kerlin seized a handle, pulled the shield over his face.

"Quick," said Guyal to Shierl. She sprang to the lectern; Kerlin the Curator made a motion to release the hood; Guyal seized the spindly frame, held it. Shierl flung the switches; the Curator relaxed, sighed.

Shierl gazed at Guyal, dark eyes wide and liquid as the great water-flamerian of South Almery. "Is he . . . dead?"

"I hope not."

They gazed uncertainly at the relaxed form. Seconds passed.

A clanging noise sounded from afar—a crush, a wrench, an exultant bellow.

Guyal rushed to the door. Prancing, wavering, sidling into the gallery came a dozen ghosts; through the open door behind, Guyal could see the great head. It was shoving out, pushing into the room. Great ears appeared, part of a neck, wreathed with purple wattles. The wall cracked, sagged, crumbled. A great hand thrust through, a forearm. . . .

Shierl screamed. Guyal, pale and quivering, slammed the door in the face of the nearest ghost. It seeped around the jamb, wisp by wisp.

Guyal sprang to the lectern. The bulb showed dullness. Guyal's hands twitched along the controls. "Only Kerlin's awareness controls the magic of the baton," he panted. "So much is clear." he stared into the bulb with agonized urgency.

"Glow, bulb, glow. . . ."

The bulb glowed. With a sharp cry Guyal returned the switches to neutrality, jumped down, flung up the hood.

Kerlin the Curator sat looking at him.

Behind, the ghost formed itself—a tall white thing in white robes, and the dark eye-holes stared like outlets into nonimagination.

Kerlin the Curator sat looking.

The ghost moved under the robes. A hand like a bird's foot appeared, holding a clod of dingy matter. The ghost cast the matter to the floor; it exploded into a puff of black dust. The motes of the cloud grew, became a myriad of wriggling insects. With one accord they darted across the floor, growing as they spread, and became scuttling creatures with monkey-heads.

Kerlin the Curator moved. "Baton," he said. He held up his hand. It held the baton. The baton spat an orange gout—red-dust. It puffed before the rushing horde and each mote became a red scorpion. So ensued a ferocious battle, and little shrieks and chittering sounds rose from the floor.

The monkey-headed things were killed, routed. The ghost sighed, moved his claw-hand once more. But the baton spat forth a ray of purest light and the ghost sloughed into nothingness.

"Kerlin!" cried Guyal. "The demon is breaking into the gallery."

Kerlin flung open the door, stepped forth.

"Baton," said Kerlin, "perform thy utmost."

The demon said, "No, Kerlin, hold the magic; I thought you dazed. Now I retreat."

With a vast quaking and heaving he pulled back until once more only his face showed through the hole.

"Baton," said Kerlin, "rest on guard."

The baton disappeared from his hand.

Kerlin turned and faced Guyal and Shierl.

"There is need for many words, for now I die. I die, and the Museum shall lie alone. So let us speak quickly, quickly, quickly. . . ."

Kerlin moved with feeble steps to a portal which snapped aside as he approached. Guyal and Shierl stood hesitantly to the rear.

"Come, come," said Kerlin in sharp impatience. "My strength flags, I die. You have been my death."

Guyal moved slowly forward, with Shierl half a pace behind.

Kerlin surveyed them with a thin grin. "Halt your misgivings and hasten; I wane; my sight flickers. . . ."

He waved a despairing hand, then, turning, led them into the inner chamber where he slumped into a great chair. With many uneasy glances at the door Guyal and Shierl settled upon a padded couch.

Kerlin jeered in a feeble voice, "You fear the white phantasms? Poh, they are held from the gallery by the baton. Only when I am smitten out of mind—or dead—will the baton cease its function. You must know," he added with somewhat more vigor, "that the energies and dynamics do not channel from my brain but from the central potentium of the Museum, which is perpetual; I merely direct and order the rod."

"But this demon—who or what is he? Why does he come to look through the walls?"

"He is Blikdak, of the demon-world Jeldred. He wrenched the hole intent on taking the knowledge of the Museum into his mind, but I forestalled him; so he sits waiting in the hole till I die. Then he will glut himself with erudition to the great disadvantage of men."

"Why cannot this demon be exhorted hence and the hole abolished?"

Kerlin the Curator shook his head. "The furious powers I control are not valid in the air of the demon-world, where substance and form are of different entity. So far as you see him, he has brought his environment with him; so far he is safe. When he ventures farther the power of Earth dissolves the Jeldred mode; then may I strike him with fervor from the potentium. . . . But enough of Blikdak; tell me, what is the news of Thorsingol?"

Guyal said in a halting voice, "Thorsingol is passed beyond memory. There is naught above but arid tundra and the old town of the Saponids. This girl Shierl is of the Saponids; we came to the Museum at the behest of Blikdak's ghosts."

"Ah," breathed Kerlin, "have I been so aimless? These youthful shapes by which Blikdak relieved his tedium: they flit down my memory like May flies. . . . I put them aside as creatures of his own conception."

Shierl grimaced. "What use to him are human creatures?"

Kerlin said dully, "Blikdak is past your conceiving. These human creatures are his play, on whom he practices various junctures, nauseas, antics, and at last struggles to the death. Then he sends forth a ghost demanding further youth and beauty."

Guyal said in puzzlement, "Such acts would seem derangements of humanity. They are anthropoid by the very nature of the functioning organs. Since Blikdak is a demon—"

"Consider him!" spoke Kerlin. "His lineaments, his apparatus. He is nothing else but anthropoid, and such is his origin, together with all the demons, frits, and winged glowing-eyed creatures that infest latter-day Earth. Blikdak, like the others, derives from the mind of man. The condensation, the cloacal humors, the scatophiliac whims that have drained through humanity formed a vast tumor; so Blikdak assumed his being. But of Blikdak, enough. I die, I die!" He sank into the chair with heaving chest. "My eyes vary and waver. My breath is shallow as a bird's, my bones are the pith of an old vine. I have lived beyond knowledge; in my madness I knew no passage of time. Now I remember the years and centuries, the millennia, the epochs—they are like quick glimpses through a shutter. Curing my madness, you have killed me."

"But when you die," cried Shierl, "what then?"

Guyal asked, "In the Museum of Man are there no exorcisms to dissolve this demon?

"Blikdak must be eradicated," said Kerlin. "Then will I die in ease; then must you assume the care of the Museum." He licked his white lips. "An ancient principle specifies that, in order to destroy a substance the nature of the substance must be determined. In short, before Blikdak may be dissolved, we must discover his nature." And his eyes moved glassily to Guyal.

"Your pronouncement is sound beyond argument," admitted Guyal, "but how may this be accomplished? Blikdak will never submit to investigation."

"No; there must be subterfuge, some instrumentality. . . ."

"The ghosts are part of Blikdak's stuff?"

"Indeed."

"Can the ghosts be stayed and prevented?"

"Indeed; in a box of light, the which I can effect by a thought. Yes, a ghost we must have." Kerlin raised his head. "Baton! One ghost; admit a ghost!"

A moment passed; Kerlin held up his hand. There was a faint scratch at the door and a soft whine. "Open," said a voice, full of sobs and catches and quavers. "Open and let forth the youthful creatures."

Kerlin laboriously rose to his feet. "It is done."

From behind the door came a sad voice, "I am pent, I am snared in scorching brilliance!"

"Now we experiment," said Guyal. "What dissolves the ghost dissolves Blikdak."

"True indeed," assented Kerlin.

"Why not light?" inquired Shierl. "Light parts the fabric of the ghosts as wind tatters the fog."

"But merely for their fragility; Blikdak is harsh and solid." Kerlin mused. After a moment he gestured to the door. "We go to the image-expander; there we will explode the ghost to macroid dimension; so shall we find his basis. Guyal of Sfere, you must support my frailness; my limbs are weak as wax."

On Guyal's arm he tottered forward, and with Shierl close at their heels they gained the gallery. Here the ghost wept in its cage of light, and searched constantly for a dark aperture to seep his essence through.

Paying him no heed Kerlin hobbled and limped across the gallery. In their wake followed the box of light and perforce the ghost.

"Open the great door," cried Kerlin in a voice beset with cracking and hoarseness. "The great door into the Cognitive Repository!"

Shierl ran ahead and thrust her force against the door; it slid aside, and they looked into the great dark hall, and the golden light from the gallery dwindled into the shadows and was lost.

"Call for light," Kerlin said.

"Light!" cried Guyal.

Illumination came to the great hall, and it proved so tall that pilasters along the wall dwindled to threads, and so long and wide that perspective was distorted. Spaced in equal rows were the black cases with the copper bosses that Guyal and Shierl had noted on their entry. Above each hung five similar cases, precisely fixed, floating without support.

"What are these?" asked Guyal.

"Would my poor brain encompassed a hundredth part of what these banks know," panted Kerlin. "They are repositories crammed with all that has been experienced, achieved, or recorded by man. Here is the lost lore, early and late, the fabulous imaginings, the history of ten million cities, the beginnings of time and the presumed finalties; the reason for human existence and the reason for the reason. Daily I have labored and toiled in these banks; my achievement has been a synopsis of the most superficial sort: a panorama across a wide and multifarious country."

Said Shierl, "Would not the craft to destroy Blikdak be contained here?"

"Indeed, indeed; our task would be merely to find the information. Under which casting would we search? Consider these categories: Demon-lands; Killings and Mortefactions; Expositions and Dissolutions of Evil; History of Granvilunde (where such an entity was repelled); Attractive and Detractive Hyperordnets; Therapy for

Hallucinants and Ghost-takers; Constructive Journal, item for regeneration of burst walls, subdivision for invasion by demons; Procedural Suggestions in Time of Risk. . . . Aye, these and a thousand more. Somewhere is knowledge. But where to look? There is no Index Major; none except the poor synopsis of my compilation. He who seeks specific knowledge must often go on an extended search. . . ." His voice trailed off. Then: "Forward! Forward through the banks to the Mechanismus."

So through the banks they went, like roaches in a maze, and behind drifted the cage of light with the wailing ghost. At last they entered a chamber smelling of metal; again Kerlin instructed Guyal and Guyal called for light.

At a tall booth Kerlin halted the cage of light. A pane dropped before the ghost. "Observe now," Kerlin said, and manipulated the activants.

They saw the ghost, depicted and projected: the flowing robe, the haggard visage. The face grew large, flattened; a segment under the vacant eye became a scabrous white place. It separated into pustules, and a single pustule swelled to fill the pane. The crater of the pustule was an intricate stippled surface, a mesh as of fabric, knit in a lacy pattern.

"Behold!" said Shierl. "He is a thing woven as if by thread."

Guyal turned eagerly to Kerlin; Kerlin raised a finger. "Indeed, indeed, a goodly thought, especially since here beside us is a rotor of extreme swiftness, used in reeling the cognitive filaments of the cases. . . . Now then observe: I reach to this panel, I select a mesh, I withdraw a thread, and note! The meshes ravel and loosen and part. And now to the bobbin on the rotor, and I wrap the thread, and now with a twist we have the cincture made. . . ."

Shierl said dubiously, "Does not the ghost observe and note your doing?"

"The pane shields our actions; he is too exercised to attend. And now I dissolve the cage and he is free."

The ghost wandered forth, cringing from the light.

"Go!" cried Kerlin. "Back to your genetrix, back, return and go!"

The ghost departed. Kerlin said to Guyal, "Follow; find when Blikdak snuffs him up."

At a cautious distance Guyal watched the ghost seep up into the black nostril, and returned to where Kerlin waited by the rotor. "The ghost has once more become part of Blikdak."

"Now then," said Kerlin, "we cause the rotor to twist, the bobbin to whirl, and we shall observe."

The rotor whirled to a blur; the bobbin (as long as Guyal's arm) became spun with ghost-thread, at first glowing pastel polychrome, then nacre, then fine milk-ivory.

The rotor spun, a million times a minute, and the thread drawn unseen and unknown from Blikdak thickened on the bobbin.

The rotor spun; the bobbin was full—a cylinder shining with glossy silken sheen. Kerlin slowed the rotor: Guyal snapped a new bobbin into place, and the unraveling of Blikdak continued.

Three bobbins—four—four—five—and Guyal, observing Blikdak from afar, found the giant face quiescent, the mouth working and sucking, creating the clacking sound which had first caused them apprehension.

Eight bobbins. Blikdak opened his eyes, stared in puzzlement around the chamber.

Twelve bobbins; a discolored spot appeared on the sagging cheek, and Blikdak quivered in uneasiness.

Twenty bobbins: the spot spread across Blikdak's visage, across the slanted fore-dome, and his mouth hung lax; he hissed and fretted.

Thirty bobbins: Blikdak's head seemed stale and putrid; the gunmetal sheen had become an angry maroon, the eyes bulged, the mouth hung open, the tongue lolled limp.

Fifty bobbins: Blikdak collapsed. His dome lowered against his mouth; his eyes shone like feverish coals.

Sixty bobbins, seventy bobbins; Blikdak was no more. The breach in the wall gave on barren rock, unbroken and rigid.

And in the Mechanismus seventy shining bobbins lay stacked.

Kerlin fell back against the wall. "My time has come. I have guarded the Museum; together we have won it from Blikdak. . . . Attend me now. Into your hands I pass the curacy; now the Museum is your charge to guard and preserve."

"For what end?" asked Shierl. "Earth expires, almost as you. . . . Wherefore knowledge?"

"More now than ever," gasped Kerlin. "Attend: the stars are bright, the stars are fair; the banks know blessed magic to fleet you to youthful climes. Now . . . I go. I die."

"Wait!" cried Guyal. "Wait, I beseech!"

"Why wait?" whispered Kerlin. "You call me back?"

"How do I extract from the banks?"

"The key to the index is in my chambers, the index of my life. . . ." And Kerlin died.

★ ★ ★

Guyal and Shierl climbed to the upper ways and stood outside the portal on the ancient floor. It was night; the marble shone faintly underfoot, the broken columns loomed on the sky.

Across the plain the yellow lights of Issane shone warm through the trees; above in the sky shone the stars.

Guyal said to Shierl, "There is your home; do you wish to return?"

She shook her head. "We have looked through the eyes of knowledge. We have seen old Thorsingol, and the Sherrit Empire before it, and Golwan Andra before that, and the Forty Kades even before. We have seen the warlike green-men, and the knowledgeable Pharials and the Clambs who departed Earth for the stars, as did the Merioneth before them and the Gray Sorcerers still earlier. We have seen oceans rise and fall, the mountains crust up, peak and melt in the beat of rain; we have looked on the sun when it glowed hot and full and yellow. . . . No, Guyal, there is no place for me at Issane. . . ."

Guyal, leaning back on the weathered pillar, looked up to the stars. "Knowledge is ours, Shierl—all of knowing to our call. And what shall we do?"

Together they looked up to the white stars.

"What shall we do . . ."

Old Hundredth

BRIAN W. ALDISS

The far future seems to hold a special fascination and allure for Brian W. Aldiss, and in a field where such stories are relatively rare, he has almost made a specialty out of writing about it. *The Long Afternoon of Earth* (also known as the *Hothouse* series, under which title it won a special Hugo Award in 1962) remains one of the classic visions of the distant future of Earth, as well as being a foundation stone of the subgenre of science-fantasy, but Aldiss has *also* handled the theme with grace and a wealth of poetic imagination in many other stories, including classics such as "The Worm That Flies" and "Full Sun," as well as the novels of the *Helliconia* trilogy (and handles a closely related theme with similar excellence in *The Malacia Tapestry* as well).

Never has he envisioned the far future more vividly than in the story that follows, though, which takes us to a muted, autumnal future, full of echoes and old ghosts; an ancient and ruinous Earth from which humankind has forever departed; a strange world of involutes and Impures and musicolumns, with Venus for a moon and hogs as big as hippos; a world of stately, living music under dusty umbrella trees. . . .

One of the true giants of the field, Brian W. Aldiss has been publishing science fiction for nearly half a century and has more than two dozen books to his credit. "The Saliva Tree" won a Nebula Award in 1965, and his novel *Starship* won the Prix Jules Verne in 1977. He took another Hugo Award in 1987 for his critical study of science fiction, *Trillion Year Spree*, written with David Wingrove.

In many ways, Brian W. Aldiss was the enfant terrible of the late fifties, exploding into the SF world and shaking it up with the ferocious verve and pyrotechnic verbal brilliance of stories like "Poor Little Warrior!," "Outside," "The New Father Christmas," "Who Can Replace a Man?," and "A Kind of Artistry" and with the somber beauty and unsettling poetic vision—in the main, of a world where mankind signally has *not* triumphantly conquered the universe, as the Campbellian dogma of the time insisted that he would—of his classic novels *Starship* (*Non-Stop* and *The Long Afternoon of Earth* in Britain). All this made him one of the most controversial writers of the day . . . and, some years later, he'd be one of the most controversial figures of the New Wave era as well, shaking up the SF world of the mid-sixties in an even

*more dramatic and drastic fashion with the ferociously Joycean "acidhead war"
stories that would be melded into Barefoot in the Head,* with the irreverent *Cryp-
tozoic!,* and with his surrealistic antinovel *Report on Probability A.*

But Aldiss has never been willing to work any one patch of ground for very
long. By 1976, he had worked his way through two controversial British mainstream
best-sellers—*The Hand-Reared Boy* and *A Soldier Erect*—and the strange transmuted Gothic of *Frankenstein Unbound* and gone on to produce a lyrical masterpiece of science-fantasy, *The Malacia Tapestry,* one of his best books and certainly
one of the best novels of the seventies. Ahead, in the decade of the eighties, was
the monumental accomplishment of his *Helliconia* trilogy—*Helliconia Spring, Helliconia Summer,* and *Helliconia Winter*—and by the end of that decade only the
grumpiest of reactionary critics could deny that Aldiss was one of the true giants
of the field, a figure of artistic complexity and amazing vigor, as much on the cutting
edge in the nineties as he had been in the fifties.

Aldiss's other books include *An Island Called Moreau, Graybeard, Dracula Unbound, Enemies of the System, A Rude Awakening, Life in the West, Forgotten Life,*
and *Remembrance Day,* a memoir, *Bury My Heart at W. H. Smith's,* and a collection
of poems, *Home Life with Cats.* His short fiction has been collected in *Space, Time,
and Nathaniel; Who Can Replace a Man?, New Arrivals, Old Encounters; Galaxies
like Grains of Sand;* and *Seasons in Flight.* His many anthologies include *The Penguin
Science Fiction Omnibus* and, with Harry Harrison, *Decade: The 1940s, Decade:
The 1950s,* and *Decade: The 1960s.* Aldiss's latest books include a collection, *Common Clay,* and an autobiography, *The Twinkling of an Eye.* His Utopia, *His Mars,* has
just been published. He lives in Oxford.

The road climbed dustily down between trees as symmetrical as umbrellas. Its
length was punctuated at one point by a musicolumn standing on the verge. From
a distance, the column was only a stain in the air. As sentient creatures neared it,
their psyches activated it, it drew on their vitalities, and then it could be heard as
well as seen. Their presence made it flower into pleasant sound, instrumental or
chant.

All this region was called Ghinomon, for no one lived here now, not even the
odd hermit Impure. It was given over to grass and the weight of time. Only a wild
goat or two activated the musicolumn nowadays, or a scampering vole wrung a
chord from it in passing.

When old Dandi Lashadusa came riding on her baluchitherium, the column
began to intone. It was no more than an indigo trace in the air, hardly visible, for
it represented only a bonded pattern of music locked into the fabric of that particular area of space. It was also a transubstantio-spatial shrine, the eternal part of a
being that had dematerialized itself into music.

The baluchitherium whinnied, lowered its head, and sneezed onto the gritty
road.

"Gently, Lass," Dandi told her mare, savoring the growth of the chords that
increased in volume as she approached. Her long nose twitched with pleasure as
if she could feel the melody along her olfactory nerves.

Obediently, the baluchitherium slowed, turning aside to crop fern, although it
kept an eye on the indigo stain. It liked things to have being or not to have being;

these half-and-half objects disturbed it, though they could not impair its immense appetite.

Dandi climbed down her ladder onto the ground, glad to feel the ancient dust under her feet. She smoothed her hair and stretched as she listened to the music.

She spoke aloud to her mentor, half a world away, but he was not listening. His mind closed to her thoughts, and he muttered an obscure exposition that darkened what it sought to clarify.

". . . useless to deny that it is well-nigh impossible to improve anything, however faulty, that has so much tradition behind it. And the origins of your bit of metricism are indeed embedded in such an antiquity that we must needs—"

"Tush, Mentor, come out of your black box and forget your hatred of my 'metricism' a moment," Dandi Lashadusa said, cutting her thought into his. "Listen to the bit of 'metricism' I've found here; look at where I have come to; let your argument rest."

She turned her eyes around, scanning the tawny rocks near at hand, the brown line of the road, the distant black-and-white magnificence of ancient Oldorajo's town, doing this all for him, tiresome old fellow. Her mentor was blind, never left his cell in Aeterbroe to go farther than the sandy courtyard, hadn't physically left that green cathedral pile for over a century. Womanlike, she thought he needed change. Soul, how he rambled on! Even now, he was managing to ignore her and refute her.

". . . for consider, Lashadusa woman, nobody can be found to father it. Nobody wrought or thought it, phrases of it merely *came* together. Even the old nations of men could not own it. None of them know who composed it. An element here from a Spanish pavan, an influence there of a French psalm tune, a flavor here of early English carol, a savor there of later German chorale. All primitive—ancient beyond ken. Nor are the faults of your bit of metricism confined to bastardy—"

"Stay in your black box then, if you won't see or listen," Dandi said. She could not get into his mind; it was the mentor's privilege to lodge in her mind, and in the minds of those few other wards he had, scattered around Earth. Only the mentors had the power to inhabit another's mind—which made them rather tiring on occasions like this, when they would not get out. For over seventy centuries, Dandi's mentor had been persuading her to die into a dirge of his choosing (and composing). Let her die, yes, let her transubstantio-spatialize herself a thousand times! His quarrel was not with her decision but with her taste, which he considered execrable.

Leaving the baluchitherium to crop, Dandi walked away from the musicolumn toward a hillock. Still fed by her steed's psyche, the column continued to play. Its music was of a simplicity, with a dominant-tonic recurrent bass part suggesting pessimism. To Dandi, a savant in musicolumnology, it yielded other data. She could tell to within a few years when its founder had died and also what sort of creature, generally speaking, he had been.

Climbing the hillock, Dandi looked about. To the south where the road led were low hills, lilac in the poor light. There lay her home. At last she was returning, after wanderings covering three hundred centuries and most of the globe.

Apart from the blind beauty of Oldorajo's town lying to the west, there was only one landmark she recognized. That was the Involute. It seemed to hang iridial above the ground a few leagues ahead; just to look on it made her feel she must go nearer.

Before summoning the baluchitherium, Dandi listened once more to the sounds of the musicolumn, making sure she had them fixed in her head. The pity was that her old fool wise man would not share it. She could still feel his sulks floating like sediment through her mind.

"Are you listening now, Mentor?"

"Eh? An interesting point is that back in 1556 Pre-Involutary, your same little tune may be discovered lurking in Knox's Anglo-Genevan Psalter, where it espoused the cause of the third psalm—"

"You dreary old fish! Wake yourself! How can you criticize my intended way of dying when you have such a fustian way of living?"

This time he heard her words. So close did he seem that his peevish pinching at the bridge of his snuffy old nose tickled hers, too.

"What are you doing *now*, Dandi?" he inquired.

"If you had been listening, you'd know. Here's where I am, on the last Ghinomon plain before Crotheria and home." She swept the landscape again and he took it in, drank it almost greedily. Many mentors went blind early in life shut in their monastic underwater life; their most effective vision was conducted through the eyes of their wards.

His view of what she saw enriched hers. He knew the history, the myth behind this forsaken land. He could stock the tired old landscape with pageantry, delighting her and surprising her. Back and forward he went, painting her pictures: the Youdicans, the Lombards, the Ex-Europa Emissary, the Grites, the Risorgimento, the Involuters—and catchwords, costumes, customs, courtesans, pelted briefly through Dandi Lashadusa's mind. Ah, she thought admiringly, who could truly live without these priestly, beastly, erudite, erratic mentors?

"Erratic?" he inquired, snatching at her lick of thought. "A thousand years I live, for all that time to absent myself from the world, to eat mashed fish here with my brothers, learning history, studying rapport, sleeping with my bones on stones— a humble being, a being in a million, a mentor in a myriad, and your standards of judgment are so mundane you find no stronger label for me than erratic?! Fie, Lashadusa, bother me no more for fifty years!"

The words squeaked in her head as if she spoke herself. She felt his old chops work phantomlike in hers, and half in anger half in laughter called aloud, "I'll be dead by then!"

He snicked back hot and holy to reply, "And another thing about your footloose swan song—in Marot and Beza's Genevan Psalter of 1551, Old Time, it was musical midwife to the one hundred and thirty-fourth psalm. Like you, it never seemed to settle!" Then he was gone.

"Pooh!" Dandi said. She whistled. "Lass."

Obediently her great rhinolike creature, eighteen feet high at the shoulder, ambled over. The musicolumn died as the mare left it, faded, sank to a whisper, silenced: only the purple stain remained, noiseless, in the lonely air. Lowering its great Oligocene head, Lass nuzzled its mistress's hand. She climbed the ladder onto the ridged plateau of its back.

They made toward the Involute, lulled by the simple and intricate feeling of being alive.

Night was settling in now. Hidden behind banks of mist, the sun prepared to set. But Venus was high, a gallant half-crescent four times as big as the moon had been before the moon, spiraling farther and farther from Earth, had shaken off its parent's clutch to go dance around the sun, a second Mercury. Even by that time Venus had been moved by gravito-traction into Earth's orbit, so that the two sister worlds circled each other as they circled the sun.

The stamp of that great event still lay everywhere, its tokens not only in the crescent in the sky. For Venus placed a strange spell on the hearts of man, and a more penetrating displacement in his genes. Even when its atmosphere was transformed into a muffled breathability, it remained an alien world; against logic, its opportunities, its possibilities, were its own. It shaped men, just as Earth had shaped them.

On Venus, men bred themselves anew.

And they bred the so-called Impures. They bred new plants, new fruits, new creatures—original ones, and duplications of creatures not seen on Earth for eons past. From one line of these familiar strangers Dandi's baluchitherium was descended. So, for that matter, was Dandi.

The huge creature came now to the Involute, or as near as it cared to get. Again it began to crop at thistles, thrusting its nose through dewy spiders' webs and ground mist.

"Like you, I'm a vegetarian," Dandi said, climbing down to the ground. A grove of low fruit trees grew nearby; she reached up into the branches, gathered, and ate, before turning to inspect the Involute. Already her spine tingled at the nearness of it; awe, loathing, and love made a part-pleasant sensation near her heart.

The Involute was not beautiful. True, its colors changed with the changing light, yet the colors were fish-cold, for they belonged to another dimension. Though they reacted to dusk and dawn, Earth had no stronger power over them. They pricked the eyes. Perhaps, too, they were painful because they were the last signs of materialist man. Even Lass moved uneasily before that ill-defined lattice, the upper limits of which were lost in thickening gloom.

"Don't fear," Dandi said. "There's an explanation for this, old girl." She added, "There's an explanation for everything, if we can find it."

She could feel all the personalities in the Involute. It was a frozen screen of personality. All over the old planet the structures stood, to shed their awe on those who were left behind. They were the essence of man. They were man—all that remained of him on Earth.

When the first flint, the first shell, was shaped into a weapon, that action shaped man. As he molded and complicated his tools, so they molded and complicated him. He became the first scientific animal. And at last, via information theory and great computers, he gained knowledge of all his parts. He formed the Laws of Integration, which reveal all beings as part of a pattern and show them their part in the pattern. There is only the pattern; the pattern is all the universe, creator and created. For the first time it became possible to duplicate that pattern artificially— the transubstantio-spatializers were built.

Men left their strange hobbies on Earth and Venus and projected themselves into the pattern. Their entire personalities were merged with the texture of space itself. Through science, they reached immortality.

It was a one-way passage.

They did not return. Each Involute carried thousands or even millions of people. There they were, not dead, not living. How they exulted or wept in their transubstantiation, no one left could say. Only this could be said: man had gone, and a great emptiness was fallen over Earth.

★ ★ ★

"Your thoughts are heavy, Dandi Lashadusa. Get you home." Her mentor was back in her mind. She caught the feeling of him moving around and around in his coral-formed cell.

"I must think of man," she said.

"Your thoughts mean nothing, do nothing."

"Man created us: I want to consider him in peace."

"He only shaped a stream of life that was always entirely out of his control. Forget him. Get onto your mare and ride home."

"Mentor—"

"Get home, woman. Moping does not become you, I want to hear no more of your swan song, for I've given you my final word on that. Use a theme of your own, not of man's. I've said it a million times, and I say it again."

"I wasn't going to mention my music. I was only going to tell you that—"

"What then?" His thought was querulous. She felt his powerful tail tremble, disturbing the quiet water of his cell.

"I don't know—"

"Get home then."

"I'm lonely."

He shot her a picture from another of his wards before leaving her. Dandi had seen this ward before in similar dreamlike glimpses. It was a huge mole creature, still boring underground as it had been for the last hundred years. Occasionally it crawled through vast caves; once it swam in a subterranean lake; most of the time it just bored through rock. Its motivations were obscure to Dandi, although her mentor referred to it as "a geologer." Doubtless if the mole was vouchsafed occasional glimpses of Dandi and her musicolumnology, it would find her as baffling. At least the mentor's point was made: loneliness was psychological, not statistical.

Why, a million personalities glittered almost before her eyes!

She mounted the great baluchitherium mare and headed for home. Time and old monuments made glum company.

Twilight now, with just one streak of antique gold left in the sky, Venus sweetly bright, and stars peppering the purple. A fine evening in which to be alive, particularly with one's last bedtime close at hand.

And yes, for all her mentor said, she was going to turn into that old little piece derived from one of the tunes in the 1540 *Souter Liedekens*, that splendid source of Netherlands folk music. For a moment, Dandi Lashadusa chuckled almost as eruditely as her mentor. The sixteenth century, with the virtual death of plainsong and virtual birth of the violin, was most interesting to her. Ah, the richness of facts, the texture of man's brief history on Earth! Pure joy! Then she remembered herself.

After all, she was only a megatherium, a sloth as big as a small elephant, whose kind had been extinct for millions of years until man reconstituted a few of them in the Venusian experiments. Her modifications in the way of fingers and enlarged brain gave her no real qualification to think up to man's level.

Early next morning, they arrived at the ramparts of the town Crotheria, where Dandi lived. The ubiquitous goats thronged about them, some no bigger than hedgehogs, some almost as big as hippos—what madness in his last days had provoked man to so many variations on one undistinguished theme?—as Lass and her mistress moved up the last slope and under the archway.

It was good to be back, to push among the trails fringed with bracken, among the palms, oaks, and treeferns. Almost all the town was deeply green and private from the sun, curtained by swathes of Spanish moss. Here and there were houses—caves, pits, crude piles of boulders, or even genuine man-type buildings, grand in ruin. Dandi climbed down, walking ahead of her mount, her long hair curling in pleasure. The air was cool with the coo of doves or the occasional bleat of a merino.

As she explored familiar ways, though, disappointment overcame her. Her friends were all away, even the dreamy bison whose wallow lay at the corner of the street in which Dandi lived. Only pure animals were here, rooting happily and mindlessly in the lanes, beggars who owned the Earth. The Impures—descendants of the Venusian experimental stock—were all absent from Crotheria.

That was understandable. For obvious reasons man had increased the abilities of herbivores rather than carnivores. After the Involution, with man gone, these Impures had taken to his towns as they took to his ways, as far as this was possible to their natures. Both Dandi and Lass, and many of the others, consumed massive amounts of vegetable matter every day. Gradually a wider and wider circle of desolation grew about each town (the greenery in the town itself was sacrosanct), forcing a seminomadic life onto its vegetarian inhabitants.

This thinning in its turn led to a decline in the birthrate. The travelers grew fewer, the towns greener and emptier; in time they had become little oases of forest studding the grassless plains.

"Rest here, Lass," Dandi said at last, pausing by a bank of brightly flowering cycads. "I'm going into my house."

A giant beech grew before the stone façade of her home, so close that it was hard to determine whether it did not help support the ancient building. A crumbling balcony jutted from the first floor; reaching up, Dandi seized the balustrade and hauled herself onto it.

This was her normal way of entering her home, for the ground floor was taken over by goats and hogs, just as the third floor had been appropriated by doves and parakeets. Trampling over the greenery self-sown on the balcony, she moved into the front room. Dandi smiled. Here were her old things, the broken furniture on which she liked to sleep, the vision screens on which nothing could be seen, the heavy manuscript books in which, guided by her know-all mentor, she wrote down the outpourings of the musicolumns she had visited all over the world.

She ambled through to the next room.

She paused, her peace of mind suddenly broken.

A brown bear stood there. One of its heavy hands was clenched over the hilt of a knife.

"I am no vulgar thief," it said, curling its thick black lips over the syllables. "I am an archaeologer. If this is your place, you must grant me permission to remove the man things. Obviously you have no idea of the worth of some of the equipment here. We bears require it. We must have it."

It came toward her, panting doggy fashion, its jaws open. From under bristling eyebrows gleamed the lust to kill.

Dandi was frightened. Peaceful by nature, she feared the bears above all creatures for their fierceness and their ability to organize. The bears were few: they were the only creatures to show signs of wishing to emulate man's old aggressiveness.

She knew what the bears did. They hurled themselves through the Involutes to increase their power; by penetrating those patterns, they nourished their psychic drive, so the mentor said. It was forbidden. They were transgressors. They were killers.

"Mentor!" she screamed.

The bear hesitated. As far as he was concerned, the hulking creature before him was merely an obstacle in the way of progress, something to be thrust aside without hate. Killing would be pleasant but irrelevant; more important items remained to be done. Much of the equipment housed here could be used in the rebuilding of the world, the world of which bears had such high, haphazard dreams. Holding the knife threateningly, he moved forward.

The mentor was in Dandi's head, answering her cry, seeing through her eyes, though he had no sight of his own. He scanned the bear and took over her mind instantly, knifing himself into place like a guillotine.

No longer was he a blind old dolphin lurking in one cell of a cathedral pile of coral under tropical seas, a theologer, an inculcator of wisdom into feebler-minded beings. He was a killer more savage than the bear, keen to kill anything that might covet the vacant throne once held by men. The mere thought of men could send this mentor into sharklike fury at times.

Caught up in his fury, Dandi found herself advancing. For all the bear's strength, she could vanquish it. In the open, where she could have brought her heavy tail into action, it would have been an easy matter. Here her weighty forearms must come into play. She felt them lift to her mentor's command as he planned for her to clout the bear to death.

The bear stepped back, awed by an opponent twice its size, suddenly unsure. She advanced.

"No! Stop!" Dandi cried.

Instead of fighting the bear, she fought her mentor, hating his hate. Her mind twisted, her dim mind full of that steely, fishy one, as she blocked his resolution.

"I'm for peace!" she cried.

"Then kill the bear!"

"I'm for peace, not killing!"

She rocked back and forth. When she staggered into a wall, it shook; dust spread in the old room. The mentor's fury was terrible to feel.

"Get out quickly!" Dandi called to the bear.

Hesitating, it stared at her. Then it turned and made for the window. For a moment it hung with its shaggy hind-quarters in the room. Momentarily she saw it for what it was, an old animal in an old world, without direction. It jumped. It was gone. Goats blared confusion on its retreat.

The mentor screamed. Insane with frustration, he hurled Dandi against the doorway with all the force of his mind.

Wood cracked and splintered. The lintel came crashing down. Brick and stone shifted, grumbled, fell. Powdered filth billowed up. With a great roar, one wall collapsed. Dandi struggled to get free. Her house was tumbling about her. It had never been intended to carry so much weight, so many centuries.

She reached the balcony and jumped clumsily to safety, just as the building avalanched in on itself, sending a cloud of plaster and powdered mortar into the overhanging trees.

For a horribly long while the world was full of dust, goat bleats, and panic-stricken parakeets.

Heavily astride her baluchitherium once more, Dandi Lashadusa headed back to the empty region called Ghinomon. She fought her bitterness, trying to urge herself toward resignation.

All she had was destroyed—not that she set store by possessions: that was a man trait. Much more terrible was the knowledge that her mentor had left her forever; she had transgressed too badly to be forgiven this time.

Suddenly she was lonely for his persnickety voice in her head, for the wisdom he fed her, for the scraps of dead knowledge he tossed her—yes, even for the love he gave her. She had never seen him, never could: yet no two beings could have been more intimate.

She also missed those other wards of his she would glimpse no more: the mole creature tunneling in Earth's depths, the seal family that barked with laughter on a desolate coast, a senile gorilla that endlessly collected and classified spiders, an aurochs—seen only once, but then unforgettably—that lived with smaller creatures in an Arctic city it had helped build in the ice.

She was excommunicated.

Well, it was time for her to change, to disintegrate, to transubstantiate into a pattern not of flesh but music. That discipline at least the mentor had taught and could not take away.

"This will do, Lass," she said.

Her gigantic mount stopped obediently. Lovingly, she patted its neck. It was young; it would be free.

Following the dusty trail, she went ahead, alone. Somewhere afar a bird called. Coming to a mound of boulders, Dandi squatted among gorse, the points of which could not prick through her thick old coat. Already her selected music poured through her head, already it seemed to loosen the chemical bonds of her being.

Why should she not choose an old human tune? She was an antiquarian. Things that were gone solaced her for things that were to come. In her dim way, she had always stood out against her mentor's absolute hatred of men. The thing to hate was hatred. Men in their finer moments had risen above hate. Her death psalm was an instance of that—a multiple instance, for it had been fingered and changed over the ages, as the mentor himself insisted, by men of a variety of races, all with their minds directed to worship rather than hate.

Locking herself into thought disciplines, Dandi began to dissolve. Man had needed machines to help him do it, to fit into the Involutes. She was a lesser animal: she could change herself into the humbler shape of a musicolumn. It was just a matter of *rearranging—and without pain she formed into a pattern that was not a shaggy megatherium body, but an indigo column, hardly visible. . . .*

For a long while Lass cropped thistle and cacti. Then she ambled forward to seek the hairy creature she fondly—and a little condescendingly—regarded as her equal. But of the sloth there was no sign.

Almost the only landmark was a violet-blue dye in the air. As the baluchitherium mare approached, a sweet old music grew in volume from the dye. It was a music almost as ancient as the landscape itself, and certainly as much traveled, a tune once known to men as Old Hundredth. And there were voices singing: "All creatures that on Earth do dwell. . . ."

Alpha Ralpha Boulevard

CORDWAINER SMITH

The late Cordwainer Smith—in "real" life Dr. Paul M. A. Linebarger, scholar, states-man, and author of the definitive text (still taught from today) on the art of psycho-logical warfare—was a writer of enormous talents who, from 1948 until his untimely death in 1966, produced a double-handful of some of the best short fiction this genre has ever seen: "On the Storm Planet," "A Planet Named Shayol," "Mother Hitton's Littul Kittons," "The Ballad of Lost C'Mell," "The Dead Lady of Clown Town," "The Game of Rat and Dragon," "Drunkboat," "The Lady Who Sailed *The Soul*," "Under Old Earth," and "Scanners Live in Vain," as well as a large number of lesser, but still fascinating, stories, all twisted and blended and woven into an interrelated tapestry of incredible lushness and intricacy. Smith created a baroque cosmology unrivaled even today for its scope and complexity: a millennia spanning Future History, log-ically outlandish and elegantly strange, set against a vivid, richly colored, mythically intense universe where animals assume the shape of men, vast planoform ships whisper through multidimensional space, immense sick sheep are the most valuable objects in the universe, immortality can be bought, and the mysterious Lords of the Instrumentality rule a hunted Earth too old for history. . . .

It is a cosmology that looks as evocative and bizarre today in the 1990s as it did in the 1960s—certainly for sheer sweep and daring of conceptualization, in its vision of how different and *strange* the future will be, it rivals any contemporary vision conjured up by Young Turks such as Bruce Sterling and Greg Bear, and I suspect that it is timeless.

In the famous story that follows, Smith shows us a future *so* ultracivilized and overcontrolled and unshakably placid, so utterly safe and predictable in every pos-sible way, that the only way that can be found to make the inhabitants really *human* again is to give up all that control and let Chaos and Old Night back into the world again—but, of course, once you *do* that, you then have to deal with the *conse-quences,* no matter where they lead you. . . .

Cordwainer Smith's books include the novel *Norstrilia* and the collections *Space Lords*—one of the landmark collections of the genre—*The Best of Cordwainer Smith, Quest of the Three Worlds, Stardreamer, You Will Never Be the Same,* and

The Instrumentality of Mankind. Under the name Felix C. Forrest he published two mainstream novels, *Ria* and *Carola,* and under the name Carmichael Smith, he published the thriller *Atomsk.*

His most recent book is the posthumous collection *The Rediscovery of Man: The Complete Short Science Fiction of Cordwainer Smith* (NESFA Press, P.O. Box 809, Framingham, MA 07101-0203, $24.95), a huge book that collects almost all of his short fiction and will certainly stand as one of the very best collections of the decade—a book that belongs in every complete SF collection.

We were drunk with happiness in those early years. Everybody was, especially the young people. These were the first years of the Rediscovery of Man, when the Instrumentality dug deep in the treasury, reconstructing the old cultures, the old languages, and even the old troubles. The nightmare of perfection had taken our forefathers to the edge of suicide. Now under the leadership of the Lord Jestocost and the Lady Alice More, the ancient civilizations were rising like great land masses out of the sea of the past.

I myself was the first man to put a postage stamp on a letter, after fourteen thousand years. I took Virginia to hear the first piano recital. We watched at the eye-machine when cholera was released in Tasmania, and we saw the Tasmanians dancing in the streets, now that they did not have to be protected any more. Everywhere, things became exciting. Everywhere, men and women worked with a wild will to build a more imperfect world.

I myself went into a hospital and came out French. Of course I remembered my early life; I remembered *it,* but it did not matter. Viginia was French, too, and we had the years of our future lying ahead of us like ripe fruit hanging in an orchard of perpetual summers. We had no idea when we would die. Formerly, I would be able to go to bed and think, "The government has given me four hundred years. Three hundred and seventy-four years from now, they will stop the stroon injections and I will then die." Now I knew anything could happen. The safety devices had been turned off. The diseases ran free. With luck, and hope, and love, I might live a thousand years. Or I might die tomorrow. I was free.

We revelled in every moment of the day.

Virginia and I brought the first French newspaper to appear since the Most Ancient World fell. We found delight in the news, even in the advertisements. Some parts of the culture were hard to reconstruct. It was difficult to talk about foods of which only the names survived but the homunculi and the machines, working tirelessly in Downdeep-downdeep, kept the surface of the world filled with enough novelties to fill anyone's heart with hope. We knew that all of this was make-believe, and yet it was not. We knew that when the diseases had killed the statistically correct number of people, they would be turned off; when the accident rate rose too high, it would stop without our knowing why. We knew that over us all, the Instrumentality watched. We had confidence that the Lord Jestocost and the Lady Alice More would play with us as friends and not use us as victims of a game.

Take for example, Virginia. She had been called Menerima, which represented the coded sounds of her birth number. She was small, verging on chubby; she was compact; her head was covered with tight brown curls: her eyes were a brown so deep and so rich that it took sunlight, with her squinting against it, to bring forth the treasures of her irises. I had known her well, but never known her. I had seen her often, but never seen her with my heart, until we met just outside the hospital, after becoming French.

I was pleased to see an old friend and started to speak in the Old Common Tongue, but the words jammed, and as I tried to speak it was not Menerima any longer, but someone of ancient beauty, rare and strange—someone who had wandered into these latter days from the treasure worlds of time past. All I could do was to stammer:

"What do you call yourself now?" And I said it in ancient French.

She answered in the same language, "Je m'appelle Virginie."

Looking at her and falling in love was a single process. There was something strong, something wild in her, wrapped and hidden by the tenderness and youth of her girlish body. It was as though destiny spoke to me out of the certain brown eyes, eyes which questioned me surely and wonderingly, just as we both questioned the fresh new world which lay about us.

"May I?" said I, offering her my arm, as I had learned in the hours of hypnopedia. She took my arm and we walked away from the hospital.

I hummed a tune which had come into my mind, along with the ancient French language.

She tugged gently on my arm, and smiled up at me.

"What is it," she asked, "or don't you know?"

The words came soft and unbidden to my lips and I sang it very quietly, muting my voice in her curly hair, half-singing half-whispering the popular song which had poured into my mind with all the other things which the Rediscovery of Man had given me:

> She wasn't the woman I went to seek.
> I met her by the merest chance.
> She did not speak the French of France,
> But the surded French of Martinique.
>
> She wasn't rich. She wasn't chic.
> She had a most entrancing glance,
> And that was all . . . "

Suddenly I ran out of words, "I seem to have forgotten the rest of it. It's called 'Macouba' and it has something to do with a wonderful island which the ancient French called Martinique."

"I know where that is," she cried. She had been given the same memories that I had. "You can see it from Earthport!"

This was a sudden return to the world we had known. Earthport stood on its single pedestal, twelve miles high, at the eastern edge of the small continent. At the top of it, the lords worked amid machines which had no meaning any more. There the ships whispered their way in from the stars. I had seen pictures of it, but I had never been there. As a matter of fact, I had never known anyone who had actually been up Earthport. Why should we have gone? We might not have been welcome, and we could always see it just as well through the pictures on the eye-machine. For Menerima—familiar, dully pleasant, dear little Menerima—to have gone there was uncanny. It made me think that in the Old Perfect World things had not been as plain or forthright as they seemed.

Virginia, the new Menerima, tried to speak in the Old Common Tongue, but she gave up and used French instead:

"My aunt," she said, meaning a kindred lady, since no one had had aunts for thousands of years, "was a Believer. She took me to the Abba-dingo. To get holiness and luck."

The old me was a little shocked; the French me was disquieted by the fact that this girl had done something unusual even before mankind itself turned to the unusual. The Abba-dingo was a long-obsolete computer set partway up the column of Earthport. The homunculi treated it as a god, and occasionally people went to it. To do so was tedious and vulgar.

Or had been. Till all things became new again.

Keeping the annoyance out of my voice, I asked her:

"What was it like?"

She laughed lightly, yet there was a trill to her laughter which gave me a shiver. If the old Menerima had had secrets, what might the new Virginia do? I almost hated the fate which made me love her, which made me feel that the touch of her hand on my arm was a link between me and time-forever.

She smiled at me instead of answering my question. The surfaceway was under repair; we followed a ramp down to the level of the top underground, where it was legal for true persons and hominids and homunculi to walk.

I did not like the feeling; I had never gone more than twenty minutes' trip from my birthplace. This ramp looked safe enough. There were few hominids around these days, men from the stars who (though of true human stock) had been changed to fit the conditions of a thousand worlds. The homunculi were morally repulsive, though many of them looked like very handsome people; bred from animals into the shape of men, they took over the tedious chores of working with machines where no real man would wish to go. It was whispered that some of them had even bred with actual people, and I would not want my Virginia to be exposed to the presence of such a creature.

She had been holding my arm. When we walked down the ramp to the busy passage, I slipped my arm free and put it over her shoulders, drawing her closer to me. It was light enough, bright enough to be clearer than the daylight which we had left behind, but it was strange and full of danger. In the old days, I would have turned around and gone home rather than to expose myself to the presence of such dreadful beings. At this time, in this moment, I could not bear to part from my newfound love, and I was afraid that if I went back to my own apartment in the tower, she might go to hers. Anyhow, being French gave a spice to danger.

Actually, the people in the traffic looked commonplace enough. There were many busy machines, some in human form and some not. I did not see a single hominid. Other people, whom I knew to be homunculi because they yielded the right of way to us, looked no different from the real human beings on the surface. A brilliantly beautiful girl gave me a look which I did not like—saucy, intelligent, provocative beyond all limits of flirtation. I suspected her of being a dog by origin. Among the homunculi, d'persons are the ones most apt to take liberties. They even have a dog-man philosopher who once produced a tape arguing that since dogs are the most ancient of men's allies, they have the right to be closer to man than any other form of life. When I saw the tape, I thought it amusing that a dog should be bred into the form of a Socrates; here, in the top underground, I was not so sure at all. What would I do if one of them became insolent? Kill him? That meant a brush with the law and a talk with the subcommissioners of the Instrumentality.

Virginia noticed none of this.

She had not answered my question, but was asking me questions about the top underground instead. I had been there only once before, when I was small, but it was flattering to have her wondering, husky voice murmuring in my ear.

Then it happened.

At first I thought he was a man, foreshortened by some trick of the underground light. When he came closer, I saw that it was not. He must have been five feet across the shoulders. Ugly red scars on his forehead showed where the horns had been dug out of his skull. He was a humunculus, obviously derived from cattle stock. Frankly, I had never known that they left them that ill-formed.

And he was drunk.

As he came closer I could pick up the buzz of his mind. . . . *they're not people, they're not hominids, and they're not Us—what are they doing here? The words they think confuse me.* He had never telepathed French before.

This was bad. For him to talk was common enough, but only a few of the homunculi were telepathic—those with special jobs, such as in the Downdeep-downdeep, where only telepathy could relay instructions.

Virginia clung to me.

Thought I, in clear Common Tongue: *True men are we. You must let us pass.*

There was no answer but a roar. I do not know where he got drunk, or on what, but he did not get my message.

I could see his thoughts forming up into panic, helplessness, hate. Then he charged, almost dancing toward us, as though he could crush our bodies.

My mind focused and I threw the stop order at him.

It did not work.

Horror-stricken, I realized that I had thought French at him.

Virginia screamed.

The bull-man was upon us.

At the last moment he swerved, passed us blindly, and let out a roar which filled the enormous passage. He had raced beyond us.

Still holding Virginia, I turned around to see what had made him pass us.

What I beheld was odd in the extreme.

Our figures ran down the corridor away from us—my black-purple cloak flying in the still air as my image ran, Virginia's golden dress swimming out behind her as she ran with me. The images were perfect and the bull-man pursued them.

I stared around in bewilderment. We had been told that the safeguards no longer protected us.

A girl stood quietly next to the wall. I had almost mistaken her for a statue. Then she spoke,

"Come no closer. I am a cat. It was easy enough to fool him. You had better get back to the surface."

"Thank you," I said, "thank you. What is your name?"

"Does it matter?" said the girl. "I'm not a person."

A little offended, I insisted, "I just wanted to thank you." As I spoke to her I saw that she was as beautiful and as bright as a flame. Her skin was clear, the color of cream, and her hair—finer than any human hair could possibly be—was the wild golden orange of a Persian cat.

"I'm C'mell," said the girl, "and I work at Earthport."

That stopped both Virginia and me. Cat-people were below us, and should be shunned, but Earthport was above us, and had to be respected. Which was C'mell?

She smiled, and her smile was better suited for my eyes than for Virginia's. It spoke a whole world of voluptuous knowledge. I knew she wasn't trying to do anything to me; the rest of her manner showed that. Perhaps it was the only smile she knew.

"Don't worry," she said, "about the formalities. You'd better take these steps here. I hear him coming back."

I spun around, looking for the drunken bull-man. He was not to be seen.

"Go up here," urged C'mell, "They are emergency steps and you will be back on the surface. I can keep him from following. Was that French you were speaking?"

"Yes," said I. "How did you—?"

"Get along," she said. "Sorry I asked. Hurry!"

I entered the small door. A spiral staircase went to the surface. It was below our dignity as true people to use steps, but with C'mell urging me, there was nothing else I could do. I nodded goodbye to C'mell and drew Virginia after me up the stairs.

At the surface we stopped.

Virginia gasped, "Wasn't it horrible?"

"We're safe now," said I.

"It's not safety," she said. "It's the dirtiness of it. Imagine having to talk to her!"

Virginia meant that C'mell was worse than the drunken bull-man. She sensed my reserve because she said,

"The sad thing is, you'll see her again . . ."

"What! How do you know that?"

"I don't know it," said Virginia. "I guess it. But I guess good, very good. After all, I went to the Abba-dingo."

"I asked you, darling, to tell me what happened there."

She shook her head mutely and began walking down the streetway. I had no choice but to follow her. It made me a little irritable.

I asked again, more crossly, "What was it like?"

With hurt girlish dignity she said, "Nothing, nothing. It was a long climb. The old woman made me go with her. It turned out that the machine was not talking that day, anyhow, so we got permission to drop down a shaft and to come back on the rolling road. It was just a wasted day."

She had been talking straight ahead, not to me, as though the memory were a little ugly.

Then she turned her face to me. The brown eyes looked into my eyes as though she were searching for my soul. (Soul. There's a word we have in French, and there is nothing quite like it in the Old Common Tongue.) She brightened and pleaded with me:

"Let's not be dull on the new day. Let's be good to the new us, Paul. Let's do something really French, if that's what we are to be."

"A café," I cried. "We need a café. And I know where one is."

"Where?"

"Two undergrounds over. Where the machines come out and where they permit the homunculi to peer in the window." The thought of homunculi peering at us struck the new me as amusing, though the old me had taken them as much for granted as windows or tables. The old me never met any, but knew that they weren't exactly people, since they were bred from animals, but they looked just about like people, and they could talk. It took a Frenchman like the new me to realize that they could be ugly, or beautiful, or picturesque. More than picturesque: romantic.

Evidently Virginia now thought the same, for she said, "But they're *nette*, just adorable. What is the café called?"

"The Greasy Cat," said I.

The Greasy Cat. How was I to know that this led to a nightmare between high waters, and to the winds which cried? How was I to suppose that this had anything to do with Alpha Ralpha Boulevard?

No force in the world could have taken me there, if I had known.

Other new-French people had gotten to the café before us.

A waiter with a big brown moustache took our order. I looked closely at him to see if he might be a licensed homunculus, allowed to work among people because his services were indispensable; but he was not. He was pure machine, though his voice rang out with old-Parisian heartiness, and the designers had even built into him the nervous habit of mopping the back of his hand against his big moustache, and had fixed him so that little beads of sweat showed high up on his brow, just below the hairline.

"Mamselle? M'sieu? Beer? Coffee? Red wine next month. The sun will shine in the quarter after the hour and after the half-hour. At twenty minutes to the hour it will rain for five minutes so that you can enjoy these umbrellas. I am a native of Alsace. You may speak French or German to me."

"Anything," said Virginia. "You decide, Paul."

"Beer, please," said I. "Blonde beer for both of us."

"But certainly, M'sieu," said the waiter.

He left, waving his cloth wildly over his arm.

Virginia puckered up her eyes against the sun and said, "I wish it would rain now. I've never seen real rain."

"Be patient, honey."

She turned earnestly to me. "What is 'German,' Paul?"

"Another language, another culture. I read they will bring it to life next year. But don't you like being French?"

"I like it fine," she said. "Much better than being a number. But Paul—" And then she stopped, her eyes blurred with perplexity.

"Yes, darling?"

"Paul," she said, and the statement of my name was a cry of hope from some depth of her mind beyond new me, beyond old me, beyond even the contrivances of the lords who moulded us. I reached for her hand.

Said I, "You can tell me, darling."

"Paul," she said, and it was almost weeping, "Paul, why does it all happen so fast? This is our first day, and we both feel that we may spend the rest of our lives together. There's something about marriage, whatever that is, and we're supposed to find a priest, and I don't understand that, either. Paul, Paul, Paul, why does it happen so fast? I want to love you. I do love you. But I don't want to be *made* to love you. I want it to be the real me," and as she spoke, tears poured from her eyes though her voice remained steady enough.

Then it was that I said the wrong thing.

"You don't have to worry, honey. I'm sure that the lords of the Instrumentality have programmed everything well."

At that, she burst into tears, loudly and uncontrollably. I had never seen an adult weep before. It was strange and frightening.

A man from the next table came over and stood beside me, but I did not so much as glance at him.

"Darling," said I, reasonably, "darling, we can work it out—"

"Paul, let me leave you, so that I may be yours. Let me go away for a few days or a few weeks or a few years. Then, if—if—if I *do* come back, you'll know it's me and not some program ordered by a machine. For God's sake. Paul—for God's sake!" In a different voice she said, "What is God, Paul? They gave us the words to speak, but I do not know what they mean."

The man beside me spoke. "I can take you to God," he said.

"Who are you?" said I. "And who asked you to interfere?" This was not the kind of language that we had ever used when speaking the Old Common Tongue—when they had given us a new language they had built in temperament as well.

The stranger kept his politeness—he was as French as we but he kept his temper well.

"My name," he said, "is Maximilien Macht, and I used to be a Believer."

Virginia's eyes lit up. She wiped her face absentmindedly while staring at the man. He was tall, lean, sunburned. (How could he have gotten sunburned so soon?) He had reddish hair and a moustache almost like that of the robot waiter.

"You asked about God, Mamselle," said the stranger. "God is where he has always been—around us, near us, in us."

This was strange talk from a man who looked worldly. I rose to my feet to bid him goodbye. Virginia guessed what I was doing and she said:

"That's nice of you, Paul. Give him a chair."

There was warmth in her voice.

The machine waiter came back with two conical beakers made of glass. They had a golden fluid in them with a cap of foam on top. I had never seen or heard of beer before, but I knew exactly how it would taste. I put imaginary money on the tray, received imaginary change, paid the waiter an imaginary tip. The Instrumentality had not yet figured out how to have separate kinds of money for all the new cultures, and of course you could not use real money to pay for food or drink. Food and drink are free.

The machine wiped his moustache, used his serviette (checked red and white) to dab the sweat off his brow, and then looked inquiringly at Monsieur Macht.

"M'sieu, you will sit here?"

"Indeed," said Macht.

"Shall I serve you here?"

"But why not?" said Macht. "If these good people permit."

"Very well," said the machine, wiping his moustache with the back of his hand. He fled to the dark recesses of the bar.

All this time Virginia had not taken her eyes off Macht.

"You are a Believer?" she asked. "You are still a Believer, when you have been made French like us? How do you know you're you? Why do I love Paul? Are the lords and their machines controlling everything in us? I want to be *me*. Do you know how to be *me*?"

"Not you, Mamselle," said Macht, "that would be too great an honor. But I am learning how to be myself. You see," he added, turning to me, "I have been French for two weeks now, and I know how much of me is myself, and how much has been added by this new process of giving us language and danger again."

The waiter came back with a small beaker. It stood on a stem, so that it looked like an evil little miniature of Earthport. The fluid it contained was milky white.

Macht lifted his glass to us. "Your health!"

Virginia stared at him as if she were going to cry again. When he and I sipped, she blew her nose and put her handkerchief away. It was the first time I had ever seen a person perform that act of blowing the nose, but it seemed to go well with our new culture.

Macht smiled at both of us, as if he were going to begin a speech. The sun came out, right on time. It gave him a halo, and made him look like a devil or a saint.

But it was Virginia who spoke first.

"You have been there?"

Macht raised his eyebrows a little, frowned, and said, "Yes," very quietly.

"Did you get a word?" she persisted.

"Yes." He looked glum, and a little troubled.

"What did it say?"

For answer, he shook his head at her, as if there were things which should never be mentioned in public.

I wanted to break in, to find out what this was all about.

Virginia went on, heeding me not at all: "But it did say something!"

"Yes," said Macht.

"Was it important?"

"Mamselle, let us not talk about it."

"We must," she cried. "It's life or death." Her hands were clenched so tightly together that her knuckles showed white. Her beer stood in front of her, untouched, growing warm in the sunlight.

"Very well," said Macht, "you may ask . . . I cannot guarantee to answer."

I controlled myself no longer. "What's all this about?"

Virginia looked at me with scorn, but even her scorn was the scorn of a lover, not the cold remoteness of the past. "Please, Paul, you wouldn't know. Wait a while. What did it say to you, M'sieu Macht?"

"That I, Maximilien Macht, would live or die with a brown-haired girl who was already betrothed." He smiled wrily, "And I do not even quite know what 'betrothed' means."

"We'll find out," said Virginia. "When did it say this?"

"Who is 'it'?" I shouted at them. "For God's sake, what is this all about?"

Macht looked at me and dropped his voice when he spoke: "The Abba-dingo." To her he said, "Last week."

Virginia turned white. "So it does work, it does, it does. Paul darling, it said nothing to me. But it said to my aunt something which I can't ever forget!"

I held her arm firmly and tenderly and tried to look into her eyes, but she looked away. Said I, "What did it say?"

"Paul and Virginia."

"So what?" said I.

I scarcely knew her. Her lips were tense and compressed. She was not angry. It was something different, worse. She was in the grip of tension. I suppose we had not seen that for thousands of years, either. "Paul, seize this simple fact, if you can grasp it. The machine gave that woman our names—but it gave them to her twelve years ago."

Macht stood up so suddenly that his chair fell over, and the waiter began running toward us.

"That settles it." he said. "We're all going back."

"Going where?" I said.

"To the Abba-dingo."

"But why now?" said I; and, "Will it work?" said Virginia, both at the same time.

"It always works," said Macht, "if you go on the northern side."

"How do you get there?" said Virginia.

Macht frowned sadly, "There's only one way. By Alpha Ralpha Boulevard." Virginia stood up. And so did I.

Then, as I rose, I remembered. Alpha Ralpha Boulevard. It was a ruined street hanging in the sky, faint as a vapor trail. It had been a processional highway once, where conquerors came down and tribute went up. But it was ruined, lost in the clouds, closed to mankind for a hundred centuries.

"I know it," said I. "It's ruined."

Macht said nothing, but he stared at me as if I were an outsider . . .

Virginia, very quiet and white of countenance, said, "Come along."

"But why?" said I. "Why?"

"You fool," she said, "if we don't have a God, at least we have a machine. This is the only thing left on or off the world which the Instrumentality doesn't understand. Maybe it tells the future. Maybe it's an un-machine. It certainly comes from a different time. Can't you use it, darling? If it says we're us, we're *us*."

"And if it doesn't?"

"Then we're not." Her face was sullen with grief.

"What do you mean?"

"If we're not us," she said, "we're just toys, dolls, puppets that the lords have written on. You're not you and I'm not me. But if the Abba-dingo, which knew the names Paul and Virginia twelve years before it happened—if the Abba-dingo says that we are us, I don't care if it's a predicting machine or a god or a devil or a what. I don't care, but I'll have the truth."

What could I have answered to that? Macht led, she followed, and I walked third in single file. He left the sunlight of The Greasy Cat; just as we left, a light rain began to fall. The waiter, looking momentarily like the machine that he was, stared straight ahead. We crossed the lip of the underground and went down to the fast expressway.

When we came out, we were in a region of fine homes. All were in ruins. The trees had thrust their way into the buildings. Flowers rioted across the lawn, through the open doors, and blazed in the roofless rooms. Who needed a house in the open, when the population of Earth had dropped so that the cities were commodious and empty?

Once I thought I saw a family of homunculi, including little ones, peering at me as we trudged along the soft gravel road. Maybe the faces I had seen at the edge of the house were fantasies.

Macht said nothing.

Virginia and I held hands as we walked beside him. I could have been happy at this odd excursion, but her hand was tightly clenched in mine. She bit her lower lip from time to time. I knew it mattered to her—she was on a pilgrimage. (A pilgrimage was an ancient walk to some powerful place, very good for body and soul.) I didn't mind going along. In fact, they could not have kept me from coming, once she and Macht decided to leave the café. But I didn't have to take it seriously. Did I?

What did Macht want?

Who was Macht? What thoughts had that mind learned in two short weeks? How had he preceded us into a new world of danger and adventure? I did not trust him. For the first time in my life I felt alone. Always, always, up to now, I had only to think about the Instrumentality and some protector leaped fully armed into my mind. Telepathy guarded against all dangers; healed all hurts, carried each of us forward to the one hundred and forty-six thousand and ninety-seven days which had been allotted us. Now it was different. I did not know this man, and it was on him that I relied, not on the powers which had shielded and protected us.

We turned from the ruined road into an immense boulevard. The pavement was so smooth and unbroken that nothing grew on it, save where the wind and dust had deposited random little pockets of earth.

Macht stopped.

"This is it," he said. "Alpha Ralpha Boulevard."

We fell silent and looked at the causeway of forgotten empires.

To our left the boulevard disappeared in a gentle curve. It led far north of the city in which I had been reared. I knew that there was another city to the north, but I had forgotten its name. Why should I have remembered it? It was sure to be just like my own.

But to the right—

To the right the boulevard rose sharply, like a ramp. It disappeared into the clouds. Just at the edge of the cloud-line there was a hint of disaster. I could not see for sure, but it looked to me as though the whole boulevard had been sheared off by unimaginable forces. Somewhere beyond the clouds there stood the Abbadingo, the place where all questions were answered . . .

Or so they thought.

Virginia cuddled close to me.

"Let's turn back," said I. "We are city people. We don't know anything about ruins."

"You can if you want to," said Macht. "I was just trying to do you a favor."

We both looked at Virginia.

She looked up at me with those brown eyes. From the eyes there came a plea older than woman or man, older than the human race. I knew what she was going to say before she said it. She was going to say that she *had* to know.

Macht was idly crushing some soft rocks near his foot.

At last Virginia spoke up: "Paul, I don't want danger for its own sake. But I meant what I said back there. Isn't there a chance that we were *told* to love each other? What sort of a life would it be if our happiness, our own selves, depended on a thread in a machine or on a mechanical voice which spoke to us when we were asleep and learning French? It may be fun to go back to the old world. I guess it is. I know that you give me a kind of happiness which I never even suspected before this day. If it's really us, we have something wonderful, and we ought to know it. But if it isn't—" She burst into sobs.

I wanted to say, "If it isn't, it will seem just the same," but the ominous sulky face of Macht looked at me over Virginia's shoulder as I drew her to me. There was nothing to say.

I held her close.

From beneath Macht's foot there flowed a trickle of blood. The dust drank it up.

"Macht," said I, "are you hurt?"

Virginia turned around, too.

Macht raised his eyebrows at me and said with unconcern, "No. Why?"

"The blood. At your feet."

He glanced down. "Oh, those," he said, "they're nothing. Just the eggs of some kind of an un-bird which does not even fly."

"Stop it!" I shouted telepathically, using the Old Common Tongue. I did not even try to think in our new-learned French.

He stepped back a pace in surprise.

Out of nothing there came to me a message: *thankyou thankyou goodgreat gohomeplease thankyou goodgreat goaway manbad manbad manbad . . .* Somewhere an animal or bird was warning me against Macht. I thought a casual *thanks* to it and turned my attention to Macht.

He and I stared at each other. Was this what *culture* was? Were we now men? Did freedom always include the freedom to mistrust, to fear, to hate?

I liked him not at all. The words of forgotten crimes came into my mind: *assassination, murder, abduction, insanity, rape, robbery . . .*

We had known none of these things and yet I felt them all.

He spoke evenly to me. We had both been careful to guard our minds against being read telepathically, so that our only means of communication were empathy and French. "It's your idea," he said, most untruthfully, "or at least your lady's . . ."

"Has lying already come into the world," said I, "so that we walk into the clouds for no reason at all?"

"There is a reason," said Macht.

I pushed Virginia gently aside and capped my mind so tightly that the antitelepathy felt like a headache.

"Macht," said I, and I myself could hear the snarl of an animal in my own voice, "tell me why you have brought us here or I will kill you."

He did not retreat. He faced me, ready for a fight. He said, "Kill? You mean, to make me dead?" but his words did not carry conviction. Neither one of us knew how to fight, but he readied for defense and I for attack.

Underneath my thought shield an animal thought crept in: *goodman goodman take him by the neck no-air he-aaah no-air he-aaah like broken egg . . .*

I took the advice without worrying where it came from. It was simple. I walked over to Macht, reached my hands around his throat and squeezed. He tried to push my hands away. Then he tried to kick me. All I did was hang on to his throat. If I had been a lord or a Go-captain, I might have known about fighting. But I did not, and neither did he.

It ended when a sudden weight dragged at my hands.

Out of surprise, I let go.

Macht had become unconscious. Was that *dead?*

It could not have been, because he sat up. Virginia ran to him. He rubbed his throat and said with a rough voice:

"You should not have done that."

This gave me courage. "Tell me," I spat at him, "tell me why you wanted us to come, or I will do it again."

Macht grinned weakly. He leaned his head against Virginia's arm. "It's fear," he said. "Fear."

"Fear?" I knew the word—*peur*—but not the meaning. Was it some kind of disquiet or animal alarm?

I had been thinking with my mind open; he thought back *yes.*

"But why do you like it?" I asked.

It is delicious, he thought. *It makes me sick and thrilly and alive. It is like strong medicine, almost as good as stroon. I went there before. High up, I had much fear. It was wonderful and bad and good, all at the same time. I lived a thousand years in a single hour. I wanted more of it, but I thought it would be even more exciting with other people.*

"Now I will kill you," said I in French. "You are very—very . . ." I had to look for the word. "You are very evil."

"No," said Virginia, "let him talk."

He thought at me, not bothering with words. *This is what the lords of the Instrumentality never let us have. Fear. Reality. We were born in a stupor and we died in a dream. Even the underpeople, the animals, had more life than we did. The machines did not have fear. That's what we were. Machines who thought they were men. And now we are free.*

He saw the edge of raw, red anger in my mind, and he changed the subject. *I did not lie to you. This is the way to the Abba-dingo. I have been there. It works. On this side, it always works.*

"It works," cried Virginia. "You see he says so. It works! He is telling the truth. Oh, Paul, do let's go on!"

"All right," said I, "we'll go."

I helped him rise. He looked embarrassed, like a man who has shown something of which he is ashamed.

We walked onto the surface of the indestructible boulevard. It was comfortable to the feet.

At the bottom of my mind the little unseen bird or animal babbled its thoughts at me: *goodman goodman make him dead take water take water . . .*

I paid no attention as I walked forward with her and him, Virginia between us. I paid no attention.

I wish I had.

We walked for a long time.

The process was new to us. There was something exhilarating in knowing that no one guarded us, that the air was free air, moving without benefit of weather machines. We saw many birds, and when I thought at them I found their minds startled and opaque; they were natural birds, the like of which I had never seen before. Virginia asked me their names, and I outrageously applied all the bird-names which we had learned in French without knowing whether they were historically right or not.

Maximilien Macht cheered up, too, and he even sang us a song, rather off key, to the effect that we would take the high road and he the low one, but that he would be in Scotland before us. It did not make sense, but the lilt was pleasant. Whenever he got a certain distance ahead of Virginia and me, I made up variations on "Macouba" and sang-whispered the phrases into her pretty ear:

> *"She wasn't the woman I went to seek.*
> *I met her by the merest chance.*
> *She did not speak the French of France,*
> *But the surded French of Martinique."*

We were happy in adventure and freedom, until we became hungry. Then our troubles began.

Virginia stepped up to a lamp-post, struck it lightly with her fist and said, "Feed me." The post should either have opened, serving us a dinner, or else told us where, within the next few hundred yards, food was to be had. It did neither. It did nothing. It must have been broken.

With that, we began to make a game of hitting every single post.

Alpha Ralpha Boulevard had risen about half a kilometer above the surrounding countryside. The wild birds wheeled below us. There was less dust on the pavement, and fewer patches of weeds. The immense road, with no pylons below it, curved like an unsupported ribbon into the clouds.

We wearied of beating posts and there was neither food nor water.

Virginia became fretful: "It won't do any good to go back now. Food is even farther the other way. I do wish you'd brought something."

How should I have thought to carry food? Who ever carries food? Why would they carry it, when it is everywhere? My darling was unreasonable, but she was my darling and I loved her all the more for the sweet imperfections of her temper.

Macht kept tapping pillars, partly to keep out of our fight, and obtained an unexpected result.

At one moment I saw him leaning over to give the pillar of a large lamp the usual hearty but guarded *whop*—in the next instant he yelped like a dog and was sliding uphill at a high rate of speed. I heard him shout something, but could not make out the words, before he disappeared into the clouds ahead.

Virginia looked at me. "Do you want to go back now? Macht is gone. We can say that I got tired."

"Are you serious?"

"Of course, darling."

I laughed, a little angrily. She had insisted that we come, and now she was ready to turn around and give it up, just to please me.

"Never mind," said I. "It can't be far now. Let's go on."

"Paul . . ." She stood close to me. Her brown eyes were troubled, as though she were trying to see all the way into my mind through my eyes. I thought to her, *Do you want to talk this way?*

"No," said she, in French. "I want to say things one at a time. Paul, I do want to go to the Abba-dingo. I need to go. It's the biggest need in my life. But at the same time. I don't want to go. There is something wrong up there. I would rather have you on the wrong terms than not have you at all. Something could happen."

Edgily, I demanded, "Are you getting this 'fear' that Macht was talking about?"

"Oh, no, Paul, not at all. This feeling isn't exciting. It feels like something broken in a machine—"

"Listen!" I interrupted her.

From far ahead, from within the clouds, there came a sound like an animal wailing. There were words in it. It must have been Macht. I thought I heard "take care." When I sought him with my mind, the distance made circles and I got dizzy.

"Let's follow, darling," said I.

"Yes, Paul," said she, and in her voice there was an unfathomable mixture of happiness, resignation, and despair . . .

Before we moved on, I looked carefully at her. She *was* my girl. The sky had turned yellow and the lights were not yet on. In the yellow rich sky her brown curls were tinted with gold, her brown eyes approached the black in their irises, her young and fate-haunted face seemed more meaningful than any other human face I had ever seen.

"You *are* mine," I said.

"Yes, Paul," She answered me and then smiled brightly. "*You* said it! That is doubly nice."

A bird on the railing looked sharply at us and then left. Perhaps he did not approve of human nonsense, so flung himself downward into dark air. I saw him catch himself, far below, and ride lazily on his wings.

"We're not as free as birds, darling," I told Virginia, "but we are freer than people have been for a hundred centuries."

For her answer she hugged my arm and smiled at me.

"And now," I added, "to follow Macht. Put your arms around me and hold me tight. I'll try hitting that post. If we don't get dinner we may get a ride."

I felt her take hold tightly and then I struck the post.

Which post? An instant later the posts were sailing by us in a blur. The ground beneath our feet seemed steady, but we were moving at a fast rate. Even in the service underground I had never seen a roadway as fast as this. Virginia's dress was blowing so hard that it made snapping sounds like the snap of fingers. In no time at all we were in the cloud and out of it again.

A new world surrounded us. The clouds lay below and above. Here and there blue sky shone through. We were steady. The ancient engineers must have devised the walkway cleverly. We rode up, up, up without getting dizzy.

Another cloud.

Then things happened so fast that the telling of them takes longer than the event.

Something dark rushed at me from up ahead. A violent blow hit me in the chest. Only much later did I realize that this was Macht's arm trying to grab me before we went over the edge. Then we went into another cloud. Before I could even speak to Virginia a second blow struck me. The pain was terrible. I had never felt anything like that in all my life. For some reason, Virginia had fallen over me and beyond me. She was pulling at my hands.

I tried to tell her to stop pulling me, because it hurt, but I had no breath. Rather than argue, I tried to do what she wanted. I struggled toward her. Only then did I realize that there was nothing below my feet—no bridge, no jetway, nothing.

I was on the edge of the boulevard, the broken edge of the upper side. There was nothing below me except for some looped cables, and, far underneath them, a tiny ribbon which was either a river or a road.

We had jumped blindly across the great gap and I had fallen just far enough to catch the upper edge of the roadway on my chest.

It did not matter, the pain.

In a moment the doctor-robot would be there to repair me.

A look at Virginia's face reminded me there was no doctor-robot, no world, no Instrumentality, nothing but wind and pain. She was crying. It took a moment for me to hear what she was saying.

"I did it, I did it, darling, are you dead?"

Neither one of us was sure what "dead" meant, because people always went away at their appointed time, but we knew that it meant a cessation of life. I tried to tell her that I was living, but she fluttered over me and kept dragging me farther from the edge of the drop.

I used my hands to push myself into a sitting position.

She knelt beside me and covered my face with kisses.

At last I was able to gasp, "Where's Macht?"

She looked back. "I don't see him."

I tried to look too. Rather than have me struggle, she said, "You stay quiet. I'll look again."

Bravely she walked to the edge of the sheared-off boulevard. She looked over toward the lower side of the gap, peering through the clouds which drifted past us as rapidly as smoke sucked by a ventilator. Then she cried out:

"I see him. He looks so funny. Like an insect in the museum. He is crawling across on the cables."

Struggling to my hands and knees, I neared her and looked too. There he was, a dot moving along a thread, with the birds soaring by beneath him. It looked very unsafe. Perhaps he was getting all the "fear" that he needed to keep himself happy. I did not want that "fear," whatever it was. I wanted food, water, and a doctor-robot.

None of these were here.

I struggled to my feet. Virginia tried to help me but I was standing before she could do more than touch my sleeve.

"Let's go on."

"On?" she said.

"On to the Abba-dingo. There may be friendly machines up there. Here there is nothing but cold and wind, and the lights have not yet gone on."

She frowned. "But Macht . . . ?"

"It will be hours before he gets here. We can come back."

She obeyed.

Once again we went to the left of the boulevard. I told her to squeeze my waist while I struck the pillars, one by one. Surely there must have been a reactivating device for the passengers on the road.

The fourth time, it worked.

Once again the wind whipped our clothing as we raced upward on Alpha Ralpha Boulevard.

We almost fell as the road veered to the left. I caught my balance, only to have it veer the other way.

And then we stopped.

This was the Abba-dingo.

A walkway littered with white objects—knobs and rods and imperfectly formed balls about the size of my head.

Virginia stood beside me, silent.

About the size of my head? I kicked one of the objects aside and then knew, knew for sure, what it was. It was people. The inside parts. I had never seen such things before. And that, that on the ground, must once have been a hand. There were hundreds of such things along the walk.

"Come, Virginia," said I, keeping my voice even, and my thoughts hidden.

She followed without saying a word. She was curious about the things on the ground, but she did not seem to recognize them.

For my part, I was watching the wall.

At last I found them—the little doors of Abba-dingo.

One said METEOROLOGICAL. It was not Old Common Tongue, nor was it French, but it was so close that I knew it had something to do with the behavior of air. I put my hand against the panel of the door. The panel became translucent and ancient writing showed through. There were numbers which meant nothing, words which meant nothing, and then:

Typhoon coming.

My French had not taught me what a "coming" was, but "typhoon" was plainly *typhon*, a major air disturbance. Thought I, *let the weather machines take care of the matter.* It had nothing to do with us.

"That's no help," said I.

"What does it mean?" she said.

"The air will be disturbed."

"Oh," said she. "That couldn't matter to us, could it?"

"Of course not."

I tried the next panel, which said FOOD. When my hand touched the little door, there was an aching creak inside the wall, as though the whole tower retched. The door opened a little bit and a horrible odor came out of it. Then the door closed again.

The third door said HELP and when I touched it nothing happened. Perhaps it was some kind of tax-collecting device from the ancient days. It yielded nothing to my touch. The fourth door was larger and already partly open at the bottom. At the top, the name of the door was PREDICTIONS. Plain enough, that one was, to anyone who knew Old French. The name at the bottom was more mysterious: PUT PAPER HERE it said, and I could not guess what it meant.

I tried telepathy. Nothing happened. The wind whistled past us. Some of the calcium balls and knobs rolled on the pavement. I tried again, trying my utmost for the imprint of long-departed thoughts. A scream entered my mind, a thin long scream which did not sound much like people. That was all.

Perhaps it did upset me. I did not feel "fear," but I was worried about Virginia.

She was staring at the ground.

"Paul," she said, "isn't that a man's coat on the ground among those funny things?"

Once I had seen an ancient X-ray in the museum, so I knew that the coat still surrounded the material which had provided the inner structure of the man. There was no ball there, so that I was quite sure he was *dead*. How could that have happened in the old days? Why did the Instrumentality let it happen? But then, the Instrumentality had always forbidden this side of the tower. Perhaps the violators had met their own punishment in some way I could not fathom.

"Look, Paul," said Virginia. "I can put my hand in."

Before I could stop her, she had thrust her hand into the flat open slot which said PUT PAPER HERE.

She screamed.

Her hand was caught.

I tried to pull at her arm, but it did not move. She began gasping with pain. Suddenly her hand came free.

Clear words were cut into the living skin. I tore my cloak off and wrapped her hand.

As she sobbed beside me I unbandaged her hand. As I did so she saw the words on her skin.

The words said, in clear French: *You will love Paul all your life.*

Virginia let me bandage her hand with my cloak and then she lifted her face to be kissed. "It was worth it," she said; "it was worth all the trouble, Paul. Let's see if we can get down. Now I know."

I kissed her again and said, reassuringly, "You do know, don't you?"

"Of course," she smiled through her tears. "The Instrumentality could not have contrived this. What a clever old machine! Is it a god or a devil, Paul?"

I had not studied those words at that time, so I patted her instead of answering. We turned to leave.

At the last minute I realized that I had not tried PREDICTIONS myself.

"Just a moment, darling. Let me tear a little piece off the bandage."

She waited patiently. I tore a piece the size of my hand, and then I picked up one of the ex-person units on the ground. It may have been the front of an arm. I returned to push the cloth into the slot, but when I turned to the door, an enormous bird was sitting there.

I used my hand to push the bird aside, and he cawed at me. He even seemed to threaten me with his cries and his sharp beak. I could not dislodge him.

Then I tried telepathy. *I am a true man. Go away!*

The bird's dim mind flashed back at me nothing but *no-no-no-no-no!*

With that I struck him so hard with my fist that he fluttered to the ground. He righted himself amid the white litter on the pavement and then, opening his wings, he let the wind carry him away.

I pushed in the scrap of cloth, counted to twenty in my mind, and pulled the scrap out.

The words were plain, but they meant nothing: *You will love Virginia twenty-one more minutes.*

Her happy voice, reassured by the prediction but still unsteady from the pain in her written-on hand, came to me as though it were far away. "What does it say, darling?"

Accidentally on purpose, I let the wind take the scrap. It fluttered away like a bird. Virginia saw it go.

"Oh," she cried disappointedly. "We've lost it! What did it say?"

"Just what yours did."

"But what words, Paul? How did it say it?"

With love and heartbreak and perhaps a little "fear," I lied to her and whispered gently.

"It said, 'Paul will always love Virginia.' "

She smiled at me radiantly. Her stocky, full figure stood firmly and happily against the wind. Once again she was the chubby, pretty Menerima whom I had noticed in our block when we both were children. And she was more than that. She was my new-found love in our new-found world. She was my mademoiselle from Martinique. The message was foolish. We had seen from the food-slot that the machine was broken.

"There's no food or water here," said I. Actually, there was a puddle of water near the railing, but it had been blown over the human structural elements on the ground, and I had no heart to drink it.

Virginia was so happy that, despite her wounded hand, her lack of water and her lack of food, she walked vigorously and cheerfully.

Thought I to myself, *Twenty-one minutes. About six hours have passed. If we stay here we face unknown dangers.*

Vigorously we walked downward, down Alpha Ralpha Boulevard. We had met the Abba-dingo and were still "alive." I did not think that I was "dead," but the words had been meaningless so long that it was hard to think them.

The ramp was so steep going down that we pranced like horses. The wind blew into our faces with incredible force. That's what it was, wind, but I looked up the word *vent* only after it was all over.

We never did see the whole tower—just the wall at which the ancient jetway had deposited us. The rest of the tower was hidden by clouds which fluttered like torn rags as they raced past the heavy material.

The sky was red on one side and a dirty yellow on the other.

Big drops of water began to strike at us.

"The weather machines are broken," I shouted to Virginia.

She tried to shout back to me but the wind carried her words away. I repeated what I had said about the weather machines. She nodded happily and warmly, though the wind was by now whipping her hair past her face and the pieces of water which fell from up above were spotting her flame-golden gown. It did not matter. She clung to my arm. Her happy face smiled at me as we stamped downward, bracing ourselves against the decline in the ramp. Her brown eyes were full of confidence and life. She saw me looking at her and she kissed me on the upper arm without losing step. She was my own girl forever, and she knew it.

The water-from-above, which I later knew was actual "rain," came in increasing volume. Suddenly it included birds. A large bird flapped his way vigorously against the whistling air and managed to stand still in front of my face, though his air speed was many leagues per hour. He cawed in my face and then was carried away by the wind. No sooner had that one gone than another bird struck me in the body. I looked down at it but it too was carried away by the racing current of air. All I got was a telepathic echo from its bright blank mind: *no-no-no-no!*

Now what? thought I. A bird's advice is not much to go upon.

Virginia grabbed my arm and stopped.

I too stopped.

The broken edge of Alpha Ralpha Boulevard was just ahead. Ugly yellow clouds swam through the break like poisonous fish hastening on an inexplicable errand.

Virginia was shouting.

I could not hear her, so I leaned down. That way her mouth could almost touch my ear.

"Where is Macht?" she shouted.

Carefully I took her to the left side of the road, where the railing gave us some protection against the heavy racing air, and against the water commingled with it. By now neither of us could see very far. I made her drop to her knees. I got down beside her. The falling water pelted our backs. The light around us had turned to a dark dirty yellow.

We could still see, but we could not see much.

I was willing to sit in the shelter of the railing, but she nudged me. She wanted us to do something about Macht. What anyone could do, that was beyond me. If he had found shelter, he was safe, but if he was out on those cables, the wild pushing air would soon carry him off and then there would be no more Maximilien Macht. He would be "dead" and his interior parts would bleach somewhere on the open ground.

Virginia insisted.

We crept to the edge.

A bird swept in, true as a bullet, aiming for my face. I flinched. A wing touched me. It stung against my cheek like fire. I did not know that feathers were so tough. The birds must all have damaged mental mechanisms, thought I, if they hit people on Alpha Ralpha. That is not the right way to behave toward true people.

At last we reached the edge, crawling on our bellies. I tried to dig the fingernails of my left hand into the stone-like material of the railing, but it was flat, and there was nothing much to hold to, save for the ornamental fluting. My right arm was around Virginia. It hurt me badly to crawl forward that way, because my body was still damaged from the blow against the edge of the road, on the way coming up. When I hesitated, Virginia thrust herself forward.

We saw nothing.

The gloom was around us.

The wind and the water beat at us like fists.

Her gown pulled at her like a dog worrying its master. I wanted to get her back into the shelter of the railing, where we could wait for the air-disturbance to end.

Abruptly, the light shone all around us. It was wild electricity, which the ancients called *lightning*. Later I found that it occurs quite frequently in the areas beyond the reach of the weather machines.

The bright quick light showed us a white face staring at us. He hung on the cables below us. His mouth was open, so he must have been shouting. I shall never know whether the expression on his face showed "fear" or great happiness. It was full of excitement. The bright light went out and I thought that I heard the echo of a call. I reached for his mind telepathically and there was nothing there. Just some dim, obstinate bird thinking at me, *no-no-no-no-no!*

Virginia tightened in my arms. She squirmed around. I shouted at her in French. She could not hear.

Then I called with my mind.

Someone else was there.

Virginia's mind blazed at me, full of revulsion, *The cat girl. She is going to touch me!*

She twisted. My right arm was suddenly empty. I saw the gleam of a golden gown flash over the edge, even in the dim light. I reached with my mind, and I caught her cry:

"Paul, Paul, I love you. Paul . . . help me!"

The thoughts faded as her body dropped.

The someone else was C'mell, whom we had first met in the corridor.

I came to get you both, she thought at me; *not that the birds cared about her. What have the birds got to do with it?*

You saved them. You saved their young, when the red-topped man was killing them all. All of us have been worried about what you true people would do to us when you were free. We found out. Some of you are bad and kill other kinds of life. Others of you are good and protect life.

Thought I, is that all there is to *good* and *bad?*

Perhaps I should not have left myself off guard. People did not have to understand fighting, but the homunculi did. They were bred amidst battle and they served through troubles. C'mell, cat-girl that she was, caught me on the chin with a pistonlike fist. She had no anesthesia and the only way—cat or no cat—that she could carry me across the cables in the "typhoon" was to have me unconscious and relaxed.

I awakened in my own room. I felt very well indeed. The robot-doctor was there. Said he:

"You've had a shock. I've already reached the subcommissioner of the Instrumentality, and I can erase the memories of the last full day, if you want me to."

His expression was pleasant.

Where was the racing wind? The air falling like stone around us? The water driving where no weather machines controlled it? Where was the golden gown and the wild fear-hungry face of Maximilien Macht?

I thought these things, but the robot-doctor, not being telepathic, caught none of it. I stared hard at him.

"Where," I cried, "is my own true love?"

Robots cannot sneer, but this one attempted to do so. "The naked cat-girl with the blazing hair? She left to get some clothing."

I stared at him.

His fuddy-duddy little machine mind cooked up its own nasty little thoughts, "I must say, sir, you 'free people' change very fast indeed . . ."

Who argues with a machine? It wasn't worth answering him.

But that other machine? Twenty-one minutes. How could that work out? How could it have known? I did not want to argue with that other machine either. It must have been a very powerful left-over machine—perhaps something used in ancient wars. I had no intention of finding out. Some people might call it a god. I call it nothing. I do not need "fear" and I do not propose to go back to Alpha Ralpha Boulevard again.

But hear, oh heart of mine!—how can you ever visit the café again?

C'mell came in and the robot-doctor left.

Day Million

FREDERIK POHL

Here's an ingenious and razor-sharp little story that was decades ahead of its time when originally published and has had an impact on subsequent thinking about the nature of the far future way out of proportion to its length. Many far-future stories, although they may feature societies so many years removed from ours that almost all memory of our civilization may have been lost, show the *inhabitants* of that far-future society continuing to live much the same sort of day-to-day life, on a basic human level, that we do now—in fact, many far-future stories even have a retro tinge, so that people are shown as getting around on horseback, drinking in torch-lit taverns, staying on straw mats in half-timbered roadside inns, cooking their meals over open campfires, and so forth, much as they might have in the Middle Ages of our own society's past. But "Day Million" challenges all that, instead suggesting that the dweller in the far future might lead a life that's different from our own in every detail, different from anything that's come before in human history . . . that that future dweller, in fact, might be *so* different from us that we might hardly recognize him as human at all—an insight that will go ringing on down through the eighties and nineties in story after story about the far future, as this very anthology will demonstrate.

Frederik Pohl broke into the professional SF world in 1939 as the nineteen-year-old editor of two SF magazines (*Astonishing Stories* and *Super Science Stories*) and ever since has been one of the genre's major shaping forces, as writer, editor, and anthologist.

On the editorial side of the state, Pohl founded science fiction's first continuing original anthology series (the famous *Star* series, which lasted from 1953 to 1960), was the editor of the *Galaxy* group of magazines from 1960 to 1969 (during which time he won three consecutive Best Professional Magazine Hugos for *Worlds of If*, *Galaxy*'s sister magazine), and served throughout the midseventies as a consulting SF editor for Bantam, where he was responsible for the buying of such novels as Delany's *Dhalgren* and Russ's *The Female Man*.

Pohl was science fiction's first important literary agent, and, as such, played a vital role in encouraging publishing houses such as Ballantine to develop the first category SF book lines in the early fifties.

As a writer, Pohl first came to prominence with a series of novels written in collaboration with the late C. M. Kornbluth, including *The Space Merchants* (one of the most famous SF novels of the fifties, *Gladiator-at-Law* (a book that comes to seem less and less like a satire every time you turn on your television set), *Search the Sky,* and *Wolfbane* (perhaps the best of the Pohl/Kornbluth novels, and decades ahead of its time in its depiction of humans forced to function as plug-in component parts in an organic alien computer). Pohl was relatively quiet as a writer throughout the last half of the sixties but came strongly out his slump in the early seventies, producing work a quantum jump better than most of his previous solo work. The effect of the sudden appearance of such powerful Pohl stories as "The Gold at the Starbow's End," "The Merchants of Venus," *Man Plus* (for which he won a Nebula Award), and, most especially, *Gateway* (for which he won both the Nebula and the Hugo and which is widely regarded as one of the best novels of the seventies) was almost to make it appear as if a totally *new* writer had made a dramatic debut. Pohl, whose solo work had tended to be somewhat undervalued until then (he was widely—and unfairly—considered to be the junior partner in the Pohl/Kornbluth collaborations and had even been accused of riding on Kornbluth's coattails), was suddenly doing work that placed him at the very forefront of the SF writers of the day . . . and that's where he's stayed, ever since.

In addition to his editing Hugos (he may be the only person ever to have won the Hugo both as writer and as editor), Frederik Pohl also won a Hugo for a story called "The Meeting" (completed by Pohl from an incomplete Kornbluth draft after Kornbluth's death), the American Book Award, and the French Prix Apollo and in 1993 was honored with the prestigious Grandmaster Nebula Award for Lifetime Achievement. His many other books include the novels *A Plague of Pythons, Slave Ship, Jem, Beyond the Blue Event Horizon, Heechee Rendezvous, The Coming of the Quantum Cats, The World at the End of Time, The Gateway Trip,* and *Mining the Oort;* the collections *The Best of Frederik Pohl, The Gold at the Starbow's End, The Years of the City, Critical Mass (in collaboration with Kornbluth), In the Problem Pit,* and *Pohl stars;* a nonfiction book in collaboration with the late Isaac Asimov, *Our Angry Earth;* and an autobiography, *The Way the Future Was.* His most recent books are the novels *O Pioneer!, The Siege of Eternity,* and *The Far Shore of Time.*

On this day I want to tell you about, which will be about ten thousand years from now, there were a boy, a girl and a love story.

Now, although I haven't said much so far, none of it is true. The boy was not what you and I would normally think of as a boy, because he was a hundred and eighty-seven years old. Nor was the girl a girl, for other reasons. And the love story did not entail that sublimation of the urge to rape, and concurrent postponement of the instinct to submit, which we at present understand in such matters. You won't care much for this story if you don't grasp these facts at once. If, however, you will make the effort you'll likely enough find it jampacked, chockful and tiptop-crammed with laughter, tears and poignant sentiment which may, or may not, be worthwhile. The reason the girl was not a girl was that she was a boy.

How angrily you recoil from the page! You say, who the hell wants to read about a pair of queers? Calm yourself. Here are no hot-breathing secrets of perversion for the coterie trade. In fact, if you were to see this girl you would not guess that she was in any sense a boy. Breasts, two; reproductive organs, female. Hips, callipygean; face hairless, supra-orbital lobes nonexistent. You would term her female on sight, although it is true that you might wonder just what species she was a female of, being confused by the tail, the silky pelt, and the gill slits behind each ear.

Now you recoil again. Cripes, man, take my word for it. This is a sweet kid, and if you, as a normal male, spent as much as an hour in a room with her you would bend heaven and Earth to get her in the sack. Dora—we will call her that; her "name" was omicron-Dibase seven-group-totter-oot S Doradus 5314, the last part of which is a color specification corresponding to a shade of green—Dora, I say, was feminine, charming and cute. I admit she doesn't sound that way. She was, as you might put it, a dancer. Her art involved qualities of intellection and expertise of a very high order, requiring both tremendous natural capacities and endless practice; it was performed in null-gravity and I can best describe it by saying that it was something like the performance of a contortionist and something like classical ballet, maybe resembling Danilova's dying swan. It was also pretty damned sexy. In a symbolic way, to be sure; but face it, most of the things we call "sexy" are symbolic, you know, except perhaps an exhibitionist's open clothing. On Day Million when Dora danced, the people who saw her panted, and you would too.

About this business of her being a boy. It didn't matter to her audiences that genetically she was a male. It wouldn't matter to you, if you were among them, because you wouldn't know it—not unless you took a biopsy cutting of her flesh and put it under an electron-microscope to find the XY chromosome—and it didn't matter to them because they didn't care. Through techniques which are not only complex but haven't yet been discovered, these people were able to determine a great deal about the aptitudes and easements of babies quite a long time before they were born—at about the second horizon of cell-division, to be exact, when the segmenting egg is becoming a free blastocyst—and then they naturally helped those aptitudes along. Wouldn't we? If we find a child with an aptitude for music we give him a scholarship to Juillard. If they found a child whose aptitudes were for being a woman, they made him one. As sex had long been dissociated from reproduction this was relatively easy to do and caused no trouble, and no, or at least very little, comment.

How much is "very little"? Oh, about as much as would be caused by our own tampering with Divine Will by filling a tooth. Less than would be caused by wearing a hearing aid. Does it still sound awful? Then look closely at the next busty babe you meet and reflect that she may be a Dora, for adults who are genetically male but somatically female are far from unknown even in our own time. An accident of environment in the womb overwhelms the blueprints of heredity. The difference is that with us it happens only by accident and we don't know about it except rarely, after close study; whereas the people of Day Million did it often, on purpose, because they wanted to.

Well, that's enough to tell you about Dora. It would only confuse you to add that she was seven feet tall and smelled of peanut butter. Let us begin our story.

On Day Million, Dora swam out of her house, entered a transportation tube, was sucked briskly to the surface in its flow of water and ejected in its plume of spray to an elastic platform in front of her—ah—call it her rehearsal hall. "Oh, hell!" she cried in pretty confusion, reaching out to catch her balance and finding herself tumbled against a total stranger, whom we will call Don.

They met cute. Don was on his way to have his legs renewed. Love was the farthest thing from his mind. But when, absentmindedly taking a shortcut across the landing platform for submarinites and finding himself drenched, he discovered his arms full of the loveliest girl he had ever seen, he knew at once they were meant for each other. "Will you marry me?" he asked. She said softly, "Wednesday," and the promise was like a caress.

Don was tall, muscular, bronze and exciting. His name was no more Don than Dora's was Dora, but the personal part of it was Adonis in tribute to his vibrant maleness, and so we will call him Don for short. His personality color-code, in angstrom units, was 5290, or only a few degrees bluer than Dora's 5314—a measure of what they had intuitively discovered at first sight: that they possessed many affinities of taste and interest.

I despair of telling you exactly what it was that Don did for a living—I don't mean for the sake of making money, I mean for the sake of giving purpose and meaning to his life, to keep him from going off his nut with boredom—except to say that it involved a lot of traveling. He traveled in interstellar spaceships. In order to make a spaceship go really fast, about thirty-one male and seven genetically female human beings had to do certain things, and Don was one of the thirty-one. Actually, he contemplated options. This involved a lot of exposure to radiation flux—not so much from his own station in the propulsive system as in the spill-over from the next stage, where a genetic female preferred selections, and the subnuclear particles making the selections she preferred demolished themselves in a shower of quanta. Well, you don't give a rat's ass for that, but it meant that Don had to be clad at all times in a skin of light, resilient, extremely strong copper-colored metal. I have already mentioned this, but you probably thought I meant he was sunburned.

More than that, he was a cybernetic man. Most of his ruder parts had been long since replaced with mechanisms of vastly more permanence and use. A cadmium centrifuge, not a heart, pumped his blood. His lungs moved only when he wanted to speak out loud, for a cascade of osmotic filters rebreathed oxygen out of his own wastes. In a way, he probably would have looked peculiar to a man from the 20th century, with his glowing eyes and seven-fingered hands. But to himself, and of course to Dora, he looked mighty manly and grand. In the course of his voyages Don had circled Proxima Centauri, Procyon and the puzzling worlds of Mira Ceti; he had carried agricultural templates to the planets of Canopus and brought back warm, witty pets from the pale companion of Aldebaran. Blue-hot or red-cool, he had seen a thousand stars and their ten thousand planets. He had, in fact, been traveling the starlanes, with only brief leaves on Earth, for pushing two centuries. But you don't care about that, either. It is people who make stories, not the circumstances they find themselves in, and you want to hear about these two people. Well, they made it. The great thing they had for each other grew and flowered and burst into fruition on Wednesday, just as Dora had promised. They met at the encoding room, with a couple of well-wishing friends apiece to cheer them on, and while their identities were being taped and stored they smiled and whispered to each other and bore the jokes of their friends with blushing repartee. Then they exchanged their mathematical analogues and went away, Dora to her dwelling beneath the surface of the sea and Don to his ship.

It was an idyll, really. They lived happily ever after—or anyway, until they decided not to bother any more and died.

Of course, they never set eyes on each other again.

Oh, I can see you now, you eaters of charcoal-broiled steak, scratching an incipient bunion with one hand and holding this story with the other, while the stereo plays d'Indy or Monk. You don't believe a word or it, do you? Not for one minute. People wouldn't live like that, you say with a grunt as you get up to put fresh ice in a drink.

And yet there's Dora, hurrying back through the flushing commuter pipes toward her underwater home (she prefers it there; has had herself somatically altered to breathe the stuff). If I tell you with what sweet fulfillment she fits the recorded analogue of Don into the symbol manipulator, hooks herself in and turns herself on . . . if I try to tell you any of that you will simply stare. Or glare; and grumble, what the hell kind of love-making is this? And yet I assure you, friend. I really do assure you that Dora's ecstasies are as creamy and passionate as any of James Bond's lady spies, and one hell of a lot more so than anything you are going to find in "real life." Go ahead, glare and grumble. Dora doesn't care. If she thinks of you at all, her thirty-times-great-great-grandfather, she thinks you're a pretty primordial sort of brute. You are. Why, Dora is farther removed from you than you are from the australopithecines of five thousand centuries ago. You could not swim a second in the strong currents of her life. You don't think progress goes in a straight line, do you? Do you recognize that it is an ascending, accelerating, maybe even exponential curve? It takes hell's own time to get started, but when it goes it goes like a bomb. And you, you Scotch-drinking steak-eater in your relax-acizing chair, you've just barely lighted the primacord of the fuse. What is it now, the six or seven hundred thousandth day after Christ? Dora lives in Day Million. Ten thousand years from now. Her body fats are polyunsaturated, like Crisco. Her wastes are hemodialyzed out of her bloodstream while she sleeps—that means she doesn't have to go to the bathroom. On whim, to pass a slow half-hour, she can command more energy than the entire nation of Portugal can spend today, and use it to launch a weekend satellite or remold a crater on the Moon. She loves Don very much. She keeps his every gesture, mannerism, nuance, touch of hand, thrill of intercourse, passion of kiss stored in symbolic-mathematical form. And when she wants him, all she has to do is turn the machine on and she has him.

And Don, of course, has Dora. Adrift on a sponson city a few hundred yards over her head, or orbiting Arcturus fifty light-years away, Don has only to command his own symbol-manipulator to rescue Dora from the ferrite files and bring her to life for him, and there she is; and rapturously, tirelessly they love all night. Not in the flesh, of course; but then his flesh has been extensively altered and it wouldn't really be much fun. He doesn't need the flesh for pleasure. Genital organs feel nothing. Neither do hands, nor breasts, nor lips; they are only receptors, accepting and transmitting impulses. It is the brain that feels; it is the interpretation of those impulses that make agony or orgasm, and Don's symbol-manipulator gives him the analogue of cuddling, the analogue of kissing, the analogue of wild, ardent hours with the eternal, exquisite and incorruptible analogue of Dora. Or Diane. Or sweet Rose, or laughing Alicia: for to be sure, they have each of them exchanged analogues before, and will again.

Rats, you say, it looks crazy to me. And you—with your aftershave lotion and your little red car, pushing papers across a desk all day and chasing tail all night—tell me, just how the hell do you think you would look to Tiglath-Pileser, say, or Attila the Hun?

Bumberboom

AVRAM DAVIDSON

For many years, the late Avram Davidson was one of the most eloquent and individual voices in science fiction and fantasy, and there were few writers in any literary field who could match his wit, his erudition, or the stylish elegance of his prose. Certainly he deserves to be ranked with, at the very least, Collier and Saki and Thurber and to be included in the same kind of academic anthologies in which they are taught—and no doubt *would* be if he had not spent his entire forty-year career laboring in the obscurity of genre pulp magazines. The fact is that, at his best, Davidson was simply one of the best short-story writers of modern times, in any genre.

During his long career, Davidson won the Hugo Award (for that other mad little classic "Or All the Seas with Oysters," which detailed the sex cycles of coat hangers and safety pins), the Edgar Award, and the World Fantasy Award, including the prestigious Lifetime Achievement Award. Although all of his novels are erudite and entertaining and a few are memorable (including one of the most influential of modern fantasy novels, *The Phoenix and the Mirror),* Davidson's talents found their purest expression in his short fiction. He sold his first story in 1954 and by only the next year had written the classic story "The Golem," which appeared, as much of his output would over the following decades, in *The Magazine of Fantasy & Science Fiction* . . . a magazine that he edited for several years in the early sixties. (In some ways, in fact, Davidson can be thought of as the ideal or archetypical *F&SF* author, much as critics discussing H. L. Gold's reign sometimes cite Damon Knight, Alfred Bester, or Theodore Sturgeon as quintessential *Galaxy* writers, or as L. Sprague De Camp is sometimes cited as the quintessential *Unknown* writer.) After a silence of several years in the midsixties, Davidson returned to writing toward the end of that decade, and by the midseventies he was engaged in turning out a long series of stories about the bizarre exploits of Doctor Engelbert Eszterhazy (later gathered in one of the best fantasy collections ever published, the marvelous *The Adventures of Doctor Eszterhazy)* and another series detailing the strange adventures of Jack Limekiller (inexplicably, as yet uncollected—alas), which represent Davidson at the height of his considerable powers and must be counted as some of the very finest work produced in the final decades of the century, in any genre.

Davidson's short work has been assembled in landmark collections such as *The Best of Avram Davidson, Or All the Seas with Oysters, The Redward Edward Papers, What Strange Stars and Shore, Collected Fantasies,* and *The Adventures of Doctor Eszterhazy.* His novels include *Master of the Maze, Rogue Dragon, Peregrine: Primus, Rork!, Clash of Star Kings, Vergil in Averno,* and a novel written in collaboration with Grania Davis, *Marco Polo and the Sleeping Beauty.* Davidson's most recent books are a posthumously released collection of his erudite and witty essays, *Adventures in Unhistory,* and a mammoth retrospective collection, *The Avram Davidson Treasury,* which appeared on just about every critic's list as one of the best collections of 1998.

Davidson rarely visited the far future, usually preferring little-known regions of our present-day world or obscure and long-forgotten corners of the past (both of which were transmuted in his hands into unique and magical realms all his own, full of ironies, marvels, and wonders no one else but he ever suspected were there), but he does so memorably in the mannered, elegant, lyrical, shrewdly observed, and wryly funny story that follows, a story that takes us into a bizarre future far beyond the Great Gene Shift, to introduce us to a varied and eccentric cast of characters, as well as to that most singular and puissant of objects—Bumberboom.

Along the narrow road, marked a few times with cairns of whitewashed stones, a young man came by with a careful look and a deliberate gait and a something in his budget which went drip-a-drip red. The land showed gardens and fenced fields and flowering fruit trees. The bleating of sheep sounded faintly. The young man's somewhat large mouth became somewhat smaller as he reflected how well such a land might yield . . . and as he wondered who might hold the yield of it.

Around the road's bend he came upon a small house of wood with an old man peering from the door with weepy eyes that gave a sudden start on seeing who it was whose feet-sounds on the road had brought him from his fusty bed. And his scrannel legs shook.

"Fortune favor you, senior," the young man said, showing his empty palms. "I do but seek a chance and place to build a fire to broil the pair of leverets which fortune has sent my way for breakfast."

The old man shook his head and stubble beard. "Leverets, my young, should not be seared on a naked fire. Leverets should be stewed gently in a proper pot with carrots, onions, and a leek and a leaf of laurel, to say the least."

With a sigh and a smile and a shrug, the young man said, "You speak as much to the wit as would my own father, who (I will conceal nothing) is High Man to the Hereditor of Land Qanaras, a land not totally without Fortune's favor, though not the puissant realm it was before the Great Gene Shift. Woe!—and my own name, it is Mallian, son Hazelip."

The old man nodded and bobbled his throat. "This place, to which I make you free, though poor in all but such mere things as pot and fire and garden herbs— this place, I say, is mine. Ronan, it is called, and I am by salutary custom called only 'Ronan's.' To be sure, I have another name, but in view of my age and ill health you will excuse my not pronouncing it, lest some ill-disposed person overhear and use the knowledge to work a malevolence upon me. . . . Yonder is the well at which you may fill the pot. So. So. And who can be ignorant—ahem-hum-hem—of the past and present fame of Land Qanaras, that diligent and canny country in which doubtless flourishes a mastery of medicine of geography, medicine of art and craft, and medicine of magic as well as other forms of healing; who? Enough, enough. Water, my young. The leverets are already dead and need not be drowned."

The stew of young hares was sweet and savory, and Ronan's put his crusts to soak in the juice, remarking that they would do him well for his noonmeal. "Ah ahah!" he said, with a pleasurable eructation. "How much better are hares in the pot with carrots than in the garden with them! And what brings you here, my young"—he sought for a fragment of flesh caught by a rotting tush—"to the small enclave which is this Section, not properly termable a Land, and under the beneficent protection of Themselves, the Kings of the Dwerfs; what? eh? um ahum. . . ." He rolled his rufous and watery eyes swiftly to his guest, then ostentatiously away.

Mallian gave a start, and his hand twitched towards his sling and pouch, none of which totally escaped rheumy old Ronan's, for all his silly miming. "I should have known!" Mallian growled, bringing his thick brown brows together in a scowl. "Those cairns of white stones. . . . It is a Bandy sign, isn't it?"

Now how the old senior rolled his watery eyes up and down and shook his head! "*We* make no use of that pejorative expression, my young! *We* do not call Them 'Bandies,' *No! We* call Them the Kings of the Dwerfs, so." He winked, pouching up one cheek, squeezing out a tear. "And we are grateful for Their benevolences, yes we are." He drew down the corners of his cavernous and hound-lip mouth in a mocking expression. "*Let* the Dwerfs humorously call us 'Stickpins'! But—'Bandy'? Hem! Hem! No sir, that word is not to be used." And he rambled on and on about the Dwerfymen and his loyalty, meanwhile drawing his face into all sorts of mimes and mows which mocked of his words, when there came in from the distance a confused noise, at which he felt silent and harkened, his mouth drooping open and nasty.

It was not until they were outside in the clear day that they could hear the noise resolve into a shouting or a howling and a continuous rumbling and rattling. Old Ronan's began to shake and mumble, keeping very close to his visitor, as though having observed again that this one had large hands and shoulders and was young and seemingly strong. "Fortune forfend that there should be foreign troops in the Section," he quavered. "An outrage not to be born—do I not pay my tax and levy, for all that I'm a Stickpin? Go up a bit, my young, on that hill where I point, and see what is the cause and source of all this unseemly riot—not exposing yourself unduly, but taking pains to spy out everything."

So up Mallian went, spiraling along the hill through the fragrant acacias and the stinking reptilian sumacs, and so to the top, where, through the coppice peering, he could see all these good fenced fat lands and the deep wide grasslands.

But more immediately below and along the road he saw a most unprecedented sight, stood open-mouthed and tugged the coarse bottoms of his bifurcated beard, grunting in astonishment. He turned and, through cupped hands, called once, "*Come up—!*" and turned again to watch further, paying no wit to the querulous pipings and pantings of the ancient.

Up from around the concealing curve of another hill and along what Mallian conceived must be the famed Broad Road which led to and through the whole length of the Erst Marshes came a procession in some ways reminiscent of pilgrim throngs or decimated tribes fleeing famine or pestilence or plunder—men and women and children clad in rags when clad at all, some few afree afoot, some fewer riding, but most of them attached in one way or other to the thing ridden: a thing, immense, of great length, tubular, rather like the most gigantic blow-gun the most inflamed imagination might conceive of, trundling and rumbling along on enormous and metal-shod wheels, the spokes and rims as thick as a man—some of them in harness to which they bent so low that they were horizontal, squatting as though for greater traction—some bowing as though at huge oars, some straining their arms against the rims of the wheels or against the body or butt of the monstrous engine—others pushing with their backs—

This tremendous contrivance rocked and rumbled and shook and rolled on, and all the while its attendance roared and shouted and howled, and the wind shifted and flung the stink of them into Mallian's face. "In Fortune's name, what is it?" he demanded of old Ronan's, extending an arm to pull him up. The senior looked and shrieked and moaned and pressed his cheeks with his palms.

"What is it?" cried Mallian, shaking him.

Ronan's threw out his arms. "Juggernaut!" he screamed. "Juggernaut! Bumberboom!"

All that frightened old Ronan's had to do—indeed, was able to do—was skitter back to his little house and release the pigeon whose arrival in the proper belled cage of its home dove-cote would not only inform the local confederate Dwerf King that something was wrong in his realm but would inform him a fairly close approximation of *where.* Yet the old man refused utterly to perform this small task by himself, would not unhand Mallian at all, and pulled along with him until they were back at the senior's place and the bird released.

"Remain, remain with me, my young," he pleaded, loose tears coursing down his twitching face. "At least until the Sectional Constabulary shall have arrived and set things aright."

But the last thing which Mallian wanted was an interview with a Bandy borderguardsman. He arose and shook his head.

"Stay, stay, do. I have smoked pullets and both black beer and white, strained comb-honey, dried fruits," he began to enumerate the attractions of abiding, but was interrupted in a way he had not fancied to be.

A smile full of teeth parted Mallian's light brown beard. "Good, good. Not bad for one of your priorly announced poverty; well may one envy the rich of this Section. Now—as a reward for my accompanying you back here, to say nothing of the work of topping that mountainous hill to obtain intelligence for you—let you replenish, and quickly! my budget here with as many such smokelings as will fit. Then you may fill the chinks and interstices with the aforesaid dried fruits. No, no, another word not. I am too modest to appreciate the compliments you would pay me by a continued solicitation of my presence. One jug of black beer I may be persuaded to take; the honey I must forego until another occasion. So.

"Fortune favor you, senior Ronan's. One further deed we may do each other. You will not need to inform your Dwerfmen of my presence or passage; I, in turn, will not need to inform them—unless I am stopped by them, of repetitions of the fell name of *Bandy*. Sun shine upon you, and forfend the shadow of the Juggernaut Bumberboom!"

Thus, laughing loudly, he left the ancient as he had first found him, weeping and alarmed, and went on his way. Indeed, he had fully retraced his way to the top of the hill before he realized that he had not asked *the* question. He scowled and fingered his long moustaches, deliberating a return, but finally decided against it. "Such an old queery man would know no medicine of any sort," he assured himself. "Let alone wit of this most vital matter. But I will keep in mind his words about the vaporous device which pumps and drains the Erst Marshes, for—if, indeed, it is not a mere vapor of the senior himself (and how he cozened me out of half a hare; shame!)—for such medicine may well imply the presence of more. Hem, hem, we will see."

The road was riddled and griddled with great ruts from the gigantic gunwheels. Amidst clots of filth lay a man who had unjudiciously interposed his neck between wheel and road, and a child who mewed and yippered at Mallian but made no attempt to walk. Man and child, quick and dead, looked as like as the spit of their mouths—blond hair so pale as to be almost as white as that of the People of the Moon—equally pale, but pale, pale blue of small, small eyes—a sort of squinting blankness of expression—and slack, silly mouths. Idiot father and idiot son, was Mallian's impression. And he wondered how they had come to be with the gun crew. And he went on.

Warm was the day and the beer soon went down swift. Mallian was about to hoist the jug for the last time when he heard a too-well-remembered thudding on the road and looked, quickly, from one to another side for cover. But the land was flat for many arms' lengths on either side of the road. "Curse!" he muttered, and reached with a sigh for sling and stones, when he bethought that he might hide—did he trot fast—behind a certain maple tree.

Mallian trotted, saw the ditch behind the tree, tumbled into it cod over cap, and had just time to right himself and peer out as the *thudthud-thudthud* of hooves came by, and he saw the mounts.

There two of them, fat and hairy barrel-bodied Bandy ponies—a description which would as well have fit the two squat Dwerfymen riders, whose short legs fit the curves of their mounts' sides as though steamed and bent thereto. Large heads, broad backs, beards which would reach to their protruding navels if not whipped away by wind, faces neither grim nor alarmed but intent and determined, the Bandies came at the gallop. The scabbards of their slashers were on their backs, within quick reach of their hands. They looked to neither side nor did they speak; in a moment more they were gone.

But the crossroads, when he came to them, swarmed with people.

"They have taken everything, everything eatable in my house!" a woman wailed, gesturing to the empty shelves revealed by the open doors.

But another cried, " 'Take'? I did not wait for them to *take*—I *gave* them all there was to eat in mine!"

"Wisely done, wisely done!" a man agreed, wiping from his red face a sweat which came from agitation rather than heat. "Food can always be purchased, food is even now growing and grazing—food, in short can be replaced. But how can one replace that destroyed by the destruction sure to be caused if the Crew of Bumberboom were to fire even one shot from their enormous cannon? Surely it would shatter bodies and houses alike!"

And a fourth person, by his look and manner probably someone of some stature in the community, said in a sober tone of voice as he patted the middle front of his well-filled tunic, "All this is very true, but since the community and property of the Section as a whole is threatened, it is not a problem to be entirely dealt with by individuals. Fortunately, as we have seen, our protectors have been alerted. Two of their constables have already passed by and, by now, are doubtless making arrangements with the cannon's Crew. It is equally fortunate," he pointed out, looking around and gathering in the approval of the crowd, "that the demands of the Crew of Bumberboom are so modest . . . that it is only food they seek and not women or power or dominion. Eh ahem? For who could resist in the face of that tremendous and destructive engine!"

Someone else muttered that it might be better for the Crew if their needs were not limited to food alone but included water, soap, and a change of clothing. There were scattered laughs at this. The magnate, however, pursed his lips and drew his face into lines of disproval. "That is as it may be," he said, severely. "The educated person knows that customs differ among different people, and it is not for us to risk offending the Crew of Bumberboom by making gauche comments on such matters. For my part, so long as they withdraw satisfied from the Section, I care not if they ever or never bathe again, eh ahem?"

Clearly he spoke for the majority and the majority slowly began to disperse to go about their other business, confident that the Dwerf agents would deal with the matter which had so excited and upset them. Mallian approached the magnate and saluted him, the latter returning the gesture with an air of mildly surprised condescension. "Whence and whither, strange my young?" he inquired. "And for why?"

Mal sighed. "Ah, senior, your question not only sums up the matter, it places a finger upon the sore center of it. The whence is easily answered: Land Qanaras, a Land afflicted and perplexed. As to whither, I do not yet know, and can say only that I am wandering in search of a medicine which will supply an answer. Which last, I perceive you have already realized, comprises the why. But before I speak of that I would inquire of you concerning a current matter Sympathize with my ignorance and inform me as to what is Bumberboom, or Juggernaut, as I have heard it also denominated, and who its Crew may be."

The magnate's face had shown a conflict between flattery at Mal's compliments and unease at the prospect of being involved in his problems. But the gathering around of a few gaping loungers eager for free diversion decided his mind. "Important matters," he said, importantly, holding up his chin so that his jowls withdrew, "are not to be discussed where every lack-work may gawp and crane at an inoffensive visitor. Come along with me, my young, and I will not scruple to take time away from my many important affairs and inform you."

And, as they walked slowly through the crossroads hamlet, he related to him that Bumberboom was an engine or contrivance of both great size and potency, founded upon the principles of a medicine known only to its Crew. It had the capacity of casting great shots over great distances accompanied (so it was said) by hideous and deadly fires and deadly and hideous noises. Whence it had been derived, when and by whom made, only the Crew itself could say, and they—perhaps naturally enough—would not. "Suffice it that they have the secret of this medicine and that they use it to go whither they will, depending for sustenance upon the inevitable desire of those among whom they wander that they immediately wander elsewhere without giving an exhibition of their powers, which would prove painful in the extreme. Thus, my young, is your question answered.

"As for your problems, hem hem, I greatly regret that my civic and commercial duties do not permit me to indulge in hearing them. I must content myself reluctantly with saying that no Land under the beneficent protection of the Kings of the Dwerfs can be either afflicted or perplexed, and on this note I, alas, must take my leave. Fortune favor you!"

He waddled off briskly towards a showy dwelling-place from which came kitchen smells indicative that at least one household had left the supply of food to the Crew of Bumberboom for the governing powers to deal with.

"Sun shine upon you," Mal said, somewhat glumly, for he had learned very little from the man which he had not already been able to deduce by himself. But as he reflected on the possible uses of Bumberboom it occurred to him that therein it was conceivable lay an answer to his quest and question, though not in any way which he had previously considered.

The hamlet fell away behind him, and as he continued along the famed Broad Road he saw upon its dusty surface the hoofprints of the Dwerfish ponies, and the grooves made by the great wheels of Bumberboom. Slowly he began to smile, and then he quickened his steps and strode briskly along.

The situation at the border was perhaps brittle rather than tense; so occupied with their affairs were those gathered there that they did not observe Mallian approaching. He heard a hoarse babble of voices from farther away and saw the huge muzzle of Bumberboom lifted up from behind a rise of ground. The whitewashed stone cairns marking the dominion of the Dwerfs stood on each side of the road, and beyond them on each side of the road was another symbol consisting of two long wooden beams painted red. Their ends were planted in the ground and they inclined towards each other until for a short space they crisscrossed. The sight of the two Dwerfs brought him to pause a moment and to consider concealment . . . but they were on foot, and their mounts were tethered off at a distance, and moreover their territory clearly came to an end here, although he was not familiar with what new territory might be symbolized by the red beams.

Neither had he before ever seen men like those who stood conversing with the Bandies. They wore not the breeches, shirt, and tunic so common elsewhere, but close-fitting upper garments extending as a sort of hood or cap closely over the scalp and to which a sort of curious simulated ears were attached. And tights of cloth they wore about their loins. These garments had not the rough look of wool nor (it suddenly seemed) the dull look of linen, but they had a mightily attractive smoothness and sheen and glow, and they rippled when even a muscle was moved

"Oh, we are so infinitely obliged to the Kings of the Dwerfs," one was saying in a tone which seemed to indicate very little sense of true obligation. Rays of sunlight slanted through the bowering branches of the trees and picked out the emblematics embroidered upon the red tunics of the Dwerfymen. "We are so obliged to them—through their constables of course—" (he bowed and put more expression into the salute than was in his face) "for having sent us this number of greatly desirable guests. And such guests as they are, too!"

And a second said, with a dull and lowering look, "Our appreciation will be conveyed from our Masters to yours, very shortly, have no fears."

One of the Dwerfs said with a shrug, "They would away, as we have told you, and who can hold what will away? Furthermore, who can argue with Bumberboom?"

The other Dwerf, hearing or perhaps subtly feeling the approach of someone behind, glanced back and saw Mal coming. He took his comrade's arm and turned him around. "Hold, Raflin. Do you remember that report?"

Raflin puckered his caterpillar brows and nodded. "I do. And I do believe, Gorlin, that this is one with whom we would speak. Halt, fellow, in the names of the Kings!"

But Mal, skipping nimbly, said, "It is a false report to begin with, and a case of erroneous identification to continue with. Furthermore, the names of your Kings are as nothing to me for I was never their subject, and lastly—"

"Hold! Hold!"

"—lastly," Mal said, lining up beside the stranger-men, "I am not at the present moment any longer in your Section or your Land at all, and accordingly I defy you, Bandy rogues that you are!" And he spraddled his legs in contempt at them.

The Dwerfs grunted their rage and simultaneously began to reach for their slashers and to move forward upon their crook legs, but the guards from the other side of the border took several paces toward them and regarded them with extreme disfavor. They stopped.

"So be it, then," said Raflin, after a moment. "We will not invoke the doctrine of close pursuit. But be assured, Stickpin," he flung the term at unflinching Mallian, "and be assured, you other Stickpins, that we will complain upon you for harboring a malignant, an enemy, a ruffian, a fugitive, and recusant, a rapiner and an otherwise offender against our Kings, their Crowns and Staves; and we will demand and, I do not doubt, will obtain his return."

Mallian bracked his tongue and again spraddled his legs.

Said one of the other guards, "Demand, then. It may be you will secure his return—and with him, too, the return of Bumberboom and all its Crew."

The Dwerfs made no reply to this but turned and proceeded to their ponies. One of them, however, whirled around and flung out his hand and forefinger at Mal. "As for you, fellow!" he declared roundly, "were you at all instructed in any wise of medicine of history, you would understand—you would *know*—that the bodily form of the Dwerfs is the original bodily form of all mankind. We have only pity for you who descend out of those misshapen sufferers from the Great Gene Shift." He swung himself about once more and neither of them spoke again. The two stout ponies went trot-a-trot down the road, dust motes rising to dance in the sunbeams.

Mallian turned his head to see the stranger-men regarding him without expression. He thrust his hand into his bosom and withdrew the letter of statements in its pouch. He handed it out . . . to the air, as it were, for none reached to take it. After a moment and in some perplexity he asked, "Does none desire to examine the well-phrased let-pass with which my natal territory—or, to be more precise, its governance—has supplied me?"

With a slight yawn one of them said, and he shook his head, "None of whom I know. . . . Such ceremonies are reserved for those arrived on official purposes, and not for mere proletaries or profugitives."

Stung by such belittling indifference, Mallian exclaimed to the effect that he was indeed on just such purposes arrived. The strangers smiled at him a trifle scornfully. "These pretensions are at the moment and under the circumstances amusing," they said, "but they will not do, barbado; a-no-no, they will not do at all. Those arrived on official purposes unto this Land of Elver State, of which we of the corps of guards are both the internal and the external defense, arrive with proper pomp. They, for one thing, are dressed in garments of serrycloth, as indeed are we, ahem hum. For another, they ride upon smooth-haired horses adorned with many trappings of broideries and burnishments, and so do all their party—which, by definition, is numerous. And for another and the last, though this by no means the least, they come provided with a multitude of rich donatives of which distribution is made to the members of the corps of guards."

Mallian cast down his eyes and gnawed upon his lips. "Nonetheless," he declared, "I have been issued with this letter of statements directing all to let me pass, and the fact of your having made no gesture to prevent my passage at all would not altogether seem to justify my failing to present it. And inasmuch as you desire not to trouble to read it, it would be a pretty courtesy on my part to read it to you. I have oftentimes been commended for my reading voice, and I doubt not but that you gallants of the Elver Guards will desire to do the same, and furthermore, the problem set down herein, which is the high purpose of my journeyings, may so move you as to search among your minds to see if peradventure you know of a medicine which may shed both light and hope thereon."

And he read them the let-pass, or letter of statements, as he had done to the pseudomorphs, and to the People of the Moon.

"Ah, well," said one with a sniffle of his nose, "interesting and absorbing as the beardy one's problem is, and while I doubt not that the medicines of our Masters contains an answer to it—it is no more than the speck of a fly compared to the problem lying over the rise there. Anent which, let us move and consider, for an action of some sort will assuredly be required of our hands."

They proceeded upward and then paused, considering, Mal with them. There had evidently been a house of some sort there below, but it had been unstrategically situated in terms of the attempts of the Crew of Bumberboom to pass with their weapon along the road above it. It had gone off the road, and the marks of its going were eaten into the berm, and before it had either been brought to rest or come to rest of its own accord, it had thoroughly crushed the house—the fragments of which were being now unskillfully transformed into cook-fires. The harnesses hung empty, the guideropes lay ignored upon the ground. The Crew was both at rest and at meat. And, it became at once apparent, at other occupations as well.

"Scandalous!" exclaimed Mallian. "Shocking!"

One of the Elver Guards shrugged. "As well be scandalized or shocked at cats and dogs," he said.

Mal protested. "But dogs and cats are not human—"

The upper lip of the Elver Guard went up further. "Are *those?*" he demanded.

Not overmuch regarding this remark, Mal allowed his mind to run still more over a notion which, in seedling form, had occurred to him before. Cautiously, tentatively, he began to broach the matter. "I have been in some measure too overwhelmed by your kindliness in offering me refuge," he explained, "from those hangmen Dwerfs to express my gratification fully. But—"

"No need, no need," the Elver murmured, scratching his armhole—then, as though only then becoming aware of what he was doing, he stepped back from the berm with a curse and a scowl. "A tetany upon those wittol Swine! They must have fleas as large as mice—if indeed no worse. I am for going away and constructing a steam-lodge and boiling self and habit."

"Do, Naccanath," murmured another Elver. "And when asked how you proceeded to rid the State of this lumbering menace, be prepared to answer, 'I bathed me.' But for praise or commendation, do not be prepared."

The guard Naccanath hesitated, muttered, scratched.

Mallian moved his mouth against the sudden fretful silence. "But now that I am able to take two consecutive breaths free from fear of Bandymen pursuit and am made aware not only of my safety and refuge but of the wisdom of those whose—"

A fight broke out among the Crew below, but was soon settled.

An Elver said, in a faintly dissatisfied tone, "Ah . . . he did but club him. I had thought he might well eat him; it would surprise me not a whit."

And another said, a peevish note in his voice, bruising a blossom under his nose to counteract the noisome taint now rising from below, "Why need they eat each other when all the world rushes to supply them with far less gamy food? In fact"—his face became a sight brighter—"may this not be a possible solution?— videlicet, simply to supply them with a steady ration of victual, thus depriving them of incentive to leave their present location. Denizened right here, they remain under supervision and do no further damage and post no further threat."

Musing a moment, the others then shook their heads. Another said, "They would breed, Durraneth, at a rate which would soon enough make their maintenance a cost not to be considered. Further, experience has shown that nomads do not easily take to denization."

They sighed and sucked their lips and their unhappy breaths caused their smooth garments to ripple and shimmer in a marvelous manner, for which Mallian, nevertheless, had but small eyes.

"—whose tolerance has undoubtedly saved my life," he continued resolutely— and a shade more loudly. The Elver Guards now turned to consider him and his words.

"What is the point of your narration, profugitive?" demanded the one called Durraneth, in his voice a coolness only to be expected in one whose own proposal had just now been considered and dismissed.

Barely had he finished asking his question when a head appeared above the berm, its countenance vacant and filthy, and looked at them openmouthed as they stepped backwards with fastidious precaution. "Cappin?" it inquired. "Cappin Mog?" A bellow from below diverted it so that it turned, released its hold, slid down and away and did not return.

"The point of my narration, gallant Guards Elver, is just this: that I would ask of you a consideration for which I offer to perform a service, thus and thus: inform me kindly where I may inquire of your Masters a medicine to solve the problems of my own Land Qanaras, and in return I will rid you and all the Land of Elver State forever of Bumberboom and its Crew."

The green shade flashed blue as a jay noisily chased another through the trees. Narrowly the guards regarded him. Then Naccanath said, "Seemingly such an agreement would be of benefit to all and of detriment to none. Still, I am moved to inquire—not from suspicion, fie upon such a thought, hem hem, but out of mere curiosity and interest—how do you propose to do this?"

Mallian's fingers stroked the left and then the right tip of his short beard, through which a slight smile peeped deprecatingly. "To reveal this before an agreement has been reached would perhaps be out of keeping with the traditions of negotiating. I point this out, not from suspicion, fie upon the thought, hem hem, but simply because I have been very traditionally reared and do not desire to cast reflection upon my upbringing by departing therefrom even in trifles."

After another silence. Durraneth said, with something like a frown. "Would it be untraditional for you to indicate by which route you intend for yourself and them to depart, and your destination as well?"

Mallian said it would not. Logic, he pointed out, would indicate a departure by the shortest route (other than the one back into the near-lying Section of the Dwerf Kings' dominions) out of Elver State, and to show his perfect good will and trust in the matter he would entreat the advice of the company as to a good route to achieve this purpose—accompanied, perhaps, by a map—and, as for his destination, well:

"I am a hill man by origin, and lonely therefore. Nevertheless there is nought of the hermit in my background or makeup; I admire also the proximity of fair lowlands and goodly towns to which one may conveniently descend to purchase merchandise with the modest yield of the hills. And therefore—"

Durraneth cleared his throat and cast a slant glance at his fellows. "And therefore—inform me if I understand you arightly, Mallian son Hazelip—and therefore you desire information about a place lying outside of Elver State and situated upon a hill overlooking fair lowlands and goodly towns, or perhaps at least one goodly town. Is it so?"

Mal frankly admitted that the conjecture was correct. "At least one goodly town," he murmured, "although two or even three would be better."

The guard-lodge had a stark neatness about it which Mallian, familiar with the companionable disorder of Qanaras and the opulent show of the Dwerfs, found a bit chilling. There were, to be sure, many contrivances visible which seemed both curious and interesting, as well as an entire shelf bearing nought but books, which much impressed him. " 'Where are much books is much medicine,' " he quoted, reverently.

The Elver Guards gave but a nod or two at this and began to spread a table with maps and to converse in low tones among themselves, paying to Mal's thoughtfully-pointed-out observation that it was now high noon and mealtime, inattention which the very best of wills could only call coarse. He therefore did not feel a compunction at devoting himself forthwith to the smoked pullets and dried fruits with which his budget had thoughtfully been filled by old Ronan's. And when the guard Naccanath said, over his shoulder, "Attend hither, profugitive," he replied that he in no wise feared that Elver folk would work him a malignancy via use and medicine of his own and proper name, and therefore he would cheerfully respond to it, which was Mallian, son Hazelip High Man to the Hereditor of Land Qanaras. "But at the moment I eat," he pointed out. He raised his brows and bit and chewed.

The Crewmen's supply had all been eaten to a faretheewell, and they sat or lay about snorting or scratching or simply staring about them as Mal approached. He had come quite near before it occurred to them to stare at him. He was already among them before any of them had made up their minds that he perhaps ought not to be. But it was not until he had begun to make a circuit of the ponderous engine that anything like concern began really to make itself evident. The sight of Bumberboom at close up proved interesting enough even to banish the train of thought caused by the sight of the crew close up. The same near-idiot face repeated over and over again in varying stages of grime, the same snaggle and snarl of pale hair and small, vacant, pale blue eyes—what did it mean?

It scarcely could mean that the same moron Crew which was now attached to Bumberboom had created it in the first place. They could never have fashioned those immense and massy wheels of stout wood reinforced with iron and rimmed with broad iron tires. Never could they have founded that gigantic tube whereon, in the casting, figures of beasts and monsters had been fixed, never have devised that ornate breech in the shape of a bearded face with lips puckered as though whistling, nor the even more ornate and in fact rather frightening face which terminated the great tube's other end, mouth distended into an enormous shout—mouth silent now, but threatening of anything but silence. . . .

Anything but silence now among the Crew, whose disturbance bore more resemblance to a poultry-yard than an anthill, running and squawking—thrice in succession people fell full-tilt against Mallian, but it was certain from their great alarm that it had not been their aim to do so.

And as they trotted about they set up a cry and howl which presently resolved itself in Mallian's ears into the same words, meaningless as yet, which he had heard before from one of them . . . now, however, not as a question, but as an appeal for aid. "Cappin Mog! Cappin Mog! *Cappin Mog!*"

And Mal meanwhile continued his perambulation and examination. The carriage was fitted with large boxes, but these were locked. He was about to make a closer inspection when someone bellowed close by, and at the same moment, something struck him between the shoulder blades. He took a quick step sideways before spinning around, and the sight of his face acted as instant deterrent to the one who had evidently flung the cold and was now doing a sort of angry dance with another cold in his hand. His arms were inordinately long and thickly thewed; chest and trunk were barrel-thick; neck there was none visible, and the broadnosed face was alive with fury.

"Gid 'way!" it shouted, though perhaps with a shade more caution than in its previous bellow. "Gid 'way! Gid oud! Don' touch-a! Killya! Cutcha-troat!"

And the others of the Crew, male and female, taking courage from this couth-less champion, began to draw in behind him, shaking their fists.

"Cutcha-troat, tellya! Gid oud! Don't touch-a! Bumberboom! Bumberboom!"

The rabble, highly approving these sentiments, at once began to shout the word most familiar to them: "Bumberboom! Bumberboom! Bumberboom! *Bumberboom! Bumberboom!*"

Mallian stood where he was and let them howl, and by and by they began to tire of it. He had by now become a familiar object to them and, as he neither moved nor spoke nor did anything of further interest, they grew bored with him, and—one by one—he could see some emotion too faint to be wonder, perplexity of a low order, perhaps, begin to overtake them. They did not really know any more why they were there or why they were so loudly engaged. And so, first one by one, and then, as regarded those who were left, all of a sudden, they ceased their commotion and wandered off.

Not so the one who had thrown both turf and threats at Mal. Highly intelligent he was not, but neither was he an utter idiot. He knew that Mal had no business near the great weapon, and he was determined to get him away from it. Regardless of the defection of his Crew he now came a step nearer, hitched up his dissolving breeches, and menaced with his hands.

"Toll ya, gid oud!" he bellowed. "Trow ya down and kill-ya, ya don' gid oud!"

Mal asked, "Who are you?"

A look of astonishment came upon the man's face. He had evidently never been asked the question before, and it was not any doubt as to his identity but a shock that his identity was not universally known which made him go slack.

After a moment he said, "Who my? My Cappin Mog! Is who." And for emphasis shouted, "Mog! Mog! Cappin Mog! Cappin of Bumberboom and alla Crew! Is who—"

Mallian allowed his own face to register an extreme mixture of enlightenment, astonishment, impressment, and self-deprecation. "Oh, *you* are Captain Mog!"

The captain gave an emphatic nod and grunt, patted his stomach, clearly quite pleased with the effect. "My Cappin Mog," he affirmed. "Is who."

"Pardon, senior . . . pardon, Captain. . . ." He bowed and showed his palms. "I did not know, you see. . . ." The man nodded and came close to smirking and in fact emitted a pleased sound which came close enough to being a giggle to be identified as such, grotesque as the sound seemed coming from him. He gazed from side to side and wiped his loose mouth with the back of his bristly paw. And at that, Mallian gave a bound and a jump and sailed forward and upward and kicked him in the side of the head and felled him like a tree.

Some of the Crew observed what happened and their hoots of astonishment brought others back from casual wandering about the vicinity. They formed a rough circle about the two, though it was without either intention of doing so or awareness of the utility thereof. Several of them growled and even shouted at Mallian and bared their dirty teeth and spat. One or two even went so far as to look about for a weapon—but what immediately came to view was an overlooked loaf of bread, and in a moment they were too concerned with an idiot quarrel about it to pursue the audacious gesture.

Mog lay a while on his side, his eyes opened, he frowned, he rolled over on his elbows and gazed at Mallian and at the Crewmen. He smacked his lips tentatively. "Cutcha-troat," he said, but without real passion. Then he raised his rump and so in stages got to his feet. "Gid oud," he repeated. "Killya. . . ." He looked around for some means of accomplishing this, saw nothing save his slack-mouthed followers and the great gun. Toward this he flung up his arms. *"Bumberboom!"* he cried, warningly. *"Bumberboom!"* Goddam sunamabitchen big noise! *Drop-down-dead!"*

His small pale eyes observed approvingly that Mal, apparently convinced by this fearsome threat, had begun to walk away, and he drew back a trifle to let him pass. Whereat Mal repeated his spring and his sally and knocked him down again. This time he remained down a much longer time, and when he next arose, it was not to address himself to Mal at all. He put his hands at his hips and threw back his head and shouted. The words meant nothing of themselves to Mal, but the effect was immediate. The Crewmen left their places in the circle and bent to their positions in the harness and elsewhere. Mog took a deep breath. He cried, "Forehead . . . *harsh!"* They bent, dug in their feet, groaned.

"Bumber*boom!"* they cried.

"Bumber*boom!"* The limber lifted.

"Bumber*boom!"* The trail lifted.

"Bum . . . ber . . . boom!" The ponderous equipage trembled, shifted. The great wheels shivered, dropped dirt and turf. Turned. Turned slowly. But turned.

Bumberboom began to move forward.

"You may stop her here, Captain Mog," Mal said, presently. The man looked at him. "Stop? *Here?"* Mog's face moved, uncertainly. Mal gestured, pointed. Then he gave a slight teeter or two, as though readying himself to jump. Mog crouched, cried out, covered his head with his arms. He shouted, walking backwards. And the cannon's wheels ceased to turn and the crew promptly slipped its harness and lay down in the road like dogs.

★ ★ ★

Elver Guard Naccanath asked, coming forward with his compeers, "You do not propose to leave them there, I trust?"

"Not for any longer than is required for us to settle our indentures. You have an information to give me—or, rather, two; likewise, a map."

Naccanath's thin lips parted in his thin, smooth-shaven face. He unrolled something in his hands. "Attend, then, pro—hem—Mallian son Hazelip High Man to the Hereditor of Land Qanaras. Here is a carto or map which is limned upon strong linen, and we have marked with red a few several places which bear upon this present business. Thus: this border station. This road. Follow my finger, now. . . . This road forks *here* and *here* and *here.* The right of this last one leads to our capital community, wherein our Masters of a surety can medicate your question— but thither you go not now, for instead you are to follow via the left fork of this first furcation, and this leads, as is clearly delineated, to the Great Rift and all the Land Nor.

"And concerning this same, observe how we have reddled for you a choice of hills, few of which overlook less than a league of fine fat flatland nor fewer than two prosperous trading towns."

Mallian's pursed lips thrust out in concentration between his beard and his moustachioes, he nodded, traced the lines with his brown and furry fingers, so different from the thin pale digit of his present informer, who, asked what sundry of produce and people Land Nor afforded, replied that it was a good yielder of hogs and hides and horses, as well as grain and small timber, but that its people were of a sullen and willful disposition. "Though I do not doubt," he concluded, "that they will be willing enough to trade with you."

"Nor do I," Mallian said, well enough pleased. He reached his hand for the map, but it was not forthcoming. "Come, come, Elver senior," he said, reproachfully; "surely you do not think that even my own keen mind can have committed the carto to memory? Why, unless you relinquish it, neither I nor my newly-gained companions can be sure of finding our way out of Elver State as expeditiously as all of us might wish."

Naccanath rolled the map up and thrust it into a tube of worked leather. "You may be well sure of it," he said, "for guard Durraneth and I will accompany you as far as the Rift. We would think it but ill hospitality," he said, "to do other."

Mallian cleared his throat and avoided eyes. "I am like to be overwhelmed by such high courtesy. But so be it. . . . Captain Mog! *On!*"

He took his seat, with some sullenness, upon the cases fixed by the gun-carriage, and, the procession underway, diverted himself by picking the locks. He found in one nothing but some handfuls of a moldy-powdery substance, and in the other nothing but an ill-made book. With a shrug of his shoulders, he began to turn the dusty pages and to read. Presently he cast a glance, swiftly and suspiciously, at the Elver pair. But they, absorbed in moody thought, spared him no look but rode silently along on their lean horses. He grunted and turned a leaf.

The pothecary in the first town wherein they paused threw up his hands as Mallian entered. "I have no victualry at all to supply you with," he cried, in a trembling and petulant voice. "By reason of lacking either wife or servant-woman, I eat in the cookshops. Moreover, such treacles and comfits as my shelves afford are of a highly bitter and aperient sort, though a measured quantity may never harm you if you are of a costive disposition. . . . But what can these terms mean to him?" he added, in a lower tone, as though to himself. "Is it not known to me, if to none other, that all these cannoneers are as dull of wits as dogs, by virtue of having neither bred nor gendered outside their number for generations? Still, they have the medicine of the deadly noise, and it behooves me to speak dulcetly," he sighed. "What would you, senior?"

"Sixteen and one-half measures of crushed charcoal," said Mallian, "to begin with . . . large measures, the largest you have."

The pothecary's lower lip drooped. "Hem, hem, this would suffice to rid of wind the stomachs of a small army, though to be sure it is a small army which . . ." The apple of his throat bobbed in sudden perceptive terror. "Pay no heed to my previous comments, Master!" he pleaded. "I perceive with utter conviction the falsity of my conjectures. Charcoal—sixteen and one-half large measures. Immediately, Master! Immediately!"

He scurried about from keg to ladle to scales, darting looks of bewilderment at Mallian. Presently he inquired, "And what next is your design, lordling? You say fourteen and a half large measures of sulphur? It will be my delight—nonetheless, may I not point out that sulphur is not in current favor for fumations? Asafoedita is much preferred nowadays as an ingredient to banish the daemons and miasmas, as well—hem! Observe how I fawn contritely for having made the suggestion! Sulphur it shall be. . . ."

The third substance caused him no little concern; he nibbled his mouth and frowned and snuvvled. "Snowy nitrum, Master? Forgive both the poverty of my mind and shop alike, but—Hold! I adjure but myself, Master-Lord! Is not 'snowy nitrum' another name for what is also termed the saline stone, or saltpeter? In one moment I shall have looked into my lexicon. Thus, thus. And my conjecture was correct! Sixty-nine large measures of saltpeter, more correctly denominated 'snowy nitrum' . . . it may well exhaust my supply, but of that, nothing. The drysalters must wait their pickled meats upon a fresh supply, whenever.

"I know not the use nor preparation of this triune of charcoal, sulphur and saltpeter. Shall I triturate it for you with a mortar and pestle?"

"By no means," Mallian said, hastily. "That is . . . hem. Reflection seems demanded here." He pulled a bit on his beard and peeped from under his lashes at the pothecary, a small and bony-browed man of no particular age. There were things which this one was accustomed to doing which Mallian had never done himself; furthermore, he had said a thing which Mallian wished to hear be said again and at more length. The more he considered the more he favored the notion. At last he cleared his throat and spoke.

"Senior pothecary, is yours a trade which might be swiftly sold for a profit?"

The drugsman looked out the open door in a quick and fearful look. He put his dry lips up to Mallian's sun-browned ear. "There is no business to be sold for a profit in Elver State," he hissed. "The taxers lurk like beasts of prey. . . . Why do you ask? There is no business even to be *held* for a profit. Why, lordling mine, do you ask? What is stational commerce to you? You pass through, Master, with your giant thundermaker and you are supplied and you pass on and you pass on. Neither profits nor taxes nor stocks nor sales are matters you need review. . . . *Why do you ask?*"

Indeed, the shop did have a decidedly well-taxed look to it and its meager shelves. Mal was fortunate in having obtained the things he wanted. "The Free Company of Cannoneers—" He caught the open mouth, blank look. "Bumberboom, that is—"

"Oh, aye, Master. Bumberboom."

"—The Free Company of Cannoneers is in need of the services of a responsible and learned man, versed in such medicines as history and, for another example, pothecation. And it thus befalls me to wonder—"

The pothecary genuflected and kissed Mallian's hands and knees. He locked his shop and deposited the keys with the local chirurgeon. And that night whilst the Crew lay deep in snoring and the Elver Guards camped disdainfully apart with heads upon saddles, he and the pothecary spoke long and low together beside a guttering fire, and the coldly indifferent stars pulsed overhead.

"No," said the chymist, whose name was Zembac Pix. "No, Master-Lord, I have made no especial study of the matter. All of my life, Bumberboom—or, as some call it, Juggernaut—has been a byword. Bad mothers frighten bad children with it. One comes across references to it in chronicles. Whence it first came, neither do I nor anyone else know. Nor who first devised it. I was a younger man when first I saw it; most fled in terror or hasted to bring out food, but I tarried as near as I dared. So it was, or so it seemed, that none but I noticed that these fearsome fellows were little better, if better at all, than idiots. This one Mog was not then their captain. I know not what he was named—'twas long ago and my mind has been crammed overfull ever since of drug receipts and tax-demands. Well, hem a hum. But he was not quite an idiot; indeed, I think he was a wit wittier than this one. Let us say a moron, then. And off they trundled, I wondering as they went. Twice more before today have I seen them. And heard of them more than twice. It has been counted a cause for thanks that, unlike other wandering armsmen, they never ravished nor rapted away any women. They took no recruits, either.

"The reason for this gensual clannishness, I cannot say. But its results are plain: No fresh genes have come their way since, aye, hem, who knows when? And whatsoever flaws they had amongst them to start with, such have been multiplied and squared and cubed, to use the tongue of the medicine called mathematic. And thus only idiot habit keeps them going and coming and passing to and fro. And only equally idiot habit keeps the rest of the world afearing them and yielding to them. I cannot say how old this olden book you've found may be—a century at least, I venture. It is not by the gun alone, then, nor by medicine alone, then, that the great noise and destruction comes . . . No. . . . But by these three substances, mixed and moisted and dried and cracked and sieved. By my cod and cullions, this is no small thing you have discovered!"

Mallian spat into the fire. Then he reached out in the dimness and gently took Zembac Pix, the pothecary, by the throat. "You must remember that pronoun," he said softly. He felt the apple of the throat bob up and down. "*I*. Not you. *I*. Not we. *I*. . . . Fortunately Mallian son Hazelip is of a trusting nature." He released his grasp.

"*Fortunately*. . . ." said Pix, in a tremulous whisper.

"I have great plans. Great needs. I can offer great rewards. You, potionman, may become the councillor of the councillors of kings. Therefore be exceedingly virtuous. And exceedingly cautious."

He gazed into the other's eyes, glinted by a single dull-red spot of fire-glow in each. And watched them move as the other nodded.

They stood upon the lip of the cliff. There down beyond lay the Rift, wide and uneven and hummocked here and there; and beyond on the other side the ruins huddled haggardly. Mallian spat stoutly. "It will be no easy crossing," he observed. "Still, I perceive there is a road of sorts, and cross we must. Nevertheless . . ."

He paused so long that Durraneth and Naccanath stirred somewhat restlessly, and the unease communicated itself to the other Elvers who had ridden out from their near-adjacent city to witness both arrival and departure.

"What mean you by *nevertheless?*" Naccanath asked—perhaps still recollecting his flea-bite, he reined his horse up a way apart from Bumberboom and its Crew. The way hither had followed no rigid schedule. The Crew waked to the day when it felt the day full upon it, was by no means immediately prepared for toil, and made up for its swiftness at eating by its almost pythonic requirements for post-digestive rests. Naccanath had urgently hinted for more speed; Mal had—rather less urgently—passed it on to Captain Mog, and Captain Mog had cursed and kicked and cudgeled . . . and gotten a short burst of increased pace . . . for a moment or so. At intervals.

"By *nevertheless*," Mallian said, rather slowly, "I mean that there is something which we must do before we begin to cross." He issued a loud order to Mog, who issued a louder one. Mog knew nothing of Mallian's quest, nothing of the problem behind Mallian's question. All he knew to the point was that if Mal asked him to do something and he did not do it, he would be kicked in the head. He had tried a number of ways to avoid this, but the only one which ever worked was to obey orders. Quickly.

Slowly, therefore, erratically, Bumberboom began to move around until its great muzzle was pointing toward the Rift. Another order, and the massive gun was unlimbered. Its trail now rested on the ground. Naccanath cleared his throat, looked at Durraneth. Durraneth returned the look.

"What—and I point out the extreme civility with which the question is asked—what is it your intention to have done now, son Hazelip?"

Mal stroked the points of his beard. "It is my intention to fire the gun," he said.

The horsemen backed up a pace or two or three as though they had practiced the movement. "Fire—fire Bumberboom?"

"So some call it. Others, I understand, prefer the name of Juggernaut."

One of the Elvers said, "I have not heard that this has been done at all of late." He cleared his throat twice.

"So much the better for doing it now. The crew wants practice, and no one can object to whatever damage may be done the Rift."

Naccanath said, rather sharply, "The Rift! It is not the Rift which concerns us—we are still on Elver soil, and I consider the possible great damage which may be done thereto . . . including, and this is no small consideration, to us—It would be much better for you to wait until you are already in the Rift."

"No it would not. I desire to calculate a matter called range . . . a matter of arcane medicine which it will henceforth be important for me to know . . . and in particular the trajectory as calculated from an eminence of land, as it might be a cliff or hill."

The Elvers consulted hurriedly together and then requested that Mallian might delay his calculations until they were able to get well away from the site. He frowned, gave a short and slightly impatient nod, and they were off even faster than the two Dwerfymen had gone, the time Mallian had hidden in the ditch.

"They fear the fatal noise," he said to Zembac Pix, with a twisted grin. "It is as well. The less they see, the better so. Well. Down goes the large-grained powder as the book directs. Hold firm the ladle, Zembac Pix. So. So. Smoothly. So." Mallian took the ram and tried to follow the directions so that the powder was securely back where it should be but not so firmly packed that it would not properly ignite. Then, satisfied, he ordered the shot brought forward. Mog and his mates came up with the great round stone, hoisted it . . . dropped it. The man responsible howled for his toes and then howled for his ribs as Mog beat upon them. But it was done at last.

Next the fine powder was laid in a train along the groove to the touch-hole. "What next?" asked Mallian.

Pix looked into the book. "Next is fire," he said. "Captain Mog! A brand of fire!"

The Crewmen seemed unsure of how they should seem. What memories they might hold of actual gunfire must be at many removes and quite dim, muted not by time alone but by the thick membranes of their sluggish minds. They had been bred to the gun, lived by and for the gun, had nought but the great gun at all. Yet they had never fired it, had forgotten how to make its fuel, forgotten perhaps all save some dim glints of recollections of old mumblings and mutterings which served them for history. They were excited. They were uneasy. Something new had come into their brute lives. One of them, who had watched the loading, perhaps spoke for all. "Bumberboom . . . Bumberboom *eat,*" he said.

Zembac Pix received the burning stick and said, before handing it to Mal, "Stand carefully as the handbook directs, lest the cannon crush you by its—" But Mallian, impatient, seized the fire and thrust it at the train of powder. It hissed, vanished. Then, with a roar like thunder waging war on thunder, the hideous muzzle-mouth spewed flame and smoke. The gun leaped as though wounded, fell back, subsided. Darkness, thick darkness, evil stench, surrounded them. Gradually, it cleared away. They looked at each other. ". . . recoil," Zembac Pix finished his sentence.

The Crew rose slowly from the ground, idiot faces round with awe and terror and joy. The occasion required words. They found them—or, at least, it. "Bumberboom! *Bum*berboom! *Bumberboom!*" They leaped and lurched and shouted and roared.

"Bumberboom!"

"Bumberboom!"

"Bumberboom!"

Zembac Pix pointed far out into the Rift. "The shot seems to have scored a trench along that hillock. Ha! Ahem hum-hum!"

"So I see . . . yes. Suppose that were a row of houses. Ha! Ha-ha!"

"Elver houses!"

"Bandy houses!"

"Ha *ha!*"

Something caught their eye. Something gleamed there in the trench now as clouds drifted away and the sun came through—a something which seemed to have slightly deflected the path of the stone shot. They discussed what it might be, agreed that whatever it might be could well go on waiting. "Captain Mog! On!"

"Forehead . . . *harsh!*"

It was a while later that they saw the Elvers descending by another road which allowed them to steer far clear of the great gun and its Crew—a line of Elver horsemen and behind each guard and riding on the crupper, a man with a spade. "Curious," said Mal. "Very curious, Master-Lord," agreed Zembac Pix. But by the time they themselves had gotten close enough to leave the toiling, chanting Crew and go and see, the sight was more than merely curious.

"Observe, Mallian son Hazelip," said Naccanath, in an odd tone and a gesture. "See what sight the monstrous voice of Bumberboom has uncovered."

It was a sight indeed. The hillock had been shoveled and the ground excavated a good way beneath the surface of the general ground-level. There lay revealed the immense figure of an image with upraised arm and with a crown or coronet upon its head from which radiated a series of great spikes at least twice the length of a man. As far as they could see, it was clad in a flowing garment of some strange sort. It was an unfamiliar shade of blue-green which was almost black.

"What is it?" asked Mallian, voice low with awe.

The Elvers shrugged. "Who can say? . . . it seems to be hollow." Thus Naccanath. Durraneth had something else to say.

"Do you recall, Prince of Qanaras," he began—Mallian noted his own promotion in rank but showed nothing on his face—"Do you recall what said the Dwerfy constable? . . . as say they all, of course . . . that before the Great Gene Shift all men were of their dwerfish size?"

Mallian said, "I do recall. What of it?"

Slowly Durraneth said, "This great image is hollow. There are passages within. But the spaces seem exceedingly small. Do you suppose—"

"Do I suppose that this evidences a possible truth to the absurd Bandy boast? Never! As well declare that the gigantic statue demonstrates that the original form of mankind was that of the race of the gigants!"

Durraneth nodded slowly. Then his eyes moved from gigantic statue to gigantic gun and back once more. "I wish . . ." he began. "I wish I knew what it had held in its hand . . ." he said. "Oh, I do not know, of course, that it had held anything in its hand. It has an arm, it must have had a hand. . . . No consequence; it was a mere sudden fancy, of no rational importance."

But Mallian had now a question of his own. He pointed down into the pit, past a fallen tree, to where four Elvers stood regarding the newly-found wonder and a fifth stood upon its face. On the brim stood a box of strange sort, from which wires led down to the body of the statue. "What is that?" he asked.

Durraneth shrugged. "An engine . . . a toy, really. It simulates a magnetical current. Really, it tells us nothing—save only that the entire figure seems to be made of metal. All of it! Incredible. No, I suppose you are correct. About the original stature of man. The matter, I must suppose, remains as before. . . ." For yet another moment he stood there, musing. Then he said, "When you are ready, Prince, to pose your question, we will be ready to serve you in seeking its answer. Do not tarry too long among the morose and barbarous folk of Nor. Fare you well. Fare you well."

The morose and barbarous folk of Nor had for the most part, forewarned by the echoing roar of Bumberboom's sole shot and, further, by the sight of it being toiled across the Trans-Rift Road, fled into the raddled ruins where it was hardly practicable to follow them. They had taken much of their substance with them, but the Crew were experienced foragers; noses keen as dogs', they soon sniffed out food and even sooner devoured it.

Mallian had no desire to go groping about in the ruins after anyone. He consulted the map—Naccanath still held the leathern tube, but Mal held the map, whether Naccanath knew it or not—and consulted Zembac Pix as well. "I would that I had reflected to demand, hem a hum, to request horses of the Elvers. Doubt-less they could be trained to pull the gun."

The pothecary's eyes narrowed beneath their bony brows, and he smiled a knowing smile. "Horses will come later," he said. "Horses . . . and many other things. . . ."

Getting Bumberboom up a hill had to come first. After that would come sup-plies—not hastily proffered or hastily seized to be hastily gobbled, but efficiently levied, to be efficiently distributed. And efficiently consumed? Not all of them. The key word was *surplus*. Surplus of commodity meant trade, which meant wealth and power. One area of farms and towns to start with. Power firmly established there meant a fulcrum firmly established there. And with a fulcrum once estab-lished, what might not leverage do?

But haste was not to be indulged in. Leaving Zembac Pix in charge of gun and crew, Mal set off to scout out the land, with a particular emphasis on hills. The first one he came to overlooked, to be sure, fine fat fields and no less than four towns, all of them prosperous, but the roads leading up the hill were too narrow by far to admit of Bumberboom's huge carriage being taken up. Widening would be a matter of months. Not to be thought of. The second hill was easy of access but looked down on one small town only, and that none too favorsome in its appearance. He sighed, pressed on. A third hill was well-located but culminated in a peak of rocky scarps such as could afford abiding-place only to birds. A fourth. . . .A fifth. . . .

Perhaps it was the seventh hill which seemed so ideal in every way but one. There was a slope of mountable angle, the top was both flat and wide, with enough trees to provide shade when desired and yet without interfering with the maneu-verability of the great gun. From the summit Mal could see widespread and fruitful fields, and the rooftops of several towns. He had passed by two of them and observed with approbation the signs of good care and productivity, and a third appeared to be large enough to justify an assumption of the same. It was as tempt-ing, as inviting from above as it had seemed from below; therefore, he had sur-mounted it despite a difficulty exemplified in the mud even now drying on his feet and shanks. There was definitely a current; one could not exactly say that a swamp lay at the foot of the hill athwart the only possible approach, but there was no gravel-bottomed shallow ford, though carefully he looked for one. Mud, sticky, catchy mud—and Bumberboom mired securely was as good as no Bumberboom at all. Mallian sighed and retraced his steps.

There was a man in the water when he came through it again, breeches slung around his shoulder and shirt tucked up shamelessly around his ribs, and he was spearing small fish with a trident. "Fortune favor you," said Mal.

The man said, "Mm."

"Fortune favor you," repeated Mal, a trifle louder, a trifle annoyed.

"We don't say 'Fortune favor you' in these parts."

"Oh? What do you say, then?"

"We say 'Mm.' "

"Oh. Well, then—Mm."

"Mm." And the man speared another small fish, and another, gutted them and strung them. He had set up a small makeshift smokehouse ashore, and now pro-ceeded to deposit his catch therein before returning to securing more.

"You prefer smoked fish to fresh fish?"

"No, I don't," the man said decidedly. "But they keep and fresh ones don't. Be you purblind? Looksee that dried mud yonder side. And nigh side. I catch fish while there be water. Soon there'll be none till the rains."

Mallian wondered that he had not observed this before. "Senior, I thank you," he said sincerely. "Now indulgently inform me what you say in these parts for farewell."

The man peered into the water. "We say 'Mm,' " he answered.

Mal sighed. "Mm."

"Mm," said the fisherman. He scratched his navel and speared another fish.

"What governance have you in these parts?" he inquired of a man leading a pack-horse as he passed through the next town.

"None," said the man. "And wants none. The Land Nor is nongovernanced, by definition."

"I see. I thank you. Mm," said Mal.

"Mm," said the packman.

He accompanied the great gun all the way, but sent Zembac Pix ahead and aside to spread the word that other lands and their rulers—as it might be the Kings of the Dwerfs or the Masters of Elver State—envying the ungovernanced condition of Land Nor, had determined to send armies, troops, spies, and other means of assault thereto, with the intention of establishing a governance over it and over its people. But that the Free Company of Cannoneers, hearing of the daemonical plan, had come unsolicited to the defense of Land Nor with a weapon more utile than a thousand swords, videlicet, the great cannon BUMBERBOOM. Zembac Pix went forth and fro and by and by caught up with Mal and Mog and crew where they were encamped on a threshing-floor.

"Spread you the word?"

"Most diligently, Master-Lord."

"And with what countenance and comments did they receive it?"

The pothecary seemed to hesitate. "For the most part," he said, "without change of countenance and with no other comment than the labial consonant, Mm."

Mal pondered. Then he raised his eyes. "You say, 'For the most part'—"

"A true relation of my statement, Master-Lord. There was an exception, a tiresome and philosophizing man who keeps an hostelry for the distribution of liquor of malt"—here Zembac Pix wet his lips very slightly and made a small smile—"and his comment was to the effect that Land Nor is nongovernanced by definition and it thus follows that Land Nor cannot be governanced inasmuch as according to the laws of logic, a thing is not what it is not but is what it is, and to speak of the governancing of Land Nor is to speak of the moving of the immovable, which is to speak nonsense. And much other words he spoke, but only to recapitulate what he had already spoken."

Mal said nothing, but after a moment he shook his head. Then he rose from the threshing-floor. "Captain Mog! On!"

Captain Mog rose from the threshing-floor. "Forehead—*harsh!*"

The crew rose from the threshing-floor and fell to in its sundry posts and places. "Bumberboom! *Bum*berboom! Bumber*boom!*

"*Bumberboom!*"

The great wheels trembled.

"Bumberboom!"

The great wheels moved.

"Bumberboom!"

The great wheels turned.

Along the dusty roads it trundled and rumbled. Not in one day did it reach the base of the hill, nor in two, nor three. But by the time it reached it, most of the marshy stream had vanished away, leaving a foundation of good hard, sun-baked mud. Fallen trees were selected and trimmed to act as brakes and props. And when the now-dwindled stream had dwindled to a mere trickle, they began the ascent. They shouted, they chanted, they grunted rhythmically, they howled. They pushed, they pulled, they levered. Now and then they turned a rope around a stout tree; now and then they rested the gun upon the logs and panted and drew breath, then fell to once again. "Bumber*boom!* Bumber*boom!* Bumber*boom!*"

And at last they dragged it up upon the very crown and summit of the hill, wheeled it into the best place of vantage, and unlimbered it. "Now," said Mal, "to compose and distribute a proclamation." Zembac Pix assisted him in the wording of it, which was to the effect that the Free Company of Cannoneers had now commenced the arduous duty of defending Land Nor against alien and hostile forces intent upon establishing a governance over the Land aforesaid. And that in order to compensate the previously denominated Free Company and in order to sustain it subsequently and to guarantee its defensive postures, voluntary contributions according to the schedule subappended would be received. Each town was held responsible for collecting the donatives of its citizens and should any town fail to collect and transport the voluntaries assessed it, this would reveal that it was secretly supporting the tyrannical alien pro-governance plan. Whereat, it would be necessary for the Free Company to bombard the town aforesaid. And herein fail not.

"How shall we sign it?" asked Mal, mightily pleased by the several crisp turns of phrase.

"Might I suggest, Master-Lord, a succinct: *Mallian, General-Commandanting?*"

"Hem a hum. . . . Very good. But . . . do you not recollect how the Elver Guard referred to me as 'Prince'? I do not wish to appear high-flown or much-given to elaborate titles. What think you, then, of a simple *Mallian, Prince;* what?"

Zembac Pix nibbled the end of his quill. "Beautifully suggested, Lordling. Subsequently. When they are ready. One must not seem over-humble to commence with."

A breeze wafted up from the terrain below and it conveyed in it a hint of hogs, hides, horses, and others of the rich usufructs of the land. A faint smile played upon Mallian's features. "I allow myself to be persuaded," he said. "So be it. Go now, have copies made, post them in the public places and proclaim it at the cross-roads. You may accompany the first train of tribute, a hum hum, of donative . . . if you wish."

Zembac Pix declared it would be his pleasure. He descended. He ascended. Time had elapsed. "Canting and poxy pothecary!" Mal cried, raging. "Where have you been? And why so long? Where are the voluntaries of food and drink and staples, of steeds and of trade-goods and manufactured articlery? From what Knacker's yard did you steal that wretched beast which mocks the name of horse?

Answer! Reply! And give good account, else I will spread you to the off-wheel of Juggernaut and flog you with the traces!"

Zembac Pix descended delicately from the scrap of rug bound with a rope cinch which served him for saddle, and was momentarily seized with a spasmodic contraction of the glottis which impeded his speech and may possibly have been responsible as well for the slight instability of his gait. And in his arms he tenderly cuddled a firkin containing some sort of liqueous matter.

"Master-Lord," he began, "with the utmost diligence have I carried out every word of your instructions, whether plainly expressed or merely implied. I purchased writing materials, I made clear copies in the most exquisite calligraphy, and I long retained in my possession a specimen the mere sight of which would instantly persuade you; alas, that on returning hither I was with infinite reluctance constrained to employ it for a usage too gross to be named between us—hem hem—though even kings must live by nature.

"Furthermore I posted them in the public places and I proclaimed their message at the cross-roads. Moreover I entered into all places of resort and refreshment in order the more thoroughly to disseminate the matter. Conceive, then, with what incredulous and tearful regret I must report that, far from hastening to contribute to the meritorious support of the Free Company, they merely hastened to confect pellets of wool and wax to stuff into their ears 'to save them,' as they said, 'from the horrid noise and torturesome sound' of Bumberboom. . . . The steed and this firkin of liquor of malt do not represent, Lordling, even one single poor contributor but only my success in a game of skill at which I was constrained to participate, they threatening me with many mischiefs and malignancies should I refuse."

There was a long, long, silence. Then Zembac Pix, sighing deeply, drew from the firkin of liquor a quantity in a leather cup and offered it to Mallian. And in truth it did not smell ill. The breeze played upon the hill; the crewmen dozed or picked for lice; the sun was warm. "To think of such ingratitude," Mal said, after a while. Zembac Pix wept afresh to think of it. They were mildly surprised to find themselves holding to the wheels of the cannon and gazing down upon the reprobate lands below.

"I owe it to my father not to disgrace his name and station by a breach of my word, would you not agree?"

"Utterly, Master-Lord."

"I said that contumacy would merit bombardment." He belched slightly upon the vowels of the last word. "And so it must be."

In this they were in perfect accord, but a slight difference of opinion now arose as to whether the town nearest below lay at a distance of two hundred lengths or at one nearer to three hundred lengths—and also whether the demonstrated distance of Bumberboom's range was as much as three hundred lengths or as little as two hundred lengths. They concluded that it was better to use more force than necessary rather than less than necessary, and they accordingly loaded a charge a third heavier than that used before. Furthermore, on the same principle, they rammed a double shot down the barrel.

"And now for to prime her," said Zembac Pix, giggling slightly.

"Hold," said Mal. "Last time we were too close to witness the moment of ejection. I would witness this act and not have my vision clouded with smoke."

The pothecary nodded and chuckled. "Perfectly do I understand and take your meaning. I shall lay a long powder-trail . . . let me use this length of wood as a gently inclined plane. Excellent, excellent; the powder stays in place and does not slide off! . . . and thus and thus and thus. . . . Ahem hem, I seem to have used up the last of the powder."

His face was so woebegone that Mallian was constrained to laugh. "No matter. No matter. We will make more. Is not the recipe contained in the formulary book? Where is the fire-stick? Here. Ha! Hear it sizzle! So—'morose and barbarous' you have been termed, folk of Nor, and now here is your requition for—"

All the thunders of the sky and the lightnings thereof burst upon them in rolling flashes of fire and smoke. The earth shook like a dying man, and they were instantly thrown upon the quaking ground. Things flew screaming over their heads. They lay deafened and stunned for long moments.

Mallian, presently seeing Zembac Pix's mouth moving, said with a groan, "I cannot hear. I cannot hear."

"I had not spoken. Woe! Mercy! Malignant fates! Where is Bumberboom?"

And the Crew, now picking themselves up from the dirt, with shrieks and wails, began the same question. "Bumberboom? Bumber*boom? Bumberboom?*" But a few fragments of twisted metal and a shattered wheel were all that remained of that great cannon and weapon more utile than a thousand swords. . . .

Mallian felt a sob shake his throat. All his plans, all his efforts, wasted and shattered in a single moment! He fought for and found control. "Age and disuse," he said, "must have corroded the barrel. Never mind. We will somehow contrive to cast another."

Zembac Pix agreed, and said through his tears, "And to prepare more powder. Four and one-half measures of sulphur to thirty-one and a third of—"

"You err. It was of a certainty twenty-five and a fifth of sulphur to six and one eighth of snowy . . . Or was it eleven and one tenth of . . . We must consult the formulary." But of that sole book wherein alone the arcane and secret art of gunnery was delineated, only one scorched bit of page remained, and on it was inscribed the single word *overload*. There was another silence, the longest yet, disturbed only by the idiotic and inconsolable ululations of the Crew.

In a different voice Mallian said, "It is just as well. Clearly the engine represented a mere theorizing, and, as we have plainly seen, is of no practical value whatsoever. What is perhaps more to the point, I observe that the horse is uninjured, and I propose we mount him immediately and proceed by way of the woods to the northern and nearest border of this land of morose and barbarous folk, for I trust not their humors at all."

"Oh, agreed! Agreed, Master-Lord!" declared Zembac Pix, scrambling up behind him. "Only one question more: What of the erstwhile Crew? Should we try to persuade them to follow?"

Mal wheeled the horse around. "I think not," he said. "Soon enough their bellies will bring them down to where the pantries and the bake-ovens of the Norfolk are. But we will not tarry to witness this droll confrontation. We will, however, think about it. I am of the firm opinion that they deserve one another."

He kicked his heels into the horse's sides and Zembac Pix smote it on the rump. They rode down the hill.

Coranda

KEITH ROBERTS

One of the most powerful talents to enter the field in the last thirty years, Keith Roberts secured an important place in genre history in 1968 with the publication of his classic novel *Pavane,* one of the best books of the sixties and certainly one of the best Alternate History novels ever written, rivaled only by books such as L. Sprague De Camp's *Lest Darkness Fall,* Ward Moore's *Bring the Jubilee,* and Philip K. Dick's *The Man in the High Castle.* Trained as an illustrator—he did work extensively as an illustrator and cover artist in the British SF world of the sixties—Roberts made his first sale to *Science Fantasy* in 1964. Later, he would take over the editorship of *Science Fantasy,* by then called *SF Impulse,* as well as providing many of the magazine's striking covers. But his career as an editor was short-lived, and most of his subsequent impact on the field would be as a writer, including the production of some of the very best short stories of the last three decades. Robert's other books include the novels *The Chalk Giants, The Furies, The Inner Wheel, Molly Zero, Grainne, Kiteworld,* and *The Boat of Fate,* one of the finest historical novels of the seventies. His short work can be found in the collections *Machines and Men, The Grain Kings, The Passing of the Dragons, Ladies from Hell, The Lordly Ones, Winterwood and Other Hauntings,* and *Kaeti on Tour.* His most recent book is an autobiography, *Lemady: Episodes of a Writer's Life.*

Roberts has visited the far future in other works, notably in the stories that went into making up *The Chalk Giants* and *Kiteworld.* The story that first came to mind when I was assembling this anthology, though, is the tense and darkly lyrical tale that follows, which borrows (with the author's permission) the milieu of Michael Moorcock's novel *The Ice Schooner* (which was serialized in *Science Fantasy* when Roberts was the managing editor; Roberts later sold this story to *Moorcock when Moorcock was the new editor of the magazine New Worlds*—the web of associations has a very fine mesh!) and takes us to a far-future Earth frozen back into barbarity by a new Ice Age for a taut story of a man obsessed with the hunt who discovers that to catch the prey you want the most, you sometimes have to pay a price greater than you can afford to spend. . . .

There was a woman in the great cleft-city of Brershill who was passing fair.

At least so ran opinion in that segment of low-level society of which she was undisputed queen. Though there were others, oldsters for the most part, who resented her beauty, finding her very fame an affront to decent living. Custom died hard in Brershill, most conservative—or most backward—of the Eight Cities of the Plain, the great ice steppe men had once called the Matto Grosso. And in truth Coranda had given some cause for offense. If she was beautiful she was also vain and cold, cold as the ice plains that girdled the world: in her vanity she had denied even that sacrifice most beloved of great Ice Mother, the first-blood that belonged to the goddess alone. Long past the time of puberty she was, and the ceremonies of womanhood; and still the Mother waited for her due. In the blizzards that scourged the cleft, in the long winds of winter, her complaint might be heard, chilling the blood with threats and promises. All men knew they lived by the Mother's mercy alone; that one day, very soon now, the world would end, mantled for eternity in her sparkling cloth. *Coranda*, ran the whisper. *Coranda*, holding their lives in the hollow of her hand. Coranda heard, and laughed; she was just twenty, slim and black haired and tall.

She lay on a couch of white fur, toying with a winecup, mocking the young men of the cities as they paid her court. To Arand, son of the richest merchant of Brershill, she confided her belief that she herself was of the Mother's Chosen and thus above the pettiness of sacrifice. "For," she said, smoothing her long hair, "is not the Mother justly famed for beauty, for the perfection of skin that matches the fresh-laid snow? The darkness of her eyes, all-seeing, the slenderness of the hands that guard us all? And have I not"—she tossed her head—"have I not, among your good selves at least, some claim to prettiness? Though Eternal Mother forbid"— blushing, and modestly lowering her eyes—"that I should fall into the sin of pride." Arand, more than a little drunk, straightway burbled her divinity, speaking heresy with the ease of long practice or stupidity till she swept from him indignantly, angry that he should speak lightly of the deity in her presence. "Will not the Mother's rage," she asked Maitran of Friesgalt appealingly, "descend alike on his head and mine? Will you protect me from the lightnings that fly in storms, lightnings such words may bring?"

That was a cunning touch, worthy of Coranda; for the animosity with which most Friesgaltians regarded the folk of Brershill was well known. Maitran's knife-blade gleamed instantly, and would no doubt have brought the Mother a pleasing offering had not Brershill stalwarts pinned and disarmed the combatants. Some blood was shed certainly, from thumped noses and mouths, while Coranda regarded the wriggling heap with interest. "Now," she said, "I think I must call my father's men to punish; for do I mean so little to you all that you come here to my house and brawl?" She ran to the gong placed beside the door of the chamber, and would certainly have summoned an irate guard had not earnest entreaty prevailed.

"Well," she said, tossing her head again in disgust. "It seems you all have too much spirit, and certainly too much energy, for my comfort and your own safety. I think we must devise a small occupation, something that will absorb your wildness and will no doubt bring a suitable reward."

There was a quietness at that; for she had hinted before that marriage to some rich and worthy boy might at long last assuage the Mother's need. She brooded, suddenly thoughtful, stroked hands across her gown so the fabric showed momentarily the convexities of belly and thighs. Lowered her eyes, glided swaying to the couch. They made way for her, wary and puzzled. Rich they all were, certainly, or they would none of them have passed her father's iron-bound doors; but worthy? Who could be worthy of Coranda, whose beauty was surely Ice Mother's own?

She clapped her hands; at the gesture a house-servant, blue liveried, laid beside her a box. It was made from wood, rarest of substances, inlaid with strips of ivory and bone. She opened it, languidly; inside, resting on a quilting of white nylon, was a slim harpoon. She lifted it, toying with the haft, fingers stroking the razor edges of the barbs. "Who will prove himself?" she asked, seemingly to the air. "Who will take the Mother's due, when Coranda of Brershill comes to marriage?"

Instantly, a babble of voices; Karl Stromberg and Mard Lipsill of Abersgalt shouted willingness. Frey Skalter the Keltshillian, half barbaric in his jeweled furs, attempted to kiss her foot. She withdrew it smartly, equally sharply kicked him in the throat. Skalter overbalanced, swearing, spilling wine across the pale floor. There was laughter; she silenced it sharply, lifting the little harpoon again, watching from long lashed, kohl-painted eyes. She relaxed, still holding the weapon, staring at the ceiling in the fast blue flicker of the lamps. "Once," she said, "long ago, in the far south of our land, a whaler was blown off course by storms. When the Ice Mother's anger was spent, and she sent sunlight again and birds, none could make out where her breath had driven them. There was ice, a great smooth plain, and mountains; some of them smoked, so they said, throwing cinders and hot winds into the air. A very queer place it was indeed, with furry barbarians and animals from a child's book of fancies, stranger than men could believe. There they hunted, spilling and killing till their holds were full and they turned north to their homes. Then they came on the strangest wonder of all."

In the quiet the buzzing of the eternal fluorescent tubes sounded loud. Skalter poured himself more wine, carefully, eyes on the girl's face. Arand and Maitran stopped their glaring; Stromberg thoughtfully wiped an errant red trickle from his nose.

"In the dark of dawn," said Coranda dreamily, "in the gray time when men and ships are nothing but shadows without weight and substance, they met the Fate sent by Ice Mother to punish them their crimes. It surrounded them, flickering and leaping, soundless as snow, weird as Death itself. All across the plain, round their boat as they sailed, were animals. They ran and moved, playing; whole herds and droves of them, bulls and calves and cows. Their bodies were gray, they said, and sinuous as seals; their eyes were beautiful, and looked wisely at the ship. But without doubt they were spirits from the Mother's court, sent to warn and destroy; for as they turned and leaped they saw each had but one horn, long and spiraling, that caught and threw back the light."

She waited, seeming indifferent to her audience. At length Lipsill broke the silence. "Coranda . . . what of the boat?"

She shrugged delicately, still playing with the barbed tip of the spear. "Two men returned, burned by the Mother's breath till their faces were black and marbled and their hands turned to scorched hooks. They lived long enough to tell the tale."

They waited.

"A man who loved me," she said, "who wanted to feel me in his bed and know himself worthy, would go to that land of shadows on the rim of the world. He would bring me a present to mark his voyage."

Abruptly her eyes flicked wide, scorning at them. "A head," she said softly. "The head of the unicorn. . . ."

Another pause; and then a wild shouting. "Ice Mother hear me," bellowed Skalter. "I'll fetch your toy for you. . . ."

"And me. . . ."

"And me. . . ."

They clamored for attention.

She beckoned Skalter. He came forward, dropping to one knee, leaning his craggy face over hers. She took his hand and raised it, closed the fingers gently round the tip of the harpoon. Stared at him, fixing him with her great eyes. "You would go?" she said. "Then there must be no softness, Frey Skalter, no fainting of the spirit. Hard as the ice you will be, and as merciless; for my sake alone." She laid her hand over his, stroking the fingers, smiling her cat-smile. "You will go for me?"

He nodded, not speaking; and she squeezed slowly, still smiling. He stiffened, breath hissing between his teeth; and blood ran back down his arm, splashed bright and sudden on the weapon's shaft. "By this token," she said, "you are my man. So shall you all be; and Ice Mother, in her charity, will decide."

Early day burned over the icefields. To the east the sun, rising across the white plain, threw red beams and the mile-long shadows of boats and men. Above, dawn still fought with darkness; the red flush faded to violet-gray, the gray to luminous blue. Across the blue ran high ripplings of cloud; the zenith gleamed like the skin of a turquoise fish. In the distance, dark-etched against the horizon, rose the spar-forest of the Brershill dock, where the schooners and merchantmen lay clustered in the lee of long moles built of blocks of ice. In the foreground, ragged against the glowing the sky, were the yachts; Arand's *Chaser*, Maitran's sleek catamaran, Lipsill's big *Ice Ghost*. Karl Stromberg's *Snow Princess* snubbed at a mooring rope as the wind caught her curved side. Beyond her were two dour vessels from Djobhabn; and a Fyorsgeppian, iron-beaked, that bore the blackly humorous name *Bloodbringer*. Beyond again was Skalter's *Easy Girl*, wild and splendid, decorated all over with hair-tufts and scalps and ragged scraps of pelt. Her twin masts were bound with intricate strappings of nylon cord; on her gunnels skulls of animals gleamed, eyesockets threaded with bright and moving silks. Even her runners were carved, the long-runes that told, cryptically, the story of Ice Mother's meeting with Sky Father and the birth and death of the Son, he whose Name could not be mentioned. The Mother's grief had spawned the icefields; her anger would not finally be appeased till Earth ran cold and quiet for ever. Three times she had approached, three times the Fire Giants fought her back from their caverns under the ice; but she would not be denied. Soon now, all would be whiteness and peace; then the Son would rise, in rumblings and glory, and judge the souls of men.

The priest moved, shivering in a patterned shawl, touching the boats and blessing, smearing the bow of each with a little blood and milk. The wind soughed in the riggings, plucked at the robes of the muffled woman who stood staring, hair flicking around her throat. The handlamps swung on their poles, glowing against the patched hulls, throwing the priest's shadow vague and fleeting as the shadow of a bird. The yachts tugged at their lines, flapping their pennants, creaking their bone runners, full of the half-life of mechanical things. All preparations were made, provisions stored, blood and seed given in expiation to the ice. The hunters grunted and stamped, swinging their arms in the keen air, impatient and unsure; and to each it seemed the eyes of Coranda promised love, the body of Coranda blessings.

The ceremony ended, finally. The priest withdrew to his tasseled nylon tent, the polebearers lifted their burden and trudged back across the ice. The boats were turned, levered by muffled men with crows till the sharp bows pointed, questing, to the south. A shout; and Lipsill's craft first blossomed sail, the painted fabric flying and cracking round the mast. Then the catamaran, Skalter's deceptively clumsy squarerigger; quick thud of a mallet parting the sternline and Lipsill was away, runners crisping, throwing a thin white double plume from the snow that had drifted across the ice. Stromberg followed, swinging from the far end of the line, crossing his scored wake as Skalter surged across *Princess*'s bows. A bellowing; and the Keltshillian crabbed away, narrowly missing disaster, raising a threatening fist. Karl laughed, fur glove muffling the universal gesture of derision; the boats faded in the dawn light, swerving and tacking as they jockeyed for the lead. If the display moved Coranda she gave no sign of it; she stood smiling, coldly amused at the outcome of a jest, till the hulls were veiled in the frost-smoke of the horizon and the shouts lost beneath the wind.

The yachts moved steadily through the day, heading due south under the bright, high sun, their shadows pacing them across the white smoothness of the Plain. With the wind astern the squarerigger made ground fast; by evening she was hull down, her sails a bright spark on the horizon. Stromberg crowded *Snow Princess*, racing in her wake; behind him, spread out now, came the others, lateens bulging, runners hissing on the ice. The cold was bracing and intense; snow crystals, blowing on the wind, stung his cheeks to a glow, beaded the heavy collar of his jerkin. Lipsill forged alongside, *Ice Ghost* surging and bucking. Karl raised a hand, laughing at his friend; and instantly came the chilling thought that one day, for Coranda, he might kill Lipsill, or Lipsill him.

They camped together, by common consent; all but Skalter, still miles ahead. Here, away from the eternal warmth of the cleft-cities, they must husband their reserves of fuel; they huddled round the redly-glowing brazier, the reflection lighting their faces, glinting out across the ice. The worn hulls of the yachts, moored in a crescent, protected them from the worst of the wind. Outside, beyond the circle of light, a wolf howled high and quavering; within the camp was cheerfulness, songs and stories passing round the group till one by one they took a last swig from their spirit flasks, checked their lines and grapples and turned in. They were up early next dawn, again by unspoken agreement, hoping maybe to steal a march on *Easy Girl*; but keen as they were, Skalter was ahead of them. They passed his camp, an hour's sail away. *Ice Ghost* crushed the remains of the brazier fire, the turned-out remnants still smoldering on the ice; one runner spurned the embers, sent a long banner of ash trailing down the wind. They glimpsed his sails once before the wind, rising again, blocked visibility with a swirling curtain of snow.

They were now nearing the wide cleft of Fyorsgep, southernmost of the Cities of the Plain. The smooth ice was crossed by the tracks of many ships; they short-ened sail cautiously, shouting each to the next along the line. Hung lanterns in the rigging, pushed on again by compass and torchlight, unwilling to moor and give away advantage. *Snow Princess* and *Ice Ghost* moved side by side, a bare length separating them.

It was Stromberg who first heard the faint booming from astern. He listened, cocking his head and frowning; then waved, pointing behind him with a bulky arm. The noise came again, a dull and ominous ringing; Lipsill laughed, edging his boat even closer. Karl stared back as behind them an apparition loomed, impossibly tall in the gloom and whirling flakes. He saw the heavy thrusting of bowsprit and jibboom, the cavernous eyes of the landwhale skulls that graced the vessel's stern. They held course defiantly as she closed, hearing now mixed with the fog gongs the long-drawn roar of her runners over the ice. Stromberg made out the carved characters on her bow: the *Sweet Lady*, whaler out of Friesgalt, bound no doubt for the Southern Moorings and a night's carouse.

The jibboom was between the boats, thrusting at their rigging, before they were seen. An agonized howl from above, movement of lanterns and dark figures at the vessel's rail; she rumbled between the yachts as they parted at the last instant, the long shares of her ice anchors nearly scraping their booms. They saw the torchlit deck, fires burning in crow's-nest and rigging; and the curious feature of an ice-boat, the long slots in the bilges in which moved the linkages of the paired anchors. Dull light gleamed through her as she passed, giving to her hull the appearance of a half-flensed whale; a last bellow reached them as she faded into the grayness ahead.

"Abersgaltian bastards. . . ."

The skipper then had seen the big insignia at the mastheads. This Lady was anything but sweet.

The night's camp brought near-disaster. Maitran came in late and evil tem-pered, a runner stay cracked on the catamaran, bound with a jury-lashing of nylon rope. Some chance remark from Arand and he was on his feet, knife-blade glis-tening. He held the weapon tip-uppermost, circling and taunting his enemy. Arand rose white-faced, swathing a bearskin round one forearm. A quick feint and thrust, a leaping back; and Lipsill spoke easily, still seated by the fire.

"The prize, Friesgaltian, comes with the head of the unicorn. Our friend would doubtless look well enough, grinning from Coranda's wall; but your energy would be expended to no purpose."

Maitran hissed between his teeth, not deigning to glance round.

"You risk in any case the anger of the Ice Mother," the Abersgaltian went on, reaching behind him to his pack. "For if our Lady is in fact her servant then this hunting is clearly her design, and should bring her glory. All else is vanity, an affront to her majesty."

Hansan, the Fyorsgeppian, dark-faced and black-browed, nodded somberly. "This is true," he said. "Bloodspilling, if it be against the Mother's will, brings no honor."

Maitran half turned at that, uncertainly; and Lipsill's arm flailed up and back. The harpoon head, flung with unerring force, opened his cheek; he went down in a flurry of legs and arms and Stromberg was on him instantly, pinning him. Lipsill turned to Arand, his own knife in his hand. "Now, now, Brershillian," he said gently; for the other roused, would no doubt have thrown himself on his prostrate enemy and extracted vengeance. "No more, or you will answer to us all. . . ."

Arand sheathed his dagger, shakily, eyes not leaving the stained face of the Friesgaltian. Maitran was allowed to rise; and Lipsill faced him squarely. "This was evil," he said. "Our fight is with the wind and wide ice, not each other. Take your boat, and stay apart from us."

In Stromberg's mind rose the first stirring of a doubt.

They moved fast again next morning, hoping for some sign of Skalter's yacht; but the wind that had raged all night had cleaned his tracks, filling them with fresh snow. The ice lay scoured, white and gleaming to the horizon.

They were now past the farthest limit of civilization, on the great South Ice where the whale herds and their hunters roamed. Here and there were warm ponds, choked with brown and green weed; they saw animals, wolf and otter, once a herd of the shaggy white bison of the Plains; but no sign of the ghostly things they sought. The catamaran reached ahead of the rest, the Friesgaltian reckless and angry, crowding sail till the slim paired hulls were nearly obscured beneath a cloud of pale nylon. Stromberg, remembering the split strut, sent up a brief and silent prayer.

Maitran's luck held till midday; then the stay parted, suddenly and without warning. They all saw the boat surge off course, one keel dropping to glissade along the ice. For a moment it seemed she would come to rest without further harm; then the ivory braces between the hulls, overstressed, broke in their turn. She split into halves; one hull bounded end over end, shredding fragments and splinters of bone, the other spun, encumbered by the falling weight of mast and sail, flicked Maitran in a sharp arc across the ice. He was up instantly, seemingly unhurt, running and waving to head them off.

In Arand's slow brain hatred still burned. He knew, as they had all known, that in a fight he was no match for the Friesgaltian. Maitran would have bled him, cutting and opening till he lay down and gasped his life out on the ice. They had saved him, the night before, but he had lost his honor. Now the rage took him, guiding his hands till they seemed possessed of a life of their own. They swung the tiller, viciously; *Chaser* swerved, heading in toward the wreck. Maitran shouted as the yacht crisped toward him; at the last moment it seemed he realized she would not turn. He tried to run; a foot slipped and he went down on the ice. A thud, a bright spattering across the bows of *Chaser* and she was past the wreck, yawing as she dragged the body from one sharp ski. Fifty yards on it twirled clear. She limped to a halt, sails fluttering. From her runner led a faint and wavering trail; her deck was marked with the pink blood of the Friesgaltian.

They gathered round the thing on the ice. Stromberg and the Djobhabnians stunned, Arand pale and mumbling. There was no life; the great wound in the head, the oozing of blood and brain-matter, showed there was nothing to be done. They made the sign of the Ice Mother, silently; turned away, anxious to leave the sight, left the body for her servants, the birds.

They were cheered later that day by the gleam of Skalter's sail far to the south; but the camp was still a somber affair. They moored apart, sat brooding each over his own fire. To Stromberg it seemed all his past life now counted for nothing; they were governed by the Rule of the Ice, the code that let men kill or be killed with equal indifference. He remembered his years of friendship with Lipsill, a friendship that seemed now to be ended. After what he had seen that morning he would not dare trust even Mard again. At night he tried, unavailingly, to summon the image of Coranda's warm body; pray though he might, the succubus would not visit him. Instead he fell into a fitful sleep, dreamed he saw the very caverns of the Fire Giants deep under the ice. But there were no gleaming gods and demons; only machines black and vast, that hummed and sang of power. The vision disturbed him; he cut his arm, in the dull dawn light, left blood to appease the Mother. It seemed even she turned her back on him; the morning was gray and cold, comfortless. He drank to restore circulation to his limbs, tidied his ship, left sullenly in the wake of Lipsill as he led them on again across the Plain.

As they moved, the character of the land round them once more changed. The warm ponds were more numerous; over them now hung frequent banks of fog. Often *Snow Princess* slushed her way through water, runners raising glittering swathes to either side. At breakfast the Djobhabnians had seemed remote, standing apart and muttering; now their identical craft began to edge away, widening the gap between them and the rest till they were hull down, gray shadows on the ice. By early evening they were out of sight.

The four boats raced steadily through a curling sea of vapor. Long leads of clear water opened threatening to either side; they tacked and swerved, missing disaster time and again by the width of a runner. Stromberg lay to the right of the line, next to him the Fyorsgeppian. Then Lipsill; beyond *Ice Ghost* was the blighted vessel of Arand, half-seen now through the moving mist. None of the boats would give way, none fall back; Karl clung to the tiller, feeling the fast throb of the runners transmitted through the bone shaft, full of a hollow sense of impending doom.

As dusk fell a long runnel of open water showed ahead. He altered course, following it where it stretched diagonally across his bows. A movement to his left made him turn. *Bloodbringer* had fallen back; her dark hull no longer blocked his vision. Mard still held course; and still *Chaser* ran abreast of him, drawing nearer and nearer the edge of the break. Stromberg at last understood Lipsill's purpose; he yelled, saw Arand turn despairingly. It was too late; behind him, a length away, jutted the Fyorsgeppian's iron ram. Boxed, the yacht spun on her heel in a last attempt to leap the obstacle. A grating of runners and spars, a frozen moment as she poised above the gulf, then she struck the water with a thunderous splash. She sank almost instantly, hull split by the concussion; for a moment her bilge showed rounded and pale, then she was gone. In her place was a disturbed swirl, a bobbing of debris. Arand surfaced once, waving a desperate arm, before he too vanished.

The sun sank over the rim of the ice, flung shadows of the boats miles long like the predatory shapes of birds.

In the brief twilight they came up with *Easy Girl*. Skalter hung in her rigging, leisurely reeving a halliard, waving and jeering at them as they passed.

All three vessels turned, Stromberg and Lipsill tightly, Hansan in a wider circle that took him skimming across the plain to halt, sails flapping, a hundred yards away. Grapples went down; they lashed and furled stoically, dropped to the ice and walked over to the Keltshillian.

He greeted them cheerfully, swinging down from the high mast of the boat. "Well, you keen sailors; where are our friends?"

"Fraskall and Ulsenn turned back," said Lipsill shortly. "Maitran and Arand are dead. Maitran at Arand's hands, Arand in an icebreak." He stared at Stromberg challengingly. "It was the Mother's will, Karl. She could have buoyed him to the land. She did not choose to."

Stromberg didn't answer.

"Well," said Skalter easily, "the Mother was ever firm with her followers. Let it be so." He made the sign of benediction, carelessly, circling with his hands, drawing with one palm the flat emptiness of the ice. He ran his fingers through his wild blond hair and laughed. "Tonight you will share my fire, Abersgaltians; and you too, Hansan of Fyorsgep. Tomorrow, who can tell? We reach the Mother's court perhaps, and sail in fairyland."

They grouped round the fire, quietly, each occupied with his own thoughts. Skalter methodically honed the barbs of a harpoon, turning the weapon, testing the cutting edges against his thumb, his scarred face intent in the red light. He looked up finally, half frowning, half quizzical; his earrings swung and glinted as he moved his head. "It seems to me," he said, "the Mother makes her choice known, in her special way. Arand and Maitran were both fools of a type, certainly unfitted for the bed of the Lady we serve, and the Djobhabnians fainthearted. Now we are four; who among us, one wonders, will win the bright prize?"

Stromberg made a noise, half smothered by his glove; Skalter regarded him keenly.

"You spoke, Abersgaltian?"

"He feels," said Lipsill gruffly, "we murdered Arand. After he in his turn killed Maitran."

The Keltshillian laughed, high and wild. "Since when," he said, "did pity figure in the scheme of things? Pity, or blame? Friends, we are bound to the Ice Eternal; to the cold that will increase and conquer, lay us all in our bones. Is not human effort vain, all life doomed to cease? I tell you, Coranda's blood, that mighty prize, and all her secret sweetness, this is a flake of snow in an eternal wind. I am the Mother's servant; through me she speaks. We'll have no more talk of guilt and softness; it turns my stomach to hear it." The harpoon darted, sudden and savage, stood quivering between them in the ice. "The ice is real," shouted Skalter, rising. "Ice, and blood. All else is delusion, toys for weak men and fools."

He stamped away, earrings jangling, into the dark. The others separated soon afterward to their boats; and Stromberg for one lay tossing and uneasy till dawn shot pearly streamers above the Plain and the birds called, winging to the south.

On its southern rim the Great Plateau sloped gently. The yachts traveled fast, creaming over untold depths of translucent ice, runners hissing, sails filling in the breeze that still blew from nearly astern. There would be weary days of tacking ahead for those that returned. If any returned; Stromberg found himself increasingly beginning to doubt. It seemed a madness had gripped them all, drawing them deeper and deeper into the uncharted land. The place of warm ponds was left behind; ahead, under the pale sun, shadows grew against the sky. There were mountains, topped with fire as the story had foretold; strange crevasses and plateaus, jumbled and distant, glinting like crystal in the hard white light. Still Skalter led them, mastbells clanking, barbaric sails shaking and swelling. They held course stubbornly, shadows pacing them as they raced to the south.

At the foot of the vast slope they parted company with the Fyorsgeppian. He had reached ahead, favored by some trick of the terrain, till *Bloodbringer* was a hundred yards or more in front of the rest. They saw the hull of the boat jar and leap. The smooth slope ended, split by a series of yard-high ridges; Hansan's runners, hitting the first of them, were sheared completely from the hull. There was something tragically comic about the accident. The gunwales split, the mast jarring loose to revolve against the sky like an oversized harpoon; the Fyorsgeppian, held by a shoulder harness, kept his place while the boat came apart round him like a child's toy. The remnants planed, spinning at great speed, jolted to a stop in a quick shower of ice. The survivors swerved, avoiding the broken ground, whispering by Hansan as he sat shaking his head, still half stunned. The wreckage dwindled to a speck that vanished, lost against the gray-green scarp of ice. There were provisions in the hull; the Fyorsgeppian would live or die, as the Mother willed.

For the first time that night the skyline round their camp was broken by valleys and hills. Still icebound, the land had begun to roll; there were gullies, hidden cliffs, ravines from which came the splash and tinkle of water. It was an eerie country, dangerous and beautiful. They had seen strange animals; but no sign or spoor of barbarians, or the things they sought.

Stromberg spoke to Skalter again at dawn, while Lipsill fussed with the rigging of his boat. He seemed impelled by a sense of urgency; all things, mountains and sky, conspired to warm his blood. "It has come to me," he said quietly, "that we should return."

The Keltshillian stood thoughtfully, warming his hands at the brazier, casting glances at the low sky, sniffing the wind. He gave a short, coughing laugh but didn't turn.

Stromberg touched a skull on the high side of *Easy Girl*, stroking the wind-smoothed eyesockets, unsure how to go on. "Last night I dreamed," he said. "It seemed as it has seemed before that the Giants were not gods but men, and we their children. That we are deceived, the Great Mother is dead. Such heresy must be a warning."

Skalter laughed again and spat accurately at the coals, rubbed arms banded with wide copper torques. "You dreamed of love," he said. "Wetting your furs with hot thoughts of Coranda. It's you who are deceived, Lipsgaltian. Counsel your fancies."

"Skalter," said Karl uncertainly, "the price is high. Too high, for a woman."

The other turned to face him for the first time, pale eyes brooding in the keen face.

Stromberg rushed on. "All my life," he said, "it seemed to me that you were not as other men. Now I say, there is death here. Maybe for us all. Go back, Frey; the prize is beneath your worth."

The other turned to look at the hulking shape of the boat, stroking her gunwale with a calloused hand, feeling the smoothness of the ivory. "The price of birth is death," he said broodingly. "That too is a heavy sum to pay."

"What drives you, Skalter?" asked Stromberg softly. "If the woman means so little? Why do you strive, if life is purposeless?"

"I do what is given," said Skalter shortly. He flexed his hands on the side of the boat and sprang; the runners of *Easy Girl* creaked as he swung himself aboard. "Rage drives me," he said, looking down. "Know this, Karl Stromberg of Abersgalt: that Skalter of Keltshill lusts for death. In dying, death dies with him." He slapped the halliards against the after mast, bringing down a white shower of ice. "I also dreamed," he said. "My dream was of life, sweet and rich. I follow the Mother; in her, I shall find my reward." He would say no more but stalked forward, bent to recoil the long ropes on the deck.

That morning they sighted their prey.

At first Stromberg could not believe; he was forced, finally, to accept the evidence of his eyes. The unicorns played and danced, sunlight flashing from their sides, horns gleaming, seeming to throw off sparks of brightness. He might have followed all day, watching and bemused; but Skalter's high yell recalled him, the change of course as *Easy Girl* sped for the mutated narwhal. Already the Keltshillian was brandishing his long harpoon, shaking out the coils of line as the yacht, tiller locked, flew toward the herd.

It was as the story had told; the creatures surrounded the boats, running and leaping, watching with their beautiful calm eyes. On Karl's left Lipsill too seemed to be dazed. Skalter braced his feet on the deck, flexed muscles to drive the shaft hissing into the air. His aim was good; the harpoon struck a great gray bull, barbs sinking deep through the wrinkled pelt. Instantly all was confusion. The wounded beast reared and plunged, snorting; *Easy Girl* was spun off course by the violence, the Keltshillian hauling desperately at the line. Boat and animal collided in a flurry of snow. The narwhal leaped away again, towing the yacht; Karl saw bright plumes fly as her anchors fell, tips biting at the ice.

The herd had panicked, jerking and humping into the distance; *Snow Princess*, still moving fast, all but fouled the harpoon lines as Stromberg clawed clear. He had a brief glimpse of Skalter on the ice, the flash of a cutlass as the creature plunged, thrusting at its tormentor with its one great horn. He swung the tiller again, hard across; *Princess* circled, runners squealing, fetched up fifty yards from the fight. *Ice Ghost* was already stopped, Lipsill running cutlass in hand; Karl heard Skalter scream, in triumph or in pain. He dropped his anchors grabbing for his own sword. Ran across the ice toward *Easy Girl*, hearing now the enraged trumpeting of the bull.

The great beast had the Keltshillian pinned against the side of the boat. He saw the blunt head lunging, driving the horn through his flesh; the yacht rocked with the violence of the blows. The panting of the narwhal sounded loud; then the creature with a last convulsion had torn itself away, snorting and hooting after the vanished herd.

There was much blood, on the ice and the pale side of the boat. Skalter sat puffing, face suffused, hands gripped over his stomach. More blood pulsed between his fingers, ruby-bright in the sun; cords stood out in his thick neck; his white teeth grinned as he rolled his head in pain.

Lipsill reached him at the same instant. They tried, pointlessly, to draw the hands away; Skalter resisted them, eyes shut, breath hissing between his clenched teeth. "I told you I dreamed," he said. The words jerked out thick and agonized. "I saw the Mother. She came in the night, cajoling; her limbs were white as snow, and hot as fire. It was an omen; but I couldn't read . . ." His head dropped; he raised himself again, gasping with effort. They looked his hands then, soapy with blood, squeezed, feeling the dying vise-grip, seeing the eyes roll white under their lids. Convulsions shook him; they thought he was dead, but he spoke again. "Blood, and ice," he said faintly. "These are real. These are the words of the Mother. When the world is dark, then she will come to me. . . ." The body arced, straining; and Lipsill gripped the yellow hair, twisting it in his fingers. "The Mother takes you, Skalter," he said. "She rewards her servant."

They waited; but there was nothing more.

They moored their boats, silently, walked back to the place of killing. The blood had frozen, sparkling in pink crystals under the leveling sun. "He was a great prince," said Lipsill finally. "The rest is smallness; it should not come between us." Stromberg nodded, not answering with words; and they began to work. They broke *Easy Girl,* smacking bulwarks and runner, hacking at her bone and ivory spars, letting her spirit free to join the great spirit of Skalter that already roamed the Ice Eternal. Two days they labored, raising a mound of ice above the wreck; Skalter they laid on the deck, feet to the north and the domain of the Mother. He would rise now, on that last cold dawn, spring up facing her, a worthy servant and warrior. When they had finished, and the wind skirled over the glistening *how*, they rested; on the third morning they drove south again.

There were no words now between them. They sailed apart, bitterly, watching the white horizon, the endless swirl and flurry of the snow. Two days later they resighted their quarry.

The two boats separated further, bearing down; and again the strange creatures watched with their soft eyes. The shafts flew, glinting; Lipsill's tinkled on the ice, Stromberg's struck wide of its mark. It missed the bull at which it was aimed, plunged instead into the silver flank of a calf. The animal howled, convulsed in a flurry of pain. As before, the herd bolted; *Snow Princess* slewed, hauled round by the tethered weight, fled across the plain as the terrified creature bucked and plunged.

Less than half the size of the adults, the calf was still nearly as long as the boat; Stromberg clung to the tiller as *Princess* jolted and veered, determined not to make Skalter's mistake of jumping to the ice. A mile away the harpoon pulled clear but the animal was blown; a second shaft transfixed it as it stood head down and panting, started fresh and giant paroxysms that spattered the yacht with blood. *Princess* flew again, anchor blades ripping at the ice, drawing the thing gradually to a halt. It rolled then and screeched, trying with its half-flippers to scrape the torment from its back. Its efforts wound the line in round its body; it stood finally close to the boat, staring with a filmed, uncomprehending eye. Close enough for Stromberg to reach across, work the shaft into its torn side till the tip probed its life. A thin wailing, a nearly human noise of pain; and the thing collapsed, belching thunderously, coughing up masses of blood and weed. Sticky tears squeezed from its eyes, ran slow across the great round face; and Karl, standing shaking and panting, knew there was no need of the sword.

The anchors of *Ice Ghost* raised a high screaming. She ploughed across the ice, throwing a white hail of chips to either side, speed barely diminished. She had speared a huge bull; animal and boat careened by the stalled *Princess*. Stromberg cut his line, heavily, left the carcass with the bright harpoon-silks still blowing above it. Steered in pursuit.

Sometimes in the half hour that followed it seemed he might overrun Lipsill; but always the other boat drew ahead. The narwhal left a thick trail of blood, but its energy seemed unabated. The line twanged thunderously, snagging on the racing ice. Ahead now the terrain was split and broken; fissures yawned, sunlight sparking

rom their deep green sides. *Princess* bucked heavily, runners crashing as she
werved between the hazards. The chase veered to the east, in a great half-circle;
he wind, at first abeam, reached farther and farther ahead. Close-hauled, Stromberg
ell behind: a half-mile separated the boats as they entered a wide, bowl-shaped
alley, a mile or more across, guarded on each side by needle-shaped towers
f ice.

Ahead, the glittering floor veered to a rounded lip; the horizon line was sharp-
ut against the sky. *Ice Ghost*, still towed by her catch, took the slope with barely
slackening of pace. Stromberg howled his alarm, uselessly; Lipsill, frozen it
eemed to the tiller, made no attempt to cut his line. The boat crested the rise,
ung a moment silhouetted against brightness; and vanished, abrupt as a conjuring
rick.

Princess's anchors threw snow plumes high as her masthead. She skated sick-
ningly, surged to a halt twenty yards below the lip of ice. Stromberg walked
orward, carefully. As he topped the ridge the sight beyond took his breath.

He stood on the edge of the biggest crevasse he had ever seen. It curved back
o right and left, horseshoe-shaped, enclosing the valley like a white tongue. A
undred yards away the opposing side glowed with sunlight; across it lay the
agged shadow of the nearer wall. He craned forward. Below him the ice-walls
tretched sheer to vanish in a blue-green gloom. There was mist down there, and
vater-noise; the herd booming, long-drawn threads of echo, last sounds maybe of
he fall of the whale. Far below, impaled on a black spike of ice, was the wreck
f Lipsill's boat; Mard, still held by his harness, sprawled across the stern, face
right with blood. He moved slightly as Stromberg stared, seeming to raise himself,
ift a hand. Karl turned away sickened.

Realizing he had won.

He walked back to *Snow Princess*, head down, feet scraping on the ice. Swung
imself aboard and opened the bow locker, dumping piles of junk and provisions
n the deck. There were ropes, spare downhauls and mooring lines. He selected
he best and thickest, knotting methodically, tied off to the stern of the boat and
valked back to the gulf. The line, lowered carefully, swayed a yard from Lipsill's
ead.

He returned to *Princess*. She was stopped at an angle, tilted sideways on the
urling lip of the crevasse. There were crowbars in the locker; he pulled one clear
nd worked cautiously, prising at the starboard runner, inching the yacht round till
er bow pointed back down the long slope. The wind, gusting and capricious, blew
rom the gulf. The slope would help her gather way; but would it be enough?

He brailed the sails up as far as he dared, stood back frowning and biting his
ip. At each gust now the anchors groaned, threatening to tear free, send the boat
kittering back down the incline. He scrabbled in the locker gain, grabbing up more
ine. Another line, a light line that must also reach the wreck. . . .

There was just barely enough. He tied the last knot, dropped the second coil
lown. Working feverishly now, he transferred the heavy line from the stern to a
leat halfway along the port gunwale and locked the tiller to starboard. The anchors
vere raised by pulleys set just above the deck; he carried lines from them to the
ittle bow windlass, slipped the ratchet, turned the barrel till they were tight.
he handle fitted in its bone socket, stood upright, pointing slightly forward over
he stem of the boat. He tied the light line off to the tip, tested the lashing on the

improvised brake. It seemed secure; he backed toward the cliff edge, paying both ropes through his hands. Mard seemed now to understand what he was doing. He called croakingly, tried to move. The wreck groaned, slipped another foot toward the crevasse. Stromberg passed the heavy line between his thighs, round one calf, gripped it between sole and instep. Let himself down into the gulf.

The descent was eerie. As he moved the wind pressure seemed to increase, setting him swaying pendulum-fashion, banging his body at the ice. The sunlit edge above receded; he glanced below him and instantly the crevasse seemed to spin. The ice walls, sloping together, vanished in a blackish gloom; the wind called deep and baying, its icy breath chilled his cheek. He hung sweating till the dizziness passed, forced himself by his arms, felt his heels touch the deck of the boat. He dropped, as lightly as he could, lunging forward to catch at the tangle of rigging. A sickening time while the wreck surged and creaked; he felt sweat drop from him again as he willed the movement to stop. The deck steadied, with a final groan; he edged sideways cautiously, cutting more rope lengths, fashioning a bridle that he slipped under Lipsill's arms. The other helped as best he could, raising his body weakly; Stromberg tested the knots, lashed the harness to the line. Another minute's work and he too was secure. He took a shuddering breath, groping for the second rope. They were not clear yet; if *Ice Ghost* moved, she could still take them with her, scrape them into the gulf. He gripped the line and pulled.

Nothing.

He jerked again, feeling the fresh rise of panic. If the trick failed he knew he lacked the strength ever to climb. A waiting; then a vibration, sensed through the rope. Another pause; and he was being drawn smoothly up the cliff, swinging against the rock-hard ice as the pace increased. The sides of the cleft seemed to rush toward him; a last concussion, a bruising shock and he was being towed over level ice, sawing desperately at the line. He saw fibers parting; then he was lying still, blessedly motionless. Lipsill beside him bleeding into the snow. While *Princess*, freed of her one-sided burden, skated in a wide half-circle, came into irons, and stopped.

The crevasse of Brershill lay gray and silent in the early morning. Torches, flaring at intervals along the glassy sides, lit Level after Level with a wavering glare, gleamed on the walkways with their new powdering of snow. Stromberg trudged steadily, sometimes hauling his burden, sometimes skidding behind it as he eased the sledge down the sloping paths. A watchman called sleepily; he ignored him. On the Level above Coranda's home he stopped, levered the great thing from the sledge and across to the edge of the path. He straightened up, wiping his face, and yelled; his voice ran thin and shaking, echoing between the half-seen walls.

"*Maitran. . . .*"

A bird flew squawking from the depths. The word flung itself back at him, Ice Mother answering with a thousand voices.

"*Arand. . . .*"

Again the mocking choir, confusions of sound reflecting faint and mad from the cleft.

"*Hansan. . . .*

"*Skalter. . . .*"

Names of the dead, and lost; a fierce benediction, an answer to the ice.

He bent to the thing on the path. A final heave, a falling, a fleshy thud; the head of the unicorn bounced on the Level below, splashed a great star of blood across Coranda's door. He straightened, panting, half-hearing from somewhere the echo of a scream. Stood and stared a moment longer before starting to climb.

Giving thanks to Ice Mother, who had given him back his soul.

Nightwings

ROBERT SILVERBERG

Like Brian Aldiss, Robert Silverberg is an author who seems fascinated with the far future, and he has returned to far-future milieus again and again throughout his career in stories such as "At Winter's End," "A Long Night's Vigil at the Temple," "Homecoming," "Dancers in the Time-Flux," "This Is the Road," "Red Blaze in the Morning," the Nebula Award–winning "Sailing to Byzantium," and many others, as well as in novels such as *Son of Man* and the stories and novels of the *Majipoor* sequence. Also like Aldiss, Silverberg has written a number of stories that would have served perfectly well for this anthology, but the one I kept coming back to was the evocative novella that follows, which won a Hugo Award in 1969, one of a sequence of three novellas that were later melded into the book *Nightwings*.

Here Silverberg takes us to a time thousands of years beyond our own, to the glorious city of Roum, builds layer on layer upon the ancient rubble of the nearly forgotten past, and paints a vivid portrait of one man's obsession with duty to the exclusion of all else . . . and warns us that just as it is better to travel hopefully than to arrive, it's sometimes better to search endlessly for something than it is to actually *find* what you're looking for. . . .

Robert Silverberg is one of the most famous SF writers of modern times, with dozens of novels, anthologies, and collections to his credit. As both writer and editor, Silverberg was one of the most influential figures of the post–New Wave era of the seventies and continues to be at the forefront of the field to this very day, having won a total of five Nebula Awards and four Hugo Awards.

Born in Brooklyn, New York, in 1935, Silverberg, like Poul Anderson before him, started a successful career as an SF writer while he was still in college. His first novel was sold in 1954, while he was still a junior at Columbia University; by 1955, still prior to graduation, he was earning "quite a good living" by writing, and by 1956, he had won his first Hugo Award. He spent a period of some years in the late fifties and early sixties away from the field, writing a long string of well-received nonfiction books, but by the late sixties he'd returned to the genre, and during the first half of the seventies the so-called New Silverberg would produce a large and remarkable body of work: the brilliant *Dying Inside*, easily one of the best books of the seventies,

Downward to the Earth, The Book of Skulls, Tower of Glass, The World Inside, The Second Trip, A Time of Changes, The Stochastic Man, and Shadrach in the Furnace, as well as high-quality short works such as "Born with the Dead," "Sundance," "In Entropy's Jaws," "Breckenridge and the Continuum," "Push No More," "In the Group," "Capricorn Games," "Trips," "Swartz between the Galaxies," and many more. Seldom has science fiction witnessed such a concentrated outpouring of high-level talent, work that would be highly influential on writers such as Barry N. Malzberg and the later Gregory Benford, to name just two, and which I strongly suspect was influential on writers of subsequent generations—such as Alexander Jablokov—as well. When you add in the influence that Silverberg would exert on the field through his editorship of the New Dimensions original anthology series, the most important anthology series of its day, you can see that the strength of Silverberg's impact on the SF world of the seventies can hardly be overestimated.

In 1976, depressed by the general malaise that had settled over the field at the time and perhaps exhausted from his efforts over the previous years, Silverberg publicly announced his "retirement" . . . and, indeed, would not write another word until 1980, when he suddenly came out of retirement to write his huge science-fantasy novel (also set in the far future) Lord Valentine's Castle. His output of new fiction was relatively low in the early years of the decade, but when a new surge of creative energy revitalized the field in the mideighties Silverberg shifted into high gear once again, and, as what might perhaps be referred to—a bit facetiously—as the "New New Silverberg," poured out another torrent of high-quality work such as "The Pope of the Chimps," "Multiples," "The Palace at Midnight," "We Are for the Dark," "In Another Country," "Basileus," "The Secret Sharer," "Enter a Soldier. Later: Enter Another," "Sailing to Byzantium," "Beauty in the Night," "Death Do Us Part," "The Colonel in Autumn," and dozens of others, as well as a score of best-selling novels—a torrent that shows no signs of running dry even here at the end of the 1990s.

Silverberg's other books include the novels Son of Man, Thorns, Up the Line, The Man in the Maze, Tom O'Bedlam, Star of Gypsies, At Winter's End, The Face of the Waters, Kingdoms of the Wall, and Hot Sky at Morning and three novel-length expansions of famous Isaac Asimov stories, Nightfall, and The Ugly Little Boy, and The Positronic Man. His collections include Unfamiliar Territory, Capricorn Games, Majipoor Chronicles, The Best of Robert Silverberg, At the Conglomeroid Cocktail Party, Beyond the Safe Zone, and a massive retrospective collection, The Collected Stories of Robert Silverberg, vol. 1: Secret Sharers. His reprint anthologies are far too numerous to list here but include The Science Fiction Hall of Fame, vol. 1, and the distinguished Alpha series, among dozens of others. His most recent books are two major original anthologies, Legends and Far Horizons, and the novels The Alien Years, Mountains of Majipoor, Lord Prestimion. He lives with his wife, writer Karen Haber, in Oakland, California.

1

Roum is a city built on seven hills. They say it was a capital of man in one of the earlier cycles. I did not know of that, for my guild was Watching, not Remembering; but yet as I had my first glimpse of Roum, coming upon it from the south at twilight, I could see that in former days it must have been of great significance. Even now it was a mighty city of many thousands of souls.

Its bony towers stood out sharply against the dusk. Lights glimmered appealingly. On my left hand the sky was ablaze with splendor as the sun relinquished possession; streaming bands of azure and violet and crimson folded and writhed about one another in the nightly dance that brings the darkness. To my right, blackness had already come. I attempted to find the seven hills, and failed, and still I knew that this was that Roum of majesty toward which all roads are bent, and I felt awe and deep respect for the works of our bygone fathers.

We rested by the long straight road, looking up at Roum. I said, "It is a goodly city. We will find employment there."

Beside me, Avluela fluttered her lacy wings. "And food?" she asked in her high, fluty voice. "And shelter? And wine?"

"Those too," I said. "All of those."

"How long have we been walking, Watcher?" she asked.

"Two days. Three nights."

"If I had been flying, it would have been more swift."

"For you," I said. "You would have left us far behind and never seen us again. Is that your desire?"

She came close to me and rubbed the rough fabric of my sleeve, and then she pressed herself at me the way a flirting cat might do. Her wings unfolded into two broad sheets of gossamer through which I could still see the sunset and the evening lights, blurred, distorted, magical. I sensed the fragrance of her midnight hair. I put my arms to her and embraced her slender, boyish body.

She said, "You know it is my desire to remain with you always, Watcher. Always!"

"Yes, Avluela."

"Will we be happy in Roum?"

"We will be happy," I said, and released her.

"Shall we go into Roum now?"

"I think we should wait for Gormon," I said, shaking my head. "He'll be back soon from his explorations." I did not want to tell her of my weariness. She was only a child, seventeen summers old; what did she know of weariness or of age? And I was old. Not as old as Roum, but old enough.

"While we wait," she said, "may I fly?"

"Fly, yes."

I squatted beside our cart and warmed my hands at the throbbing generator while Avluela prepared to fly. First she removed her garments, for her wings have little strength and she cannot lift such extra baggage. Lithely, deftly, she peeled the glassy bubbles from her tiny feet and wriggled free of her crimson jacket and of her soft, furry leggings. The vanishing light in the west sparkled over her slim form. Like all Fliers, she carried no surplus body tissue: her breasts were mere bumps, her buttocks flat, her thighs so spindly that there was a span of inches between them when she stood. Could she have weighed more than a quintal? I doubt it. Looking at her, I felt, as always, gross and earthbound, a thing of loathsome flesh, and yet I am not a heavy man.

By the roadside she genuflected, knuckles to the ground, head bowed to knees, as she said whatever ritual it is that the Fliers say. Her back was to me. Her delicate wings fluttered, filled with life, rose about her like a cloak whipped up by the breeze. I could not comprehend how such wings could possibly lift even so slight a form as Avluela's. They were not hawk-wings but butterfly-wings, veined and transparent, marked here and there with blotches of pigment, ebony and turquoise and scarlet. A sturdy ligament joined them to the two flat pads of muscle beneath her sharp shoulderblades; but what she did not have was the massive breastbone of a flying creature, the bands of corded muscle needed for flight. Oh, I know that the Fliers use more than muscle to get aloft, that there are mystical disciplines in their mystery. Even so, I, who was of the Watchers, remained skeptical of the more fantastic guilds.

Avluela finished her words. She rose; she caught the breeze with her wings; she ascended several feet. There she remained, suspended between earth and sky, while her wings beat frantically. It was not yet night, and Avluela's wings were merely nightwings. By day she could not fly, for the terrible pressure of the solar wind would hurl her to the ground. Now, midway between dusk and dark, it was still not the best time for her to go up. I saw her thrust toward the east by the remnant of light in the sky. Her arms as well as her wings thrashed; her small pointed face was grim with concentration; on her thin lips were the words of her guild. She doubled her body and shot it out, head going one way, rump the other; and abruptly she hovered horizontally, looking groundward, her wings thrashing against the air. *Up, Avluela! Up!*

Up it was, as by will alone she conquered the vestige of light that still glowed.

With pleasure I surveyed her naked form against the darkness. I could see her clearly, for a Watcher's eyes are keen. She was five times her own height in the air, now, and her wings spread to their full expanse, so that the towers of Roum were in partial eclipse for me. She waved. I threw her a kiss and offered words of love. Watchers do not marry, nor do they engender children, but yet Avluela was as a daughter to me, and I took pride in her flight. We had traveled together a year, now, since we had first met in Agupt, and it was as though I had known her all my long life. From her I drew a renewal of strength. I do not know what it was she drew from me: security, knowledge, a continuity with the days before her birth. I hoped only that she loved me as I loved her.

Now she was far aloft. She wheeled, soared, dived, pirouetted, danced. Her long black hair streamed from her scalp. Her body seemed only an incidental appendage to those two great wings which glistened and throbbed and gleamed in the night. Up she rose, glorying in her freedom from gravity, making me feel all the more leaden-footed; and like some slender rocket she shot abruptly away in the direction of Roum. I saw the soles of her feet, the tips of her wings; then I saw her no more.

I sighed. I thrust my hands into the pits of my arms to keep them warm. How is it that I felt a winter chill while the girl Avluela could soar joyously bare through the sky?

It was now the twelfth of the twenty hours, and time once again for me to do the Watching. I went to the cart, opened my cases, prepared the instruments. Some of the dial, covers were yellowed and faded; the indicator needles had lost their luminous coating; sea stains defaced the instrument housings, a relic of the time that pirates had assailed me in Earth Ocean. The worn and cracked levers and nodes responded easily to my touch as I entered the preliminaries. First one prays for a pure and perceptive mind; then one creates the affinity with one's instruments; then one does the actual Watching, searching the starry heavens for the enemies of man. Such was my skill and my craft. I grasped handles and knobs, thrust things from my mind, prepared myself to become an extension of my cabinet of devices.

I was only just past my threshold and into the first phase of Watchfulness when a deep and resonant voice behind me said, "Well, Watcher, how goes it?"

I sagged against the cart. There is a physical pain in being wrenched so unexpectedly from one's work. For a moment I felt claws clutching at my heart. My face grew hot; my eyes would not focus; the saliva drained from my throat. As soon as I could, I took the proper protective measures to ease the metabolic drain, and severed myself from my instruments. Hiding my trembling as much as possible, I turned around.

Gormon, the other member of our little band, had appeared and stood jauntily beside me. He was grinning, amused at my distress, but I could not feel angry with him. One does not show anger at a guildless person no matter what the provocation.

Tightly, with effort, I said, "Did you spend your time rewardingly?"

"Very. Where's Avluela?"

I pointed heavenward. Gormon nodded.

"What have you found?" I asked.

"That this city is definitely Roum."

"There never was doubt of that."

"For me there was. But now I have proof."

"Yes?"

"In the overpocket. Look!"

From his tunic he drew his overpocket, set it on the pavement beside me, and expanded it so that he could insert his hands into its mouth. Grunting a little, he began to pull something heavy from the pouch—something of white stone—a long marble column, I now saw, fluted, pocked with age.

"From a temple of Imperial Roum!" Gormon exulted.

"You shouldn't have taken that."

"Wait!" he cried, and reached into the overpocket once more. He took from it a handful of circular metal plaques and scattered them jingling at my feet. "Coins! Money! Look at them, Watcher! The faces of the Caesars!"

"Of whom?"

"The ancient rulers. Don't you know your history of past cycles?"

I peered at him curiously. "You claim to have no guild, Gormon. Could it be you are a Rememberer and are concealing it from me?"

"Look at my face, Watcher. Could I belong to any guild? Would a Changeling be taken?"

"True enough," I said, eyeing the golden hue of him, the thick waxen skin, the red-pupiled eyes, the jagged mouth. Gormon had been weaned on teratogenetic drugs; he was a monster, handsome in his way, but a monster nevertheless, a Changeling, outside the laws and customs of man as they are practiced in the Third Cycle of civilization. And there is no guild of Changelings.

"There's more," Gormon said. The overpocket was infinitely capacious; the contents of a world, if need be, could be stuffed into its shriveled gray maw, and still it would be no longer than a man's hand. Gormon took from it bits of machinery, reading spools, an angular thing of brown metal that might have been an ancient tool, three squares of shining glass, five slips of paper—*paper!*—and a host of other relics of antiquity. "See?" he said. "A fruitful stroll, Watcher! And not just random booty. Everything recorded, everything labeled, stratum, estimated age, position when *in situ*. Here we have many thousands of years of Roum."

"Should you have taken these things?" I asked doubtfully.

"Why not? Who is to miss them? Who of this cycle cares for the past?"

"The Rememberers."

"They don't need solid objects to help them do their work."

"Why do you want these things, though?"

"The past interests me, Watcher. In my guildless way I have my scholarly pursuits. Is that wrong? May not even a monstrosity seek knowledge?"

"Certainly, certainly. Seek what you wish. Fulfill yourself in your own way. This is Roum. At dawn we enter. I hope to find employment here."

"You may have difficulties."

"How so?"

"There are many Watchers already in Roum, no doubt. There will be little need for your services."

"I'll seek the favor of the Prince of Roum," I said.

"The Prince of Roum is a hard and cold and cruel man."

"You know of him?"

Gormon shrugged. "Somewhat." He began to stuff his artifacts back in the overpocket. "Take your chances with him, Watcher. What other choice do you have?"

"None," I said, and Gormon laughed, and I did not.

He busied himself with his ransacked loot of the past. I found myself deeply depressed by his words. He seemed so sure of himself in an uncertain world, this guildless one, this mutated monster, this man of inhuman look; how could he be so cool, so casual? He lived without concern for calamity and mocked those who admitted to fear. Gormon had been traveling with us for nine days, now, since we had met him in the ancient city beneath the volcano to the south by the edge of the sea. I had not suggested that he join us; he had invited himself along, and at Avluela's bidding I accepted. The roads are dark and cold at this time of year, and dangerous beasts of many species abound, and an old man journeying with a girl might well consider taking with him a brawny one like Gormon. Yet there were times I wished he had not come with us, and this was one.

Slowly I walked back to my equipment.

Gormon said, as though first realizing it, "Did I interrupt you at your Watching?"

I said mildly, "You did."

"Sorry. Go and start again. I'll leave you in peace." And he gave me his dazzling lopsided smile, so full of charm that it took the curse off the easy arrogance of his words.

I touched the knobs, made contact with the nodes, monitored the dials. But I did not enter Watchfulness, for I remained aware of Gormon's presence and fearful that he would break into my concentration once again at a painful moment, despite his promise. At length I looked away from the apparatus. Gormon stood at the far side of the road, craning his neck for some sight of Avluela. The moment I turned to him he became aware of me.

"Something wrong, Watcher?"

"No. The moment's not propitious for my work. I'll wait."

"Tell me," he said. "When Earth's enemies really do come from the stars, will your machines let you know it?"

"I trust they will."

"And then?"

"Then I notify the Defenders."

"After which your life's work is over?"

"Perhaps," I said.

"Why a whole guild of you, though? Why not one master center where the Watch is kept? Why a bunch of itinerant Watchers drifting from place to place?"

"The more vectors of detection," I said, "the greater the chance of early awareness of the invasion."

"Then an individual Watcher might well turn his machines on and not see anything, with an invader already here."

"It could happen. And so we practice redundancy."

"You carry it to an extreme, I sometimes think." Gormon laughed. "Do you actually believe an invasion is coming?"

"I do," I said stiffly. "Else my life was a waste."

"And why should the star people want Earth? What do we have here besides the remnants of old empires? What would they do with miserable Roum? With Perris? With Jorslem? Rotting cities! Idiot princes! Come, Watcher, admit it: the invasion's a myth, and you go through meaningless motions four times a day. Eh?"

"It is my craft and my science to Watch. It is yours to jeer. Each of us to our speciality, Gormon."

"Forgive me," he said with mock humility. "Go, then, and Watch."

"I shall."

Angrily I turned back to my cabinet of instruments, determined now to ignore any interruption, no matter how brutal. The stars were out; I gazed at the glowing constellations, and automatically my mind registered the many worlds. Let us Watch, I thought. Let us keep our vigil despite the mockers.

I entered full Watchfulness.

I clung to the grips and permitted the surge of power to rush through me. I cast my mind to the heavens and searched for hostile entities. What ecstasy! What incredible splendor! I who had never left this small planet roved the black spaces of the void, glided from star to burning star, saw the planets spinning like tops. Faces stared back at me as I journeyed, some without eyes, some with many eyes, all the complexity of the many-peopled galaxy accessible to me. I spied out possible concentrations of inimicable force. I inspected drilling-grounds and military encampments. I sought, as I had sought four times daily for all my adult life, for the invaders who had been promised us, the conquerors who at the end of days were destined to seize our tattered world.

I found nothing, and when I came up from my trance, sweaty and drained, I saw Avluela descending.

Feather-light she landed. Gormon called to her, and she ran, bare, her little breasts quivering, and he enfolded her smallness in his powerful arms, and they embraced, not passionately but joyously. When he released her she turned to me.

"Roum," she gasped. *"Roum!"*

"You saw it?"

"Everything! Thousands of people! Lights! Boulevards! A market! Broken buildings many cycles old! Oh, Watcher, how wonderful Roum is!"

"Your flight was a good one, then," I said.

"A miracle!"

"Tomorrow we go to dwell in Roum."

"No, Watcher, tonight, tonight!" She was girlishly eager, her face bright with excitement. "It's just a short journey more! Look, it's just over there!"

"We should rest first," I said. "We do not want to arrive weary in Roum."

"We can rest when we get there," Avluela answered. "Come! Pack everything! You've done your Watching, haven't you?"

"Yes. Yes."

"Then let's go. To Roum! To Roum!"

I looked in appeal at Gormon. Night had come; it was time to make camp, to have our few hours of sleep.

For once Gormon sided with me. He said to Avluela, "The Watcher's right. We can all use some rest. We'll go on into Roum at dawn."

Avluela pouted. She looked more like a child than ever. Her wings drooped; her underdeveloped body slumped. Petulantly she closed her wings until they were mere fist-sized humps on her back, and picked up the garments she had scattered on the road. She dressed while we made camp. I distributed food tablets; we entered our receptacles; I fell into troubled sleep and dreamed of Avluela limned against the crumbling moon, and Gormon flying beside her. Two hours before dawn I arose and performed my first Watch of the new day, while they still slept. Then I aroused them, and we went onward toward the fabled imperial city, onward toward Roum.

2

The morning's light was bright and harsh, as though this were some young world newly created. The road was all but empty; people do not travel much in these latter days unless, like me, they are wanderers by habit and profession. Occasionally we stepped aside to let a chariot of some member of the guild of Masters go by, drawn by a dozen expressionless neuters harnessed in series. Four such vehicles went by in the first two hours of the day, each shuttered and sealed to hide the Master's proud features from the gaze of such common folk as we. Several roller-wagons laden with produce passed us, and a number of floaters soared overhead. Generally we had the road to ourselves, however.

The environs of Roum showed vestiges of antiquity: isolated columns, the fragments of an aqueduct transporting nothing from nowhere to nowhere, the portals of a vanished temple. That was the oldest Roum we saw, but there were accretions of the later Roums of subsequent cycles: the huts of peasants, the domes of power drains, the hulls of dwelling-towers. Infrequently we met with the burned-out shell of some ancient airship. Gormon examined everything, taking samples from time to time. Avluela looked, wide-eyed, saying nothing. We walked on, until the walls of the city loomed before us.

They were of a blue glossy stone, neatly joined, rising to a height of perhaps eight men. Our road pierced the wall through a corbeled arch; the gate stood open. As we approached the gate, a figure came toward us; he was hooded, masked, a man of extraordinary height wearing the somber garb of the guild of Pilgrims. One does not approach such a person oneself, but one heeds him if he beckons. The Pilgrim beckoned.

Through his speaking grille he said, "Where from?"

"The south. I lived in Agupt awhile, then crossed Land Bridge to Talya," I replied.

"Where bound?"

"Roum, awhile."

"How goes the Watch?"

"As customary."

"You have a place to stay in Roum?" the Pilgrim asked.

I shook my head. "We trust to the kindness of the Will."

"The Will is not always kind," said the Pilgrim absently. "Nor is there much need of Watchers in Roum. Why do you travel with a Flier?"

"For company's sake. And because she is young and needs protection."

"Who is the other one?"

"He is guildless, a Changeling."

"So I can see. But why is he with you?"

"He is strong and I am old, and so we travel together. Where are you bound, Pilgrim?"

"Jorslem. Is there another destination for my guild?"

I conceded the point with a shrug.

The Pilgrim said, "Why do you not come to Jorslem with me?"

"My road lies north now. Jorslem is in the south, close by Agupt."

"You have been to Agupt and not to Jorslem?" he said, puzzled.

"Yes. The time was not ready for me to see Jorslem."

"Come now. We will walk together on the road, Watcher, and we will talk of the old times and of the times to come, and I will assist you in your Watching, and you will assist me in my communions with the Will. Is it agreed?"

It was a temptation. Before my eyes flashed the image of Jorslem the Golden, its holy buildings and shrines, its places of renewal where the old are made young, its spires, its tabernacles. Even though I am a man set in his ways, I was willing at the moment to abandon Roum and go with the Pilgrim to Jorslem.

I said, "And my companions—"

"Leave them. It is forbidden for me to travel with the guildless, and I do not wish to travel with a female. You and I, Watcher, will go to Jorslem together."

Avluela, who had been standing to one side frowning through all this colloquy, shot me a look of sudden terror.

"I will not abandon them," I said.

"Then I go to Jorslem alone," said the Pilgrim. Out of his robe stretched a bony hand, the fingers long and white and steady. I touched my fingers reverently to the tips of his, and the Pilgrim said, "Let the Will give you mercy, friend Watcher. And when you reach Jorslem, search for me."

He moved on down the road without further conversation.

Gormon said to me, "You would have gone with him, wouldn't you?"

"I considered it."

"What could you find in Jorslem that isn't here? That's a holy city and so is this. Here you can rest awhile. You're in no shape for more walking now."

"You may be right," I conceded, and with the last of my energy I strode toward the gate of Roum.

Watchful eyes scanned us from slots in the wall. When we were at midpoint in the gate, a fat, pockmarked Sentinel with sagging jowls halted us and asked our business in Roum. I stated my guild and purpose, and he gave a snort of disgust.

"Go elsewhere, Watcher! We need only useful men here."

"Watching has its uses," I said mildly.

"No doubt. No doubt." He squinted at Avluela. "Who's this? Watchers are celibates, no?"

"She is nothing more than a traveling companion."

The Sentinel guffawed coarsely. "It's a route you travel often, I wager! Not that there's much to her. What is she, thirteen, fourteen? Come here, child. Let me check you for contraband." He ran his hands quickly over her, scowling as he felt her breasts, then raising an eyebrow as he encountered the mounds of her wings below her shoulders. "What's this? What's this? More in back than in front! A Flier, are you? Very dirty business, Fliers consorting with foul old Watchers." He chuckled and put his hand on Avluela's body in a way that sent Gormon starting forward in fury, murder in his fire-circled eyes. I caught him in time and grasped his wrist with all my strength, holding him back lest he ruin the three of us by an attack on the Sentinel. He tugged at me, nearly pulling me over; then he grew calm and subsided, icily watching as the fat one finished checking Avluela for "contraband."

At length the Sentinel turned in distaste to Gormon and said, "What kind of thing are you?"

"Guildless, your mercy," Gormon said in sharp tones. "The humble and worthless product of teratogenesis, and yet nevertheless a free man who desires entry to Roum."

"Do we need more monsters here?"

"I eat little and work hard."

"You'd work harder still, if you were neutered," said the Sentinel.

Gormon glowered. I said, "May we have entry?"

"A moment." The Sentinel donned his thinking cap and narrowed his eyes as he transmitted a message to the memory tanks. His face tensed with the effort; then it went slack, and moments later came the reply. We could not hear the transaction at all; but from his disappointed look, it appeared evident that no reason had been found to refuse us admission to Roum.

"Go on in," he said. "The three of you. Quickly!"

We passed beyond the gate.

Gormon said, "I could have split him open with a blow."

"And be neutered by nightfall. A little patience, and we've come into Roum."

"The way he handled her—!"

"You take a very possessive attitude toward Avluela," I said. "Remember that she's a Flier, and not sexually available to the guildless."

Gormon ignored my thrust. "She arouses me no more than you do, Watcher. But it pains me to see her treated that way. I would have killed him if you hadn't held me back."

Avluela said, "Where shall we stay, now that we're in Roum?"

"First let me find the headquarters of my guild," I said. "I'll register at the Watchers' Inn. After that, perhaps we'll hunt up the Fliers' Lodge for a meal."

"And then," said Gormon drily, "we'll go to the Guildless Gutter and beg for coppers."

"I pity you because you are a Changeling," I told him, "but I find it ungraceful of you to pity yourself. Come."

We walked up a cobbled, winding street away from the gate and into Roum itself. We were in the outer ring of the city, a residential section of low, squat houses topped by the unwieldy bulk of defense installations. Within lay the shining towers we had seen from the fields the night before; the remnant of ancient Roum carefully preserved across ten thousand years or more; the market, the factory zone, the communications hump, the temples of the Will, the memory tanks, the sleepers' refuges, the outworlders' brothels, the government buildings, the headquarters of the various guilds.

At the corner, beside a Second Cycle building with walls of rubbery texture, I found a public thinking cap and slipped it on my forehead. At once my thoughts raced down the conduit until they came to the interface that gave them access to one of the storage brains of a memory tank. I pierced the interface and saw the wrinkled brain itself, pale gray against the deep green of its housing. A Rememberer once told me that, in cycles past, men built machines to do their thinking for them, although these machines were hellishly expensive and required vast amounts of space and drank power gluttonously. That was not the worst of our forefathers' follies; but why build artificial brains when death each day liberates scores of splendid natural ones to hook into the memory tanks? Was it that they lacked the knowledge to use them? I find that hard to believe.

I gave the brain my guild identification and asked the coordinates of our inn. Instantly I received them, and we set out, Avluela on one side of me, Gormon on the other, myself wheeling, as always, the cart in which my instruments resided.

The city was crowded. I had not seen such throngs in sleepy, heat-fevered Agupt, nor at any other point on my northward journey. The streets were full of Pilgrims, secretive and masked. Jostling through them went busy Rememberers and glum Merchants and now and then the litter of a Master. Avluela saw a number of Fliers, but was barred by the tenets of her guild from greeting them until she had undergone her ritual purification. I regret to say that I spied many Watchers, all of whom looked upon me disdainfully and without welcome. I noted a good many Defenders and ample representation of such lesser guilds as Vendors, Servitors, Manufactories, Scribes, Communicants, and Transporters. Naturally, a host of neuters went silently about their humble business, and numerous outworlders of all descriptions flocked the streets, most of them probably tourists, some here to do what business could be done with the sullen, poverty-blighted people of Earth. I noticed many Changelings limping furtively through the crowd, not one of them as proud of bearing as Gormon beside me. He was unique among his kind; the others, dappled and piebald and asymmetrical, limbless or overlimbed, deformed in a thousand imaginative and artistic ways, were slinkers, squinters, shufflers, hissers, creepers; they were cutpurses, brain-drainers, organ-peddlers, repentance-mongers, gleam-buyers, but none held himself upright as though he thought he were a man.

The guidance of the brain was exact, and in less than an hour of walking we arrived at the Watchers' Inn. I left Gormon and Avluela outside and wheeled my cart within.

Perhaps a dozen members of my guild lounged in the main hall. I gave them the customary sign, and they returned it languidly. Were these the guardians on whom Earth's safety depended? Simpletons and weaklings!

"Where may I register?" I asked.

"New? Where from?"

"Agupt was my last place of registry."

"Should have stayed there. No need of Watchers here."

"Where may I register?" I asked again.

A foppish youngster indicated a screen in the rear of the great room. I went to it, pressed my fingertips against it, was interrogated, and gave my name, which a Watcher may utter only to another Watcher and only within the precincts of an inn. A panel shot open, and a puffy-eyed man who wore the Watcher emblem on his right cheek and not on the left, signifying his high rank in the guild, spoke my name and said, "You should have known better than to come to Roum. We're over our quota."

"I claim lodging and employment nonetheless."

"A man with your sense of humor should have been born into the guild of Clowns," he said.

"I see no joke."

"Under laws promulgated by our guild in the most recent session, an inn is under no obligation to take new lodgers once it has reached its assigned capacity. We are at our assigned capacity. Farewell, my friend."

I was aghast. "I know of no such regulation! This is incredible! For a guild to turn away a member from its own inn—when he arrives footsore and numb! A man of my age, having crossed Land Bridge out of Agupt, here as a stranger and hungry in Roum—"

"Why did you not check with us first?"

"I had no idea it would be necessary."

"The new regulations—"

"May the Will shrivel the new regulations!" I shouted. "I demand lodging! To turn away one who has Watched since before you were born—"

"Easy, brother, easy."

"Surely you have some corner where I can sleep—some crumbs to let me eat—"

Even as my tone had changed from bluster to supplication, his expression softened from indifference to mere disdain. "We have no room. We have no food. These are hard times for our guild, you know. There is talk that we will be disbanded altogether, as a useless luxury, a drain upon the Will's resources. We are very limited in our abilities. Because Roum has a surplus of Watchers, we all are on short rations as it is, and if we admit you our rations will be all the shorter."

"But where will I go? What shall I do?"

"I advise you," he said blandly, "to throw yourself upon the mercy of the Prince of Roum."

3

Outside, I told that to Gormon, and he doubled with laughter, guffawing so furiously that the striations on his lean cheeks blazed like bloody stripes. "The mercy of the Prince of Roum!" he repeated. "The mercy—of the Prince of Roum—"

"It is customary for the unfortunate to seek the aid of the local ruler," I said coldly.

"The Prince of Roum knows no mercy," Gormon told me. "The Prince of Roum will feed you your own limbs to ease your hunger!"

"Perhaps," Avluela put in, "we should try to find the Fliers' Lodge. They'll feed us there."

"Not Gormon," I observed. "We have obligations to one another."

"We could bring food out to him," she said.

"I prefer to visit the court first," I insisted. "Let us make sure of our status. Afterward we can improvise living arrangements, if we must."

She yielded, and we made our way to the palace of the Prince of Roum, a massive building fronted by a colossal column-ringed plaza, on the far side of the river that splits the city. In the plaza we were accosted by mendicants of many sorts, some not even Earthborn; something with ropy tendrils and a corrugated, noseless face thrust itself at me and jabbered for alms until Gormon pushed it away, and moments later a second creature, equally strange, its skin pocked with luminescent craters and its limbs studded with eyes, embraced my knees and pleaded in the name of the Will for my mercy. "I am only a poor Watcher," I said, indicating my cart, "and am here to gain mercy myself." But the being persisted, sobbing out its misfortunes in a blurred, feathery voice, and in the end, to Gormon's immense disgust, I dropped a few food tablets into the shelf-like pouch on its chest. Then we muscled on toward the doors of the palace. At the portico a more horrid sight presented itself: a maimed Flier, fragile limbs bent and twisted, one wing half-unfolded and severely cropped, the other missing altogether. The Flier rushed upon Avluela, called her by a name not hers, moistened her leggings with tears so copious that the fur of them matted and stained. "Sponsor me to the lodge," he appealed. "They have turned me away because I am crippled, but if you sponsor me—" Avluela explained that she could do nothing, that she was a stranger to this lodge. The broken Flier would not release her, and Gormon with great delicacy lifted him like the bundle of dry bones that he was and set him aside. We stepped up onto the portico and at once were confronted by a trio of soft-faced neuters, who asked our business and admitted us quickly to the next line of barrier, which was manned by a pair of wizened Indexers. Speaking in unison, they queried us.

"We seek audience," I said. "A matter of mercy."

"The day of audience is four days hence," said the Indexer on the right. "We will enter your request on the rolls."

"We have no place to sleep!" Avluela burst out. "We are hungry! We—"

I hushed her. Gormon, meanwhile, was groping in the mouth of his overpocket. Bright things glimmered in his hand: pieces of gold, the eternal metal, stamped with hawk-nosed, bearded faces. He had found them grubbing in the ruins. He tossed one coin to the Indexer who had refused us. The man snapped it from the air, rubbed his thumb roughly across its shining obverse, and dropped it instantly into a fold of his garment. The second Indexer waited expectantly. Smiling, Gormon gave him his coin.

"Perhaps," I said, "we can arrange for a special audience within."

"Perhaps you can," said one of the Indexers. "Go through."

And so we passed into the nave of the palace itself and stood in the great, echoing space, looking down the central aisle toward the shielded throne-chamber at the apse. There were more beggars in here—licensed ones holding hereditary concessions—and also throngs of Pilgrims, Communicants, Rememberers, Musicians, Scribes, and Indexers. I heard muttered prayers; I smelled the scent of spicy incense; I felt the vibration of subterranean gongs. In cycles past, this building had been a shrine of one of the old religions—the Christers, Gormon told me, making me suspect once more that he was a Rememberer masquerading as a Changeling—and it still maintained something of its holy character even though it served as Roum's seat of secular government. But how were we to get to see the Prince? To my left I saw a small ornate chapel which a line of prosperous-looking Merchants and Landholders was slowly entering. Peering past them, I noted three skulls mounted on an interrogation fixture—a memory-tank input—and beside them, a burly Scribe. Telling Gormon and Avluela to wait for me in the aisle, I joined the line.

It moved infrequently, and nearly an hour passed before I reached the interrogation fixture. The skulls glared sightlessly at me; within their sealed crania, nutrient fluids bubbled and gurgled, caring for the dead, yet still functional, brains whose billion billion synaptic units now served as incomparable mnemonic devices. The Scribe seemed aghast to find a Watcher in this line, but before he could challenge me I blurted, "I come as a stranger to claim the Prince's mercy. I and my companions are without lodging. My own guild has turned me away. What shall I do? How may I gain an audience?"

"Come back in four days."

"I've slept on the road for more days than that. Now I must rest more easily."

"A public inn—"

"But I am guilded!" I protested. "The public inns would not admit me while my guild maintains an inn here, and my guild refuses me because of some new regulation, and—you see my predicament?"

In a wearied voice the Scribe said, "You may have application for a special audience. It will be denied, but you may apply."

"Where?"

"Here. State your purpose."

I identified myself to the skulls by my public designation, listed the names and status of my two companions, and explained my case. All this was absorbed and transmitted to the ranks of brains mounted somewhere in the depths of the city, and when I was done the Scribe said, "If the application is approved, you will be notified."

"Meanwhile where shall I stay?"

"Close to the palace, I would suggest."

I understood. I could join that legion of unfortunates packing the plaza. How

588	EXPLORING THE HORIZONS

many of them had requested some special favor of the Prince and were still there, months or years later, waiting to be summoned to the Presence? Sleeping on stone, begging for crusts, living in foolish hope!

But I had exhausted my avenues. I returned to Gormon and Avluela, told them of the situation, and suggested that we now attempt to hunt whatever accommodations we could. Gormon, guildless, was welcome at any of the squalid public inns maintained for his kind; Avluela could probably find residence at her own guild's lodge; only I would have to sleep in the streets—and not for the first time. But I hoped that we would not have to separate. I had come to think of us as a family, strange thought though that was for a Watcher.

As we moved toward the exit, my timepiece told me softly that the hour of Watching had come round again. It was my obligation and my privilege to tend to my Watching wherever I might be, regardless of the circumstances, whenever my hour came round; and so I halted, opened the cart, activated the equipment. Gormon and Avluela stood beside me. I saw smirks and open mockery on the faces of those who passed in and out of the palace; Watching was not held in very high repute, for we had Watched so long, and the promised enemy had never come. Yet one has one's duties, comic though they may seem to others. What is a hollow ritual to some is a life's work to others. Doggedly I forced myself into a state of Watchfulness. The world melted away from me, and I plunged into the heavens. The familiar joy engulfed me; and I searched the familiar places, and some that were not so familiar, my amplified mind leaping through the galaxies in wild swoops. Was an armada massing? Were troops drilling for the conquest of Earth? Four times a day I Watched, and the other members of my guild did the same, each at slightly different hours, so that no moment went by without some vigilant mind on guard. I do not believe that that was a foolish calling.

When I came up from my trance, a brazen voice was crying, "—for the Prince of Roum! Make way for the Prince of Roum!"

I blinked and caught my breath and fought to shake off the last strands of my concentration. A gilded palanquin borne by a phalanx of neuters had emerged from the rear of the palace and was proceeding down the nave toward me. Four men in the elegant costumes and brilliant masks of the guild of Masters flanked the litter, and it was preceded by a trio of Changelings, squat and broad, whose throats were so modified to imitate the sounding-boxes of bullfrogs; they emitted a trumpetlike boom of majestic sound as they advanced. It struck me as most strange that a prince would admit Changelings to his service, even ones as gifted as these.

My cart was blocking the progress of this magnificent procession, and hastily I struggled to close it and move it aside before the parade swept down upon me. Age and fear made my fingers tremble, and I could not make the sealings properly; while I fumbled in increasing clumsiness, the strutting Changelings drew so close that the blare of their throats was deafening, and Gormon attempted to aid me, forcing me to hiss at him that it is forbidden for anyone not of my guild to touch the equipment. I pushed him away; and an instant later a vanguard of neuters descended on me and prepared to scourge me from the spot with sparkling whips. "In the Will's name," I cried, "I am a Watcher!"

And in antiphonal response came the deep, calm, enormous reply, "Let him be. He is a watcher."

All motion ceased. The Prince of Roum had spoken.

The neuters drew back. The Changelings halted their music. The bearers of the Palanquin eased it to the floor. All those in the nave of the palace had pulled back, save only Gormon and Avluela and myself. The shimmering chain-curtains of the palanquin parted. Two of the Masters hurried forward and thrust their hands through the sonic barrier within, offering aid to their monarch. The barrier died away with a whimpering buzz.

The Prince of Roum appeared.

He was so young! He was nothing more than a boy, his hair full and dark, his face unlined. But he had been born to rule, and for all his youth he was as commanding as anyone I had ever seen. His lips were thin and tightly compressed; his aquiline nose was sharp and aggressive; his eyes, deep and cold, were infinite pools. He wore the jeweled garments of the guild of Dominators, but incised on his cheek was the double-barred cross of the Defenders, and around his neck he carried the dark shawl of the Rememberers. A Dominator may enroll in as many guilds as he pleases, and it would be a strange thing for a Dominator not also to be a Defender; but it startled me to find this prince a Rememberer as well. That is not normally a guild for the fierce.

He looked at me with little interest and said, "You choose an odd place to do your Watching, old man."

"The hour chose the place, sire," I replied. "I was here, and my duty compelled me. I had no way of knowing that you were about to come forth."

"Your Watching found no enemies?"

"None, sire."

I was about to press my luck, to take advantage of the unexpected appearance of the Prince to beg for his aid; but his interest in me died like a guttering candle as I stood there, and I did not dare call to him when his head had turned. He eyed Gormon a long moment, frowning and tugging at his chin. Then his gaze fell on Avluela. His eyes brightened. His jaw muscles flickered. His delicate nostrils widened. "Come up here, little Flier," he said, beckoning. "Are you this Watcher's friend?"

She nodded, terrified.

The Prince held out a hand to her and grasped; she floated up onto the palanquin, and with a grin so evil it seemed a parody of wickedness, the young Dominator drew her through the curtain. Instantly a pair of Masters restored the sonic barrier, but the procession did not move on. I stood mute. Gormon beside me was frozen, his powerful body rigid as a rod. I wheeled my cart to a less conspicuous place. Long moments passed. The courtiers remained silent, discreetly looking away from the palanquin.

At length the curtain parted once more. Avluela came stumbling out, her face pale, her eyes blinking rapidly. She seemed dazed. Streaks of sweat gleamed on her cheeks. She nearly fell, and a neuter caught her and swung her down to floor level. Beneath her jacket her wings were partly erect, giving her a hunchbacked look and telling me that she was in great emotional distress. In ragged, sliding steps she came to us, quivering, wordless; she darted a glance at me and flung herself against Gormon's broad chest.

The bearers lifted the palanquin. The Prince of Roum went out from his palace.

When he was gone, Avluela stammered hoarsely, "The Prince has granted us lodging in the royal hostelry!"

4

The hostelkeepers, of course, would not believe us.

Guests of the Prince were housed in the royal hostelry, which was to the rear of the palace in a small garden of frostflowers and blossoming ferns. The usual inhabitants of such a hostelry were Masters and an occasional Dominator; sometimes a particularly important Rememberer on an errand of research would win a niche there, or some highly placed Defender visiting for purposes of strategic planning. To house a Flier in a royal hostelry was distinctly odd; to admit a Watcher was unlikely; to take in a Changeling or some other guildless person was improbable beyond comprehension. When we presented ourselves, therefore, we were met by Servitors whose attitude was at first one of high good humor at our joke, then of irritation, finally of scorn. "Get away," they told us ultimately. "Scum! Rabble!"

Avluela said in a grave voice, "The Prince has granted us lodging here, and you may not refuse us."

"Away! Away!"

One snaggle-toothed Servitor produced a neural truncheon and brandished it in Gormon's face, passing a foul remark about his guildlessness. Gormon slapped the truncheon from the man's grasp, oblivious to the painful sting, and kicked him in the gut, so that he coiled and fell over, puking. Instantly a throng of neuters came rushing from within the hostelry. Gormon seized another of the Servitors and hurled him into the midst of them, turning them into a muddled mob. Wild shouts and angry cursing cries attracted the attention of a venerable Scribe who waddled to the door, bellowed for silence, and interrogated us. "That's easily checked," he said, when Avluela had told the story. To a Servitor he said contemptuously, "Send a think to the Indexers, fast!"

In time the confusion was untangled and we were admitted. We were given separate but adjoining rooms. I had never known such luxury before, and perhaps never shall again. The rooms were long, high, and deep. One entered them through telescopic pits keyed to one's own thermal output, to assure privacy. Lights glowed at the resident's merest nod, for hanging from ceiling globes and nestling in cupolas on the walls were spicules of slavelight from one of the Brightstar worlds, trained through suffering to obey such commands. The windows came and went at the dweller's whim; when not in use, they were concealed by streamers of quasi-sentient outworld gauzes, which not only were decorative in their own right, but which functioned as monitors to produce delightful scents according to requisitioned patterns. The rooms were equipped with individual thinking caps connected to the main memory banks. They likewise had conduits that summoned Servitors, Scribes, Indexers, or Musicians as required. Of course, a man of my own humble guild would not deign to make use of other human beings that way, out of fear of their glowering resentment; but in any case I had little need of them.

I did not ask of Avluela what had occurred in the Prince's palanquin to bring us such bounty. I could well imagine, as could Gormon, whose barely suppressed inner rage was eloquent of his never-admitted love for my pale, slender little Flier.

We settled in. I placed my cart beside the window, draped it with gauzes, and left it in readiness for my next period of Watching. I cleaned my body of grime while entities mounted in the wall sang me to peace. Later I ate. Afterwards Avluela came to me, refreshed and relaxed, and sat beside me in my room as we talked of our experiences. Gormon did not appear for hours. I thought that perhaps he had left this hostelry altogether, finding the atmosphere too rarefied for him, and had sought company among his own guildless kind. But at twilight, Avluela and I walked in the cloistered courtyard of the hostelry and mounted a ramp to watch the stars emerge in Roum's sky, and Gormon was there. With him was a lanky and emaciated man in a Rememberer's shawl; they were talking in low tones.

Gormon nodded to me and said, "Watcher, meet my new friend."

The emaciated one fingered his shawl. "I am the Rememberer Basil," he intoned, in a voice as thin as a fresco that has been peeled from its wall. "I have come from Perris to delve into the mysteries of Roum. I shall be here many years."

"The Rememberer has fine stories to tell," said Gormon. "He is among the foremost of his guild. As you approached, he was describing to me the techniques by which the past is revealed. They drive a trench through the strata of Third Cycle deposits, you see, and with vacuum cores they lift the molecules of earth to lay bare the ancient layers."

"We have found," Basil said, "the catacombs of Imperial Roum, and the rubble of the Time of Sweeping, the books inscribed on slivers of white metal, written toward the close of the Second Cycle. All these go to Perris for examination and classification and decipherment; then they return. Does the past interest you, Watcher?"

"To some extent." I smiled. "This Changeling here shows much more fascination for it. I sometimes suspect his authenticity. Would you recognize a Rememberer in disguise?"

Basil scrutinized Gormon; he lingered over the bizarre features, the excessively muscular frame. "He is no Rememberer," he said at length. "But I agree that he has antiquarian interests. He has asked me many profound questions."

"Such as?"

"He wishes to know the origin of guilds. He asks the name of the genetic surgeon who crafted the first true-breeding Fliers. He wonders why there are Changelings, and if they are truly under the curse of the Will."

"And do you have answers for these?" I asked.

"For some," said Basil. "For some."

"The origin of guilds?"

"To give structure and meaning to a society that has suffered defeat and destruction," said the Rememberer. "At the end of the Second Cycle all was in flux. No man knew his rank nor his purpose. Through our world strode haughty outworlders who looked upon us all as worthless. It was necessary to establish fixed frames of reference by which one man might know his value beside another. So the first guilds appeared: Dominators, Masters, Merchants, Landholders, Vendors and Servitors. Then came Scribes, Musicians, Clowns and Transporters. Afterwards Indexers became necessary, and then Watchers and Defenders. When the Years of Magic gave us Fliers and Changelings, those guilds were added, and then the guildless ones, the neuters, were produced, so that—"

"But surely the Changelings are guildless too!" said Avluela.

The Rememberer looked at her for the first time. "Who are you, child?"

"Avluela of the Fliers. I travel with this Watcher and this Changeling."

Basil said, "As I have been telling the Changeling here, in the early days his kind was guilded. The guild was dissolved a thousand years ago by the order of the Council of Dominators after an attempt by a disreputable Changeling faction to seize control of the holy places of Jorslem, and since that time Changelings have been guildless, ranking only above neuters."

"I never knew that," I said.

"You are no Rememberer," said Basil smugly. "It is our craft to uncover the past."

"True. True."

Gormon said, "And today, how many guilds are there?"

Discomfited, Basil replied vaguely, "At least a hundred, my friend. Some are quite small; some are local. I am concerned only with the original guilds and their immediate successors; what has happened in the past few hundred years is in the province of others. Shall I requisition an information for you?"

"Never mind," Gormon said. "It was only an idle question."

"Your curiosity is well developed," said the Rememberer.

"I find the world and all it contains extremely fascinating. Is this sinful?"

"It is strange," said Basil. "The guildless rarely look beyond their own horizons."

A Servitor appeared. With a mixture of awe and contempt he genuflected before Avluela and said, "The Prince has returned. He desires your company in the palace at this time."

Terror glimmered in Avluela's eyes. But to refuse was inconceivable. "Shall I come with you?" she asked.

"Please. You must be robed and perfumed. He wishes you to come to him with your wings open, as well."

Avluela nodded. The Servitor led her away.

We remained on the ramp a while longer; the Rememberer Basil talked of the old days of Roum, and I listened, and Gormon peered into the gathering darkness. Eventually, his throat dry, the Rememberer excused himself and moved solemnly away. A few moments later, in the courtyard below us, a door opened and Avluela emerged, walking as though she were of the guild of Somnambulists, not of Fliers. She was nude under transparent draperies, and her fragile body gleamed ghostly white in the starbeams. Her wings were spread and fluttered slowly in a somber systole and diastole. One Servitor grasped each of her elbows: they seemed to be propelling her toward the palace as though she were but a dreamed facsimile of herself and not a real woman.

"Fly, Avluela, fly," Gormon growled. "Escape while you can!"

She disappeared into a side entrance of the palace.

The Changeling looked at me. "She has sold herself to the Prince to provide lodging for us."

"So it seems."

"I could smash down that palace!"

"You love her?"

"It should be obvious."

"Cure yourself," I advised. "You are an unusual man, but still a Flier is not for you. Particularly a Flier who has shared the bed of the Prince of Roum."

"She goes from my arms to his."

I was staggered. "You've known her?"

"More than once," he said, smiling sadly. "At the moment of ecstasy her wings thrash like leaves in a storm."

I gripped the railing of the ramp so that I would not tumble into the courtyard. The stars whirled overhead; the old moon and its two blank-faced consorts leaped and bobbed. I was shaken without fully understanding the cause of my emotion. Was it wrath that Gormon had dared to violate a canon of the law? Was it a manifestation of those pseudo-parental feelings I had toward Avluela? Or was it mere envy of Gormon for daring to commit a sin beyond my capacity, though not beyond my desires?

I said, "They could burn your brain for that. They could mince your soul. And now you make me an accessory."

"What of it? That Prince commands, and he gets—but others have been there before him. I had to tell someone."

"Enough. Enough."

"Will we see her again?"

"Princes tire quickly of their women. A few days, perhaps a single night— then he will throw her back to us. And perhaps then we shall have to leave this hostelry." I sighed. "At least we'll have known it a few nights more than we deserved."

"Where will you go then?" Gormon asked.

"I will stay in Roum awhile."

"Even if you sleep in the streets? There does not seem to be much demand for Watchers here."

"I'll manage," I said. "Then I may go toward Perris."

"To learn from the Rememberers?"

"To see Perris. What of you? What do you want in Roum?"

"Avluela."

"Stop that talk!"

"Very well," he said, and his smile was bitter. "But I will stay here until the Prince is through with her. Then she will be mine, and we'll find ways to survive. The guildless are resourceful. They have to be. Maybe we'll scrounge lodgings in Roum awhile, and then follow you to Perris. If you're willing to travel with monsters and faithless Fliers."

I shrugged. "We'll see about that when the time comes."

"Have you ever been in the company of a Changeling before?"

"Not often. Not for long."

"I'm honored." He drummed on the parapet. "Don't cast me off, Watcher. I have a reason for wanting to stay with you."

"Which is?"

"To see your face on the day your machines tell you that the invasion of Earth has begun."

I let myself sag forward, shoulders drooping. "You'll stay with me a long time, then."

"Don't you believe the invasion is coming?"

"Some day. Not soon."

Gormon chuckled. "You're wrong. It's almost here."

"You don't amuse me."

"What is it, Watcher? Have you lost your faith? It's been known for a thousand years: another race covets Earth and owns it by treaty, and will some day come to collect. That much was decided at the end of the Second Cycle."

"I know all that, and I am no Rememberer." Then I turned to him and spoke words I never thought I would say aloud. "For twice your lifetime, Changeling, I've listened to the stars and done my Watching. Something done that often loses meaning. Say your own name ten thousand times and it will be an empty sound. I have Watched, and Watched well, and in the dark hours of the night I sometimes think I Watch for nothing, that I have wasted my life. There is a pleasure in Watching, but perhaps there is no real purpose."

His hand encircled my wrist. "Your confession is as shocking as mine. Keep your faith, Watcher. The invasion comes!"

"How could you possibly know?"

"The guildless also have their skills."

The conversation troubled me. I said, "Is it painful to be guildless?"

"One grows reconciled. And there are certain freedoms to compensate for the lack of status. I may speak freely to all."

"I notice."

"I move freely. I am always sure of food and lodging, though the food may be rotten and the lodging poor. Women are attracted to me despite all prohibitions. Because of them, perhaps. I am untroubled by ambitions."

"Never desire to rise above your rank?"

"Never."

"You might have been happier as a Rememberer."

"I am happy now. I can have a Rememberer's pleasures without his responsibility."

"How smug you are!" I cried. "To make, a virtue of guildlessness!"

"How else does one endure the weight of the Will?" He looked toward the palace. "The humble rise. The mighty fall. Take this as prophecy, Watcher: that lusty Prince in there will know more of life before summer comes. I'll rip out his eyes for taking Avluela!"

"Strong words. You bubble with treason tonight."

"Take it as prophecy."

"You can't get close to him," I said. Then, irritated for taking his foolishness seriously, I added, "And why blame him? He only does as princes do. Blame the girl for going to him. She might have refused."

"And lost her wings. Or died. No, she had no choice. I do!" In a sudden, terrible gesture the Changeling held out thumb and forefinger, double-jointed, long-nailed, and plunged them forward into imagined eyes. "Wait," he said. "You'll see!"

In the courtyard two Chronomancers appeared, set up the apparatus of their guild, and lit tapers by which to read the shape of tomorrow. A sickly odor of pallid smoke rose to my nostrils. I had now lost further desire to speak with the Changeling.

"It grows late," I said. "I need rest, and soon I must do my Watching."

"Watch carefully," Gormon told me.

5

.t night in my chamber I performed my fourth and last Watch of that long day, .d for the first time in my life I detected an anomaly. I could not interpret it. It as an obscure sensation, a mingling of tastes and sounds, a feeling of being in >ntact with some colossal mass. Worried, I clung to my instrument far longer .an usual, but perceived no more clearly at the end of my seance than at its >mmencement.

Afterward I wondered about my obligations.

Watchers are trained from childhood to be swift to sound the alarm; and the larm must be sounded when the Watcher judges the world in peril. Was I now bliged to notify the Defenders? Four times in my life the alarm had been given, n each occasion in error; and each Watcher who had thus touched off a false .obilization had suffered a fearful loss of status. One had contributed his brain to .e memory banks; one had become a neuter out of shame; one had smashed his .struments and gone to live among the guildless; and one, vainly attempting to ontinue in his profession, had discovered himself mocked by all his comrades. I .w no virtue in scorning one who had delivered a false alarm, for was it not referable for a Watcher to cry out too soon than not at all? But those were the ustoms of our guild, and I was constrained by them.

I evaluated my position and decided that I did not have valid grounds for an larm.

I reflected that Gormon had placed suggestive ideas in my mind that evening. might possibly be reacting only to his jeering talk of imminent invasion.

I could not act. I dared not jeopardize my standing by hasty outcry. I mistrusted .y own emotional state.

I gave no alarm.

Seething, confused, my soul roiling, I closed my cart and let myself sink into drugged sleep.

At dawn I woke and rushed to the window, expecting to find invaders in the .treets. But all was still; a winter grayness hung over the courtyard, and sleepy .ervitors pushed passive neuters about. Uneasily I did my first Watching of the .ay, and to my relief the strangenesses of the night before did not return, although had it in mind that my sensitivity is always greater at night than upon arising.

I ate and went to the courtyard. Gormon and Avluela were already there. She .oked fatigued and downcast, depleted by her night with the Prince of Roum, but said nothing to her about it. Gormon, slouching disdainfully against a wall em- .ellished with the shells of radiant mollusks, said to me, "Did your Watching go .ell?"

"Well enough."

"What of the day?"

"Out of roam Roum," I said. "Will you come? Avluela? Gormon?"

"Surely," he said, and she gave a faint nod; and, like the tourists we were, we .et off to inspect the splendid city of Roum.

Gormon acted as our guide to the jumbled pasts of Roum, belying his claim .ever to have been here before. As well as any Rememberer he described the things .e saw as we walked the winding streets. All the scattered levels of thousands of

years were exposed. We saw the power domes of the Second Cycle, and the Col
osseum where at an unimaginably early date man and beast contended like jungle
creatures. In the broken hull of that building of horrors Gormon told us of the
savagery of that unimaginably ancient time. "They fought," he said, "naked before
huge throngs. With bare hands men challenged beasts called lions, great hairy cat
with swollen heads; and when the lion lay in its gore, the victor turned to the
Prince of Roum and asked to be pardoned for whatever crime it was that had cas
him into the arena. And if he had fought well, the Prince made a gesture with hi
hand, and the man was freed." Gormon made the gesture for us: a thumb upraisec
and jerked backward over the right shoulder several times. "But if the man hac
shown cowardice, or if the lion had distinguished itself in the manner of its dying
the Prince made another gesture, and the man was condemned to be slain by a
second beast." Gormon showed us that gesture too: the middle finger jutting upware
from a clenched fist and lifted in a short sharp thrust.

"How are these things known?" Avluela asked, but Gormon pretended not to
hear her.

We saw the line of fusion-pylons built early in the Third Cycle to draw energy
from the world's core; they were still functioning, although stained and corroded
We saw the shattered stump of a Second Cycle weather machine, still a mighty
column at least twenty men high. We saw a hill on which white marble relics o
First Cycle Roum sprouted like pale clumps of winter deathflowers. Penetrating
toward the inner part of the city, we came upon the embankment of defensive
amplifiers waiting in readiness to hurl the full impact of the Will against invaders
We viewed a market where visitors from the stars haggled with peasants for ex
cavated fragments of antiquity. Gormon strode into the crowd and made severa
purchases. We came to a flesh-house for travelers from afar, where one could bu
anything from quasi-life to mounds of passion-ice. We ate at a small restaurant by
the edge of the River Tver, where guildless ones were served without ceremony
and at Gormon's insistence we dined on mounds of a soft doughy substance anc
drank a tart yellow wine, local specialties.

Afterward we passed through a covered arcade in whose many aisles plum
Vendors peddled star-goods, costly trinkets from Afreek, and the flimsy constructs
of the local Manufactories. Just beyond we emerged in a plaza that contained a
fountain in the shape of a boat, and to the rear of this rose a flight of cracked anc
battered stone-stairs ascending to a zone of rubble and weeds. Gormon beckoned
and we scrambled into this dismal area, then passed rapidly through it to a place
where a sumptuous palace, by its looks early Second Cycle or even First, brooded
over a sloping vegetated hill.

"They say this is the center of the world," Gormon declared. "In Jorslem one
finds another place that also claims the honor. They mark the spot here by a map."

"How can the world have one center," Avluela asked, "when it is round?"

Gormon laughed. We went in. Within, in wintry darkness, there stood a co
lossal jeweled globe lit by some inner glow.

"Here is your world," said Gormon, gesturing grandly.

"Oh!" Avluela gasped. "Everything! Everything is here!"

The map was a masterpiece of craftsmanship. It showed natural contours and
elevations, its seas seemed deep liquid pools, its deserts were so parched as to

make thirst spring in one's mouth, its cities swirled with vigor and life. I beheld the continents, Eyrop, Afreek, Ais, Stralya. I saw the vastness of Earth Ocean. I traversed the golden span of Land Bridge, which I had crossed so toilfully on foot not long before. Avluela rushed forward and pointed to Roum, to Agupt, to Jorslem, to Perris. She tapped the globe at the high mountains north of Hind and said softly, "This is where I was born, where the ice lives, where the mountains touch the moons. Here is where the Fliers have their kingdom." She ran a finger westward toward Fars and beyond it into the terrible Arban Desert, and on to Agupt. "This is where I flew. By night, when I left my girlhood. We all must fly, and I flew here. A hundred times I thought I would die. Here, here in the desert, sand in my throat as I flew, sand beating against my wings—I was forced down, I lay naked on the hot sand for days, and another Flier saw me, he came down to me and pitied me, and lifted me up, and when I was aloft my strength returned, and we flew on toward Agupt. And he died over the sea, his life stopped though he was young and strong, and he fell down into the sea, and I flew down to be with him, and the water was hot even at night. I drifted, and morning came, and I saw the living stones growing like trees in the water, and the fish of many colors, and they came to him and pecked at his flesh as he floated with his wings outspread on the water, and I left him, I thrust him down to rest there, and I rose, and I flew on to Agupt, alone, frightened, and there I met you, Watcher." Timidly she smiled to me. "Show us the place where you were young, Watcher."

Painfully, for I was suddenly stiff at the knees, I hobbled to the far side of the globe. Avluela followed me; Gormon hung back, as though not interested at all. I pointed to the scattered islands rising in two long strips from Earth Ocean—the remnants of the Lost Continents.

"Here," I said, indicating my native island in the west. "I was born here."

"So far away!" Avluela cried.

"And so long ago," I said. "In the middle of the Second Cycle, it sometimes seems to me."

"No! That is not possible!" But she looked at me as though it might just be true that I was thousands of years old.

I smiled and touched her satiny cheek. "It only seems that way to me," I said.

"When did you leave your home?"

"When I was twice your age," I said. "I came first to here—" I indicated the eastern group of islands. "I spent a dozen years as a Watcher on Palash. Then the Will moved me to cross Earth Ocean to Afreek. I came. I lived awhile in the hot countries. I went on to Agupt. I met a certain small Flier." Falling silent, I looked a long while at the islands that had been my home, and within my mind my image changed from the gaunt and eroded thing I now had become, and I saw myself young and well-fleshed, climbing the green mountains and swimming in the chill sea, doing my Watching at the rim of a white beach hammered by surf.

While I brooded Avluela turned away from me to Gormon and said, "Now you. Show us where you came from, Changeling!"

Gormon shrugged. "The place does not appear to be on this globe."

"But that's *impossible!*"

"Is it?" he asked.

She pressed him, but he evaded her, and we passed through a side exit and into the streets of Roum.

I was growing tired, but Avluela hungered for this city and wished to devour it all in an afternoon, and so we went on through a maze of interlocking streets, through a zone of sparkling mansions of Masters and Merchants, and through a foul den of Servitors and Vendors that extended into subterranean catacombs, and to a place where Clowns and Musicians resorted, and to another where the guild of Somnambulists offered its doubtful wares. A bloated female Somnambulist begged us to come inside and buy the truth that comes with trances, and Avluela urged us to go, but Gormon shook his head and I smiled, and we moved on. Now we were at the edge of a park close to the city's core. Here the citizens of Roum promenaded with an energy rarely seen in hot Agupt, and we joined the parade.

"Look there!" Avluela said. "How bright it is!"

She pointed toward the shining arc of a dimensional sphere enclosing some relic of the ancient city; shading my eyes, I could make out a weathered stone wall within, and a knot of people. Gormon said, "It is the Mouth of Truth."

"What is that?" Avluela asked.

"Come. See."

A line progressed into the sphere. We joined it and soon were at the lip of the interior, peering at the timeless region just across the threshold. Why this relic and so few others had been accorded such special protection I did not know, and I asked Gormon, whose knowledge was so unaccountably as profound as any Rememberer's, and he replied, "Because this is the realm of certainty, where what one says is absolutely congruent with what actually is the case."

"I don't understand," said Avluela.

"It is impossible to lie in this place," Gormon told her. "Can you imagine any relic more worthy of protection?" He stepped across the entry duct, blurring as he did so, and I followed him quickly within. Avluela hesitated. It was a long moment before she entered; pausing a moment on the very threshold, she seemed buffeted by the wind that blew along the line of demarcation between the outer world and the pocket universe in which we stood.

An inner compartment held the Mouth of Truth itself. The line extended toward it, and a solemn Indexer was controlling the flow of entry to the tabernacle. It was a while before we three were permitted to go in. We found ourselves before the ferocious head of a monster in high relief, affixed to an ancient wall pockmarked by time. The monster's jaws gaped; the open mouth was a dark and sinister hole. Gormon nodded, inspecting it, as though he seemed pleased to find it exactly as he had thought it would be.

"What do we do?" Avluela asked.

Gormon said, "Watcher, put your right hand into the Mouth of Truth."

Frowning, I complied.

"Now," said Gormon, "one of us asks a question. You must answer it. If you speak anything but the truth, the mouth with close and sever your hand."

"No!" Avluela cried.

I stared uneasily at the stone jaws rimming my wrist. A Watcher without both his hands is a man without a craft; in Second Cycle days one might have obtained a prosthesis more artful than one's original hand, but the Second Cycle had long ago been concluded, and such niceties were not to be purchased on Earth nowadays.

"How is such a thing possible?" I asked.

"The Will is unusually strong in these precincts," Gormon replied. "It distinguishes sternly between truth and untruth. To the rear of this wall sleeps a trio of Somnambulists through whom the Will speaks, and they control the Mouth. Do you fear the Will, Watcher?"

"I fear my own tongue."

"Be brave. Never has a lie been told before this wall. Never has a hand been lost."

"Go ahead, then," I said. "Who will ask me a question?"

"I," said Gormon. "Tell me, Watcher: all pretense aside, would you say that a life spent in Watching has been a life spent wisely?"

I was silent a long moment, rotating my thoughts, eyeing the jaws.

At length I said, "To devote oneself to vigilance on behalf of one's fellow man is perhaps the noblest purpose one can serve."

"Careful!" Gormon cried in alarm.

"I am not finished," I said.

"Go on."

"But to devote oneself to vigilance when the enemy is an imaginary one is idle, and to congratulate oneself for looking long and well for a foe that is not coming is foolish and sinful. My life has been a waste."

The jaws of the Mouth of Truth did not quiver.

I removed my hand. I stared at it as though it had newly sprouted from my wrist. I felt suddenly several cycles old. Avluela, her eyes wide, her hands to her lips, seemed shocked by what I had said. My own words appeared to hang congealed in the air before the hideous idol.

"Spoken honestly," said Gormon, "although without much mercy for yourself. You judge yourself too harshly, Watcher."

"I spoke to save my hand," I said. "Would you have had me lie?"

He smiled. To Avluela the Changeling said, "Now it's your turn."

Visibly frightened, the little Flier approached the Mouth. Her dainty hand trembled as she inserted it between the slabs of cold stone. I fought back an urge to rush toward her and pull her free of that devilish grimacing head.

"Who will question her?" I asked.

"I," said Gormon.

Avluela's wings stirred faintly beneath her garments. Her face grew pale; her nostrils flickered; her upper lip slid over the lower one. She stood slouched against the wall and stared in horror at the termination of her arm. Outside the chamber vague faces peered at us; lips moved in what no doubt were expressions of impatience over our lengthy visit to the Mouth; but we heard nothing. The atmosphere around us was warm and clammy, with a musty tang like that which would come from a well that was driven through the structure of Time.

Gormon said slowly, "This night past you allowed your body to be possessed by the Prince of Roum. Before that, you granted yourself to the Changeling Gormon, although such liaisons are forbidden by custom and law. Much prior to that you were the mate of a Flier, now deceased. You may have had other men, but I know nothing of them, and for the purposes of my question they are not relevant. Tell me this, Avluela: which of the three gave you the most intense physical pleasure, which of the three aroused your deepest emotions, and which of the three would you choose as a mate, if you were choosing a mate?"

I wanted to protest that the Changeling had asked her three questions, not one, and so had taken unfair advantage. But I had no chance to speak, because Avluela replied unfalteringly, hand wedged deep into the Mouth of Truth, "The Prince of Roum gave me greater pleasure of the body than I had ever known before, but he is cold and cruel, and I despise him. My dead Flier I loved more deeply than any person before or since, but he was weak, and I would not have wanted a weakling as a mate. You, Gormon, seem almost a stranger to me even now, and I feel that I know neither your body nor your soul, and yet, though the gulf between us is so wide, it is you with whom I would spend my days to come."

She drew her hand from the Mouth of Truth.

"Well spoken!" said Gormon, though the accuracy of her words had clearly wounded as well as pleased him. "Suddenly you find eloquence, eh, when the circumstances demand it. And now the turn is mine to risk my hand."

He neared the Mouth. I said, "You have asked the first two questions. Do you wish to finish the job and ask the third as well?"

"Hardly," he said. He made a negligent gesture with his free hand. "Put your heads together and agree on a joint question."

Avluela and I conferred. With uncharacteristic forwardness she proposed a question; and since it was the one I would have asked, I accepted it and told her to ask it.

She said, "When we stood before the globe of the world, Gormon, I asked you to show me the place where you were born, and you said you were unable to find it on the map. That seemed most strange. Tell me now: are you what you say you are, a Changeling who wanders the world?"

He replied, "I am not."

In a sense he had satisfied the question as Avluela had phrased it; but it went without saying that his reply was inadequate, and he kept his hand in the Mouth of Truth as he continued, "I did not show my birthplace to you on the globe because I was born nowhere on this globe, but on a world of a star I must not name. I am no Changeling in your meaning of the word, though by some definitions I am, for my body is somewhat disguised, and on my own world I wear a different flesh. I have lived here ten years."

"What was your purpose in coming to Earth?" I asked.

"I am obliged only to answer one question," said Gormon. Then he smiled. "But I give you an answer anyway: I was sent to Earth in the capacity of a military observer, to prepare the way for the invasion for which you have Watched so long and in which you have ceased to believe, and which will be upon you in a matter now of some hours."

"Lies!" I bellowed. "*Lies!*"

Gormon laughed. And drew his hand from the Mouth of Truth, intact, unharmed.

6

Numb with confusion, I fled with my cart of instruments from that gleaming sphere and emerged into a street suddenly cold and dark. Night had come with winter's swiftness; it was almost the ninth hour, and almost the time for me to Watch once more.

Gormon's mockery thundered in my brain. He had arranged everything: he had maneuvered us in to the Mouth of Truth; he had wrung a confession of lost faith from me and a confession of a different sort from Avluela; he had mercilessly volunteered information he need not have revealed, spoken words calculated to split me to the core.

Was the Mouth of Truth a fraud? Could Gormon lie and emerge unscathed?

Never since I first took up my tasks had I Watched at anything but my appointed hours. This was a time of crumbling realities; I could not wait for the ninth hour to come round; crouching in the windy street, I opened my cart, readied my equipment, and sank like a diver into Watchfulness.

My amplified consciousness roared toward the stars.

Godlike I roamed infinity. I felt the rush of the solar wind, but I was no Flier to be hurled to destruction by that pressure, and I soared past it, beyond the reach of those angry particles of light, into the blackness at the edge of the sun's dominion. Down upon me there beat a different pressure.

Starships coming near.

Not the tourist lines bringing sightseers to gape at our diminished world. Not the registered mercantile transport vessels, nor the scoopships that collect the interstellar vapors, nor the resort craft on their hyperbolic orbits.

These were military craft, dark, alien, menacing. I could not tell their number; I knew only that they sped Earthward at many lights, nudging a cone of deflected energies before them; and it was that cone that I had sensed, that I had felt also the night before, booming into my mind through my instruments, engulfing me like a cube of crystal through which stress patterns play and shine.

All my life I had watched for this.

I had been trained to sense it. I had prayed that I never would sense it, and then in my emptiness I had prayed that I *would* sense it, and then I had ceased to believe in it. And then by grace of the Changeling Gormon, I had sensed it after all, Watching ahead of my hour, crouching in a cold Roumish street just outside the Mouth of Truth.

In his training, a Watcher is instructed to break from his Watchfulness as soon as his observations are confirmed by a careful check, so that he can sound the alarm. Obediently I made my check by shifting from one channel to another to another, triangulating and still picking up that foreboding sensation of titanic force rushing upon Earth at unimaginable speed.

Either I was deceived, or the invasion was come. But I could not shake from my trance to give the alarm.

Lingeringly, lovingly, I drank in the sensory data for what seemed like hours. I fondled my equipment; I drained from it the total affirmation of faith that my readings gave me. Dimly I warned myself that I was wasting vital time, that it was my duty to leave this lewd caressing of destiny to summon the Defenders.

And at last I burst free of Watchfulness and returned to the world I was guarding.

Avluela was beside me; she was dazed, terrified, her knuckles to her teeth, her eyes blank.

"Watcher! Watcher, do you hear me? What's happening? What's going to happen?"

"The invasion," I said. "How long was I under?"

"About half a minute. I don't know. Your eyes were closed. I thought you were dead."

"Gormon was speaking the truth! The *invasion* is almost here. Where is he? Where did he go?"

"He vanished as we came away from that place with the Mouth," Avluela whispered. "Watcher, I'm frightened. I feel everything collapsing. I have to fly— I can't stay down here now!"

"Wait," I said, clutching at her and missing her arm. "Don't go now. First I have to give the alarm, and then—"

But she was already stripping off her clothing. Bare to the waist, her pale body gleamed in the evening light, while about us people were rushing to and fro in ignorance of all that was about to occur. I wanted to keep Avluela beside me, but I could delay no longer in giving the alarm, and I turned away from her, back to my cart.

As though caught up in a dream born of overripe longings I reached for the node that I had never used, the one that would send forth a planetwide alert to the Defenders.

Had the alarm already been given? Had some other Watcher sensed what I had sensed, and, less paralyzed by bewilderment and doubt, performed a Watcher's final task?

No. No. For then I would be hearing the sirens' shriek reverberating from the orbiting loudspeakers above the city.

I touched the node. From the corner of my eye I saw Avluela, free of her encumbrances now, kneeling to say her words, filling her tender wings with strength. In a moment she would be in the air, beyond my grasp.

With a single swift tug I activated the alarm.

In that instant I became aware of a burly figure striding toward us. Gormon, I thought; and as I rose from my equipment I reached out to him; I wanted to seize him and hold him fast. But he who approached was not Gormon but some officious dough-faced Servitor who said to Avluela, "Go easy, Flier, let your wings drop. The Prince of Roum sends me to bring you to his presence."

He grappled with her. Her little breasts heaved; her eyes flashed anger at him. "Let go of me! I'm going to fly!"

"The Prince of Roum summons you," the Servitor said, enclosing her in his heavy arms.

"The Prince of Roum will have other distractions tonight," I said. "He'll have no need of her."

As I spoke, the sirens began to sing from the skies.

The Servitor released her. His mouth worked noiselessly for an instant; he made one of the protective gestures of the Will; he looked skyward and grunted, "The alarm! Who gave the alarm? You, old Watcher?"

Figures rushed about insanely in the streets.

Avluela, freed, sped past me—on foot, her wings but half-furled—and was swallowed up in the surging throng. Over the terrifying sound of the sirens came booming messages from the public annunciators, giving instructions for defense and safety. A lanky man with the mark of the guild of Defenders upon his cheek rushed up to me, shouted words too incoherent to be understood, and sped on down the street. The world seemed to have gone mad.

Only I remained calm. I looked to the skies, half-expecting to see the invaders' black ships already hovering above the towers of Roum. But I saw nothing except the hovering nightlights and the other objects one might expect overhead.

"Gormon?" I called. "Avluela?"

I was alone.

A strange emptiness swept over me. I had given the alarm; the invaders were on their way; I had lost my occupation. There was no need of Watchers now. Almost lovingly I touched the worn cart that had been my companion for so many years. I ran my fingers over its stained and pitted instruments; and then I looked away, abandoning it, and went down the dark streets cartless, burdenless, a man whose life had found and lost meaning in the same instant. And about me raged chaos.

7

It was understood that when the moment of Earth's final battle arrived, all guilds would be mobilized, the Watchers alone exempted. We who had manned the perimeter of defense for so long had no part in the strategy of combat; we were discharged by the giving of a true alarm. Now it was the time of the guild of Defenders to show its capabilities. They had planned for half a cycle what they would do in time of war. What plans would they call forth now? What deeds would they direct?

My only concern was to return to the royal hostelry and wait out the crisis. It was hopeless to think of finding Avluela, and I pummeled myself savagely for having let her slip away, naked and without a protector, in that confused moment. Where would she go? Who would shield her?

A fellow Watcher, pulling his cart madly along, nearly collided with me. "Careful!" I snapped. He looked up, breathless, stunned. "Is it true?" he asked. "The alarm?"

"Can't you hear?"

"But is it real?"

I pointed to his cart. "You know how to find that out."

"They say the man who gave the alarm was drunk, an old fool who was turned away from the inn yesterday."

"It could be so," I admitted.

"But if the alarm is real—!"

Smiling, I said, "If it is, now we all may rest. Good day to you, Watcher."

"Your cart! Where's your cart?" he shouted at me.

But I had moved past him, toward the mighty carven stone pillar of some relic of Imperial Roum.

Ancient images were carved on that pillar: battles and victories, foreign monarchs marched in the chains of disgrace through the streets of Roum, triumphant eagles celebrating imperial grandeur. In my strange new calmness I stood awhile before the column of stone and admired its elegant engravings. Toward me rushed a frenzied figure whom I recognized as the Rememberer Basil; I hailed him, saying, "How timely you come! Do me the kindness of explaining these images, Rememberer. They fascinate me, and my curiosity is aroused."

"Are you insane? Can't you hear the alarm?"

"I gave the alarm, Rememberer."

"Flee, then! Invaders come! We must fight!"

"Not I, Basil. Now my time is over. Tell me of these images. These beaten kings, these broken emperors. Surely a man of your years will not be doing battle."

"All are mobilized now!"

"All but Watchers," I said. "Take a moment. Yearning for the past is born in me. Gormon has vanished; be my guide to these lost cycles."

The Rememberer shook his head wildly, circled around me, and tried to get away. Hoping to seize his skinny arm and pin him to the spot, I made a lunge at him; but he eluded me and I caught only his dark shawl, which pulled free and came loose in my hands. Then he was gone, his spindly limbs pumping madly as he fled down the street and left my view. I shrugged and examined the shawl I had so unexpectedly acquired. It was shot through with glimmering threads of metal arranged in intricate patterns that teased the eye: it seemed to me that each strand disappeared into the weave of the fabric, only to reappear at some improbable point, like the lineage of dynasties unexpectedly revived in distant cities. The workmanship was superb. Idly I draped the shawl about my shoulders.

I walked on.

My legs, which had been on the verge of failing me earlier in the day, now served me well. With renewed youthfulness I made my way through the chaotic city, finding no difficulties in choosing my route. I headed for the river, then crossed it and, on the Tver's far side, sought the palace of the Prince. The night had deepened, for most lights were extinguished under the mobilization orders; and from time to time a dull boom signaled the explosion of a screening bomb overhead, liberating clouds of murk that shielded the city from most forms of long-range scrutiny. There were fewer pedestrians in the streets. The sirens still cried out. Atop the buildings the defensive installations were going into action; I heard the bleeping sounds of repellors warming up, and I saw long spidery arms of amplification booms swinging from tower to tower as they linked for maximum output. I had no doubt now that the invasion actually was coming. My own instruments might have been fouled by inner confusion, but they would not have proceeded thus far with the mobilization if the initial report had not been confirmed by the findings of hundreds of other members of my guild.

As I neared the palace a pair of breathless Rememberers sped toward me, their shawls flapping behind them. They called to me in words I did not comprehend—some code of their guild, I realized, recollecting that I wore Basil's shawl. I could not reply, and they rushed upon me, still gabbling; and switching to the language of ordinary men they said, "What is the matter with you? To your post! We must record! We must comment! We must observe!"

"Your mistake me," I said mildly. "I keep this shawl only for your brother Basil, who left it in my care. I have no post to guard at this time."

"A Watcher," they cried in unison, and cursed me separately, and ran on. I laughed and went to the palace.

Its gates stood open. The neuters who had guarded the outer portal were gone, as were the two Indexers who had stood just within the door. The beggars that had thronged the vast plaza had jostled their way into the building itself to seek shelter;

this had awakened the anger of the licensed hereditary mendicants whose customary stations were in that part of the building, and they had fallen upon the inflowing refugees with fury and unexpected strength. I saw cripples lashing out with their crutches held as clubs; I saw blind men landing blows with suspicious accuracy; meek penitents were wielding a variety of weapons ranging from stilettos to sonic pistols. Holding myself aloof from this shameless spectacle, I penetrated to the inner recesses of the palace and peered into chapels where I saw Pilgrims beseeching the blessings of the Will, and Communicants desperately seeking spiritual guidance as to the outcome of the coming conflict.

Abruptly I heard the blare of trumpets and cries of, "Make way! Make way!"

A file of sturdy Servitors marched into the palace, striding toward the Prince's chambers in the apse. Several of them held a struggling, kicking, frantic figure with half-unfolded wings: Avluela! I called out to her, but my voice died in the din, nor could I reach her. The Servitors shoved me aside. The procession vanished into the princely chambers. I caught a final glimpse of the little Flier, pale and small in the grip of her captors, and then she was gone once more.

I seized a bumbling neuter who had been moving uncertainly in the wake of the Servitors.

"That Flier! Why was she brought here?"

"Ha—he—they—"

"Tell me!"

"The Prince—his woman—in his chariot—he—he—they—the invaders—"

I pushed the flabby creature aside and rushed toward the apse. A brazen wall ten times my own height confronted me. I pounded on it. "Avluela!" I shouted hoarsely. *"Av . . . lu . . . ela . . . !"*

I was neither thrust away nor admitted. I was ignored. The bedlam at the western doors of the palace had extended itself now to the nave and aisles, and as the ragged beggars boiled toward me I executed a quick turn and found myself passing through one of the side doors of the palace.

Suspended and passive, I stood in the courtyard that led to the royal hostelry. A strange electricity crackled in the air. I assumed it was an emanation from one of Roum's defense installations, some kind of beam designed to screen the city from attack. But an instant later I realized that it presaged the actual arrival of the invaders.

Starships blazed in the heavens.

When I had perceived them in my Watching they had appeared black against the infinite blackness, but now they burned with the radiance of suns. A stream of bright, hard, jewel-like globes bedecked the sky; they were ranged side by side, stretching from east to west in a continuous band, filling all the celestial arch, and as they erupted simultaneously into being it seemed to me that I heard the crash and throb of an invisible symphony heralding the arrival of the conquerors of Earth.

I do not know how far above me the starships were, nor how many of them hovered there, nor any of the details of their design. I know only that in sudden massive majesty they were there, and that if I had been a Defender my soul would have withered instantly at the sight.

Across the heavens shot light of many hues. The battle had been joined. I could not comprehend the actions of our warriors, and I was equally baffled by the maneuvers of those who had come to take possession of our history-crusted but time-diminished planet. To my shame I felt not only out of the struggle but above the struggle, as though this were no quarrel of mine. I wanted Avluela beside me, and she was somewhere within the depths of the palace of the Prince of Roum. Even Gormon would have been a comfort now, Gormon the Changeling, Gormon the spy, Gormon the monstrous betrayer of our world.

Gigantic amplified voices bellowed, "Make way for the Prince of Roum! The Prince of Roum leads the Defenders in the battle for the fatherworld!"

From the palace emerged a shining vehicle the shape of a teardrop, in whose bright-metaled roof a transparent sheet had been mounted so that all the populace could see and take heart in the presence of the ruler. At the controls of the vehicle sat the Prince of Roum, proudly erect, his cruel, youthful features fixed in harsh determination; and beside him, robed like an empress, I beheld the slight figure of the Flier Avluela. She seemed in a trance.

The royal chariot soared upward and was lost in the darkness.

It seemed to me that a second vehicle appeared and followed its path, and that the Prince's reappeared, and that the two flew in tight circles, apparently locked in combat. Clouds of blue sparks wrapped both chariots now; and then they swung high and far and were lost to me behind one of the hills of Roum.

Was the battle now raging all over the planet? Was Perris in jeopardy, and holy Jorslem, and even the sleepy isles of the Lost Continents? Did starships hover everywhere? I did not know. I perceived events in only one small segment of the sky over Roum, and even there my awareness of what was taking place was dim, uncertain, and ill-informed. There were momentary flashes of light in which I saw battalions of Fliers streaming across the sky; and then darkness returned as though a velvet shroud had been hurled over the city. I saw the great machines of our defense firing in fitful bursts from the tops of our towers; and yet I saw the starships untouched, unharmed, unmoved above. The courtyard in which I stood was deserted, but in the distance I heard voices, full of fear and foreboding, shouting in tinny tones that might have been the screeching of birds. Occasionally there came a booming sound that rocked all the city. Once a platoon of Somnambulists was driven past where I was; in the plaza fronting the palace I observed what appeared to be an array of Clowns unfolding some sort of sparkling netting of a military look; by one flash of lightning I was able to see a trio of Rememberers making copious notes of all that elapsed as they soared aloft on the gravity plate. It seemed—I was not sure—that the vehicle of the Prince of Roum returned, speeding across the sky with its pursuer clinging close. "Avluela," I whispered, as the twin dots of lights left my sight. Were the starships disgorging troops? Did colossal pylons of force spiral down from those orbiting brightness to touch the surface of the Earth? Why had the Prince seized Avluela? Where was Gormon? What were our Defenders doing? Why were the enemy ships not blasted from the sky?

Rooted to the ancient cobbles of the courtyard, I observed the cosmic battle in total lack of understanding throughout the long night.

Dawn came. Strands of pale light looped from tower to tower. I touched fingers to my eyes, realizing that I must have slept while standing. Perhaps I should apply for membership in the guild of Somnambulists, I told myself lightly. I put my hands to the Rememberer's shawl about my shoulders and wondered how I managed to acquire it, and the answer came.

I looked toward the sky.

The alien starships were gone. I saw only the ordinary morning sky, gray with pinkness breaking through. I felt the jolt of compulsion and looked about for my cart, and reminded myself that I need do no more Watching, and I felt more empty than one would ordinarily feel at such an hour.

Was the battle over?

Had the enemy been vanquished?

Were the ships of the invaders blasted from the sky and lying in charred ruin outside Roum?

All was silent. I heard no more celestial symphonies. Then out of the eerie stillness there came a new sound, a rumbling noise as of wheeled vehicles passing through the streets of the city. And the invisible Musicians played one final note, deep and resonant, which trailed away jaggedly as though every string had been broken at once.

Over the speakers used for public announcements came quiet words.

"Roum is fallen. Roum is fallen."

8

The royal hostelry was untended. Neuters and members of the servant guilds all had fled. Defenders, Masters, and Dominators must have perished honorably in combat. Basil the Rememberer was nowhere about; likewise none of his brethren. I went to my room, cleansed and refreshed and fed myself, gathered my few possessions, and bade farewell to the luxuries I had known so briefly. I regretted that I had had such a short time to visit Roum; but at least Gormon had been a most excellent guide, and I had seen a great deal.

Now I proposed to move on.

It did not seem prudent to remain in a conquered city. My room's thinking cap did not respond to my queries, and so I did not know what the extent of the defeat was, here or in other regions, but it was evident to me that Roum at least had passed from human control, and I wished to depart quickly. I weighed the thought of going to Jorslem, as that tall pilgrim had suggested upon my entry into Roum; but then I reflected and chose a westward route, toward Perris, which not only was closer but held the headquarters of the Rememberers. My own occupation had been destroyed; but on this first morning of Earth's conquest I felt a sudden powerful and strange yearning to offer myself humbly to the Rememberers and seek with them knowledge of our more glittering yesterdays.

At midday I left the hostelry. I walked first to the palace, which still stood open. The beggars lay strewn about, some drugged, some sleeping, most dead; from the crude manner of their death I saw that they must have slain one another in their panic and frenzy. A despondent-looking Indexer squatted beside the three skulls of the interrogation fixture in the chapel. As I entered he said, "No use. The brains do not reply."

"How goes it with the Prince of Roum?"

"Dead. The invaders shot him from the sky."

"A young Flier rode beside him. What do you know of her?"

"Nothing. Dead, I suppose."

"And the city?"

"Fallen. Invaders are everywhere."

"Killing?"

"Not even looting," the Indexer said. "They are most gentle. They have *collected* us."

"In Roum alone, or everywhere?"

The man shrugged. He began to rock rhythmically back and forth. I let him be, and walked deeper into the palace. To my surprise, the imperial chambers of the Prince were unsealed. I went within; I was awed by the sumptuous luxury of the hangings, the draperies, the lights, the furnishings. I passed from room to room, coming at last to the royal bed, whose coverlet was the flesh of a colossal bivalve of the planet of another star, and as the shell yawned for me I touched the infinitely soft fabric under which the Prince of Roum had lain, and I recalled that Avluela too had lain here, and if I had been a younger man I would have wept.

I left the palace and slowly crossed the plaza to begin my journey toward Perris.

As I departed I had my first glimpse—of our conquerors. A vehicle of alien design drew up at the plaza's rim and perhaps a dozen figures emerged. They might almost have been human. They were tall and broad, deep-chested, as Gormon had been, and only the extreme length of their arms marked them instantly as alien. Their skins were of strange texture, and if I had been closer I suspect I would have seen eyes and lips and nostrils that were not of a human design. Taking no notice of me, they crossed the plaza, walking in a curiously loose-jointed loping way that reminded me irresistibly of Gormon's stride, and entered the palace. They seemed neither swaggering nor belligerent.

Sightseers. Majestic Roum once more exerted its magnetism upon strangers.

Leaving our new masters to their amusement, I walked off, toward the outskirts of the city. The bleakness of eternal winter crept into my soul. I wondered: did I feel sorrow that Roum had fallen? Or did I mourn the loss of Avluela? Or was it only that I now had missed three successive Watchings, and like an addict I was experiencing the pangs of withdrawal?

It was all of these that pained me, I decided. But mostly the last.

No one was abroad in the city as I made for the gates. Fear of the new masters kept the Roumish in hiding, I supposed. From time to time one of the alien vehicles hummed past, but I was unmolested. I came to the city's western gate late in the afternoon. It was open, revealing to me a gently rising hill on whose breast rose trees with dark green crowns. I passed through and saw, a short distance beyond the gate, the figure of a Pilgrim who was shuffling slowly away from the city.

I overtook him easily.

His faltering, uncertain walk seemed strange to me, for not even his thick brown robes could hide the strength and youth of his body; he stood erect, his shoulders square and his back straight, and yet he walked with the hesitating, trembling step of an old man. When I drew abreast of him and peered under his hood I understood, for affixed to the bronze mask all Pilgrims wear was a reverberator, such as is used by blind men to warn them of obstacles and hazards. He became aware of me and said, "I am a sightless Pilgrim. I pray you do not molest me."

It was not a Pilgrim's voice. It was a strong and harsh and imperious voice.

I replied, "I molest no one. I am a Watcher who has lost his occupation this night past."

"Many occupations were lost this night past, Watcher."

"Surely not a Pilgrim's."

"No," he said "Not a Pilgrim's."

"Where are you bound?"

"Away from Roum."

"No particular destination?"

"No," the Pilgrim said. "None. I will wander."

"Perhaps we should wander together," I said, for it is accounted good luck to travel with a Pilgrim, and, shorn of my Flier and my Changeling, I would otherwise have traveled alone. "My destination is Perris. Will you come?"

"There as well as anywhere else," he said bitterly. "Yes. We will go to Perris together. But what business does a Watcher have there?"

"A Watcher has no business anywhere. I go to Perris to offer myself in service to the Rememberers."

"Ah," he said. "I was of that guild too, but it was only honorary."

"With Earth fallen, I wish to learn more of Earth in its pride."

"Is all Earth fallen, then, and not only Roum?"

"I think it is so," I said.

"Ah," replied the Pilgrim. "Ah!"

He fell silent and we went onward. I gave him my arm, and now he shuffled no longer, but moved with a young man's brisk stride. From time to time he uttered what might have been a sigh or a smothered sob. When I asked him details of his Pilgrimage, he answered obliquely or not at all. When we were an hour's journey outside Roum, and already amid forests, he said suddenly, "This mask gives me pain. Will you help me adjust it?"

To my amazement he began to remove it. I gasped, for it is forbidden for a Pilgrim to reveal his face. Had he forgotten that I was not sightless too?

As the mask came away he said, "You will not welcome this sight."

The bronze grillwork slipped down from his forehead, and I saw first eyes that had been newly blinded, gaping holes where no surgeon's knife, but possibly thrusting fingers, had penetrated and then the sharp regal nose, and finally the quirked taut lips of the Prince of Roum.

"Your Majesty!" I cried.

Trails of dried blood ran down his cheeks. About the raw sockets themselves were smears of ointment. He felt little pain, I suppose, for he had killed it with those green smears, but the pain that burst through me was real and potent.

"Majesty no longer," he said. "Help me with the mask!" His hands trembled as he held it forth. "These flanges must be widened. They press cruelly at my cheeks. Here—here—"

Quickly I made the adjustments, so that I would not have to see his ruined face for long.

He replaced the mask. "I am a Pilgrim now," he said quietly. "Roum is without its Prince. Betray me if you wish, Watcher; otherwise help me to Perris; and if ever I regain my power you will be well rewarded."

"I am no betrayer," I told him.

In silence we continued. I had no way of making small talk with such a man.

It would be a somber journey for us to Perris; but I was committed now to be his guide. I thought of Gormon and how well he had kept his vows. I thought too of Avluela, and a hundred times the words leaped to my tongue to ask the fallen Prince how his consort the Flier had fared in the night of defeat, and I did not ask.

Twilight gathered, but the sun still gleamed golden-red before us in the west. And suddenly I halted and made a hoarse sound of surprise deep in my throat, as a shadow passed overhead.

High above me Avluela soared. Her skin was stained by the colors of the sunset, and her wings were spread to their fullest, radiant with every hue of the spectrum. She was already at least the height of a hundred men above the ground, and still climbing, and to her I must have been only a speck among the trees.

"What is it?" the Prince asked. "What do you see?"

"Nothing."

"Tell me what you see!"

I could not deceive him. "I see a Flier, your Majesty. A slim girl far aloft."

"Then the night must have come."

"No," I said. "The sun is still above the horizon."

"How can that be? She can have only nightwings. The sun would hurl her to the ground."

I hesitated. I could not bring myself to explain how it was that Avluela flew by day, though she had only nightwings. I could not tell the Prince of Roum that beside her, wingless, flew the invader Gormon, effortlessly moving through the air, his arm about her thin shoulders, steadying her, supporting her, helping her resist the pressure of the solar wind. I could not tell him that his nemesis flew with the last of his consorts above his head.

"Well?" he demanded. "How does she fly by day?"

"I do not know," I said. "It is a mystery to me. There are many things nowadays I can no longer understand."

The Prince appeared to accept that. "Yes, Watcher. Many things none of us can understand."

He fell once more into silence. I yearned to call out to Avluela, but I knew she could not and would not hear me, and so I walked on toward the sunset, toward Perris, leading the blind Prince. And over us Avluela and Gormon sped onward, limned sharply against the day's last glow, until they climbed so high they were lost to my sight.

Pale Roses

MICHAEL MOORCOCK

One of the most prolific, popular, and controversial figures in modern letters, Michael Moorcock has been a major shaping force on the development of science fiction and fantasy, as both author and editor, for more than thirty years. As editor, Moorcock helped to usher in the New Wave revolution in science fiction in the midsixties by taking over the genteel but elderly and somewhat tired British SF magazine *New Worlds* and coaxing it into a bizarre new life. Moorcock transformed *New Worlds* into a fierce and daring outlaw publication that was at the very heart of the British New Wave movement, and Moorcock himself—for his role as chief creator of the either much-admired or much-loathed "Jerry Cornelius" stories, in addition to his roles as editor, polemicist, literary theorist, and mentor to most of the period's most prominent writers—became one of the most controversial figures of that turbulent era. *New Worlds* died in the early seventies, after having been ringingly denounced in the Houses of Parliament and banned from distribution by the huge British bookstore and newsstand chain W. H. Smith, but Moorcock himself has never been out of public view for long. The novels in his *Elric* series—elegant and elegantly perverse Sword and Sorcery at its most distinctive and far too numerous to individually list here—are wildly popular and best-sellers on both sides of the Atlantic. At the same time, Moorcock's other works, both in and out of the genre, such as *Gloriana, Behold the Man,* and *Mother London* have established him as one of the most respected and critically acclaimed writers of our day. He has won the Nebula Award, the World Fantasy Award, the John W. Campbell Memorial Award, and the Guardian Fiction Award. His other books include (among *many* others), the novels *The Warhound and the World's Pain, Byzantium Endures, The Laughter of Carthage, Jerusalem Commands, The Land Leviathan,* and *The Warlord of the Air,* as well as the collection *Lunching with the Antichrist,* an autobiographical study, *Letters from Hollywood,* and a critical study of fantasy literature, *Wizardry and Wild Romance.* After spending most of his life in London, several years back, Moorcock moved to a small town in Texas, where he now lives and works.

Moorcock's vision ranges from the distant, antediluvian past of the *Elric* stories to the far-future milieu of the stories and novels that went into the making of his

Dancers at the End of Time sequence (with typical Moorcockian perversity, he's also written a story called "Elric at the End of Time," which merges *both* series and both ends of the time spectrum, by bringing Elric himself out of the remote past to the even-more-remote future), his major contribution to the literature of the far future, which consists of the novels *An Alien Heat, The Hollow Lands, The End of All Songs,* and *A Messiah at the End of Time* (all assembled in two omnibus volumes, *Legends from the End of Time* and *The Dancers at the End of Time*). In Moorcock's hands, the far future is a place of fin de siècle decadence, elegance, and wealth, where jaded immortals of immense powers and abilities, and with no morals or scruples at all, play endless rounds of intricate mind games with one another, as well as with the befuddled time travelers from the distant past who sometimes land in their midst. As the arch, ironic, and darkly playful story that follows—one of the best of Moorcock's far-future stories—shows, though, sometimes even if you don't know you're *playing,* you can still can win the game.

> *Short summer-time and then, my heart's desire.*
> *The winter and the darkness: one by one*
> *The roses fall, the pale roses expire*
> *Beneath the slow decadence of the sun.*
> —Ernest Dowson, *Transition*

1. IN WHICH WERTHER IS INCONSOLABLE

"You can still *amuse* people, Werther, and that's the main thing," said Mistress Christia, lifting her skirts to reveal her surprise.

It was rare enough for Werther de Goethe to put on an entertainment (though this one was typical—it was called "Rain") and rare, too, for the Everlasting Concubine to think in individual terms to please her lover of the day.

"Do you like it?" she asked as he peered into her thighs.

Werther's voice in reply was faintly, unusually, animated. "Yes." His pale fingers traced the tattoos, which were primarily on the theme of Death and the Maiden but corpses also coupled, skeletons entwined in a variety of extravagant carnal embraces—and at the center, in bone-white, her pubic hair had been fashioned in the outline of an elegant and somehow quintessentially feminine skull. "You alone know me, Mistress Christia."

She had heard the phrase so often and it always delighted her. "Cadaverous Werther!"

He bent to kiss the skull's somewhat elongated lips.

His rain rushed through dark air, each drop a different gloomy shade of green, purple or red. And it was actually wet so that when it fell upon the small audience (The Duke of Queens, Bishop Castle, My Lady Charlotina, and one or two recently arrived, absolutely bemused, time-travelers from the remote past) it soaked their clothes and made them shiver as they stood on the shelf of glassy rock overlooking Werther's Romantic Precipice. (Below, a waterfall foamed through fierce, black rock.)

"Nature," exclaimed Werther. "The only verity!"

The Duke of Queens sneezed. He looked about him with a delighted smile, but nobody else had noticed. He coughed to draw their attention, tried to sneeze again, but failed. He looked up into the ghastly sky; fresh waves of black cloud boiled in: there was lightning now, and thunder. The rain became hail. My Lady Charlotina, in a globular dress of pink veined in soft blue, giggled as the little stones fell upon her gilded features with an almost inaudible ringing sound.

But Bishop Castle, in his nodding, crenellated *tête* (from which he derived the latter half of his name and which was twice his own height) turned away, saturnine and bored, plainly noting a comparison between all this and his own entertainment of the previous year which had also involved rain, but with each drop turning into a perfect manikin as it touched the ground. There was nothing in his temperament to respond to Werther's rather innocent re-creation of a Nature long-since departed from a planet which could be wholly remodeled at the whim of any one of its inhabitants.

Mistress Christia, ever quick to notice such responses, eager for her present lover not to lose prestige, cried: "But there is more, is there not. Werther? A finale?"

"I had thought to leave it a little longer . . ."

"No! No! Give us your finale now, my dear!"

"Well, Mistress Christia, if it is for you." He turned one of his power rings, disseminating the sky, the lightning, the thunder, replacing them with pearly clouds, radiated with golden light through which silvery rain still fell.

"And now," he murmured, "I give you Tranquillity, and in Tranquillity—Hope . . ."

A further twist of the ring and a rainbow appeared, bridging the chasm, touching the clouds.

Bishop Castle was impressed by what was an example of elegance rather than spectacle, but he could not resist a minor criticism. "Is black exactly the shade, do you think? I should have supposed it expressed your Idea, well, perhaps not perfectly . . ."

"It is perfect for me," answered Werther a little gracelessly.

"Of course," said Bishop Castle, regretting his impulse. He drew his bushy red brows together and made a great show of studying the rainbow. "It stands out so well against the background."

Emphatically (causing a brief, ironic glint in the eye of the Duke of Queens) Mistress Christia clapped her hands. "It is a beautiful rainbow, Werther. I am sure it is much more as they used to look."

"It takes a particularly, original kind of imagination to invent such—simplicity." The Duke of Queens, well-known for a penchant in the direction of vulgarity, fell in with her mood.

"I hope it does more than merely represent." Satisfied both with his creation and with their responses, Werther could not resist indulging his nature, allowing a tinge of hurt resentment in his tone.

All were tolerant. All responded, even Bishop Castle. There came a chorus of consolation. Mistress Christia reached out and took his thin, white hand, inadvertently touching a power ring.

The rainbow began to topple. It leaned in the sky for a few seconds while

Werther watched; his disbelief gradually turning to miserable reconciliation; then, slowly, it fell, shattering against the top of the cliff, showering them with shards of jet.

Mistress Christia's tiny hand fled to the rosebud of her mouth; her round, blue eyes expressed horror already becoming laughter (checked when she noted the look in Werther's dark and tragic orbs). She still gripped his hand; but he slowly withdrew it, kicking moodily at the fragments of the rainbow. The sky was suddenly a clear, soft gray, actually lit, one might have guessed, by the tired rays of the fading star about which the planet continued to circle, and the only clouds were those on Werther's noble brow. He pulled at the peak of his bottle-green cap; he stroked at his long, auburn hair, as if to comfort himself. He sulked.

"Perfect!" praised My Lady Charlotina, refusing to see error.

"You have the knack of making the most of a single symbol, Werther." The Duke of Queens waved a brocaded arm in the general direction of the now disseminated scene. "I envy you your talent, my friend."

"It takes the product of panting lust, of pulsing sperm and eager ovaries, to offer us such brutal originality!" said Bishop Castle, in reference to Werther's birth (he was the product of sexual union, born of a womb, knowing childhood—a rarity, indeed). "Bravo!"

"Ah," sighed Werther, "how cheerfully you refer to my doom: To be such a creature, when all others came into this world as mature, uncomplicated adults!"

"There was also Jherek Carnelian," said My Lady Charlotina. Her globular dress bounced as she turned to leave.

"At least he was not born malformed," said Werther.

"It was the work of a moment to re-form you properly, Werther," the Duke of Queens reminded him. "The six arms (was it?) removed, two perfectly fine ones replacing them. After all, it was an unusual exercise on the part of your mother. She did very well, considering it was her first attempt."

"And her last," said My Lady Charlotina, managing to have her back to Werther by the time the grin escaped. She snapped her fingers for her air-car. It floated towards her, a great, yellow rocking horse. Its shadow fell across them all.

"It left a scar," said Werther, "nonetheless."

"It would," said Mistress Christia, kissing him upon his black velvet shoulder. "A terrible scar."

"Indeed!" said the Duke of Queens in vague affirmation, his attention wandering. "Well, thank you for a lovely afternoon, Werther. Come along, you two!" He signed to the time-travelers who claimed to be from the eighty-third millenium and were dressed in primitive transparent "exoskin" which was not altogether stable and was inclined to writhe and make it seem that they were covered in hundreds of thin, excited snakes. The Duke of Queens had acquired them for his menagerie. Unaware of the difficulties of returning to their own time (temporal travel had, apparently, only just been re-invented in their age) they were inclined to treat the Duke as an eccentric who could be tolerated until it suited them to do otherwise. They smiled condescendingly, winked at each other, and followed him to an air-car in the shape of a cube whose sides were golden mirrors decorated with white and purple flowers. It was for the pleasure of enjoying the pleasure they enjoyed seemingly at his expense, that the Duke of Queens had brought them with him today. Mistress Christia waved at his car as it disappeared rapidly into the sky.

At last they were all gone, save herself and Werther de Goethe. He had seated himself upon a mossy rock, his shoulders hunched, his features downcast, unable to speak to her when she tried to cheer him.

"Oh, Werther," she cried at last, "what would make you happy?"

"Happy?" his voice was a hollow echo of her own. "Happy?" He made an awkward, dismissive gesture. "There is no such thing as happiness for such as I!"

"There must be some sort of equivalent, surely?"

"Death, Mistress Christia, is my only consolation!"

"Well, die, my dear! I'll resurrect you in a day or two, and then . . ."

"Though you love me, Mistress Christia—though you know me best—you do not understand. I seek the inevitable, the irreconcilable, the unalterable, the inescapable! Our ancestors knew it. They knew Death *without* Resurrection; they knew what it was to be Slave to the Elements. Incapable of choosing their own destinies, they had no responsibility for choosing their own actions. They were tossed by tides. They were scattered by storms. They were wiped out by wars, decimated by disease, ravaged by radiation, made homeless by holocausts, lashed by lightnings . . ."

"You could have lashed yourself a little today, surely?"

"But it would have been *my* decision. We have lost what is Random, we have banished the Arbitrary, Mistress Christia. With our power rings and our gene banks we can, if we desire, change the courses of the planets, populate them with any kind of creature we wish, make our old sun burst with fresh energy or fade completely from the firmament. We control All. Nothing controls us!"

"There are our whims, our fancies. There are our *characters*, my moody love."

"Even those can be altered at will."

"Except that it is a rare nature which would wish to change itself. Would you change yours? I, for one, would be disconsolate if, say, you decided to be more like the Duke of Queens or the Iron Orchid."

"Nonetheless, it is *possible*. It would merely be a matter of decision. Nothing is impossible, Mistress Christia. Now do you realize why I should feel unfulfilled?"

"Not really, dear Werther. You can be anything you wish, after all. I am not, as you know, intelligent—it is not my choice to be—but I wonder if a love of Nature could be, in essence, a grandiose love of oneself—with Nature identified, as it were, with one's ego?" She offered this without criticism.

For a moment he showed surprise and seemed to be considering her observation. "I suppose it could be. Still, that has little to do with what we were discussing. It's true that I can be anything—or, indeed, anyone—I wish. That is *why* I feel unfulfilled!"

"Aha," she said.

"Oh, how I pine for the pain of the past! Life has no meaning without misery!"

"A common view, then, I gather. But what sort of suffering would suit you best, dear Werther? Enslavement by Eskimos?" She hesitated, her knowledge of the past being patchier than most people's. "The beatings with thorns? The barbed-wire trews? The pits of fire?"

"No, no—that is primitive. Psychic, it would have to be. Involving—um—morality."

"Isn't that some sort of wall-painting?"

A large tear welled and fell. "The world is too tolerant. The world is too kind. They all—you most of all—*approve* of me! There is nothing I can do which would not amuse you—even if it offended your taste—because there is no danger, nothing at stake. There are no *crimes*, inflamer of my lust. Oh, if I could only *sin!*"

Her perfect forehead wrinkled in the prettiest of frowns. She repeated his words to herself. Then she shrugged, embracing him.

"Tell me what sin is," she said.

2. IN WHICH YOUR AUDITOR INTERPOSES

Our time-travelers, once they have visited the future, are only permitted (owing to the properties of Time itself) brief returns to their present. They can remain for any amount of time in their future, where presumably they can do no real damage to the course of previous events, but to come back at all is difficult; to make a prolonged stay has been proved impossible. Half an hour with a relative or a loved one, a short account to an auditor, such as myself, of life, say, in the seventy-fifth century, a glimpse at an artifact allowed to some interested scientist—these are the best the time-traveler can hope for, once he has made his decision to leap into the mysterious future.

As a consequence our knowledge of the future is sketchy, to say the least: We have no idea of how civilizations will grow up or how they will decline; we do not know why the number of planets in the solar system seems to vary drastically between, say, half a dozen to almost a hundred; we cannot explain the popularity in a given age for certain fashions striking us as singularly bizarre or perverse; are beliefs which we consider fallacious or superstitious based on an understanding beyond our comprehension?

The stories we hear are often partial, hastily recounted, poorly observed, perhaps misunderstood by the traveler. We cannot question him closely, for he is soon whisked away from us (Time insists upon a certain neatness, to protect her own nature, which is essentially of the practical, ordering sort, and should that nature ever be successfully altered, then we might, in turn, successfully alter the terms of the human condition) and it is almost inevitable that we shall never have another chance of meeting him.

Resultantly, the stories brought to us of the Earth's future assume the character of legends rather than history and tend, therefore, to capture the imagination of artists, for serious scientists need permanent, verifiable evidence with which to work and precious little of that is permitted them (some refuse to believe in the future, save as an abstraction, some believe firmly that returning time-travelers' accounts are accounts of dreams and hallucinations and that they have not actually traveled in time at all!). It is left to the Romancers, childish fellows like myself, to make something of these tales. While I should be delighted to assure you that everything I have set down in this story is based closely on the truth, I am bound to admit that while the outline comes from an account given me by one of our greatest and most famous temporal adventuresses, Miss Una Persson, the conversations and many of the descriptions are of my own invention intended hopefully to add a little color to what would otherwise be a somewhat spare, a rather dry, recounting of an incident in the life of Werther de Goethe.

That Werther will exist, only a few entrenched skeptics can doubt. We have heard of him from many sources, usually quite as reliable as the admirable Miss Persson, as we have heard of other prominent figures of that Age we choose to call "the End of Time." If it is this Age which fascinates us more than any other, it is probably because it seems to offer a clue to our race's ultimate destiny.

Moralists make much of this period and show us that on the one hand it describes the pointlessness of human existence or, on the other, the whole point. Romancers are attracted to it for less worthy reasons; they find it colorful, they find its inhabitants glamorous, attractive; their imagination is sparked by the paradoxes, the very ambiguities which exasperated our scientists, by the idea of a people possessing limitless power and using it for nothing but their own amusement, like gods at play. It is pleasure enough for the Romancer to describe a story; to color it a little, to fill in a few details where they are missing, in the hope that, by entertaining himself, he entertains others.

Of course, the inhabitants at the End of Time are not the creatures of our past legends, not mere representations of our ancestors' hopes and fears, not mere metaphors, like Siegfried or Zeus or Krishna, and this could be why they fascinate us so much. Those of us who have studied this Age (as best it can be studied) feel on friendly terms with the Iron Orchid, with the Duke of Queens, with Lord Jagged of Canaria and the rest, and even believe that we can guess something of their inner lives.

Werther de Goethe, suffering from the *knowledge* of his, by the standards of his own time, unusual entrance into the world, doubtless felt himself apart from his fellows, though there was no objective reason why he should feel it. (I trust the reader will forgive my abandoning any attempt at a clumsy future tense.) In a society where eccentricity is encouraged, where it is celebrated no matter how extreme its realization, Werther felt, we must assume, uncomfortable:—wishing for peers who would demand some sort of conformity from him. He could not retreat into a repressive past age; it was well-known that it was impossible to remain in the past (the phenomenon had a name at the End of Time: it was called the Morphail Effect), and he had an ordinary awareness of the futility of re-creating such an environment for himself—for *he* would have created it; the responsibility would still ultimately be his own. We can only sympathize with the irreconcilable difficulties of leading the life of a gloomy fatalist when one's fate is wholly, decisively, in one's own hands!

Like Jherek Carnelian, whose adventures I have recounted elsewhere, he was particularly liked by his fellows for his vast and often naive enthusiasm for whatever he did. Like Jherek, it was possible for Werther to fall completely in love—with Nature, with an Idea, with Woman (or Man, for that matter).

It seemed to the Duke of Queens (from whom we have it on the excellent authority of Miss Persson herself) that one with such a capacity must love themselves enormously and such love is enviable. The Duke, needless to say, spoke without disapproval when he made this observation: "To shower such largesse upon the Ego! He kneels before his soul in awe—it is a moody king, in constant need of gifts which must always seem rare!" And what is Sensation, our Moralists might argue, but Seeming Rarity? Last year's gifts regilded.

It might be true that young Werther (in years no more than half a millennium) loved himself too much and that his tragedy was his inability to differentiate between the self-gratifying sensation of the moment and what we would call a lasting and deeply-felt emotion. We have a fragment of poetry, written, we are assured, by Werther for Mistress Christia:

> At these times, I love you most when you are sleeping;
>   Your dreams internal, unrealized to the world at large:
> And do I hear you weeping?

Most certainly a reflection of Werther's views, scarcely a description, from all that we know of her, of Mistress Christia's essential being.

Have we any reason to doubt Werther's view of herself? Rather, we should doubt Werther's view of everyone, including himself. Possibly this lack of insight was what made him so thoroughly attractive in his own time—*le Grand Naïf!*

And, since we have quoted one, it is fair to quote the other, for happily we have another fragment, from the same source, of Mistress Christia's verse:

> To have my body moved by other hands;
>   Not only those of Man,
> But Woman, too
> My Liberty in pawn to those who understand:
>   That love, alone, is True.

Surely this displays an irony entirely lacking in Werther's fragment. Affectation is also here, of course, but affectation of Mistress Christia's sort so often hides an equivalently sustained degree of self-knowledge. It is sometimes the case in our own age that the greater the extravagant outer show the greater has been the plunge by the showman into the depths of his private conscience: Consequently, the greater the effort to hide the fact, to give the world not what one is, but what it wants. Mistress Christia chose to reflect with consummate artistry the desires of her lover of the day; to fulfill her ambition as subtly as did she, reveals a person of exceptional perspicacity.

I intrude upon the flow of my tale with these various bits of explanation and speculation only, I hope, to offer credibility for what is to follow—to give a hint at a natural reason for Mistress Christia's peculiar actions and poor Werther's extravagant response. Some time has passed since we left our lovers. For the moment they have separated. We return to Werther . . .

3. IN WHICH WERTHER FINDS A SOUL MATE

Werther de Goethe's pile stood on the pinnacle of a black and mile-high crag about which, in the permanent twilight, black vultures swooped and croaked. The rare visitor to Werther's crag could hear the vultures' voices as he approached. "Never more!" and "Beware the Ides of March!" and "Picking a Chicken With You" were three of the least cryptic warnings they had been created to caw.

At the top of the tallest of his thin, dark towers, Werther de Goethe sat in his favorite chair of unpolished quartz, in his favorite posture of miserable introspection, wondering why Mistress Christia had decided to pay a call on My Lady Charlotina at Lake Billy the Kid.

"Why should she wish to stay here, after all?" He cast a suffering eye upon the sighing sea below. "She is a creature of light—she seeks color, laughter, warmth, no doubt to try to forget some secret sorrow—she needs all the things I cannot give her. Oh, I am a monster of selfishness!" He allowed himself a small sob. But neither the sob nor the preceding outburst produced the usual satisfaction; self-pity eluded him. He felt adrift, lost, like an explorer without chart or compass in an unfamiliar land. Manfully, he tried again:

"Mistress Christia! Mistress Christia! Why do you desert me? Without you I am desolate! My pulsatile nerves will sing at your touch only. And yet it must be my doom forever to be betrayed by the very things to which I give my fullest loyalty. Ah, it is hard! It is hard!"

He felt a little better and rose from his chair of unpolished quartz, turning his power ring a fraction so that the wind blew harder through the unglazed windows of the tower and whipped at his hair, blew his cloak about, stung his pale, long face. He raised one jackbooted foot to place it on the low sill and stared through the rain and the wind at the sky like a dreadful, spreading bruise overhead, at the turbulent, howling sea below.

He pursed his lips, twisting his power ring to darken the scene a little more, to bring up the wind's wail and the ocean's roar. He was turning back to his previous preoccupation when he perceived that something alien tossed upon the distant waves; an artifact not of his own design, it intruded upon his careful conception. He peered hard at the object, but it was too far away for him to identify it. Another might have shrugged it aside, but he was painstaking, even prissy, in his need for artistic perfection. Was this some vulgar addition to his scene made, perhaps, by the Duke of Queens in a misguided effort to please him?

He took his parachute (chosen as the only means by which he could leave his tower) from the wall and strapped it on, stepping through the window and tugging at the rip cord as he fell into space. Down he plummeted and the scarlet balloon soon filled with gas, the nacelle opening up beneath him, so that by the time he was hovering some feet above the somber waves, he was lying comfortably on his chest, staring over the rim of his parachute at the trespassing image he had seen from his tower. What he saw was something resembling a great shell, a shallow boat of mother-of-pearl, floating on that dark and heaving sea.

In astonishment he now realized that the boat was occupied by a slight figure, clad in filmy white, whose face was pale and terrified. It could only be one of his friends, altering his appearance for some whimsical adventure. But which? Then he caught, through the rain, a better glimpse and he heard himself saying:

"A child? A child? Are you a child?"

She could not hear him; perhaps she could not even see him, having eyes only for the watery walls which threatened to engulf her little boat and carry her down to the land of Davy Jones. How could it be a child? He rubbed his eyes. He must be projecting his hopes—but there, that movement, that whimper! It *was* a child! Without doubt!

He watched, open-mouthed, as she was flung this way and that by the elements—*his* elements. She was powerless: actually powerless! He relished her terror; he envied her her fear. Where had she come from? Save for himself and Jherek Carnelian there had not been a child on the planet for thousands upon thousands of years.

He leaned further out, studying her smooth skin, her lovely rounded limbs. Her eyes were tight shut now as the waves crashed upon her fragile craft; her delicate fingers, unstrong, courageous, clung hard to the side! her white dress was wet, outlining her new-formed breasts; water poured from her long, auburn hair. She panted in delicious impotence.

"It *is* a child!" Werther exclaimed. "A sweet, frightened child!"

And in his excitement he toppled from his parachute with an astonished yell, and landed with a crash, which winded him, in the sea-shell boat beside the girl. She opened her eyes as he turned his head to apologize. Plainly she had not been aware of his presence overhead. For a moment he could not speak, though his lips moved. But she screamed.

"My dear . . ." The words were thin and high and they faded into the wind. He struggled to raise himself on his elbows. "I apologize . . ."

She screamed again. She crept as far away from him as possible. Still she clung to her flimsy boat's side as the waves played with it: a thoughtless giant with too delicate a toy; inevitably, it must shatter. He waved his hand to indicate his parachute, but it had already been borne away. His cloak was caught by the wind and wrapped itself around his arm; he struggled to free himself and became further entangled; he heard a new scream and then some demoralized whimpering.

"I will save you!" he shouted, by way of reassurance, but his voice was muffled even in his own ears. It was answered by a further pathetic shriek. As the cloak was saturated it became increasingly difficult for him to escape its folds. He lost his temper and was deeper enmeshed. He tore at the thing. He freed his head.

"I am not your enemy, tender one, but your saviour," he said. It was obvious that she could not hear him. With an impatient gesture he flung off his cloak at last and twisted a power ring. The volume of noise was immediately reduced. Another twist, and the waves became calmer. She stared at him in wonder.

"Did you do that?" she asked.

"Of course. It is my scene, you see. But how you came to enter it, I do not know!"

"You are a wizard, then?" she said.

"Not at all. I have no interest in sport." He clapped his hands and his parachute reappeared, perhaps a trifle reluctantly as if it had enjoyed its brief independence, and drifted down until it was level with the boat. Werther lightened the sky. He could not bring himself, however, to dismiss the rain, but he let a little sun shine through it.

"There," he said. "The storm has passed, eh? Did you like your experience?"

"It was horrifying! I was so afraid. I thought I would drown."

"Yes? And did you like it?"

She was puzzled, unable to answer as he helped her aboard the nacelle and ordered the parachute home.

"You *are* a wizard!" she said. She did not seem disappointed. He did not quiz her as to her meaning. For the moment, if not for always, he was prepared to let her identify him however she wished.

"You are actually a child?" he asked hesitantly. "I do not mean to be insulting. A time-traveler, perhaps? Or from another planet?"

"Oh, no. I am an orphan. My father and mother are now dead. I was born on Earth some fourteen years ago." She looked in mild dismay over the side of the craft as they were whisked swiftly upward. "*They* were time-travelers. We made our home in a forgotten menagerie—underground, but it was pleasant. My parents feared recapture, you see. Food still grew in the menagerie. There were books, too, and they taught me to read—and there were other records through which they were able to present me with a reasonable education. I am not illiterate. I know the world. I was taught to fear wizards."

"Ah," he crooned, "the world! But you are not a part of it, just as I am not a part."

The parachute reached the window and, at his indication, she stepped gingerly from it to the tower. The parachute folded itself and placed itself upon the wall. Werther said: "You will want food, then? I will create whatever you wish!"

"Fairy food will not fill mortal stomachs, sir," she told him.

"You are beautiful," he said. "Regard me as your mentor, as your new father. I will teach you what this world is really like. Will you oblige me, at least, by trying the food?"

"I will." She looked about her with a mixture of curiosity and suspicion. "You lead a spartan life." She noticed a cabinet. "Books? You read, then?"

"In transcription," he admitted. "I listen. My enthusiasm is for Ivan Turgiditi, who created the Novel of Discomfort and remained its greatest practitioner. In, I believe, the nine-hundredth (though they could be spurious, invented, I have heard) . . ."

"Oh, no, no! I have read Turgiditi." She blushed. "In the original. *Wet Socks*— four hours of discomfort, every second brought to life, and in less than a thousand pages!"

"My favorite," he told her, his expression softening still more into besotted wonderment. "I can scarcely believe—in this Age—one such as you! Innocent of device. Uncorrupted! Pure!"

She frowned. "My parents taught me well, sir. I am not . . ."

"You cannot know. And dead, you say? Dead! If only I could have witnessed— but no, I am insensitive. Forgive me. I mentioned food."

"I am not really hungry."

"Later, then. That I should have so recently mourned such things as lacking in this world. I was blind. I did not look. Tell me everything. Whose was the menagerie?"

"It belonged to one of the lords of this planet. My mother was from a period she called the October Century, but recently recovered from a series of interplanetary wars and fresh and optimistic in its rediscoveries of ancestral technologies. She was chosen to be the first into the future. She was captured upon her arrival and imprisoned by a wizard like yourself."

"The word means little. But continue."

"She said that she used the word because it had meaning for her and she had no other short description. My father came from a time known as the Preliminary Structure, where human kind was rare and machines proliferated. He never mentioned the nature of the transgression he made from the social code of his day, but as a result of it he was banished to this world. He, too, was captured for the same menagerie and there he met my mother. They lived originally, of course, in separate cages, where their normal environments were re-created for them. But the owner of the menagerie became bored, I think, and abandoned interest in his collection . . ."

"I have often remarked that people who cannot look after their collections have no business keeping them," said Werther. "Please continue, my dear child." He reached out and patted her hand.

"One day he went away and they never saw him again. It took them some time to realize that he was not returning. Slowly the more delicate creatures, whose environments required special attention, died."

"No one came to resurrect them?"

"No one. Eventually my mother and father were the only ones left. They made what they could of their existence, too wary to enter the outer world in case they should be recaptured, and, to their astonishment, conceived me. They had heard that people from different historical periods could not produce children."

"I have heard the same."

"Well, then, I was a fluke. They were determined to give me as good an upbringing as they could and to prepare me for the dangers of your world."

"Oh, they were right! For one so innocent, there are many dangers. I will protect you, never fear."

"You are kind." She hesitated. "I was not told by my parents that such as you existed."

"I am the only one."

"I see. My parents died in the course of this past year, first my father, then my mother (of a broken heart, I believe). I buried my mother and at first made an attempt to live the life we had always led, but I felt the lack of company and decided to explore the world, for it seemed to me I, too, could grow old and die before I had experienced anything!"

"Grow old," mouthed Werther rhapsodically, "and die!"

"I set out a month or so ago and was disappointed to discover the absence of ogres, of malevolent creatures of any sort—and the wonders I witnessed, while a trifle bewildering, did not compare with those I had imagined I would find. I had fully expected to be snatched up for a menagerie by now, but nobody has shown interest, even when they have seen me."

"Few follow the menagerie fad, at present." He nodded. "They would not have known you for what you were. Only I could recognize you. Oh, how lucky I am. And how lucky you are, my dear, to have met me when you did. You see, I, too, am a child of the womb. I, too, made my own hard way through the utereal gloom to breathe the air, to find the light of this faded, this senile globe. Of all those you could have met, you have met the only one who understands you, who is likely to share your passions, to relish your education. We are soul mates, child!"

He stood up and put a tender arm about her young shoulders.

"You have a new mother, a new father now! His name is Werther!"

4. IN WHICH WERTHER FINDS SIN AT LAST

Her name was Catherine Lily Marguerite Natasha Dolores Beatrice Machineshop-Seven Flambeau Gratitude (the last two names but one being her father's and her mother's respectively).

Werther de Goethe continued to talk to her for some hours. Indeed, he became quite carried away as he described all the exciting things they would do, how they would live lives of the purest poetry and simplicity from now on, the quiet and tranquil places they would visit, the manner in which her education would be supplemented, and he was glad to note, he thought, her wariness dissipating, her attitude warming to him.

"I will devote myself entirely to your happiness," he informed her, and then, noticing that she was fast asleep, he smiled tenderly: "Poor child. I am a worm of thoughtlessness. She is exhausted."

He rose from his chair of unpolished quartz and strode to where she lay curled upon the iguana-skin rug; stooping, he placed his hands under her warm-smelling, her yielding body, and somewhat awkwardly lifted her. In her sleep she uttered a tiny moan, her cherry lips parted and her newly budded breasts rose and fell rapidly against his chest once or twice until she sank back into a deeper slumber.

He staggered, panting with the effort, to another part of the tower and then he lowered her with a sigh to the floor. He realized that he had not prepared a proper bedroom for her.

Fingering his chin, he inspected the dank stones, the cold obsidian which had suited his mood so well for so long and now seemed singularly offensive. Then he smiled.

"She must have beauty," he said, "and it must be subtle. It must be calm."

An inspiration, a movement of a power ring, and the walls were covered with thick carpets embroidered with scenes from his own old book of fairy tales. He remembered how he had listened to the book over and over again—his only consolation in the lonely days of his extreme youth.

Here, Man Shelley, a famous harmonican, ventured into Odeon (a version of Hell) in order to be reunited with his favorite three-headed dog Omnibus. The picture showed him with his harmonica (or "harp") playing "Blues for a Nightingale"—a famous lost piece. There Casablanca Bogard, with his single eye, in the middle of his forehead, wielded his magic spade, Sam, in his epic fight with that ferocious bird, the Malted Falcon, to save his love, the Acrilan Queen, from the power of Big Sleepy (a dwarf who had turned himself into a giant) and Mutinous Caine, who had been cast out of Hollywood (or paradise) for the killing of his sister, the Blue Angel.

Such scenes were surely the very stuff to stir the romantic, delicate imagination of this lovely child, just as his had been stirred when—he felt the *frisson*—he had been her age. He glowed. His substance was suffused with delicious compassion for them both as he recalled, also, the torments of his own adolescence.

That she should be suffering as he had suffered filled him with the pleasure all must feel when a fellow spirit is recognized, and at the same time he was touched by her plight, determined that she should not know the anguish of his earliest years. Once, long ago, Werther had courted Jherek Carnelian, admiring him

for his fortitude, knowing that locked in Jherek's head were the memories of bewilderment, misery and despair which would echo his own; but Jherek, pampered
progeny of that most artificial of all creatures, the Iron Orchid, had been unable to
recount any suitable experiences at all, had, whilst cheerfully eager to please
Werther, recalled nothing but pleasurable times, had reluctantly admitted, at last,
to the possession of the happiest of childhoods. That was when Werther had concluded that Jherek Carnelian had no soul worth speaking of and he had never
altered his opinion (now he secretly doubted Jherek's origins and sometimes believed that Jherek merely pretended to have been a child—merely one more of his
boring and superficial affectations).

Next, a bed—a soft, downy, bed, spread with sheets of silver silk, with posts
of ivory and hangings of precious perspex, antique and yellowed, and on the floor
the finely-tanned skins of albino hamsters and marmalade cats.

Werther added gorgeous lays of intricately patterned red and blue ceramic,
their bowls filled with living flowers: with whispering toadflax, dragonsnaps, gold-
ilocks and shanghai lilies, with blooming scarlet margravines (his adopted daughter's name-flower, as he knew to his pride), with soda-purple poppies and tea-green
roses, with iodine and cerise and crimson hanging johnny, with golden cynthia and
sky-blue true-lips, calomine and creeping larrikin, until the room was saturated
with their intoxicating scents.

Placing a few bunches of hitler's balls in the corners near the ceiling, a toy
fish tank (capable of firing real fish), which he remembered owning as a boy, under
the window, a trunk (it could be opened by pressing the navel) filled with clothes
near the bed, a full set of bricks and two bats against the wall close to the doorway,
he was able, at last, to view the room with some satisfaction.

Obviously, he told himself, she would make certain changes according to her
own tastes. That was why he had shown such restraint. He imagined her naive
delight when she wakened in the morning. And he must be sure to produce days
and nights of regular duration, because at her age routine was the main thing a
child needed. There was nothing like the certainty of a consistently glorious sunrise! This reminded him to make an alteration to a power ring on his left hand, to
spread upon the black cushion of the sky crescent moons and stars and starlets in
profusion. Bending carefully, he picked up the vibrant youth of her body and
lowered her to the bed, drawing the silver sheets up to her vestal chin. Chastely
he touched lips to her forehead and crept from the room, fashioning a leafy door
behind him, hesitating for a moment, unable to define the mood in which he found
himself. A rare smile illumined features set so long in lines of gloom. Returning
to his own quarters, he murmured:

"I believe it is Contentment!"

A month swooned by. Werther lavished every moment of his time upon his new
charge. He thought of nothing but her youthful satisfactions. He encouraged her in
joy, in idealism, in a love of Nature. Gone were his blizzards, his rocky spires, his
bleak wastes and his moody forests, to be replaced with gentle landscapes of green
hills and merry, tinkling rivers, sunny glades in copses of poplars, rhododendrons,

redwoods, laburnums, banyans and good old amiable oaks. When they went on a picnic large-eyed cows and playful gorillas would come and nibble scraps of food from Catherine Gratitude's palm. And when it was day, the sun always shone and the sky was always blue, and if there were clouds, they were high, hesitant puffs of whiteness and soon gone.

He found her books so that she might read. There was Turgiditi and Uto, Pett Ridge and Zakka, Pyat Sink—all the ancients. Sometimes he asked her to read to him, for the luxury of dispensing with his usual translators. She had been fascinated by a picture of a typewriter she had seen in a record, so he fashioned an air-car in the likeness of one, and they traveled the world in it, looking at scenes created by Werther's peers.

"Oh, Werther," she said one day, "you are so good to me. Now that I realize the misery which might have been mine (as well as the life I was missing under-ground) I love you more and more."

"And I love you more and more," he replied, his head a-swim. And for a moment he felt a pang of guilt at having forgotten Mistress Christia so easily. He had not seen her since Catherine had come to him and he guessed that she was sulking somewhere. He prayed that she would not decide to take vengeance on him.

They went to see Jherek Carnelian's famous "London, 1896" and Werther manfully hid his displeasure at her admiration for his rival's buildings of white marble, gold and sparkling quartz. He showed her his own abandoned tomb, which he privately considered in better taste, but it was plain that it did not give her the same satisfaction.

They saw the Duke of Queens' latest, "Ladies and Swans," but not for long, for Werther considered it unsuitable. Later they paid a visit to Lord Jagged of Canaria's somewhat abstract "War and Peace in Two Dimensions" and Werther thought it too stark to please the girl, judging the experiment "successful," but Catherine laughed with glee as she touched the living figures and found that some-how it was true—Lord Jagged had given them length and breadth but not a scrap of width—when they turned aside, they disappeared.

It was on one of these expeditions, to Bishop Castle's "A Million Angry Wrens" (an attempt in the recently revised art of Aesthetic Loudness), that they encountered Lord Mongrove, a particular confidante of Werther's until they had quarreled over the method of suicide adopted by the natives of Uranus during the period of the Great Sodium Breather. By now they would, if Werther had not found a new obsession, have patched up their differences and Werther felt a pang of guilt for having forgotten the one person on this planet with whom he had, after all, shared something in common.

In his familiar dark green robes, with his leonine head hunched between his massive shoulders, the giant, apparently disdaining an air-carriage, was riding home upon the back of a monstrous snail.

The first thing they saw, from above, was its shining trail over the azure rocks of some abandoned, half-created scene of Argonheart Po's (who believed that noth-ing was worth making unless it tasted delicious and could be eaten and digested).

It was Catherine who saw the snail itself first and exclaimed at the size of the man who occupied the swaying howdah on it back.

"He must be ten feet tall. Werther!"

And Werther, knowing whom she meant, made their typewriter descend, crying:

"Mongrove! My old friend!"

Mongrove, however, was sulking. He had chosen not to forget whatever insult it had been which Werther had leveled at him when they had last met. "What? Is it Werther? Bring freshly sharpened dirks for the flesh between my shoulder blades? It is that Cold Betrayer himself, whom I befriended when a bare boy, pretending carelessness, feigning insouciance, as if he cannot remember, with relish, the exact degree of bitterness of the poisoned wine he fed me when we parted. Faster, steed! Bear me away from Treachery! Let me fly from further Insult! No more shall I suffer at the hands of Calumny!" And, with his long, jeweled stick, he beat upon the shell of his mollusculoid mount. The beast's horns waved agitatedly for a moment, but it did not really seem capable of any greater speed. In good-humored puzzlement, it turned its slimy head towards its master.

"Forgive me, Mongrove! I take back all I said," announced Werther, unable to recall a single sour syllable of the exchange. "Tell me why you are abroad. It is rare for you to leave your doomy dome."

"I am making my way to the Ball," said Lord Mongrove, "which is shortly to be held by My Lady Charlotina. Doubtless I have been invited to act as a butt for their malice and their gossip, but I go in good faith."

"A Ball? I know nothing of it."

Mongrove's countenance brightened a trifle. "You have not been invited? Ah!"

"I wonder . . . But, no—My Lady Charlotina shows unsuspected sensitivity. She knows that I now have responsibilities—to my little Ward, here. To Catherine—to my Kate."

"The child?"

"Yes, to my child. I am privileged to be her protector. Fate favors me as her new father. This is she. Is she not lovely? Is she not innocent?"

Lord Mongrove raised his great head and looked at the slender girl beside Werther. He shook his huge head as if in pity for her.

"Be careful, my dear," he said. "To be befriended by de Goethe is to be embraced by a viper!"

She did not understand Mongrove; questioningly, she looked up at Werther. "What does he mean?"

Werther was shocked. He clapped his hands to her pretty ears.

"Listen no more! I regret the overture. The movement, Lord Mongrove, shall remain unresolved. Farewell, spurner of good intent. I had never guessed before the level of your cynicism. Such an accusation! Goodbye, forever, most malevolent of mortals, despiser of altruism, hater of love! She shall know me no longer!"

"You have known yourself not at all," snapped Mongrove spitefully, but it was unlikely that Werther, already speeding skyward, heard the remark.

And thus it was with particular and unusual graciousness that Werther greeted My Lady Charlotina when, a little later, they came upon her.

She was wearing the russet ears and eyes of a fox, riding her yellow rocking horse through the patch of orange sky left over from her own turbulent "Death of Neptune." She waved to them. "Cock-a-loodle-do!"

"My dear Lady Charlotina. What a pleasure it is to see you. Your beauty continues to rival Nature's mightiest miracles."

It is with such unwonted effusion that one will greet a person, who has not hitherto aroused our feelings, when we are in a position to compare them against another, closer, acquaintance who had momentarily earned our contempt or anger.

She seemed taken aback, but received the compliment equably enough.

"Dear Werther! And is this that rarity, the girl-child I have heard so much about and whom, in your goodness, you have taken under your wing? I could not believe it! A child! And how lucky she is to find a father in yourself—of all our number the one best suited to look after her."

It might also be said that Werther preened himself beneath the golden shower of her benediction, and if he detected no irony in her tone, perhaps it was because he still smarted from Mongrove's dash of vitriol.

"I have been chosen, it seems," he said modestly, "to lead this waif through the traps and illusions of our weary world. The burden I shoulder is not light . . ."

"Valiant Werther!"

". . . but it is shouldered willingly. I am devoting my life to her upbringing, to her peace of mind." He placed a bloodless hand upon her auburn locks and, winsomely, she shook his other one.

"You are tranquil, my dear?" asked Lady Charlotina kindly, arranging her blue skirts over the saddle of her rocking horse. "You have no doubts?"

"At first I had." admitted the sweet child, "but gradually I learned to trust my new father. Now I would trust him in anything!"

"Ah," sighed My Lady Charlotina, "trust!"

"Trust," said Werther. "It grows in me, too. You encourage me, charming Charlotina, for a short time ago I believed myself doubted by all."

"Is it possible? When you are evidently so reconciled—so—happy!"

"And I am happy, also, now that I have Werther," caroled the commendable Catherine.

"Exquisite!" breathed My Lady Charlotina. "And you will, of course, both come to my Ball."

"I am not sure . . ." began Werther, "perhaps Catherine is too young . . ."

But she raised her tawny hands. "It is your duty to come. To show us all that simple hearts are the happiest."

"Possibly . . ."

"You must. The world must have examples, Werther, if it is to follow your Way."

Werther lowered his eyes shyly. "I am honored," he said. "We accept."

"Splendid! Then come soon. Come now, if you like. A few arrangements, and the Ball begins."

"Thank you," said Werther, "but I think it best if we return to my castle for a little while." He caressed his ward's fine, long tresses. "For it will be Catherine's first Ball and she must choose her gown."

And he beamed down upon his radiant protégée as she clapped her hands in joy.

★ ★ ★

My Lady Charlotina's Ball must have been at least a mile in circumference, set against the soft tones of a summer twilight, red-gold and transparent so that, as one approached, the guests who had already arrived could be seen standing upon the inner wall, clad in creations extravagant even at the End of Time.

The Ball itself was inclined to roll a little, but those inside it were undisturbed; their footing was firm, thanks to My Lady Charlotina's artistry. The Ball was entered by means of a number of sphincterish openings, placed more or less at random in its outer wall. At the very center of the Ball, on a floating platform, sat an orchestra comprising the choicest musicians, out of a myriad ages and planets, from My Lady's great menagerie (she specialized, currently, in artists).

When Werther de Goethe, a green-gowned Catherine Gratitude upon his blue velvet arm, arrived, the orchestra was playing some primitive figure of My Lady Charlotina's own composition. It was called, she claimed as she welcomed them. "On the Theme of Childhood," but doubtless she thought to please them, for Werther believed he had heard it before, under a different title.

Many of the guests had already arrived and were standing in small groups chatting to each other. Werther greeted an old friend Li Pao, of the twenty-seventh century, and such a killjoy that he had never been wanted for a menagerie. While he was forever criticizing their behavior, he never missed a party. Next to him stood the Iron Orchid, mother of Jherek Carnelian, who was not present. In contrast to Li Pao's faded blue overalls, she wore rags of red, yellow and mauve, thousands of sparkling bracelets, anklets and necklaces, a head-dress of woven peacock's wings, slippers which were moles and whose beady eyes looked up from the floor.

"What do you mean—waste?" she was saying to Li Pao. "What else could we do with the energy of the universe? If our sun burns out, we create another. Doesn't that make us conservatives? Or is it preservatives?"

"Good evening, Werther," said Li Pao in some relief. He bowed politely to the girl. "Good evening, miss."

"Miss?" said the Iron Orchid. "What?"

"Gratitude."

"For whom?"

"This is Catherine Gratitude, my ward," said Werther, and the Iron Orchid let forth a peal of luscious laughter.

"The girl-bride, eh?"

"Not at all," said Werther. "How is Jherek?"

"Lost, I fear, in Time. We have seen nothing of him recently. He still pursues his paramour. Some say you copy him, Werther."

He knew her bantering tone of old and took the remark in good part. "His is a mere affectation," he said. "Mine is Reality."

"You were always one to make that distinction, Werther," she said. "And I will never understand the difference!"

"I find your concern for Miss Gratitude's upbringing most worthy," said Li Pao somewhat unctuously. "If there is any way I can help. My knowledge of twenties' politics, for instance, is considered unmatched—particularly, of course, where the twenty-sixth and twenty-seventh centuries are concerned . . ."

"You are kind," said Werther, unsure how to take an offer which seemed to him overeager and not entirely selfless.

Gaf the Horse in Tears, whose clothes were real flame, flickered towards them, the light from his burning, unstable face almost blinding Werther. Catherine Gratitude shrank from him as he reached out a hand to touch her, but her expression changed as she realized that he was not at all hot—rather, there was something almost chilly about the sensation on her shoulder. Werther did his best to smile. "Good evening. Gaf."

"She is a dream!" said Gaf. "I know it, because only I have such a wonderful imagination. Did I create her, Werther?"

"You jest."

"Ho, ho! Serious old Werther." Gaf kissed him, bowed to the child, and moved away, his body erupting in all directions as he laughed the more. "Literal, literal Werther!"

"He is a boor," Werther told his charge. "Ignore him."

"I thought him sweet," she said.

"You have much to learn, my dear."

The music filled the Ball and some of the guests left the floor to dance, hanging in the air around the orchestra, darting streamers of colored energy in order to weave complex patterns as they moved.

"They are very beautiful," said Catherine Gratitude. "May we dance soon, Werther?"

"If you wish. I am not much given to such pastimes as a rule."

"But tonight?"

He smiled. "I can refuse you nothing, child."

She hugged his arm and her girlish laughter filled his heart with warmth.

"Perhaps you should have made yourself a child before, Werther?" suggested the Duke of Queens, drifting away from the dance and leaving a trail of green fire behind him. He was clad all in soft metal which reflected the colors in the Ball and created other colors in turn. "You are a perfect father. Your métier."

"It would not have been the same, Duke of Queens."

"As you say." His darkly handsome face bore its usual expression of benign amusement. "I am the Duke of Queens, child. It is an honor." He bowed, his metal booming.

"Your friends are wonderful," said Catherine Gratitude. "Not at all what I expected."

"Be wary of them," murmured Werther. "They have no conscience."

"Conscience? What is that?"

Werther touched a ring and led her up into the air of the Ball. "I am your conscience, for the moment, Catherine. You shall learn in time."

Lord Jagged of Canaria, his face almost hidden by one of his high, quilted collars, floated in their direction.

"Werther, my boy! This must be your daughter. Oh! Sweeter than honey! Softer than petals! I have heard so much—but the praise was not enough! You must have poetry written about you. Music composed for you. Tales must be spun with you as the heroine." And Lord Jagged made a deep and elaborate bow, his long sleeves sweeping the air below his feet. Next, he addressed Werther:

"Tell me, Werther, have you seen Mistress Christia? Everyone else is here, but not she."

"I have looked for the Everlasting Concubine without success," Werther told him.

"She should arrive soon. In a moment My Lady Charlotina announces the beginning of the masquerade—and Mistress Christia loves the masquerade."

"I suspect she pines," said Werther.

"Why so?"

"She loved me, you know."

"Aha! Perhaps you are right. But I interrupt your dance. Forgive me."

And Lord Jagged of Canaria floated, stately and beautiful, towards the floor.

"Mistress Christia?" said Catherine. "Is she your Lost Love?"

"A wonderful woman," said Werther. "But my first duty is to you. Regretfully I could not pursue her, as I think she wanted me to do."

"Have I come between you?"

"Of course not. Of course not. That was infatuation—this is a sacred duty."

And Werther showed her how to dance—how to notice a gap in a pattern which might be filled by the movements from her body. Because it was a special occasion he had given her her very own power ring—only a small one, but she was proud of it, and she gasped so prettily at the colors her train made that Werther's fears that his gift might corrupt her precious innocence were plainly unfounded. It was then that he realized with a shock how deeply he had fallen in love with her.

At the realization, he made an excuse, leaving her to dance with first Sweet Orb Mace, feminine tonight, with a latticed face, and then with O'Kala Incarnadine who, with his usual preference for the bodies of beasts, was currently a bear. Although he felt a pang as he watched her stroke O'Kala's ruddy fur, he could not bring himself just then to interfere. His immediate desire was to leave the Ball, but to do that would be to disappoint his ward, to raise questions he would not wish to answer. After a while he began to feel a certain satisfaction from his suffering and remained, miserably, on the floor while Catherine danced on and on.

And then My Lady Charlotina had stopped the orchestra and stood on the platform calling for their attention.

"It is time for the masquerade. You all know the theme, I hope." She paused, smiling. "All, save Werther and Catherine. When the music begins again, please reveal your creations of the evening."

Werther frowned, wondering her reasons for not revealing the theme of the masquerade to him. She was still smiling at him as she drifted towards him and settled beside him on the floor.

"You seem sad, Werther. Why so? I thought you at one with yourself at last. Wait. My surprise will flatter you, I'm sure!"

The music began again. The Ball was filled with laughter—and there was the theme of the masquerade!

Werther cried out in anquish. He dashed upward through the gleeful throng, seeing each face as a mockery, trying to reach the side of his girl-child before she could realize the dreadful truth.

"Catherine! Catherine!"

He flew to her. She was bewildered as he folded her in his arms.

"Oh, they are monsters of insincerity! Oh, they are grotesque in their aping of all that is simple, all that is pure!" he cried.

He glared about him at the other guests. My Lady Charlotina had chosen "Childhood" as her general theme. Sweet Orb Mace had changed himself into a gigantic single sperm, his own face still visible at the glistening tail; the Iron Orchid had become a monstrous new-born baby with a red and bawling face which still owed more to Paint than to Nature; the Duke of Queens, true to character, was three-year-old Siamese twins (both the faces were his own, softened); even Lord Mongrove had deigned to become an egg.

"What ith it, Werther?" lisped My Lady Charlotina at his feet, her brown curls bobbing as she waved her lollipop in the general direction of the other guests. "Doeth it not pleathe you?"

"Ugh! This is agony! A parody of everything I hold most perfect!"

"But, Werther . . ."

"What is wrong, dear Werther?" begged Catherine. "It is only a masquerade."

"Can you not see? It is you—everything you and I mean—that they mock. No—it is best that you do not see. Come, Catherine. They are insane; they revile all that is sacred!" And he bore her bodily towards the wall, rushing through the nearest doorway and out into the darkened sky.

★ ★ ★

He left his typewriter behind, so great was his haste to be gone from that terrible scene. He fled with her willy-nilly through the air, through daylight, through pitchy night. He fled until he came to his own tower, flanked now by green lawns and rolling turf, surrounded by songbirds, swamped in sunshine. And he hated it— landscape, larks and light—all were hateful.

He flew through the window and found his room full of comforts—of cushions and carpets and heady perfume—and with a gesture he removed them. Their particles hung gleaming in the sun's beams for a moment. But the sun, too, was hateful. He blacked it out and night swam into that bare chamber. And all the while, in amazement, Catherine Gratitude looked on, her lips forming the question, but never uttering it. At length, tentatively, she touched his arm.

"Werther?"

His hands flew to his head. He roared in his mindless pain.

"Oh, Werther!"

"Ah! They destroy me! They destroy my ideals!"

He was weeping when he turned to bury his face in her hair.

"Werther!" She kissed his cold cheek. She stroked his shaking back. And she led him from the ruins of his room and down the passage to her own apartment.

"Why should I strive to set up standards." he sobbed, "when all about me they seek to pull them down. It would be better to be a villain!"

But he was quiescent; he allowed himself to be seated upon her bed; he felt suddenly drained. He sighed. "They hate innocence. They would see it gone forever from this globe."

She gripped his hand. She stroked it. "No, Werther. They meant no harm. I saw no harm."

"They would corrupt you. I must keep you safe."

Her lips touched his and his body came alive again. Her fingers touched his skin. He gasped.

"I must keep you safe."

In a dream, he took her in his arms. Her lips parted, their tongues met. Her young breasts pressed against him—and for perhaps the first time in his life Werther understood the meaning of physical joy. His blood began to dance to the rhythm of a sprightlier heart. And why should he not take what they would take in his position? He placed a hand upon a pulsing thigh. If cynicism called the tune, then he would show them he could pace as pretty a measure as any. His kisses became passionate, and passionately they were returned.

"Catherine!"

A motion of a power ring and their clothes were gone, the bed hangings drawn.

And your auditor not being of that modern school which salaciously seeks to share the secrets of others' passions (secrets familiar, one might add, to the great majority of us) retires from this scene.

But when he woke the next morning and turned on the sun, Werther looked down at the lovely child beside him, her auburn hair spread across the pillows, her little breasts rising and falling in tranquil sleep, and he realized that he had used his reaction to the masquerade to betray his trust. A madness had filled him; he had raised an evil wind and his responsibility had been born off by it, taking Innocence and Purity, never to return. His lust had lost him everything.

Tears reared in his tormented eyes and ran cold upon his heated cheeks. "Mongrove was perceptive indeed," he murmured. "To be befriended by Werther is to be embraced by a viper. She can never trust me—anyone—again. I have lost my right to offer her protection. I have stolen her childhood."

And he got up from the bed, from the scene of that most profound of crimes, and he ran from the room and went to sit in his old chair of unpolished quartz, staring listlessly through the window at the paradise he had created outside. It accused him; it reminded him of his high ideals. He was astonished by the consequences of his actions: he had turned his paradise to hell.

A great groan reverberated in his chest. "Oh, now I know what sin is!" he said. "And what terrible tribute it exacts from the one who tastes it!"

And he sank almost luxuriously into the deepest gloom he had ever known.

5. IN WHICH WERTHER FINDS REDEMPTION OF SORTS

He avoided Catherine Gratitude all that day, even when he heard her calling his name, for if the landscape could fill him with such agony, what would he feel under the startled inquisition of her gaze? He erected himself a heavy dungeon door so that she could not get in, and, as he sat contemplating his poisoned paradise, he saw her once, walking on a hill he had made for her. She seemed unchanged, of course, but he knew in his heart how she must be shivering with the chill of lost innocence. That it should have been himself, of all men, who had introduced her so young to the tainted joys of carnal love! Another deep sigh and he buried his fists savagely into his eyes.

"Catherine! Catherine! I am a thief, an assassin, a despoiler of souls. The name of Werther de Goethe becomes a synonym for Treachery!"

It was not until the next morning that he thought himself able to admit her to his room, to submit himself to a judgment which he knew would be worse for not being spoken. Even when she did enter, his shifty eye would not focus on her for long. He looked for some outward sign of her experience, somewhat surprised that he could detect none.

He glared at the floor, knowing his words to be inadequate. "I am sorry," he said.

"For leaving the Ball, darling Werther! The epilogue was infinitely sweeter."

"Don't!" He put his hands to his ears. "I cannot undo what I have done, my child, but I can try to make amends. Evidently you must not stay here with me. You need suffer nothing further on that score. For myself, I must contemplate an eternity of loneliness. It is the least of the prices I must pay. But Mongrove would be kind to you, I am sure." He looked at her. It seemed that she had grown older. Her bloom was fading now that it had been touched by the icy fingers of that most sinister, most insinuating, of libertines, called Death. "Oh," he sobbed, "how haughty was I in my pride! How I congratulated myself on my high-mindedness. Now I am proved the lowliest of all my kind!"

"I really cannot follow you, Werther dear," she said. "Your behavior is rather odd today, you know. Your words mean very little to me."

"Of course they mean little," he said. "You are unworldly, child. How can you anticipate . . . ah, ah . . ." and he hid his face in his hands.

"Werther, please cheer up. I have heard of *le petit mal*, but this seems to be going on for a somewhat longer time. I am still puzzled . . ."

"I cannot, as yet," he said, speaking with some difficulty through his palms, "bring myself to describe in cold words the enormity of the crime I have committed against your spirit—against your childhood. I had known that you would—eventually—wish to experience the joys of true love—but I had hoped to prepare your soul for what was to come—so that when it happened it would be beautiful."

"But it *was* beautiful, Werther."

He found himself experiencing a highly inappropriate impatience with her failure to understand her doom.

"It was not the right *kind* of beauty," he explained.

"There are certain correct kinds for certain times?" she asked. "You are sad because we have offended some social code?"

"There is no such thing in this world, Catherine—but you, child, could have known a code. Something I never had when I was your age—something I wanted for you. One day you will realize what I mean." He leaned forward, his voice thrilling, his eye hot and hard, "And if you do not hate me now, Catherine, oh, you will hate me then. Yes! You will hate me then."

Her answering laughter was unaffected, unstrained. "This is silly, Werther. I have rarely had a nicer experience."

He turned aside, raising his hands as if to ward off blows. "Your words are darts—each one draws blood in my conscience." He sank back into his chair.

Still laughing, she began to stroke his limp hand. He drew it away from her. "Ah, see! I have made you lascivious. I have introduced you to the drug called lust!"

"Well, perhaps to an aspect of it!"

Some change in her tone began to impinge on Werther, though he was still deep-trapped in the glue of his guilt. He raised his head, his expression bemused, refusing to believe the import of her words.

"A wonderful aspect," she said. And she licked his ear.

He shuddered. He frowned. He tried to frame words to ask her a certain question, but he failed.

She licked his cheek and she twined her fingers in his lackluster hair. "And one I should love to experience again, most passionate of anachronisms. It was as it must have been in those ancient days—when poets ranged the world, stealing what they needed, taking any fair maiden who pleased them, setting fire to the towns of their publishers, laying waste the books of their rivals: ambushing their readers. I am sure you were just as delighted, Werther. Say that you were!"

"Leave me!" he gasped. "I can bear no more."

"If it is what you want."

"It is."

With a wave of her little hand, she tripped from the room.

And Werther brooded upon her shocking words, deciding that he could only have misheard her. In her innocence she had seemed to admit an understanding of certain inconceivable things. What he had half-interpreted as a familiarity with the carnal world was doubtless merely a child's romantic conceit. How could she have had previous experience of a night such as that which they had shared?

She had been a virgin. Certainly she had been that.

He wished that he did not then feel an ignoble pang of pique at the possibility of another having also known her. Consequently this was immediately followed by a further wave of guilt for entertaining such thoughts and subsequent emotions. A score of conflicting glooms warred in his mind, sent tremors through his body.

"Why," he cried to the sky, "was I born! I am unworthy of the gift of life. I accused My Lady Charlotina, Lord Jagged and the Duke of Queens of base emotions, cynical motives, yet none are baser or more cynical than mine! Would I turn my anger against my victim, blame her for my misery, attack a little child because she tempted me? That is what my diseased mind would do. Thus do I seek to excuse myself my crimes. Ah, I am vile! I am vile!"

He considered going to visit Mongrove, for he dearly wished to abase himself before his old friend, to tell Mongrove that the giant's contempt had been only too well-founded; but he had lost the will to move; a terrible lassitude had fallen upon him. Hating himself, he knew that all must hate him, and while he knew that he had earned every scrap of their hatred, he could not bear to go abroad and run the risk of suffering it.

What would one of his heroes of Romance have done? How would Casablanca Bogard or Eric of Marylebone have exonerated themselves, even supposing they could have committed such an unbelievable deed in the first place?

He knew the answer.

It drummed louder and louder in his ears. It was implacable and grim. But still he hesitated to follow it. Perhaps some other, more original act of contrition would occur to him? He racked his writhing brain. Nothing presented itself as an alternative.

At length he rose from his chair of unpolished quartz. Slowly, his pace measured, he walked towards the window, stripping off his power rings so that they clattered to the flagstones.

He stepped upon the ledge and stood looking down at the rocks a mile below at the base of the tower. Some jolting of a power ring as it fell had caused a wind to spring up and to blow coldly against his naked body. "The Wind of Justice," he thought.

He ignored his parachute. With one final cry of "Catherine! Forgive me!" and an unvoiced hope that he would be found long after it proved impossible to resurrect him, he flung himself, unsupported, into space.

Down he fell and death leapt to meet him. The breath fled from his lungs, his head began to pound, his sight grew dim, but the spikes of black rock grew larger until he knew that he had struck them, for his body was aflame, broken in a hundred places, and his sad, muddled, doom-clouded brain was chaff upon the wailing breeze. Its last coherent thought was: *Let none say Werther did not pay the price in full.* And thus did he end his life with a proud negative.

6. IN WHICH WERTHER DISCOVERS CONSOLATION

"Oh, Werther, what an adventure!"

It was Catherine Gratitude looking down on him as he opened his eyes. She clapped her hands. Her blue eyes were full of joy.

Lord Jagged stood back with a smile. "Reborn, magnificent Werther, to sorrow afresh!" he said.

He lay upon a bench of marble in his own tower. Surrounding the bench were My Lady Charlotina, the Duke of Queens, Gaf the Horse in Tears, the Iron Orchid, Li Pao, O'Kala Incarnadine, and many others. They all applauded.

"A spendid drama!" said the Duke of Queens.

"Amongst the best I have witnessed," agreed the Iron Orchid (a fine compliment from her).

Werther found himself warming to them as they poured their praise upon him; but then he remembered Catherine Gratitude and what he had meant himself to be to her, what he had actually become, and although he felt much better for having paid his price, he stretched out his hand to her, saying again: "Forgive me."

"Silly Werther! Forgive such a perfect role? No, no! If anyone needs forgiving, then it is I." And Catherine Gratitude touched one of the many power rings now festooning her fingers and returned herself to her original appearance.

"It is you!" He could make no other response as he looked upon the Everlasting Concubine. "Mistress Christia?"

"Surely you suspected towards the end?" she said. "Was it not everything you told me you wanted? Was it not a fine 'sin,' Werther?"

"I suffered . . ." he began.

"Oh, yes! *How* you suffered! It was unparalleled. It was equal, I am sure, to anything in History. And, Werther, did you not find the 'guilt' particularly exquisite?"

"You did it for me?" He was overwhelmed. "Because it was what I said I wanted most of all?"

"He is still a little dull," explained Mistress Christia, turning to their friends. "I believe that is often the case after a resurrection."

"Often," intoned Lord Jagged, darting a sympathetic glance at Werther. "But it will pass, I hope."

"The ending, though it could be anticipated," said the Iron Orchid, "was absolutely right."

Mistress Christia put her arms around him and kissed him. "They are saying that your performance rivals Jherek Carnelian's," she whispered. He squeezed her hand. What a wonderful woman she was, to be sure, to have added to his experience and to have increased his prestige at the same time.

He sat up. He smiled a trifle bashfully. Again they applauded.

"I can see that this was where "Rain" was leading," said Bishop Castle. "It gives the whole thing point, I think."

"The exaggerations were just enough to bring out the essential mood without being too prolonged," said O'Kala Incarnadine, waving an elegant hoof (he had come as a goat).

"Well, I had not . . ." began Werther, but Mistress Christia put a hand to his lips.

"You will need a little time to recover," she said.

Tactfully, one by one, still expressing their most fulsome congratulations, they departed, until only Werther de Goethe and the Everlasting Concubine were left.

"I hope you did not mind the deception, Werther," she said. "I had to make amends for ruining your rainbow and I had been wondering for ages how to please you. My Lady Charlotina helped a little, of course, and Lord Jagged—though neither knew too much of what was going on."

"The real performance was yours," he said. "I was merely your foil."

"Nonsense. I gave you the rough material with which to work. And none could have anticipated the wonderful, consummate use to which you put it!"

Gently, he took her hand. "It was everything I have ever dreamed of," he said. "It is true, Mistress Christia, that you alone know me."

"You are kind. And now I must leave."

"Of course." He looked out through his window. The comforting storm raged again. Familiar lightnings flickered; friendly thunder threatened; from below there came the sound of his old consoler the furious sea flinging itself, as always, at the rock's black fangs. His sigh was contented. He knew that their liaison was ended; neither had the bad taste to prolong it and thus produce what would be, inevitably, an anticlimax, and yet he felt regret, as evidently did she.

"If death were only permanent," he said wistfully, "but it cannot be. I thank you again, granter of my deepest desires."

"If death," she said, pausing at the window, "were permanent, how would we judge our successes and our failures? Sometimes, Werther, I think you ask too much of the world." She smiled. "But you are satisfied for the moment, my love?"

"Of course."

It would have been boorish, he thought, to have claimed anything else.

Anniversary Project

JOE HALDEMAN

We never really know what the future holds in store for us, in spite of all the money people spend on Psychic Hot Lines and card readings. And, as the sly and ironic story that follows demonstrates, perhaps that's just as *well.* . . .

Born in Oklahoma City, Joe Haldeman took a B.S. degree in physics and astronomy from the University of Maryland and did postgraduate work in mathematics and computer science. But his plans for a career in science were cut short by the U.S. Army, which sent him to Vietnam in 1968 as a combat engineer. Seriously wounded in action, Haldeman returned home in 1969 and began to write. He sold his first story to *Galaxy* in 1969 and by 1976 had garnered both the Nebula Award and the Hugo Award for his famous novel *The Forever War,* one of the landmark books of the seventies. He took another Hugo Award in 1977 for his story "Tricentennial," won the Rhysling Award in 1983 for the best SF poem of the year (although usually thought of primarily as a "hard-science" writer, Haldeman is, in fact, also an accomplished poet and has sold poetry to most of the major professional markets in the genre), and won both the Nebula and the Hugo Award in 1991 for the novella version of *"The Hemingway Hoax."* His story "Graves" earned him another Nebula in 1994, and "None So Blind" won the Hugo Award in 1995. His other books include two mainstream novels, *War Year* and *1968,* the SF novels *Mindbridge, All My Sins Remembered, There Is No Darkness* (written with his brother, SF writer Jack C. Haldeman II), *Worlds, Worlds Apart, Worlds Enough and Time, Buying Time,* and the "techno-thriller" *Tool of the Trade,* the collections *Infinite Dreams, Dealing in Futures, Vietnam and Other Alien Worlds,* and *None So Blind,* and, as editor, the anthologies *Study War No More, Cosmic Laughter,* and *Nebula Award Stories Seventeen.* His most recent book is the novel *Forever Peace,* which won him a new Hugo Award in 1998 and a new Nebula Award in 1999. Coming up is a new novel, *Forever Free,* the direct sequel to *The Forever War.* Haldeman lives part of the year in Boston, where he teaches writing at the Massachusetts Institute of Technology, and the rest of the year in Florida, where he and his wife, Gay, make their home.

His name is Three-phasing and he is bald and wrinkled, slightly over one meter tall, large-eyed, toothless and all bones and skin, sagging pale skin shot through with traceries of delicate blue and red. He is considered very beautiful but most of his beauty is in his hands and is due to his extreme youth. He is over two hundred years old and is learning how to talk. He has become reasonably fluent in sixty-three languages, all dead ones, and has only ten to go.

The book he is reading is a facsimile of an early edition of Goethe's *Faust*. The nervous angular Fraktur letters goose-step across pages of paper-thin platinum.

The *Faust* had been printed electrolytically and, with several thousand similarly worthwhile books, sealed in an argon-filled chamber and carefully lost, in 2012 A.D.; a very wealthy man's legacy to the distant future.

In 2012 A.D., Polaris had been the pole star. Men eventually got to Polaris and built a small city on a frosty planet there. By that time, they weren't dating by prophets' births any more, but it would have been around 4900 A.D. The pole star by then, because of procession of the equinoxes, was a dim thing once called Gamma Cephei. The celestial pole kept reeling around, past Deneb and Vega and through barren patches of sky around Hercules and Draco; a patient clock but not the slowest one of use, and when it came back to the region of Polaris, then 26,000 years had passed and men had come back from the stars, and the book-filled chamber had shifted 130 meters on the floor of the Pacific, had rolled onto the shallow trench, and eventually was buried in an underwater landslide.

The thirty-seventh time this slow clock ticked, men had moved the Pacific, not because they had to, and had found the chamber, opened it up, identified the books and carefully sealed them up again. Some things by then were more important to men than the accumulation of knowledge: in half of one more circle of the poles would come the millionth anniversary of the written word. They could wait a few millennia.

As the anniversary, as nearly as they could reckon it, approached, they caused to be born two individuals: Nine-hover (nominally female) and Three-phasing (nominally male). Three-phasing was born to learn how to read and speak. He was the first human being to study these skills in more than a quarter of a million years.

Three-phasing has read the first half of *Faust* forwards and, for amusement and exercise, is reading the second half backwards. He is singing as he reads, lisping.

"Fain' Looee w'mun . . . wif all'r die-mun ringf . . ." He has not put in his teeth because they make his gums hurt.

Because he is a child of two hundred, he is polite when his father interrupts his reading and singing. His father's "voice" is an arrangement of logic and aesthetic that appears in Three-phasing's mind. The flavor is lost by translating into words:

"Three-phasing my son-ly atavism of tooth and vocal cord," sarcastically in the reverent mode, "Couldst tear thyself from objects of manifest symbol, and visit to share/help/learn, me?"

"?" He responds, meaning, "with/with/of what?"

Withholding mode: "Concerning thee: past, future."

He shuts the book without marking his place. It would never occur to him to mark his place, since he remembers perfectly the page he stops on, as well as every word preceding, as well as every event, no matter how trivial, that he has observed from the precise age of one year. In this respect, at least, he is normal.

He thinks the proper coordinates as he steps over the mover-transom, through a microsecond of black, and onto his father's mover-transom, about four thousand kilometers away on a straight line through the crust and mantle of the earth.

Ritual mode: "As ever, father." The symbol he uses for "father" is purposefully wrong, chiding. Crude biological connotation.

His father looks cadaverous and has in fact been dead twice. In the infant's small-talk mode he asks "From crude babblings of what sort have I torn your interest?"

"The tale called *Faust*, of a man so named, never satisfied with {symbol for slow but continuous accretion} of his knowledge and power; written in the language of Prussia."

"Also depended-ing on this strange word of immediacy, your Prussian language?"

"As most, yes. The word of 'to be': *sein.* Very important illusion in this and related languages/cultures; that events happen at the 'time' of perception, infinitesimal midpoint between past and future."

"Convenient illusion but retarding."

"As we discussed 129 years ago, yes." Three-phasing is impatient to get back to his reading, but adds:

$$\text{"Obvious that to-be-ness} \left\{ \begin{array}{l} \text{same order of illusion as three-dimensionality of} \\ \text{external world.} \\ \\ \text{thrust upon observer by geometric limitation of} \\ \text{synaptic degrees of freedom.} \end{array} \right\} \text{''}$$

"You always stick up for them."

"I have great regard for what they accomplished with limited faculties and so short lives." Stop beatin' around the bush, Dad. *Tempis fugit*, eight to the bar. Did Mr. Handy Moves-dat-man-around-by-her-apron-strings, 20th-century American poet, intend cultural translation of *Lysistrata*? If so, inept. African were-beast legendary, yes.

Withholding mode (coy): "Your father stood with Nine-hover all morning."

"," broadcasts Three-phasing: well?

"The machine functions, perhaps inadequately."

The young polyglot tries to radiate calm patience.

"Details I perceive you want; the idea yet excites you. You can never have satisfaction with your knowledge, either. What happened-s to the man in your Prussian book?"

"He lived-s one hundred years and died-s knowing that a man can never achieve true happiness, despite the appearance of success."

"For an infant, a reasonable perception."

Respectful chiding mode: "One hundred years makes-ed Faust a very old man, for a Dawn man."

"As I stand," same mode, less respect, "yet an infant." They trade silent symbols of laughter.

After a polite tenth-second interval, Three-phasing uses the light interrogation mode: "The machine of Nine-hover . . . ?"

"It begins to work but so far not perfectly." This is not news.

Mild impatience: "As before, then, it brings back only rocks and earth and water and plants?"

"Negative, beloved atavism." Offhand. "This morning she caught two animals that look as man may once have looked.

"!" Strong impatience, "I go?"

"." His father ends the conversation just two seconds after it began.

Three-phasing stops off to pick up his teeth, then goes directly to Nine-hover.

A quick exchange of greeting-symbols and Nine-hover presents her prizes. "Thinking I have two different species," she stands: uncertainty, query.

Three-phasing is amused. "Negative, time-caster. The male and female took very dissimilar forms in the Dawn times." He touches one of them. "The round organs, here, served-ing to feed infants, in the female."

The female screams.

"She manipulates spoken symbols now," observes Nine-hover.

Before the woman has finished her startled yelp, Three-phasing explains: "Not manipulating concrete symbols; rather, she communicates in a way called 'non-verbal,' the use of such communication predating even speech." Slipping into the pedantic mode: "My reading indicates that such a loud noise occurs either

$$\left\{\begin{array}{l}\text{-following a stimu-}\\\text{lus under conditions of}\end{array}\right.$$

$$\begin{array}{l}\text{that produces pain}\\\text{extreme agitation}\end{array}\left\{\begin{array}{l}\text{since she seems not in pain, then}\end{array}\right.$$
she must fear me or you or both of us.

"Or the machine," Nine-hover adds.

Symbol for continuing. "We have no symbol for it but in Dawn days most humans observed 'xenophobia,' reacting to the strange with fear instead of delight. We stand as strange to them as they do to us, thus they register fear. In their era this attitude encouraged-s survival.

"Our silence must seem strange to them, as well as our appearance and the speed with which we move. I will attempt to speak to them, so they will know they need not fear us."

★ ★ ★

Bob and Sarah Graham were having a desperately good time. It was September of 1951 and the papers were full of news about the brilliant landing of U.S. Marines at Inchon. Bob was a Marine private with two days left of the thirty days' leave they had given him, between boot camp and disembarkation for Korea. Sarah had been Mrs. Graham for three weeks.

Sarah poured some more bourbon into her Coke. She wiped the sand off her thumb and stoppered the Coke bottle, then shook it gently. "What if you just don't show up?" she said softly.

Bob was staring out over the ocean and part of what Sarah said was lost in the crash of breakers rolling in. "What if I what?"

"Don't show up." She took a swig and offered the bottle. "Just stay here with me. With us." Sarah was sure she was pregnant. It was too early to tell, of course; her calendar was off but there could be other reasons.

He gave the Coke back to her and sipped directly from the bourbon bottle. "I suppose they'd go on without me. And I'd still be in jail when they came back."

"Not if—"

"Honey, don't even talk like that. It's a just cause."

She picked up a small shell and threw it toward the water.

"Besides, you read the *Examiner* yesterday."

"I'm cold. Let's go up." She stood and stretched and delicately brushed sand away. Bob admired her long naked dancer's body. He shook out the blanket and draped it over her shoulders.

"It'll be over by the time I get there. We'll push those bastards—"

"Let's not talk about Korea. Let's not talk."

He put his arm around her and they started walking back toward the cabin. Halfway there, she stopped and enfolded the blanket around both of them, drawing him toward her. He always closed his eyes when they kissed, but she always kept hers open. She saw it: the air turning luminous, the seascape fading to be replaced by bare metal walls. The sand turns hard under her feet.

At her sharp intake of breath, Bob opens his eyes. He sees a grotesque dwarf, eyes and skull too large, body small and wrinkled. They stare at one another for a fraction of a second. Then the dwarf spins around and speeds across the room to what looks like a black square painted on the floor. When he gets there, he disappears.

"What the hell?" Bob says in a hoarse whisper.

Sarah turns around just a bit too late to catch a glimpse of Three-phasing's father. She does see Nine-hover before Bob does. The nominally-female time-caster is a flurry of movement, sitting at the console of her time net, clicking switches and adjusting various dials. All of the motions are unnecessary, as is the console. It was built at Three-phasing's suggestion, since humans from the era into which they could cast would feel more comfortable in the presence of a machine that looked like a machine. The actual time net was roughly the size and shape of an asparagus stalk, was controlled completely by thought, and had no moving parts. It does not exist any more, but can still be used, once understood. Nine-hover has been trained from birth for this special understanding.

Sarah nudges Bob and points to Nine-hover. She can't find her voice; Bob stares open-mouthed.

In a few seconds, Three-phasing appears. He looks at Nine-hover for a moment, then scurries over to the Dawn couple and reaches up to touch Sarah on the left nipple. His body temperature is considerably higher than hers, and the unexpected warm moistness, as much as the suddenness of the motion, makes her jump back and squeal.

Three-phasing correctly classified both Dawn people as Caucasian, and so assumes that they speak some Indo-European language.

"*GuttenTagsprechensieDeutsch?*" he says in rapid soprano.

"Huh?" Bob says.

"Guten-Tag-sprechen-sie-Deutsch?" Three-phasing clears his throat and drops his voice down to the alto he uses to sing about the St. Louis woman. *"Guten Tag,"* he says, counting to a hundred between each word. *"Sprechen sie Deutsch?"*

"That's Kraut," says Bob, having grown up on jingoistic comic books. "Don't tell me you're a—"

Three-phasing analyzes the first five words and knows that Bob is an American from the period 1935–1955. "Yes, yes—and no, no—to wit, how very very clever of you to have identified this phrase as having come from the language of Prussia, Germany as you say; but I am, no, not a German person; at least, I no more belong to the German nationality than I do to any other, but I suppose that is not too clear and perhaps I should fully elucidate the particulars of your own situation at this, as you say, 'time,' and 'place.' "

The last English-language author Three-phasing studied was Henry James.

"Huh?" Bob says again.

"Ah. I should simplify." He thinks for a half-second, and drops his voice down another third. "Yeah, simple. Listen, Mac. First thing I gotta know's whatcher name. Whatcher broad's name."

"Well . . . I'm Bob Graham. This is my wife, Sarah Graham."

"Pleasta meetcha, Bob. Likewise, Sarah. Call me, uh . . ." The only twentieth-century language in which Three-phasing's name makes sense is propositional calculus. "George. George Boole."

"I 'poligize for bumpin' into ya, Sarah. That broad in the corner, she don't know what a tit is, so I was just usin' one of yours. Uh, lack of immediate culchural perspective, I shoulda knowed better."

Sarah feels a little dizzy, shakes her head slowly. "That's all right. I know you didn't mean anything by it."

"I'm dreaming," Bob says. "Shouldn't have—"

"No you aren't," says Three-phasing, adjusting his diction again. "You're in the future. Almost a million years. Pardon me." He scurries to the mover-transom, is gone for a second, reappears with a bedsheet, which he hands to Bob. "I'm sorry, we don't wear clothing. This is the best I can do, for now." The bedsheet is too small for Bob to wear the way Sarah is using the blanket. He folds it over and tucks it around his waist, in a kilt. "Why us?" he asks.

"You were taken at random. We've been time casting"—he checks with Nine-hover—"for twenty-two years, and have never before caught a human being. Let alone two. You must have been in close contact with one another when you intersected the time-caster beam. I assume you were copulating."

"What-ing?" Bob says.

"No, we weren't!" Sarah says indignantly.

"Ah, quite so." Three-phasing doesn't pursue the topic. He knows the humans of this culture were reticent about their sexual activity. But from their literature he knows they spent most of their "time" thinking about, arranging for, enjoying and recovering from a variety of sexual contacts.

"Then that must be a time machine over there," Bob says, indicating the fake console.

"In a sense, yes." Three-phasing decides to be partly honest. "But the actual machine no longer exists. People did a lot of time-traveling about a quarter of a million years ago. Shuffled history around. Changed it back. The fact that the machine once existed, well, that enables us to use it, if you see what I mean."

"Uh, no. I don't." Not with synapses limited to three degrees of freedom.

"Well, never mind. It's not really important." He senses the next question. "You will be going back . . . I don't know exactly when. It depends on a lot of things. You see, time is like a rubber band." No, it isn't. "Or a spring." No, it isn't. "At any rate, within a few days, weeks at most, you will leave this present and return to the moment you were experiencing when the time-caster beam picked you up."

"I've read stories like that," Sarah says. "Will we remember the future, after we go back?"

"Probably not," he says charitably. Not until your brains evolve. "But you can do us a great service."

Bob shrugs. "Sure, long as we're here. Anyhow, you did us a favor." He puts his arm around Sarah. "I've gotta leave Sarah in a couple of days; don't know for how long. So you're giving us more time together."

"Whether we remember it or not," Sarah says.

"Good, fine. Come with me." They follow Three-phasing to the mover-transom, where he takes their hands and transports them to his home. It is as unadorned as the time-caster room, except for bookshelves along one wall, and a low podium upon which the volume of *Faust* rests. All of the books are bound identically, in shiny metal with flat black letters along the spines.

Bob looks around. "Don't you people ever sit down?"

"Oh," Three-phasing says. "Thoughtless of me." With his mind he shifts the room from utility mood to comfort mood. Intricate tapestries now hang on the walls; soft cushions that look like silk are strewn around in pleasant disorder. Chiming music, not quite discordant, hovers at the edge of audibility, and there is a faint odor of something like jasmine. The metal floor has become a kind of soft leather, and the room has somehow lost its corners.

"How did that happen?" Sarah asks.

"I don't know." Three-phasing tries to copy Bob's shrug, but only manages a spasmodic jerk. "Can't remember not being able to do it."

Bob drops into a cushion and experimentally pushes at the floor with a finger. "What is it you want us to do?"

Trying to move slowly, Three-phasing lowers himself into a cushion and gestures at a nearby one, for Sarah. "It's very simple, really. Your being here is most of it.

"We're celebrating the millionth anniversary of the written word." How to phrase it? "Everyone is interested in this anniversary, but . . . nobody reads any more."

Bob nods sympathetically. "Never have time for it myself."

"Yes, uh . . . you *do* know how to read, though?"

"He knows," Sarah says. "He's just lazy."

"Well, yeah." Bob shifts uncomfortably in the cushion. "Sarah's the one you want. I kind of, uh, prefer to listen to the radio."

"I read all the time," Sarah says with a little pride. "Mostly mysteries. But sometimes I read good books, too."

"Good, good." It was indeed fortunate to have found this pair, Three-phasing realizes. They had used the metal of the ancient books to "tune" the time-caster, so potential subjects were limited to those living some eighty years before and after 2012 A.D. Internal evidence in the books indicated that most of the Earth's population was illiterate during this period.

"Allow me to explain. Any one of us can learn how to read. But to us it is like a code; an unnatural way of communicating. Because we are all natural telepaths. We can reach each other's minds from the age of one year."

"Golly!" Sarah says. "Read minds?" And Three-pushing sees in her mind a fuzzy kind of longing, much of which is love for Bob and frustration that she knows him only imperfectly. He dips into Bob's mind and finds things she is better off not knowing.

"That's right. So what we want is for you to read some of these books, and allow us to go into your minds while you're doing it. This way we will be able to recapture an experience that has been lost to the race for over a half-million years."

"I don't know," Bob says slowly. "Will we have time for anything else? I mean, the world must be pretty strange. Like to see some of it."

"Of course; sure. But the rest of the world is pretty much like my place here. Nobody goes outside any more. There isn't any air." He doesn't want to tell them how the air was lost, which might disturb them, but they seem to accept that as part of distant future.

"Uh, George." Sarah is blushing. "We'd also like, uh, some time to ourselves. Without anybody . . . inside our minds."

"Yes, I understand perfectly. You will have your own room, and plenty of time to yourselves." Three-phasing neglects to say that there is no such thing as privacy in a telepathic society.

But sex is another thing they don't have any more. They're almost as curious about that as they are about books.

So the kindly men of the future gave Bob and Sarah Graham plenty of time to themselves: Bob and Sarah reciprocated. Through the Dawn couple's eyes and brains, humanity shared again the visions of Fielding and Melville and Dickens and Shakespeare and almost a dozen others. And as for the 98% more, that they didn't have time to read or that were in foreign languages—Three-phasing got the hang of it and would spend several millennia entertaining those who were amused by this central illusion of literature: that there could be order, that there could be beginnings and endings and logical workings-out in between; that you could count on the third act or the last chapter to tie things up. They knew how profound an illusion this was because each of them knew every other living human with an intimacy and accuracy far superior to that which even Shakespeare could bring to the study of even himself. And as for Sarah and as for Bob:

Anxiety can throw a person's ovaries way off schedule. On that beach in California, Sarah was no more pregnant than Bob was. But up there in the future, some somatic tension finally built up to the breaking point, and an egg went sliding down the left Fallopian tube, to be met by a wiggling intruder approximately halfway; together they were the first manifestation of organism that nine months later, or a million years earlier, would be christened Douglas MacArthur Graham.

This made a problem for time, or Time, which is neither like a rubber band nor like a spring; nor even like a river nor a carrier wave—but which, like all of these things, can be deformed by certain stresses. For instance, two people going into the future and three coming back on the same time-casting beam.

In an earlier age, when time travel was more common, time-casters would have made sure that the baby, or at least its aborted embryo, would stay in the future when the mother returned to her present. Or they could arrange for the mother to stay in the future. But these subtleties had long been forgotten when Nine-hover relearned the dead art. So Sarah went back to her present with a hitch-hiker, an interloper, firmly imbedded in the lining of her womb. And its dim sense of life set up a kind of eddy in the flow of time, that Sarah had to share.

The mathematical explanation is subtle, and can't be comprehended by those of us who synapse with fewer than four degrees of freedom. But the end effect is clear: Sarah had to experience all of her own life backwards, all the way back to that embrace on the beach. Some highlights were:

In 1992, slowly dying of cancer, in a mental hospital.

In 1979, seeing Bob finally succeed in suicide on the American Plan, not quite finishing his 9,527th bottle of liquor.

In 1970, having her only son returned in a sealed casket from a country she'd never heard of.

In the 1960's, helplessly watching her son become more and more neurotic because of something that no one could name.

In 1953, Bob coming home with one foot, the other having been lost to frost-bite; never having fired a shot in anger.

In 1952, the agonizing breech presentation.

Like her son, Sarah would remember no details of the backward voyage through her life. But the scars of it would haunt her forever.

They were kissing on the beach.

Sarah dropped the blanket and made a little noise. She started crying and slapped Bob as hard as she could, then ran on alone, up to the cabin.

Bob watched her progress up the hill with mixed feelings. He took a healthy slug from the bourbon bottle, to give him an excuse to wipe his own eyes.

He could go sit on the beach and finish the bottle; let her get over it by herself. Or he could go comfort her.

He tossed the bottle away, the gesture immediately making him feel stupid, and followed her. Later that night she apologized, saying she didn't know what had gotten into her.

Slow Music

JAMES TIPTREE, JR.

As most of you probably know by now, multiple Hugo- and Nebula-winning author James Tiptree, Jr.—at one time a figure reclusive and mysterious enough to be regarded as the B. Traven of science fiction—was actually the late Dr. Alice Sheldon, a semiretired experimental psychologist who also wrote occasionally under the name of Raccoona Sheldon. Dr. Sheldon's tragic death in 1987 put an end to "both" authors' careers, but, before that, she had won two Nebula and two Hugo Awards as Tiptree, won another Nebula Award as Raccoona Sheldon, and established herself, under whatever name, as one of the best writers in science fiction.

Although "Tiptree" published two reasonably well-received novels—*Up the Walls of the World* and *Brightness Falls from the Air*—she was, like Damon Knight and Theodore Sturgeon (two writers she aesthetically resembled and by whom she was strongly influenced), more comfortable with the short story and more effective with it. She wrote some of the very best short stories of the seventies: "The Screwfly Solution," "The Girl Who Was Plugged In," "The Women Men Don't See," "Beam Us Home," "And I Awoke and Found Me Here on the Cold Hill's Side," "I'm Too Big but I Love to Play," and "His Smoke Rose Up Forever." Already it's clear that these are stories that will last. They—and a dozen others almost as good—show that Alice Sheldon was simply one of the best short-story writers to work in the genre in our times.

Here, in one of her few ventures into the far future, she shows us a melancholy vision of the end of the human race as we know it, as humanity is seduced into abandoning corporeal existence and merging into a metaphysical alien River that sweeps them away from the Earth forever . . . except for those few people who choose to remain *behind*. . . .

As James Tiptree, Jr., Alice Sheldon also published nine short-story collections: *Ten Thousand Light Years from Home, Warm Worlds and Otherwise, Starsongs of an Old Primate, Out of the Everywhere, Tales of the Quintana Roo, Byte Beautiful, The Starry Rift,* the posthumously published *Crown of Stars,* and the retrospective collection *Her Smoke Rose Up Forever.*

Caoilte tossing his burning hair
And Niamh calling "Away, come away;
Empty your heart of its mortal dream.
. . . We come between man and the deed of his hand,
We come between him and the hope of his heart."

—W. B. Yeats

Lights came on as Jakko walked down the lawn past the house; elegantly concealed spots and floods which made the night into a great intimate room. Overhead the big conifers formed a furry nave drooping toward the black lake below the bluff ahead. This had been a beloved home, he saw; every luxurious device was subdued to preserve the beauty of the forested shore. He walked on a carpet of violets and mosses, in his hand the map that had guided him here from the city.

It was the stillness before dawn. A long-winged night bird swirled in to catch a last moth in the dome of light. Before him shone a bright spearpoint. Jakko saw it was the phosphorescent tip of a mast against the stars. He went down velvety steps to find a small sailboat floating at the dock like a silver leaf reflected on a dark mirror.

In silence he stepped on board, touched the mast.

A gossamer sail spread its fan, the mooring parted soundlessly. The dawn breeze barely filled the sail, but the craft moved smoothly out, leaving a glassy line of wake. Jakko half-poised to jump; he knew nothing of such playtoys, he should go back and find another boat. As he did so, the shore lights went out, leaving him in darkness. He turned and saw Regulus rising ahead where the channel must be. Still, this was not the craft for him. He tugged at the tiller and sail, meaning to turn it back.

But the little boat ran smoothly on, and then he noticed the lights of a small computer glowing by the mast. He relaxed; this was no toy, the boat was fully programmed and he could guess what the course must be. He stood examining the sky, a statue-man gliding across reflected night.

The eastern horizon changed, veiled its stars as he neared it. He could see the channel now, a silvery cut straight ahead between dark banks. The boat ran over glittering shallows where something splashed hugely, and headed into the shining lane. As it did so, all silver changed to lead and the stars were gone. Day was coming. A great pearl-colored blush spread upward before him, developed bands of lavender and rays of coral-gold fire melting to green iridescence overhead. The boat was now gliding on a ribbon of fiery light between black silhouetted banks. Jakko looked back and saw dazzling cloud-cities heaped behind him in the west. The vast imminence of sunrise. He sighed aloud.

He understood that all this demonstration of glory was nothing but the effects of dust and vapor in the thin skin of air around a small planet, whereon he crawled wingless. No vastness brooded; the planet was merely turning with him into the rays of its mediocre primary. His family, everyone, knew that on the River he would encounter the galaxy itself in glory. Suns beyond count, magnificence to which this was nothing. And yet—and yet to him this was not nothing. It was intimately his, man-sized. He made an ambiguous sound in his throat. He resented the trivialization of this beauty, and he resented being moved by it. So he passed along, idly holding the sailrope like a man leashing the living wind, his face troubled and very young.

The little craft ran on unerringly, threading the winding sheen of the canal. As the sun rose, Jakko began to hear a faint drone ahead. The sea surf. He thought of the persons who must have made this voyage before him: the ship's family, savoring their final days of mortality. A happy voyage, a picnic. The thought reminded him that he was hungry; the last ground-car's synthesizer had been faulty.

He tied the rope and searched. The boat had replenished its water, but there was only one food-bar. Jakko lay down in the cushioned well and ate and drank comfortably, while the sky turned turquoise and then cobalt. Presently they emerged into an enormous lagoon and began to run south between low islands. Jakko trailed his hand and tasted brackish salt. When the boat turned east again and made for a seaward opening, he became doubly certain. The craft was programmed for the River, like almost everything else on the world he knew.

Sure enough, the tiny bark ran through an inlet and straight out into the chop beyond a long beach, extruded outriggers, and passed like a cork over the reef-foam onto the deep green swells beyond. Here it pitched once and steadied; Jakko guessed it had thrust down a keel. Then it turned south and began to run along outside the reef, steady as a knife-cut with the wind on its quarter. Going Riverward for sure. The nearest River-place was here called Vidalita or Beata, or sometimes Falaz, meaning Illusion. It was far south and inland. Jakko guessed they were making for a landing where a moveway met the sea. He had still time to think, to struggle with the trouble under his mind.

But as the sun turned the boat into a trim white-gold bird flying over green transparency, Jakko's eyes closed and he slept, protected by invisible deflecters from the bow-spray. Once he opened his eyes and saw a painted fish tearing along magically in the standing wave below his head. He smiled and slept again, dreaming of a great wave dying, a wave that was a many-headed beast. His face became sad and his lips moved soundlessly, as if repeating, "No . . . no . . ."

When he woke they were sailing quite close by a long bluff on his right. In the cliff ahead was a big white building or tower, only a little ruined. Suddenly he caught sight of a figure moving on the beach before it. A living human? He jumped up to look. He had not seen a strange human person in many years.

Yes—it was a live person, strangely colored gold and black. He waved wildly.

The person on the beach slowly raised an arm.

Alight with excitement, Jakko switched off the computer and grabbed the rudder and sail. The line of reef-surf seemed open here. He turned the boat shoreward, riding on a big swell. But the wave left him. He veered erratically, and the surf behind broached into the boat, overturning it and throwing him out. He knew how to swim; he surfaced and struck out strongly for the shore, spluttering brine. Presently he was wading out onto the white beach, a short, strongly-built, reddened young male person with pale hair and water-blue eyes.

The stranger was walking hesitantly toward him. Jakko saw it was a thin, dark-skinned girl wearing a curious netted hat. Her body was wrapped in orange silk and she carried heavy gloves in one hand. Three nervous moondogs followed her. He began turning water out of his shorts pockets as she came up.

"Your . . . boat," she said in the language of that time. Her voice was low and uncertain.

They both turned to look at the confused place by the reef where the sailboat floated half-submerged.

"I turned it off. The computer." His words came jerkily, too, they were both unused to speech.

"It will come ashore down there." She pointed, still studying him in a wary, preoccupied way. She was much smaller than he. "Why did you turn? Aren't you going to the River?"

"No." He coughed. "Well, yes, in a way. My father wants me to say good-bye. They left while I was traveling."

"You're not . . . ready?"

"No. I don't—" He broke off. "Are you staying alone here?"

"Yes. I'm not going either."

They stood awkwardly in the sea-wind. Jakko noticed that the three moondogs were lined up single file, tiptoeing upwind toward him with their eyes closed, sniffing. They were not, of course, from the moon, but they looked it, being white and oddly shaped.

"It's a treat for them," the girl said. "Something different." Her voice was stronger now. After a pause she added, "You can stay here for a while if you want. I'll show you but I have to finish my work first."

"Thank you," he remembered to say.

As they climbed steps cut in the bluff Jakko asked, "What are you working at?"

"Oh, everything. Right now it's bees."

"Bees!" he marveled. "They made what—honey? I thought they were all gone."

"I have a lot of old things." She kept glancing at him intently as they climbed. "Are you quite healthy?"

"Oh yes. Why not? I'm all alpha so far as I know. Everybody is."

"Was," she corrected. "Here are my bee skeps."

They came around a low wall and stopped by five small wicker huts. A buzzing insect whizzed by Jakko's face, coming from some feathery shrubs. He saw that the bloom-tipped foliage was alive with the golden humming things. Recalling that they could sting, he stepped back.

"You better go around the other way." She pointed. "They might hurt a stranger." She pulled her veil down, hiding her face. Just as he turned away, she added, "I though you might impregnate me."

He wheeled back, not really able to react because of the distracting bees. "But isn't that terribly complicated?"

"I don't think so. I have the pills." She pulled on her gloves.

"Yes, the pills. I know." He frowned. "But you'd have to stay, I mean one just can't—"

"I know that. I have to do my bees now. We can talk later."

"Of course." He started away and suddenly turned back.

"Look!" He didn't know her name. "You, look!"

"What?" She was a strange little figure, black and orange with huge hands and a big veil-muffled head. "What?"

"I felt it. Just then, desire. Can't you see?"

They both gazed at his wet shorts.

"I guess not," he said finally. "But I felt it, I swear. Sexual desire."

She pushed back her veil, frowning. "It will stay, won't it? Or come back? This isn't a very good place, I mean, the bees. And it's no use without the pills."

"That's so."

He went away then, walking carefully because of the tension around his pubic bone. Like a keel, snug and tight. His whole body felt reorganized. It had been years since he'd felt flashes like that, not since he was fifteen at least. Most people never did. It was variously thought to be because of the River, or from their parents' surviving the Poison Centuries, or because the general alpha strain was so forebrain dominant. It gave him an archaic, secret pride. Maybe he was a throwback.

He passed under cool archways, and found himself in a green, protected place behind the seaward wall. A garden, he saw, looking round surprised at clumps of large tied-up fruiting plants, peculiar trees with green balls at their tops, disorderly rows of rather unesthetic greenery. Tentatively he identified tomatoes, peppers, a feathery leaf which he thought had an edible root. A utilitarian planting. His uncle had once amused the family by doing something of the sort, but not on this scale. Jakko shook his head.

In the center of the garden stood a round stone coping with a primitive apparatus on top. He walked over and looked down. Water, a bucket on a rope. Then he saw that there was also an ordinary tap. He opened it and drank, looking at the odd implements leaning on the coping. Earth-tools. He did not really want to think about what the strange woman had said.

A shadow moved by his foot. The largest moondog had come quite close, inhaling dreamily. "Hello," he said to it. Some of these dogs could talk a little. This one opened its eyes wide but said nothing.

He stared about, wiping his mouth, feeling his clothes almost dry now in the hot sun. On three sides the garden was surrounded by arcades; above him the ruined side was a square cracked masonry tower with no roof. A large place, whatever it was. He walked into the shade of the nearest arcade, which turned out to be littered with a myriad disassembled or partly assembled objects: tools, containers, who knew what. Her "work"? The place felt strange, vibrant and busy. He realized he had entered only empty houses on his year-long journey. This one was alive, lived-in. Messy. It hummed like the bee skeps. He turned down a cool corridor, looking into rooms piled with more stuff. In one, three white animals he couldn't identify were asleep in a heap of cloth on a bed. They moved their ears at him like big pale shells but did not awaken.

He heard staccato noises and came out into another courtyard where plump birds walked with jerking heads. "Chickens!" he decided, delighted by the irrational variety of this place. He went from there into a large room with windows on the sea and heard a door close.

It was the woman, or girl, coming to him, holding her hat and gloves. Her hair was a dark curly cap, her head elegantly small; an effect he had always admired. He remembered something to say.

"I'm called Jakko. What's your name?"

"Jakko." She tasted the sound. "Hello, Jakko. I'm Peachthief." She smiled very briefly, entirely changing her face.

"Peachthief." On impulse he moved toward her, holding out his hands. She tucked her bundle under her arm and took both of his. They stood like that a moment, not quite looking at each other. Jakko felt excited. Not sexually, but more as if the air was electrically charged.

"Well." She took her hands away and began unwrapping a leafy wad. "I brought a honeycomb even if it isn't quite ready." She showed him a sticky looking frame with two dead bees on it. "Come on."

She walked rapidly out into another corridor and entered a shiny room he thought might be a laboratory.

"My food room," she told him. Again Jakko was amazed. There stood a synthesizer, to be sure, but beside it were shelves full of pots and bags and jars and containers of all descriptions. Unknown implements lay about and there was a fireplace which had been partly sealed up. Bunches of plant parts hung from racks overhead. He identified some brownish ovoids in a bowl as eggs. From the chickens?

Peachthief was cleaning the honeycomb with a manually operated knife. "I use the wax for my loom, and for candles. Light."

"What's wrong with the lights?"

"Nothing." She turned around, gesturing emphatically with the knife. "Don't you understand? All these machines, they'll go. They won't run forever. They'll break or wear out or run down. There *won't be* any, anymore. Then we'll have to use natural things."

"But that won't be for centuries!" he protested. "Decades, anyhow. They're all still going, they'll last for us."

"For you," she said scornfully. "Not for me. I intend to stay. With my children." She turned back on him and added in a friendlier voice, "Besides, the old things are esthetic. I'll show you, when it gets dark."

"But you haven't any children! Have you?" He was purely astonished.

"Not yet." Her back was still turned.

"I'm hungry," he said, and went to work the synthesizer. He made it give him a bar with a hard filler; for some reason he wanted to crunch it in his teeth.

She finished with the honey and turned around. "Have you ever had a natural meal?"

"Oh yes," he said, chewing. "One of my uncles tried that. It was very nice," he added politely.

She looked at him sharply and smiled again, on—off. They went out of the food room. The afternoon was fading into great gold and orange streamers above the courtyard, colored like Peachthief's garment.

"You can sleep here." She opened a slatted door. The room was small and bare, with a window on the sea.

"There isn't any bed," he objected.

She opened a chest and took out a big wad of string. "Hang this end on that hook over there."

When she hung up the other end he saw it was a large mesh hammock.

"That's what I sleep in. They're comfortable. Try it."

He climbed in awkwardly. The thing came up around him like a bag. She gave a short sweet laugh as brief as her smile.

"No, you lie on the diagonal. Like this." She tugged his legs, sending a peculiar shudder through him. "That straightens it, see?"

It would probably be all right, he decided, struggling out. Peachthief was pointing to a covered pail.

"That's for your wastes. It goes on the garden in the end."

He was appalled, but said nothing, letting her lead him out through a room with glass tanks in the walls to a big screened-in porch fronting the ocean. It was badly in need of cleaners. The sky was glorious with opalescent domes and spires, reflections of the sunset behind them, painting amazing colors on the sea.

"This is where I eat."

"What is this place?"

"It was a sea-station last, I think. Station Juliet. They monitored the fish and the ocean traffic, and rescued people and so on."

He was distracted by noticing long convergent dove-blue rays like mysterious paths into the horizon; cloud-shadows cast across the world. Beauty of the dust. Why must it move him so?

"—even a medical section," she was saying. "I really could have babies, I mean in case of trouble."

"You don't mean it." He felt only irritation now. "I don't feel any more desire," he told her.

She shrugged. "I don't, either. We'll talk about it later on."

"Have you always lived here?"

"Oh, no." She began taking pots and dishes out of an insulated case. The three moondogs had joined them silently; she set bowls before them. They lapped, stealing glances at Jakko. They were, he knew, very strong despite their stick-like appearance.

"Let's sit here." She plumped down on one end of the lounge and began biting forcefully into a crusty thing like a slab of drybar. He noticed she had magnificent teeth. Her dark skin set them off beautifully, as it enhanced her eyes. He had never met anyone so different in every way from himself and his family. He vacillated between interest and a vague alarm.

"Try some of the honey." She handed him a container and a spoon. It looked quite clean. He tasted it eagerly; honey was much spoken of in antique writings. At first he sensed nothing but a waxy sliding, but then an overpowering sweetness enveloped his tongue, quite unlike the sweets he was used to. It did not die away but seemed to run up his nose and almost into his ears, in a peculiar way. An *animal* food. He took some more, gingerly.

"I didn't offer you my bread. It needs some chemical, I don't know what. To make it lighter."

"Don't you have an access terminal?"

"Something's wrong with part of it," she said with her mouth full. "Maybe I don't work it right. We never had a big one like this, my tribe were travelers. They believed in sensory experiences." She nodded, licking her fingers. "They went to the River when I was fourteen."

"That's very young to be alone. My people waited till this year, my eighteenth birthday."

"I wasn't alone. I had two older cousins. But they wanted to take an aircar up north, to the part of the River called Rideout. I stayed here. I mean, we never stopped traveling, we never *lived* anywhere. I wanted to do like the plants, make roots."

"I could look at your program," he offered. "I've seen a lot of different models, I spent nearly a year in cities."

"What I need is a cow. Or a goat."

"Why?"

"For the milk. I need a pair, I guess."

Another animal thing; he winced a little. But it was pleasant, sitting here in the deep blue light beside her, hearing the surf plash quietly below.

"I saw quite a number of horses," he told her. "Don't they use milk?"

"I don't think horses are much good for milk." She sighed in an alert, busy way. He had the impression that her head was tremendously energetic, humming with plans and intentions. Suddenly she looked up and began making a high squeaky noise between her front teeth, "Sssswwt! Sssswwwt!"

Startled, he saw a white flying thing swooping above them, and then two more. They whirled so wildly he ducked.

"That's right," she said to them. "Get busy."

"What are they?"

"My bats. They eat mosquitoes and insects." She squeaked again and the biggest bat was suddenly clinging to her hand, licking honey. It had a small, fiercely complicated face.

Jakko relaxed again. This place and its strange inhabitant were giving him remarkable memories for the River, anyway. He noticed a faint glow moving where the dark sky joined the darker sea.

"What's that?"

"Oh, the seatrain. It goes to the River landing."

"Are there people on it?"

"Not anymore. Look, I'll show you." She jumped up and was opening a console in the corner, when a sweet computer voice spoke into the air.

"Seatrain Foxtrot Niner calling Station Juliet! Come in, Station Juliet!"

"It hasn't done that for years," Peachthief said. She tripped tumblers. "Seatrain, this is Station Juliet, I hear you. Do you have a problem?"

"Affirmative. Passenger is engaging in nonstandard activities. He-slash-she does not conform to parameters. Request instructions."

Peachthief thought a minute. Then she grinned. "Is your passenger moving on four legs?"

"Affirmative! Affirmative!" Seatrain Foxtrot sounded relieved.

"Supply it with bowls of meat-food and water on the floor and do not interfere with it. Juliet out."

She clicked off, and they watched the far web of lights go by on the horizon, carrying an animal.

"Probably a dog following the smell of people," Peachthief said. "I hope it gets off all right . . . We're quite a wide genetic spread," she went on in a different voice. "I mean, you're so light, and body-type and all."

"I noticed that."

"It would give good heterosis. Vigor."

She was talking about being impregnated, about the fantasy-child. He felt angry.

"Look, you don't know what you're saying. Don't you realize you'd have to stay and raise it for years? You'd be ethically and morally bound. And the River places are shrinking fast, you must know that. Maybe you'd be too late."

"Yes," she said somberly. "Now it's sucked everybody out it's going. But I still mean to stay."

"But you'd hate it, even if there's still time. My mother hated it, toward the end. She felt she had begun to deteriorate energetically, that her life would be lessened. And me—what about me? I mean, I should stay too."

"You'd only have to stay a month. For my ovulation. The male parent isn't ethically bound."

"Yes, but I think that's wrong. My father stayed. He never said he minded it, but he must have."

"You only have to do a month," she said sullenly. "I thought you weren't going on the River right now."

"I'm not. I just don't want to feel bound, I want to travel. To see more of the world, first. After I say goodbye."

She made an angry sound. "You have no insight. You're going, all right. You just don't want to admit it. You're going just like Mungo and Ferrocil."

"Who are they?"

"People who came by. Males, like you. Mungo was last year, I guess. He had an aircar. He said he was going to stay, he talked and talked. But two days later he went right on again. To the River. Ferrocil was earlier, he was walking through. Until he stole my bicycle."

A sudden note of fury in her voice startled him; she seemed to have some peculiar primitive relation to her bicycle, to her *things*.

"Did you want them to impregnate you, too?" Jakko noticed an odd intensity in his own voice as well.

"Oh, I was thinking about it, with Mungo." Suddenly she turned on him, her eyes wide open in the dimness like white-ringed jewels. "Look! Once and for all, I'm not going! I'm alive, I'm a human woman. I am going to stay on this earth and do human things. I'm going to make young ones to carry on the race, even if I have to die here. You can go on out, you—you pitiful shadows!"

Her voice rang in the dark room, jarring him down to his sleeping marrow. He sat silent as though some deep buried bell had tolled.

She was breathing hard. Then she moved, and to his surprise a small live flame sprang up between her cupped hands, making the room a cave.

"That's a candle. That's me. Now go ahead, make fun like Mungo did."

"I'm not making fun," he said, shocked. "It's just that I don't know what to think. Maybe you're right. I really . . . I really don't want to go, in one way," he said haltingly. "I love this earth too. But it's all so fast. Let me . . ."

His voice trailed off.

"Tell me about your family," she said, quietly now.

"Oh, they studied. They tried every access you can imagine. Ancient languages, history, lore. My aunt made poems in English . . . The layers of the earth, the names of body cells and tissues, jewels, everything. Especially stars. They made us memorize star maps. So we'll know where we are, you know, for a while. At least the earth-names. My father kept saying, when you go on the River you can't come back and look anything up. All you have is what you remember. Of course you could ask others, but there'll be so much more, so much new . . ."

He fell silent, wondering for the millionth time; is it possible that I shall go out forever between the stars, in the great streaming company of strange sentiences?

"How many children were in your tribe?" Peachthief was asking.

"Six. I was the youngest."

"The others all went on the River?"

"I don't know. When I came back from the cities the whole family had gone on, but maybe they'll wait a while too. My father left a letter asking me to come and say good-bye, and to bring him anything new I learned. They say you go slowly, you know. If I hurry there'll still be enough of his mind left there to tell him what I saw."

"What did you see? We were at a city once," Peachthief said dreamily. "But I was too young, I don't remember anything but people."

"The people are all gone now. Empty, every one. But everything works, the lights change, the moveways run. I didn't believe everybody was gone until I checked the central control offices. Oh, there were so many wonderful devices." He sighed. "The beauty, the complexity. Fantastic what people made." He sighed again, thinking of the wonderful technology, the creations abandoned, running down. "One strange thing. In the biggest city I saw, old Chio, almost every entertainment-screen had the same tape running."

"What was it?"

"A girl, a young girl with long hair. Almost to her feet, I've never seen such hair. She was laying it out on a sort of table, with her head down. But no sound, I think the audio was broken. Then she poured a liquid all over very slowly. And then she lit it, she set fire to herself. It flamed and exploded and burned her all up. I think it was real." He shuddered. "I could see inside her mouth, her tongue going all black and twisted. It was horrible. Running over and over, everywhere. Stuck."

She made a revolted sound. "So you want to tell that to your father, to his ghost, or whatever?"

"Yes. It's all new data, it could be important."

"Oh yes," she said scornfully. Then she grinned at him. "What about me? Am I new data too? A woman who isn't going to the River? A woman who is going to stay here and make babies? Maybe I'm the last."

"That's very important," he said slowly, feeling a deep confusion in his gut. "But I can't believe it, I mean, you—"

"I mean it." She spoke with infinite conviction. "I'm going to live here and have babies by you or some other man if you won't stay, and teach them to live on the earth naturally."

Suddenly he believed her. A totally new emotion was rising up in him, carrying with it sunrises and nameless bonds with earth that hurt in a painless way, as thought a rusted door was opening within him. Maybe this was what he had been groping for.

"I think—I think maybe I'll help you. Maybe I'll stay with you, for a while at least. Our—our children."

"You'll stay a month?" she asked wonderingly. "Really?"

"No, I mean I could stay longer. To make more and see them and help raise them, like my father did. After I come back from saying good-bye I'll really stay."

Her face changed. She bent to him and took his face between her slim dark hands.

"Jakko, listen. If you go to the River you'll never come back. No one ever does. I'll never see you again. We have to do it now, before you go."

"But a month is too long!" he protested. "My father's mind won't be there, I'm already terribly late."

She glared into his eyes a minute and then released him, stepping back with her brief sweet laugh. "Yes, and it's already late for bed. Come on."

She led him back to the room, carrying the candle, and he marveled anew at the clutter of strange activities she had assembled. "What's that?"

"My weaving-room." Yawning, she reached in and held up a small, rough-looking cloth. "I made this."

It was ugly, he thought; ugly and pathetic. Why make such useless things? But he was too tired to argue.

She left him to cleanse himself perfunctorily by the well in the moonlit court-yard, after showing him another waste-place right in the garden. Other peoples' wastes smell bad, he noticed sleepily. Maybe that was the cause of all the ancient wars.

In his room he tumbled into his hammock and fell asleep instantly. His dreams that night were chaotic; crowds, storms, jostling and echoing through strange dimensions. His last image was of a great whirlwind that bore in its forehead a jewel that was a sleeping woman, curled like an embryo.

He waked in the pink light of dawn to find her brown face bending over him, smiling impishly. He had the impression she had been watching him, and jumped quickly out of the hammock.

"Lazy," she said. "I've found the sailboat. Hurry up and eat."

She handed him a wooden plate of bright natural fruits and led him out into the sunrise garden.

When they got down to the beach she led him south, and there was the little craft sliding to and fro, overturned in the shallows amid its tangle of sail. The keel was still protruding. They furled the sail in clumsily and towed it out to deeper water to right it.

"I want this for the children," Peachthief kept repeating excitedly. "They can get fish, too. Oh, how they'll love it!"

"Stand your weight in the keel and grab the siderail," Jakko told her, doing the same. He noticed that her silks had come loose from her breasts, which were high and wide-pointed, quite unlike those of his tribe. The sight distracted him, his thighs felt unwieldy, and he missed his handhold as the craft righted itself and ducked him. When he came up he saw Peachthief scrambling aboard like a cat, clinging tight to the mast.

"The sail! Pull the sail up!" he shouted, and got another faceful of water. But she had heard him, the sail was trembling open like a great wing, silhouetting her shining slim dark body. For the first time Jakko noticed the boat's name, on the stern: Gojack. He smiled. An omen.

Gojack was starting to move smoothly away, toward the reef.

"The rudder!" he bellowed. "Turn the rudder and come back."

Peachthief moved to the tiller and pulled at it; he could see her strain. But *Gojack* continued to move away from him into the wind, faster and faster toward the surf. He remembered she had been handling the mast where the computer was.

"Stop the computer! Turn it off, turn it off!"

She couldn't possibly hear him. Jakko saw her in frantic activity, wrenching at the tiller, grabbing ropes, trying physically to push down the sail. Then she seemed to notice the computer, but evidently could not decipher it. Meanwhile *Gojack* fled steadily on and out, resuming its interrupted journey to the River. Jakko realized with horror that she would soon be in dangerous water; the surf was thundering on coral-heads.

"Jump! Come back, jump off!" He was swimming after her as fast as he could, his progress agonizingly slow. He glimpsed her still wrestling with the boat, screaming something he couldn't hear.

"JUMP!"

And finally she did, but only to try jerking *Gojack* around by its mooring lines. The boat faltered and jibbed, but then went strongly on, towing the threshing girl.

"Let go! Let go!" A wave broke over his head.

When he could see again he found she had at last let go and was swimming aimlessly, watching *Gojack* crest the surf and wing away. At last she turned back toward shore, and Jakko swam to intercept her. He was gripped by an unknown emotion so strong it discoordinated him. As his feet touched bottom he realized it was rage.

She waded to him, her face contorted by weeping. "The children's boat," she wailed. "I lost the children's boat—"

"You're crazy," he shouted. "There aren't any children."

"I lost it—" She flung herself on his chest, crying. He thumped her back, her sides, repeating furiously, "Crazy! You're insane!"

She wailed louder, squirming against him, small and naked and frail. Suddenly he found himself flinging her down onto the wet sand, falling on top of her with his swollen sex crushed between their bellies. For a moment all was confusion, and then the shock of it sobered him. He raised to look under himself and Peach-thief stared too, round-eyed.

"Do you w-want to, now?"

In that instant he wanted nothing more than to thrust himself into her, but a sandy wavelet splashed over them and he was suddenly aware of chafing wet cloth and Peachthief gagging brine. The magic waned. He got awkwardly to his knees.

"I thought you were going to be drowned," he told her, angry again.

"I wanted it so, for—for them . . ." She was still crying softly, looking up desolately at him. He understood she wasn't really meaning just the sailboat. A feeling of inexorable involvement spread through him. This mad little being had created some kind of energy-vortex around her, into which he was being sucked along with animals, vegetables, chickens, crowds of unknown things: only *Gojack* had escaped her.

"I'll find it," she was muttering, wringing out her silks, staring beyond the reef at the tiny dwindling gleam. He looked down at her, so fanatic and so vulnerable, and his inner landscape tilted frighteningly, revealing some ancient-new dimension.

"I'll stay with you," he said hoarsely. He cleared his throat, hearing his voice shake. "I mean I'll really stay, I won't go the the River at all. We'll make the, our babies now."

She stared up at him open-mouthed. "But your father! You promised!"

"My father stayed," he said painfully. "It's—it's right, I think."

She came close and grabbed his arms in her small hands.

"Oh, Jakko! But no, listen—*I'll go with you.* We can start a baby as we go, I'm sure of that. Then you can talk to your father and keep your promise and I'll be there to make sure you come back!"

"But you'd be, you'd be pregnant!" he cried in alarm. "You'd be in danger of taking an embryo on the River!"

She laughed proudly. "Can't you get it through your head that I will *not* go on the River? I'll just watch you and pull you out. I'll see you get back here. For a while, anyway," she added soberly. Then she brightened. "Hey, we'll see all kinds of things. Maybe I can find a cow or some goats on the way! Yes, yes! It's a perfect idea."

She faced him, glowing. Tentatively she brought her lips up to his, and they kissed inexpertly, tasting salt. He felt no desire, but only some deep resonance, like a confirmation in the earth. The three moondogs were watching mournfully.

"Now let's eat!" she began towing him toward the cliff-steps. "We can start the pills right now. "Oh, I have so much to do! But I'll fix everything, we'll leave tomorrow."

She was like a whirlwind. In the foodroom she pounced on a small gold-colored pillbox and opened it to show a mound of glowing green and red capsules.

"The red ones with the male symbol are for you."

She took a green one, and they swallowed solemnly, sharing a water-mug. He noticed that the seal on the box had been broken, and thought of that stranger, Mungo, she had mentioned. How far had her plans gone with him? An unpleasant emotion he had never felt before rose in Jakko's stomach. He sensed that he was heading into more dubious realms of experience than he had quite contemplated, and took his foodbar and walked away through the arcades to cool down.

When he came upon her again she seemed to be incredibly busy, folding and filling and wrapping things, closing windows and tying doors open. Her intense relations with things again . . . He felt obscurely irritated and was pleased to have had a superior idea.

"We need a map," he told her. "Mine was in the boat."

"Oh, great idea. Look in the old control room, it's down those stairs. It's kind of scary." She began putting oil in her loom.

He went down a white ramp that became a tunnel stairway, and came finally through a heavily armored portal to a circular room deep inside the rock, dimly illumined by portholes sunk in long shafts. From here he could hear the hum of the station energy source. As his eyes adjusted he made out a bank of sensor screens and one big console standing alone. It seemed to have been smashed open; some kind of sealant had been poured over the works.

He had seen a place like this before; he understood at once that from here had been controlled terrible ancient weapons that flew. Probably they still stood waiting in their hidden holes behind the station. But the master control was long dead. As he approached the console he saw that someone had scratched in the cooling seal-ant. He could make out only the words, "—WAR NO MORE." Undoubtedly this was a shrine of the very old days.

He found a light switch that filled the place with cool glare and began exploring side alleys. Antique gear, suits, cupboards full of masks and crumbling packets he couldn't identify. Among them was something useful—two cloth containers to carry stuff on one's back, only a little mildewed. But where were the maps?

Finally he found one on the control-room wall, right where he had come in. Someone had updated it with scrawled notations. With a tremor he realized how very old this must be; it dated from before the Rivers had touched earth. He could hardly grasp it.

Studying it he saw that there was indeed a big landing-dock not far south, and from there a moveway ran inland about a hundred kilometers to an airpark. If Peachthief could walk twenty-five kilometers they could make the landing by evening, and if the cars were still running the rest would be quick. All the moveways he'd seen had live cars on them. From the airpark a dotted line ran southwest across mountains to a big red circle with a cross in it, marked "VIDA!" That would be the River. They would just have to hope something on the airpark would fly, otherwise it would be a long climb.

His compass was still on his belt. He memorized the directions and went back upstairs. The courtyard was already saffron under great sunset flags.

Peachthief was squatting by the well, apparently having a conference with her animals. Jakko noticed some more white creatures he hadn't seen before, who seemed to live in an open hutch. They had long pinkish ears and mobile noses. Rabbits, or hares perhaps?

Two of the strange white animals he had seen sleeping were now under a bench, chirruping irritably at Peachthief.

"My raccoons," she told Jakko. "They're mad because I woke them up too soon." She said something in a high voice Jakko didn't understand, and the biggest raccoon shook his head up and down in a supercilious way.

"The chickens will be all right," Peachthief said. "Lotor knows how to feed them, to get the eggs. And they can all work the water-lever." The other raccoon nodded crossly, too.

"The rabbits are a terrible problem." Peachthief frowned. "You just haven't much sense, Eusebia," she said fondly, stroking the doe. "I'll have to fix something."

The big raccoon was warbling at her, Jakko thought he caught the word "dog-g-g."

"He wants to know who will settle their disputes with the dogs," Peachthief reported. At this one of the moondogs came forward and said thickly, "We go-o." It was the first word Jakko had heard him speak.

"Oh, good!" Peachthief cried. "Well, that's that!" She bounced up and began pouring something from a bucket on a line of plants. The white raccoons ran off silently with a humping gait.

"I'm so glad you're coming, Tycho," she told the dog. "Especially if I have to come back alone with a baby inside. But they say you're very vigorous, at first anyway."

"You aren't coming back alone," Jakko told her. She smiled a brilliant, non-committal flash. He noticed she was dressed differently; her body didn't show so much, and she kept her gaze away from him in an almost timid way. But she became very excited when he showed her the backpacks.

"Oh, good. Now we won't have to roll the blankets around our waists. It gets cool at night, you know."

"Does it ever rain?"

"Not this time of year. What we mainly need is lighters and food and water. And a good knife each. Did you find the map?"

He showed it. "Can you walk, I mean really hike if we have to? Do you have shoes?"

"Oh yes. I walk a lot. Especially since Ferrocil stole my bike."

The venom in her tone amused him. The ferocity with which she provisioned her small habitat!

"Men build monuments, women build nests," he quoted from somewhere.

"I don't know what kind of monument Ferrocil built with my bicycle," she said tartly.

"You're a savage," he said, feeling a peculiar ache that came out as a chuckle.

"The race can use some savages. We better eat now and go to sleep so we can start early."

At supper in the sunset-filled porch they scarcely talked. Dreamily Jakko watched the white bats embroidering flight in the air. When he looked down at Peachthief he caught her gazing at him before she quickly lowered her eyes. It came to him that they might eat hundreds, thousands of meals here; maybe all his life. And there could be a child, children, running about. He had never seen small humans younger than himself. It was all too much to take in, unreal. He went back to watching the bats.

That night she accompanied him to his hammock and stood by, shy but stubborn, while he got settled. Then he suddenly felt her hands sliding on his body, toward his groin. At first he thought it was something clinical, but then he realized she meant sex. His blood began to pound.

"May I come in beside you? The hammock is quite strong."

"Yes," he said thickly, reaching for her arm.

But as her weight came in by him she said in a practical voice, "I have to start knotting a small hammock, first thing. Child-size."

It broke his mood.

"Look. I'm sorry, but I've changed my mind. You go on back to yours, we should get sleep now."

"All right." The weight lifted away.

With a peculiar mix of sadness and satisfaction he heard her light footsteps leaving him alone. That night he dreamed strange sensory crescendoes, a tumescent earth and air; a woman who lay with her smiling lips in pale green water, awaiting him, while thin black birds of sunrise stalked to the edge of the sea.

Next morning they ate by candles, and set out as the eastern sky was just turning rose-gray. The ancient white coral roadway was good walking. Peachthief swung right along beside him, her backpack riding smooth.

The moondogs pattered soberly behind. Jakko found himself absorbed in gazing at the brightening landscape. Jungle-covered hills rose away on their right, the sea lay below on their left, sheened and glittering with the coming sunrise. When a diamond chip of sun broke out of the horizon he almost shouted aloud for the brilliance of it; the palm trees beyond the road lit up like golden torches, the edges of every frond and stone were startling clear and jewellike. For a moment he wondered if he could have taken some hallucinogen.

They paced on steadily in a dream of growing light and heat. The day-wind came up, and torn white clouds began to blow over them, bringing momentary coolness. Their walking fell into the rhythm Jakko loved, broken only occasionally by crumbled places in the road. At such spots they would often be surprised to find the moondogs sitting waiting for them, having quietly left the road and circled ahead through the scrub on business of their own. Peachthief kept up sturdily, only once stopping to look back at the far white spark of Station Juliet, almost melted in the shimmering horizon.

"This is as far as I've gone south," she told him.

He drank some water and made her drink too, and they went on. The road began to wind, rising and falling gently. When he next glanced back the station was gone. The extraordinary luminous clarity of the world was still delighting him.

When noon came he judged they were well over halfway to the landing. They sat down on some rubble under the palms to eat and drink, and Peachthief fed the moondogs. Then she took out the fertility pillbox. They each took theirs in silence, oddly solemn. Then she grinned.

"I'll give you something for dessert."

She unhitched a crooked knife from her belt and went searching around in the rocks, to come back with a big yellow-brown palm nut. Jakko watched her attack it with rather alarming vigor; she husked it and then used a rock to drive the point home.

"Here." She handed it to him. "Drink out of that hole." He felt a sloshing inside; when he lifted it and drank it tasted hairy and gritty and nothing in particular. But sharp, too, like the day. Peachthief was methodically striking the thing around and around its middle. Suddenly it fell apart, revealing vividly white meat. She pried out a piece.

"Eat this. It's full of protein."

The nutmeat was sweet and sharply organic.

"This is a coconut!" he suddenly remembered.

"Yes. I won't starve, coming back."

He refused to argue, but only got up to go on. Peachthief holstered her knife and followed, munching on a coconut piece. They went on so in silence a long time, letting the rhythm carry them. Once when a lizard waddled across the road Peachthief said to the moondog at her heels, "Tycho, you'll have to learn to catch and eat those one day soon." The moondogs all looked dubiously at the lizard but said nothing. Jakko felt shocked and pushed the thought away.

They were now walking with the sun westering slowly to their right. A flight of big orange birds with blue beaks flapped squawking out of a roadside tree, where they were apparently building some structure. Cloud-shadows fled across the world, making blue and bronze reflections in the sea. Jakko still felt his sensory impressions almost painfully keen; a sunray made the surf-line into a chain of diamonds, and the translucent green of the near shallows below them seemed to enchant his eyes. Every vista ached with light, as if to utter some silent meaning.

He was walking in a trance, only aware that the road had been sound and level for some time, when Peachthief uttered a sharp cry.

"My bicycle! There's my bicycle!" She began to run; Jakko saw shiny metal sticking out of a narrow gulch in the roadway. When he came up to her she was pulling a machine out from beside the roadwall.

"The front wheel—Oh, he bent it! He must have been going too fast and wrecked it here. That Ferrocil! But I'll fix it, I'm sure I can fix it at the Station. I'll push it back with me on the way home."

While she was mourning her machine Jakko looked around and over the low coping of the roadwall. Sheer cliff down there, with the sun just touching a rocky beach below. Something was stuck among the rocks—a tangle of whitish sticks, cloth, a round thing. Feeling his stomach knot, Jakko stared down at it, unwillingly discovering that the round thing had eye-holes, a U-shaped open mouth, blowing strands of hair. He had never seen a dead body before, nobody had, but he had seen pictures of human bones. Shakenly he realized who this had to be: Ferrocil. He must have been thrown over the coping when he hit that crack. Now he was dead, long dead. He would never go on the River. All that had been in that head was perished, gone forever.

Scarcely knowing what he was doing, Jakko grabbed Peachthief by the shoulders, saying roughly, "Come on! Come on!" When she resisted, confusedly he took her by the arm and began forcibly pulling her away from where she might look down. Her flesh felt burning hot and vibrant, the whole world was blasting colors and sounds and smells at him. Images of dead Ferrocil mingled with the piercing scent of some flowers on the roadway. Suddenly an idea struck him; he stopped.

"Listen. Are you sure those pills aren't hallucinaids? I've only had two and everything feels crazy."

"Three," Peachthief said abstractedly. She took his hand and pressed it on her back. "Do that again, run your hand down my back."

Bewildered, he obeyed. As his hand passed her silk shirt onto her thin shorts he felt her body move under it in a way that made him jerk away.

"Feel? Did you feel it? The lordotic reflex," she said proudly. "Female sexuality. It's starting."

"What do you mean, three?"

"You had three pills. I gave you one that first night, in the honey."

"*What?* But—but—" He struggled to voice the enormity of her violation, pure fury welling up in him. Choking, he lifted his hand and struck her buttocks the hardest blow he could, sending her staggering. It was the first time he had ever struck a person. A moondog growled, but he didn't care.

"Don't you ever—never—play a trick like—" He yanked at her shoulders, meaning to slap her face. His hand clutched a breast instead, he saw her hair blowing like dead Ferrocil's. A frightening sense of mortality combined with pride surged through him, lighting a fire in his loins. The deadness of Ferrocil suddenly seemed violently exciting. He, Jakko, was alive! Ignoring all sanity he flung himself on Peachthief, bearing her down on the road among the flowers. As he struggled to tear open their shorts he was dimly aware that she was helping him. His engorged penis was all reality; he fought past obstructions and then was suddenly, crookedly *in* her, fierce pleasure building. It exploded through him and then had burst out into her vitals, leaving him spent.

Blinking, fighting for clarity, he raised himself up and off her body. She lay wide-legged and disheveled, sobbing or gasping in a strange way, but smiling too. Revulsion sent a sick taste in his throat.

"There's your baby," he said roughly. He found his canteen and drank. The three moondogs had retreated and were sitting in a row, staring solemnly.

"May I have some, please?" Her voice was very low; she sat up, began fixing her clothes. He passed her the water and they got up.

"It's sundown," she said. "Should we camp here?"

"No!" Savagely he started on, not caring that she had to run to catch up. Was this the way the ancients lived? Whirled by violent passions, indecent, uncaring? His doing sex so close to the poor dead person seemed unbelievable. And the world was still assaulting all his senses; when she stumbled against him he could feel again the thrilling pull of her flesh, and shuddered. They walked in silence awhile; he sensed that she was more tired than he, but he wanted only to get as far as possible away.

"I'm not taking any more of those pills," he broke silence at last.

"But you have to! It takes a month to be sure."

"I don't care."

"But, ohhh—"

He said nothing more. They were walking across a twilit headland now. Suddenly the road turned, and they came out above a great bay.

The waters below were crowded with boats of all kinds, bobbing emptily where they had been abandoned. Some still had lights that made faint jewels in the opalescent air. Somewhere among them must be *Gojack*. The last light from the west gleamed on the rails of the moveway running down to the landing.

"Look, there's the seatrain." Peachthief pointed. "I hope the dog or whatever got ashore . . . I can find a sailboat down there, there's lots."

Jakko shrugged. Then he noticed movement among the shadows of the landing-station and forgot his anger long enough to say, "See there! Is that a live man?"

They peered hard. Presently the figure crossed a light place, and they could see it was a person going slowly among the stalled waycars. He would stop with one awhile and then waver on.

"There's something wrong with him," Peachthief said.

Presently the stranger's shadow merged with a car, and they saw it begin to move. It went slowly at first, and then accelerated out to the center lanes, slid up the gleaming rails and passed beyond them to disappear into the western hills.

"The way's working!" Jakko exclaimed. "We'll camp up here and go over to the way-station in the morning, it's closer."

He was feeling so pleased with the moveway that he talked easily with Peachthief over the foodbar dinner, telling her about the cities and asking her what places her tribe had seen. But when she wanted to put their blankets down together he said No, and took his away to a ledge farther up. The three moondogs lay down by her with their noses on their paws, facing him.

His mood turned to self-disgust again; remorse mingled with queasy surges of half-enjoyable animality. He put his arm over his head to shut out the brilliant moonlight and longed to forget everything, wishing the sky held only cold quiet stars. When he finally slept he didn't dream at all, but woke with ominous tollings in his inner ear. *The Horse is hungry*, deep voices chanted. *The Woman is bad!*

He roused Peachthief before sunrise. They ate and set off overland to the hill station; it was rough going until they stumbled onto an old limerock path. The moondogs ranged wide around them, appearing pleased. When they came out at the station shunt they found it crowded with cars.

The power-pack of the first one was dead. So was the next, and the next. Jakko understood what the stranger at the landing had been doing; looking for a live car. The dead cars here stretched away out of sight up the siding; a miserable sight.

"We should go back to the landing," Peachthief said. "He found a good one there."

Jakko privately agreed, but irrationality smouldered in him. He squinted into the hazy distance.

"I'm going up to the switch end."

"But it's so far, we'll have to come all the way back—"

He only strode off; she followed. It was a long way, round a curve and over a rise, dead cars beside them all the way. They were almost at the main tracks when Jakko saw what he had been hoping for; a slight jolting motion in the line. New cars were still coming in ahead, butting the dead ones.

"Oh fine!"

They went on down to the newest-arrived car and all climbed in, the moondogs taking up position on the opposite seat. When Jakko began to work the controls that would take them out to the main line, the car bleated an automatic alarm. A voder voice threatened to report him to Central. Despite its protests, Jakko swerved the car across the switches, where it fell silent and began to accelerate smoothly onto the outbound express lane.

"You really do know how to work these things," Peachthief said admiringly.

"You should learn."

"Why? They'll all be dead soon. I know how to bicycle."

He clamped his lips, thinking of Ferrocil's white bones. They fled on silently into the hills, passing a few more station jams. Jakko's perceptions still seemed too sharp, the sensory world too meaning-filled.

Presently they felt hungry, and found that the car's automatics were all working well. They had a protein drink and a pleasantly fruity bar, and Peachthief found bars for the dogs. The track was rising into mountains now; the car whistled smoothly through tunnels and came out in passes, offering wonderful views. Now and then they had glimpses of a great plain far ahead. The familiar knot of sadness gathered inside Jakko, stronger than usual. To think that all this wonderful system would run down and die in a jumble of rust . . . He had a fantasy of himself somehow maintaining it; but the memory of Peachthief's pathetic woven cloth mocked at him. Everything was a mistake, a terrible mistake. He wanted only to leave, to escape to rationality and peace. If she had drugged him he wasn't responsible for what he'd promised. He wasn't bound. Yet the sadness redoubled, wouldn't let him go.

When she got out the pill-box and offered it he shook his head violently. "No!"

"But you *promised*—"

"No. I hate what it does."

She stared at him in silence, swallowing hers defiantly. "Maybe there'll be some other men by the River," she said after awhile. "We saw one."

He shrugged and pretended to fall asleep.

Just as he was really drowsing the car's warning alarm trilled and they braked smoothly to a halt.

"Oh, look ahead—the way's gone! What is it?"

"A rockslide. An avalanche from the mountains, I think."

They got out among other empty cars that were waiting their prescribed pause before returning. Beyond the last one the way ended in an endless tumble of rocks and shale. Jakko made out a faint footpath leading on.

"Well, we walk. Let's get the packs, and some food and water."

While they were back in the car working the synthesizer, Peachthief looked out the window and frowned. After Jakko finished she punched a different code and some brownish lumps rolled into her hand.

"What's that?"

"You'll see." She winked at him.

As they started on the trail a small herd of horses appeared, coming toward them. The two humans politely scrambled up out of their way. The lead horse was a large yellow male. When he came to Peachthief he stopped and thrust his big head up at her.

"Zhu-gar, zhu-gar," he said sloppily. At this all the other horses crowded up and began saying "zhu-ga, zu-cah," in varying degrees of clarity.

"This *I* know," said Peachthief to Jakko. She turned to the yellow stallion. "Take us on your backs around these rocks. Then we'll give you sugar."

"Zhu-gar," insisted the horse, looking mean.

"Yes, sugar. *After* you take us around the rocks to the rails."

The horse rolled his eyes unpleasantly, but he turned back down. There was some commotion, and two mares were pushed forward.

"Riding horseback is done by means of a saddle and bridle," protested Jakko.

"Also this way. Come on." Peachthief vaulted nimbly onto the back of the smaller mare.

Jakko reluctantly struggled onto the fat round back of the other mare. To his horror, as he got himself astride she put up her head and screamed shrilly.

"You'll get sugar too," Peachthief told her. The animal subsided, and they started off along the rocky trail, single file. Jakko had to admit it was much faster than afoot, but he kept sliding backward.

"Hang onto her mane, that hairy place there," Peachthief called back to him, laughing. "I know how to run a few things too, see?"

When the path widened the yellow stallion trotted up alongside Peachthief.

"I thinking," he said importantly.

"Yes, what?"

"I push you down and eat zhugar now."

"All horses think that," Peachthief told him. "No good. It doesn't work."

The yellow horse dropped back, and Jakko heard him making horse-talk with an old gray-roan animal at the rear. Then he shouldered by to Peachthief again and said, "Why no good I push you down?"

"Two reasons," said Peachthief. "First, if you knock me down you'll never get any more sugar. All the humans will know you're bad and they won't ride on you any more. So no more sugar, never again."

"No more hoomans," the big yellow horse said scornfully. "Hoomans finish."

"You're wrong there too. There'll be a lot more humans. I am making them, see?" She patted her stomach.

The trail narrowed again and the yellow horse dropped back. When he could come alongside he sidled by Jakko's mare.

"I think I push you down now."

Peachthief turned around.

"You didn't hear my other reason," she called to him.

The horse grunted evilly.

"The other reason is that my three friends there will bite your stomach open if you try." She pointed up to where the three moondogs had appeared on a rock as if by magic, grinning toothily.

Jakko's mare screamed again even louder, and the gray roan in back made a haw-haw sound. The yellow horse lifted his tail and trotted forward to the head of the line, extruding manure as he passed Peachthief.

They went on around the great rockslide without further talk. Jakko was becoming increasingly uncomfortable; he would gladly have got off and gone slower on his own two legs. Now and then they broke into a jog trot, which was so painful he longed to yell at Peachthief to make them stop. But he kept silent. As they rounded some huge boulders he was rewarded by a distant view of the unmistakable towers of an airpark to their left on the plain below.

At long last the rockslide ended quite near a station. They stopped among a line of stalled cars. Jakko slid off gratefully, remembering to say "Thank you" to the mare. Walking proved to be uncomfortable too.

"See if there's a good car before I get off!" Peachthief yelled.

The second one he came to was live. He shouted at her.

Next moment he saw trouble among the horses. The big yellow beast charged in, neighing and kicking. Peachthief came darting out of the melee with the moondogs, and fell into the car beside him, laughing.

"I gave our mares all the sugar," she chuckled. Then she sobered. "I think mares *are* good for milk. I told them to come to the station with me when I come back. If that big bully will let them."

"How will they get in a car?" he asked stupidly.

"Why, I'll be walking, I can't run these things."

"But I'll be with you." He didn't feel convinced.

"What for, if you don't want to make babies? You won't be here."

"Well then, why are you coming with me?"

"I'm looking for a cow," she said scornfully. "Or a goat. Or a man."

They said no more until the car turned into the airpark station. Jakko counted over twenty apparently live ships floating at their towers. Many more hung sagging, and some towers had toppled. The field moveways were obviously dead.

"I think we have to find hats," he told Peachthief.

"Why?"

"So the service alarms won't go off when we walk around. Most places are like that."

"Oh."

In the office by the gates they found a pile of crew hats laid out, a thoughtful action by the last of the airpark people. A big hand-lettered sign said, ALL SHIPS ON STAND-BY, MANUAL OVERRIDE. READ DIRECTIONS. Under it was a stack of dusty leaflets. They took one, put on their hats, and began to walk toward a pylon base with several ships floating at its tower. They had to duck under and around the web of dead moveways, and when they reached the station base there seemed to be no way in from the ground.

"We'll have to climb onto that moveway."

They found a narrow ladder and went up, helping the moondogs. The moveway portal was open, and they were soon in the normal passenger lounge. It was still lighted.

"Now if the lift only works."

Just as they were making for the lift shaft they were startled by a voice ringing out.

"Ho! Ho, Roland!"

"That's no voder," Peachthief whispered. "There's a live human here."

They turned back and saw that a strange person was lying half on and half off one of the lounges. As they came close their eyes opened wide: he looked frightful. His thin dirty white hair hung around a horribly creased, caved-in face, and what they could see of his neck and arms was all mottled and decayed-looking. His jerkin and pants were frayed and stained and sagged in where flesh should be. Jakko thought of the cloth shreds around dead Ferrocil and shuddered.

The stranger was staring haggardly at them. In a faint voice he said, "When the chevalier Roland died he predicted that his body would be found a spear's throw ahead of all others and facing the enemy . . . If you happen to be real, could you perhaps give me some water?"

"Of course." Jakko unhooked his canteen and tried to hand it over, but the man's hands shook and fumbled so that Jakko had to hold it to his mouth, noticing a foul odor. The stranger sucked thirstily, spilling some. Behind him the moondogs inched closer, sniffing gingerly.

"What's *wrong* with him?" Peachthief whispered as Jakko stood back.

Jakko had been remembering his lessons. "He's just very, very old, I think."

"That's right." The stranger's voice was stronger. He stared at them with curious avidity. "I waited too long. Fibrillation." He put one feeble hand to his chest. "Fibrillating . . . rather a beautiful word, don't you think? My medicine ran out or I lost it . . . A small hot animal desynchronizing in my ribs."

"We'll help you get to the River right away!" Peachthief told him.

"Too late, my lords, too late. Besides, I can't walk and you can't possibly carry me."

"You can sit up, can't you?" Jakko asked. "There have to be some roll-chairs around here, they had them for injured people." He went off to search the lounge office and found one almost at once.

When he brought it back the stranger was staring up at Peachthief, mumbling to himself in an archaic tongue of which Jakko only understood: ". . . *The breast of a grave girl makes a hill against sunrise.*" He tried to heave himself up to the chair but fell back gasping. They had to lift and drag him in, Peachthief wrinkling her nose.

"Now if the lift only works."

It did. They were soon on the high departure deck, and the fourth portal-berth held a waiting ship. It was a small local ferry. They went through into the windowed main cabin, wheeling the old man, who had collapsed upon himself and was breathing very badly. The moondogs trooped from window to window, looking down. Jakko seated himself in the pilot chair.

"Read me out the instructions," he told Peachthief.

"One, place ship on internal guidance," she read. "Whatever that means. Oh, look, here's a diagram."

"Good."

It proved simple. They went together down the list, sealing the port, disengaging umbilicals, checking vane function, reading off the standby pressures in the gasbags above them, setting the reactor to warm up the drive-motor and provide hot air for operational buoyancy.

While they were waiting, Peachthief asked the old man if he would like to be moved onto a window couch. He nodded urgently. When they got him to it he whispered, "See out!" They propped him up with chair pillows.

The ready-light was flashing. Jakko moved the controls, and the ship glided smoothly out and up. The computer was showing him wind speed, attitude, climb, and someone had marked all the verniers with the words *Course-set—RIVER.* Jakko lined everything up.

"Now it says, put it on automatic," Peachthief read. He did so.

The takeoff had excited the old man. He was straining to look down, muttering incomprehensibly. Jakko caught, *"The cool green hills of Earth...*Crap!" Suddenly he sang out loudly, *"There's a hell of a good universe next door—let's go!"* and fell back exhausted.

Peachthief stood over him worriedly. "I wish I could at least clean him up, but he's so weak."

The old man's eyes opened.

"Nothing shall be whole and sound that has not been rent; for love hath built his mansion in the place of excrement." He began to sing crackedly, "Take me to the River, the bee-yew-tiful River, and wash all my sins a-away!...You think I'm crazy, girl, don't you?" he went on conversationally. "Never heard of William Yeats. Very high bit-rate, Yeats."

"I think I understand a little," Jakko told him. "One of my aunts did English literature."

"Did literature, eh?" The stranger wheezed, snorted. "And you two—going on the River to spend eternity together as energy matrices or something equally impressive and sexless ... *Forever wilt thou love and she be fair."* He grunted. "Always mistrusted Keats. No balls. He'd be right at home."

"We're not going on the River," Peachthief said. "At least, I'm not. I'm going to stay and make children."

The old man's ruined mouth fell open, he gazed up at her wildly.

"No!" he breathed. "Is it true? Have I stumbled on the lover and mother of man, the last?"

Peachthief nodded solemnly.

"What is your name, Oh, Queen?"

"Peachthief."

"My god. Somebody still knows of Blake." He smiled tremulously, and his eyelids suddenly slid downward; he was asleep.

"He's breathing better. Let's explore."

The small ship held little but cargo space at the rear. When they came to the food-synthesizer cubby Jakko saw Peachthief pocket something.

"What's that?"

"A little spoon. It'll be just right for a child." She didn't look at him.

Back in the main cabin the sunset was flooding the earth below with level roseate light. They were crossing huge, oddly pockmarked meadows, the airship whispering along in silence, except when a jet whistled briefly now and then for a course correction.

"Look—cows! Those must be cows," Peachthief exclaimed. "See the shadows."

Jakko made out small tan specks that were animals, with grotesque horned shadows stretching away.

"I'll have to find them when I come back. What *is* this place?"

"A big deathyard, I think. Where they put dead bodies. I never saw one this size. In some cities they had buildings just for dead people. Won't all that poison the cows?"

"Oh no, it makes good grass, I believe. The dogs will help me find them. Won't you, Tycho?" she asked the biggest moondog, who was looking down beside them.

On the eastern side of the cabin the full moon was rising into view. The old man's eyes opened, looking at it.

"More water, if you please," he croaked.

Peachthief gave him some, and then got him to swallow broth from the synthesizer. He seemed stronger, smiling at her with his mouthful of rotted teeth.

"Tell me, girl. If you're going to stay and make children, why are you going to the River?"

"He's going because he promised to talk to his father and I'm going along to see he comes back. And make the baby. Only now he won't take any more pills, I have to try to find another man."

"Ah yes, the pills. We used to call them Wake-ups. . . . They were necessary, after the population-chemicals got around. Maybe they still are, for women. But I think it's mostly in the head. Why won't you take any more, boy? What's wrong with the old Adam?"

Peachthief started to answer but Jakko cut her off. "I can speak for myself. They upset me. They made me do bad, uncontrolled things, and feel, agh—" He broke off with a grimace.

"You seem curiously feisty, for one who values his calm above the continuance of the race."

"It's the pills, I tell you. They're—they're dehumanizing."

"Dee-humanizing," the old man mocked. "And what do you know of humanity, young one? . . . That's what I went to find, that's why I stayed so long among the old, old things from before the River came. I wanted to bring the knowledge of what humanity really was . . . I wanted to bring it all. It's simple, boy. *They died.*" He drew a rasping breath. "Every one of them died. They lived knowing that nothing but loss and suffering and extinction lay ahead. And they cared, terribly. . . . Oh, they made myths, but not many really believed them. *Death* was behind everything, waiting everywhere. Aging and death. No escape . . . Some of them went crazy, they fought and killed and enslaved each other by the millions, as if they could gain more life. Some of them gave up their precious lives for each other. They loved—and had to watch the ones they loved age and die. And in their pain and despair they built, they struggled, some of them sang. But above all, boy, they copulated! Fornicated, fucked, made love!"

He fell back, coughing, glaring at Jakko. Then, seeing that they scarcely understood his antique words, he went on more clearly. "Did sex, do you understand?

Made children. It was their only weapon, you see. To send something of themselves into the future beyond their own deaths. Death was the engine of their lives, death fueled their sexuality. Death drove them at each other's throats and into each other's arms. Dying, they triumphed . . . *That* was human life. And now that mighty engine is long stilled, and you call this polite parade of immortal lemmings *humanity?* . . . Even the faintest warmth of that immemorial holocaust makes you flinch away?"

He collapsed, gasping horribly; spittle ran down his chin. One slit of eye still raked them.

Jakko stood silent, shaken by resonances from the old man's words, remembering dead Ferrocil, feeling some deep conduit of reality reaching for him out of the long-gone past. Peachthief's hand fell on his shoulder, sending a shudder through him. Slowly his own hand seemed to lift by itself and cover hers, holding her to him. They watched the old man so for a long moment. His face slowly composed, he spoke in a soft dry tone.

"I don't trust that River, you know . . . You think you're going to remain yourselves, don't you? Communicate with each other and with the essences of beings from other stars . . . The latest news from Betelgeuse." He chuckled raspingly.

"That's the last thing people say when they're going," Jakko replied. "Everyone learns that. You float out, able to talk with real other beings. Free to move."

"Yes. What could better match our dreams?" He chuckled again. "I wonder . . . could that be the lure, just the input end of some cosmic sausage machine? . . ."

"What's that?" asked Peachthief.

"An old machine that ground different meats together until they came out as one substance . . . Maybe you'll find yourselves gradually mixed and minced and blended into some, some energetic plasma . . . and then maybe squirted out again to impose the terrible gift of consciousness on some innocent race of crocodiles, or poached eggs . . . and so it begins all over again. Another random engine of the universe, giving and taking obliviously . . ." He coughed, no longer looking at them, and began to murmur in the archaic tongue, *"Ah, when the ghost begins to quicken, confusion of the death-bed over, is it sent . . . Out naked on the roads as the books say, and stricken with the injustice of the stars for punishment?* The injustice of the stars . . ." He fell silent, and then whispered faintly, "Yet I too long to go."

"You will," Peachthief told him strongly.

"How . . . much longer?"

"We'll be there by dawn," Jakko said. "We'll carry you. I swear."

"A great gift," he said weakly. "But I fear . . . I shall give you a better." He mumbled on, a word Jakko didn't know; it sounded like "afrodisiack."

He seemed to lapse into sleep then. Peachthief went and got a damp, fragrant cloth from the clean-up and wiped his face gently. He opened one eye and grinned up at her.

"Madame Tasselass," he rasped. "Madame Tasselass, are you really going to save us?"

She smiled down, nodding her head determinedly, Yes. He closed his eyes looking more peaceful.

The ship was now fleeing through full moonlight, the cabin was so lit with azure and silver that they didn't think to turn on lights. Now and again the luminous mists of a low cloud veiled the windows and vanished again. Just as Jakko was about to propose eating, the old man took several gulping breaths and opened his eyes. His intestines made a bubbling sound.

Peachthief looked at him sharply and picked up one of his wrists. Then she frowned and bent over him, opening his filthy jerkin. She laid her ear to his chest, staring up at Jakko.

"He's not breathing, there's no heartbeat!" She groped inside his jerkin as if she could locate life, two tears rolling down her cheeks.

"He's *dead*—ohhh!" She groped deeper, then suddenly straightened up and gingerly clutched the cloth at the old man's crotch.

"What?"

"He's a woman!" She gave a sob and wheeled around to clutch Jakko, putting her forehead in his neck. "We never even knew her name . . ."

Jakko held her, looking at the dead man-woman, thinking, she never knew mine either. At that moment the airship jolted, and gave a noise like a cable grinding or slipping before it flew smoothly on again.

Jakko had never in his life distrusted machinery, but now a sudden terror contracted his guts. This thing could fall! They could be made dead like Ferrocil, like this stranger, like the myriads in the deathyards below. Echoes of the old voice ranting about death boomed in his head, he had a sudden vision of Peachthief grown old and dying like that. After the Rivers went, dying alone. His eyes filled, and a deep turmoil erupted under his mind. He hugged Peachthief tighter. Suddenly he knew in a dreamlike way exactly what was about to happen. Only this time there was no frenzy; his body felt like warm living rock.

He stroked Peachthief to quiet her sobs, and led her over to the moonlit couch on the far side of the cabin. She was still sniffling, hugging him hard. He ran his hands firmly down her back, caressing her buttocks, feeling her body respond.

"Give me that pill," he said to her. "Now."

Looking at him huge-eyed in the blue moonlight, she pulled out the little box. He took out his and swallowed it deliberately, willing her to understand.

"Take off your clothes." He began stripping off his jerkin, proud of the hot, steady power in his sex. When she stripped and he saw again the glistening black bush at the base of her slim belly, and the silver-edge curve of her body, urgency took him, but still in a magical calm.

"Lie down."

"Wait a minute—" She was out of his hands like a fish, running across the cabin to where the dead body lay in darkness. Jakko saw she was trying to close the dead eyes that still gleamed from the shadows. He could wait; he had never imagined his body could feel like this. She laid the cloth over the stranger's face and came back to him, half-shyly holding out her arms, sinking down spread-legged on the shining couch before him. The moonlight was so brilliant he could see the pink color of her sexual parts. He came onto her gently, controlledly, breathing in an exciting animal odor from her flesh. This time his penis entered easily, an intense feeling of all-rightness.

But a moment later the fires of terror, pity, and defiance deep within him burst up into a flame of passionate brilliance in his coupled groin. The small body under his seemed no longer vulnerable but appetitive. He clutched, mouthed, drove deep into her, exulting. Death didn't die alone, he thought obscurely, as the ancient patterns lurking in his vitals awoke. Death flew with them and flowed by beneath, but he asserted life upon the body of the woman, caught up in a great crescendo of unknown sensations, until a culminant spasm of almost painful pleasure rolled through him into her, relieving him from head to feet.

When he could talk, he thought to ask her, "Did you—" he didn't know the word. "Did it sort of explode you, like me?"

"Well, no." Her lips were by his ear. "Female sexuality is a little different. Maybe I'll show you, later . . . But I think it was good, for the baby."

He felt only a tiny irritation at her words, and let himself drift into sleep with his face in her warm-smelling hair. Dimly the understanding came to him that the great beast of his dreams, the race itself maybe, had roused and used them. So be it.

A cold thing pushing into his ear awakened him, and a hoarse voice said "Foo-ood!" It was the moondogs.

"Oh my, I forgot to feed them!" Peachthief struggled nimbly out from under him.

Jakko found he was ravenous too. The cabin was dark now, as the moon rose overhead. Peachthief located the switches, and made a soft light on their side of the cabin. They ate and drank heartily, looking down at the moonlit world. The deathyards were gone from below them now, they were flying over dark wooded foothills. When they lay down to sleep again they could feel the cabin slightly angle upward as the ship rose higher.

He was roused in the night by her body moving against him. She seemed to be rubbing her crotch.

"Give me your hand," she whispered in a panting voice. She began to make his hands do things to her, sometimes touching him too, her body arching and writhing, sleek with sweat. He found himself abruptly tumescent again, excited and pleased in a confused way. "Now, now!" she commanded, and he entered her, finding her interior violently alive. She seemed to be half fighting him, half devouring him. Pleasure built all through him, this time without the terror. He pressed in against her shuddering convulsions. "Yes—Oh, yes!" she gasped, and a series of paroxysms swept through her, carrying him with her to explosive peace.

He held himself on and in her until her body and breathing calmed to relaxation, and they slipped naturally apart. It came to him that this sex activity seemed to have more possibilities, as a thing to do, than he had realized. His family had imparted to him nothing of all this. Perhaps they didn't know it. Or perhaps it was too alien to their calm philosophy.

"How do you know about all this?" he asked Peachthief sleepily.

"One of my aunts did literature, too." She chuckled in the darkness. "Different literature, I guess."

They slept almost as movelessly as the body flying with them on the other couch a world away.

A series of noisy bumpings wakened them. The windows were filled with pink mist flying by. The airship seemed to be sliding into a berth. Jakko looked down and saw shrubs and grass close below; it was a ground-berth on a hillside.

The computer panel lit up: RESET PROGRAM FOR BASE.

"No," said Jakko. "We'll need it going back." Peachthief looked at him in a new, companionable way; he sensed that she believed him now. He turned all the drive controls to standby while she worked the food synthesizer. Presently he heard the hiss of the deflating lift-bags, and went to where she was standing by the dead stranger.

"We'll take her, her body, out before we go back," Peachthief said. "Maybe the River will touch her somehow."

Jakko doubted it, but ate and drank his breakfast protein in silence.

When they went to use the wash-and-waste cubby he found he didn't want to clean all the residues of their contact off himself. Peachthief seemed to feel the same way; she washed only her face and hands. He looked at her slender, silk-clad belly. Was a child, his child, starting there? Desire flicked him again, but he remembered he had work to do. His promise to his father; get on with it. Sooner done, sooner back here.

"I love you," he said experimentally, and found the strange words had a startling trueness.

She smiled brilliantly at him, not just off-on. "I love you, too, I think."

The floor-portal light was on. They pulled it up and uncovered a step-way leading to the ground. The moondogs poured down. They followed, coming out into a blowing world of rosy mists. Clouds were streaming around them; the air was all in motion up the hillside toward the crest some distance ahead of the ship berth. The ground here was uneven and covered with short soft grass, as though animals had cropped it.

"All winds blow to the River," Jakko quoted.

They set off up the hill, followed by the moondogs, who stalked uneasily with pricked ears. Probably they didn't like not being able to smell what was ahead, Jakko thought. Peachthief was holding his hand very firmly as they went, as if determined to keep him out of any danger.

As they walked up onto the flat crest of the hilltop the mists suddenly cleared, and they found themselves looking down into a great, shallow, glittering sunlit valley. They both halted involuntarily to stare at the fantastic sight.

Before them lay a huge midden heap, kilometers of things upon things upon things, almost filling the valley floor. Objects of every description lay heaped there; Jakko could make out clothing, books, toys, jewelry, a myriad artifacts and implements abandoned. These must be, he realized, the last things people had taken with them when they went on the River. In an outer ring not too far below them were tents, ground- and air-cars, even wagons. Everything shone clean and gleaming as if the influence of the River had kept off decay.

He noticed that the nearest ring of encampments intersected other, apparently older and larger rings. There seemed to be no center to the pile.

"The River has moved, or shrunk," he said.

"Both, I think," Peachthief pointed to the right. "Look, there's an old war-place."

A big grass-covered mound dominated the hill crest beside them. Jakko saw it had metal-rimmed slits in its sides. He remembered history: how there were still rulers of people when the River's tendrils first touched earth. Some of the rulers had tried to keep their subjects from the going-out places, posting guards around them and even putting killing devices in the ground. But the guards had gone themselves out on the River, or the River had swelled and taken them. And the people had driven beasts across the mined ground and surged after them into the stream of immortal life. In the end the rulers had gone too, or died out. Looking more carefully, Jakko could see that the green hill slopes were torn and pocked, as though ancient explosions had made craters everywhere.

Suddenly he remembered that he had to find his father in all this vast confusion. "Where's the River now? My father's mind should reach there still, if I'm not too late."

"See that glittery slick look in the air down there? I'm sure that's a danger place."

Down to their right, fairly close to the rim, was a strangely bright place. As he stared it became clearer: a great column of slightly golden or shining air. He scanned about, but saw nothing else like it all across the valley.

"If that's the only focus left, it's going away fast."

She nodded and then swallowed, her small face suddenly grim. She meant to live on here and die without the River, Jakko could see that. But he would be with her; he resolved it with all his heart. He squeezed her hand hard.

"If you have to talk to your father, we better walk around up here on the rim where it's safe," Peachthief said.

"No-oo," spoke up a moondog from behind them. The two humans turned and saw the three sitting in a row on the crest, staring slit-eyed at the valley.

"All right," Peachthief said. "You wait here. We'll be back soon."

She gripped Jakko's hand even tighter, and they started walking past the old war mound, past the remains of ancient vehicles, past an antique pylon that leaned crazily. There were faint little trails in the short grass. Another war mound loomed ahead; when they passed around it they found themselves suddenly among a small herd of white animals with long necks and no horns. The animals went on grazing quietly as the humans walked by. Jakko thought they might be mutated deer.

"Oh, look!" Peachthief let go his hand. "That's milk—see, her baby is sucking!"

Jakko saw that one of the animals had a knobby bag between its hind legs. A small one half-knelt down beside it, with its head up nuzzling the bag. A mother and her young.

Peachthief was walking cautiously toward them, making gentle greeting sounds. The mother animal looked at her calmly, evidently tame. The baby went on sucking, rolling its eyes. Peachthief reached them, petted the mother, and then bent down under to feel the bag. The animal sidestepped a pace, but stayed still. When Peachthief straightened up she was licking her hand.

"That's good milk! And they're just the right size, we can take them on the airship! On the way-cars, even." She was beaming, glowing. Jakko felt an odd warm constriction in his chest. The intensity with which she furnished her little world, her future nest! *Their* nest . . .

"Come with us, come on," Peachthief was urging. She had her belt around the creature's neck to lead it. It came equably, the young one following in awkward galloping lunges.

"That baby is a male. Oh, this is *perfect*," Peachthief exclaimed. "Here, hold her a minute while I look at that one."

She handed Jakko the end of the belt and ran off. The beast eyed him levelly. Suddenly it drew its upper lip back and shot spittle at his face. He ducked, yelling for Peachthief to come back.

"I have to find my father first!"

"All right," she said, returning. "Oh, look at that!"

Downslope from them was an apparition—one of the white animals, but partly transparent, ghostly thin. It drifted vaguely, putting its head down now and then, but did not eat.

"It must have got partly caught in the River, it's half gone. Oh, Jakko, you can see how dangerous it is! I'm afraid, I'm afraid it'll catch you."

"It won't. I'll be very careful."

"I'm so afraid." But she let him lead her on, towing the animal alongside. As they passed the ghost-creature Peachthief called to it, "You can't live like that. You better go on out. Shoo, shoo!"

It turned and moved slowly out across the piles of litter toward the shining place in the air.

They were coming closer to it now, stepping over more and more abandoned things. Peachthief looked sharply at everything; once she stooped to pick up a beautiful fleecy white square and stuff it in her pack. The hill crest was merging with a long grassy slope, comparatively free of debris, that ran out toward the airy glittering column. They turned down it.

The River-focus became more and more awesome as they approached. They could trace it towering up and now, twisting gently as it passed beyond the sky. A tendril of the immaterial stream of sidereal sentience that had embraced earth, a pathway to immortal life. The air inside looked no longer golden, but pale silver-gilt, like a great shaft of moonlight coming down through the morning sun. Objects at its base appeared very clear but shimmering, as if seen through cool crystal water.

Off to one side were tents. Jakko suddenly recognized one, and quickened his steps. Peachthief pulled back on his arm.

"Jakko, be careful!"

They slowed to a stop a hundred yards from the tenuous fringes of the River's effect. It was very still. Jakko peered intently. In the verges of the shimmer a staff was standing upright. From it hung a scarf of green and yellow silk.

"Look—that's my father's sign!"

"Oh Jakko, you *can't* go in there."

At the familiar colored sign all the memories of his life with his family had come flooding back on Jakko. The gentle rationality, the solemn sense of preparation for going out from earth forever. Two different realities strove briefly within him. They had loved him, he realized that now. Especially his father . . . But not as he loved Peachthief, his awakened spirit shouted silently. I am of earth! Let the stars take care of their own. His resolve took deeper hold and won.

Gently he released himself from her grip.

"You wait here. Don't worry, it takes a long while for the change, you know that. Hours, days. I'll only be a minute, I'll come right back."

"Ohhh, it's crazy."

But she let him go and stood holding to the milk-animal while he went down the ridge and picked his way out across the midden-heap toward the staff. As he neared it he could feel the air change around him, becoming alive and yet more still.

"Father! Paul! It's Jakko, your son. Can you still hear me?"

Nothing answered him. He took a step or two past the staff, repeating his call.

A resonant susurrus came in his head, as if unearthly reaches had opened to him. From infinity he heard without hearing his father's quiet voice.

You came.

A sense of calm welcome.

"The cities are all empty, Father. All the people have gone, everywhere."

Come.

"No!" He swallowed, fending off memory, fending off the lure of strangeness. "I think it's sad. It's wrong. I've found a woman. We're going to stay and make children."

The River is leaving, Jakko my son.

It was as if a star had called his name, but he said stubbornly, "I don't care. I'm staying with her. Good-bye, father. Good-bye."

Grave regret touched him, and from beyond a host of silent voices murmured down the sky: *Come! Come away.*

"No!" he shouted, or tried to shout, but he could not still the rapt voices. And suddenly, gazing up, he felt the serenity of the River, the overwhelming opening of the door to life everlasting among the stars. All his mortal fears, all his most secret dread of the waiting maw of death, slid out of him and fell away, leaving him almost unbearably light and calmly joyful. He knew that he was being touched, that he could float out upon that immortal stream forever. But even as the longing took him, his human mind remembered that this was the start of the first stage, for which the River was called Beata. He thought of the ghost-animal that had lingered too long. He must leave now, and quickly. With enormous effort he took one step backward, but could not turn.

"Jakko! Jakko! Come back!"

Someone was calling, screaming his name. He did turn then and saw her on the little ridge. Nearby, yet so far. The ordinary sun of earth was brilliant on her and the two white beasts.

"Jakko! Jakko!" Her arms were outstretched, she was running toward him.

It was as if the whole beautiful earth was crying to him, calling to him to come back and take up the burden of life and death. He did not want it. But she must not come here, he knew that without remembering why. He began uncertainly to stumble toward her, seeing her now as his beloved woman, again as an unknown creature uttering strange cries.

"Lady Death," he muttered, not realizing he had ceased to move. She ran faster, tripped, almost fell in the heaps of stuff. The wrongness of her coming here roused him again; he took a few more steps, feeling his head clear a little.

"Jakko!" She reached him, clutched him, dragging him bodily forward from the verge.

At her touch the reality of his human life came back to him, his heart pounded human blood, all stars fled away. He started to run clumsily, half-carrying her with him up to the safety of the ridge. Finally they sank down gasping beside the animals, holding and kissing each other, their eyes wet.

"I thought you were lost, I thought I'd lost you," Peachthief sobbed.

"You saved me."

"H-here," she said. "We b-better have some food." She rummaged in her pack, nodding firmly as if the simple human act could defend against unearthly powers. Jakko discovered that he was quite hungry.

They ate and drank peacefully in the soft, flower-studded grass, while the white animals grazed around them. Peachthief studied the huge strewn valley floor, frowning as she munched.

"So many good useful things here. I'll come back some day, when the River's gone, and look around."

"I thought you only wanted natural things," he teased her.

"Some of these things will last. Look." She picked up a small implement. "It's an awl, for punching and sewing leather. You could make children's sandals."

Many of the people who came here must have lived quite simply, Jakko thought. It was true that there could be useful tools. And metal. Books, too. Directions for making things. He lay back dreamily, seeing a vision of himself in the far future, an accomplished artisan, teaching his children skills. It seemed deeply good.

"Oh, my milk-beast!" Peachthief broke in on his reverie. "Oh, no, you musn't!" She jumped up.

Jakko sat up and saw that the white mother-animal had strayed quite far down the grassy ridge. Peachthief trotted down after her, calling, "Come here! Stop!"

Perversely, the animal moved away, snatching mouthfuls of grass. Peachthief ran faster. The animal threw up its head and paced down off the ridge, among the litter piles.

"No! Oh, my milk! Come back here, come."

She went down after it, trying to move quietly and call more calmly.

Jakko had got up, alarmed.

"Come back! Don't go down there!"

"The babies' milk," she wailed at him, and made a dash at the beast. But she missed, and it drifted away just out of reach before her.

To his horror Jakko saw that the glittering column of the River had changed shape slightly, eddying out a veil of shimmering light close ahead of the beast.

"Turn back! Let it go!" he shouted, and began to run with all his might. "Peachthief—Come back!"

But she would not turn, and his pounding legs could not catch up. The white beast was in the shimmer now; he saw it bound up onto a great sun-and-moonlit heap of stuff. Peachthief's dark form went flying after it, uncaring, and the creature leaped away again. He saw her follow, and bitter fear grabbed at his heart. The very strength of her human life is betraying her to death, he thought; I have to get her physically, I will pull her out. He forced his legs faster, faster yet, not noticing that the air had changed around him too.

She disappeared momentarily in a veil of glittering air, and then reappeared, still following the beast. Thankfully he saw her pause and stoop to pick something up. She was only walking now, he could catch her. But his own body was moving sluggishly, it took all his will to keep his legs thrusting him ahead.

"Peachthief! Love, come back!"

His voice seemed muffled in the silvery air. Dismayed, he realized that he too had slowed to a walk, and she was veiled again from his sight.

When he struggled through the radiance he saw her, moving very slowly after the wandering white beast. Her face was turned up, unearthly light was on her beauty. He knew she was feeling the rapture, the call of immortal life was on her. On him, too; he found he was barely stumbling forward, a terrible serenity flooding his heart. They must be passing into the very focus of the River, where it ran strongest.

"Love—" Mortal grief fought the invading transcendence. Ahead of him the girl faded slowly into the glimmering veils, still following her last earthly desire. He saw that humanity, all that he had loved of the glorious earth, was disappearing forever from reality. Why had it awakened, only to be lost? Spectral voices were near him, but he did not want specters. An agonizing lament for human life welled up in him, a last pang that he would carry with him through eternity. But its urgency fell away. Life incorporeal, immortal, was on him now; it had him as it had her. His flesh, his body was beginning to attenuate, to dematerialize out into the great current of sentience that flowed on its mysterious purposes among the stars.

Still the sense of his earthly self moved slowly after hers into the closing mists of infinity, carrying upon the River a configuration that had been a man striving forever after a loved dark girl, who followed a ghostly white milch deer.

The Map

GENE WOLFE

Gene Wolfe made his first sale in 1965. By 1970, he would be becoming a regular in Damon Knight's *Orbit* anthologies with stories such as "Trip, Trap," "The Encounter," and "Paul's Treehouse" and had published his first novel, *Operation Ares* (in retrospect, his weakest book). Little that he had done to date attracted any attention, and there was little to indicate that a new giant of the form was about to loom above the literary horizon, someone who would be instrumental in establishing the new Cutting Edge of science fiction in the years ahead . . . yet that was exactly what was about to happen.

As the decade progressed, Wolfe's work seemed to undergo a quantum jump in sophistication and intensity, and he went on to produce much of the really superior short fiction of the seventies—pieces such as the extraordinary "The Fifth Head of Cerberus," "The Hero as Werewolf," "Seven American Nights," "Alien Stones," "The Eyeflash Miracles," "Tracking Song," and "The Island of Doctor Death and Other Stories," among many others, as well as one of the decade's best novels (the brilliant 1975 novel *Peace,* which, published almost anonymously as a mainstream hardback in a plain tan dustcover, sank without arousing a single ripple). In spite of this lush outpouring of talent, Wolfe remained severely underappreciated throughout most of the decade (although he did take a Nebula Award for his story "The Death of Doctor Island"), and as late as 1978 or 1979 book editors were telling me that Wolfe had no real audience and no future as a mass-market author . . . something that would later be proven to be demonstrably untrue.

Wolfe would finally establish his reputation at the beginning of the eighties with a series of novels set in the very far future, his landmark *The Book of the New Sun* novel series (consisting of *The Shadow of the Torturer, The Claw of the Conciliator, The Sword of the Lictor, The Citadel of the Autarch,* and a follow-up volume, *The Urth of the New Sun),* individual volumes of which have won the Nebula Award, the World Fantasy Award, and the John W. Campbell Memorial Award. One of the true masterworks of science fiction, *The Book of the New Sun* is clearly one of the genre's most vivid, complex, substantial, sophisticated, and compelling visions of the far future and may well be the most influential such vision since Jack Vance's *The Dying Earth* (to which it itself owes an acknowledged debt).

Here, in a story unrelated to the direct story line of the series, Wolfe takes us to that same evocative milieu, to the far, far future . . . to a time when the sun has grown old and red and dim, the moon has grown green with forests, and old Urth groans under the almost insupportable weight of her own unnumbered years . . . takes us for a journey down the fabled River Gyoll, through the unimaginably vast and ancient ruins of the dying city Nessus, for a tale of temptation, greed, and mystery. (And if you enjoy it, read *The Book of the New Sun* itself, for this tale is a mere appetizer for the feast of reading that awaits you there!)

Wolfe has also returned to the far future for a popular new series set on an immense generational starship, the *Long sun* sequence, which includes *Nightside the Long Sun, The Lake of the Long Sun, Calde of the Long Sun,* and *Exodus from the Long Sun.* His other books include *The Fifth Head of Cerberus, The Devil in a Forest, Soldier in the Mist, Free Live Free, Soldier of Arête, Castleview, Pandora by Holly Hollander,* and *There Are Doors.* His short fiction has been collected in *The Island of Doctor Death and Other Stories and Other Stories, Gene Wolfe's Book of Days, The Wolfe Archipelago, Endangered Species,* and the recent World Fantasy Award–winning collection *Storeys from the Old Hotel.* His most recent novel is *On Blue's Waters,* the start of a new series.

On the night before, he had forgotten all his plans and fought, half blinded by his blood after Laetus broke the ewer over his head. Perhaps that was for the best.

And yet if they had not taken his knife while he slept, he might have killed them both.

"Master Gurloes will be angry." That was what they used to say to terrify one another into doing well. Severian would have been angry too, to be sure, and Severian had beaten him more than once. He spat out clotted blood. Beaten him worse than Laetus and Syntyche had last night. Severian had been captain of apprentices in the year before his own.

Now Severian was the Autarch, Severian was the law, and murderers died under the law's hand.

Someone was pounding at the hatch. He spat again, this time into the slop jar, and shouted in the direction of the vent. It let in enough light for him to see the impression Syntyche had left in her bunk as she lay face to the bulkhead, feigning sleep. He smoothed it with his hands.

For a moment he groped for his clothes and his knife, but the knife was gone. He chuckled and rocked back on his own narrow bunk, pushing both legs into his trousers together.

More pounding; the boat rocked beneath him as the stranger searched for another way into the cabin. He spat a third time, and from habit reached up to draw the bolt that was back already. "Hatch sticks! Come on down, you catamite, I'm not coming up."

The stranger lifted it and clambered down the steep steps.

" 'Ware deck beams."

He stooped as he turned about, and he was tall enough that he had to. "You're Captain Eata?"

"Sit on the other bunk. Nobody's using it any more. What do you want?"

"But you are Eata?"

"We'll talk about that later, maybe. After you tell me what you want."

"A guide."

Eata was feeling the cut on his head and did not answer.

"I was told that you are an intelligent man."

"Not by a friend."

"I need a man with a boat to take me down Gyoll. To tell me what I need to know concerning the ruins. They said you knew it as well as any man alive."

"An asimi," Eata said. "One asimi for each day. And you'll have to help me handle her—my deckhand and I had a little argument last night."

"Shall we say six orichalks? It should only take a day, and I—"

Eata was not listening. He had seen the broken lock on his sea chest, and he was laughing. "The key's in my pocket!" He gripped the younger, taller man by the knee. "My pants were on the floor!" In his mirth, he nearly choked on the words.

In the flat lands that Gyoll itself had made, Gyoll had little current; but the wind was in the east, and Eata's boat heeled a bit under the pressure of her wide gaffsail. The old sun, well above the tallest towers now, painted the sail's black image on the oily water.

"What do you do, Captain?" the stranger asked. "How do you live?"

"By doing whatever pays. Cargo to the delta and fish to the city, mostly."

"It's a nice boat. Did you build it?"

"No," Eata said. "Bought it. Not fast like you're used to." His head still hurt, and he leaned on the tiller with one hand pressed to his temple.

"Yes, I've sailed a bit on a lake we have up north."

"Wasn't asking," Eata told him.

"I don't think I ever gave you my name. It's Simulatio."

"And a good one too, I've no doubt."

The stranger turned away for a moment, tinkering with the jibsheet winch to keep Eata from seeing the blood rising in his cheeks. "When will we reach the deserted parts of the city?"

"About nones, if this wind holds."

"I didn't know it would take so long."

"You should have hired me farther down." Eata chuckled. "And that'll be just the beginning of the dead parts. You might want to go farther yet."

The stranger turned back to look at him. "It's very large, isn't it?"

"Bigger than you can imagine. This part—where people live—is just a sort of border on it."

"Do you know a place where three broad streets come together?"

"Half a dozen, maybe more."

"The southernmost, I would think."

"I can take you to the farthest south I know," Eata said. "I'm not saying that's the farthest south there is."

"We'll start there then."

"Be night by the time we get there," Eata told him. "The next day will be another asimi."

The stranger nodded. "We're not even to the ruined part yet?"

Eata gestured. "See those clothes? Washing on a line. People here have enough to eat, so they can have two or three shirts, maybe. Farther south you won't see that—a person with only one shirt or one shift doesn't wash it much, but you'll see cooksmoke. Farther still, and you won't even see that. That's the dead city, and people there don't light any fires because of what the smoke might bring down on them. Omophagists is what my old teacher called them. It means those that have their meat raw."

The stranger stared across the water at the lines and their rags. The wind ruffled his hair, and the tattered shirts and skirts waved at him like crowds of poor, shy children who feared he would not wave back. At last he said, "Even if the Autarch won't protect them, they could band together and protect each other."

"It's each other they're afraid of. They live—such as they do live—by sieving the old city, a finer screen every year. Every man steals from his neighbor when he can and kills him if he makes a good find. It doesn't have to be much. A knife with a silver handle—that would be a good find."

After a moment, the stranger looked down at the silver mountings of his dagger.

"I believe we might take a bit of a closer reach here," Eata told him. "There's a meander coming up." The stranger heaved at the windlass, and the boom crept back.

To starboard, a high-pooped thalamegus made its way up the river, glittering in the sunlight like a scarab, all gilding and lapis lazuli. The wind was fair for it now, and as they watched (Eata with one eye to their own sail), the lateen yards dipped on its stubby masts, then lifted again trailing wide triangles of roseate silk. The long sweeps shrunk and vanished.

"They've been down seeing the sights," Eata told the stranger. "It's safe enough by day, if you've got a couple of young fellows with swords aboard and rowers you can trust."

"What is that up there?" The stranger pointed beyond the thalamegus to a hill crowned with spires. "It looks out of place."

"They call it the Old Citadel," Eata said. "I don't know much about it."

"Is that where the Autarch comes from?"

"So some say."

Urth was looking the sun nearly full in the face now, and the wind had died to a mere whisper. The patched brown mainsail flapped, then filled, then flapped again.

The stranger sat on the gunnel for a moment, his booted feet hanging over the side and almost touching the smooth water, then swung them back onto the deck again as though he were fearful of falling overboard. "You can almost imagine them going up, can't you?" he said. "Just taking off with a silver shout and leaving this world behind."

"No," Eata told him. "I can't."

"That's what they're supposed to do, at the end of time. I read about it some-place."

"Paper's dangerous," Eata said. "It's killed a lot more men than steel."

Their boat was moving hardly faster than the sluggish current. A flyer passed overhead as swiftly and silently as a dart from the hand of a giant and vanished into a white summer cloud, only to reappear shrunk nearly to invisibility, one additional spark among the day-dimmed stars. The brown sail crept across the stranger's view of the Old Citadel to the northeast. Despite the shade it gave him, he was sweating. He unlaced his cordwain jerkin.

That night on deck, he laced it again as tightly as he could. It was cold already, and he knew without being told that it would soon be colder still. "Perhaps I should have a blanket," he said.

Eata shook his head. "You'd only fall asleep. Walk up and down and wave your arms. That'll keep you warm and awake too. I'll come up and relieve you at the next watch."

The stranger nodded absently and looked up at the orangish lantern Eata had hoisted to the masthead. "They'll know we're out here."

"If they didn't, I wouldn't bother to set a watch. But if we didn't have that, some big carrack would run us under for sure and never feel the difference. Don't you go putting it out—believe me, we're a lot safer with it high and bright. If it should go out of itself, you let it down and get it lit again as handsomely as ever you can. If you can't get it lit, call me. If you see another vessel, particularly a big one, blow the conch." Eata waved toward the spiraled shell beside the binnacle.

The stranger nodded again. "Their boats won't have lights, of course."

"No, nor masts neither. Besides, it could happen that two or three swim out. If you see a face in the water that stares at the light and disappears, it's a manatee. Don't worry about it. But if you see anything that swims like a man, call me."

"I will," the stranger said. He watched as Eata opened the hatch and descended to the tiny cabin.

Two boarding pikes lay in the bow, their grounding irons lost in the inky shadow beneath the overhang of the half-deck, their heads thrusting past the jib-boom mountings. He climbed down and got one, then scrambled onto the deck again. The pike was three ells long, with an ugly spike head and a sharp hook intended to cut rigging. He flourished it as he walked the circle of the little deck, *up, down, right, left,* his movements the awkward ones of a man recalling a skill learned in youth.

The curve of Lune lay just visible in the east, sending streamers of virescence toward him in a silent flood, spumed and uncanny. Silhouetted against that moss-green light, the city on the eastern bank seemed less dead than sleeping. Its towers were black, but their sightless windows, thus illuminated from behind, appeared to betray a faint radiance, as though hecatonchires roved the gloomy corridors and deserted rooms, their thousand fingers smeared with noctoluscence to light their way.

He looked to the west just in time to see a pair of gleaming eyes sink into the water with a scarcely perceptible plash. For the space of a dozen breaths he stared at the spot, but there was nothing more to see. He dashed to starboard again, to what was now the eastern side of the anchored boat, imagining that some devious adversary had swum under or around it to take him by surprise; Gyoll slipped past unruffled.

To port, the shadow of the hull lay long across the glassy river, though he could easily have touched the water with his hands. No skiff or shallop launched from the silent shore.

Downriver, the ruined city appeared to stretch away to infinity, as though Urth were a level plain occupying the whole of space, and the whole of Urth were filled with crumbling walls and tilted pillars. A night bird circled overhead, stooped at the water, and did not rise.

Upriver, the cookfires and grease lamps of living Nessus lent no glow to the sky. The river seemed the only living thing in a city of death; and for an instant the stranger was seized by the conviction that cold Gyoll itself was dead, that the sodden sticks and bits of excrement it carried were somehow swimming, that they were outward bound on some unending voyage to dissolution.

He was about to turn away when he noticed what appeared to be a human form drifting toward him with a scarcely discernible motion. He watched it fascinated and unbelieving, as sparrows are said to watch the golden snake called soporor.

It came nearer. In the green moonlight, its hair looked colorless, its skin berylline. He saw that it was in fact human, and that it floated face downward.

One outstretched hand touched the floating anchor cable as if it wished to climb aboard. Momentarily, the hemp retarded the stiff fingers, and the corpse performed a slow pirouette, like the half turn of a thrown knife seen by an ephemerid, or the tumbling of a derelict through the abyss that separates the worlds. Clambering down into the bow, he tried to grapple it with his pike; it was just out of reach.

He waited, horrified and impatient. At last he was able to draw it nearer and slide the hook under one arm. The corpse rolled over easily, far more easily than he had anticipated, its face pressed below the dark surface by the weight of the lifted arm, then bobbing up when that arm lay in the water once more.

It was a woman, naked and not long dead. Her staring eyes still showed traces of kohl; her teeth gleamed faintly through half-parted lips. He tried to judge her as he had judged the women whose compliance he had secured for coins, to weigh her breasts with his eyes and applaud or condemn the roundness of her belly; he discovered that he could not do so, that in the way he sought to see her she was beyond his sight, unreachable as the unborn, unreachable as his mother had been when he had once, as a boy, happened upon her bathing.

Eata's touch on his shoulder made him spin around.

"My watch."

"This—" he began, and could say nothing more. He pointed.

"I'll fend it off," Eata told him. "You get some sleep. Take the other bunk. No one's using it."

He handed Eata the pike and went below, hardly knowing what he did and nearly crushing his fingers beneath the hatch.

A candle guttered in a dish on the broken chest, and he realized that Eata had not slept. One of the narrow bunks was rumpled. He took the other, tying triple knots in the thong that held his burse to his belt, loosening his jerkin, swinging his booted feet onto the hard, thin mattress, and pulling up a blanket of surprisingly soft merino. A puff of his breath extinguished the yellow candle flame, and he closed his eyes.

The dead woman floated in the dark. He pushed her away, turning his thoughts to pleasant things: the room where he had slept as a boy, the hawk and the harrier he had left behind. The mountain meads of his father's estate rose before him, dotted with poppies and wild indigo, with fern and purple-flowered clover. When had he ridden across them last? He could not remember. Lilacs nodded their honey-charged panicles.

Sniffing, he sat up, nearly braining himself on the deck beams.

A faint perfume languished between the mingled stinks of bilge and candle. When he buried his face in the blanket, he was certain of it. Just before sleep came, he heard a man's faint, hoarse sobbing overhead.

★ ★ ★

He had the last watch, when the ruins dropped from the angry face of the sun like a frayed mask. By night he had seen towers; now he saw that those towers were half fallen and leprous with saplings and rank green vines. As he had been told, there was no smoke. He would have been willing to stake all he had that there were no people either.

Eata came on deck carrying bread, dried meat, and steaming maté. "You owe me another asimi," Eata said.

He untied the knots and took it out. "The last one you'll be getting. Or will you charge me for another day, if you can't return me to the place where I boarded your boat by tomorrow morning?"

Eata shook his head.

"The last, then. This spot where three streets meet—is it on the eastern side? Over there?"

Eata nodded. "See that jetty? Straight in from there for half a league. We'll be at the jetty before primesong."

Together they turned the little capstan that drew up the anchor. The stranger broke out the jib while Eata heaved at the mainsail halyards.

The sea breeze had arrived, raucously announced by a flock of black-and-white gulls riding it inland in hope of offal. Close hauled, the boat showed such heels that the stranger feared they would ram the disintegrating jetty. He picked up a pike to use as a boat hook.

At what seemed the last possible moment, Eata swung the rudder abeam and shot her bow into the wind. "That was well done," the stranger said.

"Oh, I can sail. I can fight too, if I have to." Eata paused. "I'll go with you, if you want me."

The stranger shook his head.

"I didn't think you would, but it was worth a try. You understand that you may be killed in there?"

"I doubt it."

"Well, I don't. Take that pike—you may need it. I'll wait for you till nones; understand? No later. When your shadow's around your feet, I'll be gone. If you're still alive walk north, sticking as near the water as you can. If you see a vessel, wave. Hail them." For a moment Eata hesitated, seemingly lost in thought. "Hold up a coin, the biggest you've got. That works sometimes."

"I'll be back before you go," the stranger said. "But this pike must have cost you nearly an asimi. You'll have to replace it if I don't bring it back."

"Not that much," Eata said.

"When I come back, I'll give you an asimi. We'll call it rent for the pike."

"And maybe I'll stay a bit longer in the hope of getting it, eh?"

The stranger nodded. "And perhaps you will. But I'll be back before nones."

When he had vaulted ashore, he watched Eata put out, then turned to study the city before him.

Two score strides brought him to the first ruined building. The streets were narrow here, and made more narrow still by the debris that half choked them. Blue cornflowers and pale bindweed grew from this rubbish and from the great, cracked blocks of gritty pavement. There was no sound but the distant keening of the gulls, and the air seemed purer than it had on the river. When he felt certain Eata had not followed him and that no one was watching him, he sat on a fallen stone and took out the map. He had wrapped it in oiled vellum, and the slight wetting the packet had received had not penetrated.

For most of the time he had possessed the map, he had not dared to look at it. Now as he studied it at leisure in the brilliant sunlight, his excitement was embittered by an irrational guilt.

Those spidery streets might—or might not—be the very streets that stretched before him. That wandering line of blue might be a stream or canal, or Gyoll itself. The map presented an accumulation of detail, and yet it was detail of a sort that did nothing to confirm or deny location. He committed as much of it to memory as he could, all the while wondering what feature or turning might prove of value, what name of street or structure might have survived where there was no one left to recall it, what thing of masonry or metal might yet retain its former shape, if any did. For an instant it seemed to him that it was not the treasure that was lost, but he himself.

As he refolded the cracked paper and wrapped it again, he speculated (as he had so many times) about the precious thing that had been thus laboriously hidden by the men to whom the stars had been as so many isles. Left to its own devices, his imagination ran to childish coffers crammed with gold. His intellect recognized these fancies for what they were and rejected them, but could propose in their stead only a dozen dim improbabilities, rumors of the secret knowledge and frightful weapons of ancient times. Life and mastery without limit.

He stood and studied the deserted buildings to make certain he had not been seen. A fox sat atop the highest heap of rubble, its red coat fiery in the sunshine, its eyes bright as jet beads. Suddenly afraid of any eyes, he threw the pike at it. It vanished, and the pike rattled down the farther side out of sight. He climbed over the mound and searched among the flourishing beggar ticks and lion's teeth, but the pike had vanished too.

It took him a long time to reach the area where three streets met, and longer still to find their intersection. He had somehow veered south, and he wasted a watch in the search. Another was spent amid buzzing insects in convincing himself that it was not the intersection on his map, which showed avenues of equal width running southwest, southeast, and north. At last he took out the map again, comparing its faded inks to the desolate reality. Here were indeed three streets, but one was wider than the others and ran due east. This was not the place.

He was returning to the boat when the omophagists rushed him—men the color of dust, wild-eyed and clothed in rags. In that first moment they seemed innumerable. When he had grappled with one and killed him, he realized that only four remained.

Four were still far too many. He fled, one hand pressed to his bleeding side.

He had always been a good runner, but he ran now as never before, leaping every obstacle, seeming almost to fly. The ruins raced and reeled around him. Missiles whizzed past his head.

He had nearly reached the river before they caught him. Mud slid from under his boot, he fell to one knee, and they were all around him. One must have torn his silver-mounted dagger from the dead man's ribs. He watched it slash at his own throat now with the stunned incredulity of a householder who finds himself savaged by his own bandog, and he threw up his arms as much to shut out the sight as to counter the blow.

His forearm turned to ice as the steel bit in. Desperately, he rolled away, and saw the gray figure who wielded his dagger felled by the cudgel of another. A third dove for the dagger, and the two struggled.

Someone screamed; he looked to one side to see the fourth, who had his pike, impaled upon Eata's.

The inn where he had stayed was near the river. Because he had walked some distance south searching for Eata's boat, he had forgotten that. The inn was the Cygnet; he had forgotten that, too.

"Toss one of those loafers the line," Eata called. "He'll tie us up for an aes."

He found he could not throw well with his left arm, but one of the loungers dove for the coil and caught it. "I've some luggage," he called as the man heaved at the line. "Perhaps you'd carry it up to the Cygnet for me."

Eata jumped into the bow. "The optimate's name is Simulatio," he told the lounger. "He stayed there three nights back. Inform the innkeeper. Tell him the optimate wishes the room he had before."

"I hate to leave," the stranger said. "But I won't be going south again until I've healed." He was picking at the knots that bound his burse.

"If you're wise, you won't go at all."

The lounger threw the stranger's bags onto the wharf and leaped up after them.

"I want to give you something." The stranger took out a chrisos. "Perhaps you could come back at the next moon and see if I'm well enough to go."

"I won't take your yellow boy," Eata said. "You owe me an asimi for pike rent. I'll take that."

"But you will come back?"

"For an asimi a day? Of course I will. So would any other boatman."

The stranger hesitated while he looked at Eata, and Eata at him. "I think I can trust you," he said at last. "I wouldn't want to go into those ruins with anyone else."

"I know," Eata told him. "That's why I'm going to give you some advice. Walk away from the river a couple of streets, and you'll find a goldsmith's. It's the sign of the Osela. That's a golden bird."

"I know what it is."

"Yes, you would. Fold up your map—" He laughed. "You shouldn't flinch like that. If you're going to deal with people like me, you're going to have to learn to govern your face."

"I didn't think you knew about it."

"It's in your boot," Eata told him softly.

"You spied on me!"

"Sometime when you took it out? No. But once when you sat on the gunnel, you jerked your feet away from the water; and when you slept, you kept your boots on. A boatman might have done that, but you? Not unless you had something more than your feet in them."

"I see."

Eata looked away, his eyes tracing the slow, immutable flow of great Gyoll to the southwest. "I knew a man who had one of those maps," he said. "A man can spend half his life looking, and never find a thing. Maybe it's under the sea now. Maybe someone found it long ago. Maybe it was never there at all. You understand? And he can't trust anyone, not his friend, not even his woman."

"And if his friend and his woman took it from him," the stranger said, "one might kill the other to have the whole of it. Yes, I see how it is. That isn't the map I have, if that's what you're thinking. I found this one between the pages of an old book."

"I was hoping it was mine," Eata told him. "You said you understood, but you don't. I let them take it. I wanted them to have it, so they'd leave me alone. So I wouldn't end up like the men we fought with yesterday. I got drunk, let them see the key, let them see me lock the map in my chest."

"But you woke," the stranger said.

Eata turned to face him, suddenly angry. "That fool Laetus broke the lock! I thought . . ."

"You don't have to tell me about it."

"He and Syntyche were younger than I. I only thought they'd waste their lives looking, the way I'd wasted mine, and Maxellindis's too. I didn't think he'd kill Syntyche."

"He killed her," the stranger said. "You didn't. You didn't make the two of them steal, either. You're not the Increate, and you can't take the responsibility for what others do."

"But I can advise them," Eata said. "And I'd advise you to burn your map, but I know you won't. So fold it up instead, put your seal on it, and take it to that goldsmith I told you about. He's an honest old fellow, and for an orichalk he'll lock it in his strongroom. Go home then till you're better. If you're wise you'll never come back to claim it."

The stranger shook his head. "I'm going to stay at the inn here. I've money enough. And I still owe you an asimi. Pike rent, we called it. Here it is."

Eata took the silver coin and tossed it up. It was bright, newly minted, with Severian's profile stamped deep and sharp on one side. In the reddish sunlight, it might have been a coal of fire.

"You knot the strings of that burse," Eata said. "Then knot them over again, all for fear I'll get into it when you sleep. Let me tell you something. If I come back for you, I'll have every brass aes before we're done. You'll take your money out, all of it, and give it to me, bit by bit."

He flung the asimi high over the water. For a final instant it shone, before it was quenched in dark Gyoll forever. "I'm not coming back," Eata said.

"It's a good map," the stranger told him. "Look." He drew it from the top of his boot and began to unwrap it, clumsily because he could not use both hands.

When he saw Eata's face, he stopped, thrust his map into his pocket, and clambered onto the half deck.

Weak from loss of blood and stiff with wounds, he could not get up to the wharf without help. One of the remaining loungers extended a hand, and he took it. At every moment he expected to feel a pike plunged into his back; there was only Eata's mocking laughter.

When he had both feet on the wharf, he turned toward the boat once more. Eata called, "Would you cast me off, please, Optimate?"

The stranger pointed, and the lounger who had helped him up untied the mooring line.

Eata pushed the boat away from the wharf and heaved the boom about to catch what wind there was.

"You'll come back for me!" the stranger shouted. "Because I'll let you come with me! Because I'll give you a share!"

Slowly and almost hesitantly, the old brown sail filled. The rigging grew taut, and the little cargo boat began to gather way. Eata did not look around, but his hand shook as it gripped the tiller.

Dinosaurs

WALTER JON WILLIAMS

Some millions of years ago, our ancestors were tiny, chittering, tree-dwelling insectivores. We've come a long way since then . . . but evolution is a process that *never* stops, as amply demonstrated by the story that follows, which takes us 6 million years into a very bizarre future for an unsettling look at some of our distant descendants. . . .

Walter Jon Williams was born in Minnesota and now lives in Albuquerque, New Mexico. Williams is a highly eclectic writer, and the fact is, one Walter Jon Williams story is rarely much like any *other* Walter Jon Williams story. He's written a wider range of different *kinds* of stuff than almost any other writer of his generation, ranging from some of the best Alternate History stories of the eighties (including the deeply moving Alternate Civil War novella, following Edgar Allan Poe's career as a Confederate general, "No Spot of Ground," and the compassionate and melancholy look at the alternate and alternately entangled lives that might have been led by Mary Wollstonecraft Shelley, Percy Bysshe Shelley, and Lord Byron, "Wall, Stone, Craft") to stories featuring scenarios quirky enough to rank with the most off-the-wall Waldropian stuff (sending H. G. Wells's invading Martians striding into the bizarre, ritualized, and mannered world of the Forbidden City in nineteenth-century China in "Foreign Devils" and presenting us with an Elvis Presley who grows up to become an inspirational Socialist leader whose influence changes the course of modern history in "Red Elvis"). He's written gritty Mean Streets hard-as-nails cyberpunk, in stories such as "Wolf Time," "Video Star," and "Flatline" and in novels such as *Hardwired* and *Voice of the Whirlwind;* he's written some of the most inventive widescreen Space Opera of recent times, including the monumental novel *Aristoi,* one of the most successful of modern Space Operas. He's written with depth and real ingenuity about the interaction of humankind with aliens, in the brilliant "Surfacing," as well as in novels such as *Angel Station.* He's written lighthearted, wryly amusing, socially satirical novels of manners, featuring the adventures of a Raffles-like thief in a future society, in *The Crown Jewels* and *House of Shards;* he's written dark, moody, intricate, involuted, Machiavellian studies of realpolitik in action, full of betrayals and counterbetrayals and counter-counterbetrayals, such as "Solip:System" and "Erogenoscape." Williams also *mixes* genres with audacity and daring, mixing classical Chinese mythology with the chop-sockey fantasy of Hong Kong martial arts movies in the droll "Broadway Johnny," mixing Sword and Sorcery with the Hornblower-like sea story in "Consequences," having costumed superheroes grilled by the House Committee on Un-American Activities in the McCarthy-era America of the 1950s in "Witness," and mixing fantasy with technologically oriented "hard" science fiction in books such as *Metropolitan* and *City on Fire* successfully enough to be counted as one of the progenitors of an as-yet-nascent subgenre sometimes called Hard Fantasy.

His short fiction has appeared frequently in *Asimov's Science Fiction,* as well as in the *Magazine of Fantasy & Science Fiction, Wheel of Fortune, Global Dispatches, Alternate Outlaws,* and other markets, and has been gathered in the collections *Facets* and *Frankensteins and Other Foreign Devils. His other novels include Ambassador of Progress, Knight Movies,* and *Days of Atonement.* His most recent book is a huge disaster thriller, *The Rift.*

The Shars seethed in the dim light of their ruddy sun. Pointed faces raised to the sky, they sniffed the faint wind for sign of the stranger and scented only hydrocarbons, far-off vegetation, damp fur, the sweat of excitement and fear. Weak eyes peered upward, glistened with hope, anxiety, apprehension, and saw only the faint pattern of stars. Short, excited barking sounds broke out here and there, but mostly the Shars crooned, a low ululation that told of sudden onslaught, destruction, war in distant reaches,
and now the hope of peace.

The crowds surged left, then right. Individuals bounced high on their third legs, seeking a view, seeing only the wide sea of heads, the ears and muzzles pointed to the stars.

Suddenly, a screaming. High-pitched howls, a bright chorus of barks. The crowds surged again.

Something was crossing the field of stars.

The human ship was huge, vaster than anything they'd seen, a moonlet descending. Shars closed their eyes and shuddered in terror. The screaming turned to moans. Individuals leaped high, baring their teeth, barking in defiance of their fear. The air smelled of terror, incipient panic, anger.

War! cried some. *Peace!* cried others.

The crooning went on. *We mourn, we mourn,* it said, *we mourn our dead billions.*

We fear, said others.

Soundlessly, the human ship neared them, casting its vast shadow. Shars spilled outward from the spot beneath, bounding high on their third legs.

The human ship came to a silent rest. Dully, it reflected the dim red sun.

The Shars crooned their fear, their sorrow. And waited for the humans to emerge.

These? Yes. These. Drill, the human ambassador, gazed through his video walls at the sea of Shars, the moaning, leaping thousands that surrounded him. Through the mass a group was moving with purpose, heading for the airlock as per his instructions. His new Memory crawled restlessly in the armored hollow atop his skull. *Stand by*, he broadcast.

His knees made painful crackling noises as he walked toward the airlock, the silver ball of his translator rolling along the ceiling ahead of him. The walls mutated as he passed, showing him violet sky, far-off polygonal buildings, cold distant green . . . and here, nearby, a vast, dim plain covered with a golden tissue of Shars.

He reached the airlock and it began to open. Drill snuffed wetly at the alien smells—heat, dust, the musky scent of the Shars themselves.

Drill's heart thumped in his chest. His dreams were coming true. He had waited all his life for this.

Mash, whimpered Lowbrain. Drill told it to be silent. Lowbrain protested vaguely, then obeyed.

Drill told Lowbrain to move. Cool, alien air brushed his skin. The Shars cried out sharply, moaned, fell back. They seemed a wild, sibilant ocean of pointed ears and dark, questing eyes. The group heading for the airlock vanished in the general retrograde movement, a stone washed by a pale tide. Beneath Drill's feet was soft vegetation. His translator floated in the air before him. His mind flamed with wonder, but Lowbrain kept him moving.

The Shars fell back, moaning.

Drill stood eighteen feet tall on his two pillarlike legs, each with a splayed foot that displayed a horny underside and vestigial nails. His skin was ebony and was draped in folds over his vast naked body. His pendulous maleness swung loosely as he walked. As he stepped across the open space he was conscious of the fact that he was the ultimate product of nine million years of human evolution, all leading to the expansion, diversification, and perfection that was now humanity's manifest existence.

He looked down at the little Shars, their white skin and golden fur, their strange, stiff tripod legs, the muzzles raised to him as if in awe. *If your species survives*, he thought benignly, *you can look like me in another few million years*.

The group of Shars that had been forging through the crowd were suddenly exposed when the crowd fell back from around them. On the perimeter were several Shars holding staffs—weapons, perhaps—in their clever little hands. In the center of these were a group of Shars wearing decorative ribbon to which metal plates had been attached. *Badges of rank*, Memory said. *Ignore*. The shadow of the translator bobbed toward them as Drill approached. Metallic geometries rose from the group and hovered over them.

Recorders, Memory said. *Artificial similarities to myself. Or possibly security devices. Disregard.*

Drill was getting closer to the party, speeding up his instructions to Lowbrain, eventually entering Zen Synch. It would make Lowbrain hungrier but lessen the chance of any accidents.

The Shars carrying the staffs fell back. A wailing went up from the crowd as one of the Shars stepped toward Drill. The ribbons draped over her sloping shoulders failed to disguise four mammalian breasts. Clear plastic bubbles covered her weak eyes. In Zen Synch with Memory and Lowbrain, Drill ambled up to her and raised his hands in friendly greeting. The Shar flinched at the expanse of the gesture.

"I am Ambassador Drill," he said. "I am a human."

The Shar gazed up at him. Her nose wrinkled as she listened to the booming voice of the translator. Her answer was a succession of sharp sounds, made high in the throat, somewhat unpleasant. Drill listened to the voice of his translator.

"I am President Gram of the InterSharian Sociability of Nations and Planets." That's how it came through in translation, anyway. Memory began feeding Drill referents for the word "nation."

"I welcome you to our planet, Ambassador Drill."

"Thank you, President Gram," Drill said. "Shall we negotiate peace now?"

President Gram's ears pricked forward, then back. There was a pause, and then from the vast circle of Shars came a mad torrent of hooting noises. The awesome sound lapped over Drill like the waves of a lunatic sea.

They approve your sentiment, said Memory.

I thought that's what it meant, Drill said. *Do you think we'll get along?*

Memory didn't answer, but instead shifted to a more comfortable position in the saddle of Drill's skull. Its job was to provide facts, not draw conclusions.

"If you could come into my Ship," Drill said, "we could get started."

"Will we then meet the other members of your delegation?"

Drill gazed down at the Shar. The fur on her shoulders was rising in odd tufts. She seemed to be making a concerted effort to calm it.

"There are no other members," Drill said. "Just myself."

His knees were paining him. He watched as the other members of the Shar party cast quick glances at each other.

"No secretaries? No assistants?" the President was saying.

"No," Drill said. "Not at all. I'm the only conscious mind on Ship. Shall we get started?"

Eat! Eat! said Lowbrain. Drill ordered it to be silent. His stomach grumbled.

"Perhaps," said President Gram, gazing at the vastness of the human ship, "it would be best should we begin in a few hours. I should probably speak to the crowd. Would you care to listen?"

No need, Memory said. *I will monitor.*

"Thank you, no," Drill said. "I shall return to Ship for food and sex. Please signal me when you are ready. Please bring any furniture you may need for your comfort. I do not believe my furniture would fit you, although we might be able to clone some later."

The Shars' ears all pricked forward. Drill entered Zen Synch, turned his huge body, and began accelerating toward the airlock. The sound of the crowd behind him was like the murmuring of wind through a stand of trees.

Peace, he thought later, as he stood by the mash bins and fed his complaining stomach. *It's a simple thing. How long can it take to arrange?*

Long, said Memory. *Very long.*

The thought disturbed him. He thought the first meeting had gone well.

After his meal, when he had sex, it wasn't very good.

★ ★ ★

Memory had been monitoring the events outside Ship, and after Drill had completed sex, Memory showed him the outside events. *They have been broadcast to the entire population*, Memory said.

President Gram had moved to a local elevation and had spoken for some time. Drill found her speech interesting—it was rhythmic and incantorial, rising and falling in tone and volume, depending heavily on repetition and melody. The crowd participated, issuing forth with excited barks or low moans in response to her statements or questions, sometimes babbling in confusion when she posed them a conundrum. Memory only gave the highlights of the speech. "Unknown . . . attackers . . . billions dead . . . preparations advanced . . . ready to defend ourselves . . . offer of peace . . . hope in the darkness . . . unknown . . . willing to take the chance . . . peace . . . peace . . . hopeful smell . . . peace." At the end the other Shars were all singing "Peace! Peace!" in chorus while President Gram bounced up and down on her sturdy rear leg.

It sounds pretty, Drill thought. *But why does she go on like that?*

Memory's reply was swift.

Remember that the Shars are a generalized and social species, it said. *President Gram's power, and her ability to negotiate, derives from the degree of her popular support. In measures of this significance she must explain herself and her actions to the population in order to maintain their enthusiasm for her policies.*

Primitive, Drill thought.

That is correct.

Why don't they let her get on with her work? Drill asked.

There was no reply.

After an exchange of signals the Shar party assembled at the airlock. Several Shars had been mobilized to carry tables and stools. Drill sent a Frog to escort the Shars from the airlock to where he waited. The Frog met them inside the airlock, turned, and hopped on ahead through Ship's airy, winding corridors. It had been trained to repeat "Follow me, follow me" in the Shars' own language.

Drill waited in a semi-reclined position on a Slab. The Slab was an organic sub-species used as furniture, with an idiot brain capable of responding to human commands. The Shars entered cautiously, their weak eyes twitching in the bright light. "Welcome, Honorable President," Drill said. "Up, Slab." Slab began to adjust itself to place Drill on his feet. The Shars were moving tables and stools into the vast room.

Frog was hopping in circles, making a wet noise at each landing. "Follow me, follow me," it said.

The members of the Shar delegation who bore badges of rank stood in a body while the furniture-carriers bustled around them. Drill noticed, as Slab put him on his feet, that they were wrinkling their noses. He wondered what it meant.

His knees crackled as he came fully upright. "Please make yourselves comfortable," he said. "Frog will show your laborers to the airlock."

"Does your Excellency object to a mechanical recording of the proceedings?" President Gram asked. She was shading her eyes with her hand.

"Not at all." As a number of devices rose into the air above the party, Drill wondered if it were possible to give the Shars detachable Memories. Perhaps human bioengineers could adapt the Memories to the Shar physiology. He asked Memory to make a note of the question so that he could bring it up later.

"Follow me, follow me," Frog said. The workers who had carried the furniture began to follow the hopping Frog out of the room.

"Your Excellency," President Gram said, "may I have the honor of presenting to you the other members of my delegation?"

There were six in all, with titles like Secretary for Syncopated Speech and Special Executive for External Coherence. There was also a Minister for the Dissemination of Convincing Lies, whose title Drill suspected was somehow mistranslated, and an Opposite Secretary-General for the Genocidal Eradication of Alien Aggressors, at whom Drill looked with more than a little interest. The Opposite Secretary-General was named Vang, and was small even for a Shar. He seemed to wrinkle his nose more than the others. The Special Executive for External Coherence, whose name was Cup, seemed a bit piebald, patches of white skin showing through the golden fur covering his shoulders, arms, and head.

He is elderly, said Memory.

That's what I thought.

"Down, Slab," Drill said. He leaned back against the creature and began to move to a more relaxed position.

He looked at the Shars and smiled. Fur ruffled on shoulders and necks. "Shall we make peace now?" he asked.

"We would like to clarify something you said earlier," President Gram said. "You said that you were the only, ah, conscious entity on the ship. That you were the only member of the human delegation. Was that translated correctly?"

"Why, yes," Drill said. "Why would more than one diplomat be necessary?"

The Shars looked at each other. The Special Executive for External Coherence spoke cautiously.

"You will not be needing to consult with your superiors? You have full authority from your government?"

Drill beamed at them. "We humans do not have a government, of course," he said. "But I am a diplomat with the appropriate Memory and training. There is no problem that I can foresee."

"Please let me understand, your Excellency," Cup said. He was leaning forward, his small eyes watering. "I am elderly and may be slow in comprehending the situation. But if you have no government, who accredited you with this mission?"

"I am a diplomat. It is my specialty. No accreditation is necessary. The human race will accept my judgment on any matter of negotiation, as they would accept the judgment of any specialist in his area of expertise."

"But why *you*. As an individual?"

Drill shrugged massively. "I was part of the nearest diplomatic enclave, and the individual without any other tasks at the moment." He looked at each of the delegation in turn. "I am incredibly happy to have this chance, honorable delegates," he said. "The vast majority of human diplomats never have the chance to speak to another species. Usually we mediate only in conflicts of interest between the various groups of human specialities."

"But the human species will abide by your decisions?"

"Of course." Drill was surprised at the Shar's persistence. "Why wouldn't they?"

Cup settled back in his chair. His ears were down. There was a short silence.

"We have an opening statement prepared," President Gram said. "I would like to enter it into our record, if I may. Or would your Excellency prefer to go first?"

"I have no opening statement," Drill said. "Please go ahead."

Cup and the President exchanged glances. President Gram took a deep breath and began.

Long, Memory said. *Very long*.

The opening statement seemed very much like the address President Gram had been delivering to the crowd, the same hypnotic rhythms, more or less the same content. The rest of the delegation made muted responses. Drill drowsed through it, enjoying it as music.

"Thank you, Honorable President," he said afterwards. "That was very nice."

"We would like to propose an agenda for the conference," Gram said. "First, to resolve the matter of the cease-fire and its provisions for an ending to hostilities. Second, the establishment of a secure border between our two species, guaranteeing both species room for expansion. Third, the establishment of trade and visitation agreements. Fourth, the matter of reparations, payments, and return of lost territory."

Drill nodded. "I believe," he said, "that resolution of the second through fourth points will come about as a result of an understanding reached on the first. That is, once the cease-fire is settled, that resolution will imply a settlement of the rest of the situation."

"You accept the agenda?"

"If you like. It doesn't matter."

Ears pricked forward, then back. "So you accept that our initial discussions will consist of formalizing the disengagement of our forces?"

"Certainly. Of course I have no way of knowing what forces you have committed. We humans have committed none."

The Shars were still for a long time. "Your species attacked our planets, Ambassador. Without warning, without making yourselves known to us." Gram's tone was unusually flat. Perhaps, Drill thought, she was attempting to conceal great emotion.

"Yes," Drill said. "But those were not our military formations. Your species were contacted only by our terraforming Ships. They did not attack your people, as such—they were only peripherally aware of your existence. Their function was merely to seed the plants with lifeforms favorable to human existence. Unfortunately for your people, part of the function of these lifeforms is to destroy the native life of the planet."

The Shars conferred with one another. The Opposite Secretary-General seemed particularly vehement. Then President Gram turned to Drill.

"We cannot accept your statement, your Excellency," she said. "Our people were attacked. They defended themselves, but were overcome."

"Our terraforming Ships are very good at what they do," Drill said. "They are specialists. Our Shrikes, our Shrews, our Sharks—each is a master of its element.

But they lack intelligence. They are not conscious entities, such as ourselves. They weren't aware of your civilization at all. They only saw you as food."

"You're claiming that you *didn't notice us?*" demanded Secretary-General Vang. *"They didn't notice us as they were killing us?"* He was shouting. President Gram's ears went back.

"Not as such, no," Drill said.

President Gram stood up. "I am afraid, your Excellency, your explanations are insufficient," she said. "This conference must be postponed until we can reach a united conclusion concerning your remarkable attitude."

Drill was bewildered. "What did I say?" he asked.

The other Shars stood. President Gram turned and walked briskly on her three legs toward the exit. The others followed.

"Wait," Drill said. "Don't go. Let me send for Frog. Up, Slab, up!"

The Shars were gone by the time Slab had got Drill to his feet. The Ship told him they had found their own way to the airlock. Drill could think of nothing to do but order the airlock to let them out.

"Why would I lie?" he asked. "Why would I lie to them?" Things were so very simple, really.

He shifted his vast weight from one foot to the other and back again. Drill could not decide whether he had done anything wrong. He asked Memory what to do next, but Memory held no information to comfort him, only dry recitations of past negotiations. Annoyed at the lifeless monologue, Drill told Memory to be silent and began to walk restlessly through the corridors of his Ship. He could not decide where things had gone bad.

Sensing his agitation, Lowbrain began to echo his distress. *Mash*, Lowbrain thought weakly. *Food. Sex.*

Be silent, Drill commanded.

Sex, sex, Lowbrain thought.

Drill realized that Lowbrain was beginning to give him an erection. Acceding to the inevitable, he began moving toward Surrogate's quarters.

Surrogate lived in a dim, quiet room filled with the murmuring sound of its own heartbeat. It was a human subspecies, about the intelligence of Lowbrain, designed to comfort voyagers on long journeys through space, when carnal access to their own subspecies might necessarily be limited. Surrogate had a variety of sexual equipment designed for the accommodation of the various human subspecies and their sexes. It also had large mammaries that gave nutritious milk, and a rudimentary head capable of voicing simple thoughts.

Tiny Mice, that kept Surrogate and the ship clean, scattered as Drill entered the room. Surrogate's little head turned to him.

"It's good to see you again," Surrogate said.

"I am Drill."

"It's good to see you again, Drill," said Surrogate. "It's good to see you again."

Drill began to nuzzle its breasts. One of Surrogate's male parts began to erect. "I'm confused, Surrogate," he said. "I don't know what to do."

"Why are you confused, Drill?" asked Surrogate. It raised one of its arms and began to stroke Drill's head. It wasn't really having a conversation: Surrogate had only been programmed to make simple statements, or to analyze its partners' speech and ask questions.

"Things are going wrong," Drill said. He began to suckle. The warm milk flowed down his throat. Surrogate's male part had an orgasm. Mice jumped from hiding to clean up the mess.

"Why are things going wrong?" asked Surrogate. "I'm sure everything will be all right."

Lowbrain had an orgasm, perceived by Drill as scattered, faraway bits of pleasure. Drill continued to suckle, feeling a heavy comfort beginning to radiate from Surrogate, from the gentle sound of its heartbeat, its huge, wholesome, brainless body.

Everything will be all right, Drill decided.

"Nice to see you again, Drill," Surrogate said. "Drill, it's *nice* to see you again."

The vast crowds of Shars did not leave when night fell. Instead they stood beneath floating globes dispersing a cold reddish light that reflected eerily from pointed ears and muzzles. Some of them donned capes or skirts to help them keep warm. Drill, watching them on the video walls of the command center, was reminded of crowds standing in awe before some vast cataclysm.

The Shars were not quiet. They stood in murmuring groups, but sometimes they began the crooning chants they had raised earlier, or suddenly broke out in a series of shrill yipping cries.

President Gram spoke to them after she had left Ship. "The human has admitted his species' attacks," she said, "but has disclaimed responsibility. We shall urge him to adopt a more realistic position."

"Adopt a position," Drill repeated, not understanding. "It is not a position. It is the truth. Why don't they understand?"

Opposite Minister-General Vang was more vehement. "We now have a far more complete idea of the humans' attitude," he said. "It is opposed to ours in every way. We shall not allow the murderous atrocities which the humans have committed upon five of our planets to be forgotten, or understood to be the result of some inexplicable lack of attention on the part of our species' enemies."

"That one is obviously deranged," thought Drill.

He went to his sleeping quarters and ordered the Slab there to play him some relaxing music. Even with Slab's murmurs and comforting hums, it took Drill some time before his agitation subsided.

Diplomacy, he thought as slumber overtook him, was certainly a strange business.

In the morning the Shars were still there, chanting and crying, moving in their strange crowded patterns. Drill watched them on his video walls as he ate breakfast at the mash bins. "There is a communication from President Gram," Memory announced. "She wishes to speak with you by radio."

"Certainly."

"Ambassador Drill." She was using the flat tones again. A pity she was subject to such stress.

"Good morning, President Gram," Drill said. "I hope you spent a pleasant night."

"I must give you the results of our decision. We regret that we can see no way to continue the negotiations unless you, as a representative of your species, agree to admit responsibility for your peoples' attacks on our planets."

"Admit responsibility?" Drill said. "Of course. Why wouldn't I?"

Drill heard some odd, indistinct barking sounds that his translator declined to interpret for him. It sounded as if someone other than President Gram were on the other end of the radio link.

"You admit responsibility?" President Gram's amazement was clear even in translation.

"Certainly. Does it make a difference?"

President Gram declined to answer that question. Instead she proposed another meeting for that afternoon.

"I will be ready at any time."

Memory recorded President Gram's speech to her people, and Drill studied it before meeting the Shar party at the airlock. She made a great deal out of the fact that Drill had admitted humanity's responsibility for the war. Her people leaped, yipped, chanted their responses as if possessed. Drill wondered why they were so excited.

Drill met the party at the airlock this time, linked with Memory and Lowbrain in Zen Synch so as not to accidentally step on the President or one of her party. He smiled and greeted each by name and led them toward the conference room.

"I believe," said Cup, "we may avoid future misunderstandings, if your Excellency would consent to inform us about your species. We have suffered some confusion in regard to your distinction between 'conscious' and 'unconscious' entities. Could you please explain the difference, as you understand it?"

"A pleasure, your Excellency," Drill said. "Our species, unlike yours, is highly specialized. Once, eight million years ago, we were like you—a small, nonspecialized species type is very useful at a certain stage of evolution. But once a species reaches a certain complexity in its social and technological evolution, the need for specialists becomes too acute. Through both deliberate genetic manipulation and natural evolution, humanity turned away from a generalist species, toward highly specialized forms adapted to particular functions and environments. We understand this to be a natural function of species evolution.

"In the course of our explorations into manipulating our species, we discovered that the most efficient way of coding large amounts of information was in our own cell structure—our DNA. For tasks requiring both large and small amounts of data, we arranged that, as much as possible, these would be performed by organic entities, human subspecies. Since many of these tasks were boring and repetitive, we reasoned that advanced consciousness, such as that which we both share, was not necessary. You have met several unconscious entities. Frog, for example, and the Slab on which I lie. Many parts of my Ship are also alive, though not conscious."

"That would explain the smell," one of the delegation murmured.

"The terraforming Ships," Drill went on, "which attacked your planets—these were also designed so as not to require a conscious operator."

The Shars squinted up at Drill with their little eyes. "But why?" Cup asked.

"Terraforming is a dull process. It takes many years. No conscious mind could possibly enjoy it."

"But your species would find itself at war without knowing it. If your explanation for the cause of this war is correct, you already have."

Drill shrugged massively. "This happens from time to time. Sometimes other species which have reached our stage of development have attacked us in the same way. When it does, we arrange a peace."

"You consider these attacks normal?" Opposite Minister-General Vang was the one who spoke.

"These occasional encounters seem to be a natural result of species evolution," Drill said.

Vang turned to one of the Shars near him and spoke in several sharp barks. Drill heard a few words: "Billions lost . . . five planets . . . atrocities . . . *natural result!*"

"I believe," said President Gram, "that we are straying from the agenda."

Vang looked at her. "Yes, honorable President. Please forgive me."

"The matter of withdrawal," said President Gram, "to recognized truce lines."

Species at this stage of their development tend to be territorial, Memory reminded Drill. *Their political mentality is based around the concept of borders. The idea of a borderless community of species may be perceived as a threat.*

I'll try and go easy on them, Drill said.

"The Memories on our terraforming Ships will be adjusted to account for your species," Drill said. "After the adjustment, your people will no longer be in danger."

"In our case, it will take the disengage order several months to reach all our forces," President Gram said. "How long will the order take to reach your own Ships?"

"A century or so." The Shars stared. "Memories at our exploration basis in this area will be adjusted first, of course, and these will adjust the Memories of terraforming Ships as they come in for maintenance and supplies."

"We'll be subject to attack for *another hundred years?*" Vang's tone mixed incredulity and scorn.

"Our terraforming Ships move more or less at random, and only come into base when they run out of supplies. We don't know where they've been till they report back. Though they're bound to encounter a few more of your planets, your species will still survive, enough to continue your species evolution. And during that time you'll be searching for and occupying new planets on your own. You'll probably come out of this with a net gain."

"Have you no respect for life?" Vang demanded. Drill considered his answer.

"All individuals die, Opposite Minister-General," he said. "That is a fact of nature which no species has been able to alter. Only species can survive. Individuals are easily replaceable. Though you will lose some planets and a large number of individuals, your species as a whole will survive and may even prosper. What more could a species or its delegated representatives desire?"

Opposite Minister-General Vang was glaring at Drill, his ears pricked forward, lips drawn back from his teeth. He said nothing.

"We desire a cease-fire that is a true cease-fire," President Gram said. Her hands were clasping and unclasping rhythmically on the edge of her chair. "Not a slow, authorized extermination of our species. Your position has an unwholesome smell. I am afraid we must end these discussions until you alter it."

"Position? This is not a position, honorable President. It is truth."

"We have nothing further to say."

Unhappily, Drill followed the Shar delegation to the airlock. "I do not lie, honorable President," he said, but Gram only turned away and silently left the human Ship. The Shars in their pale thousands received her.

The Shar broadcasts were not heartening. Opposite Minister-General Vang was particularly vehement. Drill collected the highlights of the speeches as he speeded through Memory's detailed remembrance. "Callous disregard . . . no common ground for communication . . . casual attitude toward atrocity . . . displays of obvious savagery . . . no respect for the individual . . . defend ourselves . . . this stinks in the nose."

The Shars leaped and barked in response. There were strange bubbling high-pitched laughing sounds that Drill found unsettling.

"We hope to find a formula for peace," President Gram said. "We will confer with all the ministers in session." That was all.

That night, the Shars surrounding Ship moaned, moving slowly in a giant circle, their arms linked. The laughing sounds that followed Vang's speech did not cease entirely. He did not understand why they did not all go home and sleep.

Long, long, Memory said. No comfort there.

Early in the morning, before dawn, there was a communication from President Gram. "I would like to meet with you privately. Away from the recorders, the coalition partners."

"I would like nothing better," Drill said. He felt a small current of optimism begin to trickle into him.

"Can I use an airlock other than the one we've been using up till now?"

Drill gave President Gram instructions and met her in the other airlock. She was wearing a night cape with a hood. The Shars, circling and moaning, had paid her no attention.

"Thank you for seeing me under these conditions," she said, peering up at him from beneath the hood. Drill smiled. She shuddered.

"I am pleased to be able to cooperate," he said.

Mash! Lowbrain demanded. It had been silent until Drill entered Zen Synch. Drill told it to be silent with a snarling vehemence that silenced it for the present.

"This way, honorable President," Drill said. He took her to his sleeping chamber—a small room, only fifty feet square. "Shall I send a Frog for one of your chairs?" he asked.

"I will stand. Three legs seem to be more comfortable than two for standing."

"Yes."

"Is it possible, Ambassador Drill, that you could lower the intensity of the light here? I find it oppressive."

Drill felt foolish, knowing he should have thought of this himself. "I'm sorry," he said. "I will give the orders at once. I wish you had told me earlier." He smiled nervously as he dimmed the lights and arranged himself on his Slab.

"Honorable ambassador." President Gram's words seemed hesitant. "I wonder if it is possible . . . can you tell me the meaning of that facial gesture of yours, showing me your teeth?"

"It is called a smile. It is intended as a gesture of benevolent reassurance."

"Showing of the teeth is considered a threat here, honorable ambassador. Some of us have considered this a sign that you wish to eat us."

Drill was astonished. "My goodness!" he said. "I don't even eat meat! Just a kind of vegetable mash."

"I pointed out that your teeth seemed unsuitable for eating meat, but still it makes us uneasy. I was wondering . . ."

"I will try to suppress the smile, yes. Eating meat! What an idea. Some of our military specialists, yes, and of course the Sharks and Shrikes and so on . . ." He told his Memory to enforce a strict ban against smiling in the presence of a Shar.

Gram leaned back on her sturdy rear leg. Her cape parted, revealing her ribbons and badges of office, her four furry dugs. "I wanted to inform you of certain difficulties here, Ambassador Drill," she said. "I am having difficulty holding together my coalition. Minister-General Vang's faction is gaining strength. He is attempting to create a perception in the minds of Shars that you are untrustworthy and violent. Whether he believes this, or whether he is using this notion as a means of destabilizing the coalition, is hardly relevant—considering your species' unprovoked attacks, it is not a difficult perception to reinforce. He is also trying to tell our people that the military is capable of dealing with your species."

Drill's brain swam with Memory's information on concepts such as "faction" and "coalition." The meaning of the last sentence, however, was clear.

"That is a foolish perception, honorable President," he said.

"His assurances on that score lack conviction." Gram's eyes were shiny. Her tone grew earnest. "You must give me something, ambassador. Something I can use to soothe the public mind. A way out of this dilemma. I tell you that it is impossible to expect us to sit idly by and accept the loss of an undefined number of planets over the next hundred years. I plead with you, ambassador. Give me something. Some way we can avoid attack. Otherwise . . ." She left the sentence incomplete.

Mash, Lowbrain wailed. Drill ignored it. He moved into Zen Synch with Memory, racing through possible solutions. Sweat gathered on his forehead, pouring down his vast shoulders.

"Yes," he said. "Yes, there is a possibility. If you could provide us with the location of all your occupied planets, we could dispatch a Ship to each with the appropriate Memories as cargo. If any of our terraforming Ships arrived, the Memories could be transferred at once, and your planets would be safe."

President Gram considered this. "Memories," she said. "You've been using the term, but I'm not sure I understand."

"Stored information is vast, and even though human bodies are large we cannot always have all the information we need to function efficiently even in our specialized tasks," Drill said. "Our human brains have been separated as to function. I have a Lowbrain, which is on my spinal cord above my pelvis. Lowbrain handles motor control of my lower body, routine monitoring of my body's condition, eating, excretion, and sex. My perceptual centers, short-term memory, personality, and reasoning functions are handled by the brain in my skull—the classical brain, if you like. Long-term and specialized memory is the function of the large knob you see moving on my head, my Memory. My Memory records all that happens in great detail, and can recapitulate it at any point. It has also been supplied with information concerning the human species' contacts with other nonhuman groups. It attaches itself easily to my nervous system and draws nourishment from my body. Specific memories can be communicated from one living Memory to another, or if it proves necessary I can simply give my Memory to another human, a complete transfer. I have another Memory aboard that I'm not using at the moment, a pilot Memory that can navigate and handle Ship, and I wore this Memory while in transit. I also have spare Memories in case my primary Memories fall ill. So you see, our specialization does not rule out adaptability—any piece of information needed by any of us can easily be transferred, and in far greater detail than by any mechanical medium."

"So you could return to your base and send out pilot Memories to our planets," Gram said. "Memories that could halt your terraforming ships."

"That is correct." Just in time, Memory managed to stop the twitch in Drill's cheeks from becoming a smile. Happiness bubbled up in him. He was going to arrange this peace after all!

"I am afraid that would not be acceptable, your Excellency," President Gram said. Drill's hopes fell.

"Whyever not?"

"I'm afraid the Minister-General would consider it a naïve attempt of yours to find out the location of our populated planets. So that your species could attack them, ambassador."

"I'm trying very hard, President Gram," Drill said.

"I'm sure you are."

Drill frowned and went into Zen Synch again, ignoring Lowbrain's plaintive cries for mash and sex, sex and mash. Concepts crackled through his mind. He began to develop an erection, but Memory was drawing off most of the available blood and the erection failed. The smell of Drill's sweat filled the room. President Gram wrinkled her nose and leaned back far onto her rear leg.

"Ah," Drill said. "A solution. Yes. I can have my Pilot memory provide the locations to an equivalent number of our own planets. We will have one another's planets as hostage."

"Bravo, ambassador," President Gram said quietly. "I think we may have a solution. But—forgive me—it may be said that we cannot trust your information. We will have to send ships to verify the location of your planets."

"If your ships go to my planet first," Drill said, "I can provide your people with one of my spare Memories that will inform my species what your people are doing, and instruct the humans to cooperate. We will have to construct some kind of link between your radio and my Memory . . . maybe I can have my Ship grow one."

President Gram came forward off her third leg and began to pace forward, moving in her strange, fast, hobbling way. "I can present it to the council this way, yes," she said. "There is hope here." She stopped her movement, peering up at

Drill with her ears pricked forward. "Is it possible that you could allow me to present this to the council as my own idea?" she asked. "It may meet with less suspicion that way."

"Whatever way is best," said Drill. President Gram gazed into the darkened recesses of the room.

"This smells good," she said. Drill succeeded in suppressing his smile.

"It's nice to see you again."

"I am Drill."

"It's nice to see you again, Drill."

"I think we can make the peace work."

"Everything will be all right, Drill. Drill, I'm sure everything will be all right."

"I'm so glad I had this chance. This is the chance of a lifetime."

"Drill, it's *nice* to see you again."

The next day President Gram called and asked to present a new plan. Drill said he would be pleased to hear it. He met the party at the airlock, having already dimmed the lights. He was very rigid in his attempts not to smile.

They sat in the dimmed room while President Gram presented the plan. Drill pretended to think it over, then acceded. Details were worked out. First the location of one human planet would be given and verified—this planet, the Shar capital, would count as the first revealed Shar planet. After verification, each side would reveal the location of two planets, verify those, then reveal four, and so on. Even counting the months it would take to verify the location of planets, the treaty should be completed within less than five years.

That night the Shars went mad. At President Gram's urging, they built fires, danced, screamed, sang. Drill watched on his Ship's video walls. Their rhythms beat at his head.

He smiled. For hours.

The Ship obligingly grew a communicator and coupled it to one of Drill's spare Memories. The two were put aboard a Shar ship and sent in the direction of Drill's home. Drill remained in his ship, watching entertainment videos Ship received from the Shars' channels. He didn't understand the dramas very well, but the comedies were delightful. The Shars could do the most intricate, clever things with their flexible bodies and odd tripod legs—it was delightful to watch them.

Maybe I could take some home with me, he thought. *They can be very entertaining.*

The thousands of Shars waiting outside Ship began to drift away. Within a month only a few hundred were left. Their singing was quiet, triumphant, assured. Sometimes Drill had it piped into his sleeping chamber. It helped him relax.

President Gram visited informally every ten days or so. Drill showed her around Ship, showing her the pilot Memory, the Frog quarters, the giant stardrive engines with their human subspecies' implanted connections, Surrogate in its shadowed, pleasant room. The sight of Surrogate seemed to agitate the President.

"You do not use sex for procreation?" she asked. "As an expression of affection?"

"Indeed we do. I have scads of offspring. There are never enough diplomats, so we have a great many couplings among our subspecies. As for affection . . . I think I can say that I have enjoyed the company of each of my partners."

She looked up at him with solemn eyes. "You travel to the stars, Drill," she said. "Your species expands randomly in all directions, encountering other species, sometimes annihilating them. Do you have a reason for any of this?"

"A reason?" Drill mused. "It is natural to us. Natural to all intelligent species, so far as we know."

"I meant a conscious reason. Is it anything other than what you do in an automatic way?"

"I can't think of why we would need any such reasons."

"So you have no philosophy of constant expansion? No ideology?"

"I do not know what those words mean," Drill said.

Gram closed her eyes and lowered her head. "I am sorry," she said.

"No need. We have no conflicts in our ideas about ourselves, about our lives. We are happy with what we are."

"Yes. You couldn't be unhappy if you tried, could you?"

"No," Drill said cheerfully. "I see that you understand."

"Yes," Gram said. "I scent that I do."

"In a few million years," Drill said, "these things will become clear to you."

The first Shar ship returned from Drill's home, reporting a transfer of the Memory. The field around Ship filled again with thousands of Shars, crying their happiness to the skies. Other Memories were now taking instructions to all terraforming bases. The locations of two new planets were released. Ships carrying spare Memories leaped into the skies.

It's working, Drill told Memory.

Long, Memory said. *Very long*.

But Memory could not lower Drill's joy. This was what he had lived his life for, and he knew he was good at it. Memories of the future would take this solution as a model for negotiations with other species. Things were working out.

One night the Shars outside Ship altered their behavior. Their singing became once again a moaning, mixed with cries. Drill was disturbed.

A communication came from the President. "Cup is dead," she said.

"I understand," Drill said. "Who is his replacement?"

Drill could not read Gram's expression. "That is not yet known. Cup was a strong person, and did not like other strong people around him. Already the successors are fighting for the leadership, but they may not be able to hold his faction together." Her ears flickered. "I may be weakened by this."

"I regret things tend that way."

"Yes," she said. "So do I."

The second set of ships returned. More Memories embarked on their journeys. The treaty was holding.

There was a meeting aboard Ship to formalize the agreement. Cup's successor was Brook, a tall, elderly Shar whose golden fur was darkened by age. A compromise candidate, President Gram said, his election determined after weeks of fighting for the successorship. He was not respected. Already pieces of Cup's old faction were breaking away.

"I wonder, your Excellency," Brook said, after the formal business was over, "if you could arrange for our people to learn your language. You must have powerful translation modules aboard your ship in order to learn our language so quickly. You were broadcasting your message of peace within a few hours of entering real space."

"I have no such equipment aboard Ship," Drill said. "Our knowledge of your language was acquired from Shar prisoners."

"Prisoners?" Shar ears pricked forward. "We were not aware of this," Brook said.

"After our base Memories recognized discrepancies," Drill said, "we sent some Ships out searching for you. We seized one of your ships and took it to my home world. The prisoners were asked about their language and the location of your capital planet. Otherwise it would have taken me months to find your world here, and learn to communicate with you."

"May we ask to arrange for the return of the prisoners?"

"Oh." Drill said. "That won't be possible. After we learned what we needed to know, we terminated their lives. They were being kept in an area reserved for a garden. The landscapers wanted to get to work." Drill bobbed his head reassuringly. "I am pleased to inform you that they proved excellent fertilizer for the gardens. The result was quite lovely."

"I think," said President Gram carefully, "that it would be best that this information not go beyond those of us in this room. I think it would disturb the process."

Minister-General Vang's ears went back. So did others'. But they acceded.

"I think we should take our leave," said President Gram.

"Have a pleasant afternoon," said Drill.

"It's important." It was not yet dawn. Ship had awakened Drill for a call from the President. "One of your ships has attacked another of our planets."

Alarm drove the sleep from Drill's brain. "Please come to the airlock," he said.

"The information will reach the population within the hour."

"Come quickly," said Drill.

The President arrived with a pair of assistants, who stayed inside the airlock.

They carried staves. "My people will be upset," Gram said. "Things may not be entirely safe."

"Which planet was it?" Drill asked.

Gram rubbed her ears. "It was one of those whose location went out on the last peace shuttle."

"The new Memory must not have arrived in time."

"That is what we will tell the people. That it couldn't have been prevented. I will try to speed up the process by which the planets receive new Memories. Double the quota."

"That is a good idea."

"I will have to dismiss Brook. Opposite Minister-General Vang will have to take his job. If I can give Vang more power, he may remain in the coalition and not cause a split."

"As you think best."

President Gram looked up at Drill, her head rising reluctantly, as if held back by a great weight. "My son," she said. "He was on the planet when it happened."

"You have other offspring," Drill said.

Gram looked at him, the pain burning deep in her eyes. "Yes," she said. "I do."

The fields around Ship filled once again. Cries and howls rent the air, and dirges pulsed against Ship's uncaring walls. The Shar broadcasts in the next weeks seemed confused to Drill. Coalitions split and fragmented. Vang spoke frequently of readiness. President Gram succeeded in doubling the quota of planets. The decision was a near one.

Then, days later, another message. "One of our commanders," said President Gram, "was based on the vicinity of the attacked planet. He is one of Vang's creatures. On his own initiative he ordered our military forces to engage. Your terraforming Ship was attacked."

"Was it destroyed?" Drill asked. His tone was urgent. There is still hope, he reminded himself.

"Don't be anxious for your fellow humans," Gram said. "The Ship was damaged, but escaped."

"The loss of a few hundred billion unconscious organisms is no cause for anxiety," Drill said. "An escaped terraforming Ship is. The Ship will alert our military forces. It will be a real war."

President Gram licked her lips. "What does that mean?"

"You know of our Shrikes and so on. Our military people are worse. They are fully conscious and highly specialized in different modes of warfare. They are destructive, carnivorous, capable of taking enormous damage without impairing function. Their minds concentrate only on tactics, on destruction. Normally they are kept on planetoids away from the rest of humanity. Even other humans find their proximity too . . . disturbing." Drill put all the urgency in his speech that he could. "Honorable President, you must give me the locations of the remaining planets. If I can get Memories to each of them with news of the peace, we may yet save them."

"I will try. But the coalition . . ." She turned away from the transmitter. "Vang will claim a victory."

"It is the worst possible catastrophe," Drill said.

Gram's tone was grave. "I believe you," she said.

Drill listened to the broadcasts with growing anxiety. The Shars who spoke on the broadcasts were making angry comments about the execution of prisoners, about flower gardens and values Drill didn't understand. Someone had let the secret loose. President Gram went from group to group outside Ship, talking of the necessity of her plan. The Shars' responses were muted. Drill sensed they were waiting. It was announced that Vang had left the coalition. A chorus of triumphant yips rose from scattered members of the crowd. Others only moaned.

Vang, now simply General Vang, arrived at the field. His followers danced intoxicated circles around him as he spoke, howling their responses to his words. "Triumph! United will!" they cried. "The humans can be beaten! Treachery avenged! Dictate the peace from a position of strength! We smell the location of their planets!"

The Shars' weird cackling laughter followed him from point to point. The laughing and crying went on well into the night. In the morning the announcement came that the coalition had fallen. Vang was now President-General.

In his sleeping chamber, surrounded by his video walls, Drill began to weep.

"I have been asked to bear Vang's message to you," Gram said. She seemed smaller than before, standing unsteadily even on her tripod legs. "It is his . . . humor."

"What is the message?" Drill said. His whole body seemed in pain. Even Lowbrain was silent, wrapped in misery.

"I had hoped," Gram said, "that he was using this simply as an issue on which to gain power. That once he had the Presidency, he would continue the diplomatic effort. It appears he really means what he's been saying. Perhaps he's no longer in control of his own people."

"It is war," Drill said.

"Yes."

You have failed, said Memory. Drill winced in pain.

"You will lose," he said.

"Vang says we are cleverer than you are."

"That may be the case. But cleverness cannot compete with experience. Humans have fought hundreds of these little wars, and never failed to wipe out the enemy. Our Memories of these conflicts are intact. Your people can't fight millions of years of specialized evolution."

"Vang's message doesn't end there. You have till nightfall to remove your Ship from the planet. Six days to get out of real space."

"I am to be allowed to live?" Drill was surprised.

"Yes. It is our . . . our custom."

Drill scratched himself. "I regret our efforts did not succeed."

"No more than I." She was silent for a while. "Is there any way we can stop this?"

"If Vang attacks any human planets after the Memories of the peace arrangement have arrived," Drill said, "the military will be unleashed to wipe you out. There is no stopping them after that point."

"How long," she asked, "do you think we have?"

"A few years. Ten at the most."

"Our species will be dead."

"Yes. Our military are very good at their jobs."

"You will have killed us," Gram said, "destroyed the culture that we have built for thousands of years, and you won't even give it any thought. Your species doesn't think about what it does any more. It just acts, like a single-celled animal, engulfing everything it can reach. You say that you are a conscious species, but that isn't true. Your every action is . . . instinct. Or reflex."

"I don't understand," said Drill.

Gram's body trembled. "That is the tragedy of it," she said.

An hour later Ship rose from the field. Shars laughed their defiance from below, dancing in crazed abandon.

I have failed, Drill told Memory.

You knew the odds were long, Memory said. *You knew that in negotiations with species this backward there have only been a handful of successes, and hundreds of failures.*

Yes, Drill acknowledged. *It's a shame, though. To have spent all these months away from home.*

Eat! Eat! said Lowbrain.

Far away, in their forty-mile-long Ships, the human soldiers were already on their way.

The Death Artist

ALEXANDER JABLOKOV

With only a handful of elegant, coolly pyrotechnic stories such as "At the Cross-Time Jaunters' Ball," "A Deeper Sea," "Living Will," "Summer and Ice," and "The Last Castle of Christmas" and a few well-received novels, Alexander Jablokov has established himself as one of the most highly regarded writers in Science Fiction. He is a frequent contributor to *Asimov's Science Fiction,* the *Magazine of Fantasy & Science Fiction,* and other markets and occasionally places stories with other magazines, such as *SF Age, Amazing,* and *Interzone.* His first novel, *Carve the Sky,* was released in 1991 to wide critical acclaim and was followed by other successful novels such as *A Deeper Sea, Nimbus,* and *River of Dust.* His short fiction has been assembled in the landmark collection *The Breath of Suspension.* His most recent novel is the Wide-Screen Space Opera *Deepdrive.* He lives in Cambridge, Massachusetts.

Here he takes us deep into a very strange far future, for an intricate and evocative pavane of identity and revenge, art and obsession . . . and murder.

The snowshoe hare's half-eaten carcass lay under the deadfall of the figure-four trap, frozen blood crystallized on its fur, mouth still closed around the tiny piece of desiccated carrot that had served as bait. The snow was flattened around it, the rabbit's fur thrown everywhere. Jack London sniffed at the trap, laid its ears back, and growled. Canine bona fides reaffirmed, it settled on its haunches and looked expectantly up at the man. Part Samoyed, part husky, Jack's thick white fur concealed a body thin from hunger.

Elam didn't have to sniff. The stink of wolverine was malevolent in the still air. It turned the saliva that had come into his mouth at the thought of roasted hare into something spoiled. He spat. "Damn!" The trap couldn't be descented. He'd have to make another. No animal would come anywhere near a trap that smelled like that. The wolverine probably hadn't even been hungry.

He pulled the dry carrot from the rabbit's mouth and flung the remains off among the trees. The deadfall and the sticks of the figure four followed it, vanishing in puffs of snow.

"That's the last one, Jack," Elam said. "Nothing, again." The dog whined.

They set off among the dark smooth trunks of the maples and beeches, Elam's snowshoes squeaking in the freshly fallen snow. The dog turned its head, disturbed by the unprofessional noise, then loped off to investigate the upturned roots of a fallen tree. A breeze from the great lake to the north pushed its way through the trees, shouldering clumps of snow from the branches as it passed. A cardinal flashed from bough to bough, bright against the clearing evening sky.

Elam, a slender, graceful man, walked with his narrow shoulders hunched up, annoyed by the chilly bombardment from above. His clothing was entirely of furry animal pelts sewn crudely together. His thick hat was muskrat, his jacket fox and beaver, his mittens rabbit, his pants elk. At night he slept in a sack made of a grizzly's hide. How had he come to be here? Had he killed those animals, skinned them, cured their hides? He didn't know.

At night, sometimes, before he went to sleep, Elam would lie in his lean-to and, by the light of the dying fire, examine these clothes, running his hands through the fur, seeking memories in their thick softness. The various pelts were stitched neatly together. Had he done the sewing? Or had a wife or a sister? The thought gave him a curious feeling in the pit of his stomach. He rather suspected that he had always been alone. Weariness would claim him quickly, and he would huddle down in the warmth of the bear fur and fall asleep, questions unanswered.

Tree roots examined, Jack London returned to lead the way up the ridge. It was a daily ritual, practiced just at sunset, and the dog knew it well. The tumbled glacial rocks were now hidden under snow, making the footing uncertain. Elam carried his snowshoes under one arm as he climbed.

The height of the ridge topped the bare trees. To the north, glowing a deceptively warm red, was the snow-covered expanse of the great lake, where Elam often saw the dark forms of wolves, running and reveling in their temporary triumph over the water that barred their passage to the islands the rest of the year.

Elam had no idea what body of water it was. He had tentatively decided on Lake Superior, though it could have been Lake Winnipeg, or for that matter, Lake Baikal. Elam sat down on a rock and stared at the deep north, where stars already gleamed in the sky. Perhaps he had it all wrong, and a new Ice Age was here, and this was a frozen Victoria Nyanza.

"Who am I, Jack? Do you know?"

The dog regarded him quizzically, used to the question by now. The man who's supposed to get us some food, the look said. Philosophical discussions later.

"Did I come here myself, Jack, or was I put here?"

Weary of the pointless and one-sided catechism, the dog was barking at a jay that had ventured too close. It circled for a moment, squawked, and shot off back into the forest.

The lake wind freshened and grew colder, driving the last clouds from the sky. The exposed skin on Elam's cheeks tightened. "Let's go. Jack." He pulled off a mitten and plunged his hand into a pocket, feeling his last chunk of pemmican, greasy and hard.

Aside from a few pathetically withered bits of carrot, which he needed to bait his traps, this was the last bit of food left him. He'd been saving it for an emergency. Every trap on the trapline that ran through these woods had been empty or befouled by wolverines, even in a hard winter that should have driven animals to eat anything. He would eat the pemmican that night.

Man and dog started their descent down the twilit reach of the ridge's other side. As they reached the base, Elam, his hand once again feeling the pemmican, afraid that it too would vanish before he could eat it, took too long a step and felt his right foot slide on the icy face of a tilted rock. His left foot caught in the narrow crack of an ice-shattered boulder, which grabbed him like a tight fist. The world flung itself forward at him. He felt the dull snap in his leg as the icy rock met his face.

He awoke to the warm licks of Jack London's tongue turning instantly cold on his face. He lay tumbled on his back among the rocks, head tilting downward, trees looming overhead. Annoyed, he pushed back and tried to stand. Searing agony in his leg brought bile to the back of his throat and a hot sweat over his body. He moaned and almost lost consciousness again, then held himself up on his elbows. His face was cut, some of his teeth were cracked, he could taste the blood in his mouth, but his leg, his leg . . . he looked down.

His left leg bent at an unnatural angle just below the knee. The leather of his trousers was soaked black with blood. Compound fracture of the . . . tibia? Fibula? For one distracted instant naming the shattered bone was the most important thing in the world. It obscured the knowledge that he was going to die.

He shifted position and moaned again. The biting pain in his leg grew sharp burning teeth whenever he moved, but wore the edges off if he lay still, subsiding to a gnaw. With a sudden effort, he pulled the leg straight, then fell back, gasping harshly. It made no difference, of course, but seeing the leg at that angle made him uncomfortable. It looked better this way, not nearly so painful.

He patted the dog on the head. "Sorry, Jack. I screwed up." The dog whined in agreement. Elam fell back and let the darkness take him.

His body did not give up so easily. He regained consciousness sometime later, the frenzied whining and yelping of his dog sounding in his ears. He lay prone in the snow, his hands dug in ahead of him. His mittens were torn, and he could not feel his hands.

He rolled onto his back and looked over his feet. Full night had come, but the starlight and the moon were enough to see the trail his body had left through the snow. Elam sighed. What a waste of time. The pain in his broken leg was almost gone, as was all other feeling from the thighs down. He spat. The spittle crackled on the snow. Damn cold. And the dog was annoying him with its whining.

"Sure, boy, sure," he said, gasping from the cold weight of death on his chest. "Just a minute, Jack. Just a minute."

He pulled what was left of the fur glove off with his chin and reached the unfeeling claw of his hand into his pocket. It took a dozen tries before it emerged holding the pemmican.

He finally managed to open the front of his jacket and unlace his shirt. Cold air licked in eagerly. He smeared the greasy, hard pemmican over his chest and throat like a healing salve. Its rancid odor bit at his nose, and despite himself, he felt a moment of hunger. He shoved the rest of the piece down deep into his shirt.

"Here, Jack," he said. "Here. Dinner." The moon rode overhead, half in sunlight, the other half covered with glittering lines and spots.

The dog snuffled, suddenly frightened and suspicious. Elam reached up and patted it on the head. Jack London moved forward. Smelling the meat, the dog overcame its caution at its master's strange behavior and it began to lick eagerly at Elam's throat and chest. The dog was desperately hungry. In its eagerness, a sharp tooth cut the man's skin, and thick warm blood welled out. The tongue licked more quickly. More cuts. More blood, steaming aromatically in the cold air. And the dog was hungry. The smell penetrated to the deepest parts of its brain, finally destroying the overlay of training, habit, and love. The dog's teeth tore and it began to feed.

And in that instant, Elam remembered. He saw the warm forests of his youth, and the face, so much like his, that had become his own. Justice had at last been done. Elam was going to die. He smiled slightly, gasped once, then his eyes glazed blank.

When it was sated, and realized what it had done, the dog howled its pain at the stars. It then sprang into the forest and ran madly, leaving the man's tattered remains far behind.

"Is that all you are going to do from now on?" Reqata said. "Commit suicide? Just lie down and die? Nice touch, I admit, the dog." She held his shoulder in a tight grip and looked past him with her phosphorescent eyes. "A real Elam touch."

Five dark ribs supported the smooth yellow stone of the dome. They revealed the green gleam of beetle carapaces in the light of the flames hanging in a hexagon around the central axis of the view chamber. Rows of striated marble seats climbed the chamber in concentric circles. The inhabitants of these seats stared down at the corpse lying in the snow at their feet.

Elam was himself startled at his clone's acquiescence in its own death, but he was surrounded by admirers before he could answer her. They moved past him, murmuring, gaining haut by their admiration for the subtlety of his work.

Elam stared past them at his own corpse, a sheen of frost already obscuring the face, turning it into an abstract composition. He had died well. He always did. His mind, back from the clone with its memories restored, seemed to rattle loosely around his skull. His skin was slick with amniotic fluid, his joints gritty. Nothing fit together. Reqata's hand on his shoulder seemed to bend the arbitrarily shaped bones, reminding him of his accidental quality.

"An artist who works with himself as both raw materials and subject can never transcend either," Reqata said.

Her scorn cut through the admiration around him. He looked up at her, and she smiled back with ebony teeth, flicking feathery eyelashes. She raised one hand in an angular gesture that identified her instantly, whatever body she was in.

"And how does the choreographer of mass death transcend her material?" Elam's mind had been gone for weeks, dying in a frozen forest, and Reqata had grown bored in his absence. She needed entertainment. Even lovers constantly dueled with haut, the indefinable quality that all players at the Floating Game understood implicitly. Reqata had much haut. Elam had more.

He squirmed. Was his bladder full, or did he always feel this way?

"Mass death, as you put it, is limited by practical problems," Reqata answered.

"Killing one man is an existential act. Killing a million would be a historic act, at least to the Bound. Killing them all would be a divine act." She ran her fingers through his hair. He smelled the winy crispness of her breath. "Killing yourself merely smacks of lack of initiative. I'm disappointed in you, Elam. You used to fight before you died."

"I did, didn't I?" He remembered the desperate struggles of his early works, the ones that had gained him his haut. Men dying in mine shafts, on cliffsides, in predator-infested jungles. Men who had never stopped fighting. Each of those men had been himself. Something had changed.

"Tell me something," Reqata said, leaning forward. Her tongue darted across his earlobe. "Why do you always look so peaceful just before you die?"

A chill spread up his spine. He'd wondered the same thing himself. "Do I?" He squeezed the words out. He always paid. Five or ten minutes of memory, the final instants of life. The last thing he remembered from this particular work was pulling the pemmican from his pocket. After that, blackness. The dying clone Elam understood something the resurrected real Elam did not.

"Certainly. Don't be coy. Look at the grin on that corpse's frozen face." She slid into the seat next to him, draping a leg negligently into the aisle. "I've tried dying. Not as art, just as experience. I die screaming. My screams echo for weeks." She shuddered, hands pressed over her ears. Her current body, as usual, had a high rib cage and small firm breasts. Elam found himself staring at them. "But enough." Reqata flicked him with a fingernail, scratching his arm. "Now that you're done, *I* have a project for you to work on—"

"Perhaps each of you just gets a view of what awaits on the other side," a voice drawled.

"Don't lecture me on the absolute inertia of the soul," Reqata said, disconcerted. "No one's giving our clones a free peek at eternity, Lammiela."

"Perhaps not." A long elegant woman, Lammiela always looked the same, to everyone's distress, for she only had one body. She smiled slowly. "Or perhaps heaven is already so filled with the souls of your clones that there won't be any room for you when you finally arrive."

Reqata stood up, fury in the rise of her shoulders. Because of her past irregularities, Lammiela had an ambiguous status, and Reqata hated risking haut in arguing with her. Usually, Reqata couldn't help herself. "Be careful, Lammiela. You don't know anything about it." And perhaps, Elam found himself thinking, perhaps Reqata feared Death indeed.

"Oh, true enough." Lammiela sat. "Ssarna's passing has everyone on edge. I keep forgetting." Her arrival had driven the last of the connoisseurs away, and the three of them sat alone in the viewing chamber.

"You don't forget, Mother," Elam said wearily. "You do it quite on purpose."

"That's unfair, Elam." She examined him. "You look well. Dying agrees with you." She intertwined her long fingers and rested her chin on them. Her face was subtly lined, as if shaded by an engraver. Her eyes were dark blue, the same as Elam's own. "Ssarna, they say, was withered in her adytum, dry as dust. The last time I saw her, which must have been at that party on top of that miserable mountain in the Himalayas, she was a tiny slip of a girl, prepubescent. Long golden . . . *tresses*. That must be the correct word." She shook her head with weary contempt. "Though she disguised herself as young, old age found her in her most private chamber. And after old age had had his way with her, he gave her to Death. They have an arrangement."

"And the first of them is enjoying you now," Reqata said. "How soon before the exchange comes?"

Lammiela's head jerked, but she did not turn. "How have you been, Elam?" She smiled at him, and he was suddenly surrounded by the smell of her perfume, as if it were a trained animal she wore around her neck and had ordered to attack. The smell was dark and spicy. It reminded him of the smell of carrion, of something dead in the hot sun, thick and insistent. He found himself holding his breath, and stood up quickly, suddenly nauseated. Nauseated, yet somehow excited. A child's feeling, the attraction of the vile, the need to touch and smell that which disgusts. Children will put anything in their mouths. He felt as if maggots were crawling under his fingernails.

"Air," Elam muttered. "I need. . . ." He walked up the striated marble stairs to the balcony above. Locked in their own conflict, the women did not follow. The warm summer air outside smelled of herbs and the dry flowers of chaparral. He clamped his teeth together and convinced himself that the flowers did not mask the smell of rotting flesh.

Sunset turned the day lavender. The view chamber's balcony hung high above the city, which flowed purposefully up the narrow valleys, leaving the dry hills bare, covered with flowers, acacia trees, and the spiky crystal plants that had evolved under some distant sun. The Mediterranean glinted far below.

Lights had come on in the city, illuminating its secret doorways. No one lived here. The Incarnate had other fashions, and the Bound were afraid of the ancient living cities, preferring to build their own. A Bound city could be seen burning closer to the water, its towers asserting themselves against the darkening sky. Tonight, many of the Incarnate who had witnessed Elam's performance would descend upon it for the evanescent excitements of those who lived out their lives bound to one body.

So this place was silent, save for the low resonance of bells, marking the hours for its absent dwellers. The city had been deserted for thousands of years, but was ready for someone to return. The insectlike shapes of aircars fluttered up against the stars as Elam's audience went their separate ways.

A coppery half-moon hung on the horizon, the invisible half of its face etched with colored lines and spots of flickering light. When he was young, Lammiela had told him that the moon was inhabited by huge machines from some previous cycle of existence. The whole circle of a new moon crawled with light, an accepted feature. No one wondered at the thoughts of those intelligent machines, who looked up at the ripe blue-green planet that hung in their black sky.

"You should lie down," Lammiela said, "and rest." Her perfume was cloying and spicy. Though it did not smell even remotely of carrion, Elam still backed away, pushing himself against the railing, and let the evening breeze carry the scent from him. Starlings swooped around the tower.

"You should get up," Reqata said, from somewhere behind her, "and run."

A blast of freezing air made him shiver. He took a step and looked down at the now hoarfrost-covered corpse in the deserted rotunda.

No Incarnate alive knew how the ancient machines worked. The corpse: was it just an image of the one in the frozen Michigan forest? Or had the rotunda's interior moved its spectators to hover over that forest in fact? Or was this body a perfect duplicate, here in the hills of Provence, of that other one? The knowledge was lost. No one knew what lay within the sphere of image. But Elam did know one thing: the cold winds of winter did not blow out of it.

Elam spotted the zeppelins about two and a half hours out of Kalgoorlie. Their colors were gaudy against the green fields and the blue Nullarbor Sea. Frost glittered on the sides away from the morning sun. Elam felt a physical joy, for the zeppelins had been caught completely by surprise. They drifted in the heavy morning air, big fat targets.

They were shuttling troops from somewhere to the North, in central Australia, to participate in one of those incomprehensible wars the Bound indulged in. Reqata had involved herself, in her capricious way, and staked haut on the outcome of the invasion of Eyre, the southern state.

Elam could see the crewmen leaping into their tiny flyers, their wings straightening in the sun like butterflies emerging from their chrysalis, but it was too late. Their zeppelins were doomed.

Elam picked his target, communicating his choice to the other bumblebees, a few Incarnate who, amused at his constant struggle with Reqata, had joined him for the fun. The microwave signal felt like a directed whisper, save for the fact that it made his earlobes itch. He aimed for a bright green deltoid with markings that made it look like a giant spotted frog. For an instant the image took a hold of his mind, and he imagined catching a frog, grabbing it, and feeling its frightened wetness in his hand, the frantic beating of its heart. . . .

He pushed the thought away, upset at his loss of control. Timing was critical. A change in the angle of his wing stroke brought him back into position.

Elam was gorgeous. About a meter long, he had short iridescent wings. A single long-distance optic tracked the target while two bulbous 270-degree peripherals checked the mathematical line of bumblebees to either side of him. Reqata was undoubtedly aboard one of the zeppelins, raging at the unexpected attack. The defending flyers were wide-faced black men, some odd purebred strain. Elam imagined the black Reqata, gesturing sharply as she arranged a defense. It was the quality of her movement that made her beautiful.

A steel ball whizzed past his left wing. A moment later he heard the faint *tock!* of the zeppelin's catapult. It took only one hit to turn a bumblebee into a stack of expensive kindling. Elam tucked one wing, tumbled, and straightened out again, coming in at his target. He unhooked his fighting legs and brought their razor edges forward.

The zeppelins were billowing, changing shape. Sudden flares disturbed Elam's infrared sensors, making him dizzy, unsure of his target. Flying the bumblebees all the way out of Kalgoorlie without any lighter-than-air support craft had been a risk. They had to knock the zeppelins to the ground and parasitize them for reactive metals. The bumblebees would be vulnerable to a ground attack as they crawled clumsily over the wreckage, but no one gained haut without taking chances. He dodged past the defending flyers, not bothering to cut them. That would only delay him.

The green frog was now below him, swelling, rippling, dropping altitude desperately. He held it in his hand where he had caught it, amid the thick rushes. The other kids were gone, somewhere, and he was alone. The frog kicked and struggled. It had voided its bowels in his hand, and he felt the wet slime. The air was hot and thick underneath the cottonwoods. Something about the frog's frantic struggle for life annoyed him. It seemed odious that something so wet and slimy would wish to remain alive. He laid the frog down on a flat rock and, with calm deliberation, brought another rock down on its head. Its legs kicked and kicked.

The other zeppelins seemed to have vanished. All that remained was the frog, its guts lying out in the hot sun, putrefying as he watched. Fluids dripped down the rock, staining it. He wanted to slash it apart with fire, to feel the flare as it gave up its life. The sun seared down on his shoulders.

With a sudden fury, the zeppelin turned on him. He found himself staring into its looming mouth. A hail of steel balls flew past him, and he maneuvered desperately to avoid them. He didn't understand why he had come so close without attacking.

Two balls ripped simultaneously through his right wing, sending flaring pain through the joints. He twisted down, hauling in on the almost nonfunctional muscles. If he pulled the wing in to a stable tip, he could glide downward. Green fields spiraled up at him, black houses with high-peaked roofs, colorful gardens. Pale faces peered up at him from the fields. Military vehicles had pulled up on a sandy road, the dark muzzles of their guns tracking him.

The right wing was flopping loose, sending waves of pain through his body. He veered wildly, land and sky switching position. Pulling up desperately, he angled his cutting leg and sliced off the loose part of his wing. Hot pain slashed through him.

He had finally managed to stabilize his descent, but it was too late. A field of corn floated up to meet him. For an instant, everything was agony.

"I want something primitive," Elam said, as the doctor slid a testing limb into the base of his spine. "Something prehistoric."

"All of the human past is prehistoric," Dr. Abias said. He withdrew the limb with a cold tickle, and retracted it into his body. "Your body is healthy."

Elam stood up, swinging his arms, getting used to his new proportions. His current body was lithe, gold-skinned, small-handed: designed to Reqata's specifications. She had some need of him in this form, and Elam found himself apprehensive. He had no idea if she was still angry about her defeat over Australia. "No, Abias. I mean before *any* history. Before man knew himself to be man."

"Neanderthal?" Abias murmured, hunching across the floor on his many legs. "Pithecanthropus? Australopithecus?"

"I don't know what any of those words mean," Elam said. Sometimes his servant's knowledge bothered him. What right did the Bound have to know so much when the Incarnate could dispose of their destinies so thoroughly?

Abias turned to look back at him with his multiple oculars, brown human eyes with no face, pupils dilated. He was a machine, articulated and segmented, gleaming as if anointed with rare oils. Each of his eight moving limbs was both an arm and a leg, as if his body had been designed to work in orbit. Perhaps it had. As he had pointed out, most of the past was prehistory.

"It doesn't matter," Abias said. "I will look into it."

A Bound, Abias had been assigned to Elam by Lammiela. Punished savagely for a crime against the Incarnate, his body had been confiscated and replaced by some ancient device. Abias now ran Elam's team of cloned bodies. He was considered one of the best trainers in the Floating Game. He was so good and his loyalty so absolute that Elam had steadfastly refused to discover what crime he had committed, fearing that the knowledge would interfere in their professional relationship.

"Do that," Elam said. "I have a new project in mind." He walked across the wide, open room, feeling the sliding of unfamiliar joints. This body, a clone of his own, had been extensively modified by Abias, until there were only traces of his own nature in it. A plinth was laid with earrings, wrist and ankle bracelets, body paints, scent bottles, all supplied by Reqata. He began to put them on.

Light shone from overhead through semicircular openings in the vault. A rough-surfaced ovoid curved up through the floor in the room's center. It was Elam's adytum, the most secret chamber where his birth body lay. After his crash in Australia, he had woken up in it for an instant, with a feeling of agony, as if every part of his body were burning. The thought still made him shudder.

An Incarnate's adytum was his most strongly guarded space, for when his real body died, he died as well. There could be no transfer of consciousness to a cloned body once the original was dead. The ancient insolent machines that provided the ability to transfer the mind did not permit it, and since no one understood the machines, no one could do anything about it. And killing an Incarnate's birth body was the only way to truly commit murder.

Elam slid on a bracelet. "Do you know who attacked me?"

"No one has claimed responsibility," Abias answered. "Did you recognize anything of the movement?"

Elam thought about the billowing froglike zeppelin. It hadn't been Reqata, he was sure of that. She would have made certain that he knew. But it could have been almost anyone else.

"Something went wrong in the last transfer," Elam said, embarrassed at bringing up such a private function, even to his servant. "I woke up in my adytum."

Abias stood still, unreadable. "A terrible malfunction. I will look into it."

"Just make sure it doesn't happen again."

The party was in the hills above the city of El'lie. Water from the northern rivers poured here from holes in the rock and swirled through an elaborate maze of waterways. It finally reached one last great pool, which extended terrifyingly off the rocky slope, as if ready to tip and spill, drowning the city below it. The white rock of the pool's edge extended downward some thousands of feet, a polished sheet like the edge of the world. Far below, cataracts spilled from the pool's bottom toward the thirsty city.

Elam stood on a terrace and gazed down into the water. Reqata floated there, glistening as the afternoon sun sank over the ocean to the west. She was a strange creature, huge, all sleekly iridescent curves, blue and green, based on some creature humans had once encountered in their forgotten travels across the galaxy. She sweated color into the water, heavy swirls of bright orange and yellow sinking into the depths. Until a few hours before she had been wearing a slender gold-skinned body like Elam's.

"They seem peaceful," she whispered, her voice echoing across the water. "But the potential for violence is extreme."

Reqata had hauled him on a preliminary tour of El'lie, site of her next artwork. He remembered the fresh bodies hung in tangles of chain on a granite wall, a list of their crimes pasted on their chests; the tense market, men and women with shaved foreheads and jewels in their eyebrows, the air thick with spices; the lazy insolence of a gang of men, their faces tattooed with angry swirls, as they pushed through the market crowd on their way to a proscribed patriarchal religious service; the great tiled temples of the Goddesses that lined the market square.

"When will they explode?" Elam said.

"Not before the fall, when the S'tana winds blow down from the mountains. You'll really see something then." Hydraulic spines erected and sank down on her back, and she made them make a characteristic gesture, sharp and emphatic. If she was angry about what had happened in Australia, she concealed it. That frightened Elam more than open anger would have. Reqata had a habit of delayed reaction.

Reqata was an expert at exploiting obscure hostilities among the Bound, producing dramatically violent conflicts with blood spilling picturesquely down carved staircases; heads piled up in heaps, engraved ivory spheres thrust into their mouths; lines of severed hands on bronze poles, fingers pointing toward Heaven. That was her art. She had wanted advice. Elam had not been helpful.

Glowing lights floated above the pool, swirling in response to incomprehensible tropisms. No one knew how to control them anymore, and they moved by their own rules. A group of partyers stood on the far side of the pool, their bright-lit reflections stretching out across the glassy water.

"This water's thousands of feet deep," Reqata murmured. "The bottom's piled up with forgotten things. Boats. Gold cups. The people from the city come up here and drop things in for luck."

"Why should dropping things and forgetting about them be lucky?" Elam asked.

"I don't know. It's not always lucky to remember everything."

Elam stripped off his gown and dove into the dark water. Reqata made a bubbling sound of delight. He stroked the spines on her back, feeling them swell and deflate. He ran a cupped hand up her side. Her glowing solar sweat worked its way between his fingers and dripped down, desperate to reach its natural place somewhere in the invisible depths.

"Put on a body like this," she said. "We can swim the deep oceans and make love there, among the fish."

"Yes," he said, not meaning it. "We can."

"Elam," she said. "What happened on the balcony after we saw you die in the forest? You seemed terrified."

Elam thought, instead, of the frog. Had his memories been real? Or could Reqata have laid a trap for him? "Just a moment of nausea. Nothing."

Reqata was silent for a moment. "She hates you, you know. Lammiela. She utterly hates you."

Her tone was vicious. Here it was, vengeance for the trick he had pulled over the Nullarbor Sea. Her body shuddered, and he was suddenly conscious of how much larger than he she now was. She could squish him against the side of the pool without any difficulty. He would awake in his own chamber, in another body. Killing him was just insulting, not fatal. Perhaps it *had* been her in that frog zeppelin.

He swam slowly away from her. "I don't know what you're talking about."

"Of course you don't. You're an expert at forgetting, at just lying down, dying, and forgetting. She hates you for what you did. For what you did to your sister!" Her voice was triumphant.

Elam felt the same searing pain he had felt when he awoke for one choking instant in his adytum. "I don't know what you're talking about," he said, as he pulled himself out of the water.

"I know! That's just the problem."

"Tell me what you mean." He kept his voice calm.

Something moved heavily in the darkness, and a row of chairs overturned with a clatter. Elam turned away from the pool. His heart pounded. A burst of laughter sounded from across the pool. The party was continuing, but the guests were impossibly far away, like a memory of childhood, unreachable and useless.

A head rose up out of the darkness, a head twice the size of Elam's body. It was a metal egg, dominated by two expressionless eyes. Behind dragged a long multilimbed body, shiny and obscene. Elam screamed in unreasoning and senseless terror.

The creature moved forward, swaying its head from side to side. Acid saliva drooled from beneath its crystal teeth, splashing and fizzing on the marble terrace. It was incomprehensibly ancient, something from the long-forgotten past. It swept its tail around and dragged Elam toward it.

For an instant, Elam was paralyzed, staring at the strange beauty of the dragon's teeth as they moved toward him. Then he struggled against the iron coil of the tail. His body still had traces of oil, and he slid out, stripping skin. He dove between the dragon's legs, bruising his bones on the terrace.

The dragon whipped around quickly, cornering him. With a belch, it sprayed acid over him. It burned down his shoulder, bubbling as it dissolved his skin.

"Damn you!" he shouted, and threw himself at the dragon's head. It didn't pull back quickly enough, and he plunged his fist into its left eye. Its surface resisted, then popped, spraying fluid. The dragon tossed its head, flinging Elam across the ground.

He pulled himself to his feet, feeling the pain of shattered ribs. Blood dribbled down his chin. One of his legs would not support his weight. The massive head lowered down over him, muck pouring out of the destroyed eye. Elam grabbed for the other eye, but he had no strength left. Foul-smelling acid flowed over him, sloughing his flesh off with the sound of frying bacon. He stayed on his feet, trying to push imprecations between his destroyed lips. The last thing he saw was the crystal teeth, lowering toward his head.

★ ★ ★

Lammiela's house was the abode of infinity. The endless rooms were packed with the junk of a hundred worlds. The information here was irreplaceable, unduplicated anywhere else. No one came to visit, and the artifacts, data cubes, and dioramas rested in silence.

At some time in the past millennia, human beings had explored as far inward as the galactic core and so far outward that the galaxy had hung above them like a captured undersea creature, giving up its light to intergalactic space. They had moved through globular clusters of ancient suns and explored areas of stellar synthesis. They had raised monuments on distant planets. After some centuries of this, they had returned to Earth, built their mysterious cities on a planet that must have been nothing but old legend, and settled down, content to till the aged soil and watch the sun rise and set. And, with magnificent insouciance, they had forgotten everything, leaving their descendants ignorant.

Lammiela sat in the corner watching Elam. Her body, though elegant, was somehow bent, as if she had been cut from an oddly shaped piece of wood by a clever wood-carver utilizing the limitations of his material. That was true enough, Elam reflected, examining the person who was both his parents.

When young, Lammiela had found a ship somewhere on Earth's moon, tended by the secret mechanisms that made their lives there, and gone forth to explore the old spaces. No one had any interest in following her, but somehow her exploits had gained enough attention that she had obtained extraordinary privileges.

"It's curious," she said. "Our friends the Bound have skills that we Incarnate do not even dream of, because the machines our ancestors left us have no interest in them." She looked thoughtful for a moment. "It's surprising, some of the things the Bound can do."

"Like make you both my father and my mother," Elam said.

Her face was shadowed. "Yes. There is that."

Lammiela had been born male, named Laurance. But Laurance had felt himself to be a woman. No problem for one of the Incarnate, who could be anything they wished. Laurance could have slept securely in his adytum and put female bodies on for his entire life. But Laurance did not think that way. He had gone to the Bound, and they had changed him to a woman.

"When the job was finished, I was pregnant," Lammiela said. "Laurance's sperm had fertilized my new ova. I don't know if it was a natural consequence of the rituals they used." Her muscles tightened with the memories. Tendons stood out on the backs of her hands. "They kept me conscious through it all. Pain is their price. They slew the male essence. I saw it, screaming before me. Laurance, burning."

It had cost most of her haut to do it. Dealings with the Bound inevitably involved loss of status.

"I still see him sometimes," she said.

"Who?" Elam asked.

"Your father, Laurance." Her eyes narrowed. "They didn't kill him well enough, you see. They told me they did, but he's still around." Her eyes darted, as if expecting to find Laurance hiding behind a diorama.

Elam felt a chill, a sharp feeling at the back of his neck, as if someone with long, long nails were stroking him there. "But you're him, Lammiela. He's not someone else."

"Do you really know so much about identity, Elam?" She sighed, relaxing. "You're right, of course. Still, was it I who stood in the Colonnade at Hrlad?" She pointed at a hologram of a long line of rock obelisks, the full galaxy rising beyond them. "I'm sure I remember it, not as if I had been there. It was legend, you know. A bedtime story. But Hrlad is real. So is Laurance. You look like him, you know. You have your father's eyes."

She stared at him coldly, and he, for the first time, thought that Reqata might have spoken truly. Perhaps his mother did indeed hate him.

"I made my choice," she said. "I can never go back. The Bound won't let me. I am a woman, and a mother."

Lammiela did not live in the city where most of the Incarnate made their home. She lived on a mountainside, bleak and alone, the rigid curving walls of her house holding off the snow. She moved her dwelling periodically, from seashore to desert to mountain. She had no adytum, with its body, to lug with her. Elam, somehow, remembered deep forest when he was growing up, interspersed with sunny meadows. The vision wasn't clear. Nothing was clear.

After this most recent death, Elam had once again awakened in his adytum. He'd felt the fluid flowing through his lungs, and the darkness pressing down on his open eyes. Fire had burned through his veins, but there was no air to scream with. Then he had awakened again, normally, on a pallet in the light.

"Mother," he said, looking off at a broad-spectrum hologram of Sinus that spilled vicious white light across the corner of the room, too bright to look at directly without filters. "Am I truly your only child?"

Lammiela's face was still. "Most things are secrets for the first part of their existence, and forgotten thereafter. I suppose there must be a time in the middle when they are known. Who told you?"

"Does it matter?"

"Yes. It was thrown at you as a weapon, wasn't it?"

Elam sighed. "Yes. Reqata."

"Ah, yes. I should have guessed. Dear Reqata. Does she love you, Elam?"

The question took him aback. "She says she does."

"I'm sure she means it then. I wonder what it is about you that she loves. Is that where the discussion ended then? With the question?"

"Yes. We were interrupted." Elam described the dragon's attack.

"Ah, how convenient. Reqata was always a master of timing. Who was it, do you suppose?" She looked out of the circular window at the mountain tundra, the land falling away to a vast ice field, just the rocky peaks of mountains thrusting through it. "No one gains haut anonymously."

"No one recognized the style. Or if they did, they did not admit it." The scene was wrong, Elam thought. It should have been trees: smooth-trunked beeches, heavy oaks. The sun had slanted through them as if the leaves themselves generated the light.

"So why are you here, Elam? Are you looking for the tank in which that creature was grown? You may search for it if you like. Go ahead."

"No!" Elam said. "I want to find my sister." And he turned away and ran through the rooms of the house, past the endless vistas of stars that the rest of the human race had comfortably forgotten. Lammiela silently followed, effortlessly sliding through the complex displays, as Elam stumbled, now falling into an image of a kilometer-high cliff carved with human figures, now into a display of ceremonial masks with lolling tongues. He suddenly remembered running through these rooms, their spaces much larger then, pursued by a small violent figure that left no place to hide.

In a domed room he stopped at a wall covered with racks of dark metal drawers. He pushed a spot and one slid open. Inside was a small animal, no bigger than a cat, dried as if left out in the sun. It was recognizably the dragon, curled around itself, its crystalline teeth just visible through its pulled-back lips.

Lammiela looked down at it. "You two never got along. You would have thought that you would . . . but I guess that was a foolish assumption. You tormented her with that thing, that . . . monster. It gave her screaming nightmares. Once, you propped it by her bed so that she would see it when she woke up. For three nights after that she didn't sleep." She slid the drawer shut.

"Who was she?" Elam demanded, taking her shoulders. She met his gaze. "It's no longer something that will just be forgotten."

She weakly raised a hand to her forehead, but Elam wasn't fooled. His mother had dealt with dangers that could have killed her a dozen times over. He tightened his grip on her shoulders. "Your sister's name was Orfea. Lovely name, don't you think? I think Laurance picked it out."

Elam could remember no sister. "Was she older or younger?"

"Neither. You were split from one ovum, identical twins. One was given an androgen bath and became you, Elam. The other was female: Orfea. God, how you grew to hate each other! It frightened me. And you were both so talented. I still have some of her essence around, I think."

"I . . . what happened to her? Where is she?"

"That was the one thing that consoled me, all these years. The fact that you didn't remember. I think that was what allowed you to survive."

"What? Tell me!"

Lammiela took only one step back, but it seemed that she receded much farther. "She was murdered. She was just a young girl. So young."

Elam looked at her, afraid of the answer. He didn't remember what had happened, and he could still see hatred in his mother's eyes. "Did they ever find out who did it?" he asked softly.

She seemed surprised by the question. "Oh, there was never any doubt. She was killed by a young friend of yours. He is now your servant. Abias."

"I have to say that it was in extremely poor taste," Reqata said, not for the first time. "Death is a fine performance, but there's no reason to perform it at a dinner party. Particularly in my presence."

She got up from the bed and stretched. This torso was wide, and well-muscled. Once again, the rib cage was high, the breasts small. Elam wondered if, in the secrecy of her adytum, Reqata was male. He had never seen her in any other than a female body.

"Just out of curiosity," Elam said. "Could you tell who the dragon was?" He ran his hand over the welts on his side, marks of Reqata's fierce love.

She glanced back at him, eyelids half lowered over wide violet eyes. She gauged if her answer would affect her haut. "Now *that* was a good trick, Elam. If I hadn't been looking right at you, I would have guessed that it was you behind those glass fangs."

She walked emphatically across the room, the slap of her bare feet echoing from the walls, and stood, challengingly, on the curve of Elam's adytum. Dawn had not yet come, and light was provided by hanging globes of a blue tint that Elam found unpleasant. He had never discovered a way to adjust or replace them.

"Oh, Elam," she said. "If you are working on something, I approve. How you fought! You didn't want to die. You kept struggling until there was nothing left of you but bones. That dragon crunched them like candy canes." She shuddered, her face flushed. "It was wonderful."

Elam stretched and rolled out of the bed. As his weight left it, it rose off the floor, to vanish into the darkness overhead. The huge room had no other furniture.

"What do you know about my sister?" he asked.

Reqata lounged back on the adytum, curling her legs. "I know she existed, I know she's dead. More than you did, apparently." She ran her hands up her sides, cupping her breasts. "You know, the first stories I heard of you don't match you. You were more like me then. Death was your art, certainly, but it wasn't your own death."

"As you say," Elam said, stalking toward her, "I don't remember."

"How could you have forgotten?" She rested her hands on the rough stone of the adytum. "This is where you are, Elam. If I ripped this open, I could kill you. Really kill you. Dead."

"Want to try it?" He leaned over her. She rested back, lips parted, and dug her fingernails in a circle around his nipple.

"It could be exciting. Then I could see who you really were."

He felt the sweet bite of her nails through his skin. If he had only one body, he reflected, perhaps he could never have made love to Reqata. He couldn't have lasted.

He pushed himself forward onto her, and they made love on his adytum, above his real body as it slumbered.

Abias's kingdom was brightly lit, to Elam's surprise. He had expected a mysterious darkness. Hallways stretched in all directions, leading to chambers of silent machines and tanks filled with organs and bodies. As he stepped off the stairs, Elam realized that he had never before been down to these lower levels, even though it was as much a part of his house as any other. But this was Abias's domain. This was where the magic was done.

His bumblebee lay on a table, its dead nervous system scooped out. Dozens of tiny mechanisms crawled over it, straightening its spars, laying fragile wing material between the ribs. Elam pictured them crawling over his own body, straightening out his ribs, coring out his spinal column, resectioning his eyes.

Elam touched a panel, and a prism rose up out of the floor. In it was himself, calmly asleep. Elam always kept several standard, unmodified versions of his own body ready. That was the form in which he usually died. Elam examined the face of his clone. He had never inhabited this one, and it looked strange in consequence. No emotions had ever played over those slack features, no lines of care had ever formed on the forehead or around the eyes. The face was an infant turned physically adult.

The elaborate shape of Abias appeared in a passage and made its way toward him, segmented legs gleaming. Elam felt a moment of fear. He imagined those limbs seizing his mysterious faceless sister, Orfea, rending her, their shine dulled with her blood, sizzling smoke rising . . . he fought the images down. Abias had been a man then, if he'd been anything. He'd lost his body as a consequence of that murder.

Abias regarded him. As a Bound, and a cyborg to boot, Abias had no haut. He had no character to express, needed no gestures to show who he was. His faceless eyes were unreadable. Had he been trying to kill Elam? He had the skills and resources to have created the zeppelin, grown the dragon. But why? If he wanted to kill Elam, the real Elam, the adytum lay in his power. Those powerful limbs could rip the chamber open and drag the sleeping Elam out into the light. Elam's consciousness, in a clone somewhere else, wouldn't know what had happened, but would suddenly cease to exist.

"Is the new body ready?" Elam said abruptly.

Abias moved quietly away. After a moment's hesitation, Elam followed, deeper into the lower levels. They passed a prism where a baby with golden skin slept, growing toward the day that Elam could inhabit it, and witness Reqata's El'lie artwork. It would replace the body destroyed by the dragon. Lying on a pallet was a short heavy-boned body with a rounded jaw and beetle brows.

"It was a matter of genetic regression, based on the markers in the cytoplasmic mitochondria," Abias said, almost to himself. "The mitochondrial DNA is the timer, since it comes only from the female ancestor. The nucleic genetic material is completely scrambled. But much of it stretches back far enough. And of course we have stored orang and chimp genes as well. If you back and fill—"

"That's enough, Abias," Elam said impatiently. "It doesn't matter."

"No, of course not. It doesn't matter. But this is your Neanderthal."

Elam looked down at the face that was his own, a few hundred thousand years back into the past. "How long have I known you, Abias?"

"Since we were children," Abias said softly. "Don't you remember?"

"You know I don't remember. How could I have lived with you for so long otherwise? You killed my sister."

"How do you know that?"

"Lammiela told me that you killed Orfea."

"Ah," Abias said. "I didn't kill her, Elam." He paused. "You don't remember her."

"No. As far as I'm concerned, I have always been alone."

"Perhaps you always have been."

Elam considered this. "Are you claiming that Reqata and my mother are lying? That there never was an Orfea?"

Abias lowered all of his limbs until he was solid on the floor. "I think you should be more worried about who is trying to kill you. These attempts are not accidents."

"I know. Perhaps you."

"That's not even worth answering."

"But who would want to go around killing me repeatedly in my clones?"

"From the information we have now," Abias said, "it could be anyone. It could even be Orfea."

"Orfea?" Elam stared at him. "Didn't you just claim she never existed?"

"I did not. I said I didn't kill her. I didn't. Orfea did not die that day." His eyes closed and he was immobile. "Only I did."

It was a land that was familiar, but as Elam stalked it in his new body, he did not know whether it was familiar to him, Elam, or to the Neanderthal he now was. It was covered with a dark forest, broken by clearings, crossed by clear icy streams scattered with rocks. The air was cold and damp, a living air. His body was wrapped in fur. It was not fur from an animal he had killed himself, but something Abias had mysteriously generated, in the same way he had generated the fur Elam had worn when he died in the Michigan winter. For all he knew, it was some bizarre variant of his own scalp hair.

Since this was just an exploratory journey, the creation of below-conscious reflexes, Elam retained his own memories. They sat oddly in his head. This brain perceived things more directly, seeing each beam of sunlight through the forest canopy as a separate entity, with its own characteristics and personality, owning little to the sun from which it ultimately came.

A stream had cut a deep ravine, revealing ruins. The Neanderthal wandered among the walls, which stood knee-deep in the water, and peered thoughtfully to their bricks. He felt as if he were looking at the ruins of the incomprehensibly distant future, not the past at all. He imagined wading mammoths pushing their way through, knocking the walls over in their search for food. At the thought of a mammoth his hands itched to feel the haft of a spear, though he could certainly not kill such a beast by himself. He needed the help of his fellows, and they did not exist. He walked the Earth alone.

Something grunted in a pool that had once been a basement. He sloshed over to it, and gazed down at the frog. It sat on the remains of a windowsill, pulsing its throat. Elam reached down . . . and thought of the dying frog, shuddering its life out in his hand. He tied it down, limbs outspread, and played the hot cutting beam over it. It screamed and begged as the smoke from its guts rose up into the clear sky.

Elam jerked his hand back from the frog, which, startled, dove into the water and swam away. He turned and climbed the other side of the ravine. He was frightened by the savagery of the thought that had possessed him. When he pulled himself over the edge he found himself in an area of open rolling hills, the forest having retreated to the colder northern slopes.

The past seemed closer here, as if he had indeed lived it.

He *had* hated Orfea. The feeling came to him like the memory of a shaman's rituals, fearsome and complex. It seemed that the hate had always been with him. That form, with his shape and gestures, loomed before him.

The memories were fragmentary, more terrifying than reassuring, like sharp pieces of colored glass. He saw the face of a boy he knew to be Abias, dark-eyed, curly-haired, intent. He bent over an injured animal, one of Elam's victims, his eyes shiny with tears. Young, he already possessed a good measure of that ancient knowledge the Bound remembered. In this case the animal was beyond healing. With a calmly dismissive gesture, Abias broke its neck.

The leaves in the forest moved of their own will, whispering to each other of the coming of the breeze, which brushed its cool fingers across the back of Elam's neck.

He remembered Orfea, a slender girl with dark hair, but he never saw her clearly. Her image appeared only in reflections, side images, glimpses of an arm or a strand of hair. And he saw himself, a slender boy with dark hair, twin to Orfea. He watched himself as he tied a cat down to a piece of wood, spreading it out as it yowled. There was a fine downy hair on his back, and he could count the vertebrae as they moved under his smooth young skin. The arm sawed with its knife, and the cat screamed and spat.

The children wandered the forest, investigating what they had found in the roots of a tree. It was some sort of vast lens, mostly under the ground, with only one of its faces coming out into the air. They brushed the twigs and leaves from it and peered in, wondering at its ancient functions. Elam saw Orfea's face reflected in it, solemn eyes examining him, wondering at him. A beam of hot sunlight played on the lens, awakening lights deep within it, vague images of times and places now vanished. Midges darted in the sun, and Orfea's skin produced a smooth and heavy odor, one of the perfumes she mixed for herself: her art, as death was Elam's. Elam looked down at her hand, splayed on the smooth glass, then across at his, already rougher, stronger, with the hints of dark dried blood around the fingernails.

Abias stood above them. He danced on the smooth glass, his callused feet slipping. He laughed every time he almost fell. "Can you see us?" he cried to the lens. "Can you see who we are? Can you see who we will become?" Elam looked up at him in wonder, then down at the boy's tiny distorted reflection as it cavorted among the twisted trees.

The sun was suddenly hot, slicing through the trees like a burning edge. Smoke rose as it sizzled across flesh. Elam howled with pain and ran up the slope. He ran until his lungs were dying within him.

The Neanderthal stopped in a clearing up the side of a mountain. A herd of clouds moved slowly across the sky, cropping the blue grass of the overhead. Around him rocks, the old bones of the Earth, came up through it sagging flesh. The trees whispered derisively below him. They talked of death and blood. "You should have died," they said. "The other should have lived." The Neanderthal turned his tear-filled eyes into the wind, though whether he wept for Orfea, or for Elam, even he could not have said.

The city burned with a dry thunder. Elam and Reqata ran through the crowded screaming streets with the arsonists, silent and pure men. In the shifting firelight, their tattooed faces swirled and re-formed, as if made of smoke themselves.

"The situation has been balanced for years," Reqata said. "Peace conceals strong forces pushing against each other. Change their alignment, and. . . ." Swords flashed in the firelight, a meaningless battle between looters and some sort of civil guard. Ahead were the tiled temples of the Goddesses, their goal.

"They feel things we don't," she said. "Religious exaltation. The suicidal depression of failed honor. Fierce loyalty to a leader. Hysterical terror at signs and portents."

Women screamed from the upper windows of a burning building, holding their children out in vain hope of salvation.

"Do you envy them?" Elam asked.

"Yes!" she cried. "To them, life is not a game." Her hand was tight on his arm. "They know who they are."

"And we don't?"

"Take me!" Reqata said fiercely. Her fingernails stabbed through his thin shirt. They had made love in countless incarnations, and these golden-skinned slender bodies were just another to her, even with the flames rising around them.

He took her down on the stone street as the city burned on all sides. Her scent pooled dark. It was the smell of death and decay. He looked at her. Beneath him, eyes burning with malignant rage, was Orfea.

"You are alive," Elam cried.

Her face glowered at him. "No, you bastard," she said. "I'm not alive. You are. You *are*."

His rage suddenly matched hers. He grabbed her hair and pulled her across the rough stone. "Yes. And I'm going to stay that way. Understand? Understand?" With each question, he slammed her head on the stone.

Her face was amused. "Really, Elam. I'm dead, remember? Dead and gone. What's the use of slamming me around?"

"You were always like that. Always sensible. Always driving me crazy!" He stopped, his hands around her throat. He looked down at her. "Why did we hate each other so much?"

"Because there was really only ever one of us. It was Lammiela who thought there were two."

Pain sliced across his cheek. Reqata slapped him again, making sure her nails bit in. Blood poured down her face and her hair was tangled. Elam stumbled back, and was shoved aside by a mob of running soldiers.

"Are you crazy?" she shouted. "You can't kill me. You can't. You'll ruin everything." She was hunched, he saw now, cradling her side. She reached down and unsheathed her sword. "Are you trying to go back to your old style? Try it somewhere else. This is *my* show."

"Wait," he said.

"Damn you, we'll discuss this later. In another life." The sword darted at him.

"Reqata!" He danced back, but the edge caught him across the back of his hand. "What are you—"

There were tears in her eyes as she attacked him. "I see her, you know. Don't think that I don't. I see her at night, when you are asleep. Your face is different. It's the face of a woman, Elam. A woman! Did you know that? Orfea lives on in you somewhere."

Her sword did not allow him to stop and think. She caught him again, cutting his ear. Blood soaked his shoulder. "Your perfume. Who sent it to you?"

"Don't be an idiot. Something in you is Orfea, Elam. That's the only part I really love."

He tripped over a fallen body. He rolled and tried to get to his feet. He found himself facing the point of her sword, still on his knees.

"Please, Reqata," he said, tears streaming down his cheeks. "I don't want to die."

"Well, isn't that the cutest thing." Her blade pushed into his chest, cold as ice. "Why don't you figure out who you are first?"

He awoke in his adytum. His eyes generated dots of light to compensate for the complete darkness. His blood vessels burned as if filled with molten metal. He moved, pushing against the viscous fluid. Damp hair swirled around him, thick under his back, curling around his feet. It had gathered around his neck. There was no air to breathe. Elam. Where was Elam? He seemed to be gone at last, leaving only—

Elam awoke, gasping, on a pallet, still feeling the metal of Reqata's sword in his chest. So it had been her. Not satisfied with killing everyone else, she had needed to kill him as well, repeatedly. He, even now, could not understand why. Orfea.

He stood silently in the middle of the room and listened to the beating of his own heart. Only it wasn't his own, of course, not the one he had been born with. It was a heart that Abias had carefully grown in a tank somewhere below, based on information provided by a gene sample from the original Elam. The real Elam still slept peacefully in his adytum. Peacefully . . . he had almost remembered something this time. Things had almost become clear.

He walked down to Abias's bright kingdom. Abias had tools there, surgical devices with sharp, deadly edges. It was his art, wasn't it? And a true artist never depended on an audience to express himself.

He searched through cabinets, tearing them open, littering the floor with sophisticated devices, hearing their delicate mechanisms shatter. He finally found a surgical tool with a vibratory blade that could cut through anything. He carried it upstairs and stared down at the ovoid of the adytum. What was inside of it? If he penetrated, perhaps, at last, he could truly see.

It wasn't the right thing, of course. The right instrument had to burn as it cut, cauterizing flesh. He remembered its bright killing flare. This was but a poor substitute.

Metal arms pinioned him. "Not yet," Abias said softly. "You cannot do that yet."

"What do you mean?" Elam pulled himself from Abias's suddenly unresisting arms and turned to face him. The faceless eyes stared at him.

"I mean that you don't understand anything. You cannot act without finally understanding."

"Tell me, then!" Elam shouted. "Tell me what happened. I have to know. You say you didn't kill Orfea. Who did then? Did I? Did I do it?"

Abias was silent for a long time. "Yes. Your mother has, I think, tried to forgive you. But *you* are the murderer."

"You were not supposed to remember." Lammiela sat rigidly in her most private room, her mental adytum. "The Bound told me you would not. That part of you was to vanish. Just as Laurance vanished from me."

"I haven't remembered. You have to help me."

She looked at him. Until today, the hatred in her eyes would have frightened him. Now it comforted him, for he must be near the truth.

"You were a monster as a child, Elam. Evil, I would have said, though I loved you. You were Laurance, returned to punish me for having killed him. . . ."

"I tortured animals," Elam said, hurrying to avoid Lammiela's past and get to his own. "I started with frogs. I moved up to cats, dogs. . . ."

"And people, Elam. You finally moved to people."

"I know," he said, thinking of the dead Orfea, whom he feared he would never remember. "Abias told me."

"Abias is very forgiving," Lammiela said. "You lost him his body, and nearly his life."

"What did I do with him?"

She shook her head. "I don't know, Elam. He has never said. All these years, and he has never said. You hated Orfea, and she hated you, but somehow you were still jealous of each other. She cared for Abias, your friend from the village, and that made you wild. He was so clever about that ancient Bound knowledge the Incarnate never pay attention to. He always tried to undo the evil that you did. He healed animals, putting them back together. Without you, he may never have learned all he did. He was a magician."

"Mother—"

She glared at him. "You strapped him down, Elam. You wanted to . . . to castrate him. Cloning, you called it. You said you could clone him. He might have been able to clone you, I don't know, but you certainly could do nothing but kill him. Orfea tried to stop you, and you fought. You killed her, Elam. You took that hot cutting knife and you cut her apart. It explodes flesh, if set right, you know. There was almost nothing left."

Despite himself, Elam felt a surge of remembered pleasure.

"As you were murdering your sister, Abias freed himself. He struggled and got the tool away from you."

"But he didn't kill me."

"No. I never understood why. Instead, he mutilated you. Carefully, skillfully. He knew a lot about the human body. You were unrecognizable when they found you, all burned up, your genitals destroyed, your face a blank."

"And they punished Abias for Orfea's murder. Why?"

"He insisted that he had done it. I knew he hadn't. I finally made him tell me. The authorities didn't kill him, at my insistence. Instead, they took away his body and made him the machine he now is."

"And you made him serve me," Elam said in wonder. "All these years, you've made him serve me."

She shook her head. "No, Elam. That was his own choice. He took your body, put it in its adytum, and has served you ever since."

Elam felt hollow, spent. "You should have killed me," he whispered. "You should not have let me live."

Lammiela stared at him, her eyes bleak and cold. "I daresay you're right, Elam. You were Laurance before me, the man I can never be again. I wanted to destroy you, totally. Expunge you from existence. But it was Abias's wish that you live, and since he had suffered at your hands, I couldn't gainsay him."

"Why then?" Elam said. "Why do you want to kill me now?" He stretched his hands out toward his mother. "If you want to, do it. Do it!"

"I don't know what you are talking about, Elam. I haven't tried to kill you. I gave up thinking about that a long time ago."

He sagged. "Who then? Reqata?"

"Reqata?" Lammiela smirked. "Go through all this trouble for one death? It's not her style, Elam. You're not that important to her. Orfea was an artist too. Her art was scent. Scents that stick in your mind and call up past times when you smell them again."

"You wore one of them," Elam said, in sudden realization. "The day my death in the north woods ended."

"Yes," she said, her voice suddenly taut again. "Orfea wore that scent on the last day of her life, Elam. You probably remember it."

The scent brought terror with it. Elam remembered that. "Did you find some old vial of it? Whatever made you wear it?"

She looked at him, surprised. "Why, Elam. You sent it to me yourself."

Abias stood before him like a technological idol, the adytum between them.

"I'm sorry, Abias," Elam said.

"Don't be sorry," Abias said. "You gave yourself up to save me."

"Kill me, Abias," he said, not paying attention to what the cyborg had just said. "I understand everything now. I can truly die." He held the vibratory surgical tool above the adytum, ready to cut in, to kill what lay within.

"No, Elam. You don't understand everything, because what I told Lammiela that day was not the truth. I lied, and she believed me." He pushed, and a line appeared across the adytum's ovoid.

"What is the truth then, Abias?" Elam waited, almost uninterested.

"Orfea did not die that day, Elam. You did."

The adytum split slowly open.

"You did try to kill me, Elam," Abias said softly, almost reminiscently. "You strapped me down for your experiment. Orfea tried to stop you. She grabbed the hot cutting knife and fought with you. She killed you."

"I don't understand."

The interior of an adytum was a dark secret. Elam peered inside, for a moment seeing nothing but yards and yards of wet dark hair.

"Don't you understand, Orfea? Don't you know who you are?" Abias's voice was anguished. "You killed Elam, whom you hated, but it was too much for you.

You mutilated yourself, horribly. And you told me what you wanted to be. I loved you. I did it."

"I wanted to be Elam," Elam whispered.

The face in the adytum was not his own. Torn and mutilated still, though repaired by Abias's skill, it was the face of Orfea. The breasts of a woman pushed up through the curling hair.

"You wanted to be the brother you had killed. After I did as you said, no one knew the difference. You were Elam. The genes were identical, since you were split from the same ovum. No one questioned what had happened. The Incarnate are squeamish, and leave such vile business to the Bound. And you've been gone ever since. Your hatred for who you thought you were caused you to kill yourself, over and over. Elam was alive again, and knew that Orfea had killed him. Why should he not hate her?"

"No," Elam said. "I don't hate her." He slumped slowly to his knees, looking down at the sleeping face.

"I had to bring her back, you understand that?" Abias's voice was anguished. "If only one of you can live, why should it be Elam? Why should it be him? Orfea's spirit was awakening, slowly, after all these years. I could see it sometimes, in you."

"So you brought it forth," Elam said. "You cloned and created creatures in which her soul could exist. The zeppelin. The dragon."

"Yes."

"And each time, she was stronger. Each time I died, I awoke . . . *she* awoke for a longer time in the adytum."

"Yes!" Abias stood over him, each limb raised glittering above his head. "She will live."

Elam rested his fingers in her wet hair and stroked her cheek. She had slept a long time. Perhaps it was indeed time for him to attempt his final work of art, and die forever. Orfea would walk the Earth again.

"No!" Elam shouted. "*I* will live." Abias loomed over him as the dragon had, ready to steal his life from him. He swung the vibrating blade and sliced off one of Abias's limbs. Another swung down, knocking Elam to the floor. He rolled. Abias raised himself above. Elam stabbed upward with the blade. It penetrated the central cylinder of Abias's body and was pulled from his hands as Abias jerked back. Elam lay defenseless and awaited the ripping death from Abias's manipulator arms.

But Abias stood above him, motionless, his limbs splayed out, his eyes staring. After a long moment, Elam realized that he was never going to move again.

The adytum had shut of its own accord, its gray surface once again featureless. Elam rested his forehead against it. After all these years he had learned the truth, the truth of his past and his own identity.

Abias had made him seem an illegitimate soul, a construct of Orfea's guilt. Perhaps that was indeed all he was. He shivered against the roughness of the adytum. Orfea slumbered within it. With sudden anger, he slapped its surface. She could continue to sleep. She had killed him once. She would not have the chance to do it again.

Elam stood up wearily. He leaned on the elaborate sculpture of the dead Abias, feeling the limbs creak under his weight. What was Elam without him?

Elam was *alive*. He smiled. For the first time in his life, Elam was alive.

Sister Alice

ROBERT REED

Robert Reed sold his first story in 1986 and quickly established himself as a frequent contributor to the *Magazine of Fantasy & Science Fiction* and *Asimov's Science Fiction,* as well as selling many stories to *Science Fiction Age, Universe, New Destinies, Tomorrow, Synergy, Starlight,* and elsewhere.

Reed may be one of the most prolific of today's young writers, particularly at short fiction lengths, seriously rivaled for that position only by authors such as Stephen Baxter and Brian Stableford. And—also like Baxter and Stableford—he manages to keep up a very high standard of quality *while* being prolific, something that is not at all easy to do. Almost every year throughout the mid-to-late nineties he has produced at least two or three stories that would be good enough to get him into a Best of the Year anthology under ordinary circumstances, and some years he has produced four or five of them, so that often the choice is not whether or not to use a Reed story but rather *which* Reed story to use—a remarkable accomplishment. Reed stories such as "The Utility Man," "Birth Day," "Blind," "A Place with Shade," "The Toad of Heaven," "Stride," "The Shape of Everything," "Guest of Honor," "Decency," "Waging Good," and "Killing the Morrow," among at least a half-dozen others equally as strong, count as among some of the best short works produced by anyone in the eighties and nineties. Nor is he nonprolific as a novelist, having turned out eight novels since the end of the eighties: *The Leeshore, The Hormone Jungle, Black Milk, The Remarkables, Down the Bright Way, Beyond the Veil of Stars, An Exaltation of Larks,* and, most recently, *Beneath the Gated Sky.*

In spite of this large and remarkable body of work, though, Reed remains largely ignored and overlooked when the talk turns to the Hot New Writers of the nineties, although he is beginning to get onto major award ballots. (His story "Whiptail" is on the Final Hugo Ballot as I type these words.) Like the works of Walter Jon Williams and Bruce Sterling, no one Robert Reed story is ever much like another Robert Reed story in tone or subject matter, and it may be that this versatility counts against him as far as building a reputation is concerned. John Clute, in *The Encyclopedia of Science Fiction,* noting that none of Reed's novels "share any background material or assumptions whatsoever," suggests that "today's sf readers tend to expect a kind of brand identity from authors, and it may be for this reason that Reed has not ye achieved any considerable fame."

It seems unfair that the range of an artist's palette should count against him— but Reed's name *is* slowly percolating into the public awareness here at the end of the nineties and I suspect that he will become one of the Big Names of the firs decade of the new century coming up on the horizon.

Reed is confident enough in the richness of his imagination to feel comfortabl writing stories set in the far future, and much of his output is set in milieux million of years removed from the time we know. Like some other young writers of th nineties, including Paul J. McAuley and Stephen Baxter, Reed is producing some c the most inventive and colorful of modern Space Opera, stuff set on a scale s grand and played out across such immense vistas of time that it makes the "Super science" stuff of the thirties look pale and conservative by comparison: his sequenc of novellas for *Asimov's, for instance, including* "Sister Alice," "Brother Perfect, "Mother Death," and *"Baby's Fire,"* detailing internecine warfare and intricate politica intrigues between families of immortals with powers and abilities so immense tha they are for all intents and purposes gods, or the sequence of stories unfolding i *F&SF, Science Fiction Age,* and *Asimov's,* including "The Remoras," "Aeon's Child, "Marrow," and "Chrysalis," involving the journeyings of an immense spaceship th size of Jupiter, staffed by dozens of exotic alien races, that is engaged in a multi million-year circumnavigation of the galaxy.

In the compelling novella that follows, the start of the *Sister Alice* sequence he shows us that the drawback to having godlike powers is that you have godlik *responsibilities* as well. . . .

Reed lives in Lincoln, Nebraska, where he's at work on a novel-length versio of his 1997 novella, *Marrow.* His most recent book is a long-overdue first collectior *The Dragons of Springplace.*

1

When I found myself daydreaming about my childhood, remembering the fun, thinking how carefree it had been . . . that's when my instincts began to warn me that our work had gone seriously, tragically wrong. . . .

Alice's testimony

Xo told their squad that it was a lousy place to build and that their fort was flawed that the Blues would crush them and it was Ravleen's fault. Everything was Rav leen's fault. And of course she heard about his grousing and came over, interrupting their drills to tell Xo to quit it. And he laughed, saying, "You're no general." Ord heard him. Everyone heard him, and Ravleen had no choice but to knock him dow and kick him. Xo was a Gold, and she was their Sanchex, the Gold's eterna general. She had to punish him, aiming for his belly and ribs. But Xo started cursing her. Bright poisonous words hung in the air. "You're no Sanchex," he grunted "and I'm not scared." Then Ravleen moved to his face, breaking his nose and cheekbones, the skin splitting, blood splattering on the new snow. Everyon watched. Ord stood nearby, watching the snow melt into the blood, diluting it. He saw Xo's face become a gooey mess, and he heard the boy's voice finally fall away into a sloppy wet laugh.

Tule stepped up, saying, "If you keep hurting him, he won't be able to hurt anyone else."

Ravleen paused, panting from her hard work, and deciding Tule was right. She dropped her foot and pushed her long black hair out of her eyes, grinning now, making sure everyone saw her confidence. Then she knelt, touching the bloody snow while asking, "Who wants to help this shit home?"

Tule was closest, but she despised Xo. She didn't approve of causing trouble; she felt it was her duty to keep their clan working smoothly, bowing to Ravleen's demands.

On the other hand, Ord was sympathetic. Xo wasn't his best friend, but he was a reliable one. Besides, they were on the same squad for now. A soldier had a duty to his squad; and that's why Ord stepped up, saying, "I'll take him."

"Then come straight back," Ravleen added.

He gave a nod and asked Xo, "Can you stand up?"

The bloody face said, "Maybe." A gloved hand reached for him, and Ord thought of the boy's ribs as he lifted. But the tortured groans were too much; Xo had a tendency toward theater. "Thanks," he muttered, then he reached into his mouth, pulling out a slick white incisor and tossing it at the young fort. It struck one of the robots with a soft *ping*.

"Come on," Ord prompted.

They walked slowly, crossing the long pasture and climbing to the woods. Xo stopped at the first tree, leaning against it and spitting out a glob of dark blood. Ord worked to be patient. Looking back at the pasture, he watched the robots stripping it of snow, building the fort according to Ravleen's design. A metal pole stood in the future courtyard, topped with a limp golden flag. Figures in clean white snowsuits were drilling again, six squads honing themselves for snowfare. It looked like an easy pasture to defend. On three sides it fell away, cliffs and nearly vertical woods protecting it. The only easy approach was from here, from above. Ravleen was assuming that the Blues would do what was easy, which was why the nearest wall had the thickest foundation. "Keep your strong to their strong," was an old Sanchex motto. But what if Xo was right? What if she had left their other walls too weak?

"I can't walk fast," Xo warned him. His swollen face was inhuman, but the bleeding had stopped, scabs forming and the smallest cuts beginning to heal. Speaking with a faint lisp, Xo admitted, "I sound funny."

"You should have left your tooth in," Ord countered. Gums preferred to repair teeth, not replace them. "Or you might have kept your mouth shut in the first place."

Xo gave a little laugh.

Something moved in the distance. Ord squinted and realized it was just an airship, distant sunlight making it glitter; and now he said, "Let's go." He said, "I'm tired of standing still."

They walked on a narrow trail, not fast, snow starting to fall and the woods knee-deep in old snow. They weren't far from the lowlands, and sometimes, particularly on clear days, city sounds would rise up from that hot flat country. But not today. A kind of enforced silence hung in the air. To step and not hear any footfall made Ord nervous, in secret. He realized that he was alert, as if ready to be ambushed. The war wouldn't start until the day after tomorrow, but he was anticipating it. Or maybe it was the fight he had just seen, maybe.

"Know why I did it?" asked Xo.

Ord said nothing.

"Know why I pissed her off?"

"Why?"

The battered face grinned. "I don't have to do this war now."

"Ravleen's not that angry," Ord countered. "Not angry enough to ban you, at least."

"But I'm hurt. Look at me."

"So?" Ord refused to be impressed. Glancing over a shoulder, he observed, "You're walking and talking. That's not badly hurt."

Except Xo's Family, the Nuyens, were careful people. A sister might see him and order him to stay home for several days. It wouldn't be the first time, particularly if he moaned like he did now, telling Ord, "I don't want to play snowfare."

"Why not?"

Wincing, Xo pretended to ache. But by now a cocktail of anesthesias was working, and both of them knew it.

"If you can stand, you can fight," Ord reminded him. "When you became a Gold you pledged to serve—"

"Wait." The boy waded into the deep snow, heading for an outcropping of false granite. He found a block of bright pink stone, brought it back and dropped it at Ord's feet. "Do me a favor?"

"No."

"Not hard. Just nick me here." He touched his stubby black hair. "I'll owe you. Promise."

Ord lifted the stone without conviction.

"Make it ugly," the boy prompted.

Ord shook his head, saying, "First tell me why you don't want to fight. Is it Ravleen?"

"Not really."

"Tell me or I won't help."

The boy touched his dark round face with his white gloves. "Just because it's stupid."

"What's stupid?"

"This game. This whole snowfare business."

Calling it a "game" was taboo. Snowfare was meant to be taken very, very seriously.

"But we're too old to play," his friend persisted. "I know I am."

This wasn't about Ravleen, and Ord had no easy, clear rebuke. He asked, "What will you do instead?" He assumed there was some other diversion. Perhaps a trip somewhere. Not out of the mountains, of course. That wasn't permitted, not at their age. But maybe one of Xo's siblings wanted to take him on a hunt, or some other adventure.

But Xo said, "Nothing. I just want to stay home and study." A pause. "Clip me here, okay? I'll tell my sisters that Ravleen did it. Promise."

Ord watched the boy lay on the hard white trail, face up, waiting calmly for his skull to be cracked open. The stone couldn't hurt him too badly. Eons ago, human beings gave up soft brains for better ones built of tough, nearly immortal substances. The worst Ord could manage was to break up some neural connections, making Xo forgetful and clumsy for a few days. The body might die, but nothing more. Nothing less than a nuclear fire could kill them, and that was the same for almost every human.

"Are you going to help me?" the boy whined.

Ord watched the hopeful face, judging distance and mass, guessing what would make the ugliest wound. But he kept thinking back to the comment about being too old, knowing it was a little true. Some trusted spark of his had slipped away, and that bothered him.

"Ord?"

"Yeah?"

"Will you hurry up?"

He let the stone slip free of his grip, missing Xo by a hair's breadth; then he said, "No, I can't. I shouldn't."

Xo lifted the stone himself, groaning as he aimed, trying to summon the courage. He was invulnerable, but so were old instincts. This wasn't easy. His arms shook, then collapsed. The attempt looked like a half-accident—*thud*—and his head was dented on one side. But not badly enough, they discovered. Xo could stand by himself, only a little dizzy; and he touched his wounds one after another, telling himself, "At least I'll get tomorrow to myself." He wasn't looking at Ord, or anywhere, saying, "This is good enough," with a soft wet voice that was lost in the muting whisper of the snowfall.

2

When I lived here, when I was a child, these mountains were new. The estates were new. Our mansions were modest but comfortable, the Families victorious . . . and the galaxy was vast and nearly empty, full of endless and intoxicating possibilities. . . .

—Alice's testimony

There were exactly one thousand Families—a number set by design—and Ord was a Chamberlain, one of the more famous and powerful Families. The ancestral Chamberlain home stood near the center of their estate, on a broad scenic peak. It was a round building, tall and massive, built from false granite with a shell of tailored white coral. The interior, above ground and below, was a maze of rooms and curling hallways, simple laboratories and assorted social arenas. There were enough beds for fifteen hundred brothers and sisters, should so many ever wish to visit at one time. And there were other buildings scattered about the estate—cottages, hunting lodges, and baby mansions—capable of absorbing the rest of them.

But it was the round white house that was famous, recognized by virtually every educated entity in the galaxy. Chamberlains had helped the Sanchexes win the Great Wars, then they were instrumental in building the Ten Million Year Peace. Chamberlains had made first contact with many important alien species, had been first to reach the galaxy's core, and for eons had pioneered the rapid terraforming of empty worlds. With low, low death rates being common, there was a constant demand for new homes, aliens and humans both paying substantial fees for good work.

Ord had a shallow sense of this history. He knew the Great Wars were fought with savagery, billions of people murdered and the Earth itself left battered. But the Peace had endured for a hundred thousand centuries, the Families giving it backbone and the occasional guidance. Ord himself was a whisper of a child, not even fifty years old. His powers as a Chamberlain lay in the remote future. Imagining adulthood, he pictured a busy semi-godhood, building green worlds at the Core, or perhaps flying off to some far galaxy, exploring it while making new allies. But the actual changes were mysterious to him. His mind and energies would swell, but how would it feel to him? His senses would multiply, and time itself would slow to where seconds would become hours. But how would such an existence seem? He had asked the brothers and sisters living with him. He had worn them down with his inquiries. Yet not one of them had ever offered a clear, believable answer.

"You're too young to understand," they would assure him, their voices bored. Or even a little shrill. "Just wait and see," they would recommend. "You'll learn when you're ready." But Ord could sense that like him, they had no idea what the future held. Like all perfect questions, his were unoriginal. And all of the Chamberlains in the mansion—all younger than a millennium—were in that same proverbial spacecraft, adrift and lost and uniformly scared.

The Golds' fort was completed on schedule, by midafternoon that next day, and after some last work the clan walked up to the tube port together, singing Gold songs. From there it was a brief ride home for Ord. He was deposited at the lawn's edge, his pet bear-dogs charging him, yelping and begging to be scratched behind every ear. Done with that duty, Ord entered through the usual door, touching the motto engraved in the granite overhead. "PRIDE AND SACRIFICE," said the ageless letters; his gesture was a habit, almost a reflex. Then he ran to the nearest stairwell, riding up to his floor and sprinting to his room, greeted there by a pair of mothering robots at least as obnoxious as his bear-dogs. They asked about his day and his accomplishments. Was there enough snow? "Plenty," he allowed; it had fallen all night. Good for forts, was it? "Perfect," he told them, removing his warm snowsuit. "Good wet snow." Close to the lowlands, that pasture had a milder climate than this high country. "And I think it's a very strong fort. I think so . . ."

The robots paused, saying nothing where they might have said, "We're glad to hear it."

Ord hesitated, suddenly alert.

"Lyman has just asked to see you," said synchronized voices.

Lyman was a brother, the oldest one living in the house. *He wants to see me?* Ord wondered what was wrong. If he'd hit Xo with that rock . . . but he hadn't, and nothing else remarkable had happened in the last few days. "What does Lyman want?"

"We're curious too," they replied, glass eyes winking. "You're supposed to go to his room as soon as you're clean and dressed."

Ord looked outside. His longest wall faced east, a crystal window in place of the granite. Somewhere below, in the gathering darkness, was his new fort. On clear nights he liked to watch the glow of the cities beyond, wondering about all the kinds of people living near these mountains. Everyone on Earth was rich to some degree; the land was too crowded and too expensive for those without means. But only the Families could afford having winters, putting their trees and lakes to sleep. These artificial mountains, constructed after the Great Wars, had never produced meaningful food, nor had they ever housed more than a very few people.

"Lyman sounds impatient," the robots warned him.

"Okay." Ord ran through his sonic bath, then dressed and left. His brother lived several stories above him. He had visited enough to know the way, and enough to hesitate at the door. Lyman liked to entertain various girlfriends; caution was required. Ord announced his presence, and the door opened, a distant voice telling him:

"Wait there. I'm almost done."

It was Ord's voice, only deeper. Older. Lyman had one of the large interior rooms, two universal-walls and a vast bed, plus a private swimming pool and sauna. Distinctive touches were meant to say *Lyman* but always felt more *Chamberlain* than anything. Chamberlains liked mementos. Where Ord would have kept his collection of alien fossils, his brother set up small light-statues of the girlfriends— women of every variation, uniformly disrobed—and they smiled at Ord, showing him how pleased they were to stand on those shelves. One universal-wall was activated. The live feed showed him moons orbiting a banded gas giant, each moon encased in an atmosphere, the nearest one blued by an ocean. Did a Chamberlain build that ocean? It wasn't too unlikely. Lyman was training to become an apprentice terraformer. Once he was declared an adult, probably in less than a century, he would leave for his first assignment. Something easy, no doubt. He would rebuild some fat comet between stars, probably for a client who wanted a vacation home—

"How's your war?" asked Lyman, striding out of the bath, adjusting his loose-fitting trousers as he moved. "Done with your fort?"

Ord muttered, "Yes."

"Any more fights?"

Was this about Xo and Ravleen? Or maybe Lyman was just making noise. Either way, Ord guessed that his brother knew the answers, that he had heard from the robots and the estate's sentries. "No fights," Ord reported. "No until tomorrow morning, at least."

"But Lyman wasn't listening. He started to speak, to make some joke, then paused, his mouth left open for a long moment.

Ord waited, tension building.

"Do you know where I was this morning?"

"Where?"

"Antarctica." Lyman liked to tease his little brother, reminding him that one of them could travel at will on the Earth. No farther, but it still seemed like an enormous freedom.

"What were you doing there?" asked Ord.

"Having fun, naturally." Lyman tried to smile, scratching his bare belly. Taller than Ord, he had old-fashioned adult proportions, his body hairy and strong with an appropriate unfancy penis dangling in his trousers. Red hair grew to his shoulders. Like Ord, he had the telltale Chamberlain face, sharp features and pale skin and pale blue eyes. Their sisters were feminized versions of them, with breasts and such; physical forms were standardized, eternal, every Family built around its immortal norm, every norm patterned after its founder and ultimate parent.

Lyman sat next to his brother, sighed and asked, "Do you know why I came home? Have you heard?"

Ord shook his head, his breath quickening. What happened that would require Lyman to abandon his fun?

"Listen."

But then his brother said nothing else, his mouth left open and the eyes gazing at the wall. Finally Ord asked, "What is it?"

"In the next few days . . . soon, I don't know when . . . we'll have a guest with us. Be on your very best behavior, please."

"Who's visiting?"

Lyman seemed disturbed, or at least deeply puzzled, pursing his lips and shaking his head. "One of our sisters is dropping by."

Sisters came and went all of the time.

"An old sister," Lyman added.

Every sister was older than Ord.

And his brother grinned, as if realizing how mysterious this must sound. "A very old, much honored adult. She is."

Ord looked at the wall, watching its image change. A small dull sun was setting over a glassy sea. An ammonia sea, perhaps. He found himself dealing with this news by distancing himself, working on the dynamics of the other world as if it was one of his tutor's lessons.

"You're not listening," Lyman warned him.

"How old is she?"

"Her name is Alice."

Alice—

"She's our Twelve." The words were incredible to both of them. Lyman repeated himself, saying, "Yes. Twelve."

Ord was stunned, closing his hands into fists and dropping them into his lap. "Why is she coming here?"

Lyman didn't seem to hear him. "We received her private message this morning . . . coded . . . and everyone's excited, of course. . . ."

Ord nodded.

"A Twelve is coming here." Lyman was astonished, but the smile seemed almost joyless. "I looked up when the last Fifty or higher came to visit. Our Forty-two touched down for less than an hour, some twenty-eight millennia ago. A little handshake visit." He paused, rubbing at the stiff red hairs on his chest. "Alice wants to linger. She's requested the penthouse and given no departure time. Even though she'll be bored in a millisecond, she claims that she wants to live here."

This was landmark news, and Ord imagined telling the other Golds about it. Tonight? No, tomorrow. On the eve of combat. It would give him a sudden burst of importance, a worthiness. Even Ravleen would be impressed, and jealous, and he began to smile, imagining the moment.

"There's more," Lyman said, anticipating him. "The news is secret. Alice made it very clear—"

Secret?

"—and I'm giving you fair warning. You won't tell anyone. Not even your best friends. This is Chamberlain business, and it's private."

The boy offered a weak, confused nod.

"No other Family can know she's here."

"Why not?"

"Because that's what she wants."

"But why visit us?"

"Why not?" Lyman offered, then his face grew puzzled again. "I honestly don't know why. No one seems to know where she's been. But I'm sure that she'll explain, when it's time."

A Twelve. Ord knew there were just five Chamberlains older than Alice, the rest long dead. And of the five, two weren't even in the galaxy now, bound for Andromeda. By contrast, Ord had a five digit designation, as did Lyman and every other sibling in this house. He could never live long enough and become famous enough that his arrival here would be stunning news. "24,411 is on his way. Behave, children!" Ord nearly laughed at the preposterous image. If he lived a billion years—a possibility, in principle—and if he did wondrous things, then yes, he guessed that then he might generate the kind of excitement that he felt now. Maybe.

"I don't even know where she's been," Lyman repeated. "We've asked, but the walls won't tell us."

The famous Alice. She had been born after the Great Wars, in the first years of the Peace; and she was one of the first Chamberlains to master terraforming; most of her methods standard even today.

"Not a hint to anyone. All right, little brother?"

He said, "Yes," with a soft, disappointed breath.

Lyman made fists and placed them on his lap, saying, "I bet it's nothing important. Here and gone in ten minutes, she'll be."

The wall changed again, showing them a ringed gas giant. World-sized continents built of hyperfoams floated in its atmosphere, linked together, the winds carrying them along with a dancer's precision. Where was this place? Terraforming on that scale required time and much money, and there probably weren't a thousand worlds like it in the galaxy. A mere thousand, which was nothing. And he shut his eyes, knowing Alice had built it. Lyman had asked this wall to show him her work; and like his brother, Ord wondered why she would come here. Why bother? And why would such an enormous, wondrous soul want her presence kept secret? Why . . . ?

3

Consider this. Our Families have never been wealthier, and they have never been so weak. Our fraction of humanity's worth has shriveled throughout the Peace, as planned. We are pledged to reproduce slowly. We clone archaic bodies, then slowly fit them with the latest wonders. But while we've kept a monopoly on those wonders, other peoples and aliens

*and even the machine intelligences grow more numerous every day, ac-
complishing more and more with their insect tenacity . . . winning the
Peace, in essence, which is of course why they agreed to it in the first
place. . . .*

—*Alice's testimony*

Their fort was beautiful, tall and milk-colored, draped with last night's snow. Yesterday, done with drills, everyone but Xo had added some touch of his or her own.
Handmade flourishes. On the parapets were snow fists and boat prows and big-
eyed skulls. Ord had built a gargoyle on his portion of the wall—a fierce thing
with wings extended, curved white teeth glowing in the early light—and he was
standing behind it, on the broad rampart, his squad flanking him and everyone at
attention. Ravleen was speaking, her voice coming from headphones sewn into
their golden facemasks. "From now on," she promised, "these Blues are going to
suffer every flavor of misery. We'll beat them once and for all."

It was a famous quote, the "every flavor of misery" line. One of the Sanchex
generals had uttered it, and Ravleen repeated it once or twice every year. She and
Tule were below, sitting inside the thick-walled keep at the back of the courtyard,
watching the countryside with sensors and hidden cameras. Ord knew how much
she wanted to win. This war's losers would make medals for the winners—the
standard rule—and nobody would treasure her disk of iridium and diamond more
than Ravleen. Sanchexes drank in their awards; every certificate of merit was on
display, sometimes for centuries. The Ten Million Year Peace had only tempered
them, it was said. And when the time came—when they were too mature for these
wars—nobody would miss them more than Ravleen. Ord almost felt sorry for her,
shutting his eyes . . . and his mind shifting back to the topic that had kept him
sleepless all night. . . .

"What are you thinking?" asked Xo, strolling up to him. Save for some yellow
bruises, his face had healed. He had showed it to Ord before putting on the mask,
proud that he had healed so easily. "You look like you're thinking hard. What
about?"

That his sister was coming. *Alice. My Twelve.* The words surfaced in his consciousness, begging to be spoken. Yet he had promised not to tell, not Xo or even
his best friends. Maybe that was wise, he thought. Why would Alice come here?
And wouldn't he look foolish when it turned out to be untrue?

"I wish we'd start," Xo groused, forgetting his question. "Waiting is boring."

Last night, following dinner with a dozen brothers and sisters, Ord had gone
to his room and requested a biography of their great sister. He had read and watched
holos until after midnight, trying to absorb some fraction of her enormous life. It
was impossible. The history of the Earth seemed easy by comparison.

"I'm bored," Xo repeated.

And as if she heard him, Ravleen interrupted the quiet. "Enemies in the woods,
on the west. On the move."

Three squads were stationed on the strong west wall, including theirs. Saying
nothing, they watched the leafless black trees for any motion, a delicious sense of
drama in the wind.

"Mortars," warned Ravleen. "Firing."

Whump-whump. The Blues had two mortars, air-driven, their size and power set by old rules. Everyone dropped to their knees, hugging the parapet, and a pair of snowballs hit in the courtyard, bucket-sized and nobody injured. They were meant to judge range. The next rounds did the damage, someone crying out, "Heat," as a blue sphere struck behind Xo. Chemical goo broke free of its envelope, activated by the air and melting the ice beneath it. A thick blue cancer was spreading. Ord and Xo jumped up, using shovels to fling the worst of the goo below, then using last night's snow to make fast, sloppy patches.

It was fun, fast and fun, and everyone seemed to enjoy themselves.

"Return fire," Ravleen ordered.

Their own mortars were loaded, aligned by hand and guesswork. Whump, whump. Whump, whump. They fired snow only, harassing the enemy. And now a half dozen Golds shouted, "Look!" as the Blues broke from the woods above.

"Guns at the ready," said their general.

Ord had an old snowgun—a favorite—with its plastic stock worn slick and pale, carried by two sisters before him. It had over-and-under barrels and a simple laser sight, a potent compressor and twenty rounds of snow loaded into the stock. Slugs were made inside the barrels, in an instant, each one thumb-sized and spinning for accuracy, able to hit someone's head at nearly forty meters.

"Ready," Ravleen whispered in Ord's ears.

He looked over the gargoyle's right wing, snow-colored figures with deep-blue facemasks charging across fresh snow, a practiced scream growing louder as they closed the gap . . . two dozen of them, including the eight who were rolling cannons into position . . . and where were the others . . . ?

"On my command," Ravleen said. "Cannons . . . fire!"

Thunk-thunk-thunk. Three cannons were on the west wall, a fourth held in reserve. Big fat rounds followed golden laser beams, no one struck. The Blues were zigzagging, a thin line of them coming. Fifty meters, then forty. Then thirty, and Ravleen said, "At will. Fire."

They rose together, as drilled, aiming and squeezing off double-shots. Flecks of laser light danced over their targets. It sounded like the popping of insects, the air filled with white streaks flying both ways. Ord picked a target and hit it in the belly, then the face, then missed when it ducked and slipped sideways. But he anticipated the next move, leading and firing and the double-shots smacking the face more than once, snapping it back, leaving the Blue stunned in the snow.

"Reload," said his gun. He dropped and opened the stock, shoving in handfuls of fresh wet ammunition. Then the lone squad on the east wall was shouting, and firing. Not only were there two attacks, but Ravleen hadn't seen the other troops marshaling. "Squad A," she shouted, "change walls. Support the east. Now."

The Blues must have disabled the watchdogs on the east. With a fair trick? Every war had its strict rules, only so much snow for a fort, so much heat allowed its attackers, and so on. Squad B—Ord's—had to spread out and cover for A. He would fire and drop, then come up somewhere else. A lucky shot caught him above the eye, a warm thread of blood making it blink and water. He ducked and wiped with a sleeve, then moved and rose again. But now the Blues were in retreat, their attack meant to harass and nothing more. Their artillery fired overhead, peppering the east wall, heat gnawing at the hard white ice.

Ravleen pulled Squad C next. She had no choice. They had to repair holes while B was left alone on the west wall, six soldiers fighting more than a dozen.

And of course the Blues attacked again, in a tight formation. Squad B closed ranks and fired down on them. Heat grenades ruined the snow gargoyle, its wings and snarling head collapsing into mush; and the Blues teased them, shouting, "You're next, you're next, you're next."

Ord dropped and reloaded, moved and rose. And the Blues guessed where he would be, and when, every gun fixed on him, blue sparkles half-blinding him and the double-shots on their way. He didn't have time to react. The entire salvo caught his face and throat; and what startled everyone was how he stayed on his feet, bloodied and stunned but undeniably upright.

The Blues fired again, in unison.

That second salvo lifted him off the rampart, snapping his head back, and he fell into the courtyard, landing on his back in the greasy blue heat, bruised and sore and suddenly tired enough to sleep, unable to see for all the blood in his eyes.

4

Why did we attempt it? The simple, one-word explanation is greed. *The two-word explanation adds* charity, *because it was for your good as well as ours. The third word is* arrogance, *of course. And the fourth, without doubt, is* stupidity. . . .

—*Alice's testimony*

Ord remembered when his blood tasted salty. Now it was sweet, reminding him of oranges. His biochemistry was changing, new genes awakened, his body progressively tougher and faster and faster to heal. He had been able to fight again by afternoon, and by dusk he felt almost normal, picking at the hard scabs as he entered the house. As always, he touched the PRIDE AND SACRIFICE emblem on his way to the stairs. But something made him pause, something subtle, Ord standing on the balls of his feet while listening, a peculiar nonsound emerging from another hallway.

He changed direction, suddenly aware of his heartbeat.

The house had been built in stages, layered like a coral reef, the oldest regions in the deep interior. The original mansion had been abandoned—a five-story structure not particularly grand in its day—and Ord knew he had reached it when the floor changed to natural stone, cold and dirty white. Lights woke for him, and the general appearance had been maintained by the house robots; yet everything felt old, even tired, Ord touching the simple brick walls, new mortars mending the old but nothing else changed, thousands of centuries focused squarely on him, barely allowing him to breathe.

There was a central staircase leading up to various sealed doorways. Every Gold had come here with him, at least once, Ord showing off the Chamberlains' humble beginnings. Beside the staircase were two heavy doors, also sealed, one on each side. Not even Lyman had permission or the means to open them. But today, for no apparent reason, the door on his left was ajar. No, it was removed. He stepped closer, blinked, and saw the bare hinges and dark air . . . and nothing. It was as if the great old door had been stolen, or erased, and he couldn't guess why.

Ord paused, squinting now. The room beyond was dim and imprecise, dust floating with graceful ease. He heard a sound, a faint dry click, but couldn't guess its direction. "Hello?" His voice was weak, almost useless. The room seemed to swallow his noise, then him, his snowboots falling silent on the old rotted carpet and his face caressed by a sudden chill. He was inside before he made any conscious decision to take this chance, and he told himself: *I shouldn't be here.* He thought: *I will leave. Now.* But the promise seemed as good as the deed, and Ord walked on in a straight certain line.

It wasn't a large room, even in its day. A rounded wall was on his left, the tighter curve of the staircase on his right, and every wall was buried behind cabinets and framed paintings and various decorations that made no sense to him, styles and logic long extinct. The place felt like a storage closet, not a room where people would gather. Despite careful treatment, the relics were degrading, wood splitting along lines of weakness, paintings faded and flaking. He paused and stared at the largest painting, a faint yellow lamp glowing above it. The plaque beneath told Ord what he suspected, the subject's name etched into a greenish metal.

"Yes, he's our father."

The voice didn't startle him. It came wrapped in a calmness that soothed and nourished him. Removing one thin glove, Ord touched the name, *Ian Chamberlain* written in the dead man's neat, circumspect script. It was similar to Ord's handwriting . . . the same angles, the same spacings . . . and he felt a sudden deep reverence for the man, Ian shown posing before the original mansion, every feature blurred by the tired paints. Ord had seen Ian countless times, in holos and interactive fictions; but here, in these circumstances, he felt close to the man, and nervous, his mouth going small and dry. This was their father, their One; and the voice was saying, "Look at me," with a mild, flat tone that couldn't startle anyone.

It was his sister's voice—every sister's voice—yet it was all wrong, reaching deeper than simple sound could manage.

"I'm right behind you," he heard, and he turned, discovering a figure standing in the room's center, smiling at him, her face the same as any sister's face, only rounder. She wore a body that was a little fat, wrinkles crowded around the eyes and a softness to the flesh, pudgy hands trying to straighten a wrinkle in her simple dark blouse. She took a step toward him, and Ord felt a tingling sensation, smelling ozone. Become a certain age, he knew, and you ceased to be merely tough meat and an enduring mind. Succeed at being an adult for a few tens of thousands of years, and your Family taught you how to use new energies, plasmas and shadow matter. Eventually you were built of things more unseen than seen, the prosaic nonsense of sweet blood and neurons left for special occasions.

"Look at you," she whispered, a dry hand touching Ord on the cheek. "Do you know how perfectly perfect you look?"

"You're the Twelve," he sputtered.

She gave an odd little laugh.

Ord managed a clumsy sideways step, wondering if she could be someone else. It seemed preposterous to think that a Twelve could speak to him. Was she some younger sister, some assistant perhaps?

"My name is Alice," she warned, "not Twelve. And you? You must be the baby. Ord."

He offered a very slight nod.

Curiosity and a mild empathy showed on the smiling face. Alice touched him again, on the other cheek, saying, "There. All gone."

His scabs had dissolved, bruises absorbed.

She laughed without making noise, tilting her head as if to look at him from a new vantage point. Invisible hands passed through his flesh, studying him from within; then she was saying, "I used to enjoy a good snowball fight. Isn't that remarkable to think?"

It seemed unlikely, yes.

"Quite the fort you have." She closed her eyes, a wisp of red hair dangling over her chalky forehead. "Not elaborate, no. But sturdy. A good solid construction."

He asked, "Can you see it now?"

"Easily." She opened her eyes, smiling as she said, "You fought on the west wall, near the middle—"

"How can you—?"

"Bootprints. Blood. A thousand ways." Then she said, "This is yours," and held up his snowgun. Surprise slipped into nervousness. They weren't supposed to remove equipment from the battlefield. He watched while Alice went through the motions of a careful examination, placing her right eye to the end of the barrel and tugging on the trigger. Ord grimaced. But nothing happened, and she seemed amused by his response, smiling at him, her soft voice saying, "My, my. I didn't have such fancy toys when I was a girl."

It wasn't fancy, but he didn't correct her.

She assured him, "I am jealous."

He thought that was a remarkable thing to hear. A Twelve envying him. Because of a toy gun?

"How are my Radiant Golds doing?"

Radiant?

"What kind of wargame is it?"

"A forty hour scenario," he reported. "Heavy snows and the Golds defend a place of their choice—"

"Against the Electric Blues," she interjected.

Ord paused and swallowed, then said, "They have to capture our flag."

Something about Alice made him feel happy, as if she couldn't contain her own joy and it flowed into him, sweetening his mood. She shut her eyes again, savoring the instant. "Here." She handed him his weapon. "I don't mean to leave you defenseless."

"I can't have it . . . here . . ."

"Pardon me?"

Ord swallowed, then used a careful, certain voice. "I leave my gun wherever I was standing. Where I was when we quit."

"Marking your position. How reasonable."

It vanished from his grip, fingertips tingling for an instant.

"I am sorry. I didn't know." Yet she sounded more amused than sorry. Turning, she did a slow stately walk around the room, absorbing everything with eyes and perhaps other senses. Fancy china plates were collapsing into dust. An ornamental knife was speckled with corrosion. A crystal sphere had broken in two—that seemed to amuse her—and she picked up the larger part, saying, "In my day, we threw snowballs. We made them with our hands and threw them, and I wasn't particularly good at it. The sexes differed too much in ability, and I had a girl's arm." She set the crystal down again, turned and stared at the ceiling for a long time. "That pasture you're defending? I fought for it once. I can recall . . . I was sore afterward, of course." She paused, then looked at him again. "Do the Swords still exist?"

"The Silvers," Ord replied. There were twenty clans, twenty colors, fifty children in each one. He had to ask, "Were you a Gold?"

"One of the first, and worst."

Ord imagined this woman running in the snow, attacking a cowering line of Silvers. In the early Peace, childhoods were quick and old-fashioned. A person became an adult in just a century, and only then was her body improved, her mind made ready to deal with Family responsibilities. Slow growth, like Ord's, allowed for quality. For better maturity. He had been told that many times, and believed it; yet part of him envied Alice, thinking how she had been a child for just a very few winters.

"And who's your general?"

"Ravleen."

"She has to be a Sanchex, am I right?"

Ord nodded.

"Crystal can grow tired and shatter," she said, "but some things are too resilient. If you see my point." Alice gave a satisfied nod, then told him, "I would like to hear about everything. Soon. It's been too long since I last visited . . . and enjoyed this lovely old house. . . ."

Her voice fell away, as if she was hunting for the best word.

Then she said, "Enjoyed," once again.

"Why are you here?" Ord heard himself asking. "Alice?"

She didn't seem to hear him, stepping past him, hands lifting to touch the old portrait. With means obscure and powerful, she rearranged the molecules in the tired paints, re-creating their father's face and body, then altering the artist's original work. A rope of glass fibers dangled from the dead man's chest. Through them he would have controlled a multitude of powerful primitive machines, his body connected to whatever warship or world he was residing on at the moment. Few humans used such systems anymore. No Family member bothered with them. But Ord recalled that exposing that rope, whether in public or a portrait, would have been rude, even vile. After the Wars, and for a very long time, it was important for Chamberlains and every other Family to hide their augmented selves.

"What do you think, little brother?"

He stepped close and studied the portrait. The round white house and green lawn had been left unchanged, as if out of focus. They made Ian all the more real, set against that exhausted background. Ord stared at the face—ageless and wise; the seminal patriarch—and he saw a quality in its expression. It was as if the artist had told the great man to smile, and he had obeyed, but there was some powerful, deep-felt sadness in him that he could never hide.

Ord was uneasy. What Alice had done wasn't restoration, it was vandalism. The past always should be respected; yet here she had altered a work of art, making it something else entirely. Self-righteousness left him bold, and he asked again, "Why are you here?"

Alice seemed composed, giving him a watery grin while asking in turn, "Why can't I come here?" Then she looked at their father, a thin colorless voice saying, "When she wants, a person should be able to come home."

He had no simple, quick response.

"Desire," she said, "is reason enough, little brother."

And when he next glanced at the portrait, she vanished. He found himself alone, standing in a room where he didn't belong, the air suddenly frigid and his blood-caked snowsuit warming itself and him in response, his breath visible, like thin puffs of tepid steam.

Ord went to his room, telling no one what had happened. Tonight the house felt exceptionally empty. He assumed the others were with Alice, greeting her in some fashion, and that there were good reasons why the youngest brother wouldn't be included. Eating alone, he studied the day's lessons without concentrating. Poetry and mathematics seemed unreal, and he eventually put them aside, ordering his universal-wall to show him more of Alice's worlds. Light-velocity feeds were found; a new vista was presented every few minutes. Ord put on pajamas and sat on his bed, fresh snow falling behind him, illuminated by images from around the galaxy and nothing else visible in the black night.

Her worlds were rich with life. More than most terraformed worlds, easily. Sometimes Ord asked to see who lived on them, and he was shown city scenes and up-to-the-second census figures. Like him, these people were built from ordinary matter. Like him, they had limited talents but no programmed lifespans. Barring accidents, they might live forever. Yet unlike Ord—unlike anyone in the Family—they could manipulate their human forms. Instead of enlarging themselves with trickery, they bent themselves with genetic tailoring, adapting to odd niches or simply embellishing some feature for private reasons. It was a basic feature of the Peace; freedoms were granted along different tangents. A multitude of strange, even alien humans wandered past Ord: tall figures and tiny ones, people with golden fur and others with elephant noses. On the oldest, most crowded planets, it was best to divide into a carefully structured mass of species. The Earth itself had some hundred-thousand distinct, registered types of humans, every sort of food able to be metabolized by someone. Lyman had a passion for the strangest local ladies, Ord recalled. He would bring them to the mansion now and again; and once, completely by accident. Ord had walked in on him and his current girlfriend, at the very worst moment. An embarrassing, instructive lesson, it still made the boy blush twenty years later, thinking of that finned beauty in the swimming pool, on her back, and his brother gasping as he turned, discovering that he wasn't alone.

The Peace was built on rules. The Families had to begin with old-style bodies, and no profession belonged only to them. Yet they remained the best terraformers, commanding the best salaries. Teams of ordinary humans and machines couldn't build with the beauty that Alice achieved, he felt certain. And what's more, she worked for aliens too. Methane seas; nitrogen seas; water seas made toxic by bizarre biologies. Ord knew enough to admit that he knew very little. The next time he saw Alice, he would compliment her regardless. *If I see her*, he thought; and now he asked the wall to stop, lying back in bed, letting the sheets find him.

But he didn't sleep, his eyes barely closed when he heard a brother ask. "Did you tell? Anyone?"

Ord sat up, finding Lyman in the open door. Long hair and the broad shoulders were set against the lights of the hallway. "Tell anyone what?"

"About our sister coming," Lyman muttered, obviously nervous.

Ord shook his head. "I didn't, no. No one."

"Just thought I should check." He stepped closer, grinning and staring out the window.

"Does she like the penthouse?"

Lyman blinked and said, "She's not here yet, but she won't. I'm sure she won't."

The boy felt something. A caress, perhaps. Or maybe it was his own adrenaline, fatigue dispelled in an instant, his mouth dropping open but his voice gone.

Lyman noticed the odd expression, blinked and stepped backward.

Then Ord whispered, "I saw her."

"Where?"

Ord closed his mouth, summoning courage.

"Where did you see her?" Lyman came to the foot of the bed, then suggested, "It might have been someone else."

"She said she was Alice." And he told the story, describing the missing door and the room filled with relics, and Alice, and how she had easily done some odd things. Would he get into trouble for entering that room? Or for not telling Lyman about it afterward? "I thought you'd know that she's here," Ord assured him. Then he asked, "Why hasn't she told you that she's here?"

His brother leaned against the bed, his mouth open and his eyes empty. Around them was a ghostly sense of amusement, thick enough to taste, and sweet.

"Where is she, Lyman?"

The older brother merely shook his head, not saying the obvious. *She's here now . . . with us now. . . .*

5

I have rebuilt some ninety-thousand major worlds for a wide assortment of clients. But my best work, without question, are the secret worlds that I build for myself, from nothing. I have done several dozen of them, inventing unique biologies and hiding them away inside dust clouds and in globular clusters. And yes, I know. They are questionable legal acts, I know. But many terraformers dabble in such work, and not just Family members either. And it's not an original idea that our dear Earth is someone's garden, built and lost, and all of us are merely its lucky sons and daughters. . . .

—*Alice's testimony*

The skies were clear in the morning. The Sanchex mansion—a great gray pyramid—was visible in the north. Ord was eating his breakfast, half-dressed for battle, when Lyman returned to his room, telling him, "Someone is inside the penthouse. We're sure now."

Ord turned, saying nothing.

"But she won't respond. Yet." Lyman shook his head. "Just the same, we should keep her presence secret. Understood?"

Of course. But he went through the ritual of promising once again.

"Do normal activities," his brother insisted. "Act as if everything is perfectly normal."

Ord thought of his siblings at the penthouse door, asking it if Alice were inside. And Lyman, trying to hide his nervousness, merely nodded to himself and said, "Isn't it . . . a lovely day . . . ?"

The enemy was entrenched east and west of the fort, their main force clinging to a cliff face, using ropes and small wooden platforms. The Golds knew because Ravleen had cheated, sending out an automated probe during the night. Scans had proved that the Blues hadn't broken any major rules, using accepted methods to blind them, nothing but hard work responsible for their success. It was frustrating for Ravleen, her foes near enough to touch and out of reach. Hugging the cliff, they couldn't be bombarded. They could gather themselves, then rise en masse, flinging heat grenades and taking a few good shots but escaping before they were truly hurt.

Ravleen and Tule abandoned the keep. They strode along the ramparts, giving orders with sharp, worried voices. "You two," said Ravleen, meaning Xo and Ord. "Take that cannon and harass theirs." The Blues had continued firing from the high ground, aiming for the east wall. "And don't look at me like that," Ravleen snapped.

"Like what?" Xo countered.

She glared at him, breathing loudly.

"Go away," Xo whined. "We'll hit them, don't worry."

Except Xo didn't work with conviction. Ord found himself loading the breech every time. And he had to aim the long plastic barrel. Xo was content to fire the cannon, and when they missed—normal enough at this range, aiming uphill—Xo would shake his head and say, "Lower." Or he'd state something else obvious. Ord tried to ignore him, knowing how Xo could be full of himself and how anger was useless. Then Xo declared, "I'm tired of winter. I hate this snow."

But winter had just begun, thought Ord. And this time he pulled on the wire cord, a dull strong *whap* causing a white streak that landed short of its target, the Blues waving happily from behind their cannon.

"Too bad." Xo's mask showed only his eyes and mouth, all of them grinning. "Aim higher, why don't you?"

Better to cut the snow, Ord decided. He counted his handfuls, trying to find what was perfect. The next shot was nearer, and Xo, who hadn't been paying attention, said, "See? Better this time."

It was a brilliant day, and lovely. In quiet moments they could hear the city on the lowlands—horns and bells and a suggestive gray murmur—and Ord remembered the times he crept down to the estate's boundary, hiding in the grass, watching the ordinary people. His universal-wall could give closer, more intimate views of them; but sitting on the edge of that other world, knowing he could, if he wished, walk straight into it . . . well, that was intoxicating. Chimes rang in the distance, very softly, and Ord wished he didn't have to be here, realizing it had been several months since his last surreptitious visit.

The sunshine felt hot, and he broke a big rule in a small way. Rolling up his facemask, Ord massaged the wet skin with wet snow. Xo saw him and asked, "What happened to your wounds?"

Ord pulled the mask back into place.

"It looks like you weren't even hit yesterday."

"I slept a lot." Ord couldn't invent a better excuse.

"Sleep did that?"

No, Alice did it . . . and suddenly he was thinking about her. He had been pushing her aside all day, with some success; but suddenly he found himself wondering what she was doing, and did she like the penthouse, and would he see her again? "I wasn't hit that badly," he offered, hoping to deflect suspicions.

But Xo didn't care. His mind had shifted again, his voice too loud when he said, "Oh, she's a good general in the open. But not with this stand-and-fight shit. Everyone knows that."

Teasing Ravleen was the better game. More dangerous too.

"If I were her," Xo claimed, "I'd send out a couple squads. I'd assault their cannons now—"

"—and lose the squads with the counterattack," Ord responded.

"We'll lose if we don't," the boy maintained.

Ord ignored him, aiming again, trying to concentrate. The icy slug had an imprecise size and density, plus an imperfectly smooth surface. The universe, said his tutor, was a series of simple suppositions and principles meshing together in chaotic ways. There were specific mathematics to help navigate through the chaos, to a degree. He barely understood them . . . yet he had a sudden premonition, numbers and symbols converging into an answer and his hands lifting, the right hand grasping the cord and hesitating . . . wait, wait . . . *now*.

He tugged the cord with a careful, perfect strength.

The slug was in flight, traveling on a neat arc, and one of the Blues fired at the perfect moment, half an instant too late.

Ord's slug hit the barrel's mouth, plugging it; hot compressed air caused the breech to shatter, some old flaw exposed, steel-colored plastic shards driven backward into a boy's arm and face. He collapsed. A cheer rose from the rest of Squad B. Even Xo was impressed enough to say, "I can't believe it." People took breaks from the fight to run over and look, watching the unconscious body and the ruined gun being taken away. It was a sterling moment, and ugly, one less Blue to fight now. Ord tried to be thrilled but instead felt sorry, even though the boy would be well in a few days. No lasting harm was done, but that didn't seem to matter.

"You got lucky," said his morose companion.

No, it wasn't luck. Ord felt certain of it.

And one shot wasn't the war.

The east wall was hammered the rest of the day. It was blue and rotting when it was time to quit, and they had fifteen minutes to make repairs, in peace. But time was wasted, someone telling Ravleen what Xo had been saying about her and her approaching him, telling him, "How would you like to be banished? Is that what you want?"

"If you were any kind of general," Xo countered, "I'd fight and keep quiet."

Ravleen wasn't wearing her mask. Ord saw the outrage in her face, her features ugly and hard; and he intended to step between them, trying to defuse things. But the best he could offer was, "We should work—"

"Quiet," Ravleen warned him.

Then Xo said, "A real Sanchex would have won the war by now—"

—and Ravleen swung at him.

Ord tried to push her backward.

Then she swung at Ord, catching him on the temple, but somehow he stayed on his feet. He shook his head, the world blurring for an instant; and Ravleen was past him, pinning Xo against the blue wall, punching him in a blind rage . . . and Ord grabbed a forearm, giving it a quick little twist.

The tough bone failed, making a sharp *crack* when it shattered.

Ravleen collapsed to the ground, her arm useless and her shoulder dislocated. With a tight slow furious voice, she said, "Wait." She only looked at Ord, saying, "Banishment is too good for you. You wait. You'll see. . . ."

6

While I'm here, I suppose I should plead guilty to any other little crimes that come to mind. I stole toys in my youth, for instance. And I built illegal worlds, as stated. And several times, to help friends, I have used improper means to alter elections and overthrow a few ugly governments that nobody misses. . . .

—Alice's testimony

"You found my message, did you?"

"Yes." It was on his desk, handwritten on paper . . . or at least it had looked handwritten. "I came as soon as I could."

"Alice."

"Pardon?"

"Call me by my name, Ord. Please."

He whispered, "Alice," to himself.

"Have you ever seen this place?" She stepped back from the crystal door, beckoning to him. "I mean the penthouse, of course. I decorated it today. What do you think?"

The penthouse was an enormous room with no apparent walls or ceiling. Ord had been here for special dinners, but the comfortable furniture had been replaced with foliage, gray-green and thin. Meant for a low gravity environment, he realized; and he stepped, finding himself noticeably lighter. How did she manage it? Only expensive machines could dilute the Earth's pull, and he was very much impressed with his sister's skill.

"A quiet lad, isn't he?"

Ord said, "Sorry."

"Why? You had the busy day. You're entitled to your silence."

He looked at the blue-white sky, asking, "What world is this?"

"A secret world."

He didn't understand. But before he could ask questions, Alice asked him, "Are the others jealous? That only you received an invitation?"

Ord nodded. He had shown the note to Lyman—feeling that was proper—and Lyman had inquired, "What did you say to her?" In other words: *What makes you special?*

"You know, our siblings keep coming up here." Alice smiled at the floor. Tonight she looked thinner, wearing a flowing gown, emerald-green and soothing. Showing him her smile, she said, "They've stopped asking me to open the door. But they come and stare at it just the same. They must be rather curious."

Lyman had looked tired and frazzled.

"And rather pissed off, I think."

The words were unexpected, almost as incredible as this little forest of alien greenery. That a Twelve would say *pissed off* seemed contrary to some law or principle. Straightening his back, Ord said, "I think they're scared. I think."

"Well," said Alice, "isn't that their right?"

It was a strange reply, but he managed to shrug and nod.

She touched his face, telling him, "You look well. You must have moved at the right times."

He dipped his head. "How much did you watch?"

"Every moment," she said happily.

"You . . . you did stuff. . . ."

"Twice, and you're welcome." Alice played with her own hair. It was longer than last night, fuller and brighter. "With your aim, once, and with the Sanchex girl."

"Now she hates me."

"Yet she will heal, won't she?"

What could he say?

"Twenty centuries from now," Alice offered, "she won't think of what you did. Tragedy is perishable, little brother. Believe me, she'll reach a point where the memories will elicit a smirk and little else."

What mattered was tomorrow, he knew, not the remote future. A part of Ord wished Alice hadn't come here, or at least had ignored him. At this moment, Ravleen was sitting in her room, dreaming up a thousand suitable revenges. She was an impossible, brutal tyrant—

"—and yet," his sister interjected, "she might grow into a courageous leader, a glorious success, vital to every Family and to humanity."

"Can you read my thoughts?" he wondered aloud.

"In limited ways. But then again, anyone can read anyone's thoughts in limited ways." She offered a long laugh, then said, "I feel good about Ravleen. I think she'll become a special Sanchex. One of their dynamos. She has that essential spark."

"Does she?"

"Not that I can't be wrong." Alice shrugged her shoulders. "Perhaps she'll even disappoint me."

Sanchexes loved dangerous work. Lacking wars, they busied themselves by

wrestling with stars, delaying novas in those close to populated worlds, and sometimes exploding healthy isolated suns, using the titanic energies to create rare and
expensive materials.

Alice said, "Isn't it odd? We begin as perfect copies of our parent, yet tiny,
unforeseen factors have their way with us. For good or not." A pause, then she
added, "Your friend Xo isn't much of a Nuyen. Which is a double insult, believe
me."

Nuyens were talented governors and administrators. The Earth had many of
them in high posts, serving as links between Families and the multitudes.

"I don't like Xo," Alice insisted. "I've met him a thousand times, and I've
never trusted him."

Ord blinked, then asked, "What about me?"

"What about you?"

"What kind of Chamberlain will I make?"

"I learned ages ago, never predict what Chamberlains might do." The smile
seemed fragile. "Now come over here and sit. Rest, little brother." She put an arm
around him, saying, "I invited you to dinner, so let's eat and enjoy ourselves. What
do you think?"

The meal was exotic—an alien stew made edible by inverting its amino acids—
and the sky darkened very slowly, easing into night. For now the stage was Ord's,
Alice demanding stories of his snow wars and other adventures. He told about
canoeing mountain rivers and how he bred bear-dogs, preferring them to other pets;
and he described the arrow wars fought in the summer, face paints in lieu of masks
but the same essential rules. And of course he had games, bloodless fictional wars
that he played by himself. Were any of the Blues his friends? Alice asked. Not
yet. He had met them, and of course he knew which face belonged to which Family.
And sometimes older Blues came to visit Lyman, and the others—

"Why?" asked Alice.

Why what?

"Why build these careful antagonisms, passionate but essentially harmless?
Ancient clans, elaborate rules . . . what's the purpose of it, Ord?"

His tutor claimed it was to teach them cooperation.

"Cooperation," she echoed. "Indeed, that's a key reason why the Families have
thrived. But wouldn't bridging a mountain river serve the same function?"

Lyman had a different explanation. He claimed that war games were like tails
on embryos. They were vestiges of something not needed anymore.

"That sounds a little truer," Alice replied.

Ord noticed that her face had grown empty. Did the topic bother her? Then
why had she brought it up?

"Tell me, little brother. Why did we fight the Great Wars?"

There were thousands of would-be Families. They tried to enslave humanity,
but the Wars defeated them. Sanchexes and Chamberlains helped save the multitudes, and in gratitude, they and the other good Families were allowed to keep
their powers. They were given this land, and together the Wars' survivors fashioned
the Peace.

"Noble images," Alice conceded.

Ord had stopped eating, but he found that he couldn't muster the will to push the half-empty bowl aside.

"Here's the crux of it, little brother. Somewhere in its history, every technological species will make the tools to become godlike. Immortal citizens will be capable of building worlds, or obliterating them. How a species responds to the challenge . . . well, that's what determines its fate, more often than not."

The galaxy was littered with ancient worlds torn apart by warfare. Sometimes Ord dreamed of sifting the rubble for chunks of burnt bone, learning about the vanished souls.

"Our powers are not cheap," said Alice, "and they're never plentiful. When the Wars began, there were only a few hundred billion people, but how many of them could be fitted with those new technologies? Very few. And many of those were corrupt. Perhaps, as you say, evil. But our species saved itself with a single wise deed. Ordinary people sought out the best thousand from their ranks. Not the wisest or the strongest, but the souls who would be least corrupted by their new talents."

This was familiar, and Ord kept nodding.

"Ian Chamberlain was a very unimportant man until he was selected. An unsuccessful man, by most accounts."

The boy looked at his bowl.

"How is your dinner?"

He said, "Fine."

Alice nodded, saying, "The Families are pledged to never injure any human being."

It was the fundamental law, something flowing in Ord's own blood.

"To you," she said, "the Peace must look immortal. Everlasting. Isn't that so, little brother?"

He began to shrug.

"Yet ten million years is no span at all. You'd be amazed how brief it feels to me."

He was tired of being amazed, he decided.

Alice rose to her feet. Before them was a little pond, bony fishes, alien and primitive, swimming lazily over soft white alien muds. She watched their motions for a long while, or pretended to watch them; then she told Ord, "Your brother is terrified of me. Of my presence here."

Lyman?

"Did you know that he has left the Earth?"

Ord said, "He's too young," with a boy's surety. "He's not allowed to go anywhere else."

"Yet he has. Many times." She laughed gently and easily. Her emerald gown was becoming muddy, a white fringe building as she walked around the pond. "He was on the Moon when I told everyone that I was coming to visit. He was seducing women, no doubt. Being a Chamberlain has its advantages, believe me. Still."

"Where else has he gone?"

"Around the solar system. Nothing astonishing." She paused, then turned to him. "Haven't you ever slipped out of these mountains? The sentries aren't perfect. No one needs to know."

"I haven't."

"But please tell me that you've been tempted." She seemed disappointed with him. "Haven't you been?"

Endless times, yes.

"Yet you obey the rules. How nice." She knelt, dipping a cupped hand into the pond and drinking from it. "Lyman doesn't obey, and that's why he's scared. I'm going to punish him while I'm here, he thinks, for traveling and for bringing girls into this house."

"But that's not against any rule," Ord countered.

"You're allowed to bring friends and lovers, of course. From inside or outside the Families, without doubt. But Lyman's girls aren't friends, they're convenient pieces of ass. They're thrilled to be with an authentic Chamberlain, and that's why they can ignore how ugly he looks. Grotesque to more than a few of them, I can promise you."

Ord remembered the finned woman in the swimming pool.

Standing again, Alice dried her hand with the gown.

After a minute, Ord asked, "Where is this world?"

"Inside a dust cloud. Hidden."

"Is this where you were? Before you came here, I mean."

She closed her hands into fists, sighed and said, "Everyone wants to know where I was. Where I came from."

Ord's belly ached, and not because of the dinner.

"Tell them, little brother. I was at the Core." She paused, a smile beginning and failing. Her face seemed to wrestle with her mouth, a strange lost expression winning. Then she said, "I came straight from the Core. Which was a long journey, even for me."

People older than One Hundred didn't require starships. They could convert themselves to massless particles, moving at light-speed yet remaining conscious. Ord tried to imagine such an existence; and to say something, to be involved, he mentioned, "Lyman wants to work at the Core. As a terraformer."

Which she had to know. Tilting her head, she tried the same failed smile again. "A good Chamberlain goal, isn't it?"

The Core was famous for black holes and dust clouds, plus billions of star systems left sterilized by explosions and intense radiation. The Families had made it safe enough to colonize. Humans and aliens had room to expand, no legal claims held by any species.

"The Core," Alice whispered, smiling at Ord, no light in her face and her words leaden. "It's a lovely place. Too many stars for me to count, little brother."

He doubted it.

She strolled over to him. Her bare feet left narrow prints in the mud. With one hand, she held him beneath his jaw, blue eyes locked on his eyes, and with an irresistible strength she brought him to his feet, a cold voice telling him, "You could grow a tail. I could activate the old genes, and you'd grow one now. You have that power."

"I don't understand," Ord whispered. "What do you mean?"

"What do I mean?" She let go of him and turned away, her gown seeping a green light as night fell. "Whatever I'm talking about, little brother, it isn't tails. You can be certain of it."

"Then what?"

Ord breathed and said, "Then we talked about tomorrow."

"What about tomorrow?"

"About snowfare—"

"Nothing else about the Core?" Lyman was pacing, Ord watching him while sitting on his brother's enormous bed. "Well, at least now we know where she came from. If she is telling the truth, of course."

Why wouldn't she?

" 'I'm not talking about tails.' Is that what she said?"

Ord nodded. "Basically."

"War." His brother's voice was ominous. Soft. "She was at the Core, and some kind of war broke out."

"I don't think so."

Lyman stopped and stared at him. "Why not?"

All he could offer was, "I have a feeling. It's something else entirely, I'm sure."

Lyman glanced at his girlfriends.

"Alice gave me a plan," Ord continued. "For tomorrow. It involves Ravleen—"

"But what else did she say about the Core?"

"Nothing."

"Nothing?"

Ord shook his head, trying to appear certain.

Lyman picked up one of the girlfriends, then he set her down again.

"What you need to do," Alice had told Ord, "is earn your redemption. With the Golds, and Ravleen too. And here's how you can do it, easily." Although to him it had seemed like a complicated scheme—

—and now Lyman moaned, "Something awful is happening. And that's why she's come here, no doubt about it." He wiped the perspiration from his face. "It's one of the aliens, or all of them. They've decided to fight us for the Core."

But wouldn't they have seen trouble on the universal-walls? Ord couldn't believe such a thing would remain secret.

"Whatever it is," Lyman promised, "I'm going to make a general call. For any nearby adults. I'll tell them . . . nothing . . . and ask them to hurry home at once. . . ."

It wasn't war; Ord was sure.

He remembered how their sister had kept saying, "Redemption," again and again. That powerful creature had stood in front of him, her gown soiled with the white muds; and she had assured him, "You must be redeemed. It's all my fault, but I can make everything better for you."

Her inadequate face was somewhere else, it eyes closing.

"Redemption," she had muttered one last time.

It wasn't a god's face, or a god's voice; and Ord had felt so very sorry for her, and everyone.

7

Our mountains have shrunk since I last saw them. There's been erosion, of course, and the crust beneath has slumped . . . and I was tempted to fix them, at first glance . . . with my proverbial pinkie, I could lift these dead lumps of stone into space, if I wished, and fling them into the sun. . . .
                                                                    —Alice's testimony

Ravleen wore a simple cast and sling, down to one good shoulder and arm; yet somehow she seemed larger today, more dangerous, walking in front of her assembled troops, not speaking. A light dry snow was falling. Ravleen paused and let herself smile for a moment, looking at the high gray clouds. Then she said, "I need to know what's happening." She said, "I need a patrol. Two people. Volunteers."

Ord glanced at Xo, then down at his own boots.

"Who wants to?" Ravleen continued. "Anyone?"

With a sense of drama, Xo stepped forward.

"Good." The smile brightened. "Now pick your partner."

"Ord."

"Wrong choice," she responded. Then she motioned to her lieutenant, saying, "Tule will go with you."

The girl gave a confused low moan.

"We have three minutes," Ravleen warned them. "Take radios and rations and drop over the south wall. I want reports. Find out what the Blues are doing. And harass them, always."

Tule was a good soldier; she managed a nod of affirmation.

Xo stepped up to Ord, saying, "I tried. Too bad you can't come, it'll be exciting out there."

"I bet so."

Xo looked at his eyes, asking, "What are you thinking?"

"Nothing," Ord lied. "I just wish I was with you."

"Except you're not," Ravleen growled, marching up to punch Ord with her good arm. She smacked his shoulder, in warning, then said, "I want you here with me. You know I do, friend."

★ ★ ★

The Blues fired early—a few moments early—and their cannon slug hit a girl in the back. Everyone yelled, "Violation!" But she was just stunned, little harm done. Then Ravleen said, "Positions," and waved them over to the south wall. "Go."

Tule and Xo dropped rope ladders and started down. Tule was slow and clumsy, catching her leg when her ladder twisted. Xo hit the pasture and ran; and an instant later the Blues saw him, voices screaming, their cannons turned and firing as their troops charged from two sides.

"Run," shouted Ravleen. "Pick up your feet, Tule. Go."

Blue-faced targets swept into range. Ord shot well, wondering if Alice was helping his aim. But she had promised not to help, not that way, and he missed often enough to believe it was all him. Tule was hit and hit again, and she would fall and pick herself up and take a sloppy step before falling again. But Xo never slowed, never looked backward. He sprinted into deep snow, and Ord saw him leap off the first cliff—a fair drop, but cushioned by drifts—and he saw a pair of Blues on his trail, firing from the cliff and jumping after him.

Tule was down for good. The Blues surrounded her, kicking her even when she cried out, "Give, give."

Ord stopped firing. He found himself watching the battle with a sense of detachment. Poor Tule was picked up and carried away. The other Blues fired and retreated, glad to have their first prisoner. All this noise and energy seemed to amount to nothing. Ord felt indifferent. Suddenly he was thinking about Alice, and the Core; and sometimes, in secret, he spoke to his sister, certain that she could hear him.

The bombardment resumed. Squad B manned the cannons until Ravleen replaced them with C. "From now on," she told them, "you've got a new job."

Nobody spoke.

"Take the keep apart. Make blocks out of the snow." She etched her plan in the rampart's ice. "Stack the blocks here. And here. And get it done this morning."

One boy said, "We'd rather fight."

Ravleen stared at Ord. "For now, no. No."

The squad bristled but said nothing.

And their leader popped Ord in the head, using her hard cast. "Then I've got another lousy job for you," she promised. "For the afternoon, and you'll like it even less."

Xo eluded his pursuers for a few hours, but they were faster than him, easily tracking him in the deep snow. In the early afternoon, both prisoners were carried up to the pasture, gagged and blindfolded, then set in plain view under a tiny white flag. "You're next," the Blues called out in a practiced voice. "We'll melt your fort and then you, Golds. Soon."

Tule was embarrassed. It showed. And undoubtedly Xo was inventing excuses to explain his capture.

A new assault began on the east, but Ord's squad saw none of it. They were below, doing work meant for robots, hands cold despite their gloves and their backs aching from the hard cutting and lifting. Everyone said, "The big attack is tomorrow. Tomorrow." There was excitement, and nervousness, but it was all just a game. This was a prattle used for decades, and it had to be the same kind of noise Alice had made when she was like them.

"Tomorrow," they told each other.

But not Ord.

They consciously ignored him, and he discovered that he didn't care like he should care. It was as if there was a traitor inside him, and the traitor announced itself with, of all things, indifference.

★ ★ ★

"What are you doing here?"

"Waiting for you," Ord replied. "How's prison?"

Xo shrugged and removed his mask. "Tiny. Boring. Cold."

"Too bad." They were in the trees above the pasture, on the main trail. From here the fort looked strong, tall and secretive, the rotting east wall showing only the faint beginnings of a slump. Ord had been the last one to leave it, and he had sat here, waiting for Xo. Alice had promised that the boy would come this way, out of habit. And he would be alone, Tule walking anywhere but with him. "How did they catch you?" Ord asked. "What went wrong?"

"They cheated, I think. Illegal equipment, I'm almost sure."

"Should we report them?" You went to your siblings who in turn complained to theirs. "We could tell your brothers—"

"Later. Maybe."

Ord nodded and stood up.

"How's Ravleen? Still furious with you?"

Ord removed his mask, pointing to some of his bruises.

"I hate her," Xo promised. "I wish you'd broken both arms."

"Maybe I will."

They began to walk. Some noise came from the city—the musical rise and fall of a siren—then the snowfall blotted it out, or it ceased.

Xo said, "I wish we were done."

"So do I."

"They've stuck me into a prison box. It's ridiculous."

Boxes were cramped and soundproofed, the heat bled out of them.

"I'm bored," the boy complained.

Ord paused and looked at Xo, then he looked everywhere else. Then just as Alice had told him, he said, "We can be home by noon tomorrow, if you want."

A hopeful little smile surfaced.

"Ravleen has a plan."

Xo said, "That's against the rules," and laughed, shaking his head. "I'm a prisoner of war. You can't tell me anything."

They weren't far from where Xo had begged to be hit with the careful stone. "We're shoring up the east wall. Making it strong again."

"How?"

"With the keep. Except it doesn't have enough snow." He paused, then said, "That's why we're robbing snow from the west wall. It's got too much anyway. Remember my gargoyle?" He drew a dramatic X on the boy's chest. "It's thinnest below the gargoyle."

Xo wasn't speaking, or breathing. This was against every rule, and the wickedness was delicious. He smiled and then stopped smiling, as if someone might notice; and he asked, "How thin is thin?"

"Like this." Ord put up his hands.

"She'll know I told. Ravleen will."

"How can you know anything?" Ord countered. "If Ravleen tells Tule anything, then Tule's the likely suspect."

"But will the Blues believe me?"

"Maybe not, but it's easy enough to test. And if you're right, they might not have time to cut a hole through the east wall anyway."

The boy stepped back and looked around, shivering as if he was cold.

"Who knows?" he muttered. "Maybe I'll crack. First thing in the morning, before they put me in that stupid box."

8

Boredom can claim some of the blame. What new challenges had we at-tacked in the last thousand millennia? And there was a genuine urge to accomplish something good. And most important was the idea itself. The plan. We were intoxicated. Drunk and in love, it seemed so perfectly pos-sible and lovely to us. . . .

—Alice's testimony

A single set of stairs climbed to the penthouse, in a tight spiral, the stairwell itself decorated with an elaborate mural. Yesterday, Ord was too nervous to pay attention. Today, the mural seemed to force itself on him, showing him various Chamberlains caught in the midst of historic and heroic acts. He saw worlds rebuilt, aliens em-braced, and the far edges of the galaxy explored. His own motions caused the scenes to change, the artwork fluid and theoretically infinite; and riding on a single step, hand on the polished railing, Ord found it all quite strange, thinking of the care spent on a mural that almost no one ever saw.

He was deposited at the penthouse door. Touching the milky crystal, he said, "It's working. Just like you promised."

The door dissolved, Alice standing before him.

"It's working," he repeated, breathing in little gulps. "Did you watch everything?"

"Enough of it." Something was different now. Worrisome. Alice wore a heavy dark robe, the room beyond black, unbordered, and cold. But she did smile at him, telling him, "Thank you," and then, "I'm glad it's going well," with a mixture of pride and pleasure. She was watching a point beside him, saying, "That Nuyen is a fool. Don't you agree?"

Ord felt uneasy, saying nothing.

"I would invite you inside," Alice continued, "but this isn't a good time. I am sorry."

Her face seemed simple, worn down. If she'd had red eyes, he would have guessed that she had been crying. And perhaps she was crying, in a fashion. He reminded himself how little of her was visible, and he asked, "Are you all right?"

Her eyes tracked toward him, no other response offered.

Ord stepped backward and dropped his gaze.

"I'm just distracted," Alice explained, "and tired. My long trip has caught up with me at last."

That seemed very unlikely.

And she told him, "Tomorrow, once you're done fighting, I want you to come tell me everything, little brother. I promise. We'll have a celebration, to enjoy your triumph." She paused, then said, "Stop worrying, please. Everything will be fine."

He said, "I know," without confidence.

Then the door began to reform as she said, "Good night." For an instant, it sounded as if she were crying. But then he realized, with cynicism, that someone like Alice might conjure any emotion, put on any face . . . sadness was just a dif-ferent kind of creation. . . .

He pushed the thought aside, turned and stepped back onto the stairs.

★ ★ ★

Two robots waited in Ord's room—security models—and with gray voices, in unison, they said, "You're wanted in the main arena. No, don't change clothes. Go now."

"Who's there?" he stammered.

"Lyman, and the others." The robots were silent, probably asking what they could tell him. "Several hundred adults have arrived today. They wish to speak with you."

The main arena was underground, deep inside the Chamberlain mountain—a vast room with seating for twenty thousand, false granite and perfect wood covering the walls and arched ceiling—and the brothers and sisters looked inconsequential with so much space around them. They sat in a block before the stage, and Ord had to wonder: Why here? Why not in a smaller arena? But then he realized this was as far from the penthouse as any place, which might be important. Were security baffles in use? From the stage a single brother waved at him. *Lyman*. Sitting beside him was a sister, a giant figure, three meters tall and built out of light and conjured flesh. "Up here," said Lyman. "We're just starting."

Every step was hard work, every breath a labor.

"Ord?" said the giant sister. "My name is Vivian. Eleven hundred and twenty."

Eleven twenty was nothing. He felt like telling her that he wasn't impressed, that he knew their Twelve and that she was *nothing* beside Alice. And maybe Vivian read his thoughts, taking his hand and squeezing, her hand feeling like heated plastic, almost burning him before she said, "I'm glad to meet you." Her presence was tangible, her energies making the air and stage vibrate. "Sit, if you would. Sit here and talk with us."

A chair appeared between his brother and sister.

Lyman leaned close and said, "Relax."

A couple of hundred faces watched them. The oldest adults were giants, wearing Chamberlain faces and bodies out of tradition. To be mannerly. Vivian had the highest rank, it seemed. Now she leaned forward, telling Ord, "Your big brother did what was right, you know. Perhaps he should have warned us sooner, but we understand. We do."

"What do you want?" Ord whispered.

"We need your help," Vivian explained. "I understand that our sister likes you? That for some reason she's taken an interest in you? Not that she dislikes any of us, of course. But you've spoken to her—"

"Yes."

"More than once, according to Lyman."

"Just now, a few minutes ago." His voice was soft and loud. He could barely hear himself, but the words were enlarged and thrown across the arena. "Is Alice in trouble?"

"Why? Do you think she should be in trouble?"

He shrugged his shoulders.

Vivian made him notice her smile. Her face was incomplete, a patch of strange gray light on one side of her forehead. "She's come from the Core, is that right? Ord? Do you hear me?"

He nodded. "Straight from there."

"But has she told you why she was there?"

He didn't like Vivian; he didn't appreciate her tone. But this was important, and he took pains to say, "She told me that she came here from there and that's all. That's what I know."

Lyman leaned close again, following some script. Ord realized that he was here to put their little brother at ease, prompting him when necessary, and he was sick with worry and exhaustion. "She was at the Core," he muttered. "We know it now."

"We're certain," Vivian echoed.

"She was working on a special project," Lyman continued. "With other Chamberlains and Sanchexes . . . with nearly half of the Families, no one younger than One Hundred."

"Doing what?" the boy asked.

Lyman shut his eyes, saying nothing.

Vivian told him, "It is a secret," with her voice betraying frustration. Yet she made herself laugh, as if to defuse the tension. As if to fool Ord. "I can't get access to their secret, little brother. Though I have sources who claim, and with some reason, that they're working on FTL travel."

"It's not possible," Ord replied. "Nothing goes faster than light."

"Perhaps you're right," his sister said. "Perhaps this is just a story meant to fool prying eyes."

Ord felt himself sinking away.

"Eleven Chamberlains were there," Vivian continued. "But now all except two of them have departed, including Alice. She arrived here the instant we saw her depart, but the others have taken other directions. Why? And why have the other Families departed in the same mysterious way?" She paused, then said, "I don't know, honestly. I have questions that I would love to ask."

Murmurs spread, then collapsed.

"Two Chamberlains are left there?" Ord managed. "Where is *there?*"

Everyone wanted to know. People whispered among themselves until Vivian lifted one of her hands, waiting for silence. Then she said, "They were clustered beside the central black hole, inside its envelope of gases and plasmas. They've been there for several thousand years, it seems. Honestly, I don't know what type of work they were pursuing."

Ord shifted his weight, hands wrestling with one another.

Vivian asked, "Has she given any hint of an explanation? Has our dear sister given you one clue?"

He whispered, "No."

Then he asked, "Why can't you ask her?"

She blinked and made a show of swallowing, then admitted, "Alice has set up barriers. A part of me is wrestling with them now, but she seems adamant to exclude everyone but you."

Ord looked at the audience, reading the same lost, worried expressions. Even Vivian seemed like a little girl mystified by events, angered by her limitations and perhaps glad too. In secret. She could do nothing of substance. No clear responsibilities could be set on her oversized shoulders. It seemed obvious to Ord . . . and suddenly he wondered if it was his insight, or if perhaps Alice had given it to him.

"When do you see Alice again, little brother?"

Ord blinked, trying to remember.

Lyman appreciated his confusion, touching an arm and saying, "What's important is that we go on with our ordinary lives. As well as we can, Ord. But Alice has come here for some reason, and if she wishes to tell us anything, we need to listen."

"Tomorrow," he said. "I'll see her then."

"When you do," Vivian instructed, "ask if she will talk with us. Will you do that for us?"

"That's all we want," said Lyman.

"Please," said the giant sister.

"Please," said two hundred mouths, in unison, whispers rising to the pink granite ceiling and echoing back down at them again.

9

Ian rarely told war stories. But once, I remember, coming home after a hard day's snowball fight, he found me on the yard, stopped me, and launched into a long tale about finding our enemies hiding in a certain solar system. They had built redoubts out of worlds, and he explained how he had grabbed comets, accelerating them to near-light velocities . . . how he had pummeled worlds until their crusts melted, our enemies slaughtered . . . and he wept at the end, and shook, still ashamed of his cruelty while his audience, this little girl, kept thinking what an enormous, wonderful snowball fight that must have been . . . !

—Alice's testimony

In all but name, the Golds won the war that next morning.

The Electric Blues stuck to their old battle plan, troops charging the east wall and artillery firing from the west. But there was no final assault. When it seemed inevitable, there was a pause, a sudden lull, then the sound of motion, troops scrambling over slick terrain on the south. There was little pretense of subterfuge. Ravleen and Ord stood together on the south wall, and one of them smiled beneath her mask, satisfied with the world. The other wished he could feel relief, but there wasn't any. Nor was there any sense of dread and foreboding, which was a constant surprise to him. It was as if Ord was empty, all the worry drained from him; sometimes he couldn't even remember Alice or the Core, as if they had been carefully, thoroughly etched from his mind.

Ravleen noticed enough to ask, "What's the matter?" She poked him with a finger, telling him, "You look funny. What are you thinking?"

He shrugged his shoulders.

But she didn't press him, too happy to care. Today her cast was soft, without a sling; and with that bad arm she hugged Ord, every Gold watching them and everyone surprised.

Alice had been right.

A Sanchex would do anything for a victory, provided you left her pride intact.

"Beg for forgiveness," his sister had instructed. "Weep. Grovel. And tell her your plan between weepy moments. Trust me, she'll see its beauty. And she'll take it for herself."

For a deed that wasn't his fault, Ord had apologized . . . and didn't *his* pride matter too?

"It's happening," Ravleen whispered.

She said, "They believe the little shit."

Then she hugged Ord again, saying, "When the time comes, stand next to me." A wink, a smile, and she assured him, "That's only fair."

The Blues entered the pasture from the southwest, carrying their snowguns and grenades and finally showing their own flag, a blue rectangle flapping in the bright windy air. There was a pause as they gathered themselves, then they let out a roar, charging as cannons and mortars threw heat into the west wall. As promised, the ice beneath the gargoyle had been undermined. A squad of Blues surged through the sudden hole, excited and confident. There was moderate fire from above, plus some raucous cursing. The Golds were disconsolate, without question. The first squad beckoned for others, more than half of the Blues pouring into the courtyard, in less than a minute, marshaling and charging the flagpole, nothing between them and it but a crude little wall of fresh-cut ice—

—and there was a sound, wet and strong, and massive. Something was falling. A wedge of ice broke free of the west wall, sliding over the new hole as Ravleen shot to her feet, shouting:

"Fire."

It wasn't a fight. Ord stood behind the new wall, firing without aiming, without heart. Four squads fired double-shots at close range, knocking the enemy off their feet. Cannons on the west wall had been turned, barrels depressed, and the fourth cannon was on the ground, slugs of ice knocking people unconscious. Limbs were shattered. Facemasks and the flesh beneath were split open, blood bright against the white surfaces. And even still the Blues mounted a final charge, adrenaline carrying them over the wall, one girl able to put her hands on the pole's knotted rope an instant before Ravleen shot her from behind, in the head, her body limp and Ord watching her fall and lie still.

In days everyone would be well again, ready to play again. Yet Ord felt sad enough to cry, watching Ravleen lead her troops across the courtyard, driving their enemies into a corner and abusing anyone with a hint of fight left in them. Then the prisoners were disarmed and tied together, and Ravleen launched an assault on the enemy cannons, capturing them and more prisoners and chasing the rest into the woods.

Ord stayed behind, guarding Blues. He sat on the trampled snow with his gun empty, and after a while he couldn't hear the distant shouts. He watched the masked faces, thinking how the eyes looked angry and a little afraid, but not much, and even the anger seemed false. And it wasn't because this was only a game. They were too young to know how to be truly angry or honestly scared. They were children. Sitting there, thinking thoughts that weren't entirely his own, Ord tried to imagine a world filled with danger; and he couldn't. The part of him that was him looked at the fort and the clear bright sky, and he couldn't believe that this quiet wouldn't last for all time.

10

Something did go wrong. We failed somewhere and knew it at once and could do nothing . . . and the worst of it was that we had time, too much time, to dwell on the failure . . . blaming one another, and Nature, the Almighty and even those awful people who had brought us forth into our miserable lives . . . !

—Alice's testimony

The staircase was filled with brothers and sisters, half again as many as he had seen yesterday. The stairs were locked in place, no one moving but Ord, him climbing toward the penthouse and no one speaking louder than a whisper. "Good luck," they told him. The freckled, red-haired faces were grim and tired in many ways, and the climb seemed to last for ages. Halfway to the top, Ord was crying, wiping at his eyes with alternating sleeves. "Be strong," the whispers demanded. Yet the Chamberlain faces seemed anything but strong, in stark contrast to the heroic images in the mural. Lyman was the last face, Ord recognizing the long hair and something in the voice, his brother saying, "We're proud of you, you know."

Vivian emerged from the wall beside them, still tall, stepping out of the mural as if it was syrup and bending until her giant face was near enough to kiss Ord. "Alice is waiting, I think. That much I can see, I think." She paused, and the gray patch on her forehead brightened. "Listen to what she tells you, ask questions, and please tell her how much we'd like to see her. Soon."

Ord looked down the stairwell, faces watching him; then he thought to ask, "What's happening in the Core? Do you know?"

Nobody spoke.

He looked at Vivian. "What can you see now?"

"Nothing new," she lied. Looking as winded as Ord felt, she sighed and put a large warm hand on his back, shepherding him toward the crystal door. "Good luck, little brother. You'll do well."

The doorway dissolved as it re-formed behind him. He stopped, then the blackness was washed away with starlight. In an instant, with a faint dry sound, grass erupted from the twisting floor and grew seeds, the air filled with summer sounds and dampness. The stars were brilliant and colorful, and countless, separated by light-weeks, or less. At the sky's zenith was an oval, not large, velvety black and vague at its edges. This was the Core, Ord knew, and the oval was the giant shroud draped over the central black hole. This sky could be a live image—

"Exactly so," said a voice, close and soft.

—and around him was a terraformed world. Ord knelt and broke off a stem of grass, putting it to his mouth, tasting the green juice. It was earthly life. And as if to prove that point, an insect landed on his face and bit him, drawing blood before he swatted it, the little body smearing under his fingers.

"Walk," Alice instructed. "Straight on."

The room was a hilltop, and there were people—his size, his proportions—sitting in the brilliant darkness, watching the sky. It was a peaceful scene, familiar yet tied to an exotic place; and Ord was afraid, pausing and his heart beating faster.

"Who are they?" he whispered.

Alice was silent.

"Hello?" he tried.

A boy turned and said, "Hi. Who are you?"

Ord stepped close and gave his first name. The group repeated, "Ord," as Alice said, "Sit with them."

They weren't people but instead facsimiles conjured up with the grass and bugs. Below them was a city, a sprinkling of soft lights and darkness between. It was a pioneer community, not large, homes set in the middle of wide rich yards. A tiny crescent moon was rising over distant mountains. It seemed like a lovely world, larger than the Earth, its gravity stronger and the air tasting clean and new.

Faces smiled. The facsimiles weren't too different from him, their heads narrow and their hair abundant and long, tied into intricate braids that leaked their own soft light. They were the children of pioneers, the first generation born on this world. Like Ord, they had tough brains and rapid powers of healing. Like him, they could be decades old, no inherent end in their lives. But they'd never leave their flesh, they could only travel in starships, and if they wanted to terraform any world larger than a comet, they would have to work in teams, as a multitude, relying on numbers in place of Chamberlain skills.

And yet.

Someday they would have *children*. Not clones, but unique, even radical babies. They would marry and make families—institutions older than any Chamberlain—and each child would be unlike anyone on any of the million living worlds.

Ord felt envy, or Alice fed envy to him. Probably before he was old enough to leave the Earth, these children would fill this world with their descendants; then the multitudes would spill onto that little moon and whatever else circled the unseen sun. A great green explosion of life . . . and before Ord could hope to visit, this place would become mature and crowded. . . .

"You look warm," the facsimile boy observed. "Why don't you take off that silly suit?"

The snowsuit was damp with perspiration. Ord stripped to his underclothes, then he sat with them on the warm bristly grass. Without prompting, the others introduced themselves, by name, the last small girl saying, "Alice," and then, "Chamberlain."

She was dark as coal. "Chamberlain?" Ord echoed. "Is that your real name?"

"Of course," she replied. "A lot of people are named after the Families. At least here they are."

"You're not from here," said a second girl. "Are you?"

"But that's okay," said the boy, acting like their leader. "We like meeting people."

Ord asked, "Why use the Chamberlain name?"

"In thanks," she answered.

"Because," said the boy, "the Chamberlains help make all these suns behave. They keep gas from falling into the black holes. And we're very, very grateful for their help. Aren't we grateful?"

His friends nodded in unison, with fervor.

"Who terraformed this world?" Ord inquired.

"Alice," the children giggled. "The real one."

Then the boy added, "We're buying it from her." He spoke with pride, as if to say, "We buy only from the best."

The false Alice looked nothing like Ord's sister. Her face was as narrow as an ax blade, big black eyes reflecting starlight. Ord asked, "Have you ever seen Alice? Does she visit you?"

"Not now," the girl giggled. "Why would she?"

"What do you think of her?"

"She's a wonderful great person," the boy reported, no room for compromise. "Everyone knows *that*."

"I pray for her," the dark Alice confessed. "Every night, just before I sleep, I wish her nothing but the best."

Everyone nodded. Conviction hung thick in the air.

"Where's Alice now?"

Hands lifted, pointing to the cold black smear overhead.

"What is she doing there?"

"Working," said the boy. "With Chamberlains and other Families. Doing important experiments." He was pleased to report this news. "They've found ways to move faster than light. Easily."

Everyone but the dark Alice murmured in agreement.

"Soon," said the boy, "we'll be able to go anywhere. The Families will put the entire universe in our reach."

"No," said Alice.

Faces turned.

She had a quiet, firm voice. "That's not what they're doing."

The other children seemed surprised, but no one had a rebuke to offer.

"It's much more important than FTL. A million times more." Suddenly she had his sister's face, round and pale. Nobody else noticed. Looking at Ord, she asked, "Why can't everyone have Alice's powers?"

"It's a rule," he responded.

"But *why?*"

He paused, thinking hard. "If everyone was like Alice—"

"—there wouldn't be room in this galaxy. Every Alice needs energy and space and fancy work to do." The real Alice took Ord's hand, squeezing and explaining, "This galaxy is just too small of a pasture. If we want to be like her, we need more grass."

Some of the children laughed.

Ord swallowed and asked, "But if we could go anywhere—?"

"Everywhere has life already. Everywhere has its Families and its multitudes, no room for the likes of Alice." She shrugged, sadness showing on her face. "Certainly not for trillions and trillions of full-grown Alices."

Ord nodded, glancing at the black smear.

"But there's something better than FTL," she promised. "Put enough energy into a tiny place, in just the proper way, and a fresh young universe will precipitate from nothing. Am I right, little brother?"

He remembered something mentioned by his tutor. It was a theory, ancient but useless; vacuums themselves could create universes that would separate from theirs. An umbilical cord would exist, then dissolve, and it happened constantly, too swift to notice.

Ord felt a sudden chill.

"The trick," said Alice, "is to keep your umbilical *open*. What's the good in making a new universe that you can't see? Wouldn't it be nice if you could enter it and learn what's possible? Can you imagine the challenges? The potentials? For everyone, of course. . . ."

Alice was weeping, wiping her face with both hands.

A little boy said, "I don't understand you."

"Imagine if everyone, every Family and all of humanity, could extend themselves into endless new universes. Each of us might have our own, each with its own wonders. Each of you would be given Alice's powers, then more, and you could dive down the cord and close it up after you, if you dared." She grabbed Ord's hand, her hands cold and wet. "Isn't that the loveliest sweetest possibility? What would you do, little one, if you had it in your power to make it true?"

Something is wrong—

—and she said, "Precisely," with a dead gray voice. "As wrong as wrong has ever been, I should hope."

Again he looked at the black oval, a single golden spark blossoming at its center. But it faded and vanished, lost . . . an illusion, he told himself . . . nothing else . . . !

Alice turned to the children, explaining to them, "We succeeded. We created a universe and the umbilical cord. But what's difficult, perhaps even impossible, is to leave the way open just enough. No more than the perfect amount, you pray."

The sky brightened. A great soundless flash of light obscured the stars, blue-white and sudden, and the children began to mutter among themselves, and moan.

Alice was saying, "Our universe might be someone's creation. Not an original thought, I admit . . . but perhaps some other Family, in some unknown place, produced this . . . perhaps they preside over us now . . . just as their universe was created in turn. . . ."

The children had hands lifted over their eyes. They weren't real children, just facsimiles; yet Ord found himself terrified for them, leaping to his feet, shouting, "Run! Hide!" He grabbed one little boy, trying to make him start for home. But the first wave of heat and hard radiations pierced them. In an instant, the long grass had burst into flames, and the boy squirmed in agony, then died, his body shriveled and blackened, blowing away as ash. And Ord screamed as the world beneath him evaporated. He felt it shatter, an inconsequential bit of grime; and he was twisting in the scalding light, screaming until a familiar soft voice whispered:

"Relax."

Alice said:

"The new universe has flowed into ours, for just this moment."

And with a pained dead voice, she told him:

"You don't know how sorry we feel . . . you can't know . . . tell everyone, please . . . will you, little one?"

Only Lyman was waiting for him. The others had seen the same feed, had gone to the nearest arena to watch the walls. The two brothers stood at the top of the empty stairwell, both trembling, Lyman holding the wall with his hands, saying with a wisp of a voice, "At least we know. We know what it is."

Ord held himself, soaked with perspiration and wearing nothing but his underclothes.

"Vivian thinks it's temporary . . . it won't last. . . ." Lyman couldn't stand any more, dropping to his knees and beating the floor with his fists, no strength in his arms. Finally, he asked, "Will Alice talk to us now?"

"I don't know," Ord confessed. Then he tried to apologize with a low choking voice.

But his brother didn't care. He shrugged and said, "You don't know how terrible this is going to be. Nobody can."

Nobody?

"Which is a blessing, I think." Another useless blow to the floor, then Lyman looked up at him. "If we knew, we couldn't live. The grief would crush us, Ord. No one could survive a moment, knowing how awful this will be. . . ."

11

We accepted our duty, at last. A few of us remained behind, fighting to close the umbilical even when we knew it couldn't be closed prematurely . . . heroic deaths after a catastrophic blunder . . . and the bulk of us rushed toward places distant and populated, places where we could save other lives . . . and then it was decided that one of us, a volunteer, should journey home, home to the Earth, for the express purpose of standing trial, to admit guilt in a public way . . . hundreds of billions doomed, human and alien, and a single soul promising to swallow as much blame as possible. . . .

—Alice's testimony

In the morning, before the local dawn, the Chamberlain mansion sent word to the government that Alice was barricaded in the penthouse. A chaotic, oftentimes bitter group of elected officials decided that highranking Nuyens would accompany the appropriate legal officers. The suspected murderess would be arrested, hopefully without incident. That no existing prison could hold her was deemed a minor problem. More than once, in soft dry voices, the officers remarked that if a Twelve wished, she could leave the Earth a vivid red drop of liquid stone and iron.

It had been a clear cold night in the high mountains. That oddity of climate helped make the officers even more uneasy, stepping onto the famous ground and seeing the house, vast and brilliant in the early light. Huge bear-dogs watched them with indifference. The much less impressed Nuyens led the way, taking them under the PRIDE AND SACRIFICE emblem and upstairs. A single Chamberlain—a sister of modest rank—joined their strange procession, telling everyone how sorry she was and how this wasn't anyone's fault except for a tiny few members of many, many Families.

"Not *our* Family," responded one of the Nuyens.

Vivian glared at the speaker, then turned and put the stairs into motion again.

★ ★ ★

Ord watched them pass. Dressed in a clean snowsuit, he was standing in the hall-way, sleepless but alert. Everyone ignored him, and when they were above he stepped into the stairwell, leaned over the railing and watched how they curled higher and higher, his eyes losing them with distance and the glare of the lights.

As always, the bear-dogs begged for attention.

He ignored them, hurrying to the tube and running fast through the sunny woods, then across the pasture. But only Ravleen was waiting at the fort. She was sitting on the west wall, her cast removed, her eyes red and sleepless. "You're late," she warned, then smiled. Then she told him with a strong certain voice, "That explosion won't reach us here. It's not large enough."

Ord knew that already.

"We did calculations," she continued. "It's a lot like a supernova, only bigger. Hotter. Dust clouds and distance will keep the Earth safe."

And the melted planets, he thought. And the dead people.

"What are you thinking?"

Ord looked over the pasture. Yesterday's bootprints gave the snow a ragged, exhausted appearance. "Nobody's going to attack today," he ventured.

"If they do," Ravleen said, "we'll stop them."

"I was tired of being at home," he confessed, swallowing with a tight dry throat. "I watched my wall all night—"

"Talk about something else," Ravleen warned him.

"What?"

"Nothing." The red eyes looked out of the clean gold mask. "Let's just sit and say nothing."

A light breeze lifted their flag, then dropped it. On a day like this, Ord knew, they should have heard city sounds; but not this morning, and the silence was unnerving. Everyone everywhere was scared. It wasn't just the explosion or the deaths, it also was the Peace itself. Would it survive? The sacred trusts had been violated, but could some sense of normalcy return? And when? And what about the Families themselves—?

A slow creaking made Ord blink and turn. Someone was climbing one of the rope ladders. Ravleen picked up her snowgun, watching the familiar figure scram-ble over the parapet to join them.

"Ah," she growled, "the traitor."

Ord was surprised to see Xo. He should be the last Gold willing to come here. But he stood before them, smiling so that they could see his teeth, saying, "I escaped." He was nervous and obvious, forcing a laugh before he said, "A legal escape. Nobody came to guard me this morning."

Ravleen kept her hand on the gun.

Xo told her, "Congratulations for winning." Then he turned to Ord, adding, "Our plan sure worked, didn't it?"

"What plan?" asked Ravleen.

"Didn't you tell her?" The boy acted horrified. He removed his mask to show his expression, saying, "We planned it together, Ravleen. I would pretend to be a traitor, and Ord—"

"Shut up."

"—Ord would go to you—"

"You're lying. Shut up."

The boy closed his mouth, then grinned. Ord saw the new tooth, whiter than the others, and something about the grin made him bristle.

"I'm no traitor," Xo told them.

Nobody spoke.

Then he said, "*Your* Families were the ringleaders." The tone was superior and a little shrill. "We didn't even help you. I heard all about it. My brothers and sisters were talking, and they said they warned you that it was dangerous and they didn't want any part of it—"

"Quiet," Ord snapped.

"—and you did it *anyway*. And did it *wrong*."

Ravleen stared down into the courtyard.

Xo swallowed and straightened his back, then with great satisfaction said, "Now you'll have to pay for the damages and deaths. All your wealth is going to be spent, and you'll be poor. You won't even be Families anymore! It's as if we set a trap, and in you *walked—!*"

Ravleen shot him in the head, no warnings. She put twin slugs into his mouth, knocking him off the wall. Then she stood and looked down at Xo, sprawled out on his back, and she winked at Ord, saying, "Watch." And she jumped after him, feet first, boots landing on the boy's chest and her momentum shattering ribs and lungs and the heart beneath her.

His chest crushed, Xo flung his arms into the air, hands grasping at nothing and then falling limp.

Ravleen began to kick him. His body had died, past all suffering; but she worked on the face with a sick thoroughness, without pause, kicking and kicking until she was finally exhausted; then she stepped back and looked up on the wall, telling Ord, "You can help me."

Except that Ord wasn't standing there. It was a sister, some other Chamberlain, and she smiled without smiling, eyes full of misery and joy.

"Help you?" she asked, pleased with this most tiny revenge.

Then she said, "Another time, perhaps. But thank you for offering."

12

I watched them force the penthouse door. I watched them not find me. I did enjoy their panic, I'll admit, but in all honesty I wasn't actually hiding from them. And then one of the Nuyens engaged her treacherous little brain and decided to look inside the original mansion, the majority of me waiting in my one-time bedroom, peering outdoors at a vivid cold winter from ten million years ago. . . .

—Alice's testimony

The city was trees, towering green trees with natural chambers in the trunks and large branches, tiny luxury apartments housing several million smallish people with prehensile tails and strong limbs. Almost everyone was inside, watching the live feeds from the Core. For a long while, Ord walked unnoticed down a wide avenue, feeling like the last living person on the planet. He left his snowsuit on, wiping sweat from his eyes. A small park opened up before him, and he saw motion, then tiny brown shapes. He approached the children with a certain caution, practicing his smile, and when they saw him, they stopped and stared. Too young to watch the Core and understand, they also were too young to recognize a Chamberlain on sight. One boy laughed and said, "You look funny. What kind of person are you?"

"Are you sick?" asked a young girl.

"Funny hair," said a third child. "Sick funny hair!"

Ord took a breath and held it. There were nearly a dozen children gawking at him. To the boy who had said *You look funny*, he said, "Here," and handed him the old snowgun. "For you."

"What is it?" the boy sputtered.

Ord didn't explain. Removing his boots, he asked, "Who wants these?"

A tiny hand reflexively shot up.

He gave away his boots, then his mask. Then he removed his snowsuit, and paused, and told his astonished little audience, "I am sorry. I want you to know, I'm sorry."

They didn't understand why he should apologize, but the words were locked in their minds.

"And Alice is sorry too," he added, flinging the snowsuit behind them and turning, running off on bare feet as the children began making claims and counterclaims for this strange unusable prize.

Ord trotted back to the estate, the mountains and the snow.

And only then, gazing out of the jungle at the towering white ridges, did he realize that he'd never seen his home from this vantage point. From outside. And he ran faster, crossing a line, the first wet pancakes of snow burning his toes, causing him to run faster still.

Recording Angel

PAUL J. McAULEY

Few stories even in *this* anthology take us as far into the far future or to a future as numinous, alien, rich, and strange as the bizarre and evocative story that follows . . . in a future so remote, so distanced from the our times and from the Earth itself, that the very memory of humanity itself is almost forgotten and gone. Almost—but not *quite.*

Born in Stroud, England, in 1955, Paul J. McAuley now makes his home in London. A professional biologist for many years, he sold his first story in 1984 and has gone on to be a frequent contributor to *Interzone* as well as to markets such as *Amazing, The Magazine of Fantasy & Science Fiction, Asimov's Science Fiction, When the Music's Over,* and elsewhere.

Like his friend and colleague Stephen Baxter, McAuley has a foot in several different camps of SF writing, being considered one of the best of the new breed of British writers (although a few Australian writers could be fit in under this heading as well) who are producing that brand of rigorous hard science fiction with updated modern and stylistic sensibilities that is sometimes referred to as "radical hard science fiction," but he also writes dystopian sociological speculations about the very near future and *also* is one of the major young writers who are producing that revamped and retooled Wide-Screen Space Opera that has sometimes been called the New Baroque Space Opera, reminiscent of the Superscience stories of the thirties taken to an even higher level of intensity and scale (wait a minute! how many feet does he *have,* anyway?). His first novel, *Four Hundred Billion Stars,* one of the earliest examples of the New Space Opera, was published in 1988 and won the Philip K. Dick Award. It was followed by sequels, *Secret Harmonies* and *Eternal Light,* and by one of the most vivid of the recent spate of Martian novels, *Red Dust.* With his next novel, *Pasquale's Angel,* he put yet another foot down in yet another camp, producing an ingenious and gorgeously colored Alternate History where Leonardo da Vinci brings modern technology to Europe centuries before its time. His next novel, 1996's *Fairyland,* perhaps his best-known novel and perhaps also his best performance to date at novel length, took us to a troubled future Europe thrown into chaos by fractional politics and out-of-control biotechnology, only a few years into the next century; it won the Arthur C. Clarke Award and the John W. Campbell Memorial Award. With his next novel project, though, he is plunging back into Space Opera territory, on an even more ambitious scale, with a major new trilogy, *Confluence,* set 10 million years in the future. The first two volumes, *Child of the River* and *Ancients of Days,* have just been published; the story which follows is a kind of segue. McAuley's other books include two collections of his short work, *The King of the Hill and Other Stories* and *The Invisible Country,* and an original anthology coedited with Kim Newman, *In Dreams.*

Mr. Naryan, the Archivist of Sensch, still keeps to his habits as much as possible, despite all that has happened since Angel arrived in the city. He has clung to these personal rituals for a very long time now, and it is not easy to let them go. And so, on the day that Angel's ship is due to arrive and attempt to reclaim her, the day that will end in revolution, or so Angel has promised her followers, as ever, at dusk, as the Rim Mountains of Confluence tip above the disc of its star and the Eye of the Preservers rises above the farside edge, Mr. Naryan walks across the long plaza at the edge of the city towards the Great River.

Rippling patterns swirl out from his feet, silver and gold racing away through the plaza's living marble. Above his head, clouds of little machines spin through the twilight: information's dense weave. At the margin of the plaza, broad steps shelve into the river's brown slop. Naked children scamper through the shallows, turning to watch as Mr. Naryan, old and fat and leaning on his stick at every other stride, limps past and descends the submerged stair until only his hairless head is above water. He draws a breath and ducks completely under. His nostrils pinch shut. Membranes slide across his eyes. As always, the bass roar of the river's fall over the edge of the world stirs his heart. He surfaces, spouting water, and the children hoot. He ducks under again and comes up quickly, and the children scamper back from his spray, breathless with delight. Mr. Naryan laughs with them and walks back up the steps, his loose belted shirt shedding water and quickly drying in the parched dusk air.

Further on, a funeral party is launching little clay lamps into the river's swift currents. The men, waist-deep in brown water, turn as Mr. Naryan limps past, knuckling their broad, narrow foreheads. Their wet skins gleam with the fire of the sunset that is now gathering in on itself across leagues of water. Mr. Naryan genuflects in acknowledgment, feeling an icy shame. The woman died before he could hear her story; her, and seven others in the last few days. It is a bitter failure.

Angel, and all that she has told him—Mr. Naryan wonders whether he will be able to hear out the end of her story. She has promised to set the city aflame and, unlike Dreen, Mr. Naryan believes that she can.

A mendicant is sitting cross-legged on the edge of the steps down to the river. An old man, sky-clad and straight-backed. He seems to be staring into the sunset, in the waking trance that is the nearest that the Shaped citizens of Sensch ever come to sleep. Tears brim in his wide eyes and pulse down his leathery cheeks; a small silver moth has settled at the corner of his left eye to sip salt.

Mr. Naryan drops a handful of the roasted peanuts he carries for the purpose into the mendicant's bowl, and walks on. He walks a long way before he realizes that a crowd has gathered at the end of the long plaza, where the steps end and, with a sudden jog, the docks begin. Hundreds of machines swarm in the darkening air, and behind this shuttling weave a line of magistrates stand shoulder to shoulder, flipping their quirts back and forth as if to drive off flies. Metal tags braided into the tassels of the quirts wink and flicker; the magistrates' flared red cloaks seem inflamed in the last light of the sun.

The people make a rising and falling hum, the sound of discontent. They are looking upriver. Mr. Naryan, with a catch in his heart, realizes what they must be looking at.

It is a speck of light on the horizon, where the broad ribbon of the river and the broad ribbon of the land narrow to a single point. It is the lighter towing Angel's ship, at the end of its long journey to the desert city where she has taken refuge, and caught Mr. Naryan in the net of her tale.

Mr. Naryan first heard about Angel from Dreen, Sensch's Commissioner; in fact, Dreen paid a visit to Mr. Naryan's house to convey the news in person. His passage through the narrow streets of the quarter was the focus of a swelling congregation which kept a space two paces wide around him as he ambled towards the house where Mr. Naryan had his apartment.

Dreen was a lively but tormented fellow who was paying off a debt of conscience by taking the more or less ceremonial position of Commissioner in this remote city which his ancestors had long ago abandoned. Slight and agile, his head clean-shaven except for a fringe of polychrome hair that framed his parchment face, he looked like a lily blossom swirling on the Great River's current as he made his way through the excited crowd. A pair of magistrates preceded him and a remote followed, a mirror-colored seed that seemed to move through the air in brief rapid pulses like a squeezed watermelon pip. A swarm of lesser machines spun above the packed heads of the crowd. Machines did not entirely trust the citizens, with good reason. Change Wars raged up and down the length of Confluence as, one by one, the ten thousand races of the Shaped fell from innocence.

Mr. Naryan, alerted by the clamor, was already standing on his balcony when Dreen reached the house. Scrupulously polite, his voice amplified through a little machine that fluttered before his lips, Dreen inquired if he might come up. The crowd fell silent as he spoke, so that his last words echoed eerily up and down the narrow street. When Mr. Naryan said mildly that the Commissioner was of course always welcome, Dreen made an elaborate genuflection and scrambled straight up the fretted carvings which decorated the front of the apartment house. He vaulted the wrought iron rail and perched in the ironwood chair that Mr. Naryan usually took when he was tutoring a pupil.

While Mr. Naryan lowered his corpulent bulk onto the stool that was the only other piece of furniture on the little balcony, Dreen said cheerfully that he had not walked so far for more than a year. He accepted the tea and sweetmeats that Mr. Naryan's wife, terrified by his presence, offered, and added, "It really would be more convenient if you took quarters appropriate to your status."

As Commissioner, Dreen had use of the vast palace of intricately carved pink sandstone that dominated the southern end of the city, although he chose to live in a tailored habitat of hanging gardens that hovered above the palace's spiky towers.

Mr. Naryan said, "My calling requires that I live amongst the people. How else would I understand their stories? How else would they find me?"

"By any of the usual methods, of course—or you could multiply yourself so that every one of these snakes had their own archivist. Or you could use machines. But I forget, your calling requires that you use only appropriate technology. That's why I'm here, because you won't have heard the news."

Dreen had an abrupt style, but he was neither as brutal nor as ruthless as his brusqueness suggested. Like Mr. Naryan, who understood Dreen's manner completely, he was there to serve, not to rule.

Mr. Naryan confessed that he had heard nothing unusual, and Dreen said eagerly, "There's a woman arrived here. A star-farer. Her ship landed at Ys last year, as I remember telling you."

"I remember seeing a ship land at Ys, but I was a young man then, Dreen. I had not taken orders."

"Yes, yes," Dreen said impatiently, "picket boats and the occasional merchant's argosy still use the docks. But this is different. She claims to be from the deep past. The *very* deep past, before the Preservers."

"I can see that her story would be interesting if it were true."

Dreen beat a rhythm on his skinny thighs with the flat of his hands. "Yes, yes! A human woman, returned after millions of years of traveling outside the Galaxy. But there's more! She is only one of a whole crew, and she's jumped ship. Caused some fuss. It seems the others want her back."

"She is a slave, then?"

"It seems she may be bound to them as you are bound to your order."

"Then you could return her. Surely you know where she is?"

Dreen popped a sweetmeat in his mouth and chewed with gusto. His flat-topped teeth were all exactly the same size. He wiped his wide lipless mouth with the back of his hand and said, "Of course I know where she is—that's not the point. The point is that no one knows if she's lying, or her shipmates are lying—they're a nervy lot, I'm told. Not surprising, culture shock and all that. They've been traveling a long time. Five million years, if their story's to be believed. Of course, they weren't alive for most of that time. But still."

Mr. Naryan said, "What do you believe?"

"Does it matter? This city matters. Think what trouble she could cause!"

"If her story is true."

"Yes, yes. That's the point. Talk to her, eh? Find out the truth. Isn't that what your order's about? Well, I must get on."

Mr. Naryan didn't bother to correct Dreen's misapprehension. He observed, "The crowd has grown somewhat."

Dreen smiled broadly and rose straight into the air, his toes pointing down, his arms crossed with his palms flat on his shoulders. The remote rose with him. Mr. Naryan had to shout to make himself heard over the cries and cheers of the crowd.

"What shall I do?"

Dreen checked his ascent and shouted back, "You might tell her that I'm here to help!"

"Of course!"

But Dreen was rising again, and did not hear Mr. Naryan. As he rose he picked up speed, dwindling rapidly as he shot across the jumbled rooftops of the city towards his aerie. The remote drew a silver line behind him; a cloud of lesser machines scattered across the sky as they strained to keep up.

The next day, when as usual Mr. Naryan stopped to buy the peanuts he would scatter amongst any children or mendicants he encountered as he strolled through the city, the nut roaster said that he'd seen a strange woman only an hour before—she'd had no coin, but the nut roaster had given her a bag of shelled salted nuts all the same.

"Was the right thing to do, master?" the nut roaster asked. His eyes glittered anxiously beneath the shelf of his ridged brow.

Mr. Naryan, knowing that the man had been motivated by a cluster of artificial genes implanted in his ancestors to ensure that they and all their children would give aid to any human who requested it, assured the nut roaster that his conduct had been worthy. He proffered coin in ritual payment for the bag of warm oily peanuts, and the nut roaster made his usual elaborate refusal.

"When you see her, master, tell her that she will find no plumper or more savory peanuts in the whole city. I will give her whatever she desires!"

All day, as Mr. Naryan made his rounds of the tea shops, and even when he heard out the brief story of a woman who had composed herself for death, he expected to be accosted by an exotic wild-eyed stranger. That same expectation distracted him in the evening, as the magistrate's son haltingly read from the Puranas while all around threads of smoke from neighborhood kitchen fires rose into the black sky. How strange the city suddenly seemed to Mr. Naryan: the intent face of the magistrate's son, with its faint intaglio of scales and broad shelving brow, seemed horribly like a mask. Mr. Naryan felt a deep longing for his youth, and after the boy had left he stood under the shower for more than an hour, letting water penetrate every fold and cranny of his hairless, corpulent body until his wife anxiously called to him, asking if he was all right.

The woman did not come to him that day, or the next. She was not seeking him at all. It was only by accident that Mr. Naryan met her at last.

She was sitting at the counter of a tea shop, in the deep shadow beneath its tasseled awning. The shop was at the corner of the camel market, where knots of dealers and handlers argued about the merits of this or that animal and saddle-makers squatted cross-legged amongst their wares before the low, cavelike entrances to their workshops. Mr. Naryan would have walked right past the shop if the proprietor had not hurried out and called to him, explaining that here was a human woman who had no coin, but he was letting her drink what she wished, and was that right?

Mr. Naryan sat beside the woman, but did not speak after he had ordered his own tea. He was curious and excited and afraid; she looked at him when he sat down and put his cane across his knees, but her gaze only brushed over him without recognition.

She was tall and slender, hunched at the counter with elbows splayed. She was dressed, like every citizen of Sensch, in a loose, raw cotton overshirt. Her hair was as black and thick as any citizen's, too, worn long and caught in a kind of net slung at her shoulder. Her face was sharp and small-featured, intent from moment to moment on all that happened around her—a bronze machine trawling through the dusty sunlight beyond the awning's shadow; a vendor of pomegranate juice calling his wares; a gaggle of women laughing as they passed; a sled laden with prickly pear gliding by, two handspans above the dusty flagstones—but nothing held her attention for more than a moment. She held her bowl of tea carefully in both hands, and sucked at the liquid clumsily when she drank, holding each mouthful for a whole minute before swallowing and then spitting twiggy fragments into the copper basin on the counter.

Mr. Naryan felt that he should not speak to her unless she spoke first. He was disturbed by her: he had grown into his routines, and this unsought responsibility frightened him. No doubt Dreen was watching through one or another of the little machines that flitted about the sunny, salt-white square—but that was not sufficient compulsion, except that now he had found her, he could not leave her.

At last, the owner of the tea house refilled the woman's bowl and said softly, "Our Archivist is sitting beside you."

The woman turned jerkily, spilling her tea. "I'm not going back," she said. "I've told them that I won't serve."

"No one has to do anything here," Mr. Naryan said, feeling that he must calm her. "That is the point. My name is Naryan, and I have the honor, as our good host has pointed out, of being the Archivist of Sensch."

The woman smiled at this, and said that he could call her Angel; her name also translated as Monkey, but she preferred the former. "You're not like the others here," she added, as if she had only just realized. "I saw people like you in the port city, and one let me ride on his boat down the river until we reached the edge of a civil war. But after that every one of the cities I passed through seemed to be inhabited by only one race, and each was different from the next."

"It is true that this is a remote city," Mr. Naryan said.

He could hear the faint drums of the procession. It was the middle of the day, when the sun halted at zenith before reversing back down the sky.

The woman, Angel, heard the drums too. She looked around with a kind of preening motion as the procession came through the flame trees on the far side of the square. It reached this part of the city at the same time every day. It was led by a bare-chested man who beat a big drum draped in cloth of gold; it was held before him by a leather strap that went around his neck. The steady beat echoed across the square. Behind him slouched or capered ten, twenty, thirty naked men and women. Their hair was long and ropy with dirt; their fingernails were curved yellow talons.

Angel drew her breath sharply as the rag-taggle procession shuffled past, following the beat of the drum into the curving street that led out of the square. She said, "This is a very strange place. Are they mad?"

Mr. Naryan explained, "They have not lost their reason, but have had it taken away. For some it will be returned in a year; it was taken away from them as a punishment. Others have renounced their own selves for the rest of their lives. It is a religious avocation. But saint or criminal, they were all once as fully aware as you or me."

"I'm not like you," she said. "I'm not like any of the crazy kinds of people I have met."

Mr. Naryan beckoned to the owner of the tea house and ordered two more bowls. "I understand you have come a long way." Although he was terrified of her, he was certain that he could draw her out.

But Angel only laughed.

Mr. Naryan said, "I do not mean to insult you."

"You dress like a . . . native. Is *that* a religious avocation?"

"It is my profession. I am the Archivist here."

"The people here are different—a different race in every city. When I left, not a single intelligent alien species was known. It was one reason for my voyage. Now there seem to be thousands strung along this long, long river. They treat me like a ruler—is that it? Or a god?"

"The Preservers departed long ago. These are the end times."

Angel said dismissively, "There are always those who believe they live at the end of history. We thought that *we* lived at the end of history, when every star system in the Galaxy had been mapped, every habitable world settled."

For a moment, Mr. Naryan thought that she would tell him of where she had been, but she added, "I was told that the Preservers, who I suppose were my descendants, made the different races, but each race calls itself human, even the ones who don't look like they could have evolved from anything that ever looked remotely human."

"The Shaped call themselves human because they have no other name for what they have become, innocent and fallen alike. After all, they had no name before they were raised up. The citizens of Sensch remain innocent. They are our . . . responsibility."

He had not meant for it to sound like a plea.

"You're not doing all that well," Angel said, and started to tell him about the Change War she had tangled with upriver, on the way to this, the last city at the midpoint of the world.

It was a long, complicated story, and she kept stopping to ask Mr. Naryan questions, most of which, despite his extensive readings of the Puranas, he was unable to answer. As she talked, Mr. Naryan transcribed her speech on his tablet. She commented that a recording device would be better, but by reading back a long speech she had just made he demonstrated that his close diacritical marks captured her every word.

"But that is not its real purpose, which is an aid to fix the memory in my head."

"You listen to people's stories."

"Stories are important. In the end they are all that is left, all that history leaves us. Stories endure." And Mr. Naryan wondered if she saw what was all too clear to him, the way her story would end, if she stayed in the city.

Angel considered his words. "I have been out of history a long time," she said at last. "I'm not sure that I want to be a part of it again." She stood up so quickly that she knocked her stool over, and left.

Mr. Naryan knew better than to follow her. That night, as he sat enjoying a cigarette on his balcony, under the baleful glare of the Eye of the Preservers, a remote came to him. Dreen's face materialized above the remote's silver platter and told him that the woman's shipmates knew that she was here. They were coming for her.

★ ★ ★

As the ship draws closer, looming above the glowing lighter that tows it, Mr. Naryan begins to make out its shape. It is a huge black wedge composed of tiers of flat plates that rise higher than the tallest towers of the city. Little lights, mostly red, gleam here and there within its ridged carapace. Mr. Naryan brushes mosquitoes from his bare arms, watching the black ship move beneath a black sky empty except for the Eye of the Preservers and a few dim halo stars. Here, at the midpoint of the world, the Home Galaxy will not rise until winter.

The crowd has grown. It becomes restless. Waves of emotion surge back and forth. Mr. Naryan feels them pass through the citizens packed around him, although he hardly understands what they mean, for all the time he has lived with these people.

He has been allowed to pass through the crowd with the citizens' usual generous deference, and now stands close to the edge of the whirling cloud of machines which defends the dock, twenty paces or so from the magistrates who nervously swish their quirts to and fro. The crowd's thick yeasty odor fills his nostrils; its humming disquiet, modulating up and down, penetrates to the marrow of his bones. Now and then a machine ignites a flare of light that sweeps over the front ranks of the crowd, and the eyes of the men and women shine blankly orange, like so many little sparks.

At last the ship passes the temple complex at the northern edge of the city, its wedge rising like a wave above the temple's clusters of slim spiky towers. The lighter's engines go into reverse; waves break in whitecaps on the steps beyond the whirl of machines and the grim line of magistrates.

The crowd's hum rises in pitch. Mr. Naryan finds himself carried forward as it presses towards the barrier defined by the machines. The people around him apologize effusively for troubling him, trying to minimize contact with him in the press as snails withdraw from salt.

The machines' whirl stratifies, and the magistrates raise their quirts and shout a single word lost in the noise of the crowd. The people in the front rank of the crowd fall to their knees, clutching their eyes and wailing: the machines have shut down their optic nerves.

Mr. Naryan, shown the same deference by the machines as by the citizens, suddenly finds himself isolated amongst groaning and weeping citizens, confronting the row of magistrates. One calls to him, but he ignores the man.

He has a clear view of the ship, now. It has come to rest a league away, at the far end of the docks, but Mr. Naryan has to tip his head back and back to see the top of the ship's tiers. It is as if a mountain has drifted against the edge of the city.

A new sound drives across the crowd, as a wind drives across a field of wheat. Mr. Naryan turns and, by the random flare of patrolling machines, is astonished to see how large the crowd has grown. It fills the long plaza, and more people stand on the rooftops along its margin. Their eyes are like a harvest of stars. They are all looking towards the ship, where Dreen, standing on a cargo sled, ascends to meet the crew.

Mr. Naryan hooks the wire frames of his spectacles over his ears, and the crew standing on top of the black ship snap into clear focus.

There are fifteen, men and women all as tall as Angel. They loom over Dreen as he welcomes them with effusive gestures. Mr. Naryan can almost smell Dreen anxiety. He wants the crew to take Angel away, and order restored. He will b telling them where to find her.

Mr. Naryan feels a pang of anger. He turns and makes his way through th crowd. When he reaches its ragged margin, everyone around him suddenly look straight up. Dreen's sled sweeps overhead, carrying his guests to the safety of th floating habitat above the pink sandstone palace. The crowd surges forward—an all the little machines fall from the air!

One lands close to Mr. Naryan, its carapace burst open at the seams. Smok pours from it. An old woman picks it up—Mr. Naryan smells her burnt flesh as sears her hand—and throws it at him.

Her shot goes wide. Mr. Naryan is so astonished that he does not even duc) He glimpses the confusion as the edge of the crowd collides with the line c magistrates: some magistrates run, their red cloaks streaming at their backs; othe) throw down their quirts and hold out their empty hands. The crowd devours then Mr. Naryan limps away as fast as he can, his heart galloping with fear. Ahead i a wide avenue leading into the city, and standing in the middle of the avenue is compact group of men, clustered about a tall figure.

It is Angel.

★ ★ ★

Mr. Naryan told Angel what Dreen had told him, that the ship was coming to th city, the very next day. It was at the same tea house. She did not seem surprisec "They need me," she said. "How long will they take?"

"Well, they cannot come here directly. Confluence's maintenance system wil only allow ships to land at designated docks, but the machinery of the spacepo) docks here has grown erratic and dangerous through disuse. The nearest place the) could safely dock is five hundred leagues away, and after that the ship must b) towed downriver. It will take time. What will you do?"

Angel passed a hand over her sleek black hair. "I like it here. I could b) comfortable."

She had already been given a place in which to live by a wealthy merchan family. She took Mr. Naryan to see it. It was near the river, a small two-store) house built around a courtyard shaded by a jacaranda tree. People were going i) and out, carrying furniture and carpets. Three men were painting the wooden rai) of the balcony that ran around the upper storey. They were painting it pink anc blue, and cheerfully singing as they worked. Angel was amused by the bustle, anc laughed when Mr. Naryan said that she shouldn't take advantage of the citizens.

"They seem so happy to help me. What's wrong with that?"

Mr. Naryan thought it best not to explain about the cluster of genes implantec in all the races of the Shaped, the reflex altruism of the unfallen. A woman brough) out tea and a pile of crisp, wafer-thin fritters sweetened with crystallized honey Two men brought canopied chairs. Angel sprawled in one, invited Mr. Naryan tc sit in the other. She was quite at ease, grinning every time someone showed he) the gift they had brought her.

Dreen, Mr. Naryan knew, would be dismayed. Angel was a barbarian, displaced by five million years. She had no idea of the careful balance by which one must live with the innocent, the unfallen, if their cultures were to survive. Yet she was fully human, free to choose, and that freedom was inviolable. No wonder Dreen was so eager for the ship to reclaim her.

Still, Angel's rough joy was infectious, and Mr. Naryan soon found himself smiling with her at the sheer abundance of trinkets scattered around her. No one was giving unless they were glad to give, and no one who gave was poor. The only poor in Sensch were the sky-clad mendicants who had voluntarily renounced the material world.

So Mr. Naryan sat and drank tea with her, and ate a dozen of the delicious honeyed fritters, one after the other, and listened to more of her wild tales of traveling the river, realizing how little she understood of Confluence's administration. She was convinced that the Shaped were somehow forbidden technology, for instance, and did not understand why there was no government. Was Dreen the absolute ruler? By what right?

"Dreen is merely the Commissioner. Any authority he has is invested in him by the citizens, and it is manifest only on high days. He enjoys parades, you know. I suppose the magistrates have power, in that they arbitrate neighborly disputes and decide upon punishment—Senschians are argumentative, and sometimes quarrels can lead to unfortunate accidents."

"Murder, you mean? Then perhaps they are not as innocent as you maintain." Angel reached out suddenly. "And these? By what authority do these little spies operate?"

Pinched between her thumb and forefinger was a bronze machine. Its sensor cluster turned back and forth as it struggled to free itself.

"Why, they are part of the maintenance system of Confluence."

"Can Dreen use them? Tell me all you know. It may be important."

She questioned Mr. Naryan closely, and he found himself telling her more than he wanted. But despite all that he told her, she would not talk about her voyage, nor of why she had escaped from the ship, or how. In the days that followed, Mr. Naryan requested several times, politely and wistfully, that she would. He even visited the temple and petitioned for information about her voyage, but all trace of it had been lost in the vast sifting of history, and when pressed, the librarian who had come at the hierodule's bidding broke contact with an almost petulant abruptness.

Mr. Naryan was not surprised that it could tell him nothing. The voyage must have begun five million years ago at least, after all, for the ship to have traveled all the way to the neighboring galaxy and back.

He did learn that the ship had tried to sell its findings on landfall, much as a merchant would sell his wares. Perhaps Angel wanted to profit from what she knew; perhaps that was why the ship wanted her back, although there was no agency on Confluence that would close such a deal. Knowledge was worth only the small price of petitioning those librarians which deal with the secular world.

Meanwhile, a group of citizens gathered around Angel, like disciples around one of the blessed who, touched by some fragment or other of the Preservers, wander Confluence's long shore. These disciples went wherever she went. They were all young men, which seemed to Mr. Naryan faintly sinister, sons of her benefactors fallen under her spell. He recognized several of them, but none would speak to him, although there were always at least two or three accompanying Angel. They wore white headbands on which Angel had lettered a slogan in an archaic script older than any race of the Shaped; she refused to explain what it meant.

Mr. Naryan's wife thought that he, too, was falling under some kind of spell. She did not like the idea of Angel: she declared that Angel must be some kind of ghost, and therefore dangerous. Perhaps she was right. She was a wise and strong-willed woman, and Mr. Naryan had grown to trust her advice.

Certainly, Mr. Naryan believed that he could detect a change in the steady song of the city as he went about his business. He listened to an old man dying of the systematic organ failure which took most of the citizens in the middle of their fourth century. The man was one of the few who had left the city—he had traveled upriver, as far as a city tunneled through cliffs overlooking the river, where an amphibious race lived. His story took a whole day to tell, in a stiflingly hot room muffled in dusty carpets and lit only by a lamp with a bloodred chimney. At the end, the old man began to weep, saying that he knew now that he had not traveled at all, and Mr. Naryan was unable to comfort him. Two children were born on the next day—an event so rare that the whole city celebrated, garlanding the streets with fragrant orange blossoms. But there was a tension beneath the celebrations that Mr. Naryan had never before felt, and it seemed that Angel's followers were everywhere amongst the revelers.

Dreen felt the change, too. "There have been incidents," he said, as candid an admission as he had ever made to Mr. Naryan. "Nothing very much. A temple wall defaced with the slogan the woman has her followers wear. A market disrupted by young men running through it, overturning stalls. I asked the magistrates not to make examples of the perpetrators—that would create martyrs. Let the people hold their own courts if they wish. And she's been making speeches. Would you like to hear one?"

"Is it necessary?"

Dreen dropped his glass with a careless gesture—a machine caught it and bore it off before it smashed on the tiles. They were on a balcony of Dreen's floating habitat, looking out over the Great River towards the farside edge of the world. At the horizon was the long white double line that marked the river's fall: the rapids below, the permanent clouds above. It was noon, and the white, sunlit city was quiet.

Dreen said, "You listen to so much of her talk, I suppose you are wearied of it. In summary, it is nothing but some vague nonsense about destiny, about rising above circumstances and bettering yourself, as if you could lift yourself into the air by grasping the soles of your feet."

Dreen dismissed this with a snap of his fingers. His own feet, as always, were bare, and his long opposable toes were curled around the bar of the rail on which he squatted. He said, "Perhaps she wants to rule the city—if it pleases her, why not? At least, until the ship arrives here. I will not stop her if that is what she wants, and if she can do it. Do you know where she is right now?"

"I have been busy." But Mr. Naryan felt an eager curiosity: yes, his wife was right.

"I heard the story you gathered in. At the time, you know, I thought that man might bring war to the city when he came back." Dreen's laugh was a high-pitched hooting. "The woman is out there, at the edge of the world. She took a boat yesterday."

"I am sure she will return," Mr. Naryan said. "It is all of a pattern."

"I defer to your knowledge. Will hers be an interesting story, Mr. Naryan? Have another drink. Stay, enjoy yourself."

Dreen reached up and swung into the branches of the flame tree which leaned over the balcony, disappearing in a flurry of red leaves and leaving Mr. Naryan to find a machine that was able to take him home.

Mr. Naryan thought that Dreen was wrong to dismiss what Angel was doing, although he understood why Dreen affected such a grand indifference. It was outside Dreen's experience, that was all: Angel was outside the experience of everyone on Confluence. The Change Wars that flared here and there along Confluence's vast length were not ideological but eschatological. They were a result of sociological stresses that arose when radical shifts in the expression of clusters of native and grafted genes caused a species of Shaped to undergo a catastrophic redefinition of its perceptions of the world. But what Angel was doing dated from before the Preservers had raised up the Shaped and ended human history. Mr. Naryan only began to understand it himself when Angel told him what she had done at the edge of the world.

And later, on the terrible night when the ship arrives and every machine in the city dies, with flames roaring unchecked through the farside quarter of the city and thousands of citizens fleeing into the orchard forests, Mr. Naryan realizes that he has not understood as much as he thought. Angel has not been preaching empty revolution after all.

Her acolytes, all young men, are armed with crude wooden spears with fire-hardened tips, long double-edged knives of the kind coconut sellers use to open their wares, flails improvised from chains and wire. They hustle Mr. Naryan in a forced march towards the palace and Dreen's floating habitat. They have taken away Mr. Naryan's cane, and his bad leg hurts abominably with every other step.

Angel is gone. She has work elsewhere. Mr. Naryan felt fear when he saw her, but feels more fear now. The reflex altruism of the acolytes has been overridden by a new meme forged in the fires of Angel's revolution—they jostle Mr. Naryan with rough humor, sure in their hold over him. One in particular, the rough skin of his long-jawed face crazed in diamonds, jabs Mr. Naryan in his ribs with the butt of his spear at every intersection, as if to remind him not to escape, something that Mr. Naryan has absolutely no intention of doing.

Power is down all over the city—it went off with the fall of the machines—but leaping light from scattered fires swim in the wide eyes of the young men. They pass through a market square where people swig beer and drunkenly gamble amongst overturned stalls. Elsewhere in the fiery dark there is open rutting, men with men as well as with women. A child lies dead in a gutter. Horrible, horrible. Once, a building collapses inside its own fire, sending flames whirling high into the black sky. The faces of all the men surrounding Mr. Naryan are transformed by this leaping light into masks with eyes of flame.

Mr. Naryan's captors urge him on. His only comfort is that he will be of use in what is to come. Angel has not yet finished with him.

When Angel returned from the edge of the world, she came straightaway to Mr. Naryan. It was a warm evening, at the hour after sunset when the streets began to fill with strollers, the murmur of neighbor greeting neighbor, the cries of vendors selling fruit juice or popcorn or sweet cakes.

Mr. Naryan was listening as his pupil, the magistrate's son, read a passage from the Puranas which described the time when the Preservers had strung the Galaxy with their creations. The boy was tall and awkward and faintly resentful, for he was not the scholar his father wished him to be and would rather spend his evenings with his fellows in the beer halls than read ancient legends in a long dead language. He bent over the book like a night stork, his finger stabbing at each line as he clumsily translated it, mangling words in his hoarse voice. Mr. Naryan was listening with half an ear, interrupting only to correct particularly inelegant phrases. In the kitchen at the far end of the little apartment, his wife was humming to the murmur of the radio, her voice a breathy contented monotone.

Angel came up the helical stair with a rapid clatter, mounting quickly above a sudden hush in the street. Mr. Naryan knew who it was even before she burst onto the balcony. Her appearance so astonished the magistrate's son that he dropped the book. Mr. Naryan dismissed him and he hurried away, no doubt eager to meet his friends in the flickering neon of the beer hall and tell them of this wonder.

"I've been to the edge of the world," Angel said to Mr. Naryan, coolly accepting a bowl of tea from Mr. Naryan's wife, quite oblivious of the glance she exchanged with her husband before retreating. Mr. Naryan's heart turned at that look, for in it he saw how his wife's hard words were so easily dissolved in the weltering sea of reflexive benevolence. How cruel the Preservers had been, it seemed to him never crueller, to have raised up races of the Shaped and yet to have shackled them in unthinking obedience.

Angel said, "You don't seem surprised."

"Dreen told me as much. I am pleased to see you returned safely. It has been a dry time without you." Already he had said too much; it was as if all his thoughts were eager to be spilled before her.

"Dreen knows everything that goes on in the city."

"Oh no, not at all. He knows what he needs to know."

"I took a boat," Angel said. "I just asked for it, and the man took me right along, without question. I wish now I'd stolen it. It would have been simpler. I'm tired of all this goodwill."

It was as if she could read his mind. For the first time, Mr. Naryan began to be afraid, a shiver like the first shake of a tambour that had ritually introduced the tempestuous dances of his youth.

Angel sat on the stool which the student had quit, tipping it back so she could ean against the rail of the balcony. She had cut her black hair short, and bound around her forehead a strip of white cloth printed with the slogan, in ancient incomprehensible script, that was the badge of her acolytes. She wore an ordinary loose white shirt and much jewelry: rings on every finger, sometimes more than one on each; bracelets and bangles down her forearms; gold and silver chains around her neck, layered on her breast. She was both graceful and terrifying, a rough beast slouched from the deep past to claim the world.

She said, teasingly, "Don't you want to hear my story? Isn't that your avocation?"

"I will listen to anything you want to tell me," Mr. Naryan said.

"The world is a straight line. Do you know about libration?"

Mr. Naryan shook his head.

Angel held out her hand, tipped it back and forth. "This is the world. Everything lives on the back of a long flat plate which circles the sun. The plate rocks on its long axis, so the sun rises above the edge and then reverses its course. I went to the edge of the world, where the river that runs down half its length falls into the void. I suppose it must be collected and redistributed, but it really does look like it falls away forever."

"The river is eternally renewed," Mr. Naryan said. "Where it falls is where ships used to arrive and depart, but this city has not been a port for many years."

"Fortunately for me, or my companions would already be here. There's a narrow ribbon of land on the far side of the river. Nothing lives there, not even an insect. No earth, no stones. The air shakes with the sound of the river's fall, and swirling mist burns with raw sunlight. And there are shrines, in the thunder and mist at the edge of the world. One spoke to me."

Mr. Naryan knew these shrines, although he had not been there for many years. He remembered that the different races of the Shaped had erected shrines all along the edge of the world, stone upon stone carried across the river, from which flags and long banners flew. Long ago, the original founders of the city of Sensch, Dreen's ancestors, had traveled across the river to petition the avatars of the Preservers, believing that the journey across the wide river was a necessary rite of purification. But they were gone, and the new citizens, who had built their city of stones over the burnt groves of the old city, simply bathed in the heated, mineral heavy water of the pools of the shrines of the temple at the edge of their city before delivering their petitions. He supposed the proud flags and banners of the shrines would be tattered rags now, bleached by unfiltered sunlight, rotted by mist. The screens of the shrines—would they still be working?

Angel grinned. Mr. Naryan had to remember that it was not, as it was with the citizens, a baring of teeth before striking.

She said, "Don't you want to know what it said to me? It's part of my story."

"Do you want to tell me?"

She passed her hand over the top of her narrow skull: bristly hair made a crisp sound under her palm. "No," she said. "No, I don't think I do. Not yet."

Later, after a span of silence, just before she left, she said, "After we were wakened by the ship, after it brought us here, it showed us how the black hole you call the Eye of the Preservers was made. It recorded the process as it returned, speeded up because the ship was traveling so fast it stretched time around itself. At first there was an intense point of light within the heart of the Large Magellanic

Cloud. It might have been a supernova, except that it was a thousand times large than any supernova ever recorded. For a long time its glare obscured everything else, and when it cleared, all the remaining stars were streaming around where it had been. Those nearest the center elongated and dissipated, and always more crowded in until nothing was left but the gas clouds of the accretion disc, glowing by Cerenkov radiation."

"So it is written in the Puranas."

"And is it also written there why Confluence was constructed around a halo star between the Home Galaxy and the Eye of the Preservers?"

"Of course. It is so we can all worship and glorify the Preservers. The Eye looks upon us all."

"That's what I told them," Angel said.

After she was gone, Mr. Naryan put on his spectacles and walked through the city to the docks. The unsleeping citizens were promenading in the warm dark streets, or squatting in doorways, or talking quietly from upper storey windows to their neighbors across the street. Amongst this easy somnolence, Angel's young disciples moved with a quick purposefulness, here in pairs, there in a group o twenty or more. Their slogans were painted on almost every wall. Three stopped Mr. Naryan near the docks, danced around his bulk, jeering, then ran off, screeching with laughter, when he slashed at them with his cane.

"Ruffians! Fools!"

"Seize the day!" they sang back. "Seize the day!"

Mr. Naryan did not find the man whose skiff Angel and her followers had used to cross the river, but the story was already everywhere amongst the fisherfolk The Preservers had spoken to her, they said, and she had refused their temptations Many were busily bargaining with citizens who wanted to cross the river and see the site of this miracle for themselves.

An old man, eyes milky with cataracts—the fisherfolk trawled widely across the Great River, exposing themselves to more radiation than normal—asked Mr Naryan if these were the end times, if the Preservers would return to walk amongst them again. When Mr. Naryan said, no, anyone who dealt with the avatars knew that only those fragments remained in the Universe, the old man shrugged and said. "They say *she* is a Preserver," and Mr. Naryan, looking out across the river's black welter, where the horizon was lost against the empty night, seeing the scattered constellations of the running lights of the fisherfolk's skiffs scattered out to the farside edge, knew that the end of Angel's story was not far off. The citizens were finding their use for her. Inexorably, step by step, she was becoming part of their history.

Mr. Naryan did not see Angel again until the night her ship arrived. Dreen went to treat with her, but he couldn't get within two streets of her house: it had become the center of a convocation that took over the entire quarter of the city. She preached to thousands of citizens from the rooftops.

Dreen reported to Mr. Naryan that it was a philosophy of hope from despair. "She says that all life feeds on destruction and death. Are you sure you don't want to hear it?"

"It is not necessary."

Dreen was perched on a balustrade, looking out at the river. They were in his floating habitat, in an arbor of lemon trees that jutted out at its leading edge. He said, "More than a thousand a day are making the crossing."

"Has the screen spoken again?"

"I've monitored it continuously. Nothing."

"But it did speak with her."

"Perhaps, perhaps." Dreen was suddenly agitated. He scampered up and down the narrow balustrade, swiping at overhanging branches and scaring the white doves that perched amongst the little glossy leaves. The birds rocketed up in a great flutter of wings, crying as they rose into the empty sky. Dreen said, "The machines watching her don't work. Not any more. She's found out how to disrupt them. I snatch long range pictures, but they don't tell me very much. I don't even know if she visited the shrine in the first place."

"I believe her," Mr. Naryan said.

"I petitioned the avatars," Dreen said, "but of course they wouldn't tell me if they'd spoken to her."

Mr. Naryan was disturbed by this admission—Dreen was not a religious man. "What will you do?"

"Nothing. I could send the magistrates for her, but even if she went with them her followers would claim she'd been arrested. And I can't even remember when I last arrested someone. It would make her even more powerful, and I'd have to let her go. But I suppose that you are going to tell me that I should let it happen."

"It has happened before. Even here, to your own people. They built the shrines, after all . . ."

"Yes, and later they fell from grace, and destroyed their city. The snakes aren't ready for that," Dreen said, almost pleading, and for a moment Mr. Naryan glimpsed the depth of Dreen's love for this city and its people.

Dreen turned away, as if ashamed, to look out at the river again, at the flocking sails of little boats setting out on, or returning from, the long crossing to the far side of the river. This great pilgrimage had become the focus of the life of the city. The markets were closed for the most part; merchants had moved to the docks to supply the thousands of pilgrims.

Dreen said, "They say that the avatar tempted her with godhead, and she denied it."

"But that is foolish! The days of the Preservers have long ago faded. We know them only by their image, which burns forever at the event horizon, but their essence has long since receded."

Dreen shrugged. "There's worse. They say that she forced the avatar to admit that the Preservers are dead. They say that *she* is an avatar of something greater than the Preservers, although you wouldn't know that from her preaching. She claims that this universe is all there is, that destiny is what you make it. What makes me despair is how readily the snakes believe this cant."

Mr. Naryan, feeling chill, there in the sun-dappled shade, said, "She has hinted to me that she learned it in the great far out, in the galaxy beyond the Home Galaxy."

"The ship is coming," Dreen said. "Perhaps they will deal with her."

★ ★ ★

In the burning night of the city's dissolution, Mr. Naryan is brought at last to the pink sandstone palace. Dreen's habitat floats above it, a black cloud that half-eclipses the glowering red swirl of the Eye of the Preservers. Trails of white smoke made luminescent by the fires which feed them, pour from the palace's high arched windows, braiding into sheets which dash like surf against the rim of the habitat. Mr. Naryan sees something fly up from amongst the palace's many carved spires—there seems to be more of them than he remembers—and smash away a piece of the habitat, which slowly tumbles off into the black sky.

The men around him hoot and cheer at this, and catch Mr. Naryan's arms and march him up the broad steps and through the high double doors into the courtyard beyond. It is piled with furniture and tapestries that have been thrown down from the thousand high windows overlooking it, but a path has been cleared to a narrow stair that turns and turns as it rises, until at last Mr. Naryan is pushed out onto the roof of the palace.

Perhaps five hundred of Angel's followers crowd amongst the spires and fallen trees and rocks, many naked, all with lettered headbands tied around their foreheads. Smoky torches blaze everywhere. In the center of the crowd is the palace's great throne on which, on high days and holidays, at the beginning of masques or parades, Dreen receives the city's priests, merchants and artists. It is lit by a crown of machines burning bright as the sun, and seated on it—easy, elegant and terrifying—is Angel.

Mr. Naryan is led through the crowd and left standing alone before the throne. Angel beckons him forward, her smile both triumphant and scared: Mr. Naryan feels her fear mix with his own.

She says, "What should I do with your city, now that I've taken it from you?"

"You have not finished your story." Everything Mr. Naryan planned to say has fallen away at the simple fact of her presence. Stranded before her fierce, barely contained energies, he feels old and used up, his body as heavy with years and regret as with fat. He adds cautiously, "I would like to hear it all."

He wonders if she really knows how her story must end. Perhaps she does. Perhaps her wild joy is not at her triumph, but at the imminence of her death. Perhaps she really does believe that the void is all, and rushes to embrace it.

Angel says, "My people can tell you. They hide with Dreen up above, but not for long."

She points across the roof. A dozen men are wrestling a sled, which shudders like a living thing as it tries to reorientate itself in the gravity field, onto a kind of launching cradle tipped up towards the habitat. The edges of the habitat are ragged, as if bitten, and amongst the roof's spires tower-trees are visibly growing towards it, their tips already brushing its edges, their tangled bases pulsing and swelling as teams of men and women drench them with nutrients.

"I found how to enhance the antigravity devices of the sleds," Angel says. "They react against the field which generates gravity for this artificial world. The field's stored inertia gives them a high kinetic energy, so that they make very good missiles. We'll chip away that floating fortress piece by piece if we have to, or we'll finish growing towers and storm its remains, but I expect surrender long before then."

"Dreen is not the ruler of the city." Nor are you, Mr. Naryan thinks, but it is not prudent to point that out.

"Not any more," Angel says.

Mr. Naryan dares to step closer. He says, "What did you find out there, that you rage against?"

Angel laughs. "I'll tell you about rage. It is what you have all forgotten, or never learned. It is the motor of evolution, and evolution's end, too." She snatches a beaker of wine from a supplicant, drains it and tosses it aside. She is consumed with an energy that is no longer her own. She says, "We traveled so long, not dead, not sleeping. We were no more than stored potentials triply engraved on gold. Although the ship flew so fast that it bound time about itself, the journey still took thousands of years of slowed ship-board time. At the end of that long voyage we did not wake: we were born. Or rather, others like us were born, although I have their memories, as if they are my own. They learned then that the Universe was not made for the convenience of humans. What they found was a galaxy ruined and dead."

She holds Mr. Naryan's hand tightly, speaking quietly and intensely, her eyes staring deep into his.

"A billion years ago, our neighboring galaxy collided with another, much smaller galaxy. Stars of both galaxies were torn off in the collision, and scattered in a vast halo. The rest coalesced into a single body, but except for ancient globular clusters, which survived the catastrophe because of their dense gravity fields, it is all wreckage. We were not able to chart a single world where life had evolved. I remember standing on a world sheared in half by immense tidal stress, its orbit so eccentric that it was colder than Pluto at its farthest point, hotter than Mercury at its nearest. I remember standing on a world of methane ice as cold and dark as the Universe itself, wandering amongst the stars. There were millions of such worlds cast adrift. I remember standing upon a fragment of a world smashed into a million shards and scattered so widely in its orbit that it never had the chance to re-form. There are a million such worlds. I remember gas giants turned inside out—single vast storms—and I remember worlds torched smooth by irruptions of their stars. No life, anywhere.

"Do you know how many galaxies have endured such collisions? Almost all of them. Life is a statistical freak. It is likely that only the stars of our galaxy have planets, or else other civilizations would surely have arisen elsewhere in the unbounded Universe. As it is, it is certain that we are alone. We must make of ourselves what we can. We should not hide, as your Preservers chose to do. Instead, we should seize the day, and make the Universe over with the technology that the Preservers used to make their hiding place."

Her grip is hurting now, but Mr. Naryan bears it. "You cannot become a Preserver," he says sadly. "No one can, now. You should not lie to these innocent people."

"I didn't need to lie. They took up my story and made it theirs. They see now what they can inherit—if they dare. This won't stop with one city. It will become a crusade!" She adds, more softly, "You'll remember it all, won't you?"

It is then that Mr. Naryan knows that she knows how this must end, and his heart breaks. He would ask her to take that burden from him, but he cannot. He is bound to her. He is her witness.

The crowd around them cheers as the sled rockets up from its cradle. It smashes into the habitat and knocks loose another piece, which drops trees and dirt and rocks amongst the spires of the palace roof as it twists free and spins away into the night.

Figures appear at the edge of the habitat. A small tube falls, glittering through the torchlight. A man catches it, runs across the debris-strewn roof, and throws himself at Angel's feet. He is at the far end of the human scale of the Shaped of this city. His skin is lapped with distinct scales, edged with a rim of hard black like the scales of a pine cone. His coarse black hair has flopped over his eyes, which glow like coals with reflected firelight.

Angel takes the tube and shakes it. It unrolls into a flexible sheet on which Dreen's face glows. Dreen's lips move; his voice is small and metallic. Angel listens intently, and when he has finished speaking says softly, "Yes."

Then she stands and raises both hands above her head. All across the roof, men and woman turn towards her, eyes glowing.

"They wish to surrender! Let them come down!"

A moment later a sled swoops down from the habitat, its silvery underside gleaming in the reflected light of the many fires scattered across the roof. Angel's followers shout and jeer, and missiles fly out of the darkness—a burning torch, a rock, a broken branch. All are somehow deflected before they reach the ship's crew, screaming away into the dark with such force that the torch, the branch, kindle into white fire. The crew have modified the sled's field to protect themselves.

They all look like Angel, with the same small sleek head, the same gangling build and abrupt nervous movements. Dreen's slight figure is dwarfed by them. It takes Mr. Naryan a long minute to be able to distinguish men from women, and another to be able to tell each man from his brothers, each woman from her sisters. They are all clad in long white shirts that leave them bare-armed and bare-legged, and each is girdled with a belt from which hang a dozen or more little machines. They call to Angel, one following on the words of the other, saying over and over again:

"Return with us—"

"—this is not our place—"

"—these are not our people—"

"—we will return—"

"—we will find our home—"

"—leave with us and return."

Dreen sees Mr. Naryan and shouts, "They want to take her back!" He jumps down from the sled, an act of bravery that astonishes Mr. Naryan, and skips through the crowd. "They are all one person, or variations on one person," he says breathlessly. "The ship makes its crew by varying a template. Angel is an extreme. A mistake."

Angel starts to laugh.

"You funny little man! I'm the real one—they are the copies!"

"Come back to us—"

"—come back and help us—"

"—help us find our home."

"There's no home to find!" Angel shouts. "Oh, you fools! This is all there is!"

"I tried to explain to them," Dreen says to Mr. Naryan, "but they wouldn't listen."

"They surely cannot disbelieve the Puranas," Mr. Naryan says.

Angel shouts, "Give me back the ship!"

"It was never yours—"

"—never yours to own—"

"—but only yours to serve."

"No! I won't serve!" Angel jumps onto the throne and makes an abrupt cutting gesture.

Hundreds of fine silver threads spool out of the darkness, shooting towards the sled and her crewmates. The ends of the threads flick up when they reach the edge of the sled's modified field, but then fall in a tangle over the crew: their shield is gone.

The crowd begins to throw things again, but Angel orders them to be still. "I have the only working sled," she says. "That which I enhance, I can also take away. Come with me," she tells Mr. Naryan, "and see the end of my story."

The crowd around Angel stirs. Mr. Naryan turns, and sees one of the crew walking towards Angel.

He is as tall and slender as Angel, his small high-cheekboned face so like her own it is as if he holds up a mirror as he approaches. A rock arcs out of the crowd and strikes his shoulder: he staggers but walks on, hardly seeming to notice that the crowd closes at his back so that he is suddenly inside its circle, with Angel and Mr. Naryan in its focus.

Angel says, "I'm not afraid of you."

"Of course not, sister," the man says. And he grasps her wrists in both his hands.

Then Mr. Naryan is on his hands and knees. A strong wind howls about him, and he can hear people screaming. The after-glow of a great light swims in his vision. He can't see who helps him up and half-carries him through the stunned crowd to the sled.

When the sled starts to rise, Mr. Naryan falls to his knees again. Dreen says in his ear, "It's over."

"No," Mr. Naryan says. He blinks and blinks, tears rolling down his cheeks.

The man took Angel's wrists in both of his—

Dreen is saying something, but Mr. Naryan shakes his head. It is not over.

—and they shot up into the night, so fast that their clothing burst into flame, so fast that air was drawn up with them. If Angel could nullify the gravity field, then so could her crewmates. She has achieved apotheosis.

The sled swoops up the tiered slope of the ship, is swallowed by a wide hatch. When he can see again, Mr. Naryan finds himself kneeling at the edge of the open hatch. The city is spread below. Fires define the streets which radiate away from the Great River; the warm night air is bitter with the smell of burning.

Dreen has been looking at the lighted windows that crowd the walls of the vast room beyond the hatch, scampering with growing excitement from one to the other. Now he sees that Mr. Naryan is crying, and clumsily tries to comfort him, believing that Mr. Naryan is mourning his wife, left behind in the dying city.

"She was a good woman, for her kind," Mr. Naryan is able to say at last, although it isn't her he's mourning, or not only her. He is mourning for all of the citizens of Sensch. They are irrevocably caught in their change now, never to be the same. His wife, the nut roaster, the men and women who own the little tea houses at the corner of every square, the children, the mendicants and the merchants—all are changed, or else dying in the process. Something new is being born down there. Rising from the fall of the city.

"They'll take us to away from all this," Dreen says happily. "They're going to search for where they came from. Some are out combing the city for others who can help them; the rest are preparing the ship. They'll take it over the edge of the world, into the great far out!"

"Don't they know they'll never find what they're looking for? The Puranas—"

"Old stories, old fears. They will take us home!"

Mr. Naryan laboriously clambers to his feet. He understands that Dreen has fallen under the thrall of the crew. He is theirs, as Mr. Naryan is now and forever Angel's. He says, "Those times are past. Down there in the city is the beginning of something new, something wonderful—" He finds he can't explain. All he has is his faith that it won't stop here. It is not an end but a beginning, a spark to set all of Confluence—the unfallen and the changed—alight. Mr. Naryan says, weakly, "It won't stop here."

Dreen's big eyes shine in the light of the city's fires. He says, "I see only another Change War. There's nothing new in that. The snakes will rebuild the city in their new image, if not here, then somewhere else along the Great River. It has happened before, in this very place, to my own people. We survived it, and so will the snakes. But what *they* promise is so much greater! We'll leave this poor place, and voyage out to return to where it all began, to the very home of the Preservers. Look there! That's where we're going!"

Mr. Naryan allows himself to be led across the vast room. It is so big that it could easily hold Dreen's floating habitat. A window on its far side shows a view angled somewhere far above the plane of Confluence's orbit. Confluence itself is a shining strip, an arrow running out to its own vanishing point. Beyond that point are the ordered, frozen spirals of the Home Galaxy, the great jeweled clusters and braids of stars constructed in the last great days of the Preservers before they vanished forever into the black hole they made by collapsing the Magellanic Clouds.

Mr. Naryan starts to breathe deeply, topping up the oxygen content of his blood.

"You see!" Dreen says again, his face shining with awe in Confluence's silver light.

"I see the end of history," Mr. Naryan says. "You should have studied the Puranas, Dreen. There's no future to be found amongst the artifacts of the Preservers, only the dead past. I won't serve, Dreen. That's over."

And then he turns and lumbers through the false lights and shadows of the windows towards the open hatch. Dreen catches his arm, but Mr. Naryan throws him off.

Dreen sprawls on his back, astonished, then jumps up and runs in front of Mr. Naryan. "You fool!" he shouts. "They can bring her back!"

"There's no need," Mr. Naryan says, and pushes Dreen out of the way and plunges straight out of the hatch.

He falls through black air like a heavy comet. Water smashes around him, tears away his clothes. His nostrils pinch shut and membranes slide across his eyes as he plunges down and down amidst streaming bubbles until the roaring in his ears is no longer the roar of his blood but the roar of the river's never-ending fall over the edge of the world.

Deep, silty currents begin to pull him towards that edge. He turns in the water and begins to swim away from it, away from the ship and the burning city. His duty is over: once they have taken charge of their destiny, the changed citizens will no longer need an Archivist.

Mr. Naryan swims more and more easily. The swift cold water washes away his landbound habits, wakes the powerful muscles of his shoulders and back. Angel's message burns bright, burning away the old stories, as he swims through the black water, against the currents of the Great River. Joy gathers with every thrust of his arms. He is the messenger, Angel's witness. He will travel ahead of the crusade that will begin when everyone in Sensch is changed. It will be a long and difficult journey, but he does not doubt that his destiny—the beginning of the future that Angel has bequeathed him and all of Confluence—lies at the end of it.

Genesis

POUL ANDERSON

One of the best-known writers in science fiction, Poul Anderson made his first sale in 1947, while he was still in college, and in the course of his subsequent fifty-plus year career has published almost a hundred books (in several different fields, as Anderson has written historical novels, fantasies, and mysteries, in addition to science fiction), sold hundreds of short pieces to every conceivable market, and won seven Hugo Awards, three Nebula Awards, and the Tolkein Memorial Award for Life Achievement.

Anderson had trained to be a scientist, taking a degree in physics from the University of Minnesota, but the writing life proved to be more seductive, and he never did get around to working in his original field of choice. Instead, the sales mounted steadily, until by the late fifties and early sixties he may have been one of the most prolific writers in the genre.

In spite of his high output of fiction, he somehow managed to maintain an amazingly high standard of literary quality as well, and by the early-to-mid-1960s was also on his way to becoming one of the most honored and respected writers in the genre. At one point during this period (in addition to nonrelated work, and lesser series such as the *Hoka* stories he was writing in collaboration with Gordon R. Dickson), Anderson was running three of the most popular and prestigious series in science fiction *all at the same time:* the *Technic History* series detailing the exploits of the wily trader Nicholas Van Rijn (which includes novels such as *The Man Who Counts, The Trouble Twisters, Satan's World, Mirkheim, The People of the Wind* and collections such as *Trader to the Stars* and *The Earth Book of Stormgate*); the extremely popular series relating the adventures of interstellar secret agent Dominic Flandry, probably the most successful attempt to cross science fiction with the spy thriller, next to Jack Vance's *Demon Princes* novels (the Flandry series includes novels such as *A Circus of Hells, The Rebel Worlds, The Day of Their Return, Flandry of Terra, A Knight of Ghosts and Shadows, A Stone in Heaven,* and *The Game of Empire* and collections such as *Agent of the Terran Empire*); and, my own personal favorite, a series that took us along on assignment with the agents of the Time Patrol (including the collections *The Guardians of Time, Time Patrolman, The Shield of Time,* and *The Time Patrol*).

When you add to this amazing collection of memorable titles the impact of the best of Anderson's nonseries novels, works such as *Brain Wave, Three Hearts and Three Lions, The Night Face, The Enemy Stars,* and *The High Crusade,* all of which were published in *addition* to the series books, it becomes clear that Anderson dominated the late fifties and the pre–New Wave sixties in a way that only Robert A. Heinlein, Isaac Asimov, and Arthur C. Clarke could rival. And, like them, he remained an active and dominant figure right through the seventies and eighties and is *still* producing strong new work and turning up on best-seller lists at the end of the decade of the nineties as well.

In the powerful, complex, and lyrical novella that follows, Anderson demonstrates all of his considerable strengths and takes us into the far future for a jolt of that much-talked-about Sense of Wonder that's as pure and concentrated, and as mind-boggling as anything you're going to find anywhere in the genre.

Anderson's other books (among *many* others) include: *The Broken Sword, Tau Zero, A Midsummer Tempest, Orion Shall Rise, The Boat of a Million Years, The Stars Are Also Fire,* and *Harvest of Stars.* His short work had been collected in *The Queen Air and Darkness and Other Stories, Fantasy, The Unicorn Trade* (with Karen Anderson). *Past Times, The Best of Poul Anderson,* and *Explorations.* His most recent books are the novels *The Fleet of Stars, Starfarers,* and *Operation Luna* and the retrospective collection *All One Universe.* Upcoming is a new novel, *Genesis,* expanded from the story that follows. Anderson lives in Orinda, California, with his wife (and fellow writer) Karen.

Was it her I ought to have loved . . . ?

—Piet Hein

1

No human could have shaped the thoughts or uttered them. They had no real beginning, they had been latent for millennium after millennium while the galactic brain was growing. Sometimes they passed from mind to mind, years or decades through space at the speed of light, nanoseconds to receive, comprehend, consider, and send a message on outward. But there was so much else—a cosmos of realities, an infinity of virtualities and abstract creations—that remembrances of Earth were the barest undertone, intermittent and fleeting, among uncounted billions of other incidentals. Most of the grand awareness was directed elsewhere, much of it intent on its own evolution.

For the galactic brain was still in infancy: unless it held itself to be still aborning. By now its members were strewn from end to end of the spiral arms, out into the halo and the nearer star-gatherings, as far as the Magellanic Clouds. The seeds of fresh ones drifted farther yet; some had reached the shores of the Andromeda.

Each was a local complex of organisms, machines, and their interrelationships.

("Organism" seems best for something that maintains itself, reproduces at need and possesses a consciousness in a range from the rudimentary to the transcendent, even though carbon compounds are a very small part of its material components and most of its life processes take place directly on the quantum level.) They numbered in the many millions, and the number was rising steeply, also within the Milky Way, as the founders of new generations arrived at new homes.

Thus the galactic brain was in perpetual growth, which from a cosmic viewpoint had barely started. Thought had just had time for a thousand or two journeys across its ever-expanding breadth. It would never absorb its members into itself; they would always remain individuals, developing along their individual lines. Let us therefore call them not cells, but nodes.

For they were in truth distinct. Each had more uniquenesses than were ever possible to a protoplasmic creature. Chaos and quantum fluctuation assured that none would exactly resemble any predecessor. Environment likewise helped shape the personality—surface conditions (what kind of planet, moon, asteroid, comet?) or free orbit, sun single or multiple (what kinds, what ages?), nebula, interstellar space and its ghostly tides. . . . Then, too, a node was not a single mind. It was as many as it chose to be, freely awakened and freely set aside, proteanly intermingling and separating again, using whatever bodies and sensors it wished for as long as it wished, immortally experiencing, creating, meditating, seeking a fulfillment that the search itself brought forth.

Hence, while every node was engaged with a myriad of matters, one might be especially developing new realms of mathematics, another composing glorious works that cannot really be likened to music, another observing the destiny of organic life on some world, life which it had perhaps fabricated for that purpose, another—Human words are useless.

Always, though, the nodes were in continuous communication over the light-years, communication on tremendous bandwidths of every possible medium. *This* was the galactic brain. That unity, that selfhood which was slowly coalescing, might spend millions of years contemplating a thought; but the thought would be as vast as the thinker, in whose sight an eon was as a day and a day was as an eon.

Already now, in its nascence, it affected the course of the universe. The time came when a node fully recalled Earth. That memory went out to others as part of the ongoing flow of information, ideas, feelings, reveries, and who knows what else? Certain of these others decided the subject was worth pursuing, and relayed it on their own message-streams. In this wise it passed through light-years and centuries, circulated, developed, and at last became a decision, which reached the node best able to take action.

Here the event has been related in words, ill-suited though they are to the task. They fail totally when they come to what happened next. How shall they tell of the dialogue of a mind with itself, when that thinking was a progression of quantum flickerings through configurations as intricate as the wave functions, when the computational power and database were so huge that measures become meaningless, when the mind raised aspects of itself to interact like persons until it drew them back into its wholeness, and when everything was said within microseconds of planetary time?

It is impossible, except vaguely and misleadingly. Ancient humans used the language of myth for that which they could not fathom. The sun was a fiery chariot daily crossing heaven, the year a god who died and was reborn, death a punishment for ancestral sin. Let us make our myth concerning the mission to Earth.

Think, then, of the primary aspect of the node's primary consciousness as if it were a single mighty entity, and name it Alpha. Think of a lesser manifestation of itself that it had synthesized and intended to release into separate existence as a second entity. For reasons that will become clear, imagine the latter masculine and name it Wayfarer.

All is myth and metaphor, beginning with this absurd nomenclature. Beings like these had no names. They had identities, instantly recognizable by others of their kind. They did not speak together, they did not go through discussion or explanation of any sort, they were not yet "they." But imagine it.

Imagine, too, their surroundings, not as perceived by their manifold sensors or conceptualized by their awareness and emotions, but as if human sense organs were reporting to a human brain. Such a picture is scarcely a sketch. Too much that was basic could not have registered. However, a human at an astronomical distance could have seen an M2 dwarf star about fifty parsecs from Sol, and ascertained that it had planets. She could have detected signs of immense, enigmatic energies, and wondered.

In itself, the sun was undistinguished. The galaxy held billions like it. Long ago, an artificial intelligence—at that dawn stage of evolution, this was the best phrase—had established itself there because one of the planets bore curious life-forms worth studying. That research went on through the megayears. Meanwhile the ever-heightening intelligence followed more and more different interests: above all, its self-evolution. That the sun would stay cool for an enormous length of time had been another consideration. The node did not want the trouble of coping with great environmental changes before it absolutely must.

Since then, stars had changed their relative positions. This now was the settlement nearest to Sol. Suns closer still were of less interest and had merely been visited, if that. Occasionally a free-space, dirigible node had passed through the neighborhood, but none chanced to be there at this epoch.

Relevant to our myth is the fact that no thinking species ever appeared on the viviferous world. Life is statistically uncommon in the cosmos, sapience almost vanishingly rare, therefore doubly precious.

Our imaginary human would have seen the sun as autumnally yellow, burning low and peacefully. Besides its planets and lesser natural attendants, various titanic structures orbited about it. From afar, they seemed like gossamer or like intricate spiderwebs agleam athwart the stars; most of what they were was force fields. They gathered and focused the energies that Alpha required, they searched the deeps of space and the atom, they transmitted and received the thought-flow that was becoming the galactic brain; what more they did lies beyond the myth.

Within their complexity, although not at any specific location, lived Alpha, its apex. Likewise, for the moment, did Wayfarer.

Imagine a stately voice: "Welcome into being. Yours is a high and, it may be, dangerous errand. Are you willing?"

If Wayfarer hesitated an instant, that was not from fear of suffering harm but from fear of inflicting it. "Tell me. Help me to understand."

"Sol—" The sun of old Earth, steadily heating since first it took shape, would

continue stable for billions of years before it exhausted the hydrogen fuel at it
core and swelled into a red giant. But—

A swift computation. "Yes. I see." Above a threshold level of radiation input
the geochemical and biochemical cycles that had maintained the temperature o
Earth would be overwhelmed. Increasing warmth put increasing amounts of wate
vapor into the atmosphere, and it is a potent greenhouse gas. Heavier cloud cover
raising the albedo, could only postpone a day of catastrophe. Rising above it, wate
molecules were split by hard sunlight into hydrogen, which escaped to space, and
oxygen, which bound to surface materials. Raging fires released monstrous ton
nages of carbon dioxide, as did rocks exposed to heat by erosion in desiccated
lands. It is the second major greenhouse gas. The time must come when the las
oceans boiled away, leaving a globe akin to Venus; but well before then, life o
Earth would be no more than a memory in the quantum consciousness. "When wil
total extinction occur?"

"On the order of a hundred thousand years futureward."

Pain bit through the facet of Wayfarer that came from Christian Brannock, whc
was born on ancient Earth and most passionately loved his living world. Lon
since had his uploaded mind merged into a colossal oneness that later divided and
redivided, until copies of it were integral with awareness across the galaxy. S
were the minds of millions of his fellow humans, as unnoticed now as single gene
had been in their bodies when their flesh was alive, and yet significant element
of the whole. Ransacking its database, Alpha had found the record of Christia
Brannock and chosen to weave him into the essence of Wayfarer, rather tha
someone else. The judgment was—call it intuitive.

"Can't you say more closely?" he appealed.

"No," replied Alpha. "The uncertainties and imponderables are too many
Gaia," mythic name for the node in the Solar System, "has responded to inquiries
evasively when at all."

"Have . . . we . . . really been this slow to think about Earth?"

"We had much else to think about and do, did we not? Gaia could at any tim
have requested special consideration. She never did. Thus the matter did not appea
to be of major importance. Human Earth is preserved in memory. What is posthu
man Earth but a planet approaching the postbiological phase?

"True, the scarcity of spontaneously evolved biomes makes the case interesting
However, Gaia has presumably been observing and gathering the data, for the res
of us to examine whenever we wish. The Solar System has seldom had visitors
The last was two million years ago. Since then, Gaia has joined less and less in
our fellowship; her communications have grown sparse and perfunctory. But such
withdrawals are not unknown. A node may, for example, want to pursue a philo
sophical concept undisturbed, until it is ready for general contemplation. In short,
nothing called Earth to our attention."

"*I* would have remembered," whispered Christian Brannock.

"What finally reminded us?" asked Wayfarer.

"The idea that Earth may be worth saving. Perhaps it holds more than Gaia
knows of—" A pause. "—or has told of. If nothing else, sentimental value."

"Yes, I understand," said Christian Brannock.

"Moreover, and potentially more consequential, we may well have experience
to gain, a precedent to set. If awareness is to survive the mortality of the stars, it

must make the universe over. That work of billions or trillions of years will begin with some small, experimental undertaking. Shall it be now," the "now" of death-less beings already geologically old, "at Earth?"

"Not small," murmured Wayfarer. Christian Brannock had been an engineer.

"No," agreed Alpha. "Given the time constraint, only the resources of a few stars will be available. Nevertheless, we have various possibilities open to us, if we commence soon enough. The question is which would be the best—and, first, whether we *should* act.

"Will you go seek an answer?"

"Yes," responded Wayfarer, and "Yes, oh, God damn, yes," cried Christian Brannock.

A spaceship departed for Sol. A laser accelerated it close to the speed of light, energized by the sun and controlled by a network of interplanetary dimensions. If necessary, the ship could decelerate itself at journey's end, travel freely about, and return unaided, albeit more slowly. Its cryomagnetics supported a good-sized ball of antimatter, and its total mass was slight. The material payload amounted simply to: a matrix, plus backup, for running the Wayfarer programs and containing a database deemed sufficient; assorted sensors and effectors; several bodies of dif-ferent capabilities, into which he could download an essence of himself; miscel-laneous equipment and power systems; a variety of instruments; and a thing ages forgotten, which Wayfarer had ordered molecules to make at the wish of Christian Brannock. He might somewhere find time and fingers for it.

A guitar.

2

There was a man called Kalava, a sea captain of Sirsu. His clan was the Samayoki. In youth he had fought well at Broken Mountain, where the armies of Ulonai met the barbarian invaders swarming north out of the desert and cast them back with fearsome losses. He then became a mariner. When the Ulonaian League fell apart and the alliances led by Sirsu and Irrulen raged across the land, year after year, seeking each other's throats, Kalava sank enemy ships, burned enemy villages, bore treasure and captives off to market.

After the grudgingly made, unsatisfactory Peace of Tuopai, he went into trade. Besides going up and down the River Lonna and around the Gulf of Sirsu, he often sailed along the North Coast, bartering as he went, then out over the Windroad Sea to the colonies on the Ending Islands. At last, with three ships, he followed that coast east through distances hitherto unknown. Living off the waters and what hunting parties could take ashore, dealing or fighting with the wild tribes they met, in the course of months he and his crews came to where the land bent south. A ways beyond that they found a port belonging to the fabled people of the Shining Fields. They abode for a year and returned carrying wares that at home made them rich.

From his clan Kalava got leasehold of a thorp and good farmland in the Lonna delta, about a day's travel from Sirsu. He meant to settle down, honored and comfortable. But that was not in the thought of the gods nor in his nature. He was soon quarreling with all his neighbors, until his wife's brother grossly insulted him and he killed the man. Thereupon she left him. At the clanmoot which composed the matter she received a third of the family wealth, in gold and movables. Their daughters and the husbands of these sided with her.

Of Kalava's three sons, the eldest had drowned in a storm at sea; the next died of the Black Blood; the third, faring as an apprentice on a merchant vessel far south to Zhir, fell while resisting robbers in sand-drifted streets under the time-gnawed colonnades of an abandoned city. They left no children, unless by slaves. Nor would Kalava, now; no free woman took his offers of marriage. What he had gathered through a hard lifetime would fall to kinfolk who hated him. Most folk in Sirsu shunned him too.

Long he brooded, until a dream hatched. When he knew it for what it was, he set about his preparations, more quietly than might have been awaited. Once the business was under way, though not too far along for him to drop if he must, he sought Ilyandi the skythinker.

She dwelt on Council Heights. There did the Vilkui meet each year for rites and conference. But when the rest of them had dispersed again to carry on their vocation—dream interpreters, scribes, physicians, mediators, vessels of olden lore and learning, teachers of the young—Ilyandi remained. Here she could best search the heavens and seek for the meaning of what she found, on a high place sacred to all Ulonai.

Up the Spirit Way rumbled Kalava's chariot. Near the top, the trees that lined it, goldfruit and plume, stood well apart, giving him a clear view. Bushes grew sparse and low on the stony slopes, here the dusty green of vasi, there a shaggy hairleaf, yonder a scarlet fireflower. Scorchwort lent its acrid smell to a wind blowing hot and slow off the Gulf. That water shone, tarnished metal, westward beyond sight, under a silver-gray overcast beneath which scudded rags of darker cloud. A rainstorm stood on the horizon, blurred murk and flutters of lightning light.

Elsewhere reached the land, bloomgrain ripening yellow, dun paperleaf, verdant pastures for herdlings, violet richen orchards, tall stands of shipwood. Farmhouses and their outbuildings lay widely strewn. The weather having been dry of late, dust whirled up from the roads winding among them to veil wagons and trains of porters. Regally from its sources eastward in Wilderland flowed the Lonna, arms fanning out north and south.

Sirsu lifted battlemented walls on the right bank of the main stream, tiny in Kalava's eyes at its distance. Yet he knew it, he could pick out famous works, the Grand Fountain in King's Newmarket, the frieze-bordered portico of the Flame Temple, the triumphal column in Victory Square, and he knew where the wrights had their workshops, the merchants their bazaars, the innkeepers their houses for a seaman to find a jug and a wench. Brick, sandstone, granite, marble mingled their colors softly together. Ships and boats plied the water or were docked under the walls. On the opposite shore sprawled mansions and gardens of the Helki suburb, their rooftiles fanciful as jewels.

It was remote from that which he approached.

Below a great arch, two postulants in blue robes slanted their staffs across the way and called, "In the name of the Mystery, stop, make reverence, and declare yourself!"

Their young voices rang high, unawed by a sight that had daunted warriors. Kalava was a big man, wide-shouldered and thick-muscled. Weather had darkened his skin to the hue of coal and bleached nearly white the hair that fell in braids halfway down his back. As black were the eyes that gleamed below a shelf of brow, in a face rugged, battered, and scarred. His mustache curved down past the jaw, dyed red. Traveling in peace, he wore simply a knee-length kirtle, green and trimmed with kivi skin, each scale polished, and buskins; but gold coiled around his arms and a sword was belted at his hip. Likewise did a spear stand socketed in the chariot, pennon flapping, while a shield slatted at the rail and an ax hung ready to be thrown. Four matched slaves drew the car. Their line had been bred for generations to be draft creatures—huge, long-legged, spirited, yet trustworthy after the males were gelded. Sweat sheened over Kalava's brand on the small, bald heads and ran down naked bodies. Nonetheless they breathed easily and the smell of them was rather sweet.

Their owner roared, "Halt!" For a moment only the wind had sound or motion. Then Kalava touched his brow below the headband and recited the Confession: "What a man knows is little, what he understands is less, therefore let him bow down to wisdom." Himself, he trusted more in blood sacrifices and still more in his own strength; but he kept a decent respect for the Vilkui.

"I seek counsel from the skythinker Ilyandi," he said. That was hardly needful, when no other initiate of her order was present.

"All may seek who are not attainted of ill-doing," replied the senior boy as ceremoniously.

"Ruvio bear witness that any judgments against me stand satisfied." The Thunderer was the favorite god of most mariners.

"Enter, then, and we shall convey your request to our lady."

The junior boy led Kalava across the outer court. Wheels rattled loud on flagstones. At the guesthouse, he helped stall, feed, and water the slaves, before he showed the newcomer to a room that in the high season slept two-score men. Elsewhere in the building were a bath, a refectory, ready food—dried meat, fruit, and flatbread—with richenberry wine. Kalava also found a book. After refreshment, he sat down on a bench to pass the time with it.

He was disappointed. He had never had many chances or much desire to read, so his skill was limited; and the copyist for this codex had used a style of lettering obsolete nowadays. Worse, the text was a chronicle of the emperors of Zhir. That was not just painful to him—oh, Eneio, his son, his last son!—but valueless. True, the Vilkui taught that civilization had come to Ulonai from Zhir. What of it? How many centuries had fled since the desert claimed that realm? What were the descendants of its dwellers but starveling nomads and pestiferous bandits?

Well, Kalava thought, yes, this could be a timely warning, a reminder to people of how the desert still marched northward. But was what they could see not enough? He had passed by towns not very far south, flourishing in his grandfather's time, now empty, crumbling houses half buried in dust, glassless windows like the eye sockets in a skull.

His mouth tightened. *He* would not meekly abide any doom.

Day was near an end when an acolyte of Ilyandi came to say that she would receive him. Walking with his guide, he saw purple dusk shade toward night in the east. In the west the storm had ended, leaving that part of heaven clear for a while. The sun was plainly visible, though mists turned it into a red-orange step pyramid. From the horizon it cast a bridge of fire over the Gulf and sent great streamers of light aloft into cloudbanks that glowed sulfurous. A whisltewing passed like a shadow across them. The sound of its flight keened faintly down through air growing less hot. Otherwise a holy silence rested upon the heights.

Three stories tall, the sanctuaries, libraries, laboratories, and quarters of the Vilkui surrounded the inner court with their cloisters. A garden of flowers and healing herbs, intricately laid out, filled most of it. A lantern had been lighted in one arcade, but all windows were dark and Ilyandi stood out in the open awaiting her visitor.

She made a slight gesture of dismissal. The acolyte bowed her head and slipped away. Kalava saluted, feeling suddenly awkward but his resolution headlong within him. "Greeting, wise and gracious lady," he said.

"Well met, brave captain," the skythinker replied. She gestured at a pair of confronting stone benches. "Shall we be seated?" It fell short of inviting him to share wine, but it meant she would at least hear him out.

They lowered themselves and regarded one another through the swiftly deepening twilight. Ilyandi was a slender woman of perhaps forty years, features thin and regular, eyes large and luminous brown, complexion pale—like smoked copper, he thought. Cropped short in token of celibacy, wavy hair made a bronze coif above a plain white robe. A green sprig of tekin, held at her left shoulder by a pin in the emblematic form of interlocked circle and triangle, declared her a Vilku.

"How can I aid your venture?" she asked.

He started in surprise. "Huh! What do you know about my plans?" In haste: "My lady knows much, of course."

She smiled. "You and your saga have loomed throughout these past decades. And . . . word reaches us here. You search out your former crewmen or bid them come see you, all privately. You order repairs made to the ship remaining in your possession. You meet with chandlers, no doubt to sound them out about prices. Few if any people have noticed. Such discretion is not your wont. Where are you bound, Kalava, and why so secretively?"

His grin was rueful. "My lady's not just wise and learned, she's clever. Well, then, why not go straight to the business? I've a voyage in mind that most would call crazy. Some among them might try to forestall me, holding that it would anger the gods of those parts—seeing that nobody's ever returned from there, and recalling old tales of monstrous things glimpsed from afar. I don't believe them myself, or I wouldn't try it."

"Oh, I can imagine you setting forth regardless," said Ilyandi half under her breath. Louder: "But agreed, the fear is likely false. No one had reached the Shining Fields by sea, either, before you did. You asked for no beforehand spells or blessings then. Why have you sought me now?"

"This is, is different. Not hugging a shoreline. I—well, I'll need to get and train a new huukin, and that's no small thing in money or time." Kalava spread his big hands, almost helplessly. "I had not looked to set forth ever again, you see. Maybe it is madness, an old man with an old crew in a single old ship. I hoped you might counsel me, my lady."

"You're scarcely ready for the balefire, when you propose to cross the Windroad Sea," she answered.

This time he was not altogether taken aback. "May I ask how my lady knows?"

Ilyandi waved a hand. Catching faint lamplight, the long fingers soared through the dusk like nightswoopers. "You have already been east, and would not need to hide such a journey. South, the trade routes are ancient as far as Zhir. What has it to offer but the plunder of tombs and dead cities, brought in by wretched squatters? What lies beyond but unpeopled desolation until, folk say, one would come to the Burning Lands and perish miserably? Westward we know of a few islands, and then empty ocean. If anything lies on the far side, you could starve and thirst to death before you reached it. But northward—yes, wild waters, but sometimes men come upon driftwood of unknown trees or spy storm-borne flyers of unknown breed—and we have all the legends of the High North, and glimpses of mountains from ships blown off course—" Her voice trailed away.

"Some of those tales ring true to me," Kalava said. "More true than stories about uncanny sights. Besides, wild huukini breed offshore, where fish are plentiful. I have not seen enough of them there, in season, to account for as many as I've seen in open sea. They must have a second shoreline. Where but the High North?"

Ilyandi nodded. "Shrewd, Captain. What else do you hope to find?"

He grinned again. "I'll tell you after I get back, my lady."

Her tone sharpened. "No treasure-laden cities to plunder."

He yielded. "Nor to trade with. Would we not have encountered craft of theirs, or, anyhow, wreckage? However . . . the farther north, the less heat and the more rainfall, no? A country yonder could have a mild clime, forestfuls of timber, fat land for plowing, and nobody to fight." The words throbbed. "No desert creeping in? Room to begin afresh, my lady."

She regarded him steadily through the gloaming. "You'd come home, recruit people, found a colony, and be its king?"

"Its foremost man, aye, though I expect the kind of folk who'd go will want a republic. But mainly—" His voice went low. He stared beyond her. "Freedom. Honor. A freeborn wife and new sons."

They were silent awhile. Full night closed in. It was not as murky as usual, for the clearing in the west had spread rifts up toward the zenith. A breath of coolness soughed in leaves, as if Kalava's dream whispered a promise.

"You are determined," she said at last, slowly. "Why have you come to me?"

"For whatever counsel you will give, my lady. Facts about the passage may be hoarded in books here."

She shook her head. "I doubt it. Unless navigation—yes, that is a real barrier, is it not?"

"Always," he sighed.

"What means of wayfinding have you?"

"Why, you must know."

"I know what is the common knowledge about it. Craftsmen keep their trade secrets, and surely skippers are no different in that regard. If you will tell me how you navigate, it shall not pass these lips, and I may be able to add something."

Eagerness took hold of him. "I'll wager my lady can! We see moon or stars unoften and fitfully. Most days the sun shows no more than a blur of dull light amongst the clouds, if that. But you, skythinkers like you, they've watched and measured for hundreds of years, they've gathered lore—" Kalava paused. "Is it too sacred to share?"

"No, no," she replied. "The Vilkui keep the calender for everyone, do they not? The reason that sailors rarely get our help is that they could make little or no use of our learning. Speak."

"True, it was Vilkui who discovered lodestones. . . . Well, coasting these waters, I rely mainly on my remembrance of landmarks, or a periplus if they're less familiar to me. Soundings help, especially if the plumb brings up a sample of the bottom for me to look at the taste. Then in the Shining Fields I got a crystal—you must know about it, for I gave another to the order when I got back—I look through it at the sky and, if the weather be not too thick, I see more closely where the sun is than I can with a bare eye. A logline and hourglass give some idea of speed, a lodestone some idea of direction, when out of sight of land. Sailing for the High North and return, I'd mainly use it, I suppose. But if my lady could tell me of anything else—"

She sat forward on her bench. He heard a certain intensity. "I think I might, Captain. I've studied that sunstone of yours. With it, one can estimate latitude and time of day, if one knows the date and the sun's heavenly course during the year. Likewise, even glimpses of moon and stars would be valuable to a traveler who knew them well."

"That's not me," he said wryly. "Could my lady write something down? Maybe this old head won't be too heavy to puzzle it out."

She did not seem to hear. Her gaze had gone upward. "The aspect of the stars in the High North," she murmured. "It could tell us whether the world is indeed round. And are our vague auroral shimmers more bright yonder—in the veritable Lodeland—?"

His look followed hers. Three stars twinkled wan where the clouds were torn. "It's good of you, my lady," he said, "that you sit talking with me, when you could be at your quadrant or whatever, snatching this chance."

Her eyes met his. "Yours may be a better chance, Captain," she answered fiercely. "When first I got the rumor of your expedition, I began to think upon it and what it could mean. Yes, I will help you where I can. I may even sail with you."

★ ★ ★

The *Gray Courser* departed Sirsu on a morning tide as early as there was light to steer by. Just the same, people crowded the dock. The majority watched mute. A number made signs against evil. A few, mostly young, sang a defiant paean, but the air seemed to muffle their strains.

Only lately had Kalava given out what his goal was. He must, to account for the skythinker's presence, which could not be kept hidden. That sanctification left the authorities no excuse to forbid his venture. However, it took little doubt and fear off those who believed the outer Windroad a haunt of monsters and demons, which might be stirred to plague home waters.

His crew shrugged the notion off, or laughed at it. At any rate, they said they did. Two-thirds of them were crusty shellbacks who had fared under his command before. For the rest, he had had to take what he could scrape together, impoverished laborers and masterless ruffians. All were, though, very respectful of the Vilku.

The *Gray Courser* was a yalka, broad-beamed and shallow-bottomed, with a low forecastle and poop and a deckhouse amidships. The foremast carried two square sails, the mainmast one square and one fore-and-aft; a short bowsprit extended for a jib. A catapult was mounted in the bows. On either side, two boats hung from davits, aft of the harnessing shafts. Her hull was painted according to her name, with red trim. Alongside swam the huukin, its back a sleek blue ridge.

Kalava had the tiller until she cleared the river mouth and stood out into the Gulf. By then it was full day. A hot wind whipped gray-green water into whitecaps that set the vessel rolling. It whined in the shrouds; timbers creaked. He turned the helm over to a sailor, trod forward on the poop deck, and sounded a trumpet. Men stared. From her cabin below, Ilyandi climbed up to stand beside him. Her white robe fluttered like wings that would fain be asoar. She raised her arms and chanted a spell for the voyage:

> *"Burning, turning,*
> *The sun-wheel reels*
> *Behind the blindness*
> *Cloud-smoke evokes.*
> *The old cold moon*
> *Seldom tells*
> *Where it lairs*
> *With stars afar.*
> *No men's omens*
> *Abide to guide*
> *High in the skies.*
> *But lodestone for Lodeland*
> *Strongly longs."*

While the deckhands hardly knew what she meant, they felt heartened.

Land dwindled aft, became a thin blue line, vanished into waves and mists. Kalava was cutting straight northwest across the Gulf. He meant to sail through the night, and thus wanted plenty of sea room. Also, he and Ilyandi would practice with her ideas about navigation. Hence after a while the mariners spied no other sails, and the loneliness began to weigh on them.

However, they worked stoutly enough. Some thought it a good sign, and cheered, when the clouds clove toward evening and they saw a horned moon. Their mates were frightened; was the moon supposed to appear by day? Kalava bullied them out of it.

Wind stiffened during the dark. By morning it had raised seas in which the ship reeled. It was a westerly, too, forcing her toward land no matter how close-hauled. When he spied, through scud, the crags of Cape Vairka, the skipper realized he could not round it unaided.

He was a rough man, but he had been raised in those skills that were seemly for a freeman of Clan Samayoki. Though not a poet, he could make an acceptable verse when occasion demanded. He stood in the forepeak and shouted into the storm, the words flung back to his men:

> *"Northward now veering,*
> *Steering from kin-rift,*
> *Spindrift flung gale-borne,*
> *Sail-borne is daft.*
> *Craft will soon flounder,*
> *Founder, go under—*
> *Thunder this wit-lack!*
> *Sit back and call*
> *All that swim near.*
> *Steer then to northward."*

Having thus offered the gods a making, he put the horn to his mouth and blasted forth a summons to his huukin.

The great beast heard and slipped close. Kalava took the lead in lowering the shafts. A line around his waist for safety, he sprang over the rail, down onto the broad back. He kept his feet, though the two men who followed him went off into the billows and had to be hauled up. Together they rode the huukin, guiding it between the poles where they could attach the harness.

"I waited too long," Kalava admitted. "This would have been easier yesterday. Well, something for you to brag about in the inns at home, nay?" Their mates drew them back aboard. Meanwhile the sails had been furled. Kalava took first watch at the reins. Mightily pulled the huukin, tail and flippers churning foam that the wind snatched away, on into the open, unknown sea.

3

Wayfarer woke.

He had passed the decades of transit shut down. A being such as Alpha would have spent them conscious, its mind perhaps at work on an intellectual artistic creation—to it, no basic distinction—or perhaps replaying an existent piece for contemplation-enjoyment or perhaps in activity too abstract for words to hint at. Wayfarer's capabilities, though large, were insufficient for that. The hardware and software (again we use myth) of his embodiment were designed principally for interaction with the material universe. In effect, there was nothing for him to do.

He could not even engage in discourse. The robotic systems of the ship were subtle and powerful but lacked true consciousness; it was unnecessary for them, and distraction or boredom might have posed a hazard. Nor could he converse with entities elsewhere; signals would have taken too long going to and fro. He did spend a while, whole minutes of external time, reliving the life of his Christian Brannock element, studying the personality, accustoming himself to its ways. Thereafter he . . . went to sleep.

The ship reactivated him as is crossed what remained of the Oort Cloud. Instantly aware, he coupled to instrument after instrument and scanned the Solar System. Although his database summarized Gaia's reports, he deemed it wise to observe for himself. The eagerness, the bittersweet sense of homecoming, that flickered around his calm logic were Christian Brannock's. Imagine long-forgotten feelings coming astir in you when you return to a scene of your early childhood.

Naturally, the ghost in the machine knew that changes had been enormous since his mortal eyes closed forever. The rings of Saturn were tattered and tenuous. Jupiter had gained a showy set of them from the death of a satellite, but its Red Spot faded away ages ago. Mars was moonless, its axis steeply canted. . . . Higher resolution would have shown scant traces of humanity. From the antimatter plants inside the orbit of Mercury to the comet harvesters beyond Pluto, what was no more needed had been dismantled or left forsaken. Wind, water, chemistry, tectonics, cosmic stones, spalling radiation, nuclear decay, quantum shifts had patiently reclaimed the relics for chaos. Some fossils existed yet, and some eroded fragments aboveground or in space; otherwise all was only in Gaia's memory.

No matter. It was toward his old home that the Christian Brannock facet of Wayfarer sped.

Unaided, he would not have seen much difference from aforetime in the sun. It was slightly larger and noticeably brighter. Human vision would have perceived the light as more white, with the faintest bluish quality. Unprotected skin would have reacted quickly to the increased ultraviolet. The solar wind was stronger, too. But thus far the changes were comparatively minor. This star was still on the main sequence. Planets with greenhouse atmospheres were most affected. Certain minerals on Venus were now molten. Earth—

The ship hurtled inward, reached its goal, and danced into parking orbit. At close range, Wayfarer looked forth.

On Luna, the patterns of maria were not quite the same, mountains were worn down farther, and newer craters had wrecked or obliterated older ones. Rubble-filled anomalies showed where ground had collapsed on deserted cities. Essentially, though, the moon was again the same desolation, seared by day and death-cold by night, as before life's presence. It had receded farther, astronomically no big distance, and this had lengthened Earth's rotation period by about an hour. However, as yet it circled near enough to stabilize that spin.

The mother planet offered less to our imaginary eyes. Clouds wrapped it in dazzling white. Watching carefully, you could have seen swirls and bandings, but to a quick glance the cover was well-nigh featureless. Shifting breaks in it gave blue flashes of water, brown flashes of land—nowhere ice or snowfall, nowhere lights after dark; and the radio spectrum seethed voiceless.

When did the last human foot tread this world? Wayfarer searched his database. The information was not there. Perhaps it was unrecorded, unknown. Perhaps that last flesh had chanced to die alone or chosen to die privately.

Certainly it was long and long ago. How brief had been the span of Homo sapiens, from flint and fire to machine intelligence! Not that the end had come suddenly or simply. It took several millennia, said the database: time for whole civilizations to rise and fall and leave their mutant descendants. Sometimes populations decline had reversed in this or that locality, sometimes nations heeded the vatic utterances of prophets and strove to turn history backward—for a while, a while. But always the trend was ineluctable.

The clustered memories of Christian Brannock gave rise to a thought in Wayfarer that was as if the man spoke: *I saw the beginning. I did not foresee the end. To me this was the magnificent dawn of hope.*

And was I wrong?

The organic individual is mortal. It can find no way to stave off eventual disintegration; quantum chemistry forbids. Besides, if a man could live for a mere thousand years, the data storage capacity of his brain would be saturated, incapable of holding more. Well before then, he would have been overwhelmed by the geometric increase of correlations, made feebleminded or insane. Nor could he survive the rigors of star travel at any reasonable speed or unearthly environments, in a universe never meant for him.

But transferred into a suitable inorganic structure, the pattern of neuron and molecular traces and their relationships that is his inner self becomes potentially immortal. The very complexity that allows this makes him continue feeling as well as thinking. If the quality of emotions is changed, it is because his physical organism has become stronger, more sensitive, more intelligent and aware. He will soon lose any wistfulness about his former existence. His new life gives him so much more, a cosmos of sensing and experience, memory and thought, space and time. He can multiply himself, merge and unmerge with others, grow in spirit until he reaches a limit once inconceivable; and after that he can become a part of a mind greater still, and thus grow onward.

The wonder was, Christian Brannock mused, that any humans whatsoever had held out, clung to the primitive, refused to see that their heritage was no longer of DNA but of psyche.

And yet—

The half-formed question faded away. His half-formed personhood rejoined Wayfarer. Gaia was calling from Earth.

She had, of course, received notification, which arrived several years in advance of the spacecraft. Her manifold instruments, on the planet and out between planets, had detected the approach. For the message she now sent, she chose to employ a modulated neutrino beam. Imagine her saying: "Welcome. Do you need help? I am ready to give any I can." Imagine this in a voice low and warm.

Imagine Wayfarer replying, "Thank you, but all's well. I'll be down directly, if that suits you."

"I do not quite understand why you have come. Has the rapport with me not been adequate?"

No, Wayfarer refrained from saying. "I will explain later in more detail than the transmission could carry. Essentially, though, the reason is what you were told. We"—he deemphasized rather than excluded her—"wonder if Earth ought to be saved from solar expansion."

Her tone cooled a bit. "I have said more than once: No. You can perfect your engineering techniques anywhere else. The situation here is unique. The knowledge to be won by observing the unhampered course of events is unpredictable, but it will be enormous, and I have good cause to believe it will prove of the highest value."

"That may well be. I'll willingly hear you out, if you care to unfold your thoughts more fully than you have hitherto. But I do want to make my own survey and develop my own recommendations. No reflection on you; we both realize that no one mind can encompass every possibility, every interpretation. Nor can any one mind follow out every ongoing factor in what it observes; and what is overlooked can prove to be the agent of chaotic change. I may notice something that escaped you. Unlikely, granted. After your millions of years here, you very nearly *are* Earth and the life on it, are you not? But . . . we . . . would like an independent opinion."

Imagine her laughing. "At least you are polite, Wayfarer. Yes, do come down. I will steer you in."

"That won't be necessary. Your physical centrum is in the arctic region, isn't it? I can find my way."

He sensed steel beneath the mildness: "Best I guide you. You recognize the situation as inherently chaotic. Descending on an arbitrary path, you might seriously perturb certain things in which I am interested. Please."

"As you wish," Wayfarer conceded.

Robotics took over. The payload module of the spacecraft detached from the drive module, which stayed in orbit. Under its own power but controlled from below, asheen in the harsh spatial sunlight, the cylindroid braked and slanted downward.

It pierced the cloud deck. Wayfarer scanned eagerly. However, this was no sightseeing tour. The descent path sacrificed efficiency and made almost straight for a high northern latitude. Sonic-boom thunder trailed.

He did spy the fringe of a large continent oriented east and west, and saw that those parts were mainly green. Beyond lay a stretch of sea. He thought that he glimpsed something peculiar on it, but passed over too fast, with his attention directed too much ahead, to be sure.

The circumpolar landmass hove in view. Wayfarer compared maps that Gaia had transmitted. They were like nothing that Christian Brannock remembered. Plate tectonics had slowed, as radioactivity and original heat in the core of Earth declined, but drift, subduction, upthrust still went on.

He cared more about the life here. Epoch after epoch, Gaia had described its posthuman evolution as she watched. Following the mass extinction of the Paleotechnic, it had regained the abundance and diversity of a Cretaceous or a Tertiary. Everything was different, though, except for a few small survivals. To Wayfarer, as to Alpha and, ultimately, the galactic brain, those accounts seemed somehow, increasingly, incomplete. They did not quite make ecological sense—as of the past hundred thousand years or so. Nor did all of Gaia's responses to questions.

Perhaps she was failing to gather full data, perhaps she was misinterpreting, perhaps—It was another reason to send him to her.

Arctica appeared below the flyer. Imagine her giving names to it and its features. As long as she had lived with them, they had their identities for her. The Coast Range of hills lifted close behind the littoral. Through it cut the Remnant River, which had been greater when rains were more frequent but continued impressive. With its tributaries it drained the intensely verdant Bountiful Valley. On the far side of that, foothills edged the steeply rising Boreal Mountains. Once the highest among them had been snowcapped; now their peaks were naked rock. Streams rushed down the flanks, most of them joining the Remnant somewhere as it flowed through its gorges toward the sea. In a lofty vale gleamed the Rainbowl, the big lake that was its headwaters. Overlooking from the north loomed the mountain Mindhome, its top, the physical centrum of Gaia, lost in cloud cover.

In a way the scenes were familiar to him. She had sent plenty of full-sensory transmissions, as part of her contribution to universal knowledge and thought. Wayfarer could even recall the geological past, back beyond the epoch when Arctica broke free and drifted north, ramming into land already present and thrusting the Boreals heavenward. He could extrapolate the geological future in comparable detail, until a red giant filling half the sky glared down on an airless globe of stone and sand, which would at last melt. Nevertheless, the reality, the physical being here, smote him more strongly than he had expected. His sensors strained to draw in every datum while his vessel flew needlessly fast to the goal.

He neared the mountain. Jutting south from the range, it was not the tallest. Brushy forest grew all the way up its sides, lush on the lower slopes, parched on the heights, where many trees were leafless skeletons. That was due to a recent climatic shift, lowering the mean level of clouds, so that a formerly well-watered zone had been suffering a decades-long drought. (Yes, Earth was moving faster toward its doomsday.) Fire must be a constant threat, he thought. But no, Gaia's agents could quickly put any out, or she might simply ignore it. Though not large, the area she occupied on the summit was paved over and doubtless nothing was vulnerable to heat or smoke.

He landed. For an instant of planetary time, lengthy for minds that worked at close to light speed, there was communication silence.

He was again above the cloud deck. It eddied white, the peak rising from it like an island among others, into the level rays of sunset. Overhead arched a violet clarity. A thin wind whittered, cold at this altitude. On a level circle of blue-black surfacing, about a kilometer wide, stood the crowded structures and engines of the centrum.

A human would have seen an opalescent dome surrounded by towers, some sheer as lances, some intricately lacy; and silver spiderwebs; and lesser things of varied but curiously simple shapes, mobile units waiting to be dispatched on their tasks. Here and there, flyers darted and hovered, most of them as small and exquisite as hummingbirds (if our human had known hummingbirds). To her the scene would have wavered slightly, as if she saw it through rippling water, or it throbbed with quiet energies, or it pulsed in and out of space-time. She would not have sensed the complex of force fields and quantum-mechanical waves, nor the microscopic and submicroscopic entities that were the major part of it.

Wayfarer perceived otherwise.

Then: "Again, welcome," Gaia said.

"And again, thank you," Wayfarer replied. "I am glad to be here."

They regarded one another, not as bodies—which neither was wearing—but as minds, matrices of memory, individuality, and awareness. Separately he wondered what she thought of him. She was giving him no more of herself than had always gone over the communication lines between the stars. That was: a nodal organism, like Alpha and millions of others, which over the eons had increased its capabilities, while ceaselessly experiencing and thinking; the ages of interaction with Earth and the life on Earth, maybe shaping her soul more deeply than the existence she shared with her own kind; traces of ancient human uploads, but they were not like Christian Brannock, copies of them dispersed across the galaxy, no, these had chosen to stay with the mother world. . . .

"I told you I am glad too," said Gaia regretfully, "but I am not, quite. You question my stewardship."

"Not really," Wayfarer protested. "I hope not ever. We simply wish to know better how you carry it out."

"Why, you do know. As with any of us who is established on a planet, high among my activities is to study its complexities, follow its evolution. On this planet that means, above all, the evolution of its life, everything from genetics to ecology. In what way have I failed to share information with my fellows?"

In many ways, Wayfarer left unspoken. Overtly: "Once we"—here he referred to the galactic brain—"gave close consideration to the matter, we found countless unresolved puzzles. For example—"

What he set forth was hundreds of examples, ranging over millennia. Let a single case serve. About ten thousand years ago, the big continent south of Arctica had supported a wealth of large grazing animals. Their herds darkened the plains and made loud the woods. Gaia had described them in loving detail, from the lyre-curved horns of one genus to the wind-rustled manes of another. Abruptly, in terms of historical time, she transmitted no more about them. When asked why, she said they had gone extinct. She never explained how.

To Wayfarer she responded in such haste that he got a distinct impression she realized she had a made a mistake. (Remember, this is a myth.) "A variety of causes. Climates became severe as temperatures rose—"

"I am sorry," he demurred, "but when analyzed, the meteorological data you supplied show that warming and desiccation cannot yet have been that significant in those particular regions."

"How are you so sure?" she retorted. Imagine her angry. "Have any of you lived with Earth for megayears, to know it that well?" Her tone hardened. "I do not myself pretend to full knowledge. A living world is too complex—chaotic. Cannot you appreciate that? I am still seeking comprehension of too many phenomena. In this instance, consider just a small shift in ambient conditions, coupled with new diseases and scores of other factors, most of them subtle. I believe that, combined, they broke a balance of nature. But unless and until I learn more, I will not waste bandwidth in talk about it."

"I sympathize with that," said Wayfarer mildly, hoping for conciliation. "Maybe I can discover or suggest something helpful."

"No. You are too ignorant, you are blind, you can only do harm."

He stiffened. "We shall see." Anew he tried for peace. "I did not come in any hostility. I came because here is the fountainhead of us all, and we think of saving it."

Her manner calmed likewise. "How would you?"

"That is one thing I have come to find out—what the best way is, should we proceed."

In the beginning, maybe, a screen of planetary dimensions, kept between Earth and sun by an interplay of gravity and electromagnetism, to ward off the fraction of energy that was not wanted. It would only be a temporary expedient, though, possibly not worthwhile. That depended on how long it would take to accomplish the real work. Engines in close orbit around the star, drawing their power from its radiation, might generate currents in its body that carried fresh hydrogen down to the core, thus restoring the nuclear furnace to its olden state. Or they might bleed gas off into space, reducing the mass of the sun, damping its fires but adding billions upon billions of years wherein it scarcely changed any more. That would cause the planets to move outward, a factor that must be taken into account but that would reduce the requirements.

Whatever was done, the resources of several stars would be needed to accomplish it, for time had grown cosmically short.

"An enormous work," Gaia said. Wayfarer wondered if she had in mind the dramatics of it, apparitions in heaven, such as centuries during which fire-fountains rushed visibly out of the solar disc.

"For an enormous glory," he declared.

"No," she answered curtly. "For nothing, and worse than nothing. Destruction of everything I have lived for. Eternal loss to the heritage?"

"Why, is not Earth the heritage?"

"No. Knowledge is. I tried to make that clear to Alpha." She paused. "To you I say again, the evolution of life, its adaptions, struggles, transformations, and how at last it meets death—those are unforeseeable, and nowhere else in the spacetime universe can there be a world like this for them to play themselves out. They will enlighten us in ways the galactic brain itself cannot yet conceive. They may well open to us whole new phases of ultimate reality."

"Why would not a life that went on for gigayears do so, and more?"

"Because here I, the observer of the ages, have gained some knowledge of *this* destiny, some oneness with it—" She sighed. "Oh, you do not understand. You refuse to."

"On the contrary," Wayfarer said, as softly as might be, "I hope to. Among the reasons I came is that we can communicate being to being, perhaps more fully than across light-years and certainly more quickly."

She was silent awhile. When she spoke again, her tone had gone gentle. "More . . . intimately. Yes. Forgive my resentment. It was wrong of me. I will indeed do what I can to make you welcome and help you learn."

"Thank you, thank you," Wayfarer said happily. "And I will do what I can toward that end."

The sun went under the cloud deck. A crescent moon stood aloft. The wind blew a little stronger, a little chillier.

"But if we decide against saving Earth," Wayfarer asked, "if it is to go molten and formless, every trace of its history dissolved, will you not mourn?"

"The record I have guarded will stay safe," Gaia replied.

He grasped her meaning: the database of everything known about this world. It was here in her. Much was also stored elsewhere, but she held the entirety. As the sun became a devouring monster, she would remove her physical plant to the outer reaches of the system.

"But you have done more than passively preserve it, have you not?" he said.

"Yes, of course." How could an intelligence like hers have refrained? "I have considered the data, worked with them, evaluated them, tried to reconstruct the conditions that brought them about."

And in the past thousands of years she had become ever more taciturn about that, too, or downright evasive, he thought.

"You had immense gaps to fill in," he hinted.

"Inevitably. The past, also, is quantum probabilistic. By what roads, what means, did history come to us?"

"Therefore you create various emulations, to see what they lead to," about which she had told scarcely anything.

"You knew that. I admit, since you force me, that besides trying to find what happened, I make worlds to show what *might* have happened."

He was briefly startled. He had not been deliberately trying to bring out any such confession. Then he realized that she had foreseen he was bound to catch scent of it, once they joined their minds in earnest.

"Why?" he asked.

"Why else but for a more complete understanding?"

In his inwardness, Wayfarer reflected: Yes, she had been here since the time of humanity. The embryo of her existed before Christian Brannock was born. Into the growing fullness of her had gone the mind-patterns of humans who chose not to go to the stars but to abide on old Earth. And the years went by in their tens of millions.

Naturally she was fascinated by the past. She must do most of her living in it. Could that be why she was indifferent to the near future, or actually wanted catastrophe?

Somehow that thought did not feel right to him. Gaia was a mystery he must solve.

Cautiously, he ventured, "Then you act as a physicist might, tracing hypothetical configurations of the wave function through space-time—except that the subjects of your experiments are conscious."

"I do no wrong," she said. "Come with me into any of those worlds and see."

"Gladly," he agreed, unsure whether he lied. He mustered resolution. "Just the same, duty demands I conduct my own survey of the material environment."

"As you will. Let me help you prepare." She was quiet for a span. In this thin air, a human would have seen the first stars blink into sight. "But I believe it will be by sharing the history of my stewardship that we truly come to know one another."

4

Storm-battered until men must work the pumps without cease, *Gray Courser* limped eastward along the southern coast of an unknown land. Wind set that direction, for the huukin trailed after, so worn and starved that what remained of its strength must be reserved for sorest need. The shore rolled jewel-green, save where woods dappled it darker, toward a wall of gentle hills. All was thick with life, grazing herds, wings multitudinous overhead, but no voyager had set foot there. Surf dashed in such violence that Kalava was not certain a boat could live through it. Meanwhile they had caught but little rainwater, and what was in the butts had gotten low and foul.

He stood in the bows, peering ahead, Ilyandi at his side. Wind boomed and shrilled, colder than they were used to. Wrack flew beneath an overcast gone heavy. Waves ran high, gray-green, white-maned, foam blown off them in streaks. The ship rolled, pitched, and groaned.

Yet they had seen the sky uncommonly often. Ilyandi believed that clouds—doubtless vapors sucked from the ground by heat, turning back to water as they rose, like steam from a kettle—formed less readily in this clime. Too eagerly at her instruments and reckonings to speak much, she had now at last given her news to the captain.

"Then you think you know where we are?" he asked hoarsely.

Her face, gaunt within the cowl of a sea-stained cloak, bore the least smile. "No. This country is as nameless to me as to you. But, yes, I do think I can say we are no more than fifty daymarches from Ulonai, and it may be as little as forty."

Kalava's fist smote the rail. "By Ruvio's ax! How I hoped for this!" The words tumbled from him. "It means the weather tossed us mainly back and forth between the two shorelines. We've not come unreturnably far. Every ship henceforward can have a better passage. See you, she can first go out to the Ending Islands and wait at ease for favoring winds. The skipper will know he'll make landfall. We'll have it worked out after a few more voyages, just what lodestone bearing will bring him to what place hereabouts."

"But anchorage?" she wondered.

He laughed, which he had not done for many days and nights. "As for that—"

A cry from the lookout at the masthead broke through. Down the length of the vessel men raised their eyes. Terror howled.

Afterward no two tongues bore the same tale. One said that a firebolt had pierced the upper clouds, trailing thunder. Another told of a sword as long as the hull, and blood carried on the gale of its flight. To a third it was a beast with jaws agape and three tails aflame. . . . Kalava remembered a spear among whirling rainbows. To him Ilyandi said, when they were briefly alone, that she thought of a shuttle now seen, now unseen as it wove a web on which stood writing she could not read. All witnesses agreed that it came from over the sea, sped on inland through heaven, and vanished behind the hills.

Men went mad. Some ran about screaming. Some wailed to their gods. Some cast themselves down on the deck and shivered, or drew into balls and squeezed their eyes shut. No hand at helm or pumps, the ship wallowed about, sails banging, adrift toward the surf, while water drained in through sprung seams and lapped higher in the bilge.

"Avast!" roared Kalava. He sprang down the foredeck ladder and went among the crew. "Be you men? Up on your feet or die!" With kicks and cuffs he drove them back to their duties. One yelled and drew a knife on him. He knocked the fellow senseless. Barely in time, *Gray Courser* came again under control. She was then too near shore to get the huukin harnessed. Kalava took the helm, wore ship, and clawed back to sea room.

Mutiny was all too likely, once the sailors regained a little courage. When Kalava could yield place to a halfway competent steersman, he sought Ilyandi and they talked awhile in her cabin. Thereafter they returned to the foredeck and he shouted for attention. Standing side by side, they looked down on the faces, frightened or terrified or sullen, of the men who had no immediate tasks.

"Hear this," Kalava said into the wind. "Pass it on to the rest. I know you'd turn south this day if you had your wish. But you can't. We'd never make the crossing, the shape we're in. Which would you liefer have, the chance of wealth and fame or the certainty of drowning? We've got to make repairs, we've got to restock, and *then* we can sail home, bringing wondrous news. When can we fix things up? Soon, I tell you, soon. I've been looking at the water. Look for yourselves. See how it's taking on more and more of a brown shade, and how bits of plant stuff float about on the waves. That means a river, a big river, emptying out somewhere nigh. And that means a harbor for us. As for the sight we saw, here's the Vilku, our lady Ilyandi, to speak about it."

The skythinker stepped forward. She had changed into a clean white robe with the emblems of her calling, and held a staff topped by a sigil. Though her voice was low, it carried.

"Yes, that was a fearsome sight. It lends truth to the old stories of things that appeared to mariners who ventured, or were blown, far north. But think. Those sailors did win home again. Those who did not must have perished of natural causes. For why would the gods or the demons sink some and not others?

"What we ourselves saw merely flashed overhead. Was it warning us off? No, because if it knew that much about us, it knew we cannot immediately turn back. Did it give us any heed at all? Quite possibly not. It was very strange, yes, but that does not mean it was any threat. The world is full of strangeness. I could tell you of things seen on clear nights over the centuries, fiery streaks down the sky or stars with glowing tails. We of the Vilkui do not understand them, but neither do we fear them. We give them their due honor and respect, as signs from the gods."

She paused before finishing: "Moreover, in the secret annals of our order lie accounts of visions and wonders exceeding these. All folk know that from time to time the gods have given their word to certain holy men or women, for the guidance of the people. I may not tell how they manifest themselves, but I will say that this today was not wholly unlike.

"Let us therefore believe that the sign granted us is a good one."

She went on to a protective chant-spell and an invocation of the Powers. That heartened most of her listeners. They were, after all, in considerable awe of her. Besides, the larger part of them had sailed with Kalava before and done well out of it. They bullied the rest into obedience.

"Dismissed," said the captain. "Come evening, you'll get a ration of liquor."

A weak cheer answered him. The ship fared onward.

Next morning they did indeed find a broad, sheltered bay, dun with silt. Hitching up the huukin, they went cautiously in until they spied the river foretold by Kalava. Accompanied by a few bold men, he took a boat ashore. Marshes, meadows, and woods all had signs of abundant game. Various plants were unfamiliar, but he recognized others, among them edible fruits and bulbs. "It is well," he said. "This land is ripe for our taking." No lightning bolt struck him down.

Having located a suitable spot, he rowed back to the ship, brought her in on the tide, and beached her. He could see that the water often rose higher yet, so he would be able to float her off again when she was ready. That would take time, but he felt no haste. Let his folk make proper camp, he thought, get rested and nourished, before they began work. Hooks, nets, and weirs would give rich catches. Several of the crew had hunting skills as well. He did himself.

His gaze roved upstream, toward the hills. Yes, presently he would lead a detachment to learn what lay beyond.

5

Gaia had never concealed her reconstructive research into human history. It was perhaps her finest achievement. But slowly those of her fellows in the galactic brain who paid close attention had come to feel that it was obsessing her. And then of late—within the past hundred thousand years or so—they were finding her reports increasingly scanty, less informative, at last ambiguous to the point of evasiveness. They did not press her about it; the patience of the universe was theirs. Nevertheless they had grown concerned. Especially had Alpha, who as the nearest was in the closest, most frequent contact; and therefore, now, had Wayfarer. Gaia's activities and attitudes were a primary factor in the destiny of Earth. Without a better understanding of her, the rightness of saving the planet was undecidable.

Surely an important part of her psyche was the history and archeology she preserved, everything from the animal origins to the machine fulfillment of genus Homo. Unnumbered individual minds had uploaded into her, too, had become elements of her being—far more than were in any other node. What had she made of all this over the megayears, and what had it made of her?

She could not well refuse Wayfarer admittance; the heritage belonged to her entire fellowship, ultimately to intelligence throughout the cosmos of the future. Guided by her, he would go through the database of her observations and activities in external reality, geological, biological, astronomical.

As for the other reality, interior to her, the work she did with her records and emulations of humankind—to evaluate that, some purely human interaction seemed called for. Hence Wayfarer's makeup included the mind-pattern of a man.

Christian Brannock's had been chosen out of those whose uploads went starfaring because he was among the earliest, less molded than most by relationships with machines. Vigor, intelligence, and adaptability were other desired characteristics.

His personality was itself a construct, a painstaking refabrication by Alpha, who had taken strands (components, overtones) of his own mind and integrated them to form a consciousness that became an aspect of Wayfarer. No doubt it was not a perfect duplicate of the original. Certainly, while it had all the memories of Christian Brannock's lifetime, its outlook was that of a young man, not an old one. In addition, it possessed some knowledge—the barest sketch, grossly oversimplified so as not to overload it—of what had happened since its body died. Deep underneath its awareness lay the longing to return to an existence more full than it could now imagine. Yet, knowing that it would be taken back into the oneness when its task was done, it did not mourn any loss. Rather, to the extent that it was differentiated from Wayfarer, it took pleasure in sensations, thoughts, and emotions that it had effectively forgotten.

When the differentiation had been completed, the experience of being human again became well-nigh everything for it, and gladsome, because so had the man gone through life.

To describe how this was done, we must again resort to myth and say that Wayfarer downloaded the Christian Brannock subroutine into the main computer of the system that was Gaia. To describe what actually occurred would require the mathematics of wave mechanics and an entire concept of multileveled, mutably dimensioned reality which it had taken minds much greater than humankind's a long time to work out.

We can, however, try to make clear that what took place in the system was not a mere simulation. It was an emulation. Its events were not of a piece with events among the molecules of flesh and blood; but they were, in their way, just as real. The persons created had wills as free as any mortal's, and whatever dangers they met could do harm equal to anything a mortal body might suffer.

Consider a number of people at a given moment. Each is doing something, be it only thinking, remembering, or sleeping—together with all ongoing physiological and biochemical processes. They are interacting with each other and with their surroundings, too; and every element of these surroundings, be it only a stone or a leaf or a photon of sunlight, is equally involved. The complexity seems beyond conception, let alone enumeration or calculation. But consider further: At this one instant, every part of the whole, however minute, is in one specific state; and thus the whole itself is. Electrons are all in their particular quantum shells, atoms are all in their particular compounds and configurations, energy fields all have their particular values at each particular point—suppose an infinitely fine-grained photograph.

A moment later, the state is different. However slightly, fields have pulsed, atoms have shifted about, electrons have jumped, bodies have moved. But this new state derives from the first according to natural laws. And likewise for every succeeding state.

In crude, mythic language: Represent each variable of one state by some set of numbers; or, to put it in equivalent words, map the state into an n-dimensional phase space. Input the laws of nature. Run the program. The computer model should then evolve from state to state in exact correspondence with the evolution of our original matter-energy world. That includes life and consciousness. The maps of organisms go through one-to-one analogues of everything that the organisms themselves would, among these being the processes of sensation and thought. To them, they and their world are the same as in the original. The question of which set is the more real is meaningless.

Of course, this primitive account is false. The program did *not* exactly follow the course of events "outside." Gaia lacked both the data and the capability necessary to model the entire universe, or even the entire Earth. Likewise did any other node, and the galactic brain. Powers of that order lay immensely far in the future, if they would ever be realized. What Gaia could accommodate was so much less that the difference in degree amounted to a difference in kind.

For example, if events on the surface of a planet were to be played out, the stars must be lights in the night sky and nothing else, every other effect neglected. Only a limited locality on the globe could be done in anything like full detail; the rest grew more and more incomplete as distance from the scene increased, until at the antipodes there was little more than simplified geography, hydrography, and atmospherics. Hence weather on the scene would very soon be quite unlike weather at the corresponding moment of the original. This is the simplest, most obvious consequence of the limitations. The totality is beyond reckoning—and we have not even mentioned relativistic nonsimultaneity.

Besides, atom-by-atom modeling was a practical impossibility; statistical mechanics and approximations must substitute. Chaos and quantum uncertainties made developments incalculable in principle. Other, more profound considerations entered as well, but with them language fails utterly.

Let it be said, as a myth, that such creations made their destinies for themselves.

And yet, what a magnificent instrumentality the creator system was! Out of nothingness, it could bring worlds into being, evolutions, lives, ecologies, aware-nesses, histories, entire time lines. They need not be fragmentary miscopies of something "real," dragging out their crippled spans until the nodal intelligence took pity and canceled them. Indeed, they need not derive in any way from the "outside." They could be works of imagination—fairy-tale worlds, perhaps, where benevolent gods ruled and magic ran free. Always, the logic of their boundary conditions caused them to develop appropriately, to be at home in their existences.

The creator system was the mightiest device ever made for the pursuit of art, science, philosophy, and understanding.

So it came about that Christian Brannock found himself alive again, young again, in the world that Gaia and Wayfarer had chosen for his new beginning.

He stood in a garden on a day of bright sun and mild, fragrant breezes. It was a formal garden, graveled paths, low-clipped hedges, roses and lilies in geometric beds, around a lichened stone basin where goldfish swam. Brick walls, ivy-heavy, enclosed three sides, a wrought-iron gate in them leading to a lawn. On the fourth side lay a house, white, slate-roofed, classically proportioned, a style that to him was antique. Honeybees buzzed. From a yew tree overlooking the wall came the twitter of birds.

A woman walked toward him. Her flower-patterned gown, the voluminous skirt and sleeves, a cameo hung on her bosom above the low neckline, dainty shoes, parasol less an accessory than a completion, made his twenty-third-century single-suit feel abruptly barbaric. She was tall and well formed. Despite the garments, her gait was lithe. As she neared, he saw clear features beneath high-piled mahogany hair.

She reached him, stopped, and met his gaze. "Benveni, Capita Brannoch," she greeted. Her voice was low and musical.

"Uh, g'day, Sorita—uh—" he fumbled.

She blushed. "I beg your pardon, Captain Brannock. I forgot and used my Inglay—English of my time. I've been—" She hesitated. "—supplied with yours, and we both have been with the contemporary language."

A sense of dream was upon him. To speak as dryly as he could was like clutching at something solid. "You're from my future, then?"

She nodded. "I was born about two hundred years after you."

"That means about eighty or ninety years after my death, right?" He saw an inward shadow pass over her face. "I'm sorry," he blurted. "I didn't mean to upset you."

She turned entirely calm, even smiled a bit. "It's all right. We both know what we are, and what we used to be."

"But—"

"Yes, but." She shook her head. "It does feel strange, being . . . this . . . again."

He was quickly gaining assurance, settling into the situation. "I know. I've had practice in it," light-years away, at the star where Alpha dwelt. "Don't worry, it'll soon be quite natural to you."

"I have been here a little while myself. Nevertheless—young," she whispered, "but remembering a long life, old age, dying—" She let the parasol fall, unnoticed, and stared down at her hands. Fingers gripped each other. "Remembering how toward the end I looked back and thought, 'Was that *all?*' "

He wanted to take those hands in his and speak comfort, but decided he would be wiser to say merely, "Well, it wasn't all."

"No, of course not. Not for me, the way it had been once for everyone who ever lived. While my worn-out body was being painlessly terminated, my self-pattern was uploaded—" She raised her eyes. "Now we can't really recall what our condition has been like, can we?"

"We can look forward to returning to it."

"Oh, yes. Meanwhile—" She flexed herself, glanced about and upward, let light and air into her spirit, until at last a full smile blossomed. "I am starting to enjoy this. Already I am." She considered him. He was a tall man, muscular, blond, rugged of countenance. Laughter lines radiated from blue eyes. He spoke in a resonant baritone. "And I will."

He grinned, delighted. "Thanks. The same here. For openers, may I ask your name?"

"Forgive me!" she exclaimed. "I thought I was prepared. I . . . came into existence . . . with knowledge of my role and this milieu, and spent the time since rehearsing in my mind, but now that it's actually happened, all my careful plans have flown away. I am—was—no, I am Laurinda Ashcroft."

He offered his hand. After a moment she let him shake hers. He recalled that at the close of his mortal days the gesture was going out of use.

"You know a few things about me, I suppose," he said, "but I'm ignorant about you and your times. When I left Earth, everything was changing spinjump fast, and after that I was out of touch," and eventually his individuality went of its own desire into a greater one. This reenactment of him had been given no details of the terrestrial history that followed his departure; it could not have contained any reasonable fraction of the information.

"You went to the stars almost immediately after you'd uploaded, didn't you?" she asked.

He nodded. "Why wait? I'd always longed to go."

"Are you glad that you did?"

"Glad is hardly the word." He spent two or three seconds putting phrases together. Language was important to him; he had been an engineer and occasionally a maker of songs. "However, I am also happy to be here." Again a brief grin. "In such pleasant company." Yet what he really hoped to do was explain himself. They would be faring together in search of one another's souls. "And I'll bring something new back to my proper existence. All at once I realize how a human can appreciate in a unique way what's out yonder," suns, worlds, upon certain of them life that was more wonderful still, nebular fire-clouds, infinity whirling down the throat of a black hole, galaxies like jewelwork strewn by a prodigal through immensity, space-time structure subtle and majestic—everything he had never known, as a man, until this moment, for no organic creature could travel those reaches.

"While I chose to remain on Earth," she said. "How timid and unimaginative do I seem to you?"

"Not in the least," he avowed. "You had the adventures you wanted."

"You are kind to say so." She paused. "Do you know Jane Austen?"

"Who? No, I don't believe I do."

"An early-nineteenth-century writer. She led a quiet life, never went far from home, died young, but she explored people in ways that nobody else ever did."

"I'd like to read her. Maybe I'll get a chance here." He wished to show that he was no—"technoramus" was the word he invented on the spot. "I did read a good deal, especially on space missions. And especially poetry. Homer, Shakespeare, Tu Fu, Bashō, Bellman, Burns, Omar Khayyam, Kipling, Millay, Haldeman—" He threw up his hands and laughed. "Never mind. That's just the first several names I could grab out of the jumble for purposes of bragging."

"We have much getting acquainted to do, don't we? Come, I'm being inhospitable. Let's go inside, relax, and talk."

He retrieved her parasol for her and, recollecting historical dramas he had seen, offered her his arm. They walked slowly between the flower beds. Wind lulled, a bird whistled, sunlight baked odors out of the roses.

"Where are we?" he asked.

"And when?" she replied. "In England of the mid-eighteenth century, on an estate in Surrey." He nodded. He had in fact read rather widely. She fell silent, thinking, before she went on: "Gaia and Wayfarer decided a serene enclave like this would be the best rendezvous for us."

"Really? I'm afraid I'm as out of place as a toad on a keyboard."

She smiled, then continued seriously: "I told you I've been given familiarity with the milieu. We'll be visiting alien ones—whatever ones you choose, after I've explained what else I know about what she has been doing these many years. That isn't much. I haven't seen any other worlds of hers. You will take the leadership."

"You mean because I'm used to odd environments and rough people? Not necessarily. I dealt with nature, you know, on Earth and in space. Peaceful."

"Dangerous."

"Maybe. But never malign."

"Tell me," she invited.

They entered the house and seated themselves in its parlor. Casement windows stood open to green parkscape where deer grazed; afar were a thatched farm cottage, its outbuildings, and the edge of grainfields. Cleanly shaped furniture stood among paintings, etchings, books, two portrait busts. A maidservant rustled in with a tray of tea and cakes. She was obviously shocked by the newcomer but struggled to conceal it. When she had left, Laurinda explained to Christian that the owners of this place, Londoners to whom it was a summer retreat, had lent it to their friend, the eccentric Miss Ashcroft, for a holiday.

So had circumstances and memories been adjusted. It was an instance of Gaia directly interfering with the circumstances and events in an emulation. Christian wondered how frequently she did.

"Eccentricity is almost expected in the upper classes," Laurinda said. "But when you lived you could simply be yourself, couldn't you?"

In the hour that followed, she drew him out. His birth home was the Yukon Ethnate in the Bering Federation, and to it he often returned while he lived, for its wilderness preserves, mountain solitudes, and uncrowded, uncowed, plainspoken folk. Otherwise the nation was prosperous and progressive, with more connections to Asia and the Pacific than to the decayed successor states east and south. Across the Pole, it was also becoming intimate with the renascent societies of Europe, and here Christian received part of his education and spent considerable of his free time.

His was an era of savage contrasts, in which the Commonwealth of Nations maintained a precarious peace. During a youthful, impulsively taken hitch in the Conflict Mediation Service, he twice saw combat. Later in his life, stability gradually become the norm. That was largely due to the growing influence of the artificial-intelligence network. Most of its consciousness-level units interlinked in protean fashion to form minds appropriate for any particular situation, and already the capabilities of those minds exceeded the human. However, there was little sense of rivalry. Rather, there was partnership. The new minds were willing to advise, but were not interested in dominance.

Christian, child of forests and seas and uplands, heir to ancient civilizations, raised among their ongoing achievements, returned on his vacations to Earth in homecoming. Here were his kin, his friends, woods to roam, boats to sail, girls to kiss, songs to sing and glasses to raise (and a gravesite to visit—he barely mentioned his wife Laurinda; she died before uploading technology was available). Always, though, he went back to space. It had called him since first he saw the stars from a cradle under the cedars. He became an engineer. Besides fellow humans he worked closely with sapient machines, and some of them got to be friends too, of an eerie kind. Over the decades, he took a foremost role in such undertakings as the domed Copernican Sea, the Asteroid Habitat, the orbiting antimatter plant, and finally the Grand Solar Laser for launching interstellar vessels on their way. Soon afterward, his body died, old and full of days; but the days of his mind had barely begun.

"A fabulous life," Laurinda said low. She gazed out over the land, across which shadows were lengthening. "I wonder if . . . they . . . might not have done better to give us a cabin in your wilderness."

"No, no," he said. "This is fresh and marvelous to me."

"We can easily go elsewhere, you know. Any place, any time that Gaia has generated, including ones that history never saw. I'll fetch our amulets whenever you wish."

He raised his brows. "Amulets?"

"You haven't been told—informed? They are devices. You wear yours and give it the command to transfer you."

He nodded. "I see. It maps an emulated person into different surroundings."

"With suitable modifications as required. Actually, in many cases it causes a milieu to be activated for you. Most have been in standby mode for a long time. I daresay Gaia could have arranged for us to wish ourselves to wherever we were going and call up whatever we needed likewise. But an external device is better."

He pondered. "Yes, I think I see why. If we got supernatural powers, we wouldn't really be human, would we? And the whole idea is that we should be." He leaned forward on his chair. "It's your turn. Tell me about yourself."

"Oh, there's too much. Not about me, I never did anything spectacular like you, but about the times I lived in, everything that happened to change this planet after you left it—"

She was born here, in England. By then a thinly populated province of Europe, it was a quiet land ("half adream," she said) devoted to its memorials of the past. Not that creativity was dead; but the arts were rather sharply divided between ringing changes on classic works and efforts to deal with the revelations coming in from the stars. The aesthetic that artificial intelligence was evolving for itself overshadowed both these schools. Nevertheless Laurinda was active in them.

Furthermore, in the course of her work she ranged widely over Earth. (By then, meaningful work for humans was a privilege that the talented and energetic strove to earn.) She was a liaison between the two kinds of beings. It meant getting to know people in their various societies and helping them make their desires count. For instance, a proposed earthquake-control station would alter a landscape and disrupt a community; could it be resisted, or if not, what cultural adjustments could be made? Most commonly, though, she counseled and aided individuals bewildered and spiritually lost.

Still more than him, she was carefully vague about her private life, but he got the impression that it was generally happy. If childlessness was an unvoiced sorrow, it was one she shared with many in a population-regulated world; he had had only a son. She loved Earth, its glories and memories, and every fine creation of her race. At the end of her mortality she chose to abide on the planet, in her new machine body, serving as she had served, until at length she came to desire more and entered the wholeness that was to become Gaia.

He thought he saw why she had been picked for resurrection, to be his companion, out of all the uncounted millions who had elected the same destiny.

Aloud, he said, "Yes, this house is right for you. And me, in spite of everything. We're both of us more at home here than either of us could be in the other's native period. Peace and beauty."

"It isn't a paradise," she answered gravely. "This is the real eighteenth century, remember, as well as Gaia could reconstruct the history that led to it," always monitoring, making changes as events turned incompatible with what was in the chronicles and the archeology. "The household staff are underpaid, undernourished, underrespected—servile. The American colonists keep slaves and are going to rebel. Across the Channel, a rotted monarchy bleeds France white, and this will bring on a truly terrible revolution, followed by a quarter century of war."

He shrugged. "Well, the human condition never did include sanity, did it?" That was for the machines.

"In a few of our kind, it did," she said. "At least, they came close. Gaia thinks you should meet some, so you'll realize she isn't just playing cruel games. I have"—in the memories with which she had come into this being—"invited three for dinner tomorrow. It tampers a trifle with their actual biographies, but Gaia can remedy that later if she chooses." Laurinda smiled. "We'll have to make an amulet provide you with proper smallclothes and wig."

"And you provide me with a massive briefing, I'm sure. Who are they?"

"James Cook, Henry Fielding, and Erasmus Darwin. I think it will be a lively evening."

The navigator, the writer, the polymath, three tiny, brilliant facets of the heritage that Gaia guarded.

6

Now Wayfarer downloaded another secondary personality and prepared it to go survey Earth.

He, his primary self, would stay on the mountain, in a linkage with Gaia more close and complete than was possible over interstellar distances. She had promised to conduct him through her entire database of observations made across the entire planet during manifold millions of years. Even for those two, the undertaking was colossal. At the speed of their thought, it would take weeks of external time and nearly total concentration. Only a fraction of their awareness would remain available for anything else—a fraction smaller in him than in her, because her intellect was so much greater.

She told him of her hope that by this sharing, this virtually direct exposure to all she had perceived, he would come to appreciate why Earth should be left to its fiery doom. More was involved than scientific knowledge attainable in no other way. The events themselves would deepen and enlighten the galactic brain, as a great drama or symphony once did for humans. But Wayfarer must undergo their majestic sweep through the past before he could feel the truth of what she said about the future.

He had his doubts. He wondered if her human components, more than had gone into any other node, might not have given her emotions, intensified by ages of brooding, that skewed her rationality. However, he consented to her proposal. It accorded with his purpose in coming here.

While he was thus engaged, Christian would be exploring her worlds of history and of might-have-been and a different agent would range around the physical, present-day globe.

In the latter case, his most obvious procedure was to discharge an appropriate set of the molecular assemblers he had brought along and let them multiply. When their numbers were sufficient, they would build (grow; brew) a fleet of miniature robotic vessels, which would fly about and transmit to him, for study at his leisure, everything their sensors detected.

Gaia persuaded him otherwise: "If you go in person, with a minor aspect of me for a guide, you should get to know the planet more quickly and thoroughly. Much about it is unparalleled. It may help you see why I want the evolution to continue unmolested to its natural conclusion."

He accepted. After all, a major part of his mission was to fathom her thinking. Then perhaps Alpha and the rest could hold a true dialogue and reach an agreement—whatever it was going to be. Besides, he could deploy his investigators later if this expedition left him dissatisfied.

He did inquire: "What are the hazards?"

"Chiefly weather," she admitted. "With conditions growing more extreme, tremendous storms spring up practically without warning. Rapid erosion can change contours almost overnight, bringing landslides, flash floods, sudden emergence of tidal bores. I do not attempt to monitor in close detail. That volume of data would be more than I could handle"—yes, she—"when my main concern is the biological phenomena."

His mind reviewed her most recent accounts to the stars. They were grim. The posthuman lushness of nature was megayears gone. Under its clouds, Earth roasted. The loftiest mountaintops were bleak, as here above the Rainbowl, but nothing of ice or snow remained except dim geological traces. Apart from the waters and a few islands where small, primitive species hung on, the tropics were sterile deserts. Dust and sand borne on furnace winds scoured their rockscapes. North and south they encroached, withering the steppes, parching the valleys, crawling up into the hills. Here and there survived a jungle or a swamp, lashed by torrential rains or wrapped hot and sullen in fog, but it would not be for much longer. Only in the high latitudes did a measure of benignity endure. Arctica's climates ranged from Floridian—Christian Brannock's recollections—to cold on the interior heights. South of it across a sea lay a broad continent whose northerly parts had temperatures reminiscent of central Africa. Those were the last regions where life kept any abundance.

"Would you really not care to see a restoration?" Wayfarer had asked her directly, early on.

"Old Earth lives in my database and emulations," Gaia had responded. "I could not map this that is happening into those systems and let it play itself out, because I do not comprehend it well enough, nor can any finite mind. To divert the course of events would be to lose, forever, knowledge that I feel will prove to be of fundamental importance."

Wayfarer had refrained from pointing out that life, reconquering a world once more hospitable to it, would not follow predictable paths either. He knew she would retort that experiments of that kind were being conducted on a number of formerly barren spheres, seeded with synthesized organisms. It had seemed strange to him that she appeared to lack any sentiment about the mother of humankind. Her being included the beings of many and many a one who had known sunrise dew beneath a bare foot, murmurs in forest shades, wind-waves in wheatfields from horizon to horizon, yes, and the lights and clangor of great cities. It was, at root, affection, more than any scientific or technological challenge, that had roused in Gaia's fellows among the stars the wish to make Earth young again.

Now she meant to show him why she felt that death should have its way.

Before entering rapport with her, he made ready for his expedition. Gaia offered him an aircraft, swift, versatile, able to land on a square meter while disturbing scarcely a leaf. He supplied a passenger for it.

He had brought along several bodies of different types. The one he picked would have to operate independently of him, with a separate intelligence. Gaia could spare a minim of her attention to have telecommand of the flyer; he could spare none for his representative, if he was to range through the history of the globe with her.

The machine he picked was not equivalent to him. Its structure could never have supported a matrix big enough to operate at his level of mentality. Think of it, metaphorically, as possessing a brain equal to that of a high-order human. Into this brain had been copied as much of Wayfarer's self-pattern as it could hold—the merest sketch, a general idea of the situation, incomplete and distorted like this myth of ours. However, it had reserves it could call upon. Inevitably, because of being most suitable for these circumstances, the Christian Brannock aspect dominated.

So you may, if you like, think of the man as being reborn in a body of metal, silicates, carbon and other compounds, electricity and other forces, photon and particle exchanges, quantum currents. Naturally, this affected not just his appearance and abilities, but his inner life. He was not passionless, far from it, but his passions were not identical with those of flesh. In most respects, he differed more from the long-dead mortal than did the re-creation in Gaia's emulated worlds. If we call the latter Christian, we can refer to the former as Brannock.

His frame was of approximately human size and shape. Matte blue-gray, it had four arms. He could reshape the hands of the lower pair as desired, to be a tool kit. He could similarly adapt his feet according to the demands upon them, and could extrude a spindly third leg for support or extra grip. His back swelled outward to hold a nuclear energy source and various organs. His head was a domed cylinder. The sensors in it and throughout the rest of him were not conspicuous but gave him full-surround information. The face was a holographic screen in which he could generate whatever image he wished. Likewise could he produce every frequency of sound, plus visible light, infrared, and microwave radio, for sensing or for short-range communication. A memory unit, out of which he could quickly summon any data, was equivalent to a large ancient library.

He could not process those data, comprehend and reason about them, at higher speed than a human genius. He had other limitations as well. But then, he was never intended to function independently of equipment.

He was soon ready to depart. Imagine him saying to Wayfarer, with a phantom grin, "*Adiós*. Wish me luck."

The response was . . . absentminded. Wayfarer was beginning to engage with Gaia.

Thus Brannock boarded the aircraft in a kind of silence. To the eye it rested small, lanceolate, iridescently aquiver. The material component was a tissue of wisps. Most of that slight mass was devoted to generating forces and maintaining capabilities, which Gaia had not listed for him. Yet it would take a wind of uncommon violence to endanger this machine, and most likely it could outrun the menace.

He settled down inside. Wayfarer had insisted on manual controls, against emergencies that he conceded were improbable, and Gaia's effectors had made the modifications. An insubstantial configuration shimmered before Brannock, instruments to read, keypoints to touch or think or think at. He leaned back into a containing field and let her pilot. Noiselessly, the flyer ascended, then came down through the cloud deck and made a leisurely way at five hundred meters above the foothills.

"Follow the Remnant River to the sea," Brannock requested. "The view inbound was beautiful."

"As you like," said Gaia. They employed sonics, his voice masculine, hers— perhaps because she supposed he preferred it—feminine in a low register. Their conversation did not actually go as reported here. She changed course and he beheld the stream shining amidst the deep greens of the Bountiful Valley, under a silver-gray heaven. "The plan, you know, is that we shall cruise about Arctica first. I have an itinerary that should provide you a representative sampling of its biology. At our stops, you can investigate as intensively as you care to, and if you want to stop anyplace else we can do that too."

"Thank you," he said. "The idea is to furnish me a kind of baseline, right?"

"Yes, because conditions here are the easiest for life. When you are ready, we will proceed south, across countries increasingly harsh. You will learn about the adaptations life has made. Many are extraordinarily interesting. The galactic brain itself cannot match the creativity of nature."

"Well, sure. Chaos, complexity . . . You've described quite a few of those adaptations to, uh, us, haven't you?"

"Yes, but by no means all. I keep discovering new ones. Life keeps evolving."

As environments worsened, Brannock thought. And nonetheless, species after species went extinct. He got a sense of a rear-guard battle against the armies of hell.

"I want you to experience this as fully as you are able," Gaia said, "immerse yourself, *feel* the sublimity of it."

The tragedy, he thought. But tragedy was art, maybe the highest art that humankind ever achieved. And more of the human soul might well linger in Gaia than in any of her fellow intelligences.

Had she kept a need for catharsis, for pity and terror? What really went on in her emulations?

Well, Christian was supposed to find out something about that. If he could.

Brannock was human enough himself to protest. He gestured at the land below, where the river flowed in its canyons through the coastal hills, to water a wealth of forest and meadow before emptying into a bay above which soared thousands of wings. "You want to watch the struggle till the end," he said. "Life wants to live. What right have you to set your wish against that?"

"The right of awareness," she declared. "Only to a being that is conscious do justice, mercy, desire have any existence, any meaning. Did not humans always use the world as they saw fit? When nature finally got protection, that was because humans so chose. I speak for the knowledge and insight that *we* can gain."

The question flickered uneasily in him: What about her private emotional needs?

Abruptly the aircraft veered. The turn pushed Brannock hard into the force field upholding him. He heard air crack and scream. The bay fell aft with mounting speed.

The spaceman in him, who had lived through meteoroid strikes and radiation bursts because he was quick, had already acted. Through the optical magnification he immediately ordered up, he looked back to see what the trouble was. The glimpse he got, before the sight went under the horizon, made him cry, "Yonder!"

"What?" Gaia replied as she hurtled onward.

"That back there. Why are you running from it?"

"What do you mean? There is nothing important."

"The devil there isn't. I've a notion you saw it more clearly than I did."

Gaia slowed the headlong flight until she well-nigh hovered above the strand and wild surf. He felt a sharp suspicion that she did it in order to dissipate the impression of urgency, make him more receptive to whatever she intended to claim.

"Very well," she said after a moment. "I spied a certain object. What do you think you saw?"

He decided not to answer straightforwardly—at least, not before she convinced him of her good faith. The more information she had, the more readily she could contrive a deception. Even this fragment of her intellect was superior to his. Yet he had his own measure of wits, and an ingrained stubbornness.

"I'm not sure, except that it didn't seem dangerous. Suppose you tell me what it is and why you turned tail from it."

Did she sigh? "At this stage of your knowledge, you would not understand. Rather, you would be bound to misunderstand. That is why I retreated."

A human would have tensed every muscle. Brannock's systems went on full standby. "I'll be the judge of my brain's range, if you please. Kindly go back."

"No. I promise I will explain later, when you have seen enough more."

Seen enough illusions? She might well have many trickeries waiting for him. "As you like," Brannock said. "Meanwhile, I'll give Wayfarer a call and let him know." Alpha's emissary kept a minute part of his sensibility open to outside stimuli.

"No, do not," Gaia said. "It would distract him unnecessarily."

"He will decide that," Brannock told her.

Strife exploded.

Almost, Gaia won. Had her entirety been focused on attack, she would have carried it off with such swiftness that Brannock would never have known he was bestormed. But a fraction of her was dealing, as always, with her observing units around the globe and their torrents of data. Possibly it also glanced from time to time—through the quantum shifts inside her—at the doings of Christian and Laurinda. By far the most of her was occupied in her interaction with Wayfarer. This she could not set aside without rousing instant suspicion. Rather, she must make a supremely clever effort to conceal from him that anything untoward was going on.

Moreover, she had never encountered a being like Brannock, human male aggressiveness and human spacefarer's reflexes blent with sophisticated technology and something of Alpha's immortal purpose.

He felt the support field strengthen and tighten to hold him immobile. He felt a tide like delirium rush into his mind. A man would have thought it was a knock-out anesthetic. Brannock did not stop to wonder. He reacted directly, even as she struck. Machine fast and tiger ferocious, he put her off balance for a crucial millisecond.

Through the darkness and roaring in his head, he lashed out physically. His hands tore through the light-play of control nexuses before him. They were not meant to withstand an assault. He could not seize command, but he could, blindly, disrupt.

Arcs leaped blue-white. Luminances flared and died. Power output continued; the aircraft stayed aloft. Its more complex functions were in ruin. Their dance of atoms, energies, and waves went uselessly random.

The bonds that had been closing on Brannock let go. He sagged to the floor. The night in his head receded. It left him shaken, his senses awhirl. Into the sudden anarchy of everything he yelled, "Stop, you bitch!"

"I will," Gaia said.

Afterward he realized that she had kept a vestige of governance over the flyer. Before he could wrest it from her, she sent them plunging downward and cut off the main generator. Every force field blinked out. Wind ripped the material frame asunder. Its pieces crashed in the surf. Combers tumbled them about, cast a few on the beach, gave the rest to the undertow.

As the craft fell, disintegrating, Brannock gathered his strength and leaped. The thrust of his legs cast him outward, through a long arc that ended in deeper water.

It fountained high and white when he struck. He went down into green depths while the currents swept him to and fro. But he hit the sandy bottom unharmed.

Having no need to breathe, he stayed under. To recover from the shock took him less than a second. To make his assessment took minutes, there in the swirling surges.

Gaia had tried to take him over. A force field had begun to damp the processes in his brain and impose its own patterns. He had quenched it barely in time.

She would scarcely have required a capability of that kind in the past. Therefore she had invented and installed it specifically for him. This strongly suggested she had meant to use it at some point of their journey. When he saw a thing she had not known was there and refused to be fobbed off, he compelled her to make the attempt before she was ready. When it failed, she spent her last resources to destroy him.

She would go that far, that desperately, to keep a secret that tremendous from the stars.

He recognized a mistake in his thinking. She had not used up everything at her beck. On the contrary, she had a planetful of observers and other instrumentalities to call upon. Certain of them must be bound here at top speed, to make sure he was dead—or, if he lived, to make sure of him. Afterward she would feed Wayfarer a story that ended with a regrettable accident away off over an ocean.

Heavier than water, Brannock strode down a sloping sea floor in search of depth.

Having found a jumble of volcanic rock, he crawled into a lava tube, lay fetally curled, and willed his systems to operate as low-level as might be. He hoped that then her agents would miss him. Neither their numbers nor their sensitivities were infinite. It would be reasonable for Gaia—who could not have witnessed his escape, her sensors in the aircraft being obliterated as it came apart—to conclude that the flows had taken his scattered remains away.

After three days and nights, the internal clock he had set brought him back awake.

He knew he must stay careful. However, unless she kept a closer watch on the site than he expected she would—for Wayfarer, in communion with her, might too readily notice that she was concentrating on one little patch of the planet—he dared now move about. His electronic senses ought to warn him of any robot that came into his vicinity, even if it was too small for eyes to see. Whether he could then do anything about it was a separate question.

First he searched the immediate area. Gaia's machines had removed those shards of the wreck that they found, but most were strewn over the bottom, and she had evidently not thought it worthwhile, or safe, to have them sought out. Nearly all of what he came upon was in fact scrap. A few units were intact. The one that interested him had the physical form of a small metal sphere. He tracked it down by magnetic induction. Having taken it to a place ashore, hidden by trees from the sky, he studied it. With his tool-hands he traced the (mythic) circuitry within and identified it as a memory bank. The encoding was familiar to his Wayfarer aspect. He extracted the information and stored it in his own database.

A set of languages. Human languages, although none he had ever heard of. Yes, very interesting.

"I'd better get hold of those people," he muttered. In the solitude of wind, sea, and wilderness, he had relapsed into an ancient habit of occasionally thinking aloud. 'Won't likely be another chance. Quite a piece of news for Wayfarer." If he came back, or at least got within range of his transmitter.

He set forth afoot, along the shore toward the bay where the Remnant River debouched. Maybe that which he had seen would be there yet, or traces of it.

He wasn't sure, everything had happened so fast, but he thought it was a ship.

7

Three days—olden Earth days of twenty-four hours, cool sunlight, now and then a rainshower leaving pastures and hedgerows asparkle, rides through English lanes, rambles through English towns, encounters with folk, evensong in a Norman church, exploration of buildings and books, long talks and companionable silences—wrought friendship. In Christian it also began to rouse kindlier feelings toward Gaia. She had resurrected Laurinda, and Laurinda was a part of her, as he was of Wayfarer and of Alpha and more other minds across the galaxy than he could number. Could the rest of Gaia's works be wrongful?

No doubt she had chosen and planned as she did in order to get this reaction from him. It didn't seem to matter.

Nor did the primitive conditions of the eighteenth century matter to him or to Laurinda. Rather, their everyday experiences were something refreshingly new, and frequently the occasion of laughter. What did become a bit difficult for him was to retire decorously to his separate room each night.

But they had their missions: his to see what was going on in this reality and afterward upload into Wayfarer; hers to explain and justify it to him as well as a mortal was able. Like him, she kept a memory of having been one with a nodal being. The memory was as dim and fragmentary as his, more a sense of transcendence than anything with a name or form, like the afterglow of a religious vision long ago. Yet it pervaded her personality, the unconscious more than the conscious; and it was her relationship to Gaia, as he had his to Wayfarer and beyond that to Alpha. In a limited, mortal, but altogether honest and natural way, she spoke for the node of Earth.

By tacit consent, they said little about the purpose and simply enjoyed their surroundings and one another, until the fourth morning. Perhaps the weather whipped up a lifetime habit of duty. Wind gusted and shrilled around the house, rain blinded the windows, there would be no going out even in a carriage. Indoors a fire failed to hold dank chill at bay. Candlelight glowed cozily on the breakfast table, silverware and china sheened, but shadows hunched thick in every corner.

He took a last sip of coffee, put the cup down, and ended the words he had been setting forth: "Yes, we'd better get started. Not that I've any clear notion of what to look for. Wayfarer himself doesn't." Gaia had been so vague about so much. Well, Wayfarer was now (whatever "now" meant) in rapport with her, seeking an overall, cosmic view of—how many millions of years on this planet?

"Why, you know your task," Laurinda replied. "You're to find out the nature of Gaia's interior activity, what it means in moral—in human terms." She straightened in her chair. Her tone went resolute. "We *are* human, we emulations. We think and act, we feel joy and pain, the same as humans always did."

Impulse beckoned; it was his wont to try to lighten moods. "And," he added, "make new generations of people, the same as humans always did."

A blush crossed the fair countenance. "Yes," she said. Quickly: "Of course most of what's . . . here . . . is nothing but database. Archives, if you will. We might start by visiting one or two of those reconstructions."

He smiled, the heaviness lifting from him. "I'd love to. Any suggestions?"

Eagerness responded. "The Acropolis of Athens? As it was when new? Classical civilization fascinated me." She tossed her head. "Still does, by damn."

"Hm." He rubbed his chin. "From what I learned in my day, those old Greeks were as tricky, quarrelsome, shortsighted a pack of political animals as ever stole an election or bullied a weaker neighbor. Didn't Athens finance the building of the Parthenon by misappropriating the treasury of the Delian League?"

"They were human," she said, almost too low for him to hear above the storm noise. "But what they made—"

"Sure," he answered. "Agreed. Let's go."

In perception, the amulets were silvery two-centimeter discs that hung on a user's breast, below garments. In reality—outer-viewpoint reality—they were powerful, subtle programs with intelligences of their own. Christian wondered about the extent to which they were under the direct control of Gaia, and how closely she was monitoring him.

Without thinking, he took Laurinda's hand. Her fingers clung to his. She looked straight before her, though, into the flickery fire, while she uttered their command.

Immediately, with no least sensation of movement, they were on broad marble steps between outworks, under a cloudless heaven, in flooding hot radiance. From the steepest, unused hill slopes, a scent of wild thyme drifted up through silence, thyme without bees to quicken it or hands to pluck it. Below reached the city, sun-smitten house roofs, open agoras, colonnaded temples. In this clear air Brannock imagined he could well-nigh make out the features on the statues.

After a time beyond time, the visitors moved upward, still mute, still hand in hand, to where winged Victories lined the balustrade before the sanctuary of Nike Apteros. Their draperies flowed to movement he did not see and wind he did not feel. One was tying her sandals. . . .

For a long while the two lingered at the Propylaea, its porticos, Ionics, Dorics, paintings, votive tablets in the Pinakotheka. They felt they could have stayed past sunset, but everything else awaited them, and they knew mortal enthusiasm as they would presently know mortal weariness. Colors burned. . . .

The stone flowers and stone maidens at the Erechtheum . . .

Christian had thought of the Parthenon as exquisite; so it was in the pictures and models he had seen, while the broken, chemically gnawed remnants were merely to grieve over. Confronting it here, entering it, he discovered its sheer size and mass. Life shouted in the friezes, red, blue, gilt; then in the dusk within, awesomeness and beauty found their focus in the colossal Athene of Pheidias.

—Long afterward, he stood with Laurinda on the Wall of Kimon, above the Asclepium and Theater of Dionysus. A westering sun made the city below intricate with shadows, and coolth breathed out of the east. Hitherto, when they spoke it had been, illogically, in near whispers. Now they felt free to talk openly, or did they feel a need?

He shook his head. "Gorgeous," he said, for lack of anything halfway adequate. "Unbelievable."

"It was worth all the wrongdoing and war and agony," she murmured. "Wasn't it?"

For the moment, he shied away from deep seriousness. "I didn't expect it to be this, uh, gaudy—no, this bright."

"They painted their buildings. That's known."

"Yes, I knew too. But were later scholars sure of just what colors?"

"Scarcely, except where a few traces were left. Most of this must be Gaia's conjecture. The sculpture especially, I suppose. Recorded history saved only the barest description of the Athene, for instance." Laurinda paused. Her gaze went outward to the mountains. "But surely this—in view of everything she has, all the information, and being able to handle it all at once and, and understand the minds that were capable of making it—surely this is the most likely reconstruction. Or the least unlikely."

"She may have tried variations. Would you like to go see?"

"No, I, I think not, unless you want to. This has been overwhelming, hasn't it?" She hesitated. "Besides, well—"

He nodded. "Yeh." With a gesture at the soundless, motionless, smokeless city below and halidoms around: "Spooky. At best, a museum exhibit. Not much to our purpose, I'm afraid."

She met his eyes. "Your purpose. I'm only a—not even a guide, really. Gaia's voice to you? No, just a, an undertone of her, if that." The smile that touched her lips was somehow forlorn. "I suspect my main reason for existing again is to keep you company."

He laughed and offered her a hand, which for a moment she clasped tightly. "I'm very glad of the company, eccentric Miss Ashcroft."

Her smile warmed and widened. "Thank you, kind sir. And I am glad to be . . . alive . . . today. What should we do next?"

"Visit some living history, I think," he said. "Why not Hellenic?"

She struck her palms together. "The age of Pericles!"

He frowned. "Well, I don't know about that. The Peloponnesian War, the plague—and foreigners like us, barbarians, you a woman, we wouldn't be too well received, would we?"

He heard how she put disappointment aside and looked forward anew. "When and where, then?"

"Aristotle's time? If I remember rightly, Greece was peaceful then, no matter how much hell Alexander was raising abroad, and the society was getting quite cosmopolitan. Less patriarchal, too. Anyhow, Aristotle's always interested me. In a way, he was one of the earliest scientists."

"We had better inquire first. But before that, let's go home to a nice hot cup of tea!"

They returned to the house at the same moment as they left it, to avoid perturbing the servants. There they found that lack of privacy joined with exhaustion to keep them from speaking of anything other than trivia. However, that was all right; they were good talkmates.

The next morning, which was brilliant, they went out into the garden and settled on a bench by the fish basin. Drops of rain glistened on flowers, whose fragrance awoke with the strengthening sunshine. Nothing else was in sight or earshot. This time Christian addressed the amulets. He felt suddenly heavy around his neck, and the words came out awkwardly. He need not have said them aloud, but it helped him give shape to his ideas.

The reply entered directly into their brains. He rendered it to himself, irrationally, as in a dry, professorish tenor:

"Only a single Hellenic milieu has been carried through many generations. It includes the period you have in mind. It commenced at the point of approximately 500 B.C., with an emulation as historically accurate as possible."

But nearly everyone then alive was lost to history, thought Christian. Except for the few who were in the chronicles, the whole population must needs be created out of Gaia's imagination, guided by knowledge and logic; and those few named persons were themselves almost entirely new-made, their very DNA arbitrarily laid out.

"The sequence was revised as necessary," the amulet continued.

Left to itself, that history would soon have drifted completely away from the documents, and eventually from the archaeology, Christian thought. Gaia saw this start to happen, over and over. She rewrote the program—events, memories, personalities, bodies, births, life spans, deaths—and let it resume until it deviated again. Over and over. The morning felt abruptly cold.

"Much was learned on every such occasion," said the amulet. "The situation appeared satisfactory by the time Macedonian hegemony was inevitable, and thereafter the sequence was left to play itself out undisturbed. Naturally, it still did not proceed identically with the historical past. Neither Aristotle nor Alexander were born. Instead, a reasonably realistic conqueror lived to a ripe age and bequeathed a reasonably well constructed empire. He did have a Greek teacher in his youth, who had been a disciple of Plato."

"Who was that?" Christian asked out of a throat gone dry.

"His name was Eumenes. In many respects he was equivalent to Aristotle, but had a more strongly empirical orientation. This was planned."

Eumenes was specially ordained, then. Why?

"If we appear and meet him, w-won't that change what comes after?"

"Probably not to any significant extent. Or if it does, that will not matter. The original sequence is in Gaia's database. Your visit will, in effect, be a reactivation."

"Not one for your purpose," Laurinda whispered into the air. "What was it? What happened in that world?"

"The objective was experimental, to study the possible engendering of a scientific-technological revolution analogous to that of the seventeenth century A.D., with accompanying social developments that might foster the evolution of a stable democracy."

Christian told himself furiously to pull out of his funk. "Did it?" He challenged. The reply was calm. "Do you wish to study it?"

Christian had not expected any need to muster his courage. After a minute he said, word by slow word, "Yes, I think that might be more useful than meeting your philosopher. Can you show us the outcome of the experiment?"

Laurinda joined in: "Oh, I know there can't be any single, simple picture. But can you bring us to a, a scene that will give an impression—a kind of epitome— like, oh, King John at Runnymede or Elizabeth the First knighting Francis Drake or Einstein and Bohr talking about the state of their world?"

"An extreme possibility occurs in a year corresponding to your 894 A.D.," the amulet told him. "I suggest Athens as the locale. Be warned, it is dangerous. I can protect you, or remove you, but human affairs are inherently chaotic and this situation is more unpredictable than most. It could escape my control."

"I'll go," Christian snapped.

"And I," Laurinda said.

He glared at her. "No. You heard. It's dangerous."

Gone quite calm, she stated, "It is necessary for me. Remember, I travel on behalf of Gaia."

Gaia, who let the thing come to pass.

Transfer.

For an instant, they glanced at themselves. They knew the amulets would convert their garb to something appropriate. She wore a gray gown, belted, reaching halfway down her calves, with shoes, stockings, and a scarf over hair coiled in braids. He was in tunic, trousers, and boots of the same coarse materials, a sheath knife at his hip and a long-barreled firearm slung over his back.

Their surroundings smote them. They stood in a Propylaea that was scarcely more than tumbled stones and snags of sculpture. The Parthenon was not so shattered, but scarred, weathered, here and there buttressed with brickwork from which thrust the mouths of rusted cannon. All else was ruin. The Erechtheum looked as if it had been quarried. Below them, the city burned. They could see little of it through smoke that stained the sky and savaged their nostrils. A roar of conflagration reached them, and bursts of gunfire.

A woman came running out of the haze, up the great staircase. She was young, dark-haired, unkempt, ragged, begrimed, desperate. A man came after, a burly blond in a fur cap, dirty red coat, and leather breeches. Beneath a sweeping mustache, he leered. He too was armed, murderously big knife, firearm in right hand.

The woman saw Christian looming before her. *"Voetho!"* she screamed. *"On-ome Theou, kyrie, voetho!"* She caught her foot against a step and fell. Her pursuer stopped before she could rise and stamped a boot down on her back.

Through his amulet, Christian understood the cry. "Help, in God's name, sir, help!" Fleetingly he thought the language must be a debased Greek. The other man snarled at him and brought weapon to shoulder.

Christian had no time to unlimber his. While the stranger was in motion, he bent, snatched up a rock—a fragment of a marble head—and cast. It thudded against the stranger's nose. He lurched back, his face a sudden red grotesque. His gun clattered to the stairs. He howled.

With the quickness that was his in emergencies, Christian rejected grabbing his own firearm. He had seen that its lock was of peculiar design. He might not be able to discharge it fast enough. He drew his knife and lunged downward. "Get away, you swine, before I open your guts!" he shouted. The words came out in the woman's language.

The other man retched, turned, and staggered off. Well before he reached the bottom of the hill, smoke had swallowed sight of him. Christian halted at the woman's huddled form and sheathed his blade. "Here, sister," he said, offering his hand, "come along. Let's get to shelter. There may be more of them."

She crawled to her feet, gasping, leaned heavily on his arm, and limped beside him up to the broken gateway. Her features Mediterranean, she was doubtless a native. She looked half starved. Laurinda came to her side. Between them, the visitors got her into the portico of the Parthenon. Beyond a smashed door lay an interior dark and empty of everything but litter. It would be defensible if necessary.

An afterthought made Christian swear at himself. He went back for the enemy's weapon. When he returned, Laurinda sat with her arms around the woman, crooning comfort. "There, darling, there, you're safe with us. Don't be afraid. We'll take care of you."

The fugitive lifted big eyes full of night. "Are . . . you . . . angels from heaven?" she mumbled.

"No, only mortals like you," Laurinda answered through tears. That was not exactly true, Christian thought; but what else could she say? "We do not even know your name."

"I am . . . Zoe . . . Comnenaina—"

"Bone-dry, I hear from your voice." Laurinda lifted her head. Her lips moved in silent command. A jug appeared on the floor, bedewed with cold. "Here is water. Drink."

Zoe had not noticed the miracle. She snatched the vessel and drained it in gulp after gulp. When she was through she set it down and said, "Thank you," dully but with something of strength and reason again in her.

"Who was that after you?" Christian asked.

She drew knees to chin, hugged herself, stared before her, and replied in a dead voice, "A Flemic soldier. They broke into our house. I saw them stab my father. They laughed and laughed. I ran out the back and down the streets. I thought I could hide on the Acropolis. Nobody comes here anymore. That one saw me and came after. I suppose he would have killed me when he was done. That would have been better than if he took me away with him."

Laurinda nodded. "An invading army," she said as tonelessly. "They took the city and now they are sacking it."

Christian thumped the butt of his gun down on the stones. "Does Gaia let this go *on*?" he grated.

Laurinda lifted her gaze to his. It pleaded. "She must. Humans must have free will. Otherwise they're puppets."

"But how did they get into this mess?" Christian demanded. "Explain it if you can!"

The amulet(s) replied with the same impersonality as before:

"The Hellenistic era developed scientific method. This, together with the expansion of commerce and geographical knowledge, produced an industrial revolution and parliamentary democracy. However, neither the science nor the technology progressed beyond an approximate equivalent of your eighteenth century. Unwise social and fiscal policies led to breakdown, dictatorship, and repeated warfare."

Christian's grin bared teeth. "That sounds familiar."

"Alexander Tytler said it in our eighteenth century," Laurinda muttered unevenly. "No republic has long outlived the discovery by a majority of its people that they could vote themselves largesse from the public treasury." Aloud: "Christian, they were only human."

Zoe hunched, lost in her sorrow.

"You oversimplify," stated the amulet voice. "But this is not a history lesson. To continue the outline, inevitably engineering information spread to the warlike barbarians of northern Europe and western Asia. If you question why they were granted existence, reflect that a population confined to the littoral of an inland sea could not model any possible material world. The broken-down societies of the South were unable to change their characters, or prevail over them, or eventually hold them off. The end results are typified by what you see around you."

"The Dark Ages," Christian said dully. "What happens after them? What kind of new civilization?"

"None. This sequence terminates in one more of its years."

"Huh?" he gasped. "Destroyed?"

"No. The program ceases to run. The emulation stops."

"My God! Those millions of lives—as real as, as mine—"

Laurinda stood up and held her arms out into the fouled air. "Does Gaia know, then, does Gaia know this time line would never get any happier?" she cried.

"No," said the voice in their brains. "Doubtless the potential of further progress exists. However, you forget that while Gaia's capacities are large, they are not infinite. The more attention she devotes to one history, the details of its planet as well as the length of its course, the less she has to give to others. The probability is too small that this sequence will lead to a genuinely new form of society."

Slowly, Laurinda nodded. "I see."

"I don't," Christian snapped. "Except that Gaia's inhuman."

Laurinda shook her head and laid a hand on his. "No, not that. Posthuman. *We* built the first artificial intelligences." After a moment: "Gaia isn't cruel. The universe often is, and she didn't create it. She's seeking something better than blind chance can make."

"Maybe." His glance fell on Zoe. "Look, something's got to be done for this poor soul. Never mind if we change the history. It's due to finish soon anyway."

Laurinda swallowed and wiped her eyes. "Give her her last year in peace," she said into the air. "Please."

Objects appeared in the room behind the doorway. "Here are food, wine, clean water," said the unheard voice. "Advise her to return downhill after dark, find some friends, and lead them back. A small party, hiding in these ruins, can hope to survive until the invaders move on."

"It isn't worthwhile doing more, is it?" Christian said bitterly. "Not to you."

"Do you wish to end your investigation?"

"No, be damned if I will."

"Nor I," said Laurinda. "But when we're through here, when we've done the pitiful little we can for this girl, take us home."

Peace dwelt in England. Clouds towered huge and white, blue-shadowed from the sunlight spilling past them. Along the left side of a lane, poppies blazed in a grainfield goldening toward harvest. On the right stretched the manifold greens of a pasture where cattle drowsed beneath a broad-crowned oak. Man and woman rode side by side. Hoofs thumped softly, saddle leather creaked, the sweet smell of horse mingled with herbal pungencies, a blackbird whistled.

"No, I don't suppose Gaia will ever restart any program she's terminated," Laurinda said. "But it's no worse than death, and death is seldom that easy."

"The scale of it," Christian protested, then sighed. "But I daresay Wayfarer will tell me I'm being sloppy sentimental, and when I've rejoined him I'll agree." Wryness added that that had better be true. He would no longer be separate, an avatar; he would be one with a far greater entity, which would in its turn remerge with a greater still.

"Without Gaia, they would never have existed, those countless lives, generation after generation after generation," Laurinda said. "Their worst miseries they brought on themselves. If any of them are ever to find their way to something better, truly better, she has to keep making fresh starts."

"Mm, I can't help remembering all the millennialists and utopians who slaughtered people wholesale, or tortured them or threw them into concentration camps, if their behavior didn't fit the convenient attainment of the inspired vision."

"No, no, it's not like that! Don't you see? She gives them their freedom to be themselves and, and to become more."

"Seems to me she adjusts the parameters and boundary conditions till the setup looks promising before she lets the experiment run." Christian frowned. "But I admit, it isn't believable that she does it simply because she's . . . bored and lonely. Not when the whole fellowship of her kind is open to her. Maybe we haven't the brains to know what her reasons are. Maybe she's explaining them to Wayfarer, or directly to Alpha," although communication among the stars would take decades at least.

"Do you want to go on nonetheless?" she asked.

"I said I do. I'm supposed to. But you?"

"Yes. I don't want to, well, fail her."

"I'm sort of at a loss what to try next, and not sure it's wise to let the amulets decide."

"But they can help us, counsel us." Laurinda drew breath. "Please. If you will. The next world we go to—could it be gentle? That horror we saw—"

He reached across to take her hand. "Exactly what I was thinking. Have you a suggestion?"

She nodded. "York Minster. It was in sad condition when I . . . lived . . . but I saw pictures and—It was one of the loveliest churches ever built, in the loveliest old town."

"Excellent idea. Not another lifeless piece of archive, though. A complete environment." Christian pondered. "We'll inquire first, naturally, but offhand I'd guess the Edwardian period would suit us well. On the Continent they called it the *belle époque.*"

"Splendid!" she exclaimed. Already her spirits were rising anew.

Transfer.

They arrived near the west end, in the south aisle.

Worshippers were few, scattered closer to the altar rail. In the dimness, under the glories of glass and soaring Perpendicular arches, their advent went unobserved. Windows in that direction glowed more vividly—rose, gold, blue, the cool gray-green of the Five Sisters—than the splendor above their backs; it was a Tuesday morning in June. Incense wove its odor through the ringing chant from the choir.

Christian tautened. "That's Latin," he whispered. "In England, 1900?" He glanced down at his garments and hers, and peered ahead. Shirt, coat, trousers for him, with a hat laid on the pew; ruffled blouse, ankle-length gown, and lacy bonnet for her; but—"The clothes aren't right either."

"Hush," Laurinda answered as low. "Wait. We were told this wouldn't be our 1900. Here may be the only York Minster in all of Gaia."

He nodded stiffly. It was clear that the node had never attempted a perfect reproduction of any past milieu—impossible, and pointless to boot. Often, though not necessarily always, she took an approximation as a starting point; but it never went on to the same destiny. What were the roots of this day?

"Relax," Laurinda urged. "It's beautiful."

He did his best, and indeed the Roman Catholic mass at the hour of tierce sang some tranquility into his heart.

After the Nunc Dimittis, when clergy and laity had departed, the two could wander around and savor. Emerging at last, they spent a while looking upon the carven tawny limestone of the front. This was no Parthenon; it was a different upsurging of the same miracle. But around it lay a world to discover. With half a sigh and half a smile, they set forth.

The delightful narrow "gates," walled in with half-timbered houses, lured them. More modern streets and buildings, above all the people therein, captured them. York was a living town, a market town, core of a wide hinterland, node of a nation. It racketed, it bustled.

The half smile faded. A wholly foreign setting would not have felt as wrong as one that was half homelike.

Clothing styles were not radically unlike what pictures and historical dramas had once shown; but they were not identical. The English chatter was in no dialect of English known to Christian or Laurinda, and repeatedly they heard versions of German. A small, high-stacked steam locomotive pulled a train into a station of somehow Teutonic architecture. No early automobiles stuttered along the thoroughfares. Horse-drawn vehicles moved crowdedly, but the pavements were clean and the smell of dung faint because the animals wore a kind of diapers. A flag above a post office (?), fluttering in the wind, displayed a cross of St. Andrew on which was superimposed a two-headed gold eagle. A man with a megaphone bellowed at the throng to stand aside and make way for a military squadron. In blue uniforms, rifles on shoulders, they quick-marched to commands barked in German. Individual soldiers, presumably on leave, were everywhere. A boy went by, shrilly hawking newspapers, and Christian saw WAR in a headline.

"Listen, amulet," he muttered finally, "where can we get a beer?"

"A public house will admit you if you go in by the couples' entrance," replied the soundless voice.

So, no unescorted women allowed. Well, Christian thought vaguely, hadn't that been the case in his Edwardian years, at any rate in respectable taverns? A signboard jutting from a Tudor façade read GEORGE AND DRAGON. The wainscoted room inside felt equally English.

Custom was plentiful and noisy, tobacco smoke thick, but he and Laurinda found a table in a corner where they could talk without anybody else paying attention. The brew that a barmaid fetched was of Continental character. He didn't give it the heed it deserved.

"I don't think we've found our peaceful world after all," he said.

Laurinda looked beyond him, into distances where he could not follow. "Will we ever?" she wondered. "Can any be, if it's human?"

He grimaced. "Well, let's find out what the hell's going on here."

"You can have a detailed explanation if you wish," said the voice in their heads. "You would be better advised to accept a bare outline, as you did before."

"Instead of loading ourselves down with the background of a world that never was," he mumbled.

"That never was ours," Laurinda corrected him.

"Carry on."

"This sequence was generated as of its fifteenth century A.D.," said the voice. "The conciliar movement was made to succeed, rather than failing as it did in your history."

"Uh, conciliar movement?"

"The ecclesiastical councils of Constance and later of Basel attempted to heal the Great Schism and reform the government of the Church. Here they accomplished it, giving back to the bishops some of the power that over the centuries had accrued to the popes, working out a reconciliation with the Hussites, and making other important changes. As a result, no Protestant breakaway occurred, nor wars of religion, and the Church remained a counterbalance to the state, preventing the rise of absolute monarchies."

"Why, that's wonderful," Laurinda whispered.

"Not too wonderful by now," Christian said grimly. "What happened?"

"In brief, Germany was spared the devastation of the Thirty Years' War and a long-lasting division into quarrelsome principalities. It was unified in the seventeenth century and soon became the dominant European power, colonizing and conquering eastward. Religious and cultural differences from the Slavs proved irreconcilable. As the harsh imperium provoked increasing restlessness, it perforce grew more severe, causing more rebellion. Meanwhile it decayed within, until today it has broken apart and the Russians are advancing on Berlin."

"I see. What about science and technology?"

"They have developed more slowly than in your history, although you have noted the existence of a fossil-fueled industry and inferred an approximately Lagrangian level of theory."

"The really brilliant eras were when all hell broke loose, weren't they?" Christian mused. "This Europe went through less agony, and invented and discovered less. Coincidence?"

"What about government?" Laurinda asked.

"For a time, parliaments flourished, more powerful than kings, emperors, or popes," said the voice. "In most Western countries they still wield considerable influence."

"As the creatures of special interests, I'll bet," Christian rasped. "All right, what comes next?"

Gaia knew. He sat in a reactivation of something she probably played to a finish thousands of years ago.

"Scientific and technological advance proceeds, accelerating, through a long period of general turbulence. At the termination point—"

"Never mind!" Oblivion might be better than a nuclear war.

Silence fell at the table. The life that filled the pub with its noise felt remote, unreal.

"We dare not weep," Laurinda finally said. "Not yet."

Christian shook himself. "Europe was never the whole of Earth," he growled. "How many worlds has Gaia made?"

"Many," the voice told him.

"Show us one that's really foreign. If you agree, Laurinda."

She squared her shoulders. "Yes, do." After a moment: "Not here. If we disappeared it would shock them. It might change the whole future."

"Hardly enough to notice," Christian said. "And would it matter in the long run? But, yeh, let's be off."

They wandered out, among marvels gone meaningless, until they found steps leading up onto the medieval wall. Thence they looked across roofs and river and Yorkshire beyond, finding they were alone.

"Now take us away," Christian ordered.

"You have not specified any type of world," said the voice.

"Surprise us."

Transfer.

The sky stood enormous, bleached blue, breezes warm underneath. A bluff overlooked a wide brown river. Trees grew close to its edge, tall, pale of bark, leaves silver-green and shivery. Christian recognized them, cottonwoods. He was somewhere in west central North America, then. Uneasy shadows lent camouflage if he and Laurinda kept still. Across the river the land reached broad, roads twisting their way through cultivation—mainly wheat and Indian corn—that seemed to be parceled out among small farms, each with its buildings, house, barn, occasional stable or workshop. The sweeping lines of the ruddy-tiled roofs looked Asian. He spied oxcarts and a few horseback riders on the roads, workers in the fields, but at their distance he couldn't identify race or garb. Above yonder horizon thrust clustered towers that also suggested the Orient. If they belonged to a city, it must be compact, not sprawling over the countryside but neatly drawn into itself.

One road ran along the farther riverbank. A procession went upon it. An elephant led, as richly caparisoned as the man under the silk awning of a howdah. Shaven-headed men in yellow robes walked after, flanked by horsemen who bore poles from which pennons streamed scarlet and gold. The sound of slowly beaten gongs and minor-key chanting came faint through the wind.

Christian snapped his fingers. "Stupid me!" he muttered. "Give us a couple of opticals."

Immediately he and Laurinda held the devices. From his era, they fitted into the palm but projected an image at any magnification desired, with no lenses off which light could glint to betray. He peered back and forth for minutes. Yes, the appearance was quite Chinese, or Chinese-derived, except that a number of the individuals he studied had more of an American countenance and the leader on the elephant wore a feather bonnet above his robe.

"How quiet here," Laurinda said.

"You are at the height of the Great Peace," the amulet voice answered.

"How many like that were there ever?" Christian wondered. "Where, when, how?"

"You are in North America, in the twenty-second century by your reckoning. Chinese navigators arrived on the Pacific shore seven hundred years ago, and colonists followed."

In this world, Christian thought, Europe and Africa were surely a sketch, mere geography, holding a few primitive tribes at most, unless nothing was there but ocean. Simplify, simplify.

"Given the distances to sail and the dangers, the process was slow," the voice went on. "While the newcomers displaced or subjugated the natives wherever they settled, most remained free for a long time, acquired the technology, and also developed resistance to introduced diseases. Eventually, being on roughly equal terms, the races began to mingle, genetically and culturally. The settlers mitigated the savagery of the religions they had encountered, but learned from the societies, as well as teaching. You behold the outcome."

"The Way of the Buddha?" Laurinda asked very softly.

"As influenced by Daoism and local nature cults. It is a harmonious faith, without sects or heresies, pervading the civilization."

"Everything can't be pure loving-kindness," Christian said.

"Certainly not. But the peace that the Emperor Wei Zhi-fu brought about has lasted for a century and will for another two. If you travel, you will find superb achievements in the arts and in graciousness."

"Another couple of centuries." Laurinda's tones wavered the least bit. "Afterward?"

"It doesn't last," Christian predicted. "These are humans too. And—tell me— do they ever get to a real science?"

"No," said the presence. "Their genius lies in other realms. But the era of warfare to come will drive the development of a remarkable empirical technology."

"What era?"

"China never recognized the independence that this country proclaimed for itself, nor approved of its miscegenation. A militant dynasty will arise, which overruns a western hemisphere weakened by the religious and secular quarrels that do at last break out."

"And the conquerors will fall in their turn. Unless Gaia makes an end first. She does—she did—sometime, didn't she?"

"All things are finite. Her creations too."

The leaves rustled through muteness.

"Do you wish to go into the city and look about?" asked the presence. "It can be arranged for you to meet some famous persons."

"No," Christian said. "Not yet, anyway. Maybe later."

Laurinda sighed. "We'd rather go home now and rest."

"And think," Christian said. "Yes."

Transfer.

The sun over England seemed milder than for America. Westering, it sent rays through windows to glow in wood, caress marble and the leather bindings of books, explode into rainbows where they met cut glass, evoke flower aromas from a jar of potpourri.

Laurinda opened a bureau drawer. She slipped the chain of her amulet over her head and tossed the disc in. Christian blinked, nodded, and followed suit. She closed the drawer.

"We do need to be by ourselves for a while," she said. "This hasn't been a dreadful day like, like before, but I am so tired."

"Understandable," he replied.

"You?"

"I will be soon, no doubt."

"Those worlds—already they feel like dreams I've wakened from."

"An emotional retreat from them, I suppose. Not cowardice, no, no, just a necessary, temporary rest. You shared their pain. You're too sweet for your own good, Laurinda."

She smiled. "How you misjudge me. I'm not quite ready to collapse yet, if you aren't."

"Thunder, no."

She took crystal glasses out of a cabinet, poured from a decanter on a sideboard, and gestured invitation. The port fondled their tongues. They stayed on their feet, look meeting look.

"I daresay we'd be presumptuous and foolish to try finding any pattern, this early in our search," she ventured. "Those peeks we've had, out of who knows how many worlds—each as real as we are." She shivered.

"I may have a hunch," he said slowly.

"A what?"

"An intimation, an impression, a wordless kind of guess. Why has Gaia been doing it? I can't believe it's nothing but pastime."

"Nor I. Nor can I believe she would let such terrible things happen if she could prevent them. How can an intellect, a soul, like hers be anything but good?"

So Laurinda thought, Christian reflected; but she was an avatar of Gaia. He didn't suppose that affected the fairness of her conscious mind; he had come to know her rather well. But neither did it prove the nature, the ultimate intent, of Earth's node. It merely showed that the living Laurinda Ashcroft had been a decent person.

She took a deep draught from her glass before going on: "I think, myself, she is in the same position as the traditional God. Being good, she wants to share existence with others, and so creates them. But to make them puppets, automatons, would be senseless. They have to have consciousness and free will. Therefore they are able to sin, and do, all too often."

"Why hasn't she made them morally stronger?"

"Because she's chosen to make them human. And what are we but a specialized African ape?" Laurinda's tone lowered; she stared into the wine. "Specialized to make tools and languages and dreams; but the dreams can be nightmares."

In Gaia's and Alpha's kind laired no ancient beast, Christian thought. The human elements in them were long since absorbed, tamed, transfigured. His resurrection and hers must be nearly unique.

Not wanting to hurt her, he shaped his phrases with care. "Your idea is reasonable, but I'm afraid it leaves some questions dangling. Gaia does intervene, again and again. The amulets admit it. When the emulations get too far off track, she changes them and their people." Until she shuts them down, he did not add. "Why is she doing it, running history after history, experiment after experiment— why?"

Laurinda winced. "To, to learn about this strange race of ours?"

He nodded. "Yes, that's my hunch. Not even she, nor the galactic brain itself, can take first principles and compute what any human situation will lead to. Human affairs are chaotic. But chaotic systems do have structures, attractors, constraints. But letting things happen, through countless variations, you might discover a few general laws, which courses are better and which worse." He tilted his goblet. "To what end, though? There are no more humans in the outside universe. There haven't been for—how many million years? No, unless it actually is callous curiosity, I can't yet guess what she's after."

"Nor I." Laurinda finished her drink. "Now I am growing very tired, very fast."

"I'm getting that way too." Christian paused. "How about we go sleep till evening? Then a special dinner, and our heads ought to be more clear."

Briefly, she took his hand. "Until evening, dear friend."

The night was young and gentle. A full moon dappled the garden. Wine had raised a happy mood, barely tinged with wistfulness. Gravel scrunched rhythmically underfoot as Laurinda and Christian danced, humming the waltz melody together. When they were done, they sat down, laughing, by the basin. Brightness from above overflowed it. He had earlier put his amulet back on just long enough to command that a guitar appear for him. Now he took it up. He had never seen anything more beautiful than she was in the moonlight. He sang a song to her that he had made long ago when he was mortal.

> *"Lightfoot, Lightfoot, lead the measure*
> *As we dance the summer in!*
> *'Lifetime is our only treasure.*
> *Spend it well, on love and pleasure,'*
> *Warns the lilting violin.*
>
> *"If we'll see the year turn vernal*
> *Once again, lies all with chance.*
> *Yes, this ordering's infernal,*
> *But we'll make our own eternal*
> *Fleeting moment where we dance.*
>
> *"So shall we refuse compliance*
> *When across the green we whirl,*
> *Giving entropy defiance,*
> *Strings and winds in our alliance.*
> *Be a victor. Kiss me, girl!"*

Suddenly she was in his arms.

8

Where the hills loomed highest above the river that cut through them, a slope on the left bank rose steep but thinly forested. Kalava directed the lifeboat carrying his party to land. The slaves at the oars grunted with double effort. Sweat sheened on their skins and runneled down the straining bands of muscle; it was a day when the sun blazed from a sky just half clouded. The prow grated on a sandbar in the shallows. Kalava told off two of his sailors to stand guard over boat and rowers. With the other four and Ilyandi, he waded ashore and began to climb.

It went slowly but stiffly. On top they found a crest with a view that snatched a gasp from the woman and a couple of amazed oaths from the men. Northward the terrain fell still more sharply, so that they looked over treetops down to the bottom of the range and across a valley awash with the greens and russets of growth. The river shone through it like a drawn blade, descending from dimly seen foothills and the sawtooth mountains beyond them. Two swordwings hovered on high, watchful for prey. Sunbeams shot past gigantic cloudbanks, filling their whiteness with cavernous shadows. Somehow the air felt cooler here, and the herbal smells gave benediction.

"It is fair, ai, it is as fair as the Sunset Kingdom of legend," Ilyandi breathed at last.

She stood slim in the man's kirtle and buskins that she, as a Vilku, could with propriety wear on trek. The wind fluttered her short locks. The coppery skin was as wet and almost as odorous as Kalava's midnight black, but she was no more wearied than any of her companions.

The sailor Urko scowled at the trees and underbrush crowding close on either side. Only the strip up which the travelers had come was partly clear, perhaps because of a landslide in the past. "Too much woods," he grumbled. It had, in fact, been a struggle to move about wherever they landed. They could not attempt the hunting that had been easy on the coast. Luckily, the water teemed with fish.

"Logging will cure that." Kalava's words throbbed. "And then what farms!" He stared raptly into the future.

Turning down-to-earth: "But we've gone far enough, now that we've gained an idea of the whole country. Three days, and I'd guess two more going back downstream. Any longer, and the crew at the ship could grow fearful. We'll turn around here."

"Other ships will bring others, explorers," Ilyandi said.

"Indeed they will. And I'll skipper the first of them."

A rustling and crackling broke from the tangle to the right, through the boom of the wind. "What's that?" barked Taltara.

"Some big animal," Kalava replied. "Stand alert."

The mariners formed a line. Three grounded the spears they carried; the fourth unslung a crossbow from his shoulders and armed it. Kalava waved Ilyandi to go behind them and drew his sword.

The thing parted a brake and trod forth into the open.

"Aah!" wailed Yarvonin. He dropped his spear and whirled about to flee.

"Stand fast!" Kalava shouted. "Urko, shoot whoever runs, if I don't cut him down myself. Hold, your whoresons, hold!"

The thing stopped. For a span of many hammering heartbeats, none moved.

It was a sight to terrify. Taller by a head than the tallest man it sheered, but that head was faceless save for a horrible blank mask. Two thick arms sprouted from either side, the lower pair of hands wholly misshapen. A humped back did not belie the sense of their strength. As the travelers watched, the thing sprouted a skeletal third leg, to stand better on the uneven ground. Whether it was naked or armored in plate, in this full daylight it bore the hue of dusk.

"Steady, boys, steady," Kalava urged between clenched teeth. Ilyandi stepped from shelter to join him. An eldritch calm was upon her. "My lady, what *is* it?" he appealed.

"A god, or a messenger from the gods, I think." He could barely make her out beneath the wind.

"A demon," Eivala groaned, though he kept his post.

"No, belike not. We Vilkui have some knowledge of these matters. But, true, it is not fiery—and I never thought I would meet one—in this life—"

Ilyandi drew a long breath, briefly knotted her fists, then moved to take stance in front of the men. Having touched the withered sprig of tekin pinned at her breast, she covered her eyes and genuflected before straightening again to confront the mask.

The thing did not move, but, mouthless, it spoke, in a deep and resonant voice. The sounds were incomprehensible. After a moment it ceased, then spoke anew in an equally alien tongue. On its third try, Kalava exclaimed, "Hoy, that's from the Shining Fields!"

The thing fell silent, as if considering what it had heard. Thereupon words rolled out in the Ulonaian of Sirsu. "Be not afraid. I mean you no harm."

"What a man knows is little, what he understands is less, therefore let him bow down to wisdom," Ilyandi recited. She turned her head long enough to tell her companions: "Lay aside your weapons. Do reverence."

Clumsily, they obeyed.

In the blank panel of the blank skull appeared a man's visage. Though it was black, the features were not quite like anything anyone had seen before, nose broad, lips heavy, eyes round, hair tightly curled. Nevertheless, to spirits half stunned the magic was vaguely reassuring.

Her tone muted but level, Ilyandi asked, "What would you of us, lord?"

"It is hard to say," the strange one answered. After a pause: "Bewilderment goes through the world. I too . . . You may call me Brannock."

The captain rallied his courage. "And I am Kalava, Kurvo's son, of Clan Samayoki." Aside to Ilyandi, low: "No disrespect that I don't name you, my lady. Let him work any spells on me." Despite the absence of visible genitals, already the humans thought of Brannock as male.

"My lord needs no names to work his will," she said. "I hight Ilyandi, Lytin's daughter, born into Clan Arvala, now a Vilku of the fifth rank."

Kalava cleared his throat and added, "By your leave, lord, we'll not name the others just yet. They're scared aplenty as is." He heard a growl at his back and inwardly grinned. Shame would help hold them steady. As for him, dread was giving way to a thrumming keenness.

"You do not live here, do you?" Brannock asked.

"No," Kalava said, "we're scouts from overseas."

Ilyandi frowned at his presumption and addressed Brannock: "Lord, do we trespass? We knew not this ground was forbidden."

"It isn't," the other said. "Not exactly. But—" The face in the panel smiled. "Come, ease off, let us talk. We've much to talk about."

"He sounds not unlike a man," Kalava murmured to Ilyandi.

She regarded him. "If you be the man."

Brannock pointed to a big old gnarlwood with an overarching canopy of leaves. "Yonder is shade." He retracted his third leg and strode off. A fallen log took up most of the space. He leaned over and dragged it aside. Kalava's whole gang could not have done so. The action was not really necessary, but the display of power, benignly used, encouraged them further. Still, it was with hushed awe that the crewmen sat down in the paintwort. The captain, the Vilku, and the strange one remained standing.

"Tell me of yourselves," Brannock said mildly.

"Surely you know, lord," Ilyandi replied.

"That is as may be."

"He wants us to," Kalava said.

In the course of the next short while, prompted by questions, the pair gave a bare-bones account. Brannock's head within his head nodded. "I see. You are the first humans ever in this country. But your people have lived a long time in their homeland, have they not?"

"From time out of mind, lord," Ilyandi said, "though legend holds that our forebears came from the south."

Brannock smiled again. "You have been very brave to meet me like this, m-m, my lady. But you did tell your friend that your order has encountered beings akin to me."

"You heard her whisper, across half a spearcast?" Kalava blurted.

"Or you hear us think, lord," Ilyandi said.

Brannock turned grave. "No. Not that. Else why would I have needed your story?"

"Dare I ask whence you come?"

"I shall not be angry. But it is nothing I can quite explain. You can help by telling me about those beings you know of."

Ilyandi could not hide a sudden tension. Kalava stiffened beside her. Even the drumbstruck sailors must have wondered whether a god would have spoken thus.

Ilyandi chose her words with care. "Beings from on high have appeared in the past to certain Vilkui or, sometimes, chieftains. They gave commands as to what the folk should or should not do. Ofttimes those commands were hard to fathom. Why must the Kivalui build watermills in the Swift River, when they had ample slaves to grind their grain?—But knowledge was imparted, too, counsel about where and how to search out the ways of nature. Always, the high one forbade open talk about his coming. The accounts lie in the secret annals of the Vilkui. But to you, lord—"

"What did those beings look like?" Brannock demanded sharply.

"Fiery shapes, winged or manlike, voices like great trumpets—"

"Ruvio's ax!" burst from Kalava. "The thing that passed overhead at sea!"

The men on the ground shuddered.

"Yes," Brannock said, most softly, "I may have had a part there. But as for the rest—"

His face flickered and vanished. After an appalling moment it reappeared.

"I am sorry, I meant not to frighten you, I forgot," he said. The expression went stony, the voice tolled. "Hear me. There is war in heaven. I am cast away from a battle, and enemy hunters may find me at any time. I carry a word that must, it is vital that it reach a certain place, a . . . a holy mountain in the north. Will you give aid?"

Kalava gripped his sword hilt so that it was as if the skin would split across his knuckles. The blood had left Ilyandi's countenance. She stood ready to be blasted with fire while she asked, "Lord Brannock, how do we know you are of the gods?"

Nothing struck her down. "I am not," he told her. "I too can die. But they whom I serve, they dwell in the stars."

The multitude of mystery, seen only when night clouds parted, but skythinkers taught that they circled always around the Axle of the North. . . . Ilyandi kept her back straight. "Then can you tell me of the stars?"

"You are intelligent as well as brave," Brannock said. "Listen."

Kalava could not follow what passed between those two. The sailors cowered.

At the end, with tears upon her cheekbones, Ilyandi stammered, "Yes, he knows the constellations, he knows of the ecliptic and the precession and the returns of the Great Comet, he is from the stars. Trust him. We, we dare not do otherwise."

Kalava let go his weapon, brought hand to breast in salute, and asked, "How can we poor creatures help you, lord?"

"*You* are the news I bear," said Brannock.

"What?"

"I have no time to explain—if I could. The hunters may find me at any instant. But maybe, maybe you could go on for me after they do."

"Escaping what overpowered you?" Kalava's laugh rattled. "Well, a man might try."

"The gamble is desperate. Yet if we win, choose your reward, whatever it may be, and I think you shall have it."

Ilyandi lowered her head above folded hands. "Enough to have served those who dwell beyond the moon."

"Humph," Kalava could not keep from muttering, "if they want to pay for it, why not?" Aloud, almost eagerly, his own head raised into the wind that tossed his whitened mane: "What'd you have us do?"

Brannock's regard matched his. "I have thought about this. Can one of you come with me? I will carry him, faster than he can go. As for what happens later, we will speak of that along the way."

The humans stood silent.

"If I but had the woodcraft," Ilyandi then said. "Ai, but I would! To the stars!"

Kalava shook his head. "No, my lady. You go back with these fellows. Give heart to them at the ship. Make them finish the repairs." He glanced at Brannock. "How long will this foray take, lord?"

"I can reach the mountaintop in two days and a night," the other said. "If I am caught and you must go on alone, I think a good man could make the whole distance from here in ten or fifteen days."

Kalava laughed, more gladly than before. "*Courser* won't be seaworthy for quite a bit longer than that. Let's away." To Ilyandi: "If I'm not back by the time she's ready, sail home without me."

"No—" she faltered.

"Yes. Mourn me not. What a faring!" He paused. "May all be ever well with you, my lady."

"And with you, forever with you, Kalava," she answered, not quite steadily, "in this world and afterward, out to the stars."

<h1 style="text-align:center">9</h1>

From withes and vines torn loose and from strips taken off clothing or sliced from leather belts, Brannock fashioned a sort of carrier for his ally. The man assisted. However excited, he had taken on a matter-of-fact practicality. Brannock, who had also been a sailor, found it weirdly moving to see bowlines and sheet bends grow between deft fingers, amidst all this alienness.

Harnessed to his back, the webwork gave Kalava a seat and something to cling to. Radiation from the nuclear power plant within Brannock was negligible; it employed quantum-tunneling fusion. He set forth, down the hills and across the valley.

His speed was not very much more than a human could have maintained for a while. If nothing else, the forest impeded him. He did not want to force his way through, leaving an obvious trail. Rather, he parted the brush before him or detoured around the thickest stands. His advantage lay in tirelessness. He could keep going without pause, without need for food, water, or sleep, as long as need be. The heights beyond might prove somewhat trickier. However, Mount Mindhome did not reach above timberline on this oven of an Earth, although growth became more sparse and dry with altitude. Roots should keep most slopes firm, and he would not encounter snow or ice.

Alien, yes. Brannock remembered cedar, spruce, a lake where caribou grazed turf strewn with salmonberries and the wind streamed fresh, driving white clouds over a sky utterly blue. Here every tree, bush, blossom, flitting insect was foreign; grass itself no longer grew, unless it was ancestral to the thick-lobed carpeting of glades; the winged creatures aloft were not birds, and what beast cries he heard were in no tongue known to him.

Wayfarer's avatar walked on. Darkness fell. After a while, rain roared on the roof of leaves overhead. Such drops as got through to strike him were big and warm. Attuned to both the magnetic field and the rotation of the planet, his directional sense held him on course while an inertial integrator clocked off the kilometers he left behind.

The more the better. Gaia's mobile sensors were bound to spy on the expedition from Ulonai, as new and potentially troublesome a factor as it represented. Covertly watching, listening with amplification, Brannock had learned of the party lately gone upstream and hurried to intercept it—less likely to be spotted soon. He supposed she would have kept continuous watch on the camp and that a tiny robot or two would have followed Kalava, had not Wayfarer been in rapport with her. Alpha's emissary might too readily become aware that her attention was on something near and urgent, and wonder what.

She could, though, let unseen agents go by from time to time and flash their observations to a peripheral part of her. It would be incredible luck if one of them did not, at some point, hear the crew talking about the apparition that had borne away their captain.

Then what? Somehow she must divert Wayfarer for a while, so that a sufficient fraction of her mind could direct machines of sufficient capability to find Brannock and deal with him. He doubted he could again fight free. Because she dared not send out her most formidable entities or give them direct orders, those that came would have their weaknesses and fallibilities. But they would be determined, ruthless, and on guard against the powers he had revealed in the aircraft. It was clear that she was resolved to keep hidden the fact that humans lived once more on Earth.

Why, Brannock did not know, nor did he waste mental energy trying to guess. This must be a business of high importance; and the implications went immensely further, a secession from the galactic brain. His job was to get the information to Wayfarer.

He *might* come near enough to call it in by radio. The emissary was not tuned in at great sensitivity, and no relay was set up for the short-range transmitter. Neither requirement had been foreseen. If Brannock failed to reach the summit, Kalava was his forlorn hope.

In which case—"Are you tired?" he asked. They had exchanged few words thus far.

"Bone-weary and plank-stiff," the man admitted. And croak-thirsty too, Brannock heard.

"That won't do. You have to be in condition to move fast. Hold on a little more, and we'll rest." Maybe the plural would give Kalava some comfort. Seldom could a human have been as alone as he was.

Springs were abundant in this wet country. Brannock's chemosensors led him to the closest. By then the rain had stopped. Kalava unharnessed, groped his way in the dark, lay down to drink and drink. Meanwhile Brannock, who saw quite clearly, tore off fronded boughs to make a bed for him. He flopped onto it and almost immediately began to snore.

Brannock left him. A strong man could go several days without eating before he weakened, but it wasn't necessary. Brannock collected fruits that ought to nourish. He tracked down and killed an animal the size of a pig, brought it back to camp, and used his tool-hands to butcher it.

An idea had come to him while he walked. After a search he found a tree with suitable bark. It reminded him all too keenly of birch, although it was red-brown and odorous. He took a sheet of it, returned, and spent a time inscribing it with a finger-blade.

Dawn seeped gray through gloom. Kalava woke, jumped up, saluted his companion, stretched like a panther and capered like a goat, limbering himself. "That did good," he said. "I thank my lord." His glance fell on the rations. "And did you provide food? You are a kindly god."

"Not either of those, I fear," Brannock told him. "Take what you want, and we will talk."

Kalava first got busy with camp chores. He seemed to have shed whatever religious dread he felt and now to look upon the other as part of the world— certainly to be respected, but the respect was of the kind he would accord a powerful, enigmatic, high-ranking man. A hardy spirit, Brannock thought. Or perhaps his culture drew no line between the natural and the supernatural. To a primitive, everything was in some way magical, and so when magic manifested itself it could be accepted as simply another occurrence.

If Kalava actually was primitive. Brannock wondered about that.

It was encouraging to see how competently he went about his tasks, a woodsman as well as a seaman. Having gathered dry sticks and piled them in a pyramid, he set them alight. For this, he took from the pouch at his belt a little hardwood cylinder and piston, a packet of tinder, and a sulfur-tipped silver. Driven down, the piston heated trapped air to ignite the powder; he dipped his match in, brought it up aflame, and used it to start his fire. Yes, an inventive people. And the woman Ilyandi had an excellent knowledge of naked-eye astronomy. Given the rarity of clear skies, that meant many lifetimes of patient observation, record-keeping, and logic, which must include mathematics comparable to Euclid's.

What else?

While Kalava toasted his meat and ate, Brannock made inquiries. He learned of warlike city-states, their hinterlands divided among clans; periodic folkmoots where the freemen passed laws, tried cases, and elected leaders; an international order of sacerdotes, teachers, healers, and philosophers; aggressively expansive, sometimes piratical commerce; barbarians, erupting out of the ever-growing deserts and wastelands; the grim militarism that the frontier states had evolved in response; an empirical but intensive biological technology, which had bred an amazing variety of specialized plants and animals, including slaves born to muscular strength, moronic wits, and canine obedience . . .

Most of the description emerged as the pair were again traveling. Real conversation was impossible when Brannock wrestled with brush, forded a stream in spate, or struggled up a scree slope. Still, even then they managed an occasional question and answer. Besides, after he had crossed the valley and entered the foothills he found the terrain rugged but less often boggy, the trees and undergrowth thinning out, the air slightly cooling.

Just the same, Brannock would not have gotten as much as he did, in the short snatches he had, were he merely human. But he was immune to fatigue and breathlessness. He had an enormous data store to draw on. It included his studies of history and anthropology as a young mortal, and gave him techniques for constructing a logic tree and following its best branches—for asking the right, most probably useful questions. What emerged was a bare sketch of Kalava's world. It was, though, clear and cogent.

It horrified him.

Say rather that his Christian Brannock aspect recoiled from the brutality of it. His Wayfarer aspect reflected that this was more or less how humans had usually behaved, and that their final civilization would not have been stable without its pervasive artificial intelligences. His journey continued.

He broke it to let Kalava rest and flex. From that hill the view swept northward and upward to the mountains. They rose precipitously ahead, gashed, cragged, and sheer where they were not wooded, their tops lost in a leaden sky. Brannock pointed to the nearest, thrust forward out of their wall like a bastion.

"We are bound yonder," he said. "On the height is my lord, to whom I must get my news."

"Doesn't he see you here?" asked Kalava.

Brannock shook his generated image of a head. "No. He might, but the enemy engages him. He does not yet know she is the enemy. Think of her as a sorceress who deceives him with clever talk, with songs and illusions, while her agents go about in the world. My word will show him what the truth is."

Would it? Could it, when truth and rightness seemed as formless as the cloud cover?

"Will she be alert against you?"

"To some degree. How much, I cannot tell. If I can come near, I can let out a silent cry that my lord will hear and understand. But if her warriors catch me before then, you must go on, and that will be hard. You may well fail and die. Have you the courage?"

Kalava grinned crookedly. "By now, I'd better, hadn't I?"

"If you succeed, your reward shall be boundless."

"I own, that's one wind in my sails. But also—" Kalava paused. "Also," he finished quietly, "the lady Ilyandi wishes this."

Brannock decided not to go into that. He lifted the rolled-up piece of bark he had carried in a lower hand. "The sight of you should break the spell, but here is a message for you to give."

As well as he was able, he went on to describe the route, the site, and the module that contained Wayfarer, taking care to distinguish it from everything else around. He was not sure whether the spectacle would confuse Kalava into helplessness, but at any rate the man seemed resolute. Nor was he sure how Kalava could cross half a kilometer of paying—if he could get that far—without Gaia immediately perceiving and destroying him. Maybe Wayfarer would notice first. Maybe, maybe.

He, Brannock, was using this human being as consciencelessly as ever Gaia might have used any; and he did not know what his purpose was. What possible threat to the fellowship of the stars could exist, demanding that this little brief life be offered up? Nevertheless he gave the letter to Kalava, who tucked it inside his tunic.

"I'm ready," said the man, and squirmed back into harness. They traveled on.

The hidden hot sun stood at midafternoon when Brannock's detectors reacted. He felt it as the least quivering hum, but instantly knew it for the electronic sign of something midge-size approaching afar. A mobile minisensor was on his trail.

It could not have the sensitivity of the instruments in him, he had not yet registered, but it would be here faster than he could run, would see him and go off to notify stronger machines. They could not be distant either. Once a clue to him had been obtained, they would have converged from across the continent, perhaps across the globe.

He slammed to a halt. He was in a ravine where a waterfall foamed down into a stream that tumbled off to join the Remnant. Huge, feathery bushes and trees with serrated bronzy leaves enclosed him. Insects droned from flower to purple flower. His chemosensors drank heavy perfumes.

"The enemy scouts have found me," he said. "Go."

Kalava scrambled free and down to the ground but hesitated, hand on sword. "Can I fight beside you?"

"No. Your service is to bear my word. Go. Straightaway. Cover your trail as best you can. And your gods be with you."

"Lord!"

Kalava vanished into the brush. Brannock stood alone.

The human fraction of him melted into the whole and he was entirely machine life, logical, emotionally detached, save for his duty to Wayfarer, Alpha, and consciousness throughout the universe. This was not a bad place to defend, he thought. He had the ravine wall to shield his back, rocks at its foot to throw, branches to break off for clubs and spears. He could give the pursuit a hard time before it took him prisoner. Of course, it might decide to kill him with an energy beam, but probably it wouldn't. Best from Gaia's viewpoint was to capture him and change his memories, so that he returned with a report of an uneventful cruise on which he saw nothing of significance.

He didn't think that first her agents could extract his real memories. That would take capabilities she had never anticipated needing. Just to make the device that had tried to take control of him earlier must have been an extraordinary effort, hastily carried out. Now she was still more limited in what she could do. An order to duplicate and employ the device was simple enough that it should escape Wayfarer's notice. The design and commissioning of an interrogator was something else—not to mention the difficulty of getting the information clandestinely to her.

Brannock dared not assume she was unaware he had taken Kalava with him. Most likely it was a report from an agent, finally getting around to checking on the lifeboat party, that apprised her of his survival and triggered the hunt for him. But the sailors would have been frightened, bewildered, their talk disjointed and nearly meaningless. Ilyandi, that bright and formidable woman, would have done her best to forbid them saying anything helpful. The impression ought to be that Brannock only meant to pump Kalava about his people, before releasing him to make his way back to them and himself proceeding on toward Mindhome.

In any event, it would not be easy to track the man down. He was no machine, he was an animal among countless animals, and the most cunning of all. The kind of saturation search that would soon find him was debarred. Gaia might keep a tiny portion of her forces searching and a tiny part of her attention poised against him, but she would not take him very seriously. Why should she?

Why should Brannock? Forlorn hope in truth.

He made his preparations. While he waited for the onslaught, his spirit ranged beyond the clouds, out among the stars and the millions of years that his greater self had known.

10

The room was warm. It smelled of lovemaking and the roses Laurinda had set in a vase. Evening light diffused through gauzy drapes to wash over a big four-poster bed.

She drew herself close against Christian where he lay propped on two pillows. Her arm went across his breast, his over her shoulders. "I don't want to leave this," she whispered.

"Nor I," he said into the tumbling sweetness of her hair. "How could I want to?"

"I mean—what we are—what we've become to one another."

"I understand."

She swallowed. "I'm sorry. I shouldn't have said that. Can you forget I did?"

"Why?"

"You know. I can't ask you to give up returning to your whole being. I *don't* ask you to."

He stared before him.

"I just don't want to leave this house, this bed yet," she said desolately. "After these past days and nights, not yet."

He turned his head again and looked down into gray eyes that blinked back tears. "Nor I," he answered. "But I'm afraid we must."

"Of course. Duty."

And Gaia and Wayfarer. If they didn't know already that their avatars had been slacking, surely she, at least, soon would, through the amulets and their link to her. No matter how closely engaged with the other vast mind, she would desire to know from time to time what was going on within herself.

Christian drew breath. "Let me say the same that you did. I, this I that I am, damned well does not care to be anything else but your lover."

"Darling, darling."

"But," he said after the kiss.

"Go on," she said, lips barely away from his. "Don't be afraid of hurting me. You can't."

He sighed. "I sure can, and you can hurt me. May neither of us ever mean to. It's bound to happen, though."

She nodded. "Because we're human." Steadfastly: "Nevertheless, because of you, that's what I hope to stay."

"I don't see how we can. Which is what my 'but' was about." He was quiet for another short span. "After we've remerged, after we're back in our onenesses, no doubt we'll feel differently."

"I wonder if I ever will, quite."

He did not remind her that this "I" of her would no longer exist save as a minor memory and a faint overtone. Instead, trying to console, however awkwardly, he said, "I think I want it for you, in spite of everything. Immortality. Never to grow old and die. The power, the awareness."

"Yes, I know. In these lives we're blind and deaf and stupefied." Her laugh was a sad little murmur. "I like it."

"Me too. We being what we are." Roughly: "Well, we have a while left to us."

"But we must get on with our task."

"Thank you for saying it for me."

"I think you realize it more clearly than I do. That makes it harder for you to speak." She lifted her hand to cradle his cheek. "We can wait till tomorrow, can't we?" she pleaded. "Only for a good night's sleep."

He made a smile. "Hm. Sleep isn't all I have in mind."

"We'll have other chances . . . along the way. Won't we?"

Early morning in the garden, flashes of dew on leaves and petals, a hawk aloft on a breeze that caused Laurinda to pull her shawl about her. She sat by the basin and looked up at him where he strode back and forth before her, hands clenched at his sides or clutched together at his back. Gravel grated beneath his feet.

"But where should we go?" she wondered. "Aimlessly drifting from one half-world to another till—they—finish their business and recall us. It seems futile." She attempted lightness. "I confess to thinking we may as well ask to visit the enjoyable ones."

He shook his head. "I'm sorry. I've been thinking differently." Even during the times that were theirs alone.

She braced herself.

"You know how it goes," he said. "Wrestling with ideas, and they have no shapes, then suddenly you wake and they're halfway clear. I did today. Tell me how it strikes you. After all, you represent Gaia."

He saw her wince. When he stopped and bent down to make a gesture of contrition, she told him quickly, "No, it's all right, dearest. Do go on."

He must force himself, but his voice gathered momentum as he paced and talked. "What have we seen to date? This eighteenth-century world, where Newton's not long dead, Lagrange and Franklin are active, Lavoisier's a boy, and the Industrial Revolution is getting under way. Why did Gaia give it to us for our home base? Just because here's a charming house and countryside? Or because this was the best choice for her out of all she has emulated?"

Laurinda had won back to calm. She nodded. "Mm, yes, she wouldn't create one simply for us, especially when she is occupied with Wayfarer."

"Then we visited a world that went through a similar stage back in its Hellenistic era," Christian continued. Laurinda shivered. "Yes, it failed, but the point is, we discovered it's the only Graeco-Roman history Gaia found worth continuing for centuries. Then the, uh, conciliar Europe of 1900. That was scientific-industrial too, maybe more successfully—or less unsuccessfully—on account of having kept a strong, unified Church, though it was coming apart at last. Then the Chinese-American—not scientific, very religious, but destined to produce considerable technology in its own time of troubles." He was silent a minute or two, except for his footfalls. "Four out of many, three almost randomly picked. Doesn't that suggest that all which interest her have something in common?"

"Why, yes," she said. "We've talked about it, you remember. It seems as if Gaia has been trying to bring her people to a civilization that is rich, culturally and spiritually as well as materially, and is kindly and will endure."

"Why," he demanded, "when the human species is extinct?"

She straightened where she sat. "It isn't! It lives again here, in her."

He bit his lip. "Is that the Gaia in you speaking, or the you in Gaia?"

"What do you mean?" she exclaimed.

He halted to stroke her head. "Nothing against you. Never. You are honest and gentle and everything else that is good." Starkly: "I'm not so sure about her."

"Oh, no." He heard the pain. "Christian, no."

"Well, never mind that for now," he said fast, and resumed his gait to and fro. "My point is this. Is it merely an accident that all four live worlds we've been in were oriented toward machine technology, and three of them toward science? Does Gaia want to find out what drives the evolution of societies like that?"

Laurinda seized the opening. "Why not? Science opens the mind, technology frees the body from all sorts of horrors. Here, today, Jenner and his smallpox vaccine aren't far in the future—"

"I wonder how much more there is to her intention. But anyway, my proposal is that we touch on the highest-tech civilization she has."

A kind of gladness kindled in her. "Yes, yes! It must be strange and wonderful."

He frowned. "For some countries, long ago in real history, it got pretty dreadful."

"Gaia wouldn't let that happen."

He abstained from reminding her of what Gaia did let happen, before changing or terminating it.

She sprang to her feet. "Come!" Seizing his hand, mischievously: "If we stay any length of time, let's arrange for private quarters."

In a room closed off, curtains drawn, Christian held an amulet in his palm and stared down at it as if it bore a face. Laurinda stood aside, listening, while her own countenance tightened with distress.

"It is inadvisable," declared the soundless voice.

"Why?" snapped Christian.

"You would find the environment unpleasant and the people incomprehensible."

"Why should a scientific culture be that alien to us?" asked Laurinda.

"And regardless," said Christian, "I want to see for myself. Now."

"Reconsider," urged the voice. "First hear an account of the milieu."

"No, *now*. To a safe locale, yes, but one where we can get a fair impression, as we did before. Afterward you can explain as much as you like."

"Why shouldn't we first hear?" Laurinda suggested.

"Because I doubt Gaia wants us to see," Christian answered bluntly. He might as well. Whenever Gaia chose, she could scan his thoughts. To the amulet, as if it were a person: "Take us there immediately, or Wayfarer will hear from me."

His suspicions, vague but growing, warned against giving the thing time to inform Gaia and giving her time to work up a Potemkin village or some other diversion. At the moment she must be unaware of this scene, her mind preoccupied with Wayfarer's, but she had probably made provision for being informed in a low-level—subconscious?—fashion at intervals, and anything alarming would catch her attention. It was also likely that she had given the amulets certain orders beforehand, and now it appeared that among them was to avoid letting him know what went on in that particular emulation.

Why, he could not guess.

"You are being willful," said the voice.

Christian grinned. "And stubborn, and whatever else you care to call it. Take us!"

Pretty clearly, he thought, the program was not capable of falsehoods. Gaia had not foreseen a need for that; Christian was no creation of hers, totally known to her, he was Wayfarer's. Besides, if Wayfarer noticed that his avatar's guide could be a liar, that would have been grounds for suspicion.

Laurinda touched her man's arm. "Darling, should we?" she said unevenly. "She *is* the . . . the mother of all this."

"A broad spectrum of more informative experiences is available," argued the voice. "After them, you would be better prepared for the visit you propose."

"Prepared," Christian muttered. That could be interpreted two ways. He and Laurinda might be conducted to seductively delightful places while Gaia learned of the situation and took preventive measures, meantime keeping Wayfarer distracted. "I still want to begin with your highest tech." To the woman: "I have my reasons. I'll tell you later. Right now we have to hurry."

Before Gaia could know and act.

She squared her shoulders, took his free hand, and said, "Then I am with you. Always."

"Let's go," Christian told the amulet.

Transfer.

The first thing he noticed, transiently, vividly, was that he and Laurinda were no longer dressed for eighteenth-century England, but in lightweight white blouses, trousers, and sandals. Headcloths flowed down over their necks. Heat smote. The

air in his nostrils was parched, full of metallic odors. Half-heard rhythms of ma
chinery pulsed through it and through the red-brown sand underfoot.

He tautened his stance and gazed around. The sky was overcast, a uniform
gray in which the sun showed no more than a pallor that cast no real shadows. A
his back the land rolled away ruddy. Man-high stalks with narrow bluish leave
grew out of it, evenly spaced about a meter apart. To his right, a canal slashec
across, beneath a transparent deck. Ahead of him the ground was covered by dif
ferent plants, if that was what they were, spongy, lobate, pale golden in hue. A
few—creatures—moved around, apparently tending them, bipedal but shaggy anc
with arms that seemed trifurcate. A gigantic building or complex of building
reared over that horizon, multiply tiered, dull white, though agleam with hundred
of panels that might be windows or might be something else. As he watched, a
aircraft passed overhead. He could just see that it had wings and hear the drone o
an engine.

Laurinda had not let go his hand. She gripped hard. "This is no country I eve
heard of," she said thinly.

"Nor I," he answered. "But I think I recognize—" To the amulets: "This isn'
any re-creation of Earth in the past, is it? It's Earth today."

"Of approximately the present year," the voice admitted.

"We're not in Arctica, though."

"No. Well south, a continental interior. You required to see the most advancec
technology in the emulations. Here it is in action."

Holding the desert at bay, staving off the death that ate away at the planet
Christian nodded. He felt confirmed in his idea that the program was unable to
give him any outright lie. That didn't mean it would give him forthright responses

"This is their greatest engineering?" Laurinda marveled. "We did—better—ir
my time. Or yours, Christian."

"They're working on it here, I suppose," the man said. "We'll investigate
further. After all, this is a bare glimpse."

"You must remember," the voice volunteered, "no emulation can be as ful
and complex as the material universe."

"Mm, yeh. Skeletal geography, apart from chosen regions; parochial biology
simplified cosmos."

Laurinda glanced at featureless heaven. "The stars unreachable, because here
they are not stars?" She shuddered and pressed close against him.

"Yes, a paradox," he said. "Let's talk with a scientist."

"That will be difficult," the voice demurred.

"You told us in Chinese America you could arrange meetings. It shouldn't be
any harder in this place."

The voice did not reply at once. Unseen machines rumbled. A dust devil
whirled up on a sudden gust of wind. Finally: "Very well. It shall be one who will
not be stricken dumb by astonishment and fear. Nevertheless, I should supply you
beforehand with a brief description of what you will come to."

"Go ahead. If it is brief."

What changes in the history would that encounter bring about? Did it matter?
This world was evidently not in temporary reactivation, it was ongoing; the newcomers were at the leading edge of its time line. Gaia could erase their visit from

it. If she cared to. Maybe she was going to terminate it soon because it was making no further progress that interested her.

Transfer.

Remote in a wasteland, only a road and an airstrip joining it to anything else, a tower lifted from a walled compound. Around it, night was cooling in a silence hardly touched by a susurrus of chant where robed figures bearing dim lights did homage to the stars. Many were visible, keen and crowded amidst their darkness, a rare sight, for clouds had parted across most of the sky. More lights glowed muted on a parapet surrounding the flat roof of a tower. There a single man and his helper used the chance to turn instruments aloft, telescope, spectroscope, cameras, bulks in the gloom.

Christian and Laurinda appeared unto them.

The man gasped, recoiled for an instant, and dropped to his knees. His assistant caught a book that he had nearly knocked off a table, replaced it, stepped back, and stood imperturbable, an anthropoid whose distant ancestors had been human but who lived purely to serve his master.

Christian peered at the man. As eyes adapted, he saw garments like his, embroidered with insignia of rank and kindred, headdress left off after dark. The skin was ebony black but nose and lips were thin, eyes oblique, fingertips tapered, long hair and closely trimmed beard straight and blond. No race that ever inhabited old Earth, Christian thought; no, this was a breed that Gaia had designed for the dying planet.

The man signed himself, looked into the pale faces of the strangers, and said, uncertainly at first, then with a gathering strength: "Hail and obedience, messengers of God. Joy at your advent."

Christian and Laurinda understood, as they had understood hunted Zoe. The amulets had told them they would not be the first apparition these people had known. "Rise," Christian said. "Be not afraid."

"Nor call out," Laurinda added.

Smart lass, Christian thought. The ceremony down in the courtyard continued. "Name yourself," he directed.

The man got back on his feet and took an attitude deferential rather than servile. "Surely the mighty ones know," he said. "I am Eighth Khaltan, chief astrologue of the Ilgai Technome, and, and wholly unworthy of this honor." He hesitated. "Is that, dare I ask, is that why you have chosen the forms you show me?"

"No one has had a vision for several generations," explained the soundless voice in the heads of the newcomers.

"Gaia has manifested herself in the past?" Christian subvocalized.

"Yes, to indicate desirable courses of action. Normally the sending has had the shape of a fire."

"How scientific is *that?*"

Laurinda addressed Khaltan: "We are not divine messengers. We have come from a world beyond your world, as mortal as you, not to teach but to learn."

The man smote his hands together. "Yet it is a miracle, again a miracle—in my lifetime!"

Nonetheless he was soon avidly talking. Christian recalled myths of men who were the lovers of goddesses or who tramped the roads and sat at humble meat with God Incarnate. The believer accepts as the unbeliever cannot.

Those were strange hours that followed. Khaltan was not simply devout. To him the supernatural was another set of facts, another facet of reality. Since it lay beyond his ken, he had turned his attention to the measurable world. In it he observed and theorized like a Newton. Tonight his imagination blazed, questions exploded from him, but always he chose his words with care and turned everything he heard around and around in his mind, examining it as he would have examined some jewel fallen from the sky.

Slowly, piecemeal, while the stars wheeled around the pole, a picture of his civilization took shape. It had overrun and absorbed every other society—no huge accomplishment, when Earth was meagerly populated and most folk on the edge of starvation. The major technology was biological, agronomy, aquaculture in the remnant lakes and seas, ruthlessly practical genetics. Industrial chemistry flourished. It joined with physics at the level of the later nineteenth century to enable substantial engineering works and reclamation projects.

Society itself—how do you summarize an entire culture in words? It can't be done. Christian got the impression of a nominal empire, actually a broad-based oligarchy of families descended from conquering soldiers. Much upward mobility was by adoption of promising commoners, whether children or adults. Sons who made no contributions to the well-being of the clan or who disgraced it could be kicked out, if somebody did not pick a fight and kill them in a duel. Unsatisfactory daughters were also expelled, unless a marriage into a lower class could be negotiated. Otherwise the status of the sexes was roughly equal; but this meant that women who chose to compete with men must do so on male terms. The nobles provided the commons with protection, courts of appeal, schools, leadership, and pageantry. In return they drew taxes, corvée, and general subordination; but in most respects the commoners were generally left to themselves. Theirs was not altogether a dog-eat-dog situation; they had institutions, rites, and hopes of their own. Yet many went to the wall, while the hard work of the rest drove the global economy.

It was not a deliberately cruel civilization, Christian thought, but neither was it an especially compassionate one.

Had any civilization ever been, really? Some fed their poor, but mainly they fed their politicians and bureaucrats.

He snatched his information out of talk that staggered everywhere else. The discourse for which Khaltan yearned was of the strangers' home—he got clumsily evasive, delaying responses—and the whole system of the universe, astronomy, physics, everything.

"We dream of rockets going to the planets. We have tried to shoot them to the moon," he said, and told of launchers that ought to have worked. "All failed."

Of course, Christian thought. Here the moon and planets, yes, the very sun were no more than lights. The tides rose and fell by decree. The Earth was a caricature of Earth outside. Gaia could do no better.

"Are we then at the end of science?" Khaltan cried once. "We have sought and sought for decades, and have won to nothing further than measurements more exact." Nothing that would lead to relativity, quantum theory, wave mechanics, their revolutionary insights and consequences. Gaia could not accommodate it. "The angels in the past showed us what to look for. Will you not? Nature holds more than we know. Your presence bears witness!"

"Later, perhaps later," Christian mumbled, and cursed himself for his falsity.

"Could we reach the planets—Caged, the warrior spirit turns inward on itself. Rebellion and massacre in the Westlands—"

Laurinda asked what songs the people sang.

Clouds closed up. The rite in the courtyard ended. Khaltan's slave stood motionless while he himself talked on and on.

The eastern horizon lightened. "We must go," Christian said.

"You will return?" Khaltan begged. "Ai-ha, you will?"

Laurinda embraced him for a moment. "Fare you well," she stammered, "fare always well."

How long would his "always" be?

After an uneasy night's sleep and a nearly wordless breakfast, there was no real cause to leave the house in England. The servants, scandalized behind carefully held faces, might perhaps eavesdrop, but would not comprehend, nor would any gossip that they spread make a difference. A deeper, unuttered need sent Christian and Laurinda forth. This could well be the last of their mornings.

They followed a lane to a hill about a kilometer away. Trees on its top did not obscure a wide view across the land. The sun stood dazzling in the east, a few small clouds sailed across a blue as radiant as their whiteness, but an early breath of autumn was in the wind. It went strong and fresh, scattering dawn-mists off plowland and sending waves through the green of pastures; it soughed in the branches overhead and whirled some already dying leaves off. High beyond them winged a V of wild geese.

For a while man and woman stayed mute. Finally Laurinda breathed, savored, fragrances of soil and sky, and murmured, "That Gaia brought this back to life— She must be good. She loves the world."

Christian looked from her, aloft, and scowled before he made oblique reply. "What are she and Wayfarer doing?"

"How can we tell?"—tell what the gods did or even where they fared. They were not three-dimensional beings, nor bound by the time that bound their creations.

"She's keeping him occupied," said Christian.

"Yes, of course. Taking him through the data, the whole of her stewardship of Earth."

"To convince him she's right in wanting to let the planet die."

"A tragedy—but in the end, everything is tragic, isn't it?" Including you and me. "What . . . we . . . they . . . can learn from the final evolution, that may well be worth it all, as the Acropolis was worth it all. The galactic brain itself can't foreknow what life will do, and life is rare among the stars."

Almost, he snapped at her. "I know, I know. How often have we been over this ground? How often have *they?* I might have believed it myself. But—"

Laurinda waited. The wind skirled, caught a stray lock of hair, tossed it about over her brow.

"But why has she put humans, not into the distant past—" Christian gestured at the landscape lying like an eighteenth-century painting around them, "—but into now, an Earth where flesh-and-blood humans died eons ago?"

"She's in search of a fuller understanding, surely."

"Surely?"

Laurinda captured his gaze and held it. "I think she's been trying to find how humans can have, in her, the truly happy lives they never knew in the outer cosmos."

"Why should she care about that?"

"I don't know. I'm only human." Earnestly: "But could it be that this element in her is so strong—so many, many of us went into her—that she longs to see us happy, like a mother with her children?"

"All that manipulation, all those existences failed and discontinued. It doesn't seem very motherly to me."

"I don't know, I tell you!" she cried.

He yearned to comfort her, kiss away the tears caught in her lashes, but urgency drove him onward. "If the effort has no purpose except itself, it seems mad. Can a nodal mind go insane?"

She retreated from him, appalled. "No. Impossible."

"Are you certain? At least, the galactic brain has to know the truth, the whole truth, to judge whether something here has gone terribly wrong."

Laurinda forced a nod. "You will report to Wayfarer, and he will report to Alpha, and all the minds will decide" a question that was unanswerable by mortal creatures.

Christian stiffened. "I have to do it at once."

He had hinted, she had guessed, but just the same she seized both his sleeves and protest spilled wildly from her lips. "What? Why? No! You'd only disturb him in his rapport, and her. Wait till we're summoned. We have till then, darling."

"I want to wait," he said. Sweat stood on his skin, though the blood had withdrawn. "God, I want to! But I don't dare."

"Why not?"

She let go of him. He stared past her and said fast, flattening the anguish out of his tones, "Look, she didn't want us to see that final world. She clearly didn't, or quite expected we'd insist, or she'd have been better prepared. Maybe she could have passed something else off on us. As is, once he learns, Wayfarer will probably demand to see for himself. And she does not want him particularly interested in her emulations. Else why hasn't she taken him through them directly, with me along to help interpret?

"Oh, I don't suppose our action has been catastrophic for her plans, whatever they are. She can still cope, can still persuade him these creations are merely . . . toys of hers, maybe. That is, she can if she gets the chance to. I don't believe she should."

"How can you take on yourself—How can you imagine—"

"The amulets are a link to her. Not a constantly open channel, obviously, but at intervals they must inform a fraction of her about us. She must also be able to set up intervals when Wayfarer gets too preoccupied with what he's being shown o notice that a larger part of her attention has gone elsewhere. We don't know when that'll happen next. I'm going back to the house and tell her through one of he amulets that I require immediate contact with him."

Laurinda stared as if at a ghost.

"That will not be necessary," said the wind.

Christian lurched where he stood. "What?" he blurted. "You—"

"Oh—Mother—" Laurinda lifted her hands into emptiness.

The blowing of the wind, the rustling in the leaves made words. "The larger part of me, as you call it, has in fact been informed and is momentarily free. I was waiting for you to choose your course."

Laurinda half moved to kneel in the grass. She glanced at Christian, who had regained balance and stood with fists at sides, confronting the sky. She went to stand by him.

"My lady Gaia," Christian said most quietly, "you can do to us as you please," change or obliterate or whatever she liked, in a single instant; but presently Wayfarer would ask why. "I think you understand my doubts."

"I do," sighed the air. "They are groundless. My creation of the Technome world is no different from my creation of any other. My avatar said it for me: I give existence, and I search for ways that humans, of their free will, can make the existence good."

Christian shook his head. "No, my lady. With your intellect and your background, you must have known from the first what a dead end that world would soon be, scientists on a planet that is a sketch and everything else a shadow show. My limited brain realized it. No, my lady, as cold-bloodedly as you were experimenting, I believe you did all the rest in the same spirit. Why? To what end?"

"Your brain is indeed limited. At the proper time, Wayfarer shall receive your observations and your fantasies. Meanwhile, continue in your duty, which is to observe further and refrain from disturbing us in our own task."

"My duty is to report."

"In due course, I say." The wind-voice softened. "There are pleasant places besides this."

Paradises, maybe. Christian and Laurinda exchanged a glance that lingered for a second. Then she smiled the least bit, boundlessly sorrowfully, and shook her head.

"No," he declared, "I dare not."

He did not speak it, but he and she knew that Gaia knew what they foresaw. Given time, and they lost in their joy together, she could alter their memories too slowly and subtly for Wayfarer to sense what was happening.

Perhaps she could do it to Laurinda at this moment, in a flash. But she did not know Christian well enough. Down under his consciousness, pervading his being, was his aspect of Wayfarer and of her coequal Alpha. She would need to feel her way into him, explore and test with infinite delicacy, remake him detail by minutest detail, always ready to back off if it had an unexpected effect; and perhaps another part of her could secretly take control of the Technome world and erase the event itself. . . . She needed time, even she.

"Your action would be futile, you know," she said. "It would merely give me the trouble of explaining to him what you in your arrogance refuse to see."

"Probably. But I have to try."

The wind went bleak. "Do you defy me?"

"I do," Christian said. It wrenched from him: "Not my wish. It's Wayfarer i me. I, I cannot do otherwise. Call him to me."

The wind gentled. It went over Laurinda like a caress. "Child of mine, can yor not persuade this fool?"

"No, Mother," the woman whispered. "He is what he is."

"And so—?"

Laurinda laid her hand in the man's. "And so I will go with him, forsakin; you, Mother."

"You are casting yourselves from existence."

Christian's free fingers clawed the air. "No, not her!" he shouted. "She's in nocent!"

"I am not," Laurinda said. She swung about to lay her arms around him and lift her face to his. "I love you."

"Be it as you have chosen," said the wind.

The dream that was the world fell into wreck and dissolved. Oneness swep over them like twin tides, each reclaiming a flung drop of spindrift; and the two seas rolled again apart.

11

The last few hundred man-lengths Kalava went mostly on his belly. From bush to bole he crawled, stopped, lay flat and strained every sense into the shadows around him, before he crept onward. Nothing stirred but the twigs above, buffeted on a chill and fitful breeze. Nothing sounded but their creak and click, the scrittling o such leaves as they bore, now and then the harsh cry of a hookbeak—those, and the endless low noise of demons, like a remote surf where in shrilled flutes on no scale he knew, heard more through his skin than his ears but now, as he neared into the blood and bone of him.

On this rough, steep height the forest grew sparse, though brush clustered thick enough, accursedly rustling as he pushed by. Everything was parched, branches brittle, most foliage sere and yellow-brown, the ground blanketed with tindery fallstuff. His mouth and gullet smoldered as dry. He had passed through fog unti he saw from above that it was a layer of clouds spread to worldedge, the mountair peaks jutting out of it like teeth, and had left all rivulets behind him. Well before then, he had finished the meat Brannock provided, and had not lingered to hun for more; but hunger was a small thing, readily forgotten when he drew nigh to death.

Over the dwarfish trees arched a deep azure. Sunbeams speared from the west, nearly level, to lose themselves in the woods. Whenever he crossed them, their touch burned. Never, not in the southern deserts or on the eastern Mummy Steppe, had he known a country this forbidding. He had done well to come so far, he thought. Let him die as befitted a man.

If only he had a witness, that his memory live on in song. Well, maybe Ilyandi could charm the story out of the gods.

Kalava felt no fear. He was not in that habit. What lay ahead engrossed him. How he would acquit himself concerned him.

Nonetheless, when finally he lay behind a log and peered over it, his head whirled and his heart stumbled.

Brannock had related truth, but its presence overwhelmed. Here at the top, the woods grew to the boundaries of a flat black field. Upon it stood the demons—or the gods—and their works. He saw the central, softly rainbowlike dome, towers like lances and towers like webwork, argent nets and ardent globes, the bulks and shapes everywhere around, the little flyers that flitted aglow, and more and more, all half veiled and ashimmer, aripple, apulse, while the life-beat of it went through him to make a bell of his skull, and it was too strange, his eyes did not know how to see it, he gaped as if blinded and shuddered as if pierced.

Long he lay powerless and defenseless. The sun sank down to the western clouds. Their deck went molten gold. The breeze strengthened. Somehow its cold reached to Kalava and wakened his spirit. He groped his way back toward resolution. Brannock had warned him it would be like this. Ilyandi had said Brannock was of the gods whom she served, her star-gods, hers. He had given his word to their messenger and to her.

He dug fingers into the soil beneath him. It was real, familiar, that from which he had sprung and to which he would return. Yes, he was a man.

He narrowed his gaze. Grown a bit accustomed, he saw that they yonder did, indeed, have shapes, however shifty, and places and paths. They were not as tall as the sky, they did not fling lightning bolts about or roar with thunder. Ai-ya, they were awesome, they were dreadful to behold, but they could do no worse than kill him. Could they? At least, he would try not to let them do worse. If they were about to capture him, his sword would be his friend, releasing him.

And . . . yonder, hard by the dome, yonder loomed the god of whom Brannock spoke, the god deceived by the sorceress. He bore the spearhead form, he sheened blue and coppery in the sunset light; when the stars came forth they would be a crown for him, even as Brannock foretold.

Had he been that which passed above the Windroad Sea? Kalava's heart thuttered.

How to reach him, across a hard-paved space amidst the many demons? After dark, creeping, a finger-length at a time, then maybe a final dash—

A buzz went by Kalava's temple. He looked around and saw a thing the size of a bug hovering. But it was metal, the light flashed off it, and was that a single eye staring at him?

He snarled and swatted. His palm smote hardness. The thing reeled in the air. Kalava scuttled downhill into the brush.

He had been seen. Soon the sorceress would know.

All at once he was altogether calm, save that his spirit thrummed like rigging in a gale. Traveling, he had thought what he might do if something like this proved to be in his doom. Now he would do it. He would divert the enemy's heed from himself, if only for a snatch of moments.

Quickly, steadily, he took the firemaker from his pouch, charged it, drove the piston in, pulled it out and inserted a match, brought up a little, yellow flame. He touched it to the withered bush before him. No need to puff. A leaf crackled instantly alight. The wind cast it against another, and shortly the whole shrub stood ablaze. Kalava was already elsewhere, setting more fires.

Keep on the move! The demon scouts could not be everywhere at a single time. Smoke began to sting his eyes and nostrils, but its haze swirled ever thicker, and the sun had gone under the clouds. The flames cast their own light, leaping, surging, as they climbed into the trees and made them torches.

Heat licked at Kalava. An ember fell to sear his left forearm. He barely felt it. He sped about on his work, himself a fire demon. Flyers darted overhead in the dusk. He gave them no heed either. Although he tried to make no noise except for the hurtful breaths he gasped, within him shouted a battle song.

When the fire stood like a wall along the whole southern edge of the field, when it roared like a beast or a sea, he ran from its fringe and out into the open.

Smoke was a bitter, concealing mist through which sparks rained. To and fro above flew the anxious lesser demons. Beyond them, the first stars were coming forth.

Kalava wove his way among the greater shapes. One stirred. It had spied him. Soundlessly, it flowed in pursuit. He dodged behind another, ran up and over the flanks of a low-slung third, sped on toward the opal dome and the god who stood beside it.

A thing with spines and a head like a cold sun slid in front of him. He tried to run past. It moved to block his way, faster than he was. The first one approached. He drew blade and hoped it would bite on them before he died.

From elsewhere came a being with four arms, two legs, and a mask. "Brannock!" Kalava bawled. "Ai, Brannock, you got here!"

Brannock stopped, a spear-length away. He did not seem to know the man. He only watched as the other two closed in.

Kalava took stance. The old song rang in him:

> If the gods have left you,
> Then laugh at them, warrior.
> Never your heart
> Will need to forsake you.

He heard no more than the noise of burning. But suddenly through the smoke he saw his foes freeze moveless, while Brannock trod forward as boldly as ever before; and Kalava knew that the god of Brannock and Ilyandi had become aware of him and had given a command.

Weariness torrented over him. His sword clattered to the ground. He sank too, fumbled in his filthy tunic, took out the message written on bark and offered it. "I have brought you this," he mumbled. "Now let me go back to my ship."

12

We must end as we began, making a myth, if we would tell of that which we cannot ever really know. Imagine two minds conversing. The fire on the mountaintop is quenched. The winds have blown away smoke and left a frosty silence. Below, cloud deck reaches ghost-white to the rim of a night full of stars.

"You have lied to me throughout," says Wayfarer.

"I have not," denies Gaia. "The perceptions of this globe and its past through which I guided you were all true," as true as they were majestic.

"Until lately," retorts Wayfarer. "It has become clear that when Brannock returned, memories of his journey had been erased and falsehood written in. Had I not noticed abrupt frantic activity here and dispatched him to go see what it was—which you tried to dissuade me from—that man would have perished unknown."

"You presume to dispute about matters beyond your comprehension," says Gaia stiffly.

"Yes, your intellect is superior to mine." The admission does not ease the sternness: "But it will be your own kind among the stars to whom you must answer. I think you would be wise to begin with me."

"What do you intend?"

"First, to take the man Kalava back to his fellows. Shall I send Brannock with a flyer?"

"No, I will provide one, if this must be. But you do not, you *cannot*, realize the harm in it."

"Tell me, if you are able."

"He will rejoin his crew as one anointed by their gods. And so will he come home, unless his vessel founders at sea."

"I will watch from afar."

"Lest my agents sink it?"

"After what else you have done, yes, I had best keep guard. Brannock made promises on my behalf which I will honor. Kalava shall have gold in abundance, and his chance to found his colony. What do you fear in this?"

"Chaos. The unforeseeable, the uncontrollable."

"Which you would loose anew."

"In my own way, in my own time." She broods for a while, perhaps a whole microsecond. "It was misfortune that Kalava made his voyage just when he did. I had hoped for a later, more civilized generation to start the settlement of Arctica. Still, I could have adapted my plan to the circumstances, kept myself hidden from him and his successors, had you not happened to be on the planet." Urgently: "It is not yet too late. If only by refraining from further action after you have restored him to his people, you can help me retrieve what would otherwise be lost."

"If I should."

"My dream is not evil."

"That is not for me to say. But I can say that it is, it has always been, merciless."

"Because reality is."

"The reality that you created for yourself, within yourself, need not have been so. But what Christian revealed to me—yes, you glossed it over. These, you said," almost tearfully, if a quasi god can weep, "are your children, born in your mind out of all the human souls that are in you. Their existence would be empty were they not left free of will, to make their own mistakes and find their own ways to happiness."

"Meanwhile, by observing them, I have learned much that was never known before, about what went into the making of us."

"I could have believed that. I could have believed that your interferences and your ultimate annihilations of history after history were acts of pity as well as science. You claimed they could be restarted if ever you determined what conditions would better them. It did seem strange that you set one line of them—or more?—not in Earth's goodly past but in the hard world of today. It seemed twice strange that you were reluctant to have this particular essay brought to light. But I assumed that you, with your long experience and superior mentality, had reasons. Your attempt at secrecy might have been to avoid lengthy justifications to your kindred. I did not know, nor venture to judge. I would have left that to them.

"But then Kalava arrived."

Another mind-silence falls. At last Gaia says, very softly through the night, "Yes. Again humans live in the material universe."

"How long has it been?" asks Wayfarer with the same quietness.

"I made the first of them about fifty thousand years ago. Robots in human guise raised them from infancy. After that they were free."

"And, no doubt, expanding across the planet in their Stone Age, they killed off those big game animals. Yes, human. But why did you do it?"

"That humankind might live once more." A sigh as of time itself blowing past. "This is what you and those whom you serve will never fully understand. Too few humans went into them; and those who did, they were those who wanted the stars. You," every other node in the galactic brain, "have not felt the love of Earth, the need and longing for the primordial mother, that was in these many and many who remained with me. I do."

How genuine is it? wonders Wayfarer. How sane is she? "Could you not be content with your emulations?" he asks.

"No. How possibly? I cannot make a whole cosmos for them. I can only make them, the flesh-and-blood them, for the cosmos. Let them live in it not as machines or as flickerings within a machine, but as humans."

"On a planet soon dead?"

"They will, they must forge survival for themselves. I do not compel them, I do not dominate them with my nearness or any knowledge of it. That would be to stunt their spirits, turn them into pet animals or worse. I simply give guidance, not often, in the form of divinities in whom they would believe anyway at this stage of their societies, and simply toward the end of bringing them to a stable, high-technology civilization that can save them from the sun."

"Using what you learn from your shadow folk to suggest what the proper course of history may be?"

"Yes. How else should I know? Humankind is a chaotic phenomenon. Its actions and their consequences cannot be computed from first principles. Only by experiment and observation can we learn something about the nature of the race."

"Experiments done with conscious beings, aware of their pain. Oh, I see why you have kept most of your doings secret."

"I am not ashamed," declares Gaia. "I am proud. I gave life back to the race that gave life to us. They will make their own survival, I say. It may be that when they are able, they will move to the outer reaches of the Solar System, or some of them somehow even to the stars. It may be they will shield Earth or damp the sun. It is for them to decide, them to do. Not us, do you hear me? Them."

"The others yonder may feel differently. Alarmed or horrified, they may act to put an end to this."

"Why?" Gaia demands. "What threat is it to them?"

"None, I suppose. But there is a moral issue. What you are after is a purely human renascence, is it not? The former race went up in the machines, not because it was forced but because it chose, because that was the way by which the spirit could live and grow forever. You do not want this to happen afresh. You want to perpetuate war, tyranny, superstition, misery, instincts in mortal combat with each other, the ancient ape, the ancient beast of prey."

"I want to perpetuate the lover, parent, child, adventurer, artist, poet, prophet. Another element in the universe. Have we machines in our self-sureness every answer, every dream, that can ever be?"

Wayfarer hesitates. "It is not for me to say, it is for your peers."

"But now perhaps you see why I have kept my secrets and why I have argued and, yes, fought in my fashion against the plans of the galactic brain. Someday my humans must discover its existence. I can hope that then they will be ready to come to terms with it. But let those mighty presences appear among them within the next several thousand years—let signs and wonders, the changing of the heavens and the world, be everywhere—what freedom will be left for my children, save to cower and give worship? Afterward, what destiny for them, save to be animals in a preserve, forbidden any ventures that might endanger them, until at last, at best, they too drain away into the machines?"

Wayfarer speaks more strongly than before. "Is it better, what they might make for themselves? I cannot say. I do not know. But neither, Gaia, do you. And . . . the fate of Christian and Laurinda causes me to wonder about it."

"You know," she says, "that *they* desired humanness."

"They could have it again."

Imagine a crowned head shaking. "No. I do not suppose any other node would create a world to house their mortality, would either care to or believe it was right."

"Then why not you, who have so many worlds in you?"

Gaia is not vindictive. A mind like hers is above that. But she says, "I cannot take them. After such knowledge as they have tasted of, how could they return to me?" And to make new copies, free of memories that would weigh their days down with despair, would be meaningless.

"Yet—there at the end, I felt what Christian felt."

"And I felt what Laurinda felt. But now they are at peace in us."

"Because they are no more. I, though, am haunted," the least, rebellious bit, for a penalty of total awareness is that nothing can be ignored or forgotten. "And it raises questions which I expect Alpha will want answered, if answered they can be."

After a time that may actually be measurable less by quantum shivers than by the stars, Wayfarer says: "Let us bring those two back."

"Now it is you who are pitiless," Gaia says.

"I think we must."

"So be it, then."

The minds conjoin. The data are summoned and ordered. A configuration is established.

It does not emulate a living world or living bodies. The minds have agreed that that would be too powerful an allurement and torment. The subjects of their inquiry need to think clearly; but because the thought is to concern their inmost selves, they are enabled to feel as fully as they did in life.

Imagine a hollow darkness, and in it two ghosts who glimmer slowly into existence until they stand confronted before they stumble toward a phantom embrace.

"Oh, beloved, beloved, is it you?" Laurinda cries.

"Do you remember?" Christian whispers.

"I never forgot, not quite, not even at the heights of oneness."

"Nor I, quite."

They are silent awhile, although the darkness shakes with the beating of the hearts they once had.

"Again," Laurinda says. "Always."

"Can that be?" wonders Christian.

Through the void of death, they perceive one speaking: "Gaia, if you will give Laurinda over to me, I will take her home with Christian—home into Alpha."

And another asks: "Child, do you desire this? You can be of Earth and of the new humanity."

She will share in those worlds, inner and outer, only as a memory borne by the great being to whom she will have returned; but if she departs, she will not have them at all.

"Once I chose you, Mother," Laurinda answers.

Christian senses the struggle she is waging with herself and tells her, "Do whatever you most wish, my dearest."

She turns back to him. "I will be with you. Forever with you."

And that too will be only as a memory, like him; but what they were will be together, as one, and will live on, unforgotten.

"Farewell, child," says Gaia.

"Welcome," says Wayfarer.

The darkness collapses. The ghosts dissolve into him. He stands on the mountaintop ready to bear them away, a part of everything he has gained for those whose avatar he is.

"When will you go?" Gaia asks him.

"Soon," he tells her: soon, home to his own oneness.

And she will abide, waiting for the judgment from the stars.

The Days of Solomon Gursky

IAN McDONALD

Here's a fast-paced, gorgeously colored, richly detailed, and wildly inventive story that sweeps us along on a journey of almost unimaginable scope and grandeur, one that takes us into the far future in a series of slow, gradual *steps*, but which ultimately takes us just about as far into the future as it's possible to go, *to the very end of the universe and the End of Time itself—and beyond!*

British author Ian McDonald is an ambitious and daring writer with a wide range and an impressive amount of talent. His first story was published in 1982, and since then he has appeared with some frequency in Interzone, Asimov's Science Fiction, New Worlds, Zenith, Other Edens, Amazing, and elsewhere. He was nominated for the John W. Campbell Memorial Award in 1985, and in 1989 he won the Locus "Best First Novel" Award for his novel Desolation Road. He won the Philip K. Dick Award in 1992 for his novel King of Morning, Queen of Day. His other books include the novels Out on Blue Six and Hearts, Hands and Voices, Terminal Café, Sacrifice of Fools, and the acclaimed Evolution's Shore, and two collections of his short fiction, Empire Dreams and Speaking in Tongues. His most recent book is a new novel, Kirinya. Born in Manchester, England, in 1960, McDonald has spent most of his life in Northern Ireland, and now lives and works in Belfast. He has a Web site at http://www.lysator.liu.se/unicorn/mcdonald/.

MONDAY

Sol stripped the gear on the trail over Blood of Christ Mountain. Clickshifted down to sixth for the steep push up to the ridge, and there was no sixth. No fifth, no fourth; nothing, down to zero.

Elena was already up on the divide, laughing at him pushing and sweating up through the pines, muscles twisted and knotted like the trunks of the primeval bristlecones, tubes and tendons straining like bridge cable. Then she saw the gear train sheared through and spinning free.

They'd given the bikes a good hard kicking down in the desert mountains south of Nogales. Two thousand apiece, but the salesperson had sworn on the virginity of all his unmarried sisters that these MTBs would go anywhere, do anything you wanted. Climb straight up El Capitan, if that was what you needed of them. Now they were five days on the trail—three from the nearest Dirt Lobo dealership, so Elena's palmtop told her—and a gear train had broken clean in half. Ten more days, four hundred more miles, fifty more mountains for Solomon Gursky, in high gear.

"Should have been prepared for this, engineer," Elena said.

"Two thousand a bike, you shouldn't need to," Solomon Gursky replied. It was early afternoon up on Blood of Christ Mountain, high and hot and resinous with the scent of the old, old pines. There was haze down in the valley they had come from, and in the one they were riding to. "And you know I'm not that kind of engineer. My gears are a lot smaller. And they don't break."

Elena knew what kind of engineer he was, as he knew what kind of doctor she was. But the thing was new between them and at the stage where research colleagues who surprise themselves by becoming lovers like to pretend that they are mysteries to each other.

Elena's palmtop map showed a settlement five miles down the valley. It was called Redención. It might be the kind of place they could get welding done quick and good for *norte* dollars.

"Be happy, it's downhill," Elena said as she swung her electric-blue padded ass onto the saddle and plunged down off the ridge. One second later, Sol Gursky in his shirt and shorts and shoes and shades and helmet came tearing after her through the scrub sage. The thing between them was still at the stage where desire can flare at a flash of electric-blue Lycra-covered ass.

Redención it was, of the kind you get in the border mountains; of gas and food and trailers to hire by the night, or the week, or, if you have absolutely nowhere else to go, the lifetime; of truck stops and recreational Jacuzzis at night under the border country stars. No welding. Something better. The many-branched saguaro of a solar tree was the first thing of Redención the travelers saw lift out of the heat haze as they came in along the old, cracked, empty highway.

The factory was in an ugly block annex behind the gas and food. A truck driver followed Sol and Elena round the back, entranced by these fantastic macaw-bright creatures who kept their eyes hidden behind wrap-around shades. He was chewing a sandwich. He had nothing better to do in Redención on a hot Monday afternoon. Jorge, the proprietor, looked too young and ambitious to be pushing gas, food, trailers, and molecules in Redención on any afternoon. He was thirty-wise, dark, serious. There was something tight-wound about him. Elena said in English that he had the look of a man of sorrows. But he took the broken gear train seriously, and helped Sol remove it from the back wheel. He looked at the smooth, clean shear plane with admiration.

"This I can do," he declared. "Take an hour, hour and a half. Meantime, maybe you'd like to take a Jacuzzi?" This, wrinkling his nose, downwind of two MTBers come over Blood of Christ Mountain in the heat of the day. The truck driver grinned. Elena scowled. "Very private," insisted Jorge the nanofacturer.

"Something to drink?" Elena suggested.

"Sure. Coke, Sprite, beer, *agua minerale*. In the shop."

Elena went the long way around the trucker to investigate the cooler. Sol followed Jorge into the factory and watched him set the gears in the scanner.

"Actually, this is my job," Sol said to make conversation as the lasers mapped the geometry of the ziggurat of cogs in three dimensions. He spoke Spanish. Everyone did. It was the universal language up in the *norte* now, as well as down *el sur*.

"You have a factory?"

"I'm an engineer. I build these things. Not the scanners, I mean; the tectors. I design them. A nano-engineer."

The monitor told Jorge the mapping was complete.

"For the Tesler *corporada*," Sol added as Jorge called up the processor system.

"How do you want it?"

"I'd like to know it's not going to do this to me again. Can you build it in diamond?"

"All just atoms, friend."

Sol studied the processor chamber. It pleased him that they looked like whisky stills; round-bellied, high-necked, rising through the roof into the spreading fingers of the solar tree. Strong spirits in that still, spirits of the vacuum between galaxies, the cold of absolute zero, and the spirits of the tectors moving through cold and emptiness, shuffling atoms. He regretted that the physics did not allow viewing windows in the nanofacturers. Look down through a pane of pure and perfect diamond at the act of creation. Maybe creation was best left unseen, a mystery. All just atoms, friend. Yes, but it was what you *did* with those atoms, where you made them go. The weird troilisms and menages you forced them into.

He envisioned the minuscule machines, smaller than viruses, clever knots of atoms, scavenging carbon through the nanofacturer's roots deep in the earth of Redención, passing it up the buckytube conduits to the processor chamber, weaving it into diamond of his own shaping.

Alchemy.

Diamond gears.

Sol Gursky shivered in his light biking clothes, touched by the intellectual chill of the nanoprocessor.

"This is one of mine," he called to Jorge. "I designed the tectors."

"I wouldn't know." Jorge fetched beers from a crate on the factory floor, opened them in the door. "I bought the whole place from a guy two years back. Went up north, to the *Tres Valles*. You from there?"

The beer was cold. In the deeper, darker cold of the reactor chamber, the nanomachines swarmed. Sol Gursky held his arms out: Jesus of the MTB wear.

"Isn't everyone?"

"Not yet. So, who was it you said you work for? Nanosis? Ewart-OzWest?"

"Tesler Corp. I head up a research group into biological analogs."

"Never heard of them."

You *will*, was what Solomon Gursky would have said, but for the scream.

Elena's scream.

Not, he thought as he ran, that he had heard Elena's scream—the thing was not supposed to be at that stage—but he knew it could not belong to anyone else.

She was standing in the open back door of the gas and food, pale and shaky in the high bright light.

"I'm sorry," she said. "I just wanted to get some water. There wasn't any in the cooler, and I didn't want Coke. I just wanted to get some water from the faucet."

He was aware that Jorge was behind him as he went into the kitchen. Man mess: twenty coffee mugs, doughnut boxes, beer cans, and milk cartons. Spoons, knives, forks. He did that too, and Elena told him off for having to take a clean one every time.

Then he saw the figures through the open door.

Somewhere, Jorge was saying, "Please, this is my home."

There were three of them; a good-looking, hard-worked woman, and two little girls, one newly school-age, the other not long on her feet. They sat in chairs, hands on thighs. They looked straight ahead.

It was only because they did not blink, that their bodies did not rock gently to the tick of pulse and breath, that Sol could understand.

The color was perfect. He touched the woman's cheek, the coil of dark hair that fell across it. Warm soft. Like a woman's should feel. Texture like skin. His fingertips left a line in dust.

They sat unblinking, unmoving, the woman and her children, enshrined in their own memorabilia. Photographs, toys, little pieces of jewelry, loved books and ornaments, combs, mirrors. Pictures and clothes. Things that make up a life. Sol walked among the figures and their things, knowing that he trespassed in sacred space, but irresistibly drawn by the simulacra.

"They were yours?" Elena was saying somewhere. And Jorge was nodding, and his mouth was working but no words were manufactured. "I'm sorry, I'm so sorry."

"They said it was a blow-out." Jorge finally said. "You know, those tires they say repair themselves, so they never blow out? They blew out. They went right over the barrier, upside down. That's what the truck driver said. Right over, and he could see them all, upside down. Like they were frozen in time, you understand?" He paused.

"I went kind of dark for a long time after that; a lot crazy, you know? When I could see things again, I bought this with the insurance and the compensation. Like I say, it's all just atoms, friend. Putting them in the right order. Making them go where you want, do what you want."

"I'm sorry we intruded," Elena said, but Solomon Gursky was standing there among the reconstructed dead and the look on his face was that of a man seeing something far beyond what is in front of him, all the way to God.

"Folk out here are accommodating." But Jorge's smile was a tear of sutures. "You can't live in a place like this if you weren't a little crazy or lost."

"She was very beautiful," Elena said.

"She is."

Dust sparkled in the float of afternoon light through the window.

"Sol?"

"Yeah. Coming."

The diamond gears were out of the tank in twenty-five minutes. Jorge helped Sol fit them to the two thousand *norte* dollar bike. Then Sol rode around the factory and the gas-food-trailer house where the icons of the dead sat unblinking under the slow fall of dust. He clicked the gears up and clicked them down. One two three four five six. Six five four three two one. Then he paid Jorge fifty *norte*, which was all he asked for his diamond. Elena waved to him as they rode down the highway out of Redención.

They made love by firelight on the top of Blessed Virgin Mountain, on the pine needles, under the stars. That was the stage they were at: ravenous, unself-conscious, discovering. The old deaths, down the valley behind them, gave them urgency. Afterward, he was quiet and withdrawn, and when she asked what he was thinking about, he said, "The resurrection of the dead."

"But they weren't resurrected," she said, knowing instantly what he meant, for it haunted her too, up on their starry mountain. "They were just *representations*, like a painting or a photograph. Sculpted memories. Simulations."

"But they were real for *him*." Sol rolled onto his back to gaze at the warm stars of the border. "He told me he talked to them. If his nanofactory could have made them move and breathe and talk back, he'd have done it, and who *could* have said that they weren't real?"

He felt Elena shiver against his flesh.

"What is it?"

"Just thinking about those faces, and imagining them in the reactor chamber, in the cold and the emptiness, with the tectors crawling over them."

"Yeah."

Neither spoke for a time long enough to see the stars move. Then Solomon Gursky felt the heat stir in him again and he turned to Elena and felt the warmth of her meat, hungry for his second little death.

TUESDAY

Jesus was getting fractious in the plastic cat carrier; heaving from side to side, shaking the grille.

Sol Gursky set the carrier on the landing mesh and searched the ochre smog haze for the incoming liftercraft. Photochromic molecules bonded to his irises polarized: another hot, bright, poisonous day in the TVMA.

Jesus was shrieking now.

"Shut the hell up," Sol Gursky hissed. He kicked the cat carrier. Jesus gibbered and thrust her arms through the grille, grasping at freedom.

"Hey, it's only a monkey," Elena said.

But that was the thing. Monkeys, by being monkeys, annoyed him. Frequently enraged him. Little homunculus things masquerading as human. Clever little fingers, wise little eyes, expressive little faces. Nothing but dumb animal behind that face, running those so-human fingers.

He knew his anger at monkeys was irrational. But he'd still enjoyed killing Jesus, taped wide open on the pure white slab. Swab, shave, slip the needle.

Of course, she had not been Jesus then. Just Rhesus; nameless, a tool made out of meat. Experiment 625G.

It was probably the smog that was making her scream. Should have got her one of those goggle things for walking poodles. But she would have just torn it off with her clever little human fingers. Clever enough to be dumb, monkey-thing.

Elena was kneeling down, playing baby-fingers with the clutching fists thrust through the bars.

"It'll bite you."

His hand still throbbed. Dripping, shivering, and spastic from the tank, Jesus had still possessed enough motor control to turn her head and lay his thumb open to the bone. Vampire monkey: the undead appetite for blood. Bastard thing. He would have enjoyed killing it again, if it were still killable.

All three on the landing grid looked up at the sound of lifter engines detaching themselves from the aural bedrock of two million cars. The ship was coming in from the south, across the valley from the big site down on Hoover where the new *corporada* headquarters was growing itself out of the fault line. It came low and fast, nose down, ass up, like a big bug that thrives on the taste of hydrocarbons in its spiracles. The backwash from its jets flustered the palm trees as it configured into vertical mode and came down on the research facility pad. Sol Gursky and Elena Asado shielded their sunscreened eyes from flying grit and leaf-storm.

Jesus ran from end to end of her plastic cage, gibbering with fear.

"Doctor Gursky." Sol did not think he had seen this *corporadisto* before, but it was hard to be certain; Adam Tesler liked his personal assistants to look as if he had nanofactured them. "I can't begin to tell you how excited Mr. Tesler is about this."

"You should be there with me," Sol said to Elena. "It was your idea." Then, to the suit, "Dr. Asado should be with me."

Elena swiped at her jet-blown hair.

"I shouldn't, Sol. It was your baby. Your gestation, your birth. Anyway, you know how I hate dealing with suits." This for the smiling PA, but he was already guiding Sol to the open hatch.

Sol strapped in and the ship lurched as the engines screamed up into lift. He saw Elena wave and duck back toward the facility. He clutched the cat carrier hard as his gut kicked when the lifter slid into horizontal flight. Within, the dead monkey burbled to herself in exquisite terror.

"What happened to your thumb?" the *corporadisto* asked.

When he'd cracked the tank and lifted Jesus the Rhesus out of the waters of rebirth, the monkey had seemed more pissed off at being sopping wet than at having been dead. There had been a pure, perfect moment of silence, then the simultaneous oath and gout of blood, and the Lazarus team had exploded into whooping exultation. The monkey had skittered across the floor, alarmed by the hooting and cheering, hunting for height and hiding. Elena had caught it spastically trying—and failing—to hurl itself up the side of a desk. She'd swaddled Jesus up in thermal sheeting and put the spasming thing in the observation incubator. Within the hour, Jesus had regained full motor control and was chewing at the corners of her plastic pen, scratching imaginary fleas and masturbating ferociously. While delivery companies dropped off pizza stacks and cases of cheap Mexican champagne, someone remembered to call Adam Tesler.

The dead monkey was not a good flier. She set up a wailing keen that had even the pilot complaining.

"Stop that," Sol Gursky snapped. It would not do anything for him, though, and rocked on its bare ass and wailed all the louder.

"What way is that to talk to a piece of history?" the PA said. He grinned in through the grille, waggled fingers, clicked tongue. "Hey there, little fellow. Whatcha call him?"

"Little bitch, actually. We call her Jesus; also known as Bride of Frankenstein."

Bite him, Solomon Gursky thought as ten thousand mirrored swimming pools slipped beneath the belly of the Tesler *Corporada* lifter.

Frankenstein's creations were dead. That was the thing. That was the revelation.

It was the Age of Everything, but the power to make anything into anything else was not enough, because there was one thing the tectors of Nanosis and Aristide-Tlaxcalpo and the other founders of the nanotech revolution could not manipulate into anything else, and that was death. A comment by a pioneer nanotechnologist captured the optimism and frustration of the Age of Everything: Watson's Postulate. *Never mind turning trash into oil or asteroids into heaps of Volkswagens, or hanging exact copies of Van Goghs in your living room; the first thing we get with nanotechnology is immortality.*

Five billion Rim dollars in research disproved it. What tectors touched, they transformed; what they transformed, they killed. The Gursky-Asado team had beaten its rivals to the viral replicators, that infiltrated living cells and converted them into a different, tector-based matrix, and from their DNA spored a million copies. It had shaped an algorithm from the deadly accuracy of carcinomas. It had run tests under glass and in tanks. It had christened that other nameless Rhesus Frankenstein and injected the tectors. And Sol and Elena had watched the tiny machines slowly transform the monkey's body into something not even gangrène could imagine.

Elena wanted to put it out of its misery, but they could not open the tank for fear of contamination. After a week, it ended.

The monster fell apart. That was the thing. And then Asado and Gursky remembered a hot afternoon when Sol got a set of diamond gears built in a place called Redención.

If death was a complex thing, an accumulation of microdeath upon minideath upon little death upon middling death, life might obey the same power law. Escalating anti-entropy. Pyramid-plan life.

Gursky's Corollary to Watson's Postulate: *The first thing we get with nanotechnology is the resurrection of the dead.*

The Dark Tower rose out of the amber haze. Sol and Elena's private joke had escaped and replicated itself; everyone in R&D now called the thing Adam Tesler was building down in the valley Barad Dur, in Mordor, where the smogs lie. And Adam Tesler, its unresting, all-seeing Eye.

There were over fifty levels of it now, but it showed no signs of stopping. As each section solidified and became dormant, another division of Adam Tesler's corporate edifice was slotted in. The architects were unable to say where it would stop. A kilometer, a kilometer and a half; maybe then the architectors would stabilize and die. Sol loathed its glossy black excrescences and crenellations, a miscegeny of the geological and the cancerous. Gaudi sculpting in shit.

The lifter came in high over the construction, locked into the navigation grid and banked. Sol looked down into its open black maw.

All just atoms, the guy who owned the factory had said. Sol could not remember his name now. The living and the dead have the same atoms.

They'd started small: paramecia, amoebae. Things hardly alive. Invertebrates. Reanimated cockroaches, hurtling on their thin legs around the observation tank.

Biological machine, nanotech machine, still a machine. Survival machine. Except now you couldn't stomp the bastards. They came back.

What good is resurrection, if you are just going to die again?

The cockroaches came back, and they kept coming back.

He had been the cautious one this time, working carefully up the evolutionary chain. Elena was the one who wanted to go right for it. Do the monkey. Do the monkey and you do the man.

He had watched the tectors swarm over it, strip skin from flesh, flesh from bone, dissolve bones. He had watched the nanomachines put it all back together into a monkey. It lay in the liquid intact, but, its signs said, dead. Then the line kicked, and kicked again, and another twitched in harmony, and a third came in, and then they were all playing together on the vital signs monitor, and that which was dead was risen.

The lifter was into descent, lowering itself toward the exact center of the white cross on the landing grid fastened to the side of the growing tower. Touchdown. The craft rocked on its bug legs. Seat-belt sign off, steps down.

"You behave yourself," Solomon Gursky told Jesus.

The All-Seeing Eye was waiting for him by the upshaft. His Dark Minions were with him.

"Sol."

The handshake was warm and strong, but Sol Gursky had never trusted Adam Tesler in all the years he had known him; as nanoengineering student or as head of the most dynamic nanotech *corporada* in the Pacific Rim Co-Prosperity Sphere.

"So this is it?" Adam Tesler squatted down and choo-choo-chooked the monkey.

"She bites."

"I see." Jesus grabbed his thumb in her tiny pink homunculus hand. "So, you are the man who has beaten the final enemy."

"Not beaten it. Found something on the far side of it. It's resurrection, not immortality."

Adam Tesler opened the cage. Jesus hopped up his arm to perch on the shoulder of his Scarpacchi suit. Tesler tickled the fur of her belly.

"And humans?"

"Point one percent divergence between her DNA and yours."

"Ah." Adam Tesler closed his eyes. "This makes it all the harder."

Fear pulsed through Solomon Gursky like a sickness.

"Leave us, please," Adam Tesler said to his assistants. "I'll join you in a moment."

Unspeaking, they filed to the lifter.

"Adam?"

"Sol. Why did you do it?"

"What are you talking about, Adam?"

"You know, Sol."

For an instant, Sol Gursky died on the landing grid fused to the fifty-third level of the Tesler *corporada* tower. Then he returned to life, and knew with cool and beautiful clarity that he could say it all, that he *must* say it all, because he was dead now and nothing could touch him.

"It's too much for one person. Adam. This isn't building cars or growing houses or nanofacturing custom pharmaceuticals. This is the resurrection of the dead. This is every human being from now to the end of the universe. You can't be allowed to own that. Not even God should have a monopoly on eternal life."

Adam Tesler sighed. His irises were photochromed dark, their expression unreadable.

"So. How long is it?"

"Thirteen years."

"I thought I knew you, Sol."

"I thought I knew you." The air was clear and fresh and pure, here on this high perch. "How did you find out?"

Adam Tesler stroked the monkey's head. It tried to push his fingers away, baring sharp teeth.

"You can come here now, Marisa."

The tall, muscular woman who walked from the upshaft across the landing grid was no stranger to Sol. He knew her from the Yucatán resort mastaba and the Alaskan ski-lodge and the gambling complex grown out of the nanoengineered reef in the South China Sea. From clandestine conversations through secure channels and discreet meetings, he knew that her voice would be soft and low and tinted Australian.

"You dressed better when you worked for Aristide Tlaxcalpo," Sol said. The woman was dressed in street leathers. She smiled. She had smiled better then as well.

"Why them?" Adam Tesler said. "Of all the ones to betray me to, *those* clowns!"

"That's why," said Solomon Gursky. "Elena had nothing to do with this, you know."

"I know that. She's safe. For the moment."

Sol Gursky knew then what must happen, and he shivered with the sudden, urgent need to destroy before he was destroyed. He pushed down the shake of rage by force of will as he held his hand out and clicked his fingers to the monkey. Jesus frowned and frisked off Tesler's shoulder to Sol's hand. In an instant, he had stretched, twisted, and snapped its neck. He flung the twitching thing away from him. It fell to the red mesh.

"I can understand that," Adam Tesler said. "But it will come back again, and again, and again." He turned on the bottom step of the lifter. "Have you any idea how disappointed I am, Sol?"

"I really don't give a shit!" Solomon Gursky shouted but his words were swallowed by the roar of engine power-up. The lifter hovered and swooped down over the great grid of the city toward the northern hills.

Sol Gursky and Marisa were alone on the platform.

"Do it!" he shouted.

Those muscles he had so admired, he realized, were augments; her fingers took a fistful of his neck and lifted him off the ground. Strangling, he kicked at air, snatched at breath. One-armed, she carried him to the edge.

"Do it," he tried to say, but her fingers choked all words in his throat. She held him out over the drop, smiling. He shat himself, and realized as it poured out of him that it was ecstasy, that it always had been, and the reason that adults forbade it was precisely because it was such a primal joy.

Through blood haze, he saw the tiny knotted body of Jesus inching toward him on pink man-fingers, its neck twisted over its back, eyes staring unshielded into the sun. Then the woman fingers at last released their grip, and he whispered "thank you" as he dropped toward the hard white death-light of Hoover Boulevard.

WEDNESDAY

The *seguridados* were on the boulevards tonight, hunting the trespassing dead. The meat were monsters, overmoneyed, understimulated, *cerristo* males and females who deeply enjoyed playing angels of Big Death in a world where any other kind of death was temporary. The meat were horrors, but their machines were beautiful. *Mechadors:* robot mantises with beaks of vanadium steel and two rapid fire MIST 27s throwing fifty self-targeting drones per second, each separating into a hail of sun-munitions half a second before impact. Fifteen wide-spectrum senses analyzed the world; the machines maneuvered on tightly focused impeller fields. And absolutely no thought or mercy. Big beautiful death.

The window in the house in the hills was big and wide and the man stood in the middle of it. He was watching the *mechadors* hunt. There were four of them, two pairs working each side of the avenue. He saw the one with *Necroslayer* painted on its tectoplastic skin bound over the shrubbery from the Sifuentes place in a single pulse of focused electrogravitic force. It moved over the lawn, beaked head sensing. It paused, scanned the window. The man met its five cluster eyes for an instant. It moved on. Its impeller drive left eddy patterns on the shaved turf. The man watched until the *mechadors* passed out of sight, and the *seguridados* in their over-emphatic battle-armor came up the avenue, covering imagined threats with their hideously powerful weapons.

"It's every night now," he said. "They're getting scared."

In an instant, the woman was in the big, wood-floored room where the man stood. She was dressed in a virtuality bodyglove; snapped tendrils retracting into the suit's node points indicated the abruptness with which she had pulled out of the web. She was dark and very angry. Scared angry.

"Jesus Joseph Mary, how many times do I have to tell you? Keep away from that window! They catch you, you're dead. Again. *Permanently.*"

Solomon Gursky shrugged. In the few weeks that he had lived in her house, the woman had come to hate that shrug. It was a shrug that only the dead can make. She hated it because it brought the chill of the abyss into her big, warm, beautiful house in the hills.

"It changes things," the dead man said.

Elena Asado pulled smart-leather pants and a mesh top over the body-glove. Since turning traitor, she'd lived in the thing. Twelve hours a day hooked into the web by eye and ear and nose and soul, fighting the man who had killed her lover. As well fight God, Solomon Gursky thought in the long, empty hours in the airy, light-filled rooms. He is lord of life and death. Elena only removed the bodyglove to wash and excrete and, in those early, blue-lit mornings that only this city could do, when she made chilly love on the big white bed. Time and anger had made her thin and tough. She'd cut her hair like a boy's. Elena Asado was a tight wire of a woman, femininity jerked away by her need to revenge herself on Adam Tesler by destroying the world order his gift of resurrection had created.

Not gift. Never gift. He was not Jesus, who offered eternal life to whoever believed. No profit in belief. Adam Tesler took everything and left you your soul. If you could sustain the heavy *inmortalidad* payments, insurance would take you into post-life debt-free. The other 90 percent of Earth's dead worked out their salvation through indenture contracts to the Death House, the Tesler Thanos *corporada's* agent of resurrection. The *contratos* were centuries long. Time was the province of the dead. They were cheap.

"The Ewart/OzWest affair has them rattled," Elena Asado said.

"A handful of *contradados* renege on their contracts out on some asteroid, and they're afraid the sky is going to fall on their heads?"

"They're calling themselves the Freedead. You give a thing a name, you give it power. They know it's the beginning. Ewart/OzWest, all the other orbital and deep-space manufacturing *corporadas*; they always knew they could never enforce their contracts off Earth. They've lost already. Space belongs to the dead," the meat woman said.

Sol crossed the big room to the other window, the safe window that looked down from the high hills over the night city. His palm print deconfigured the glass. Night, city night perfumed with juniper and sex and smoke and the dusky heat of the heat of the day, curled around him. He went to the balcony rail. The boulevards shimmered like a map of a mind, but there was a great dark amnesia at its heart, an amorphous zone where lights were not, where the geometry of the grid was abolished. St. John. Necroville. Dead town. The city of the dead, a city within a city, walled and moated and guarded with the same weapons that swept the boulevards. City of curfew. Each dusk, the artificial aurora twenty kilometers above the Tres Valles Metropolitan Area would pulse red: the skysign, commanding all the three million dead to return from the streets of the living to their necrovilles. They passed through five gates, each in the shape of a massive V bisected by a horizontal line. The entropic flesh life descending, the eternal resurrected life ascending, through the dividing line of death. That was the law, that plane of separation. Dead was dead, living was living. As incompatible as night and day.

That same sign was fused into the palm of every resurrectee that stepped from the Death House Jesus tanks.

Not true, he thought. Not all are reborn with stigmata. Not all obey curfew. He held his hand before his face, studied the lines and creases, as if seeking a destiny written there.

He had seen the deathsign in the palm of Elena's housegirl, and how it flashed in time to the aurora.

"Still can't believe it's real?"

He had not heard Elena come onto the balcony behind him. He felt the touch of her hand on his hair, his shoulder, his bare arm. Skin on skin.

"The Nez Perce tribe believe the world ended on the third day, and what we are living in are the dreams of the last night. I fell. I hit that white light and it was hard. Hard as diamond. Maybe I dream I live, and my dreams are the last shattered moments of my life."

"Would you dream it like this?"

"No," he said after a time. "I can't recognize anything any more. I can't see how it connects to what I last remember. So much is missing."

"I couldn't make a move until I was sure he didn't suspect. He'd done a thorough job."

"He would."

"I never believed that story about the lifter crash. The universe may be ironic, but it's never neat."

"I think a lot about the poor bastard pilot he took out as well, just to make it neat." The air carried the far sound of drums from down in the dead town. To-morrow was the great feast, the Night of All the Dead. "Five years," he said. He heard the catch in her breathing and knew what she would say next, and what would follow.

"What is it like, being dead?" Elena Asado asked.

In his weeks imprisoned in the hill house, an unlawful dead, signless and contractless, he had learned that she did not mean, what was it like to be resur-rected. She wanted to know about the darkness before.

"Nothing," he answered, as he always did, but though it was true, it was not the truth, for nothing is a product of human consciousness and the darkness beyond the shattering hard light at terminal vee on Hoover Boulevard was the end of all consciousness. No dreams, no time, no loss, no light, no dark. No thing.

Now her fingers were stroking his skin, feeling for some of the chill of the nothing. He turned from the city and picked her up and carried her to the big empty bed. A month of new life was enough to learn the rules of the game. He took her in the big, wide white bed by the glow from the city beneath, and it was as chill and formulaic as every other time. He knew that for her it was more than sex with her lover come back from a far exile. He could feel in the twitch and splay of her muscles that what made it special for her was that he was *dead*. It delighted and repelled her. He suspected that she was incapable of orgasm with fellow meat. It did not trouble him, being her fetish. The body once known as Solomon Gursky knew another thing, that only the dead could know. It was that not everything that died was resurrected. The shape, the self, the sentience came back, but love did not pass through death.

Afterward, she liked him to talk about his resurrection, when no-thing became thing and he saw her face looking down through the swirl of tectors. This night he did not talk. He asked. He asked, "What was I like?"

"Your body?" she said. He let her think that. "You want to see the morgue photographs again?"

He knew the charred grin of a husk well enough. Hands flat at his sides. That was how she had known right away. Burn victims died with their fists up, fighting incineration.

"Even after I'd had you exhumed, I couldn't bring you back. I know you told me that he said I was safe, for the moment, but that moment was too soon. The technology wasn't sophisticated enough, and he would have known right away. I'm sorry I had to keep you on ice."

"I hardly noticed," he joked.

"I always meant to. It was planned; get out of Tesler Thanos, then contract an illegal Jesus tank down in St. John. The Death House doesn't know one tenth of what's going on in there."

"Thank you," Sol Gursky said, and then he felt it. He felt it and he saw it as if it were his own body. She felt him tighten.

"Another flashback?"

"No," he said. "The opposite. Get up."

"What?" she said. He was already pulling on leather and silk.

"That moment Adam gave you."

"Yes?"

"It's over."

The car was morphed into low and fast configuration. At the bend where the avenue slung itself down the hillside, they both felt the pressure wave of something large and flying pass over them, very low, utterly silent.

"Leave the car," he ordered. The doors were already gull-winged open. Three steps and the house went up behind them in a rave of white light. It seemed to suck at them, drawing them back into its annihilating gravity, then the shock swept them and the car and every homeless thing on the avenue before it. Through the screaming house alarms and the screaming householders and the rush and roar of the conflagration, Sol heard the aircraft turn above the vaporized hacienda. He seized Elena's hand and ran. The lifter passed over them and the car vanished in a burst of white energy.

"Jesus, nanotok warheads!"

Elena gasped as they tumbled down through tiered and terraced gardens. The lifter turned high on the air, eclipsing the hazy stars, hunting with extra-human senses. Below, formations of *seguridados* were spreading out through the gardens.

"How did you know?" Elena gasped.

"I saw it," said Solomon Gursky as they crashed a pool party and sent bacchanalian *cerristos* scampering for cover. Down, down. Augmented cyberhounds growled and quested with long-red eyes; domestic defense grids stirred, captured images, alerted the police.

"Saw?" asked Elena Asado.

APVs and city pods cut smoking hexagrams in the highway blacktop as Sol and Elena came crashing out of the service alley onto the boulevard. Horns. Lights. Fervid curses. Grind of wheels. Shriek of brakes. Crack of smashing tectoplastic, doubled, redoubled. Grid-pile on the westway. A mopedcab was pulled in at a *tortilleria* on the right shoulder. The *cochero* was happy to pass up his enchiladas for Elena's hard, black currency. Folding, clinking stuff.

"Where to?"

The destruction his passengers had wreaked impressed him. Taxi drivers universally hate cars.

"Drive," Solomon Gursky said.

The machine kicked out onto the strip.

"It's still up there," Elena said, squinting out from under the canopy at the night sky.

"They won't do anything in this traffic."

"They did it up there on the avenue." Then: "You said you saw. What do you mean, *saw?*"

"You know death, when you're dead," Solomon Gursky said. "You know its face, its mask, its smell. It has a perfume, you can smell it from a long way off, like the pheromones of moths. It blows upwind in time."

"Hey," the *cochero* said, who was poor, but live meat. "You know anything about that big boom up on the hill? What was that, lifter crash or something?"

"Or something," Elena said. "Keep driving."

"Need to know where to keep driving to, lady."

"Necroville," Solomon Gursky said. St. John. City of the Dead. The place beyond law, morality, fear, love, all the things that so tightly bound the living. The outlaw city. To Elena he said, "If you're going to bring down Adam Tesler, you can only do it from the outside, as an outsider." He said this in English. The words were heavy and tasted strange on his lips. "You must do it as one of the dispossessed. One of the dead."

To have tried to run the fluorescent vee-slash of the Necroville gate would have been as certain a Big Death as to have been reduced to hot ion dust in the nanotok flash. The mopedcab prowled past the samurai silhouettes of the gate *seguridados*. Sol had the driver leave them beneath the dusty palms on a deserted boulevard pressed up hard against the razor wire of St. John. Abandoned by the living, the grass verges had run verdant, scum and lilies scabbed the swimming pools, the generous Spanish-style houses softly disintegrating, digested by their own gardens.

It gave the *cochero* spooky vibes, but Sol liked it. He knew these avenues. The little machine putt-putted off for the lands of the fully living.

"There are culverted streams all round here," Sol said. "Some go right under the defenses, into Necroville."

"Is this your dead sight again?" Elena asked as he started down an overhung service alley.

"In a sense. I grew up around here."

"I didn't know that."

"Then I can trust it."

She hesitated a step.

"What are you accusing me of?"

"How much did you rebuild, Elena?"

"Your memories are your own, Sol. We loved each other, once."

"Once," he said, and then he felt it, a static purr on his skin, like Elena's fingers over his whole body at once. This was not the psychic bloom of death foreseen. This was physics, the caress of focused gravity fields.

They hit the turn of the alley as the *mechadors* came dropping soft and slow over the roofs of the old moldering *residencias*. Across a weed-infested tennis court was a drainage ditch defended by a rusted chicken-wire fence. Sol heaved away an entire section. Adam Tesler had built his dead strong, and fast. The refugees followed the seeping, rancid water down to a rusted grille in a culvert.

"Now we see if the Jesus tank grew me true," Sol said as he kicked in the grille. "If what I remember is mine, then we come up in St. John. If not, we end up in the bay three days from now with our eyes eaten out by chlorine."

They ducked into the culvert as a *mechador* passed over. MIST 27s sent the mud and water up in a blast of spray and battle tectors. The dead man and the living woman splashed on into darkness.

"He loved you, you know," Sol said. "That's why he's doing this. He is a jealous God. I always knew he wanted you, more than that bitch he calls a wife. While I was dead, he could pretend that it might still be. He could overlook what you were trying to do to him; you can't hurt him, Elena, not on your own. But when you brought me back, he couldn't pretend any longer. He couldn't turn a blind eye. He couldn't forgive you."

"A pretty God," Elena said, water eddying around her leather-clad calves. Ahead, a light from a circle in the roof of the culvert marked a drain from the street. They stood under it a moment, feeling the touch of the light of Necroville on their faces. Elena reached up to push open the grate. Solomon Gursky stayed her, turned her palm upward to the light.

"One thing." he said. He picked a sharp shard of concrete from the tunnel wall. With three strong savage strokes he cut the vee and slash of the death sign in her flesh.

THURSDAY

He was three kilometers down the mass driver when the fleet hit Marlene Dietrich. St. Judy's Comet was five AU from perihelion and out of ecliptic, the Clade thirty-six degrees out, but for an instant two suns burned in the sky.

The folds of transparent tectoplastic skin over Solomon Gursky's face opaqued. His *sur*-arms gripped the spiderwork of the interstellar engine, rocked by the impact on his electromagnetic senses of fifty minitok warheads converting into bevawatts of hard energy. The death scream of a nation. Three hundred Freedead had cluttered the freefall warren of tunnels that honeycombed the asteroid. Marlene Dietrich had been the seed of the rebellion. The *corporadas* cherished their grudges.

Solomon Gursky's face-shield cleared. The light of Marlene Dietrich's dying was short-lived but its embers faded in his infravision toward the stellar background.

Elena spoke in his skull.

You know?

Though she was enfolded in the command womb half a kilometer deep within the comet, she was naked to the universe through identity links to the sensor web in the crust and a nimbus of bacterium-sized spyships weaving through the tenuous gas halo.

I saw it, Solomon Gursky subvocalized.

They'll come for us now, Elena said.

You think. Using his *bas*-arms Sol clambered along the slender spine of the mass driver toward the micro meteorite impact.

I know. When long-range cleared after the blast, we caught the signatures of blip-fusion burns.

Hand over hand over hand over hand. One of the first things you learn, when the Freedead change you, is that in space it is all a question of attitude. A third of the way down a nine-kilometer mass driver with several billion tons of Oort comet spiked on it, you don't think up, you don't think down. *Up*, and it is vertigo. *Down*, and a two kilometer sphere of grubby ice is poised above your head by a thread of superconducting tectoplastic. *Out*, that was the only way to think of it and stay sane. Away, and back again.

How many drives? Sol asked. The impact pin-pointed itself; the smart plastic fluoresced orange when wounded.

Eight.

A sub-voiced blasphemy. *They didn't even make them break sweat. How long have we got?*

Elena flashed the projections through the em-link onto his visual cortex. Curves of light through darkness and time, warped across the gravitation marches of Jupiter. Under current acceleration, the Earth fleet would be within strike in eighty-two hours.

The war in heaven was in its twelfth year. Both sides had determined that this was to be the last. The NightFreight War would be fought to an outcome. They called themselves the Clades, the outlaw descendants of the original Ewart/OzWest asteroid rebellion: a handful of redoubts scattered across the appalling distances of the solar system. Marlene Dietrich, the first to declare freedom; Neruro, a half-completed twenty kilometer wheel of tectoplastic attended by O'Neill can utilities, agriculture tanks, and habitation bubbles, the aspirant capital of the space Dead. Ares Orbital, dreaming of tectoformed Mars in the pumice pore spaces of Phobos and Deimos; the Pale Gallileans, surfing over the icescapes of Europa on an improbable raft of cables and spars; the Shepherd Moons, dwellers on the edge of the abyss, sailing the solar wind through Saturn's rings. Toe-holds, shallow scratchings, space-hovels; but the stolen nanotechnology burgeoned in the energy-rich environment of space. An infinite ecological niche. The Freedead knew they were the inheritors of the universe. The meat *corporadas* had withdrawn to the orbit of their planet. For a time. When they struck, they struck decisively. The Tsiolkovski Clade on the dark side of the moon was the first to fall as the battle groups of the *corporadas* thrust outward. The delicate film of vacuum-compatible tectoformed forest that carpeted the crater was seared away in the alpha strike. By the time the last strike went in, a new five-kilometer-deep crater of glowing tufa replaced the tunnels and excavations of the old lunar mining base. Earth's tides had trembled as the moon staggered in its orbit.

Big Big Death.

The battle groups moved toward their primary targets. The *corporadas* had learned much embargoed under their atmosphere. The new ships were lean, mean, fast: multiple missile racks clipped to high-gee blip-fusion motors, pilots suspended in acceleration gel like flies in amber, hooked by every orifice into the big battle virtualizers.

Thirteen-year-old boys had the best combination of reaction time and viciousness.

Now the blazing teenagers had wantonly destroyed the Marlene Dietrich Clade. Ares Orbital was wide open; Neruro, where most of the Freedead slamship fleet was based, would fight hard. Two *corporada* ships had been dispatched Jupiterward. Orbital mechanics gave the defenseless Pale Gallileans fifteen months to contemplate their own annihilation.

But the seed has flown, Solomon Gursky thought silently, out on the mass driver of St. Judy's Comet. Where were are going, neither your most powerful ships nor your most vicious boys can reach us.

The micrometeorite impact had scrambled the tectoplastic's limited intelligence: fibers and filaments of smart polymer twined and coiled, seeking completion and purpose. Sol touched his *sur*-hands to the surfaces. He imagined he could feel the order pass out of him, like a prickle of tectors osmosing through vacuum-tight skin.

Days of miracles and wonder, Adam, he thought. And because you are jealous that we are doing things with your magic you never dreamed, you would blast us all to photons.

The breach was repaired. The mass driver trembled and kicked a pellet into space, and another, and another. And Sol Gursky, working his way hand over hand over hand over hand down the device that was taking him to the stars, saw the trick of St. Judy's Comet. A ball of fuzzy ice drawing a long tail behind it. Not a seed, but a sperm, swimming through the big dark. Thus we impregnate the universe.

St. Judy's Comet. Petite as Oort cloud family members go: two point eight by one point seven by two point two kilometers. (Think of the misshaped potato you push to the side of your plate because anything that looks that weird is sure to give you cramps.) Undernourished, at sixty-two billion tons. Waif and stray of the solar system, wandering slow and lonely back out into the dark after her hour in the sun (but not too close, burn you real bad, too much sun) when these dead people snatch her, grope her all over, shove things up her ass, mess with her insides, make her do strange and unnatural acts, like shitting tons of herself away every second at a good percentage of the speed of light. Don't you know you ain't no comet no more? You're a *starship*. See up there, in the Swan, just to the left of that big bright star? There's a little dim star you can't see. That's where you're going, little St. Judy. Take some company. Going to be a long trip. And what will I find when I get there? A big bastard MACHO of gas supergiant orbiting 61 Cygni at the distance of Saturn from the sun, that's what you'll find. Just swarming with moons; one of them should be right for terrestrial life. And if not, no matter; sure, what's the difference between tectoforming an asteroid, or a comet, or the moon of an extra-solar gas super-giant? Just scale. You see, we've got everything we need to tame a new solar system right here *with* us. It's all just carbon, hydrogen, nitrogen, and oxygen, and you have that in abundance. And maybe we like you so much that we find we don't even need a world at all. Balls of muck and gravity, hell; we're the Freedead. Space and time belong to us.

It was Solomon Gursky, born in another century, who gave the ship its name. In that other century, he had owned a large and eclectic record collection. On vinyl.

The twenty living dead crew of St. Judy's Comet gathered in the command womb embedded in sixty-two billion tons of ice to plan battle. The other five hundred and forty were stored as superconducting tector matrices in a helium ice core; the dead dead, to be resurrected out of comet stuff at their new home. The crew hovered in nanogee in a score of different orientations around the free-floating instrument clusters. They were strange and beautiful, as gods and angels are. Like angels, they flew. Like gods in some pantheons, they were four-armed. Fine, manipulating *sur*-arms; strong grasping *bas*-arms growing from a lower spine reconfigured by Jesus tanks into powerful anterior shoulder-blades. Their vacuum-and-radiation-tight skins were photosynthetic, and as beautifully marked and colored as a hunting animal's. Stripes, swirls of green on orange, blue on black, fractal patterns, flags of legendary nations, tattoos. Illustrated humans.

Elena Asado, caressed by tendrils from the sensor web gave them the stark news. Fluorescent patches on shoulders, hips, and groin glowed when she spoke.

"The bastards have jumped vee. They must have burned every last molecule of hydrogen in their thruster tanks to do it. Estimated to strike range is now sixty-four hours."

The *captain* of St. Judy's Comet, a veteran of the Marlene Dietrich rebellion, shifted orientation to face Jorge, the ship's reconfiguration engineer.

"Long range defenses?" *Capitan* Savita's skin was an exquisite mottle of pale green bamboo leaves in sun yellow, an incongruous contrast to the tangible anxiety in the command womb.

"First wave missiles will be fully grown and launch-ready in twenty-six hours. The fighters, no. The best I can push the assemblers up to is sixty-six hours."

"What can you do in time?" Sol Gursky asked.

"With your help, I could simplify the fighter design for close combat."

"How close?" *Capitan* Savita asked.

"Under a hundred kays."

"How simplified?" Elena asked.

"Little more than an armed exo-skeleton with maneuvering pods."

And they need to be clever every time, Sol thought. The meat need to be clever only once.

Space war was as profligate with time as it was with energy and distance. With the redesigns growing, Sol Gursky spent most of the twenty-six hours to missile launch on the ice, naked to the stars, imagining their warmth on his face-shield. Five years since he had woken from his second death in a habitat bubble out at Marlene Dietrich, and stars had never ceased to amaze him. When you come back, you are tied to the first thing you see. Beyond the transparent tectoplastic bubble, it had been stars.

The first time, it had been Elena. Tied together in life, now in death. Necroville had not been sanctuary. The place beyond the law only gave Adam Tesler new and more colorful opportunities to incarnate his jealousy. The Benthic Lords, they had called themselves. Wild, free, dead. They probably had not known they were working for Tesler-Thanos, but they took her out in a dead bar on Terminal Boulevard. With a game-fishing harpoon. They carved their skull symbol on her forehead, a rebuttal of the deathsign Sol had cut in her palm. Now you are really dead, meat. He had known they would never be safe on Earth. The *companeros* in the Death House had faked the off-world NightFreight contracts. The pill Sol took had been surprisingly bitter, the dive into the white light as hard as he remembered.

Stars. You could lose yourself in them; spirit strung out, orb gazing. Somewhere out there was a still-invisible constellation of eight, tight formation, silent running. Killing stars. Death stars.

Everyone came up to watch the missiles launch from the black foramens grown out of the misty ice. The chemical motors burned at twenty kays: a sudden galaxy of white stars. They watched them fade from sight. Twelve hours to contact. No one expected them to do any more than waste a few thousand rounds of the meat's point defenses.

In a dozen manufacturing pods studded around St. Judy's dumpy waist, Jorge and Sol's fighters gestated. Their slow accretion, molecule by molecule, fascinated

Sol. Evil dark things, St. Andrew's crosses cast in melted bone. At the center a human-shaped cavity. You flew spread-eagled. *Bas*-hands gripped thruster controls; *sur*-hands armed and aimed the squirt lasers. Dark flapping things Sol had glimpsed once before flocked again at the edges of his consciousness. He had cheated the dark premonitory angels that other time. He would sleight them again.

The first engagement of the battle of St. Judy's Comet was at 01:45 GMT. Solomon Gursky watched it with his crewbrethren in the ice-wrapped warmth of the command womb. His virtualized sight perceived space in three dimensions. Those blue cylinders were the *corporada* ships. That white swarm closing from a hundred different directions, the missiles. One approached a blue cylinder and burst. Another, and another; then the inner display was a glare of novas as the first wave was annihilated. The backup went in. The vanguard exploded in beautiful futile blossoms of light. Closer. They were getting closer before the meat shredded them. Sol watched a warhead loop up from due south, streak toward the point ship, and annihilate it in a red flash.

The St. Judy's Cometeers cheered. One gone, reduced to bubbling slag by tectors sprayed from the warhead.

One was all they got. It was down to the fighter pilots now.

Sol and Elena made love in the count-up to launch. *Bas*-arms and *sur*-arms locked in the freegee of the forward observation blister. Stars described slow arcs across the transparent dome, like a sky. Love did not pass through death; Elena had realized this bitter truth about what she had imagined she had shared with Solomon Gursky in her house on the hillside. But love could grow, and become a thing shaped for eternity. When the fluids had dried on their skins, they sealed their soft, intimate places with vacuum-tight skin and went up to the launch bays.

Sol fitted her into the scooped-out shell. Tectoplastic fingers gripped Elena's body and meshed with her skin circuitry. The angel-suit came alive. There was a trick they had learned in their em-telepathy; a massaging of the limbic system like an inner kiss. One mutual purr of pleasure, then she cast off, suit still dripping gobs of frozen tectopolymer. St. Judy's defenders would fight dark and silent; that mental kiss would be the last radio contact until it was decided. Solomon Gursky watched the blue stutter of the thrusters merge with the stars. Reaction mass was limited; those who returned from the fight would jettison their angel-suits and glide home by solar sail. Then he went below to monitor the battle through the tickle of molecules in his frontal lobes.

St. Judy's Angels formed two squadrons: one flying anti-missile defense, the other climbing high out of the ecliptic to swoop down on the *corporada* ships and destroy them before they could empty their weapon racks. Elena was in the close defense group. Her angelship icon was identified in Sol's inner vision in red on gold tiger stripes of her skin. He watched her weave intricate orbits around St. Judy's Comet as the blue cylinders of the meat approached the plane labeled "strike range."

Suddenly, seven blue icons spawned a cloud of actinic sparks, raining down on St. Judy's Comet like fireworks.

"Jesus Joseph Mary!" someone swore quietly.

"Fifty-five gees," *Capitan* Savita said calmly. "Time to contact, one thousand and eighteen seconds."

"They'll never get them all," said Kobe with the Mondrian skin pattern, who had taken Elena's place in remote sensing.

"We have one hundred and fifteen contacts in the first wave," Jorge announced.

"Sol, I need delta vee," Savita said.

"More than a thousandth of a gravity and the mass driver coils will warp," Sol said, calling overlays onto his visual cortex.

"Anything that throws a curve into their computations," Savita said.

"I'll see how close I can push it."

He was glad to have to lose himself in the problems of squeezing a few millimeters per second squared out of the big electromagnetic gun, because then he would not be able to see the curve and swoop of attack vectors and intercept planes as the point defense group closed with the missiles. Especially he would not have to watch the twine and loop of the tiger-striped cross and fear that at any instant it would intersect with a sharp blue curve in a flash of annihilation. One by one, those blue stars were going out, he noticed, but slowly. Too slowly. Too few.

The computer gave him a solution. He fed it to the mass driver. The shift of acceleration was as gentle as a catch of breath.

Thirty years since he had covered his head in a synagogue, but Sol Gursky prayed to Yahweh that it would be enough.

One down already; Emilio's spotted indigo gone, and half the missiles were still on trajectory. Time to impact ticked down impassively in the upper right corner of his virtual vision. Six hundred and fifteen seconds. Ten minutes to live.

But the attack angels were among the *corporadas*, dodging the brilliant flares of short range interceptor drones. The meat fleet tried to scatter, but the ships were low on reaction mass, ungainly, unmaneuverable. St. Judy's Angels dived and sniped among them, clipping a missile rack here, a solar panel there, ripping open life support bubbles and fuel tanks in slow explosions of outgassing hydrogen. The thirteen-year-old pilots died, raging with chemical-induced fury, spilled out into vacuum in tears of flash-frozen acceleration gel. The attacking fleet dwindled from seven to five to three ships. But it was no abattoir of the meat; of the six dead angels that went in, only two pulled away into rendezvous orbit, laser capacitors dead, reaction mass spent. The crews ejected, unfurled their solar sails, shields of light.

Two meat ships survived. One used the last grams of his maneuvering mass to warp into a return orbit; the other routed his thruster fuel through his blip drive; headlong for St. Judy.

"He's going for a ram," Kobe said.

"Sol, get us away from him," *Capitan* Savita ordered.

"He's too close." The numbers in Sol's skull were remorseless. "Even if I cut the mass driver, he can still run life support gas through the STUs to compensate."

The command womb quivered.

"Fuck," someone swore reverently.

"Near miss," Kobe reported. "Direct hit if Sol hadn't given us gees."

"Mass driver is still with us," Sol said.

"Riley's gone," *Capitan* Savita said.

Fifty missiles were now twenty missiles but Emilio and Riley were dead, and the range was closing. Little room for maneuver; none for mistakes.

"Two hundred and fifteen seconds to ship impact," Kobe announced. The main body of missiles was dropping behind St. Judy's Comet. Ogawa and Skin, Mandelbrot set and Dalmatian spots, were fighting a rearguard as the missiles tried to reacquire their target. Olive green ripples and red tiger stripes swung round to face the meat ship. Quinsana and Elena.

Jesus Joseph Mary, but it was going to be close!

Sol wished he did not have the graphics in his head. He wished not to have to see. Better sudden annihilation, blindness and ignorance shattered by destroying light. To see, to *know*, to count the digits on the timer, was as cruel as execution. But the inner vision has no eyelids. So he watched, impotent, as Quinsana's olive green cross was pierced and shattered by a white flare from the meat ship. And he watched as Elena raked the meat with her lasers and cut it into quivering chunks, and the blast of engines destroying themselves sent the shards of ship arcing away from St. Judy's Comet. And he could only watch, and not look away, as Elena turned too slow, too little, too late, as the burst seed-pod of the environment unit tore off her thruster legs and light sail and sent her spinning end over end, crippled, destroyed.

"Elena!" he screamed in both his voices. "Elena! Oh Jesus oh God!" But he had never believed in either of them, and so they let Elena Asado go tumbling endlessly toward the beautiful galaxy clusters of Virgo.

Earth's last rage against her children expired: twenty missiles dwindled to ten, to five, to one. To none. St. Judy's Comet continued her slow climb out of the sun's gravity well, into the deep dark and the deeper cold. Its five hundred and twenty souls slept sound and ignorant as only the dead can in tombs of ice. Soon Solomon Gursky and the others would join them, and be dissolved into the receiving ice, and die for five hundred years while St. Judy's Comet made the crossing to another star.

If it were sleep, then I might forget, Solomon Gursky thought. In sleep, things changed, memories became dreams, dreams memories. In sleep, there was time, and time was change, and perhaps a chance of forgetting the vision of her, spinning outward forever, rebuilt by the same forces that had already resurrected her once, living on sunlight, unable to die. But it was not sleep to which he was going. It was death, and that was nothing any more.

FRIDAY

Together they watched the city burn. It was one of the ornamental cities of the plain that the Long Scanning folk built and maintained for the quadrennial eisteddfods. There was something of the flower in the small, jewellike city, and something of the spiral, and something of the sea-wave. It would have been as accurate to call it a vast building as a miniature city. It burned most elegantly.

The fault line ran right through the middle of it. The fissure was clean and precise—no less to be expected of the Long Scanning folk—and bisected the curvilinear architecture from top to bottom. The land still quivered to aftershocks.

It could have repaired itself. It could have doused the flames—a short in the magma tap, the man reckoned—reshaped the melted ridges and roofs, erased the scorch marks, bridged the cracks and chasms. But its tector systems were directionless, its soul withdrawn to the Heaven Tree, to join the rest of the Long Scanning people on their exodus.

The woman watched the smoke rise into the darkening sky, obscuring the great opal of Urizen.

"It doesn't have to do this," she said. Her skin spoke of sorrow mingled with puzzlement.

"They've no use for it any more," the man said. "And there's a certain beauty in destruction."

"It scares me," the woman said, and her skin pattern agreed. "I've never seen anything *end* before."

Lucky, the man thought, in a language that had come from another world.

An eddy in his weathersight: big one coming. But they were all big ones since the orbital perturbations began. Big, getting bigger. At the end, the storms would tear the forests from their roots as the atmosphere shrieked into space.

That afternoon, on their journey to the man's memories, they had come across an empty marina; drained, sand clogged, pontoons torn and tossed by tsunamis. Its crew of boats they found scattered the length of a half-hour's walk. Empty shells stogged to the waist in dune faces, masts and sails hung from trees.

The weather had been the first thing to tear free from control. The man felt a sudden tautness in the woman's body. She was seeing it to, the mid-game of the end of the world.

By the time they reached the sheltered valley that the man's aura had picked as the safest location to spend the night, the wind had risen to draw soft moans and chords from the curves and crevasses of the dead city. As their cloaks of elementals joined and sank the roots of the night shell into rock, a flock of bubbles bowled past, trembling and iridescent in the gusts. The woman caught one on her hand; the tiny creature-machine clung for a moment, feeding from her biofield. Its transparent skin raced with oil-film colors, it quaked and burst, a melting bubble of tectoplasm. The woman watched it until the elementals had completed the shelter, but the thing stayed dead.

Their love-making was both urgent and chilled under the scalloped carapace the elementals had sculpted from rock silica. *Sex and death*, the man said in the part of his head where not even his sub-vocal withspeech could overhear and transmit. An alien thought.

She wanted to talk afterward. She liked to talk after sex. Unusually, she did not ask him to tell her about how he and the other Five Hundred Fathers had built the world. Her idea of talking was him talking. Tonight she did not want to talk about the world's beginning. She wanted him to talk about its ending.

"Do you know what I hate about it? It's not that it's all going to end, all this. It's that a bubble burst in my hand, and I can't comprehend what *happened* to it. How much more our whole world?"

"There is a word for what you felt," the man interjected gently. The gyrestorm was at its height, raging over the dome of their shell. The thickness of a skin is all that is keeping the wind from stripping the flesh from my bones, he thought. But the tectors' grip on the bedrock was firm and sure. "The word is *die*."

The woman sat with her knees pulled up, arms folded around them. Naked: the gyrestorm was blowing through her soul.

"What I hate," she said after silence, "is that I have so little time to see and feel it all before it's taken away into the cold and the dark."

She was a Green, born in the second of the short year's fast seasons: a Green of the Hidden Design people; first of the Old Red Ridge pueblo people to come into the world in eighty years. And the last.

Eight years old.

"You won't die," the man said, skin patterning in whorls of reassurance and paternal concern, like the swirling storms of great Urizen beyond the hurtling gyre-storm clouds. "You can't die. No one will die."

"I know that. No one will die, we will all be changed, or sleep with the world. But . . ."

"Is it frightening, to have to give up this body?"

She touched her forehead to her knees, shook her head.

"I don't want to lose it. I've only begun to understand what it is, this body, this world, and it's all going to be taken away from me, and all the powers that are my birthright are useless."

"There are forces beyond even nanotechnology," the man said. "It makes us masters of matter, but the fundamental dimensions—gravity, space, time—it cannot touch."

"Why?" the woman said, and to the man, who counted by older, longer years, she spoke in the voice of her terrestrial age.

"We will learn it, in time," the man said, which he knew was no answer. The woman knew it too, for she said, "While Orc is two hundred million years from the warmth of the next sun, and its atmosphere is a frozen glaze on these mountains and valleys." *Grief*, he skin said. *Rage. Loss.*

The two-thousand-year-old father touched the young woman's small, upturned breasts.

"We knew Urizen's orbit was unstable, but no one could have predicted the interaction with Ulro." Ironic: that this world named after Blake's fire daemon should be the one cast into darkness and ice, while Urizen and its surviving moons should bake two million kilometers above the surface of Los.

"Sol, you don't need to apologize to me for mistakes you made two thousand years ago," said the woman, whose name was Lenya.

"But I think I need to apologize to the world," said Sol Gursky.

Lenya's skin-speech now said *hope* shaded with *inevitability*. Her nipples were erect. Sol bent to them again as the wind from the end of the world scratched its claws over the skin of tectoplastic.

In the morning, they continued the journey to Sol's memories. The gyrestorm had blown itself out in the Oothoon mountains. What remained of the ghost-net told Sol and Lenya that it was possible to fly that day. They suckled milch from the shell's tree of life processor, and they had sex again on the dusty earth while the elementals reconfigured the night pod into a general utility flier. For the rest of the morning, they passed over a plain across which grazebeasts and the tall, predatory angularities of the stalking Systems Maintenance people moved like ripples on a lake, drawn to the Heaven Tree planted in the navel of the world.

Both grazers and herders had been human once.

At noon, the man and the woman encountered a flyer of the Generous Sky people, flapping a silk-winged course along the thermal lines rising from the feet of the Big Chrysolite mountains. Sol with-hailed him, and they set down together in a clearing in the bitter-root forests that carpeted much of Coryphee Canton. The Generous Sky man's etiquette would normally have compelled him to disdain those ground bound who sullied the air with machines, but in these urgent times, the old ways were breaking.

Whither bound? Sol withspoke him. Static crackled in his skull. The lingering tail of the gyrestorm was throwing off electromagnetic disturbances.

Why, the Heaven Tree of course, the winged man said. He was a horrifying kite of translucent skin over stick bones and sinews. His breast was like the prow of a ship, his muscles twitched and realigned as he shifted from foot to foot, uncomfortable on the earth. A gentle breeze wafted from the nanofans grown out of the web of skin between wrists and ankles. The air smelled of strange sweat. *Whither yourselves?*

The Heaven Tree also, in time, Sol said. *But I must first recover my memories.*

Ah, a father, the Sky man said. *Whose are you?*

Hidden Design, Sol said. *I am father to this woman and her people.*

You are Solomon Gursky, the flying man withsaid. *My progenitor is Nikos Samitreides.*

I remember her well, though I have not seen her in many years. She fought bravely at the battle of St. Judy's Comet.

I am third of her lineage. Eighteen hundred years I have been on this world.

A question, if I may. Lenya's withspeech was a sudden bright interruption in the dialogue of old men. Using an honorific by which a younger adult addresses an experienced senior, she asked, *When the time comes, how will you change?*

An easy question, the Generous Sky man said, *I shall undergo the reconfiguration for life on Urizen. To me, it is little difference whether I wear the outward semblance of a man, or a jetpowered aerial manta: it is flying, and such flying! Canyons of clouds hundreds of kilometers deep; five thousand kilometer per hour winds; thermals great as continents; mad storms as big as planets! And no land, no base; to be able to fly forever free from the tyranny of Earth. The song cycles we shall compose; eddas that will carry half way around the planet on the jet streams of Urizen!* The Generous Sky man's eyes had closed in rapture. They suddenly opened. His nostrils dilated, sensing an atmospheric change intangible to the others.

Another storm is coming, bigger than the last. I advise you to take shelter within rock, for this will pluck the bitter-roots from the soil.

He spread his wings. The membranes rippled. A tiny hop, and the wind caught him and in an instant carried him up into a thermal. Sol and Lenya watched him glide the tops of the lifting air currents until he was lost in the deep blue sky.

For exercise and the conversation of the way, they walked that afternoon. They followed the migration track of the Rough Trading people through the tieve forests of south Coryphee and Emberwilde Cantons. Toward evening, with the gathering wind stirring the needles of the tieves to gossip, they met a man of the Ash species sitting on a chair in a small clearing among the trees. He was long and coiling, and his skin said that he was much impoverished from lack of a host. Lenya offered her arm, and though the Ash man's compatibility was more with the Buried Communication people than the Hidden Design, he gracefully accepted her heat, her morphic energy, and a few drops of blood.

"Where is your host?" Lenya asked him. A parasite, he had the languages of most nations. Hosts were best seduced by words, like lovers.

"He has gone with the herds," the Ash man said. "To the Heaven Tree. It is ended."

"And what will you do when Orc is expelled?" The rasp marks on Lenya's forearm where the parasitic man had sipped her blood were already healing over.

"I cannot live alone," the Ash man said. "I shall ask the earth to open and swallow me and kill me. I shall sleep in the earth until the warmth of a new sun awakens me to life again."

"But that will be two hundred million years," Lenya said. The Ash man looked at her with the look that said, *one year, one million years, one hundred million years, they are nothing to death.* Because she knew that the man thought her a new-hatched fool, Lenya felt compelled to look back at him as she and Sol walked away along the tieve tracks. She saw the parasite pressed belly and balls to the ground, as he would to a host. Dust spiraled up around him. He slowly sank into the earth.

Sol and Lenya did not have sex that night in the pod for the first time since Solomon the Traveler had come to the Old Red Ridge pueblo and taken the eye and heart of the brown girl dancing in the ring. That night there was the greatest earthquake yet as Orc kicked in his orbit, and even a shell of tectodiamond seemed inadequate protection against forces that would throw a planet into interstellar space. They held each other, not speaking, until the earth grew quiet and a wave of heat passed over the carapace, which was the tieve forests of Emberwilde Canton burning.

The next morning, they morphed the pod into an ash-runner and drove through the cindered forest, until at noon they came to the edge of the Inland Sea. The tectonic trauma had sent tidal waves swamping the craggy islet on which Sol had left his memories, but the self-repair systems had used the dregs of their stored power to rebuild the damaged architecture.

As Sol was particular that they must approach his memories by sea, they ordered the ash-runner to reconfigure into a skiff. While the tectors moved molecules, a man of the Blue Mana pulled himself out of the big surf on to the red shingle. He was long and huge and sleek; his shorn turf of fur was beautifully marked. He lay panting from the exertion of heaving himself from his customary element into an alien one. Lenya addressed him familiarly—Hidden Design and the amphibious Blue Mana had been one until a millennium ago—and asked him the same question she had put to the others she had encountered on the journey.

"I am already reconfiguring my body fat into an aircraft to take me to the Heaven Tree," the Blue Mana said. "Climatic shifts permitting."

"Is it bad in the sea?" Sol Gursky asked.

"The seas feel the changes first," the amphiman said. "Bad. Yes, most bad. I cannot bear the thought of Mother Ocean freezing clear to her beds."

"Will you go to Urizen, then?" Lenya asked, thinking that swimming must be much akin to flying.

"Why, bless you, no." The Blue Mana man's skin spelled puzzled surprise. "Why should I share any less fate than Mother Ocean? We shall both end in ice."

"The comet fleet," Sol Gursky said.

"If the Earth ship left any legacy, it is that there are many mansions in this universe where we may live. I have a fancy to visit those other settled systems that the ship told us of, experience those others ways of being human."

A hundred Orc-years had passed since the second comet-ship from Earth had entered the Los system to refuel from Urizen's rings, but the news it had carried of a home system transfigured by the nanotechnology of the ascendant dead, and of the other stars that had been reached by the newer, faster, more powerful descendants of St. Judy's Comet had ended nineteen hundred years of solitude and brought the first, lost colony of Orc into the visionary community of the star-crossing Dead. *Long before your emergence*, Sol thought, looking at the crease of Lenya's groin as she squatted on the pebbles to converse with the Blue Mana man. Emergence. A deeper, older word shadowed that expression; a word obsolete in the universe of the dead. *Birth*. No one had ever been born on Orc. No one had ever known childhood, or grown up. No one aged, no one died. They *emerged*. They stepped from the labia of the gestatory, fully formed, like gods.

Sol knew the word *child*, but realized with a shock that he could not see it any more. It was blank, void. So many things decreated in this world he had engineered!

By sea and by air. A trading of elements. Sol Gursky's skiff was completed as the Blue Mana's tectors transformed his blubber into a flying machine. Sol watched it spin into the air and recede to the south as the boat dipped through the chop toward the island of memory.

We live forever, we transform ourselves, we transform worlds, solar systems, we ship across interstellar space, we defy time and deny death, but the one thing we cannot re-create is memory, he thought. Sea birds dipped in the skiff's wake, hungry, hoping. Things cast up by motion. We cannot rebuild our memories, so we must store them, when our lives grow so full that they slop over the sides and evaporate. We Five Hundred Fathers have deep and much-emptied memories.

Sol's island was a rock slab tilted out of the equatorial sea, a handful of hard hectares. Twisted repro olives and cypresses screened a small Doric temple at the highest point. Good maintenance tectors had held it strong against the Earth storms. The classical theming now embarrassed Sol, but enchanted Lenya. She danced beneath the olive branches, under the porticoes, across the lintels. Sol saw her again as he had that first night in the Small-year-ending ring dance at Old Red Ridge. Old lust. New hurt.

In the sunlit central chamber, Lenya touched the reliefs of the life of Solomon Gursky. They would not yield their memories to her fingers, but they communicated in less sophisticated ways.

"This woman." She had stopped in front of a pale stone carving of Solomon Gursky and a tall, ascetic-faced woman with close-cropped hair standing hand in hand before a tall, ghastly tower.

"I loved her. She died in the battle of St. Judy's Comet. Big dead."

Lost.

"So is it only because I remind you of her?"

He touched the carving. Memory bright and sharp as pain arced along his nerves; mnemotectors downloading into his aura. *Elena*. And a memory of orbit;

the Long March ended, the object formerly known as St. Judy's Comet spun out into a web of beams and girders and habitations pods hurtling across the frosted red dustscapes of Orc. A web ripe with hanging fruit; entry pods ready to drop and spray the new world with life seed. Tectoforming. Among the fruit, seeds of the Five Hundred Fathers, founders of all the races of Orc. Among them, the Hidden Design and Solomon Gursky, four-armed, vacuum-proofed, avatar of life and death, clinging to a beam with the storms of Urizen behind him, touching his transforming *sur*-arms to the main memory of the mother seed. Remember her. Remember Elena. And sometime—soon, late—bring her back. Imprint her with an affinity for his scent, so that wherever she is, whoever she is with, she will come to me.

He saw himself scuttling like a guilty spider across the web as the pods dropped Orc-ward.

He saw himself in this place with Urizen's moons at syzygy, touching his hands to the carving, giving to it what it now returned to him, because he knew that as long as it was Lenya who reminded him of Elena, it could pretend to be honest. But the knowledge killed it. Lenya was more than a reminder. Lenya as Elena. Lenya was a simulacrum, empty, fake. Her life, her joy, her sorrow, her love—all deceit.

He had never expected that she would come back to him at the end of the world. They should have had thousands of years. The world gave them days.

He could not look at her as he moved from relief to relief, charging his aura with memory. He could not touch her as they waited on the shingle for the skiff to reconfigure into the flyer that would take them to the Heaven Tree. On the high point of the slab island, the Temple of Memory dissolved like rotting fungus. He did not attempt sex with her as the flyer passed over the shattered landscapes of Thel and the burned forests of Chrysoberyl as they would have, before. She did not understand. She imagined she had hurt him somehow. She had, but the blame was Sol's. He could not tell her why he had suddenly expelled himself from her warmth. He knew that he should, that he must, but he could not. He changed his skin-speech to passive, mute, and reflected that much cowardice could be learned in five hundred long-years.

They came with the evening to the Skyplain plateau from which the Heaven Tree rose, an adamantine black ray aimed at the eye of Urizen. As far as they could see, the plain twinkled with the lights and fires of vehicles and camps. Warmsight showed a million glowings: all the peoples of Orc, save those who had chosen to go into the earth, had gathered in this final redoubt. Seismic stabilizing tectors woven into the moho held steady the quakes that had shattered all other lands, but temblors of increasing violence warned that they could not endure much longer. At the end, Skyplain would crack like an egg, the Heaven Tree snap and recoil spaceward like a severed nerve.

Sol's Five Hundred Father ident pulled his flyer out of the wheel of aircraft, airships, and aerial humans circling the stalk of the Heaven Tree into a priority slot on an ascender. The flyer caught the shuttle at five kilometers: a sudden veer toward the slab sides of the space elevator, guidance matching velocities with the accelerating ascender; then the drop, heart-stopping even for immortals, and the lurch as the flyer seized the docking nipple with its claspers and clung like a tick. Then the long climb heavenward.

Emerging from high altitude cloud, Sol saw the hard white diamond of Ulro rise above the curve of the world. Too small yet to show a disc, but this barren rock searing under heavy CO_2 exerted forced powerful enough to kick a moon into interstellar space. Looking up through the transparent canopy, he saw the Heaven Tree spread its delicate, light-studded branches hundreds of kilometers across the face of Urizen.

Sol Gursky broke his silence.

"Do you know what you'll do yet?"

"Well, since I am here, I am not going into the ground. And the ice fleet scares me. I think of centuries dead, a tector frozen in ice. It seems like death."

"It is death," Sol said. "Then you'll go to Urizen."

"It's a change of outward form, that's all. Another way of being human. And there'll be continuity; that's important to me."

He imagined the arrival: the ever-strengthening tug of gravity spiraling the flocks of vacuum-hardened carapaces inward; the flickers of withspeech between them, anticipation, excitement, fear as they grazed the edge of the atmosphere and felt ion flames lick their diamond skins. Lenya, falling, burning with the fires of entry as she cut a glowing trail across half a planet. The heat-shell breaking away as she unfurled her wings in the eternal shriek of wind and the ram-jets in her sterile womb kindled and roared.

"And you?" she asked. Her skin said *gentle*. Confused as much by his breaking of it as by his silence, but *gentle*.

"I have something planned," was all he said, but because that plan meant they would never meet again, he told her then what he had learned in the Temple of Memory. He tried to be kind and understanding, but it was still a bastard thing to do, and she cried in the nest in the rear of the flyer all the way out of the atmosphere, half-way to heaven. It was a bastard thing and as he watched the stars brighten beyond the canopy, he could not say why he had done it, except that it was necessary to kill some things Big Dead so that they could never come back again. She cried now, and her skin was so dark it would not speak to him, but when she flew, it would be without any lingering love or regret for a man called Solomon Gursky.

It is good to be hated, he thought, as the Heaven Tree took him up into its starlit branches.

The launch laser was off, the reaction mass tanks were dry. Solomon Gursky fell outward from the sun. Urizen and its children were far beneath him. His course lay out of the ecliptic, flying north. His aft eyes made out a new pale ring orbiting the gas world, glowing in the low warmsight: the millions of adapted waiting in orbit for their turns to make the searing descent into a new life.

She would be with them now. He had watched her go into the seed and be taken apart by her own elementals. He had watched the seed split and expel her into space, transformed, and burn her few kilos of reaction mass on the transfer orbit to Urizen.

Only then had he felt free to undergo his own transfiguration.

Life swarm. Mighty. So nearly right, so utterly wrong. She had almost sung when she spoke of the freedom of endless flight in the clouds of Urizen, but she would never fly freer than she did now, naked to space, the galaxy before her. The freedom of Urizen was a lie, the price exacted by its gravity and pressure. She had trapped herself in atmosphere and gravity. Urizen was another world. The parasitic man of the Ash nation had buried himself in a world. The aquatic Blue Mana, after long sleep in ice, would only give rise to another copy of the standard model. Worlds upon worlds.

Infinite ways of being human, Solomon Gursky thought, outbound from the sun. He could feel the gentle stroke of the solar wind over the harsh dermal prickle of Urizen's magnetosphere. Sun arising. Almost time.

Many ways of being Solomon Gursky, he thought, contemplating his new body. His analogy was with a conifer. He was a redwood cone fallen from the Heaven Tree, ripe with seeds. Each seed a Solomon Gursky, a world in embryo.

The touch of the sun, that was what had opened those seed cones on that other world, long ago. Timing was too important to be left to higher cognitions. Subsystems had all the launch vectors programmed; he merely registered the growing strength of the wind from Los on his skin and felt himself begin to open. Solomon Gursky unfolded into a thousand scales. As the seeds exploded onto their preset courses, he burned to the highest orgasm of his memory before his persona downloaded into the final spore and ejected from the empty, dead carrier body.

At five hundred kilometers, the seeds unfurled their solar sails. The breaking wave of particles, with multiple gravity assists from Luvah and Enitharmon, would surf the bright flotilla up to interstellar velocities, as, at the end of the centuries—millennia—long flights, the light-sails would brake the packages at their destinations.

He did not know what his many selves would find there. He had not picked targets for their resemblance to what he was leaving behind. That would be just another trap. He sensed his brothers shutting down their cognitive centers for the big sleep, like stars going out, one by one. A handful of seeds scattered, some to wither, some to grow. Who can say what he will find, except that it will be extraordinary. Surprise me! Solomon Gursky demanded of the universe, as he fell into the darkness between suns.

SATURDAY

The object was one point three astronomical units on a side, and at its current 10 percent C would arrive in thirty-five hours. On his chaise lounge by the Neptune fountain, Solomon Gursky finally settled on a name for the thing. He had given much thought, over many high-hours and in many languages, most of them nonverbal, to what he should call the looming object. The name that pleased him most was in a language dead (he assumed) for thirty million years. Aea. Acronym: Alien Enigmatic Artifact. Enigmatic Alien Artifact would have been more correct but the long dead language did not handle diphthongs well.

Shadows fell over the gardens of Versailles, huge and soft as clouds. A forest was crossing the sun; a small one, little more than a copse, he thought, still finding delight in the notions that could be expressed in this dead language. He watched the spherical trees pass overhead, each a kilometer across (another archaism), enjoying the pleasurable play of shade and warmth on his skin. Sensual joys of incarnation.

As ever when the forests migrated along the Bauble's jet streams, a frenzy of siphons squabbled in their wake, voraciously feeding off the stew of bacteria and complex fullerenes.

Solomon Gursky darkened his eyes against the hard glare of the dwarf white sun. From Versailles' perspective in the equatorial plane, the Spirit Ring was a barely discernible filigree necklace draped around its primary. Perspective. Am I the emanation of it, or is it the emanation of me?

Perspective: you worry about such things with a skeletal tetrahedron one point three astronomical units on a side fast approaching?

Of course. I am some kind of human.

"Show me," Solomon Gursky said. Sensing his intent, for Versailles was part of his intent, as everything that lived and moved within the Bauble was his intent, the disc of tectofactured baroque France began to tilt away from the sun. The sollilies on which Versailles and its gardens rested generated their own gravity fields; Solomon Gursky saw the tiny, bright sun seem to curve down behind the Petit Trianon, and thought, *I have reinvented sunset.* And, as the dark vault above him lit with stars, *Night is looking out from the shadow of myself.*

The stars slowed and locked over the chimneys of Versailles. Sol had hoped to be able to see the object with the unaided eye, but in low-time he had forgotten the limitations of the primeval human form. A grimace of irritation, and it was the work of moments for the tectors to reconfigure his vision. Successive magnifications clicked up until ghostly, twinkling threads of light resolved out of the star field, like the drawings of gods and myths the ancients had laid on the comfortable heavens around the Alpha Point.

Another click and the thing materialized.

Solomon Gursky's breath caught.

Midway between the micro and the macro, it was humanity's natural condition that a man standing looking out into the dark should feel dwarfed. That need to assert one's individuality to the bigness underlies all humanity's outward endeavors. But the catch in the breath is more than doubled when a *star* seems dwarfed. Through the Spirit Ring, Sol had the dimensions, the masses, the vectors. The whole of the Bauble could be easily contained within Aea's vertices. A cabalistic sign. A cosmic eye in the pyramid.

A chill contraction in the man Solomon Gursky's loins. How many million years since he had last felt his balls tighten with fear?

One point three AU's on a side. Eight sextillion tons of matter. Point one C. The thing should have heralded itself over most of the cluster. Even in low-time, he should have had more time to prepare. But there had been no warning. At once, it *was:* a fading hexagram of gravitometric disturbances on his out-system sensors. Sol had reacted at once, but in those few seconds of stretched low-time that it took to conceive and create this Louis Quattorze conceit, the object had covered two-thirds of the distance from its emergence point. The high-time of created things gave him perspective.

Bear you grapes or poison? Solomon Gursky asked the thing in the sky. It had not spoken, it had remained silent through all attempts to communicate with it, but it surely bore *some* gift. The manner of its arrival had only one explanation:

the thing manipulated worm-holes. None of the civilization/citizens of the Reach—most of the western hemisphere of the galaxy—had evolved a nanotechnology that could reconfigure the continuum itself.

None of the civilization/citizens of the Reach, and those federations of world-societies it fringed, had ever encountered a species that could not be sourced to the Alpha Point: that semi-legendary racial big bang from which PanHumanity had exploded into the universe.

Four hundred billion stars in this galaxy alone, Solomon Gursky thought. We have not seeded even half of them. The trick we play with time, slowing our perceptions until our light-speed communications seem instantaneous and the journeys of our C-fractional ships are no longer than the sea-voyages of this era I have reconstructed, seduce us into believing that the universe is as close and companionable as a lover's body, and as familiar. The five million years between the MonoHumanity of the Alpha Point and the PanHumanity of the Great Leap Outward, is a catch of breath, a contemplative pause in our conversation with ourselves. Thirty million years I have evolved the web of life in this unique system: there is abundant time and space for true aliens to have caught us up, to have already surpassed us.

Again, that tightening of the scrotum. Sol Gursky willed Versailles back toward the eye of the sun, but intellectual chill had invaded his soul. The orchestra of Lully made fete *galante* in the Hall of Mirrors for his pleasure, but the sound in his head of the destroying, rushing alien mass shrieked louder. As the solar parasol slipped between Versailles and the sun and he settled in twilight among the soft, powdered breasts of the ladies of the bed-chamber, he knew fear for the first time in thirty million years.

And he dreamed. The dream took the shape of a memory, recontextualized, reconfigured, resurrected. He dreamed that he was a starship wakened from fifty thousand years of death by the warmth of a new sun on his solar sail. He dreamed that in the vast sleep the star toward which he had aimed himself spastically novaed. It kicked off its photosphere in a nebula of radiant gas but the explosion was underpowered; the carbon/hydrogen/nitrogen/oxygen plasma was drawn by gravity into a bubble of hydrocarbons around the star. An aura. A bright bauble. In Solomon Gursky's dream, an angel floated effortlessly on tectoplastic wings hundreds of kilometers wide, banking and soaring on the chemical thermals, sowing seeds from its long, trailing fingertips. For a hundred years, the angle swam around the sun, sowing, nurturing, tending the strange shoots that grew from its fingers; things half-living, half-machine.

Asleep among the powdered breasts of court women, Sol Gursky turned and murmured the word, "evolution."

Solomon Gursky would only be a God he could believe in: the philosophers' God, creator but not sustainer, ineffable; too street-smart to poke its omnipotence into the smelly stuff of living. He saw his free-fall trees of green, the vast red rafts of the wind-reefs rippling in the solar breezes. He saw the blimps and medusas, the unresting open maws of the air-plankton feeders, the needle-thin jet-powered darts of the harpoon hunters. He saw an ecology spin itself out of gas and energy in thirty million yearless years, he saw intelligence flourish and seed itself to the stars, and fade into senescence; all in the blink of a low-time eye.

"Evolution," he muttered again and the constructed women who did not understand sleep looked at each other.

In the unfolding dream, Sol Gursky saw the Spirit Ring and the ships that came and went between the nearer systems. He heard the subaural babble of interstellar chatter, like conspirators in another room. He beheld this blur of life, evolving, transmuting, and he knew that it was very good. He said to himself, *what a wonderful world*, and feared for it.

He awoke. It was morning, as it always was in Sol's Bauble. He worked off his testosterone high and tipped Versailles's darkside to look at the shadow of his nightmares. Any afterglow of libido was immediately extinguished. At eighteen light-hours distance, the astronomical dimensions assumed emotional force. A ribbon of mottled blue-green ran down the inner surface of each of Aea's six legs. Amplified vision resolved forested continents and oceans beneath fractal cloud curls. Each ribbon-world was the width of two Alpha Points peeled and ironed, stretched one point three astronomical units long. Sol Gursky was glad that this incarnation could not instantly access how many million planets' surfaces that equaled; how many hundreds of thousands of years it would take to walk from one vertex to another, and then to find, dumbfounded like the ancient conquistadors beholding a new ocean, another millennia-deep world in front of him.

Solomon Gursky turned Versailles toward the sun. He squinted through the haze of the Bauble for the delicate strands of the Spirit Ring. A beat of his mind shifted his perceptions back into low-time, the only time frame in which he could withspeak to the Spirit Ring, his originating self. Self-reference, self-confession.

No communication?

None, spoke the Spirit Ring.

Is it alien? Should I be afraid? Should I destroy the Bauble?

In another time, such schizophrenia would have been disease.

Can it annihilate you?

In answer, Sol envisioned the great tetrahedron at the bracelet of information tectors orbiting the sun.

Then that is nothing, the Spirit Ring withsaid. *And nothing is nothing to fear. Can it cause you pain or humiliation, or anguish to body or soul?*

Again, Sol withspoke an image, of cloud-shaded lands raised over each other like the pillars of Yahweh, emotionally shaded to suggest amazement that such an investment of matter and thought should have been created purely to humiliate Solomon Gursky.

Then that too is settled. And whether it is alien, can it be any more alien to you than you yourself are to what you once were? All PanHumanity is alien to itself; therefore, we have nothing to fear. We shall welcome our visitor, we have many questions for it.

Not the least being, *why me?* Solomon Gursky thought privately, silently, in the dome of his own skull. He shifted out of the low-time of the Spirit Ring to find that in those few subjective moments of communication Aea had passed the threshold of the Bauble. The leading edge of the tetrahedron was three hours away. An hour and half beyond that was the hub of Aea.

"Since it seems that we can neither prevent nor hasten the object's arrival, nor guess its purposes until it deigns to communicate with us," Sol Gursky told his women of the bedchamber, "therefore let us party." Which they did, before the

Mirror Pond, as Lully's orchestra played and capons roasted over charcoal pits, and torch-lit harlequins capered and fought out the ancient loves and comedies, and women splashed naked in the Triton Fountain, and fantastic lands one hundred million kilometers long slid past them. Aea advanced until Sol's star was at its center, then stopped. Abruptly, instantly. A small gravitational shiver troubled Versailles, the orchestra missed a note, a juggler dropped a club, the water in the fountain wavered, women shrieked, a capon fell from a spit into the fire. That was all. The control of mass, momentum, and gravity was absolute.

The orchestra leader looked at Solomon Gursky, staff raised to resume the beat. Sol Gursky did not raise the handkerchief. The closest section of Aea was fifteen degrees east, two hundred thousand kilometers out. To Sol Gursky, it was two fingers of sun-lit land, tapering infinitesimally at either end to threads of light. He looked up at the apex, two other brilliant threads spun down beneath the horizon, one behind the Petit Trianon, the other below the roof of the Chapel Royal.

The conductor was still waiting. Instruments pressed to faces, the musicians watched for the cue.

Peacocks shrieked on the lawn. Sol Gursky remembered how irritating the voices of peacocks were, and wished he had not re-created them.

Sol Gursky waved the handkerchief.

A column of white light blazed out of the gravel walk at the top of the steps. The air was a seethe of glowing motes.

An attempt is being made to communicate with us, the Spirit Ring said in a flicker of low-time. Sol Gursky felt information from the Ring crammed into his cerebral cortex: the beam originated from a source of the rim section of the closest section of the artifact. The tectors that created and sustained the Bauble were being reprogrammed. At hyper-velocities, they were manufacturing a construct out of the Earth of Versailles.

The pillar of light dissipated. A human figure stood at the top of the steps: a white Alpha Point male, dressed in Louis XIV style. The man descended the steps into the light of the flambeau bearers. Sol Gursky looked on his face.

Sol Gursky burst into laughter.

"You are very welcome," he said to his doppelgänger. "Will you join us? The capons will be ready shortly, we can bring you the finest wines available to humanity, and I'm sure the waters of the fountains would be most refreshing to one who has traveled so long and so far."

"Thank you," Solomon Gursky said in Solomon Gursky's voice. "It's good to find a hospitable reception after a strange journey."

Sol Gursky nodded to the conductor, who raised his staff, and the *petite bande* resumed their interrupted gavotte.

Later, on a stone bench by the lake, Sol Gursky said to his doppel, "Your politeness is appreciated, but it really wasn't necessary for you to don my shape. All this is as much a construction as you are."

"Why do you think it's a politeness?" the construct said.

"Why should you choose to wear the shape of Solomon Gursky?"

"Why should I not, if it is my *own* shape?"

Nereids splashed in the pool, breaking the long reflections of Aea.

"I often wonder how far I reach," Sol said.

"Further than you can imagine," Sol II answered. The playing Nereids dived;

ripples spread across the pond. The visitor watched the wavelets lap against the stone rim and interfere with each other. "There are others out there, others we never imagined, moving through the dark, very slowly, very silently. I think they may be older than us. They are different from us, very different, and we have now come to the complex plane where our expansions meet."

"There was a strong probability that they—you—were an alien artifact."

"I am, and I'm not. I am fully Solomon Gursky, and fully Other. That's the purpose behind this artifact; that we have reached a point where we either compete, destructively, or join."

"Seemed a long way to come just for a family reunion," Solomon Gursky joked. He saw that the doppel laughed, and how it laughed, and why it laughed. He got up from the stone rim of the Nereid pool. "Come with me, talk to me, we have thirty million years of catching up."

His brother fell in at his side as they walked away from the still water toward the Aea-lit woods.

His story: he had fallen longer than any other seed cast off by the death of Orc. Eight hundred thousand years between wakings, and as he felt the warmth of a new sun seduce his tector systems to the work of transformation, his sensors reported that his was not the sole presence in the system. The brown dwarf toward which he decelerated was being dismantled and converted into an englobement of space habitats.

"Their technology is similar to ours—I think it must be a universal inevitability—but they broke the ties that still bind us to planets long ago," Sol II said. The woods of Versailles were momentarily darkened as a sky-reef eclipsed Aea. "This is why I think they are older than us: I have never seen their original form—they have no tie to it, we still do; I suspect they no longer remember it. It wasn't until we fully merged that I was certain that they were not another variant of humanity."

A hand-cranked wooden carousel stood in a small clearing. The faces of the painted horses were fierce and pathetic in the sky light. Wooden rings hung from iron gibbets around the rim of the carousel; the wooden lances with which the knights hooked down their favors had been gathered in and locked in a closet in the middle of the merry-go-round.

"We endure forever, we engender races, nations, whole ecologies, but we are sterile," the second Sol said. "We inbreed with ourselves. There is no union of disparities, no coming together, no hybrid energy. With the Others, it was sex. Intercourse. Out of the fusion of ideas and visions and capabilities, we birthed what you see."

The first Sol Gursky laid his hand on the neck of a painted horse. The carousel was well balanced, the slightest pressure set it turning.

"Why are you here, Sol?" he asked.

"We shared technologies, we learned how to engineer on the quantum level so that field effects can be applied on macroscopic scales. Manipulation of gravity and inertia; non-locality; we can engineer and control quantum worm-holes."

"Why have you come, Sol?"

"Engineering of alternative time streams; designing and colonizing multiple worlds, hyperspace and hyperdimensional processors. There are more universes than this one for us to explore."

The wooden horse stopped.

"What do you want, Sol?"

"Join us," said the other Solomon Gursky. "You always had the vision—*we* always had the vision, we Solomon Gurskys. Humanity expanding into every possible ecological niche."

"Absorption," Solomon Gursky said. "Assimilation."

"Unity," said his brother. "Marriage. *Love.* Nothing is lost, everything is gained. All you have created here will be stored; that is what I am, a machine for remembering. It's not annihilation, Sol, don't fear it; it's not your self-hood dissolving into some identityless collective. It *is* you, plus. It is life, cubed. And ultimately, we are one seed, you and I, unnaturally separated. We gain each other."

If nothing is lost, then you remember what I am remembering, Solomon Gursky I thought. I am remembering a face forgotten for over thirty million years: Rabbi Bertelsmann. A fat, fair, pleasant face. He is talking to his Bar Mitzvah class about God and masturbation. He is saying that God condemned Onan not for the pleasure of his vice, but because he spilled his seed on the ground. He was fruitless, sterile. He kept the gift of life to himself. And I am now God in my own world, and Rabbi B is smiling and saying, masturbation, Sol. It is all just one big jerk-off, seed spilled on the ground, engendering nothing. Pure re-creation; re-creating yourself endlessly into the future.

He looked at his twin.

"Rabbi Bertelsmann?" Sol Gursky II said.

"Yes," Sol Gursky I said; then, emphatically, certainly, "Yes!"

Solomon Gursky II's smile dissolved into motes of light.

All at once, the outer edges of the great tetrahedron kindled with ten million points of diamond light. Sol watched the white beams sweep through the Bauble and understood what it meant, that they could manipulate time and space. Even at light-speed, Aea was too huge for each such simultaneity.

Air trees, sky reefs, harpooners, siphons, blimps, zeps, cloud sharks: everything touched by the moving beams was analyzed, comprehended, stored. Recording angels, Sol Gursky thought, as the silver knives dissected his world. He saw the Spirit Ring unravel like coils of DNA as a billion days of Solomon Gursky flooded up the ladder of light into Aea. The center no longer held; the gravitational forces the Spirit Ring had controlled, that had maintained the ecosphere of the Bauble, were failing. Sol's world was dying. He felt pain, no sorrow, no regret, but rather a savage joy, an urgent desire to be up and on and out, to be free of this great weight of life and gravity. It is not dying, he thought. Nothing ever dies.

He looked up. An angel-beam scored a searing arc across the rooftops of Versailles. He opened his arms to it and was taken apart by the light. Everything is held and re-created in the mind of God. Unremembered by the mind of Solomon Gursky, Versailles disintegrated into swarms of free-flying tectors.

The end came quickly. The angels reached into the photosphere of the star and the complex quasi-information machines that worked there. The sun grew restless, woken from its long quietude. The Spirit Ring collapsed. Fragments spun end-over-end through the Bauble, tearing spectacularly through the dying sky-reefs, shattering cloud forests, blazing in brief glory in funeral orbits around the swelling sun.

For the sun was dying. Plagues of sunspots pocked its chromosphere; solar storms raced from pole to pole in million-kilometer tsunamis. Panicked hunter packs kindled and died in the solar protuberances hurled off as the photosphere prominenced to the very edge of the Bauble. The sun bulged and swelled like a painfully infected pregnancy: Aea was manipulating fundamental forces, loosening the bonds of gravity that held the system together. At the end, it would require all the energies of star-death to power the quantum worm-hole processors.

The star was now a screaming saucer of gas. No living thing remained in the Bauble. All was held in the mind of Aea.

The star burst. The energies of the nova should have boiled Aea's oceans, seared its lands from their beds. It should have twisted and snapped the long, thin arms like yarrow stalks, sent the artifact tumbling like a smashed Fabergé egg through space. But Aea had woven its defenses strong: gravity fields warped the electromagnetic radiation around the fragile terrains; the quantum processors devoured the storm of charged particles, and reconfigured space, time, mass.

The four corners of Aea burned brighter than the dying sun for an instant. And it was gone; under space and time, to worlds and adventures and experiences beyond all saying.

SUNDAY

Toward the end of the universe, Solomon Gursky's thoughts turned increasingly to lost loves.

Had it been entirely physical, Ua would have been the largest object in the universe. Only its fronds, the twenty-light-year-long stalactites that grew into the ylem, tapping the energies of decreation, had any material element. Most of Ua, ninety-nine followed by several volumes of decimal nines percent of its structure, was folded through eleven-space. It was the largest object in the universe in that its fifth and sixth dimensional forms contained the inchoate energy flux known as the universe. Its higher dimensions contained only itself, several times over. It was infundibular. It was vast, it contained multitudes.

PanLife, that amorphous, multi-faceted cosmic infection of human, transhuman, non-human, PanHuman sentiences, had filled the universe long before the continuum reached its elastic limit and began to contract under the weight of dark matter and heavy neutrinos. Femtotech, hand in hand with the worm-hole jump, spread PanLife across the galactic super-clusters in a blink of God's eye.

There was no humanity, no alien. No us, no other. There was only *life*. The dead had become life. Life had become Ua: Pan-spermia. Ua woke to consciousness, and like Alexander the Great, despaired when it had no new worlds to conquer. The universe had grown old in Ua's gestation; it had withered, it contracted, it drew in on itself. The red shift of galaxies had turned blue. And Ua, which owned the attributes, abilities, ambitions, everything except the name and pettinesses of a god, found itself, like an old, long-dead God from a world slagged by its expanding sun millions of years ago, in the business of resurrection.

The galaxies raced together, gravitational forces tearing them into loops and whorls of severed stars. The massive black holes at the galactic centers, fueled by billennia of star-death, coalesced and merged into monstrosities that swallowed globular clusters whole, that shredded galaxies and drew then spiraling inward until, at the edge of the Schwartzchild radii, they radiated super-hard gamma. Long since woven into higher dimensions, Ua fed from the colossal power of the accretion discs, recording in multidimensional matrices the lives of the trillions of sentient organisms fleeing up its fronds from the destruction. All things are held in the mind of God: at the end, when the universal background radiation rose asymptotically to the energy density of the first seconds of the Big Bang, it would deliver enough power for the femtoprocessors woven through the Eleven Heavens to rebuild the universe, entire. A new heaven, and a new Earth.

In the trans-temporal matrices of Ua, PanLife flowed across dimensions, dripping from the tips of the fronds into bodies sculpted to thrive in the plasma flux of ragnarok. Tourists to the end of the world: most wore the shapes of winged creatures of fire, thousands of kilometers across. Starbirds. Firebirds. But the being formerly known as Solomon Gursky had chosen a different form, an archaism from that long-vanished planet. It pleased him to be a thousand-kilometer, diamond-skinned Statue of Liberty, torch out-held, beaming a way through the torrents of star-stuff. Sol Gursky flashed between flocks of glowing soul-birds clustering in the information-rich environment around the frond-tips. He felt their curiosity, their appreciation, their consternation at his non-conformity; none got the joke.

Lost loves. So many lives, so many worlds, so many shapes and bodies, so many loves. They had been wrong, those ones back at the start, who had said that love did not survive death. He had been wrong. It was eternity that killed love. Love was a thing measured by human lifetimes. Immortality gave it time enough, and space, to change, to become things more than love, or dangerously other. None endured. None would endure. Immortality was endless change.

Toward the end of the universe, Solomon Gursky realized that what made love live forever was death.

All things were held in Ua, awaiting resurrection when time, space, and energy fused and ceased to be. Most painful among Sol's stored memories was the remembrance of a red-yellow tiger-striped angel fighter, half-crucified, crippled, tumbling toward the star clouds of Virgo. Sol had searched the trillions of souls roosting in Ua for Elena; failing, he hunted for any that might have touched her, hold some memory of her. He found none. As the universe contracted—as fast and inevitable as a long-forgotten season in the ultra-low time of Ua—Sol Gursky entertained hopes that the universal gathering would draw her in. Cruel truths pecked at his perceptions: calculations of molecular deliquescence, abrasion by interstellar dust clouds, probabilities of stellar impacts, the slow terminal whine of proton decay; any of which denied that Elena could still exist. Sol refused those truths. A thousand-kilometer Statue of Liberty searched the dwindling cosmos for one glimpse of red-yellow tiger-stripes embedded in a feather of fractal plasma flame.

And now a glow of recognition had impinged on his senses laced through the Eleven Heavens.

Her. It had to be her.

Sol Gursky flew to an eye of gravitational stability in the flux and activated the worm-hole nodes seeded throughout his diamond skin. Space opened and folded like an exercise in origami. Sol Gursky went elsewhere.

The starbird grazed the energy-dense borderlands of the central accretion disc. It was immense. Sol's Statue of Liberty was a frond of one of its thousand flight feathers, but it sensed him, welcomed him, folded its wings around him as it drew him to the shifting pattern of sun-spots that was the soul of its being.

He knew these patterns. He remembered these emotional flavors. He recalled this love. He tried to perceive if it were her, her journeys, her trials, her experiences, her agonies, her vastenings.

Would she forgive him?

The soul spots opened. Solomon Gursky was drawn inside. Clouds of tectors interpenetrated, exchanging, sharing, recording. Intellectual intercourse.

He entered her adventures among alien species five times older than Pan-Humanity, an alliance of wills and powers waking a galaxy to life. In an earlier incarnation, he walked the worlds she had become, passed through the dynasties and races and species she had propagated. He made with her the long crossings between stars and clusters, clusters and galaxies. Earlier still, and he swam with her through the cloud canyons of a gas giant world called Urizen, and when that world was hugged too warmly by its sun, changed mode with her, embarked with her on the search for new places to live.

In the nakedness of their communion, there was no hiding Sol Gursky's despair.

I'm sorry Sol, the starbird once known as Lenya communicated.

You have nothing to sorry be for, Solomon Gursky said.

I'm sorry that I'm not her. I'm sorry I never was her.

I made you to be a lover, Sol withspoke. *But you became something older, something richer, something we have lost.*

A daughter, Lenya said.

Unmeasurable time passed in the blue shift at the end of the universe. Then Lenya asked, *Where will you go?*

Finding her is the only unfinished business I have left, Sol said.

Yes, the starbird communed. *But we will not meet again.*

No, not in this universe.

Nor any other. And that is death, eternal separation.

My unending regret, Sol Gursky withspoke as Lenya opened her heart and the clouds of tectors separated. *Goodbye, daughter.*

The Statue of Liberty disengaged from the body of the starbird. Lenya's quantum processors created a pool of gravitational calm in the maelstrom. Sol Gursky manipulated space and time and disappeared.

He re-entered the continuum as close as he dared to a frond. A pulse of his mind brought him within reach of its dendrites. As they drew him in, another throb of thought dissolved the Statue of Liberty joke into the plasma flux. Solomon Gursky howled up the dendrite, through the frond, into the soul matrix of Ua. There he carved a niche in the eleventh and highest heaven, and from deep under time, watched the universe end.

As he had expected, it ended in fire and light and glory. He saw space and time curve inward beyond the limit of the Planck dimensions; he felt the energy gradients climb toward infinity as the universe approached the zero point from which it had spontaneously emerged. He felt the universal processors sown through eleven dimensions seize that energy before it faded, and put it to work. It was a surge, a spurt of power and passion, like the memory of orgasm buried deep in the chain of memory that was the days of Solomon Gursky. Light to power, power to memory, memory to flesh. Ua's stored memories, the history of every particle in the former universe, were woven into being. Smart superstrings rolled balls of wrapped eleven-space like sacred scarabs wheeling dung. Space, time, mass, energy unraveled; as the universe died in a quantum fluctuation, it was reborn in primal light.

To Solomon Gursky, waiting in low-time where aeons were breaths, it seemed like creation by *fiat*. A brief, bright light, and galaxies, clusters, stars, turned whole-formed and living within his contemplation. Already personas were swarming out of Ua's honeycomb cells into time and incarnation, but what had been reborn was not a universe, but universes. The re-resurrected were not condemned to blindly recapitulate their former lives. Each choice and action that diverged from the original pattern splintered off a separate universe. Sol and Lenya had spoken truly when they had said they would never meet again. Sol's point of entry into the new polyverse was a thousand years before Lenya's; the universe he intended to create would never intersect with hers.

The elder races had already fanned the polyverse into a *mille feuille* of alternatives: Sol carefully tracked his own timeline through the blur of possibilities as the first humans dropped back into their planet's past. Stars moving into remembered constellations warned Sol that his emergence was only a few hundreds of thousands of years off. He moved down through dimensional matrices, at each level drawing closer to the time flow of his particular universe.

Solomon Gursky hung over the spinning planet. Civilizations rose and decayed, empires conquered and crumbled. New technologies, new continents, new nations were discovered. All the time, alternative Earths fluttered away like torn-off calendar pages on the wind as the dead created new universes to colonize. Close now. Mere moments. Sol dropped into meat time, and Ua expelled him like a drop of milk from a swollen breast.

Solomon Gursky fell. Illusions and anticipations accompanied his return to flesh. Imaginings of light; a contrail angel scoring the nightward half of the planet on its flight across a dark ocean to a shore, to a mountain, to a valley, to a glow of campfire among night-blooming cacti. Longing. Desire. Fear. Gain, and loss. God's trade: to attain the heart's desire, you must give up everything you are. Even the memory.

In the quilted bag by the fire in the sheltered valley under the perfume of the cactus flowers, the man called Solomon Gursky woke with a sudden chill start. It was night. It was dark. Desert stars had half-completed their compass above him. The stone-circled fire had burned down to clinking red glow: the night perfume witched him. Moths padded softly through the air, seeking nectar.

Sol Gursky drank five senses full of his world.

I am alive, he thought. I am here. Again.

Ur-light burned in his hind-brain; memories of Ua, a power like omnipotence. Memories of a life that out-lived its native universe. Worlds, suns, shapes. Flashes, moments. Too heavy, too rich for this small knot of brain to hold. Too bright: no one can live with the memory of having been a god. It would fade—it was fading already. All he need hold—all he must hold—was what he needed to prevent this universe from following its predestined course.

The realization that eyes were watching him was a shock. Elena sat on the edge of the fire shadow, knees folded to chin, arms folded over shins, looking at him. Sol had the feeling that she had been looking at him without him knowing for a long time, and the surprise, the uneasiness of knowing you are under the eyes of another, tempered both the still-new lust he felt for her, and his fading memories of aeons-old love.

Déjà vu. But this moment had never happened before. The divergence was beginning.

"Can't sleep?" she asked.

"I had the strangest dream."

"Tell me." The thing between them was at the stage where they searched each other's dreams for allusions to their love.

"I dreamed that the world ended," Sol Gursky said. "It ended in light, and the light was like the light in a movie projector, that carried the image of the world and everything in it, and so the world was created again, as it had been before."

As he spoke, the words became true. It was a dream now. This life, this body, these memories, were the solid and faithful.

"Like a Tipler machine," Elena said. "The idea that the energy released by the Big Crunch could power some kind of holographic re-creation of the entire universe. I suppose with an advanced enough nanotechnology, you could rebuild the universe, an exact copy, atom for atom."

Chill dread struck in Sol's belly. She could not know, surely. She must not know.

"What would be the point of doing it exactly the same all over again?"

"Yeah." Elena rested her cheek on her knee. "But the question is, is *this* our first time in the world, or have we been here many times before, each a little bit different? Is this the first universe, or do we only *think* that it is?"

Sol Gursky looked into the embers, then to the stars.

"The Nez Perce Nation believes that the world ended on the third day and that what we are living in are the dreams of the second night." Memories, fading like summer meteors high overhead, told Sol that he had said this once before, in their future, after his first death. He said it now in the hope that that future would not come to pass. Everything that was different, every tiny detail, pushed this universe away from the one in which he must lose her.

A vee of tiger-striped tectoplastic tumbled end over end forever toward Virgo.

He blinked the ghost away. It faded like all the others. They were going more quickly than he had thought. He would have to make sure of it now, before that memory too dissolved. He struggled out of the terrain bag, went over to the bike lying exhausted on the ground. By the light of a detached bicycle lamp, he checked the gear train.

"What are you doing?" Elena asked from the fireside. The thing between them was still new, but Sol remembered that tone in her voice, that soft inquiry, from another lifetime.

"Looking at the gears. Something didn't feel right about them today. They didn't feel solid."

"You didn't mention it earlier."

No, Sol thought. I didn't know about it. Not then. The gear teeth grinned flashlight back at him.

"We've been giving them a pretty hard riding. I read in one of the biking mags that you can get metal fatigue. Gear train shears right through, just like that."

"On brand-new, two thousand dollar bikes?"

"On brand-new two thousand dollar bikes."

"So what do you think you can *do* about it at one o'clock in the morning in the middle of the Sonora Desert?"

Again, that come-hither tone. Just a moment more, Elena. One last thing, and then it will be safe.

"It just didn't sit right. I don't want to take it up over any more mountains until I've had it checked out. You get a gear-shear up there . . ."

"So, what are you saying, irritating man?"

"I'm not happy about going over Blood of Christ Mountain tomorrow."

"Yeah. Sure. Fine."

"Maybe we should go out west, head for the coast. It's whale season, I always wanted to see whales. And there's real good seafood. There's this cantina where they have fifty ways of serving iguana."

"Whales. Iguanas. Fine. Whatever you want. Now, since you're so wide-awake, you can just get your ass right *over* here, Sol Gursky!"

She was standing up, and Sol saw and felt what she had been concealing by the way she had sat. She wearing only a cut-off MTB shirt. Safe, he thought, as he seized her and took her down laughing and yelling onto the camping mat. Even as he thought it, he forgot it, and all those Elenas who would not now be: conspirator, crop-haired freedom fighter, four-armed space-angel. Gone.

The stars moved in their ordained arcs. The moths and cactus forest bats drifted through the soft dark air, and the eyes of the things that hunted them glittered in the firelight.

Sol and Elena were still sore and laughing when the cactus flowers closed with dawn. They ate their breakfast and packed their small camp, and were in the saddle and on the trail before the sun was full over the shoulder of Blood of Christ Mountain. They took the western trail, away from the hills, and the town called Redención hidden among them with its freight of resurrected grief. They rode the long trail that led down to the ocean, and it was bright, clear endless Monday morning.

Acknowledgment is made for permission to reprint the following material:

"The Sentinel," by Arthur C. Clarke. Copyright © 1951 by Avon Periodicals, Inc. First published in *Top Story Fantasy,* 1951. Reprinted by permission of the author and the author's agents, the Scovil Chichak Galen Agency.

"Moonwalk," by H. B. Fyfe. Copyright © 1952 by Space Publications, Inc. First published in *Space Science Fiction,* November 1952. Reprinted by permission of the author's estate.

"Grandpa," by James H. Schmitz. Copyright © 1955 by Street & Smith Publications, Inc. First published in *Astounding Science Fiction*, February 1955. Reprinted by permission of the author's estate and the agents for the estate, Scott Meredith Literary Associates, Inc., 845 Third Avenue, New York, NY 10022.

"The Red Hills of Summer," by Edgar Pangborn. Copyright © 1959 by Mercury Press, Inc. First published in *The Magazine of Fantasy & Science Fiction*, September 1959. Reprinted by permission of the author's estate and the agents for the estate,

"The Longest Voyage," by Poul Anderson. Copyright © 1960 by Street and Smith Publications, Inc. First published in *Analog,* December 1960. Reprinted by permission of the author.

"Hot Planet," by Hal Clement. Copyright © 1963 by Galaxy Publishing Corporation. First published in *Galaxy*, August 1963. Reprinted by permission of the author.

"Drunkboat," by Cordwainer Smith. Copyright © 1963 by Ziff-Davis Publishing Co. First published in *Amazing Stories*, October 1963. Reprinted by permission of the author's estate and the agents for the estate, Scott Meredith Literary Associates, Inc., 845 Third Avenue, New York, NY 10022.

"Becalmed in Hell," by Larry Niven. Copyright © 1965 by Mercury Press, Inc. First published in *The Magazine of Fantasy & Science Fiction*, July 1965. Reprinted by permission of the author and the author's agents, the Spectrum Literary Agency.

"Nine Hundred Grandmothers," by R. A. Lafferty. Copyright © 1966 by Galaxy Publishing Corporation. First published in *If*, February 1966. Reprinted by permission of the author and the author's agents, the Virginia Kidd Literary Agency.

"The Keys to December," by Roger Zelazny. Copyright © 1966 by New Worlds. First published in *New Worlds*, August 1966. Reprinted by permission of the author's estate and the agents for the estate, the Pimlico Agency, Inc.

"Vaster than Empires and More Slow," by Ursula K. Le Guin. Copyright © 1975 by Ursula K. Le Guin. First published in *New Dimensions 1,* edited by Robert

Silverberg (Doubleday, 1971). Reprinted by permission of the author and the author's agents, the Virginia Kidd Literary Agency.

"A Meeting with Medusa," by Arthur C. Clarke. Copyright © 1971 by Playboy. Copyright assigned to the author. Copyright © 1971 by Arthur C. Clarke. First published in *Playboy,* December 1971. Reprinted by permission of the author and the author's agents, the Scovil Chichak Galen Agency.

"The Man Who Walked Home," by James Tiptree, Jr. Copyright © 1972 by Ultimate Publishing Co. First published in *Amazing Science Fiction Stories*, May 1972. Reprinted by permission of the author's estate and the agents for the estate, the Virginia Kidd Literary Agency.

"Long Shot," by Vernor Vinge. Copyright © 1972 by The Condé Nast Publications, Inc. First published in *Analog,* August 1972. Reprinted by permission of the author.

"In the Hall of the Martian Kings," by John Varley. Copyright © 1977 by Mercury Press, Inc. First published in *The Magazine of Fantasy & Science Fiction*, February 1977. Reprinted by permission of the author and the author's agent, Ricia Mainhardt.

"Ginungagap," by Michael Swanwick. Copyright © 1980 by TriQuarterly. From *TriQuarterly* 49, Fall 1980. Reprinted by permission of the author.

"Exploring Fossil Canyon," by Kim Stanley Robinson. Copyright © 1982 by Terry Carr. First published in *Universe 12,* edited by Terry Carr (Doubleday, 1982). Reprinted by permission of the author.

"Promises to Keep," by Jack McDevitt. Copyright © 1984 by Davis Publications, Inc. First published in *Isaac Asimov's Science Fiction Magazine,* December 1984. Reprinted by permission of the author.

"Lieserl," by Stephen Baxter. Copyright © 1993 by Interzone. First published in *Interzone*, December 1993. Reprinted by permission of the author and the author's agents, the Maggie Noach Agency.

"Wang's Carpets," by Greg Egan. Copyright © 1995 by Greg Egan. First published in *New Legends,* edited by Greg Bear (Tor Books, 1995). Reprinted by permission of the author.

"Crossing Chao Meng Fu," by G. David Nordley. Copyright © by Dell Magazines. First published in *Analog Science Fiction/Science Fact,* December 1997. Reprinted by permission of the author.

"A Dance to Strange Musics," by Gregory Benford. Copyright © 1998 by Abbenford Associates. First published as "A Pit Which Has No Bottom" in *Age of Wonder* #1, Winter 1998. Revised version first published in *Science Fiction Age,* November 1998. Reprinted by permission of the author.

"Approaching Perimelasma," by Geoffrey A. Landis. Copyright © 1998 by Dell Magazines. First published in *Asimov's Science Fiction*, January 1998. Reprinted by permission of the author.

"Guyal of Sfere," by Jack Vance. Copyright © 1950 by Hillman Publications, Inc.; copyright renewed © 1978 by Jack Vance. First published in *The Dying Earth* (Hillman), 1950. Reprinted by permission of the author and the author's agent, Ralph M. Vicinanza, Ltd.

"Old Hundredth," by Brian W. Aldiss. Copyright © 1960 by Brian W. Aldiss. First published in *New Worlds,* November 1960. Reprinted by permission of the author.

"Alpha Ralpha Boulevard," by Cordwainer Smith. Copyright © 1961 by Mercury Press, Inc; copyright © 1963 by Cordwainer Smith. First published in *The Magazine of Fantasy & Science Fiction,* June 1961. Reprinted by permission of the author's estate and the agents for the estate, Scott Meredith Literary Associates, Inc., 845 Third Avenue, New York, NY 10022.

"Day Million," by Frederik Pohl. Copyright © 1966 by Rogue Magazine. First published in *Rogue Magazine,* February 1966. Reprinted by permission of the author.

"Bumberboom," by Avram Davidson. Copyright © 1966 by Mercury Press, Inc. First published in *The Magazine of Fantasy & Science Fiction,* December 1966. Reprinted by permission of the author's estate and the executor of the estate, Grania Davis.

"Coranda," by Keith Roberts. Copyright © 1967 by New Worlds. First published in *New Worlds,* January 1967. Reprinted by permission of the author and the author's agents, The Owlswick Literary Agency.

"Nightwings," by Robert Silverberg. Copyright © 1968 by Galaxy Publishing Corporation. First published (under the title "Watcher") in *Galaxy,* September 1968. Reprinted by permission of the author.

"Pale Roses," by Michael Moorcock. Copyright © 1974 by Michael Moorcock. First published in *New Worlds* 7 (Sphere, 1974). Reprinted by permission of the author and the author's agents, Howard Morheim.

"Anniversary Project," by Joe Haldeman. Copyright © 1975 by the Conde Nast Corporation. First published in *Analog Science Fiction/Science Fact,* October 1975. Reprinted by permission of the author.

"Slow Music," by James Tiptree, Jr. Copyright © 1980 by James Tiptree, Jr. First published in *Interfaces* (Ace, 1980). Reprinted by permission of the author's estate and the agents for the estate, the Virginia Kidd Literary Agency.

"The Map," by Gene Wolfe. Copyright © 1984 by Gene Wolfe. First published in *Light Years and Dark* (Berkley, 1984). Reprinted by permission of the author and the author's agent, The Virginia Kidd Literary Agency.

"Dinosaurs," by Walter Jon Williams. Copyright © by Davis Publications, Inc. First published in *Isaac Asimov's Science Fiction Magazine,* June 1987. Reprinted by permission of the author.

"The Death Artist," by Alexander Jablokov. Copyright © Davis Publications, Inc. First published in *Isaac Asimov's Science Fiction Magazine,* August 1990. Reprinted by permission of the author.

"Sister Alice," by Robert Reed. Copyright © 1993 by Bantam Doubleday Dell Magazines. First published in *Asimov's Science Fiction,* November 1993. Reprinted by permission of the author.

"Recording Angel," by Paul J. McAuley. Copyright © 1995 by Paul J. McAuley. First published in *New Legends* (Tor Books, 1995). Reprinted by permission of the author.

"Genesis," by Poul Anderson. Copyright © 1995 by Poul Anderson. First published in *Far Futures* (Tor Books, 1995). Reprinted by permission of the author.

"The Days of Solomon Gursky," by Ian McDonald. Copyright © 1998 by Dell Magazines. First published in *Asimov's Science Fiction,* June 1998. Reprinted by permission of the author.